I0627361

WHITE HAVEN HUNTERS

BOOK FOUR -SEVEN

TJ GREEN

White Haven Hunters Books 4 – 7
Mountolive Publishing

PO BOX 28, Vila do Bispo CTT, Portugal, 8651-909

Copyright©2025 TJ Green

Paperback ISBN: 978-1-991313-32-4

Hardback ISBN: 978-1-991313-33-1

Cover Design by Fiona Jayde Media

Editing by Missed Period Editing

This is a work of fiction. Names, characters, businesses, places, events, locales, and incidents are either the products of the author's imagination or used in a fictitious manner. Any resemblance to actual persons, living or dead, or actual events is purely coincidental.

All rights reserved.

No portion of this book may be reproduced in any form without written permission from the publisher or author, except as permitted by U.S. copyright law.

Contents

Contents

HUNTER'S DAWN

WHITE HAVEN HUNTERS BOOK FOUR

TJ GREEN

One

"Well," Shadow said, looking around at the reinforced doors and security system cameras, "this is impressive."

Jackson smiled as he led them along the corridor. "Hazards of the Paranormal Division—and I guess government intelligence agencies in general. They have to be prepared for attack."

Gabe's eyes narrowed as he examined their surroundings. "I guess they do. It feels like a warren down here."

Harlan was walking alongside Shadow, and he nodded. "I think I'm lost already."

"I felt like that the first time I was here," Jackson admitted, "but I've got used to it."

Shadow exchanged a look with Harlan. As suspected, Jackson was very familiar with this place, and as usual, he'd underplayed his hand.

It was Wednesday morning in early July, a couple of weeks after the events with the Dark Star Astrolabe in France, and Jackson had invited Shadow, Gabe, and Harlan to the government's Paranormal Division headquarters. It was situated in the basement of the MI5 building and accessed via a rear entrance on Thornley Street. They had passed through the plain front rooms to a well-manned security checkpoint where they had been searched and scanned, and annoyingly, Shadow had to leave her weapons in the screening area—even the ones she tried to conceal.

Once through security, they used the lift to descend two floors down from street level, and found themselves in a low-ceilinged space with narrow corridors and small rooms. It felt cramped and neglected.

Harlan huffed. "It feels like you're out of sight, out of mind down here."

"That's exactly how they treat the PD, and it suits us," Jackson admitted, not looking concerned in the slightest. "The bigwigs don't really like to acknowledge what we do here. Hence the rear entrance. But there are a couple of labs here, a back entrance that leads to our own morgue, and even a few cells which we can use for a limited time. They have another entrance, too."

"I presume," Gabe said, prowling like a caged cat, "they are well guarded?"

"Of course." Jackson grinned as he stopped outside a closed door. "Anyway, time to meet our director, Waylen Adams."

Our? Shadow had a feeling they were being recruited, whether they wanted to be or not.

Jackson swung the door open into a very unusual office. The entire back wall was glass, and as they progressed into the room, Shadow could see that the vast window looked onto a couple of labs staffed with a handful of black-clad scientists. There appeared to be one old-fashioned laboratory, complete with alembic jars, glass jars, flasks, crucibles, and other equipment, and another one kitted out with state-of-the-art machinery and modern technology.

She inwardly groaned. *More alchemy and magic.* She'd pretty much had her fill of it with Black Cronos and JD, but knew it wasn't going away. However, she had very little time to take in the details, as a man rose from behind the desk and limped around to greet them as Jackson made the introductions.

Waylen was a very average man who Shadow estimated to be in his forties. Average height, average build, wearing an average suit, and with sensibly cut hair, but his eyes were a pale brown, the colour of honey, and it felt like they looked right through her.

"Good to meet you all," Waylen said, shaking their hands. "Jackson has explained how helpful you've been regarding Black Cronos." He ushered them into seats around a large, wooden table. "Your fighting skills are impressive."

"Er, not mine," Harlan said, shooting Jackson a nervous glance. "Are you sure you want me here?"

Waylen smiled, his sharp eyes narrowing. "Oh yes. You work with JD."

"Unfortunately, yes, I do. What's that got to do with anything?"

"I'll get to that." Waylen turned back to Gabe and Shadow, studying them with interest. "Not many could have killed so many of Black Cronos's...*soldiers.*"

Gabe gave him a grim smile. "As I'm sure Jackson has told you, we have a few extra skills that others don't."

Waylen nodded. "Advanced fighting ability, wings, and," his gaze slid to Shadow, "fey magic."

Shadow bristled under his stare. "I presume we're here because you want our help."

"With Black Cronos, yes. We're trying to find where Toto Dax and The Silencer of Souls have fled to, but so far are having limited success. They've covered their tracks well. But," he stood and walked over to the window to look at the labs, "in the last twenty-four hours we have identified one lead that seems to be current. I'm just waiting on an update."

Gabe nodded. "And you want our help to find them?"

"Exactly." Waylen leaned against the glass and folded his arms across his chest as he stared at them. "I had originally thought to keep our search within this division, but I have to be realistic. We need your help. What I want to do now is secure your agreement. You have brothers, I understand, and a witch who helped you in France."

Herne's horns. Shadow knew she'd have to put up with more time around Estelle, but it still grated on her.

Gabe said, "Six brothers, but not all are free to help all the time. I organise their availability." He glanced over at Harlan. "We also work with The Orphic Guild, in addition to doing a few other things."

Waylen shrugged. "That's fine. I trust you to organise who you need and when. Just be aware that you may have to move quickly."

"We can do that—for a price. I presume you offer good rates?"

"We're competitive."

Shadow butted in before anyone else could answer. "You'll have to be *very* competitive. Black Cronos is dangerous. That means hazard pay. Or no deal."

"And," Gabe added, "we want real details, not just some sketchy, scant amount of information you're happy to tell us. If we're risking our lives, it's the least you can do."

"Agreed." Waylen limped back to the table and Shadow wondered what had caused his injury. If Waylen noticed her interest, he didn't explain himself, instead saying, "I want you to be successful, so of course I'll share what we have."

Gabe leaned forward, arms resting on the table. "Are we expected to catch them or kill them?"

"That really depends on the circumstances, I guess." Waylen glanced at Jackson, who was watching the exchange. "Jackson will liaise with you."

"And where do I come into this?" Harlan asked, looking very suspicious.

"I need you to keep tabs on JD, and make sure he doesn't get in the way."

Harlan snorted. "You've got to be kidding! You want me to watch that sneaky son of a bitch? I hardly ever see him. And in case Jackson didn't tell you," he gave Jackson a long sideways glance, "we're not exactly on good terms right now."

Waylen smiled. "I understand. JD is a tricky character. Has he recovered from his experience in France?"

"Being kidnapped by Toto Dax? I think his pride was more injured. It's Mason who was affected more. He's grieving for Smythe. In fact," Harlan shuffled in his seat, "it would be fair to say he wants revenge. He's furious."

Waylen's hands steepled together, elbows on his desk, and he leaned on them, his eyes hooded. "Yes, I understand that. They've been responsible for many deaths in their time. How is Caldwell Fleet? I gather his colleague was killed, too."

"As well as can be expected," Harlan told him. "Especially considering the manner of his friend's death."

"Aubrey Cavendish," Gabe said, his voice hard, "was killed by The Silencer of Souls. You wouldn't happen to know how she kills with her lips, would you?"

Waylen sighed. "I'm afraid not. But I would dearly like to."

Gabe muttered under his breath, "Of course you don't."

Shadow knew that Gabe had been more disturbed than he'd like to admit when he was attacked by The Silencer of Souls. Not many things unnerved him, but she did. However, Waylen ignored Gabe's sarcasm and opened a slim folder, extracting several sheets of paper. He slid them across the table, one for Shadow and Gabe, and one for Harlan.

"Our contract. It outlines our terms and pay. I need your answer now, though obviously I'll give you a few minutes to go through it." He headed to the door. "I'll be back soon."

In seconds he'd gone, leaving them alone, and Shadow leapt from her chair to study the labs beyond the glass wall. Jackson joined her. "Don't you want to read the contract?"

"I'll read it in a minute. I'm more interested in those." She nodded to the men carrying out their investigations. "You obviously come here a lot. Do you know what they're doing?"

Jackson gave a lopsided grin and ruffled his shaggy hair. The last time she'd seen him he'd looked tired, exhausted from the chase. He looked better now, flushed with success. "I'm not privy to everything that happens here, you know."

Shadow stared at his mischievous expression. "Liar! You're a dark horse, Jackson Strange."

He just laughed. "It's the name of the game." His eyes travelled across her face and then back to the labs. "I know some things, but am not privy to all. Some of the scientists are trying to recreate Toto's experiments. Not on humans, you understand!"

Shadow stifled a snort. "No, of course not!"

"I'm serious. It's more the alchemical process they're interested in."

"For now." Shadow knew how these things worked. The Paranormal Division were at a disadvantage, and they didn't like it. That's why they needed them. "They've been trying for years though, right? And failing."

"But the documents we found weeks ago have changed things."

Shadow turned to look at him. "Caldwell allowed you access to his papers?"

"Of course. That was the deal that allowed the order to have access to the Dark Star Temple." Jackson pointed to a far wall where a series of objects were laid out. "A few things we retrieved. But so far, all that they prove is that Toto—or someone—is a genius. And of course, he escaped with some of the research."

"It's early days though, isn't it?"

"Very."

"And you have the bodies?"

Jackson nodded. "Yes, and the remains of those who had been dead in that temple for years. They're being examined, too."

Images of blood tests and autopsies flooded Shadow's mind. *What a fate.* Another thought struck her. "What about Stefan Hope-Robbins? Has he said much?"

"Ah! No." Jackson rubbed his jaw, his eyes brooding. "But I haven't seen him for a few days. Our security team continues to question him, though."

That sounded suitably ominous.

"Have you found the order's mole yet?" They all knew someone had betrayed Caldwell and Aubrey, despite their protestations. Shadow just hoped Caldwell wouldn't become a victim, too. He was an odd man, but she liked him.

"No. Things have been very quiet there, but we're watching and waiting."

"And this new lead?"

"Looks good."

Before she could ask any more questions, Gabe called her over. "Have a look at this, Shadow."

She walked to his side and lifted the contract, skimming through it. "I'm happy with it. I'm sure your brothers will be, too."

He nodded. "At least we retain discretion as to how we organise ourselves."

Harlan's eyes narrowed as he put his contract down. "Standard waffle," he drawled, "and the money is okay, but I earn more not having to babysit that awkward bastard, JD."

Gabe looked at him, clearly amused. "You must get paid way more than us, then. I thought the rates were pretty good."

"Maybe you're risking death more than I am and your rates are better," Harlan answered, his hand raking through his hair. "I'm just risking my sanity."

Jackson was still at the window, and he called over, "You don't mind spying on your boss, then?"

"I'm not exactly comfortable with it, but if it keeps us all a little safer, I can deal with it." He signed his contact with a flourish. "JD is borderline nuts...a loose cannon. I guess that's what immortality does to you. Gives you a damn God complex. I'll do what I can to keep an eye on him. Hell, I try anyway! I may as well get paid for it now."

"I don't envy you," Shadow confessed, sinking into her seat again.

The last time they'd seen JD was in France, and he'd left early to go to the Paris branch, leaving the rest of them in peace at the *château*. Days of bliss, in which Shadow had only reluctantly left Gabe's bed. She only wished she hadn't hesitated for so long. She glanced at him now, noting his hard jaw, firm mouth, and dark olive skin. The sun was kind to him, and he looked good.

"Seriously, though," Harlan continued, addressing Jackson. "How the hell *am I* supposed to keep tabs on that man? He does what he likes when he likes, and I've barely seen him since France. And Mason is tight-lipped about him. There may even be a rift between them."

"Perhaps," Gabe suggested, also signing their contract and passing it to Shadow, "he blames him for Smythe's death."

"Yeah. I think there's a fair bit of that."

Despite the fact that Gabe and the others had saved JD and Mason, JD had barely given them thanks. Instead he was preoccupied with the papers that Caldwell had retrieved from the Minotaur's tomb. *Ungrateful bastard.* But Shadow reminded herself that she wasn't doing this for gratitude, but for the money, and JD was unlikely to ever show gratitude for anything.

"I think," Jackson mused, "that once JD knows we have a lead, he will suddenly make himself *very* available to you. Just make sure you keep him updated."

The door swung wide as Waylen re-entered, a broad smile on his face. "I hope you're happy with your contracts, because our lead has been confirmed. Can you travel today?"

"Today!" Gabe's voice rose with surprise. "Sure. But I need to get the team together. Where are we going?"

"Scotland. A remote abbey, in fact. We'll have to fly you there. We can provide weapons, but..."

Shadow interrupted him. "We prefer our own. Are you sending a team, too?"

Waylen's smile disappeared. "There'll be an extraction team like the last time for anyone you catch. Or kill. But you go in alone."

"And we attack tonight?" Gabe asked. "My preference is to do this in darkness."

"Absolutely."

"And some of my brothers will need flights from Cornwall."

Waylen didn't hesitate. "Not a problem. I just need names." He nodded to Jackson. "Liaise with him. He will organise it all."

"And me?" Harlan asked, alarmed. "Do I need to be there?"

Gabe answered immediately. "No. It's too dangerous. But we'll let you know what we find so you can update JD."

Harlan looked relieved as a wicked grin crossed his face. "Sure. I'd like to rattle him."

"In that case," Waylen said, skimming the signed contacts and adding his own, "here are your copies. Can you be ready by late afternoon?"

"No problem," Shadow said, already eager to be out of there. "But we need details. Background."

"Of course." Waylen settled himself at the table again. "I'll tell you what we know so far. But I warn you, it's not much."

<h1 style="text-align:center">Two</h1>

N ahum ended the call with Gabe, his mind whirring with necessary preparations, and went in search of Niel, who was in the barn fighting with Ash.

The clash of metal and thumps carried across the courtyard, and he could see them easily as he approached. The weather was hot, and the barn doors were thrown wide open, revealing the dusty, straw-strewn interior. Ash was of a slimmer build than Niel, and more agile. Niel was ridiculously strong and brawny, so it was an interesting fight, and well matched for all their differences.

However, Nahum hadn't got time to indulge them. "Guys! We're flying to Scotland in a couple of hours. We need to pack and get to the airport."

Ash wiped a hand across his sweat-beaded brow and walked to his side. "Scotland? Are you kidding?"

"What for?" Niel asked, cricking his neck as he grabbed a towel and wiped himself down.

Both men were shirtless, their olive-toned bodies ripped with muscles. Niel had many tattoos, but Ash had tattoos only on his arms. Both had their hair tied up in top knots, revealing corded neck muscles.

"The Paranormal Division has got a lead on Black Cronos," Nahum told them, hoping neither had changed their mind about the pursuit of their alchemically-enhanced enemies. "It's just us going in."

A gleam of pleasure lit Niel's eyes. "Excellent. I take it negotiations went well?"

They all knew Gabe and Shadow had gone to meet Waylen Adams. "Good rates and no interference was pretty much all Gabe said. Even so, I think he was surprised we're involved so quickly."

"Are we taking Barak?" Niel asked.

"Gabe wants him," Nahum admitted. Barak was at Caspian's warehouse, flirting with Estelle no doubt. "Caspian has been good to us lately. I'm wondering how far we can abuse his generosity, though. It doesn't seem fair to keep pulling out and leaving him short-staffed."

Ash frowned. "It depends on what we find when we get to Scotland. If there are just a couple of them, it's not an issue, but if it's some kind of barracks, we'll need him. What *is* the situation?"

"Information is scant. But, they have tracked businesses and places owned by Toto Dax—tricky, it seems. Shell corporations and other such weird stuff. A lot of their leads proved to be old and useless. But then they traced an old Scottish abbey to Toto. They've been keeping a discreet eye on it, and Toto has been spotted in the area."

"Is *she* with him?" Niel asked.

Nahum knew exactly who he meant. *The Silencer of Souls.* "Yes, it seems so."

Ash groaned and started to collect some of the weapons in the barn. "Of course she is. I better head to the shower and start getting ready then." He gestured to the swords and daggers. "Can we get these on a flight?"

"You can with the permission of the government," Nahum said, glad there were some perks. "We'll need our protective vests, too. And Shadow wants her armour."

Niel smirked. "We need to go through her clothes?"

Nahum glared at him, thinking Niel might want to prank Shadow, which would be a very bad thing. "Leave that with me. Gabe is calling Caspian, so with luck Barak will be back within the hour."

He left them to prepare and headed to Shadow's room, thinking he should call Eli and Zee with an update, too. *At least leaving them behind wouldn't be a worry this time.* And they hadn't been bored while they were away, having helped the witches with their own problems.

For the next hour, Nahum kept busy packing their things, and was surprised when he heard Barak's shout and his footfalls along the hall. He appeared at the living room door, grinning with pleasure when he found Nahum packing up the large case of weapons.

"He let you go, then?" Nahum asked with a smile.

Barak headed to his side, idly picking up his own sword and running his palm along the flat of the blade. "Sounds like negotiations are up for us to be finished with Caspian in the next month or so. Just enough time for him to get more staff."

"I'm sort of sorry to hear that." Nahum took Barak's sword from him and placed it next to Shadow's armour, hoping he hadn't missed anything. "It's been steady work. Safe."

"It has, but this is better." His grin broadened, revealing white, even teeth that gleamed against his dark skin. "And Estelle is coming. She'll meet us at the airport."

"Good. We need a witch. I'm not sure you need the distraction, though."

Barak laughed. "I can concentrate."

"Really? You spend a lot of time checking her out."

"I like to show a woman that I appreciate her assets."

"I'm not entirely sure Estelle's that type of woman." The last thing Nahum and his brothers needed to deal with was a horny Gabe and Barak. "Go and pack your gear, because we need to be out of here in an hour." That wasn't strictly true, but Barak had a shower addiction and time pressure helped.

He nodded, already backing out the door. "And where are we staying?"

"No idea. It will be a surprise. Although, we might only be there for a night!"

Barak grunted and disappeared, leaving Nahum alone with his preparations, and wondering what they may face that night.

Harlan arrived at The Orphic Guild to the unfamiliar sight of Eloise Ward coming down the stairs.

She paused as she reached the bottom, greeting Harlan with a shy smile. "Hi, Harlan. Sorry, I know you only just got back, but Mason wanted to see you as soon as you arrived."

Eloise had taken over as Mason's secretary, and from all he could gather, she was having a hard time, mainly because she wasn't Smythe. She'd previously worked within the admin team, and was young and competent, and Harlan was pleased she got a promotion. She was always far more polite than Smythe when Harlan considered how he'd often greeted him with his supercilious attitude.

Pushing his uncharitable thought aside, he asked, "Is he cranky again?"

She nodded, and her blunt, dark bob fell around her flushed cheeks.

Grumpy bastard.

"It will get easier...I hope. He's like that with all of us."

She nodded and straightened her shoulders. "I know. He's grieving, but we all are." A hand flew to her cheek. "It's not often a colleague dies under such circumstances, is it?"

"No. Let's hope it's the last time, too." He started for the stairs, and added, "I'll go and see him now."

"Thank you." She gave him a smile of utter relief and hurried onwards, and Harlan was suddenly glad he wasn't in his twenties and so unsure of himself anymore. *Although, maybe a little less cynicism wouldn't go amiss.*

Because it was Eloise who'd asked so nicely, he went straight to Mason's office, took a deep breath, knocked, and went in.

Mason scowled as he looked up. "Oh, it's you."

"I thought you wanted to see me?"

"You are quicker than I expected. Have a seat."

Clenching his fists and wishing he'd stopped for a shot of caffeine on the way, Harlan forced himself to be polite. "How can I help?"

"Black Cronos. Have you heard anything?"

For a moment, Harlan's fear that he was being spied on returned, and then he shook it off. This was a regular question from Mason, but the timing was uncanny. He lied, having decided that until there was definite news, he'd say nothing. "No. There have been tentative leads, but nothing certain."

Mason banged his fist on the table. "That's not good enough! They have got away with murder!"

"You've met them, Mason. They are well organised, heavily funded, and clever. It was never going to be easy. But Jackson assures me they are searching. The government is not without its own extensive resources."

"You're keeping in touch with him, then?"

"You know I am! But that isn't my job. I hunt occult objects, remember? I have cases that keep me busy."

"This is Smythe we're talking about! One of our own!" He shot off his chair and started pacing. "He deserved a better death, and JD is giving me nothing!"

"I'm sure he knows nothing. But you see him more than I do."

"He's holed up in Mortlake Estate right now, so I have no idea what he's doing. Messing with his bloody experiments, I presume."

Yep. There was definitely a rift. "Coming up with a way to find Black Cronos, no doubt."

"Or to turn himself into some sort of superhuman!"

Harlan blinked. "You think JD wants to do that? He's old!"

Mason smacked his chest over his heart. "It doesn't stop how you feel! And he felt very frustrated at being thwarted by Toto and that bloody woman and his team of aberrations!"

Fuck. He hadn't even considered that. "Toto has years of research on superhumans, and as ambitious as JD is, I'm sure he's not anywhere close to that." He hesitated, wondering if Mason knew something he didn't. "Is he?"

"I have no idea what he cooks up in his bloody laboratory." Mason marched to his cupboard, pulled his whiskey bottle out, and poured a hefty shot, downing it in one go. "I just want justice."

No wonder Eloise looked strained. Mason was having a very bad day.

Mason hadn't finished his rant. "Do me a favour, and keep an eye on JD."

"What?" *This day was getting weirder.* "You want me to spy on him?" He almost added 'too,' but quickly clamped his mouth shut.

"Did I say spy? No! Just keep an eye on him, and let me know if he does anything sneaky."

"That's called spying." Harlan wondered why he was complaining. He'd been given permission to spy on JD, and was getting paid to do it, too. The Gods were messing with him. "Seeing as he's not here, and I'm pretty sure you've noticed that we clash—badly, how do you suggest I do that?"

"I've got some papers I need him to sign. I want you to take them to him and see what he's up to."

"What kind of papers?"

"Does it matter? Just do it. I'll get them ready, and you can go tomorrow."

Harlan knew his mouth was hanging open and that he looked like an imbecile, so he cleared his throat and composed himself. And besides, this suited him perfectly. "Absolutely. Tomorrow. See you then."

And without giving him a chance to change his mind, he left Mason stewing and went to make himself a coffee. A strong one.

Despite the undoubtedly hard night ahead, Gabe was looking forward to visiting Scotland. It was another opportunity to see more of their new world, and it was even better that someone else was paying for it.

As the plane circled over Glasgow Airport, he noted the huge, sprawling city and the water beyond it, but of more interest was the endless green of Loch Lomond and The Trossachs National Park. Somewhere in there was Arklet Abbey and Toto Dax.

Shadow nudged his arm and looked past him to peer through the tiny window. "So much green!"

He nodded, breathing in her musky scent as her face pressed close to his. "And so rugged. It's very different to Cornwall."

"Wild. Untamed." She turned her head and stared at him. "Anything could happen tonight."

"Like that worries you!"

She gave her feral grin. "I'm looking forward to killing The Silencer of Souls." Her eyes narrowed. "Unless you want to."

"I don't care who kills her. But as much as I admire your enthusiasm and skills, that won't be easy—if she's even there!"

"I know. A girl can hope." Shadow leaned back, readying herself for descent. "When do the others arrive?"

"Half hour after us."

"Good. And Jackson?"

"I'm not sure. He just said he'd be in touch when he landed." He thought back to their last conversation before they boarded the plane. "I think the extraction team was holding him up. They'll be travelling in a private plane."

"Lucky for them!" Shadow arched an eyebrow.

He laughed. "So will Nahum and the others. That's the only way they get to bring all the weapons."

"Typical. And we go commercial!"

"But we get to travel unsupervised. I have a feeling Jackson will join us just to make sure we don't screw up."

She snorted, "As if!" and then fell into silence, no doubt like him, mulling on what they may find in Arklet Abbey.

When the plane landed, they threaded through the disembarking passengers to the rental cars and picked up the keys to the two SUV's that Jackson had arranged, and had only a short wait after that to collect the rest of the team. Gabe spotted Niel first, striding easily through the crowd, a good foot taller than most people, his blond Viking-like appearance drawing stares that he was oblivious to. However, his other brothers were just as tall, all drawing looks too, as they walked purposefully through the crowd, watchful eyes darting everywhere. Estelle was with them, and although she was much shorter, her appearance was just as commanding. Gabe just hoped she and Shadow would remain civil.

Niel raised a hand when he saw Gabe and Shadow, grinning when he reached their side. "Brother! Shadow. Another interesting night ahead."

"The Gods hate us to be bored." Gabe greeted his brothers and looked at the bags they carried. "You have the weapons?"

"Right here," Barak said, pointing to a large case. "And there." He nodded to one that Nahum carried.

"We better get on." Gabe turned to lead them to the car park. "I'd like to go over our plans before we head out there later."

"Where are we staying?"

"An old house the government keeps on standby. One of many, I gather, from what Jackson said. It's close to Loch Lomond."

"And our target?" Nahum asked, falling into step next to him.

"Arklet Abbey, not far from the shores of Loch Arklet. Isolated. One road in and out."

"So, we fly in then?"

Gabe grinned. "Absolutely."

Niel studied the map spread out on the table in front of them, marvelling at the many lochs, waterways, mountains, and endless greenery that surrounded the area.

"I see what you mean by remote, Gabe," he said, studying Loch Arklet in particular. "There aren't many roads around there at all."

Ash nodded. "Perfect for Toto's purposes."

"Perfect for ours, too," Gabe said. "Not many people around to see us fly."

They had all arrived at the large stone house on the edge of Loch Lomond about an hour before, and had quickly organised rooms and weapons. It was close to seven in the evening, and they had a few hours before darkness descended. Plenty of time to plan their attack. They were all gathered around the scrubbed wooden table situated at one end of a rustic kitchen. A huge picture window was next to them, offering a stunning view of the loch, but most of them were focussed only on the map.

"I feel I've missed the details," Estelle said, leaning back in her chair and picking up her coffee. "Tell me about this abbey."

Gabe nodded. "Arklet Abbey is privately owned, sold by the Church in the last century, and the ruins of the old abbey are still there. One of the buildings was converted into a house." He dug out a couple of photos from under the map. "This is it. Toto has owned it for about thirty years, but there are very few records on it. It's at the end of a drive that lies off the road running alongside the north of the loch."

Barak was sitting next to Estelle and examined the photos with her. "So, it's just a private retreat?"

Gabe shrugged. "Perhaps. Various Paranormal Division scouts have been looking out for any sign of Black Cronos since France. They've investigated any buildings or businesses that belong to them—but it's been hard. Toto covers his tracks well. The one sighting they had of him yesterday is the only one anyone has had yet. We have to hope he's still there."

Niel felt disappointed. "I thought this was going to be a bunker where some of his soldiers were holed up."

"It might be, idiot!" Shadow said scathingly. "We don't know!"

Niel glared at her. "Yes, I gather that. Thank you for your sarcasm. So," he turned back to Gabe, "what's the plan?"

"I think a couple of us should circle the place first. It's not far from here. We can assess it properly, and then all of us can head over."

"Too risky," Barak said immediately. "I think we should all go and surround the place—move in slowly. If we're spotted overhead, they could leave."

Gabe's jaw tightened. "You were shot and poisoned the last time we went in blind. I'd like to avoid that."

"I know. But whether we have two trips or one, the risks are the same."

Nahum, always Gabe's right-hand man, sided surprisingly with Barak. "He's right, Gabe. The element of surprise is all we've got. I know you want to be safe, but Barak's idea is better."

"Agreed," Shadow said, taking the photos from Estelle to study them. "We have no idea what surveillance systems are there. Once in and out is easiest."

Niel was pleased her relationship with Gabe meant she still held her own opinions, and she was good at strategising. He knew Gabe liked independent thinking, too. Gabe's gaze dropped to the map, and the others exchanged speculative glances. Niel appreciated safety, but this was no time to be slow, and everyone knew it.

Finally, Gabe said, "You're all happy to go in sight unseen? That map and old photos are all we have. The layout could have changed."

Ash spoke for them. "Toto and Black Cronos are slippery. We strike once—hard."

"What about the extraction team?" Nahum asked. "Where are they?"

Gabe shrugged. "Arriving later with Jackson. We move without them. They have to catch up—Jackson's instructions."

"And Jackson?" Barak asked.

"Will be with them, well out of our way." Gabe rolled his broad shoulders, his expression still tight, and Niel knew he wasn't happy. Gabe was a planner, and this was sketchy. "Preferably we want Toto alive, and anyone else with him, but we all know that's unlikely. If your lives are at risk, their death is the only option. With luck, however, we'll find something of use in the house or grounds. But we clear it first!" He stared around the table. "Let's split into groups. Me and Shadow will take the front of the house. Barak and Estelle, you can take the rear. Nahum, Ash, and Niel, the abbey's remains."

Niel nodded, pleased. Black Cronos felt like unfinished business, and he was keen to put an end to their dangerous experiments. "Good. Now for some food," he said, rising to his feet. "I can't fight on an empty stomach."

Three

S hadow slipped from Gabe's grip on the outskirts of a bare garden under the shadows of a huge tree, and watched the old, stone-built building on Arklet Abbey's grounds.

The abbey was situated at the head of a small valley, the hills rippling around them. It was a well-protected area, nestled in its spot that would probably be sheltered from wind. There was no sign of the loch from here, but she'd had a good view of it as they flew overhead. Fortunately for their safety, it was a cloudy night with little moonlight, and the air was cool and damp.

Their initial scan of the area had shown no movement, but they hadn't lingered, sweeping in low instead, the others doing the same. The building was more mansion than house, the ornate, gothic arched windows adding a chill to its appearance. Beyond were the remnants of the abbey, its huge, ruined buttresses rearing into the night sky.

Gabe leaned close to her ear. "That building over there looks to be a garage."

"No lights anywhere, though. It's a big place."

They stood for a moment more, trying to discern any noises disturbing the night, but there was only utter silence. If she hadn't known about the rest of their team, Shadow would have assumed they were alone.

"Come on," Gabe said, drawing his sword. "Let's take this slowly."

Keeping to the border of the poorly maintained lawn, they edged their way to the drive and garage. Shadow felt naked without her bow. She was looking for a new one, but so far, nothing she'd seen suited her. Instead, she pulled both swords free and followed Gabe, keeping watch while he looked inside the garage, converted from an outbuilding.

Moments later, he returned. "One car inside, but that's all. Let's hope that means Toto is here."

They prowled around the front of the house inspecting all the windows and doors, but everything was sealed tight. Shadow looked up to the floors above, and on the second floor spotted a partially open window. She nudged Gabe and pointed. In seconds he had extended his wings and holding her tightly, soared upwards. She opened the window wider, and Gabe set her on the sill. After assessing the darkened room, she dropped inside, Gabe quickly following.

They were in a bedroom, in the centre of which was a four-poster bed draped with heavy material. Evidence of female clothes and toiletries were strewn around, and Shadow saw Gabe's eyes light up.

Someone was here—perhaps The Silencer of Souls.

Again they waited, breath held, but still hearing nothing they passed into the corridor. A low light burned at the end, but it was an inner corridor, with no windows to reveal the glow. Gabe headed left and she went right, easing open doors to peer inside the rooms, but the whole house was unnervingly silent.

They congregated on the landing, and together they progressed downward. They would search floor by floor, and room by room. Toto had to be here somewhere.

Barak grimaced. "It's too quiet."

"Did you think they'd be having a party?" Estelle looked at him, amused.

"What the hell else would you do around here? Oh, wait." A big grin spread across his face. "I can think of something."

"Your mind is in the gutter again. *Focus.*"

She turned away, but she was smiling, and Barak knew she liked his flirting. *Good. He wasn't planning on stopping.* He was in this for the long game, and so far she'd kept him at arm's length, but he sensed her resolve weakening as she began to trust him. Estelle was wary of men and relationships, and he didn't know if it was because of a bad experience, or just her normal defensiveness. Whatever it was, he was prepared to wait.

But she was also right. He needed to focus. The rear of the house was a walled kitchen garden, and once no doubt it would have been magnificent. A glasshouse lay to one side, but now most of its windows were broken, and the garden beds had run to weeds. It was also huge, and at one point it had probably fed the entire abbey.

Estelle however was focussing on the house, and she pointed at a ground floor window where a chink of light was visible. She put her finger to her lips, and they crept across the grounds, keeping to the shadows. But once outside the window there was no sound from within. Barak edged to the back door and turned the handle. It was open, and he felt both excited and wary. He had a horrible feeling that they'd been spotted and were walking into a trap.

Nevertheless, he pushed the door open and stepped inside, Estelle on his heels.

"Another building consecrated to a God who doesn't care," Ash said, shaking his head as he stepped beneath the ruined arches. "What a waste. All that time spent worshipping when they could have been doing something more useful."

Niel snorted so softly he sounded like a horse snickering. "It soothed their soul, you heathen."

"Heathen yourself," Ash shot back, and the damp air swallowed his words.

"Will you both shut up?" Nahum hissed. "We're supposed to be finding Black Cronos."

Ash stepped into the deep shadows and studied the remnants of old walls lost within long grass, the silence settling around them. "No one's been here for a long time, brother. It's too eerie. Look at the grass—no footprints. Untended grounds. Slabs broken into rubble with weeds and time."

"This place may be for the ghosts, but the house is intact," Nahum pointed out. "Let's pan out in a line and sweep our way towards the house. Step carefully in case there are traps."

"I'm not a novice," Niel complained.

"Then get on with it!" Nahum said.

Ash subdued a smile and walked to the far corner to begin his sweep, but his foot caught on something, and he stumbled. Crouching, he saw an iron ring sticking out of a stone slab, only the edges covered by grass. "Nahum!"

Nahum spun around, his eyes widening as he focussed on the spot, and he summoned Niel, all three of them examining the ground together.

"There's no sign of footprints around this, either," Ash noted.

"But," Nahum said, poking the turf, "the grass isn't embedded in the stone."

Niel nodded. "As if it's been partially maintained." He lifted his gaze. "And it's in the corner of the grounds. Easy to get into the woods from here."

Nahum's eyes gleamed in the darkness as he studied the treeline only a short distance away. "An escape route, perhaps." A smile spread. "Keep watch, Ash, and we'll head to the house."

Ash looked up at the ruined walls and shells of window frames, and high above him saw the perfect spot. A ledge within the curve of the ruined gothic arch. "I'll be up there. Happy hunting."

Within moments he was settled on the cold stone, the window edge at his back, the abbey remains spread below him, and placing the crossbow on his knees, he settled in to wait and watch.

Gabe scanned the dark kitchen, his excellent night vision easily seeing used pots and pans stacked on the side. *Someone was definitely here, but where were they now?*

As he and Shadow progressed through the house, they had found another bedroom in use, and once on the ground floor, increasing evidence of people living there. Newspapers left in a darkened lounge, the remnants of a fire, boots and coats in the hall. The silence, however, was unnerving.

Gripping his sword tightly, Gabe stepped back into the hall where Shadow was standing, virtually invisible in the darkness. A sound up ahead startled both of them, and as they progressed down the long corridor, a chink of light came through a partially closed door, and then the murmur of voices.

Gabe raised his sword and flung the door open. It banged against the wall, sounding like a gunshot in the silence, and he leapt through, sword raised, only to come to a skidding halt as he faced Barak's sword and Estelle with fire balling in her palms.

"Herne's bloody horns!" he exclaimed. "I thought you were Toto!"

Barak sheathed his weapon with a sheepish grin. "Sorry, brother. I thought *you* were!"

Gabe panned around the room, taking in the well-stocked bookshelves and desk laden with papers. "A library." He frowned at Barak. "Why did you put the light on?"

"We didn't," Estelle answered in her usual sharp tone, and once again Gabe wondered what Barak saw in her. "It was the only room with a light on. We found the back door open and searched the entire ground floor, but there's no sign of anyone here."

Shadow hadn't sheathed her weapons, and instead stood just inside the room looking back into the darkened corridor. "We found the same upstairs. But two bedrooms show signs of occupation. They must have heard us arrive...or were warned." She swung her gaze back to the room. "But why is this light on?"

"And why is the car in the garage?" Gabe asked as he headed to the desk and shuffled through the papers on it. "It's not rusty or dusty. I think it arrived here recently."

Barak grimaced. "They're hiding. They must be. On the grounds, perhaps?"

Gabe shook his head. "In the ruins? I doubt it. The others must have had time to search by now, and we would have surely heard something if they'd found anyone." A sudden image of his brothers lying dead in the ruins had him swinging around. "I'm going to look outside. Keep searching in here, Barak. These papers may give us a clue as to where they've gone."

"I'll come with you," Shadow said.

In moments they stood at the threshold of the back door, but before they could step outside, they heard Nahum's soft call. "It's us, brother." He stepped out of the shadows of the far wall, Niel with him, and headed to their side.

"Where's Ash?" Gabe asked, looking behind them.

"Watching the grounds from above," Niel said, "and what may be a possible escape route. That's all we found. You?"

Gabe explained what they'd discovered, adding, "It's freakishly quiet, and I don't like it." An uncomfortable prickle crept along his skin as he considered their options, still feeling like there was a trap waiting to be sprung. "I don't understand why this door was left open, when everything else is locked tight."

"It's a walled garden. Secure," Shadow pointed out as she studied the space. "They could just feel safe here...or, it's a lure."

Unable to shake off his worry, Gabe said, "Come inside, and we'll talk in there."

When they returned to the library, Estelle was examining shelves and pulling out books, and Barak was searching the desk. Both looked relieved to see Niel and Nahum.

"Tell us about the escape route," Gabe said immediately.

"Ash found a stone slab in the earth with a ring set into it," Nahum explained. "It's big enough that someone could get through it, and it's in the far corner of the ruins. It seemed suspicious."

Shadow nodded. "It's likely that an old abbey would have passages or cellars beneath it."

"And perhaps access from here," Barak said, pausing in his search. "Perhaps there's a hidden door in this room."

Niel nodded. "It would explain why this has the only light on. Maybe it's their after-dinner activity."

"An underground lab?" Gabe asked. "That might mean more people are down there, but I doubt it. It's too quiet, and there are not enough cars parked." His gaze swept around the room again, and he noted Shadow had joined the search, pulling books out and tapping the panelling while Niel and Nahum looked at him expectantly. "You want to lift the slab, don't you?"

Niel grinned. "Of course. We need to flush them out. *If* they're there!"

"They're here somewhere, I know it! And I'd rather *them* be on the end of a trap than us. Which it could be!" He rubbed his jaw. "Okay. Niel, you and Ash lift that slab, and if there's something under there, head inside—carefully. We either flush them out to here, or if we find an entrance, we pincer them in. Nahum, go with Niel just to see what they find, and then report back."

As they left the room, Estelle said, "I could try a finding spell, it's one of my specialties, but I'd need something of theirs. Something very personal."

"There'd be something in the bedrooms," Shadow suggested, clearly eager to get on with it.

"Let's focus on searching this room thoroughly first," Gabe said, finally sheathing his sword. "Anything interesting in the papers, Barak?"

"Nothing much. Alchemical documents, books on ancient civilisations—all too varied to narrow them down..." Barak was crouching as he searched through the drawers and he paused, his lips tightening. "I can feel something."

Everyone stopped and stared as a small click broke the silence, and a section of the bookcase opened a few inches. Estelle was closest and she pulled it open carefully, revealing a hollow wall behind it and dark stairs leading downwards.

Four

A sh had been walking through the deserted passages beneath the abbey for several minutes when something snarled in the darkness, and then flew at him.

It landed on his chest, throwing him to the ground as jaws snapped at his face, drool splattering everywhere. His sword clattered out of his right hand, and he fumbled for it, while his left hand pushed against the beast's neck, suspending it above him. It was a dog, hugely muscled, with an enormous head and jaw, and glowing red eyes.

He yelled, "Niel! *Help!*"

Niel came running from a side passage, and within seconds, the animal was dead as his sword pierced its side. "What the fuck, brother?"

But Ash didn't have a chance to answer, as the clattering of claws on stone announced more. He had barely thrust the dead body off him when a second one leapt from the darkness. Ash fumbled for his sword, angling it upwards so that as the dog leapt, it landed on his upturned blade, again pinning him to the ground.

Niel leapt over him, axe swinging as he faced the others racing towards them. Ash scrambled from under the weight of the beast, cursing profusely, and trying to maintain a tight grip on his sword, the pommel now slick with blood. He managed to find his feet as another dog leapt from a side passage behind him. *What was this place? A kennel for demon dogs?*

"Are you with me?" Niel yelled, the crunch of his axe sounding brutal as it bit into another dog.

"Yes! Keep moving!"

Back-to-back, they battled down the passage, gore splattering, bodies strewn in their wake, trying not to stumble over the dead animals. The sharp smell of blood and confined beasts was strong, and their snarling filled the air with menace, but a startled yelp heralded the last of them as they entered a long, low room.

Finally able to draw breath, Ash scanned the space, noting the open cages down each side and a camera in the corner. "Niel. Up there. There must be other cameras we missed. They would have seen us enter."

Niel groaned. "Fuckers. There's a control room somewhere."

"Has to be down here...unless it's hidden in the house."

Niel grunted as he headed to the corner, looked into the camera, and roared, "I'm coming for you!" He smashed the camera and marched to the next exit. "Onwards, brother. There's more killing to do."

Barak had barely progressed down the first passage beneath the house when he felt something click beneath his feet.

He threw himself backwards, crashing into Gabe behind him as he yelled, "Everyone down!"

They dived to the ground as sharp metal spikes catapulted out of the walls ahead, zinging across the passage and thudding into the other side. No one moved as they waited for something else to happen, Estelle and Shadow also crouching in anticipation.

But when silence fell, Barak struggled to his feet and pulled Gabe up. "It's a bloody death trap! Sorry, brother."

"I'd rather be squashed than you impaled."

Estelle threw a couple of witch-lights down the stone corridor, illuminating the long spikes embedded in the opposite wall, all at head and chest height.

He exchanged a wary glance with Estelle, and she pointed at the rectangular stone on the floor that Barak had stepped on, now a couple of inches below the others it was set into. "This whole place could be booby trapped, and it doesn't look that different from the rest of the floor."

Shadow had been at the rear, but she shouldered her way forward. "Let me. I'm lighter on my feet."

"But not weightless!" Gabe protested.

"I have an idea," Estelle said. "Let's see if I can trigger anything else. Let's face it, if they're down here, they'll know we're here by now."

Conjuring balls of energy into her palms, she launched them down the corridor, using them like cannon balls, and as they ricocheted off the walls and ground, spikes flew from hidden recesses and pits opened up the whole way down. At the end was a wooden door.

"They really want to keep us out of here," Shadow said, almost sounding impressed.

Barak still wanted revenge for the injury that had almost killed him, and he gripped his sword even tighter. "Well, they won't. Nice job, Estelle. Let's get this over with."

Estelle laid a hand on his arm. "Hold on. Why don't I open the door from here?"

She hurled more balls of energy directly at the door, her lips moving with a noiseless spell, and it blew off its hinges with a splintering crash. A deeper boom came from beyond it, and flames shot through the doorway. *Another booby trap.* While dust and debris billowed out, Barak used it as cover for his approach. He stepped carefully but confidently across sprung traps and around the spikes, finally pausing at the doorway and the ruins within, the others right behind him.

It was a control room, a handful of screens on the wall, all of which had been destroyed. Only one door lay on the other side, and it opened onto another corridor.

"Damn it," Gabe said. "They're on the move. Estelle, want to do the honours again?"

She didn't answer, instead just stepping up and hurling her cannon balls of energy down the next corridor. Nothing was triggered, but they saw multiple passages opening, and the slam of a door echoed from the far end.

Barak gave chase, the others on his heels.

"Shit!" Niel exclaimed as a boom echoed down the corridor, the ground rumbling beneath their feet, and Ash echoed his sentiment.

They were progressing slowly through the few empty rooms they found beyond the kennels, deciding to stick together for safety, but all they found were the detritus of desks and research stations. It seemed that although the dogs had been fed and looked after, the rest of the place had fallen into disuse.

Now they picked up the pace, Niel's thoughts with his brothers approaching from the other end.

They entered the next corridor and soon found their way blocked by a reinforced gate with heavy steel beams, another passage on the far side. He studied the rock that the gate was set into. It looked solid, and there were no obvious signs of a mechanism to open it.

"Think we can move this?" he asked Ash.

Ash ran his hands around it, frowning. "Odd. There has to be a way to open it."

"I'm happy to try brute force," Niel said, putting his axe down and gripping the bars.

Ash joined him, and together they pulled, muscles straining with the effort, but nothing budged.

And then footsteps sounded, and light bloomed on the other side, illuminating Toto Dax and The Silencer of Souls running towards them. Both carried bulky bags and were breathing heavily. Toto barely glanced at them, skidding to his left, and disappearing down another passage, but the woman paused, and a smile spread across her face.

She pulled an object from her pocket and pointed it at them, and Niel felt himself being yanked back by Ash before an explosion ripped through the air, throwing them backwards as rock rained down on them.

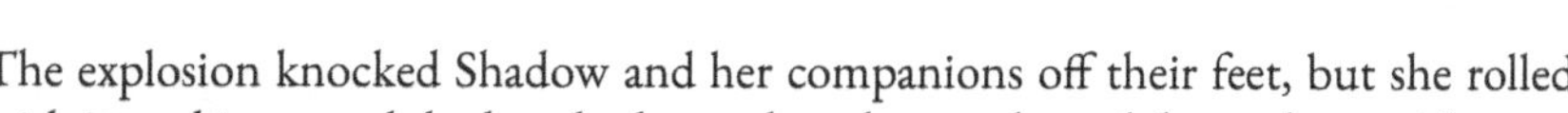

The explosion knocked Shadow and her companions off their feet, but she rolled with it, and in seconds had vaulted over the others and raced down the corridor.

They had cornered their enemies, and Shadow was not about to lose them, even when she careened into a well-lit room covered with maps and images of stone tablets. She gave it barely a glance and raced onwards, the passage beyond snaking away.

Shadow reached a section filled with dust, and hesitated for a second before seeing a clear passage on her left, and she ran again. If they were ahead of her, then the route must be safe. She was vaguely aware of Gabe calling from behind her, but she ignored him, rounding a corner before finally skidding to a halt. The Silencer of Souls was a short distance away, waiting for them. A bag rested at her feet, and she clutched something in her hand.

Shadow studied the ground, wondering what new level of Hell was between them. The corridor was plain stonework, floor and walls smooth and unadorned. Still Shadow waited, her eyes locked with The Silencer of Souls, who wore an enigmatic smile. Shadow itched to wipe it off her face, and she clenched her swords.

But something was wrong.

Gabe arrived, breathless, at her side. "What's..."

The Silencer of Souls smiled as she lifted her hand. Shadow felt a searing pain in her chest as she flew backwards. A boom filled the air, and then utter darkness fell.

Nahum hovered over the abbey grounds, the dull booms below him making him more and more worried, especially when a wall crumbled before his eyes, masonry thudding to the ground. The booms were powerful. *What was going on down there?*

He kept a close eye on the dark hole that had been revealed when they moved the stone slab, but no one emerged. Nahum suddenly made up his mind. He couldn't wait any longer.

He dropped to the ground and descended the stone staircase, very quickly stumbling across dead dogs in the dust-filled air. With increasing panic, he raced onwards, barely noticing the rooms he ran through, and finally saw Ash pulling Niel out from under a pile of rubble.

Nahum raced to help, lifting chunks of rock and hauling them out of the way. "What happened?"

"Toto and The Silent Bitch. Who else?" Ash said bitterly, coughing as he spoke. "The whole damn place is booby trapped."

"Stop yakking and get me out of here," Niel complained, struggling to get one arm clear.

As Nahum moved another chunk of rock, Ash grunted and finally pulled Niel free. He was covered in cuts and dust, but his eyes were furious as he staggered to his feet, his right arm limp at his side.

Niel's voice was a growl as he asked, "Where is she?"

"Gone, brother," Ash answered.

Niel groaned and coughed, hacking up dusty spit as he leaned his left hand on his knee. He peered up at Nahum. "Tell me you found them."

"I came looking for *you*!"

"Nahum, find me that bitch right now!"

There was a dangerous glint in Niel's eyes. A berserker glint he'd seen before, and the end was never pretty. "What are you going to do?"

"Move this rubble and get through."

"No, you're not. The search is over on this end. You move that and it will all come down on your heads. *Again.* Ash, make him see sense! I need to check on the others."

Ash nodded, and Nahum ran for the exit, hearing Niel yell, "I am not stopping now!"

Gabe saw the blast hit Shadow, and an explosion of fury ripped through him.

As she flew past him, he raced forward, and he saw the shock in The Silencer's eyes as she retreated. She thought she'd take them both out. He was happy to prove her wrong.

She turned her weapon on him, but he was too quick, and he threw himself at her. Unfortunately, the bag that was on the ground tripped him up, and his momentum wasn't as great as he'd planned. Instead of tackling her around the waist, he caught her legs instead.

They both landed with a thud, but she kicked her way out of his grasp, her boot striking his jaw. Gabe's head snapped back, and blood filled his mouth. He staggered to his feet, whipping his sword from his scabbard. But she had gained precious seconds.

Her weapon—something small and metallic—had skidded across the ground, and with lightning-quick reflexes, she rolled and grabbed the weapon in one slick move, shooting at Gabe. He dived out of the way, and he saw her eyes dart to the bag. But he was between her and it, and leaping to his feet again, he charged at her.

She turned and ran, firing multiple shots behind her. One struck the roof of the passage, and with a thunderous roar, it collapsed, dust billowing out. Once again Gabe found himself on his back. He blinked several times and brushed dust from his eyes and face, desperate to see his surroundings. But when the air cleared, he saw that the way ahead was completely blocked. The Silencer of Souls had gone.

He regained his feet, slower this time. Everything ached, and his head pounded. He studied the other direction, and to his horror saw that Shadow was motionless. "Shadow!" His voice sounded muffled in his ears, as if he was deep underwater. The explosion had deafened him.

He skidded to Shadow's side, but she didn't move. She'd hit the wall and was lying in a crumpled heap, a huge dent in her breast plate. His heart almost stopped when he saw blood trickling from Shadow's slack mouth. He'd always thought of her as indestructible. She was such a force of nature. But right now... Lifting Shadow as carefully as he could, he limped back down the corridor to the main chamber where he'd left Barak and Estelle.

Barak met him just beyond the entrance, words dying on his lips as he took in the sight of Shadow in his arms. "In here, on the table." He ran before him, sweeping everything onto the floor so Gabe could lie her down.

In the light of the bare bulbs hanging from the ceiling, he could see Shadow's injuries more clearly. The massive dent in her fey armour ended in a sharp point, but it hadn't broken. Blood smeared her forehead from where rubble had struck it, and her breathing was shallow. He quickly loosened her breastplate, cursing his shaking fingers. Gabe could barely think straight. Or hear. His ears were still ringing, and everything sounded muffled around him.

"Let me," Estelle said, resting her hand on his. He saw her mouth the words rather than heard them, and he blinked the dust from his eyes and stepped back.

She was deft as she commanded Barak to help her, freeing the fastening that secured the armour and quickly stripping it away to reveal Shadow's supple leather jacket beneath it. Estelle also unzipped that, just enough to see a huge bruise already spreading across Shadow's chest. Estelle laid a hand on bare skin and said a spell, and Shadow took a sharp intake of breath. Estelle nodded to herself, and then did a quick sweep of Shadow's other injuries, magic swirling across her skin.

Satisfied, she turned to Gabe who stood stupefied, wishing he could think straight. He was used to keeping a clear head in battle, and wasn't sure if the blast had addled his brain, or if it was his worry about Shadow. Whichever, it infuriated him. Estelle forced him into a chair and laid hands on either side of his head. Barak watched, arms folded across his chest. Gabe's eyes idly travelled around the room as he felt her magic wash over him like a cool breeze. The underground chamber had a couple of large tables, chairs, and work benches around the edges, as well as drawings and maps on the walls. It looked as if things had been evacuated hurriedly. There were bare patches in places, and papers scattered across the floor, but several images caught his attention—photos of a stone tablet. He tried to rise to his feet, but Estelle forced him back with a frown.

"Just wait! Bloody men," she muttered under her breath, and he subdued a smile as he realised his hearing was returning.

Barak wagged a finger at him and winked.

"Can you do me a favour, Barak?" Gabe asked, suddenly realising he'd abandoned their weapons and the bag. "Can you find our swords and her bag? Head to the left once—"

Barak interrupted him, already walking to the door. "No problem. Stay put!"

After another few moments, during which his hearing improved, Estelle straightened and lowered her hands. "There you go. That's as much as I can manage right now."

He smiled at her. "You're a miracle worker. I feel much better. What about Shadow?"

"She's a stubborn, hardy madam," Estelle said, returning to her side. "I'll work on her head now, since you're fixed and she's breathing."

Gabe headed to the images that had caught his attention, but knew he needed to thank Estelle properly. "Look, Estelle, I know we don't always see eye to eye, but you've been fantastic tonight. The way you triggered those traps, and then healing us..."

She met his eyes, her expression sincere. "Thank you for letting me join you. You've given me a lifeline I didn't know I needed." And with that enigmatic statement, she turned her attention back to Shadow.

Gabe stared at her a moment longer and decided not to pursue it, instead studying the photos of the stone tablet. They were taken from various angles, but one in particular showed how big it was. The writing on it was tiny cuneiform, and he strained to read it. A few words, however, caught his attention immediately, and he groaned with dismay. *The Igigi. What did Black Cronos want with them?*

Nahum spent a good while flying over the abbey grounds and surrounding area, his keen eyes investigating every moving branch, twitching shadow, and swaying grassy patch. But there was no sign of Toto or The Silencer of Souls.

He checked the garage a couple of times and made sure the car was still there, but eventually had to conclude they'd either holed up underground, or had an escape route that led them far from the abbey.

Anxious to check on his brothers, he finally returned to the passageway, finding that Niel and Ash had cleared the way, and had used the huge, metal-barred gate to wedge into the weakened roof. *Clever.* Casting a wary glance at it as he passed beneath, Nahum pressed onwards, finally hearing Niel's strident boom.

"The bloody *Igigi*? You have got to be kidding me!"

A glow of light up ahead illuminated Barak standing by a door, armed with two swords and a grim expression, and Nahum shouted, "It's just me!"

His posture relaxed. "Good hunting, brother?"

"No. You?"

Barak stepped aside, allowing him to enter the room. "Nothing but images and papers they abandoned after a concerted attempt to kill us all. We did manage to get her bag, though." He gestured to a holdall that was half unpacked on a table, papers spewing out of it.

Everyone was clustered around a series of photos. All except for Shadow, who was sitting in a chair, a mixture of pain and fury on her face, and Nahum asked, "Did I hear the Igigi mentioned?"

Barak rolled his eyes and nodded to the photos. "Yes. It seems that tablet provides a way to find them."

Disbelief rolled through Nahum. "Impossible."

"See for yourself. I've had my fill for now, and just want to get out of here." He lowered his voice, but there was no chance of anyone hearing him anyway over the heated debate. "Gabe is not himself."

Nahum nodded at his warning, and not feeling ready to argue with Gabe right now, crouched next to Shadow, noting her damaged armour on the floor. "What happened to you?"

Her violet eyes that were normally so teasing were now hard, pain lurking behind them. "Guess."

Nahum exhaled. "Anyone else injured?"

"Gabe, Niel, Ash—all less than me, fortunately."

Maybe it was because Nahum had only just entered the chambers and the others were used to them, or maybe it was because he hadn't got swept up in the Igigi talk, he wasn't sure, but he knew they needed to leave. He suddenly wished he hadn't left the entrances unguarded.

He stood abruptly. "Gabe. Now isn't the time. We need to take what you need and get out of here." Gabe turned to him, startled, a huge bruise darkening his cheek and blood staining his lips. He looked feral. The raised voices died as the others faced him, too. Under the bright lights, Nahum could see Niel holding his right arm awkwardly, he and Ash splattered with blood, cuts, and grime, and Gabe didn't look much better. Only Estelle and Barak were unharmed. Most of his brothers seemed to have been possessed by some collective madness. "What is the matter with you all? I can't find Black Cronos, and for all I know they'll be back with reinforcements. The last thing we need is to be trapped down here like cornered rats." He clicked his fingers angrily. "Focus!"

Reason returned to Gabe's eyes. "Of course. You're right."

"I'm going to sweep above the house and grounds, and I'll see you back at our rental in fifteen minutes. Agreed?"

Gabe nodded, and as Nahum turned on his heel and left, he said to Barak, "Get them moving."

Five

Ash called Jackson, relieved when he answered the phone. He left the group in the kitchen and wandered onto the slabbed patio, glad of the peace and the night breeze that kept away the midges.

"Where are you, Jackson?"

"In a van on our way to the abbey, why?"

"I suggest you come here instead." He quickly summarised the events of the night.

Jackson's normally confident tone faltered. "They've escaped? *Again?*"

"Honestly, we're not sure where they are. They're either circling back, or have a well-planned escape route."

"Did you get anything?"

Ash sighed as he remembered the scant items they'd been able to salvage. "Look, come here and we can explain better. Preferably without your team."

He listened to the mumble of voices while Jackson conferred, and then he said, "I'll be with you soon."

Ash turned to watch the drama playing out in the kitchen, the bright yellow lights showing the tableau of activity. Niel was doing what he always did when faced with a crisis—he cooked. Right now he was cooking up a storm, a very apt word for it too, because the crash of pans was like thunder. Gabe was having a heated debate with Nahum, both of them wearing stern expressions, both gesturing at the papers they'd rescued that were placed on the table and the images now secured to the kitchen walls. Barak was leaning on the counter, arms folded across his mammoth chest as he watched and listened, the quiet centre of the space. Estelle and Shadow were elsewhere in the house, Estelle tending Shadow's wounds. *Yet another worry.*

In the cool of the garden, unseen, he studied the images of the stone tablet, pondering on the references to the Igigi. They were their contemporaries a lifetime ago—half man, half beast. Some of whom could fly. *No wonder Black Cronos was interested in these hybrid creatures.* They were created by the Sumerian Gods, the Anunnaki, for labour, and were treated as slaves. Monstrously strong, considered demons by some, they eventually fought back and fled across the desert, before vanishing without a trace. At the time, rumours were varied. Some said they were dead, their bodies buried where no one would find them. Others said they had made a new life for themselves. Even if they had survived, in theory they would have died later in the flood.

Taking another deep breath, Ash returned to the kitchen, took a seat at the table, and pulled the papers towards him, hoping not to get dragged into the argument.

Too late.

"Ash! You're the scholar amongst us!" Gabe said, his expression tight. "What do you think this passage means?"

"I've barely looked at it, so I can't say right now. Maybe when I've had a chance to read it properly..."

"Read it now! It's legible!"

Ash's gaze slid to Nahum, whose eyes held a warning, and then back to Gabe. "It's a large amount of text. We'd be unwise to jump to conclusions."

"But if Black Cronos know where they are..."

"*Were*," Nahum corrected him. "They still have to find the place, and that won't be easy!"

Gabe rounded on him. "But they could have been studying that text for months!"

"Or mere days," Ash said calmly. "Obviously they thought the stone tablet important enough to hide within a booby-trapped bunker, but it doesn't mean they've found anything."

"If anything," Barak added, "it means they're only just starting to translate it. Look at it! The photos are clear, but the writing is tiny. Certain words are weathered and damaged. Even we who translate easily would have to make calculated guesses to interpret it properly."

Ash shot Barak a grateful glance. They had all been shaken by mention of the Igigi, but he was glad to see that most of his brothers were calming down now. "Exactly. We need to take these home and study them properly. What I'd like to know is where that stone tablet is."

Nahum nodded. "I'd like to see the original too, but that would seem impossible right now."

A knock at the door disturbed them, and Ash stood. "That will be Jackson. I'll get it."

Barak waved him down. "Let me."

Instead of sitting again, Ash left Nahum to reason with Gabe, and headed to the fridge to get a beer. He wished he could go to bed, but knew they needed to talk a few things through before then. Their nerves were all on edge after the night they'd had. He was aching from the earlier explosion, and grimy with dust and dirt. He grabbed several bottles, placing one on the counter next to Niel. "Are you okay?"

Niel grunted as he flipped the steaks using his left hand, his right arm now in a sling. "I'm more annoyed that we got bested by that bloody woman than the Igigi."

"How's your arm?"

"Sore, but I can feel it getting better already. Muscle damage to my shoulder—not a break."

Ash nodded. One of their abilities was understanding their bodies' injuries, as well as healing them quickly. "Good. We'll come across her again, there's no doubt about that. You'll get your revenge. We all will."

As he crossed the kitchen to the table with the other beers, Barak returned with Jackson, Estelle, and Shadow. Whatever healing magic Estelle had used on Shadow had worked. She looked to be her normal feisty, self—well, almost.

Shadow turned down Ash's offered beer, instead heading for the fridge. "Gin for me."

"Me too, please!" Estelle called after her as she sat at the table. She and Shadow still didn't seem that comfortable together, but at least their blatant animosity had waned.

Shadow nodded and prepared their drinks, but Jackson paused at the door to the kitchen, his sharp eyes sweeping over them. "If you don't mind me saying so, tensions seem to be high tonight, and many of you look injured. What happened?"

Ash tapped the chair next to him. "Take a seat. This will take a while."

"You all need to sit," Niel's commanding voice said. "Food is ready. We can talk while we eat."

Jackson laughed. "Steak and chips at three in the morning! I haven't done that since my student years. Is there enough for me?"

Ash laughed too, glad to feel the atmosphere brightening as they all found a seat. "You've clearly never experienced Niel's cooking before. He prepares enough for a small army."

Between them they summarised the night's events, and Jackson made notes on a pad he pulled from his pocket, jotting down points while he ate, and asking the odd question as they went. When they finished, he exhaled heavily. "Potentially, every place of theirs that we might find could have similar traps. That's worrying."

Gabe pushed his empty plate away. "I'm not sure the abbey is safe, even now. There are a few corridors we didn't explore. I'm not sure it's okay for your men."

"Agreed," Nahum said. "They could be planning to return, too."

"Nevertheless, we have to search it." Jackson's gaze swung to the images of the tablet. "Are those everything you found?"

Ash shook his head. "No, we just took the essentials. There are more papers down there, abandoned rooms, dead dogs, and of course Toto escaped with a bag."

"Dangerous or not, we have to go, but we'll proceed carefully," Jackson said, sipping his beer. "However, what I'm more interested in right now is the Igigi. What's the big deal with them?"

"I'd like to know that, too," Shadow said, staring at the Nephilim accusingly, especially Gabe. "You're all very cagey, and I want to know why!"

Ash felt sorry for her. Shadow hated to be left out of the loop, and her injury had side-lined her for a short while. "Because," he told her, "they are superhumans. Well, half human, half beast. Made by the Sumerian Gods for labour."

"And what are Sumerians?" she asked, eyes narrowing.

"An ancient Mesopotamian people who lived in the south of the region—now the Middle East. It was a collection of city states more than anything else. But they were clever, inventive people, highly respected. They invented the concept of time—literally the way the day is structured, and the concepts of cities and farming.

And," Ash added, staring at the tablet, "they invented writing. Cuneiform, it's called now."

Nahum gave a dry laugh. "Yes. The world literally changed around us. And as we lived for a long time, we saw how those changes civilised everyone."

Jackson leaned back in his chair, tapping his notebook. "The Sumerians were undiscovered until the nineteenth century. They were lost to time until then."

All of the Nephilim were shocked at that, their heads jerking around to stare at Jackson.

"Are you serious?" Gabe asked, confusion clouding his features. "They were a powerhouse. It seems impossible that they would have disappeared."

"Really, brother?" Niel said sceptically. "Many civilisations are buried beneath deserts, jungles, and modern cities. What remains is paltry. The British Museum, and I'm sure many like it, prove that. Mere fragments remain."

Ash hated this talk as much as he loved it. To think of their own time utterly destroyed was unnerving and fascinating.

Jackson continued, "Their existence was discovered by scholars who were anxious to prove the Bible's stories. What they found challenged everything. It proved the Bible wrong, for one thing. It pushed history back...or I should say, civilisations. A place referenced in the Bible—Shinar—puzzled scholars for years. It turned out to be Sumer."

"Because *that* book is full of stories," Estelle said, amused. "Interesting for the light they shed on a certain time and place, but that's all."

Ash watched Jackson, intrigued. He had paused in his note taking, and was leaning forward, studying them all intently. Ash voiced his thoughts. "You seem well-informed on this topic, Jackson. How come?"

"I'm a collector, like Harlan and Olivia. I like knowing about old things. Sumer is one of the more fascinating places. It has its own flood history, too. It was documented in the Epic of Gilgamesh, which I admit to having only a passing knowledge of."

Ash was familiar with it. "I've done much reading on the flood since our return. It seems the Sumerian Gods colluded with our own God in wanting to rid the world of humans. One of their men was able to build an ark, as well." He looked at his brothers. "Either way, it wiped us out."

"A universal flood myth?" Shadow asked, intrigued.

"It appears in many histories," Ash told her. "Time and time again. We weren't the only civilisation at the time. But as we've said before, I doubt it was a worldwide flood. Maybe just most of the Mediterranean and the Middle East. How would we know, though? It killed us." Ash's last memory surfaced of him standing on a hill watching a gigantic wave roll in, smashing everything in its path. He had considered taking flight, but he was far from the mountains. He had waited with the others besides him, resigned to his fate, and feeling like he had deserved it for some of his activities. He, like his brothers, now felt their time on Earth was a chance to rectify past behaviours. A type of atonement.

Shadow was single-minded, however, her questions dragging him from his reverie. "And the Igigi? Where do they fit in?"

"The Sumerians," Niel said, "had their own Gods, like many civilisations did. Each of their city states had one. The Gods created the Igigi to build their cities and do the heavy work. That's why they were so powerful. They could work tirelessly for hours."

Nahum cut in, "Until they decided they didn't want to. They rebelled."

"And," Gabe added, "our own God became twitchy at their rebellion. Some of us were sent to subdue them. We failed, and they disappeared."

Ash had not been part of that, but knew why Gabe was so troubled. He, Niel, Zee, and Nahum had fought them, and it had been hard and dangerous. Some of the Nephilim had died. Barak, like Ash and Eli, had not been involved.

Estelle asked, "Their own Gods couldn't subdue them?"

"It seemed not," Gabe answered bleakly. "And we never found them once they escaped."

"But that tablet," she pointed beyond his ear to the wall, "points the way?"

They all turned to stare at it as Gabe's low voice rumbled around the room. "It seems to tell the remnants of their history, and yes, suggests a resting place. But that's just my initial interpretation."

"A resting place that Black Cronos is searching for?" Shadow asked.

"It appears so." Gabe gave a dry laugh. "They're powerful enough already, without recruiting the Igigi to their side."

"You think they're still alive?" Estelle asked, alarmed.

"I sincerely hope not," Niel said, "but equally I wouldn't rule it out." He glanced at his brothers as he started to collect the empty plates together. "I doubt, however, that they could have kept their existence so quiet over so many millennia. They must be dead."

"Agreed," Barak rumbled.

Jackson folded his notebook and put it in his pocket. "It's maybe just their bones that Toto wants. We have no idea how they fit into his plans. Yet. But we do need to stop him." He looked around the table, weighing them up one by one. "Are you interested in helping?"

Gabe didn't even consider their opinion when he answered, and Ash knew why. It was unfinished business. All of it.

"Of course, we will."

Six

Harlan set out early on Thursday morning, eager to get his visit with JD over with.

He wasn't particularly pleased to be Mason's messenger boy, but it suited his needs, and to be honest, he was intrigued by Mason's attitude. Once again, he felt on shifting ground, and wished he could have seen Olivia. He valued her opinion, and besides, she let him complain without judgement, usually adding her own complaints, too. It was a general bitching session that suited both of them. With luck, he'd catch up with her later.

Once at JD's Tudor mansion, Anna, JD's assistant, met him at the door, a frown on her face. "I'm not sure this is a good time, Harlan. He's very busy."

He waved the papers secured in an envelope at her. "He's got to sign these. Mason's instructions."

She let him in, edging the door open with obvious reluctance. "Doesn't he have admin staff for that kind of thing?"

He smiled and lied. "I'm down this way on business. It was convenient. Didn't Mason warn you I was coming?"

"Of course." Her voice was brusque. "He knows he must. JD is a busy man." She waved him into a comfortably old-fashioned reception room with French doors that looked onto the garden. "Let me see if he's ready to see you."

She didn't give him a chance to argue his case. He wanted to see where JD was working and what he was up to, but he also believed Anna wouldn't have the slightest problem throwing him out if he didn't behave, so instead he walked to the open doors and stepped on to the patio to admire the garden. He presumed JD had a gardener. The garden was a riot of summer colour. An elaborate Elizabethan knot garden was in front of him, and from here he could see what looked to be a well-planned herb garden in the distance. Harlan smiled. It seemed JD still liked to surround himself with things from his youth.

Fortunately, he didn't have to wait long. Anna returned after a few minutes, saying, "He'll see you downstairs. He's in the middle of something and he said it's tricky timing."

Intrigued, Harlan followed her down the hall to where a door lay open, previously disguised in the panelling. Wall lights illuminated steps descending beneath the house, and she directed, "Down there. Don't touch anything!"

With her words ringing in his ears like he was some kind of wayward child, he went cautiously, emerging onto a small landing with a heavy door. Pushing his way inside, he gasped with surprise. It was a long, low-ceilinged laboratory, lined with bottles, jars, Bunsen burners, and lots of equipment he didn't even recognise, as well as some more modern technology in one corner.

There was no natural light at all. Instead, electric bulbs illuminated the space well. It was also extremely clean—clinical, even. Cupboards and shelves lined one wall, and if it wasn't for some of the more modern items and the lighting, Harlan would have thought he'd stepped back in time. He was in an alchemist's laboratory.

JD was oblivious to his arrival, watching a series of jars linked with tubes, some stacked above each other, all filled with bubbling liquids of various colours, while making notes on a large pad of paper. As Harlan walked closer, he realised the paper was illegible to him, filled with odd symbols and tiny handwriting.

"I'll be with you in a moment," JD said, not taking his eyes from one jar whose contents were bubbling down to a solid lump of...*something*. After another few seconds he whipped the jar off the heat and placed it on the counter to cool. He finally looked at Harlan, his eyes narrowing and his lips puckering with distaste. "I can spare a few moments only. I would have thought Mason would have sent someone else."

"I was down this way on business," Harlan said, repeating his earlier lie and not bothering with pleasantries. If JD couldn't be bothered, why should he? "I have some papers..."

"Yes, yes, yes." He thrust his hand out. "Let's get this over with."

Harlan's fury suddenly bubbled over. "Hey, JD! Stop being a dick. I'm doing you a favour!" He slapped the envelope on the counter rather than in JD's hand. "You should work on your manners!"

JD froze, eyes locked with Harlan's, then he snorted, grabbed the envelope, and ripped it open. "As I suspected. This could have waited. Stupid contracts. Have you been sent to spy on me?"

Harlan folded his arms across his chest. "It seems that I am caught between your and Mason's stupid feud! I don't care for it. Sign the damn paper so I can go. I couldn't give a shit what has happened between you two. All I know is that your behaviour a few weeks ago was infantile and dangerous. You and Mason could have been killed! And I felt compelled to try to help—risking my life, too!"

JD drew himself fully upright, shoulders back. "Liar. You couldn't wait to get out there and see what was happening."

"You're right. I was interested, but I was worried about Mason. He's not good in the field, and you took him with you! If you wanted help, you should have asked me. It's what I'm good at. Mason is traumatised, and Smythe—not only his secretary, but his good friend—is dead! He's very upset right now."

"Which is not my fault!" JD jabbed him in the chest with his finger. "Black Cronos killed him, not me."

Harlan grabbed JD's hand, squeezing it within his own. "Don't you ever touch me again." He stared into JD's eyes and had the feeling he was talking to a sociopath. "If this is what immortality does to you, I want none of it. You're a monster, JD.

Mason is supposed to be your friend. I fully realise you are not mine, and I'm more than happy with that if this is how you treat them."

JD clenched his jaw, and he stepped back, wrenching his hand free. "I had a good reason for finding Toto Dax. What he's doing is against all the principles of alchemy. He's subverting it, sullying it. It is meant for finer things. I want to stop him."

"We all want to stop him, but getting your friends killed in the process is not the way." Harlan studied the jars currently bubbling away. "Seeing as how you disapprove of Toto's actions, I take it you are not trying to become superhuman yourself?"

"Are you insane? Of course not!"

"Then what are you doing? You've been keeping your head down, which means everyone's making assumptions. Especially knowing you were looking at the research found in the Dark Star Temple."

"What do you mean, *everyone*?"

"The Paranormal Division, Jackson, the Nephilim, me!" He decided to leave Mason out of it. "Your attitude isn't instilling confidence."

JD looked incredulous. "I am trying to find an antidote, you imbecile!"

Harlan was so astonished, he forgot to be angry about being called an imbecile. "You're doing *what*?"

"An. Antidote." He said it slowly and loudly, as if Harlan was deaf.

"An antidote to their superhuman abilities?"

"Of course!"

"Is that even possible?" Harlan's gaze swept across the array of jars. "Is that what this is?"

"These are the early stages of my experiments, yes." JD wiped a hand across his brow and closed his eyes for a moment, before fixing Harlan with an impatient stare. "As to whether it's possible, I have no idea. If I don't try, I won't know."

Harlan's annoyance evaporated, and he sat on the closest stool. "That's amazing."

"Nothing is amazing yet. I've barely begun."

"Why haven't you told anyone? The Paranormal Division, for example. They'd want to know. I know you know them."

"I don't like to share my experiments until I know I'm making progress, and so far, I'm making none."

Harlan fell into silence while JD continued to tinker with the Bunsen burners and his jars. He'd turned his back as if Harlan wasn't even there, and for a few moments, Harlan watched, fascinated, thinking through what he knew about Black Cronos. "But JD, Toto or whoever was before him have been doing these experiments for years. Why have you only just started to look for an antidote now? I know you were involved in the search for them during the war."

He shook his head and muttered under his breath, "You have been sent to try my patience."

"I'm genuinely curious."

"Of course I've tried before...multiple times. But until I saw them recently—actually saw them," he swung around to look at Harlan, "I had no idea what they'd achieved. I'm horrified. It's so much more than I'd imagined. And…" He stopped and seemed to summon his courage. "And I have to admit that I thought I was brilliant, but I confess that I find myself impressed by their achievements."

Ah. So that was it. JD, for all of his brilliance, couldn't work out how they'd done it.

"But you didn't have any of this old research before," Harlan said.

"And I have mere fragments of it now. This will be no easy task." He gestured towards a row of metals on the bench, small and large chunks of what Harlan recognised as iron, silver, copper, and gold, and others he didn't know. His fingers ran across his lip as he stared at them. "It's some ingenious use of these. Some way of fusing them…" His voice trailed off.

"How would the antidote work? I mean, how would we administer it?"

"Too soon to say. Far too soon."

"Working with the Paranormal Division might help. They have labs—"

JD cut him off. "They're not alchemists. They will have no idea."

"They're scientists. That's what alchemists are, right?"

"We are so much more than that." He grabbed his pen and signed the papers Harlan had given him, and then thrust them back. "There you go. How is Mason?"

"Angry. You should call him."

JD didn't respond, instead returning to his work, and Harlan left him to it, happy to leave feeling at least slightly victorious. At least he knew what JD was up to now.

Shadow woke late on Thursday morning, cocooned next to Gabe's sprawling body in their bedroom in the Scottish house. His arm lay across her back, and she rolled over, trying not to disturb him.

She immediately winced as she felt the pain within her chest, and lifting the duvet, saw the dark purple bruise that started on her sternum and spread across her breasts and down to her abdomen. *Shit.* If not for her fey armour, she'd likely be dead.

Gabe heard her stir, and still sleepy, pulled her close.

"Not so tight," she murmured.

His eyes flew wide open at that. "Are you okay?"

"Hideously bruised. Maybe a cracked rib or two." She snuggled into him despite her discomfort, and showered kisses along his jaw. "I haven't been so badly injured for a long time."

He propped himself up on his elbow and pulled the duvet back, his eyes widening with horror at her bruise. "That's worse than last night."

"It's to be expected. Estelle did something to draw the bruise out. It eased my breathing, whatever she did." She pulled the duvet back and studied his face. "What about you? How's your head?"

"Fine. Just scratches and minor bruises now. They've almost healed already." He grunted. "And my pride, of course."

"I don't know why. The Silencer of Souls is a worthy opponent. I just wish I knew what weapon she was using."

"Do you admire her?"

"To an extent. She's fast, strong, clever... What's not to admire?" She teased him. "Not as fast as me, though. I am fey."

"She might not be as fast as you, but she got first strike last night."

"Her weapon gave her an advantage. Something handheld." Shadow tried to remember if she'd seen anything within her clenched fist. "It was metal, I think. Small, whatever it was."

"And deadly. At least she didn't kiss you."

Gabe's eyes always took on a faraway, glazed expression when he thought of that almost deadly embrace, and she knew it wasn't from lust. She had genuinely unnerved him, and not much did. In fact, Black Cronos had unnerved all of them. Which reminded her of the stone tablet. "Tell me about the Igigi. You were holding something back last night."

"Not really." He sank back on to the pillows, pulling her gently against his chest, and she rested her hand on him, feeling the soft rise and fall of his chest. "Honestly, we fought so many campaigns, sometimes it's hard to distinguish them. But no doubt *they* were different. I suppose thinking about it now, the Minotaur we encountered at the temple was of a similar height and build. Some of the Igigi had the legs of horses, some the heads of lions, others the strength of apes. Some had the trunk of an elephant on a human face and elephantine feet. Some had wings and the upper bodies of eagles. Some were intelligent, though most were not, bred only for slavery. It was the intelligent ones who led the revolt, of course."

"Against the Gods?"

"Enlil, to be precise. The God of air, wind, earth and storms, and most senior of all of the Sumerian Gods."

Shadow thought her own world had too many Gods, but Earth's past seemed to have thousands. "He rivalled your God."

He looked at her and raised his eyebrow, amused. "*My* God? No. I worshiped none, even though he was the leader and father of the angels, even the Fallen."

"Which makes him your grandfather."

"Ha!" Gabe's laugh rumbled deep within his chest. "I've never thought of him like that before. But he wasn't, not really. Not in the true sense of the word."

"Why didn't the angels battle the Igigi?"

"They couldn't walk on Earth, not properly. When they fell, the Fallen had to take different forms that were not sustainable. To look upon the true face of an angel would cause madness or death. And they certainly couldn't mate with a human woman without taking a human shape."

Shadow was more confused than ever. "Then why fall in the first place, if they couldn't live on Earth?"

"To encourage descension, distrust, meddle, or, as they saw it, spread enlightenment. We were their servants, bred to do their dirty work as the Igigi were bred to do their Gods' work."

"But you said they were called demons."

"For their appearance, more than their actions, at least initially."

"And this stone tablet? What did you really read?"

He looked down at her. "I need to study it properly. My brothers were right. It is barely legible in places, but what I can read talks of a final resting place. Anyway," he sat up, easing away from her, "we have a plane to catch, and plenty of homework to do."

"We're going to find them, right?"

"Of course we are." He grinned. "We need to beat Black Cronos at their own game."

Seven

When Harlan returned to London, the first thing he did once he'd dropped the contract off with administration was find Olivia and take her to the closest pub. He was putting off speaking to Mason.

She was looking at him now, eyes wide. "JD is doing *what*? I can't get my head around any of it!"

"I know! I mean, he had all these jars bubbling away. What do they call it? Distilling stuff? Precipitating things?" He waved his hands ineffectually. "I don't know. And there were these modern, scientific instruments on one bench, too."

Olivia sipped her wine and stared at him over the rim of her glass. "But it's a lifetime's work...more than a lifetime, really. Do you think Toto is immortal, or has at least lengthened his own lifespan?"

"Possibly. Either that or they have some kind of alchemical apprenticeship where one picks up the work of another, always adding and building. That makes sense, right?"

"Sure. So, what's next for you?"

"Good question. I heard from Gabe earlier. They had a rough night." He filled her in on their brief conversation. "I'm hoping to hear more from him later, but what do you know about the Sumerians?"

"They were fascinating. Clever. There's some very interesting information on them in the British Museum, but obviously there's more elsewhere...Berlin, America. During the Gulf War thousands of ancient objects were stolen from the Iraq Museum in Baghdad. It was heart-breaking. Most have never been found."

"So maybe this tablet came from that collection."

"Possibly. I'm sure there are many private collections that have swelled from those thefts." Olivia leaned forward. "You say they only have images?"

He nodded. "Yes. Reasonably good quality, but they'd rather see the actual tablet."

"Good luck with that!"

"Any suggestions?"

She laughed, incredulous. "Whoever has anything looted from Iraq won't be advertising it."

"But have any of your clients got an interest in that era?"

Her eyes narrowed and she tapped her glass. "A couple. But the tablet could be anywhere in the world. There's a huge interest in that subject."

"Anything you can find will be useful. I'll ask Aiden, too. If I ever see him." Aiden was the third collector for The Orphic Guild, but of the three of them, he travelled the most. "Any idea where he is?"

"Cumbria. On the trail of an illuminated manuscript."

"Maybe I should call him, then."

Olivia smiled. "You don't think you're being followed anymore?"

He looked over his shoulder, and then dropped his voice, teasing her. "I don't think so, but I'll book right back into The Oriental if I suspect anything."

"You just like flash hotels."

"Who doesn't?"

They paused while a waiter delivered their food, and then Olivia said, "I'm sorry to hear that Mason and JD aren't getting on, but I'm not surprised. Mason is furious about Robert's death. He's dealing with it very badly."

"He blames JD."

Olivia shook her head. "He blames himself. He trusted Robert with everything, and everyone knew that." She picked at her food, distracted. "I was in the office with him the other day, talking about my new case, actually, and he could barely concentrate. I asked him if he was okay, and he nearly snapped my head off. Then he apologised, all tearful, and said he hasn't been sleeping." She speared a piece of tomato off her salad. "I tried to console him when he opened up a little, but he won't forgive himself."

"And we had one lead, but now they've disappeared again," Harlan said, thinking of the fight in Scotland. "What if we never get another one? What if that's it, for years?"

"But you said the Paranormal Division had got that professor guy, right? And you thought the order had a mole."

Harlan was so startled he almost dropped his fork. He'd forgotten he told Olivia about the Paranormal Division. He'd blurted it out after a few bourbons when he was telling her about France. "You're right. I should ask Jackson if they've made progress with that."

"Jackson?"

Harlan froze.

Olivia sniggered. "Oh, you should see your face. You'd be a terrible spy."

"Shit. I should have kept that quiet. I should really have kept it all quiet."

"Too late now." She patted his hand. "It's lucky you can trust me. Consider me impressed that you're involved in all of this cloak and dagger stuff."

"It's not all it's cracked up to be. I'm paranoid most of the time now."

"You'll get used to it. I must admit, Jackson's involvement intrigues me." She had another mouthful of her chicken salad. "I always knew there was more going on with him. At least you haven't managed to upset Sam from The Alley Cat. I'm still trying to get back into his good books."

Harlan laughed. "Of course. Your little problem with Caspian and Newton when they tried to trap Harry."

Olivia looked sheepish. "It didn't go as smoothly as we planned."

"He'll forgive you. Eventually." Harlan finished off his burger, wondering how Olivia survived on just salads. "Anyway, I'd better call Jackson and let him know what JD is up to. I feel like my life's gotten very complicated."

She winked. "Just stay off the bourbon. I don't think it's your friend when you have secrets. And by the way, I don't blame you for spying on JD. I know it seems like he's acting for the best, but I still don't trust him."

"No. Strangely enough, neither do I."

Gabe surveyed his brothers, Estelle, and Shadow, who were gathered in the living room of the farmhouse, trying to gauge the mood.

They had arrived back from Scotland a few hours earlier, and Eli and Zee had returned from work. A few of them were playing video games to relax, and he could understand that. It had been an intense twenty-four hours. Niel and Ash had recovered from their injuries, and although Shadow still winced sometimes, she seemed much better. She visited Briar as soon as they'd returned home, and as usual, the earth witch had used her magic to heal Shadow's injuries.

She was now examining her dented breastplate under the light, her lips pursed, and he knew she was planning on visiting Dante, the blacksmith, with El. She hoped he could repair it. They all laughed at her when she extolled the virtues of her armour, but not anymore, and Gabe was never more grateful for it. In the small amount of time they'd been together, his feelings for her had multiplied beyond his expectations. The thought of her dying was too much to bear.

He was more surprised that Estelle had joined them again after a quick visit to her home in Harecombe. She was sitting on the sofa watching Barak play on the console against Niel, amused by their good-natured banter. Although Barak had offered her the controller a few times, she'd declined, but Gabe was pretty sure she'd relent at some point. He wasn't quite sure what was happening between her and Barak, but it seemed to be suiting her. She'd lost her pinched expression—well, mostly—and she and Shadow seemed to have reached a truce, which was something.

They were all killing time, he knew, waiting for the discussion to begin, so he raised his voice to be heard over the game. "Hey, guys! Let's talk about the tablet."

"One minute," Barak complained as a volley of grunts and loud music filled the room, "while I smash Niel's head in!"

Gabe rolled his eyes and turned to look at the images of the tablet pinned to the back wall. Ash was already studying them. "What do you think of it?" Gabe asked him. "Is it genuine?"

"It's hard to know from the photo, but I'd say so just from the fact that Toto has it. He strikes me as a man who does his homework."

Gabe nodded in agreement. "I've been thinking about how we find it, and I keep coming back to the mole."

Ash's head whipped around. "From The Order of the Midnight Sun?"

"We both know they have one, and although Jackson hasn't mentioned them..."

"He must have been following it up," Ash said, finishing his sentence. He smiled broadly, his white teeth looking even whiter against his tanned skin. "We must call him."

"I figure he'll be calling us first," Gabe said, nodding at the tablet. "We've all got unfinished business."

A whoop and a roar of laughter ripped around the room, and Gabe gathered that the game had finished. He looked around, amused to see Barak punching the air, as Niel's character lay bloodied on the screen.

Niel was already complaining. "I demand another game."

Gabe interrupted them. "Later. I need your brains on this." They shuffled around to look at the back wall of the room, and when they'd quieted, he said, "As you know, we found this last night in Scotland, at Arklet Abbey—Toto's place. This was in a bag they were trying to escape with."

"One bit of luck, then," Zee said as he stared at the image.

"Not luck," Gabe replied. "Hard won. It almost killed us. The whole place was a bloody boobytrap."

"And the bitch blew us up!" Niel added, grimacing.

"Have you had a chance to look at these?" Gabe gestured to the images of the tablet.

Eli shrugged. "I had a quick glance at it. But what's the interest? It speaks of things we've long known, and that history talks of. The flight of the Igigi."

Ash tapped a section of the writing. "The first part does. But then it mentions a place that I've never heard associated with them before—Izalla. Have you?"

All of the Nephilim shook their heads, but Estelle asked, "Can you do me a favour and translate it? I know you've talked about it, but you haven't really explained what it says."

"I'll summarise it, because it's wordy," Ash said. "It essentially outlines the revolt the Igigi had against the Anunnaki, their Gods. It tells of a terrible battle in which cities were laid to waste as they tried to escape, and that armies were sent against them." Ash raised an eyebrow. "That would include us."

Gabe added, "We caused quite a bit of trouble, because we had been ordered in by our fathers, and it clashed with the Anunnaki's plans. They wanted their slaves back. We were trying to kill them, and banish them for good. It got messy."

Nahum was perched on the arm of the chair, and he grunted. "It always did."

"Anyway," Ash said, continuing, "the tablet obviously skips details, but says the Igigi gathered together and fled Sumer for the borders, seeking a place to call their own. And they finally found it, according to this. A place where they could live their long life free from persecution...a place close to Izalla. In our time, this city was on a trade route through to Mesopotamia, in the north of the country. It was on a hill overlooking the Tigris and Mesopotamian planes. Anyway, this is where it gets interesting. It speaks of a city of giants in an oasis in the desert. There the Igigi built castles, waterways, and canals, grew vegetables, and bred their children."

Estelle sat cross-legged in her jeans, her arms resting on her knees. "They made a sanctuary? How wonderful."

Barak nodded. "I guess it is. They built cities for the Anunnaki. Why not use that knowledge to build their own?"

"Indeed," Ash said. He paused, as if summoning his courage, and then looked at Gabe as he tapped the image again. "I couldn't work out what was bothering me about the wording on this last night, but I've studied it all day, and I now think this account is written by them. It's their own history."

Gabe's mouth gaped as he stared at Ash. "*What*? You didn't mention this earlier!"

He flashed him an apologetic smile. "Sorry. I've been second-guessing myself. I thought I was imagining it, but…"

"Holy shit!" Niel exclaimed, almost upending his beer. "That means this tablet could have come from that city!"

"Not could have," Ash said. "*Must* have! They would have had a records library of some sort. Or a commemoration of the city being built."

Gabe's mind was whirling with ideas, and he tried to keep things in perspective. "Hold on! Say you're right, Ash, and they founded their own city. That is amazing news. But grave robbers and archaeologists have been raiding such sites for years. Someone could have found this centuries ago and stripped whatever remains were there." He looked around at his brothers, their expressions a mix of excitement, puzzlement, or worry. "It does not mean there's anything to find *now*. And surely, the Igigi are long dead."

"Perhaps the flood swept them away, like it did everything," Eli reminded them.

That immediately sobered everyone. Well, everyone except Shadow. "The very fact that Toto was studying it and tried to hide it means *something* survived. Maybe the city, or at least remnants of it. Their cemeteries or memorials."

"If they buried their dead," Estelle pointed out to her. She addressed the Nephilim in general. "What did Sumerians do with their dead?"

Zee confirmed the suggestion. "They buried them, wrapped in baskets, usually. Children were sometimes placed in jars. They did not mummify them."

"Which," Eli said, "means their bones are probably dust by now. What possible use can the ruins of a city be to Toto?"

A light kindled deep within Ash's eyes as he stared at Eli. "Because it's not just any city. It's the *Igigi's* city. Supernatural, hybrid creatures are what Black Cronos is obsessed with. Toto is interested. *Very* interested. Perhaps he has information that suggests there is something useful there! Like Shadow said, he tried to hide this from us. No doubt he's furious right now that he failed."

The books and notes that were in the bag they'd retrieved were on the coffee table, and Niel leaned forward and shuffled through them. "These are books on Sumerian history, religion, and their myths, and there are multiple notes that look like translations of the tablet's text. But no maps or suggestions of where the city could be."

"I've given them a cursory read," Ash said, "and there are a few notes in the margins of some books that bear further examination."

"Okay," Nahum said, stirring into action. "If Black Cronos is interested, that means we are, too. Our main lead is that they built a city near Izalla. I remember the place well. It sat on a slope, buildings rising on top of one another. I bet that's long gone, too."

"But it isn't," Ash said, fairly humming with excitement now, unusual for the normally reserved Greek. "It still exists. It's called Mardin now, and it's in Turkey. Just across the border from Syria and Iraq." He shrugged at their puzzled faces. "Google is a wonderful thing."

"Have you looked at the terrain?" Gabe asked, always impressed with Ash's research.

"Briefly, on the internet."

"Let me," Nahum said, standing and stretching before heading to the bookshelf where they kept several maps and history tomes.

"What are you proposing, Gabe?" Barak asked, looking amused. "Another plane trip?"

Gabe didn't answer for a moment, instead studying the words and phrases of the tablet, his curiosity piqued. He finally turned back to him. "I think if we can find more clues as to where their city was, it might be worth it."

Shadow cleared her throat. "While I hate to smother everyone's excitement, I think I should remind you that you're talking about a city that disappeared thousands of years ago—along with all mention of the Igigi. How can you hope to find it when archaeologists only discovered Sumer recently?"

Estelle cast her a sidelong glance. "Shadow is right. And you're up against Black Cronos. They must have a lead, and they'll move quickly now that we have this information."

"All excellent points," Gabe admitted. "But Black Cronos still has a mole in The Midnight Sun. I suggest we find him and haul him in for questioning."

"I'd forgotten about him," Niel mused, looking impressed. "But I like that plan. If we know who it is."

Gabe had already made his mind up. "I'm going to speak to Jackson. They must have discovered who it is by now. Maybe they're watching him."

Ash shrugged. "We all want leads. And I'm sure Waylen Adams would fund us, too."

"You'd come to Turkey?"

"Try to stop me."

Nahum called them over to the coffee table where he'd spread the map. "I've found it." He jabbed his finger on the page. *Mardin.* "And it's still surrounded by desert."

Eli was scrolling through his phone. "It's a beautiful place. The old town is a UNESCO World Heritage Site."

Estelle had leaned forward to look at the map. "You're lucky it's in Turkey. Any further south and you'd have been searching a war zone."

Gabe walked over to stare at the map, noting the close borders of Syria and Iraq. "Very lucky. But that's a big expanse of desert."

"But a lot of small towns, too," Nahum pointed out. "And a couple of National Forests. That means a good water supply."

Niel grinned. "Old oases. Excellent."

Gabe was fired up now. "It's better than nothing, but it still leaves us a lot to do to get there before Toto. And to be honest, we can't afford to fail."

Eight

Harlan stared at Barnaby Armstrong's flat, and remembering how he'd been chased by Black Cronos soldiers only weeks before from this spot, turned to Jackson. "This might not be a good idea."

Jackson was leaning against a wall, his coat collar pulled up around his ears, looking like an old-fashioned gumshoe in his well-worn trench coat as he surveyed Armstrong's building. "This is the best bet. We go in quietly. He knows me, so he should let us in."

"He was being watched by Black Cronos the last time I was here. They nearly caught me!"

"An agent has been watching all day. He got home from the order an hour ago, unescorted. No one's guarding him." He winked. "And we've got the door code, too."

It was twilight on Thursday evening, and Jackson had called Harlan a couple of hours before asking for his help. According to their investigations, their initial suspicions had been proven correct. Barnaby was the mole. Large sums of money were regularly deposited in his account, and his hacked emails revealed he had been sending information about the order's alchemy research to an account belonging to someone named Beautiful Mother.

"You know he'll deny everything," Harlan said. "And he may be armed."

Jackson shook his head. "He's a pencil pusher and a sneak. He won't be dangerous." He straightened up, gesturing to the black van parked on the kerb. "We'll stick him in the back and take him to headquarters."

"Why aren't you using some kind of covert operative to do this?'

Jackson laughed. "We are the covert operatives, you pillock."

"That was not in the contract I signed! That was only to spy on JD!"

Jackson grinned. "Yeah, but this is fun, right?"

"That is yet to be determined. What am I supposed to do?"

"Let me do the talking and block the exit. Come on."

Harlan should have known Jackson was going to drag him into everything, and although he wasn't sure that it was fun, it *was* different. Jackson was already striding across the street, so he caught up with him, and together they walked up the path to the flat's front door and Jackson entered the code into the keypad. The door clicked open, and he led them upstairs and knocked on the door to the first floor flat.

When the door swung open, a short man with thinning, dark hair stood before them. He wore corduroy trousers and a knitted vest over his shirt, and Harlan thought he looked like the most unlikely spy ever. Barnaby looked at them with surprise, and then recognition. "Jackson? What are you doing here?"

Ever affable, Jackson said, "Sorry to swing by so late, but I have a question about a sensitive issue, and thought you could help?"

"Me?" Barnaby looked puzzled, and then suspicious. "Well, er, I suppose I could, but couldn't it wait?"

"It's really quite urgent. I've found some documents and really need your assistance with them. I was in the area, you see..."

"And this is?" He stared at Harlan.

"Harlan Beckett, with The Orphic Guild. I don't think you've met."

Harlan shook his hand as Barnaby said, "Ah! Harlan. I've heard of you. You helped us immensely only a few weeks ago. Of course, come in."

For all of his politeness, Barnaby looked flustered, but he ushered them in and down the hall to a richly furnished living room lined with books. The flat might not look ostentatious from the outside, but the inside was filled with high-end antiques and a few first editions, from what Harlan could see of the books.

"Fantastic books," Harlan murmured, pausing to inspect them so that he was close to the door. "May I?"

"Of course, just be gentle with them. Please, take a seat, Jackson." Jackson sat in a leather armchair while Barnaby headed to a side table where he had a few bottles of spirits and mixers lined up, and wiggled the bottle of gin. "Would you like one?"

Both declined, but they waited patiently while Barnaby finished fixing his drink and sat down.

Jackson pulled some papers from his pocket, and passed them to Barnaby. "These are the papers I want your opinion on. I wondered if you could tell me who the recipient of your email is. You seem to have been passing them some very interesting information."

Barnaby was so startled that he leapt to his feet, upending the side table next to him, and sending his drink crashing to the floor. Jackson was still waving the papers at him. "Don't you want to look?"

"How have you accessed my emails?"

Jackson's arm dropped and he leaned back in the chair, the papers resting on his lap. "I have my ways. Why don't you sit, and we can talk civilly?"

"I have nothing to talk about. I suggest you leave."

His eyes darted to the door, but Harlan stepped in front of it, arms folded across his chest, feeling like Jackson's enforcer.

Jackson continued, "I can't leave. You see, we suspect that you are working with Black Cronos, and they are a very dangerous organisation. That makes you dangerous, too."

"Me? Don't be ridiculous. I'm the secretary for the order and a middle-grade alchemist. I have nothing to do with Black whoever-they-are."

"You are a Senior Adept with The Order of the Midnight Sun, privy to the Inner Temple and all of their most secret plans, and that makes you very knowledgeable." Jackson's voice hardened. "I'm not an idiot, Barnaby, although admittedly you fooled us for a long time—and Caldwell, of course. Sit down."

Barnaby's eyes darted around the room, his lips twitching, and then he finally sat again. "You have no proof of anything. This is all ridiculous conjecture. I shall phone my solicitor first thing in the morning."

"How do you explain the large sums of money deposited in your account?"

"I do private consultancy work."

"Then please write down who you consult for, and we can confirm your story. It doesn't completely explain the emails, though. You advised Beautiful Mother that the Dark Star Astrolabe had been found, where it was stored, and the best time to steal it. Need I say more?" Jackson looked around the luxurious flat. "Some very nice goods here. Your betrayal certainly earns you an enviable lifestyle. Tell me, do you feel any guilt at all about Aubrey Cavendish's death?"

Barnaby clenched his hands into fists. "I had nothing to do with that."

Jackson leaned forward. "Of course you did. If Black Cronos hadn't been at the Dark Star Temple, he'd still be alive. They were there because you leaked the information about the Dark Star Astrolabe. The thief was killed, did you know? Blaze. A young man with much to live for."

Barnaby was silent for a moment, and then his eyes adopted a calculating expression. "Who do *you* work for? I thought you were an occult collector."

"I am. But like you, I have a side-line. I'm not a killer, though. You could receive a lot of jail time for your crimes. You might never see your flat again. Or any of that lovely money in your bank account."

"What if I cooperated fully?"

Jackson smiled and leaned back. "That's more like it. Who's your contact in Black Cronos, and more importantly, where is he? Or she?"

"I have no idea! It makes it safer that way. I was just given an email contact."

"But you must have met someone. This can't all have been done over the phone or through email. We're talking about a deadly organisation that certain areas of the government are very interested in."

Barnaby froze, and then a victorious light lit up his eyes. "It was Stefan Hope-Robbins. He kept in touch with me after he left. I agreed with his principles, but didn't leave with him."

"That does go back a long way. But unfortunately, that's not who your contact is, because Stefan has been in our custody for quite a while with zero access to email, and yet you are still sending them and receiving answers."

Barnaby's lips tightened. "Stefan is much higher up than I am. He is far more valuable, and has more information about this. You don't need me."

"You seem to think you can wriggle your way out of this." Jackson leaned in, staring at Barnaby. "You can't. We will track down Toto Dax and his enhanced soldiers, and you will help us. Time to go." He stood, shoving the printed emails back in his pocket. "Let's do this quietly so you can maintain some dignity, shall we?"

Barnaby looked between Harlan and Jackson, and must have fancied his chances. "I don't think so. You have no authority to detain me, and you're not the police! I have no idea who you work for or where you're going to take me. I'm not a fool. You could be working for another organisation that wants to kill me." He stood too, shoulders back, staring Jackson down. "You need to leave." He pulled his phone from his pocket. "Or I will call for help."

Jackson reached into his pocket, withdrawing an envelope with an official seal, and passed it to Barnaby. Even from across the room, Harlan could see the gilding on it, flashing in the light. "That letter is a warrant for your arrest, and it details my authority to do it."

Barnaby eyed it suspiciously and then snatched it from Jackson's hand. Harlan was almost as surprised as Barnaby. Jackson had kept that quiet, too. However, it did make him feel they had insurance in their actions. He was starting to feel like a kidnapper.

Barnaby's hands had a tremor when he passed the letter back to Jackson, and his voice shook as he said, "You'll find you are quite mistaken, but of course I shall assist your investigations. May I get my coat?"

He was already turning to take his jacket from the back of a chair positioned next to his desk, and in one swift movement had put it on, reached into the pocket, and then pulled out something silver. In a split second, it turned into a short, silver, rapier-like blade that glistened like molten metal, and he thrust it at Jackson. Jackson leapt back, stumbling over the chair and falling to the floor. He grabbed a statue on a side table and flung it at Barnaby, catching his arm, and spinning him around. Simultaneously, Harlan darted across the room, tackling Barnaby to the ground. They caught the edge of the side table, and Harlan felt the corner scrape his ribs as he slid to the floor, pinning Barnaby beneath him.

He was still clutching the narrow blade, and he twisted his hand, trying to thrust it in Harlan's face. Harlan punched his arm again and again, and Barnaby lost his grip. Jackson was back on his feet, and kicking the blade away, stood on Barnaby's outstretched arm while Harlan used his weight to keep Barnaby down.

Jackson met Harlan's eyes as he picked up the unusual weapon that had now become a small silver ball again. "Clever things, these. I'm glad we have one to analyse." He crouched down, bringing his face close to Barnaby's. "If you have one of these weapons, you are clearly very important to Black Cronos. You can be sure that we will strip this place and find every secret you have ever harboured."

He whipped a pair of handcuffs out of his pocket, and in another ugly few seconds of furious struggling, helped Harlan keep him secure while he pulled Barnaby's arms behind his back and cuffed him. Barnaby had fallen silent, fury behind his eyes.

Harlan hauled him to his feet and carefully searched his pockets. "I can't find any other weapons. We should get him out of here—just in case he has backup." He studied the comfortable flat and hoped there were no hidden cameras or recording devices around.

"Don't worry," Jackson said, and between them they frogmarched Barnaby to the door and down the corridor to the van. "The team will be searching this place as soon as we've left."

Shadow raced across the fields surrounding the farmhouse, crouched low against Kailen's back.

When she awoke on Friday morning, it was to a cloudy, overcast day, heavy with impending rain, but she didn't care. Her meeting with Dante and El was all arranged, and she was going to ride, regardless of the weather—and her bruises.

She could feel the dull ache in her chest even now, despite Briar's magic and Eli's poultices. As she adjusted her position on Kailen's back, she felt the twinge in her ribs but ignored it, instead relishing the feeling of freedom that being on horseback gave her. The long grass that swayed in the light breeze looked like pewter in the light, and she hoped it would thunder. The weather matched her mood.

The fury she'd been feeling at having her armour damaged had been growing ever since Scotland. And she was still angry that her bow had been broken. Black Cronos, and especially The Silencer of Souls, were proving more and more dangerous every time they met. But she hadn't been lying to Gabe. She couldn't help but admire the woman's skills. And she was determined to find out more about her.

As Dante's Forge came into view, she slowed and finally stopped on the other side of the wall bordering Dante's car park. El was already there, her old, battered Land Rover parked at the side. Shadow dismounted, tying Kailen to the wall and allowing him to graze, before heading inside the forge with her armour. The heat hit her immediately as she inhaled the familiar, pleasant smell of metal, oil, steam, and fire. Skirting around the iron, she joined El and Dante where they stood next to the long bench examining a sword. Dante's powerful arms were revealed by his sleeveless t-shirt, and sweat glistened on his dark skin. His dreadlocks were bound up on his head in a colourful bandanna.

He winked as he greeted her. "Getting into trouble again, Shadow?"

"You could say that. Thanks for agreeing to help me."

El hugged her. "You know we'll try."

"I'm intrigued," Dante said, eyeing the bag with a twinkle in his eye. "I can't wait to see your *special* armour."

He didn't know Shadow was fey, but she had a feeling she might have to reveal it when he examined the metal. She extracted it and placed it under the light cast from the bare bulb. "I better not keep you in suspense, then."

Both El and Dante gasped when they saw the dent in the breastplate. It was dead centre, the bullseye narrowed to a point, the rest of the dent shallower as it radiated outward. It had damaged most of the breastplate, including the engraving in the centre.

El's eyes widened as she stared at it. "What did this?"

"Good question. We're not entirely sure. My opponent pulled something from her pocket, something small, and pointed it at me. All I know is that a wave of *something* struck me. My arm guards have a few dents in them, too. I'd appreciate you fixing all of it."

Dante ran his hand across the surface of the breastplate. "The weapon was invisible?"

She exchanged a nervous glance with El. "Essentially, yes. I should also say that I have used this armour many times, and it is rarely ever damaged. It's made of a particularly strong metal." *Dragonium, predominantly, but she wasn't about to tell Dante that.* Dragonium was a metal only available in the Otherworld, sourced from dragons, and the metal was imbued by the fey blacksmiths with special protection, too.

Dante lifted it and frowned. "It's incredibly light for something so strong. What metal?"

"It's special to the area I come from."

His lips twisted into a wry smile. "I get it. Well, whatever it is, it should respond to the usual treatment." He headed to the fire, Shadow watching him warily. If it shattered or couldn't be fixed, she'd be devastated.

El took her by the arm and led her outside to the fresh air. "Come on. Let's give him some space. Tell me more about the weapon."

El was, as usual, dressed in skinny black jeans and a t-shirt, and her makeup was bold and immaculate. The faint scent of musk and patchouli emanated from her as they sat next to each other on the wall.

"I don't know what to say," Shadow confessed. "As I said, it looked like a small silver device, but it happened so fast, and it was in her hand, so it's hard to be certain. But the wave of power from it was huge."

"Magic?"

"I'm not sure. If it was, it wasn't familiar to me. As you know I'm sensitive to magic and can usually feel it, even in small amounts."

"And these are the alchemists, right, who have been doing experiments on people?"

"Making superhumans, yes, and superweapons. It seems they've been using planets and their correspondences, among other things, but..." she shrugged. "That's as much as I understand."

El frowned. "They must have harnessed power much like we did when we put spells in bottles and other objects for Ghost Ops. I wouldn't imagine it could reproduce it like a gun, but who knows? They're inventive."

"Unfortunately, yes."

"I'm worried about you." El shuffled around to look at her properly. "I know how strong and quick you all are, but against Black Cronos..."

Shadow smiled. "We've met our match, that's for sure, but I think we're frustrating them just as much. And we think we know where Toto is heading next." She updated her on the Igigi.

"Wow! This keeps getting worse and worse. But it's also intriguing. Do you really think these creatures might still exist?"

"Surely not. But," Shadow added, finally voicing what was really worrying her, "Gabe is being cagey about the Igigi. I think there's something he's not telling me."

"He's probably trying to protect you."

"As gallant as that sounds, I don't think so. He knows better. I think he's ashamed of something, or more likely, worried." She shrugged and sighed. "I'll find out eventually. I'll just have to wear down his defences."

El giggled. "I won't ask how. But I am glad you two have got together. Now, tell me about Estelle!"

For a while they gossiped and laughed until Dante emerged from the forge, wiping sweat from his brow with the back of his hand. "That's some unusual metal, Shadow!"

Shadow's heart faltered. "You can't repair it?"

"I can, but I'm having to heat it to a very high temperature. I'll need it for a day or so to finish, okay?"

As much as she hated having to leave it with him, she had no choice. "Of course. Thank you. I'll pay, of course."

"No need. I have a feeling I'll learn something from this metal. If you ever feel like sharing, I'm all ears." And with an enigmatic smile, he headed back inside.

Niel studied the large map pinned to the wall, the photos of the tablet they'd stolen from The Silencer of Souls next to it. Or *salvaged*, as he liked to call it. His lips twisted with annoyance just thinking about her. *Damn woman.*

Ash was next to him, and he tapped the map. "I can feel your anger radiating off you. Focus on finding this place, and then you can get your revenge."

"I want to wring her neck and see the life drain from her eyes."

"Your ego is dented, that's all." Ash couldn't disguise his amusement, and it annoyed Niel even more.

"Yours should be dented, too. We both got flattened in that blast!"

"But I saw it coming." Ash turned to him with a smug smile. "I dragged you back."

"I was seething about the damn demon dogs!"

"Which distracted you. We can't afford to be distracted by their toys."

"Hardly bloody toys," Niel grumbled under his breath. But Ash was right. He did need to focus. He stared at the map that detailed the area around Mardin and exhaled. "Surely the forested areas are more likely...they fit with the story of the oasis."

"Perhaps. But landscapes change dramatically over the years. Places that we knew as very fertile valleys are now deserts. And I bet they're not heavily wooded forests, either. We *have* to find a way to narrow the search, or it will take us years."

Niel sat on the edge of the table behind him. "Then we should get out there soon. There's no other way." A feeling of excitement, but also worry, settled over him. "I'm not sure how I feel about going back to the Middle East. It will have changed beyond recognition. Right now I have my memories of places and people, but those will be shattered once we return."

Ash nodded, wariness entering his eyes. "I've considered that too, brother. I want to see Greece again, but fear I'll be disappointed by what I see. All the places I knew will have turned to dust or ruins. And there'll be places that will have sprung up after we left, and they'll be ruins, too. Whereas here," he gestured around him, "it's all new. There's nothing to compare."

"That's the best thing about Western Europe," Niel admitted. "We never came here. I feel we're beginning afresh. New life, new place. And my memories of the Igigi are bloody…" He trailed off as images flooded his thoughts. "They were worthy opponents. Strong."

"But not all were disciplined," Ash reminded him. "They weren't trained to fight like us."

"Is it a terrible thing to say that I felt guilty about attacking them? I wanted them to have their freedom."

"Of course it isn't terrible. But I'd still like to know how they disappeared so quickly and completely."

He was right. The battle had moved outside the cities and had broken into skirmishes. After a particularly vicious campaign, the Nephilim had withdrawn to regroup, and that's when the Igigi vanished.

"Perhaps," Niel mused, "someone had scouted a place and sent word out."

"But we scoured the plains and hills from the skies—for miles! They must have gone underground."

"An underground city? That's new!"

Ash shook his head and pointed at the map. "Not particularly. Cappadocia and Derinkuyu in Turkey—what was called Anatolia—are known for its cave dwellings. In fact, the authorities think the Phrygians excavated some. It could be something similar. I'll do some more reading. Old myths from after our time may reference hidden cities. What if," he turned away from the map to stare at Niel, "whoever had or still has the tablet had more information on the Igigi's city? That would help us narrow it down, too."

"But we have no idea who that is! And you said there's nothing in that handful of papers we found except endless histories of the Sumerians."

Ash nodded. "True. But the very fact they were taking them must mean something useful is in there. I must study them more closely."

Niel grunted. He liked action and movement, not endless research and speculation. "Better you than me." His thoughts returned to when he'd visited the museum with Nahum. "I wonder if it's worth returning to the British Museum. They have an extensive collection of Mesopotamian objects, including huge stone reliefs."

"I'd love to see them, but I doubt they'll offer much on this subject. Surely, hidden cities and clues to the Igigi would have been mentioned in the display notes?"

Deflating, Niel nodded. "I guess so. I certainly didn't read anything about them, but I was overwhelmed, if I'm honest. Although," he brightened as he thought of how huge the museum was, "I didn't see all of it—not by a long shot."

Ash slapped his shoulder. "Let me see how I get on, but perhaps you're right. A trip to the museum could be useful. And it might explain the photographs. Even Black Cronos would have their work cut out to steal from there." He virtually pushed Niel out the door. "Leave me in peace. I need to concentrate."

Nine

Jackson studied Barnaby Armstrong through the two-way mirror. He fidgeted and fussed, adjusting his cuffs and the collar of his now rumpled shirt as he waited to be interviewed, and the longer he waited, the more nervous he appeared—which was exactly what Jackson wanted.

He turned to Waylen Adams. "He's not looking quite as assured as he did last night."

"You did well to get him. Any injuries?"

"Some bruising from where I fell, that's all." He shrugged it off. "I think Harlan was worse. He hit the table as they went down."

"Was it a good idea to involve him?"

Jackson nodded, knowing Waylen was always wary. But his caution had served him well, and made him the director of the Paranormal Division. "Absolutely. I've known Harlan for a long time. He knows when to bend the rules and when not to. He's got good connections, and he likes the intrigue."

"How does he get on with JD?"

"Same as everyone. He drives him mad, but we all learn to tolerate him, don't we? He's brilliant, and that means we have to. JD trusts him, as much as he does anyone."

Waylen turned back to Barnaby. "What have you got planned for him?"

Jackson grinned. "I'm going to play him off against Stefan Hope-Robbins...just a little."

It wasn't normally Jackson's job to interview prisoners; they had a small team of security staff who did that. They would continue to interrogate him once he finished today. But right now, Jackson wanted information about the Igigi tablet, and Waylen had been happy to indulge him. In all of the weeks that they'd had Hope-Robbins in custody, he had kept infuriatingly mute, no doubt holding out for a rescue that wouldn't happen.

However, they were running out of time. The PD had special authority to question and detain, but only for a limited period. Soon they would have to process Stefan Hope-Robbins through the court and then he, and Barnaby when his time came, would be lost to them—or at least not available for regular access.

Jackson asked, "I presume this is being recorded?"

"Of course. There's a camera in the corner."

Jackson headed inside and sat on the plain chair opposite Barnaby, a wooden table between them. Barnaby's ankles were cuffed and chained, so even if he lunged at Jackson, he couldn't reach him properly.

"Barnaby, I hope you understand how much trouble you're in. Toto's protection is gone now. You're best to cooperate, and try to reduce your sentence."

Barnaby looked scornful. "A sentence based on *what*? Sharing the secrets of an arcane society? That's hardly breaking any laws. You have no grounds to keep me here."

"Actually, it's the fact that you're working with a corrupt, terroristic organisation that kidnaps people, commits experiments on their bodies, and attacks law-abiding societies and tries to kill them. And of course, theft of private property. You colluded with that. And the kidnapping of two individuals in France, and a full-on armed assault against others."

Barnaby paled, but still blustered. "I had nothing to do with that."

"But you do work for them. Stefan Hope-Robbins says you are a key figure in their organisation."

"He's lying!"

"Is he? He says he's known you for years, ever since he was a member of The Midnight Sun, and that you agreed to stay and spy for him." Jackson leaned forward. "And you did, as you worked your way into the Senior Adepts, gaining access to their occult knowledge. Hope-Robbins said you contacted him several months ago with news of the Dark Star Astrolabe and helped arrange it all."

Barnaby's eyes darted around the room before finally settling on Jackson again. "They threatened me...and you've seen how dangerous they are. I couldn't say no."

"Bullshit. I've seen your emails, remember? You contacted them and asked what they could provide for that information. I've seen the expensive furniture in your flat and your bank balance. It will be sad that it all has to be sold off. Unless you can help us. You may get a reduced sentence."

"I don't know anything."

"All I need to know is where Toto is going next."

"No one knows what Toto is doing! He tells no one except *her*!"

"The Silencer of Souls?"

Barnaby swallowed nervously. "Yes."

"Who is she?" Jackson was genuinely curious.

"I have no idea. All I know is that she is trusted and indispensable. And deadly."

"She was with him in Scotland. When they ran, we managed to obtain information about a stone tablet. Photos. We think they're going to the Middle East next."

Barnaby shuffled in his seat. "So, you don't need me, then."

"Where *is* the stone tablet? We'd like to see it properly."

"As I'm sure you can see from my emails, I know nothing about it!"

That was true, Jackson reflected. There were only emails about the astrolabe and the order's plans to go to France. He tried another tack. "But there were phone calls, too, to untraceable numbers. And our team found lots of research in your flat into Sumerian myths and the Igigi. I doubt that's a coincidence."

"I'm interested in myths and legends. There's nothing wrong with that."

"But it isn't a coincidence that Toto is now chasing after some Igigi legend recorded on a stone tablet."

Barnaby snorted again. "He's always searching after anything like that! Mythical creatures that blend human and animal or supernatural strengths are his obsession. He sees them as the supreme, ideal creation. Pre-natural abilities. He even was interested in vampires for a while, until he realised that they were utterly feral and uncontrollable. Above all else, Toto demands control. He coveted the ability of shifters, too."

Jackson was surprised. He didn't think Barnaby would be so well-informed about the paranormal world's creatures, despite his interest in the occult. There was something homely about him, but clearly those looks were deceiving. "You know about them?"

"I know they exist, but I don't know any personally. He's taken some of them, too."

Jackson hadn't even considered that. *What if Black Cronos had been experimenting with all sorts of creatures?* The thought made his blood run cold. "It seems you do know him quite well!"

"Only what Stefan has told me! He was his righthand man for years."

"How did they meet?"

"University, I think. He didn't elaborate."

"Toto is the head of Black Cronos?"

Barnaby's flowing chat suddenly ceased, and he sat back in his chair. "I doubt that."

"Why?"

"I don't know, actually. It's just a feeling."

"Stefan said something, didn't he?"

Barnaby sighed and closed his eyes, as if wishing everything would stop. When he opened them again, he looked resigned. "He just said something about how Toto's ambitions could push someone's nose out of joint. It made me think there was a hierarchy, and Toto wasn't at the top of it."

Jackson tried not to appear too excited. "Can you remember a name?"

"No. It was odd."

"Okay." Jackson took a breath and leaned back in his chair, mirroring Barnaby. "Thank you. You've been very helpful. If you think of a name, please tell us. Remember, it will help your own cause."

Barnaby shook his head. "It's not worth leaving here. My life is forfeit now that I've been caught. The little I know is enough to sign my death warrant." He met Jackson's eyes. "My achievements are over. So are Stefan's."

Jackson felt suddenly sorry for him. Barnaby wasn't old, nor was Stefan. Both were clever men—brilliant in their way, and now their academic lives were finished. "We were friends, of a sort, once. I don't want to be your enemy, but I don't get why you'd want to support such an endeavour."

Barnaby's eyes glazed as he stared at the desk. "It seemed like a dream to create hybrids and clever weapons. To manipulate flesh and matter. The pinnacle of alchemy and magic. Stefan told me what they'd achieved—years after he'd left the Order, of course. I was fascinated. I wanted to help them go further. Now, after hearing about France and poor Aubrey, it seems sullied."

"The reality is more dangerous than you thought?"

"I suppose so. I honestly didn't expect that anyone would die, but the attack on the order's London office did surprise me." His fingers worried his bottom lip as he talked. "Toto seems to control them now, but what if his soldiers rebel? What then?"

Barnaby's night in the cell, and maybe Aubrey's death, seemed to have chastened him. Jackson appealed to his conscience. "Then help us. The paranormal world is weird and dangerous enough without adding some magically-enhanced hybrids employed as someone's private army. In fact, I'm struggling to understand what Toto could want next. He seems to have achieved the perfect balance. His men and women are formidable."

"But they don't fly."

"What?" Jackson thought he'd misheard him.

"It's Black Cronos's next big step, but so far, it's proving impossible. His soldiers don't shift. Ever. They're strong and fast, yes, but he wants more. Always more. The Igigi had wings—some of them, anyway—and he's investigated other creatures that have wings. And then he saw *your* guys." His eyes widened, impressed. "Caldwell told me about the men he'd employed through Harlan. The huge men with wings—Nephilim. Now that Toto knows they exist, he wants to achieve that even more."

Jackson felt a horrible certainty spread over him, and he wondered why he hadn't thought of this before. "He wants to create his own Nephilim?"

"I believe so, but he knows that's virtually impossible...at the moment. But the Igigi are the first step."

Jackson's voice hardened. "Where did they find the tablet?"

"A private collection. That's all I know."

"Here? Abroad? London? *Where?*"

There was another long pause as Barnaby's eyes narrowed in thought. "A few weeks ago, before you caught Stefan, he mentioned something about a visit to Wales. He said Toto had finally found an intriguing clue to the missing Igigi. He was enigmatic. Smug, even. But that was Stefan all over."

"Just Wales? You can't narrow it down?"

He shook his head and fell silent. Jackson knew occult dealers and collectors all over the country, and there were a few in Wales. He might be able to find the right one—with Harlan's help.

"Thank you, Barnaby." He stood abruptly, pushing back his chair and gesturing to the interview room. "I'm sorry about all this."

Barnaby gave a short, barking laugh. "No, you're not. Does Caldwell know I'm here?"

"Not yet, but I'll see him today. Why?"

"Tell him I'm sorry…especially for Aubrey." He shrugged. "He'll never forgive me, but say it anyway."

And then he folded his arms across his chest and stared at the desk, and Jackson left him to his thoughts.

Harlan was in his office studying the files of his recent cases when Jackson called to update him on the interview. He was going to interview Stefan Hope-Robbins, and had asked Harlan to start the search, promising to liaise again in a couple of hours.

Harlan was happy to help. He had a comprehensive list of dealers of occult items, and that included those who bought historically significant objects, too. Many things that weren't strictly considered occult still had interest to the paranormal world, and that included ancient objects that didn't have any magical powers. Professional scholars and amateurs alike were always looking for hidden gems of knowledge, buried by history, and just waiting to be unearthed again to reveal secrets.

He opened up his files on the computer and then decided a fresh coffee would help. He winced as he moved, and gingerly felt his ribs. He was sure he'd cracked some during the fight, but was glad Armstrong had decided to talk. Harlan had volunteered to tell Caldwell the news about Barnaby's betrayal; he felt it was his case and his responsibility, and was planning to head over there soon.

Coffee made, he sat at his desk again, and started to search his database—an admittedly small one when it came to Wales, but three dealers immediately caught his attention. Although perhaps *dealers* was the wrong word. They were collectors, really, with extensive personal treasure troves of Egyptian, Assyrian, Mesopotamian, and European artifacts—all of which should belong in a museum, but didn't. And that meant they were wealthy, too.

He knew Silas Morgan from a deal a few years back. Collectors could be famously cagey about their acquisitions, but hopefully Silas would be reasonably forthcoming. However, five minutes later after a friendly, chatty conversation, Harlan had to rule him out, and with trepidation turned to the next one on his list. An octogenarian called Harry Gibson, who lived in the north of Wales and was famously cranky. As expected, the conversation was short and brutal and he was sent off with a flea in his ear, but also a flat denial. That left Countess Catarina Edevane, a formidable woman who had married the notorious Earl of Breconshire, sharing his passion for history and his collection of illicitly-obtained goods. He was older than her by some years, and in his youth he, like his father before him, had travelled extensively, essentially looting places before that became frowned upon in these enlightened times. Now it just happened in more devious ways. Although the earl was still alive, he was so frail that Harlan knew the countess dealt with the collection now.

The earl's ancestral home was in the Black Mountains, a wild area in the south of Wales, and suitably brooding for such an unusual family. And, from the little Harlan knew of British peerages, it was an old title. He exhaled heavily as he stared at the photos of the stately home. It was small compared to some, craggy and piled with towers and turrets and crenelated walls, but with extensive private grounds.

Harlan had never worked for them, but knew that other Orphic Guild employees had a few years before. Hoping that alone would stand him in good credit, he summoned his courage and dialled the number on their records. A superior voice answered—a secretary, not surprisingly—and he was put on hold before being sent to someone who was impossibly brisk and annoying.

"You cannot possibly be put through to the countess because she is extremely busy."

"Is there anyone else I can speak to?" Harlan asked in his most diplomatic tone. "I just need to ask a question about the collection of Mesopotamian objects that belong to the earl."

The voice cut in, "There are no such things! I have no idea who is giving you such information, but you are sadly misinformed and—"

"Wait!" Harlan interrupted him, fearing the uptight man who reminded him of Smythe was about to hang up on him. "I'm from The Orphic Guild. We have helped acquire such items before, and have worked with the earl in the past."

A loud, commanding voice sounded on the other end. It dripped with impatience, and Harlan fell silent, struggling to hear what was being said. In seconds a woman was on the phone.

"Who is this?" Her voice was silky but with a core of steel, her accent plummy.

His heart pounding, Harlan thought he might be speaking to the countess herself, and he quickly explained who he was and what he wanted. He'd barely finished his sentence when she said, "I wondered if someone else would call."

"You did? Why?"

She huffed, and he heard shuffling, as if she was moving. "A rather annoying, obsequious man visited a few weeks ago with a gorgeous creature who smacked of violence. A Mr Plumley. If I'd have known quite how untrustworthy he was, I might have refused the visit. Perhaps I had a sixth sense, though." She was talking as if to herself. "I sense a refusal wouldn't have gone down well."

"I think I know who you're referring to," Harlan said cautiously, afraid she might slam the phone down on him if he said the wrong thing. "Does he have white-blond hair? And was his companion a woman with long, black hair?"

"Yes, that's them. He struck me as being very devious."

Harlan wondered what Toto had done to cause such umbrage. *Surely it was more than just his manner?* "You're right. He is not to be trusted. Can I confirm that he wanted to see a stone tablet describing the flight of the Igigi?"

"You can indeed. I have no idea how he found that it was in our possession. No doubt records published years ago when the previous earl was a garrulous, bragging fool. My father-in-law, you understand."

Harlan wasn't sure what to say to that. To agree would seem rude. Instead, he just said "Oh, well, yes, your visitor is known for his extensive research. And to be honest, your father-in-law's and your husband's discoveries were renowned at the time."

"Your name, again?"

"Harlan Beckett, a collector with The Orphic Guild, based in Eaton Place." He dropped the location, knowing it carried weight and credibility.

"Ah, yes, that name is vaguely familiar. What do you want, Mr Beckett? Spit it out!"

Harlan took the plunge. "My associates and I would like to see that tablet, too. We believe that it is vitally important."

"Do you intend to search for the location—the lost city it references?"

Suspecting that lying to her would be a mistake, he said, "I believe so, yes."

"Can you be here by tonight?"

Harlan checked his watch. It was late morning, so there was plenty of time. "In Wales? Of course."

"Good. But there are conditions. If you search for it, then I must come with you."

Harlan stuttered, thinking he'd misheard. "You want to come with us?"

"Yes. It is my condition for you to see this tablet. Yes or no? It's quite simple."

"Yes, of course."

"Good. How many should I expect? You said *associates*—emphasis on the plural."

Quickly calculating who should come, he decided Gabe, Shadow, and Ash would want to be there, as well as Jackson. "Five—if that's okay?"

"Perfectly. I can accommodate you all overnight. You'll have to stay after such a journey, and we have acres of rooms here. You're all in London?"

"Some are in Cornwall."

"Even worse! Such a long drive. And besides, we need to plan. See you this evening—and dress for dinner."

Without any goodbyes, she hung up, leaving Harlan's head reeling.

Ten

G abe ended the call with Harlan and glared at his brothers and Shadow, who were clustered in the kitchen for lunch.

"What the hell does 'dress for dinner' mean? Does he suppose I'd go naked?"

Shadow's appreciative gaze ran down him, sending shivers along his spine, and he mentally gave himself a cold shower as she said, "That would be nice."

Niel mimed vomiting. "Ugh. No, thanks. I don't need to see Gabe's bare ass as I'm eating." He frowned at Shadow. "Seriously, keep those thoughts between you two."

She raised her eyebrows and grinned. "Are you a prude? Does the fact that we're having sex—a lot of sex—disturb you?"

Gabe leaned his elbow on the table and his cheek in his hand, closing his eyes in disbelief. *Not this again.* Since they'd started their relationship, that admittedly did involve lots of sex, Shadow had decided to embrace acknowledging their relationship, and now she constantly teased his brothers about it. Fortunately, they tolerated it in good humour—most of the time. Gabe, however, wished she'd shut up. She didn't hear the relentless ribbing he got when she wasn't there.

Niel glowered at her. "No, it doesn't disturb me. I'm a grown man who's had plenty of sex, thank you. But I don't need to hear about *your* sex life constantly."

She pouted. "Poor Niel. Does it remind you of what you're not getting?"

"I could have sex if I wanted to."

"With your hand?"

Nahum, Ash, and Zee almost choked on their burgers as Niel yelled, "*With a woman*! I have my charms."

She raised her eyebrows over her teasing, violet eyes. "I'm sure you do. Certainly, all this cooking would mean you'd make a fine wife."

Gabe intervened before Niel reached for his axe. "Shadow! Please stop, for the love of Herne."

"There is no love between me and Herne, but of course, *darling*. Whatever you say." She reached for her own burger with a chaste expression, although she couldn't resist shooting Niel a cheeky smirk.

"I ask again," Gabe said, trying not to laugh, because Niel was glaring daggers at Shadow, "what does 'dress for dinner' mean?"

Nahum swallowed his food, and said, "It means to wear a suit, or a tux, or something smart. Not jeans and t-shirt."

"A tux? As in, *tuxedo*? Why the hell should I dress up to eat food?"

"Perhaps," Ash said calmly, "you should explain the phone call, so we have some context?"

"Oh, that probably would help," he said, realising he'd been so flustered by the news from Harlan that he hadn't told them anything. He quickly summarised their plans. "So, my beloved one, and Ash, that means you also have to dress for dinner."

Ash's eyes widened. "I'm coming, too?"

"Yes. You're our scholar. I need your brain. So does Harlan, by the sound of it."

Shadow looked relaxed about it. "No problem. I have that black dress I borrowed from El. And the shoes. She told me I could keep them—a gift. And besides, Nahum said I looked sexy as hell in them."

Gabe glared at Nahum. "You said *what*?"

"It was merely a compliment! And well before you two were a thing!" Nahum wagged his finger at Shadow. "And you, stop shit-stirring!"

She sniggered, clearly in one of her more playful moods.

Gabe turned his attention to the most pressing matter at hand. "Well, we haven't got tuxes, but we do have smart suits, so that's something. Not that I've worn one for a while. I guess I should make sure it has no creases." He gave Shadow a knowing wink, aimed more at teasing Niel. "Perhaps I'll like dressing for dinner. And then undressing you afterwards."

"Oh, funny man!" Niel said, standing up to clear the plates. "I won't miss either of you. Stay away as long as you like!"

Ash laughed and checked his watch. "What time do we need to leave?"

Nahum was already searching his phone. "You need to allow five hours for the journey, possibly more for traffic."

Gabe nodded. "Right. We'd better get a move on. Let's pack weapons and enough clothes for a couple of days, just in case. As civilized as this sounds, I do not intend to go in empty-handed."

Barak was in the main security room at Caspian's warehouse, having just supervised the shift changeover, when Caspian entered the office.

He stood to put the kettle on as he greeted him. He hadn't seen him for a couple of weeks, and like Estelle, he seemed different, like he'd shed a weight.

"Have you recovered from your stab wound?" Barak asked him.

Caspian smiled and patted his side. "I have. Briar's magic and a lot of rest have worked wonders. It helps that we've bound the witches' powers, the ones who were behind the attacks. I sleep more easily because of it."

"Estelle told me what happened at Litha," Barak said as he prepared the mugs, presuming Caspian would want a drink. "It sounds like a sad business."

Caspian nodded as he stood in front of the monitors, absently watching the activities around the warehouse. "I hated doing it...we all did. But that's not what I wanted to talk to you about." He looked at him, a smile playing around his lips as he spoke. "I think you're the one responsible for Estelle's recent change in mood—for the better, I should add."

"I'm relieved to hear that. I'd hate to think I'd pissed her off! She can be mean when she wants to be."

Caspian gave a short laugh. "I'm well aware of that! She's asked to do less hours here. It seems she enjoyed the last job she worked on with you guys."

Barak leaned against the counter, hoping Caspian wasn't about to say it was impossible. "She was great—well, more than great. I think we already see her as part of the team. I mean, I know she can't work with us all the time..."

Caspian interrupted him as he sank into a chair. "It's fine, Barak. My own thoughts on our business are conflicted, too. It was a surprise to me to know that Estelle was so unhappy here. I suspect she's been unhappy for years, and didn't even know why."

Barak silently prepared the coffee and placed it in front of Caspian, scared of breaking a conversation that had the ring of a confession. While there was no doubt that he and Estelle had chemistry, nothing had happened beyond him flirting and Estelle tolerating it. *But she didn't rebuff him, either.* It was a dance; one he wasn't sure he knew the steps to.

Caspian continued, "All we have ever been brought up to do was to take over the business. It's been in our family for generations, and frankly, not being involved in it was unacceptable. My father was a hard taskmaster. Unforgiving. I suppose at least he was modern, and was as happy for Estelle to be involved in the business, too. I know my grandfather didn't think that way about women in the workplace." He met Barak's eyes and laughed. "Maybe she'd have preferred it!"

"I doubt it. Better to be involved than not."

"True. Anyway, neither of us has had time for anything beyond Kernow Shipping, and I think that only now are we beginning to see that as a mistake. Now the office feels like a chain."

"I get that, but what can you do? You're the CEO."

"I'm asking my cousins to pick up more of my work, and Estelle's. And we have some excellent staff who can be promoted. I will never leave the business completely, of course, and neither will Estelle. But we can arrange things so that our lives are less bound by it." He sipped his coffee and frowned at Barak. "I suppose I just wanted to ensure that using Estelle wasn't a short-term thing for you. I don't want to see her hurt."

Barak grinned. "Are you asking if my intentions towards your sister are good?"

Caspian laughed. "I trust that they are, and besides, what's between you two is your business. It's more the work. She enjoys it, despite the danger. Not that we've discussed it in depth, but I can tell."

"At the moment, there aren't enough jobs for all of us, but her magic is an asset, so she has a place. Which I guess brings us to me and Niel, and our work here..."

"Already organised. You can finish at the end of this month, if you want. If you guys have enough money."

Relief swept through Barak. "We've got enough, and I've got to be honest, I can't wait. As good as this place has been for us, especially when we really needed it, I want more."

"And you deserve it. You're too good for this role. So, you think you'll have a couple of jobs on the go at once?"

"Potentially. It's hard to say, but there's a market for our services, and the money's good, which means we don't need to work constantly, either. Are you saying *you* want to work with us?"

He shook his head. "No. I would crowd Estelle. This should be her thing. I was just curious. And who knows, I may wish to employ you in a different capacity. Sometimes we have need of more specialised services."

"You'll get good rates, I promise."

Caspian rose to his feet with his coffee. "I'll take this next door. I need to see Dean."

"Sure." Barak eased back in his seat, looking forward to telling Gabe the good news, but Caspian paused in the doorway.

"Thanks for Estelle, anyway. She looks happier...much happier. I hope things works out." And with an enigmatic smile, he left the room.

Harlan accepted a ride with Jackson to Wales, preferring to be a passenger for the long drive, rather than having to concentrate on the road. They'd had a diversion when Jackson announced he wanted JD to have the weapon they'd found, but Harlan had waited in the car while he dropped it off.

"I figure," Jackson said, navigating onto the M4 motorway that led to Wales, "that seeing as he's trying to find an antidote to their powers, the weapon might help. And besides we are baffled."

"You're kidding! Your science experts can't help?"

"It seems not, but there's a lot of magic involved in what Black Cronos does, and our scientists don't really understand that. I'm hoping JD's brain will unlock the secret."

"If he could, he might even be able to manufacture them."

Jackson laughed. "Tucking away a futuristic weapon in my coat pocket is tempting. And I imagine the military would be very interested in such a thing...should they ever find out."

"You're trying to keep it a secret?"

"Until we understand it more, yes. But Black Cronos is already making waves."

"With other government departments, you mean?"

"Not yet. Just within our own. The thing is," Jackson said, glancing over at him, "that for all the years we've been hunting Black Cronos, this is the most information we've ever found in such a short time. In the past, we discovered bits of information scattered around—fragments, that as soon as you had a lead on just seemed to evaporate. Now we feel like we have a real chance."

"Because of the Nephilim?"

"Partly. There's no doubt that their unique abilities—and Shadow's—have helped give us an advantage. But also partly because Toto seems to be the driving force that has decided to push ahead, whatever the cost. His supreme confidence suggests that he feels he will always be one step ahead."

Harlan angled himself in his seat so he could see Jackson better. "Tell me about your grandfather in the war."

Jackson gave a short laugh. "I wish I could, but I actually don't know that much. As I told you in your flat, he was sent into France after the Allied Forces were told about another faction that was operating in France. The Resistance were everywhere at the time, constantly communicating with Britain. It became clear that something else was happening, besides the German invasion. The Resistance were in the hills and countryside and privy to seeing certain things. Some men and women disappeared, and they knew it wasn't the Germans who had taken them. They always made a big deal about displaying the captured Resistance fighters. These guys were *never* seen again. My grandfather was sent in with a special team. They went missing, too."

"I'm so sorry. That must have been terrible for your grandmother and family."

"No more terrible than for anyone else at that time."

"I guess you're right. My grandfather fought too, but he came home. But why did you say that the PD runs in your family?"

"My great-uncle worked for the division, too. He survived the war, and well, I guess considering the nature of the job, the PD likes to keep their circle small. Obviously, we have new members, but if family members want to join and have the aptitude, that makes life easier. I was brought up knowing about the occult and paranormal creatures, although my parents didn't join. I think my father was bitter about my grandfather—understandable, really."

"Any other family members in the PD?"

"No. My older sister isn't interested, so it's just me."

"And of course, you know about JD. Does everyone in the PD know?" Harlan still felt a fool about that. He thought he'd been privy to a great secret, and yet Layla Gould, Waylen Adams, and Jackson knew about him, too.

"Absolutely not! JD insists we keep that information close. He's cagey, not surprisingly."

"He's a pain in the ass! He and Mason aren't talking right now... Although, I think that's Mason's doing. JD seemed oblivious."

Jackson glanced at him. "How is Mason?"

"Pissed off and grieving. But he'll come around."

"Good. So, tell me about this place we're going to."

Harlan laughed. "Breconshire House. Countess Catarina Edevane, the Countess of Breconshire, sounds crazy. I've never met her, but her husband's family is responsible for looting many ancient sites over the years. Especially between the wars, when it was all the rage. I understand the house is filled with ancient Mediterranean and Middle Eastern objects. You know what I mean."

"Stone columns, figures, reliefs, etc, etc..."

"Yep. Back when it was acceptable to have that stuff and you weren't accused of cultural theft. I think that's why the family keeps quiet about it now. They certainly don't want to give it all back."

"So, why did you speak to her and not the earl?"

"Because he's in his eighties now, and she's the one we were engaged by a few years ago."

"Not an alchemist?" Jackson asked.

"Hard to say, but I doubt it. She restored the ancestral home, too."

"They don't live in London?"

"They have a house there, but I'm not sure how often she's there. We only have Breconshire House listed to contact."

"As long as the bloody place isn't booby-trapped, it's fine," Jackson said. "Arklet Abbey was a bloody nightmare."

"I wish I could have been there," Harlan admitted. "Sounds fascinating."

"Gruesome, more like." Jackson shuddered, his hands tightening on the wheel.

"Did you find anything of use?"

"To be honest, not really. The house was full of stuff—furniture and the like—but nothing personal. The study was full of books, but nothing that could provide any clues about Black Cronos. Not obviously, anyway," he conceded. "No personal information like bank accounts, either. It could have been owned by anyone!"

"Except, of course, for the cellar of horrors."

"Yes, that. But everything was stripped bare, apart from the one room and the dogs. They must have virtually wound up their operation there."

"Someone must have been looking after the dogs."

"Well, they haven't been back since. We're still watching the place. But Toto will have warned anyone off now."

"They must have been local if they weren't living there," Harlan mused. "Or they left when Toto arrived."

"Maybe." Jackson shrugged, frustrated. "Anyway, do we know when Black Cronos took the photos of the stone tablet?"

"A couple of months ago. Well before the Dark Star Temple." Harlan considered the countess's tone. "She was unnerved enough by the visit that she expected there'd be more."

"She sounds smart." Jackson gave Harlan a knowing look. "And what else did she want?"

"What makes you ask that?" Harlan hadn't told anyone what he'd promised her, not even Gabe, although he was planning to tell him when they met at their rendezvous point.

"Because people like that—the entitled—think they can get extras."

"She does own the damn thing, and she is letting us see it!"

"Go on."

"She wants to go with the team when they try to find the city."

"I knew it! And?"

"I said yes."

"You said *what*? Ha!" Jackson threw his head back and laughed, almost swerving as he drove. "Gabe will kill you!"

"Tough shit. I made the deal. Without me, none of us would be seeing this thing."

"True. You know, I'm surprised they didn't hurt her or try to steal it."

"She's royalty…or something of the sort." Harlan was always confused by the titles of the nobility. "I would guess that must give her some life insurance. Killing a countess would get a lot of attention, and even Toto wouldn't risk that. And I'm sure she has security. I must admit, I can't wait to see the place. And her. I'm very intrigued."

"As long as you've packed a suit," Jackson said with a grin.

"Of course!" Harlan had a horrible thought. "Please tell me you have one. I never see you in anything but the scruffy shit you're wearing now." He gestured at the old trench coat, t-shirt, jeans, and sneakers that Jackson was wearing.

"Of course I do! A very nice one, too."

Harlan imagined that it was years old with moth holes, smelling of camphor. "Is it double-breasted with a kipper tie?"

"Cheeky bastard," Jackson said good naturedly. "Although, it is nylon."

"You're kidding, right?"

"If I'm not bothered, why should you be?"

Harlan wouldn't be surprised in the least. Jackson seemed like he couldn't give a crap about what he wore or what people thought of him. It was probably months since he'd last had a haircut.

"You're right," Harlan admitted. "But don't blame me if I laugh when I see it."

"And where are we meeting the team?"

"A country pub in Llanthony, on the way. We'll sort out the details then. Has Toto and The Silencer of Souls shown up yet?"

Jackson shook his head, his mouth settling into a tight line. "No. It was like they disappeared into thin air."

Harlan leaned back and looked out of the window. "Sneaky bastards."

"I'm not worrying about that right now. One step at a time. They'll show up again. Especially now that we know about the tablet."

"As long as they don't show up tonight, though I'm sure that's unlikely. I bet Toto and that woman have already left the country."

Feeling more relaxed than he had in days, Harlan settled back to enjoy the ride.

Eleven

S hadow sipped her gin and tonic as Jackson and Harlan settled into seats next to Ash and Gabe.

They were in the Black Dog pub having a private catch-up before heading to Breconshire House, and Shadow was glad to stretch her legs. The journey to south Wales had been long, and not helped by endless Friday traffic.

"How much further is the house?" Ash asked, looking relaxed as he leaned back and surveyed the room. Shadow knew his stance was misleading. His eyes were watchful, and he would leap into action as quickly as she and Gabe, should the need arise.

"About another mile or two up a winding country lane," Harlan said before sipping his pint. "Fortunately. That felt like a long drive! I have to warn you though, I'm not exactly sure what to expect."

"If we're staying overnight," Shadow said, "I'd at least like to think it's safe. The countess hasn't invited us to a trap, I hope." As she spoke, she absently played with the knives strapped to her thighs—hidden by her magic, of course. It wasn't the done thing to stride around with them on display, especially in quaint country pubs.

Harlan looked amused. "I'm pretty certain it's not a trap—unless she's a very good liar. She genuinely sounded put out by Toto's visit. And, in case I didn't mention it earlier, we've worked with her before... Well, not me personally, you understand."

"Tell me about her," Gabe said. "I want to know what we're walking into. And how you found her." He stared at Jackson. "Are you sure Barnaby isn't setting us up?"

Jackson nodded as he brushed the head from his Guinness off his top lip. "Fairly certain. He was rattled last night, tried to get away, and pulled one of their weird weapons on us. But today he seemed resigned to his fate. Troubled, even. I think Aubrey's death has pricked his conscience. He even sent his apologies to Caldwell."

Harlan snorted. "Which were not accepted. I went to see him, and he's furious. And he feels like a fool. He was utterly shocked when I told him."

"Poor guy," Ash said thoughtfully. "He'll be second-guessing everything now. Every conversation, every plan..."

"He's already amending their plans to return to France," Harlan said. "Although, Toto has what he wants from there, I guess. I'm sure he'll have the copies of the old documents that Caldwell took from the temple, too. Barnaby will have shared them."

"Of course! I'd forgot about them," Shadow confessed, remembering that the manuscripts had been split between Toto and Caldwell in the mad scramble as the Minotaur attacked them.

"The countess," Gabe reminded Harlan. "What's she like?"

"From what I can gather, she married the Earl of Breconshire when she was eighteen, and he was in his forties. It was sort of an arranged, nobility marriage. Her father is an earl, too. I doubt it was a love match, but who knows?"

He shook his head, perplexed, and Shadow thought she couldn't imagine anything worse than being married to someone she didn't love. Especially someone so much older. In fact, she hated the thought of marriage in general.

"Anyway," Harlan continued, "it seems she became as interested in the family's acquisitions as her husband. They used to travel extensively. Now, of course, the earl is in his late seventies, and from what I can gather has been unwell for years after having a stroke. She's still fit and in her forties." He cleared his throat and looked sheepish. "Which brings me to the next thing. A condition of us seeing this tablet is that if we search for the city, she comes with us. I have already agreed."

"*What*!" Gabe's voice boomed across the quiet pub, and everyone stared. His face flushed with anger, and he forced himself to lower his voice. "What the fuck were you thinking?"

Jackson retreated behind his pint, but Harlan wasn't fazed in the slightest. "We wouldn't be seeing this tablet without her permission. She gave me little choice. Besides, when she knows what's involved, she may change her mind."

"Which requires us to tell her what's involved!" Gabe looked astounded. "Do we really want to tell our business to *everyone*?"

"She's hardly everyone," Ash put in, trying to calm Gabe down.

"She's a countess! And doubtless will have a million requirements!"

Shadow inwardly rolled her eyes. *Gabe was such a drama queen sometimes*. He was obsessively private, and liked to keep his team small. To be fair, every case they had seemed to balloon, and while part of her understood his frustration, she just rolled with it.

Harlan placed his glass down. "Gabe, can we just meet her first and go from there? She may not be as bad as we think! Think of the goal!"

"That's true," Ash said. "And her family found the damn thing. That must mean they have a more accurate location than we do right now." He raised his pint to Harlan. "I'm impressed you tracked it down in such a short time."

"Barnaby's intel helped. There are only a few places in Wales it could have been. I guess there was always the possibility that it was an unknown, but sometimes the Gods smile on you!"

"But more often," Shadow said, thinking of her own experiences, "they like to screw with you."

Ash leaned forward, excitement flaring in his eyes. "I confess, I can't wait to see the tablet. To think the Igigi found a place for themselves so close to where we were looking all those years ago...it's unbelievable."

"But Ash," Gabe said, seemingly now resigned to Harlan's news about the countess, "what if they *are* still alive somehow? They were our enemies. We were supposed to kill them. I'm not feeling good about doing that anymore."

Shadow felt sorry for him, knowing he'd had sleepless nights ever since the news. Despite all of Gabe's aggression and training, he was always fair.

"Me neither," Ash agreed. "And they certainly don't deserve to be kidnapped by Black Cronos for experimentation. But they surely won't be alive. They'll be dust."

"I damn well hope they're dead," Harlan said with feeling.

Gabe leaned back and rubbed his stubble. "I'm sure they are, but if they're not, I can't see Toto being able to kidnap any Igigi. They're too strong, even for his soldiers. We should help them. Or at least save their remains from being stolen. Anyway," he shrugged, "let's not get ahead of ourselves. We need to see the tablet first. The actual thing may give us more clues."

Shadow looked at Jackson. "I hear you interviewed Stefan after Barnaby. Did he tell you anything?"

"Not a thing." Jackson's jaw tightened. "He's been mute for weeks. It's uncanny. I thought that maybe with Barnaby in custody he would talk." He shook his head in frustration. "Nothing!"

"Surely he's too valuable to Toto to leave there," Shadow said. "He's waiting to be rescued."

"I'll be impressed if they get him. He's in a very secure place. But," Jackson paused, his pint halfway to his mouth, "I guess when he's transferred to court that will be the vulnerable moment. Our special holding powers only last so long before he has to enter the regular system."

Gabe grunted with worry. "Then I suggest you have very good security on hand."

"Come on, guys," Harlan said, draining his pint. "We have a dinner to get to. Best not be late."

Ash nodded. "Agreed. But one last question. If it is a trap, what's the plan?"

"Fight, kill, and see the tablet regardless," Shadow said, relishing the chance to get her own back on Black Cronos. Her chest continued to ache, and her armour was still being repaired. "And steal the tablet, if necessary. Easy."

As they drove higher and higher into the Black Mountains, Ash found himself falling in love with the rolling hills and brooding landscape. Up here, the summer air had become colder, and long shadows stretched across the ground. It felt as if they had left the modern world behind.

Ash had done plenty of reading about British history, and knew about the wars and skirmishes that had taken place here. The fights over the border between England and Wales, the feudal kings, the castles that littered the landscape. It was intoxicating. He could almost taste the past. Looking beyond the winding roads, he could imagine the men riding into battle, the attempts to tame the wilderness, introduce farming, build homesteads. The whole place seemed untouched by time. It might not be his past, but he loved it nonetheless. Ash had been fascinated by the past even in his own time, and the civilisations that had preceded him.

He was sitting in the back seat of Gabe's SUV, happy to let Shadow and Gabe chat up front. Although, they had all fallen silent now as Gabe followed Jackson's battered Volvo off the lane and through huge, wrought iron gates with an ornate design, and what looked to be a family crest: a boar and a hawk placed on either side of a shield. The rest of the elaborate design was lost to him as they swept past it. They wound up a long drive edged by thick foliage that was interspersed with topiary designs. He saw a dragon, an elephant, an eagle, and a unicorn, among others. The gardener was clearly skilful.

The drive led them past a gatehouse and then split in two in front of an archway in a thick stone wall with battlements overhead. One road snaked to the side, which Ash presumed led to more outbuildings, and the other, the one Jackson followed, led through the archway. Suddenly, Breconshire House was in front of them, across a huge, paved courtyard.

"Herne's horns," he murmured, unable to hide his surprise and admiration. "What a building!"

Shadow sounded breathless. "It's like a fey castle! It's magnificent."

"It's a bloody mess!" Gabe exclaimed.

To be fair, Gabe was right. The building was a jumble of styles, evidence that the house had been added to over the years. There were towers of a variety of shapes and sizes, crenelated walls, narrow windows, arched windows, three wings, one clearly Tudor in origin, and an enormous, studded wooden door marked the entrance. Virginia creeper scrambled up some of the walls, and enormous pots of topiary flanked the doorway.

Ash exited the car, his eyes sweeping everywhere. It was hard to decide if the place was welcoming or intimidating. Before anyone could speak, the huge door swung open to reveal a woman with long, chestnut hair and huge, dark eyes, dressed in a figure-hugging, calf-length, dark red dress. She strode forward to meet them, hand outstretched, and Harlan stepped up to greet her.

"Welcome! You found us, then!" She shook Harlan's hand vigorously.

"Countess Edevane," Harlan started, but she waved him off.

"Catarina, for God's sake. You must be Harlan with that American accent."

He nodded, looking amused by her strident welcome, and he quickly made the introductions.

When Catarina shook Ash's hand, she looked up at him, and he found himself caught in her gaze. He had expected her to be older, more severe, but she looked younger than her years, her figure trim, her eyes mischievous.

"Follow me," she instructed as she released his hand and walked back to the house. "I wanted to welcome you myself rather than have Bryn do it." She flashed them a warm smile as they stepped into the cavernous hall. The floor was constructed of huge slabs of grey stone, and the walls were covered in dark, wooden panelling with a fireplace halfway down. "We don't stand on ceremony here—not too much, anyway. I can't be bothered with it!"

"Except the required dressing for dinner, of course," Harlan said, holding up his suit in its bag. "We have all come prepared."

"Excellent!" A challenge was in her gaze as she studied them. "One must have some pleasures, and eating good food and drinking fine wine is best appreciated when one has dressed appropriately."

"I couldn't agree more," Ash said, deciding she was impossible to dislike, and already doubting that they were walking into a trap. There was something decidedly upfront and honest about her that he respected. "You're very generous to invite us to stay."

She laughed. "You might not say that when you experience our rooms with dodgy heating. But at least it's summer. Although, sometimes it's hard to tell up here when the mists roll in. I can almost hear the shriek of past battles when that happens." She turned and shouted, "Bryn! Our guests are here."

An older man with grey hair and a paunch, but wearing a smart suit, stepped out of a room to the right and nodded. "The drinks are ready, ma'am."

"Excellent. Bryn will show you to your rooms, and when you have freshened up and changed, you can join me in there." She nodded to the room Bryn had vacated. "Drinks, dinner, and then business!"

Bryn walked to the stairs that led to the upper floors in a huge sweep. "Please follow me."

Bags in hand, they trooped after Bryn, and Ash couldn't help but think that the evening ahead was going to be a very entertaining one.

There was no doubt that the countess provided an excellent dinner, Harlan thought, as he finished the main course of perfectly cooked roast lamb with all the trimmings and picked up his glass of red wine. *And it was the perfect setting, too.*

Their pre-dinner drinks had been served in the drawing room where they had talked idly about the journey and where they had travelled from, Catarina peppering them with questions all the while. But then she had led them up to the first-floor dining room that had a breath-taking view of the garden and mountains. The room was lined with blue silk and tapestries, candles glinted everywhere, and the table was covered in a snowy white tablecloth, silverware, and sparkling glasses.

Harlan had been taken aback when they entered the dining room, suddenly very glad they had dressed for dinner. To eat in such surroundings wearing a t-shirt and jeans seemed very wrong. Now, half-listening to the conversation about the history of the area, he looked out of the window at the thickening twilight and the garden washed in shadows. The room looked over the rear gardens, and a series of terraces filled with plants led down to a lawn edged with borders. On the far side was a stone pavilion, not as old as the main house, with columns lining an outer terrace. Large windows showed glimpses of the interior, but it was too far to see inside. He could also see other buildings around the grounds, and the topiary continued. A long, high hedge had been trimmed to look like a serpent, and there were also large, clipped balls, pyramids, and even a ziggurat, once favoured by the Sumerians.

The gardens were devoted to the passions of the owners, a curious mix of styles. Classic English gardens set against a wild Welsh backdrop, and notes of the ancient Middle East and Greece. Curiously, it all worked well together. *And its owner was also a mix of styles*, he realised, as he turned back to Catarina. She was a beauty, and probably had blended ancestry. Her dark eyes and slightly olive skin suggested Italian or maybe Spanish roots, but that shouldn't be a surprise, considering her name.

And with increasing certainty, Harlan was sure she was lonely. Her chatter suggested someone who loved company but was starved of it. He took advantage of a natural break in the conversation and asked, "Catarina, forgive my curiosity, but this is a big place. Do only you and your husband live here? And your staff, of course."

She smiled, a little sadly. "Yes, just us and half a dozen staff, gardeners, and there are nursing personnel, too. A team of four who look after my husband night and day. He suffered a severe stroke several years ago and is now bedbound. A terrible tragedy for someone who loved life and travel as much as he did."

"And a tragedy for you, too."

She was matter of fact when she answered him. "It changed our lives completely. I could return to London, but that would mean leaving him, and I won't do that—except for short periods. And he will not move. He wishes to die here, in his ancestral home. Our children visit from time to time. We have three. My son, Arthur—although he likes to be called *Art*—will inherit this place then. I hope he doesn't change it too much. I haven't decided what I will do at that point. I love it here, even though it's quiet."

"You're still young," Jackson said, who, despite Harlan's worries about his suit, looked very smart. "You could do anything you want."

"I could." She smiled at him gratefully. "Still young enough to travel."

"I love it here, too," Shadow announced. "It reminds me of home."

"And where is that?" Catarina asked. "Other than Cornwall. I'm sure you are not originally from there."

"A long way from here. It's also wild and free, full of quirks and secrets. I'm sure there are many here."

The countess laughed. "Secrets? Perhaps there are."

Ash leaned forward, looking ridiculously handsome in his suit, his hair tied in a top knot revealing his strong Greek features, his eyes golden in the candlelight. "You aren't entirely English, are you? Your eyes and skin. Italian?"

She nodded, clearly delighted. "My grandmother. I was named after her. And you are Greek, I think?" At his nod, she said, "I love Greece. A wonderful country with a rich history. I shall visit again, one day. And I think you," she looked at Gabe, "are from the Middle East. I guess that brings us to the reason for you being here. Our tablet."

Harlan's pulse quickened now that they had finally arrived at the subject they had all been dancing around, politely waiting for the countess to bring it up. "I must admit," he said, his gaze taking in his companions, "we cannot wait to see it."

"It will be worth it." She gestured behind her. "It's in another wing, with several other pieces."

"Can you give us some context?" Harlan asked. "Like where it was found, and when?"

She held her hand up to pause him and rang a bell, and within seconds, Bryn appeared. "You can clear the plates and bring dessert."

He nodded, and after silently collecting the plates, he disappeared, shutting the door behind him.

"There." She smiled. "That will give us more privacy, although I'm sure he knows all of this already. My father-in-law, Jasper, participated in many digs in the Middle East, and found this particular tablet, along with a handful of statues, to the east of Mardin. It was in the 1950s, when my husband was a teenager. Anyway, Jasper immediately knew the significance of the find, but they discovered nothing else." Her eyes clouded for a moment. "My husband doesn't talk about it much. He just says that they had to cut their search short."

Gabe exchanged a worried glance with Ash, who asked, "Does he think it was looted from elsewhere and dumped for some reason?"

"He thought it unlikely. It was found with related objects. You'll see," she replied enigmatically. "It certainly excited that unpleasant man the other month."

"Toto," Harlan said, feeling dread at the mention of just his name. "Was it just him and the woman who came?"

"Yes. They certainly didn't stay here." She shuddered. "I know of you and the guild, Harlan, but from the very first phone conversation I didn't like him."

Shadow's eyebrows shot up. "Why did you show him the tablet, then?"

Catarina stared at her glass, holding the deep red wine up to the candlelight before looking back at Shadow. "It was the way he asked. He *knew* I had it. It wasn't really a request. It was a demand, couched in polite terms. I could have said no, of course, but I sensed that would be a mistake." She gestured outside the windows where night had now fallen. "This place is secure. The walls are high, and the alarm system is excellent, but I just knew he was a man not to be crossed. I played nice, ushered them in and out, answered questions, played dumb about some things, and then celebrated when they left."

Gabe smiled. "What did you play dumb about?"

"The maps." She met his smile with her own, and her eyes twinkled with mischief as she looked at her guests. "We had a fire years ago in one of the oldest parts of the house. We have photos that I showed to Toto. The damage was extensive at the time, although it's all been repaired now. I lied and said all the old documents went with it. But they didn't. I have the maps. I have everything."

Jackson raised his glass in salute. "Smart! I'm hoping you'll share those with us."

"In return for confirming my earlier request. You're going to search for the lost city, and I want to come."

Harlan turned to Gabe to see his response, as did everyone. Despite Jackson's involvement and his representation of the Paranormal Division, and Harlan's own negotiations, everyone knew that Gabe was the leader of their group. He met her gaze with his own steady one. "It will be dangerous. They'll be searching, too, and they don't play nice. And when the fighting starts, neither do we. There's a lot at stake with this tablet...this city. Are you sure you want to come?"

"I am dying here as surely as my husband is. I need to get out. I need to smell hot, dust-filled air, feel harsh sand beneath my feet, and taste authentic Turkish food again. I have to come, and I promise you won't have to look after me."

"You could die. We all could."

"I'm prepared to risk it."

Her plea was sincere, and Harlan found that he liked her, and felt sorry for her. She shouldn't be cooped up here, even it was of her own volition. He hoped Gabe thought so, too. Surely, he couldn't back out now.

Gabe was quiet as he visibly considered her words, the room silent in anticipation. And then he nodded. "It's a deal, then."

Twelve

A s soon as Gabe stepped into the long room that stretched the width of the wing, windows on either side, he saw the tablet. It was unmissable, despite the fact that the room was filled with other ancient objects.

The tablet was huge and exuded a hypnotic power. It was at least ten feet high and six feet across, the surface pitted and eroded, the cuneiform text missing in places, and the corners crumbling. It was mounted on a stone plinth and spot lit, casting the cuneiform into faint relief.

Ignoring all the other objects, he strode towards it, aware of the others flanking him. Up close he could see the cracks in the surface that indicated where it had broken into pieces and had been reconstructed.

Gabe was speechless at its size, and clearly so was Ash, because he murmured in Greek, "*Apó tous Theoús. Eínai ypérocho.*"

By the Gods. It's magnificent.

Harlan gave a dry laugh. "No wonder he didn't steal it. I had no idea it was so big!"

"The photos are deceptive," Shadow agreed as she walked around it.

Catarina stood back, allowing them space, her arms folded across her chest as she studied it and them. "It's stunning, isn't it? I come in here most days, and have to remind myself not to touch it and risk further damage."

Gabe half-listened, concentrating on the text, and a sudden vision of the past swept over him.

The fight with the Igigi had lasted for weeks but felt longer. It had moved from the cities to the desert, where the Igigi had the advantage. Although the Nephilim were certainly accustomed to the heat and deprivations of battle, the Igigi were far more comfortable in the dry, arid conditions. Despite their size, they were able to blend in with their surroundings. Men called them demons because of it.

Jackson leaned in closer and frowned. "There looks to be more text here than in the photos."

"That's because there is," Ash agreed. "We obviously only found some of the images. Toto and the Silencer must have split them between them." He cocked his head at Gabe. "Clever. It means we only had half the information."

"There are images on the back, too," Shadow said from the other side.

Gabe joined her, frowning as he took in the three figures with horns, wings, and eagle heads with a human body. "Not surprising that the eagle-headed Igigi should be carved here. They were the most intelligent of them."

"Why do you say that?" Catarina asked sharply. "I don't remember reading that anywhere."

Startled, Gabe recovered quickly. "I must have read it somewhere—I forget the source."

"What does the rest of the text say?" Jackson asked Ash, watching as he crouched and leaned forward. The stone may have been large, but the text was tiny.

"Well, the first part is what we have photos of—the story of their flight and the founding of their city near Izalla. Some sections are missing, unfortunately, either through erosion or because of the cracks, but this latter half adds to those details." He glanced up at Jackson and then across to Gabe, a smile illuminating his face. "I was right. It is a personal history. The tone makes it clear. It speaks of Zu, who led them beneath the earth and into a great cave."

"Zu!" Gabe hurried to his side. "It mentions names?"

Ash pointed to a section. "Right there. He was one of their leaders, if I remember correctly." And then as if remembering Catarina, he hurriedly added, "In that text we found. And there is Urbarra's name."

Gabe remembered Urbarra well. He had a wolf's head and legs, as well as their cunning, speed, and strength. Gabe had got close to him in battle only once, before he made his escape and vanished into the dunes like a djinn. He nodded absently. "He survived...not surprisingly." He scanned the broken text. "It says that although many died, hundreds still survived to build their city."

Catarina sat on the floor with her legs tucked to the side, close to Ash, and studied the text, too. "You seem to translate it easily. You're a scholar?"

"I guess you could say that."

She looked up at Gabe and then back at Ash, her eyes narrowing, but there was also amusement there. "I think you're downplaying your skills for some reason, but I won't pry—yet."

"What about you?" Ash asked. "Can you read cuneiform?"

"No. It was my husband who could, but it took him a while. Nothing like as quick as you. And what about the rest of you?"

Jackson, Harlan, and Shadow all shook their heads as Harlan said, "Go on, Ash. What else does it say?"

"It speaks of the pleasure of building a place for themselves. 'We hid from the Watchers deep beneath the desert, and out of darkness came light, water, peace, and prosperity. The Watchers will not pass our defences, nor shall the Anunnaki enslave us again. Should they try, our response will be swift and bloody.'"

Shadow asked, "Who are the Watchers?"

Gabe caught himself in time, about to say *us*, instead explaining, "The Nephilim. They were often called 'Watchers' because of the responsibilities given to them by their fallen fathers."

Catarina nodded. "To watch over mankind. To herd them like cattle."

Gabe bristled at her tone. It made him feel like a slave master, but then he had to admit, that was one of the things they were created for. "Amongst other things," he murmured.

"The important thing is," Shadow said in her usual, impatient tone and with her hands on her hips, "does it give more clues to where the city is?"

"I need to study it more closely," Ash said, taking his phone out to snap some photos. "The language is ornate, cryptic, which was typical of the time. Even the Igigi were prone to embellishing their achievements. They caught the habit from the Anunnaki."

Jackson was studying the image. "Behind the three eagle-headed men, there looks to be fainter carvings. Steps, perhaps? Columns?"

"Are there?" Gabe asked, annoyed with himself for not seeing that before, but realising he'd been captivated by the text. When he examined the tablet again, he saw what Jackson meant. A fainter carving in the background did show what looked like steps descending to a cavern. "You're right." He turned to Catarina. "Did your husband or father-in-law ever search for the city again?"

She shook her head. "Not to my knowledge."

"Did Toto say anything?" Jackson asked.

"Whatever conclusions he came to, he kept them to himself."

"And said nothing about his plans?"

"No. His excuse for being here was that he was writing a paper on the Sumerian Gods and that he wanted access to as much material as possible. Apparently, he'd found records of Jasper's find in old library newspaper records. We certainly don't advertise this collection publicly anymore."

Harlan smiled. "You don't want to give it back?"

"Absolutely not." Catarina looked sheepish. "Is that terrible?"

"If I thought that was terrible, I would need a new job."

"I console myself," she said, walking around her collection, "by knowing that if they were still in Iraq, they would have been looted anyway during the war."

Gabe tore his gaze away from the tablet for the first time since entering the room and took in the rest of the collection, which was arranged much like a museum. Objects were displayed on plinths and lit with spotlights. Some were encased in glass, and descriptions on small cards were next to them. The objects were a mix of small and large, stone and metal, figures, bowls, jars, ritual items, and reliefs. They weren't just Mesopotamian, either; some were Greek. All were displayed perfectly on the highly polished wooden floor. Mounted on the walls and on long cabinets down the sides were smaller objects, and what looked to be manuscripts and photographs.

Spotting a man-sized statue of a hawk-headed creature carrying a sword in one hand and a spear in the other, Gabe hurried over to examine it. It was damaged, the features blurred by time, the sword broken. He couldn't resist running his hand across the surface. "Hurin Igigi. One of the fiercest in battle—*reputedly*," he quickly added, cursing his slip.

"It's magnificent, isn't it?" Catarina said, gesturing to a few more objects. "These were found with the tablet, too."

There were half a dozen full size statues, plus numerous small ones, as well as the remains of stone columns, drinking vessels, and bowls.

Harlan was already staring at the photographs, and he asked, "Are these from Jasper's digs?"

She smiled and walked to his side. "Yes. Look at all the men. Jasper was an enthusiastic amateur, so he hired an archaeologist, who supplemented his own knowledge. I forget his name. All the excavation work was carried out by hired locals. They spent months in the desert. I know he missed it when he had to return here." She gestured at the room. "This was the old ballroom. We certainly don't throw those anymore."

She walked over to one of the cabinets and opened a door, pulling out a collection of maps and laying them out on a table in the corner. "I removed these before Toto arrived, and it was fortunate I did. He searched all the cupboards." She sniffed. "He was avaricious, and she was just odd. I'm curious to hear how you know about them?"

Jackson just grunted. "Unfortunately, we have met several times for different reasons, and none of them have been pleasant." He stared at the maps she had spread out, and Gabe and the others clustered around them.

They were years old, heavily annotated, and Catarina laid her finger on one. "These maps are from a variety of different digs in many places, but this one is of the area around Mardin. It's riddled with caves and old monasteries cut into the rocky hillsides, and it was to the east, as I mentioned earlier, where they found the tablet...but I'm not sure exactly where. My husband was always vague about it."

"It sounds like your husband was vague about a lot of things relating to that dig," Gabe said, feeling uneasy. *Someone is keeping secrets.* "It's a shame. I was hoping for better directions. How soon can you travel?"

Catarina lifted her dark eyes to his. "I can leave at any time. But surely you need to assemble a team? Men to dig? Secure a permit, even?"

Gabe shook his head impatiently. "We haven't got time for that, and with luck, no one will find out what we're doing. This is unofficial, and we have our own means." *Even if that meant digging it out with his bare hands.* But he had a feeling that wouldn't be the case. "I'll get Nahum to make the arrangements."

"Then I," Ash said, returning to the tablet, "will spend the next few hours here, working on the text."

Gabe nodded, eyes sweeping over the photographs and documents. "Good. And we'll try to glean any clues we can from these."

Catarina nodded. "In that case, I'll get Bryn to bring us more coffee and drinks here. It could be a long night."

Thirteen

Nahum ended the call with Gabe and stared at the map on the wall in the living room, his finger tracing the area to the east of Mardin.

They would need a hotel, somewhere small and unassuming where no one would notice their odd hours...unless they could camp in the desert.

"Well?" Niel asked, pausing his game with Zee as they ended a fight scene. "How are they getting on?"

Nahum sat on the sofa and reached for his beer. "Catarina has been very helpful, and we now know we need to search to the east of the city. I need to find us a base."

"It wasn't a trap, then?" Zee asked, putting the controller down and turning his back on the TV. "That's a relief."

"She sounds like an interesting woman," Nahum admitted, "but Gabe couldn't really talk properly. It sounded as if they were all together and have a long night ahead. The countess kept information back from Toto, so we might even have a head start."

"I guess that's something," Niel said. "But it's still a long shot. The city must be rubble by now."

"Maybe not. The tablet survived, and so have several other relics."

"And," Zee added, "the dry desert conditions can help preserve things."

A gleam of intrigue kindled in Niel's eyes. "I'm willing to search, anyway—despite my reservations about going there."

A troubled looked crossed Zee's face. "I'm worried that nothing will be the same. In fact, it's likely to be unrecognisable."

"I've considered that," Niel said, placing his long legs on the coffee table and reclining in his chair, "but it's like an itch I have to scratch."

"Even if it destroys our memories?" Nahum asked, interested in the fact that all of them were worried about returning, switching between excitement and trepidation. Interesting though their new life was, his thoughts often returned to their old one, especially at night when sleep refused to come. Whilst some memories were painful, others were comforting.

"Memories," Niel said abruptly, "cannot be destroyed! They're still up here." He tapped his head. "I have many that I return to...and many I shouldn't."

"Lilith?" Nahum asked, knowing how he still thought of her.

Niel huffed and nodded. "Yes. Lilith." Her name came out as a sigh.

Nahum had loved a few women in his lifetime, some with a passion he thought would never die, but he wasn't sure he had loved as deeply as Niel. Her death burned him, even now.

"Perhaps," Zee said gently, "it is time to put those memories aside, brother."

Niel stared at his beer glass. "Easier said than done. Maybe that's why I need the desert. Perhaps I can forget her there."

"It made no difference at the time," Nahum reminded him, cursing himself for mentioning her name. He could see where this was going, and so did Zee, from the concerned glance he shot Nahum. They needed to snap Niel out of it. "Let's focus on the present and stopping Toto."

"And killing The Silencer of Souls," Zee put in. "You have a score to settle, remember?"

"Like I'd forget," Niel said, rousing himself.

"And perhaps," Nahum ventured, "you need another woman to take your mind off Lilith."

Niel met his eyes with a baleful stare. "That never worked before."

"But it might work now. The trouble," Nahum said, thinking of Gabe and Shadow, "is that some of our brothers are moving on with their lives, while some of us are not. Gabe, Eli, and Barak are doing just fine."

Zee rolled his eyes. "Because they've found a woman—or *women*, in Eli's case..."

"Nothing new there," Niel pointed out. "Lover boy has always preferred a harem."

"But my point is that I'm doing just fine," Zee continued, "woman or not! It's about mindset!" He looked at Nahum with a frown. "And you're okay, too! Niel, seriously," he glared at his brother, "stop it! You get into these maudlin moments and reminisce about the good times. But they weren't all good with Lilith. Far from it!"

Nahum froze. *Zee was actually going there.*

"What does that mean?" Niel asked, a dangerous edge to his voice as he sat up.

Zee held his gaze. "You know what it means. You argued and fought. You were incensed when she started to practise magic! You said she meddled with the Gods' powers, and it would end badly. Then she abandoned you for months when she retreated to the hills with the local magi to enhance her skills. She drove you insane!"

Niel leapt to his feet, fists clenched. "That is not true."

Zee refused to stand. Instead, he leaned back in his chair, regarding Niel coolly. "You know it is. I also know you loved her and forgave her. But she wasn't perfect. No one is. What I'm saying is, keep things in perspective."

"I am." Niel's voice was almost a growl.

"You're not. You never do with her. You've always put her on a pedestal. Until you take her off it, you'll never love again."

Nahum hoped he wouldn't have to leap up to stop Niel from lunging for Zee. *Not that Zee needed his help.* He looked up at Niel defiantly, refusing to back down.

After what seemed like endless minutes of tension, but was in fact mere seconds, Niel said, "Screw you, Zee," before marching out of the room, slamming the door behind him.

"For fuck's sake," Nahum said, glaring at Zee. "What were you thinking?"

Zee grunted. "What we all think. Did you disagree?"

Nahum buried his head in his hands. "No. She's his blind spot. Always has been."

"We do him no favours by not addressing it. I decided it was time."

"He may never speak to you again."

"Of course he will. Eventually." Zee picked up the game's controller and turned back to the TV. "Want to play?"

"No. I need my bed. But I don't want to run into Niel upstairs."

Zee grinned broadly and threw him the other controller. "Then give him some space."

Shadow surveyed her companions over breakfast on Saturday morning, wondering if they would be spending all day searching through the relics and photos again. While it was interesting for a few hours, she really couldn't get as excited over them as Gabe and Ash.

They were both preoccupied even now, Ash poring over the notes he'd made that were propped next to his plate. Catarina was next to him, asking questions and nodding to his answers. Gabe was obviously only half-listening, lost in his own thoughts. He'd had a restless night. Harlan and Jackson were seated opposite them, also chatting quietly, heads together. Sighing, Shadow looked out of the window at the mist-filled landscape outside. Perhaps she'd go exploring. The Black Mountains' brooding wildness called to her. *If only she had Kailen with her...*

Her thoughts were interrupted when Harlan said, "Hey, Shadow. I heard from JD this morning. He wants to know if you can spare him some time today."

She frowned, automatically suspicious. "Why? I don't trust that funny little man."

Harlan smirked. "Neither do I, but he's been examining one of Black Cronos's weapons, and has a theory he wants you to test."

"Weapons? Now *that* sounds more interesting. Why me and not them?" She jerked her head at Gabe and Ash.

He lowered his voice and leaned close so Catarina couldn't hear. "Your fey magic intrigues him."

"As it should," she acknowledged breezily. "But what does he want me to actually do?"

"He didn't exactly spell it out, Shadow! You know JD! We're both leaving soon. There's nothing else me and Jackson can do here. Do you want to come? Weapons are your favourite hobby, right?"

Shadow studied his amused expression. "You just want to know what JD is up to."

"Of course! Don't you? But then, if studying old stones all day are your thing..."

She quickly made her up her mind. "No, it is not! But how will I get back home?"

"I'll drive you there if necessary. Coming?"

"Hold on." She nudged Gabe, who hadn't been listening. "Are you planning on staying here all day?"

He looked bewildered as he focussed on her question. "Er, yes, I think so. Or at least for the next few hours. There's a lot more I want to study before we leave."

"In that case, I'm leaving with Harlan. JD wants to see me. When are we flying to Turkey?"

"It depends on what Nahum has managed to organise. Tomorrow, maybe? Or Monday?"

Jackson intervened with his opinion. "We can't wait much longer than that."

"You want to come, too?" Gabe asked, alarmed. "I'm not sure that's a good idea."

"Of course I'm coming! I'm the ears and eyes of the PD."

"I thought that was our job now?" Gabe said, bristling. "Or don't you trust us?"

Ash and Catarina had fallen silent as they listened to the exchange.

"You know we trust you," Jackson remonstrated. "But this is of national interest. I need to be there."

Shadow knew Gabe wanted to keep the numbers down. Jackson's presence, and Catarina's, meant babysitting the non-paranormals.

Gabe groaned. "Harlan? Are you wishing to grace us with your presence, too?"

"You know what?" he drawled, taking in Gabe's resigned expression. "I don't think I will! Being almost killed last time was bad enough. I'm sure I'll keep busy here."

"Thank you!" Gabe said with exaggerated patience.

"In that case," Shadow said, rising to her feet, "I'll pack now and arrange to get back to Cornwall before you leave." She wagged a finger at Gabe. "Make sure you don't leave without me!"

He winked and blew her a kiss, and she swayed her hips as she left the room. That would leave him something to think about.

The ensuing journey to JD's home was uneventful, the time spent talking about the tablet and the photos of the old expeditions. Harlan in particular seemed quite enamoured of the old-fashioned clothing and the romanticism attached to the digs, especially those between the wars. She listened rather than talked, a useful way of extending her knowledge about her new world. She thought she would have liked that time period, if not for the horrendous sexism and racism. One of the many things she didn't have to tolerate in her own world.

When they arrived at JD's, Jackson exited the car with them, but Anna kept them at the front door, eyeing him suspiciously. "JD didn't say *you* were coming."

"I gave him the damn weapon," Jackson said, irate. "And I'm their lift!" He nodded to Shadow and Harlan.

Shadow was both amused and impressed. Jackson had a way of inviting himself into all sorts of things. It was quite a skill. Anna, however, was quite the guard dog, and was clearly undecided about letting him in. Harlan appealed to her on Jackson's behalf. "He's in the PD, Anna, you know that. Come on! He's not staying long."

Anna rolled her eyes and ushered them all in, saying to Harlan, "He's downstairs. You know the way."

She shut the door, and walked towards the back of the house, leaving them all looking at each other, amused.

Harlan lowered his voice. "I don't think she likes us much. Follow me. And don't touch anything, or she'll have something else to moan about."

"I'm a delight," Shadow said as she followed him down the hall and through a heavy wooden door. "There's something clearly wrong with her. Where are you leading us?"

"Back in time," Harlan murmured enigmatically as he led them downstairs into a huge room.

Shadow paused on the threshold, hands on her hips as she took in the space.

Jackson was similarly impressed, muttering, "Bloody hell," beneath his breath as he took in the old-fashioned laboratory.

"Excellent," JD's voice boomed out, startling Shadow. He straightened from behind a series of test tubes and bottles, all bubbling and emitting steam. "You made good time!"

"The traffic was good," Harlan explained as he headed to his side. "You've had success, then?"

"Reasonably!" He wiggled his hand. "My dear." He beamed at Shadow. "Thank you so much for coming." It was the most cheerful she had ever seen JD, which made her instantly suspicious, but JD called her over. "This way!"

Shadow weaved between the long benches, eyeing the bubbling jars with distrust. The room was warm from the heat of the burners, and in the far wall she spotted a fireplace, the coals glowing, and she was glad she only wore her jeans and t-shirt.

JD was standing in the corner of the room next to a large, round table entirely inlaid with an ornate, geometric grid. It seemed to have interlocking parts, and the many concentric rings of symbols could be moved so that different sections aligned. Unnervingly, it emitted a strange power—a low hum that made the air around it shimmer.

Shadow kept her distance. "What is that?"

"This is my alchemical grid of correspondences." His chest swelled as it always seemed to when he was pleased with himself. "It's complicated and took years—*years*—to perfect."

"Complicated?" Harlan almost stuttered. "It's nuts!"

JD shot him an impatient look. "It most certainly is not *nuts*. It's a highly systematic grid that allows me to move the various parts into almost endless matches.

There are rings of planets, metals, angels, cardinal signs, months, days, astrological signs, gemstones, and metals, and many things you would not possibly understand."

There was no doubt about that. Shadow had a headache just looking at it. But there was also no doubt that it was a work of art. Inlaid with an intriguing number of materials, it would have taken decades to complete. Or an army of skilled men. She lifted her eyes to find JD still staring at it with pride and asked, "You made this? All on your own?"

"Of course! It has enabled me to unlock this." JD opened his palm to reveal a small, spherical object in a silver material. "This is a knife."

"It doesn't look like one," Shadow said.

Jackson huffed. "It belonged to Barnaby. He did something to it and nearly stabbed me with it."

Realisation dawned as Shadow remembered being attacked by Black Cronos's soldiers. "But they all seemed to pull weapons out of thin air! I didn't see them holding anything like this."

JD shrugged. "Maybe something was tucked into their clothing or armour. Or maybe there are more weapons we have yet to discover. But I think I know how this one works."

"So soon?" Harlan asked, looking doubtful.

JD snorted. "I used my centuries of experience to analyse this." He placed the silver sphere into the centre of the geometric grid, and the sphere shimmered and morphed into a long, sleek, double-edged blade with a simple hilt.

Harlan gasped. "Holy shit! How did that happen?"

JD puffed his chest out as he preened. "I attuned the correct planetary signatures and correspondences. It took a while, admittedly. I had to play around with a variety before it worked. But..." his face fell as he picked up the knife. Instantly, it reverted to its spherical shape in his palm. "It won't last."

Jackson leaned in. "Interesting. Why not?"

"Because I need to be attuned to it!" JD looked both annoyed and impressed.

"A personalised weapon! Very cool."

"But," Harlan pointed out, "this was Barnaby's and he's human, so how does that work?"

JD rubbed his chin as he placed the knife back on the grid where it immediately changed shape again. "I'm not sure. Perhaps it was designed around his aura, or energy signature."

"So that," Jackson pointed at the grid, his eyebrows beetling together with concentration, "is Barnaby's energy reading?"

"Possibly." He shrugged. "Probably."

Still too many questions, as far as Shadow was concerned. "The superhuman soldiers had lots of enhanced abilities. Does Barnaby?"

Harlan looked at Jackson for confirmation. "He didn't seem to. We overpowered him with reasonable ease...once we got rid of the weapon."

Jackson nodded. "Agreed. The trouble is, we found no weapons from the soldiers. They disappeared with their death, or upon leaving their hands. Infuriating."

Shadow was barely listening as she stared at the sleek blade. "I like that! May I?"

"Be my guest."

Shadow picked it up, but although it held its shape longer for her, within moments it had reverted to the sphere again. "Herne's hairy balls! It's gone!"

JD slapped the bench next to him. "A pox on it! I had hoped that you would be the key."

Disappointed, Shadow still marvelled at the lightness of the sphere. "This is almost weightless. It's incredible!" She looked at JD. "How do we make it work?"

"That is the question! Potentially that particular weapon will never work for us because it's so personalised. Unless perhaps we align you to it, or try to change it to align with you?"

Harlan looked sceptical. "Change Shadow? Isn't that dangerous?"

JD spread his hands wide. "I doubt it. Was Barnaby ill in any way?"

"Not while I was interviewing him," Jackson said.

"Hmm." JD's fingers drummed on the bench. "It's not a physical change. Nothing as dull as DNA. It's about attuning your body. The more I think on it, the more I feel this is aura-based technology."

Shadow dropped the sphere back on the grid, watching it morph again. "No. I do not wish to have my aura changed." She stared at JD. "My fey magic is part of me. It allows me to shield my weapons, move silently, blend into the landscape when I choose, and makes me fast. I will not risk that. But you can make it fit me."

JD's eyes narrowed. "Have you any weapons hidden now?"

She whipped one of her knives out from the sheath on her thigh, and it popped into view in her hand.

Jackson jumped back. "Bloody hell! Where the fuck did you pull that from?"

She smirked. "I am fey."

Harlan smirked, too. "I love it when you do that!"

"So, the question is," JD said, as he took the knife from her hand, "how do we achieve this. Can you stay?"

"For a day, maybe two, but that's all."

JD beamed. "Excellent. I'll get Anna to make you a room up and then we shall begin in earnest. You two may go," he said dismissively to Harlan and Jackson.

"Can't we watch?" Harlan asked, obviously disappointed.

JD stared at him, a calculating expression in his eyes. "You may stay if you wish to participate. But only you. I cannot focus with too many people around."

Harlan grinned with relief, but Jackson rolled his eyes. "I get it. But will you share your findings?"

JD sniffed. "I'm sure an arrangement can be made."

"Thought so," Jackson grunted. "Come and get your bags then, guys." His eyes swept the room. "And be careful."

Fourteen

Ash sat back on his heels and sighed, the tablet's bulk looming above him. His eyes ached and his head buzzed with what felt like a million questions—questions that would not be resolved right now.

It was early on Saturday afternoon, and he and Gabe had been studying the antiquities since breakfast. The room was a fascinating treasure trove, and Ash loved nothing more than wrestling with their secrets. Unfortunately, the tablet was hanging on to some of them.

Ash had taken a few breaks to examine other objects, particularly fascinated with the photos of the digs. Catarina had offered to make copies of the ones they deemed most important. Gabe had also been taking photos to show their brothers. His eyes swept around the room again as he sat on the worn wooden floor, sipping water. The objects found with the tablet had been pieced back together, like the tablet, but the smaller statues were less damaged. *But if Jasper's team hadn't found the city, where had they come from?*

Catarina entered through the huge doors carrying a tray, announcing, "I've brought coffee and cake, if you're interested. My cook has made baklava and Turkish delight."

Ash lifted his head and sniffed, catching the rich smell of honey and nuts, and he quickly rose to his feet. "It smells wonderful."

She gave him a beaming smile, and once again Ash was struck by how unexpectedly attractive she was. He'd imagined someone older, stuffier, yet she was vibrant and vivacious—despite her sometimes-brusque manner. "My cook does a wonderful job, but I can't wait to get out there and buy locally."

"You and me both," Gabe admitted as he joined them. His hands were dusty, and a smear of ink streaked his cheek.

Catarina poured their coffee from the silver pot, and Ash smelled cardamom. "Arabic coffee?"

"The best." She handed him a tiny porcelain cup decorated with Arabic designs. "I hope it measures up."

Ash took a sip and sighed with pleasure. "Excellent. We make it at home sometimes. My brother particularly likes it when he smokes the hookah."

"Your brother?" She eyed them both curiously. "Just the one?"

Gabe laughed. "There are seven of us. It's quite the houseful."

"And Shadow?" she asked.

"Yes, her too. Not related, obviously," Gabe added hurriedly.

"I should hope not." Catarina had an impish grin on her face. "Your relationship would be scandalous. But I'm curious," she added, her smile slipping. "You, Ash, are Greek, and Gabe, you're not, so why call yourself brothers?"

Ash answered that easily. "We are good friends...very good. So we might not be blood brothers, but our past experiences bind us."

She pulled a stool from under the bench and sat down, and Ash and Gabe followed suit. "I understand," she said, sipping her aromatic drink. "Experiences I had in the desert meant we bonded closely—and argued intensely sometimes, too."

"Don't get me started," Gabe muttered, prompting a laugh from both of them.

Catarina proffered the sweets. "Please take one. I hope they don't disappoint."

"They certainly don't," Ash said, savouring the rich taste of the baklava. He asked something that had been bugging him all morning. "Will you be bringing security with you? A bodyguard? Or a secretary?"

Catarina looked appalled. "Absolutely not! I am not royalty, and can't abide being followed around by anyone. The size of the estate demands we have staff, but that's all. No, I travel alone. Besides," her eyes ran over them, "with you two with me, I doubt I'll need security. Are your brothers of the same build?"

Ash nodded. "They are."

She nibbled on a Turkish delight, the icing sugar dusting her chin, and she absently brushed it off. "I'd like to pay for the hotel."

"It's all sorted," Gabe told her. "Save your money."

"No. This is my way of thanking you for bringing me along." She cast her eyes to the floor briefly. "I know that what I ask is an imposition, but I've always had the feeling that the dig was unfinished business."

Gabe's eyes narrowed. "You're holding out on something."

"Not me, my husband." She studied them again, searching their faces as if wondering whether to trust them. And then she shook her head, brushing a lock of hair from her cheek. "Why is this city so important? You haven't really said."

Ash noted the stubborn lift of her jaw and her intense stare. She was too intelligent to fob off. And she was being incredibly generous and helpful. He turned to Gabe, who had fallen silent. "We may as well tell her. She'll know soon enough."

He reached for another slice of baklava. "Go on, then."

He turned back to Catarina to find her watching him avidly. "You know the myths about the Igigi and the Anunnaki, I presume?"

"Of course! I've read on them extensively. This find prompted my curiosity."

"Do you believe the Igigi are supernatural beings?"

"I believe that many thought them to be, but that myth has transformed them from powerful men and women into something else. Like the Egyptians, the images aren't real. They're art!"

"But what if they *were* real, a hybrid mix of human and beast, their bodies hidden within the city—and within them are secrets to their supernatural abilities? That is what Black Cronos believes."

Her face was pale, her coffee forgotten. "And you?"

"We believe it, too. The city—and their bodies—could hide many secrets. Secrets Toto wishes to exploit."

Catarina fell silent for a long time before she answered, but when she did, she seemed resolute. "I'm taking you to see my husband."

Gabe surveyed the man in the bed and suppressed a shudder. To end up like this would be a terrible fate.

He'd seen photos of Hugo Edevane when he was a tall, imposing man with a thick sweep of blond hair and a piercing gaze. But now he was shrunken, weak, and his right cheek and lip dropped from the effects of the stroke. *Fate was sometimes a cruel mistress*. He hoped his father's angelic status and their ability to heal meant that this never happened to him.

And the room he resided in didn't fare much better. It was elegant—high ceilings, beautiful mouldings—but it was filled with medical paraphernalia, and it smelled of age and impending death. *Surely*, Gabe thought, *he couldn't have long left*. He looked as if he were hanging onto life by a thread.

Catarina hovered by the head of the bed, where Hugo was propped up on multiple pillows. "Hugo, these are the men I was telling you about."

Gabe shook the earl's hand, wondering just how he should address him. He opted for a brusque, "Good to meet you, your lordship."

The earl's eyes were keen, but his grip was weak, as was his voice. "Forget that," he rasped, his voice thick and tricky to understand because of his stroke. "Call me Hugo."

Once the introductions were made, he and Ash settled in a seat. Hugo tried to speak and then wheezed, which set him off in a fit of coughing. Finally, he said, "You seek the city of the Igigi—Enamtila."

Gabe jolted with surprise. "You know its name?" He looked at Ash, confused, but he appeared just as baffled. "How?"

"I'll come to that. Tell me why you're looking for it."

Gabe was glad he was getting to the point. He'd wondered if they would have to spend hours waffling about nothing, but guessed that was impossible for Hugo now. Even sustaining a short conversation was an effort. "It's vitally important that we find it before anyone else."

"I'd suggest you don't go, but you look like men who are not easily swayed."

"We're not."

"Even if I tell you that finding it might kill you?"

"Why would it kill us? It's just ruins, isn't it? And," Gabe added, curious to see Hugo's response, "you found only remnants...not the city itself."

Hugo stared at Gabe and Ash, a flicker of fear behind his eyes. "I know what my wife has told me, but I want to hear it from you. Why the sudden interest in a place that has been lost for millennia?"

Ash answered. "Because of what the Igigi were. Supernatural hybrid creatures created by the Anunnaki. Some say they have the blood of the Gods. Someone wants to exploit that, and that would be a disaster."

Hugo wiped away a tear from his watering eyes, a result of the stroke. "How would they do such a thing? That would seem impossible."

"Alchemy and magic," Gabe answered bluntly. "It may sound improbable, but it isn't."

Hugo didn't laugh or scoff. "You will stop it?"

Ash nodded. "If we can. We have resources."

Hugo fell silent for a moment, sagging against his pillows, but Gabe was sure there was more to come. He looked haunted, and eaten by indecision.

Gabe leaned forward, arms on his knees. "Something happened, didn't it? You actually found the city."

Hugo sighed, closing his eyes briefly. "We found the entrance. That's where the tablet and statues were. Although, we didn't know it was the entrance at the time. It was a shallow cave, high in the hills, and very remote. Everything was in pieces, and we didn't realise at first, obviously, what we'd found." He paused to get his breath. "But then when we understood what the tablet said, we set up camp and started to explore in earnest. We were there for weeks. After an unexpected storm, the rain changed everything. The cave flooded, streams and waterfalls were everywhere. It was...bewildering. But it triggered a rockfall, revealing a ziggurat built into the rock, doors set within it. The name *Enamtila* was carved above them. When the water subsided, we managed to open them, but something happened, something terrible..."

Gabe exchanged a worried glance with Ash, but Catarina's attention was fixed on her husband, her hand resting on his shoulder.

Hugo gasped, "I need water."

Catarina held a glass to his lips, and Hugo took a few sips, clearly agitated. Gabe didn't dare speak, unwilling to rush him or put him off.

Finally, he continued. "Something came out of the rock, and three men were killed. Crushed. Thrown like dolls. Another four disappeared. It was as if the rock just swallowed them. It was mayhem, and we ran."

"*Something?*" Ash asked, not taking his eyes off Hugo. "What did it look like?"

"It was a blur of wings and a beak. Monstrous. Like a demon come to life. All shadows and feathers. I thought I was hallucinating. I was a boy at the time—in my teens, gawky and awkward—and I'm ashamed to say I ran and didn't look back. We were falling over ourselves to get out. I remember pulling my father behind me."

Gabe could imagine it. A figure from myth manifesting out of the darkness to maim and kill. Sheer terror would have sent them running. He asked, "How many escaped?"

"Barely half of us. Me, my father, the archaeologist, three assistants, and half a dozen locals. The rest were lost. Sealed inside the cave."

Gabe glanced at Ash, finding that he looked as puzzled as he was, and Gabe asked, "Sealed? Like in a rockfall?"

Hugo shook his head, his eyes clouded with confusion. "No, nothing so straightforward. It just seemed to seal itself. I don't know how, but it just did. By then, the locals had fled, leaving our small English group and half a dozen camels and horses on our own. Despite what happened, we were determined to leave nothing behind. The objects'that are now downstairs in the hall were already out of the cave, being examined in our camp. We packed up what we could and left, too. And we never went back."

"But," Ash said, edging forward in his seat, "do you have a location? Can you point it out on a map?"

"I tried to block it from my mind, and we swore never to speak of it again. My father even destroyed one of the maps. We blamed the deaths on the flood. But I think I can remember it."

"Good," Gabe said, relieved. "We'll bring you a map, and you can show us where to go."

Hugo looked bleak. "Are you sure you want to?"

"We have no choice."

As soon as Jackson returned to the division's headquarters, he headed to Waylen's office, pleased to find him at his desk.

He didn't bother with pleasantries. "We had success. We found the original tablet—which is lucky, because the photos we found only showed half of it."

Waylen eased back in his seat, hands folded across his chest. "You're sure it's the right one?"

"Absolutely. Ash translated what he could, but says some of it is cryptic. However, it seems his initial thoughts were right. It describes a history of the Igigi, and the founding of a city. It even talks of the Watchers who they hid from."

Waylen's face broke into a broad grin. "Brilliant. Then we have to get out there. Have you made any arrangements yet?"

Jackson shook his head. "Gabe wants Nahum to arrange it, and that's fair enough. We have given the lead to them. I'll check in with them later."

"What do you think? Is it really likely that the city is intact?"

"It's hard to know. I've been thinking on it all the way here, and it honestly seems impossible. I mean, we're talking three or four thousand years ago, at least!"

"But they were supernatural. They may have had magic that preserved it."

Jackson grunted a half laugh, not sure if Waylen was clutching at straws. "Maybe. But it's not just the Igigi, is it? It's Black Cronos. They may well have more information than we think. The thought of another battle with them..." he trailed off as he remembered the fight at the Dark Star Temple. *That was bad enough.*

"Walk with me," Waylen said, rising to his feet. "Let's get a drink. You look like you need one."

"Ha! You mean *you* need one!" Jackson knew Waylen too well. Come late afternoon, especially on a weekend when he was putting in extra hours, he wanted a beer or a whiskey. The PD had its own well-stocked staff area filled with tea, coffee, soft drinks, and alcohol, as well as food.

They strode down the empty corridors, and Jackson reflected on how odd he always found this place when most of the staff weren't around. Like many government departments, most staff worked Monday to Friday, nine to five, except when they had to monitor crisis situations, which was rare for them. Jackson hadn't been lying to the others. This was not a huge department, and they only had a handful of staff, including a small security team. It really was a division meant to watch, monitor, and report. Their current circumstances were very different to the normal way of things.

Jackson was updating him on the countess as they walked, who he had to admit he found very interesting, when a distant boom echoed down the corridor, shaking everything. They managed to keep their balance, until another boom threw them to their knees.

"Fuck it!" Waylen yelled. "We're under attack!"

Waylen leapt to his feet and ran down the corridor as fast as his limp would allow him, Jackson on his heels, knowing exactly where they were running to.

The cells.

"Have we still got Stefan?" Jackson asked, wishing he had some kind of weapon on him.

"Due to be moved on Monday."

They arrived at the steps leading down to the small cell block, the whole place swirling with dust. Neither hesitated, Jackson pulling his t-shirt over his mouth and nose as he descended.

It had to be Black Cronos. The only two prisoners they had belonged to their organisation. *But how had they got in?* They were several levels below the street.

They reached the bottom of the stairs and a thickly-barred gate controlled by a keypad. Just as Waylen was about to punch the number in, Jackson threw his hand out to stop him. The dust made visibility poor, which worked both ways. It would be hard to spot them, but hard to spot the enemy, too. And Waylen had not experienced Black Cronos like he had.

Jackson held a finger to his lips and for a moment, they listened. There were no shouts or footsteps to indicate anyone immediately beyond the gate, so Waylen entered the number on the pad and carefully opened it.

This part of the corridor was where the interview rooms were. The cells were at the far end, beyond another gate and a guard room normally staffed by two men—fully armed and well trained. They crept down the dust-filled corridor in a half crouch, eyes darting everywhere. Another series of smaller explosions sounded up ahead of them, and both dropped to the floor, Jackson's cheek pressed into the cool tiles covered in chunks of plaster.

After pausing for a beat, they were both back on their feet, heading to the guard room. It was central, secured with bulletproof glass that could see the cells and both parts of the corridor, a door on either side, with security screens mounted on the walls. But the far door was blown off and the glass was shattered. Waylen punched in the key code to the door on their side and Jackson pushed ahead, immediately stumbling over a body. *One dead guard, his chest blown open. Shit.* Waylen grabbed his gun, by far the better marksmen of the two because of his military background. Keeping their heads down, they checked the monitors lining the wall. None were working, the screens black.

Heart pounding, Jackson looked through the shattered doorway into the dust-filled corridor and spotted a cell door blown off its hinges. He and Waylen edged onwards, finding every cell empty—including the ones holding Stefan and Barnaby.

There was a second entrance to this level. Another barred gate and a set of stairs that led to a labyrinthine corridor and exited in a disused Tube station. From there a set of steps went to the street. At the base of the blown-out gate was the second dead guard.

"Damn it! I hate these bastards," Waylen said, checking the man's pulse before handing the second gun to Jackson. "They've gone through the station. I'm going to try to stop them."

He had barely finished his sentence before he was pounding up the stairs, but his speed was already impacted by his injured leg. Fearing it was a suicide mission, but not wanting to abandon his boss, Jackson ran after him, quickly overtaking him.

Jackson had only been in this part of the headquarters once, when he was being shown around, and he found the place equally fascinating and disturbing. There were many abandoned Tube stations in London, closed years before usually because of a lack of use, and several tours could take you around them—but not this one. This was strictly out of bounds. The MI5 building had other access points to it. One thing was certain: Black Cronos did their research.

Footsteps echoed off the bare stone walls as they ran to the station, and rounding a corner, a volley of shots ricocheted off the walls. Jackson and Waylen shot back as they dived for cover.

The station was in sight through another destroyed doorway, the rounded tile walls beyond gleaming in the flashes of torchlight. Jackson just had time to see a muscled soldier hurl what looked like a bomb at them before he ran from view.

Jackson grabbed Waylen's collar and hauled him backwards just as another explosion ripped through the passageway, blowing them off their feet.

Fifteen

Harlan watched JD place Shadow's fey blade in the centre of the grid, and with amazement, looked on as it shimmered and disappeared.

Shadow looked horrified. "What have you done to it?"

JD clapped his hands together, applauding himself. "I have found the correspondences that your blade attunes to. Your fey magic."

"But where has it gone?" She looked agitated, and in seconds her second blade was in her hands, as if she would threaten JD.

Blithely unconcerned, he said, "Nowhere. It's still there." He reached forward, seemingly grasping at nothing, and lifted the blade out. It immediately became visible again.

Harlan whistled. "Holy shit. That's a neat trick."

"No trick, you imbecile! Alchemy and magic!"

Harlan bristled. JD had very little patience, especially with Harlan, who he seemed to have decided was a borderline moron. Remaining polite, but through gritted teeth, he said, "I guess I didn't expect fey magic to have correspondences."

"Everything connects in this world—*everything*! We share the same vibrations, energies, and connections, except our combinations are different. Shadow's world is still of this one, it's just that her energies work differently to ours."

"I can honestly say," Shadow said, whipping her blade from JD's fingers, "that I have never heard it explained like that before. I don't like my magic reduced to *energies*."

JD shrugged, utterly unconcerned. "Like it or not, that's what they are. You should be pleased. It means I can now attune our unusual weapon to you. I think."

"How?" Harlan asked, genuinely curious.

"You couldn't possibly understand."

That was most likely true. "Well, what about my energies?"

"Later! This one first. Now shoo, both of you. I have more work to do. And don't wander the garden perimeter—I've activated it!"

JD had already turned his back on them, bending once more over his grid, and resisting the urge to grab one of Shadow's blades and plunge it into his back, Harlan turned away and strode across the lab, cursing under his breath.

"That damn, infuriating man!"

Shadow matched his stride, amused. "You let him get under your skin."

"He's crawled under it and taken residence, like a goddamn tick. Doesn't he drive you insane?" he asked as they arrived on the main floor and headed to the sitting room that led to the gardens.

"I find him more amusing than annoying, but I get it." Shadow headed for the drinks cabinet that Anna had shown them earlier, and pulled a bottle of gin out, along with tonic from the small fridge concealed within it. "Want one?"

"Yes, please. And make it strong!"

Harlan walked to the French doors that were wide open, allowing access to a broad, stone-flagged patio area. It was early on Saturday evening, and it was the first time he'd been out of the lab for hours. JD had laden them both with gemstones and metals, read their auras, recorded their astrological signs, and done all sorts of weird things he couldn't make heads or tails of. It felt like they'd been in the lab for days rather than one afternoon.

Before they'd started, Anna had shown them to their bedrooms to leave their bags and freshen up, pointed out where they could sit and relax, and then left them to it. Harlan wondered how she spent her time. Probably cleaning and cooking, plus pandering to JD's whims. If they could be left alone for the evening, that would suit Harlan just fine.

He took a deep breath of cool evening air and tried to relax, grateful to have Shadow push a glass into his hand, saying, "Bottoms up!"

"Cheers." He dropped into a chair and placed his feet on the chair opposite, Shadow doing the same, and he studied the garden with appreciation. "It's quite the place JD has made for himself."

She sipped her drink and nodded. "The advantage of more than the average lifespan to plan for things."

"The same as you." He looked at her graceful profile as she stared across the emerald lawns and flower beds. She'd relaxed her glamour, and her fey beauty was quite breathtaking.

She turned, her violet eyes sparkling. "I guess that's true, but I've never put down roots in one place for such a long time. I've always kept moving."

"Your life of crime, you mean?" he teased her, remembering her sometimes questionable past. *And to be honest, questionable present.*

"Exactly."

"But now? Especially now that you and Gabe..."

She raised an eyebrow. "If you think I'm the marrying kind who's likely to have a dozen kids, then you don't know me at all!"

He threw his head back, laughing. "Oh, I know that. Neither am I!"

She chinked her glass against his. "Excellent. But would I like a base to call home?" She looked around at JD's house. "Maybe. Not this big, though. Besides, the farmhouse suits us for now. We have plenty of space."

"This place has its charms," Harlan admitted. "But the city life works for me right now." He felt rather than heard his phone buzz in his pocket, and realised being in the lab had probably interfered with his signal. "Hold on. My phone's ringing."

"So is mine," Shadow said, pulling it from her pocket with a frown.

Harlan stood and walked to the end of the patio to give her some privacy. "Hey, Jackson—"

But he couldn't say anything else, because Jackson cut in. "Bloody Black Cronos has broken into the division's headquarters. Stefan and Barnaby have escaped!"

"*What?*" Harlan sank down onto the paving in a patch of sunlight. "When?"

"This afternoon, just after I got there. Waylen and I tried to stop it, but almost got blown up in the process. Well, actually, we did get blown up."

"What? Are you all right?"

"My ears are ringing, I'm a bit bruised, and I might have a concussion. I've certainly got a horrendous headache. Waylen has a broken arm, and he's aggravated his old leg wound. We were lucky, though. We could have been buried alive. The guards weren't so lucky. Two were killed in the prison area, and another two at ground level."

Harlan could imagine only too clearly the scale of destruction that Black Cronos could achieve. "Shit. Sorry to hear that, but I'm glad you're okay."

"We're pissed off more than anything. Well, that's an understatement. Waylen is furious." He went on to explain how they'd broken in, and Harlan closed his eyes in weariness. He thought the PD would be infallible. *Clearly not.*

"What about the labs?"

"Not touched. They weren't accessible from the cells. But we're on the move now that we've been compromised. Waylen is sorting out a new location."

"Really? How do you relocate an entire division?"

"We have our means, and it helps that we're small. But that brings me to my next problem."

Harlan groaned. "Your concussion."

"'Fraid so. I can't fly."

"Please don't tell me I have to go to Turkey. I'd be a hindrance!"

"You wouldn't be, but no. We still want you to stay here and keep an eye on JD, especially now that Black Cronos is on the move again. I don't know what protection JD has got at his place, but it's probably wise to increase it. And you be careful, too."

"I'll move into the hotel again if I have to, but we'll be here tonight. He said something about activating the garden perimeter—whatever that means—so hopefully we'll be safe."

"Okay. I'm going to try to sleep, although that'll probably be impossible. I'm still in the hospital. Stay safe, Harlan."

Harlan headed back to his seat after ending the call, finding Shadow watching him. "Everything okay?"

"No." He updated her on his news.

"JD might be a target," Shadow mused. "He'll be the biggest threat to Black Cronos—you know, as far as being able to match their achievements."

"Maybe. I'll warn him later. What was your call about?"

"Flights. We leave tomorrow—early. Gabe is coming to get me."

"So soon?"

Shadow nodded, idly playing with her knife in one hand, her drink in the other. "We have a much clearer idea of what we're up against, and where we're going. And it's a long flight, with multiple stops."

Harlan drained his drink and stared at the deepening twilight, worried for all of his friends, and wondering what might happen later. He stood and rattled his glass. "Time for another drink, and then you can tell me everything."

Niel was still brooding about Zee's comments on his love life, but couldn't deny he might have a point. Not that he was willing to concede that yet. *If ever.* But right now, he had other things to worry about, like the Igigi. And the very attractive woman Ash had brought home with him.

Catarina Edevane was an undeniable beauty, and vivacious and witty as well. When Ash had returned a few hours earlier and made the introductions, she had fit in with his brothers straight away. She had arrived with an overnight bag and dressed in old fatigues, a t-shirt, and sweatshirt, the exact opposite of what he'd expected of a countess. When he told her that, she had laughingly explained that it was her dig clothing, and her pack contained much of the same. Now, however, she was in bed, proclaiming tiredness and the wish to be ready for the early flight.

Gabe was collecting Shadow from JD's home, and they were expected back very soon.

Niel studied his brothers, who were readying weapons and preparing their packs in the living room that looked currently more like a war zone. They had decided everyone except Eli would travel to Turkey, Gabe thinking the more of them there, the better—although, he hadn't fully explained why on the phone. No doubt he'd update them when he arrived later. Ash hadn't discussed anything, saying it was better to talk when they were all together. It also wasn't surprising that Gabe wanted Zee to join them. He had faced the Igigi before, unlike Barak and Ash. Fortunately, Zee was happy to help, and Alex, the witch who owned The Wayward Son where Zee worked, had been willing to give him the time off.

He addressed Nahum. "I presume we can take all of our weapons because we're on a PD-approved flight?"

Nahum nodded as he straightened from a crouch on the floor, his bag at his feet. "Yep. We have special passes, and the airport is expecting us. We'll keep the weapons together, like last time. You're in charge of them, okay?"

"Suits me." Niel strode over to the weapons and started to check them off against the list he'd already made before filling the bags. "How long is the flight?"

"Long! Because of a couple of stops, it will take nearly twelve hours. We fly to Batman, it's the closest airport to Mardin. I've got some big vehicles booked."

Zee had been listening, and shocked, he repeated, "Twelve hours!"

Nahum laughed. "You heard me. Plenty of reading time."

"Or film time!" Barak added as he zipped up his bag. "I don't need to remind myself about the Igigi. I remember them all too well!"

"But you didn't fight them," Niel said, puzzled.

"I met them, though." Barak sat on the corner of the sofa. "I travelled to Bad-tibira once and saw the Igigi at work. They were memorable."

Niel said its English name. "The Fortress of the Smiths. I remember it well. The clang of metal rang across the town's bazaars."

"I went in search of weapons to furnish my men. Back when I still commanded an army." Barak laughed. "I spent a small fortune there, even when I bartered for a good price."

"For what battle?"

"Against the angels, of course. My father waged a war upon one in particular—Dantanian. They hated each other. I can't even remember why. It was bloody, as these things are."

Niel remembered those types of battles only too well. All of his brothers had been amongst the strongest Nephilim, commanding armies of other Nephilim, as they waged war upon the enemies of the Fallen, or upon each other. But that was in the early days, before they had learned to refuse. "How did you find the Igigi?"

"Sullen, for the most part. Not surprising, really. They toiled long hours."

Zee spoke up. "And vented their frustration on us when they rebelled."

"Not just us," Nahum said. "Everyone."

"Is there anything else I can do?" Barak asked, changing the subject. "I've finished my packing. My weapons are with Niel."

Nahum nodded and headed to the corner of the room. "Check the camping equipment with me. There are half a dozen tents, sleeping bags, cooking instruments, and packs of dried food. I don't expect we'll be camping for long...if at all."

For the next few minutes, they were preoccupied with checking everything, except for Ash, who was studying the tablet's inscriptions again. Zee helped Niel, unfazed by his belligerent attitude about Lilith the day before. That was not entirely surprising. Zee brushed things off with ease, which made it hard for Niel to remain angry with him. They were so preoccupied that when Gabe and Shadow swung through the door, they took everyone by surprise.

Gabe had his familiar brooding look on his face, which meant trouble. He dropped his bag on the floor, and studied his brothers' activities, hands on his hips. "Are we prepared?"

"Pretty much," Nahum said. "Just double-checking our equipment."

Gabe's eyes narrowed. "Tents?"

"The works." Nahum folded his arms across his chest. "You look shattered. Both of you."

Shadow sprawled on the sofa, declaring, "Being stuck in a car for hours is surprisingly exhausting."

"You should try driving!" Gabe shot back.

She just grunted at him, and Niel suppressed a grin. It was a bone of contention that Shadow hadn't yet learned to drive. And also surprising. She was so headstrong normally, and so independent, that no one could work out why. And she wasn't averse to technology, either. Niel had come to the conclusion that it was low on her priority list, and had decided he was going to motivate her at some point in the near future.

"The drive didn't help," Gabe conceded as he dropped into an armchair, "but I've got a headache just thinking about what we found. Have you told them?" he asked Ash.

"No. I thought it would be easier if we were all together."

Gabe scanned the room. "Where's Catarina?"

"In bed."

"And Estelle?"

Barak answered, "She'll meet us at the airport. And Shadow, El dropped your armour off. It seems that Dante fixed it, just in time."

Shadow, still reclined, gave him a thumbs up, but Gabe sighed with relief. "Good. We'll need Estelle. With luck she can hide our tents in the desert with a spell. And we'll need her help with whatever comes out of that cave."

"What the hell does that mean?" Barak asked, the tents at his feet forgotten.

"It means," Ash said, the papers slack in his hands, "that the Earl of Breconshire told us the true story of what had happened on that dig. It seems that the Igigi are still very much alive."

Sixteen

T he heat of the desert was a shock after England's weather, even at night, and Shadow angled the air conditioning in the car to point at her face.

"Oi! You're not the only one who wants the cold air," Niel pointed out, leaning over to slap her hands away and wrestle the vents in his direction.

She glared at him and slapped his hand back, restraining herself from pulling out her blades. "There are plenty of other vents! And besides, you keep saying how fantastic it is to experience proper heat!"

He glared back at her. "I may be a little unused to it, after all this time."

"Children, please," Ash scolded from the driver's seat. "Will you both shut up? It's been a long flight, and we're all tired."

Gabe was in the passenger seat, and he twisted around to stare at Shadow, amusement dancing in his eyes. "Darling, please don't upset Niel. And don't bicker in front of the guests."

Shadow switched her attention to Gabe, her eyes narrowing. When he called her *darling*, it was always with a slow drawl, aimed to provoke her, and it worked. His grin spread as he observed her building annoyance, and she decided she would have her revenge in private.

Catarina was sitting next to the window, and she tittered as she watched their exchange. "Please don't hold back on my account. Family dramas are always entertaining!"

Unwilling to be labelled a drama queen, Shadow decided to call Niel one instead. "It's his fault. He's like a fey prince without his retinue. All pouty and cross."

Catarina did a double-take. "*Fey?*"

Shadow winced. "Old family saying, that's all. Folklore nonsense."

Niel snorted, his lips twisting into a grin. "You're always full of nonsense."

Shadow decided to ignore him, and focussed instead on the view beyond him, through the window. It was Sunday evening, and they had left the city lights of Batman far behind, following a road through the desert and passing small towns and villages on the way. The surrounding landscape was pitch black beyond the settlements, but from what she'd seen in photos, it was filled with rocky terraces, scoured by wind and time.

This area, like several in Turkey, was known for the villages, monasteries, and buildings carved into rockfaces and deep into the hills. A useful way to stay out of the desert heat, and to keep warm in the winter months. "So, the Igigi," she said, voicing her curiosity, "would have been one of the first people to build their city underground here?"

"Potentially, yes," Catarina answered. She turned away from the view to look at Shadow, her expression almost invisible in the dim interior, but the gleam in her eyes was unmistakable. "It's *fascinating*, isn't it?"

"It will be if it doesn't get us killed." Shadow liked Catarina; her sense of adventure was similar to her own. "Are you sure you want to be with us?"

"Absolutely. I need this. It reminds me of the digs in my youth. Unfortunately, as my husband got older, we haven't been on one for many years. I miss it."

"You're an enthusiastic amateur, I presume?"

"I am. But I've picked things up along the way, and I've always liked to be involved as much as possible. Of course, babies got in the way, too."

Niel leaned around Shadow, who was seated in the middle. "They're older now?"

"Of course. Young adults, leading their own lives. Parents have to be careful, you know, not to lose themselves. Or else, when they leave the nest, you have nothing left. You're like a hollowed-out shell."

Niel just grunted, "Very true," and leaned back to stare out of the window again.

Once again, Shadow wondered if the Nephilim had fathered children. It was the one conversation that hadn't come up, especially between her and Gabe. All three Nephilim had fallen silent at that. *Perhaps it was time to ask Gabe. Later.*

Lights appeared ahead of them, illuminating buildings layered upon each other on a hillside, and Ash said, "That's Mardin, where our hotel is. I must admit, I'm glad we opted for this for the first couple of nights."

Gabe nodded his agreement. "Yes, scoping out the area in the daylight will be best to begin with."

They threaded through the outskirts of the town, Nahum and the others in the car behind them, and Shadow studied the streets and buildings, captivated. This was nothing like England or France, and she couldn't wait to explore.

Ash finally pulled into the carpark of a hotel in the old town, Nahum parking next to him, and within seconds they had all exited the vehicles, breathing in the city scents and warm night air. But right now, Shadow was more interested in Gabe and his brothers' reactions to the scenery. This was a type of homecoming for them, and it showed on their faces.

They had purposefully picked a boutique hotel in a traditional building, and all of them fell silent as they studied it and their surroundings. The smell of food and spices filled the air, and yellow lights blazed against the walls.

Zee took a deep breath and smiled. "This feels like home. I like it."

The tension seemed to seep away and the others nodded and grinned, Niel slapping Zee on his shoulder. "That it does, brother. Come on, let's check in, and then I vote we explore our surroundings. Now that I'm here, I've livened up. And I'm hungry. Airplane food just doesn't cut it."

Barak agreed and patted his flat, muscled stomach. "No, it does not." He winked at Estelle's amused face. "You're not too tired, Estelle?"

Estelle was dressed casually in jeans and a t-shirt, and Shadow was pleased to see she had shed her pinched expression, instead looking as curious as the rest of them. "I am, but I'm hungry, too. And I think I'm too excited to sleep."

"Excellent." He shouldered some bags and headed to the hotel door. "Time to check in."

Harlan yawned and checked his watch, not surprised to see how late it was. It felt like he'd spent days in this subterranean dungeon, instead of just Sunday.

"JD, you must be exhausted, and I know I am. Perhaps we should continue this in the morning?"

They were in JD's laboratory, JD hunched over his grid as he moved specific sections and noted reactions in a small notebook. A knife was in the centre of the grid again, this time a small silver dagger. Every now and again he grunted, clearly frustrated, and for a moment he ignored Harlan. He had measured Harlan's correspondences earlier, based on the endless questions he'd asked yesterday, and was now trying to align the two together.

JD finally said, "I suppose you're right."

"I know I am. We've been doing this for hours, and getting nowhere."

He glared at him. "Not true! I've made steady progress. It may seem tedious to you, but this is about fine-tuning correspondences and energies, and it all takes time."

"Yeah, but this is what you do. It's mumbo jumbo to me! Why am I even sitting here? I'm not doing anything!"

"Because having the subject close may help. Your energy will resonate and complement the grid."

Harlan closed his eyes, pressing his palms into his eyelids. "If you say so." When he opened his eyes, JD was looking at him, lips pursed. "What?"

"You have no curiosity about this? Unbelievable!"

"Not true! I am curious. It's fascinating in many ways, but I don't really get it. It's all starting to blur." Harlan took a breath, fearing they were about to argue again, and he couldn't afford for that to happen. "You are a genius, and I am not. I'm very good at my job, but not this."

JD sniffed. "Yes, I suppose you are."

Harlan stiffened, suspicious that JD was about to follow that grudging compliment with an insult, because that was what usually happened. Instead, however, there was a large boom from outside, and the whole room shook.

"What the hell was that?" Harlan asked leaping to his feet. And then he realised. "Black Cronos are here." The threat of imminent death had him whirling around and running to the door. "JD, my shotgun is in my room. Do you have any weapons down here?"

"Calm down, you nincompoop! Didn't you listen earlier? This place is secure!"

Harlan skidded to a halt and looked at JD strutting across the room. "But this is Black Cronos! They probably want their weapon back, or your research or something!"

"They can want it all they like, but they won't get it." A pompous grin spread across his face. "Come with me, and you'll see what I mean."

JD led the way to the main floor of the house, where Anna stood in the hall wearing her dressing gown and a worried expression. "JD! Did you hear that?"

"I'd be deaf, my dear, not to hear that. Go back to bed, and don't worry."

Another explosion rocked the house, and a flash of red light illuminated the hall. With surprise, Harlan saw all the occult symbols carved into the wood and plaster flare into life.

JD pointed at them. "See? That's what is supposed to happen. They'll never get in."

Having seen Black Cronos fight several times, Harlan wasn't so sure.

Neither was Anna. She clutched her robe to her throat. "Don't worry? We have never been attacked like this before!"

"Anna! This idiot doubts me enough, don't you start," he grumbled, striding down to the corridor, and then up the stairs to the attic room. He called over his shoulder, "If you insist on worrying and staying up, bring us some whiskey and bourbon!"

Anna scowled and scurried to the kitchen, and Harlan bounded after JD, wondering what the wily old devil had up his sleeve. As they entered the huge attic space with the long glass wall, another flare of light flashed across the grounds, and Harlan closed his eyes and averted his gaze. "Holy shit! What are they doing?"

"Trying to get past my protection. Fools."

JD hurried to a door in the panelling, and swinging it open, revealed another set of stairs winding upward. When they reached the top, Harlan gasped. They were in a room perched on the roof, the upper half of which had glass all the way around like a lighthouse, offering a 360-degree view of the gardens and surrounding countryside. Underneath the glass were panelled walls and a workstation that glittered with buttons, electronics, and monitors.

Harlan's mouth fell open as he looked at what appeared to be a high tech, state of the art defence system. "What the actual..."

JD's chest swelled. "Impressive, isn't it? I designed it myself."

"But this looks so modern! I didn't think you did modern."

"Always you underestimate me!"

"Not true! I said only minutes ago that you were a bloody genius!"

"Exactly! Should I so choose, I could be employed by any tech company in the world. I am not only a mathematical genius, but I am a master of advanced physics, chemistry, pharmaceuticals, and this century I learned all about electronics. But I do not wish to work for corporations and tech companies. The pleasure of being centuries of years old is that you accumulate knowledge and wealth, and I can do what I bloody well please. Of course, my particular brilliance is the way I blend everything with alchemy."

Harlan watched dumbfounded as JD manipulated buttons and brought up images from his security cameras of the grounds. "Well, I get that, but didn't expect *this*!"

"Of course," JD rumbled on, "I didn't pursue human experimentation and weapons, because frankly, there are boundaries. I am being forced to adjust my thinking on that!"

Alarmed though Harlan was about that statement, he couldn't ask anything else, because JD was pointing to figures on the screen by the main gate. One man lay unmoving on the ground, possibly dead, and another was trying to disable the gate controls. "Look at him! Pestilent bugbear! Watch what happens now."

As the huge man took apart the intercom, a red light emanated from it, surging outwards and touching the soldier. The man instantly dissolved and disappeared.

"Holy shit!" Harlan exclaimed. "What happened?"

"Mars happened."

"*What*?" JD ignored him and looked across to the other screens, where a team of soldiers had scaled JD's tall stone-walled boundary and were in the grounds. "Er, JD, they're inside!"

"Exactly where I want them. Keep watching."

Harlan's mouth went dry as he watched the soldiers advance. Half a dozen in total, they passed through the shrubbery to the edge of the lawn. As they spread out into a line and stepped on the grass, a shimmering grid of red lights appeared, strung across the lawn's edge. In a split-second, it exploded, a boom rocked the grounds, and the soldiers vanished.

Harlan's mouth fell open, and he blinked to see properly. "Mars again?"

"With a little Saturn thrown in."

As they stared at the other screens, seeing another two groups of soldiers get incinerated by the powerful grids, JD folded his arms across his chest and sighed. "Excellent. That actually worked better than I thought."

A noise behind him startled Harlan, but it was only Anna with their drinks. She left the tray on the side, well away from any controls, and cast JD a reproving glance. "Is it over?"

He focussed on her with a bright smile, suddenly aware of her presence. When he spoke his impatience disappeared, his voice gentle instead. "I think so, but we'll stay up here a while longer to be sure. Honestly, go to bed now. You have nothing to fear."

She nodded, and with a final anxious glance outside, hurried down the stairs again.

Harlan picked his glass up and handed JD another, pleased to see that Anna had brought the bottles, too. *Good.* This one wouldn't even touch the sides. He knocked the first shot back and topped his glass up before scanning the garden again. His adrenalin had spiked, and his hands were shaking. He took some deep breaths to calm himself down.

The grounds were dark again, a more consuming blackness than before after the flare of lights around the perimeter faded. He studied JD's profile as his gaze swept the camera feeds. "So, this is what you meant earlier, when you told me and Shadow not to wander the grounds."

JD nodded. "Yes. After France, I've been activating my protection all day. I only used to bother at night, but we are private here, and Toto's men don't follow the normal rules. I only deactivate the grids when the gardener is here."

"And you harness the power of the planets?"

"I always have. After the planetary parade I charged my crystals, realigned some, and strengthened the grids. I must admit, it works even better than I thought."

Harlan realised he had underestimated JD. He knew he was a genius, of course, but even so, he hadn't expected this. "That was pretty impressive. How does it work? The basics, I mean."

For once, JD didn't adopt a patronising tone. "It's a system made up of a variety of crystals of various sizes, with different properties and correspondences, all inter-connected and placed carefully on their correct alignment. A select few can be..." He struggled to find the right word, eventually saying, "*Muffled* best describes it. That's what turns the system off. When I want it to work, I *un-muffle* them."

A sudden flare in the corner of the grounds made them look up, and another group of soldiers dissolved in a different grid.

Worried, Harlan asked, "Could they overload the system and disable it?"

"No. It's not like electricity. The charge will last a very long time. And the crystals are buried deep beneath the earth. It's taken me a great many years to perfect."

"Perhaps you should offer this system to the PD. It would protect them from further attack."

"Perhaps. But if I'm honest," JD cocked his head at Harlan, "I tend not to offer things I fear could be misused."

"You don't trust them?"

"I don't trust the system, although Waylen and his team seem trustworthy enough." JD settled on a chair, and Harlan followed suit. "In my many years of experience, I have found that it doesn't pay to be too trusting." He shifted his gaze from the grounds to Harlan, his expression filled with disappointment. "I have been betrayed again and again, by friends, kings and queens, governments... At least enemies are predictable. You think I'm abrupt. Abrasive—"

"You are."

"You would be too if you'd experienced what I have. Immortality brings great advantages, but it has also taught me that, generally, people are petty and greedy. Generationally that never changes. It's depressing."

Harlan suddenly felt his animosity melting away as he regarded JD's usually hidden vulnerability. "I guess when you've lived through countless wars and conflicts, it can become difficult."

"Wars are one thing, but inept governments, selfish behaviour, the willingness to exploit others for personal gain—it's all very wearing." JD gestured to his house and grounds. "That's why, when it all becomes too much, I withdraw here."

"But there are positives, right?"

"Of course. I have visited many interesting places, and met many brilliant people. And of course, the chance to study—*really study*—life's great mysteries. And the knowledge—and this seems odd, I know," he said, cocking his head at Harlan, "the knowledge that I will never know everything is actually thrilling. I truly believe we will never unlock every secret of the universe."

Harlan sipped his drink. "You're right. That is odd, coming from you. Especially considering the events in The Temple of the Trinity." Harlan wondered if he should bring it up, considering they were conversing in a way they never had before, but decided to anyway. After all, JD had been obsessed with finding The Book of Raziel and the knowledge it could offer him.

"Ah, that!" JD nodded and topped up his drink. "I did not acquit myself well then. There are some things that grip you so completely, you can lose yourself. That was certainly one of them. Looking back now, I think I had a lucky escape."

"I'm glad to hear you say that, because, quite honestly, you really pissed me off. The Nephilim and Shadow, too."

JD's finger worried at his lower lip as he studied the monitors again. "The angels get in your head, you know. They worm their way in there, overwhelming your will. That is their true power." He closed his eyes briefly, and then fixed Harlan with his steely-eyed stare again. "I have stepped away from that for now. There are other things to pursue. Like Toto."

Harlan guessed that was as much an apology as he would get, and JD's excuse made sense. Angels were paranormal creatures like anything else, possessing powers he couldn't imagine. He decided to move on, too. "How is your research into an antidote to Black Cronos's powers going?"

"Badly. I am frustrated at my lack of progress, and in my eagerness to start, I think I'm going in the wrong direction. I began in completely the wrong place."

"But you said it was early days."

"Even so, you get a feeling for how things are going, and I'm sure I'm on the wrong path. They always seem one step ahead, too, which makes me wonder who is really behind them."

"You mean, other than Toto?"

"Toto is a visible figurehead, and undoubtedly clever, but there are far more involved in their experiments than just him."

"But surely their set up will be like The Order of the Midnight Sun? A group of Senior Adepts who drive it all, with Toto as the Grand Master?"

"I agree that their organisation will have a similar structure. After all, we mustn't forget that Black Cronos had the same beginnings as the order. But more and more, I truly believe that someone of a great age is behind it all."

"You mean someone *immortal*? Like you?" The idea seemed shocking to Harlan, but the more he thought about it, the more it seemed not only possible, but probable. "Another ancient alchemist."

JD nodded and tapped his glass, his expression distant. "Yes. It's crossed my mind before, but I have dismissed the idea several times. I tell myself that I would know, surely. I have known many great alchemists in my time, all brilliant men, and I've always doubted that I could be the only one to have mastered immortality. But I thought I would run into them...recognise them." He shrugged. "But why would I? I have purposefully hidden, reinvented myself, changed my name. I'm JD now, but I have completely changed my name before. And if someone was manipulating human matter, they would not want to advertise it. They could even have been an original member of Black Cronos, or they could have joined later on."

Harlan felt a horrible stirring of certainty at JD's words. *Of course that made sense. Why should JD be the only alchemist to have cracked immortality?* "Do you have some idea of who it could be?"

"Oh yes." JD fixed his acute amber eyes on Harlan, all speculation gone. "I have considered various men and women, and ended up dismissing them all, except for one. The *Comte de Saint-Germain*."

Seventeen

Gabe lay on his back, staring up at the vaulted stone ceiling above his head, listening to the sounds of the city.

Memories resurfaced that he thought he'd long forgotten. Snatches of conversations, walking through the bazaars and markets, long, decadent meals, languorous lovemaking in the heat of the afternoon, and the juicy, sweet taste of fresh figs as they burst against his tongue.

Shadow stirred beside him and wriggled closer, her hand on his chest, her leg wrapped over his. "You're awake," she murmured.

"My mind is too busy to sleep."

"And your stomach is too full of food. You ate like a horse."

He laughed and kissed the top of her head as he pulled her closer. "I always do."

"Not at midnight. And not like that!"

She was right. They had wandered the streets around their hotel, drinking in the sights, sounds, and smells, eventually stopping at a small restaurant where they crowded around a table beneath vines in a courtyard. They had ordered a feast: kisir, saksuka, koftes, a variety of kebabs, gozleme, and many others. The table had been piled high.

Gabe had tasted spices and flavours he hadn't experienced in years, and even though they cooked all sorts of food at home, it hadn't been like this. And now his gut was protesting.

"Are you glad we came?" she asked.

"Of course. I'm glad we're staying here, too. It's good to be in a more traditional place—even if it is only a semblance of the dwellings in our time."

"I know what you mean. The traditional has a feel that the modern does not." She propped herself on her elbow, and drew his chin towards her so that she could look at him properly. A faint light came through the curtains stirring lazily on the night breeze. "When children were mentioned earlier, you all fell silent. I feel we've avoided the subject, but I would like to know. Did you have children?"

A familiar ache filled his chest as he took a deep breath and sighed it out again. Even in this light, Shadow's violet eyes glowed. "I had one, and she died too young."

"I'm sorry. How young?"

"She was three years old." She was so small, and her death served to prove what the angels had promised. He sighed again, knowing he must explain it to Shadow. "We, the Nephilim, were not meant to have children. Our women did not fall pregnant, and if they somehow did, our children did not live for long. I and many others thought we could prove them wrong. But they were right all along."

"Why didn't you tell me?"

"Because it was a long time ago now. It's history."

"It's *your* history. That's important to me."

He bent his head to kiss her, savouring her soft lips and warm curves. "You're very beautiful, Shadow. I'm a lucky man."

"You are. But stop changing the subject." She rolled on top of him, legs straddling his body and elbows propped on his chest as she gazed into his eyes. "Tell me about her. And your wife."

Images flooded his mind again, and the words seemed to dry in his throat as he recalled his daughter's honey blonde locks and almond eyes, just like his wife. "I'm not sure I want to. I quite like them buried in the past. To talk about them makes it more painful."

"Because you loved them so much?"

"Yes. Also, the fact that I wasn't around as much as I should have been. I waged war when I should have been home, and I took them for granted. I wonder if they thought I didn't love them as much as I did, and that they died thinking I didn't care."

"Gabe! Don't taunt yourself with useless recriminations. I'm sure that's not the case!"

"Then why do I feel so guilty?"

She cupped his face with her hands. "Because you're a good man. Share their stories with me. I'm with you now, connected to you, as I've never been with any other man. I want that connection to be even deeper."

Desire stirred within him at those words, but he knew he wasn't the only man she had loved. "You have been with other men."

"But not like this, Gabe Malouf." She patted his heart. "This beats within me now, too. You have done something truly unexpected to me."

He caught her hands in his. His connection with Shadow had been immediate, and they had fought their growing desire for weeks before they had both finally relented to the inevitable. But Shadow rarely opened up like this, for all of the love she showered on him in bed. She kept a little piece of herself apart—until now.

"Is that right?" His voice was husky, even to his own ears.

"I won't lie about that."

He flipped her over, lying astride her, his desire now too strong to ignore. "Then I'll tell you. Later," he said, nuzzling her neck. "You have woken up another type of appetite that needs feeding now."

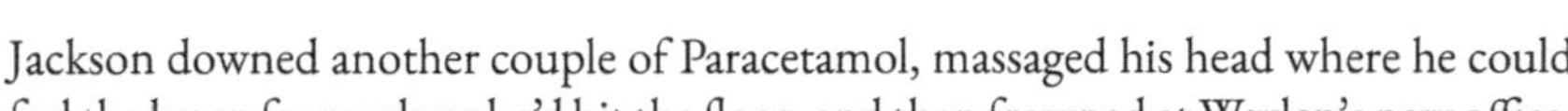

Jackson downed another couple of Paracetamol, massaged his head where he could feel the lump from where he'd hit the floor, and then frowned at Waylen's new office.

"This should work out fine, once the boxes are unpacked. I'm just amazed we're in another building already!"

Waylen grunted from behind the desk and then straightened, his arm in a sling, discomfort etched across his face. "We couldn't afford to delay. When you're compromised, you have to move fast."

"I get that. It's more the fact that there's a place to go!"

Layla Gould, the PD's doctor, was in the room with them, and she gave a dry laugh. "We've always got bolt holes and back-up places. We've just never really had to use them before—except, of course, during the World Wars. This was set up in the early twentieth century, and is the place we used then." Despite the late night and dusty surroundings, Layla was still dressed in expensive clothing and wearing elegant heels. Jackson often wondered if she spent every night at flash functions and posh restaurants. She must have caught his curious glance, because she explained, "I was at a gallery opening when I got the call. My husband is an investor." She marched to his side. "Let's check you out again." She whipped a small torch from her bag and peered into his eyes.

Jackson blinked. "Am I alive?"

"Barely. You are both very bloody lucky. I'm sorry I couldn't get here earlier." She turned to Waylen. "Where's Russell?"

"Supervising the lab move. It's a bloody nightmare." Waylen slumped in his chair. "This mess will put us back weeks."

Russell Blake was the Assistant Director of the PD, and Waylen's right-hand man. He was in his fifties, had a background in science, and oversaw the lab. They were salvaging as much as they could, but it would take time.

Jackson grunted. "Better than months. So," he said, staring at his surroundings, "early twentieth century? That explains the dust and Art Nouveau décor."

"The electricity is up to date, though, and internet connections were put in a few years ago," Waylen explained. "Beautiful furniture though, right?"

Layla stroked one of the designs on the back of the door in typical Art Nouveau style. "It's stunning. My husband would love to see this place."

"Stunning is one word," Jackson admitted. "*Unexpected* is another. Weren't these back-up places meant to be utilitarian?"

"It depends on the director and how much power he had, and when this was requisitioned, he had a lot!" Waylen told him.

They were in another subterranean series of rooms situated under Hyde Park, not far from the Serpentine, the famous lake in its centre, and also close to Kensington Palace. The winding series of brick and wood-lined passages connected to the palace at one point, but was now separated from it by a series of blast doors. In fact, all of the entrances were sealed by blast doors and anterooms, which meant these offices were far harder to get to. *They would have had to be during the wars*, Jackson reckoned. And then another thought struck him; it was highly likely that his grandfather would have worked down here at some point.

More curious because of it, Jackson studied the room again, and then stepped into the corridor, noting several doors that opened off it. The place was designed with great detail. Fine mouldings, polished finishes—although dusty now—jewel-like Art Nouveau window designs set between offices and corridors. Half a dozen staff were carrying boxes as they set up their new workspaces. The whole department had been activated to come in and help. Jackson shook his head. It was hard to believe they were so far underground.

Entering Waylen's office again, Jackson addressed the director, startling him as he emptied a box. "Who was the man who achieved all this?"

Layla snorted. "Woman, actually! A member of the aristocracy."

"Aristocracy? A royal?"

She smiled impishly, the grin taking years off her face. "Oh, yes! We had an auspicious benefactor. Princess Louise. The fourth daughter of Queen Victoria."

"You're kidding? I didn't know that!"

"She lived in Kensington Palace for years, and when her mother died, it freed her to pursue other things. Like this. She was quite the feminist, you know." Layla laughed. "I adore her. Anyway, this isn't getting my rooms sorted. I'd better get on. And you, Jackson, should get home. Rest is the best thing after a head injury."

She left, leaving the scent of floral perfume in her wake, and with a sigh, Jackson had to acknowledge she was right. He'd left the hospital that morning, disobeying doctors' orders, and had helped Waylen and the other staff make the emergency move. Now his head was pounding, and the Paracetamol wasn't touching it.

"I think she's right," he admitted to Waylen. "You should go home, too."

Waylen finished plugging in his computer and sighed. "My arm is throbbing, but I'll finish this first." He studied Jackson with narrowed eyes. "But you look like shit. Go home and sleep late. But come back tomorrow. I'll have a room for you."

"Seriously?" Jackson had only ever been a regular visitor before.

"The way this thing is going with Black Cronos, we'll need you around more than ever. Any objections?"

"None whatsoever. Thanks, Waylen."

And with a spring in his step, despite his headache, Jackson went home.

Harlan helped himself to another liberal glass of bourbon, cast an anxious glance out of the windows, settled back in his chair, and asked, "The Comte *who*?"

JD also surveyed his grounds before answering. "The *Comte de Saint-Germain*—or the Count of St Germain, as we say in English. You've seriously never heard of him?"

"Actually," Harlan mused, thinking on the name, "it does ring a bell. An alchemist, you say?"

"One of the most famous. Or should I say infamous?" JD's head dropped forward in contemplation, almost on his chest as he sank deeper into his chair. "I met him during his lifetime, by which I mean his legitimate one, several times over a close period of years. That was in the mid-1700s. I was of course *dead* by then, and going by a completely different name, and I certainly didn't reveal who I was to him. But he already had a reputation and was extremely influential. However, rumours—that he encouraged—suggested he was already over three hundred years old, even then. And then people bumped into him after years of not seeing him, and remarked on how he hadn't aged. Of course," he looked at Harlan, "I studiously avoided him after a while. I didn't want him to be aware of how I didn't age, either. And of course, I moved around a lot—careful to avoid such rumours myself. But he courted it. Despite his undoubted brilliance, I thought he was a charlatan. But now..."

Harlan shook his head, confused. "Why a charlatan? You achieved immortality. Did you really think he couldn't?"

"You think I'm arrogant about my achievements, that I believe no one else could do what I have? No. That's not it. It's the fact that he toyed with people about it. What foolish nonsense! It's almost childlike. Attention-seeking. If anyone had proved it, his life would be forfeit!"

"You think that about your own?"

"Of course! I don't wish to be kidnapped for my knowledge, or to be studied like a lab rat."

"What's changed your mind about the count?"

"Things he was talking about back then—immortality, remaining youthful, his ability to manipulate gemstones and jewels. His links to secret societies that persisted up to the nineteenth century—I have read on him extensively over the years. And then of course Black Cronos appeared. Or rather," he corrected himself, "they became more visible."

"From what I recall, we first interacted with them in the late 1800s."

"Yes, although those early meetings were sporadic. Just after I formed The Orphic Guild."

"A coincidence?"

"Perhaps. But at that time there was a resurgence of groups interested in esoteric studies. The Order of the Midnight Sun stepped out of the shadows then, and others formed—The Hermetic Order of the Golden Dawn and the Freemasons, among others. And spiritualism in general was on the rise."

Harlan leaned forward, eyes fixed on JD. "But why him?"

JD met his stare. "I think I saw him—fleetingly. And I think he saw me. I went to a talk hosted by The London Geographic Society of all places, and he was there, too—on the other side of the room. He asked a question, and I couldn't believe my eyes. His clothes were different, obviously, and his hairstyle—no longer one of those ridiculous wigs that fashion forced us to wear. But it was him. His voice...”

"You didn't stop to meet him?" Harlan thought that meeting someone else who had mastered immortality would surely be a good thing. It would lessen the feelings of loneliness.

JD shook his head vigorously. "No. There was something about him. A dangerous edge. It was always there. I sensed it when I first met him."

Harlan considered his next words carefully, and then said them anyway. "You know, you also have one of those. Your willingness to sacrifice things and people...your analytical mind. It makes you cold."

JD shrugged. "Maybe. Anyway, I have nothing but that sight of him and my intuition to go on, but I'd put money on it. He is Black Cronos's Grand Master."

Eighteen

Early on Monday morning, Nahum pulled the car off the dusty road that was surrounded by desert, and turned to Barak, who was in the passenger seat. He had Catarina's map stretched across his lap, heavily marked, with his finger on the spot identified by the earl.

Nahum asked, "Are we close?"

"According to this we are, and the GPS agrees."

They had entered the coordinates of the dig into the car's navigational system, but Catarina had warned them that they weren't exact. Although the earl couldn't remember the specific location now, they were a lot closer than they would have been only days before.

Ash leaned forward, wedged between Niel and Estelle. "Are we close enough to set the tents up?"

"A little further," Barak answered, staring ahead into the wild terrain. "There are still more people around than I would like."

Estelle leaned forward, too. "Don't forget that I can veil us in a protection spell."

"Nevertheless, I would still like us to be more off the beaten track," Nahum mused, looking through the windscreen and lowering his sunglasses back over his eyes.

The directions had led them deeper into the desert, the rocky terraces folding around them like a rumpled blanket. He tried to marry it with his recollections of the past, but it had been so long ago that it was virtually impossible. It used to be greener, and so much was missing. And of course, so much was new.

He looked to the south. "Do you remember the ziggurats towering above the city walls? The gardens within the cities? They were spectacular."

"I remember the paved roads," Niel said. "They were so flat, so perfect. And there were canals and rivers."

"It wasn't this dry then?" Estelle asked, wonder in her voice.

"Not at all." Ash's hand swept across the horizon. "You could see patches of greenery among the desert sand, far more than there is now."

"And what about Mardin?" Estelle asked, looking comfortable in the heat. Her hair was pulled back into a ponytail to keep her neck cool, and she wore a t-shirt that showed off her toned arms. "That's an ancient city."

Nahum twisted in his seat to look at her more easily. "The layout is familiar, but even so, most of the buildings are new compared to our time...even the really ancient ones. It has a familiar feel, though."

Barak tapped the driving wheel. "Come, brother. Let's get on so I can stretch my legs."

Niel grunted. "I second that!"

Nahum nodded, and checking that the road was clear he accelerated again, following the twisting asphalt that shimmered in the heat. Barak directed him on to a narrow track that led up into the hills, leaving the main road far behind. They rose higher, snaking along the contours of the terraces, passing hollows in the rock, until they finally reached the end of the path.

"Shit. It doesn't go any further," Nahum said, driving off the road and onto hard, packed earth and sand. "Are we close?"

"Hard to say," Barak said, frowning. "I think beyond this terrace, but I'm not sure."

Niel was already opening the door. "Then we need to explore on foot."

They were already high above the plane, and yet terraced rockfaces, pitted with dark crevices and cave entrances, still rose around them, casting their surroundings in deep shadow. It was deserted, too. They clambered out, and once out of the air-conditioned car, the heat felt like an oven.

Barak stretched his arms above him as he studied the landscape. "This could be a good place to camp, but I'd prefer to be out of view of the road."

Ash nodded. "I agree. Why don't you and Estelle check out beyond the ridge, and we'll investigate here?"

"Sounds good. Estelle, are you ready?"

"Sure." She swung a small pack over her back and fell into step next to Barak, heading towards the rift in the rock.

Nahum turned to Ash and Niel, disgruntled. "Look at this place! It's riddled with hollows and caves. I know we've narrowed it down, but it's still going to be hard to find."

"But we're high up," Ash said, his eyes gleaming. "And therefore, the many folds in these terraces could mean multiple entrances. The Igigi wouldn't box themselves in."

"Look around!" Nahum swung his arm wide, and despite his sunglasses, shaded the top of them as he stared around him. "Look at how ridged the whole landscape is. On first impression, it all looks the same. And down the valley there are monasteries set into these hills. We could find remnants of many old dwellings, but be in the completely wrong place!"

"Have faith in the map," Niel said, "and in the directions we were given."

Niel seemed to have forgotten his argument with Zee the other night, although he seemed not as upbeat as he usually was. Nahum hoped that being out here would do him good.

"While I don't want to come across Black Cronos," Nahum admitted, scanning the road they'd just driven up, "at least seeing them here will mean we're in the right place."

"Do you think we can risk flying?" Ash asked, almost a plea in his voice.

Nahum knew why. To glide along the desert thermals would be fantastic. "As long as we don't fly too high, we'll be fine."

He pulled his t-shirt off and flung it in the car, and then extended his wings. The rush of pleasure gave him a surge of adrenalin, and he soared upwards, catching the current. If they achieved nothing else this morning, at least he'd have flown in the sunlight. Something he hadn't done for a very long time.

The market sellers' voices assaulted Shadow's ears as she browsed the stalls in the bazaar, but she was enjoying every moment.

Mardin reminded her of the cities of the Djinn in the Realm of Fire; the rich yellow stone of the buildings gleaming in the sun, the desert stretching around it in all directions, the pungent scent of spices, and the overwhelming heat. It all triggered her senses. And what was even better was how excited Gabe was to be here.

He had eventually fallen asleep after his disturbed night, and she watched him now, aware of the grief he carried still, and wishing she could ease it more. Knowing about his child made her want to protect him. *Or at least his heart.* He was huge; he certainly didn't need her physical protection. But their talk seemed to have helped. A soft smile had played about his lips all morning, and he bartered now with obvious pleasure. She couldn't understand a word he was saying, but he seemed at ease here, as did Zee. He was a short distance away with Catarina, browsing the spices for their cooking—at Niel's insistence, while he explored with Nahum.

Shadow couldn't lose herself entirely to the moment, though. She kept a wary eye out for signs of Toto and The Silencer of Souls. If they weren't already here, they would be soon. The paperwork they had found in their bags meant they were targeting this area, too. With luck, Nahum and the others would have found a promising spot to set up camp. Shadow just hoped they wouldn't be camped out for weeks.

Gabe finished his bartering and placed the small selection of pots into his backpack before shouldering it again, and walking on to the next stalls. "Excellent find. We'll take some fresh food with us, as well. It will last a few days at least, so we don't have to survive on that reconstituted stuff." His nose wrinkled as he said it, and she laughed.

"Dried food isn't great, but it's better than nothing. Although, we won't be that far from the town anyway, will we?"

"An hour or so, maybe more. It's hard to say. I guess one of us could always come back for supplies if we need to." He echoed her own sentiment. "Hopefully we'll be there hours, rather than days."

"You're looking forward to this, aren't you?"

"The camping? Yes. The Igigi, no."

They caught up with Zee and Catarina, and Zee gestured to the bags they carried. "We managed to get a good price for these blankets, so we won't freeze at night."

Shadow was unconvinced. "Are you sure we'll need them at all? We've got sleeping bags."

"The desert is always cold at night, especially higher up, where we'll be," Catarina explained. "My husband said they had camped well above the plains."

"Fair enough," Shadow said, reaching forward to take a bag from Catarina. "Are we done here?"

"Except for some meat and a few treats," Gabe said, leading them towards the food section of the market. "Time for some authentic Turkish delight, I think. And then we'll be ready for coffee."

Fifteen minutes later they were seated at a table on the pavement in front of a small café, shaded by a colourful umbrella, with the smell of cardamom coffee wafting around them. Gabe opened the box of Turkish delight and passed them around, and Shadow selected the pistachio flavour. "Perfect, thank you."

"So, what now?" Catarina asked, lifting her hair to allow her neck to cool as she glanced down the crowded street.

"We load the car up and join the others in the hills," Gabe said. He leaned back in his chair, facing the street, so he could see their surroundings with ease. "I'll feel safer when we're away from prying eyes."

"You think they're here?" Catarina asked.

"If not now," Zee said, "then they'll be here soon. There's too much at stake to wait." He smiled at her. "You did well to hide the maps."

"I wish I could have hidden the tablet, too."

"Herne's flaming bollocks!" Shadow exclaimed, her hands already on her knives. "I think I've just seen The Silencer of Souls."

"The *who*?" Catarina asked, alarmed, her head whipping around at the same time as the others.

Zee quickly explained, "The woman with Toto."

"That's her name?" Catarina shrank in her chair. "She sounds deadly."

"She is," Shadow murmured, not taking her eyes off the deadly woman. "So far, we haven't been seen. She's at the far end of the street. She must have come out of one of the little lanes."

Gabe downed his coffee and threw the box of sweets into his pack. "Then we'll leave right now."

"You go," Shadow said, standing. "She's heading away from us. I'm going to follow her."

"No! There's no need," Gabe said, his brow creasing with worry. He had a tendency to do that lately. Ever since they'd become a couple. It was protective, caring, and also seriously annoying. "If she hasn't seen us, then we're in no danger."

Shadow stood her ground. "But knowing where they are and who she's with will help us. And she won't see me. You know she won't."

Gabe huffed and stared at Zee for support, but Zee just shrugged. "She's right. An idea of their numbers will be useful. But don't be long, Shadow. We'll pack up and be out of here within the hour."

Shadow nodded, checked her watch, and then left them, slipping through the crowd with ease as she engaged her fey magic. It wasn't as effective in towns, but it worked well enough, and unless the soul-sucker was a very good actress, Shadow remained convinced they hadn't been seen. The crowd of other café patrons had hidden them well.

Shadow reached the end of the street, momentarily puzzled. They were in the old town, halfway down the hill that Mardin was built on, and the warren of streets was both fascinating and baffling. She hadn't seen her quarry cross the road, so Shadow headed right, and was rewarded a few moments later when she caught sight of her threading through the locals and tourists, before taking a left turn. Shadow hurried after her, The Silencer of Souls leading her deeper and higher into the old town, past ancient buildings, places of worship, hotels, restaurants, and cafés. The number of people around thinned out, but the lanes wound frequently as they staggered upwards, steps mixed with gently sloping rises, and it was easy to stay out of sight. Although Shadow was on alert for any other Black Cronos members—they had a dead-eyed look to them that she'd come to recognise—she spotted no one else.

Finally, the woman slowed and turned into a building, and after waiting a few moments before getting closer, Shadow realised she had entered a traditionally de-signed boutique hotel, similar in style to their own. A narrow lane, barely more than a footpath, ran along the side, leading up steps and to more streets behind it, and Shadow realised she could climb onto a wall to see into the hotel courtyard that was undoubtedly at the rear.

She raced down it, vaulted onto ledges, and found a spot against a wall in deep shadow, hidden from the morning sun. She settled into place, drawing her fey magic around her, and concentrated on the scene below: a fountain in the centre of a stone-flagged courtyard, with potted plants scattered amongst tables. But voices from above caught her attention. A wide balcony with fretted stonework overlooked the area, the door thrown wide open. A flash of white-blond hair appeared out of the gloom of the room. Shadow was almost at eye level and she froze, trying to sink into the wall. As she focussed, The Silencer of Souls came into view, and someone was next to her. Stefan Hope-Robbins had joined them.

Barak emerged from the narrow gully that ran between a ridge of terraced rock, and found himself in a flat area surrounded on all sides by craggy rockfaces, all except for a break to their right offering a view of the desert below.

The wind dropped and he turned his face to the sun, saying, "I like this place. This would suit us well for a campsite. The top is wide enough to allow in a good amount of sunlight, and sheltered enough to protect us from the winds."

"I agree," Estelle said, already striding to the gap to look on the desert below. "The drop from here is sheer, so easy to defend, too."

He walked to her side, feeling the air cool as he plunged into shadow. But beyond, the glare of the sun on the golden sand was enough to make him pull his sunglasses firmly over his eyes. "Stunning, isn't it?"

"It has an unusual beauty. Harsh, but I like it."

"It becomes addictive after a while. It looks like nothing could live out there, but it teems with life." He smiled down at her. She was above average height for a woman, but still barely reached his chest. Her hair was still in a ponytail, and he saw the sweat glistening on her skin. A tan was already developing, and she seemed to be more relaxed than ever. "This place suits you, Estelle. You look beautiful."

Her hand brushed across her cheek, sweeping an errant hair away, suddenly self-conscious. "Thank you. You look...beautiful isn't the word. *Magnificent.*" She laughed and sighed out, "Yes, that's right."

Barak hadn't kissed her yet, but he figured there was no time like the present. They were alone, in a place of stark beauty, and she seemed to be more relaxed with him than ever before. He turned to face her and pulled her into him, her arms resting on his chest. He didn't speak. He didn't need to. She looked up at him, her gaze wary but promising, and cupping his hand around the back of her head, he leaned in to gently kiss her. She sank against him, responding fully, and their kiss grew deeper, until they broke away, both breathless.

"Well," he said, when his voice steadied, "that was worth waiting for."

A smile lit her face, but she was already pulling away. "Yes, it mostly certainly was. But we should probably find the others and set up the camp."

He pulled her back to him. "We should, but they can wait a few minutes more." The arrival of loud, noisy brothers would ensure no more intimacy for a while, so he'd get it while he could.

Nineteen

Jackson was feeling much better after a good night's sleep, so it was with a sense of excitement that he returned to The Retreat—on first impressions a ridiculous name, considering what the corridors beneath Kensington Gardens housed. It sounded like a spa.

But the more he thought on it, he decided that the name probably suited it well. After the attack on their previous headquarters, and with Black Cronos on the offensive, they needed a place of safety, especially one finished with Art Nouveau décor.

He made his way to Lancaster Gate Tube Station, and then walked to the Serpentine South Gallery, which housed one of the entrances to The Retreat. Opening a shabby looking door at the rear using the key Waylen had given him, he entered a dusty room with an abandoned filing cabinet, desk, and chair that clearly no one had used in years. Another sturdy door made of oak with iron bands was at the back of the room, and a shiny new intercom with a camera had been fitted next to it. He was relieved to see the door looked robust, and although a discreet entrance, that security was already in place. He buzzed through with his name, smiled at the camera, and in seconds the door clicked open smoothly, allowing him into an antechamber and a set of stairs leading downwards. At the bottom was a reception and security area, manned by two familiar armed security personnel.

After signing in and checking him for weapons, he was allowed through to the corridor leading to the heart of The Retreat, and this time, more alert than he'd been the day before, Jackson took his time to examine his surroundings. The winding corridor, lined with polished wood and brick, had decorative Art Nouveau embellishments, with age-appropriate light fittings. A light layer of dust coated everything, but he could already see a couple of cleaners at work, and the smell of polish and disinfectant hung in the air.

A murmur of voices came from an office, and recognising them, Jackson knocked the partially open door and stuck his head inside. There were at most a dozen people in the Paranormal Division, including Waylen, Blake, and Layla. The two people in this office were analysts who monitored paranormal events across the United Kingdom, and the rest were lab staff or security.

"Hey, guys," he said, greeting Petra and Austin.

Both seemed ridiculously young to be in this type of job, but he had to acknowledge that they were efficient and organised, and had qualifications bursting out of them. He estimated both to be in their late twenties. Petra was a petite woman of West Indian descent, with a sharp sense of humour and a cackling laugh, and Austin was a skinny man from somewhere in the Midlands. Both bonded over music that was incomprehensible to Jackson. While Petra oversaw England and Wales, Austin monitored all paranormal activity in Northern Ireland and Scotland.

"Hey, Jackson," Austin said, turning from the huge white board they had mounted on the wall. "Are you okay after the attack?"

"Well, my headache has settled after a good night's sleep." He perched on the corner of a desk. "You two are lucky you weren't there."

"You two are lucky you weren't killed," Petra pointed out. She had been reading from a piece of paper in her hands, and she placed it on the desk. "I was always told this job was monitoring and surveillance only. They lied."

Jackson tried to reassure her. Both of them, actually. They looked equally tetchy. "Not true. This *was* unusual, and we should never have kept Hope-Robbins and Armstrong at the headquarters for so long. We won't make that mistake again." He hadn't talked to Waylen about it, but was sure he'd agree—although, they had obtained information from Barnaby that they might not have otherwise learned. "In fact, I don't think this place even has cells. And this location is secure, and somewhere unexpected."

Austin laughed. "Yeah, I guess so. I feel like I'm working in a museum. Waylen reckons this is long term, too."

"It makes sense. Why try and find another place, when with a few upgrades, you get to work here? It's classy!" He gestured at the whiteboard where they recorded their current cases of interest. "I see you've brought that with you, too. Anything fun going on?"

Austin grinned and tapped the huge map of the United Kingdom pinned to the wall. "Rumours of Selkie sightings in Scotland. Right at the top."

"Selkies! For real?" Selkies were seals who were rumoured to be able to take to the land and turn into women. Some fishermen had been lured into taking selkie wives. "Are they dangerous?"

Austin shook his head. "No. Far from it. They have a gentle, almost solemn quality to them—or so the legends say. But the fact that the locals are talking about it is unusual. The police are monitoring it, just in case it means something more unsettling."

Jackson was confused. "Like what?"

"That's the question, isn't it?"

"And I am monitoring," Petra said, shaking her paper, "a pack of shifters in Cumbria. There are reports of shifter border wars. Hopefully it won't blow up, and they usually manage themselves, but the last thing we want is for the human population to be dragged into it."

"Nothing in London?" Jackson asked.

"There's always something in London! But nothing we need to worry about—other than the attack on us, of course."

"I better let you get on," Jackson said, standing and heading to the door. "Have you heard, though, that I'll be around more often?"

Austin smiled. "The boss told us. It makes sense, considering how often you're here at the moment. Welcome aboard."

When Jackson finally arrived at Waylen's office, he saw that it looked far more organised than Waylen did. Day-old stubble covered his jaw, and his hair was ruffled, but he was at least wearing a fresh shirt.

"Did you even go home?" Jackson asked by way of greeting.

Waylen looked up from his computer, startled, and then laughed. "Yes, but I appreciate that it doesn't look like I have. It was a late finish and an early morning." He gestured to a door on the far side of the room. "Fortunately, I have a private bathroom. Perhaps I should take a break for a shave."

"Don't bother on my account." Jackson nodded at the computer. "You're online already, then?"

He nodded. "As the director, it's my job to keep our back-up rooms and plans operational." He grimaced as he looked around at a few errant cobwebs. "That doesn't apply to cleaning, but we're getting there."

"It's not an easy task to uproot a whole department, so I'm impressed. But I'm also intrigued," Jackson said, voicing what he'd been musing on overnight. "You're offering me a room, but I sense there are conditions attached."

"You're right. Follow me." Waylen walked out to the corridor, his limp more pronounced than usual, and led him down a small side passage before opening a door. "This is your office. You're the head of the investigation into Black Cronos as of now. Well, you will be if you accept."

Jackson barely took in the room, staring instead at Waylen, who leaned against the doorframe watching him with a hopeful expression. "Seriously? Don't you already do that?"

"I oversee everything, including the lab. I kept an eye on Black Cronos, but it was never an issue, because they barely made waves. Now, with them actively causing problems, I need someone monitoring them, and considering your recent involvement, you're the best candidate."

Jackson had been expecting to have greater involvement with Black Cronos, but not this. "An official role, then?"

"Yes. Are you interested?"

"Of course I'm interested! Especially considering what happened with my grandfather. How will this work?"

"Let's talk inside," Waylen said, striding into the room and dusting off a chair before sitting.

Jackson followed him, taking a seat opposite. "I report to you, obviously."

"Of course. I thought your role could dovetail with Petra and Austin. Anything that sounds suspiciously like Black Cronos comes to you, and you can follow it up. Keep a database—much like they do now for paranormal issues. I'll be honest, most of Black Cronos's stuff hasn't been looked at properly in years, just because they've kept a low profile. I'm planning to share everything we have, and you can see if you can join the dots."

"In case we've missed something."

"We've definitely missed stuff. It's time to look at everything with fresh eyes, historical as well as what's happening now."

Jackson thought of Harlan. "I can see if The Orphic Guild has more information they haven't shared yet, too."

"Excellent. Any source is good. You're Harlan's main contact now, too."

"And what about Gabe and Shadow's group? They're in Turkey now. What if they need extraction teams for bodies or relics? I have no idea how to organise that."

"That's my job. I liaise with other departments for all of that. Same as we use government morgues for the bodies that Layla oversees. You just let me know what you need—and that includes logistics, like flights."

Jackson nodded, relieved to be focussing on the things he liked. "And what about my other job? Hunting for occult objects. Can I keep that up?"

"If you have time—which I doubt you will right now." Waylen laughed at Jackson's perplexed face that he obviously hadn't hidden very well. "Don't worry. You will again, I'm sure, in the future. We just happen to be having an intense period right now."

"Tell me about it!"

Waylen stood, prompting Jackson to stand, too, and they shook hands. "I'm glad you've accepted, Jackson. I'll organise the contract and send you the files we have. Some stuff is on the computer already, but you'll have to add the rest."

"That's fine. I can't wait."

And Jackson meant it. The slow-burning vengeance that he always carried over his missing grandfather and his team ignited with a sudden fury, and he was determined to find every single scrap of evidence he could.

The team had made good time out of the city, and Gabe studied their secure camp, deciding that for now, they were in the best place possible.

The tents had been set up in a circle, a firepit already constructed in the middle. The weapons had been distributed, and Estelle had cast a protection spell over the camp and their cars that they'd left at the side of the road. Zee and Barak were currently perched high on the rocky terraces, hidden within shadowy clefts to watch their surroundings.

"Good job," he said to his brothers. "And with Estelle's protection spell, I'm satisfied that Black Cronos won't find us."

"Ominous news about Stefan Hope-Robbins, though," Nahum said, his eyes roving over the rocks surrounding them before settling on Gabe again. "He's obviously very important to them if he's out here."

"It doesn't change the risks for us. I'm more worried about their soldiers than him, and Shadow didn't see how many they have with them."

"And you're sure no one followed you out of the city?"

Gabe shook his head. "No. We kept a close eye on the road, and we certainly weren't followed up this track. I guess we should take advantage and start searching for the lost city. Do we think it's in one of these terraces?"

Ash cut in, a puzzled expression on his face as he looked up from the map. "I'm not sure. We're close, but I doubt this is it. It doesn't look like the photos, but nothing I've spotted so far actually does."

The old, grainy photographs were on Catarina's lap, and she started to sift through them before passing them around the group. "Unfortunately," she said, "these rocky terraces are all so similar."

"We need landmarks," Niel said. "Odd shapes that might be more obvious from above than on the ground, perhaps."

Catarina frowned. "Do we have a plane at our disposal?"

Niel froze, as did his other brothers, but Shadow laughed. "Ah. You didn't think that one through, Niel!"

Gabe grunted with annoyance, but most of his brothers laughed too, a resigned expression on their faces as Niel said, "There's probably something about us we need to share."

This was always inevitable, and despite Gabe's initial wishes to keep their abilities a secret, it was clear that in this business it was going to prove difficult. Especially when wayward countesses insisted on coming with them. He knew he should have put his foot down.

Catarina looked at the group clustered around the firepit, a question in her eyes, as well as wariness, and Gabe realised she was probably now acutely aware of the fact that she didn't know any of them, not really, and the one person she did, Harlan, was not there.

"Well?" she asked, almost withdrawing back into her camp chair.

Gabe tried to reassure her. "It's nothing alarming. You are safe with us."

"That's good to know, because you're worrying me now!"

Estelle's expression was mischievous. "Perhaps you should show her, Niel." She turned to Catarina. "It's really quite something."

Niel shook his head as if to rebuke her, but Gabe knew he was looking forward to it. All the Nephilim loved to spread their wings, and they all loved the looks it got them, too. It stoked their egos, and Gabe couldn't deny it. He knew he loved nothing better than Shadow's admiring glances, and her hands digging deep in his feathers, especially when they were... He mentally dismissed those images, already feeling his stirrings of desire at the memory.

Niel pulled his t-shirt over his head, revealing his impressively muscled physique and more of his unusual tattoos, and stepping away from the group, his wings appeared out of nowhere. He spread them wide, turning slowly. "Sorry if it shocks you!"

Catarina gasped, and leapt to her feet, knocking the chair back as she did so. "*Shock*? Oh, my God!"

Niel's grin widened. "Not a God. Just a Nephilim."

In seconds, Catarina wobbled and her face turned a deathly white, and Ash, who was closest, reacted first, catching her before she fell.

"Oops," Niel said, looking stricken. "I didn't mean to make her faint!"

"Bloody preening pillock," Ash muttered as he lifted her effortlessly and carried her to some shade in the tent. "We have to remember that she's human! Not fey, not a witch, or a shifter. She's a countess, and an amateur archaeologist!"

Shadow smirked as she played with one of her knives, turning it over her fingers with lightning speed. "She insisted on coming. These are the consequences. And besides, she'll get over it."

"I agree with you," Estelle said, fireballs erupting into her hands. "Wait until she sees what I get up to."

Shadow narrowed her eyes, and Gabe was relieved when Shadow didn't top it with a boast of her own. The last thing he needed was Estelle and Shadow at loggerheads again.

"Please, Estelle," Gabe remonstrated. "Let's keep it to just one shock at a time. And Niel, put your bloody wings away! Perhaps we need food, too. It feels like hours since breakfast. We can plan our next move once we've studied those photos again."

Niel obliged, pulling his t-shirt on again, but there was an undeniable twinkle in his eye as he grabbed their supplies. "Yes, sir. And I'll cook. Maybe I should offer to take Catarina for a flight, later."

"Just focus on the food, for now!" Gabe told him.

And then Gabe had another thought. If it took Niel's mind off brooding about Lilith, perhaps he should entertain the countess.

Twenty

Harlan stared with disbelief at the number of books spread across JD's table in his vast library.

"There are this many volumes written about the *Comte de Saint-Germain*? That's nuts!"

"He fascinated thousands of people in his time." JD sniffed, drew himself upright, and pointed to a packed shelf. "Much like myself. There are just as many about my life, you know. Most of them full of poppycock!"

It was mid-morning on Monday, and they had both slept in after their late night and the attack on the grounds. Despite proof of JD's brilliant defence systems, Harlan had found it difficult to relax, and it was only with dawn that he had finally settled into a deep sleep.

Harlan tried to keep the incredulity from his voice and failed. "You buy books about your own life? Why?"

"I like to know what people think. I sometimes review them—under a pseudonym, of course. I can be quite scathing."

"No shit." Harlan could envisage JD reading books about himself, huffing with annoyance and uttering Shakespearean curses as he did so. He decided to change the subject before he said something rude, and picked up the closest book about the count. "Are there any you'd recommend?"

"Not that one. That's a copy of the only book he's ever written—allegedly."

Harlan glanced down at the title and frowned as he read it out loud. "*The Most Holy Trinosophophia of the Comte de Saint-Germain.* What's it about?"

"It's an allegorical account of a spiritual and alchemical initiation." JD sneered. "Not so allegorical, I'm sure."

"I thought he would have published lots of books and papers. Isn't that what you alchemists do?"

"Exactly. And that's why I always thought him to be a charlatan in those respects, despite his brilliance in other ways."

"But that's clever, surely. If he is immortal, and born earlier than he professed to be, publishing anything would destroy his mystique."

"True," JD said, picking up another couple of volumes. "But for background on him and his life, and some of his letters, I'd recommend these two books. But see what you think. Others may appeal."

"You said that no one knows his true nationality?"

"No. He was deliberately vague about his origins, although he later said he was the son of Francis Racoczi the second, Prince of Transylvania, born in 1690." JD shrugged. "But others thought he was Italian or French, or even Polish. Some asserted that he had been around since the time of Jesus." He snorted. "I don't believe that for a second!"

Harlan thought he'd misheard. "*Jesus*? You're kidding!"

"No. That's what I mean! He courted rumours back then. Encouraged them. Deliberately misled people and laid false trails. I honestly took him for a colossal fake. I've certainly come across others." Harlan wondered if he was referring to Edward Kelley, the man who JD had worked closely with, and who had scryed and contacted angels for him. Books now suggested he had fooled JD for years, but Harlan wasn't about to bring that up. JD gestured to the books and the library. "Make yourself at home. I'll need you again in an hour or so to finetune that knife. I feel I'm close to a breakthrough."

"You're going back to the lab?"

He nodded. "I'll make sure Anna brings you some lunch."

"Okay, but JD, I need to get back to London tonight. I know this is important, which is why I stayed, but I've got cases to follow up. And I need to let Jackson know about your thoughts on the count."

"Ah, yes, you should." He worried his lower lip as he stared into the distance. "Let's chat later, before you go. I may have some ideas of where we should look."

He swept through the door, closing it softly behind him. Harlan picked the books up and settled into a comfortable armchair in a patch of sunlight under the window. As much as Harlan was looking forward to curling up in JD's extensive library and reading up on an interesting character, he couldn't ignore his other work. But he had to admit that working closely with JD this weekend had gone a long way to rebuilding their relationship. He wouldn't call them friends, but at least JD was civil now, and Harlan felt he understood him better.

But if they could find the count, which sounded fairly impossible at this stage, what was next?

Nahum stood atop the highest point of the rock terraces that surrounded their camp, studying the contours of the land in the setting sun, and then frowned again at the photos in his hand.

"We're in the wrong place," he said to Zee, who stood at his side.

"You sure? I thought the GPS and map suggested we were close."

"Not close enough. The Earl of Breconshire—Jasper—deliberately destroyed the most detailed map." He sighed. "I didn't find anything below us, did you?"

"Not a thing. Most caves are shallow or narrow, more like clefts. I sensed nothing."

"Do you expect to?" Nahum asked, puzzled.

Zee shrugged. "Maybe. The Igigi were powerful creatures, with their own kind of magic. It makes me think we should feel something, even after all this time."

"Perhaps we will." Nahum lifted his head, inhaling the scent of the desert that the wind carried to him. "Dusk comes soon, and then we can fly higher. Maybe it's a good thing not to be camped too close, considering what happened to the earl's team."

"You think something might emerge from the city?"

"Don't you?" Nahum said, remembering what they'd been told of the earl's story. "It sounded like he was genuinely terrified. I don't know what came out of that cave, but it certainly wasn't friendly."

"Perhaps the Igigi set up some kind of defence system," Zee mused. "Something automated. They were clever at building things."

Nahum pocketed the photos as he thought on Zee's suggestion. "Automatons, perhaps? But the earl said the rock came to life. None of it makes sense!"

As they were speaking the sun plunged below the horizon, leaving a smear of blazing light in the west, before it began to fade. Immediately, the heat ebbed away, too.

"Let's wait here until it's dark enough, and then we'll re-join the team," Zee said. "And let's hope Catarina has recovered from the shock."

Ash stoked the fire, setting the flames blazing again before lifting the pot from the chain they had used to suspend it. The water in it was hot, and he made a cup of tea for the countess, adding plenty of sugar too, and then made one for himself.

They were the only ones in the camp, the others having separated to investigate their surroundings. All of them thought it best to offer the countess some space to get over her shock. Her faint hadn't lasted long, but when she came around, she had stared at Ash and asked, "Have you got wings, too?"

He nodded, keeping as much distance between them as possible in the small tent so as not to scare her. "All of us do, except for Shadow and Estelle."

"They're...normal?"

Ash had winced. "Er, not exactly. But let's talk more later."

He had left her to gather her thoughts, and she finally emerged from the tent when the camp had fallen quiet. Now she sat opposite Ash in silent contemplation, staring into the flames.

"Catarina, have some tea. It's good for shock. Or so the many English people I know keep telling me."

Catarina finally relaxed and smiled. "It's the mundaneness of it, I think."

"I prefer other drinks myself, but I'll drink tea with you."

"Let me guess. Ouzo?"

"Mastika, actually, but it has been a while since I tasted it."

She took the cup from his outstretched hand, sipped it, and then sighed. "I feel a fool."

"Why? It's not every day you see a Nephilim. Well, six of us, actually."

"Where are the others?"

"Giving you space. And searching for the entrance to the city, of course."

She looked him straight in the eye. "The Nephilim are supposed to be myth."

"So are the Igigi, but we're out here looking for them."

"You're supposed to be violent, too."

"We have been," Ash confessed. And then thinking of their recent exploits said, "Well, we still are, but only when we need to be. We certainly don't attack those weaker than us." He smiled. "That includes you."

"I'm glad to hear that!"

"I can take you back to the hotel if you'd prefer." She had shrunk back into her chair again, flinching at every noise.

"I had considered it, but then again, when I asked to come here—"

"Demanded, actually," Ash reminded her, amused.

She pursed her lips. "I guess that's true. Anyway, it was because I craved a distraction from my husband's illness and the small world that my life has become. I'm certainly getting that, aren't I?" Without waiting for him to answer, she said, "And besides, you're right. I came looking for the mythical Igigi. If you exist, then so must they."

Ash laughed. "I can confirm that they *did* exist, but whether they still do is another matter. We arrived here by unusual means." He gave her a brief description of their recent history.

She shook her head. "All my life I have devoured these myths and legends. I feel like I'm in a storybook now. Look where we are! In a desert, around a campfire, and a handsome Nephilim is watching over me." She met his eyes over the fire. "Now I know why you look like a Greek God."

"You can blame our angel fathers for our looks. They bestowed a certain amount of divinity upon us."

"Then they did the world a favour."

Ash's eyebrows shot up. It seemed the countess was flirting. *Fine.* He could cope with that.

"I'm hoping that means that you want to stay?"

"Yes. I've got over my shock...more or less. You'll just have to forgive me if I stare a lot." She sipped her tea again, and Ash wasn't sure if it was that or the firelight that had restored the colour to her cheeks. "I have another question. You said Shadow and Estelle were not quite human?"

"Correct. Shadow is fey, and Estelle is a witch."

"Ah! Okay. A fey and a witch. I feel suddenly inadequate."

"Don't." Ash leaned forward. "You know your husband better than anyone, and these maps and papers. You've studied them for years. Potentially, you'll find the cave quicker than us. We're close."

"I hope I can. But I admit, I'm scared."

"You'd be a fool not to be. Now," he said stirring and moving to the cooking supplies, "I promised I'd cook, and if I don't, I'll be in trouble. We all have big appetites."

Catarina smiled, threw the dregs of her tea into the fire, and stood, too. "In that case, I must help. And later, if we search again, I insist on going, too."

When Niel arrived back in the camp, he was relieved to see Catarina relaxed and chatty.

He'd stayed away from the camp for a long time, feeling guilty for scaring her—even though it was unintentional. *Ash calling him a preening pillock hadn't helped.* Although, he had enjoyed seeing Catarina's wide-eyed appreciation of his physique before she fainted.

It smelled like the meal was ready, some kind of spicy meat stew that was simmering over the fire. If they didn't find the cave in the next day or so, they'd be out of fresh food and resorting to reconstituted dried meals, and he wasn't looking forward to that.

"Niel!" Barak said, spotting him as he stepped out of the shadows. "We thought we'd lost you. We're about to eat."

The team was gathered around the fire in small groups, talking quietly. Nobody looked particularly excited, so he thought that like him, they hadn't found the cave yet.

"I thought I'd give Catarina some space," he said, looking at her with what he hoped was a contrite expression on his face. "I'm sorry. I didn't think you'd faint."

"Neither did I!" she shot back. "It's not as if I'm a giddy schoolgirl! Don't worry, I'm fine now."

"Good. Let's hope Ash isn't going to poison us."

Ash glared at him. "I think you know I can cook quite well. And besides, Catarina helped me!"

"That should be no recommendation," she confessed. "I'm not that good a cook. I just did as I was told."

Niel grunted. "Well, it smells good, and I'm starving."

"Then let's dig in," Barak said, handing out bowls.

The meal was informal, with everyone helping themselves, and tearing off hunks of bread to mop up the spicy sauce.

While they ate, Gabe asked, "Has anyone got any leads on the city?"

Everyone shook their heads.

"I've seen something," Niel confessed, not wishing to alarm Catarina in particular. "I watched a convoy of cars on the road, heading into the desert. A little further south from here. I didn't want to get too close, but it could be Toto. They were in their usual black vans, and some off-roaders, too."

"Why the hell didn't you mention this sooner?" Gabe asked, annoyed.

"I've been here five minutes, Gabe. And besides, that's another reason I'm late. I watched them set up their camp. But I was high up, so I couldn't see details."

Shadow's eyes narrowed. "Then take me there. I can get closer and listen."

Gabe glared at her, their familiar dance already starting. "Are you mad? If it's them, their soldiers will be everywhere!"

"I am fey! They will not see me, as long as that big idiot drops me far enough away so we're not spotted."

Niel bristled with annoyance. "*Idiot*? I spotted them, didn't I? And I have wings that a certain someone does not!"

Shadow poked her tongue at him before addressing Gabe. "Besides, what if they're in the right place and we're not? We need to stop them—tonight. And if not, we need to resume our own search. We can't afford to wait."

Ash asked, "How far south, Niel?"

He shrugged. "Five kilometres or so? Beyond another large ridge of rock."

"How many soldiers?" Zee asked.

"At least a dozen, probably more."

Barak turned to Gabe. "Could we try and take them out? That would eliminate the risk from the start."

Gabe shook his head. "No. Let's stay well out of their way. With luck, they won't find the city or us. We only attack if we need to."

Niel had a feeling he would say that. "That's fine for now, Gabe, but if we find the city, I don't want to get hemmed in by them. If the Igigi are alive and aggressive, we could end up trapped between two powerful groups."

Gabe nodded. "I know. We'll assess as we go, and in the meantime," he sighed deeply and looked at Shadow, "be careful. Observe only!"

She gave him her biggest smile. "Of course. I'll thank you properly later."

Gabe smirked while Niel feigned vomiting. "If you mention anything about your sex life while I'm flying you there, I'll drop you, understand?"

Shadow didn't answer, instead giving him the finger, and he silently counted to ten.

Twenty-One

I t was getting late by the time Jackson finished organising his new office and the seemingly endless files to his satisfaction.

He was pleased with his room. It had an old-world grandeur about it, with its sweeping lines and old-fashioned lamps. The cleaners had come through mid-afternoon, and now the woodwork was gleaming in the soft lamplight. A decorative window inlaid with an ornate stained-glass design was set into the wall dividing the room from the passage, and through it he saw the light from the corridor. The occasional silhouette passed by on the way to the kitchen and communal room that was at the end of the corridor, but it was impossible to see who it was.

It was because of this window that he forgot he was so far underground, despite the fact that it didn't show a view of any sort. It relieved the monotony of the wood panelling and made him feel less shut in. His phone worked, his computer worked, and he found a couple of comfortable chairs and a low table to go in the corner of the room, salvaged from a storeroom that contained all sorts of interesting pieces of furniture. Waylen had given him free reign, a benefit of being on a small team in a place able to accommodate more. It made him wonder if the Paranormal Division had been bigger at one point, or if Princess Louise just had grand aspirations.

Jackson checked his watch, and with a shock realised it was time to meet Harlan. In five minutes, he was outside Serpentine South and making his way to the now dark entrance where he saw Harlan leaning against a wall, dressed casually in jeans, boots, and a leather jacket.

"You survived your time with JD, then?" he asked Harlan by way of a greeting, his eyes sweeping over him. "You don't look like a man at the end of your tether."

Harlan laughed. "There were trying moments, no doubt about that. And it's fair to say I have a new appreciation of his talents. But first, tell me why we're outside Serpentine South at eight at night. You said we were going to your headquarters."

Jackson realised he was looking forward to this. "We are. This is the main entrance for our new place. Come and see."

He led the way back to the deserted office, through security, and along the passage to his private office, pleased to see Harlan was as impressed as he was with the PD's new headquarters.

Harlan shook his head. "It never fails to amaze me what's hidden beneath London."

"I know! Kensington Gardens, of all places. I think Waylen is still here, somewhere, and Blake and the science techs are still organising the labs. This forced move will put us back days, if not weeks. It's infuriating."

Harlan wrestled with his leather messenger bag. "I brought you a present. A couple, actually." He handed Jackson a bottle wrapped in paper. "A housewarming present to suit your fancy new office. I'm hoping you have glasses."

"Hardly fancy," he said, pleased to see a bottle of good quality whiskey. "Thanks, Harlan. Just what I need."

Harlan's gaze swept the room. "Art Nouveau? Are you kidding me? This place is fantastic." He fished in his bag. "Here's present number two—although it's a loan, really. A book for you to read."

Harlan placed it on the low table and took a seat, and Jackson joined him once he fished around in a cupboard for cups. "Forgive me. I've yet to find the cut glass and decanters."

"I'll cope."

Jackson cracked the lid and poured them a couple of fingers, raising it in a toast. It wasn't until it was blazing a warm trail down his throat that he realised how thirsty he was. And hungry. He reached forward for the book and frowned. "*The Comte de Saint-Germain.* Why are you giving me this?"

Harlan brushed his hand through his thick dark hair, a crease settling on his brow. "Have you heard of him?"

"I have, actually. He's a very interesting figure." Jackson placed his glass down and flicked through the book. It was well thumbed, a few pages marked with sticky notes, and pencilled scribbles filled the margins.

"JD thinks he's Black Cronos's Grand Master."

He fumbled the book with shock. "*What?* Are you kidding?"

"No. And the more I read today, the more I think JD is right. You know he was rumoured to be immortal in his own lifetime?"

"Sure. He's one of the most fascinating historical characters I know of. He influenced royalty, amassed loads of money, was an amazing musician, spoke multiple languages..." He trailed off, studying Harlan's serious expression. "Black Cronos?"

Harlan outlined JD's reasoning. "And it makes sense. If JD has achieved immortality, why couldn't the count? He may even be older than JD, if those rumours are correct. The many encounters with him that people have recorded all suggest he was *really* odd, and he disappeared for years on end. When he did turn up again, he hadn't aged a day. His great age could well explain how he has made his soldiers so advanced. JD is having trouble wrapping his head around what they've achieved, and that's saying something."

Jackson picked his glass up again and leaned back in his chair, rubbing his face, perplexed. "I don't know whether to think that's great news or terrible. But, if you're right, then we have something to build on." He glanced at the stack of boxes on the floor. "It also means I have a new focus for those."

"JD has a few suggestions where he thinks he may have a base, too. Places in Europe."

"Like where?"

"France, where he spent many years as the advisor and friend of King Louis XV. Or, because Spanish and Portuguese were his most fluent languages, JD suggests that maybe there's a base in one of those countries. He's still compiling a list of possible places."

"Wow. Okay, so much to think on." Jackson's excitement about his new role bubbled up again, mixed with some trepidation. "If it is him, he's a formidable opponent."

"We have formidable friends."

"True. How did JD get on with the weapon?"

"He's made some progress, but he thinks he started it all wrong and is going back to basics." Harlan huffed. "I'm going back in a couple of days. I'll get his list then, too. But for now," Harlan stood, draining his glass as he did, "I need food, and so do you. Come on, let's find a pub."

Shadow landed with Niel a short distance away from Black Cronos's camp, which, like theirs, was encompassed by rocky terraces, and although she enjoyed flying, Shadow was relieved to have the hard earth beneath her feet again.

It was odd flying with Niel, as Shadow had only ever flown with Gabe before, and it was clear that Gabe wasn't that thrilled about it from the warning glance he gave Niel before they set off. His arms felt odd around her, and although she was good friends with Niel, despite their bickering, it felt oddly intimate. Not that Niel did anything except carry her. They flew high overhead for a short while, dipping down lower and lower in a wide circle before landing on a ridge just beyond their camp, in a fold that was out of their view. The camp was comprised of half a dozen off-road vehicles, several large tents, and many soldiers.

"You're right, Niel, that definitely looks like them," she admitted, adjusting her armour breastplate that Dante had fixed.

"Shadow, please be careful. Don't get too close. There were at least a dozen soldiers there, and they may have different abilities to what we've seen before."

Shadow bristled at his advice. He was looming over her, his tree trunk arms resting on his hips. "I'm not an idiot."

"I know. You're highly skilled, but so are they. Don't get too close. I'll hover overhead to keep an eye on you."

She nodded, all too aware that her cockiness could sometimes get her into trouble. "I'll head back here when I'm done. Maybe an hour, max."

"And if you're in trouble, I'll join in. I have your back, sister."

Shadow shot him a grateful smile as she pulled her fey magic around her and melted into the desert night. The stars glittered overhead, the swathe of the Milky Way cutting a path across the sky as she headed up the rocky incline, the uneven ground not an obstacle even in the dark. The air was cool now, but she barely noticed she was so intent on her quarry.

As she reached the top of the ridge, she slowed down, and slid flat on her stomach until the camp was laid out below her. The terrace sloped sharply downward, a tumble of rock and hollows with the occasional stunted bush clinging to life. One wrong move and she would set off a rockfall, but she had to get closer.

Easing to a crouch, she edged her way down, flitting from hollow to hollow. She could see soldiers below her guarding the way that led to the road. Unfortunately, a couple were studying the sky overhead, crossbows in their hands. She thanked the Gods that Niel had flown high. It seemed they were expecting company. In total, there were at least half a dozen men and women, all dressed in familiar black clothing with protective armour, some carrying their unusual weaponry. In the centre of the camp was a large fire, and a pavilion-style tent had been erected, which seemed to be a meeting space. As she dropped lower, she could see a table inside it, covered with paperwork. Stefan and Toto were deep in conversation, heads bent over what looked like a map. The Silencer of Souls was nowhere in sight. Other large tents had been set up as a type of barracks, and a couple of soldiers were gathered around a fire.

What was of more interest was a generator and the cables plugged into it. They led into a narrow cleft in the rock, and from deep within it was a gleam of light. *Had they found the city, after all? And was that where the other soldiers were? She could see fewer than Niel's estimated numbers.*

Shadow assessed the camp again. While the centre was lit with torch light, flames flaring in the night breeze, the outskirts, particularly under the rockface were in darkness, and no one was outside the break in the rock. She needed to get in there. Edging higher, and careful not to alert the guards, she stuck to the rocky terraces, clinging like a limpet, and made her way around the camp until she was much closer to the cleft. Dropping onto the ground, and making sure she hadn't been seen, she crept inside.

The cleft was long and narrow, a pale light glowing at the far end, showing up the rough, uneven walls and sandy floor, and the entrance to a cave. The banging of metal on rock drummed around her. She would have to be careful. When she reached the end, she could be spotted. However, when she finally made it to the cave, she found the dozen or so soldiers at the far end, working under the lights to break down a section of rock. The Silencer of Souls seemed to be supervising them.

But why there?

Shadow kept to the dark edges, finally scrambling up to a secure perch with a good view of the action. The soldiers were battering at what appeared to be a gate carved into the wall of rock. It was huge, and covered in carvings of the now familiar shapes of the Igigi. Stone pillars on either side had places for torches, and now that she was higher, she could see that the ground had a series of channels in it.

But the longer she watched, the more puzzled she became. For a start, she couldn't understand why they weren't using their explosive devices to blast through the rock. *Maybe they were worried about causing too much damage and bringing down the roof on their heads.* The other problem was that she had studied the grainy photos that Catarina had brought with her, and this cave looked nothing like that one. *This was another entrance, and Black Cronos had beaten them to it.* Even worse, there was nothing she could do to stop them. There were far too many to take on. Her priority was to get back and tell the others.

Shadow was on her way back to the cave's mouth when the roar of breaking rock signalled their success in smashing through the stone gate. Rock dust filled the air, and she pulled her jacket over her nose in an effort not to sneeze.

The Silencer of Souls broke away from the main group, a triumphant smile on her face, and headed to the exit, no doubt to tell the others. There was no way Shadow could get there before her, but she could follow her, and might even be able to kill her before she reached the camp.

Shadow followed her into the narrow cleft, knives drawn, and quickened her pace. She was within knifing distance when the woman dropped, rolled, and threw a weapon at Shadow. With lightning-quick reflexes, Shadow dodged and struck back, but her opponent threw herself at Shadow, and in the narrow, confined space, Shadow had nowhere to go.

Ash circled another section of the terraced rock, trying to discern landmarks, whilst keeping a tight grip on Catarina. Not that he needed to worry. She was clinging to his arms so tightly he thought they might go numb.

"Are you okay?" he asked her.

"Fine." She sounded breathless, but from what he could see of her face, she looked elated. "This is amazing. And terrifying. I feel like Lois Lane with Superman."

He laughed. "Christopher Reeve. I saw that one. Please don't freak out like she did."

"I'm keeping it together...just."

"Focus on the search. That will take your mind off it."

She snorted in a very unladylike manner. "Like that would help!"

She wriggled back against his chest, and Ash realised this was the closest he'd been to any woman in a long time. *Or a man, for that matter.* Ash was relaxed about his lovers. He was drawn to the person, not the gender. But it was a shock for him to think of Catarina in that respect, and he blamed it on his hormones and the heat of the desert.

"I'm serious," he said, his lips close to her ear, pleased to see a blush spread across her cheeks.

"You need to drop down lower—to the right."

He did as she instructed, gliding down so they were above the next ridged valley, and it was the change of angle that triggered his memory. And for Catarina, too.

"I see it! That spur. It looks familiar."

Ash dropped lower, the shallow valley below the spur closing in, until with the lightest of landing, they were on the ground. Catarina took a moment to release herself from his hold. Her eyes were wide as she studied the odd angle of the space, and the sheer wall of rock to one side.

"Ash! This looks like the photos!"

She fumbled in her pocket and found the envelope they were contained in. Her fingers shook as she pulled them free, and Ash shined a pocket torch on them, comparing the photos to their surroundings. There was no doubt the scene was incredibly similar.

"I agree. That area in particular looks the same. That, however, does not." He pointed to the sheer rock that looked strangely smooth compared to the rest of the terrace.

"That's because it was the entrance before!" She jabbed the image of the cave's entrance. "Wait." She dropped to her knees and spread the images out, marrying them together by overlapping, and the broad expanse of the rocky terrace suddenly came together.

"Herne's bollocks, you're right. It's the same place."

Her eyes danced with excitement. "My husband said the cave sealed itself. A rockfall, perhaps?"

"That's not a rockfall. Not a natural one, anyway." Tentatively, he walked to the sheer face, Catarina next to him, and ran his fingers across the surface. "It's too smooth. Sculpted."

"By the Igigi?"

"I presume so. It's further to the east than we thought, though. We're at least two miles out."

"More remote. Is there even a road here?"

"There must be if your husband's team came here, but we'll check when we fly again."

Her shoulders dropped and she sighed as she looked up at him. "They didn't come by car. They arrived by camel. There probably is no road here!"

"Fuck it!" Ash groaned as he realised their mistake. He'd been trying to marry the directions to a road. Now he felt like a complete idiot. "But still, we followed the map as best we could."

"No matter. We've found it now, I'm sure."

"Let's check a few more photos, just to make sure. If we're going to uproot the camp, I want to make sure we're right this time."

Besides, he liked being alone with the countess under the Milky Way, with nothing but the soft susurrus of shifting sand and the wind through the rocks. Taking another few minutes alone would be no hardship. And from the long look she gave him as she turned back to the photos, he had a feeling she felt the same.

Twenty-Two

N iel watched Black Cronos's camp from above, looking for any sign that Shadow had been spotted.

She had long since disappeared from his view, and although he loved his own strength and speed, he wished he had even half of her stealth. He hunkered down on a rock, folding his wings away, and now that he was closer, he could see the men with their crossbows trained on the sky.

He considered his options, wondering if he could take some of their soldiers out, but it was too risky alone, especially with Shadow down there. The soldiers guarding the rough track that led to the paved road were all within sight and sound of each other, so it was impossible to pick them off.

A jeering shout below broke his concentration. With horror he saw The Silencer of Souls emerge from the cleft, her arm wrapped firmly around Shadow, who looked almost insensible as she was dragged into the camp. Stefan and Toto emerged from beneath the main tent to close in on them, and all the guards turned to watch, including the ones with the crossbows.

Niel seized his chance. He jumped from the outstretched rock, his wings close to his side as he dived downwards, sword in one outstretched hand.

It seemed Shadow had seized her moment, too. As soon as she cleared the cleft, she broke free of her captor and threw her knives at Toto and Stefan. As Stefan scrambled for cover, Toto fell awkwardly. Shadow didn't stop, pulling her swords and whirling them as she faced The Silencer of Souls.

Niel changed direction. He attacked the two closest guards with his sword, knocking them off their feet and inflicting deep cuts, before swooping on one of the soldiers with a crossbow. He shot a bolt at Niel, but it went wide, and Niel landed on him, flattening him to the ground. He grabbed the crossbow from his outstretched hands, whirled around, and using the stolen weapon, took out the other soldier armed with the crossbow, satisfied to see the bolt pierce his throat.

The camp was now in chaos. Toto had collapsed on the ground, and Stefan was at his side, while Shadow danced out of reach of The Silencer of Souls and the remaining guards. Her swords were a blur of motion, and despite everyone's best attempts, they couldn't get close.

Niel charged across the ground, pulling his axe free and smashing one of the main tent poles as he passed it. It collapsed onto the ground, half enveloping Stefan and adding to the confusion. Shadow ran to his side, and wrapping one free arm around her, he launched into the air again.

"Fuck me, Shadow!" he yelled as they ascended. "What happened?"

"That bitch happened, of course."

"I thought you were unconscious," he told her.

She twisted to look at him, a wicked grin on her face. "That's what she thought, too. But I have news. Bad news. They've found another entrance. I'll explain when we land."

Niel nodded, and soon they were back at their own campsite. But for some reason, everyone was packing up.

"What's going on?" he asked as he landed and released Shadow from his hold.

Ash grimaced. "We're in the wrong place, but we're sure we've found the entrance now. We're a mile or two out."

Gabe dropped the half-packed tent he was holding and hurried to their side, his eyes hard as they raked over them both. "What happened? Why are you carrying a crossbow?"

Shadow shrugged coolly. "I had an incident."

Gabe folded his arms across his chest. "An *incident*?" This time when he looked them over, he was more worried. "Are you injured?"

"I am fey! Of course not."

Estelle snorted as she joined them, the rest of their team circling around. "You're not immune, Shadow. Your chest injury proved that the other day."

She shot her an impatient look. "I was caught off-guard then. Today I had my revenge."

Gabe's voice was almost a growl. "How?"

"Niel was right. Black Cronos has set up camp a few miles south in a secluded valley, accessed only by a rough track. Toto and Stefan were distracted by paperwork, and the soldiers were busy watching the track that led to the valley. A narrow cleft in the rockface led to a cave, and I was able to sneak in. Many more soldiers were in the cave, including that bloody woman." She paused, perplexed. "There was a huge stone gate set into the rock wall. It was richly carved with images of the Igigi, stone pillars on either side. To me it looked ornamental. But they had a team with machinery and tools, and as I was there, they broke into it—put a hole right through the door. It was thick, too. At least a couple of feet."

The group looked uneasily at each other, and Zee asked, "What was on the other side?"

"I was too far away to see anything other than darkness, but it must be a way into the city." She turned to Catarina. "The photos didn't look like the cave your father-in-law found. Perhaps they discovered a rear entrance? Or a side gate?"

Catarina's eyes clouded with confusion. "Does it matter, as long as we have a way in, too? Are you sure they've found the Igigi's city? It could be something else entirely."

"The carvings on the gate were like those on the stone tablet," Shadow said. "I'm sure."

"And besides," Nahum said, "two cities or underground complexes would just be nuts. They have to be the same."

Gabe huffed with annoyance. "Agreed. The only thing that matters is that they're getting into the city and we're not." He looked at Shadow and Niel, his earlier reticence gone. "What if we follow them in and finish this now? How many soldiers are there?"

"A couple of dozen?" Shadow suggested with a shrug. "I think we're already too late. But I wounded Toto. One of my knives found its mark."

Ash cut into the conversation. "While it's annoying that they have found their own way in somehow, we have Jasper's entrance, and we need to use it. Let's get moving. The four wheel drives should make it to the new camp, even though there's no track to speak of. I'll fly and lead the way, okay?"

There was a chorus of agreement, and as everyone disbursed, Gabe grabbed Niel and pulled him aside. "Do me a favour. Follow us to the new place, and then circle back and check on Toto's camp. If we can enter from their side too, we can trap them between us."

"While I like your reasoning, Gabe, I need to warn you that the other entrance is a good few miles away. That means the city beneath us is huge. I don't think us splitting up is a good idea."

Gabe's eyes took on a faraway expression as he considered his options, and he reluctantly nodded. "Point taken, but check anyway. We can't be too careful."

Gabe studied the smooth stone wall, Nahum beside him, and grunted with frustration.

"I think Ash has gone mad!"

Nahum patted his shoulder. "Sorry Gabe, but I think he's right. The photos marry up. How we get in there is another matter."

The sun was rising, casting a rosy, pink glow over their new campsite, which they had set up quickly. After a cursory examination of the area, Gabe had instructed the others to get some sleep. It had been a long night, and he wanted to make sure they were fresh when they entered the city.

If they entered the city.

He glared at the wall again, frowning at its smooth, unyielding surface. "How in Herne's hairy bollocks did they achieve this?"

"The Igigi always had their own magic, gifted by the Gods. That's why they were such great builders. And that's why we have a witch with us."

Gabe tore his gaze from the rock and stared at Nahum, his brother's blue eyes looking even bluer against his bronzed skin. Even just a couple of days in the desert had deepened his tan. "You think she can open this up?"

"I spoke to her before she went to sleep. She has a few ideas, but she looked beat."

Gabe knew Estelle's magic was powerful, and hoped she could find a way through. He voiced his other concern next. "How did Black Cronos find another entrance? We thought we'd be ahead of them, and now they're already inside!"

"They must have found another source. But we have an advantage they don't. We know the Igigi."

"Which is no advantage at all if they're dead. For all we know, they've got a map of the place and are raiding their dead bones right now."

"Or they've been buried in a rockslide or caught in a weird Igigi trap and are all dead themselves." Nahum looked amused. "We focus on our end, not theirs."

Gabe grunted again, knowing he was being unreasonable. But frankly, he wouldn't feel happy until they were in there. "The other thing we need to decide is whether we leave someone outside on guard. What if Black Cronos finds this place and follow us in?"

"Look around. We're well off the road here, and hidden from view. We barely got the off-road vehicles here. And they haven't got wings."

"True." Gabe groaned as he ran his hands through his hair, already gritty with sand and sweat. He'd forgotten how the desert invaded all clothes and belongings. "Do you miss this?"

"The desert?" Nahum asked, startled.

"The whole place. The food, the heat, the culture..."

Nahum shrugged. "Yes and no. That was one life, this is another. And we're here now. We can travel whenever we want—and planes make it much easier now!"

Gabe nodded. "True. I guess it's just weird being back. I thought it would feel like I was coming home, but instead I just feel unsettled. So much has changed."

"And so much hasn't. We chased them across these deserts before. Well, to the south, at least. Until these hills swallowed them."

Gabe met Nahum's bright blue eyes. "The Igigi can't possibly still be alive, can they?"

"My head says no, but my heart..." Nahum shook his head and sighed. "I actually hope they are."

A shadow fell over them as they talked, and in seconds Niel landed next to them, his snowy wings streaked pink and gold by the early morning sun.

"You're pushing your luck with the light," Gabe told him.

Niel just grinned. "Someone will think I'm a big bird of prey. And the light is still dim."

"You are a big bird of prey," Nahum said, laughing. "What did you see?"

"A dozen guards protecting the entrance, and more inside. Reinforcements have arrived. I watched them go in, all armed with their strange weaponry." Niel clenched his jaw, clearly uncomfortable with what he'd seen. "They have something big planned. If we were to attack them now, I'm not sure we'd survive. We're outnumbered—especially in the open. Our only option is to stop them inside, when hopefully we'll have stealth on our side. And there's no sign of Toto or Stefan, or that bitch, either."

Niel was obviously still furious about their encounter in Scotland, which was completely understandable. Gabe was, too. "Damn it. Part of me hoped we could finish this now, but I knew it wouldn't be that straightforward. Let's ignore them for now and focus on this."

"That's presuming we can get in, and that our entrance will connect with theirs at some point," Nahum argued. "If there's been a rockfall, we're screwed anyway."

"Let's try to be positive," Gabe said. "They were excellent builders. Let's hope whatever they built is still intact, even if they are long gone."

"Have you slept while I've been gone?" Niel asked him, changing the subject.

Gabe considered his gritty eyes and befuddled brain. "No. But I'll be fine. You two should sleep, though, while we have the chance."

Nahum shook his head, directing Gabe to the tent he was sharing with Shadow. "Nope. We all need a few hours' sleep. We're under Estelle's protection spell, so we'll be safe."

"That's true," Niel nodded in agreement. "We're invisible from above. If I didn't know where you were, I wouldn't have had a clue."

"Good." Nahum was already yawning. "And besides, only Herne knows what we'll face in there. We need all the rest we can get."

Gabe reluctantly had to admit he was right, so with a final glance around the camp to make sure all was in order, he ducked into the tent he shared with Shadow. Shedding only his boots, he curled in alongside her, and it seemed he'd only laid his head down for seconds before he was asleep.

Unfortunately, his sleep wasn't dreamless. Images of the Igigi and their prolonged battles dogged his thoughts. The clash of weapons, the long days spent under a searing hot sun, the weary game of cat and mouse, and the traps and ambushes that accompanied the sure and certain knowledge that they weren't going to be successful. And even more, that they shouldn't be. And then there was the memory of a conversation with his father.

"Why are we doing this?" he demanded after a particularly hard campaign in which nothing tangible had been achieved. "You rebelled against your God! Why not let them?"

His father, all flashing eyes full of dark malice, said, "Because we have new partners now, and we have sworn to help the Anunnaki. I personally promised help."

Gabe virtually spat at him. "And yet, you aren't! I am. I have had enough. This ends now."

His father, Remiel, an archangel who was once known as 'God's Thunder' before he fell with Lucifer, was prouder and more headstrong than most. He towered over Gabe, almost blinding in his brilliance.

"It ends when I say it will."

"Then do it yourself!"

Gabe turned his back on Remiel, making to leave the cave where their encounter had taken place. But instead, he found himself pinned in place by his father's power—and his threats. "Any independence you think you have will cease if you fail to do this. And that includes your life with your beautiful wife."

Gabe's blood ran cold as he turned to face his father. "You don't need to threaten her."

"It seems I do. You have a place on Earth for one reason—and that is because I willed it."

Gabe glared at him. "You don't even know why you're here anymore! You argued with your God in the bid for independence, fled your former home, and now resent everything about the place that is your new home! You mourn your loss of privilege, and you flounder in chaos."

Remiel leaned in close. "Don't test me, Gabreel. You still have a home left to return to. Isn't the loss of your child enough?"

Gabe felt such a white-hot rage at those words that he could barely speak, but it was quickly followed by terror at what else he may lose. So, he left the cave carved from the curling dunes and returned to his team—defeated and furious. But the following weeks achieved nothing until even Remiel and the other Fallen angels who had sided with the Anunnaki had been forced to admit defeat.

And then a voice pierced Gabe's dreams that was not a memory at all.

"You failed before, Gabreel. Do not fail again."

Seconds later Gabe woke up, sweat pouring off him, and he shot up in bed, instinctively reaching for his sword, only to find that the tent was empty and Shadow was still sleeping at his side.

But there was no mistaking the voice. It belonged to his father.

Remiel.

It was with relief when Harlan entered his own office at The Orphic Guild on Tuesday morning, happy to be settling back into his normal routine.

There were a couple of cases he needed to focus on, and once he'd made coffee, he accessed the files and evaluated where he'd gotten up to. However, his peace was short-lived when his phone rang, and he cursed when he saw who the caller was.

"Maggie!" he groaned, sounding like he was dreading their conversation, but secretly loving the battle of wits he endured with her. "What crap have you called with now?"

"You're a cheeky fucker, Harlan! You constantly call me with shit that *I* have to mop up! And besides, I could be asking you to dinner."

He tried not to laugh at her caustic tone. "Are you? I'm not sure we're that well suited."

"I know we're bloody not, you smooth American bugger! No, I'm ringing about a body."

Harlan had never been called *smooth* before and wasn't sure he liked it. *However...* "A body? Why are you calling *me*? I swear I haven't murdered anyone."

"It's Barnaby bloody Armstrong. Someone spotted him floating in the Thames this morning."

"*What?*" All of the playfulness left his voice, and he sagged into his chair. "You're kidding."

"I don't kid about death, you moron." Her voice softened. "Sorry, I know you knew him. You arrested him, didn't you, for the PD?"

Harlan fumbled for his coffee, feeling suddenly nauseous. "Yes, with Jackson, only a few nights ago. But Black Cronos broke him out when they raided the old headquarters on Saturday. Did he drown?"

"No. He was already dead, a look of abject horror on his face. No obvious wounds, but remarkably like Blaze. Ring a bell?"

"The Silencer of Souls."

"Most likely. But it's not his death I'm ringing about. It's what we found in the autopsy."

"You've done that already? When did you find him?"

"Yesterday afternoon. There was a small key in his stomach."

Harlan thought he was hearing things. "A *what*?"

"A key, to a bank deposit box. And what's in it will interest you."

"He swallowed a key?"

"Well, he didn't bloody use surgery to get it in there!"

"Sorry, I'm in shock." He kept seeing Barnaby's resigned look when he finally stopped struggling, and couldn't help but feel he was responsible for his death. "What was in the box?"

"Notes on old stories about a buried city."

"Really? Because we already found stuff in his room on that. Did it mention the Igigi?"

"Something like that. But there were also notes about a bloke called Count Belle-mare. Lists of places and names. It means nothing to me, but I thought you and Jackson might be interested."

Harlan's pulse quickened at the mention of a count. "Are you sure it wasn't the Count of St Germain?"

"No. Definitely Bellemare. You can collect them if you want. I've taken copies for my own records, but I know you're looking into Black Cronos." She snorted. "Frankly, I'm too busy to deal with that crap right now."

Harlan was already standing and grabbing his jacket. "Yes, please. I'll come get them right now."

Twenty-Three

Estelle laid her hands on the smooth rock, sending her awareness out and feeling for space beyond it.

She was aware of the team watching her, but blocked their attention out. Earth magic wasn't her strength, but this was a relatively simple thing to do. Witches responded strongly to natural energies, and the earth vibrated with it. In the desert, it felt much the same as anywhere. At the moment all she could feel was solid, unyielding rock, but as she walked along the rockface, her touch detecting the imperfections in the surface, she felt a change. She stopped, pressing both hands against the rock and closed her eyes. Beyond the initial thickness loomed a huge space.

Relieved, because despite her natural faith in her abilities she was keen to impress the Nephilim and cement her place in the team, she turned to face them. "This is the spot. Beyond the rock is a cave."

Gabe was at her side in seconds, and she lifted her head to look up at him as he asked, "Did you detect any magic?"

"None...not yet, anyway. Do you want me to open it up?"

"Do you think you can?" Barak asked, approaching behind them. "What if we set off a rockfall?" His beautiful, dark eyes settled on Estelle's face. "We don't want you buried under it."

Estelle felt the now familiar flutter settle in her stomach. His look felt like a caress, and ever since their kiss yesterday, she wanted more of him—his lips, his hands... Now, however, was not the time to indulge in daydreams. She forced her voice to be steady. "If I focus on a small spot using a targeted blast, it should be relatively safe. Of course, I'll stand back, too. We all should." She looked at the rock and frowned as another idea struck her. "In fact, I should be able to carve a doorway if I use fire, too. That would strengthen the surrounding rock like a lintel."

Gabe rubbed his already thick stubble, looking at Estelle with doubt-filled eyes. And something else. He appeared more rattled than he normally did. "Is that possible?"

"Have a little faith," she said, sounding more confident than she felt.

She ushered everyone back and then sent out a pulse of magic. It was a blend of power as well as fire, designed to melt the rock and then fuse it. She cast a spell used to move obstacles, and doubled her intention. Instead of blasting the rock in a display of strength that would no doubt have caused a rockfall, she used her magic like a laser beam, and very soon a small hole appeared in the rock. Manipulating her power across a larger area, the hole grew bigger and bigger.

She couldn't help grinning with her success. The rock seemed to melt away, and in a few minutes, a doorway opened into the space beyond.

Whoops erupted from the team behind her, and she turned, still grinning, pleased to see looks of incredulity on everyone's faces. *Especially Shadow's.* "Impressed?"

"Very!" Nahum said, slapping her on the shoulder as he reached her side. "Wow. That was like watching a sculptor."

Shadow sniffed. "Not bad, I admit."

"Could you do better?" she asked, cocking an eyebrow, unable to resist baiting her. Shadow's presence was a constant thorn in her side, but one she had to tolerate. It didn't help that Shadow was a devastatingly efficient killer and tracker, and breathtakingly beautiful in an ethereal way.

Shadow shrugged and pouted, and Estelle smirked as she hurried after the others. Gabe had his sword in one hand and a torch in the other, already peering into the dark space.

"Wait!" Estelle said, pulling him back. "Let me throw some witch-lights in."

In seconds, half a dozen witch-lights were bobbing around the cave beyond, but Gabe quickly thrust her out of the way. "Let me go first."

Estelle's first instinct was to whip his legs out from under him. *Bloody Nephilim.* They were a force unto themselves, so full of ego.

Nahum followed Gabe, Niel and Ash on their heels, but Barak and Zee hung back. Shadow caught her tight expression as she joined her at the entrance.

"They're very annoying sometimes," Shadow told her. "I take my revenge by beating them at sword-fighting."

Zee must have heard her comment and laughed. Estelle didn't know Zee as well as the others. He was as tall and broad-shouldered as his brothers, with dark, almost black hair that had a slight curl to it. Like many of the other Nephilim he looked Middle Eastern, and had an angular face that seemed even more so now that his hair was pulled back into a high ponytail. His dark eyes currently flashed with humour as he teased Shadow.

"Sometimes, Princess," Zee said, tweaking her hair.

"*All* the time!" she shot back, swatting his hand away. "Have you beat me yet?"

Zee smirked. "I'm biding my time. Ladies, after you!" He extended his arm into the dark space, encompassing Catarina in his statement.

Despite Zee's teasing, Catarina looked nervous. She gestured at the newly formed doorway. "Is that safe?"

"As safe as anything more conventionally engineered," Estelle assured her, and shouldering her pack, she walked into the cave beyond. However, she paused next to Gabe and his brothers just inside the threshold, shocked at what lay beyond. "By the Gods..."

Her words trailed off as she took in the large cave and what appeared to be a ziggurat carved into the far wall. A steep ramp led to an entrance halfway up. Huge double doors that looked enormous even from here awaited them, with cuneiform writing carved above them. Its shape stood out in sharp relief from the rockface, the witch-lights also highlighting the carved faces and figures in the rock.

In seconds the others had shuffled in, and they all looked as shocked as Estelle felt.

Catarina took in a sharp breath next to her. "This is what my husband saw! We've actually found it."

"And those are from the rockfall." Ash pointed to the rocks scattered over the ground, some still on the ziggurat itself.

Estelle didn't take her eyes off the huge stone structure. "It's breathtaking. I can't believe what I'm seeing."

"It *is* impressive," Shadow admitted. "But why build such an ornate entrance if you don't want anyone to see it?"

Nahum gave Shadow a sharp, appraising glance. "That's an interesting question, but maybe it's just because they could."

"Or because they want to invite someone in…and then trap them," Gabe grunted.

Barak stood next to Estelle, his presence radiating towards her, impossible to ignore. "Keep your spells at the ready, Estelle. I don't like this." The muscles in his arm flexed as he gripped his sword. "The Igigi were swift and deadly when they attacked. And big."

"Bigger than you?" Catarina asked, wide-eyed.

"Much. And some of them had wings."

"But brother," Zee said, readying his crossbow as he studied the cave, "they were not naturally aggressive. Don't forget that. Only pursuit and slavery did that to them."

"Where are the bodies?" Niel asked. He swung around to look at Catarina. "Your husband said men were killed, right? Their bones should be here."

Catarina stuttered, her hand grasping her backpack. "I don't know. Perhaps his memory was confused, and they dragged some out?"

"No," Gabe said with certainty. "He said that they fled and the walls turned to rivers of rock. There are no rivers of rock here."

"But that," Zee said, pointing to a broad stone channel cut into the floor, "looks like a dry canal. It runs from the base of the ziggurat face to down there." He pointed to a dark hole low down on the opposite cave wall where it met the floor.

A chill ran through Estelle and she shivered, wondering what dark place the old canal led to.

Barak noticed her reaction and said, "They built waterways for kings and gods. Their expertise was like no other. Their cities were green."

"Like the Hanging Gardens of Babylon?"

"Absolutely. Stories like that have survived for a reason. No one who saw it could forget it." He pointed to the face of the ziggurat. "Each level of the ziggurat is set back from the level below, and every ledge would be filled with plants. Water channels ran everywhere…they looked magnificent."

Estelle had seen images and she knew what he meant, but before she could ask anything else, Gabe was already moving on.

"Okay," Gabe said, scanning the cave. "So there's the sort of half-ziggurat, and what looks like an entrance in it, the empty canal, and not much else. No sign of bodies, rockfalls, or old digs. But this is the place, and the ziggurat is our way in."

"Or down there," Zee suggested, looking at where the watercourse reached the hole in the rock.

Gabe looked incredulous. "Let's leave that as a last resort." He addressed Estelle. "Are your protection spells still over the camp?"

She tried not to take offense at his question. "All secure. And I can protect this entrance, too."

"And have we got all of our gear?"

There was a chorus of murmured agreement and nods. All of the Nephilim were heavily loaded, not only with weapons, but with food and basic supplies too, and the women had smaller packs. They had discussed the plans over a hasty breakfast, and while nobody wanted to be underground for too long, they wanted to prepare for every eventuality.

"Good." Gabe took a deep breath. "Then let's see if we can get farther than your husband did, Catarina. Barak, Zee, Shadow, and Estelle, keep to the rear and watch for attack from behind. But all of you—stay close."

And with that, he led them towards the steps leading to the ziggurat's entrance.

Jackson sank back into his chair, all elation at his new office and role leaching out of him as he absorbed Harlan's news.

"Barnaby is dead? Fuck me." He rubbed his hands across his jaw and closed his eyes, envisaging their last conversation. "Poor bugger. He said his life was forfeit, and to be honest, I didn't quite believe it. And now he's dead." When he opened his eyes, he found Harlan looking as guilty as he felt. "If we hadn't arrested him..."

"I've been wrestling with this news all morning, but this is not our fault. He got himself into this, and there was a price to pay."

"I know you're right, but I still feel like shit."

"But," Harlan said, leaning forward and slapping his messenger bag on Jackson's crowded desk, "he was hiding things. Things we now have."

Jackson perked up and leaned forward, eyeing the bag. "Like what?"

"Information about the Igigi and Count Bellamarre."

"Who?"

"Count Bellamarre is another name that the *Comte de Saint-Germain* used—one of his many pseudonyms."

"You're shitting me! Barnaby was researching him?"

Harlan started to pull papers out of his bag, a mix of loose sheets, notebooks, and old files. "Looks like it. Maybe he thought he could use it as a type of insurance, maybe blackmail. Or perhaps he was just curious."

"Considering how he was only too happy to betray The Order of the Midnight Sun, it wouldn't surprise me if he had something similar planned for Black Cronos. Sneaky shit." That news lifted a weight from Jackson's shoulders. "Now I don't feel quite so guilty that he's dead. How did you find out all this?"

"Maggie Milne phoned me. They discovered a safety deposit key stuck in his gut, and by checking his bank details worked out where it was for." Harlan grimaced. "They found it in the autopsy. God knows when he swallowed it."

Jackson groaned as he recalled the night they caught him. "He was fussing at that side table in his living room, remember? When he offered us a drink? Perhaps he suspected what was coming and swallowed it then."

"Oh, yeah! When he had his gin and tonic." Harlan huffed. "Some special agents we are, when we didn't even notice that."

"I was too busy checking out his room, and you were hovering by the door. It's not that surprising. Anyway, what's he written?"

Harlan spread the papers out, pushing them towards Jackson, but grabbing one file. "He has made lists on properties once associated with the count and his pseudonyms. I think he fixed on the name Bellamarre in particular, because of the name of the email address he used." Harlan's eyebrows rose, and his lips twisted into a rueful smile. "Beautiful Mother. *Bella Marre* in Spanish."

Jackson groaned, feeling like an idiot. "Of course! I thought the address was weird, but presumed it was just meant to mislead." He shuffled through some of the notes written in a crabbed hand. "This supports JD's idea."

"Unless this name is someone's idea of a gigantic hoax. A tease."

"Perhaps. What kind of properties are in there?"

"All sort of places. Castles and palaces, old townhouses, even manor homes across Europe—all the way to Romania. There are loads of them! But," Harlan pointed out, "we could cross-reference them with JD's suggestions."

Jackson leaned back, hands behind his head as he considered their options. "So potentially, one of these addresses could be a base for Black Cronos."

"Or multiple bases."

"This is brilliant! This could lead us right to the heart of their operation. And what about the Igigi? What's he got on them?"

Harlan huffed. "Some garbled notes on another historical find in Turkey when it was part of the Ottoman Empire. I started reading it and it gave me a headache, but I think it refers to a city beneath the sands. I have no idea whether it refers to the same place, or somewhere different."

"Can you spare a few hours to help?" Jackson was starting to feel overwhelmed again as he took in the enormity of the tasks ahead.

Fortunately, Harlan took pity on him and shed his jacket, placing it on the chair behind him. "I can give you a couple of hours—as long as you have lots of coffee on hand, and promise me lunch."

"Deal."

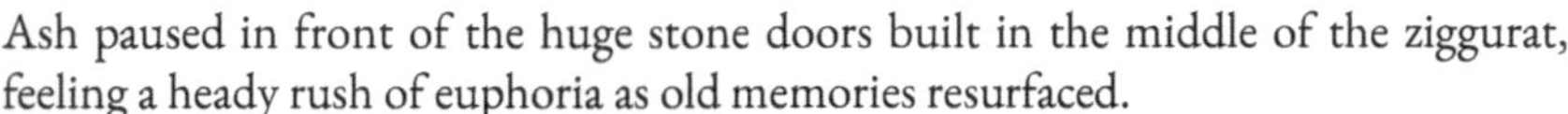

Ash paused in front of the huge stone doors built in the middle of the ziggurat, feeling a heady rush of euphoria as old memories resurfaced.

It seemed odd, but he had forgotten how imposing these buildings were. The doors in front of him were massive, towering four times his height, carved reliefs of Igigi making decorative panels. The walls stretched away on either side, and the top was lost in darkness that the witch-lights didn't penetrate. Behind him, the ramp carved out of the rock fell to the cave floor below.

He laid his hand on the rock, noting the seam where the two doors met in the middle, and he turned to Shadow. "Were these like the doors that Black Cronos broke through?"

"They were smaller, less ornate, but essentially the same." Her face wrinkled with annoyance. "They completely shattered it. I hate wanton destruction."

Niel grunted with annoyance. "Unless we can find a way of opening them, we'll be doing the same."

"Through those?" Zee asked, incredulous. "These will be several feet thick. There's no way we'll smash through them!"

Ash hastened to calm his brothers. "I'm sure we can work it out. There must be some kind of mechanism. They invented hydraulics and the wheel, after all."

"True," Barak said, heading to the far side of the left-hand door and peering upwards. "If I remember correctly, they used a series of wheels to open doors and move walls."

"That's true, brother!" Nahum shed his pack and t-shirt, extending his wings as he spoke. "The mechanisms were high on the walls."

In seconds both were flying upwards, examining the sheer walls of the ziggurat, while the others shuffled nervously below, wary of any sign of movement.

Catarina surveyed the cave, her expression one of disbelief. "I find it hard to believe this is where my husband was. Any sign of the dig has been erased."

Ash exchanged a cautious glance with Gabe as he said, "If anything, this suggests that at least some of them are still alive. Perhaps they moved the bodies."

"But if so," Gabe whispered, "where are they now?"

A muffled shout from above had them all looking up, weapons drawn. All Ash could see was the deeper shadows of his brothers' beating wings as they conferred together, and then Nahum landed next to them.

"We found a narrow gap in the rock above on either side of the doors. We can see a glimpse of cogs beyond. We're going in."

Gabe nodded, his hand clutching his sword. "Be careful!"

For what seemed like endless minutes nothing happened, and then a slow, grinding noise rumbled across the cave as the seam started to inch apart.

Catarina's breath caught and she stumbled back a pace. "They've done it!"

Ash squeezed her shoulder in reassurance, but grinned at his brothers. "After all these years, we've finally found them."

"But will we live to regret it?" Gabe turned and cautioned the others. "Let's take our time heading in. There could be traps."

The doors inched slowly open, the grind of the cogs mixing with the scraping of sand and gravel beneath the doors. Estelle once again threw witch-lights inside, and as soon as they were able to edge through the opening, their pale light revealed the broad hall that lay ahead.

Torches lined the walls, and as they stepped inside, the torches flared into life, throwing the hall into leaping firelight and shadow.

Gabe whipped around to stare at Estelle. "Was that you?"

She shook her head, her eyes wary. "No."

Gabe swallowed and gripped his sword even tighter. "A trick?"

"Or a mechanism?" Niel countered. "But if so, someone must maintain it."

"Herne's hairy balls," Ash whispered, ignoring their whispered questions. The hall was imposing, reliefs of the Igigi carved into panels that ran along either side of the room. The roof was high, the cog mechanism on a platform towering above them. Nahum and Barak flew overhead, acting as guards above them, while the others shuffled forward below.

"Another doorway," Shadow said pointing ahead to a pair of burnished copper doors at the far end of the hall.

"From what I recall of the normal structure of these buildings," Zee said, "there will be a series of anterooms before we reach the large, central chamber. But this is not a normal ziggurat, so I may be wrong."

"Exactly," Niel agreed. "Beyond there could be the city proper."

A flare of excitement flashed through Ash's body as he said, "Only one way to find out."

But they had advanced barely halfway down the hall when a strange, clanking noise had them whirling around, weapons raised. But there was nothing they could do as a huge metal gate dropped from a recess in the roof, sealing the entrance and trapping them inside.

When Harlan finally arrived back in his office, it was late afternoon. He had barely had time to make himself coffee when there was an irate knock on his door and Mason burst in.

"Here you are! You've been gone for hours!"

"I've been working!" Harlan responded, just as annoyed. Obviously, he wasn't about to disclose that he'd been helping Jackson. Besides, he had managed to devote a few hours to one of his latest cases. "Is something wrong?"

Mason was as elegantly dressed as always, but his crankiness gave him an air of dishevelment, which was at odds with his normally smooth manner. "I want to know if there's been any progress in finding Black Cronos!"

Harlan looked at him, perplexed. "We have leads, but that's all. It's going to take time finding them. They've taken the word *covert* to a whole new level."

"That's what JD said." Mason stalked across the office to stare out of the window. "It's not good enough."

Harlan pushed his irritation aside. For some reason, Mason thought he was some kind of super sleuth, and he realised Smythe's death was still weighing heavily on him. Instead, he said, "You're talking to JD now?"

"Yes. He phoned me. He's been trying to reach you, too. He wants you to return to Mortlake."

Harlan checked his phone, baffled, and realised he'd missed several calls that must have come through while he was at The Retreat. "Perhaps he's made headway with the weapon."

Mason rounded on him. "What weapon?"

"He's trying to replicate Black Cronos's weapons. I thought I told you. He's tried a few angles, but when I left him yesterday, he thought he'd found the best way."

"You're *helping* him?" Mason looked outraged. "You're supposed to be stopping him!"

Harlan took a deep breath and exhaled slowly, then walked to his espresso machine and started to prepare coffee. Yelling at Mason wasn't going to solve anything, and he needed to regain his composure. "You asked me to keep an eye on him. This is one way to do that. Besides, this might help us work out the whole superhuman thing—which, by the way, he has no interest in doing to himself!"

Mason calmed down. "That's good, I suppose."

"Better than good. We need to understand what they're doing. The Nephilim found weird super-dogs in Scotland. Who knows what else they're experimenting with! Did JD tell you that his estate had been attacked?"

"No!" Mason folded his arms across his chest. "When?"

"Sunday night. Want one?" He gestured to the coffee, but Mason shook his head. "It was serious. If JD hadn't installed such excellent defences, we'd have been killed. I suspect they're tracking down their stolen items. And it seems they want to develop superhumans with wings." He quickly updated Mason on the hunt for the Igigi, and what Gabe's team was doing.

Mason's eyes narrowed. "Why track down ancient beings who most likely don't exist when they could just capture a Nephilim? They have superhuman strength and wings, don't they? And are the sons of the Fallen." His face wrinkled with distaste. "As disgusting as their methods are, surely analysing a Nephilim would have greater value."

A chill swept over Harlan. "I hadn't even considered that. But to be honest, they're so formidable and have killed so many of Black Cronos's soldiers that surely they would avoid that idea completely."

"They're formidable as a group, but split up they're more vulnerable. How many have gone to Turkey?"

"All except for Eli." Harlan fumbled for his phone, worried for Eli's safety, and then he recalled what Gabe had told him. "The witches set up protection over the farmhouse weeks ago. He should be safe, but I'll call him anyway."

"I'll leave you to it." But halfway across the room, Mason stopped. "We haven't got any of their *'items'* here, have we? Are we in danger?"

"No. Nothing except the records we've always had. And I have bad news. Barnaby Armstrong is dead. He was the order's mole."

Mason seemed to deflate a little more. "I knew Barnaby. Not well, but... That's terrible news. What a fool, to get himself involved with such things."

"And Mason, I may have to go to JD's tonight—"

Mason cut in, "That's fine. Do what you have to do. Anything that helps find them is fine by me."

Twenty-Four

S hadow stood before another set of burnished doors, this time made from a variety of metals in a complex design, wishing the others would hurry up.

Despite their best efforts, they were unable to open the gate that had trapped them inside. The mechanism that triggered its release was hidden from view, and they had unwillingly conceded that they needed to proceed. At least they knew there was another way out—admittedly through Black Cronos. They had just spent the last ten minutes walking through another long hall decorated with carved panels depicting the Igigi's flight from the Anunnaki. The carvings were elaborate and stunningly intact, and recorded a more detailed version of the founding of their city than what had been displayed on the tablet.

Shadow was the least overawed of all of them. Catarina, Estelle, and the Nephilim had lingered, virtually speechless as they studied the images and the story. The Nephilims' wonder had been compounded by the fact that they were mentioned frequently, as were the Fallen, and she watched them wrestle with their emotions as they drank it all in.

Gabe was especially shaken. When she had woken earlier after a short but heavy sleep, it was to find Gabe wide awake, staring at the roof of the tent, a sheen of sweat on his brow that had nothing to do with the heat. His eyes held shock and anger, and it was with much effort that she had finally persuaded him to tell her what was wrong.

Remiel.

Neither could decide what that meant. *Was Gabe's father watching their every move? And if so, why hadn't he physically appeared?*

They had decided not to tell the others, but Gabe was clearly distracted, and she was sure the others had noticed, especially Nahum. Perhaps they had put it down to finding the city. For all of their wishes and expectations, it had surprised everyone. But now time was marching on, and Black Cronos was already ahead of them.

"Guys!" she shouted. "We need to get on! We can come back to this later."

While they tarried, she studied the doors. There was no sign of any cog mechanism, and she laid her hand on one of them and pushed. As if on oiled hinges, it swung open easily, and gripping both swords, she stepped into the blackness beyond.

The torch light from behind her illuminated a short distance ahead. She had stepped onto a broad balcony, but below was a black void that even her keen eyesight couldn't penetrate. On either side, a fretted stonework balcony stretched into darkness, and she sensed huge space ahead of her.

Sheathing one sword, she pulled her battery-powered torch out, but the beam barely pierced the dark. By this time the team had lined up next to her, and Estelle's witch-lights revealed that they were overlooking a vast city carved out of the rock, and in front of them a broad sweep of steps led down into its heart.

Catarina found her voice first. "Oh, my God. This is enormous. This is far more than I was expecting!"

"This surpasses anything they built for the Anunnaki," Ash murmured. "I wonder if they managed to get light into here somehow?"

The city comprised of a variety of buildings, some of which were huge, while others were smaller dwellings. Holes in the distant cave walls suggested other tunnels or even houses built into the rock itself. The buildings staggered downwards like an inverted pyramid to a flat section at the bottom. Something glassy was reflected in the witch-lights, and Shadow realised it was a series of waterways at the bottom. In addition to the buildings were enormous, carved statues—all half man, half beast, with the heads of eagles, wolves, bears, and other animals.

Barak pointed to the opposite side of the city. "There are tunnels to the rear. Perhaps they lead to other parts of the city." He turned to the others, a question in his eyes. "They must have buried their dead down here, so it may even be a burial ground."

Gabe nodded. "It makes sense that it would be beyond the city proper." He turned to Nahum and Barak, who still had their wings extended. "Fly over the city, and we'll progress on foot for now."

But as they approached the top step, torchlights flared again, illuminating the perimeter of the city, and a few spots below.

"Fuck it," Niel muttered, swinging his torch. "Things like this don't work after hundreds of years without something maintaining them. We're walking into a trap."

Ash shook his head. "I'm not so sure. They designed ingenious systems of lights and hydraulics..." But he stopped speaking, instead staring beyond Niel.

Shadow stepped to his side, wondering what he was looking at, but instead was distracted by a statue at the top of the stairs that seemed to shift in the firelight. She blinked to clear her eyes, thinking it was a trick of the light.

But it was no trick, and gripping her swords, she yelled, "The statues are coming to life!"

"They aren't bloody statues!" Gabe yelled back, lining up next to her. "It's the Igigi!"

As another huge gate dropped behind them, trapping them inside, the Igigi moved with lightning speed. He lifted the long spears in his hands and lunged at Gabe and Shadow. Both leapt out the way, weapons raised to defend rather than attack. But other Igigi where appearing out of the darkness, their immense shadows advancing before them as they hunted down the Nephilim.

Catarina screamed, and Shadow felt rather than saw the effects of Estelle's magic as she repelled another attack. But Shadow could only concentrate on her own battle.

She had seen many odd creatures in her life in the Otherworld, but there was no doubt that the Igigi advancing on her was *very* odd. It was easily eight feet tall, with the body of a man but the head of a wolf. Its skin was of burnished gold and its eyes gleaned like silver.

Its movements were so swift that Shadow barely had time to react. She needed to up her game. She drew on her fey magic, normally shielded from the others, and instantly felt her speed and perception increase. But Gabe had insisted they not kill the Igigi if they encountered them, and she kept his words in mind while she ducked and defended. *If only the Igigi knew that.*

Several Igigi were advancing on either side, and the team was trapped within the narrow confines of the balcony. Shadow had the feeling that the Igigi had purposefully waited to lure them into the city's gates before attacking.

As her opponent's spear came within millimetres of plunging into her stomach, she leapt over the balustrade and onto the rooftops below. Fortunately, the first was only a few feet beneath the balcony. The city, as she had noticed earlier, staggered downwards to the flat centre below, and she leapt from rooftop to rooftop, hoping that the Nephilim were protecting Catarina. She certainly couldn't get close to her. But she had achieved some breathing space from her attacker, because she was far nimbler than it was. She was now several levels down, trying to decide how to evade the creature and return to her team.

But then the wolf-headed Igigi bellowed and followed her onto the rooftops.

Gabe was battling his own Igigi as they almost fell down the broad set of steps. Nahum was flying overhead, and she saw him swoop down to collect Catarina, but her rescue was short-lived. An eagle-headed Igigi with enormous wings soared through the cavernous space and attacked Nahum, forcing him to veer away dramatically.

Ash, Zee, and Niel were all fighting back-to-back as half a dozen Igigi surrounded them, and Estelle, like Shadow, had dropped onto the rooftops, protecting herself with blasts of magic. Barak was nowhere to be seen.

A sudden movement from above made Shadow throw herself on the flat rooftop, face-up, and with horror she saw an eagle-headed Igigi swoop down on her. She had just enough time to roll into a gap between buildings, and found herself on the street level, dwarfed by the huge stone edifices. A warren of lanes—much like the lanes in old Mardin—spread out in a web around her.

She raced through them, trying to find a way back to the stairs, and heard Gabe yell something unintelligible in what she presumed was the Sumerian language. She followed his voice, but found the path blocked by another Igigi, its silver eyes watching her dispassionately.

Barak was high above the city in the cavernous recess of the roof, which was as beautifully finished as the rest of the city. Niches had been cut in the walls, and while many were empty, others were not.

Three Igigi emerged from their perches, their enormous wingspan buffeting the air as they advanced on Barak, weapons drawn. They came at him from all sides, but he dropped like a stone, plunging from their advance to find airspace below. His smaller size gave him greater agility, and he was thankful that he was born to fight, whereas they were not. But they were still quick and strong.

He glanced below, noting his brothers similarly embattled, and was relieved to see that Estelle was managing to defend herself. *But how long could this last, for any one of them?* They desperately didn't want to kill the Igigi, but wounding them was inevitable in their effort to get away.

Suddenly he was grabbed from behind, his wings half crushed between the steely grip of his attacker, and he yelled in Sumerian, "Stop fighting! We're here to help!"

"You should have thought of that before you invaded our home, Nephilim!"

Barak brought his fist up and smashed behind his shoulder, smacking his opponent in the face. But he didn't lose his grip, and they plunged towards the water at the base of the city.

Estelle was casting several spells, but they all seemed to bounce off the advancing Igigi like they were wearing some kind of spell-resistant armour.

She grunted with frustration, presuming it was their supernatural abilities that offered them protection. At least the blasts of power were keeping them off-guard. *Just.* Like Shadow, she scrambled across the rooftops, but nowhere near as agilely. Wishing she had Caspian's mastery of air magic, she kept running and slipping, her hands now starting to bleed as they caught on the jagged edges of tiles and rock.

This was a nightmare. And they were being driven further and further into the city. She couldn't be sure, but she had the horrible feeling they were not planning to kill them, but capture them, and that couldn't be for any good purpose.

As two Igigi advanced on her she realised she needed an ally, and unfortunately, Shadow was it. She clambered to where she had last seen her, and then dropped from the roof into the street below, shrouding herself in a shadow spell as she raced down the lane. Little light illuminated down here, and by the time the Igigi pursing her had reached where she had been, she'd be long gone and invisible.

Drawn by Gabe's voice, she rounded the corner to see Shadow up ahead, her path blocked by a wolf-headed Igigi wielding a spear in one hand, and a curved sword in the other. Estelle took a moment to study the strange being. His thighs were thick with corded muscles, as were his arms. He wore ornately engraved armour—breastplate, arm and leg guards—and a long cloth with embroidered edges was wrapped around his waist. Everything about him reminded Estelle of Anubis. He advanced on Shadow, looking impregnable, his bulk blocking the way ahead.

Shadow was backing up, but wasn't running, no doubt assessing her options. Estelle decided to help, aiming a spell at the section of wall next to the Igigi. The stone blocks exploded, blasting the creature backwards. Estelle hurled a ball of energy at him, forcing him back further.

Estelle hissed, "Shadow, over here!"

Shadow spun around, eyes narrowed, and ran to her voice, Estelle lifting her cloaking spell for the briefest of moments. "Was that your handywork?" she whispered. "Great timing."

"I know. I'm a witch." Estelle decided to answer as cockily as Shadow did. As the thundering of footsteps sounded overhead, Estelle draped them both in her shadow spell and turned. "This way."

Niel yelled at his brothers, "We need to join the others—take to the air!"

Zee grunted as he ducked and rolled. "All very well, brother, but that's not so easy right now!"

Niel swung his axe, trying to get the Igigi surrounding them to back off rather than hurt them, but that was not easy, either. "Any ideas, Ash?"

"A time machine?"

"Not funny." Niel arched backwards to avoid the brutal thrust of a spear, and swung his axe up, shattering the spearhead and earning him time and space. He glanced around him in the brief seconds of respite he had before another attack, and noticed something odd. "There are no others coming. They're either hiding, or this is it." He brought his sword up to form a cross with his axe and repelled another attack.

"A final guard, you mean?" Ash said, panting heavily now.

"Exactly. If we can get through this..."

"Gabe is on the stairs," Zee said. "We need to get to him. If we strike as one coordinated force now, we'll make enough room to escape. Let's extend our wings together—one powerful thrust will send them all back."

As they fought to give themselves enough space, Ash yelled, "Now!"

Nahum clutched Catarina to his side, noticing she felt like a wounded bird fluttering in his hands.

He was shaking her around like a rag doll, and knew he had to get her onto the ground, but he couldn't leave her. She was far too vulnerable, and he wasn't sure where the safest place was. He'd managed to fend off one attack, but noticed they were being herded to the city centre—a large square surrounded by canals.

In fact, he realised as he studied the area, *down there were no other Igigi at all*. No one was emerging from the buildings or streets. The whole place was deserted, like a ghost city. *But was it a trap?* He had a sudden idea.

"Catarina, are you okay?"

She was breathless when she answered. "Hardly, but I'll survive—thanks to you."

"I'm going to check the tunnel at the back. Hold tight."

She managed a grunting laugh. "Like I'd let go!"

He soared to the tunnel, grateful that he seemed to have passed by undetected, for now. The tunnel entrance was huge and once he arrived there, he could see passages leading off it. It was a maze down there. He strained to hear anything, but the noise of the fight in the city behind him smothered any other sounds. And if Black Cronos was down there, they weren't close...yet.

They needed a truce, but right now, Nahum wasn't sure they were going to get it.

Gabe gripped his sword and backed down the steps, aware of other Igigi advancing on him.

Scanning the area, he estimated there were at least twenty Igigi of various types moving in on them from around the city, and several more overhead. He was furious with himself. Although they had debated their existence, he had seriously doubted that they were really alive, and now they were under attack and struggling.

His first appeal had been ignored, so he tried again, speaking in their language once more. "Stop fighting us. You are under attack by another group, and we are here to help you!"

The snake-headed Igigi he was fighting laughed. "You have never helped us before, Nephilim. It is because of you we are here."

"Not true!" he shot back. "It is because of your rebellion against the Anunnaki that you are here. We had our own orders to follow."

While the Igigi wasn't actively attacking him, he kept advancing, and Gabe kept retreating down the broad stairs. A blast of falling rubble came from his right, indicating that the other Igigi had not stopped fighting, and he saw Ash, Zee, and Niel all take to the air as they forced their attackers back. Within moments, all of them landed behind him.

A flurry of wings from above had him ducking, but it was Nahum and Barak, both swooping down, with Nahum clutching Catarina tightly in one arm, his sword in the other. But Shadow and Estelle were nowhere in sight. The only clue to their whereabouts were the few Igigi fanning out across the rooftops, and he hoped they were hiding somewhere. Winged Igigi landed on the steps behind them, and Gabe realised they were surrounded.

He turned to the others, sheathing his sword and shouting, "Put your weapons away!" Niel hesitated, a mutinous expression on his face, and he added, "Niel—do it!"

Glaring at him, Niel did as he asked, but his fingers hovered over the butt of his axe—just in case.

"See!" He appealed to his opponent, extending his empty hands and gesturing to the others. "We wish you no harm. We're here to help!"

The snake-headed Igigi didn't answer, instead stepping back to make way for an enormous Igigi who landed with surprising grace for his size. He was winged and had the head of a hawk. His shoulders were huge, his wings much bigger than Gabe's own, and he cocked his head, a steely glint in his eye.

"You should be dead, Nephilim. How are you here?"

"A quirk of fate." He decided to be honest in the hope that it earned him some trust. "We died in the flood, and had a second chance when a portal allowed us to come back here. Only my six brothers and I returned."

His eyes narrowed. "Only seven from all the hundreds? Then you've fared even worse than us. Your name?"

"Gabreel of the House of Remiel. Greetings from my house to yours." He straightened up, throwing his shoulders back and drawing himself up to his full height. He often tried not to look imposing. He knew his height and build were threatening. But this was an Igigi, and trying to shrink away from who he was would do none of them any favours. "And your name?"

"Gishkim, named after my ancestor, the great Hawk Igigi who led the rebellion and the flight to independence."

Gabe nodded as the memories flashed through his mind. "I remember your ancestor. He was powerful and wise. I apologise for this intrusion, and seek permission to be in your city."

Gishkim's mouth twisted into a smile. "Gabreel, son of Remiel. You are mentioned in our stories. You and your men pursued us for weeks. Many of our dead fell at your hands."

"And many of mine at yours. We were different men in those days. They were the years when our fathers had more sway—before we sought our own independence."

"I know something of this. Scraps of news filtered down to our city when we dared venture to the surface. Before the flood that killed you." He glanced around him. "A flood that almost killed us, too."

Gabe nodded. "We had expected you to be dead." *In fact, how the hell had they survived down here without sunlight for all these years?* It seemed impossible.

Ignoring Gabe's confusion, he said, "So, you have come to raid our city."

"No! We have come to help defend you against an attack from a mutual enemy."

"Even though you thought us dead?" Gishkim looked amused. "The dead don't need defending."

"It's complicated. You are under attack right now. Your back gate has been blown wide open, and men are—"

Gishkim cut him short. "We know. Others have gone to intercept them. They will not get far—like you." He shook his head, a sneer starting on his lips. "Always so superior, Nephilim. You forget we have strengths, too."

"But those are no normal men," Gabe said, his eyes not leaving Gishkim's golden ones. "They carry odd weapons and unusual powers."

"And you are the sons of the Fallen, and yet we have captured you." He gestured to the Igigi who surrounded them, spears and swords drawn. "But your team is different. Two humans, and someone from beyond our world." He glanced around, perturbed. "She is missing, as is one of the humans. Where are they?"

"I have no idea. Hiding, I suspect, in fear for their lives." Gabe just hoped they weren't injured, or about to do something catastrophic. He fought back his impatience. "But you don't understand. It's not your riches the others want. It's *you!*"

A distant explosion rocked through the city, and everyone swung around to look towards where the tunnels led further underground. Gabe closed his eyes briefly. *Please let that not be Estelle and Shadow.*

Gishkim immediately dispatched half a dozen Igigi, and then gestured to the Nephilim. "You're coming with us."

Twenty-Five

Harlan watched JD's deft hands as he placed the small metal ball in the centre of his complex grid, and then adjusted the outer circles.

"I was going about it all wrong," JD told him, his lips pressing into a thin line. "I was trying to change the properties that the metal already has, when I should have just started afresh using the base metal."

"Okay," Harlan drawled, wondering what he was going on about. "That means what, exactly?"

JD pointed to the rows of bubbling jars that were connected by a series of tubes. "The metal is put into its base state, and then its alchemical correspondences are refined and adjusted—to you, the planets, all of it. Then I put it into a mould to make the weapon and fix those properties, and then reduce it again." He gave Harlan a wolfish grin. "I won't bore you with the details."

"Good. It's already gibberish."

"Watch." He turned the final circle, and the copper ball in the centre morphed into a copper blade. "Pick it up."

Harlan eyed it warily and then glanced at JD, who looked like an excited child. Taking a deep breath, Harlan picked it up, holding the blade on his outstretched hand as if it might bite. A strange tingling sensation started in his palm and flowed up his arm, and he almost dropped it. "What the fuck! It's doing something to me!"

"Wait!" JD instructed. "Let it settle."

Harlan glared at his arm and the dagger, willing nothing else to happen. He liked his arm just the way it was. "What now?"

"What now? You are an utter nincompoop! Look! It isn't changing."

"Oh!" Harlan suddenly realised what he meant. "It's holding its shape."

"Because it's attuned to you." JD took the blade from Harlan's palm and it changed shape again. "See? It won't hold its shape for me. No matter what I do, it will never be a weapon." He placed it back on Harlan's hand again, watching with glee as it changed shape once more.

"But Black Cronos can change their weapons' shape seemingly at will. From nothing to weapon and back again instantly. How do I do that?"

JD stared at him expectantly. "Have you *tried* changing it by will?"

"Like with my mind?" Harlan looked at him like he'd gone crazy, but JD continue to stare at him, so he focussed on the blade, willing it to change shape as he clenched his hand. "I feel like a dick. Nothing is happening."

JD's shoulders slumped again. "One step at a time. I haven't worked that bit out yet." He studied Harlan with narrowed eyes. "Maybe it's because you haven't been enhanced yet. It's attuned to you, but maybe there should be something more..."

"Oh, no!" Harlan dropped the weapon on the bench like it burned his hand and stepped away. "You are not changing me! I am not turning into one of those creatures. No way!"

"You aren't even slightly tempted? You could fight with the Nephilim on equal terms."

"I don't give a crap about that." Harlan stared at JD, horrified. "Those men and women were cold—their eyes dead. And that Silencer of Souls..." He trailed off, his horror at her memory already making his skin crawl. "They're unnatural! We don't know what it does to their mind—their soul! No way. And besides, you said they were aberrations! Have you changed your mind?"

JD looked sheepish. "No, but I thought it might be possible to just do a mild enhancement. I am intrigued about it all."

Harlan changed tack. "How are you getting on with finding an antidote?"

"I'm not. I don't know nearly enough to start doing that. My enthusiasm got the better of me the other day."

Harlan felt sorry for him. It must be frustrating to be so clever and yet not know anything about the supernatural enhancements. Another thought struck Harlan. "Barnaby Armstrong, The Order of the Midnight Sun's secretary and Inner Adept, wasn't enhanced. He was just a regular guy in bad clothes."

"Hmm, food for thought."

JD's eyes still gleamed with intrigue, and Harlan stepped back again. The only comfort he had was that he was younger, bigger, and much stronger than JD—just in case he tried to restrain him in some way.

As if he'd read his mind, JD rolled his eyes. "Calm down. I'm not about to do anything to you. I'm just frustrated. It's clever. Ingenious, even."

"You're clever, too. You'll work it out—just not by using me as a guinea pig. By the way, Barnaby was researching the *Comte de Saint-Germain*."

"Really? Interesting." JD sat on a stool, staring intently at Harlan. "Did he say why?"

Harlan grimaced. "He's dead, so no."

"Dead? Not another one! This is worrying. They seem to have abandoned their low-key activities completely."

"Well, to be fair, we don't *know* they killed him, but it's the most likely answer. Killed by The Silencer of Souls, we think."

"Her again..."

"Maggie Milne found some papers in his bank deposit box. But everything points to him maybe preparing to blackmail them, or even just safeguard his future. That didn't work, obviously."

"And what were his findings on the count?"

"We're still going through his notes, but he assembled a list of places associated with him. We thought we could cross-reference it with your ideas." He pulled a copy of the list from his messenger bag that lay on the bench and passed it to JD.

JD grunted as he read, huffing occasionally. "There are some addresses in here I've not heard of, but a few I have. There are a couple in England."

"I know. We thought we should start with those."

"He didn't like England. Had a bad experience here, apparently. However, he did carry out secret missions in England for King Louis XV of France. He was very close to him for years."

Harlan shrugged. "Whether he liked the place or not, those addresses are still worth investigating."

"Of course. He would likely do whatever would confound people." JD's face wrinkled with distaste. "Odd little man." Harlan tried not to smile as JD uttered the phrase they all used to describe him, but JD hadn't noticed and was already continuing. "How are you going to investigate them?"

"Do the basics first, like checking ownership records to see if anything odd is going on, and then some covert surveillance."

JD nodded and walked over to inspect the potions bubbling in jars. Harlan shouldered his bag, ready to leave as JD said, "I suggest you be careful. If his defence systems are anything like mine, you'd be dead before you even knew what was happening." JD shot him a speculative look. "Where are Gabe and Shadow?"

"Still in Turkey...I think. I haven't heard from them." A knot of worry tightened in his gut. "They were chasing down the lead on the Igigi and their hidden city."

"The Igigi!" JD's eyebrows shot up. "You didn't mention them."

"That's what they found beneath Arklet Abbey. We think Black Cronos is looking to find Igigi bones or something of the sort. Something else to experiment on." Surprised, he added, "You've heard of them, then?"

"Of course. Sumerian slaves to the Anunnaki." JD cocked his head on one side and tapped his lips thoughtfully. "Did you know they were the first recorded civilisation to have used crystals in magic?"

"No. Do you think it's relevant?"

"I don't know. But remember, the count liked his crystals, too." He turned away, inspecting his alembic jars again. "Something to consider, perhaps."

Harlan had been preoccupied with the weapon and the count's old haunts, and had pushed the Igigi to the back of his mind, but now he decided that they warranted further investigation. It was time to leave.

"I'll be in touch, JD," he said, taking one last look at the alchemical grid before weaving through the benches.

"If you change your mind on taking our experiments a little further, let me know."

"I can assure you, I will not."

And with JD's dubious offer ringing in his ears, Harlan hurried to the stairs, eager to leave what he was beginning to think of as JD's dungeon.

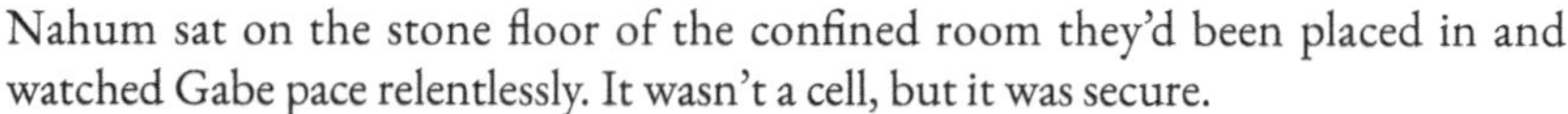

Nahum sat on the stone floor of the confined room they'd been placed in and watched Gabe pace relentlessly. It wasn't a cell, but it was secure.

The walls were constructed of huge blocks of stone, all expertly fitted together with barely a seam visible, and the roof was made of vaulted wood and lined with sheets of metal. There were no windows, and the only way in or out was through a thick, iron-barred, wooden door. But there were decorative reliefs on the walls painted in rich colours, huge designs that stretched from floor to ceiling.

Ash was talking quietly with Zee and Catarina, and Niel and Barak were investigating every single part of the room, trying to find a way to escape it.

Nahum suspected they were in a records room of some kind, although why it should be so secure, he wasn't sure. Frankly, he was too distracted right now to take any real notice of the space. Their weapons had been taken from them, and Gabe had shot them all a warning look to comply with instructions. Nahum knew he was determined to prove they were allies, but that wasn't really working right now.

"We have to find a way out of here," Niel said, abandoning his search and pounding the door with his fist.

"Not like that, you idiot," Nahum said wearily. "Save your strength. The fact that we're not dead yet bodes well. I think they want to check out our story."

"Or hunt down Estelle and Shadow and use them for leverage."

Nahum snorted. "They clearly don't know them, do they? I just hope those two haven't killed each other."

A spark gleamed in Niel's eyes. "Want to wager who would win in a fight? I think I'd go with Shadow."

Barak clearly felt he needed to defend his almost-girlfriend. "Estelle can hold her own!"

"I can barely hold my own against Shadow," Gabe pointed out. "I'd rather hope they're working together."

"Do you think the explosion was them?" Ash asked, ending his conversation with Zee and Catarina.

"I doubt it." Nahum leaned back against the wall, trying to get comfortable. "It was too far down that tunnel. There's no way they could have got there so quickly. It had to have been Black Cronos."

Catarina's eyes were wide. "They're using explosives?"

"We warned you," Ash told her as he turned away to study the carved panels. "They're relentless. I just wish the Igigi would let us help. Perhaps Shadow and Estelle are trying to get us out right now."

"With three Igigi outside?" Zee said, looking doubtful. "Unlikely. Besides, it would undermine our offer of help if we broke out. We need Gishkim to know that he needs us."

"Unless Black Cronos gets to him first," Barak pointed out. "And then it won't be him coming through that door. It will be *them*."

Shadow sat on the rooftop closest to the tunnel entrance, Estelle next to her. Both were veiled in the invisibility spell, and Shadow enhanced it with her own fey magic.

They had lost their pursuers a good ten minutes ago, and had watched Gabe and the others get locked in a building in the narrow streets at the rear of the city, close to the cavern walls.

"Gabe would not thank us for breaking him out," Shadow murmured to Estelle. "He wants to do this the right way. It's important to him."

"It would be tricky with guards posted on the door," Estelle said, "but it's doable. What worries me more is what's happening down there."

For the last few minutes, they had seen the Igigi running or flying down the tunnel, and so far, no one had returned. "If Black Cronos overrun them and end up here, we're all in trouble. I think we should go and see what's happening."

"And leave the others locked up?" Estelle's scorn dripped from her words. "They'll be furious!"

"Missing your boyfriend already?" Shadow countered, unable to keep the sarcasm from her voice.

There was a momentary pause, and then Estelle answered, her voice like ice. "He is not my boyfriend."

"Well, he should be," Shadow pointed out, miffed on Barak's behalf, even though he had never uttered one word of reproach about Estelle. But Shadow could see how he looked at her. "He won't wait forever."

"He doesn't need to wait forever! I'm just...sorting things out in my head. Besides, you and Gabe waited long enough!"

"We had business concerns."

"Bullshit. You were as worried about messing things up as I am. Anyway, this is not the time for us to be talking about our love lives—or lack of."

"There's no *lack* of on my behalf, I can assure you."

"Shadow, you are the most irritating woman. I don't know why I even rescued you!"

"*Rescued*? I didn't need rescuing!" Shadow clenched her blades. "You are infuriating."

Another blast echoed down the tunnel, this time carrying dust and shouts, and as awful as that was, Shadow was very grateful for the distraction.

"Come on. We've waited too long. They need our help," she said, slipping off the roof and landing softly on the ground.

"And the others?" Estelle asked, landing next to her.

"We can come back, if needed. And besides, Gishkim is no fool. He'll come for Gabe if he needs help. And if he doesn't, we'll have to talk him into it."

As the sound of the second explosion died away, Barak pounded on the door. "Let us out! We can help!"

He didn't advertise the fact that the main part of his worry was Estelle, although he knew his brothers sensed it. When silence greeted him, he pounded again. "We're sitting ducks in here! Let us out!"

"It sounded closer that time," Zee said, his usually calm demeanour now ruffled. "What the hell is happening out there?"

Ash turned away from the decorative panels he was studying with Catarina. "I just hope it's the dead they're raiding, and Black Cronos is not trying to capture the Igigi."

"We can't afford for either of those scenarios to happen, but I wouldn't put anything past Black Cronos, or..." Gabe paused, anger written all over his face.

"Or *who*?" Barak asked, finally stopping his banging on the door.

Gabe raked his hands through his hair. "I had a dream last night. Except, I don't think it was a dream, not really."

Nahum cast a puzzled glance at the others. "You're not making any sense, Gabe. What do you mean?"

Gabe was looking at the floor, but then he finally looked up at them. "I heard from my father last night. He said I was to finish the job—as in, kill the Igigi."

A stunned silence followed, but Ash found his voice first. "It had to be a dream, Gabe. It's just being here again that brought it all back."

"No. It was no dream. It was him. His voice passed through me, just like it always did. Like a blade." He wiped sweat from his brow. "I hoped we'd left them all behind. Have any of you heard anything from your fathers? Nahum?"

Everyone shook their heads, Barak included, and Nahum rose to his feet to grip Gabe's shoulder. "Why would our father contact you and not me?"

"I don't know! But I'm sure it wasn't just a dream. He sounded too angry."

"Dreams can feel like that," Barak pointed out. "Ever since my injury and that strange healing, I've had dreams of my father. They've woken me in a cold sweat sometimes, too." *More times than he'd care to admit, actually.* Barak, like his brothers, enjoyed his freedom in this intriguing new world, and had no wish for a battle of wills with his father again.

Gabe met Barak's eyes, fear and anger in his own. "I'm not wrong. And I'm damn sure not going to be a slave to that again. I'd rather die first."

"Woah!" Niel intervened. "There'll be no dying. They couldn't control us in the end back then, and I'm certain they can't do it now."

"And we've been here for months," Zee added, "and haven't heard a thing. Only Niel had that encounter with Chassan, and that led to nothing. And found those weapons, of course..."

Niel grunted with annoyance. "I still haven't worked out why they were there! Why put our weapons in Raziel's own temple? It doesn't make sense."

"Guys," Catarina said, breaking into their conversation, "let's focus on where we are now. There seem to be other stories on these panels...stories from after the battle."

"She's right," Ash said, turning to study them again. "These are stories about the building of their city. Look at the images of falling water, and what seems to be a light source coming from above."

They all stepped closer to examine the panels, and Barak said, "I flew to the roof of the cave earlier. Like the ceiling here, the roof is vaulted and lined with various metals, but I didn't have time to examine it properly before I was attacked. There might be some kind of light up there—something covered up right now."

"And," Zee added, "there are plenty of canals going through the city. There's no running water now, though."

Catarina pointed at the far panels. "But look—there are images of fields and irrigation systems. Rivers and lakes. Did they live above ground for a while?"

"Unlikely," Gabe said, obviously puzzled as he studied the carvings. "And look at the edges. The curve suggests a cave wall again."

Gabe was right. The edges of the panel did suggest a curve, which meant the fields and irrigation were underground.

"Seeing as you can't grow food in darkness," Barak said, "what in Herne's horns did they use for light?"

A baffled silence followed the question, until Ash directed them to another panel. "This depicts a battle in the city with creatures with wings—and it wasn't us! We never found this place!"

"This image right here," Catarina said, pointing, "depicts a body of water, and look at the huge waves that tower over the mountains. Could it be a flood? *The Flood*?"

"You're right," Barak said with certainty as he studied the expert carvings. "It has to be. The city survived it...no doubt a tribute to their engineering."

Nahum's eyes narrowed. "But the fight with the winged men occurs after that panel—after the flood. We were all dead then. And like Ash said, we never found this city."

"So, who are they fighting with?" Niel asked. "Did Nephilim survive?"

"Oh shit," Gabe groaned. "Our fathers. They must have resumed the battle after the flood. Perhaps the flood was meant to kill the Igigi, too."

Zee huffed, hands on hips. "Our fathers doing their own dirty work? Unlikely."

"Unless they were compelled to," Ash said thoughtfully. "Our God—and I use the term *our* loosely—wasn't the only God, obviously. The Anunnaki were Gods too, and while some Gods have numerous titles depending on who worships them, there were many others, all of whom had their own powers, whims, and fancies. Myths across the world talk about a giant flood. We have always harboured the belief that our God caused the flood, but what if the Gods worked together to make this happen...a chance to start again? The Igigi rebelled against their masters, just like we did. We died, they didn't."

Barak stared at Ash, disturbed at the scale of what he suggested. "You're suggesting it was a clean-up job? So why aren't the Igigi all dead?"

Nahum's eyes gleamed. "Because the Fallen are fallible. They always were. That's why they fell in the first place. The Igigi found a way to beat them, or to..." he faltered, searching for words.

Catarina finished his sentence. "To render them powerless. They removed them as a threat, somehow."

A commotion outside the door interrupted their conversation, and they turned quickly, prepared to fight.

Gishkim threw the door open, sending it crashing against the wall as he burst inside, eyes blazing with fury. "Our attackers are trying to capture us, and are desecrating the City of the Dead! Why?"

Gabe stepped up to him. "I told you. To study you and recreate you, and they'll do it any way they can. And I fear the bones of your ancestors won't be enough. It's your magic that intrigues them—your mix of brains and physicality, animal and human. They will put you in cages and study you. Is that what you want?"

Gishkim growled. "No! Does your offer of help still stand?"

"Of course it does!"

"Then follow me—except for you." He pointed at Catarina, and then at the wolf-headed Igigi behind him. "You will stay here under Urbarra's guard."

Catarina stepped back, eyes widening with fear, but Ash placed a reassuring hand on her arm. "It's for the best. We'll see you soon." But as he passed Urbarra on the way out of the room, he glared at him. "If you hurt her in any way, you'll answer to me."

Barak nodded his own reassurance at Catarina, suddenly aware of her fragility. He followed his brothers, but paused on the threshold, staring into Urbarra's cold eyes, and decided to back up Ash's threat with his own. "You'll answer to all of us."

<h1 style="text-align:center">Twenty-Six</h1>

S hadow raced down the main tunnel leading out of the city as fast as she could, while still allowing Estelle to keep up.

She was tempted to just abandon her, preferring to fight on her own, but although Estelle had plenty of magic to deal with whatever might come next, Shadow couldn't quite bring herself to let her fend for herself. *Damn it. Was she starting to like the woman?*

The tunnel was dark, lit only by the occasional flaring torch on the wall. They passed several smaller side-tunnels all of them in total darkness, but the commotion was coming from ahead. They raced around a bend and into a cloud of dust and smoke.

Shadow slowed, pulling her shirt over her mouth and nose. A section of the roof had fallen down, a mix of rubble and huge blocks of stone. She warily looked up, spotting gaping holes in the ceiling, but the solid rock beyond the stone blocks remained intact—for now.

She could sense Estelle next to her rather than see her, and said, "They're trying to seal the passage."

"We'd better get inside then before they succeed," Estelle answered, already moving forward.

In another few feet the dust cleared, revealing a series of interconnected caves ahead of them, filled with ziggurats of various sizes and designs, and Shadow presumed they were towering memorials to the dead. The tunnel emerged onto a colonnaded walkway partway up the cave wall, another just above it, reminding Shadow of cloisters. A place for reflection, perhaps, but these seemed deserted right now.

Fire provided the only light, from the torches placed on the walls to huge metal braziers casting grotesque shadows on the ground. Off to the side was another tunnel, at the entrance of which Shadow saw the bright, white-blond hair of Toto and a few soldiers. But within the burial city a fierce battle was raging. Shadow estimated two dozen Igigi were fighting Black Cronos soldiers, some in groups, others alone. A couple of Igigi were flying overhead, but the soldiers were trying to pick them off with crossbow bolts. Fortunately, the Igigi had their own longbows, but it meant the air zinged with arrows, adding to the hazards. Already there were unmoving bodies from both parties littering the ground.

Shadow pulled both her swords free—the Empusa's and the Dragonium one—and twirled them with lightning speed. She grinned at Estelle, eager to get into the fight. "May your aim be accurate, and kills be swift. Hunt well, Estelle."

Estelle returned her grin with her own tight-lipped one. "Hunt well, Shadow." She surveyed the cave with narrowed eyes, and targeting the biggest group of soldiers, launched fireball after fireball at them.

Shadow vaulted down the steps, rounded the first ziggurat, and immediately saw three soldiers battling a snake-headed Igigi. He staggered back under the onslaught, a deep cut along one heavily muscled arm, and Shadow saw his eyes glaze as he stumbled backwards.

Poisoned blades. It had to be. Much like the poisoned bolt that struck Barak.

Unseen by the soldiers who were already closing in, one of them carrying a long pole with prongs at the end, she gleefully attacked them from behind whilst cloaked in her fey magic. She stabbed one in the back, dragging her sword across him and virtually slicing him in two, decapitated the other, and as the third whipped around, alarmed, she cut his throat. In seconds, all three lay dead at her feet, and the Igigi was swaying, eyes dazed.

Shadow pointed to the dark entrance of the closest ziggurat. "You've been poisoned. Get yourself in there and hide."

She had no idea if he could understand, and she hadn't got time to hang around and find out. Gesturing once more she ran onward, her blood singing to be back in battle. This is what she was born for, and when her time came, this is how she wanted to die. But now was not that time.

Today she would take her revenge on The Silencer of Souls.

Estelle was using her shadow spell periodically, casting it on and off as she needed to like a cloak. It was no longer useful whilst hurling fireballs and spells at the battle below, but when she ran from place to place, it masked her movements, causing confusion for her pursuers.

She was already drawing the ire of the Black Cronos soldiers armed with crossbows, and she ran along the walkway, sheltering behind the thick stone columns before taking pot shots.

A soldier with a crossbow was racing up the stairs to Estelle's level, leaving her vulnerable on that side. With a well-aimed blast, Estelle took out the balustrade, hurling the stone into the soldier. The collision threw her attacker onto the ziggurat below, and she landed in a mangled heap.

Estelle ran to the left, casting her shadow spell around her again before sheltering behind a column. She edged around it, pleased to see half a dozen soldiers running to intercept her, and immediately ran in the opposite direction. She paused behind another column, this time much closer to the entrance of the tunnel where Toto watched the battle, his expression tight. She suspected the bulky area on his shoulder was a dressing over the injury that Shadow had inflicted. He certainly seemed to hold it awkwardly. A guard looked in her direction, and regardless of her spell, she ducked behind the pillar.

Estelle took a deep breath, trying to calm her racing heart, while thinking of a spell for Toto that would be both insidious and unexpected. *A spell to heat the blood would do it.* She rounded the column, the words already forming on her lips, her intent sure. But Toto had vanished, and in fury she used it on a nearby soldier instead. He roared and fell to his knees. The others whirled around, one aiming a strange weapon at her. A blast of energy struck the column next to her, the stone shattering, and she dived to the floor.

Bollocks.

Gabe and his brothers flew down the tunnel to the City of the Dead, emerging through the dust of the explosions to see the fight raging below.

Gabe's first thoughts flew to Shadow. *Where was she?* He scanned the area, but it was too dark beyond the pools of firelight, and he knew she'd be using her fey magic to conceal herself. He next wondered where all the Igigi were coming from. The city they had left was in darkness, deserted. But before he could reason through it, a bloodcurdling cry made him wheel in the air, just in time to avoid a long spear hurled from the darkness below.

Their arrival had drawn attention.

Gishkim was already shooting arrows at Black Cronos's soldiers, but many of the Igigi were struggling with the onslaught. Black Cronos were using their unusual weapons with devastating efficiency—particularly those weapons that emitted the powerful blasts that had wounded Shadow and buried Ash and Niel under a pile of rubble in Scotland.

Fortunately, the Igigi had their own armour, but it was clear that the strength of the attack was taking them by surprise.

Niel and Nahum were already assisting in a skirmish, but Zee had flown high and was using the crossbow to pin Black Cronos down. Barak wheeled to the right to join Estelle on one of the balconies, while Ash was on the ground fighting in one-to-one combat. Gabe was about to fly down to assist an Igigi below when he saw movement at the base of one of the ziggurats in the next cave, well beyond the main fight. Another muffled boom and a flash of light erupted from the spot, and he realised Black Cronos was trying to get into one of the ziggurats.

He changed direction, flying high enough to keep out of range of the crossbows, and as soon as he was close, swooped down on the Black Cronos soldiers at the ziggurat's entrance.

Gabe decapitated one before he even knew what was happening. He grabbed another by the collar, smashing him into the wall of the ziggurat, and followed it up with a thrust of his sword. The third he pinned to the wall with one wing, leaving his feet dangling off the ground. Gabe whipped his dagger from his belt, throwing it with deadly accuracy. He struck the soldier's throat, and blood splattered everywhere, including across Gabe's face and wings. Gabe dropped the man to the ground, grimacing at the feel of the hot, sticky blood on him.

Up close, Gabe saw a hole blasted through the ziggurat's thick door. *Shit.* More soldiers were inside, no doubt hunting for remains. *Grave robbers.* Gabe's fury erupted. As he advanced, a soldier emerged from the hole, others behind her. She raised her hand and blasted him using a strange device.

The power threw him backwards, and he crashed into the next building, momentarily stunned. *Bollocks.* Gabe groaned as he staggered to his feet. His chest ached and his head throbbed, and just as he was about to throw himself at her, she raised her hand, pointing the strange device at him again. He could see the power pulsing in her palm, and the malevolent gleam in her eye as she levelled it at him. His armour was already smoking, and he wasn't sure he could survive another hit that powerful.

His first preference was always to attack, but he had no choice now. The distance between them was too great. He dived behind an ornate wall that surrounded the closest ziggurat. As he landed behind it, another blast took out a chunk of it, showering him in rubble. He used his wings as a shield, but the bombardment continued.

He was pinned down, with nowhere to go.

Niel gritted his teeth as he threw off the soldier who had tackled him to the ground, his knife millimetres from Niel's ribs.

Damn Black Cronos. They were like a virus. They just kept coming, and he was sick of them. He rolled quickly, swinging his axe down with a thud, but missed as the soldier rolled away. Fortunately, Nahum's throwing knife embedded in his throat, blood spurting everywhere as he collapsed on the ground.

Niel grunted as he stood, pulling the knife free and swiping at the next soldier who raced at him. He sliced through his throat, and he too fell quickly. With no one else in sight—not alive, at least—he took a deep breath and wiped the sweat from his face, cursing loudly.

He wiped Nahum's blade on his fatigues to clean it, then passed it to him, saying, "Holy shit, brother. They must have got reinforcements. There are far more Black Cronos soldiers here than I saw outside."

"After their failed attack on the farmhouse and in France, they're taking no chances." Nahum was also covered in blood and sweat, and he nudged the nearest dead soldier with his feet. "This one did this." He gestured to the top of his left arm, and Niel saw a deep cut, saturated with blood. Fortunately, it was already congealing. "I'm lucky it wasn't worse, but it stings like a bitch. Come on. Let's help the others."

They were in a narrow alley between ziggurats, but the sounds of shouts and clanging of metal indicated many fights were still raging across the cave. And then a deeper clang sounded—something much heavier and bigger.

Something horribly ominous.

"What the hell was that?" Niel asked, alarmed.

"Nothing good. Let's get moving."

As soon as Barak entered the City of the Dead, he searched for Estelle, his heart in his throat. There were already many dead and wounded, and he was relieved not to see her body on the ground. He immediately lifted his gaze, spotting her emerge from under a pile of rubble on the first level balcony. She had barely regained her feet when she hurled a mix of fireballs and curses at the soldiers racing up the stairs.

Her well-aimed magic took out the first couple, knocking them over the stairs and taking some other soldiers out behind them. But a group was advancing on her other side too, and she would struggle to deal with both. Barak swooped in low, winging his way along the outside of the balcony, before deftly folding his wings and leaping over the rail to land behind them.

His approach was so swift, they had barely time to turn before he threw the first one over the rail to a crunching death below, and then plunged his sword into the next. The third soldier, however, was ready for him.

The next few seconds were a furious clash of blades, each grunting in the other's face, and his opponent was easily as big as Barak was. But up close, especially in the light of the smoking torches, Barak saw that his skin had a coppery sheen, just like his eyes.

Barak's blade cut the skin on his forearm, but the wound was dry, leaking no blood at all. *Fuck it.* As if sensing his frustration, the soldier smirked, incensing Barak even more. After several more clashes with neither gaining an advantage over the other, Barak had enough. He turned so that his back was to the wall, flung open his wings, and used them to propel himself and the solider he gripped through the stone balustrade. The swiftness of the move caught his opponent by surprise, and with an enormous crack, they both tumbled over the edge. Barak immediately released his opponent, watching his flailing limbs as he plummeted to the ground and landed in a mangled heap. In seconds Barak was back on the balcony, winded and covered in cuts and grazes.

Estelle raced to his side, her eyes scanning him. "Are you okay?"

"Just about. Are you?" He looked beyond her shoulder, but the way was clear—although, the stairs were smashed. "You've got rid of them all."

She smiled, but her eyes were wary. "It was tricky. They're so quick." She turned to survey the tunnel Black Cronos had arrived through. "We need to cut them off before any more arrive."

A new clanging noise resounded through the chamber, and Barak groaned. "What now?"

The immediate area in front of them was deserted, the view blocked by a row of ziggurats, but a flare of fire in the distance drew their attention, as did another loud clang.

Barak turned to Estelle, "I'm going to look."

"Take me with you!" She grabbed his arm, her hand warm and soft on his muscled forearm.

"There are men with crossbows, it's too dangerous."

"I think most are gone. They were the first that the Igigi and Zee targeted—and me, too. Besides," she wiggled her fingers, "I'll be an extra weapon for you."

He hesitated for a second, but he didn't like leaving her alone either, knowing she would make her own way to the noise. "All right. But you have the use of one hand only. You'll need the other to hold on tight." He swept her into his arms, facing her forward, and gripping her securely, leapt off the edge. He heard her sharp intake of breath and said, "Sorry. I was hoping to make our first flight together a little less dramatic."

"I can cope with drama, but maybe—"

Her words were lost as they swooped over the next ziggurats and saw the havoc below. Most of the fighting was taking place in the centre of the first cave, and dozens of Igigi and Black Cronos were engaged in battle. Barak spotted Niel and Nahum in the middle of it all, but the most horrifying sight were the three huge cages at the edge—traps for prisoners. Black Cronos soldiers were poised beside them, ready to haul them away. One of them had a motionless Igigi trapped inside, and the second contained Ash.

Zee was perched high above the City of the Dead. The roof here wasn't as well finished as in the other cave, and deep crevices provided places to wedge himself and watch, his crossbow trained below.

He had taken out the Black Cronos soldiers with crossbows, appreciating more than ever the advantage his wings gave him, and was now trying to pick off the soldiers whilst avoiding the Igigi. Not far from him, another Igigi was watching too, longbow cocked and ready. Eagle-headed and eagle-eyed, he was a good shot, but the skirmishes below were now making life tricky. And then the cages appeared, dragged in from the far tunnel.

They should have expected this. If Black Cronos wanted Igigi to experiment on, they needed to capture some alive. For some reason, Zee imagined them extracting the Igigi bound and trussed. But of course, that would always have been hard. They were huge, muscled, and built for endurance. Logically, a cage was the only way. Perhaps they had brought them here in sections after assessing the way in first. But equally, how would they get them out of the desert? Unless a large truck had arrived, and Niel hadn't mentioned that. Or...a helicopter? Something big enough for transport. *And that meant Black Cronos was far better connected and well-resourced than they knew.*

With horror, Zee saw a motionless Igigi being hauled out of the crowd of Black Cronos soldiers and thrown into a cage, the door clanging shut behind it. And with even greater horror, Ash's motionless body was thrown into the next cage.

No...

Immediately, soldiers began hauling the cages out, swiftly rolling them on hidden wheels, and Zee's initial shock turned to ice cold rage. He looked across to the Igigi, and with an unspoken agreement, they dropped from their secure perches and made a beeline for the cages as they disappeared into the tunnel.

Ash was groggy and confused, feeling only a cold floor beneath him and the sensation of moving. He filtered through his memories, trying to recall what had just happened.

Mid-fight, just as he thought he was getting the upper hand with a silver-eyed soldier with whirling blades, something hit him from behind, sending him sprawling. A jolt of pain made his body convulse, and his jaw clenched so hard he thought it would break. And then he'd passed out.

As he dragged himself upright, his vision finally clearing, he saw that he was in a cage being escorted by several soldiers, a couple carrying a long stick with electrodes on the end. Ash had done enough reading to know what that was. It wasn't any weird Black Cronos weaponry. It was a standard cattle prod. He'd been electrocuted. One soldier looked across at him, waving the prod menacingly. His intent was clear: one wrong move and he would use it again.

Ash kept very still. He had no wish to repeat that experience, and he had no weapons. Instead, he focussed on his surroundings.

They were moving at pace up a long, flat tunnel, an escort of soldiers in front and behind. Ahead was another cage with an Igigi trapped inside. The tunnel was broad and high-roofed, but rudimentary compared to the one they'd passed through earlier. Ash could only console himself that it would surely be long, and they'd have to haul them up a slope or steps to get to the surface. They'd be more distracted then, and would possibly be manhandling the cage awkwardly.

Ash settled into the middle of the cage, calmly gathering himself. That would be the moment he'd have to strike. And he hoped his brothers would be there to assist him.

<h1 style="text-align:center">Twenty-Seven</h1>

S hadow had spent the last few minutes silently stalking and killing several Black Cronos members.

Shadow liked stealth kills. They were clean and efficient. While she enjoyed combat, there was nothing more satisfying than killing someone who was completely unsuspecting, but thoroughly deserving. And Black Cronos absolutely was. They were thugs. Bred for destruction, and utterly psychopathic. And she had a grudge. After their bruising encounter under Arklet Abbey, she now had a score to settle. They all did. As soon as she could, she planned to head outside, following Black Cronos's way in, and take out as many soldiers there as she could.

However, ten minutes earlier, she saw Gabe pass swiftly overhead. She'd kept her eye on him ever since he entered the cavern, and she was glad Gishkim had finally seen sense. But then she realised Gabe had not returned. And even worse, The Silencer of Souls was heading to the next cave, in the same direction as Gabe. Dressed all in black, her eyes impassive, she had skirted around the fighting, prowling like a panther, and carrying a wooden box with a handle.

Interesting.

Shadow followed her. Once or twice the woman turned, her eyes narrowed, but Shadow froze, certain her fey magic would keep her protected. She moved on, and so did Shadow.

As they reached the next cave, Shadow realised what was happening. Well away from the fighting, one of the ziggurats had been broken into. A couple of Black Cronos members were already carrying boxes out. *Remains, or something else? Relics or weapons, perhaps?* Typical graverobbers would covet funereal tokens that might accompany the dead, but not Black Cronos. Relics had no relevance to them unless they were magical. It had to be bones...or the dust of them, at least.

Shadow increased her pace, hoping to attack The Silencer of Souls before she reached the others. Unfortunately, the woman increased her pace too, and she headed into the tomb before Shadow could reach her. Seconds later, she emerged with Toto, both drawing away to talk privately. Frustrated, Shadow hung back in the darkest shadows, watching them. Toto's arm was in a sling, but he looked otherwise well, and she cursed her wayward shot. But something had disturbed both of them, and with the bark of a command at the Black Cronos soldiers, he walked away with

The Silencer of Souls, threading through the ziggurats to the next cave, their pace quickening with every step.

Shadow's eyes narrowed. *What else was going on here?* Frozen with indecision, she debated her options, but decided that following them was more important than what was happening here. Just as she was about to leave, a blast directed at a corner of the next ziggurat commanded her attention, three soldiers closing in as they fired again and again. That could mean only one thing.

Gabe.

Her suspicions were confirmed moments later when she saw an outstretched wing flash above the wall and a chunk of rock sail over it, landing with a thunk among the advancing soldiers. Several more followed, scattering the soldiers.

This was her chance.

She ran in, grabbed the closest one from behind, and drew her blade across the soldier's throat. She fell at Shadow's feet, blood bubbling out of the wound. The remaining two soldiers were distracted by the bombardment of stone, and she swiftly killed the next. By then she was in Gabe's range too, and danced out of the way of an incoming block of stone, as did the soldier. Unseen, she ran up behind her, driving her blade up into her ribcage before cutting her throat with the other blade.

It had all happened so quickly, and the other soldiers were so preoccupied with the boxes of bones, that the exchange went unseen by anyone else. Shadow scrambled up the stone wall and vaulted over the top, hissing, "Gabe! It's me!"

"Shadow!" A broad grin split his face as he pulled her into his arms and kissed her. "I was worried about you."

She pulled back, smiling. "I've been having lots of fun. Your immediate attackers are dead now. But," her smile disappeared, "that bitch has arrived and taken Toto somewhere." She waved vaguely toward the other cave. "Something else is going on here. And they're stealing bones!"

"I know. They pinned me down before I could do anything." He ran a dusty hand across his face, smearing dirt along it. "Fuck it. How big is the group by the next ziggurat now?"

"Just a few. We can take them together. And then we need to find that bitch."

Gabe grabbed his weapons. "Good. Let's do this."

Nahum hung in the air, Niel next to him, watching a caged Ash and an Igigi vanish into the tunnel, soldiers surrounding them.

"Right, brother," he said, turning to Niel. "Ash and the Igigi are our priority. The others are withdrawing, now that they have what they want."

"Trying to," Niel corrected. "The Igigi aren't letting them go so easily."

"But they can't get close, either. That final line is holding them off." Nahum's jaw clenched. "We'd fare better in flight—especially now that we have the crossbows."

"But they have their explosive handheld devices. However," Niel shrugged, his huge shoulders shifting upwards, "what's life without a little danger?"

Nahum considered their best approach, and then spotted Zee alongside Barak who was holding Estelle. He whistled, and in seconds they were all hovering together, Estelle looking flushed. "You saw that Ash was captured?" Nahum asked.

Zee nodded, his eyes fixed on the tunnel's entrance. "We need to follow them. Now."

"But where's Gabe?" Barak asked. "I haven't seen him in a while."

"Right there." Niel pointed to where the huge, dark-winged shape of Gabe was flying towards them, Shadow in his arms. Moments later he had joined them, and Niel said, "You had us worried for a moment."

Gabe grimaced. "I got pinned down, but we took out a group in the next cave stealing remains. They're all dead."

"And I killed a lot on my way," Shadow added.

Nahum nodded. "Good. But we have bigger problems now. They've captured Ash and an Igigi. They're heading out, and we have to stop them."

Gabe paled, cursing under his breath. "And the rest of the Igigi?"

"Some dead, but others are still battling down below," Barak said. "But Black Cronos are holding them off. We need a plan."

"Right. And Shadow says Toto is on the move, too." Gabe assessed the situation quickly. "Gishkim is fighting with his men. We need to help them. If we get rid of the rear guard, we can get close to Ash. Whatever happens, they *cannot* take them."

"And there's Toto." Niel pointed to where a unit of soldiers were stealthily moving up the stairs, Toto and The Silencer of Souls in the middle of them. "They're heading to the main city."

"What can possibly be of interest to them there?" Zee asked, confused. "It's deserted. There's just Catarina and Urbarra left there."

Nahum grunted with annoyance. "Something has been bugging me since we arrived. The city is deserted, and their City of the Dead is huge. That means their main population is somewhere else. That must be where they're going." The others looked shocked. "You know it makes sense. There are a *lot* of soldiers here. And the panel in the room we were locked in shows irrigation systems and a light source. There has to be another city."

"But how do they know where to go?" Estelle asked. Her hands, Nahum noted, were gripping Barak's arms so tightly that her knuckles were white.

"The same way they knew about the other entrance. Old intel."

"I don't give a shit about the details right now," Gabe huffed. "Zee, Barak, Estelle, Nahum—you chase down Ash and the Igigi. We," he nodded at Niel and Shadow, who rested easily in his arms as if she'd done it her whole life, "will stop Toto, and join you as soon as possible. If you can, get a message to Gishkim, so he knows the plan."

Nahum met his brother's determined gaze, knowing failure was not an option. Nahum would rather die than let Ash be taken prisoner. All of them would. "Don't worry, Gabe. We won't fail."

And with a nod at the others, they wheeled around to begin another assault on Black Cronos.

Harlan was glad to get back to the peace and quiet of his own flat after what felt like a whirlwind few days.

He turned the lights on and threw the windows open to allow the cool night breeze to banish the stuffiness of his home. It carried the sounds and smells of London up to him. He made a beeline to the shower, feeling like he needed to wash off days of accumulated dirt and stress, and when he was finished, he grabbed a beer and headed to his study.

Ever since he'd left JD, he'd been thinking about the Igigi and what else they may offer Black Cronos. But logically, there'd be nothing to find in their city except bones and ruins. He'd tried to contact the Nephilim and Shadow several times, and then Catarina, but no one answered. He wasn't sure if that was good or bad. If they'd found the city and were underground, there would be no signal. *But if Black Cronos had found them...*

He shook off his worry and started to research the Igigi. He hadn't got very far before there was a knock on the door. Startled, he checked the time. It was late. Almost ten. He grabbed the baseball bat he'd taken to keeping close—like that would stop Black Cronos from killing him—and headed to his front door to peer through the spyhole. With relief, he saw only Olivia.

"Goddamn it! I thought you were Black Cronos!" he said, ushering her in.

"Like they'd knock!" Olivia looked like she'd been out to dinner. She was wearing one of her elegant dresses and high heeled shoes, and she smirked as she looked at his bat. "How very American."

"Funny," he said, leading her down the hall to the study. "It could make a big dent in someone's head if I was attacked."

"And a big dent in yours if they wrestled it off you."

"I'm disappointed that you have no faith in me. I work out!"

"And they're superhumans." She cocked an eyebrow at him. "Are you still worried they'll come for you?"

He shrugged. "Not really, I guess, or I'd be back at the Mandarin Oriental. I'm not big enough to bother them right now, which is fine by me." He nodded at the computer screen. "I am, however, looking into their latest interest. What are you doing here, anyway? All dressed up and nowhere to go?"

"I had dinner with a potential client who needed reassuring about our abilities, and now I'm checking in on you. I was worried, and I admit, I'm nosy."

He laughed. "I'll get you a drink and fill you in. Wine, gin, beer, coffee?"

"A beer is just fine with me," she said, shrugging off her light jacket and grabbing a chair.

When he returned to the study, Olivia was scrolling through his web searches, and she looked at him, puzzled. "You're still looking into the Sumerian stuff?"

It had been days since he'd last spoken to Olivia, and he'd forgotten that he told her about the tablet. "Yes. We found the original tablet in Wales. It has taken Gabe and the others to Turkey."

"*What*? I didn't know that!"

"They're looking for the city. And might have found it, too."

"It would be a wreck, right?"

"That's the thing. We don't know. And I haven't heard from them for days, which makes me worry."

"Because you think Black Cronos is there, too?"

"Yes. We're even more sure now that they want whatever they can find to experiment on." Harlan glanced at the computer screen again. "The other worrying thing is JD's theory on who's behind it all. The *Comte de Saint-Germain*."

"Oh, I've heard of him." Olivia leaned back in the chair, drank her beer, and regarded Harlan silently for a moment. "That's a hell of a theory. And the Igigi, too. Bloody hell, Harlan, I know we live and work in the strange world of the occult, but this is stretching things, even for us. A hidden city beneath the desert, and another immortal alchemist!"

"If John Dee did it, why couldn't someone else? And we know there are many old civilisations out there that have vanished with time. Look at what they're finding in South America with Lidar. And Cambodia! Evidence of ancient civilisations—extensive cities—lost beneath the jungle. Why shouldn't there be one underneath the desert?" He couldn't help but feel disappointed with Olivia. "We went to the Temple of the Trinity. I can't believe you doubt it."

"Well, that's true. And your encounter with a Minotaur in a Mithraic Chamber."

He closed his eyes at the memory. "That was horrific."

Olivia sighed. "I'm being unfair, but I'm just trying to stay grounded here. You're right, odd discoveries are made all the time. I wonder what else the Igigi could offer Black Cronos?"

"Isn't their superhuman status enough?"

"Maybe. They're the subject of many conspiracy theories."

He sipped his beer and sat next to her. "I must admit, they are not something I was that familiar with until this week. It's not really my field."

"Mine either, but I love a good conspiracy theory. They are rumoured to be aliens."

Harlan snorted, almost inhaling his beer. "You're kidding."

"Nope." She pointed at the article on the screen. "Most people who work in this field focus purely on the evidence of the Mesopotamian empire, of which the Sumerians were a part of. It was only in the last century that we found so much evidence of their existence. Studies suggest that there are seven main Sumerian Gods, called the Anunnaki. All of them lived in Heaven, and had entire cities dedicated to them. City states. Their idols were revered and treated as the living embodiment of the Gods. Their servants, the ones who built their cities, were the Igigi. However, some people—pseudoscientists—suggest they were ancient astronauts who came to Earth to spread their knowledge." She smirked. "Fun!"

"I think we should stick to the facts. JD said the Sumerians were one of the first recorded people to have used crystals in magic. And The *Comte de Saint-Germain loved* his crystals."

"So, the Igigi are part of Sumerian culture who used lots of magic based on crystals...crystals with Otherworldly powers, perhaps. Amazing builders, too. They invented so many things."

"I was chatting with Jackson about it," Harlan said, nodding. "In theory, there are many things about them that could interest Black Cronos. And that doesn't bode well for Gabe. I just hope they're okay."

Gabe turned his back on the others, trusting that they would do the best they could. Now, he focussed on Toto's group.

"I guess you want to be on the ground, Shadow?"

"Of course. That woman is mine."

"Oh no, sister," Niel put in swiftly. "After that debacle under the abbey, she's *mine.*"

Shadow gave him a twisted grin. "We'll just have to see who wins, won't we?"

Gabe inwardly groaned. There was always so much competition between them all. "Just don't forget the others while you're vying to kill her. I'm going after Toto."

Black Cronos were only a few steps away from the broad balcony that led to the tunnel. Gabe arrowed his wings and dropped quickly, swooping above the soldiers in a rush of silent speed and accuracy. "Take a few out before I drop you?" he asked, mouth to Shadow's ear.

"Of course."

Angling low, arms gripped around her waist to support her and her feet braced on his, she was able to hold both swords. As they swept above their enemies' heads, her blades despatched two without them even realising that they were coming from above. He released Shadow from his grip and she landed gracefully, blades whirling. Niel dropped in the centre of the pack, using his wings to sweep the soldiers away. They crashed into walls, and some flew over the side of the stairs, landing in a crumpled heap below.

Toto spun around, hand raised, and Gabe had just enough time to see the flash of the weapon in his palm. He dived out of the way, and the mighty blast of power surged past him, taking out a chunk of one of the huge pillars that supported the upper balcony. Rubble blasted everywhere, sending everyone diving for cover, and Gabe wrapped his wings around himself, using them as a shield.

An ominous crack emitted from the pillar as it started to crumble, and huge fault lines appeared in the balcony overhead. Everyone looked up, the soldiers scattering.

Niel and Shadow barrelled through them, racing to get into the tunnel before the balcony collapsed. Gabe was closest, and he vaulted through the opening. Toto and The Silencer of Souls were racing ahead, a handful of soldiers with them, just as a huge fall of rock descended.

A chunk of stone crashed into his back, sending him sprawling. *Fuck, fuck fuck.*

Gabe was sick of being blasted by rocks and covered in dust. His eyes stung, everything ached, and he couldn't stop coughing. But Niel and Shadow had made it through, and in seconds they were all on their feet and running after them.

And then Gabe had another thought. "Urbarra!" he yelled at the others. "We need to alert him!"

"Not me," Shadow yelled back. "I'm not letting her out of my sight." She pointed to the fleeing Silencer of Souls, who ducked down a side corridor with Toto and the others.

"And not me either," Niel argued, glaring at Shadow. "I have a score to settle."

"Fine," Gabe ground out through clenched teeth. "As far as I can see, they're all trapped anyway. It's just a matter of time. I'll get him." And besides, Urbarra might have a quicker route—plus, he needed to make sure Catarina was okay.

Leaving the others to pursue Toto, Gabe flew through the tunnel and into the city, landing outside the stone building where Catarina was being... *Protected?* He hoped so.

Urbarra was standing sentry, a spear in one hand, and a sword in the other. His eyes swept across Gabe's grubby appearance. "What's happened?"

"They're retreating—finally, but with a captured Igigi and one of my brothers. Don't worry!" He held his hand up as Urbarra's eyes filled with rage. "We're chasing them down, but..." He quickly told him about Toto, and Urbarra's growl made Gabe's hair stand on end. He started to move, eyes on the far tunnel, but Gabe stepped in front of him. "Am I right in thinking you have another city?"

He froze, eyes hardening. "What do you know about that?"

"It's a reasonable guess. Am I right?"

"Yes. It's a big one, and well protected, but even so..."

Catarina's voice disturbed them as she hammered on the door. "Urbarra! It's the light source! It has to be what they want."

He turned and flung the door open, glaring at her. "What do you know about the light source?"

Catarina looked none the worse for her captivity. "I've been studying your records—your history. You stole some kind of gemstone that powered your city. Gave it light. Am I right?"

Urbarra hesitated, and then nodded. "Yes. Our ancestors stole it from the Anunnaki. It's what has enabled us to live here for so long. The Stone of Utu."

Gabe could barely believe his ears. "Are you fucking kidding me? You stole *that*?" His shock was so huge, he felt as if the earth had shifted beneath his feet. The Stone of Utu was renowned through the Sumerian world. There had always been rumours about the Anunnaki Gods. That they wielded the powers of the universe, brought from the skies. He had never seen it, and they certainly hadn't advertised its loss. *And no wonder*. It would have weakened them in their subjects' eyes. A revelation struck him. "That's the *real* reason we had to find you. And our fathers searched for you."

Urbarra nodded. "There were six other stones, one for each God, but we only took one. Its power could be devastating in the wrong hands. And it would mean the end of us. We would die, and our city would collapse."

"Is there another way to get there? Niel and Shadow are following them, but they need help."

Urbarra nodded. "Follow me."

Catarina forced her way out of the room, glaring at Gabe. "You are *not* leaving me behind!"

He was too anxious to get moving to argue. "Then you'd better stay close."

Barak raced down the tunnel after the fleeing Black Cronos soldiers, with his brothers, Estelle, and the Igigi keeping pace alongside.

After a combined assault on the remaining Black Cronos soldiers in the City of the Dead, the stragglers ran, but they had a head start, and were annoyingly quick. Partway down the tunnel, as it started to twist and turn, they hunkered down and began blasting them again, holding them back.

With every passing minute, Ash and the captured Igigi were getting further away. Barak's worry about his brother rocketed, and he could see the rising panic in his brothers' eyes, too.

But Gishkim remained calm. "We have another route. This place is riddled with tunnels that we created many years ago for just such a scenario." He barked an order, separating his team into two groups, the other led by Dumuzi, a jackal-headed Igigi who seemed to be his second in command. "Dumuzi, you stay here. Continue the attack and make them think they're blocking us. We'll head down here." He gestured to a side passage as he addressed the Nephilim and Estelle. "This will bring us out into the main cave." A ferocious scowl split his face in two. "They'll regret ever coming here."

Barak looked at Estelle while his brothers followed Gishkim's team who were already setting a fast pace. So far, she hadn't complained once. "Are you coming with us?" He hated to lose sight of her, but she was making no move to follow them.

She shook her head. "I'll stay here. I think I'll be of more use—and I won't slow you down." Her hand cupped his cheek as she held his gaze. "Be careful."

He kissed her palm, feeling the innate strength beneath her femininity. "And you. I like…" he gestured between them, "whatever this is."

She smiled, and it lit up her face, making his heart jump. "So do I. Be safe, Barak."

He kissed her palm once more, and then ran to join the others, holding the promise in her eyes close to his heart.

Twenty-Eight

Niel couldn't believe his eyes as the enormous vista of another underground city opened up before him.

"Herne's hairy bollocks! How is this even possible?"

Even Shadow, who pretended never to be impressed by anything, pulled up short. "I have no idea. Where is the light coming from? And the heat?"

They had progressed down a roughly carved tunnel that ended at a thick wooden door, and passing through it, now stood on a stone platform high above a verdant valley. Streams and rivers flowed through fields and forests, and clusters of buildings were spread throughout, the main city appearing in the distance. Igigi moved in the fields below them and along the lanes, and following the main road, Niel spotted a huge gate set into the wall directly below them. But ahead of them was a series of stone walkways set beneath the metal-covered dome of the cavern—a mixture of silver, bronze, copper, and gold. Ahead, set into the roof, a light source blazed, and that's where Toto and The Silencer of Souls were heading.

Niel pointed. "The gate down there must be the main entrance."

Shadow nodded. "Accessed by another tunnel, somewhere below this one. This is a kind of service access. How have they found it?"

Niel shook his head. "They've obviously either found a better source than us, or have some impressive technology. But," he stared at the handful of soldiers ahead who were facing them on the huge stone walkways, weapons drawn, "we need to get rid of them to get to Toto and that bitch."

"The light source looks like it would be too big to take."

"They always do their homework, Shadow. They must be sure they can get it. That's why she's carrying a box." Niel grimaced. "There are four guards left. I'm going to fly around them, draw their fire, and take out who I can. The roof is high enough that I can get above the walkways. I'm going to make this quick."

Without waiting to hear her response, he dropped off the ledge, plummeting to the ground until he was a good way beneath them before extending his wings. He then swept up, circling fast and rolling quickly, so his wings shielded him. He felt a few blasts come close, ruffling his feathers, but he kept going, his speed and momentum too much for them to counter. As the first soldiers came into view, he levelled out, opened his wings, and headed right for them. He took two out immediately, sweeping them off the walkway to plunge to their deaths. The other two scattered, and he swung back around. They had both flattened themselves against the walkway, and keeping low, he grabbed one mid-flight, and dropped him over the side, his scream resonating through the chamber.

Shadow had used Niel's distraction to run in, and she tackled the next soldier, coming perilously close to the edge as they rolled together. Just as Niel was swooping around, she kicked out, sending the last soldier plummeting over the edge.

"Nice job, sister," he said, landing next to her. "Ready for the next two?" Toto and The Silencer of Souls were still running towards the light source, but had pulled further ahead now. He opened his arms. "I can give you a lift."

Shadow didn't hesitate. "Let's go."

Ash braced himself against the bars of his cage as Black Cronos carried it up the steep slope to the surface.

Despite their strength, they were breathless, and it was no wonder. The cages were heavy and hard to manhandle over the rough ground. This tunnel was nowhere near as finished as the one they had entered through, and he could hear grumblings and mutterings amongst his captors, especially about Stefan Hope-Robbins.

Good. With luck, infighting might break out.

He'd overheard them saying that Stefan was waiting on the surface with a team to take them away. Ash had anxiously watched behind him, and had become increasingly more despondent that his brothers weren't in sight. But it wasn't over yet, and he was now much more rested than his captors.

Fresh air swept over him as a huge gateway appeared ahead, a hole blown in it, and he realised they'd reached the gate that Shadow had seen. He hadn't got much time left. He'd have to make his move. Now.

Suddenly, a strange rushing and roaring sensation filled his ears, and he realised the breeze felt damp. *What the hell?* And then he realised what it was. *Water, a lot of it, somewhere up ahead.*

Zee was tucked safely in a narrow tunnel high above the cave floor, watching the Black Cronos soldiers emerge from the hole in the gate below and head across the cave to the narrow cleft in the rock that was the exit. He was eager to attack them, and annoyed that Gishkim had urged them to wait.

Nahum was barely reining in his patience, especially when he saw the first cage appear, and his hand tightened on his throwing knives. Barak was equally impatient, but Gishkim ignored them, he and his team instead focussing on manipulating a mechanism set into the wall—a system of cogs and gears.

When a roaring noise filled his ears, Zee immediately knew why. Water gushed out of an opening in the cave high above the gate, sluicing down into the dry canal below. Gishkim and the Igigi had opened the ancient water channels. At first, he'd thought there was only one, but within a few seconds, another three around the cave started to release water, again all several metres above the ground.

Water churned out, the noise deafening, as the waterfalls plunged below. The canals were instantly full of water, and then they started to overflow.

There were no attempts at heroics from Black Cronos soldiers now. They ran, water sloshing around their feet, a couple already losing their footing and getting washed away.

Gishkim gave them a feral grin and pointed to the cleft. "I suggest you leave through there if you wish to reach the others outside. I will go, too. I need to teach these trespassers a lesson."

Zee shook his head. "We need to get Ash out. And your Igigi."

"And you will," Gishkim said calmly. "While the rest of them drown."

Barak cricked his neck, eyes already on the exit. A few men had already entered it, but the water was overwhelming the others. "I'll come with you, Gishkim. Brothers, join us soon."

Gishkim and Barak soared across the cave, a couple of Igigi with them, while Nahum and Zee headed to the area just beyond the gate, the handful of remaining Igigi scrambling down behind them.

Confusion reigned as the water churned. The main current swept to a hole in the far wall, carrying many soldiers with it as the water level rapidly rose. The cages, both of which were now out of the tunnel and half submerged, had soldiers clinging to them like life rafts.

Zee swooped down on them, no longer needing his crossbow. The soldiers were sitting ducks.

Ash had never been so relieved to see his brothers, or the mass of water that was flooding the cave, carrying the soldiers with it.

They had been caught completely off-guard. But although Zee was flinging the other guards into the rushing current, the bastard with the cattle prod was still grimly hanging on, and determined to use it on Ash.

He couldn't use it on the cage because he'd electrocute himself, but he prodded wildly through the bars, trying to hit Ash. But the action made him unbalanced, especially now that the current was tearing at him, and he only had one hand free to hold on.

In a perfectly-timed move, Ash snatched the cattle prod from his grasp and used the blunt end to hit the soldier in the face repeatedly. His eyes rolled back, and Ash grabbed him before he could let go. He threw the prod out of the cage, and wrapping his arm around the man's throat, pinned him to the bars.

"Zee! He has the keys."

"On it, brother," Zee yelled, dropping another soldier into the swirling water before joining him. He searched his pockets, and quickly pulled a key free. "Got it. You can let him go now."

"Good," Ash grunted, watching the soldier fall into the water with a splash.

Zee inserted the key into the lock, threw open the door, and extending a hand, pulled Ash out of the cage and onto its roof. "You had me worried."

"I'd like to say I had complete faith in you, but I was getting worried, too." Ash sighed heavily, repressing a shudder. "I was desperately trying not to think of what horrible experiments I might have been subjected to. I would rather have died first." He turned to the trapped Igigi, Nahum clinging to his cage as he tried to wrench open the door. "Let's help Nahum. Hopefully the key works on that cage, too."

Nahum was drenched, the water still rising rapidly, as the amount pouring into the cave was far more than could drain away quickly. He eyed the key with relief. Fortunately, it worked on the second lock, and once they released the Igigi, he clambered onto the cage's roof, too.

The Igigi growled with relief. "I never thought I would owe the Nephilim my life."

"If I'm honest," Nahum admitted, "I never thought I'd be saving it. But your brothers have a lot to do with it. This water, for instance."

"We have built fail safes throughout our world. We can never risk losing it to enemies."

World.

That word struck Ash as odd, but now wasn't the time to ask any more questions, as the Igigi gave a series of piercing whistles that were swiftly answered by others. Immediately, the torrent issuing from the walls started to slow. The Igigi must have closed the mechanism again. The cave began to empty, as waist-high water flowed through the hole in the wall and into the darkness beyond, and continued to pour through the crevice to the outside world. For a few moments more they held on to the cages that had wedged into the narrow canal base, waiting for the current to slow, as the captured Igigi couldn't fly.

Ash looked back to the gate, which led to the city complex. "Where are the others?"

"Tackling other issues," Nahum said, looking worried, "but Estelle should be..."

He didn't need to say anything else. A few lights in the distance heralded the arrival of the others, and soon Estelle emerged through the gate with the other Igigi, grim-faced and covered in dirt.

She sighed with relief at the sight of them, the group sloshing through the remaining water toward the cage. "Thank the Gods. We've killed the rest of them. Where's Barak?"

"Out there," Zee said, already headed to the cleft. "Let's join him."

Ash jumped to the floor, stretching his cramped limbs and flexing his wings before following him. He was looking forward to exacting more revenge on Black Cronos.

Gabe studied the mechanism in the centre of space, mouth dropping open as he examined the unbelievable engineering that was around him.

It had taken what seemed to be an age to reach this place, its entrance hidden in the rear of one of the other buildings, and Gabe wondered what other features this old city hid. Urbarra had barely explained anything while on the move, and Gabe had focussed only on keeping up with him, and making sure Catarina was keeping up with *both* of them. Fortunately, she had, seemingly undaunted by their strange surroundings.

The passage had sloped upwards on a gentle gradient, the occasional side path leading off it, but Urbarra had ignored them, guiding them steadily onwards until stopping at a central space with all manner of mechanisms that disappeared into darkness on either side. It was like they had arrived in the space above a stage. Standing still, Gabe felt the hum of the machinery beneath his feet, and saw a track set in the floor that disappeared into the gloom on either side; they were at the top of a rise, the ground falling away beyond them.

It seemed Catarina was equally shocked. "What is this place?"

"I have no idea, Catarina," he said, baffled, but translated the question to Urbarra.

He smiled in response, his wolf's grin unnerving in the dim light. "There's a reason Gishkim left me to watch Catarina. I'm one of the Igigi who maintains this—it is how the Stone of Utu passes overhead, lighting our world below."

Gabe gaped. "Like the sun?"

"Yes. It disappears at the end of every cycle to simulate night, passing backwards and forwards across the sky. Essentially, the roof of the cavern is covered in metal to add to the brightness. I'm about to speed that up. It will trigger a warning."

As Gabe translated for Catarina, Urbarra manipulated a control panel, and an enormous clang resounded around them, as if coming from deep within the core of the cavern. Immediately the humming beneath Gabe's feet increased, and Urbarra nodded, satisfied. "The Stone of Utu will now head towards its night time resting place. If our attackers are seeking it, it will soon be far from their reach."

Gabe felt suddenly out of his depth. "How did you achieve this?"

"We have been here for thousands of years. Our building skills were already superior to most. We have had time to perfect them for our needs." Urbarra positioned himself above a large hatch set into the floor. "This opens to a shaft, which leads to the maintenance platforms below. That's where the tunnel the others took will lead."

"What's going on?" Catarina interrupted. "I don't understand."

"Sorry," Gabe said, forgetting that he'd been speaking ancient Sumerian, and he quickly summarised what they were doing. "And below the platforms?"

"Our world. We will be high, as if in the Heavens."

Gabe nodded. *Good.* He would go through it and find The Silencer of Souls and Toto—and with luck, kill them both...if they weren't dead already.

Shadow ignored the nausea that Niel's erratic flight was causing, focussing only on her objective.

The Silencer of Souls and Toto were both taking pot shots at them, but they were mainly focussed on their goal. The light source.

Shadow had to turn her face away, the dazzle was so bright, but their enemies had come prepared, both now strapping darkened goggles on the faces as they ran.

"Why the hell didn't I bring sunglasses with me?" Niel groaned as he dodged another blast.

"Because no one told us about a bloody great crystal," Shadow pointed out.

"I don't think I can get us any closer."

"Niel, I swear to the Gods, I shall cut your balls off if you don't drop me close enough."

"Wait! Something's happening. The light..."

He trailed off and Shadow squinted at the source, wondering what he was talking about. But he was right. The light was dimming, just as Toto and the woman were reaching the platform below it.

"Get us closer!" Shadow yelled, readying her weapons.

By now the light was dimming rapidly, night settling over the city, and Niel arrowed in on the spot. As soon as he was above the walkway, he dropped her.

She landed like a cat on all fours, quickly bounding upwards and racing towards The Silencer of Souls, who was distracted by the disappearing crystal. Shadow didn't hesitate, and she tackled her to the floor, simultaneously raising her knife to stab her. But rather than The Silencer of Souls pushing Shadow off, she grabbed her head and pulled her close, raising her lips eagerly to hers.

The momentum was unexpected, and Shadow toppled forward, her knife clattering to the floor as she lost her balance. But she had just enough strength to slide to the side, those deadly lips missing her own by inches.

As Shadow scrambled to grapple her opponent, they both ended up rolling over and over again, and the next thing she knew, they'd plunged over the side and were freefalling.

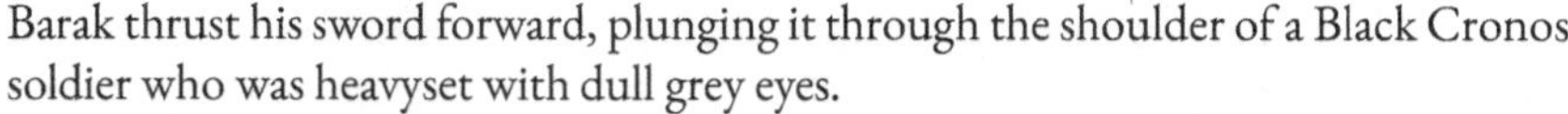

Barak thrust his sword forward, plunging it through the shoulder of a Black Cronos soldier who was heavyset with dull grey eyes.

The force of Barak's thrust was so great that it pinned him to the rock behind him. Barak restrained his other arm, and swiftly slit his throat with his dagger. As the man slumped forward, he pulled his sword free, scowling at the blade that was now pock-marked and scarred from the fight.

Warily he spun around, weapon raised, but there was no one left to fight.

All of the Black Cronos soldiers lay dead, half a dozen Igigi lying next to them. The survivors stood, winded and panting, some bent double from their exertions. Zee and Ash, both wounded from what Barak could see, were with a group of Igigi, some of whom were bleeding heavily, all looking at the sky. Another cluster of Igigi were searching through the dead bodies, no doubt checking that they really were dead, Estelle with them. But Barak couldn't see Nahum.

He looked skyward, wondering if he was flying, but then a groan drew his attention, and Barak spun around. From the midst of a few fallen dead soldiers, a figure moved. Barak flung the dead bodies aside, revealing Nahum beneath them, eyes glazed with pain.

He quickly assessed his injuries, and saw a knife sticking out from under his ribcage.

"Nahum! You've been stabbed. Don't move."

"I couldn't move if I wanted to, brother." His breaths were fast and shallow, sweat covering his face. He fumbled for the knife, his hands slick with blood and shaking.

"Don't touch it!" Barak warned, moving his hand gently away. "We're best leaving it in place right now." He shouted to the Igigi. "We need help! Have you a healer in the city?"

The shout summoned everyone, and they crowded around. Ash and Zee shoved them aside so they could get closer. Ash looked at Barak, panic in his eyes. "He's lost a lot of blood. We have to stabilise him to give him the best chance of recovery."

Estelle pushed him aside. "I can help, but we need to get him inside. Somewhere warm."

Gishkim was hanging back, watching, but now he said, "We have an infirmary, in our main city. I can take you there. In fact," his lips pursed as he took in the number of wounded, "we all need to go, apart from a few we'll leave behind to seal the entrance. I'll fly Nahum there myself. It will be quicker."

Estelle was kneeling by Nahum's side, murmuring a spell as her hand cradled over his wound.

Barak nodded and stood, allowing Gishkim to get close, and then turned to his brothers. "Has anyone escaped?"

Zee dragged his gaze away from Nahum, pointing to a distant shape in the sky. "See the lights? A helicopter took off while we were fighting—with Stefan Hope-Robbins in it, I suspect." He gestured around him. "He doesn't seem to be here."

For a moment, Barak focussed on the retreating helicopter, trying to calculate if he could reach it, but Zee squeezed his shoulder. "I've already considered it. We wouldn't get to it in time. They're gone."

"Shit," Barak huffed. "What about Toto and that bitch?"

"Still inside, I suspect. But whether they're dead or alive..."

He trailed off as Gishkim lifted Nahum effortlessly, his huge muscles rippling beneath his burnished skin. He barked out a few orders, and the Igigi who were well drew back, nodding at the command, while the others prepared to move.

It seemed it was time to leave.

As soon as the hatch was open, revealing the shaft beneath, Gabe saw a ladder attached to its side, and he leapt in front of Urbarra.

"I'm going down. Take care of Catarina."

Urbarra scowled. "I'm no babysitter. I'm going, too."

But Gabe didn't stop to argue, instead starting his descent. He had no idea where Shadow and Niel were, but he had to find out.

The shaft wasn't that long, but the light he could see below was rapidly dimming, no doubt due to the disappearing Stone of Utu. Even in the shaft he could feel the rumbling of the mechanism. As the ladder cleared the shaft, he could see the platform below, and he jumped down the last few feet, extending his wings as he did so. His gaze swept the area, taking in everything possible in the rapidly dying light.

A short distance away, Toto was firing his weapon at Niel, who was sheltering behind a column of rock. It seemed even Toto wasn't stupid enough to hit the column and risk the structure that was keeping him alive. *Although*, Gabe thought, puzzled, *where on Earth did he think he could go?* There was no escape, and defeat was inevitable.

And where was Shadow?

Niel bellowed at him, reading his mind. "Shadow has fallen off the platform with that bitch! Go get her!"

Gabe suddenly realised what was happening. Toto was pinning Niel down deliberately.

Gabe soared over the edge, heart in his mouth. *How long ago had it happened?*

A vast darkness spread below him, but lights were visible in the distance. His breath was coming quickly as his panic escalated, and he yelled, "Shadow!"

An answering shout came from beneath him, and he finally spotted two tumbling figures below.

He dived down, wings close to his side, knowing exactly how to angle them to get the most speed. Their fall was swift, but their tumbling bodies weren't as quick as his descent. It seemed to take a horribly long time to reach them though, and the ground below was getting closer. Buildings were becoming more detailed, and he could discern rivers and fields. But there was no time to wonder at the view.

Shadow and The Silencer of Souls were locked together, limbs wrapped around each other. Gabe could see Shadow desperately trying to keep the woman's face from her own, but they were inches apart. Neither seemed to have any weapons anymore.

As soon as he was close enough, Gabe grasped The Silencer of Souls by her hair with one hand, and her jacket with the other. As soon as she realised Gabe had caught her, she twisted around, grabbing him with a claw-like hand and releasing Shadow.

But Shadow wasn't letting go that easily either, wrapping her legs around the woman's waist and falling backward, like a crazy trapeze act.

Gabe had by now stopped their descent and they hung in the air, his wings outstretched, a maniacal grin on his face. He had the upper hand, and the woman knew it. Even in the dark he could see her wide-eyed expression, her pupils almost black. She was trying to twist towards him, her fingers clutching at his face. But her angle was all wrong, her back towards him, and Shadow's weight at her waist was keeping her pinned in position.

Still clutching her hair, Gabe freed his other hand, drawing his dagger from its scabbard and placing it beneath her chin. She scrabbled at him, her look of malice draining from her face, her strength no match for his own. Gabe could still feel the coldness of her lips from their last encounter, the horrible weakness she'd caused him, and he stared her down.

"Time's up, bitch."

For the first time in all their encounters, she spoke, her voice only a harsh whisper. "There are more like me. They will come for you."

"Then I'll kill them, too."

Gabe plunged his knife into her throat, and she fell limp in his arms, her blood spurting over him. Shadow scrambled over her body and clung to Gabe, and when he was sure she was secure, he dropped the woman's corpse, watching her fall to a field below. He swallowed when he realised how close they were to the ground. If he'd been there a few seconds later, Shadow would have been dead, too.

"Damn you, Gabreel Malouf! I wanted to kill her myself!" Shadow's legs were wrapped around his waist, her face inches from his, her expression furious.

"Oh, I'm sorry! I thought I just saved your life! Or can *you* fly now?"

She scowled, words battling to get out, but in the end all she managed was, "Bollocks!"

"That's my girl. Shall we go and check on Niel now?" It wasn't really a question, and he was already wheeling in the air, his wings beating as he climbed back to the distant platforms beneath the metallic sky. "Toto had him pinned down with that damn blasting weapon of theirs."

But by the time they arrived on the platform, Gabe flying in low and quick just in case of attack, it was all over.

Niel and Urbarra were standing over Toto's dead body, and even Catarina had arrived. She stood in the centre of the platform beneath the shaft, terrified to move as she took in the city below. Gabe landed softly, Shadow unwound herself to stand on her own two feet.

Niel sighed with relief. "I always knew you'd be hard to get rid of, Shadow. I trust The Silencer is dead?"

"Of course. But not by my hands." She scowled at Gabe. "He did it."

Gabe gave a mock bow, feeling a huge surge of relief that these two people who had been haunting his dreams for weeks were now gone. "And now Toto is dead, too.

"Courtesy of Urbarra," Niel said.

Urbarra gave a wolf-smile, his blade bloody in his hand. "It was my pleasure."

"Look at him," Gabe said, eyeing the dead man with distaste. "He looks pathetically small in death, and yet he was a force of nature in life." He sighed. "It's a shame we couldn't take him back for questioning."

"He would never have talked," Niel said. "In fact, once you went for Shadow, he became ever more reckless."

Gabe knew Niel was right. Toto would have been determined to take his secrets to the grave, but what did his loss mean for Black Cronos and their alchemical experiments?

Urbarra's question pulled him from his thoughts. "Will any more attack here?"

Gabe shrugged, uncertain, but it was Niel who answered. "They were the only group heading this way, so it's unlikely, but we can do a final sweep to make sure."

Urbarra nodded, relieved. "Good, and once that's done, I'll take you to the city. Hopefully we'll get some news on the others."

Twenty-Nine

S hadow accepted the wine that was offered her, sipping it gratefully as she took in their strange surroundings.

A few hours had passed since they killed Toto and The Silencer of Souls, and the other Nephilim and Igigi who had battled outside the city had joined them. They had been offered use of the public baths, a system of hot and cool pools and saunas. Their injuries were dressed, their filthy clothes, stained with blood, sweat, and dirt, had been sent to be cleaned, and they were now wearing the clothing of the Igigi. It was, admittedly, a little large. More importantly, Nahum was resting in the infirmary, his condition now stable, and Zee was keeping him company.

And now they were all seated under the stars—fake, of course—at a long wooden table, surrounded by vines that scrambled across a wooden pergola. A stone building was behind them, a hum of noise coming from the Igigi inside as they finished preparing the food. Gishkim and Urbarra were seated with them, as well as a handful of other Igigi, females included. It was, without a doubt, very surreal. The Igigi's voices sounded all too human, and yet their appearance, with their animal heads, was anything but. At least Shadow was used to satyrs and the oddness of the fey, some of whom were very different in appearance, but Catarina, for all her composure, still looked utterly shocked. Estelle seemed more at ease, but Shadow suspected that was out of sheer bloody-mindedness. She sat opposite Shadow, next to Barak, chatting to him while studying everyone intently.

The Igigi wore the traditional clothes she'd seen on the old stone carvings, although considerably more ornate and decorative, and made of fine silks and linens in gloriously rich colours. Shadow felt like she was in one of those carvings now. And the Nephilim looked...well, seeing them in their finery made her view them in a whole new light. They always exuded power and authority, especially together, but in traditional clothing, she knew exactly how they would have looked in their time. *No wonder they were kings and princes.* Their skin, like her own, was oiled and perfumed, their hair freshly washed and styled, and they were certainly at ease, chatting to the Igigi.

Shadow was sitting next to Gabe, and she turned to him, struggling to understand their conversation. "Can you translate? How does this place exist?"

Gabe looked guilty as he stopped listening to an exchange between Ash and Gishkim. "Sorry, Shadow. And you, Catarina." She sat on his other side, eyes wide.

"Excellent questions, and one we've just asked, too. I'll tell him to slow down so I can translate properly." Gabe turned to Gishkim who nodded at his words before starting again, this time more slowly as Gabe repeated everything after him. "He says that they had to flee from the Anunnaki, because despite their strength and size, their labours were killing them. And they'd had enough of working so hard for such little reward. The Anunnaki would never have agreed to let them leave, and so they rebelled. But what we didn't know was that they had the Stone of Utu."

Catarina interjected, "One of the seven Gods?"

"Exactly. Utu represented the sun, and was believed to have a sun chariot. His sister was called Inanna, and was the Queen of Heaven."

Catarina nodded, clearly excited, her voice low as she said, "Also called Ishtar."

"Exactly. Each of the seven Gods had a city dedicated to them, and the Sumerians were the first to use crystals in magic. Each God had one that mirrored its own powers." Gabe paused as he listened to Gishkim again. "They knew that if they were to succeed, they must hide deep underground, but to survive long term they needed a source of light—their own sun. So, they stole Utu's crystal."

Shadow nodded. "The stone they now use above. It's huge, surely?"

Gabe shook his head. "Not really. They looked like large eggs, highly polished, beautifully finished, about so big." He held his hands approximately twelve inches apart. "But the power they contained was enormous. And if you could use magic, as many of them did, you could manipulate that."

"The Igigi can do magic?"

"Some can—of a sort. Manipulation of the basic elements of air, water, fire, and earth. Not quite how Estelle can." He shushed them again, listening to Gishkim before continuing. "The city they built above, the old one, was their first, but they soon realised that wouldn't be sufficient. Once they explored the cave system here, they found this one. Most of it is natural. The rest they mined, connecting it to the next."

Estelle leaned across the table and said, "But the fields and irrigation systems, that seems impossible to maintain."

Gabe rapidly translated her question for the Igigi. It was another who answered this time, not Gishkim. A woman with the head of a hawk, while the human part of her body was clearly feminine. It was...odd.

Barak translated next. "They have magi, who we call magicians. Rock was transformed to earth, seeds are collected and replanted, and the water system down here is controlled to make irrigation possible. When we leave," Barak explained, "they will destroy all the tunnels to the surface. She warns us that they will never be found again. They no longer have use of the outside world, and never will again. When we have eaten our fill, offered in thanks for our help in defending their city, they will escort us to the surface. Despite our aid today, we are cautioned that if we ever try to find them again, we will die. Whatever we need to find out, we need to ask now. We'll never have another chance."

"There is something you should discuss," Shadow said, hating the fact that she was bringing up the subject, but knew she had to anyway. "You need to ask about your fathers."

Estelle met her eyes and nodded. "Yes, you're right. They do."

Shadow was surprised, but glad of her support. Gabe and Barak, however, groaned in unison.

"The last thing I want to talk about is bloody Remiel," Gabe complained.

Shadow glared at both of them. "You have to. It could be important for your lives right now!"

With a look of resignation, Gabe attracted Gishkim's attention and asked the question, and the separate conversations that had been taking place all around the table ground to a halt. Gishkim, however, looked amused when he answered, and Gabe's shoulders dropped as he leaned back in his chair.

"Well?" Shadow demanded, irate.

Gabe had a sparkle in his eye when he translated. "After the flood, the Igigi left their underground city, wondering if they could live in the desert again, seeing as the area had been wiped clean. The cities they had built were destroyed, the Sumerian Gods had retreated, and they were prepared to build afresh. But unfortunately, all that did was advertise their survival, and the Fallen came looking for them. However," Gabe smiled, "the Stone of Utu saved them. Utu is not only the God of the sun, he is also the God of justice. They used it against the Fallen, weakening their powers in this world. It stopped them taking human form completely. They couldn't march on Earth or breed with women, and their powers were blunted."

"Which means," Shadow said, "that they have no hold over you either, right?"

Gabe looked at his brothers. "That's how I interpret it. What about you?"

Niel snorted. "Sounds too good to be true, but it would explain a lot."

"Maybe," Ash suggested, "they're licking their wounds and trying to find a way back. I can't imagine they'd just accept it."

"Sounds like they had to," Barak said, amused. "But you're right, they wouldn't like to be defeated. However, it still leaves them with plenty to fight about amongst themselves. I reckon our return is insignificant, in general. You hearing Remiel, Gabe, was a desperate attempt at persuading you to help him."

"Which means," Shadow said, nudging Gabe gently, "that the next time he appears in your head, you can tell him to get lost."

Gabe's tension finally ebbed away, and he reached for his drink. "I can guarantee that I most certainly will."

With that promise ringing in their ears, the arrival of steaming plates of spiced meats and vegetables halted their conversation, and heralded the end of their stay.

Jackson emptied out the final box of papers, dust flying everywhere, and coughed, waving his hand around in a futile attempt to clear the air.

He had been in his office since six that morning, eager to get the place in shape, but that meant clearing the last few boxes of Black Cronos information. Thank the Gods, it was the final one. He was already over it.

"You all right, old man?" Harlan asked, poking his head around the door.

Harlan looked fresh, clean, and undeniably American. There was something horribly energetic about him, from his well-cut hair to his excellent tan, which he seemed to maintain despite the English weather. His expensive leather jacket oozed style as it sat on his impressive shoulders—a result of endless sessions at the gym, no doubt. And yet despite all of that, he had this roguish attractiveness that made Jackson feel like a scarecrow. Let's face it. He actually looked like a scarecrow. He wore the same thing day in and day out. He consoled himself that he had his own charm, and grinned at Harlan as if he hadn't just had such uncharitable thoughts about his good friend.

"I will be when all of this crap is out of the way," he answered. Jackson threw the old box on the floor in a fit of pique, and then checked his watch. It wasn't even nine o'clock yet. "You're up early. Everything okay?"

"Yes, I have very good news. I heard from Gabe earlier. They found the Igigi, killed a lot of Black Cronos soldiers, and in an added bonus, took out Toto and The Silencer of Souls, too."

"*What*? Are you kidding? Damn it! Couldn't we have caught one of them?" And then he realised what Harlan had said. "And what do you mean, found the Igigi? Their city, you mean?"

Harlan wiggled his hand. "Kind of. What I tell you stays between us."

Jackson groaned. Harlan seemed to be taking this cloak and dagger stuff very seriously. "We're in the top-secret Paranormal Division. Of course I'll keep it a secret."

"I mean it. No memos to Waylen, nothing documented. Only the bare essentials." Harlan raised an eyebrow, looking insufferably pleased with himself.

"He's my boss."

"And what he won't know won't kill him. It's important."

Jackson wasn't at all sure that he liked where this was going, but he nodded anyway. "Go on."

"The Igigi are alive and well, and living deep under the desert in a massive cave system. It seems Black Cronos had alternate intel that led them there. And it wasn't just their bones or bodies they wanted." He held a hand up, forestalling questions. "It seems that several hundred years ago desert nomads found their caves, and they were accepted as friends because of the fact that they avoided the cities and lived in the desert. The story of their friendship was passed down in the tribe and eventually recorded, long after that friendship had ceased to exist. That's what Barnaby found and passed on to Toto. That's what was in the papers in the bank deposit box. A name is mentioned in there, too. Another traveller that the nomads met. A Count Soltikoff." Harlan's mouth twitched in a smile.

"Oh, shit. One of the pseudonyms of the count."

"Exactly. He never visited the city, but obviously has known of its existence for years. This adds weight to our argument that he's behind Black Cronos. And Barnaby was starting to realise it, too."

Jackson stood abruptly and headed to the drink supplies and the kettle plugged in on a sideboard, switching it on. He needed tea. *Strong, sweet tea*. "It's really him."

"Unless he's got descendants. But that's unlikely."

"I've tried to pretend it wasn't real, but this is another bit of evidence. I guess it's good. Something to work on."

Harlan's face fell. "There's bad news, though. Stefan was there, but he escaped in a helicopter. We have no idea where he is. And before she died, The Silencer said there were more like her. She said they would come after us, and it wasn't over yet."

Jackson squeezed his tea bag until it was very strong, and put another spoonful of sugar in his mug just to cheer himself up. "Want one?"

Harlan looked alarmed. "Not if you're going to try and give me diabetes! Black coffee would be better."

"It's instant."

"Forget it. I'll stick to water."

Jackson sat down again, sipping his steaming drink. "Well, that settles it. We need to narrow down addresses. Having failed here, who knows what he might have planned next. Have you got any leads yet?"

"You're kidding, right? There's a mass of stuff to wade through. There are a couple of English addresses, but JD already reckons they're a dud. What about you?"

Jackson shook his head. "Not yet. I've only just emptied all the boxes. I'll begin cataloguing it all later. It's going to take a long time."

"And," Harlan shuffled in his seat, making himself more comfortable, "I have an interesting case myself. It could prove tricky."

"Fair enough." As much as Jackson wanted Harlan helping him all the time, he knew he had to keep The Orphic Guild happy. "You'd better warn Gabe and the others that they might have some stakeouts coming up."

Gabe let the cool night breeze wash over him, grateful to experience fresh air and natural night sounds again.

They had been escorted from the depths of the Igigi city to the surface a few hours earlier. Their camp was undisturbed and still protected by Estelle's spell, and their vehicles were intact. The shock of the late afternoon sun seemed to scald his eyeballs, despite the cleverness of the Igigi's light source, which had risen as they were preparing to leave.

The Igigi had kindly taken them on a brief tour of their world, an exhibition of pride and achievement, but then they had been ushered out, and Gabe knew there were many parts of it they would never get to see.

They hadn't lingered in the desert, in a hurry to get back to Mardin, and once there, they had checked back into the hotel and slept for hours. Their group had been quiet on their return, subdued even, but the good news was that Nahum was better—sort of—and they were now sitting in a rooftop restaurant not far from their hotel, their food ordered and with drinks in front of them.

"Cheer up," Nahum said to him, a hand on the site of his wound as he grimaced. "At least you weren't stabbed."

"Not as badly as you, but I'm still covered in cuts," he said, glancing down at the bandages that were wrapped around his arms. They were on his legs too, but at least those weren't visible. He'd hoped that in this new life they might not be fighting so much. *Perhaps this trip would be an anomaly.*

Niel snorted. "The whole lot of us look terrible. It's a miracle they let us in here. Well, apart from Catarina, who looks undamaged and very respectable. And you, Estelle. You escaped with only a few bruises."

He was right. They were all bruised and bandaged to varying degrees, each one making the odd wince when they moved. The restaurant staff had raised quizzical eyebrows, but their politeness and fluent Turkish saw them admitted anyway.

"My ribs ache," Estelle admitted, "from where I struck a wall, but the baths and sauna helped."

Catarina laughed as she looked down at herself. "Physically I might look fine, but I have mental scars. When we arrived here a few days ago, I had no idea that we would actually find..." she faltered. "*Them.*"

"You wanted an adventure," Shadow pointed out.

"I did. And I have plenty to share with my husband. I can assure you, their secret is safe with him." A look of uncertainty crossed her face, and Gabe knew she was wondering how long he'd have left.

"Well," Shadow huffed, "I came closer to death than I have in a long time. Something I do not wish to repeat."

Gabe squeezed her hand. While Shadow hadn't said much about her fall with The Silencer of Souls, he knew she was shaken by it. She really had been moments from death, and Gabe's heart faltered at the thought of it. But he teased her regardless, and Niel. "So much for you two arguing about who would kill her." He winked, watching Niel scowl. "It was left to me to do the honours. By the sound of her final threat, though, there are more of them like her."

"I would imagine," Ash said, "that there are a lot more of all of them. They certainly arrived with reinforcements after you two saw them." He nodded at Niel and Shadow. "And they have a helicopter."

"Private, no doubt," Zee said, signalling for more beer to the waiter. "And that means they have lots of money."

"But they're not infallible," Estelle argued. She leaned forward on the table, her hand fiddling with the napkin. "They underestimated the Igigi, despite the old records they found from the nomads. Or maybe because of them. They were friends, and assumed the Igigi were weak. And that man who heard their story...what was his name? Count Soltikoff, right?"

"The man we believe to be the *Comte de Saint-Germain*. Sounds arrogant to me," Barak said. "Just like Black Cronos. It's their Achilles heel. And the Anunnaki, for that matter."

And their fathers' Achilles heel, too, Gabe thought, and from the speculative looks around the table, his brothers thought it too, although no one wanted to say it.

He addressed Estelle next. "The last few days haven't put you off working with us, then?"

"Not at all." She glanced up at Barak, a smile on her lips. "I'm finding it a welcome challenge after dealing with boardroom antics."

Gabe felt rather than saw Shadow's resigned shuffle in her chair but ignored it, thinking he'd enjoy taking her mind off it later. "You held your own, Estelle. You're a welcome addition to the team." She beamed with pleasure, her resting bitch face vanishing. But to be honest, he hadn't seen it for a few weeks anyway. *The Barak effect*. "But I have a feeling we'll be splitting up our efforts in future."

"Why is that?" Shadow prompted.

"Harlan and Jackson need our help to search for the *Comte de Saint-Germain*, and Harlan also thinks he may need help on his next case."

Nahum held his hand up, and then winced as it pulled his side. "I'll help Harlan. I'm over Black Cronos and bloody alchemists. Damn secret societies. I'm up for a good, old-fashioned relic hunt." A grin split his face. "I might get to avoid old tombs and underground cities, too."

"You're kidding, right?" Zee said, amused. "I'm sure there'll be plenty more tombs. Any idea what Harlan wants us for?"

Gabe shook his head. "Not a clue. He said it would be a nice surprise when we got home."

Catarina was leaning on the table, listening avidly to every word. "I envy you your freedom. Your life sounds fun. When my husband passes, because I know it won't be long, I shall travel again."

Ash smiled at her. "That sounds like a good idea. You're far too young to give up on life completely. Besides, you're travelling now. Enjoy it while you're here."

"We all should," Barak said, reaching for his beer. "Let's stay a while longer, soak up the sun, and let our wounds heal before we go home." He gave Estelle a long look that she returned. "I'd like to show Estelle the sights, and I'd like to explore the place, too. I was worried that being here would be unsettling, but it's not so bad."

"I agree," Niel said, his expression resolute. "If anything, it's banished a few ghosts."

Gabe wondered if he meant Lilith, but he certainly wasn't going to ask. Instead, he raised his glass in a toast. "I think we all need to banish a few ghosts. Let's drink to that."

MIDNIGHT FIRE

WHITE HAVEN HUNTERS BOOK FIVE

TJ GREEN

One

Harlan Beckett settled behind his desk with a cup of strong espresso and looked at the files that Eloise, Mason Jacobs's new secretary, had placed on his desk. He sighed, hoping there was something more interesting in them than the current jobs he was working on. *Although, why was he complaining?* The last few weeks had been a welcome respite from the earlier turmoil.

It was a Wednesday in late August, Black Cronos had vanished, and the information on their possible whereabouts had dried up. Jackson Strange was researching files diligently, while Harlan focussed on his job with The Orphic Guild. He hated to say this, but while the jobs had been easy—he had needed to find a few alchemical manuscripts, old maps, and an unusual mirror—they were also boring. Nahum and Ash, the Nephilim, had helped him out with a few cases, and Gabe and Shadow with another, but he hadn't seen anything of them for a couple of weeks.

Restless, he headed to the window and looked down onto Eaton Place, which was lined with expensive and therefore exclusive properties, sipping his drink while he did so. He opened the window, and the sound of traffic carried inside on a wave of heat. London was hot, and it was making him claustrophobic. He had a sudden urge to get out of the city, and he returned to his desk, eager to see what new jobs he may have.

There were only a handful of files, all containing job requests from known clients, and he searched through them quickly, growing increasingly frustrated. More old documents to bid on in auctions, one grimoire to find for an out-of-town witch, and a charmed, bronze statue. He frowned at the last one. That sounded more interesting, but only just. He pinched the bridge of his nose. Dealing with Black Cronos seemed to have turned him into an adrenaline junkie.

While he was deciding on a plan of action for the day, his phone rang, the vibrations carrying it across the desk. The barking greeting of an old client made him wince.

"Morning, Theo. I'm not deaf."

"Sorry, old boy, I'm excited. I have a job for you. It's urgent."

Harlan rolled his eyes. All of Theo's jobs were *urgent* in his eyes. Theobald Henry James Carmichael was in his late seventies and rich, with a castle in Kent, a town-house in London, a house in Provence, one in Madrid, and no doubt many others. He also had a very young wife, a few ex-wives, and half a dozen children. He had made his money by trading in stocks, and now was obsessed with antiques of an unusual provenance. He was The Orphic Guild's dream client.

"All your jobs are urgent, Theo," Harlan remonstrated with him gently.

"Ha! I know. The hazards of old age. I might die before you find my latest must-have."

"You're fitter than I am. You've got a good few years left in you yet. Go on, then. What do you need now?"

"You know, I don't really want to talk about this over the phone. It's sensitive."

Immediately suspicious, Harlan asked, "Sensitive how? Does it involve stealing?"

Theo snorted. "Nothing so sordid. Any chance you can pop in for a chat?"

"Are you in London?"

"In this heat? Are you mad? No, I'm at my estate in Temple Moreton. Can you pop in?"

Harlan suppressed a laugh. You could hardly pop into Theo's estate. It was nestled in the High Weald of Kent and a good two hours' drive, but it did provide Harlan with an excuse to get out of London.

"No problem. I can be there late morning."

"Perfect. You're going to like this job, Harlan. I can feel it in my bones. This is going to be my greatest acquisition yet."

Theo hung up abruptly, as usual, and Harlan pocketed his phone, musing on what Theo wanted him to find. Suddenly energised, he turned his attention to the files on his desk, noting down the objects he needed to locate and where he should start looking for them when he returned, and then decided to find Olivia before he left the office.

Knocking on her door down the corridor from his own, he stuck his head in. "Is this a good time?"

She looked up at him and smiled. "Always time for you." Olivia James was sun-kissed, her hair gleaming gold in the light from the window, her strappy sundress revealing toned shoulders and arms.

"You're chirpy," he observed as he crossed the room and perched on her desk. "Good night last night?"

"Nice pay check this morning. Moorland paid, and I've got my commission."

"Ah! I sense more Louboutins are on the way."

She slapped his leg playfully. "Cheeky. No, actually. I'm going on holiday. I've booked a villa in Italy, and I can't wait."

He checked his watch. "It's only half-past nine. That was quick."

"Idiot. No, I did it yesterday, knowing my commission was imminent."

"Is there room for two?" He gave her his most charming smile.

"No. I'm going with my best friend. No men allowed. Well, until, of course, we start meeting handsome Italian men."

"And I'll be stuck here, coping with Mason, alone."

Olivia sniggered. "You're hardly alone. I think Eloise seems to have mastered his moods." Her expression softened. "He seems a changed man the last couple of weeks. I think he's finally put his grief over Smythe aside."

Harlan nodded. "You're right, which is good. He's also stopped harassing me about Black Cronos." He eased off the desk and into a seat. "I'm sure it won't last, but it's a welcome respite."

"And JD?"

"Suspiciously quiet. Holed up in his dungeon, I think, experimenting."

"Don't you mean his lab?"

"It feels and looks like a dungeon! You'd think the same if you saw it."

Olivia leaned forward, eyes sharp. "Has he made progress with the whole en-hanced-humans thing?"

"I'm not sure." Harlan thought about their last phone call and how cagey JD had been. "I don't think so, which is why he's quiet. I think he'd be broadcasting any success. He's finding it hard."

"Not surprising. What about his work on making weapons disappear?"

He'd told Olivia about JD's alchemical wheel and its correspondences, and how he'd made Shadow's knife resonate with her energy, and then one that worked with him. Harlan shrugged. "No word on that, either. I must admit, I didn't like the way that made me feel. If I'm honest, I've kept away, and fortunately, JD hasn't demanded my presence."

"That's fair enough." Olivia rested her chin on her long, elegant fingers. "With Black Cronos quiet, it gives him time to work, anyway."

"But it's unnerving. Where have they gone?"

"I'd like to say they're licking their wounds, but I doubt it."

"I doubt it, too," Harlan said with a sigh as he rose to his feet. "Anyway, I must go. I'm heading to Kent to see Theo. I'm hoping he has a juicy job. What have you got going on?"

"I'm tracking down a very tricky, supposedly magical reliquary. The search is becoming more convoluted by the day." Her eyes narrowed. "I was debating whether to involve Shadow and the Nephilim."

"I'm sure they'll be happy to help, although I know Barak is assisting Jackson with Black Cronos. I have no idea what the rest of them are up to. I'm sure at least one of them could help you, though."

She nodded, clearly already distracted by the idea. "Okay. I'll see how it goes."

Harlan left her to her thoughts, called Eloise to tell her where he was going, not wanting to talk to Mason, and headed out into the sunshine. *Time to see Theo and give his car a spin.*

Shadow pulled her bow string back, feeling the power and strength in it, before releasing the arrow. She watched it thump into the distant target at the edge of the field, and smiled with satisfaction as she hit the bullseye.

"Perfect," she declared. In seconds, she had shot a flurry of arrows at the target, all finding their mark, and she lowered the bow before turning to Gabe. "It's better than I hoped."

"Better than your fey-made one?"

She snorted. "Don't be an idiot! Of course not."

Gabe laughed, his teeth flashing white against his dark tan. "You are so easy to wind up." His skin was darker than normal, a result of the good weather they'd been having throughout August. His jaw was skimmed with stubble, but his warm brown eyes were hidden by his sunglasses.

She narrowed her eyes as she gave him a sidelong glance. "I am not. I am merely correcting you. Nothing made here will ever beat a fey-made weapon." She ran her hand across the carved wooden bow that was almost as tall as she was. "However, I will concede, this is excellent. It will be even better when El has strengthened it with magic."

Ever since her bow had broken when she fought against Black Cronos in France, she'd felt its loss. Her bow was an extension of her, even more than her sword. She had taken her time finding someone to make her a new one. It had to be right, and this was. She had found a craftsman in Devon to make it for her, and had chosen yew, a common wood for a long bow because of its high-tensile strength. However, the other advantage of yew was its magical properties. The tree symbolized immortality, rebirth, and protection, its connected elements were earth and water, and it was considered a guardian of the Otherworld. It was also strongly connected with the Goddess. As an added enhancement, protection runes had been carved into it.

"What material did you choose for the bowstring?" Gabe asked, taking it from her hands to examine it.

"I bowed to modernity and used Dacron. It seemed sensible. It will last longer, and it's lightweight." She shrugged. "I wanted the best bow possible. He made me some arrows, too. They're good, but I prefer my own." She sometimes spent hours making them herself, but she found it satisfying, and with her earth magic, it made it easier. "I'm going hunting tonight, when it's cooler." She lowered her sunglasses over her eyes to block out the glare of the mid-morning sun. "It's too hot now. I'll see El instead."

Gabe nodded. "Why don't I come with you? We can have a pub lunch in The Wayward Son. There's not much else to do around here."

"That's a great idea."

They strolled across the field next to the farmhouse above White Haven, heading through the side door and into the cool kitchen, where Niel was already prepping meat for the barbeque that evening.

Niel looked up as they entered, his hands covered in some kind of sauce. "Jackson has phoned Barak. He's talking to him now."

Shadow rested her bow against the wall as Gabe asked, "Black Cronos?"

"I reckon."

Barak, like Niel, was no longer working for Caspian Faversham, and he'd been eager to pick up more responsibility with their own business. Gabe had nominated him as Jackson's contact in the hunt for the shadowy organisation and their mysterious leader, who they suspected to be the immortal *Comte de Saint-Germain*. A few weeks previously, Barak and Estelle Faversham had visited The Retreat, the Paranormal Division's new headquarters, and now he and Jackson kept in regular contact. Shadow had long resigned herself to Estelle's constant presence. She would have to later, too, when she came to their barbeque. Her relationship with Barak was growing stronger every day, which was great for Barak, but painful for everyone else. At least Estelle was softening, slightly. She was like a rusty knife now, rather than a sharp one.

Before they could question Niel further, Barak bounded in, a satisfied smile on his face. "We think we have a lead!"

"Really?" Shadow asked, heading to the fridge and grabbing some beers for all of them. "You said that last time, and it went nowhere."

"And the time before that," Gabe added.

Barak shrugged, his huge shoulders rising and his chest muscles rippling beneath his t-shirt. "They're good at hiding. I suspected it would take a while. I'm actually enjoying the hunt. Besides, I'm getting to see new places with the beautiful Estelle. That's even better than finding them." He winked at Shadow, knowing it made her cranky. "Estelle is a woman with hidden depths."

"Like Loch Ness. We all know what's down there."

Barak's enthusiasm would not be subdued, and he blew her a kiss. "Tetchy madam."

"Piss off."

Gabe intervened, shooting Shadow a warning glance that she ignored. "Where are you heading?"

"Avignon. Apparently, there's another old *château* there that the *Comte* once stayed in."

"Who owns it now?" Shadow asked.

"The same people who built it centuries ago—the du Buade family. Jackson wonders if they have affiliations to Black Cronos."

Shadow leaned against the counter. "Why? Is there something suspicious about them?"

"They own a couple of businesses that Jackson thinks are dodgy. He's leaving no stone unturned."

"That's part of the problem," Gabe said, sitting at the kitchen table and raking his hand through his hair. "I think he's spreading his net too wide."

"But with no clues at all," Barak argued, "what's the alternative? We have to chase down every possible lead in the hope of a breakthrough."

Niel washed his hands, his food preparation finished, as he said, "At least Jackson is paying."

"Exactly!" Barak grinned. "And I get to see the world."

"When do you leave?" Shadow asked.

"In a couple of hours. I'll be there for three or four days, probably. It depends on what we find." He looked at the stack of meat that Niel was marinating, lips twisting with disappointment. "Unfortunately, I'll miss the barbeque."

Gabe studied him. "Don't hesitate to call for backup if you think you've found something."

Barak nodded as he put a number into his phone and headed out of the room. "Sure thing. I'll let Estelle know our plans."

Shadow patted Gabe's hand. "He'll be fine. It's like you said—they're chasing everything right now."

"But at some point they'll get lucky, and there's only two of them."

"At which time he'll call us." Shadow inwardly sighed. Gabe always worried about the others. He couldn't help it. It was even worse when he didn't have anything else to worry about, which they didn't right now. "Come on. Time to see El, and then pub." She turned to Niel. "Want to join us?"

"Nah. I'm going to the barn to spar with Nahum. He's already warming up." He flexed his arms and rolled his shoulders as he gave them a wicked grin. "I'm already feeling victorious."

Shadow tutted. "Overconfidence will cost you."

"Says the woman who is constantly overconfident!"

"It's justified. I am fey!" she proclaimed, wide-eyed, and then dodged out of the kitchen before he could retaliate, giggling as Niel swore behind her. "Come on, Gabe. Places to be!"

Two

Jackson paced his office after finishing making all the arrangements for Barak and Estelle's trip, hoping that something useful would come of the latest intel.

He always knew that this would take a long time, but he was already getting impatient. He took a deep breath, reminding himself that this search had been going on for a long time, and that they were making more progress than they had in years. *Patience.* He itched to be going with Barak, but he would be of more use here. He had more leads to follow up, and that included liaising with JD.

His gaze swept around his organised office. He'd been working at The Retreat for weeks now, and his room was arranged perfectly. There were lots of shelves stacked with books on all sorts of subjects, filing cabinets for old paperwork, a polished wooden desk and comfortable chair, plus a computer and phone. In the corner was a coffee table with armchairs for guests and relaxing, where he did much of his reading, as well as a drinks cabinet and a kettle and mugs. It was self-sufficient. He'd recently acquired a long, low sofa, perfect for sleeping on if he needed to. Although he hadn't yet, he was preparing for the fact that he may have to hole up down here if he ever felt he was being followed.

However, after his latest conversation with Waylen Adams, the Director of the Paranormal Division, it seemed that he was already addressing that particular issue. There were many unused rooms and side corridors in The Retreat, and he had decided to utilise them. Some were being converted into bedrooms, others were storage rooms, and one had become a large kitchen and staffroom that was much improved on the old one. The labs were at the far end of the complex in much larger spaces, and they were now finally up and running. Not surprisingly, they had taken the longest time to organise with all of the equipment they needed. Layla Gould's office was close by, next to Russell Blake's, the Assistant Director of the PD.

Suddenly curious as to what was happening elsewhere in the headquarters, and needing to stretch his legs, Jackson pocketed his mobile phone and headed down the corridor to find the room the analysts were based in. He liked to check the paranormal activity occurring over the UK, just in case there was something that could be traced to Black Cronos.

Petra and Austin, the two young analysts, were deep in conversation when he entered their office, but they paused and greeted him, both of them wearing a worried frown.

"Everything okay?" he asked, immediately worried, too.

"Just the usual," Petra replied. "We both seem to be having spirit trouble, and we're not sure why."

Austin barked out a laugh. "Maybe the hot weather unsettles ghosts."

Petra rolled her eyes and threw a paperclip at him. "Idiot."

He laughed, unmoved by the teasing insult. "Well, something is stirring them up. Don't worry, Jackson. It's nothing we haven't experienced before. I'm sure it will settle down."

Jackson nodded and sat in a spare chair. "Nothing to do with Black Cronos?"

"No sign of anything that could be attributed to them." Petra gave him a half smile. "Sorry, but not sorry. I'm glad they've vanished."

"Well, me too, I guess. We can all do without destruction on an epic scale," Jackson confessed. "But still, a glimpse of them would be nice. Nothing from overseas?" He had asked them to keep in touch with their foreign colleagues.

Austin shook his head. "Nothing."

"Okay." Jackson sighed and rose to his feet. "I'll drop in on Layla, see if any more post-mortem results have come in. And see if maybe the lab has had a breakthrough."

Petra smiled at him sympathetically. "Regretting taking the job?"

"Not at all. Just regretting the slow progress." He shrugged. "Nothing I didn't expect. See you later."

Harlan gaped at Temple Keep, unable to hide his shock at how impressive the beautiful stone-built building was.

As far as castles went, it wasn't that big really, but it had a lot of charm. It was set in beautiful grounds that he'd caught tantalising glimpses of as he wound along the woodland-edged drive. He'd also caught sight of the moat that encompassed half the building, before the drive switched back, bringing him to the entrance. *Wow. Theo must be loaded.*

Harlan presumed Theo was looking out for him, because he bounded out of the front door and almost ran to greet him. He was a tall, bald man, with shrewd eyes, an extravagant, grey moustache, and a beard that stretched down to his chest. He looked the epitome of a country squire, wearing tweed trousers, shirt, and waistcoat.

"Nice car, Harlan," he said, casting his gaze along it as he shook his hand. "Must have cost you a pretty packet. Worth it, though."

"It didn't cost as much as this!" Harlan gestured to the house.

Theo winked. "It's only little, but it satisfies my need to pretend I'm royalty. My house in France is bigger. Anyway, enough of such vulgar topics. I can't wait to share what I want you to find."

"Why the secrecy?" Harlan asked, his intrigue growing by the second. "I can't help thinking you have me searching for something underhanded."

"Not at all. Just old, with a very *interesting* story attached. Plus, everyone's away, and I'm on my own. I'm going slightly mad with no one to talk to. Old Chivers and his wife don't really count. They're older than I am."

"Chivers?"

"The butler and his wife, my housekeeper. They're in the kitchen at the moment, preparing a late morning tea. It will be up in a moment."

Fortunately, Theo was ahead of him, striding across the entrance hall and up the curving staircase to the next floor, so he didn't see Harlan's clenched jaw. *He'd been brought here because Theo was bored?* He took a deep breath, exhaling slowly. *It was a job.* Plus, he *had* wanted to get out of the office.

Theo, talking all the while as he pointed out rooms, oil paintings, and furnishings, led him to a comfortable sitting room that overlooked the back of the house. It was furnished with a mixture of armchairs, a squishy sofa, and a table under the window. The old, leaded-paned windows were thrown open, and the view of the moat and the grounds was dazzling. Theo, however, ignored it, leading Harlan to the table where a small, slim, book lay open, its pages yellowed with age and slightly dogeared. Next to it was an antique dagger with what looked like a bone hilt engraved with symbols.

"This is the bugger." His finger jabbed at the knife.

"A dagger? May I?"

"Of course."

Harlan picked it up, examining it closely. Some of the symbols were familiar. "What's so special about this?"

Theo gave him an almost maniacal grin. "It belonged to William de la More, the last Master of England who served the Knights Templar."

Harlan groaned. "Oh, no. I sense a long and diabolical tale." He dropped into a chair with a finely woven tapestry base, wondering if he was sitting on a small fortune.

"Harlan! You have an overactive imagination. It's not diabolical, but it is interesting. It's rumoured to lead to treasure..." He trailed off, raising an eyebrow as he studied Harlan's face.

"Everything with the Templars is supposed to lead to secrets and wealth, and it rarely does. They are all dead ends. What's so different about this one?"

Theo gestured around him with a theatrical air. "This castle once belonged to him."

"I remember you telling me." Harlan looked around with renewed interest. "Is that why you bought it?"

"Sort of." Theo dropped into a chair opposite Harlan. "I bought this place because it was beautiful, close to London, private, and very old. As you know, I love history and ancient buildings, and when this came on the market years ago, I snapped it up. Obviously, I knew about the Templar connection. The name says it all, but I hadn't realised until the estate agent told me that it actually belonged to William's family! The tower was built in the twelfth century, and then bits have been added over the years." He broke off as an ancient man shuffled into the room pushing a wheeled trolly on which was laid a morning tea service, resplendent with small cakes, scones, and pots of tea and coffee. "Thanks, Chivers. You can have a few hours rest, now."

Chivers nodded and retreated, shutting the door behind him.

"Shouldn't he be retired?"

"I tried. He looked horrified when I suggested it, so I keep them both on. I have a couple of youngsters doing most of the work now, but he likes to feel useful."

"Is he?"

"His wife's cooking is divine, so yes. Help yourself to some cakes. Coffee or tea?"

"Coffee, please." Harlan inhaled the rich scents and he realised how hungry and thirsty he was after his drive.

Theo poured the drinks, choosing tea for himself, and after loading his own plate with cakes, resumed his tale. "As I was saying, this place belonged to the de la More family. Normans, obviously, landed gentry. The men had a history of joining the Templars, once they had a son to pass the estate on to. William was no different. Of course, by the time he joined, there were no Crusades, but there were plenty of lands to administer. They were still a powerful organisation, even in the late thirteenth century. He was the Grand Commander of England from 1298 to 1307, when they were arrested. Because this castle was owned by his son, who wasn't a Templar, it was never seized, as so many Templar properties were."

Harlan sensed this could go on and on, and he could do without a complicated history lesson. "Where did you find the knife?"

"Right here! Since the day I owned this place, I've been renovating. It's a never-ending job, as you can imagine. I've updated plumbing, electrics, plaster, the roof." He rolled his eyes. "Everything. Anyway, I arranged to have part of the cellars cleared out recently. My wife wants a home cinema, and it seems the perfect spot. It's damp down there, so they've been pulling out walls, plastering, waterproofing, and they found this!"

"In the wall?"

"Yes. Bricked up and wrapped in oilskin cloth."

Harlan leaned forward, interest piqued. "Anything else in there?"

"No. Just that. I made sure that they proceeded carefully after that, and kept a close eye on things. The discovery coincided with me dropping one or two other jobs. I decided that I needed to slow down. I was a member of a few company boards, and to be honest, it was all getting very tedious. All these young men and women with their energetic ideas." He huffed. "Tiresome. So, I needed a hobby, and decided to research the castle and that knife. My wife more or less ordered me to do *something*, actually. I think I was getting under her feet." He took a bite of a fluffy scone and groaned. "Delicious. Anyway, I started doing research, quickly got bogged down, and then asked Owen, the assistant gardener to help. He's very good with the internet, and gave me a few tips. After that I headed to the local library and did a bit more research, and the lady there directed me to a whole section on the area. Fascinating!" Theo drew a breath while he had more cake, and then launched into a potted history of the castle that Harlan could barely keep track of. He finally said, "But other than a slight reference to the knife, I can find out nothing else." He looked sheepish. "I've been a bit possessed."

While Theo had been talking, Harlan studied the hilt, and recognised a couple of symbols as being Templar in origin. "Have you had it valued?"

"God, no! I didn't want anyone to get wind of it until I knew what it was—if it meant anything!"

"And does it?"

"I think it does. I think it leads to some of the Templar treasure." He picked up the old book. "This details some of the trials, and refers to a symbolic blade that was mentioned in William de la More's interrogation. He was asked about it and denied its existence. He said the one the authorities had already seized was the only ceremonial blade they used. Did you know that the Templars had hardly any weapons when they searched their holdings?"

"No. But then again, I don't know many details at all of anything Templar-related. It's a huge subject."

"You're not wrong there! Anyway, someone talked. Maybe under torture. The crown knew of this blade's existence, and were of course greedy for the order's land and money. William merely said many weapons had passed through Templar hands. How could he possibly know about all of them?"

Harlan was baffled. "That was like seven hundred years ago. Can you really read those records?"

"Yes! Well, *I* can't. Historians can, and do. They're extensive. I've read summaries. Anyway, I already had the knife, and when I read this—well, I assumed..."

Harlan nodded. "You thought this was *the* knife. It looks the part. It has emeralds on it, too. It must be valuable, especially considering the provenance. But I'm guessing you don't want to auction it?"

"No! Any treasure we find will be worth more than the knife!"

"I guess it makes sense that the final grand master would have had a part in hiding any treasure—or that it had already been hidden for safe keeping."

"Oh, yes. There were many commanders through the years, as there were in Portugal, France, Germany, Hungary, Croatia, the Holy Land, and others. They all played their part." Theo frowned. "You must know your Templar history. You're a collector!"

"I know the basics, obviously, but it's a big, convoluted subject, and I've had other things to occupy my time."

"You haven't searched for Templar treasure before?"

Harlan shook his head, amused at Theo's surprise. "There are plenty of others out there who've done that. Besides, I tend to stick to more occult subjects." He held his hand up to forestall Theo's arguments. "Yes, I know about the Holy Grail and all that, but that's not my field."

Theo leaned forward, his eyes sparkling. "But this could be lots of treasure! Gold, silver, precious gems...who knows what type of reliquaries or other fascinating things. Maybe written histories. What we find could be phenomenal."

"You really believe this?"

"I'm not discounting the possibility. Why are you?"

"Because it's the Knights Templar! They have been dissected and analysed, and still no one has found anything."

"Read it before you poo-poo it." Theo gestured at the text. "It's easier than me explaining."

"Where did you find this book?"

"It's a reprint of a book written by a local historian in the eighteenth century. I found it in the local library, squashed in the stacks. According to the author—a man called James Goodberry—the dagger, *my* dagger, had been listed as English commanders' property, and had been used in ceremonies. A knife was confiscated when they arrested William, but as I said earlier, it didn't match this description."

"1307 was when the Templars fell?"

Theo nodded. "In Europe. The Pope ordered their arrest on October 13th in France. He ordered the other countries that housed the Templars to comply. In England, the king delayed for a couple of months. He basically said the charges didn't hold up—he was right—but the pope prevailed eventually. When he did finally arrest them in December of that year, it was a loose affair. They would have had time to hide everything. Including this."

Harlan still wasn't convinced. "That means there might have been plenty of time to hide treasure, but also pass on instructions. The family probably dug the whole place up looking for it, and then either found it and spent it, or it was never there to begin with!"

"Or never found it at all!" Theo clearly wasn't going to let this go. "And we're not just talking about William's family. We're talking about the remains of the order. Please. Read the text. Humour me." He gave Harlan a toothy grin.

Harlan picked up a small, honeyed cake and chewed it thoughtfully as he scanned the page. Goodberry described the last few months before the English order fell, in what Harlan thought was a dubious leap of imagination as far as personal details went. However, he did talk about how William was a prisoner at a Templar manor, and then moved to other castles and kept in a reasonably good state, having been granted respect due to his position. He still was able to talk to other members of the order, and no doubt the few remaining members had gathered together in England to discuss strategies. That wasn't surprising though, considering they would have known what was happening on the continent. Goodberry, however, summarised other source documents that said the dagger was a family heirloom, not a Templar knife, but had recently been engraved by a local loyal to the family. The knife was then passed to a family friend, who hid it. The dagger then resurfaced years later, and Goodberry suggested it was then returned to Temple Keep, where it was hidden.

Harlan huffed as he leaned back and looked at Theo. "I grant you, it's intriguing, and considering you found the knife here, it seems Goodberry was accurate. It suggests nothing of what it may lead to, though."

"But there are connections—lots of them. And I own this place now. I put it at your disposal!"

"Surely the treasure won't be here. It would have been madness to hide it in a place that was about to be confiscated!"

"But that's the point. It *wasn't* about to be confiscated. It didn't belong to the Templars. The king couldn't legally grab it. They were only able to seize actual Templar property. If the knife is here, the treasure could be, too!" As Harlan paused, thinking about how long this could drag out, Theo added, "I'll pay well, and I'm prepared to let you look for a good while."

Harlan rubbed his jaw as his interest in finding lost treasure overcame his scepticism. Besides, he knew Mason would go nuts if he turned this down. He also knew Shadow loved treasure hunting, too. "I haven't got the time to devote to this, but I know someone—well, a few people, actually—who will be interested. As long as you don't mind them ducking in and out if more pressing needs arise." He wanted to hedge his bets, just in case Black Cronos turned up.

Theo whooped, which was unexpected from someone in his seventies, and his face creased into wrinkles. "Excellent. Who are they, and when can they start?"

Three

Gabe chatted to El Robinson and Reuben Jackson, two of the White Haven witches, while Shadow took a call from Harlan. They were seated around a table in the courtyard of The Wayward Son pub, finishing their pints after a pub lunch, and discussing the latest news on Black Cronos.

The witches were looking tanned and relaxed, both blonder than normal, and Gabe presumed the sun had lightened their hair. El had escaped from her shop after she'd enhanced Shadow's bow with magic, leaving her employee, Zoey, to manage it. Reuben, on the other hand, seemed to always have very loose hours as far as his business went. Not that Gabe could complain. They were the same. In fact, he was enjoying their days off after their harried time chasing Black Cronos and a few other easy jobs they'd done for Harlan. He was also trying not to worry about Barak and Estelle.

"I still can't believe Barak and Estelle are together," El said, face wrinkling with a mixture of horror and bewilderment. "She's a nightmare!"

"Estelle needs a firm hand, that's all," Reuben said, breezily. "Most women do. I like to think I've been a steadying hand with you and your wild ways."

Gabe almost choked on his pint. "Herne's horns, Reuben. You do like to take your life in your hands."

Reuben winked at him, a goofy expression on his face. He looked very pleased with himself—for a second, anyway, before El used magic to boil his remaining beer. He watched it steaming with an anguished expression. "Woman! Look what you've done!"

"You shouldn't test me, Reuben Jackson. Tame my wild ways, indeed."

With an almost imperceptible motion, Reuben cast another spell, cooling his beer down so quickly that the glass turned frosty. "I take it all back! Just don't touch my beer again." He turned his attention back to Gabe. "Seriously, though. Why Estelle?"

Gabe sighed. "It's something we've all wondered about. I guess it takes all sorts. She does actually seem happier, with less of a..." He hesitated to say the phrase, but El said it for him.

"Resting bitch face? Or should I say resting *witch* face?" She sniggered. "That will be the day. I thought that was her only expression."

Gabe could see Shadow in the corner of the courtyard turning back to them, as if her conversation with Harlan was coming to an end. "Please change the subject.

I have to listen to Shadow moaning all the time about her. She'll go off again if she hears this."

Reuben smirked and whispered, "Firm hand, Gabe, firm hand."

Fortunately, before El could boil his beer again, Shadow returned to the table with a flurry of goodbyes and sat in her chair again. Barely drawing breath, she said, "We've got a job."

Gabe felt himself bristle, partly in resentment at having to give up his leisure time, and partly because they should be discussing jobs before taking them. He was aware of Reuben's wide-eyed, questioning expression as if baiting him to challenge Shadow. He met his gaze and turned back to Shadow with pursed lips. *Challenge accepted.* "Darling, I thought we wanted a break."

She lifted her chin, her eyes steely. "Darling, I thought we wanted to make money."

"We have money. We've had several lucrative months."

"There is never such a thing as *too much money.*"

"There is if it means we're exhausted and vulnerable to attack by Black Cronos."

"We'll be fine, and you know it. Besides, we get to stay in a castle."

"We've stayed in a castle. A big one, in Wales."

"This is another one in Kent. Wherever that is." She arched an eyebrow, her violet eyes pinning him beneath her intense stare. "Don't you want to know what the job is?"

Reuben and El were watching in rapt silence as Gabe said, "It better be good."

She smiled triumphantly. "We're searching for treasure. Templar treasure."

"And what the hell are the Templars?"

Shadow shrugged. "Some kind of knights, I gather, who had lots of money."

"You've just accepted the job! Why didn't you ask more questions?"

"It was long-winded. I ran out of patience once I heard *big treasure*! Besides, Harlan said the man who has hired us would explain more himself."

Not caring that they had witnesses to their argument, Gabe slapped his forehead with his hand. "What if we've agreed to something with a mad man?"

"I haven't signed anything yet. It was a phone call!"

Reuben bellowed with laughter. "Seriously? You have no idea who the Knights Templar are? You two are just priceless! I love you guys, really, I do."

Gabe glared at him. "Don't start, Jackson. I have to put up with enough from Shadow."

"Me? I'm adorable!" she exclaimed, while Reuben laughed some more.

"Why would they know?" El said, remonstrating Reuben, although Gabe noted she was desperately trying not to laugh, too. "They're not from here! Honestly, Reuben, you're like a naughty child."

Reuben ignored her jibe, rubbed his hands together, and settled more comfortably in his chair. "Let me enlighten you about the Knights Templar. It's a long and tragic tale, and yes, there's lots of treasure—supposedly."

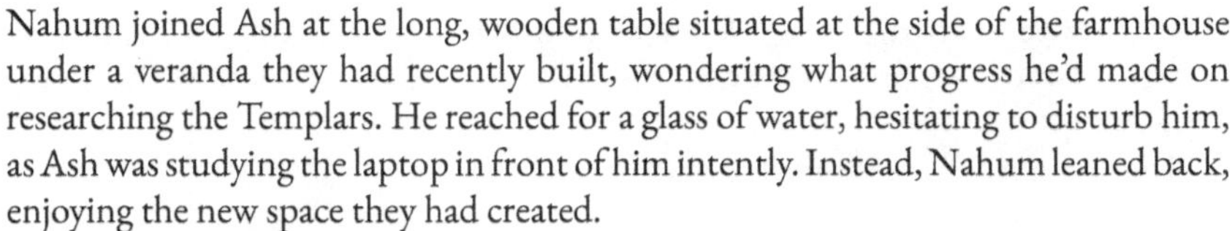

Nahum joined Ash at the long, wooden table situated at the side of the farmhouse under a veranda they had recently built, wondering what progress he'd made on researching the Templars. He reached for a glass of water, hesitating to disturb him, as Ash was studying the laptop in front of him intently. Instead, Nahum leaned back, enjoying the new space they had created.

Since they had returned from their overseas travels, especially France, where they'd enjoyed dining on the long table beneath the vine-clad pergola, the Nephilim and Shadow had wanted to repeat the experience at their home. Once they'd returned from Mardin in Turkey, they'd started work on constructing a large veranda at the side of the house, alongside the door by the kitchen that provided easy access. The area also offered a breath-taking view across the fields and moors that surrounded them, with the sea shimmering beyond.

They had used thick, wooden beams to create the structure, and to support the climbing perennials they'd planted around the edges. Fortunately, with so many of them working together, the work had been completed quickly. They'd spread a fine white gravel on the ground, and it made the whole area seem light and airy. The one thing that had threatened to take much longer was, of course, the maturity of the plants. However, Shadow had taken charge of that, and with her own and Briar's magic, the plants had grown far quicker than normal, enough to soften the hard edges of the wood and add some shade. A wooden table and an eclectic selection of chairs had completed the space, with a barbeque grill placed at the end.

Nahum sighed with satisfaction, feeling his muscles start to unwind after his fighting practice with Niel earlier that day, and the sigh disturbed Ash, who finally looked up, blinking with surprise at Nahum's presence.

"Nahum! Sorry, I was engrossed."

"It's fine. I was enjoying the peace and quiet." He nodded at the laptop. "Find anything useful?"

Ash leaned back, pushing his hair from his eyes. "Herne's balls, it's a minefield! So much information, my head is spinning. But I can understand why so many people are obsessed with the Templars."

"Does this mean you will be?"

He laughed. "Interested, yes. Obsessed? Not yet."

"*Yet*. That's what's worrying me."

"Brother, I have too many other things that interest me to become obsessed with just one thing. Plus, quite honestly, I could be reading all of this non-stop for months, probably years. There is so much information and speculation about them. Their history, the myths and rumours. Fascinating."

Nahum already knew a little bit about the Templars from what Shadow and Gabe had told them after returning from the pub. He'd searched the internet, and after reading a few basic posts had left the rest to Ash. "Exhausting, from the little I read."

"That, too."

"So, what about the new job? Likely to be successful, or not?"

"Impossible to say right now. Whatever information this Theo man has will be more than I can likely find on the net." Ash's face creased with curiosity as he stared at the laptop.

Nahum smiled. "You want to go with them."

"I think I do."

The sound of voices disturbed them as Gabe and Shadow strolled around the side of the house from the barn, and Niel entered the veranda from behind them, placing a tray of beers on the table with a gruff, "I hope you're hungry. I have a mountain of meat to cook."

Ash nodded at him. "Always. Need any help?"

"No. All in hand."

He headed to light the barbeque while Gabe and Shadow joined them at the table. Both looked flushed, with sweat coating their faces and arms. They'd been sparring in the barn, and maybe a little something else, Nahum guessed, hiding a grin. They both looked sneaky and satisfied.

Gabe reached for the beers, cracking each one open and passing them around the table, as he asked, "What do you think, Ash?"

"I've just been telling Nahum how complicated their whole history is. It's hard to say about your particular job, as the details of it won't be anywhere on the internet, I'm sure."

"We like knotty histories," Shadow declared after sipping her beer. "The last couple of jobs were easy but unsatisfying. I'd like something to get my teeth into."

Nahum understood what she meant, but easy was welcome after Black Cronos, and their dealings with them were far from over.

"You might be biting off more than you can chew," Ash warned her as Niel joined them at the table, carrying the scent of burning charcoal with him. "What are your plans?"

"We'll head to Kent tomorrow morning," Gabe said. "Temple Keep is close to a place called Temple Moreton. The original owners were the de la Mores—William was the last English Master of the Templars. Theo will show us the evidence, and we'll go from there."

Niel grunted. "From what you said earlier, there doesn't sound like much evidence."

Shadow cast him a withering glance. "There's enough to start. What do you want? A dot to dot?"

"Just saying, sister. Don't get cranky."

The trouble, Nahum reflected, was that the downtime meant they were getting under each other's feet. This job, and Barak's, would be a good thing. He asked a question before the exchange escalated. "Why does the English master sound French?"

"Because he was Norman, who were French," Ash explained, "and descended from Vikings. They had invaded England years before, ruling the country for a good while. They still owned land and held positions of power. From my initial reading, it seems by the time the Templars were arrested, the members in England were few, and most of their masters were French. But, looking at other bases, they were there, too. Maybe that's why the arrests started in France."

"I haven't had a chance to read anything," Niel said, looking confused. "Who the hell were they, and why were they arrested?"

Ash leaned back in his chair, his hand loosely clasping his beer bottle that rested on the table. "Would you like me to give a very brief summary of them?"

"I would," Gabe told him. "I'd like to know exactly what we're letting ourselves in for." He cast Shadow a sidelong glance, which she acknowledged with a sly grin.

"Essentially, the Knights Templar were a religious organisation designed to carry the Christian faith into Jerusalem and the Holy Land—which in current terms is roughly Palestine, Israel, parts of Jordan, Lebanon, and Syria. The area was Muslim, and the Christians wanted to regain control of the land, particularly Jerusalem."

Nahum shook his head. "Not so different to the wars fought over that place today."

"Unfortunately, not," Ash said with a sigh.

No one said what Nahum was sure that they were all thinking. That the old God—their God—had been responsible for some of this. He brushed it aside, knowing it was something they could do nothing about.

Ash continued. "They formed after the first Crusade, which put Jerusalem into Christian hands. After that, Christians wanted to travel there on pilgrimage. The Knights Templar protected travellers, and allowed them safe passage through Muslim areas."

"Escorts, then," Gabe said. "That's sort of what Reuben said."

"Much more than that. The Templars were strict, and their knights were expected to give up all land and possessions. This meant they usually donated large chunks of their money to the order, which was kept for their exclusive use. This made them rich. It supported their battles, and later, funded building all over Europe and the east. They were also a formidable fighting force, and their numbers grew—as did their wealth. That made them enemies that eventually led to their downfall. But I'm getting ahead of myself. The organisation essentially became the first bank. Because of their reach and strength, people trusted them with money, and they also offered loans. They traded all sorts of things, which made lots more money, and they also owned fleets of ships and land. And," Ash grinned, "they were treasure hunters."

"Really?" Niel leaned forward, eyes wide. "Hunting for what?"

"Religious artifacts. Big ones. They searched for the Ark of the Covenant, among other things."

Gabe emitted a low whistle. "Did they find it?"

"Not sure. They dug beneath what was Solomon's palace and the First Temple in Jerusalem. No one knows what they found or where it went. Although, other histories suggest that the Ark had been in Ethiopia for years. The Templars carried out lots of excavations, and found lost scrolls, too."

Nahum nodded, remembering their rudimentary knowledge of Solomon—a powerful king, who existed after their time.

"Anyway," Ash continued after sipping his beer, "kings began to worry. The Templars were essentially a well-funded, private army."

"But I thought," Niel said, "that the church—Catholic, I presume—approved of them."

"It did. But the more powerful they became, the less the pope trusted them. Rumours surfaced of their mysterious rites, and eventually they were accused of heresy."

"What kind of rites?" Shadow asked.

Ash leaned forward to read the internet page on the laptop. "Worshipping an idol, sodomy, worshipping Baphomet, who many interpreted to be a devil, but was actually a symbol of balance in many occult and gnostic organisations. However," he turned the screen so that everyone could see the image, "he does have horns and goat's feet. You can see why religious leaders would have interpreted it that way."

"The charges were made up?" Nahum asked.

"Sounds like it. By the early fourteenth century, the pope was looking for a way to disband them. He was scared of their power, and jealous of their wealth. On Friday the thirteenth in October 1307, several countries moved to arrest them. That's one of the reasons why Friday the thirteenth is considered to mean bad luck." He grimaced. "It was not a good end. They were tortured, and many were burnt at the stake. It was like an early forerunner of the witch trials. They were tortured until they confessed."

"What happened to the treasure?" Niel asked.

"No one ever found it. Rumours are that a fleet of Templar ships left France loaded with treasure the night before the arrests, but no one saw the fleet again. It's been suggested that they landed in Scotland, and even Canada, but nothing was confirmed."

Shadow's violet eyes were glowing with excitement. "So, their treasure is out there, somewhere, and this clue that Theo has could really lead to some?"

"In theory, yes. But countless people across the world have been tracking down clues for years. It's every treasure hunter and conspiracy theorist's dream."

"Which means," Gabe said, "that if it does exist, the treasure could have been found long ago."

"Perhaps, yes." Ash gave his characteristic shrug, always understated. "I should also warn you that the English king at the time did not leap to torture his captives as quickly as the Europeans did. Like during the witch trials, the English were not known for their love of torture. And the king liked the Templars. They served under house arrest for quite a while, which might mean they did spread any treasure they possessed far and wide."

Nahum was impressed. "You found out a lot in a short time."

Ash turned his golden eyes on him. "I have merely scratched the surface. I confess, I plan to buy some more books on the subject. It's interesting, for the political and religious twists alone, never mind everything else." He turned back to Gabe. "I'd like to help."

"Good," Gabe said, standing and stretching. "I'd like you to look at the paperwork and dagger and help analyse them. We'll leave early tomorrow. Right now, however, I need a shower."

"Me too," Shadow said, draining her beer. She started to walk to her room, housed in the outbuilding around the courtyard. "How long until the food's ready, Niel?"

"An hour or two yet."

"Great, see you later."

She disappeared around the side of the house, and Gabe watched her leave, his lips twisting with unspoken annoyance.

Nahum smiled, knowing Gabe was still peeved that she'd accepted the job, and that Harlan had called her first. "Something on your mind, Gabe?"

"Nope. I'm just fine," he said striding around the table and through the door into the house.

Ash sighed with amusement. "Trouble in paradise!"

Niel snorted. "Unlikely. They smelt of sex. Ugh. The only sex I like to smell is my own."

"You wish," Nahum teased him. "By the time the others leave, there'll only be me, you, Zee, and Eli. The place will feel quiet."

"Let's hope it stays that way," Niel said, rising to his feet and heading to check the barbeque, unperturbed by Nahum's comment on his lack of a love life.

"He'll be bored in two days without Shadow to annoy him," Ash observed.

"And you'll have the pleasure instead."

Ash laughed. "I'll have research to keep me busy."

"I hope, for your sake, that's true. Plus, staying in a castle has got to be good! I feel I'm missing out."

"I'm sure you'll get your chance. Besides, you used to live in one."

"Several, in fact," Nahum said, his memories suddenly full of his old palaces surrounded by high walls, and his water-filled courtyards, lush with plants. "But that was a long time ago. Maybe I should build some water features here while I have the chance."

However, even as Nahum was saying it, he had a feeling that wouldn't happen. Barak could well find some clue to the whereabouts of Black Cronos in France, and who knows what Gabe might discover in Kent.

The sun was setting as Barak surveyed the *château* situated on the rise of the hill, a vast grove of olive trees blanketing the space around it. The light caught the silvery leaves, and the building's huge stone blocks glowed a warm bronze as the sun tipped below the horizon. It was breathtakingly beautiful.

Estelle stood next to him, echoing his thoughts. "Wow. That's stunning. It's hard to think it might provide cover for Black Cronos."

"Part of me hopes that Jackson is wrong," Barak confessed, frowning at the idyllic scene. "However, we badly need a lead, and I'd like to think this is it."

Their flight had landed only a couple of hours ago, and they had picked up their hire car and driven to the hotel in the city centre. Jackson, ever the gentlemen, had booked two rooms, not presuming on the state of their relationship, but Barak hoped they wouldn't need the second room. They had slept together, several times, and yet he still sensed a reserve within Estelle that he desperately wished would go. However, patience had worked so far, and he was determined to crack whatever reservations Estelle still held regarding him.

"We should take the tour tomorrow," she suggested, disturbing his thoughts, and brushing her thick dark hair back from her face. "We can't stake out the place all night from here."

He nodded, thinking on their earlier discussion. The *château* was also a working farm, producing olive oil, a modest selection of wine, as well as preserves and cheeses. From the description on the website, a farm shop was in the grounds, and you could stroll a limited section of the gardens, as well as sign up for a tour of the olive press.

"I agree. The gardens open at ten o'clock, right?"

"Right, and the tour is at eleven." Estelle frowned at him. "You don't exactly blend in. If anyone is looking out for us, you'll stand out a mile away."

He laughed. "You think I'm on a 'most wanted' list?"

"It's very possible. I could be, too. We have all caused them lots of problems. Fortunately," she grinned, "I blend in much better than you do."

"It's a chance we'll have to take. Like Jackson said, the links could be purely historical."

"I still don't get it. The *château's* main business is the olive grove and farm. What's so suspicious about that?"

Barak realised he hadn't told Estelle his entire conversation with Jackson. They'd been too distracted with each other. "The count stayed in this place a long time ago, and according to records, was a good friend of the owner. However, it's still owned by the same family, and if he is immortal, and knew them well enough, they might still be connected. Also, during the war, there were rumours that the family was sympathetic to the Nazis."

Estelle sat on the bonnet of their rental car, a small Citroën that felt like a shoebox to Barak, nodding as she thought through the implications. "That may have offered them and Black Cronos freedom to move during the Second World War. But surely the Nazis wouldn't have wanted another group interfering in the war."

"I agree. But perhaps they didn't know." He fell silent while he considered the potential scenarios. "If this *château* and the family *was* sympathetic to the Nazis, they would have been free to continue to do their own business, which would have given cover to Black Cronos and their activities."

"But the Germans took over places like this. Turned them into their own head-quarters."

"Maybe not this one, if they were compliant. That might have been the payoff. We support you, you leave us alone."

Estelle's dark eyes turned stormy. "Awful. They were monsters to support them."

"Maybe they were scared, too. Many were." Barak had read about the atrocities of that war. Despite the centuries between this time and his own, nothing really changed. "The Nazis were too big and terrifying for many to say no to."

"But if Black Cronos were here, then they were monsters twice over."

Barak followed Estelle's gaze, studying the charming *château* in the distance, and wondered what dark secrets it could hold. He hoped they were wrong.

"Come on. Enough speculation. I need food."

Four

S hadow thought that Theo Carmichael was proving to be a very affable host, especially as he plied them with excellent coffee in the first floor sitting room.

They had made good time on their journey on Thursday morning, and had arrived close to lunch. After showing them to their rooms to freshen up, they hadn't wasted time. Theo, as enthusiastic as a teenager, had spread out the research, comprising of a couple of books and handwritten notes, before them. Shadow was examining the dagger, Ash was reading the notes, and Gabe was studying Theo himself.

Shadow dragged her attention away from the knife and looked at Gabe as he said, "I want to be completely honest with you, Theo. This could all come to nothing."

"I know that. I'm no fool, Gabe, although I may seem like a babbling idiot right now." Theo's smile disappeared. "I'm well aware of the history of the Templars, and how convoluted it is. But I truly believe that the dagger leads to the treasure, and it's here somewhere. If not on these grounds, then at least close by."

Ash turned over another page, and looked up. "I'm hoping there's more than just this to help us. This is a very useful summary of the family and events at the time, but I need details. Source materials, or as close to that as possible. And a map of the grounds and the castle, if you've got one? Something to compare references to."

Theo nodded. "There are more documents in Bodiam Village Library. The librarian refused to let me photocopy all of it. Said it wasn't allowed, and you can't remove them from the library. I made a few notes." He gestured at the small notebook on the side.

"I prefer to see them myself," Ash told him. "The originals provide context. Sometimes you need to read between the lines."

Shadow knew bringing Ash would be a good idea. He was logical and organised when it came to research. Methodical.

Theo nodded, but he looked worried. "Not a problem. I can take you there. The only thing is, some of the documents are in French—old French. Some are in Latin. Only a few are translated. I have to admit, I've been reluctant to hire someone to get them translated. People can be unscrupulous. They may not translate them correctly, or could keep information back from me. Or even pass it on elsewhere."

Ash brightened. "That's not a problem. I can translate them. I am fluent in many languages. We both are." He gestured to Gabe.

"Are you? Brilliant!" He beamed at all of them.

"Hold on." Gabe held a hand up, puzzled. "You didn't tell Harlan this? Because he didn't mention we'd need to translate. Like Ash says, it's not a problem, but if you want your best success, translation is the key. It's just lucky we can help. Not everyone could."

Theo's eyes widened, and he stumbled over his words. "I'd hoped you would manage with what I have. And I thought if we could decipher the symbols on the dagger, that would also help. But yes, this is great news!"

Ash shrugged. "No harm done. I'd like to finish reading this first, and then head to the library as soon as possible. Is it close?"

"Just a few miles down the road." Theo beamed. "I'll give you a tour of the castle and grounds, we'll have a late lunch, and then I can take you. The librarian knows me, and that should make it easier." He turned to Gabe and Shadow. "What will you two do?"

"Study the map of the castle and look around," Shadow said immediately. "I want to know every inch of this place."

"Not a problem." Theo reached for a large roll of paper that was on an armchair. "There are a few blueprints in here."

Ash moved the papers aside, allowing room for Theo to unroll the large sheets of paper. The outer one looked modern, but rolled within it were older versions. He spread them out, pointing to a floor plan that was worn thin with age. "This one is not the original. That has long vanished. This is from the sixteenth century, when additions were made. The west wing, predominantly, and the lodge in the woods."

"Lodge?" Gabe lifted his head, staring at Theo.

"Hunting lodge. The grounds used to be much bigger, and there were deer here. The place is habitable, but it needs more work."

"So that wasn't here during William's time?"

"No. But it does have some fascinating symbols in there. I think it might even have been a Masonic lodge at some point. They are supposedly linked to the Templars—though a later organisation."

Shadow had been studying the symbols on the bone-handled dagger, unable to make much sense of them. "Do any of the symbols match the ones on the hilt?"

Theo looked startled. "I'm not sure!"

Shadow tried not to roll her eyes in front of the man employing them, but seriously?

Gabe shot her a look that told her to shut up, and instead nodded, satisfied. "Thanks, Theo. We can check that. There is plenty to keep us going. I do want to reiterate that this could take a while, and we still might find nothing."

"I know. I'm prepared for the fact that this could take weeks."

"Or months," Shadow said. "And we may not be able to spare that much time." In fact, she knew she'd go loopy if she had to search that long with no result. She'd rather be fighting Black Cronos.

"I understand. I'll leave you to it, and go to make lunch arrangements. Then we'll tour the grounds." He gave them beaming smiles. "It's excellent that you could come so quickly."

Ash looked at him, puzzled. "You're very generous to let us stay here to search. It will expedite things, hopefully. But what will you do while we're here?"

"Help, of course! We're in this together!"

Shadow stifled a groan, but Ash leapt in. "Perfect, thank you. Your help will be much appreciated."

With a quick nod, Theo left the room and Gabe exhaled. "Bollocks. I suspected he'd stick around, but I hoped he'd leave us to it. I don't want him crowding us."

Ash rolled his eyes. "Gabe. He would hardly leave us in his castle unattended. Plus, he's retired. This is his baby."

"Then you can babysit him," Shadow said. The man seemed pleasant enough, but he was old, and would no doubt fuss over things and hold them up.

"He's paying us, Shadow. This is his house, his search, his dagger, and maybe his treasure. We play by his rules."

Gabe just smirked at her. "I told you to ask more questions. If there's any justice, you'll be babysitting him more than anyone."

Shadow considered a retort, and decided silence was the best option. Shooting him a scathing glance, she studied the plans instead.

Jackson was trying to concentrate on his research about *Château du Buade,* going over the details about the du Buade family in case he had missed something significant, but his mind kept drifting to Barak and Estelle.

They were there now, hopefully on the guided tour, if their plans had come to fruition. Jackson didn't know why he was so worried. A ridiculously oversized Nephilim and a powerful witch didn't need his protection, yet he couldn't help but feel he'd sent them into the lion's den. Plus, it was broad daylight in August, and the place would be packed with visitors, so of course, nothing would happen to them.

However, what was playing on his mind was the fact that the family had been collaborators, and it was the area where his grandfather had been sent during the war. A place he had never returned from. *Was he just transmitting his fears and anger about his grandfather onto the current situation? Probably.* As his eyes strayed back to the documents in front of him, though, he imagined the horrors of that time. The uncertainty, the shootings, the torture.

He had also found the original communication sent from France at the time that had led to Jackson's grandfather going in the first place. It was part of a series of communications that detailed the Resistance's efforts, and their setbacks. The one that interested him most talked about the disappearance of a half dozen fighters, all of whom had vanished over the preceding months, and none of them had been found.

Normally, captured Resistance fighters were paraded in the towns' squares—both the small villages and larger cities—so that no one was spared knowing the fate of those who dared to cross the Germans. But these four men and two women had not been made an example of. They hadn't appeared in the small villages or in Avignon itself, the largest town.

The Resistance had waited and watched, hoping the fighters themselves were in hiding and would reappear when it was safe, but eventually they had to assume they would not. They had wondered if they were dead, but their bodies were never found, either. And then one man returned—looking like a ghost. He was gaunt, hollow-eyed, and almost incomprehensible. Strange tattoos decorated his arms and chest. He talked about devils who walked among men, but that was all. Within hours he had died without being able to fully describe where he'd been.

When the English authorities were contacted, the news was passed on to the Paranormal Division, who were looking into links to the occult and the Nazis, and the news of another unknown group. They made a tentative connection between them, and that sealed Jackson's grandfather's fate. He parachuted into the area north of Avignon in March 1943. Within three days he'd vanished, along with his three companions.

When the phone rang on his desk, Jackson almost jumped out of his skin. He answered it quickly, anxious that his office should return to contemplative silence. "Jackson here."

"I have news," Layla Gould said, the PD's doctor. "Come on down to the lab."

The tour guide's droning voice was making Estelle sleepy, and she took a deep breath, trying not to yawn.

Of course, the long-winded tour wasn't the only reason for her tiredness. The previous night spent with Barak had done that. There'd been very little time for sleep. Her gaze slid to him now, and he flashed her a grin as if he knew exactly what she was thinking, his appreciative glance sliding down her toned figure. She nudged him to pay attention, deliberately staring at the man leading their group. With luck, the almost two-hour tour was coming to an end.

The group was large, a couple of dozen people, Estelle estimated, a mixture of ages and nationalities, and she and Barak had hung at the back, nodding as they listened, but they studied their surroundings carefully, both looking for a way to explore any private places without being easily spotted.

There was no doubt that the du Buade's castle was a beautiful place, but unfortunately the tour did not include the interior. Instead, they had been shown the gardens with a section for the bee hives, strolled through the olive groves, visited the squat stone building that housed the olive press, admired the vineyards and the huge vats stored in vaulted chambers, and now they were being shepherded to the ubiquitous gift shop with a café attached. With a final flurry, the tour guide smiled, nodded, and left them to it, and she drew Barak aside.

"So far so good. It all seems very respectable. But," she paused, looking across the grounds to the olive press in the distance. "I think I'd like to head back there. The door we spotted."

He nodded, eyes following her gaze. "With the electronic panel. It did seem jarring in such a rustic place. Of course, it could just be security for their stores. The building was big, and we only saw a part of it."

"But worth checking out." She looked up at him. "Considering the age of this place, there'll be extensive cellars, possibly connecting all of the outbuildings, and potentially the main building, as well. If we access one of them, we might find a way into the house."

"Agreed. Hopefully, the olive store will still be busy, and they won't notice us. It's worth a shot." Barak nodded towards the wine tasting rooms across the grounds, where for an extra charge you could sample their produce. "There will be cellars under there too, but too hard to access for us."

They had been shown inside, but there were a lot of staff there, and the doors to other rooms were behind the long counter.

"Maybe it's just paranoia," Estelle said uneasily, "but there is something unsettling about this place. Maybe it's just because I know its history." She tried to shake off her misgivings, but her magical abilities gave her more awareness than most, and she knew better than to ignore those feelings. "If it's tricky, we can come back tonight. At least we know the lay of the place now."

Barak looked longingly at the café, from which delicious, garlic-rich smells were emanating. "It almost seems a shame to miss that place, though."

"Later! Your appetite is astonishing...for many things!"

He grinned. "There were no complaints last night, though."

Knowing she had no comeback to that, she grabbed his hand and pulled him away from the café towards the far building that shimmered in the heat. A few other groups were heading that way, and they trailed behind them, happy to blend in.

The centuries-old building was split into sections. The olive press and associated equipment was in a cordoned off area, but was fully visible for the tour. There was also a small shop, and plenty of displays detailing the place's history, and once inside, they edged to the cool, shadowed recesses and the door that was almost hidden from sight. With Barak playing lookout, Estelle used her magic to disable the electronic lock and open the door, and within seconds, they had both slipped inside.

The room on the other side was large with high ceilings, rafters stretching above them. It had a couple of long, narrow windows, wooden double doors that opened to the rear, and a long counter that ran down one side. The main space was filled with crates containing bottles of olive oil, jarred olives, and stock for the shop. But set into one wall at the far end was another door with another key-coded electronic panel. Wordlessly, they crossed the room quickly, giving a cursory check in the crates that confirmed they were all olive-related products.

Fearful that someone would catch them snooping, Estelle once again used her magic to bypass security, and they slipped through the door, the brief flash of daylight illuminating a small stone landing with steps leading down into darkness.

"Excellent," Barak murmured. "Let's hope this isn't a dead end."

Estelle threw a witch-light ahead of them, and Barak led the way down the long stone staircase, his footfalls silent despite his size. When they reached the bottom, another room opened up, and Barak located the light switch and flicked it on.

The light showed another big, stone-walled room, but this one was much dustier than the one above. It had a few old crates in it, straw all over the floor, and some rickety shelving against one wall. "Damn it. Dead end," Barak murmured. "Why put an electronic lock on this?"

"There has to be something else here."

They both started looking around, Estelle focussing on the ground and the potential for a trap door, Barak tapping the walls. When he came to the shelves, he eased them aside, and gave a whoop of success. She hurried to his side, and saw a thick, wooden door set into the wall with another electronic key code panel next to it.

"At least there aren't security cameras, as well," Estelle noted as she studied the panel. She placed her hand on the door and focussed her magic, trying to discern what could be on the other side. She ran her hand across the walls before returning to the door. "A passage I think." She looked up at Barak, uncertain. "The further we go in, the harder it might be to get out."

"Second thoughts?"

"Just a consideration."

"Good. Let's do this."

Five

As promised, Ash was escorted by Theo to Bodiam Library after a delicious lunch. It was situated on one of the narrow village lanes, and was a popular place.

It had a good selection of new and old titles, browsed by a cross-section of society, but Theo bypassed the main room, taking him to the librarian behind the counter. After a polite chat, she escorted them to a series of rooms that were actually much bigger than the main, public area.

Ash looked at her, confused, and then back at the shelves. "This is more than I expected."

The librarian, Lily, gave him a beaming smile. "This place houses the documents from lots of historical houses in the area. Some hang on to their old libraries, but others have no idea what to do with their collections, so they come here."

"The books aren't sold to private buyers?"

"This place is private, sort of."

Theo chuckled. "In the 1970s, Roger Downes, who once owned Shellbrook Manor, decided to clear out his huge library, but rather than sell it all off and let the books leave the area or go to a big central library, he decided to endow Bodiam Library with the important items. He used his persuasive powers on other landowners in the area, and this place was created! A few of us, myself included, donate money regularly to maintain it. Some of the books from what was Temple Keep's library are here, too."

Lily smiled her thanks to Theo. "The usual rules apply when storing important documents. The rooms must be kept at the correct temperature, and the documents handled carefully. You also have to sign in and out. It's actually very exciting to be able to look after such an amazing collection. All sorts of people come to visit. They're not that valuable, of course. Only for local historical reasons." She gestured to a table. "Now, what was it you wanted, Theo?"

"There is the diary of Madeleine Montgomery, wife of a local landowner, a couple of local histories, and records for land that the Templars had owned in the area, and who had originally owned it." He pulled a list from his pocket. "Just a few things I'd like my friend to look over."

"Of course. Take a seat, and I'll get Adam to bring you the documents. Some of the later ones are originals, but the earlier ones are copies. The originals are too delicate for frequent inspection."

Ash frowned. "Where are they kept?"

"In the basement. I'm afraid no one touches them except experts."

Ash suppressed his annoyance. He would much rather see the originals, but the only way that would happen would be to break in. It was doable, of course, but he'd rather not. Hopefully the copies would be fine. He was itching to be able to browse the shelves, but sat where he was told, watching as Adam, an older librarian, accessed some books from a section to the rear of the room, and then placed them in front of Ash and Theo.

"These are the history books and the private diary, detailing some old searches in the eighteenth century. There was interest at the time in Templar treasure, but it never amounted to anything."

Theo nodded enthusiastically. "These are the ones I took notes from."

"Great, thanks." Ash pulled the books towards him.

Adam, however, didn't move, instead looking at Ash with open curiosity. "Are you Greek? Sorry, I heard you talking to Lily."

"I am, but I haven't lived there for a long time."

"Ah, I thought so. Are you related to the gentleman who came the other day?"

Ash found himself momentarily speechless, so it was Theo who answered, his face contorting with surprise. "Someone else has requested these documents?"

"Yes. Only a couple of days ago. He said he was a Templar scholar."

Ash felt the first stirring of unease. "No, I don't believe I'm related. What did he look like?"

"Forties perhaps, tanned, handsome. Darker haired than you."

Shit. That sounded like Nicoli. Ash made sure he still appeared calm before he spoke. Theo was purple with annoyance. "I suppose you have had quite a bit of interest in William de la More, due to his Templar links?"

"Sometimes. It seems to come in waves. Writers and students access the records the most." He shrugged, unconcerned. "Everyone's fascinated with the Templars. Of course," he glanced at Theo and laughed, "not everyone lives in a castle owned by one. I'm sure Theo has told you, however, that Temple Keep was never actually owned by the Templars."

"He did. It was private, right?"

"Yes. But other land around here was managed by them. They owned estates right across the country, but the other records you've requested list the local ones."

Ash nodded. "Great, thank you. Did the Greek visitor leave a name?"

"Of course. He was required to sign in, but I can't reveal his identity. Sorry."

"Just curious." Ash shrugged, eager that the man should leave them to it, and he pulled the old, leather-bound books towards him.

Adam continued, "I'll return soon with the copies of the land records."

Ash nodded and turned to Theo, who was looking decidedly worried. "Is there any reason someone else should be looking at these documents now, Theo?"

Theo blustered, but there was panic behind his eyes. "No, but as Adam said, many people are interested in the Templars."

"Who else have you discussed this with? Have you employed someone else?" Ash was trying to be calm, but failing. "We don't appreciate being made to compete."

"No! I haven't employed anyone else!"

Ash was not going to argue now. He needed to focus on the diary. However, he was sure Theo had said something to someone, and maybe they were searching for the treasure, too. Ash had a horrible feeling The Order of Lilith were involved, and that could make life very tricky indeed.

Before Ash could comment further, Adam returned, looking flustered. "I'm so sorry, Theo, I can't find the land records. Let me speak to Lily, in case they've been moved."

Ash watched Lily and Adam, heads bent together, frowns creasing their faces, before both of them headed to where the copies should be. Another flurry of activity and hushed conversation seemed to confirm the worst. Lily disappeared in one direction, while Adam returned to them.

"I'm so sorry, it seems they have disappeared. Perhaps they have been miscatalogued. Of course, we can always arrange for more copies. Just bear with us."

"But how can you have lost them?" Theo asked, agitated. "They were here the other day!"

"Please, Theo, just let us look." He scurried away without another word.

Ash turned to Theo again. "This is bad news, Theo. I suspect they'll find that the originals have vanished, too. Stolen."

By now their hushed voices were drawing attention, and Ash wanted Theo out of the way. "I need you to phone Gabe and let him know—just in case."

"Just in case of what?"

"Anything."

The body laid out on the mortuary table made Jackson's skin crawl.

"Did you have to bring me here?" he asked Layla.

"Yes. You want answers about Black Cronos, don't you?"

"Of course!" He stared at the frozen features of the corpse with the large, ragged hole where one eye should have been. It was further deformed by evidence of the autopsy. He took a deep breath to quell his rising bile, trying not to inhale through his nose. "I thought you said that you hadn't found anything of use, though. That the tattoos had vanished. And I also thought," he added, looking around the chill room that he'd barely had time to inspect because Layla had hustled him right to the body, "that you weren't going to have a mortuary here."

"I changed my mind." She gestured around her. "The Retreat is huge, with lots of unoccupied rooms. Why not make use of them? I was sick of going back and forth to the main mortuary. At the moment, this still needs work, but it will suffice for now."

Happily diverted from the corpse revealed by the sheet drawn back to his navel, Jackson studied the room. It was tiled from floor to ceiling, but some areas looked unfinished. "Was this a bathroom?"

"Yes, a large one. It was the easiest place to convert. It's tiled, there's a water supply, and has plenty of room for cupboards and storage. Waylen arranged the work, and as you can see, it's been stripped out and the rest of the construction will commence soon. In the meantime, I manage."

"Where do you store the bodies?"

"The room next door. I'll only need a couple of fridges, though. This place will be for those bodies I need to study in depth. This poor man is it for now."

Jackson turned to the large, muscular man, wondering who he used to be before he became a weapon for Black Cronos. "Have you identified him?"

"I have, but I'll come on to that later." Layla's bright eyes were veiled, troubled, but she pointed at the corpse. "His body is finally revealing some secrets."

"Really? How?"

"As you can see, I've performed the autopsy. He was killed by an arrow shot to the head. Instant death."

"That would be Shadow. She's deadly accurate."

"I can see, which is fortunate for me. The reason I kept this body is because there were no other major wounds. On examination, his organs were normal, as was his brain—well, what was left of it." She said this matter-of-factly, but Jackson's stomach churned. Layla continued, oblivious. "The unusual black eyes your team described have gone, leaving just his normal appearance behind. Difficult to tell now, of course. But I was curious about the tattoos you mentioned, and the strange skin some of the warriors had—the metallic skin."

Jackson nodded. "I can't forget the tattoos. They were covered in them. The general consensus was that they were imbued with magic for strength and protection. But then they vanished after death. Their metallic skin I remember vaguely, but I wasn't fighting them."

"Fortunately for you." Layla ran an appraising glance down his body. "You're not built for fighting."

Jackson glanced down at his lean form, clad in his usual old jeans and worn trainers, slightly insulted. "I brought Barnaby in, didn't I?"

"You did, but you know what I mean."

He gave a sheepish grin. "Yes. I know my limitations. But get on with it. I'm bursting with impatience!"

Layla didn't answer him. Instead she crossed to the counter and retrieved a long, hand-held lamp, before turning the lights off. She shone the light on the body, and immediately tattoos on his skin glowed in the light.

"Holy crap! Black light?" Jackson exclaimed.

"Yes. I was so frustrated that I decided to try a few different lights—they all vary—and this one worked. Tattoos normally don't just disappear. I'm annoyed I didn't try this sooner."

"There were lots of bodies, and many of them were a bloody mess. A lot to process. At least you've found them now."

"The thing is, most of the bodies have now been cremated. We couldn't possibly keep them all."

"Of course not. But what have you found out about these tattoos? The symbols?" Despite Jackson's revulsion at the body before him, he stepped closer to study the sigils. "They're complex."

"I'm afraid I don't know much about them at all, but we can take photos, study them, and I'll look at the skin around them more closely. I can take some micro samples." She strode over to the main light and flicked it back on, making Jackson squint with the brightness. "I'll have to rig up better lighting, and I've decided to call in an expert. I think it's about time JD saw this."

"That's a great idea—if you can handle his nit-picking."

"He's in my lab, so he'll do as I say!"

Layla may be an older, slender woman, but she was razor-sharp and no pushover. Jackson wouldn't dare cross her, but he knew JD would try. However, they knew each other well, and had worked together in the past.

He nodded at the corpse, recalling her earlier statement. "You said you had an ID."

"Ah, yes." Layla fell silent as she returned the light to the counter, then leaned against it to face him, arms crossed. "I confess, it's not what we expected to find, but running out of ideas, I was prepared to try anything. When DNA tests failed, I ran his fingerprints. That failed, too, until I compared them to some old records. This will come as a bit of a shock."

Jackson's chest tightened. "Go on."

"This man is James Arbuthnot. He was part of your grandfather's team that was sent into France during World War Two."

Six

G abe crossed the castle grounds in the afternoon sunshine, tension radiating through him as he studied his surroundings.

"Someone could be watching us right now!" he complained to Shadow.

"Maybe." Dark sunglasses obscured her eyes. "We'll search after nightfall. We'll have the advantage then."

"Will we? We have no idea who stole those documents."

"Besides Nicoli, you mean? His team is nothing like Black Cronos."

Gabe paused in the shade beneath a spreading oak tree on their way to the hunting lodge. Theo had given them a tour earlier, but hadn't brought them this far. "We don't know who is on his team anymore. Half of them died in Raziel's temple. He'll have recruited more...and potentially, let's face it, probably already had more team members we've never met." He leaned against the tree trunk, staring back at the castle shimmering in the heat. "I'm more curious to know who hired *him*."

"If anyone did." Shadow slid her sunglasses onto her head, turning her violet eyes on him. "He may have found out about this potential treasure all on his own. He might even have a buyer lined up."

Gabe sighed as he considered her words, rolling his tense shoulders. "Damn it. You could be right."

"And unless we can get copies of the stolen documents, we're already behind. I hate that. At least we have permission to be here!"

"That might not be to our advantage if we're searching in the wrong place." Gabe pushed away from the tree, anxious to continue. "Come on. Let's get to the lodge."

They continued across the lush grass, maintained by a series of sprinklers, and soon entered a wooded area, a glimpse of the old lodge visible through the trees.

"This is impressive," Shadow said, when they finally stood before it. "Needs work, obviously."

"That's an understatement." The two storey lodge was constructed of brick and wood, with huge beams on the outside, but the whole place was dilapidated. The wooden trim was cracked and warped, the roof sagged, and weeds were springing up in the paving around it.

Theo had given them a huge, old iron key, and Gabe twisted it in the lock, forcing the door open to get inside. The smell of mildew hit him immediately.

"Watch your step, Shadow. The floor will be rotten."

"Herne's horns. It's a mess."

Apart from a few old pieces of heavy wooden furniture, the place was empty. A staircase swept up into gloom, and a cavernous fireplace dominated most of one wall.

"I honestly think this place will have nothing to do with the treasure or the knife," Gabe said thoughtfully. "It was built well after the Templar's time."

"We shouldn't rule out anything at this stage." Shadow headed to the fireplace, standing within the empty grate and looking up the chimney.

Gabe turned away, looking for the carvings that Theo had mentioned. They weren't hard to find. Unusual symbols had been carved into the wooden panelling. Occult symbols. As his eyes adjusted to the gloom, he realised there were lots of them on the coving, the ceiling rose, and the banisters. He swung around to study the chimney, watching as Shadow pushed and pulled at the stone mouldings there.

This place was more than just a hunting lodge. It had occult overtones.

And then he heard a distinct click and Shadow yelled, "Run!" just before a huge explosion blasted him across the room.

Barak did not like this passageway beneath the *Château du Buade* one bit.

It was narrow and winding, with a few passages sloping off it, some up, some down, and others running level. They had stuck to the main tunnel, which was wider than the others. He had a good sense of direction, but even he was getting confused as to where they were headed. The air, however, was fresh, and the passages relatively dust free, which meant an air supply was getting down here, and people used it frequently.

"I think we're heading to the *château*," he whispered to Estelle, wary of his voice carrying. He pulled a compass out of his pocket, trying to envisage the grounds above him as he studied the map they had picked up on the tour. It was basic, but would suffice for their needs. "I think the tasting room and vineyards are that way." He pointed to his left. "The *château* should be straight ahead."

"There's not much to suggest Black Cronos, though, is there?"

"Not yet." He had a sudden recollection of the traps spread beneath Arklet Abbey. "Do you think this is booby trapped?"

Estelle shook her head. "With so many people above us? I doubt it. Plus, if people regularly use this, they wouldn't risk it. Arklet Abbey was evacuated. It was a last resort."

"I agree." He hurried onward, reassured, until he saw another door and another keypad set in the wall.

They crept closer and heard voices beyond it. Barak froze. There was a camera set in the door, almost imperceptible from a distance.

He started to pull Estelle back, hissing, "Get rid of your witch-light."

But it was too late. A solid metal gate slid out of the stone behind them, clanging to the floor.

They were trapped.

Ash took a deep breath, inhaling the scents of the old books, and pulled the small stack towards him. He may as well do something useful while they waited for word on the original records.

Theo had pulled up a chair next to him, plainly rattled, but he soldiered on. "The top book is written by an English scholar, and it has a large section on the English Templars. He talks about the commanders, and mentions Guillaume de la More—William, in English—and he speculates about the treasure. I liked it because it was pretty comprehensive. And he was local."

"The author?" Ash asked, thumbing through the book.

"Yes, he lived in Millcorner, a few miles away. The other book is a history of the Templars, and very interesting, but has less of a local flavour." He sighed. "I'm no scholar, so I have no idea how accurate these books are. I've read all sorts over the last few months, but as I told Harlan, it makes my head hurt. The diary is interesting, though. Madeleine Montgomery was the wife of a local landowner, and she wrote about many things. Dinners, guests, weekends, household trivia—a fascinating snapshot of the landed gentry. But she also mentions Temple Keep, and the dig on the grounds."

Ash looked at Theo, shocked. "You didn't mention that earlier!"

"But it came to nothing! I thought you might want to look at it, though."

"Absolutely." He picked up the first history book. "These are the ones you have a few photocopies of?"

"Yes—the passages that I thought were most relevant." Theo took the book from Ash and flicked through it, and then stopped, mouth open.

"What?"

"The pages have been cut out!"

Ash grabbed the book from his hand. Theo was right. A few pages had been sliced out of the book, cut close to the edge, and virtually impossible to see when the book was closed.

Bollocks.

"Someone else is also searching for this treasure, Theo, and destroying any evidence as they go." Ash quickly searched the other books and found them damaged, too. "Who have you been talking to?"

"No one! Well, my wife of course, but no details. She wouldn't be interested." His eyes widened at Ash's stare. "She's my wife! I trust her."

Ash wasn't so sure. When it came to treasure and untold wealth, allegiances sometimes vanished. "Theo, think! Why the sudden interest in this now? These books have been here for years! When were you last here?"

"Just last week, and they were intact then."

"You must have said something to someone about your recent activities."

"Just my assistant gardener!"

Ash groaned. "You have to be kidding me!"

"No!" Theo was glaring at him, eyes narrowed. "He helped me with some of the research. He's been working for me for years."

"You deal in stock and shares! You can't be that gullible."

"I'm not! I asked for some general assistance."

Ash took a deep breath, trying to calm down. "You are unfamiliar with the internet, then?"

"My dealing in stocks and shares was years ago! I had staff! I've been on boards since then—no internet necessary." Theo's lips were tight, but there was uncertainty now behind his eyes, and Ash felt suddenly sorry for him.

"I think you've underestimated the interest in all this. Perhaps you didn't say much to your gardener, but he might have looked into it further—done research of his own. He may even have employed someone to search on his behalf." *Nicoli, for example, but he kept that thought to himself.* "Is he working today?"

"Owen? Er, probably."

"We need to talk to him when we get back." And keep Shadow and her sharp knives away from him.

Before Theo could respond, Adam returned, Lily at his side, both wearing pinched expressions. This was not going to be good news.

"The originals have gone, haven't they?" Ash asked before they could speak.

Lily nodded. "I don't know how! This place is secure."

"There's no sign of a break-in?"

"None! We have alarms, cameras, key codes!" Lily was almost spluttering with indignation.

Theo was thunderous as he stood up. "This is outrageous! I demand to see the area. There might be evidence!"

"We have already called the police," Lily said, trying to calm Theo down. "We will do everything we can..."

Theo cut her off. "I demand to see it myself." He leaned in, lowering his voice. "I donate to this place. I think you owe me this much."

Lily glanced around at the inquisitive glances of other library users, unwilling to be the centre of so much attention. Ash was impressed. Theo's relaxed nature obviously hid a core of steel. And maybe he was also motivated by his own failure in judgement.

Lily, however, was no pushover. "The police said not to touch anything!"

"I won't. I just want to look!"

Ash laid a hand on Theo's arm, knowing they wouldn't find a thing. Not *now*, anyway. "It's okay, Theo. Let the police do their job and we'll do ours. We have books to study." *What was left of them.* They could report the damage later.

Theo shot him an impatient look, but at Ash's intense stare, he finally acquiesced, and Lily bobbed away, shooting Ash a grateful glance.

Without another word, Ash pulled his pen and notepad out. There was probably nothing left in the books in front of him to help their search, or they would already have been stolen, but there may be a snippet of information that would help them.

Then tonight, they could break-in themselves and investigate fully.

Seven

S hadow crashed into the curving staircase, wood shattering as she ploughed straight through it and landed, winded, on the rotten floorboards on the other side.

She landed with such force that the floorboards cracked beneath her, and she fell through the hole and onto the foundation. For a few seconds, she couldn't think straight, or see beyond the darkness compounded by her narrowed vision, and her ears were ringing.

Herne's blistering balls. What had just happened?

Then she smelled smoke, and realised she could see a billowing, black cloud above her. A roaring noise supplanted the ringing in her ears.

Her memory returned with a rush. She'd triggered a bomb, and now there was a fire, and somewhere above her was Gabe.

She staggered to her feet, every muscle in her body aching, and with shock saw that her clothes were smouldering. She patted herself down, and yelled, "Gabe!"

There was no answer, and she scrambled up the shattered planks and back to the ground floor.

A scene of horror spread before her. One entire side of the house was on fire, flames curling across the ceiling. Black, choking smoke filled the space, obscuring her vision. Gabe had been behind her, well away from the blast. "Gabe!"

She started searching, pulling her t-shirt over her mouth as she zigzagged across the floor. Finally, a groan reached her, and then a fallen table was upended as Gabe emerged from beneath it, a cut across his forehead bleeding profusely.

He glared at her. "Shadow! What the hell have you done now?"

"Me?" Her relief at seeing him turned to outrage. "This explosion is nothing to do with me, you big, winged idiot!"

An ominous crash had them both looking upwards, just in time to see a huge, flaming beam fall down on the staircase, and that burst into flames, too.

"I suggest," she yelled, "that we get out of here!"

She turned to the door, but unfortunately the entrance was blocked by another fallen beam, and the flames licked higher, trapping them inside. The windows were their only way out, and they were boarded up, but Gabe was already sprinting to one furthest from the flames, and she followed him.

Gabe ripped the boards away, using one of them to punch through the glass and smash the jagged edges. With a whoosh, the flames roared across the ceiling, fuelled by the new supply of oxygen. Gabe grabbed Shadow and pushed her through the opening, and in seconds they were both outside and sprinting from the burning building.

Only at the edge of the tree line did they stop and look back. The entire building was now burning, flames already curling out of the roof, fuelled by the tinder-dry, rotten wood.

"Well," Gabe said, wiping the blood from his forehead, and trying to stem the bleeding, "someone didn't want us looking in there." He looked up and down her body, searching for injuries. "Are you okay?"

Shadow patted herself down. "Just sore. Fortunately, I was already running when the blast caught me. Which, by the way, was *not* my fault."

He grinned, pulling her to him for a kiss. "I know. But you did trigger it, some-how."

"Accidentally!"

"You're so easy to tease!"

"Piss off!" She reached her hand to the deep cut on his forehead. "Is this your only injury?"

He nodded, his laugh disappearing. "Just this and a very sore shoulder where the damn table hit me. We were bloody lucky, Shadow. That blast was meant to kill. I doubt Theo could have got away if he'd been the one to trigger it."

"Which means he's right. There *is* something to this treasure."

He nodded, and pulled his phone from his pocket. "I'd better call the fire brigade before the whole wood is set alight. Then you can tell me what happened."

Shadow studied the lodge, wincing as the roof collapsed inwards. "Herne's hairy bollocks! There'll be nothing left of that by the time they arrive."

She waited silently while Gabe made the call, trying to recall the design of the moulding that had triggered the blast, and wondering if there was any way she could have averted it.

"Go on," Gabe said when he finished the call. "What happened?"

"I noticed there were a lot of symbols around the fireplace. Some were in the wood, others in the stone."

"I noticed that, too—all around the room, including the staircase. Theo never said there were so many."

"The outer fire-surround was enormous, solid wood, but there was a huge stone lintel underneath, and obviously at the back of the fireplace. There was a relief right in the centre, but smaller ones around the edge. One of them looked to be an eye in a triangle, and others, well, I'm not sure. Anyway," she shrugged, hoping the intricacies of the shapes would come back to her later, "I was feeling around a couple of them, and noticed one stood prouder than most. I pushed it, then pulled it, and saw wires. That's when I ran and shouted at you. I'd barely gone half a dozen paces when the explosion threw me across the room."

"What if they booby trapped the library?"

"Sounds like they've just stolen the documents, from what Theo says."

"I'd better phone Ash next."

"And I'll go and find the fire brigade," Shadow said, setting off across the grounds to direct them.

Estelle summoned her magic, power balling at the ends of her fingertips as the barrier dropped into place behind her.

Barak waited next to her, watching the door at the end of the corridor as voices grew louder. "They're coming. We either fight it out, or flee. Can you damage the camera from here? It's at the top of the door."

She saw it and hurled a blast of power at the target, reinforcing it with a spell, and with a satisfying crack, the camera shattered. The patter of footsteps slowed. "If it's Black Cronos on the other side, it will be a tough fight."

"But it's an opportunity to see what they're guarding. A risk I'm prepared to take." He levelled his dark eyes at her, uncompromising in this light.

"I agree. I'll use a spell on them—one to confuse them."

The door edged open before they could discuss it further. A flash bloomed as something shot down the passage towards them. Estelle threw a protective shield around them as she and Barak dived to the floor. Simultaneously, she hurled a fireball at the door, blasting it off its hinges and taking whoever was behind out with it.

Beyond the smouldering door frame, a man clambered to his feet in the centre of the room, something glinting in his palms. It looked suspiciously like the weapon that the Silencer of Souls had used on Shadow. Presuming the worst, Estelle aimed a blast of power at him, throwing him into the wall. She followed it up with a binding spell that wrapped his limbs to his body and sealed his mouth shut.

Neither waited to see what else would happen, opting instead to attack. They leapt to their feet and raced to the room's entrance, backs pressed flat against the wall for a brief moment as they peered inside.

One man lay insensible beneath the heavy wooden door in the middle of the room, as another groaned against the far wall. No one else was in sight, and there were no shouts or pounding feet, either.

Barak nodded in appreciation as he edged inside. "Nice work, Estelle. Fast, efficient, and effective, just as I like it. Well, not for *everything*, obviously."

He winked at her and she felt a flush creep up her cheeks like she was a schoolgirl with a crush. "Even now, that's where your mind goes?"

"Of course. However, I suppose I should focus on our immediate issue."

"Like where the hell are we and what just happened?"

The room had a bank of monitors on the wall that flickered with different scenes. A couple of doors were set in the far wall, both shut. A glass panel looked into what seemed to be a security checkpoint, with a door on either end. A low grill was set into it.

"It seems to be some kind of guard room." Estelle headed to a row of IDs and swipe cards on the wall, some of the hooks empty. "Is this just *château* security?"

Barak snorted. "Down here? I don't think so." He ignored the screens and strode over to the man immobilised by the binding spell. Grabbing him by the throat, he lifted him off his feet and seated him on an office chair. He lowered his face so he was on eye level with the man. "He doesn't look like an enhanced human. His eyes are fine."

"No tattoos, either," Estelle noted as she studied his bare arms exposed by a short-sleeved shirt. She estimated he was in his late thirties, and was wearing a uniform of smart shirt, tie, and trousers. He looked like a security guard. He glared at her, a mixture of fear and frustration in his eyes. His jaw moved, but his lips remain sealed by her spell. She remembered her own fury when Caspian cast the same spell on her. It was horrible, but the man had just tried to kill them.

"I need to question him," Barak said.

"Let me check the cameras first."

Most of the screens showed rooms rather than outdoor areas, and a few showed corridors. A couple looked to be labs that had a handful of people working in them, some appeared to be cells, and one had been recently occupied, with an unmade bed. One room looked like a theatre, and a man was lying on a trolley as people moved around him. Her unease intensified. "By the Goddess, Barak. There's a man strapped to a trolley. He might be a prisoner. There are cells here somewhere!"

Barak grabbed the man's collar again, pulling him close as he growled, "What is this place?"

Estelle said a spell to muffle sound before releasing the binding on his tongue. The man, however, refused to speak.

"I asked you a question," Barak repeated. "If you want to keep your tongue, I suggest you use it." He repeated the question in French.

The man laughed derisively and replied in heavily-accented English. "I don't need you to translate, fool."

"Then answer the question."

"My life won't be worth living."

"It isn't anyway."

Barak dragged him to his feet, hauling him in front of the cameras. He pointed at the operating room. "Who is that and why is he here?"

"I don't know. I'm just security."

"Exactly. So, you see everything."

The security guard snorted. "There are rooms here that have no cameras." He stared at Barak impassive. "There are things they don't want you to see."

Estelle repressed a shudder. "Fancy *châteaus* don't normally have hidden lairs and prisoners. We know this has to do with Black Cronos. Is the *Comte* here?"

The guard looked genuinely shocked. "Who? I have never heard of that name."

A flicker of movement caught Estelle's eye, and she looked at the screens. One of them showed two guards walking down a corridor, and she heard footsteps outside. So did the guard, and he opened his mouth to scream. She sealed it shut again and he stared at her, horrified.

"We've got company, Barak. Change of shift, I bet. We've got a couple of minutes at most."

Barak's face wrinkled with annoyance, and he punched the guard, knocking him out cold, and then stowed him under a desk in the corner. "We'll let them in, incapacitate them, and find the prisoner. Bind this guy, too, just in case." He quickly picked up the other unconscious man and threw him through the blasted doorway, and then lifted the door and put it back in position. "That will have to do."

They positioned themselves on either side of the door, and heard the click as the door opened. The guards stepped inside, chatting and laughing, distracted enough that they didn't see the other guards weren't there until the door swung shut behind them. In seconds it was all over, and both lay incapacitated on the floor.

"Right," Estelle said, satisfied. "Let's find a floor plan. Time to rescue a prisoner."

"We aren't exactly equipped to pull off a rescue mission," Barak pointed out. "And it's broad daylight."

Estelle grinned, relishing the fact that she was working with the Nephilim—especially Barak. This was just what her life had been lacking. "Then we improvise!"

Eight

Ash stared at the ruins of the lodge, horrified. It was a smoking, waterlogged mess, merely a shell of a building. A small fire crew were still onsite, one man consulting with Theo.

Gabe and Shadow stood next to Ash, both singed, stinking of smoke, and covered in sooty smears. They were sheltering under the trees that had fortunately been saved as they were well away from the smouldering ruin, able to talk quietly. "You two were lucky. That blast must have been huge."

"It was designed to kill, that's for sure," Gabe said. "Meant to cover all traces of what might be found in there. I'm sure that building was more than just a hunting lodge."

"Whoever planted that bomb must be responsible for the theft of the papers, too," Ash said thoughtfully. "Why not just burn the place down?"

Shadow shrugged, and then winced. "To create maximum damage, I guess. Risky, though. The explosion might never have been triggered."

"Unless several things were booby trapped," Ash suggested.

"Of course! Which would explain the other explosions, after we escaped," Shadow said, nodding. "I hadn't considered that."

Gabe gestured towards Theo. "I think his life is at risk."

"And Owen, the assistant gardener, must have something to do with it." Ash related his conversation with Theo. "We need to find him. Question him."

"Ha!" Shadow snorted. "After this? He'll be long gone."

"We could be jumping to conclusions," Gabe pointed out.

"Come on." Ash turned away, striding back towards the main grounds. "Theo will be tied up there for a while. Let's see what we can find out about Owen. Have they interviewed you?"

Gabe nodded. "Just the fire brigade, not the police—yet. And they checked us for injuries. We were lucky not to be carted off to hospital. What about you? Have you found out anything useful?"

"Background stuff only, but someone doctored the books—cut out the salient pages. I need to examine Theo's copies. It was lucky he took them, and made notes." He pulled up short. "We still have his stuff, right? And the knife?"

"He put everything in his safe," Shadow said, "before he left with you."

They emerged from the woods, and the castle glowed in the late afternoon sunshine. It looked peaceful in its bucolic setting. Ash hoped it was peaceful inside, too, and that Chivers and his wife were okay.

A sudden urgency quickened his pace. "I should check."

"Then we'll head to the potting sheds to find the gardener," Gabe said, turning towards the long, brick-built buildings with low roofs behind the main house. "Call us if you need us."

Jackson felt sick, stunned with Layla's news, and for a moment, he couldn't speak.

"I'm sorry." Layla pulled a stool from under the bench, and made him sit on it. "There was no easy way to tell you. I'm shocked too, but I've had some time to get used to it."

"There's no mistake?" Jackson's tongue felt thick in his mouth as he stared at the body. "He was on my grandfather's team. You're sure?"

"I'm sure." Layla pulled out another stool and sat next to him. "Bastards, aren't they?"

The implications were horrific, but he had to ask. "The other bodies, could one of them have been my grandfather? Or even the rest of his team?"

"It's possible. Unfortunately, they've been cremated now, so we'll never know, but it's unlikely." She squeezed his hand. "The odds are ridiculous. It's more likely that your grandfather died, along with the rest of the team."

"*He* didn't. James."

"But you know what they were subjected to."

Bile rose in Jackson's throat, quickly followed by fury, and he rocketed to his feet, upending the stool. The noise of it hitting the floor echoed around the room. "Fuck them. I hate Black Cronos! They're monsters." He stared at James Arbuthnot's body. "They would have suffered. Horribly."

"Perhaps. We don't know that, though. We still have no idea what they do to affect the changes. Alchemical experimentation might not be as painful as other ways of changing the body."

Jackson turned to her. Layla still looked elegant, despite the scrubs that clad her slender body, but the fine lines on her face were exaggerated now by her fierce concentration. "You don't have to lie to me."

"Of course I don't. You're an adult. I would never dream of it." Her tone was brisk as she stood, brushing her scrubs down. She headed to the cupboards, pulling out instruments, the sharp smell of formaldehyde filling his nostrils. "And now that I can see the tattoos, I'm going to take samples. Lots of them. I'm sure there are still more secrets to unlock. James may help his country, after all. You, however, need to leave me in peace. If you'd like to help me, call JD."

Jackson nodded and left the room, hurrying to his office where he poured himself a neat whiskey. He threw it back, savouring the warmth as it travelled down his throat. He poured another, hoping to ease the trembling in his hands. Adrenalin still flooded his system, and for a few minutes, all he did was pace his office, trying to subdue his fury, but he couldn't settle. He decided to call JD, as promised.

Anna, JD's housekeeper, or whatever she was—*gatekeeper was more apt*—answered the phone, her clipped, sharp tone restoring some of his equilibrium. However, she refused to put him through to JD. "He's too busy. He forbade me from disturbing him for at least another couple of hours."

"He'll want to hear this, Anna!"

"Call back later." She ended the call, and he swore loudly into his empty office.

He needed a distraction. Another drink, though one with some company. Time to call Harlan.

Harlan had never seen Jackson look so desolate. He was slumped in the corner of The Swan pub at the edge of Hyde Park, a half-drunk pint of Guinness on the table in front of him, and another two empty glasses on the side, staring into the distance.

There were plenty of seats outside under umbrellas in the sunshine, but Jackson was instead sitting in the gloomy interior. Harlan could understand why after hearing his news, and wished he'd been able to join him earlier. "I'm sorry, Jackson. I wish I could do more than just sympathise."

"It's fine. Of course you can't do anything. I just wanted someone to get drunk with."

"That might not be the best plan."

"I don't care."

Harlan sipped his own pint, considering the best course of action. "It's interesting, though. How old did James look?"

"Mid-thirties, I'd guess."

"Frozen in time, then."

Jackson looked at him, startled. "Well, yes. Of course."

"So it means that whatever alchemy does to their bodies—the enhanced strength, the metallic skin that seems to act like armour—it preserves life, too. Perhaps makes them immortal. Like the *comte*. Bloody hell. Immortal super-soldiers."

"Not unlike the Nephilim."

Harlan eased back in his chair. "They're not immortal. Just long-lived. Like Shadow." He reconsidered his assessment. "Maybe Black Cronos are long-lived too, rather than immortal. Perhaps the count wouldn't actually want his soldiers to live as long as him."

"If it is the count behind all this."

"Perhaps," Harlan mused, "that's also why Layla hasn't been able to identify most of them. They might all be very old. There'd be no DNA or fingerprints to compare them to."

"I'm sure they're still recruiting, though, somehow."

"Of course." Harlan didn't doubt that. "Let's just hope the tattoos reveal something of worth. You say you couldn't speak to JD?"

Jackson rolled his eyes as he picked up his pint. "No, Anna refused to put me through. She's worse than a GP's receptionist. Anyone would think I was trying to get an appointment with God. Not that He exists, of course."

"JD is a God, in his own head!" Harlan laughed. "And maybe Anna's. I'd love to know how she came to work for him." He sobered, wondering what JD was up to. "I must admit, I haven't spoken to him for a while. Perhaps he'll make a breakthrough...or Layla's discovery will help him to. Still no news from Barak?" Jackson had told him where he and Estelle had gone.

"No, actually." Jackson checked his watch. "They were on the tour this morning. I was expecting to hear from them by now. I'd phone, but if they're in hiding, I'd hate to give away their position."

"You say the *château* has links to the count?"

"Centuries ago. And now they have some less than transparent business dealings, despite their wholesome image as a tourist attraction." Jackson fidgeted, picking up his phone and scrolling for messages. "Nothing. At what point do I get worried? It's unlike Barak not to be in contact."

"Give it 'til nightfall. They must be following a lead. Is there backup in place if something goes wrong?"

"Nothing local, just Niel and Nahum, I guess. No involvement from the PD except extraction, perhaps. Waylen would need to arrange that. To be honest, I hadn't considered it. This was supposed to just be about watching them."

"If they saw an opportunity..."

"Damn it. Now I'm worried."

"Patience. They know what they're doing."

Jackson nodded, but he was clearly distracted. "Tell me about your latest jobs. What's happening?"

Harlan quickly summarised Theo's discovery of the knife and the search for Templar gold. "I haven't heard from them, either, but that doesn't surprise me. They've only just started the search."

Jackson frowned, and sat up straighter, staring over Harlan's shoulder at the TV next to the bar. "Did you say they were in Kent?"

"Yes, Temple Keep. Why?" He twisted to see the screen behind, horrified to see a screenshot of fire engines at the country estate, the caption, '*Fire at historic castle in Temple Moreton*' scrolling across the bottom of the page. "Holy shit!"

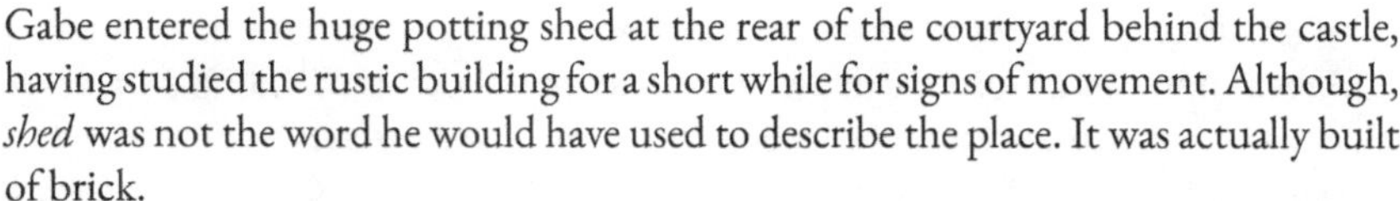

Gabe entered the huge potting shed at the rear of the courtyard behind the castle, having studied the rustic building for a short while for signs of movement. Although, *shed* was not the word he would have used to describe the place. It was actually built of brick.

On their way across the grounds, they passed about half a dozen staff gathered on the lawn in front of the house, all watching the smoke in the woods with rapt fascination, and a fair degree of worry. They hadn't lingered though, only long enough to ascertain that Owen, the assistant gardener, wasn't there, nor the head gardener, Malcolm. A couple of other junior gardeners were present, shrugging as they directed them to the courtyard.

The potting shed was surprisingly well organised, a series of interconnected spaces, most with external doors. The smell of compost hung on the air, rich and welcoming. Rows of gleaming, well-maintained tools were stored in racks along the wall, as were row upon row of plant pots—a mix of clay pots and plastic, of a variety of sizes. Seed trays were stacked up, but some were positioned under long windows, tiny shoots coming through that Gabe presumed were salad leaves for the kitchen garden.

The sound of loud music drew them through a couple of rooms, passing larger machinery such as lawnmowers and hedge-trimmers, to the end room where a middle-aged man stood at a long sink washing out plant pots and singing to the radio.

Gabe knocked on the door frame and shouted, "I'm looking for Owen!"

The man looked around, startled, water splashing everywhere. "Bloody hell! Are you trying to give me a heart attack?" His eyes narrowed with suspicion as he took in their appearance. Gabe had forgotten he looked such a sight. He placed the pot on the side and grabbed a cloth to dry his hands, then turned down the volume. "Who are you?"

"My name's Gabe, and this is Shadow. Theo hired us to help him with a project. Sorry about our appearance—we got caught in the fire." Gabe crossed the room to shake his hand, but Shadow merely nodded and stayed in the doorway, eyes darting everywhere.

"Fire? What fire?"

Gabe looked at him, incredulous. "The lodge in the wood has just blown up. Didn't you hear the fire engines? The explosion?"

"Explosion? Bloody hell!" He ran to the window looking onto the courtyard, where a plume of smoke could still be seen eddying across the grounds. "Was Theo in there? Or anyone?"

"Just us, although Theo's there now."

The man exhaled heavily. "That's all right, then. I like my music loud—you probably noticed. It must have blocked everything out." He studied them again, carefully this time, as he leaned against the sink. "You were lucky. How did it happen?"

"Hard to say right now," Gabe answered, fudging the truth. "You are?"

"Sorry, I'm Malcolm, the head gardener." A knowing look crossed his face. "You're helping Theo look for his Templar treasure!"

Gabe suppressed a groan, exchanging an annoyed glance with Shadow. *Did everyone know?* "News travels fast. Theo seemed to think it was a secret."

Malcolm laughed. "He talked to Chivers, and that man loves to gossip over his evening sherry. News gets round." Gabe clenched his jaw with annoyance, but Malcolm continued. "And of course, everyone knows about this castle's link to the Templars. It's a source of great pride and gossip—even now. I don't think anyone actually thinks there's any treasure, though. Over the years, many have looked for it and found nothing."

"What about Owen?"

"He enlisted Owen's help, didn't he? Owen's always bragging about his computer skills." He rolled his eyes. "Did you say you were looking for him?"

"Yes. I have a couple of questions for him." Gabe didn't elaborate, and wondered if there was any point, considering Chivers's gossip. However, Owen would have been more involved, and might have more information to share.

"The last time I saw him, he was supervising the junior gardeners in the greenhouse."

"They're all on the lawn now, watching the action. Except for Owen."

Malcolm shrugged. "Maybe he's still there on his own, then."

Shadow asked a question from the doorway. "Does he seem okay? Is he edgy? Worried?"

Malcolm shifted to look at her. "A bit quieter than normal, but other than that, no." He frowned. "You don't think he's got anything to do with this?"

Gabe answered first. "We're checking everything. Lodges don't normally explode."

"And Owen is not a bomber!"

"Good." Gabe turned away, collecting Shadow on his way out the door. "If you see him, tell him I want to chat."

They found the huge greenhouse in the walled garden a short distance away, but it took only a short search to see that Owen wasn't in there, either.

"He's on the run," Shadow declared. "Sneaky shit."

"We don't know that." Gabe still wasn't convinced that Owen was the source of the issue. "Malcolm said everyone knew Theo's secret after Chivers had gossiped. Anyone could have blabbed. And besides, everyone also knew about the castle's history."

Shadow idly played with her knives as she studied the plants in the greenhouse, the hot air wrapping around them. "Well, obviously Theo's interest has made someone think there are new clues, and seeing as his search isn't being broadcast on the news, someone local must have said something."

"Come on. Let's get to the main house and see how Ash is getting on, and then we should get an address for Owen. If he doesn't reappear in the next few hours, we'll go to his home. Maybe he's sick." Even as he said it, Gabe knew he was kidding himself.

"Or he's dead," Shadow said, cutting to the chase. "And then we'll know who we are really up against."

Nine

B arak opened the electronic lock using the pass they'd found in the office, and sidled through the door ahead of Estelle. Once on the other side, they paused, searching the space in front of them.

They were in a changing room. The shelves were stacked with surgical scrubs and handwashing facilities—and fortunately, no people. A room with showers and a bathroom was off to the side, and at the far end of the room was a door, partly ajar, opening onto a corridor. But there were several groups of clothing hanging on pegs, and shoes on the floor.

Barak whispered, "Half a dozen clothes—must mean half a dozen people."

"A hospital?" Estelle asked.

"A chamber of horrors, more like. But let's hope they're all medical staff and unarmed."

Before they left the guard room, they had studied a very basic floorplan that was pinned to the wall marking fire exits, and it was clear that anyone who entered the underground area had to pass through the glass-walled room adjacent to the security room. An antechamber, where they could be scanned and issued their security passes. He and Estelle had obviously entered through the back door. After walking along a couple of short passages and down a long, dank flight of stone steps, they were now in the heart of the complex.

Barak voiced the concerns that had been playing on his mind. "Why aren't the guards here enhanced soldiers, and why aren't there more people around?"

"Maybe because this is a satellite base?"

"Then why is there a prisoner here? I don't like it. Something feels off."

"It feels off *because* there's a prisoner here...maybe more than one. Perhaps he's housed here, ready for transfer to another facility? Unless," she faltered, "he could be a willing participant, and this place is a kind of barracks."

"I guess we're about to find out."

After a cursory examination of the changing room, Estelle edged to the door and looked out. She mouthed, *Voices*, and pointed to the right.

Barak joined her. The passageway ran from left to right. To the left were more doors, all shut, a couple with grills set in the top. *Cells, perhaps.* But on their right were more rooms, many with their doors open, all blazing with light and the sound of chatter. The place smelt of disinfectant and something he couldn't quite place. It gave him the chills.

Barak drew Estelle back inside the changing room. "That man must be somewhere on the right. If he's a prisoner, we should try to rescue him. But if he's not..."

"Either way, we're heading for a fight. Or we could just back out and report what we've found. We've already come this far, though."

"And," he sighed, wondering if he was mad for suggesting the next option, "we could cause a lot of disruption here."

Estelle's dark eyes brightened. "Sabotage?"

"Big time."

"I like that option better."

"We could be trapped if we get this wrong—if someone seals this exit."

Estelle shook her head, clearly considering their options. "Those doors have grills in them. They're cells, not barracks. Which means there's another way out—a route to bring prisoners in. Not through the staff area. And probably not marked on the map. I'm willing to chance it, anyway."

"Good. We take the staff out as cleanly as possible."

Barak advanced down the corridor, his booted feet silent on the stone floor, the dagger he'd strapped to his leg in his hand. But he'd barely walked three paces when the muted chatter raised in volume, and a voice shouted, "Stop him!"

An ear-piercing shriek echoed down the corridor, followed by the sounds of crashing furniture.

A man emerged from a corridor, a surgical gown flapping around him, tattoos snaking down his arms. Blood was splashed across his chest, and his eyes were wild, terrified. Right behind him was a man struggling to grip a rifle, and within seconds another couple of staff followed, all splattered with blood, all yelling.

The prisoner spotted Barak and dived into a side room. At the same time, the man with the rifle managed to secure his grip and shot at their captive—and then he saw Barak and Estelle, too. For a split second he froze, and then adjusted his aim.

Barak and Estelle hurtled through the closest doorway, but Estelle was ready to strike. A ball of fire grew in her hands, and she hurled it down the corridor, following it up with a blast of pure energy. It knocked every single member of staff off their feet, and the rifle clattered across the floor.

Barak took advantage of the lull and barrelled down the corridor, sprinting for the gun. The man who'd fired it ran in a crouch towards it. Barak released his knife with deadly accuracy, hitting the man in the chest, and he fell, unmoving.

Other staff emerged from a side room, and as Barak dived for the gun, Estelle dealt with them. A wind swept over Barak, powerful enough to force the staff back into the room. Then she said a spell. Barak felt the words of power take effect. Suddenly, the staff were trapped behind a wall of flames, and they backed to the wall, eyes wide, some with fear, others with fury.

Barak grabbed the gun and returned to Estelle. "This is a tranquilliser gun. Hold them here, I'll check the prisoner."

But before she could answer, another staff member bolted from the end room they hadn't yet secured, and ran around the corner and down the corridor the prisoner had emerged from.

"Leave him to me!" Estelle said, already giving chase.

Barak turned back to the prisoner, who wasn't taking any chances on Barak or Estelle helping him. He'd seized his opportunity as they dealt with the staff, and was running to the exit, a scalpel in his hand. But his steps were slowing, blood pouring from a wound on his thigh, a feathered dart cast aside on the floor.

Barak knew he couldn't let him escape. They needed him. And, he might give them away. He tackled him from behind, and they both hit the floor hard. Barak saw the deadly blade flash, and smacked down hard on the man's arm, crunching it into the floor.

"I'm here to help you!"

The man grunted, his face planted into the ground. "It doesn't seem like it!"

"We are getting you out of here."

"I can do it alone." The man had a French accent, but his English was good.

"Not half-drugged you can't."

Up close, the prisoner looked feverish, his face covered in sweat. His eyes had a strange sheen to them, and Barak wondered if he was suffering from some kind of physical change—courtesy of the tattoos, no doubt, as some of them looked fresh. However, he didn't have the strength that a Black Cronos soldier normally had. Maybe that was because of whatever they had drugged him with.

Making sure the scalpel was well out of reach, Barak eased up and off him in a gesture of good will. "This is not the time to argue. We all need to get out of here."

The man sat up, rubbing his head where it had struck the floor, but he eyed the staff pinned in the side-room by the flames. "Not before we deal with those."

Barak nodded, thinking through their options, and distracted by Estelle's return. She was tight-lipped with fury and radiating magic, but otherwise unharmed. "You need to see something,"

Barak stood, pulling the man to his feet, and quickly patted him down to check for other weapons. All the fight, however, seemed to have left him, and he sagged against the wall, breathing heavily and looking increasingly glassy-eyed.

Barak turned to Estelle. "We need to move the staff, get into the room they were in, and check everywhere else. We need answers—anything!"

Estelle didn't hesitate. "I can spell them to sleep and we can drag them into the cells." She glanced over her shoulder at the locked rooms at the other end of the corridor. "If that's what they are. But what if the camera feeds down here go elsewhere? Others could already be on the way. They might have even triggered an alarm we can't hear."

Barak was damn sure they weren't running out there yet, not after all this. "Then we'd best be quick."

Ten

Ash was standing at the window, staring at the smoke that drifted over the wood, when Shadow and Gabe entered the first floor sitting room.

He turned to them, amused. They were still streaked in black soot, and still wearing fire-damaged clothing. "Your smoky stench preceded you. You need a shower."

"Tough," Shadow said, scowling at his clean jeans and t-shirt before looking around the neat room. "Everything okay here?"

"Seems to be." Ash nodded at a large picture of a deer in dappled shade on the wall. "The safe is behind that, and it's sealed shut. Hopefully everything is locked within it, unless someone knows the code. Chivers certainly didn't...or so he says. Any luck finding Owen?"

"No," Gabe answered, heading to the table that was strewn with the notes Ash had taken that morning. "He's not in the potting sheds or greenhouse, but was here this morning. The head gardener, Malcolm, clearly thinks he has nothing to do with the fire. He also said," he looked up at Ash, his lips curling with annoyance, "that Chivers is a gossip, and everyone knows about the dagger anyway."

Shadow crossed to the window, looking over the moat and lush lawns. "Malcolm is wrong. He might work with Owen, but that doesn't mean he knows him well. Owen is on the run." She looked restless, her eyes darting everywhere, wild energy radiating from her. Ash was used to that now, after all the months spent living and working with her. Shadow could barely sit still once she was rattled. It was what made her so good at hunting. A fight honed her senses even more. "We need his address *now*. If we're wrong about his involvement, then no harm done. We can start looking elsewhere. Someone other than Theo must have his address. Chivers, perhaps."

Ash nodded. "Makes sense. They'll have all the staffs' addresses. If you see Chivers, go easy on him. He looked pretty shook up."

"He should be. His tattling might have caused this." Shadow was already heading to the door. "I'll go and get it. The sooner we look, the better."

"Be careful," Gabe warned her. "Meet me back here!"

But she had already gone, the door slamming behind her.

"She'll be fine," Ash said, watching Gabe as he rifled through Ash's notes.

"It's not her safety I'm worried about." He shot Ash a wry smile.

Ash laughed, glad to see Gabe's mood settling. "You two were lucky. I keep thinking about the size of that bomb—or bombs. Whoever's behind this does not want competitors. We need to get ahead, quickly. Theo must have noticed something he hasn't yet said to us."

Gabe tapped Ash's notes. "I know you've barely begun to look at these, but any ideas?"

"Nothing that stands out. The diary could be interesting, though. From the brief read I had of Theo's copy, Madeleine talks about a search on these grounds by some kind of historical society. Knowing where they searched could help us eliminate places now."

Gabe settled on the edge of the table. "So, this was a stronghold?"

"It was, but not for the Templars. William de la More's family had built this in the twelfth century, and he inherited it as the eldest son. Once William had a son, he joined the Templars as had his forefathers. It was a tradition. But the keep was always passed on to family. Only money was donated to the Templars. That was pretty common. He travelled in the Middle East for a while, and was later rewarded when he was made Master of England."

"A very grand title."

"For good reason. It came with a lot of power. The title didn't last long, though, for any individual. There were many masters, and the position seemed to change hands frequently...I have no idea why. Poor old William had the misfortune of being the final one. Something struck me, though. I suspect his family would have done what many wealthy landowners did at the time. They would have built a chapel on site. Or even maybe in the building."

"Good point." Gabe's gaze was distant as he thought through the implications. "Theo didn't mention one, or show us one on the tour."

"No. Perhaps it was destroyed during the reformation, or just disintegrated over time. Or was converted into something else."

"Or it never existed in the first place."

"Perhaps. But if there was one, maybe something was hidden there. I'll ask Theo." Ash stared over the grounds. "Do you think he's safe out there?"

"With the fire brigade there, yes, of course. Don't you?"

"He's been gone a while. Shouldn't he be back by now?"

Alarm sparked in Gabe's eyes, his jaw tightening and pulling at the cut on his forehead. It had stopped bleeding, the blood congealed into a thick line. "Don't say something else has happened. You stay here, find us something to go on." He turned, shoulders bunching with annoyance under his torn t-shirt. "I'm going to go and check. I'll find Shadow on the way."

His phone rang as he was crossing the room. He looked at the screen and ignored the call. "It's Harlan. Do me a favour and update him. I haven't got time to talk to him now. And maybe we should call in backup. Things are getting complicated."

"Sure."

"By the way," Gabe paused at the door. "Theo was right about those symbols. They were everywhere. Perhaps there's more to the Freemasons than he made out. Good hunting."

"You too, brother."

Ash's phone was already ringing as Gabe walked out. Harlan again. "Harlan," he said, answering quickly. "Brace yourself. Things have gone a little sidewards here."

"Sidewards!" Harlan muttered, still fuming at the wheel of his car as he navigated the London roads thick with traffic. "Bloody Nephilim. Masters of understatement."

"But they are okay. That's something!" Jackson gripped the side of his seat as Harlan took a sharp corner. "That fire looked big."

"Because it was a damn explosion!" Harlan repeated with disbelief, seething with both annoyance and relief. Annoyance that Nicoli might be involved, and relief that his friends weren't hurt. He told Jackson what had happened, and desperate to do something, had decided to visit Nicoli's office. Jackson had insisted on joining him. "You know, you don't have to come. It could be dangerous."

"I doubt Nicoli would be foolish enough to attack us in his office. In fact, I doubt he's even there."

"Well, we'll soon find out." Harlan grimaced as he saw the crowded streets around Nicoli's office. It had taken long enough to crawl through the traffic. "Goddamn it! There's nowhere to park."

"Why don't I jump out and go in, and you circle around?" Jackson suggested.

"No. I want to do this. I want to look into his lying eyes and see what bullshit he comes up with. *Damn it.*" He smacked the steering wheel. "Where the hell can I park?"

"In that case, why don't you jump out, and I'll circle around?"

Harlan looked at Jackson suspiciously. "Are you sober?"

"More or less. I only had a couple of sodding pints before your bloody call of doom."

"This car is my baby." Harlan stared at Jackson, making sure his eyes looked clear. "If I allow you to get behind the wheel, you are to treat it gently!"

"You've just smacked the steering wheel and driven around London like a mad man."

"But I know how to drive it!"

"I'm not an imbecile, and it is just a car."

Harlan's need to find Nicoli overcame his concern over his car. "Just be careful with it."

Jackson grinned, and with a sinking feeling, Harlan pulled to the side, double parked, and exited his car. He didn't even watch Jackson change seats, instead racing into Nicoli's offices.

Nicoli's business was on the second floor of a converted warehouse in Camden. Harlan charged up the stairs, emerging onto a landing with several doors leading off it. He spotted Nicoli's name on the wall next to a heavy-set wooden door: *Andreas*

Nicoli, Consultant. He subdued a snort. *Of course, he wouldn't put Order of Lilith on the wall. People would think he ran a cult.*

Harlan took a deep breath, preparing himself for who he might find inside, and pushed the door open. On the other side was a small reception area, richly carpeted, with art on the walls, plush seats for clients to wait on, and a desk with a computer on it and all the normal receptionist paraphernalia. There were two other doors, both shut.

A young woman sitting behind the desk looked up, startled. "Can I help you?"

"Nicoli. Where is he?"

Her eyes darted behind her to the far door, and then to the computer in front of her. "Have you got…"

"No." He marched to the door she had glanced at, throwing it open. "Andreas Nicoli. What the hell are you up to?"

Andreas was standing at the large window, a coffee cup in hand, elegantly clad in an expensive suit. He leaned against the frame, smirking at Harlan. "My, my. If it isn't my good friend, Harlan Beckett!" He gestured to the window. "I saw you arrive in your beautiful car. If only you were wearing a very nice suit to go with it, instead of…" His lips twisted with disdain as he took in Harlan's jeans and leather jacket. "*That.* You look…flustered. Coffee?"

Harlan slammed the door shut behind him. "Screw your coffee. You heard me. What were you doing in Bodiam, in Kent? And why did you plant a bomb? You could have killed someone!"

Nicoli shrugged. "That is the general idea of a bomb. But I must confess, I have no idea what you're talking about." He walked to his desk, sat down, and gestured for Harlan to do the same.

Nicoli was as well-manicured as always. His sleek brown hair was expertly cut, his face clean shaven, his tan immaculate, and his physique lean. But his eyes sparkled with malice as he smiled at Harlan.

Harlan eyed the seat warily, and then studied the room before he sat down, as if there might be a hidden trap. He had never been here before, although he had been aware of where the office was for months. The room was as well decorated as the reception area, taking advantage of the old warehouse's design features. Long, black metal-framed windows, high ceiling, sleek wood floors, bare brick walls. The warehouse conversion had been completed to a high standard. The walls were decorated with modern art, as well as older pieces. The desk was polished and a sleek laptop was open on it.

Conceding that nothing looked remotely like a trap, Harlan still refused to sit, instead pacing to the window and looking down on to the street. His car, with Jackson in it, had vanished. Nicoli twisted in his seat, watching him.

"So nervy, Harlan," he said smoothly, his Greek-accented voice like honey. "Tell me what's bothering you."

"You are, you sneaky son of a bitch." He decided to level with him. "A man matching your description was seen in Bodiam Library, shortly before the papers you were looking at disappeared." He leaned across the desk, taking in the pungent scent of Nicoli's aftershave. "You stole them."

Nicoli rolled his eyes. "I am not the only Greek man in the country, imbecile."

"Cut the crap, Nicoli. This is a rarefied field we work in, and I know many of the players. You were studying documents about the Templars, and now they're gone."

"About the Templars? Interesting. And what might I have found?"

Harlan dropped into the chair, glaring at him. "The more important question is, why are you trying to kill people? Specifically, *my* people."

"*Your* people! Ha. Whom have you got chasing Templar treasure?"

"The very people who dragged your sorry ass out of The Temple of the Trinity."

"Ah! The delightful Shadow and her companions." His lips pursed, a slight grimace of regret crossing his face before it swiftly vanished. "Unfortunate. She is an admirable creature. I trust she is all right?"

"No thanks to you! The important part is that I was employed to search for it." Harlan was over this ridiculous dance. "Why are you looking for it?"

"I believe it is a public library. I am allowed to look. Like you I am interested in many things."

"It's quite a coincidence though, isn't it? That you should be looking right now."

"Like you, I was also employed. Competition is something we have to deal with. *You* have to deal with. If I happen to find the treasure first, then so be it." Nicoli sipped his coffee, eyeing Harlan across the rim. "I have not planted any bombs."

Nicoli was slippery. Just because he hadn't done it, didn't mean he wasn't behind it. "Then you employed someone to do it. Someone could have died!" Harlan's fury returned, and he wanted to punch Nicoli. Instead, he opted for abusing his desk. He slammed it hard, pinning Nicoli in place between his desk and the chair. "This isn't funny. Theo is a good man. You've just destroyed his lodge, and nearly killed Gabe and Shadow."

Nicoli had managed to avoid spilling his coffee and he placed the cup down, eyes narrowing. "Much blood has been spilled over Templar gold. They themselves spilled oceans of it to get their treasure while pursuing their religious ideals. I am merely continuing the tradition." Nicoli gripped his desk and pushed it forcefully back, making Harlan scoot backwards. "At least we now have our cards on the table. The hunt is on. It is a hunt I intend to win."

Gabe spotted Theo with relief. He was staring at the smouldering remains of the lodge, arms crossed, watching the police tape off the area.

"Herne's bloody horns," Shadow muttered as they approached. "That's all we need—the bloody police poking around."

Gabe looked at her, exasperated. "There's been a bomb! Of course they're here."

She slowed, loitering beneath the trees. "This will delay us searching for Owen. I'm going to go alone."

"You're kidding me!"

"Nope." She was already stepping away from him, melting into the long shadows cast by the lowering sun, her fey magic helping her blend into the natural environment. "They can question me later. Right now, I need to find Owen."

He nodded, trusting her instincts. She was probably right. Owen's disappearance was ominous. "How are you going to get there? You can't drive!"

"I'll go with Ash."

"You need to learn. Ash has got other things to be doing."

She bristled at their familiar argument. "I will. I've been busy!"

"Just be careful."

"Always." She winked, and then vanished.

Gabe headed to Theo's side, thinking he was going to have to blackmail her into taking driving lessons soon. Or just leave her stranded, occasionally. That would work. "Are you all right?" he asked Theo, pushing his irritation with Shadow aside.

Theo looked like he'd aged ten years. His mouth was set in a grim line and his shoulders sagged. Even his moustache seemed to have wilted. "Not really. Look at it. It's just waterlogged beams and bits of wall now!" His eyes swept over Gabe. "And look at you! You're injured, and no doubt covered in bruises. When I started this search, I had no idea this would happen. Are you sure it wasn't an electrical fault? It was old, and desperately needed updating."

"I'm sure. Shadow saw wires set behind a relief carved around the fireplace. They had nothing to do with light fittings."

"Behind a relief? What does that mean?"

Gabe had briefly discussed it with Theo earlier, but figured the shock had made him forgetful. "We think it must have triggered something to open. A secret panel, perhaps? A hiding place." Gabe shrugged as he glanced at the smoking remains of the lodge. "Whatever it was or contained is gone now."

"Which means someone else found it first. Whatever *it* was."

"Potentially, yes."

Theo closed his eyes, fingers pressing into his brow. When he opened them again, he looked resolute, stubborn. "I will not be put off by this. This is my find—my house! If whoever's behind this thinks they're scaring me off, they don't know Theobald Henry James Carmichael." He swelled his chest out and stretched to his full height, but he was still several inches shorter than Gabe. "I have conquered the stock market, ruled over boardrooms, and made millions in my life. This just confirms what I've long suspected. Somewhere on these grounds there is Templar treasure."

"Or another clue to Templar treasure," Gabe pointed out, feeling that he needed to remind Theo of the reality of the situation.

"We will find it," Theo insisted, "or die trying!"

"Slow down, Theo!" Gabe was not happy that Theo seemed willing to risk his own life, and everyone else's. "While I admire the fact that you're not put off by this, let's not get too carried away. No one needs to die. Ash raised an interesting point earlier. William, the last English Master, would have been deeply religious, and came from a rich, religious family. It makes sense that when they built this keep, they would also have built a chapel on these grounds. Have you heard anything about one?"

A gleam filled Theo's eyes. "That's an excellent suggestion. I hadn't considered that, but as I said, I haven't got the original plans, and I haven't read everything. But..." He trailed off, deep in thought.

Gabe prompted him. "Any possibility of hidden rooms in the keep, or the remains of a building on the grounds?"

"Perhaps. There might be some reference in the records that I've missed."

"If it's there, Ash will find it."

A shout interrupted them, and a hard-eyed man wearing a suit reached their side, his eyes raking over Gabe. "DI Gibson. You're the gentleman involved in the incident?"

Gabe shook his hand. "Yes, Gabreel Malouf."

"I have a few questions for you."

Gabe forced a smile, expecting to be questioned for a long time, and suddenly glad that Shadow wasn't there to antagonise the situation. "Of course. Go right ahead."

Eleven

With every passing minute, Estelle became more nervous, wary for any noise that could indicate others were approaching.

She and Barak had secured the facility's staff in the cells along the corridor, separating as many as they could. They were all sleeping soundly, courtesy of a spell. They had found that one of the rooms they had thought was a cell was actually the entrance to another corridor, this one much broader than the others. A cursory inspection of it led to an underground garage with a van parked in it, and the wide corridor beyond suggested it ran away from the *château* and further into the grounds.

The prisoner who had tried to escape was resting on a narrow examination table in one of the medical rooms, and they'd cleared it of potential weapons. Not that the man appeared likely to attack them. He seemed exhausted, and the tranquilliser dart had taken care of the rest.

Leaving him sleeping, they had quickly examined the other rooms, working their way methodically along the corridor. Many appeared to be minor surgical rooms, but at the end corridor they also found what looked like a post-surgery recovery room, as well as an operating theatre with restraints attached to the table. However, as well as containing conventional surgical equipment, there was also an array of tattoo inks and jars containing ground metals.

Estelle picked one up, holding it under an overhead light, and then studied the mixture prepared on the side. "They're mixing the metals and ink together. I think they're tattooing with both!"

Barak was taking pictures with his phone across the room. "Stage one, perhaps, of making their skin a protective armour."

"Which would explain why some of the soldiers seem to have copper skin, and others bronze or silver. Weird. Ingenious, even." She slipped a couple of the bottles into her bag. "They must apply some kind of alchemy to the tattoos afterward."

"JD or the PD can figure that out." Barak took a few more photos. "That will have to do. There's no big lab down here, though. You know, how it sounds like JD has, and the PD."

Estelle nodded, remembering the two different labs at The Retreat: one modern, one old-fashioned, both full of alchemical paraphernalia. "This is a preparation area. Why isn't there a lab here? Seems odd."

"Perhaps this place is just to expedite local victims. They must be constantly recruiting and experimenting." A grimace of distaste flashed across Barak's face as he headed to the door. "Come on. Time to get out of here."

"There's one more room," Estelle said, cranky about what had happened in there earlier when she raced after the fleeing staff member. "But I'll destroy all of this first." Estelle stood in the doorway while Barak listened for any sign of approaching guards.

"We're good. Go on."

She cast a silence spell for good measure before she hurled ball after ball of powerful blasts of magic at the equipment. Glass jars full of ink and metals exploded, shattering their contents everywhere. She used a spell to warp the metal instruments, and earth magic to crack the ground open, swallowing part of the room. When she'd finished, the room was ruined, and with satisfaction she led Barak down the corridor, pausing at the entrance to the final room with its door blasted off its hinges. Unlike the other rooms, it wasn't a lab or a medical room. It was an office.

"This is where I chased that bloody man to. Unfortunately, he got in here before I could reach him." She paused, furious with herself. "I was only seconds behind him, but in that time, he'd smashed both computers. They're utterly ruined."

Barak squeezed her arm. "He was doing what he was trained to do. It's annoying, but we've caused a lot of trouble here today."

"But we could have got so much information from them!"

Barak examined a large cork board on the wall, bits of paper and notes all over it. He started snapping photos. "We still could yet. Look for lists, phone numbers, anything helpful."

Estelle had barely examined the room earlier. Having incapacitated the staff member, she dragged him to the corridor and left him in a binding spell on the floor before returning to Barak. Now she pulled out drawers, rifling through them for anything of interest. A list of names that made no sense was next to the phone, and she grabbed it, pushing it into her pack. Unfortunately, there were no paper patient files of any sort.

"Damn it, Barak. I fucked up. There would have been so much information on those computers."

"No, you didn't." He grabbed her hand, pulling her from the room. "Time to go. The clock's ticking."

They headed back along the corridor, destroying everything in their wake, until they arrived in the room with the prisoner. He was still unconscious on the narrow trolley bed.

"There's no way we can get him out of here," Estelle said, taking in his tall frame. "You can't carry him across the grounds like that. Too many people would spot us."

"I'm not leaving him here to become a Black Cronos soldier. Poor bastard. Besides, he could have valuable information. There must be somewhere we can hide until nightfall."

Estelle nodded, thinking through their options. "If we can get back to the store room at the olive oil place, we could hide there. I could potentially use magic, but a veiling spell is not effective in the day. If we wait until nightfall, we can get to the car park and our car."

"Which will be the only one on the car park by then, and may well have attracted attention. And if they have shift changes, they'll discover what has happened well before then. Plus, the medical staff must be due to go home soon." Barak shook his head, perplexed. "We need to use that far corridor, take the van, and hope the underground road leads somewhere private. If that's the way they bring prisoners in, it will be quiet."

"But could well have security at the other end."

"That's our only option, Estelle." He walked to her side, taking her hands and kissing them. "We can do this. We have to. I promise you, we will not become Black Cronos's next subjects."

The thought of it chilled her blood, and her magic welled up again. "No. We will not!" She wondered where they would end up, and if they would even escape. Potentially, the corridor could lead to the centre of a Black Cronos spider's web. "All right. Let's do it."

Shadow studied the small, modern terraced house from the passenger seat of Gabe's SUV. There was no movement from it, or from any neighbouring homes. The whole road seemed to be basking in the early evening heat.

"Damn it. I wish I could go through the gardens."

Ash huffed in amusement. "I can smell barbeques. Back gardens will be full right now. You'll have to do this the old-fashioned way and knock on the front door."

"I knew bringing you was a mistake."

"I brought *you*," Ash reminded her. "And I'll probably stop you from being arrested. Come on. Now that I'm here, I'm going in, too."

He exited the car, and Shadow followed him, resolving that she *would* learn to drive soon. Then she wouldn't have to be escorted everywhere by annoying Nephilim. "I need someone to teach me."

Ash looked at her, confused for a moment. "Ah! To learn to drive." He grinned. "I will. But only if you'll listen."

"I always listen."

"Let me qualify that. Only if you listen, and then do as I say."

"I can do that!"

"You can, but rarely do. And seeing as I am probably the most patient of us all, I would make the better teacher. Niel would kill you."

She snorted. "He could try."

"And would." He continued, undaunted. "So would Eli. Zee would refuse outright. Barak would laugh at the suggestion. Nahum, however, would be a good second choice. You would bicker with Gabe constantly."

"You make it sound as if I will be hard to teach."

Ash turned his golden eyes on her, full of laughter. "You will be an absolute nightmare. But I am willing to rise to the occasion."

She stopped on the pavement, rounding on him. "I'm not stupid."

"I know. You're clever and resourceful, and will no doubt pick it up in no time. But you don't like rules or boring things, and driving requires concentration, and sometimes that's very boring."

"I have watched buildings for endless hours on stakeouts. And I spend hours sparring and refining my fighting skills."

"And those have a monetary reward. This gets you from A to B."

Shadow itched to wipe the smirk off Ash's face, but knew he was right. "Fine. When we get home."

"Challenge accepted, sister." He gave her a rakish grin before turning back to the house. As they approached the front door, his voice dropped. "Do you think you can ask Owen questions without terrifying him? If he's there, of course."

"How dare you."

"I dare and double-dare."

She glared at Ash, and then rapped on the door, emitting a waft of fey glamour for good measure.

For a moment, they heard nothing, and Shadow was already deciding how best to break in without alerting suspicion, when footsteps sounded and the door opened a short way, revealing a rangy figure who looked to be in his thirties on the other side. His face was impassive, but his eyes were wary. "Yes?"

"Owen?" Shadow asked, surprised he was actually there. "My name is Shadow, and this is Ash. We're friends of Theo's, and need to chat."

"Theo Carmichael? My employer?"

Shadow immediately decided he was an idiot, but kept smiling. "Yes. He said he'd discussed a few things with you. That you'd helped him with internet searches. We have a few more questions."

He immediately tried to shut the door, and Shadow stepped forward, wedging it open. "That's not very nice, Owen. Let's talk inside."

She forced her way in, blade already in her hand, and Owen backed up the hall, arms raised.

"I have nothing here at all. Nothing worth stealing."

She glanced around dismissively, noting the poor-quality furnishing. "No, I can see that. But all I want to do is talk."

"Then why the knife?"

"Because I don't like having the door shut in my face."

"I don't like having a knife in my face, either." Owen looked behind her as Ash followed her in, his eyes widening at his size. "Is he your enforcer?"

"Don't be ridiculous. I don't need one." She put her knife away, strengthened her glamour, and with satisfaction, saw his eyes glaze. "Please, Owen, we'd just like to talk. This is important. Your life could be at risk."

His jaw tightened, but he didn't look surprised. "Because of Theo's Templar research?"

"Exactly." And she wanted to know why he'd left work, but that could wait.

He didn't answer, instead leading them through the living room and out into the garden. For a moment, Shadow stopped, attention caught by the rampant growth of plants that filled the narrow plot. The fences down either side were covered in climbing plants, but she could only see a short way, as Owen had compartmentalised his garden into rooms. Trellises broke the space up, but beyond the first one, festooned in greenery, a bustle of growth could be seen further in.

Shadow turned to him, her opinion of him softening, as it always did when faced with someone with true gardening skills. "Your garden is amazing."

He offered her a shy smile. "Thank you. I spend all of my spare time here." He gestured to a round table with a few chairs under a pergola. "Take a seat. This is about the fire, isn't it? Not just the dagger." Owen's open expression became haunted, and he stared at the table, fingers rubbing the grain.

Shadow couldn't tell if he was scared or guilty. "This conversation is about many things. You assisted Theo with his research. How much did you help him uncover?"

"Very little. All I did was teach Theo how to search the internet for Templar history. For all of his knowledge, he's not that skilled with a computer. To be honest, they were fairly basic searches. I just helped a little."

"But he told you about the knife?"

"Of course. I admit, that was news to me, but not the Templar link. Everyone knows the keep's history, and the links to William de la More." He smiled. "It's fun to think that somewhere in the area could be Templar treasure. The knife with the symbols, that's new—to me, at least."

"Who did you tell?"

"No one!" His eyes widened with surprise. "Well, no one outside of the estate."

"Did you sell your information to anyone? Employ someone to help you?"

"Look at my house! It's small. I can't afford that. I spend all of my money on plants. And I would never betray Theo. He's a good man."

Shadow exchanged a questioning glance with Ash. This was not what she'd expected from Owen. "So, who did you talk to on the estate?"

"Everyone! The gardening staff, the house staff...when I see them. We're a close-knit group. It's just chat. And Theo didn't tell me not to. And besides," he laughed, "Chivers is a gossip. He'd seen the knife before I had."

Ash interrupted him. "So, why did you leave work today? We know you know the lodge burned down. Did you have anything to do with that?"

"No! I'm not a bloody arsonist. Besides, the fire could have damaged the woods. I would never risk them."

"Then why leave?" Shadow asked. "Everyone else was standing around, watching the action."

"To be honest, something struck me about the knife and the lodge, and I wanted to come back and check it out."

"It couldn't wait until tonight?" Ash asked, incredulous.

"I thought I could sneak off and no one would know." He shrugged, apologetic. "I'll make up the work time."

Shadow was growing impatient. "What struck you that was so important?"

"The knife's bone hilt had Templar symbols on it, and what hit me when I saw the lodge in flames was that it was filled with similar symbols."

"You went in it?" Ash asked.

"I looked through the windows, between a gap in the boards. We worked in the woods, and I was curious. We all were—the gardening staff, that is."

Shadow nodded. "Yes, you're right. There were symbols everywhere." She decided not to mention the one that was wired with a bomb. "Theo mentioned the Masons, too. He said they were linked to the Templars."

"After its downfall, other organisations rose in its wake. It's believed by some people that the few remaining survivors of the Templars were behind the rise of the Masons. They were originally a group of guildsmen. Stonemasons, actually. But over the years, this group changed. It's complicated."

Ash groaned. "It always is. And what's your conclusion?"

"I think the hunting lodge was once a Masonic lodge, but I have no idea how it connects with the knife with the bone handle. They might not be connected at all. It is suspicious that it burned down now, though." He suddenly seemed to take in Shadow's appearance. "Were you there at the time?"

"Yes, and I can assure you that fire was not accidental." Shadow changed tack. "Was there anyone in the household that you spoke to who seemed more interested than others in the news of the knife?"

"I don't think so." Owen shrugged. "Sorry."

"What about the symbols?" Ash asked. "Any that particularly strike you? Or any you might have seen around the house?"

"I hardly go in the house, so no. But I can show you a few of the symbols I recognised. On my laptop. It's on the sofa."

Ash nodded. "Yes, please."

Owen stood up, and Shadow followed him. As much as she thought she'd been wrong about him, she still didn't entirely trust him. Until they were out of the house, she wasn't going to take her eyes off him.

But this might be a lead, and one they couldn't pass up.

Twelve

B arak accelerated the stolen van along the concrete-lined underground tunnel, lit by the occasional overhead light, wondering where they would end up.

Estelle was next to him, keeping an eye on the unconscious man on the back seat, while trying to get a phone signal. "Nothing yet. We're too far underground."

Barak spotted a camera on the wall and groaned. "Shit. Take that out, Estelle. We're screwed. I bet that's being monitored in the *château*. Or even somewhere ahead of us," he added.

Estelle blasted the camera as they passed it. "If—*once*—we get out, where to next?"

"We hide anywhere we can until we get hold of Jackson. An abandoned building, a *gîte*, stables, anything!"

He estimated they had travelled along the underground road at least a couple of kilometres, and with relief saw that the corridor was rising to the surface on a gradual incline, but Barak didn't slow down. That camera feed had to have alerted someone.

As he reached the top of the rise, the electric lights cut out, plunging them into darkness, and he quickly flipped the full beam of the headlights on.

"Get ready," he said to Estelle. "And keep your head down."

Estelle cast a spell, and a blue light expanded around the whole vehicle. "Extra protection," she told him, wriggling down in her seat.

The corridor levelled off, and in the brief sweep of the headlights, Barak saw a high-roofed space that looked like an underground garage or warehouse. And then a brilliant bank of white lights lit up the space in front of them, temporarily blinding him as the boom of weapons shattered the silence.

Estelle's protection spell flared, but it held, and Barak accelerated towards the lights. It was impossible to see how many people there were, or what was beyond the lights, but he wasn't stopping now.

Estelle, however, was casting spells, and one after another, all of the lights ahead exploded, plunging them into darkness, except for the narrow swathe of light cast by their headlights.

They illuminated a huge man pointing a fire-tipped weapon, and Barak drove at him. But he wasn't fast enough to stop him from shooting at them, and something exploded under the van, catapulting them into the air.

Flames erupted around them.

"What the actual fuck is going on?" Barak roared, furious. He wrestled the steering wheel pointlessly as the van started to twist towards the ground.

Time seemed to slow as torch lights flared across the room below. Barak estimated there were half a dozen people scrambling for cover, but some were definitely aiming weapons at them.

The huge man immediately below them was angling his weapon towards them, but the van crashed to the ground, half-crushing him. Metal and glass splintered around them, and only their seatbelts prevented them from being propelled through the shattered windscreen.

Barak needed to fly. He glanced at Estelle, relieved to see that although she was twisted and bloodied in her seat, she was still conscious. He yelled to be heard across the shouts, "Kill the lights!"

In seconds, he wrenched the seat belt off him, kicked the door open, extended his wings, and soared into the air, just as the sizzle of magic exploded outwards.

Barak had no idea how she'd done it, and right now he didn't care, but the torchlights vanished. He needed to stop their attackers before any more arrived. It was now pitch-black, but Barak's excellent night vision meant that he could see everything perfectly.

They were in the middle of a huge space that had another couple of vehicles in it, an office along one side, a regular doorway, as well as a huge roller door for the vehicles. All of the exits were shut tight. Half a dozen men and women were struggling to their feet and firing furiously. Shots echoed across the space, splintering the remaining windows of the van, and thudding into metal. A couple of people were motionless on the ground, but the man the van had almost crushed was still moving.

Barak swept down on them, a silent assassin in the dark, killing the closest two with his blade. Random bullets strafed through his wings, shattering fine bones and grazing his skin, but he whirled in the air, and threw his dagger across the room with unerring accuracy. It struck the third soldier in the throat and he dropped to the ground, blood splattering.

Pain rocked through Barak's body as another bullet struck his shoulder, but he couldn't stop now. He attacked the next one from behind, breaking his neck swiftly with strong hands, the *crunch* of bones loud as the shouts vanished.

In seconds, their assailants were dead. Except for one.

The van rocked on to its side, trapping Estelle inside as the man finally shouldered it aside. He was badly injured, one arm crushed and limp, but fire blazed in his eyes as he staggered to his feet. Barak ran over before he found his balance, punched him, then grabbed one leg with his own uninjured arm, lifting them both into the air as he did so. The man wriggled like an eel as he twisted to reach Barak, but Barak swung him around and smacked him against the closest wall. The sound of cracking bone was sickening. Barak dropped him to the ground, and killed him with a swift twist of his neck.

Back to the wall, he waited, chest heaving as he scanned the room for any sign of movement. When nothing stirred, he headed to the office, peering through the reinforced glass, but there were no other guards.

Grateful for the reprieve, but knowing reinforcements could arrive at any moment, he ran to the van, shouting, "All clear!"

Estelle was already scrambling up and out of the driver's buckled door, throwing a witch-light above them. Blood poured down her arm from a cut. "The prisoner is in a bad way, Barak. He's covered in bruises after all that, and there's a big wound on his head. I've stemmed the blood flow as best as I can, but he needs medical attention."

He focussed only on her, offering her his hand as she struggled to the ground. "But are you all right?"

She gave him a rueful smile. "Battered, but I'll survive." She spotted the blood pouring from his shoulder. Her eyes widened with horror. "Barak! You've been shot!"

He winced. "Yeah, it's painful, but I'll heal." To be honest, it burned like his arm was on fire, and his wings felt awkward and sore from the damage they'd sustained. He tried to ignore it and eyed their destroyed van. "We need new transport. And we need to get this back on its wheels to get the prisoner out. Over there." He nodded to the other two vehicles. One was marked with the *château's* logo, the other was a plain black transit van. "We'll use the black one. Can you find the keys while I get the van upright?"

While she searched, Barak folded his wings away, grasped the side of the van and wrenched it down, feeling every single muscle strain as he did so. Sweat broke across his face, but he took deep breaths in an effort to quell his nausea. He quickly made himself a rudimentary bandage from the remains of his t-shirt, wrapping it firmly around his shoulder.

Estelle exited the office, two sets of keys in her hand. She wiggled them, metal clinking. "Just in case."

"Great. Help me move the prisoner. I can't manage him alone."

Between them, and with Estelle using magic, they lifted the injured man from the back seat. He was still out cold, and Barak wasn't sure if it was a result of the tranquilliser or the head injury. His face was smeared with blood, both from the cut and a broken nose. The rear of their next van was kitted out with benches and they positioned him carefully, securing him with tie downs, before facing the shuttered doors that promised them a way out. *But what was beyond them? Another compound? Or a road to freedom?* A round green button marked the mechanism to open it.

"Start her up," he instructed Estelle, "and get in front of the door. Any sign of more soldiers, floor it. I'll catch up."

While she maneuvered the van into position, Barak retrieved his knife and collected a couple of weapons from the dead guards. The first was one of the metal palm-held devices, typical of Black Cronos, the other was a shotgun. Pocketing the small device, he loaded the shotgun, and then pressed the green button.

With an agonising slowness, the metal door rolled upwards and evening sunshine pierced the gloom. Barak dropped to the ground to the side of the doorframe and studied the scene beyond. All he could see was a paved area surrounded by forest. He rolled through, leapt to his feet, and raised his weapon, scanning his immediate surroundings.

All around him was a dense wall of trees with a narrow road leading away from the compound. Behind him was a series of hills that the warehouse was set into. There was no evidence of a building within it at all, other than the doors. It was breathtakingly quiet. Only the evening chorus of birds disturbed the silence. That and the van's engine, as Estelle pulled up next to him.

She leaned through the open window. "All clear then, although we must still be on the *château's* grounds."

"A back road, I hope." He closed the roller door again, sealing the facility shut, before clambering into the passenger seat. "Eyes peeled now. I'll call Jackson, and then try and find us a place to shelter."

Jackson was returning to The Retreat with Harlan when he received the call from Barak. He listened with a mixture of dread and excitement, and nodded his agreement as Barak ended the call.

"They're safe—but only just. I was right. The *château* is a front for Black Cronos."

"Shit!" Harlan glanced over at him, hands gripping the wheel. He was still fuming from his encounter with Nicoli. "What happened? How do they even know that?"

"Because they've rescued a prisoner and had to fight their way out. I need to get them out of there." Jackson was racing through contingency plans. There was a team they could call on in France, but they were nowhere near Barak and Estelle. "This was supposed to be reconnaissance. It could take hours to get someone out to them. I need to call Waylen. He could arrange something quicker than I can." His fingers fumbled for the number. "What the fuck have I done, Harlan? I'm not prepared. I could get them killed! I shouldn't even have accepted this job."

"Slow down! Barak and Estelle are resourceful. That's why they found the guy in the first place. Although, frankly, I need more details, because I'm as curious as hell! Where are they now?"

"Escaping out of the *château* grounds in a stolen Black Cronos van. Heading west, well away from the main building." Waylen's phone line started to ring, and while Jackson waited for him to answer, he twisted to look at Harlan. "They had an underground lair with an operating theatre. Estelle destroyed it."

"Wow. Go Estelle! And a lair? Like it. Very Bond!"

"Very annoying—and so not cool! These guys are like bloody termites."

"At least there were no booby-trapped passages, like in Scotland."

Jackson nodded, remembering the stench of dogs and blood, and the warren beneath Arklet Abbey. "That was a nightmare." Waylen's voice mail kicked in and Jackson slammed his hand onto the dashboard with frustration as he left a basic message to return the call.

Harlan glared at him. "Watch my car!"

"Sorry. I'm flustered." Jackson huffed, and then frowned as he looked at their surroundings. "This isn't the way to The Retreat."

"No. We're heading to my flat instead. We're going to consult a map and I'll see if I can help. The Orphic Guild has contacts in France—with a base in Paris."

"Don't you have issues of your own to deal with?"

"Oh, I'll deal with them, don't you worry! In the meantime, I have favours I can call in."

Fifteen minutes later, Jackson and Harlan sat around Harlan's computer, a map of the *château* and the surrounding area on the screen. "It must be one of these roads they're on," Jackson said, his fingers hovering over several lanes on the map. "Barak said they travelled about a couple of kilometres underground—he checked the odometer just after they escaped. But he wasn't sure where the underground medical facility was. He thinks to the west of the *château*."

Harlan leaned in, enlarging the screen. "And you say they entered via the olive oil store?" He flicked to the *château*'s website, quickly scrolling through the photos until he found a rustic stone building. "That place." He flicked back to the map and pointed at the *château*'s grounds again. "Which must be this building, here."

Jackson spotted the line of low hills on the map. "That should be where they exited. Right on the edge of the grounds, in that area of woodland. Velleron is the closest town."

Harlan reached for his phone. "I'll call the Paris branch, see if they can help."

"I'll call Waylen again. And then I'll call Barak, and see if they've found anywhere to hide."

Thirteen

"At least we know who we're up against," Gabe said to Ash, Shadow, and Theo, who were now gathered in Theo's sitting room.

Gabe had finally enjoyed a shower and changed his clothes after a long interview with the police, and then a conversation with Harlan. Shadow was still in her fire-blackened clothing.

"But we don't know who the thief is," Shadow complained. She stood at the window, looking across the grounds that were quickly disappearing in the thickening twilight. "If Nicoli is in London, then he has someone down here."

"Maybe more than one person," Ash reasoned. "And they are familiar with bombs, too."

Theo leaned back in the chair, eyes vacantly staring at the book in front of him. "I can't believe it. This is a nightmare. How has the news leaked?"

Gabe couldn't hide his frustration. "It wasn't a secret, Theo! Your staff knew about it, and people talk. Chivers talked! It could have been a completely innocuous comment. Nicoli is very good at sniffing out opportunities."

Ash had his laptop open and he pointed at the screen. "These are common Masonic images. Do any of you recognise these?"

Gabe stood behind Ash and leaned over his shoulder. "I recognise the eye, and the compass, and the G-sign. The designs were in the finials on the wooden staircase, and in some of the plasterwork."

Shadow stood next to him. "I can't see the one I moved, though. The one with the bomb behind it."

Ash looked up at her. "Can you remember what it looks like? I've barely started the search."

"It looked like a bunch of flowers or something."

"This perhaps?" Ash scrolled to another image. "The Masonic Sheaf of Corn. It represents money earned or something like that."

"Yes! That's it!"

"But what does it mean?" Theo asked, annoyed. "Why put a bomb behind it?"

"I suspect it opened a secret compartment," Shadow said. "I've come across many things like that. Or it could have opened a door to a secret room, or a small place to hide an object, papers, or a map, even."

"Another clue that could be gone!" Theo's face was turning purple with annoyance.

Ash shrugged. "Perhaps. Or it could have been a ruse, and the bomb was just to scare you or anyone else off the trail. But you and Owen are right. It does appear that it was a Masonic lodge. The symbols all suggest it. Of course, it may have nothing to do with Templar treasure."

Shadow snorted. "I don't believe that for a moment."

"However, what I need to do," Ash continued, nodding at the dagger on the table next to him, "is examine that hilt. The symbols have to mean something useful, or else why hide it?"

Gabe lifted it, feeling its weight. "It's surprisingly heavy."

Shadow nodded. "I thought that, too. It's not balanced either, but I wondered if that's because it was ceremonial. The hilt is heavy."

"And ornate," Gabe noted. Silver and gold metals were inlaid into the bone, and the emeralds glinted along the base. However, the lodge continued to distract him. "Who built the lodge, Theo? You said it was constructed years after the keep was built. Was it a descendent of William, or someone else?"

"I can't remember, but the plans are in that collection." He gestured to the sofa where he'd placed the plans after removing them from the safe.

Gabe had perused them earlier that day, but could recollect no details, and had barely looked at the plans for the lodge. Placing the knife down, he unrolled the blueprints on the table, sifting through them until he found the one he wanted. It was a photocopy of the original document, and the spidery writing was hard to make out, as was the floor plan. "This is weird." He pointed to the tangle of schematics. Stairs were marked, as were rooms, doorways, and the huge fireplace and central hall was immediately obvious. "What is that section, there? It looks like a third level." He turned to Theo. "Was there attic space?"

"Yes, I went up there years ago. But it was a shallow pitch roof and nothing was up there. No rooms, certainly."

"I don't think that's attic space, Gabe," Ash said, frowning over the drawings. "I think it's a cellar."

"A cellar?" Theo frowned. "I'm pretty sure there wasn't one of those."

"Perhaps that's what the relief triggered," Shadow suggested, her excitement obvious. "A doorway. And if it's a cellar..."

"It could still be there!" Gabe said, already walking to the door. "The bomb may not have destroyed it. We need to check."

Theo rose to his feet. "Surely the fire brigade or the police will have found it?"

"Not necessarily. The remains of the building were smouldering, and still hot. Debris was all over the place. And it was unsafe. They've barely touched it," Gabe reminded him. "They're going back tomorrow to examine it in the light, when it's cooler."

Ash grabbed his backpack, stuffing the books, notes, and the plans inside it. "These are coming with us—just in case."

Gabe turned to Shadow, knowing that what he was about to ask her would not be received well. "Shadow, I want you to stay here with Theo."

She glared at him. "Like a guard dog?"

"Exactly. If someone is watching this place, they could wait until we've left and come in. Theo could be at risk—as could the whole household. That might have been the sole point of the bomb. To distract everyone and get in here."

Ash nodded. "That's true. There are a lot of people on the grounds now. They could blend in."

"I can't guard an entire castle!"

"You could from the roof!" Theo said, eager to help. "You have a 360-degree view from the tower—through the battlements."

Shadow's expression brightened as she eyed her bow and quiver full of arrows propped against the wall. "Now you're talking, Theo."

"And," Gabe added, "either Nahum or Niel are on the way right now. I trust that you can watch this place on your own in the meantime."

"Well, *now* I can." Her violet eyes gleamed. "Lead the way, Theo. And bring me some food when I'm settled. I'm starving."

Exhausted, Estelle completed the protection spell around the dilapidated barn they had found sanctuary in, and stood for a moment, looking down the only lane that led to their location.

It was virtually dusk now, and she could see lights from a small village twinkling in the distance, and the occasional flash of headlights as cars swept along the lanes. But the approach to the barn remained devoid of traffic, and she took a deep breath of relief.

They had found this place only fifteen minutes earlier, after Barak had directed her through convoluted back lanes, eager to lose any would-be pursuers and find an unassuming shelter. They had travelled steadily west, passing towns and villages, debating their best course of action. Had it been just Barak and Estelle, they could have found a room somewhere, but that was impossible with the prisoner. It would look far too suspicious.

Fortunately, Barak had spotted the building in the slanting rays of the setting sun, set low on a hillside surrounded by olive trees, and on a whim, they headed to it. The lane ended at a rutted track, allowing Estelle to ease their van right into the barn itself. It had huge wooden doors, but one had collapsed on the ground, and portions of the roof had also disintegrated. However, the other half offered shelter from any potential helicopters that could be looking for them. Neither of them could forget the helicopter that had whisked Professor Stefan Hope-Robbins away in Turkey.

Estelle headed inside the building, and found Barak in the back of the van, tending to the prisoner.

"Is he still unconscious?"

Barak nodded as he straightened up and joined her in the barn. "Yes, but his breathing appears easier, and it seems more like a natural sleep now. I hate to think what he's gone through."

Estelle studied the prone figure. He was still in the surgical gown, but they had stolen a selection of scrubs for him to change into. It wasn't ideal, but it was better than nothing. "I know we think some soldiers were willingly recruited, but I don't think he was. How do you even start to control someone who doesn't want to be part of Black Cronos?"

"Maybe some sort of mind control? An implant? Alchemy, or magic?" He shrugged and then winced, hand flying to his shoulder. "I don't like to think of what they might do."

"Me neither. But I know what I do want. Food. Then I'll try a healing spell on him—and you. You need a scrub top to wear, too. You can't walk around looking like that—as much as I like admiring your pecs." She reached across the driver's seat and grabbed the bag of food and drinks that she had bought on a very quick stop to put petrol in the van. Barak, with his bare chest, injured shoulder, and makeshift, blood-stained dressing, had stayed in the van. "I can't think straight I'm so hungry."

Barak grabbed the picnic blankets she'd bought at the same time. "Let's sit at the barn doors, just beneath the roof, and keep watch."

They positioned themselves carefully, and for good measure, Estelle shrouded them in the veiling spell, too. She bit into a baguette with relish. "This is good."

"A bit stale now, but better than nothing." For a few minutes they ate in companiable silence before Barak said, "Thanks for your help back there. You were incredible."

"Incredible? I like that. To be fair, so were you."

"You're always incredible, Estelle. Never forget that." His voice was soft, his brown eyes full of promise.

Estelle smiled, feeling herself blushing. So close to him, she was well aware of his heat, and his size, and she had an urge to keep touching him. She clutched her food instead. "You're too good to me."

"No, I'm not. I'm as good as anyone should be." He took another bite of food, watching her thoughtfully. She felt scrutinised by his studied gaze, and glanced away. But then he spoke again. "What happened that made you so guarded? So closed off to the world?"

Her head snapped around to him. "I'm not closed off!"

His voice, like his gaze, remained gentle. "Not to me. Not anymore. Or not all of the time, at least. Don't close off to me now."

Estelle felt tears well up and she looked at the rug, angry at herself. "I'm not closing myself to you. Not intentionally, anyway. It's like flexing a muscle. I do it instinctively." She forced herself to say what she'd been thinking for weeks. "I'm comfortable with you, Barak. More than I have been with anyone for a very long time. You make me feel safe. And I don't mean just physically."

"I know what you mean." He reached across and brushed her hair back from her shoulders, caressing her cheek as he did so. She leaned into his hand, savouring his warmth. "I won't abuse you, misuse you, or harm you in any way. What happened? Because I swear, if someone did something to you, I will find him and kill him. Or her, for that matter."

She caught his hand in hers and kissed it. "He's already dead. And besides, it wasn't just him. It was a series of events that taught me not to trust."

"Who's *he*? Your father?"

At the very mention of his name, her skin crawled. "Yes, him. He was never a father figure, though. Not a kind one, anyway. He may have been modern in the sense that he encouraged education and allowed me a place in the family business—well, *insisted* I have a place in the family business, actually. But he was always, always, criticising me. Not just me, either, to be fair. Caspian received it just as much. He was sharp with his own brother—my uncle—and my cousins, too. He was a miserable bastard. I hated him."

Barak nodded, eyes watchful as he considered his words. "And the events?"

"After a childhood of constantly feeling like I was never good enough, it made me sensitive. I withdrew. From everything. School, university, even work. I was constantly protecting myself, so much so that I was accused of being frigid by boyfriends. And they were probably right." She could feel herself trembling, and she looked away, unable to meet Barak's eyes. "I've missed out on so much, because I wouldn't let myself do anything in the end. What a waste of a life."

"I'm sorry you had to put up with all of that, but your behaviour makes sense. Why put yourself out there to be constantly found wanting? I get that. But he's dead now. You are a powerful witch and a clever woman, and very beautiful, too. And, you have *not* wasted your life. You've achieved so much!"

"Money, yes. Job, sure. And I admit, I'm proud of my magical abilities. It's the one thing that sustains me when everything else feels like a prison. But there's more to life than all of that. Caspian is now realising that, too." A flash of guilt ripped through her as she thought of how her father had driven a wedge between her and Caspian. "I'm horrible to Caspian, and have said terrible things to him."

"He's already forgiven you. I can tell."

"He's still wary around me. Like most people."

"They'll change when they see *you* change. I don't understand why you hate the White Haven witches so much. They killed your father, but they did you a favour."

"I know." Her usual anger at even the mention of them didn't appear. Instead, she sighed. "They weren't intimidated by him, and I resented that—and their unwavering self-belief. And they're always so bloody happy!" She caught Barak's grin and started to laugh, too. "I know, I know! That's terrible, isn't it? I'm a monster!"

"You resented what you didn't have. It made you bitter. But that's all changing, right? You're living fully now! Maybe a little too fully!" He gestured around them. "We're sheltering in an abandoned barn, fleeing Black Cronos, with a prisoner in a van. And we're stuck."

"The thing is, though, I'm actually loving all of this! How weird is that? I'm terrified half the time, but also have never felt so alive. And I'm using my magic to its full capacity. Challenging myself constantly. It's addictive." She took a deep breath, savouring the warm evening air, the wide-open sky, and Barak, and voiced what she really felt. "I feel free."

"I'll share a secret." Barak leaned closer. "I love it, too. Most of the time, at least. I was born for it. It's in my blood."

Estelle kissed Barak, allowing herself to do so without fear of rejection or criticism, knowing that this man could be her answer to everything. This *Nephilim*. A magnificent creature of muscle and feather, of mystery and strength, and unbelievable gentleness.

For the first time in a very long time, Estelle allowed herself hope.

Fourteen

Ash stood next to Gabe at the edge of the ruined lodge, the air still thick with the stench of burnt wood, although the smoke had long vanished.

Although it was dark, the Nephilim's excellent night vision allowed him to see that portions of some walls, interior and exterior, still stood, but the roof had collapsed, leaving only the occasional beam jutting into the air. A portion of the stairs and upper floor remained, as did part of the stone fireplace, but the explosion had effectively destroyed everything else.

"Most of the floor is gone," Ash noted, peering between the joists to the earth beneath. "There's certainly no cellar in this part of the lodge."

"It's huge, though. There could be something at the back."

Ash sighed. "Look at that place! As mad as Theo's idea of this lost treasure seems, he has to be right, or this wouldn't have happened. We can't forget the theft in the library, either. I had hoped we were one step ahead, but now I feel we are way behind on this chase."

"We have the dagger. That's something."

"True." Ash felt annoyed with himself. "I've been caught up in background information when I should be analysing it. But if I'm honest, it's hard to know where to start, and getting some context on this whole situation is important. How do I know the importance of a symbol, otherwise?"

"Don't beat yourself up over it. We only arrived this morning. I know I said earlier that Nicoli only needed a bit of information to get involved, but now I think he must have been ahead of Theo, even. This bomb, the theft...that's a lot of planning."

"But he has a formidable organisation, plus money and resources. With all that behind him, it's easy to get ahead quickly. Theo was thinking that we had time, and so did Harlan. We were wrong." Ash studied his old friend's face as he turned towards him, a frown between his brows. "Right now, we just need to act, and figure it out as we go along. We've played catch-up before."

"True, but I feel there were valuable clues in there that we have now lost. But you're right, nothing we can do about that now except find the cellar."

"And the chapel, if it exists. Once we're done here, I'd like to study the grounds again—from the air. It's risky, but needs must."

Gabe pulled his t-shirt off, expanding his wings. "Agreed. It will be easier to fly at night. Hopefully, no one will see us."

Ash nodded his agreement, thankful that the police had restricted themselves to blocking the driveway, and stripped his t-shirt off and extended his wings, too. He flexed them, glad to feel the cool night air ruffling his feathers. He strapped the pack to his chest, not wanting to leave it unattended, and then soared into the air.

From above, it was easy to see the huge footprint of the lodge, but while Gabe studied the building, Ash took in their surroundings. The immediate woods stretched out around the lodge, and beyond it were the lawns and gardens, the moat glinting with lights from the keep above it. The tower where Shadow was positioned, blocked a portion of the night sky, but he couldn't see her. That wasn't surprising. No doubt she had hidden herself well. The lanes around the estate were quiet, and no one was approaching it. Not in a vehicle, at least. Ash focussed on their immediate area, searching for anyone that could be on foot, but other than the gentle stir of leaves in the breeze, nothing moved.

Gabe called to him from where he hovered above a small square of ground that looked darker than its surroundings, set close to an internal wall but partly covered by blackened beams. "I've found it. I can see steps going down, but we'll have to move the beams to get access."

Together they lifted a couple of beams aside, and folding their wings away, edged carefully down the stone stairs. The wall to one side fell away, revealing a small anteroom, beyond which was a larger room, stone-slabbed, with a vaulted stone ceiling and a series of archways overhead. The room had been protected from the fire by its position and stone structure, and Ash used his torch so he could see the details of it clearly. The beam illuminated an altar at the far side.

"Gabe! Look. From what I've read, the Masons would have had an altar. This must have been a hidden inner sanctum."

"And the same symbols that we saw above are down here." Gabe played his own torch along the walls and ceiling, picking out the reliefs. "Look. They're everywhere."

Ash couldn't help but be disappointed. "But there's nothing else here. It's been completed cleared out."

"But maybe there are hidden rooms or compartments...if we want to risk searching it. This place could be wired to a bomb, too." Gabe's lips were set in a thin line. "I think we have to look, though. We might not get another chance."

Ash nodded, and wordlessly, they started the search.

Harlan paced his study, phone in one hand and bourbon in the other, nodding as he listened to Pierre at the other end. Satisfied, he said goodbye and ended the call.

"Well?" Jackson asked. He was sitting in front of the computer, cradling a glass of whiskey.

"There's an apartment above a small supermarket that we've used before, in Méthamis, and Barak and Estelle can use it. Pierre says the keys are in a lock box on the property. I have the code. You can send your extraction team there. It's up to Barak and Estelle as to whether they stay at the barn overnight, or head there now."

"From the last conversation I had with them, they're staying at the barn. It's isolated, and they feel safe there. Plus, they're exhausted." Jackson sipped his drink and smacked his lips. "I needed that. I still can't believe it. That they actually broke in to the *château*! It's incredible."

"They're resourceful. That's what's so good about them," Harlan said, easing into his seat again, and realising he was also exhausted. "But you have decisions to make now. What are you going to do about the *château* and the owners, now you've confirmed their involvement? And what are you going to do with your prisoner? Not that he's really *your* prisoner."

"Great questions! As far as the *château* goes, I'm torn. We could take this higher, get a team together to raid the place, but that will take time. I honestly wasn't anticipating this, and after Barak and Estelle swept through there, I imagine that they will be clearing everything out and destroying any evidence of what they were doing. Unfortunately, they'll likely be destroying *anything* that could link them to Black Cronos. It doesn't change what we know, though. Tomorrow I'll start an in-depth investigation into the family—their associates, money, assets...everything."

"You're right," Harlan conceded. "But you've identified a link in the chain, and it could inadvertently lead you to another."

"Let's hope so. In the meantime," Jackson sighed, a hand rubbing his eyes, "how do we keep the prisoner safe? Black Cronos will want him back, surely. He'll have secrets to share that we badly need."

Harlan shook his head. "I doubt he will. Not unless he's been privy to certain conversations. I think you'll find he can tell you nothing."

"But anything could help! Where he was abducted from, or if he was moved between facilities."

Harlan noted the grim determination on Jackson's face. "Please don't tell me you're thinking of going over there." They'd argued about that earlier, and worried about the team, Jackson had been prepared to fly in there single-handedly. Now, however, he just looked resigned.

"No. I'll meet them at the airport here instead. Waylen has arranged for a medic to be part of the extraction team, and they'll transport them to a private plane."

"At Avignon?"

"No, a private airport to the north of the city. They're on the way now."

"Good. Black Cronos might search the main airport. Hell, they might watch all of them." He considered his next words carefully. "You know, we might have rattled them too much. They might well come after us—harder, this time."

"I've considered that, but I don't think they will. With luck, they won't know who has infiltrated them—not for sure, anyway. For all we know, they've made lots of different enemies. As a consequence, I doubt they'll start an all-out war with us. It will bring them too much attention, and covert is their entire way of operating."

"What about picking us off, one by one?"

Jackson stared balefully at him. "It's possible."

"That settles it. I'm moving into the Mandarin Oriental again."

"Why are you so worried? You had nothing to do with this!"

"Because I'm associated with you and the Nephilim. You should move into The Retreat—just in case." Harlan had a better idea. "Actually, I know what I'm going to do. I'm going to Kent to stay with Theo. I think I should help with the search for Templar treasure." Harlan felt the stir of familiar excitement that appeared with all the most intriguing jobs, and this one, despite his earlier scoffing, was shaping up to be a beauty.

Jackson snorted. "So you're putting yourself in the path of a bomber and Nicoli? Yes, much safer!"

"Safer than Black Cronos!" Nicoli's smug face flashed into his brain. "Besides, that irritating bastard has annoyed the crap out of me. I do not intend to let him win. And that means I need to be in Kent."

"Or are you better off watching him? He's pulling strings from here."

"He'll be extra careful from now on. I could watch his office all week and still see nothing of relevance."

"I told you not to go charging in there."

"At least now I know for sure he's involved. I still can't believe he was behind the bomb, though."

"If I'm honest, neither can I." There was a deep crease between Jackson's brows as he raked his hands through his shaggy hair. "Nicoli is sneaky and underhanded, but very determined. Theft, assault, blackmail, subterfuge—all of those are Nicoli's calling cards. But a bomb? Did he really admit to that?"

Harlan scratched his jaw, and a prickle of discomfort ran down his spine as he considered their heated conversation. "Actually, not exactly. He said he hadn't planted it or something of the sort, and I accused him of hiring someone. You know how pedantic he is. He didn't deny that."

"I wonder if there's a third player in all this. Someone who really planted the bomb."

"Like who?"

"I don't know. Maybe I'm just paranoid. Tiredness does that to me." Jackson finished his drink, placed his glass on the table and stood. "I'm shattered, and I have a lot to process about Layla's news and everything else, so I'm going home. I need to be fresh in the morning. Although..." he hesitated, deep in thought.

"You're changing your mind, aren't you? About going to France."

Jackson nodded. "I feel I should meet them and escort them out of there. I head this investigation! I could still get a late flight and be part of the extraction team."

"Don't you trust your team?"

"Of course I do, but after Layla's news, I want answers."

"And you'll get them."

Jackson scowled as he wrestled with his emotions, but when he met Harlan's eyes, he looked resolute. "I'm going."

Despite his misgivings, Harlan knew Jackson wouldn't be dissuaded, and he understood why, too. Sitting here seemed...lazy. "Do you need a lift?"

"No, thanks. I'll walk or get the tube or something. I'll keep you informed, Harlan."

"Good luck."

Harlan topped up his drink and moved to the window, watching Jackson exit the building and lope down the street. Jackson's decision goaded him into action, too. *What if there was another dangerous group searching for Templar gold?* He knew he couldn't stay here, far from the action. He'd go to Theo's. *Right now.*

Shadow rested her cheek against the cool stone parapet as she watched the driveway below.

Theo was right. Up here offered the perfect place to survey the grounds. The parapets were high, offering plenty of space to shelter behind, with narrow gaps to aim her bow through. She could see all approaches to the keep, but the moon, a silvered crescent, provided a wealth of shadows. Complete darkness cloaked parts of the drive and areas of the grounds that were scattered with trees. The wood was dense and impenetrable from here, but she could see the break in the canopy, revealing where the lodge had been.

She studied the drive again, and then crept around the tower, surveying the lanes that bordered the grounds. Only the occasional car and its headlights provided illumination there. Moving again, she studied the string of courtyards below with their collection of outbuildings, and the greenhouse set inside the walled garden.

If she were a thief—which she was, on occasion—she wouldn't approach via the drive or anywhere near it. Plus, a patrol car was parked at the gate. She'd cross the grounds from the lane, sticking to the edges of the lawns and the huge, perennial borders that at this time of year were thick with flowers. Or she'd arrive in the day with the crowds of emergency personnel and hide somewhere, emerging only when no one expected it.

The sound of an approaching car disturbed her thoughts, and she swung around to the front of the house. She raised her bow, sighting the car along the arrow as it sped up the drive. There was no subtlety of approach here, and with a sigh of relief, she realised why. It was Nahum's car, and Niel was in the passenger seat. She smirked. It appeared that neither could decide who should come, and they both had. She waited until they stopped in front of the keep, and then released an arrow at Niel's feet as he exited the car.

He yelled and then scowled as he looked up, raising his middle finger in salute. The subtle moonlight gave his blond hair and beard a silvery glow. Shadow returned his one-fingered greeting, and dropped back with a grin, out of sight, continuing to survey her surroundings.

Within ten minutes, both had joined her up on the wide, round roof of the tower, Theo with them, and they clustered behind a thick pillar of stone.

Niel grimaced as he handed her the arrow. "You're funny, Shadow."

"I know. Your face was a picture."

"Now, now," Nahum chided, although he couldn't hide his amusement. "Please don't start already."

Theo looked confused, and nervously stroked his luxuriant moustache. "Is there a problem? You are acquainted? Gabe said..."

Nahum smiled. "Shadow just likes to tease Niel. Ignore them both."

Theo still looked uncertain. "I feel you should settle in. You've had a long journey."

Niel stopped him. "We're here to help, and Nahum almost killed us, he drove so quickly to get here. It would be a waste to rest. We're just fine, Theo."

"He's right." Shadow nodded to the doorway that led to the steps and the lower floors. "You can head back downstairs, Theo. Is the place locked up? Every door? Every window?"

Theo nodded. "Yes, and all the outbuildings too, just as you asked."

"Good. Head back down and keep searching those records." Shadow had learned that Theo needed to be kept busy to stay out of her way. "Particularly the symbols on the knife's hilt!"

Theo agreed and retreated, leaving them alone, and Shadow returned to her watch, Nahum and Niel following her, keeping well out of sight.

"You were risky, taking that shot," Niel observed. "You could have been spotted."

"Unlikely, from that angle. If anyone is coming tonight, they won't approach from that side. It will be from the grounds. There are places along the lane where you can get over the walls, or through the hedge. We also wondered if someone had sneaked in when there were a lot of emergency services here."

"Good point," Nahum said, nodding. "Nothing so far?"

"No. Although, your arrival might have put them off."

"Where's the lodge?" Niel asked, scanning the grounds.

Shadow pointed it out. "Gabe and Ash are there now."

Nahum settled himself into position. "We may as well watch with you for a while."

They fell silent for several minutes, focussing on the grounds below them, with only the sound of a distant barking dog to disturb the quiet.

Then Niel called softly. "I see something." In seconds Shadow was at his side, Nahum on her left. "Down there, in the shadow of the wall." Shadow raised her bow, focussing on the spot Niel had directed her to. His voice was low in her ear. "By the rhododendron."

"What the fuck is a rhododendron?"

"The big, bloody bush on the far, right corner!"

She waited, marginally distracted by Niel's gardening knowledge, and was finally rewarded as a creeping figure edged towards the house.

Nahum put his mouth to her ear on her other side. "Don't kill him. We need to talk to whoever it is."

"I'm not an idiot. I'll injure the intruder. Will you two shut up and let me focus?" *Why in the great Goddess's name had she let them watch with her?*

She waited for her eyes to adjust to the light, discerning what was plant from person. A leg injury would bleed a lot, but it would immobilise him. Unfortunately, the thick bushes were impeding her sight, unless she guessed at his position.

As she aimed her arrow, her finger ready to release, a blast rocked the grounds, and a plume of fire lit up the sky, directly where the lodge had been.

Fifteen

A groan summoned Barak from thoughtful contemplation. He was leaning against the rotten doorframe at the entrance to the barn, nursing his injured shoulder, and feeling grateful for Estelle's magic and his own healing abilities that had eased some of the pain. Already he could feel the flesh and bone knitting back together.

He looked around at the van, seeing movement within. Their prisoner was stirring, the blankets shifting off him as he struggled to sit up. The noise roused Estelle from her light slumber, too.

He took a moment before responding, not wanting to rush their guest, but also enjoying the view of Estelle stretching like a cat as she yawned, her eyes flickering open. They had talked a lot earlier that evening, and he was glad of it. Estelle had opened up to him properly for the first time in months. Despite their recent physical closeness, she had always kept something back. However, now he felt the change in her, and he'd watched her sleeping, easy in his heart at their newfound honesty. She blinked up at him, her eyes warm.

He squeezed her hand. "Our guest is awake. Stay here, and keep an eye on the road." Barak crossed the barn. "Easy," he said, stepping into the van and crouching at the man's side in an attempt to subdue the man's noticeable rising panic. "You were drugged."

The man groaned again, his voice rasping, making his French accent stronger. "Not for the first time." He tried to focus, eyes blinking rapidly. "*Merde*. Where am I?"

"Somewhere safe. We're hiding in a barn, well away from the *château*." Barak handed him a bottle of water. "Here. Drink up. It's just water."

The man sniffed at the bottle, then squinted at Barak. "I don't know if I can trust you!"

"You're alive, aren't you? And not tied up, either. You've been sleeping for hours. I could have killed you plenty of times by now."

He nodded and downed the water, finishing the bottle in one long drink, before wiping his mouth with the back of his hand. "I still feel dizzy."

"The after-effects of the drug. You need food, too." He pointed to the scrubs stacked at the side. "Get changed, and then come and join us."

Barak backed out and gave the man a moment of privacy, then watched him test his strength before exiting the van. He took a deep breath and looked around, his chest rising and falling. He flexed his fingers and stretched as he took his bearings. He was tall, around six feet, slimly built with a wiry, muscular frame. His head was shaved, although he had stubble across his jaw. He spotted Estelle sitting quietly by the door, and frowned. "Who's that?"

"My friend, Estelle. She was at the facility, remember? She helped you escape. I'm Barak." He extended his hand, and the man shook it with a firm grip.

"Lucien." Tension seeped out of him. "Yes. Sorry. My memory is hazy."

"Not surprising, all things considered. Come and join us." Barak was now sure that Lucien wasn't a threat. Even if he was, they should be able to handle him easily.

Barak sat next to Estelle on the rug, and they both gave Lucien plenty of room. He stood for a moment, looking down the lane, before finally sitting and introducing himself to Estelle.

Estelle handed him a pre-packed baguette. "Sorry. It's all we had time to buy."

"Anything right now is fine. Tell me what's going on."

They had already discussed how much to tell him when he finally woke up, both reluctant to disclose too much. Estelle started. "We work with an organisation investigating the paranormal. In recent months, we've discovered some individuals who have developed unusual physical enhancements. They seem to be associated with a powerful group who have few morals. Through various means, we found *Château du Buade*." She succinctly explained how they discovered Lucien at the facility, finally asking, "Do you know who captured you?"

"No, but I know why they did. I've been working at the *château* for the last few months—a temporary summer job." He shrugged at Barak's questioning expression. "I was looking for a change. Life has been tricky lately. The *château* seemed like a good place to try something new. Anyway, I was staying on site, in one of the workers' cottages, helping in the shops and café, and getting ready for the olive harvest later in the year. Then I saw something I shouldn't."

"Like what?" Barak asked.

"I don't sleep that well, so sometimes I explore the grounds at night. I found a large door set into a hill, and I saw vans coming and going. I went back a few times after that, thinking at first that it was supplies for the *château*, but it didn't make sense. Why not take vans to the front? I see delivery vans there all the time. And why deliver in the middle of the night? I knew this was something different." He shrugged. "I was careless. They spotted me. I think they shot at me. The next thing I know, I was in that underground lab being endlessly questioned. 'Who did I work for? Was someone else with me? Why was I there?'" His gaze became distant as he looked, unseeing, down the lane. "They didn't believe me at first. Then they asked about *me*. Where I was from. My family. My friends. When they realised that I had no one close in the area, that my life had...changed," he hesitated over the word, his eyes haunted, "they said they had a new job for me, helping them in their research. I refused." He huffed. "Turns out, they didn't like that. I didn't really have a choice."

"Then what?" Barak asked, as Lucien hesitated again.

"It was only a week or so ago, but I feel it's been months. They ran a whole load of tests on me, and," he glanced down at his arms, "they did this."

"Were there others with you at any point?"

"One man and one woman, but not for long. They disappeared within days of my arrival. I never spoke to them. They were careful to keep us separated." He finished his food, and brushed crumbs off his chest. "I need to go now. I can't stay here. They'll be looking for us. They won't stop. They made that *very* clear."

Barak held his hand out in a stop sign. "We have a plan to get out of here. Out of France. That includes you, too. But we'd like your help in exchange. There are things you must have heard in there. We suspect that the facility is one of many. We aim to shut them down, for good." He gestured at the tattoos. "Those, we think, are stage one of a kind of transformation."

"What sort of transformation?"

"Enhanced strength, speed, longevity. And potentially some kind of mind control. Something that would have made you compliant."

"The big man. The main doctor. He talked about stages in the process." Lucien's eyes clouded as he struggled to remember. "I was drugged at the time. These tattoos are everywhere. They took time to do." He lifted his shirt. "They cover my chest and my back, and they feel odd. They tingle, on occasion." He closed his eyes tightly, as if to block the memory. "They ran energy pulses over me. Over *them*."

"Like electrocution?" Estelle asked, eyes widening in alarm.

He flexed his arm muscles. "No, something different. I have no idea."

Barak leaned forward, now more certain than ever that this man could help them. His captors were trying to activate or prime his tattoos. But another thought struck him, something that should have occurred to him far sooner. He glanced down the lane, expecting to hear car engines and the screech of tires. "Did you have a tracker implanted on you?"

"Who knows? Maybe?"

Estelle turned to Barak. "Potentially, if there is one, my spell will disrupt it."

"Spell?" Lucien edged back. "What are you talking about?"

"Just something that protects us." Estelle's magic was already rising, ready to subdue Lucien, but he was too exhausted to fight.

"I just want to get out of here."

Barak came to a quick decision. If Lucien did have a tracker implanted somewhere on his body, Black Cronos would have followed them part of the way, even if Estelle's spell was blanketing it now. They could be waiting somewhere on the lanes for them to move again, and travelling at night would be better than daylight. "Let's get moving now, just in case. We have a rendezvous anyway in a few hours. Can you protect us while we travel, Estelle?"

"I can protect Lucien. No problem. The van, while we're moving, is harder."

He nodded. "Do what you can. Anything to buy us more time will be good."

Nahum dived off the keep's tower, extending his wings and soaring towards the woods, not caring who saw him. His priority was his brothers.

Niel swooped next to him, but headed towards where they had seen the intruder. Shadow remained behind, still watching the grounds.

Another roar heralded a column of flames shooting up above the wood, and Nahum circled around it. The fire illuminated the sprawled figures of Gabe and Ash on the ground beyond the house. Nahum dropped to their side, calling their names.

"We're fine!" Gabe said, sitting up and rubbing his head. "It was a controlled explosion."

"Controlled? You're kidding, right? Your feathers are singed!"

Gabe reached over, quelling the red glow on his wing tips. "No. We used that!" He pointed at a long, wooden beam that was burning at one end. "That was our trigger."

Ash staggered to his feet. "It was still a big blast, though. And now we've destroyed the Inner Sanctum, too."

Nahum stared at them, exasperated. "What the hell are you two doing? You could have been killed! And what the hell is the Inner Sanctum?"

"It's a ruse. The whole place is! The explosion...everything!" Gabe groaned as he stood up. "We think this was meant to distract us from the real place we should be looking. The chapel."

Nahum had only received a garbled message earlier, and there was no mention of Inner Sanctums. "Keep explaining, please. I'm playing catch up here!"

The distant flashing of red and blue lights, accompanied by the whine of engines tearing down the lanes made them all stop.

Gabe led them into the woods. "This way."

"Shadow thinks you're dead."

Gabe winced, and pulled his phone out of his pocket. "Shit. Go ahead. I'll call her."

Ash took over the lead, weaving through the trees, away from the castle, setting a quick pace. He talked as he walked. "The knife that Theo found hidden in the walls of his cellar is marked with Templar symbols."

"Which started this whole thing off. I get that. How did he find it?"

"Constructing a cinema room."

"Nice!"

"I guess so. Anyway, he thinks that the symbols on its hilt are a coded message, a type of map."

"To treasure."

"Yes, because Temple Keep used to belong to the final English Commander."

"What if it's a fake?"

Ash shook his head. "I know weapons. It's old. I've studied the symbols a little, but so far, they make little sense. I'm trying to get my head around it all."

"Where does the exploding lodge come into this?"

Ash paused in a clearing, a shaft of moonlight illuminating his pinched expression. "The lodge was built centuries after the keep, but had lots of symbols carved into it. However, they are more Masonic in origin, an organisation believed to have formed from the ashes of the Knights Templar."

"And what are they? What did they do?"

"Not did. *Do*! They're still around. Originally, hundreds of years ago, they were a guild of stonemasons. Men with businesses helping other men get ahead. It evolved over time. Became more secretive. They had rituals and secret handshakes." Ash rolled his eyes. "Nothing new, really."

Nahum laughed. "No. Secret organisations have been around for millennia. What's the link with the dagger?"

"It's murky. When the Templars were rounded up and tortured, their treasure disappeared. Maybe it was hidden in one place. Maybe it was separated. Anyway, the organisation's property was split up, their possessions shared out. Other organisations developed from it, and the Masons are thought to be one of them. The Knights Hospitaller benefitted most—I think. However, the treasure vanished, but there *were* survivors, as I mentioned before. Men who ran before the net closed and the Templars were arrested for heresy. It's believed that their knowledge was passed down, potentially knowledge about the missing treasure, maybe also their rituals. After discovering the knife with the carved hilt, Theo believes it's a new clue to the cache of English treasure that was hidden somewhere around here. It seems Theo's lodge, built well after the main castle, was probably a Masonic lodge."

"Which is why you were searching it."

"Yes." Ash plunged into the trees again, still talking. "It made sense to check it out. But when Gabe and Shadow investigated it, *boom*!" He quickly summarised how Shadow had found and activated the trigger. "But we reasoned it must be a trigger to something! A hidden room or hiding place. We examined the blueprint of the building and found a cellar in the foundation."

Nahum understood Ash's reasoning. "You thought the bomb had been planted to hide the cellar."

"Initially, yes. That's what Gabe and I were doing. Checking it out. But the room was empty, and footprints were visible on the ground. Someone had already been there. We knew that potentially if something was there, it had been removed, or it was a false trail. We spotted a carved relief that was slightly protruding from the wall behind the altar. It looked suspicious."

"Too suspicious?"

"Exactly! So, we prodded it with a big stick."

Nahum couldn't hide his surprise. "I thought you liked to preserve things. You didn't have to set it off. You could have avoided it!"

Ash stopped again as they reached the top of the rise and a break in the trees. He put his hands on his hips as he studied the surrounding gardens. He finally faced him, his eyes glittering with pleasure as Gabe joined them again. "We could have avoided it, of course. But someone is watching us. Or watching the castle, or Theo. We decided not to disappoint them."

Nahum knew that expression well. His brothers were hunting, and the chase was intriguing.

However, before he could ask more questions, Gabe interrupted their conversation. "I gather that Niel is here. He's given chase to the intruder."

"Intruder?" Ash's eyes widened as he stared at Nahum. "You kept *that* quiet."

"You were on a roll." He turned back to Gabe. "Has he found the suspect?"

"Not so far. Shadow virtually told me to get lost while she watched him. After giving me an earful of abuse for scaring her." He looked sheepish. "She was worried."

"We all were! Which brings me back to your insane idea to trigger the explosion. Please tell me you have a plan! Are you planning on pretending you're dead or something?"

"No! That would be far too inconvenient," Gabe said with a frown. "We will let Theo spread the word that we have given up. That all clues have been destroyed, and we fear there is no way forward now. Let the opposition relax."

"And in the meantime?" Nahum asked.

Ash pointed across the ground to a colonnaded folly with a domed roof surrounded by shrubbery and plants. "We investigate *that*."

"Why?"

He smiled. "Follow me."

Niel had been planning on flying low over the walled garden in an attempt to spot their intruder, but the flash of lights and wail of sirens had made that impossible.

As soon as the bomb exploded, all three of them had lost track of the suspect as they turned to watch the flames tear up the night sky. Shadow swore as her aim went wide, and her arrow thudded into the wall. Similarly furious with himself, Niel focussed on the ground again, and made a split-second decision to pursue the figure while Nahum raced in the other direction.

He landed in the shadow of the wall, his back to the stone, folded his wings behind him, and waited. Nothing stirred. The intruder was stealthy and quick. Niel plucked Shadow's arrow out of the wall, and proceeded along the back of the wide border, the large perennials and climbing plants at the rear serving both to mask his movements and thwart his every step.

He finally reached the gate into the walled kitchen garden. He edged inside, waiting in the doorframe. A flicker of movement against the far wall caught his eye. He crouched and crept down the gravelled path, but no matter how hard he tried, every now and again the crunch of gravel gave him away. Abandoning all pretence, he ran instead, sprinting along the paths by the most direct route. Unfortunately, by the time he reached the spot, no one was there.

But a large tree was overhanging the garden wall.

Niel leapt up and grabbed a branch, hoping it wouldn't snap beneath his weight, and then clambered up and along it. On the other side of the wall was the park-like grounds, dotted with trees. He waited and watched again. While he studied the dappled shade, he reflected on the figure he'd seen, and the niggling suspicion of who he thought it might be.

It had been hard to judge from atop the tower, but on the ground, the brief glimpse of the figure had revealed they were slight of build and short. The suspect's movements had been deft, and had hardly caused any damage when progressing along the border. He recalled the almond eyes and petite build of the intruder at the farmhouse. *Mouse.* He was sure it was the same person.

But Mouse had been working for The Orphic Guild, recruited by Mason and JD to interfere with the hunt for the Dark Star Astrolabe. They wouldn't have recruited her this time. She was obviously a freelancer, which perhaps meant Nicoli had employed her. *Maybe she had broken into the library, too. But was she the bomber?*

Niel considered his conversation with her. *No.* If he was any judge of character, she wasn't a bomber. Although, maybe he just didn't want her to be one. He may have seen her only once, and briefly at that, but her eyes were imprinted in his thoughts. And if it was her, he wanted to catch her for several reasons.

Unfortunately, however, the longer he sat there searching the grounds, the more certain he was that she had escaped. He slipped from his perch and set off on foot, determined to find something.

Sixteen

E stelle spotted a dark van exit a side road and pull onto the lane behind them, barely a couple of miles from the barn.

"Barak!"

"I see it. I can't risk going any faster, or we'll crash."

Lucien leaned forward, head poking between the seats. "Is it them? What did you call them? Black Cronos?"

"Yep. And their trademark black van—just like the one we're in." Barak glanced at Estelle. "Your spell?"

"In place!" But the words *trademark black van* took ominous shape in her head. "They're tracking our van. They must be!"

Barak swore, but remained focussed on the road. Estelle consulted the map on her phone. It was still dark, hours away from dawn, and she wondered if they'd done the right thing by moving, but it was too late to debate that now.

"In another couple of miles, we'll be on the outskirts of a small town. Lots of winding roads. We might be able to lose them and swap cars."

Barak cocked an eye at her. "Are you suggesting we steal a car?"

"Do you have a better idea?"

"No."

Lucien stared at them. "Who the hell are you two? International spies?"

Estelle liked the sound of that. It was glamourous, if dangerous. She hedged. "Not exactly. Our job is varied. Right now, you're the priority. But I'd like to see Barak in a tuxedo at a casino. He'd look good as 007."

"And you wearing a floor-length evening gown, draped in diamonds? I could handle that."

"*Mon Dieu*. At least you love your work." Lucien seemed to have recovered from his earlier shock, despite the fact that he kept glancing nervously out of the tinted windows behind him. "I have no idea what I will do...if I survive. That van is getting closer."

"Love is a questionable word right now!" Barak braked hard to take the next turn before accelerating again. A break in the vineyards showed another lane on the left, another van travelling swiftly along it, ready to intercept them.

"Barak!" Estelle shouted. "Floor it!"

A boom shook the back of the van, and the rear wheels snaked across the road before Barak could wrest it back under control.

"What the hell was that?" Lucien asked, his voice rising with fear.

Estelle twisted in her seat, just about able to see the flash of a weapon in an outstretched hand coming out of the passenger-side window. "One of their weird weapons!"

Barak gave her a sidelong glance. "Any magic you can use to help us?"

"Lucien," she warned, "you may wish to look away."

Estelle wound down the window, and promptly blasted the hedge behind her. It erupted into flames, and with a grasping motion, she pulled part of the hedge out of the ground and flung the shrubs across the road. She magnified the fire, making a huge wall of flames. Not even seeing the van's response, she looked ahead. The other black van was racing to intercept them, and they were due to hit the intersection at the same time.

Estelle didn't have time for finesse, and while travelling in a moving vehicle, performing any kind of earth magic was hard. She also couldn't see the drivers, which made it difficult to cast any kind of spell on them. She liked to see who she was aiming at. She opted for the most straightforward plan of attack.

"Barak, open your window!"

"I'm driving!"

"Fine! I'll do it my way!"

When they reached the intersection, mere seconds ahead of the enemy van, she hurled a white-hot ball of energy just under Barak's nose. It shattered the driver's side window and hurtled through the other van's windshield, causing the van to veer through the hedge and into the vineyard, where it thudded to a stop in a plume of earth and splattering plants. Barak didn't stop, racing onwards down the dark lane towards the twinkle of street lights.

Lucien leaned forward again, staring at her. "What was that?"

She studied his expression. He wasn't scared. He was curious. "Magic. I'm a witch. A good one."

"Glad you're on my side."

"They have plenty of tricks up their sleeve. We're not out of it, yet."

"No, we're not." Lucien pointed to a van bouncing along a rutted track at the edge of a vineyard to their right. "There's another one."

"For fuck's sake," Barak said. "They'll reach the road ahead of us."

Estelle knew she didn't have the power to lift the whole van out of their way, and even if she blasted it, it would still block their path. "Stop the van."

"Are you insane?"

"No. Do it."

Barak screeched to a halt, and Estelle leapt out and ran in front of their van as Black Cronos crashed through a gate and onto the lane. A flash of a weapon gave her split-second warning, and she threw up a protective shield just as a fireball roared towards her. It stopped as if it had hit a wall only feet away.

The van swerved towards them, and Estelle braced herself. She had one chance to get this right, because she had no doubt that the van would block their way as the soldiers attacked them. She threw two balls of pure energy under the van, then lifted her hands and used the power she had just released and the vehicle's own momentum to lift it. She almost staggered from the concentration it required, but she couldn't stop now. The van lifted higher, but it was still on a collision course and not nearly high enough to clear their own vehicle.

It was going to crash right into them.

And then a flash of darkness to her left almost took her breath away.

Barak exploded from the driver's side of the van like a bullet, wings shooting outwards as he leapt beneath the van and lifted it himself. He flipped it aside, and it landed on its roof in the vineyard, glass shattering and metal groaning from the impact. Estelle followed it up with a blast of fire.

"Get in!" Lucien yelled. "I see more on the hill!"

On the narrow rise above them, headlights raced along an unseen lane.

Wordlessly, they both leapt back into the van, and Barak accelerated.

Estelle focussed on the road, heart hammering and hands shaking. "Head for the centre of town. We need a car park or something."

In a few more moments they were on the outskirts of the town, and unless Estelle was imagining it, curtains were twitching. The last attack had to have been audible from here. Barak slowed down in the town so as not to attract more attention. The roads were lined with shops, houses, and parked cars. He took a sharp turn down a narrow alley that cut between roads, and parked behind a row of shops so they were well out of sight. He pointed to a battered, silver four-door Citroen. "Everyone out. That one will do. Estelle?"

"It will be my pleasure."

She used magic to unlock the car, and after searching the van for anything that would give them away, they swapped vehicles. Seconds later, they were easing away from the alley. Once again, she secured the protection spell around Lucien.

For a few minutes, they were silent and watchful as Barak drove along the quiet streets. It was still dark, but a few other cars were around at this hour. Hopefully, they would blend in.

Estelle leaned back, sighing with relief. She'd never been so terrified or exhilarated in her life. "I think we're okay."

"So where to now?" Lucien asked.

"The safehouse. And our rescue, hopefully." She pulled her phone out again. "I'll pull up the directions."

For what felt like the hundredth time, Harlan explained who he was to the policeman at the end of Theo's drive.

"I'm a friend of Theo's. I've come to help!"

"At two in the morning?" The police officer looked sceptical.

"That's what friends do!"

With a stern frown and a sweeping glance of disapproval, the officer radioed through to a colleague. Harlan waited, his fingers drumming the steering wheel as he studied the blaze of light in the distance. He could only see the castle tower above the trees, illuminated with flashing red and blue lights.

After Jackson had left, Harlan had tipped his bourbon down the sink, packed a bag, and driven to Kent. He hoped Theo would be understanding at the hour of his arrival. He could also check in on JD from there, as he lived only a short distance away. He wanted to know what the wily old dog was up to. Right now, however, he wondered what was going on at the castle. He'd tried to ring Theo, and then Gabe, Ash, and Shadow, but no one answered. Dread settled in the pit of his stomach. He glared at the tight-lipped police officer again. However, with a curt nod, the officer pulled the police tape away, and Harlan was allowed to enter.

Theo was waiting for him outside the huge wooden doors. Everything about him sagged, from his moustache to the old cardigan he'd thrown on over a rumpled shirt. Regardless, he shook Harlan's hand vigorously. "I'm glad to see you. Things have taken a turn for the worse!"

"And then some!" Harlan marvelled at English understatement. "Is everyone okay? What's on fire?"

"There was another explosion at the lodge, but Gabe and Ash are fine. Gabe called Shadow."

"And where's she?"

Theo pointed upwards. "The tower roof. Their two colleagues have arrived." He frowned. "They're all so huge!"

Harlan spotted Nahum's car. "Nahum and Niel, I presume?"

Theo nodded. "Nahum is with Gabe and Ash, Niel is with Shadow. Come in. Get some tea."

"Anything stronger available?"

Theo barked a dry laugh as he herded Harlan inside, masking an almost maniacal desperation. "Of course. I'll join you."

As they reached the entrance hallway, lit only by lamps, Chivers appeared at the end of the hall looking like a spectral apparition, and Theo requested their drinks. "Bring them up to the sitting room, please." He led them up the staircase. "Are you planning on staying, Harlan?"

Harlan looked at him, feeling guilty. "I was hoping to. My bag is in the trunk of my car, but I can stay in the village. I guess you already have a full house. It was presumptuous of me, sorry. I acted on impulse."

"Not at all. The more the merrier. I have enough rooms here to accommodate an army. The way this search is going, I may have to."

He flung open the door of the sitting room, and Harlan gasped. The room was in darkness, but the curtains were wide open, revealing the flashing lights of the fire engines and police cars in the woods.

"Holy shit, Theo. That's a lot of people."

"It's not every day I have *two* bombs exploding on my property." He stood at the window, arms crossed and lips pressed tight. "I've started something I never expected."

"But it means you're right. You doubted yourself earlier. You can't anymore. The theft at the library, the bombed lodge, Nicoli's involvement, and possibly others." Harlan grinned at him, unable to hide his enthusiasm, despite the night's events.

Theo nodded, a twinkle returning to his eyes. "You're right, of course. I'm just tired."

"Shouldn't you be down there?"

"There's nothing I can do. I saw enough this afternoon. Actually, yesterday afternoon."

"Where have Gabe and the others gone now?"

"To the pavilion. I don't know why. Ash had an idea, apparently."

Harlan nodded, gazing across the grounds. *What were they looking for now?*

Gabe stood at the entrance to the pavilion, finally understanding what Ash had seen earlier. "I see it now. The old marks on the ground. Looks like foundations. Tricky to make out from here, though."

Nahum was walking across the dry, sun-baked grass, brown and stubbly from the hot summer weather. "But what's the significance of them?" And then a knowing smile crossed his face. "The old chapel."

Ash nodded. "I think so. The hot weather has dried the ground so much that it's exposing the old foundation. It would be easier to see from above, but that's impossible in the day, and it certainly is right now." He nodded to the flashing lights of the emergency vehicles across the park. "They'll search the grounds soon. It's inevitable."

Gabe nodded, staring beyond them to Temple Keep. "The castle, too. Although, I doubt there'll be a bomb in there, not with all the staff around."

"It depends who planted the bombs and how determined they are. And what's at stake," Nahum reasoned. "So, what do we do with these foundations?"

Ash paced across the faint outline of the depression in the grass. "I wanted to see if perhaps there was something underground, that might now be under the pavilion."

"Like a crypt?" Nahum asked, looking doubtful.

"Possibly."

While his brothers investigated the old site marked on the grass, Gabe studied the inside of the pavilion. It had a huge porch entrance supported by pillars, and set within it were two wooden doors that were currently wedged open. Three of the walls had large windows set into them, offering views of the gardens and a pond, and the centre of the space was filled with wicker furniture and rugs. The perfect summer spot for relaxing. Maybe Ash was right, and the pavilion had been the chapel, a decent distance away from the house. *But why knock it down?*

He examined the floor. It was lined with huge stone tiles, and was elevated off the ground by about a foot. High foundations, which could hide all sorts of things. *But...* He stepped to the doorway again. "This is probably a concrete foundation, Ash. It's nuts. We can't destroy the pavilion just to get under it on a whim!"

Ash was already heading around the side, but he paused to answer Gabe. "I'm not saying we dig it up, but I am curious. I think we should eliminate it."

"Or find a good reason to dig it up," Nahum added. "You need more than a hunch, otherwise it's a gigantic waste of time. Did you even see a chapel on the maps of the grounds? This could have been anything. Maybe another old summerhouse that was knocked down to make way for this one."

Ash shook his head, looking more doubtful by the moment. Gabe knew he'd been excited about this possibility, but now... Glancing around the grounds again and seeing no one approaching, Gabe flew to the flat roof above. He crouched at the end and peered over the side.

"I can see the old foundations clearly from here. They *do* seem to disappear under this building."

"But," Nahum argued, "it could have been *anything*. You guys have gone mad. The bombs have addled your brain."

Gabe didn't answer. *Maybe they were going about this wrong.* They'd been here less than twenty-four hours, and in that time, he'd already been nearly killed twice. Although it was important to act quickly, they also needed to be smart about it. He stood up, surveying his surroundings. The summer house was to the rear of the grounds. Only a short distance away was the hamlet of Temple Moreton, named after the keep and the family who owned it. The cluster of rooftops huddled close together. If he remembered correctly, Theo had said that land had been sold from the estate years before. Perhaps the village had once been part of the grounds—owned by William de More and his descendants. Perhaps there was a chapel there, or something worth searching in one of the houses—if any of the original ones were still standing.

Seeing lights moving towards them from the woods, he ducked and dropped to the ground on the far side of the pavilion. "I've had another idea," he announced to his brothers.

"What idea?" Nahum asked suspiciously. "I'm knackered, and wasn't expecting to be digging up the grounds in the middle of the bloody night."

Gabe grinned as he slapped his shoulder, directing his brothers back towards the house. "There'll be no digging tonight! Don't worry, sleeping beauty, your bed awaits. This can wait until tomorrow."

Seventeen

Jackson studied Lucien Moreau, noting the man looked as exhausted as he felt. *Not surprising, really.* Both of them had been up most of the night trying to reach the safehouse, and he was struggling to keep his eyes open. *At least*, Jackson reflected, *he hadn't been shot at.*

It was just before seven on Friday morning, and they were in the living area of a small apartment in Méthamis. Jackson and a team of six armed men and women, one of them with medical training, had arrived only fifteen minutes earlier. Four of the team members were out on the street, looking inconspicuous as they surveyed the area. A couple were in the apartment. Estelle and Barak had summarised their story, surprised to see Jackson with the team. The medic checked over Lucien and dressed his head wound while they talked.

"Where are you taking me?" Lucien asked. "And can you keep me safe?"

"We have another safehouse in London," Jackson told him, trying to look like this was something he arranged every day. "It will also be guarded by a small team at all times, but you need to confirm that you'll comply. If you leave on your own—as in, sneak off—we can't guarantee your safety."

"I have no wish to die! Or be recaptured! But equally, I do not wish to be experimented on by you, either!" Lucien's French accent was strong, but his English was excellent. His pale brown eyes were sharp, and Jackson felt he was being assessed, as were the rest of the team. Under these circumstances, he would do the same.

But although Jackson could sympathise, he was also frustrated. "We're not monsters, but we do need to check you over. Try to understand what they were doing with those tattoos." The symbols and sigils were entwined so closely, it was hard to see where one ended and the other began. "However, in order to understand them properly, we'd like you to stay at our headquarters for a while. You won't see where it is, or how you enter, but you will be safe there. Secure."

"Another lab?"

Barak answered first. "Not like the facility you were in. I've been there, and I can vouch for Jackson. You'll have your own room, too."

Lucien looked at Barak and Estelle. "Is that where you were given your powers? Your wings?"

"You mean my magic?" Estelle looked shocked for a moment, and then her stance softened. "No, I was born with it. I doubt anything anyone could do to you would give you my powers."

"And nothing will give you my wings, either," Barak added.

Jackson could only imagine the conversation they'd had following their attack. The fact that they had both shown their paranormal abilities to Lucien indicated how much pressure they had been under. He was also getting nervous with all the explaining, but he knew that to force Lucien would be the wrong thing now. He wasn't a prisoner; he was an asset. A valuable one.

Jackson tried to be reasonable. "Look, Lucien, I desperately want you to come with us. Black Cronos are dangerous, and I have my own personal reasons for getting involved in searching for them. But at the end of the day, I'm not going to force you to comply. This is an extraction team—that's all. We're taking you to safety. If you're not happy, you can walk out of that door right now. I won't stop you. I will, however, wish you luck, because Barak and Estelle will no longer be your body guards."

Lucien nodded, his eyes dropping to the floor for a brief moment before addressing Barak and Estelle again. "You two are coming, too?"

"Actually, no," Barak answered.

Jackson's head whipped around to stare at them. "You're not? Why?"

"Estelle and I have been thinking. We'd like to keep searching here. We've rattled them now. We might be able to find out more. And we have those notes we'd like to investigate."

"But they've seen you! They may even still be searching for you."

"They *might* have seen us. We knocked out all of their cameras, and were fighting mostly in the dark. It's a risk we're prepared to take." Estelle smiled. "Plus, we are better equipped than most to deal with them. And I have connections here. I've already sourced us somewhere secure to stay, and a car. I won't tell you where, though. Not yet."

Jackson studied their set expressions. He knew better than to try to talk them out of it. "I won't deny that I'm worried, but equally, anything else you can find out will be fantastic. Obviously, on our end, we'll keep investigating the family and their connections. You need to send me copies of what you found in the office, too."

Barak nodded. "Thanks, Jackson. After seeing that place, we are doubly motivated to keep going. We'll keep you informed, and you need to let us know how Lucien is doing, too. Do you need us to go with you to the airport?"

Jackson glanced around to the team leader, David Miller, standing behind him. Miller was ex-military. He had a sidearm under his jacket, but as Waylen had stressed, the team was there for protection only. They were not an assault team. He wasn't sure Miller would make the distinction, though. He made Jackson nervous just looking at him, even though he knew he was on his side. "Do we need extra help?" he asked him.

He shook his head. "We're just fine."

"In that case, bring the van around," Jackson instructed him.

While the man radioed his team, and his companion instructed Lucien as to their next steps, Jackson moved aside to speak to Barak and Estelle privately. "Are you sure you know what you're doing?"

Barak laughed. "That's a matter to debate, but we know *who* we're up against."

"What will you do next?"

"Go to Estelle's place, and get some sleep first." He pointed at his eyes, which to Jackson looked perfectly fine. "See these bags? I'm shattered! There's only so much excitement even a Nephilim can take. Then we'll work on our next move." He lowered his voice, shooting a glance at Lucien before continuing. "From what Lucien said to us earlier, I think that if you play this right, he'll join the cause."

"Why? What did he say?"

"He's running from something. Looking for a change. He seemed...excited by what we did. He even said he had no idea what he was going to do next."

Jackson looked over at Lucien, excitement stirring at the possibilities. "That would be useful, especially if we could activate those tattoos somehow. I'll need to investigate him first, though."

Estelle leaned in. "You're going to involve JD, I presume?"

"Once we've run our own tests. Although, I'm worried what JD will say—or do. I don't want to scare Lucien. But..."

Barak finished his sentence. "JD is your best shot. And he'll be way ahead of your team."

Jackson nodded, already planning his next step. The Retreat, background checks, blood tests, scans, everything health-related, then JD. *If* he could convince Lucien. He needed to play it right.

Shadow stretched luxuriously across Gabe's chest, listening to the steady thumping of his heart that was always so reassuring, even when he was snoring. And even when he smelled of smoke and fire, like he did now.

Not that she smelled much better. They had both showered before bed, sluicing off the black soot that had been ingrained on their skin and in their hair. It had infiltrated her nose and her ears, and she could still taste it.

She studied Gabe, noting the slightly singed edge of his thick, dark hair. It was lucky he and Ash had escaped from the second blast with so little damage. They had arrived back at the castle with a determined swagger to their stride, discussing their plans for the next day. Not that they could discuss them for long. The police had arrived, asking plenty of questions. Fortunately, Gabe and Ash had managed to shower first, and had successfully denied being anywhere near the second blast. The grounds would be teaming with people today. Apparently, a bomb disposal squad was going to sweep the castle. It was only because Theo was rich and influential that they were able to stay at the keep overnight. The police had warned them that they were there at their own risk until the morning.

And then there was the intruder. She had watched from the tower as Niel continued to search on foot, but the blast had allowed the would-be thief to vanish. He had told her of his theory, but as Shadow had never met Mouse, she had to trust his judgement. They hadn't told the police about the intruder. That was something *they* would deal with.

Shadow rolled onto her back and stared at the high ceiling, thinking they needed to get up. The trail was going cold. Just as she was about to roll out of bed, Gabe's hand snaked out and pinned her down.

"Where do you think you're going?" He nuzzled into her neck, stretching against her.

"I was going to have another shower, because I still stink of smoke. As do you."

"Good. We can both stink together." He opened one eye, squinting at her. "We can shower together, too."

"We have things to do! Lots of things. Like tracking down bombers and thieves, and discovering what the dagger's mysterious symbols mean. And finding gold, of course." She showered kisses along his neck as she said, "Lots...of...lovely...gold."

"Yes, but there'll be more bombs, and threats, and also the police. Lots of police." He kissed behind her ear. "Staying here is better."

She giggled. "Like all of that would put you off the hunt! Besides, if we don't get out of here quickly, the police will question us for hours."

"They've already questioned us for hours. How much more can they ask?"

Shadow may be new to this world of police and rules and bomb squads, but she knew enough to realise that this was serious, and despite the fact that Theo had employed them, they looked suspicious. "We arrived twenty-four hours ago, and there have been two bombs set off since then."

Gabe grunted, finally opening both eyes. "We were nearly killed. They can't possibly think we're to blame."

"But it looks bad! They were asking Theo all sorts of questions last night—especially about the Templar gold. It sounded like they thought he'd gone mad."

Gabe propped himself up on one elbow, looking down at her. "How do you know that?"

"I eavesdropped after the second bomb, which by the way—" she poked him hard in the chest, "scared the crap out of me! You could have called first!"

"Sorry." He leaned in and kissed her. "We were excited."

"Excited? You're madder than I am."

"And that's why we're perfect together." His eyes flamed with desire, but curiosity won over. "Go on."

"I watched the action from the tower for some time, wondering if anyone would appear to witness the destruction."

"The bomber, you mean?"

"Yes, or the mysterious intruder."

"They might have been one and the same."

"Perhaps. Unfortunately, all the emergency vehicles and police made that impossible. I noticed the village lights going on, and the casual passer-by in a car gawking from the lane, but nothing suspicious was happening. The intruder had vanished, and Niel was coming back to the keep. I went downstairs then. I was thinking I should listen to the staff gossip, but ended up overhearing Theo instead. And then I bumped into Harlan."

Harlan had gone to bed by the time Gabe had arrived back, and he said, "How's he doing?"

"He was worried about us, and furious with Nicoli. But he's fine. Just knackered. He had news about Barak, too."

"Barak?" Gabe tensed. "Is he okay?"

"Yes, but it's a long story."

"In that case," Gabe leaned in for another kiss, his hand sliding down her body, "you can tell me later. I've got other things on my mind right now."

She teased him a little. "You don't want to know about their encounter with Black Cronos?"

He tensed again. "But they're okay?"

"Yes."

"Then no. Later." And with that, he lowered his head, and she surrendered to the moment.

Breakfast, Niel decided, felt more like a council of war. It was fortunate that the food was excellent, or he might have complained about the subject matter.

Harlan, Shadow, and his brothers were all dressed casually in either khakis or jeans, but Theo wore a shirt, trousers, and plaid waistcoat. They were sitting around a wooden table in an informal dining room on the ground floor of the castle that overlooked the moat. The windows were open wide to welcome in the warm breeze, and he could hear the gentle lap of the water against the stone walls.

Harlan was scowling at the other end of the table, having just described his encounter with Nicoli. "Unfortunately," he said, savagely buttering his toast, "I don't think that Nicoli did plant the bombs. Jackson was right. It's not his style."

"Any idea who might have?" Gabe asked. He looked calm and in control, despite the events of the previous few hours. Gabe did not rattle easily.

"Not yet. I'm running through potential rivals. Unfortunately, or perhaps fortunately, none of them are usually this overtly violent."

"A new player?" Nahum asked.

"Perhaps. Or an old one that is very motivated."

Theo was twirling his moustache, and despite his obvious worry, was looking more animated this morning. "I shall just be much happier when the police have searched the house today. The thought of there being a bomb in here is quite terrifying."

Niel stared at him, bacon halfway to his mouth. "And yet you didn't want to move out last night?"

"Absolutely not! I will not be driven from my home by these thugs!" He banged the table with his fist.

Niel had to give the old man credit. He was belligerent, and not easily intimidated. Not many would be willing to stick around after two bombs had exploded on his property.

"As much as I would like to investigate the possibility of hidden rooms in this house," Ash said, "I think that would be a bad idea until the whole place has been thoroughly investigated."

"You think something else is hidden here?" Shadow asked.

"It's possible. The blade was hidden here. I doubt the treasure will be, though."

Niel snorted. "No. That would be far too easy."

"There might be other clues to its whereabouts, though."

Theo's fingers drummed on the table. "But don't forget that I have refurbished much of this castle over the years. I found a priest hole in one of the bedrooms, but that would have been added much later. Most of the cellars were converted to the cinema room, and all have been damp-proofed." He grimaced. "The moat makes life difficult."

A thought struck Niel. "The moat is original, then?"

"Oh, yes. It was part of the original castle."

Niel peered out of the window at it. The water looked black in the shadow of the building, the sun still behind it at this hour. It looked low as a result of the recent dry weather, and he could see where the water level had been. The stones that were revealed were old and stained with lichen and mosses. "Has it ever been drained?"

"No, but I've had it cleaned occasionally."

"Thinking of having a swim?" Ash asked Niel, his eyes dancing with laughter.

Niel shrugged. "It just struck me that hiding something in the brickwork of the moat could be a possibility."

Shadow's nose wrinkled with dislike. "It looks dirty! You wouldn't be able to see a thing down there."

"And it's big," Harlan added. "That would take a long time to search."

"Unless you drained it," Nahum suggested.

"Drain my moat?" Theo looked outraged. "That would be a nightmare! And expensive. Not to mention messy. No!"

Niel could feel outrage flowing from Theo, but mainly amusement and incredulity from everyone else, and he held up his hand for calm. "Chill out, people. I just thought I'd throw it into the mix. Besides, some moats can be constructed of dirt, too. Parts of this one could be." He stared down into the water again, wishing he'd never mentioned it. Certainly no one was going to volunteer to swim in it, and he didn't want to, either. "Forget it! Just a question."

Gabe eyed him speculatively, and Niel waited for the inevitable, but then he just shrugged and poured himself more coffee. "Which is why I want to focus on the village, Temple Moreton. Theo, in the records you've read, there are a lot of details about the Templars and their contacts. Is there anything about who William de la More would have trusted?"

"Well, there were other knights, of course, and sergeants. I can refresh my memory. And his son and family, naturally."

"Good. What about servants?"

"Perhaps, but I doubt their names would have been recorded. They wouldn't have been considered important enough. Why?"

"The hamlet was once on these lands, right? Part of the feudal system that existed then?"

Theo nodded. "And still does, although not quite in the same way. Many grand estates still own vast tracts of lands and villages, and those who live there are tenants."

Harlan huffed with astonishment. "You think something is hidden in the village? In a house?"

"Perhaps," Gabe reasoned. "I could be completely wrong, but some of the houses might be as old as this castle. A church, perhaps."

Theo brightened. "There is a church there, of course. I'm not sure of its age, but I think it's as old as the castle. I'm not a religious man, but have been in there once when I first bought the estate."

Ash nodded, leaning forward. "I thought there might once have been a chapel on the grounds. There are old foundations out by the pavilion, and the only reason we can see them now is because of the weeks of sunshine that has dried the ground. But Gabe thinks it's unlikely, and he could be right. The other option is that we look at William's associates. Other manor houses in the area, perhaps. We were talking last night, and wondered if the bombs were meant to kill us, scare us, or just make us think we are too late."

"What if we *are* too late?" Harlan asked. "Say someone has other clues that have given them a way forward."

"But we have the dagger," Theo protested.

"Yes, we do," Niel said, spearing a forkful of scrambled eggs. It wasn't as delicious as one of his breakfasts, but it was pretty good. "And we wouldn't have had an intruder trying to break in last night if it was unimportant."

"Of course. I'd forgotten about the intruder," Harlan said.

"Which brings me to my observation," Niel said, staring at Harlan. "From the admittedly brief glance I had of the potential thief last night, it looked suspiciously like Mouse."

"Mouse!" Harlan crashed his mug on the table. "But we use her!"

"That's what I thought. But she's freelance, right?"

Theo was looking between them, bewildered. "A mouse?"

"Not *a* mouse. Mouse." Niel held his hand up. "About yay big, petite, stealthy—almond eyes."

Shadow grinned. "Memorable, were they?"

"Actually, yes!"

Before she could make any further comment, Harlan sighed. "She's one of the best in the business. We have to be careful if you're right and it is her."

"It will be my pleasure to keep watch," Niel said, smiling broadly at Shadow's smirk.

"Which means," Ash said, "that the dagger has to be my focus today. I also need to look at those notes I made yesterday, check Theo's information, and cross-reference everything we have."

"In which case," Gabe said, "the rest of us need to get out of the house; let the police do their thing. We'll head to the village."

Anxious to search for signs of Mouse, Niel said, "I was going to check the grounds in the daylight. I might learn something new. Try to confirm it was Mouse."

"Why don't we help search the village first, and then I'll join you later?" Nahum suggested. "Two of us will make light work of it."

"Fair enough," Niel said, pushing his plate away. "Harlan, did you say that Nicoli is the one who stole those papers from the library? Do we need to steal them back?"

Ash intervened. "Not yet. See how I fare today."

"Well, I'm aiming to help you guys, but I need to see JD first," Harlan said, finishing his coffee and looking wistfully at the empty cafetière. "I have other things to discuss."

Niel knew what he was cryptically referring to. He had managed to speak to Barak before breakfast, and was reassured to hear that he and Estelle were both unharmed. Unfortunately, Barak had given him only the briefest rundown of what had happened, and said he'd be in touch when they were settled elsewhere and had rested.

Theo stood. "I'll leave you all to it. I realise you have things you may wish to talk about privately. I'll be in my study looking for those names, if anyone wants me."

Ash nodded. "I'll join you soon."

As soon as Theo left the room, everyone turned to Harlan, but Nahum asked the question that they all wanted to know. "What's happening with the prisoner?"

"Jackson has collected him this morning, and they are on their way back to London." He checked his watch. "The flight is due to leave soon. I'm just hoping Black Cronos hasn't tracked them down again. But he's not *our* prisoner."

"Well, no," Shadow agreed, "but he's hardly likely to be safe walking the streets."

"He'll have to learn to hide from them," Gabe mused. "Disguise himself, somehow. Or be prepared to fight them."

"Or join them," Nahum suggested, clearly distrustful of the man already.

"Or join *us*," Niel added. "Barak mentioned that he could be interested in joining the PD—if approached correctly."

Harlan nodded. "Jackson mentioned something similar, but our conversation was brief."

"And JD?" Nahum asked. "What will he do in all this?"

"That's exactly what I want to find out!" Harlan stood, his chair scraping back. "Wish me luck, and let's hope he doesn't piss me off as much as he usually does."

Eighteen

Harlan was surprised to find that JD wasn't in his lab, but in the glass-walled room at the top of his house.

It was very hot, despite the open windows and lowered blinds. JD was wearing an informal shirt with huge, billowing sleeves that made him look like a renaissance artist, his glasses perched on the end of his nose as he studied a star chart.

"Looking for something in particular, JD?" Harlan asked, standing next to him.

"I'm working on a formula that you wouldn't understand, something that needs a certain planetary alignment. I need to time it perfectly."

Harlan was glad he hadn't bothered to describe the details. "Fair enough. How are the weapon experiments going?"

JD snorted. "They're going, that's about as much as I can say. I take two steps forward and one step back all the time. Some progress, at least." He scribbled some notes on a pad, placed his glasses into his top pocket, and finally focussed on Harlan. "You look pensive. Is there an issue?"

"Sort of. I have news." He relayed Barak and Estelle's success.

"*Château du Buade*! I remember that place during the war. Second one, that is. We had the owner under surveillance, but found nothing to link him to Black Cronos. Collaborators, though." JD's eyes clouded with memories.

"So I gather."

"Many were. Unpleasant, but people did what they needed to do to survive. Horrible news from Layla, though." JD led him to a table where Anna had left them iced water laced with sliced lemons, and poured two glasses, handing Harlan one. "I gather Jackson is upset."

"Very. Which is why he's so pleased by Barak's success." He hadn't yet told him the biggest news, and he watched JD closely. "They found a prisoner, and took him with them. Jackson is taking him to London." He outlined what had happened.

"Good God." JD started pacing. "This could change everything! I want him here."

"I think Jackson would rather you go there. And he has to consent!"

"I know that. I'm not a bloody fool!"

"He's covered in tattoos. Barak thinks it was the start of their process of transformation. He said they had a kind of operating theatre. Estelle found pots of ground metals they mixed with inks."

"Intriguing. I wonder what Layla will find when she analyses the skin around the tattoos on James's body. Good to know they haven't completely vanished after all. Did they find anything alchemical in the facility?"

"I don't think so, but they're forwarding a few things on to Jackson. There was an office there, with a list of what looked like codenames."

"Intriguing. I'd like that list, too. But it will be no good me going to The Retreat. Their equipment is juvenile compared to mine. Lucien needs to come here."

"Well, you might want to rethink that approach, considering we don't know anything about him, but that's between you and Jackson." Harlan was more than happy to stay out of that argument. "Look, I can't stay long. This Templar business is sucking up my time. It's taken an ugly turn. But, is there anything I can do for you before I go?" *Please don't take me to the lab.*

To his utter relief, JD shook his head. "No. What kind of Templar business? What ugly turn?"

"Sorry, I presumed Mason would have told you."

"We don't live in each other's pockets, you imbecile!"

Harlan clenched his fists. This man was infuriating. He took a deep breath and related their latest job.

JD stared at Harlan, frozen in shock. "He found the dagger? In the keep?"

"*The* dagger? Yes. You knew about it?"

"Of course! I searched for it back in the 1800s. Dug half the damn grounds up and found nothing!"

Harlan could feel his mouth gaping open, both of them staring at each other in a ridiculous tableau. "You did? Why?"

"I was part of the search party." JD frowned and rubbed his head. "I can't remember the exact circumstances, but I'll give it some thought. I've been caught up in a few Templar-related treasure hunts. None of them ever yielded anything. They're sneaky buggers."

Why the hell hadn't he thought to ask JD sooner? As far as treasure and religious artefacts were concerned, of course JD would have been interested. "JD, anything you can remember will be immensely helpful. Ruling things out is imperative if we're to get ahead of the competition. We think Nicoli has contracted Mouse to steal the dagger. And, well, I'm sure you've heard about the explosions."

"That was Theo's place?"

"Yes. They blew up his hunting lodge."

"That bloody Masonic monstrosity? Good. But no, it wouldn't have been there. I was a member of a secret society for a while, you know. Well, a couple actually, at different times. Got tired of it. All that ritual, secret nonsense."

Harlan was struggling to find his words. "Unbelievable."

"Everyone of import seemed to be in one at some point, and probably still are. Powerful men get kicks out of secret knowledge. There's a certain crossover with alchemy, you know. Symbols, a hierarchy of knowledge, internal levels of initiation. Much like The Order of the Golden Dawn and The Order of the Midnight Sun."

"What was the group called?"

"The one I was in at the time of the treasure hunt was called The Order of Illumination."

"Are you for real?"

"Of course!"

"Are they still around?"

"Not that I know of. Our mission was the acquisition of knowledge, obviously, particularly pertaining to Templar wealth. But we combined it with religious knowledge—I was still trying to communicate with angels at that point. Of course, I had a completely different name."

Harlan sank down onto the closest chair. *That made perfect sense.* All the links between the organisations and aspirations of higher knowledge, and power. "Surely the freemasons and the Templars were about monetary acquisitions, though."

"Not always. Why do you think they coveted certain religious artifacts? Esoteric knowledge was important to them, and us. Although, obviously the Templars were before my time, they continued in one form or another."

"Including the Order of Illumination?"

"Oh, no. That was no old order. It was started by a member of the aristocracy in 1789."

Harlan wished he could read JD's mind. *On second thought, maybe not.* "What aren't you telling me?"

"Something is percolating at the back of my mind."

"Are you well-versed in Masonic and Templar symbology?"

"I was. I'd need a refresher."

"I'm sure Ash will work it out."

"Ah, yes. The Greek scholar." JD's eyes narrowed. "Who do you think the bomber is?"

"We don't know, but we doubt it's Nicoli."

"No. Too inelegant for that viper." JD ran his fingers across his lower lip. "I need to think on this. I'll call you if anything strikes me."

His eyes were clouded as he turned to the window, and effectively dismissed, Harlan left him to his thoughts.

It had taken approximately half an hour to walk around the village, and Nahum leaned on the lychgate that led into the churchyard, waiting for the chapel to be opened up. They had already strolled all around the graveyard after leaving Shadow and Gabe to investigate the inn, and Nahum and Niel were awaiting the arrival of the vicar after seeing a timetable on the main door.

"Well, it's slim pickings here," Nahum observed.

Niel grunted, shifting his weight against the stone pillar that was part of the lychgate, shadows from the plant-wrapped archway falling across his face. "When

Theo said the village was small, he wasn't kidding. He's right about the church, too."
He nodded at the old stone building at the end of the path. "It looks the same age as
the castle. It's bigger than I expected, too."

"As befitting an English commander." Nahum studied the roofline. "It will have
been refurbished. That looks like a new roof. I have trouble thinking anything could
be hidden in that." Movement to his right caught his eye, and he saw the vicar cross
the graveyard from another lane to the side. "There he is. Let's see if we can get in."

The vicar was making his way to the side entrance, and Nahum and Niel quickened their pace to reach him, arriving just in time to see him pushing his way through
the heavy door. He was a trim man of medium height with a thatch of thick grey hair,
who looked to be in his sixties. His eyes widened with alarm as his gaze swept over
them. "Can I help you?"

Nahum extended his hand. "I'm Nahum, this is Niel. We're friends of Theo's
from Temple Keep."

He visibly relaxed as he shook their hands. "Colin Roberts. Vicar of Temple
Church, and a few of the surrounding churches, actually. Terrible business with the
fire. Is Theo okay?"

"He's fine," Nahum reassured him. "But busy with the police and the fire investigation team. It was quite a shock—for all of us." Nahum looked down the side path
and out to the lane, wondering if there was a vicarage they'd missed. "Do you live in
the village?"

"No. In Bodiam. We rotate our services through the surrounding villages, however, and this Sunday the service will be here. I'm checking to make sure everything
is in order." He grimaced. "Good timing, I think. The parishioners will be in need
of support after the recent events."

"Indeed, they will." Niel nodded to the corridor beyond the open door. "We were
hoping we could come in, Father. We're interested in the church's architecture."

"Really? You're men of God?"

Nahum nodded. "Of a sort. It's been a while since we've offered our respects.
Being caught up in the events at Theo's has prompted our wish to be here today."
Not exactly a lie.

"Of course. The Lord's house will always offer sanctuary and respite in troubled
times. If you head to the main door, I'll open it up for you." He bobbed his head and
smiled before heading inside.

Niel snorted as they walked to the main entrance. "Offer our respects! I hope you
don't think I'll be doing *that*."

"Just be polite, at least!"

"Of course. Colin seems a perfectly nice man. Misguided, obviously, but I won't
disillusion him."

"Good." Niel seemed more belligerent than usual. "What's got your goat?"

"Just the feeling that we're barking up the wrong tree. From what Theo has said,
this area must have been researched a million times as regards to lost treasure. We're
covering old ground."

"But with fresh eyes! And besides, we need to get an objective view of everything to move forward." Nahum lowered his voice. "Two bombs, Niel! Theo is on to something."

The door to the church opened before Niel could respond, and Colin welcomed them in, wedging the door open and allowing the sunshine to pour into the vestibule. "Welcome to Temple Church. It's a fine old building. A struggle to maintain, obviously, although Theo is a charitable donor." Colin led them inside, his arms thrown wide. "Isn't it beautiful?"

Nahum took in the rows of wooden pews, the soaring columns leading to a vaulted roof, the elaborate pulpit, and the ornate, stained glass windows. A large altar was at the far end, a towering cross above it, a choir area behind, and a small chapel to either side. A door to the right led to a private area, where Nahum assumed the side entrance was.

"We were saying outside," Nahum said, obviously impressed, "that it's bigger than we expected for a small village."

Colin smiled. "But it's a small village with a big history! The name says it all."

"Do you know much about the Templars?" Niel asked.

"The basics, just like everyone else, I guess. This was constructed by the de la More family at the same time as the keep, but it was added to in later years. Made more elaborate." He shrugged. "All of the men joined the Templars, you know, after they had produced a male heir."

Niel shook his head. "I didn't know that."

Colin nodded enthusiastically, walking down the nave, and they followed him. "The Templars only really wanted older soldiers who had already been married and were prepared to dedicate their life to the order, and poverty. William de la More was typical in that sense. He was a wealthy man, born into nobility, and followed the family tradition. The hamlet and this church were on the grounds for hundreds of years."

Nahum was confused. "So, William was older when he joined, which means he wasn't a Templar long. How did he get to be the master?"

"Oh no, he was with them for years. His wife died young, and he left the children in the care of his sister. All his lands were left to his oldest son. It meant that men like him had no distractions, were mature, and dedicated to the cause. Although, of course by the time William joined them, they were an order known less for the Crusades than their banking. William added to this place, too, you know, once he became the Grand Master."

Nahum looked at the church with renewed interest. "Really? What did he add?"

"The pulpit used to be simpler. He wanted something larger. And the altar was made bigger, too."

"Interesting." Did that mean he had concealed something?

"But you said he made a vow of poverty?" Niel asked.

"They all did. It was a condition of them joining. It was common that many Templars donated large amounts of money or land to the order, some even their entire property; other knights donated smaller amounts and passed on their wealth and property to family. Of course, this made the Templars as an organisation very rich, even though the individual knights were poor. On top of that, they banked other peoples' money and charged *rent*." Colin laughed. "Which meant interest, although they couldn't call it that. William was master for nine years. From 1298 to 1307. This building was added to in 1300." Colin turned and led the way to a small side chapel. There were half a dozen pews and a modest altar at the front. "This was the de la Mores' private chapel." He raised his eyebrows conspiratorially. "Not many know that, actually. We don't advertise it. It seems irrelevant. Catholic, of course, at the time. All of it was."

Nahum tried to quell his rising excitement. *Surely this new information meant something.* "Is it different in any way from the main church?"

"Not particularly. Simpler, of course, but intimate." He pointed to the heavy wooden door. "The family could shut out everything for private worship, although obviously would have joined the main congregation at Sunday Mass. William added the stained-glass window, too. It wasn't the original." The design was of a knight kneeling at the side of a horse, the Templar cross unfurling on a flag, a huge cross dominated the scene. "Simple, but beautiful."

"He did all this, despite his vow of poverty?" Niel repeated, clearly as confused as Nahum.

Colin shrugged. "Perhaps it was deemed Templar business. Or maybe it was done under the auspices of his family. His son was an adult by then, so it didn't reflect on William directly. You have to understand that records are scant to non-existent. However," he pointed up to the vaulted ceiling. "If you look closely, you will see Templar symbols are carved into the stonework."

Something else struck Nahum. "Was the entire village, keep, and church renamed, or was it always called Temple Moreton and Temple Keep?"

"Good question, Nahum! Yes, it was renamed, in honour of William. This hamlet was originally Moreton—'ton' actually means farm or hamlet—and the keep was Moreton Keep."

"Let me guess," Niel said dryly. "The Church was called Moreton Church."

"Our Lady of Moreton Chapel, actually. Then Our Lady of Temple Church. With the dissolution of the monasteries and all things Catholic being banned, it became just Temple Church. 'Our Lady' has strong Catholic overtones."

Nahum studied the church as Colin led them back into the main nave. Such division from Catholicism to the Church of England, and it all came down to divorce, power, and money. Money was never far from any decision. *But was there significance in the renaming and additions to the church, and was it anything to do with treasure?*

"Of course," Colin continued, "The Templars had many buildings and places named after them. Anything with the name 'Temple' in is undoubtedly linked to the Templars. We are certainly not unique."

Niel said, "We walked around the graveyard, but didn't see any graves that might have belonged to the family."

"Oh no, you won't." Colin laughed, his finger running along his white clerical collar. "They were landed gentry." He tapped the ground with his foot. "They are buried below us, in the crypt."

Nahum blinked with surprise, and tried to keep the excitement out of his voice. "There's a crypt? Is the whole family there?"

"I believe so. I confess, I haven't examined the place in detail. It gets cleaned a few times a year." As if anticipating their next question, he said, "We keep it locked, and do not allow the public to go down there. I'm not sure the stonework is that safe, really." Colin checked his watch. "If you don't mind, I really need to check on a few things for Sunday."

"Of course, but one more question," Nahum said quickly. "William de la More died in the Tower of London. Is he down there?"

"No, unfortunately. Only his predecessors and descendants. I can't quite recall when the last one was interred there, though." Colin's eyes narrowed. "This is no casual interest, is it? Is this about Templar treasure?"

"It's a recent interest of Theo's, that's all."

"And the fire? Is that related to this new interest?"

"Perhaps. A bomb was planted in Theo's lodge. Two, actually. He didn't make any secret of his new search. Not locally, anyway."

Colin's joviality vanished, his eyes hardening. "So, others are involved?"

"It seems so."

"I wonder..." For a moment, Colin didn't speak, and he stood in front of the main altar, staring up at the image of Christ on the cross, as if wrestling with something. Nahum exchanged another worried glance with Niel, but they waited silently. Something was troubling the vicar. After a few moments of silent contemplation, he turned back to them. "I think someone broke in here the other week."

"Why?" Niel asked. "Damaged locks? Something stolen?"

"Nothing. That's the thing, so I didn't report it. But things were misplaced. I popped in to pick up some vestments I had left here. The door to the vestry had been left open, and I always shut everything. There was also an unusual air to the place. Something different. I decided that perhaps the cleaner hadn't been as meticulous as usual, but then I found out she hadn't been in. She'd been sick. Never mind. I'm being paranoid."

Nahum had a sudden vision of the bomber sneaking around the church looking for the most likely spot to plant something. "Or perhaps not." He placed his hand on Colin's shoulder, turning him gently towards the door. "I think we should leave. *Now.*"

Nineteen

B arak studied the list they had printed out, a headache settling between his eyes. "This is gibberish."

"It's a code!" Estelle leaned over and kissed his cheek. "We'll work it out."

"We need a key for that, and we haven't got one."

"Yet!"

"You're enjoying this, aren't you?"

"It's a puzzle. I like puzzles."

"I'd rather be naked with you." He kissed her again.

"And you will be," she eventually answered when he released her. "But we need to get somewhere with this. It dictates where we go next!"

"Bed sounds good."

"You have a one-track mind."

"Only with you, Estelle." She smelled delicious. *Apples and honey. Like a pie.* He wanted to eat her up.

She pointed at the list, laughing. "Focus!"

They were in a small *gîte* south of Avignon that belonged to a business friend of Estelle's, and although it was nowhere near as grand as the *château* they had first stayed in, it was beautifully decorated in a rustic French fashion, and very intimate. It was also nestled deep within an olive grove, and while Barak would have preferred something with a view for safety purposes, the flipside was that it was hidden away. Fortunately, it was well supplied with a computer and printer, and they had printed off all the photos they had taken of the facility's office.

They had left the safehouse without any difficulties, and used a taxi to return to their hotel in Avignon. They had retrieved their belongings, left immediately in another taxi, and were dropped off to collect a new rental car from a different company. They hadn't dared risk retrieving the other one at the *château*, and Barak had phoned the company with a terrible excuse as to why they'd had to abandon the car.

"The trouble is," Barak said with a sigh, his attention returning reluctantly to their current problems, "is that whoever, or wherever these places are, they will have been alerted by now."

"Perhaps. But if these are big facilities, then they won't be able to shut down so easily. They'll just increase their security instead."

"Great! Even better!"

She poked him in the ribs. "Or, they will feel sufficiently safe with their code names and current security that they might not feel threatened at all."

"True. They haven't survived this long without being smart and taking precautions. But perhaps we're approaching this the wrong way. If we *are* right, and this is about old connections to the count, then we should cross-reference known places with these names. See if we can identify a link."

Estelle nodded thoughtfully. "That makes sense. Sort of reverse engineer it. It's worth trying."

"But have we brought anything about the count with us? I know I haven't. I travelled light."

"Me, too. But we have the internet. And Jackson. He can send us a list of what he's found so far, and we can start with that."

Barak checked his watch. "It will probably be a few hours before he can speak to us. He'll be busy with Lucien. We can buy a few books, though. I could do with familiarising myself with the count properly. I feel I need to sink into his mind, try to get a feel for the man we're pursuing. And it might distract me from worrying about my brothers, too."

His phone call with Niel had disturbed him. His brothers were well able to look after themselves, but it sounded as if they had run into another powerful enemy.

Estelle squeezed his thigh in an attempt to reassure him. "They'll be okay. Let's focus on our problems. You can always phone them again later."

He sighed, knowing she was right. And besides, he was too far away to help them. Instead, he looked to the bright sunshine outside, and the seating area beneath the trees. "That looks like the perfect spot."

"Coffee and croissants?"

"Even better."

He watched her easy sway of hips as she headed to the kitchen, and felt extremely content. He could get used to this. He just hoped that she could, too.

Gabe stretched his long legs out in front of him, and studied the winding lanes surrounding The Knight's Rest, the inn in Temple Moreton, reflecting on the fact that you'd have to be an idiot not to know this place was connected to the Templars.

He lifted the coffee cup to his lips and sipped it. At least they made good coffee, not that he should be surprised. This might be a small village, but the inn had a reputation as a gastro pub, and there was a large car park to accommodate its visitors. Today, bathed in late August sunshine, it already had a fair number of people drinking coffee in its courtyard area.

The pub had originally had a stable block, and although it had been converted and built on over the years, parts of the building still looked like stables, with its long, low roof that had skylight windows built into it. Gabe was partial to good food and wondered if he should book a table there for him and Shadow. It would be nice to ditch his brothers for a few hours and spend some time alone with her. As big as the castle was, it was starting to feel crowded. He looked around, wondering if she'd managed to see anything interesting after she'd volunteered to scout the place out.

He spotted her sauntering around the side of the building, and within moments she was sitting next to him, a disgruntled look on her face as she reached for her coffee.

"No luck, I take it?" he asked her.

"Not really. There aren't any unusual symbols etched into beams, stonework, or anything else! The main dining area is deserted at this hour, but I passed through it on the way to the toilets and loitered. There's an old stone fireplace in there, but there are no tempting symbols at all."

"Not surprising, really. This place has been renovated to within an inch of its life. Nicely done, but anything original will have been extensively investigated years ago."

"And that's the trouble with this whole thing, isn't it?" Shadow sipped her coffee, her eyes sweeping the courtyard and customers. "Anything that has strong links with the Templars has been investigated by treasure hunters several times over, and no one has ever found *anything*."

"Not that's been publicly acknowledged. Who's to say it hasn't already been found, and is now in some very secure vault somewhere? But I don't actually believe that."

Shadow cocked her head at him. "Why not?"

"If treasure hunters had found it, they would have shouted about it."

"Would they? I wouldn't. I would have kept quiet and sold it off, bits at a time, on the black market. Or kept it in my own secure vault to admire at leisure."

He laughed. "Would you have rolled around in it?"

"Maybe. Probably naked. All that gold and jewels on my bare skin." She gave him an impish grin.

Images flooded his mind and ended in his jeans. "Behave. I'm in public." All she did was laugh, and he focussed on other things. "I've been trying to imagine what kind of treasure it is, though. They were, understandably for a religious order, obsessed with religious artifacts. What if they really did find the Ark of the Covenant or the Holy Grail? Or lost scrolls? Or magical books..." He trailed off, trying to imagine what else they may have found.

"Tell me again what the significance of the Ark of the Covenant is?"

"It contains God's ten commandments, written down by Moses on two stone tablets and encased in a wooden box, covered in gold."

"And was that in your time?"

"Yes. But I never saw them, or had anything to do with them. I was busy elsewhere." *Fighting.* He didn't need to say it. They both knew his history. "The Ark also contained Aaron's Rod, which is a walking stick with mythical properties, and *manna*—a food that can sustain someone over long periods. Now I did try that, and it was impressive. Designed by angels."

Shadow shrugged. "The gold part sounds interesting. Stone tablets, not so much."

"But if you were religious, and deeply devout, that would be quite something, right?"

"I guess so."

Gabe subdued a grin. *At least Shadow was refreshingly honest.* "But there are lots of relics from that time that the Templars might have looked for. Powerful weapons that we carried, for example, or books of power such as that which Raziel made. I mean, honestly, it's endless. They spent years in the Middle East, in all of those places where we lived, loved, and waged war."

"But like you said before, so much would be dust."

"But powerful objects have ways of hiding themselves and remaining annoyingly intact to wreak havoc later on. And gold doesn't disappear, or jewels."

"Thank Herne for that."

Gabe's brain ached with the possibilities. No wonder the Templar history and their fabled treasure had fascinated people for over seven hundred years. He was starting to see why. And powerful organisations didn't just disappear overnight. They just changed and adapted. However, before he could muse on it further, a fire engine and police car sped past them, and his phone pealed on the table.

Nahum.

Ash turned the knife over again, feeling the age in it, and wondered how he could unlock its secrets. He tried to banish all his pre-conceptions, and studied it with cold, analytical eyes.

A Damascus steel blade, double-edged, dull, and its edge blunt. Ceremonial then, not a weapon as such. The bone hilt was yellowed with age, but felt as hard as iron. It was inlaid with a selection of metals in a curling design that framed the symbols, with a row of small emeralds edging the base where it met the blade.

The symbols on the hilt had been burned into it. He could swear he scented the burnt odour of bone from its inscription, but knew that after all this time, he must be imagining it. The largest symbol was the image of two knights on one horse, a typical Templar image, but without writing around it. There was also the de la More family crest, the Star of David, and the cross and the crown. Nothing that remotely suggested where he should go next. Maybe this *was* just a ceremonial knife. It was certainly interesting, but perhaps that was all it was. He had tentatively pushed and prodded some of the symbols, but that was pointless. They were just engravings.

Theo called over from across the room where he sat in a shaft of sunlight. "I have a magnifying glass, if that helps."

"I'm worried I'll break it." He studied it again, turning it over in his hands, the bone warming beneath his touch. "The blade is Damascus steel, you know. That makes it one of the earliest examples. It must have cost a lot at the time. Never mind the emeralds and precious metals set into it."

Theo stood, rummaged in a drawer, and then handed him a small magnifying glass. "All it's worth to me is the information it contains. Why hide a ceremonial knife? I feel sure it means something."

Ash bent his head over it again, and then jerked in shock. "There *is* writing around the two men on a horse image. Herne's balls! It's tiny. I thought it was just an abstract pattern."

"You know what has just struck me," Theo said, almost breathlessly as he sank into the chair next to him. "The two knights on a horse symbol was never used as a seal in England. Only France. The Grand Masters here used the *Agnus Dei*. The lamb of God. Other countries had other seals."

Ash jerked up in shock, staring at Theo, the writing momentarily forgotten. "Is that right? Are you sure?"

"Very. It's what I've just been reading about. All the Grand Masters, or Grand Commanders, as they were also called, had a seal. They used the same seal always—no matter who was the commander. There might have been slight variations, but always *Agnus Dei* in England."

"So, the English commanders, no matter who it was, should have *always* used the *Agnus Dei*?"

"Yes." Theo rose from his chair, grabbed his book, and handed it to Ash as he sat again. "See? A lamb with a crossed foreleg and the cross. It has the cross of St George on it, too."

"Holy shit." Ash handed the book back and picked up the knife again. "Then this is significant. A sign. Either this isn't William's knife, and it has something to do with the French order, or the seal is a clue. But the fact that the family crest is there... The two men on a horse emblem denotes poverty, is that right?"

"Yes. It developed very early on in Templar history. It essentially demonstrates that the knights were so poor that they had to share a horse. I guess it also shows brotherly loyalty. However, one of the many Templar rules forbade two men on the same horse. They were, in actual fact, also allowed to own up to three. The image is just symbolic and does not reflect the truth."

Ash sat back, filtering through the information before finally looking at Theo. "We're on to something, Theo." He lifted the hilt and the magnifying glass again and moved to the window where the light was brighter.

Theo followed him, clasping his hands together almost in prayer. "Can you read it?"

"Not yet." Ash bent over the handle, hardly daring to breathe. Then the words floated into focus, and he realised they were Latin. "Two brothers, united under God." *What the hell did that mean? Two knights? A knight and his sergeant? Two masters?* He bent his head again, and noticed a deeper indentation around the seal than the other marks, and also down an inlaid metallic wavy line running along the length of the hilt, skilfully hidden within the other elaborate designs. He stared at Theo. "I'm going to try something. Something risky."

"Perhaps we should take photos first?"

"Yes, excellent plan."

Ash waited impatiently while Theo took photos, and then picked up Theo's fine-bladed letter opener. He ran it around the edge of the seal, clearing out centuries' old dirt, and exposing the seam even more. With great care, he pushed the seal down. When nothing happened, he hit it harder. Still nothing happened.

"Just whack it!" Theo said, equally impatient next to him.

"Wait!" Ash wanted to do this cleanly.

Earlier, Ash had used an oiled cloth to polish the hilt and blade, and he picked up the bottle of oil and dribbled some around the seal and along what appeared to be a seam. After waiting a few moments for it to soak in, he picked up a pen from the table, fitting the head of the pen neatly over the seal, and used the end of the magnifying glass like a hammer. He cracked it downward, and the seal clicked down. The curving seam that ran the length of the hilt along the silver and gold metalwork split open by mere millimetres.

Theo squealed like a child. "You did it!"

Hardly daring to speak, Ash inserted the fine blade of the letter opener into the seam and eased it open, exposing an ornate key beneath the bone hilt. It was carved from iron, and screwed to the blade.

"I've done *something*, Theo. But what does it open?"

Twenty

Jackson watched a security guard run another metal detector over Lucien's body, and then usher him through the scanner that looked like something you'd find in an airport.

It was a recent installation at The Retreat, and although Jackson resented having to pass through it every day, he had to admit that it made him feel safer.

Lucien lifted his arms obediently and spread his legs wide, and then stepped through at a nod from the guard. "All clear, Jackson."

"You know this is the fourth time I've been scanned," Lucien complained to everyone.

Jackson sighed as he led him down the corridor, four members of the extraction team marching behind them. "I was there every time. I know. But I told you it would happen. At least you're not blindfolded anymore."

Jackson finally felt himself relax, his shoulders loosening from the knots that seemed welded into place from his neck downwards. It had been a tense trip from France to The Retreat, all of them on alert for signs of attack. However, no one had followed them from the safehouse, and they had carefully travelled along main roads with lots of traffic to take them to the private airport. At that point, Lucien had been blindfolded until they stepped into The Retreat's corridors.

Now he looked around, curious at his surroundings. "This is impressive. Your base?"

"Yes, and your home for a while."

"And these men? They're staying, too?"

"For now."

"But you said I wasn't a prisoner."

"They're here to protect this place and those who work in it from you." Jackson's eyes swept over him. Lucien was still wearing the baggy green scrubs and Crocs from the facility, the short sleeves revealing the full range of tattoos on his skin. His sharp face and keen eyes gave him a dangerous air, and Jackson still wasn't sure how much to trust him. He was considering all options, including the possibility that he could be a plant who was activated by Barak and Estelle's unexpected arrival and suddenly put into action. On the journey, Jackson had mulled on the fact that his attempted escape had been suspiciously well-timed, and Jackson was wary of such things. But perhaps the Gods were smiling on them, for once.

A cynical curl of Lucien's lip preceded a snort. "Semantics."

"This is our headquarters. What do you expect? I want to trust you, but there's too much I don't know about you. Would you behave any differently?"

"Perhaps not." Lucien's expression was guarded, but his eyes still flitted everywhere, and Jackson suddenly had misgivings at ever bringing him here. But where else could he go? Not another safehouse...not yet, at least.

"Why are you wearing scrubs?"

"Barak stole them for me. I was in a surgical gown when I tried to escape."

Jackson nodded. Something else to check with Barak and Estelle. He should have asked more questions when he had the time, but everything was so unexpected.

Jackson turned down a side corridor that led to the labs and morgue, and opening a door, gestured him inside a room with a reinforced glass window, an observation room on the other side. "I won't be long."

The guards remained with Lucien while Jackson continued to Layla's medical suite.

She was already in her examination room, her equipment ready—camera, sample kits, and other things Jackson didn't recognise—and was wearing a white lab coat over her clothes. "He's here?"

"In the holding room. Look, I'm worried he might be a plant. I may be paranoid, but..."

"That's okay. I'll keep the guards handy and run lots of tests. I'll take samples of his tattoos too, compare them to the ones I took from James. What's your gut telling you?"

"That he's genuine, but I'm worried to trust my instincts right now. I don't know whether I'm coming or going. Barak and Estelle are convinced he's trustworthy. Said he was shot with a tranquilliser gun and out cold for hours."

"That's good to know. I'll run tox reports." Layla squeezed his arm reassuringly. "I'll chat with him while I work. I have a surprisingly good bedside manner. I'll get some background on him, too."

Jackson smiled and took a deep breath. "Thanks. I have the basics. Last known address, date of birth, full name. I'll see what I can find and let you know. I asked him about conversations he might have heard, but he denied hearing anything, really."

"I'll try again. He's been stressed, as well as drugged. It plays havoc with memory. How long are we keeping him here?"

"Great question. If we think he's untrustworthy in any way, then not long at all. But he could be a valuable asset. A way in. I guess we play it by ear."

"I want you to go home, Jackson. Sleep. Rest. You'll function better afterward. You have also had a big shock in the past day or so."

Jackson nodded, knowing she was right, but time was against him. "There's too much to do first."

"It can wait a couple of hours."

"I'm not sure it can. Be careful."

Jackson's steps quickened as he reached his office, but as he passed Waylen's open door, he heard a shout. "Jackson! You're back."

Jackson leaned on the doorframe, unwilling to step inside and be delayed even more. "Back, but shattered, and with plenty to check up on."

"I can see you're tired." Waylen was wearing his familiar suit and white shirt, and stood and rounded his desk, perching on the edge. "You did well, though."

"Let's hope so."

"You're not convinced?"

"I'm worried he's a plant." He outlined his fears, and then stifled a yawn. "I'm going to run background checks now."

"When was the last time you slept?"

"Maybe the night before last?"

"Then go home and sleep first."

"It will take too long. Barak and Estelle are out there, searching and going through code stuff—which they have hopefully sent to me by now. They risked their lives for this. I can't just sleep. And going home will take too long!"

"That settles it." Waylen headed back around the desk, rummaged in his drawer, then handed Jackson a key. "We're a small team. We work together. I may have put you in charge of this thing, but that doesn't mean I'm about to abandon you. Head down the west corridor, through another locked door. You'll find new sleeping quarters there. Grab the room you like; it's yours from now on—not that I expect you to use it often! List?" He held his hand out expectantly.

Jackson dug into the deep pockets of his long mac, finding sweet wrappers, bits of paper, and sticks of gum, before finally landing on his little pocket book. He pulled it out and ripped out Lucien's details. "These all need checking."

"Good. I'll do it now. Now go. Everything's fine here."

Jackson turned away, feeling his burden lifted. But a new heaviness now dogged his steps. Were Black Cronos searching for them? Was his home still a safe place to be? And worse, would he be living in The Retreat forever?

I t was a raucous dinner that night at Temple Keep, everyone interrupting each other's conversations, and Harlan could barely think straight.

All four Nephilim, Shadow, Theo, and himself, were seated in the informal dining room overlooking the moat, the sun low on the horizon. The atmosphere was a result of the elation of Ash's discovery, and the fact that they'd found another bomb.

"Seriously, guys," he remonstrated, shouting to be heard above the din, "can we all stop yelling? I can't hear a thing except Niel bellowing about bombs! We have a lead! What are we doing with it?"

Niel continued to grumble. "There's a lunatic bomber out there who could have wired a bomb to *anything*. I have every reason to moan! I like all of my limbs exactly where they are. And my ruggedly handsome face needs to stay that way."

Shadow spit her drink out, a spray of wine landing across the remnants of food on her plate. "Did you say that you were *ruggedly handsome*? Have you been reading soft porn or something?"

"I have a mirror, and women stare. A lot."

"Deluded women."

"The lady doth protest too much, methinks."

Gabe glared at him. "Which means what, Niel?"

"Which means that while she may have eyes only for you, she cannot be blind to this!" His hand swept around his face, as if presenting a work of art.

"I most certainly can be, you giant oaf," Shadow protested. "Talk to your hand, why don't you? Perhaps while you're thinking of Mouse!"

Did she mean what Harlan thought she meant?

Now Gabe glared at Shadow. "Seriously? Again? We're in company!"

Theo looked amused. "Don't mind me. I've heard worse around conference tables."

Nahum cocked his head at Niel, unable to hide a smirk. "At least we found the bomb before it went off this time. And I told you not to linger!"

"I took photos! I thought it was important!" Niel was belligerent.

"And," Gabe added, wagging his fork at Niel, "the whole house has been swept. There are no bombs in here."

Harlan massaged his forehead, feeling the tension behind his eyes. He'd grabbed a couple of hours sleep that afternoon after returning from JD's house, but it didn't seem to be helping. "Where was the bomb in the church?"

"In the pulpit," Nahum told him. "Wired to the top step."

"Shit. They meant to kill the vicar? That seems harsh!"

"Apparently," Niel said, rolling his eyes, "it wasn't a big bomb. Enough for a little scare. Like, oh, that's just my leg missing. I'll survive. Do you get my concern now?"

"I doubt it was meant for the vicar," Shadow said. She was twirling her dinner knife with the same dexterity as she twirled her daggers, and Theo was watching, mesmerised. "It was meant for us—or Theo. It was obvious we would have searched the church. I don't like being one step behind."

"At least it gives us a timeframe for the bombs," Harlan said. "It crossed my mind that they could have been planted a while ago, but if the vicar comes here every month, then that can't be the case."

Nahum nodded. "Excellent point, which suggests Theo finding the dagger has triggered everything."

"And now we have the chance to be ahead," Ash told them. "We just have to work out what the key opens."

The dagger was on the table, now in three pieces—the hilt, the blade, and the key that had been unscrewed from a slim metal shaft atop the blade.

"Yes, so easy." Shadow gave him a side-long glare.

Ash continued regardless, but he looked edgy. "We just have to be smart. I've been thinking on those symbols all afternoon, and I have a theory. It's a leap, but possible."

"Do you want a drumroll?" Niel asked.

Ash ignored him. "The symbols are the key. The family crest clearly links the knife to William de la More. But here at Temple Keep? Or at an older family estate—which is where? Does it even exist anymore? Where was he buried? Is that even useful?"

"He wasn't buried at the local church," Nahum said. "But as I mentioned earlier, there is a crypt containing other family members. I'm not sure how many, though. The vicar said it was unsafe, and the public weren't allowed down there. Something to investigate later, perhaps."

"I confess, I never knew about that," Theo said, looking vexed.

"Clearly it's something they don't wish to advertise," Gabe mused.

Ash jotted a note down. "I'll think on that. Which brings me to my next point. The writing around the seal: 'Two brothers united under God'. I thought it might be like a brotherhood, meaning two knights. But it could mean two actual brothers. Did William have a brother? Or did he have two sons?"

"We can check in the family crypt," Theo said.

"Exactly. But more intriguing is why is the Star of David, a Jewish symbol, on the knife hilt?"

Gabe shrugged. "Would it be something to do with Jerusalem, and the Temple Mount where the Templars stayed for a while?"

"Perhaps, but that was well before William's time. But I've had another idea. You won't like it. The Star of David is also the alchemical sign meaning 'as above, so below'."

Harlan was so shocked that he fumbled his fork and it clattered against his plate. "Goddamn it, Ash! That's not funny."

"It's not meant to be." Ash's golden-brown eyes were deadly serious. "What if that's another clue to what the key leads to? Something alchemical. The Templars were all over the Middle East, north Africa, Europe. They were avaricious in their search for powerful objects—usually religious, but not always. The other clue is the emeralds around the base of the hilt." He stared around the table meaningfully.

Gabe groaned, dropping his head on the table, and Theo looked at him and then the rest of them in shock. "What?"

It took Harlan a moment to catch on and then his eyes widened. "You think it's the Emerald Tablet of Hermes Trismegistus. The actual *original* tablet?"

"It's possible, right?" Ash said.

Nahum frowned. "But everyone knows what it says! Translations are available, and have been for years."

"But they aren't the original tablet." Ash pushed his plate aside and pulled his notebook towards him. "The text is available in multiple languages, both shortened and longer versions. It's cryptic and odd. But the phrase, 'That which is above is like to that which is below, and that which is below is like to that which is above,' comes from that document. From my admittedly limited understanding, it underpins all alchemical principles." He picked up the hilt, which opened like a book on tiny hidden hinges. "It has emeralds on it. Why emeralds, out of all the gems you could pick? It's a sign. The original document is thought to be inscribed on actual emerald—hence the name. It could contain all sorts of coded messages."

A horrible fear settled in Harlan's stomach, and from the grim look on Ash's face, he hadn't shared all of his thoughts. Harlan huffed, thinking of JD's news that he had yet to disclose. "You think other alchemists are after this? Is this Black Cronos again? The count?"

"Oh, fuck! Don't tell me it's *them* again!" Niel was red-faced and furious. "I came here for a treasure hunt, not to fight some bomb-wielding Black Cronos mercenary!"

"Let them come!" Shadow said. "I relish it."

"Slow down!" Ash held his hand up. "I have been reviewing a few things this afternoon. The Count of St Germain was known to be involved in many things. We believe he is behind Black Cronos, but we don't know for sure. Barak and Estelle's progress suggests that yes, it looks more likely. But the count was also linked with several secret societies. The Freemasons, the Templars, the Rosicrucians, the Illuminati, and more. Rumours? Perhaps. Can we discount them? No." His fingers drummed the table. "A lot is made of the Templar trials, and with good reason. Many were arrested, tortured, and tried. Some were burned at the stake. But the majority of knights, sergeants, and others were absorbed into other orders, or their orders changed names. Their knowledge would have been passed down. Maybe the count was in an order that was once the Templars. In Portugal, a place he was suspected to be a native of, the organisation literally just changed names. What if the count diversified, and has several groups running?"

Nahum had a resigned expression on his face as he leaned his chin into his left hand, his right resting on his wine glass. "I reluctantly admit, there is a certain logic to that. He has his experimental, alchemical branch and a treasure-seeking branch."

"No way!" Harlan looked around at the mix of expressions—resignation, excitement, belligerence, wariness, and just plain baffled. He was well aware he needed to share JD's news, but couldn't with Theo there. They'd probably said too much already. "We're paranoid—for good reason—but not everything comes back to our old friend. However, Ash, you could well be right about another Templar organisation that still keeps watch for news of lost treasure. They would be very motivated to reclaim what they would see as theirs."

"But," Shadow countered, "if it was theirs, wouldn't they know where it was anyway?"

"Not necessarily." Ash leaned forward, warming to his subject. "In France there was a finite amount of time to hide gold and treasure. England, Portugal, and Spain had a little longer. But they all had to move quickly. Suddenly, kings they'd had good relationships with for years were put in precarious positions by the pope and King Philip the Fourth of France. They had an agenda. They wanted Templar money and their power. So, the Templars put plans into place, and treasure and money were hidden. But we all know how things get lost, or clues get convoluted over time. Wars interfere, changes of governments, popes—you name it. The dissolution of the monasteries here in England, perhaps. Especially if the treasure was split up. All these years later, maybe the descendants of the Templars are as confused as everyone else. Prepared to follow up every lead—and this is a good one."

"They're our bombers," Gabe said with a grim certainty.

"I would put money on it."

Theo took a large sip of wine, and his hand seemed to shake, but seemingly more from excitement than worry. Harlan had seen that look on his face before. "My God. An actual secret Templar organisation is here, in Temple Moreton, searching for *that*!" He pointed at the key.

"No." Shadow shook her head. "They are looking for what that opens—or what's on the other side of what that opens. And let's face it. They like bombs. Who says they need a key?"

"If they want what is beyond it to be intact, they won't use a bomb," Ash reasoned.

Gabe reached for the wine bottle and topped up his drink, as if preparing for a long discussion. "Then we need to make a decision. Where do we go next?" He glanced over at Niel and Nahum. "The church?"

"Unlikely, despite the bomb," Niel said. "But we could go back after dark and check it out properly. Colin, the vicar, pointed out some Templar designs carved into the stonework close to the roof."

Gabe nodded. "That's a good idea. Despite Colin's doubts, we shouldn't rule it out."

"The other ideas I want to explore," Ash said, "are why use the seal of the two knights on horseback. I feel sure there's a message concealed in there. And it's a Damascus steel blade. Could that be a clue?"

"But the key is made from iron, right?" Niel asked.

"Yes."

"I can help follow up some things," Theo said, eager to help. "I can look at William's family and associate knights. Try to work out what 'Two brothers under God' could reference."

Ash smiled at him. "That would be really useful. Thanks, Theo."

"I have something to share," Harlan said, topping his own glass up. He looked at Theo apologetically. "I'm afraid it's a bit sensitive, Theo, and this feels really rude, but..."

Theo held his hand up. "I understand, although I admit to feeling a little aggrieved. I'll head back to my study and continue my research."

"Thank you." Harlan felt horrible. He had imposed himself on Theo, and now thrown him out of the discussion, but his news was important. He waited until the door had shut behind him and Theo's footsteps had faded down the corridor. "I had an intriguing discussion with JD earlier. He said he was a member of a secret society in the 1800s, before he got sick of it all. He was part of the group that searched these grounds back then. The same search outlined in the diary by Lady Madeleine Montgomery."

A stunned silence fell around the table, before Ash finally spoke. "JD was part of that search? Why didn't we know this before?"

"He didn't know what was happening here. He only vaguely knew about the bomb. He lives in his own world, you know."

Gabe muttered something unintelligible under his breath, his jaw clenching. "Has he any useful insights?"

"Not so far. Just that they searched everything and found nothing." Harlan grimaced as he apologised. "I guess it was a long time ago. He also says he's rusty on Templar symbology."

"Well, that just proves what a shit search they did," Niel pointed out. "They missed the dagger!"

Nahum shook his head, amused. "Well, this just gets weirder by the minute. I guess if JD can offer some useful insights, then great, but essentially we now have a clue—a big one—that they didn't. We need to follow that and not get distracted by anything else."

"Exactly," Shadow agreed. "I've experienced more than one treasure hunt that became confusing because of too many details. We have to remain focussed. Forget the bombs and previous searches, and all of that tedious information about Templar politics."

"We can't forget *everything*," Gabe reminded her. "We have an unknown thief who was on the grounds last night, and a bomber who may well be part of an old Templar organisation who is prepared to kill to get their way."

"But who they are," she argued, "doesn't matter. We just need to be better than them."

Gabe turned to Harlan. "What was the name of JD's secret society?"

"The Order of Illumination." He glanced around the table. "Does that ring a bell with anyone?" There was a general shaking of heads. "Okay. So, what now? What can I do to help?"

"We split up and follow what little clues we have," Gabe said decisively. "Niel, I think you should keep watch for our intruder. If it's Mouse, you seem to have a connection."

Niel mock saluted. "On it. I'll set up where I think she came in last night. Nahum and I searched the grounds again this afternoon, and found a likely spot where she climbed over the wall. I'll find a place to hole up."

"Good. Nahum, are you okay to search Temple Church? I think those symbols are worth investigating, as well as the crypt. Harlan, want to go with him?"

"Sure. I *love* crypts." He turned to Nahum. "Okay with you?"

"Happy to have help."

"Shadow," Gabe said, "you're with me. We'll search the old potting sheds here. According to the plans, they would have been the old stable block. I'm wondering if that seal with the two knights and the horse could have another meaning."

"It's worth exploring. I," Ash said, rising to his feet, "will join Theo for yet more research."

Shadow stood, too. "Should any of us be searching for errant knights with bombs?"

"Maybe that's something we should all do," Gabe said, as chairs scraped back and everyone prepared to leave. "I guess they must be here, somewhere. Watching and waiting. We need to be careful."

As Harlan joined Nahum, he wondered if staying in London might have been his safest option.

Twenty-Two

E stelle stretched out on the rug and gazed at the stars that were just beginning to appear. The sun had dropped below the horizon, and twilight was thickening, especially at the *gîte*, surrounded by olive groves.

Barak was next to her, hands behind his head as he too looked at the sky. They had both been struck by apathy and despondency, caused by their lack of progress and the events of the day before that were catching up with them.

Barak rolled onto his side, head propped on one hand to look at her. "What are we going to do? None of this list makes any sense to us!"

"Yet." She turned to look at him. "They're not stupid. They wouldn't give obvious names that anyone would make a connection with, but I'm sure we'll work it out. Tiredness doesn't help us think. Besides, Jackson may have a breakthrough."

"I think my brain is stuck in a rut. All we do is circle the same old things."

Estelle nodded, staring at the stars again, and letting her thoughts drift. "We're not thinking like they are. Or like he is. The *comte*. We need to put ourselves in his shoes."

Barak huffed as he also settled on his back again, hands behind his head once more. "I don't think I can. Or want to."

"We have to. We need to focus on what the count wants. What he's trying to achieve."

"The perfect warrior, created with alchemy. Or the perfect enhanced human."

"But isn't it more than that?"

Estelle fell silent as the stars became brighter against the backdrop of the night sky. She stared at them, thinking of astrology, the planets and their correspondences, and how practitioners of alchemy and magic saw connections in everything. As a witch she experienced these connections every day, and almost took them for granted, they came so naturally to her. She could feel her connection with the unseen energy of the world even stronger now that she was spreadeagled on the earth, relishing the hum of ancient magic in the soil.

Earth, air, fire, water—the fundamentals of life and the profound connection with the psyche could not be separated. Water was in the air and the earth, it ran through humans, animals, and plants. Air carried water and the heat of the sun, and the sun's heat penetrated the earth and enabled everything to grow. Within the earth were precious metals and crystals, birthed by the planet's energies. She could feel it all, a web that couldn't be broken. Her strength was fire, but it didn't mean she wasn't connected to the other elements. It was impossible not to be connected. The psyche drew it all together, and for some, like Alex, the White Haven witch, they saw beyond this realm and into the next. Other worlds, where spirits and demons walked. And the Nephilim. That's where they had been for millennia. She glanced at Barak, who was lost in his own thoughts.

The elemental energies were all around her. It just took a moment to feel for them. It wasn't hard. What was hard was manipulating them. That needed power that only a few had. Like she'd told Lucien, she had been born with it. But it took practice to hone her skills and maintain them. For men like JD and the *Comte de Saint-Germain*, and many other men and women like them, they had no natural abilities. For them, it was decades of hard work. And they needed power to draw on for that. They desired to master the elements. Her thoughts focussed, penetrating beyond that. She and other witches wielded power, and manipulated it through spells and complex language. It was a type of creation. She was in a sense no different to alchemists. But, perhaps while she accepted magic and her ability to use it, it seemed that alchemists—or some of them, at least—tried to see beyond that. To find the language of creation.

"Barak," she said, turning to him again, propping her head on her hand. "You're a Nephilim, the son of a Fallen Angel. Do you believe that the language of a God or angels is written in our DNA or, I don't know, *everything*? I read about that somewhere."

"Herne's horns, Estelle! That's a big question!" He mirrored her actions and turned to face her again. "Why? Do you?"

"No, actually. Not like *the* God. Yours. I'm not a creationist. I firmly believe that magic is everywhere, and it has nothing to do with Gods. They're a part of it, not the cause of it."

"Interesting." His eyebrow lifted. "Why would I believe any different?"

"Because of who your father is. I'm trying to think how an alchemist does. Like JD, who studied the language of angels. They are seeking the language of creation. To become one with the universe. To see beyond the mechanics of it, I suppose. Is that possible?"

He grinned. "I love that you have just asked me that insanely big question! Like I'd know the answer!"

She prodded his chest and wished she hadn't. It was like pushing solid rock. "But your father was an angel—at the right hand of your God. You pursued the Book of Raziel, that was supposedly the foundational grimoire."

"*One* of them. And I didn't, actually. I was stuck at home—thankfully. Sounded like a bloody nightmare. But no, my father was no one's right hand. He was part of an army of angels. They exist on a different plane, and by the sound of it after what the Igigi said, they are stuck in it."

"But they aren't corporeal," she persisted.

"No, they are light and energy. But I guess it's fair to say that they tap into the fundamental elements of our existence. Don't ask me how, though. As you know, my father has healing skills, but was far more interested in destruction."

Barak rarely spoke of his father. He never appeared tense about him, just resigned, and somehow dismissive. "But Nahum said he could show remarkable kindness when he chose to heal."

"Probably for an ulterior motive, like them needing to keep fighting. But," Barak smiled, "maybe I'm being harsh. He wasn't a father figure...not how people expect one to be."

"Well, I guess we both share that experience."

"Where's this going, Estelle? Angels are just another paranormal creature, like we are—maybe with better connections. Some of us have more strength than others, or different strengths."

"I'm just trying to fathom the count's motives."

"I think it's simple, and it's something I've talked about a few times with my brothers. He—like JD—wants to harness the power of creation, to position himself as a God. He's trying to crack a formula. But you know what? It's too big. The formula is too great and varied, and ancient, powerful magic beyond what we can ever fathom, is behind it all. The Green Man conjured Ravens' Wood out of thin air!"

Estelle was baffled. "What are you talking about? Ravens' Wood in White Haven is ancient woodland, and has been there for millennia. I remember playing in it as a child."

Barak smiled enigmatically. "That's what he wants you to believe. But according to Shadow—poof! Came out of nowhere."

Estelle felt dizzy and confused, her mind at war with itself. "When?"

"At Imbolc. This year."

"Impossible."

"And yet, it happened. I remember it being here when I arrived. But it actually wasn't. So, my point is, the alchemists can all try as much as they want. They will only ever achieve a portion of what the Gods can do. They will never tap into ancient magic. *Never.*"

Estelle pushed aside the endless questions she had on Ravens' Wood, and focussed on the count. "But he's had success, of a sort."

"Of course he has."

"So, bear with me. Have you seen JD's lab?"

"No, why?"

"I just wondered about his grid of correspondences. You know, that enormous, complex wheel that Harlan and Shadow talked about."

"Where he manipulated weapons and tried to experiment on poor Harlan? I remember. No, I haven't seen it."

"So, as you've just said, JD is an alchemist, and so is the Count of St Germain. But they don't have real magic like witches, or the innate magic that you or Shadow have.

They have to force nature to work for them. That's why the creation of a superior being is so hard."

"But we couldn't create an enhanced human, even with our natural magic. Mine is limited. Yes, I have wings and can speak any language, living or dead, but I can't wield the elements. Neither can Shadow. And *you* couldn't create a super being, either. Or could you?"

"No, actually, I couldn't. And wouldn't want to, either."

"But if you did," he asked, shuffling to get comfortable, "how would you do it?"

"I have no idea! I suppose I would have to create a spell to do it, but that would be incredibly complex. I wouldn't even know where to begin."

"Exactly. Because it's ancient, powerful magic beyond our ken, mixed with generations of adaption and change."

"But I guess," she reluctantly admitted, "that is partly what the count has done. Which brings me to my point. The metals ground into tattoo ink, for example, to create the metallic skin and weapons that seem to spring from nowhere. They must be activated somehow. The count must have a bigger alchemical correspondence wheel...or something of the sort."

Barak nodded. His expression, barely visible in the dim light, looked thoughtful. "So, it would need to be man-sized or something bigger. And," he added, his voice quickening with excitement, "he would need to power it somehow, like in the cave beyond Mithras Temple."

"The Dark Star Chamber. Yes. That had rudimentary batteries." Estelle shuddered at the thought. She could still feel the enormous power that she'd drawn on and that had almost killed her. The mere thought of it made the fine hair on her arms rise off her skin. "The power you broke before it consumed me. Did I ever thank you properly for that? You saved my life."

He leaned forward and kissed her. "And I would do it again in a heartbeat. I've read *Frankenstein*, you know. It was like Dr Frankenstein's lab. He animated the creature with lightning."

"You see, that's what I mean! I think he's based his giant wheel—if that's what he's got—at a centre of enormous power. Like a ley line or something!"

"That's an intriguing thought. But the lab we raided wasn't on one."

"Have we checked? Maybe it was! Or, maybe it didn't need to be. It seemed to be a preparation station." Estelle started to feel excited and sat up. "We think Black Cronos has a spider's web of places, but a spider's web has a centre. There can't be many places where they would complete whatever they do to make their superhumans. And maybe they do other things there!" She shrugged, putting aside questions about the existence of the universe and the powers of the Gods. "Whatever. The count needs power to draw on. Huge power. That's what we need to search for."

"Places where power gathers. Like stone circles and ley lines." Barak sat up, too. "That is definitely worth investigating. But the code names?"

"Maybe they will make more sense once we look into this." She stood and extended her hand. "Come on. Time to search the internet again."

Twenty-Three

T he shadows were long beneath the trees behind the walled garden when Niel started to search for a place to hide and watch for their intruder.

This area was far more open than the wood, the trees placed further apart. In fact, he realised as he strolled through them in the evening gloaming, they were all fruit trees. A mixture of apple, pear, plum, and cherry varieties. He hadn't noticed that when he was there earlier with Nahum, after they had escaped the tedium of the bomb squad and the encounter with the irate Detective Inspector. Then they had been preoccupied with where the intruder had exited the grounds—and where he or she might enter again.

Trust Theo to have his own orchard. Fruit was hanging ready, and come September, he imagined the kitchen would be in a frenzy of storing for the winter. He sighed. He used to have orchards. In the spring, the air would be rich with the scent of blossoms, and if he narrowed his eyes, he could imagine how this orchard would look, thick with pink and white flowers. It made him slightly homesick, but he shook it off. He wasn't here to dwell on the past. As his brothers had annoyingly pointed out, he was prone to it.

Instead, he focussed on his quarry. He was well aware that Mouse, if that's who it was, may not come back that night, or might even search for another place through which to enter Temple Keep's grounds. Sections of the wall had hedges alongside it, and large tree branches overhung some parts. He had climbed one earlier to view the country lane on the other side with a narrow verge full of wild flowers.

Now he paused, inhaling the rich, grassy scent that was magnified by the warmth of the evening, and searched for the part of the boundary wall they had spotted earlier. It was accessible because of the slightly bulging bricks at the base, distended by tree roots. Seeing it to his right, he headed to the closest tree with the thickest branches, and climbed high into the canopy. He scrambled around the central trunk until he found the perfect spot. A large branch, smothered in overhanging leaves, that offered a good place to see a large portion of the boundary.

As he eased his back against the trunk, his legs bracing against the branch, he considered Mouse's almond eyes. In their brief, but memorable, encounter, he'd shared a kinship. Maybe that word was too strong. *A connection.* He liked her. He'd imagined what she might look like without her black balaclava. Hopefully, in a few hours, he might not have to wonder anymore.

Even better, perhaps he could persuade her to work *with* them.

Shadow placed her hands on her hips as she stared at the potting sheds.

"I can't believe this is my Friday night! At least if it was still a stable, there'd be horses here." She was missing Kailen, and his familiar scent.

"Well, I was planning on wining and dining you at The Knight's Rest, and then thought, Shadow doesn't care about that! She'd love to search for Templar treasure instead!"

She turned to look at Gabe. His right eyebrow was raised, and his lips were twisted in an annoying smirk that she wanted to wipe right off his face. "I would be excited if I thought we'd actually find any. Instead, I'm going to stink of compost and old wellington boots."

"Sexy."

"Funny."

"I tell you what." He leaned in, nuzzling her neck, his hands sliding over her hips. "I'll help you wash every single bit of compost smell off you later. Deal?"

"Only if you let me run my hands through your deliciously thick feathers."

His eyes darkened to a stormy black and he almost growled. "Deal."

Teasing him, she pulled away, and sashayed to the main doors that were locked for the night. She turned back, pleased to see him watching her hips. "Come on, then. Our bath awaits."

Using the key Theo had provided them, she unlocked the door, progressed into the dark interior of the shed, and flicked the light on. It threw the shelves, work surfaces, and rows of gardening implements into stark relief. Interconnected rooms marched away on either side of them. Nothing looked remotely intriguing. "This is a seriously massive waste of time."

"We don't know that unless we check thoroughly. We barely glanced at the place when we were here earlier. According to the oldest plans Theo has, this building looks virtually unchanged—except for the interior layout, of course. The foundations are the same and could hide a tunnel or something. I mean, look at the ancient stonework." He walked over to the back wall mostly hidden by shelving and stacks of pots, and crouched to move them, exposing the base. "That is old, thick stone. Some of the walls look as if they have been repaired. These do not."

Shadow studied his vaguely hopeful expression. "You're not convincing me, or yourself."

"Shadow. Please. The two knights on horseback have to signify something. This was a stable block. It's also close enough to the house that they might be connected in some way." He pointed to either side. "The interior walls look more recent, but we have to check everything. Even the stone slabs on the floor. There could be symbols in the stonework."

"Did they sweep for bombs in here?"

"Yes. I checked and double checked."

She huffed. "All right. We may as well get this over with. I'll start at the other end, where we found Malcolm."

Nahum stood with his hands on hips in the middle of Temple Church's main nave. It was dark, with only a few stripes of light from a distant street light illuminating the interior.

"So, where do we start? The unstable crypt or the symbols?"

"Let's leave the most exciting part until last, shall we?" Harlan's drawl was unmistakably sarcastic. "Let's start with the symbols."

"Not thrilled at searching through old tombs?"

"The last time that happened, I was being pursued by zombies."

Nahum grinned. "Ah, yes. Old Haven Church. That was fun."

"So. Much. Fun. And the last time I was in a church, Jackson was hanging me upside down by my ankles over the pulpit."

"Well, the advantage of wings is that I can handle all of that."

"Good." Harlan flicked his torch on and aimed it down at the floor, shielding it with his hand. "Are you sure the door is locked behind us? I don't want a crazy, errant knight sneaking up on me."

"You could have stayed with Ash and Theo, you know. I can manage alone."

Harlan cocked his head at him. "Okay, I'll shut up and just get on with it. I'll start in the family chapel."

Nahum stretched out his wings, glad that the main nave of Temple Church was a good size. "In which case, you'll find me up there."

The vaulted stone roof comprised of a series of arches sweeping out of pillars. Templar symbols as well as traditional church carvings dotted the stonework, especially where the arches intersected with the pillars. Nahum spotted several Green Man carvings, not uncommon in churches, as well as a variety of Templar crosses, a couple of *Agnus Deis*, and a carving of two knights on horseback again.

He briefly considered whether he should touch any of the carvings, seeing as the bomb squad could hardly had examined up here, but that also meant it was unlikely their adversaries could have planted a bomb, either. Besides, these were grubby from centuries of grime and dust and clearly hadn't been tampered with. He worked his way methodically around the entire roof, pushing and pulling, but nothing budged.

Exhausting the roof, he joined Harlan, finding him on his hands and knees under the stained glass window in the private chapel. "Find anything?"

Harlan stood up, turned his torch off, and dusted off his knees and hands. "Actually, yes. I kept thinking about the fact that this stained glass image is the French seal."

They both stared up at it, able to see it relatively clearly because of the streetlights outside. The colours were muted, but still visible. "I know it's a traditional Templar sign, but why not put the *Agnus Dei* into stained glass? Why this? It makes me think that like the symbol on the dagger's hilt, this must mean something."

Nahum nodded. "That actually makes a lot of sense. The image is different, though. Only one knight is on the horse, the other is kneeling."

"I know, right? Does that mean something, too?"

"I saw the two-knight image carved in the ceiling, but it was solid. They all were. Nothing budged, no matter how much I tried to move them. Why were you looking at the floor?"

"The stone slabs are a slightly different size under the window. They're bigger than the rest of the floor. Not obviously so, but..."

Nahum studied the ground, comparing the slabs as he paced across the floor. "Herne's balls. You're right. But, could it just be because they edge the outer wall?"

"Maybe. But the different image, and the stone slabs... It bothers me."

"Any other important symbols here?"

"Nope. I've poked around the altar, and inspected the slabs. There's nothing on them, either. Unless age has completely erased them, or the pews obscured them." He pointed upwards. "That's the only part I couldn't manage."

"I can do that," Nahum said, already flexing his wings. "After I've checked here, I'll move on to the other small chapel. Think you can check the ground floor of the main nave for me? I want to exhaust everything up here before we find the crypt. If there is something hidden in here, the trigger for it must be somewhere else." He scanned the family chapel again, a prickle of unease sliding down his spine. "Now that I'm here again, at night, in the dark, I feel the press of years here. Secrets. I dismissed this place earlier. Now, I'm not so sure."

Harlan slapped his shoulder. "I hope you're right, my friend. Frankly, if I'm going to spend hours of my life in here getting covered in dust and shit, I want it to be worth something."

And with that, he strode away, leaving Nahum to his thoughts.

Theo's voice jolted Ash out of his contemplative study, and he looked up, bringing himself out of the dusty Templar past with its secrets, murky politics, and betrayals, to the present.

"Two brothers. It could refer to William's two sons." Theo tapped the page. "I found a passing reference in one of these history books, and Lady Madeleine mentions them, too. Apparently, there was a lot of interest in the crypt below Temple Church when the Order of Illumination searched for the treasure."

"He had two sons?"

"The heir and the spare. And one daughter."

Ash leaned back in his chair, his own research temporarily forgotten. "And they're in the crypt?"

"Yes. But nothing remotely resembling treasure, or the clue to treasure, was found there."

"Damn it." Although he couldn't say as much to Theo, he felt sure JD would have been thorough. "I need to keep searching for clues to William's burial. He has to be somewhere. Even though he died in the Tower, he would have been respectfully laid to rest."

"Could he have been buried in the Tower grounds?"

"Perhaps. But from everything I have read, that was reserved for those who were killed there. He died of natural causes."

Theo headed to a side cabinet, pulled out two cutglass tumblers, and offered Ash a drink. "Whiskey?"

"Perfect. Are you sure you haven't missed any hidden rooms in the castle over the course of your renovations?"

Theo handed him the glass and stood at the leaded windows overlooking the grounds. The heavy damask curtains had been left slightly open, but in the lamplight, Ash could see nothing beyond their own reflections.

Theo shook his head. "I can't be one hundred percent sure, obviously, but I'm as sure as I can be. We stripped walls back, left some stonework on show, plastered over others. Other than the priest hole, which was obviously a later addition, and the compartment in the cellar wall, it has revealed only old fireplaces which were bricked up or made smaller. Oh, and the pantry off the kitchen had a false wall, but when we knocked that down, we found nothing exciting."

"It's accessible now?"

"Yes, of course. But we pulled up the old floor and laid a new one. There was nothing there."

"Not even in the old fire surrounds?"

"'Fraid not."

"Damn it!" Ash took a sip of the smooth malt whiskey, thinking of what Shadow had said earlier. "It's easy for Shadow to say we need to dismiss all the other history and conjecture, but it's not that simple. William had two knights who he stayed in close contact with, even after his arrest. What if the knights on horseback refers to them? They're two brothers of a different sort!"

Theo didn't answer, lost in his own thoughts, and Ash fell silent, too. It was easy to let his thoughts drift to the past in the ancient keep. As he sipped his whiskey, he imagined what the castle would be like when it was first built. The oldest part of the keep, the tower and the square building attached to it, had small windows throughout, including in this study, which was on the second floor of the tower. The light would have been dim, the candles and oil lamps providing scant light. Fires would have blazed for most of the year. Sweet-smelling rushes mixed with herbs would have covered the floors, and servants would have scurried everywhere. Trusted servants who would have been well paid, perhaps, to keep their silence in a castle owned by several generations of Templars. The moat would have sealed them all in, keeping them safe from attack. Except it couldn't really, because it was only on one side.

He circled back to the images on the hilt. The family crest. The two knights on horseback. The cross and the crown. The Star of David—or the alchemical symbol, as he thought of it now: *as above, so below.*

"Theo, what's beneath the oldest part of the keep? Is that where the cellar is?"

"No, that's under the east wing of the castle. The later addition. It was built over what was the other half of the moat."

"So the moat went all the way around, originally?"

"Yes, but it hasn't for hundreds of years. That's why the cellars are so deep under the east wing. They used the old moat. Then they refilled the remaining part that you can see now."

"So, what's under the keep and original hall?"

"A square, very dank hole of nothingness. You can access it through the laundry room."

"Nobody builds a dank hole of nothingness for no good reason, Theo." Ash drained his whiskey and stood up, grabbing the bone hilt and placing it in his pocket.

"Now?" Theo's moustache quivered with horror. "It's horrible down there. Probably flooded. I haven't been down there in years. The builders cemented the slabs in."

"Then we'll just have to break through them." Ash suppressed his impatience. "Do you want to find this treasure or not?"

"Yes."

"Then we have to search it." Not knowing what they might find, Ash strapped on his sword that was placed on a chair.

Theo had nervously glanced at it earlier, but ignored it. Now he clearly couldn't resist asking, "Why do you carry a sword?"

Ash laughed in an attempt to make light of it. "It comforts me. It's a family thing. I've had fencing lessons for years."

"That's hardly a foil." He cocked an eyebrow at him. "It's a full sword, and deadly sharp. I checked. Your team carry them, too. And that Shadow…" His eyes widened. "She manipulates her daggers like a professional."

"We *are* professionals. We work in security, as well as this kind of thing. Blades are our weapon of choice."

"Niel has an axe."

Ash scratched his neck, and decided honesty was best. "At least we're on your side, Theo."

Theo reluctantly got to his feet. "All right. Follow me. But trust me, it won't be pleasant."

Niel saw the shadow slide over the wall and ease to the ground. If he hadn't been watching so closely, he'd have presumed that the shadow was caused by a cloud passing over the moon.

He let the intruder cross the stretch of grass below him, noting the petite form and deft movements that suggested a female, and smiled. *Mouse.* She passed beneath him and, wondering where she would go, decided to follow at a distance. He finally slipped to the ground, as stealthy as she had been, and pursued her on foot.

She kept to the shadows, but followed a more or less straight line to the walled garden, opened the gate, and passed through it. Niel couldn't even hear the snick of the gate as it shut. The walled garden was close to the house, the gate at the other side exited close to the drive and the stables. If she wasn't careful, Mouse would run into Gabe and Shadow. Actually, that was the last thing he wanted.

He ran across the grass and vaulted up the wall to crouch at the top. He saw her weave across the gravelled paths, again utterly silent, her footsteps sure and quick. Unless she was planning to swim, which was highly unlikely, she'd have to circle behind the keep, past the tower. Or go the long way around and intersect the drive.

But then she diverted her path, heading away from the gate. Instead, she headed to a section of wall that was closest to the keep, and thick with espaliered fruit trees. She effortlessly climbed them before reaching the top of the wall and dropping down to the other side. As soon as she was out of sight, he ran along the top of the wall to the corner. She had already reached the side of the moat. He was tempted to intercept her right then, but curious, he watched as she pulled a lightweight rope out of her pack that was fixed to a small device with a grappling hook on the end. She aimed for the top of the tower.

She was a good shot. With a tiny clink, it caught on the ramparts, and after tugging it a couple of times to make sure it was secure, she wound up the rope to shorten it, stepped back and took a running jump. She tucked her legs up and swung over the water, hit the wall, and steadied herself. Then she hit a button on her device, and within seconds, she was being pulled up the wall, walking up it like a monkey.

Niel could barely believe his eyes. She was good. Very good. And impressively silent and quick. But he wasn't there to admire her. *Well, not totally.* It was clear she was heading for the top of the keep. *Good.* He would meet her there. He stepped from his hiding place, extended his wings, and swooping around the back of the tower, landed softly beyond the parapet. Trying not to feel like an exultant stalker, he slipped inside the unlocked door built into the wall of the tower and waited at the top of the stairs for her arrival.

Twenty-Four

Harlan stood on the top step leading down to the crypt, the entrance in a concealed part of the choir that was well away from the nave where the public went, and hoped the roof wasn't about to fall in on them.

"There won't be zombies down there, you know," Nahum said, prodding him gently in the shoulder. "Get a move on."

"But the roof might fall on my head."

"If it was that dangerous, the whole church would be closed. Plus, the bomb squad was down here earlier. I saw Colin give them the keys and direct them where to go." He shook the keys he'd taken from the sacristy. "These ones. Shall I go first?"

"No." Harlan took the keys. "I'm good. It reminds me of my old treasure hunting days. They were nowhere near as dignified as my current jobs."

"There you go, then. A chance to relive your youth."

Harlan descended the dozen steps to a sturdy wooden door that sealed the crypt. With a deep breath, he placed the key in the lock, expecting it would be stiff from lack of use, but it turned easily, and he swung it open.

A musty, damp smell enveloped them, and he paused just inside the entrance to take his bearings. His flashlight showed a huge room that ran almost halfway under the nave, and was almost as wide. Pillars ran the length of the space, supporting a simple roof arranged in a series of squares. Beneath it were at least a dozen tombs, surrounded by a variety of metal grills.

"Holy shit. I didn't expect this." Harlan stepped further inside, reassured by the solidity of the space.

Nahum headed towards an oil lamp and a box of matches to the right of the entrance on a stone shelf, and lit the wick. A warm, orange glow dispelled the darkness, and also showed a series of lamps and candles around the room. As Harlan started to examine an eye-catching tomb on the second row, Nahum lit all of the lights, and soon the crypt felt far more welcoming that it had only moments before.

"Unbelievable," Harlan mumbled as he stared at the full-sized figure of a knight resting on the tomb in front of him. "This is amazing. I can see the detail on his chainmail. This is incredibly well preserved."

"I guess that's what happens in a private tomb. No grubby hands wearing the design away." Nahum looked unsettled for a moment, cocking his head as if straining to hear something.

"What's wrong?"

Nahum gave a slow smile. "The voices of the dead. I hear them murmuring."

Harlan gave an involuntary shudder as goose bumps erupted along his skin. He stared into the dark corners, as if something was stirring there. "Can you see spirits?"

"No. I can't even discern what they're saying." He shrugged it off. "It's a skill, for want of a better word, that I share with Gabe."

"They're not telling you where the treasure is? That would be nice!"

Nahum shook his head as he started to examine the tombs. "No, I'm afraid not."

Harlan's attention returned to the tomb in front of him, taking in the stone carving of the armour, the helmet, and the long sword resting between the knight's hands that ran the length of his body. "Robert de la More. Died 1278. He must have been a Knight Templar, too."

"William's father, perhaps? Or maybe an uncle?" Nahum moved away to investigate another tomb, this one much simpler with the family crest on it. "This is Henri de la More, who died in 1267." He hesitated, looking at Nahum. "Someone who wasn't a Templar, by the look of it."

"Hard to say. Presumably not all of them became Templars, or I guess they would all have knights on their tombs. I only have the names of the sons." Harlan pulled his notebook from his pocket, scanning the hasty notes he'd made before they left. "The oldest son was called Henri, and the youngest was Olivier."

They both started to explore, Nahum heading one way and Harlan the other. Nahum said, "Neither would have been knights, so their tombs should be simpler."

"Depends on your version of simple, I guess." Harlan used his torch to highlight details. Some had angels carved atop them, others ornate crosses mounted on a variety of plinths. Others had flowers carved around them, particularly those tombs belonging to women. He also realised, as he progressed through the crypt, that there were a series of recesses in the wall where yet more tombs lay, and he checked the dates. "There are several generations here. All the way up to the sixteenth century. I wonder what happened then."

"Perhaps the family moved, or they all died. No heirs at all." Nahum suddenly stopped. "Over here! I've found the brothers."

Harlan hurried to his side, his footfall echoing through the chamber, and for a moment he thought he heard footsteps above. He stopped abruptly to listen, but was greeted only by silence. Shaking off his nerves, he continued to Nahum's side. Both brothers' tombs were heavily carved with an inscription running down the tomb lid. Both also had crosses mounted at the head, and symbols of the Templars were also engraved into the lid and sides.

Harlan ran his fingers over the cold surface of Henri's tomb. "You're right. The dates and names fit." He started to push on the different symbols, hoping something would give. "Damn it. All these are solid."

Nahum was similarly engaged, and for minutes there was silence as they thoroughly investigated. Then Nahum stood, shoulders dropping. "Nothing. But..." he pointed upwards. "There are more symbols above."

Harlan had been so side-tracked by the tombs that he hadn't spent more than cursory moments inspecting the roof, but now he saw that Nahum was right. More Templar symbols were carved into certain points of the ceiling. "But Nahum, surely JD's team, the Order of Illumination, would have done all of this a few hundred years ago. What could we find that they didn't?"

"You know what they couldn't do then, but we can? Open the tombs."

"Are you nuts?"

"No. They would have been watched by the church, and probably wouldn't have had permission to open them. We can." He laughed at Harlan's expression. "I don't like it either, but they'll all be dust now. No bodies left at all. I'll check the ceiling just in case, and you can search Henri's tomb."

Harlan grumbled under his breath as he and Nahum heaved the lid to the side, twisting it to reveal the inside rather than removing it completely. Wincing at the scrape of stone that rumbled around them, Harlan was grateful that Nahum was with him. His strength made light work of it.

And then Harlan was aware of a change in the light as the candles flickered. Harlan and Nahum whipped around, just in time to see a small, round object bouncing towards them, and a huge hooded figure in the entrance of the crypt before it fled.

Their unknown assailant had thrown a grenade, and they had nowhere to go.

Gabe straightened up, and finally admitted defeat. There was nothing to suggest there was anything hidden in the old stable block.

He steeled himself as Shadow huffed next to him, hand on hips, leg tapping the floor and violet eyes wide. "Can we go now? This is pointless!"

"It is not pointless. We have ruled it out!"

"Yes, we most certainly have. Can we go to the church now?"

"You don't want to join Niel on intruder watch?"

She cocked her head at him. "And deny him his reunion? I don't think so."

"And what if it's a brutish male intruder with a face like a bulldog?"

"Then he'll still enjoy the fight. I want to search for treasure!"

Unable to suppress his own curiosity, Gabe extended his arm and gestured to the door. "Then let's go, my beloved."

In minutes they were striding across the grounds towards the pavilion, the shortest route Gabe estimated to the village.

"You know," he whispered, "we need to be quiet, just in case our intruder is still finding her way inside. We don't want to scare her off."

"In that case, we should fly. There's hardly any moon."

Gabe considered their options. They certainly didn't want to get caught in Niel's stakeout, and he was itching to get to the church. He quickly pulled his shirt off and extended his wings. "All right. Let's do it."

In seconds Shadow's lithe form was wrapped around his body, and he ascended to a good height before wheeling around and heading to the church. He studied the ground, wondering if there was something they might spot from up here that could give them a clue. However, everything was quiet. He could see the fluttering yellow tape around the bombed lodge, and the police car still parked at the entrance to the drive, but if there were any secrets hiding in the darkness, they weren't revealing themselves now.

Within minutes, the village of Temple Moreton was below them, the occasional light showing in the windows of the houses. The inn was closed at this hour, and Gabe realised they had been in the barn longer than he had anticipated. Shadow was facing him, her legs wrapped around his waist, her familiar scent enveloping him. She lifted her lips to his ear. "Gabe. I see figures below, in the graveyard. It's not Harlan or Nahum."

Startled, he twisted to stare below him. She was right. A couple of tall people stood just inside the lychgate, and... He waited, hovering, looking for signs of movement. Shuffling shadows revealed another couple standing at the entrance to the side path.

Within seconds he had perched on the bell tower and released Shadow, who whispered, "Bollocks. I've left my bow at the keep."

"They might not be our enemy. Best not to kill them—yet." Aware that Nahum and Harlan were inside the church, and worried for their safety, he studied the grounds again, finally spotting another couple of figures at the side entrance to the church. They had easy sight of the side gate. They were dressed in black, and appeared to be wearing long cloaks. "I see six in total. You?"

"Same, two at each gate, two at the side entrance. But who knows how many more are inside? They certainly aren't friends."

"Agreed. I'm going to drop down on the far side of the tower where no one can see us. If we take out the two at the church's side door, they won't spot whoever heads to the side gate."

"Fine." Shadow's blade was already in hand. "I'll take the side gate once we're done."

"Just don't kill them until we know who they are! Maybe try to take one alive."

Shooting him an impatient look, Shadow wrapped herself around him again. He swung over the tower's roof and glided to the ground. As soon as he landed, they rounded the corner together, weaving between the tombs so that the long grass masked their steps.

They dropped behind a huge tombstone as the side entrance came into view. The two guards were draped in long, sweeping cloaks, cowl hoods drawn up over their heads so that their faces were pools of darkness. Their backs were to the door, and they faced towards the graveyard. Their gloved hands gripped the hilt of huge swords, the points resting on the ground.

Modern day knights, and potentially their bombers.

Gabe knew these men would be skilled fighters. He glanced at Shadow, and she gestured to indicate that she would circle around. In seconds she had vanished like a wraith between the graves, and Gabe edged well to the side, trying to mask his approach. He only needed to give her a moment to get in position. Just as he was about to make his attack, a deep boom sounded within the church, and the ground shuddered beneath him.

Shit.

Ash stared into the deep cellar that, to be honest, looked more like a pit of death beneath the keep's tower, and wrinkled his nose at the dank smell.

"Bloody hell, Theo. You weren't wrong about this."

"It's gross. But I think the water has dropped since the last time I looked. Probably because the dry weather has lowered the moat level."

Ash studied the ground, noting a pool of dark water that even his torch light didn't penetrate. "I need to get down there and check the floor. Let's position the ladder."

"Are you mad?" Theo looked at him, appalled. "It stinks down there."

Ash had been crouching to get a better view, but now he straightened up. "It's the oldest part of the castle, and according to you, there is no other cellar—not of this age, anyway. All of these castles usually had private exits that would allow someone to escape in the event they were surrounded. I'm sure this castle is no different. This is the only place you haven't renovated or explored. I think that down there must be an entrance to a passageway."

"But what has that to do with Templar treasure?"

"I don't know. Maybe nothing. But we're running out of options, and we need to check. If I'm wrong, fine. I'll just have a hot shower after. You stay here."

With obvious reluctance, Theo helped Ash position the ladder, and Ash quickly descended. The cellar was only about ten square feet, and the water was a foot deep and icy cold. Ash tentatively tested his footing, shining his torch into the water. It was brackish, and probably full of bugs. It was also slimy beneath, and the walls glistened with moisture.

Theo was right, though. There was clearly a line showing where the water level had been. Ash examined the walls with great care, but there were no doorways marked here. Not surprising. They were probably level with the moat. If there was a passage, it would run beneath it. Turning his attention to the floor, he gave up on trying to keep clean and instead ran his hands across the uneven floor. It seemed to be made of both earth and stone. Probably covered by a layer of silt. He wished he'd thought to bring a spade, but the only thing he had picked up was a crowbar. Testing and prodding the floor methodically, he finally had success. He was tapping the floor with the bar, when the sound changed to a slighter deeper, more hollow noise.

"Hey, Theo! I've found something!"

Tracing the edge of the stone, Ash identified the large stone slab. He wedged the crowbar into place and lifted. For long moments nothing happened, until finally, with a sucking sound, the huge stone slab lifted up a few millimetres. Ash doubled his efforts, until finally it lifted properly and the water gurgled through the gap to whatever was below. Wedging the crowbar in the gap, Ash lifted the edge with his bare hands and flipped the slab over. With luck, Theo would be so astonished at his find, he wouldn't question Ash's inhuman strength.

Theo was already descending the ladder. He hurried to his side and peered into the square hole. "I can't believe it! This was here all along!"

"Well, we don't know where it goes yet. Don't get your hopes up. It could be blocked, or flooded."

Ash stuck his head through the gap and shined his torch around. The hole led to the start of a narrow stone-lined passage that ran away from the castle towards the grounds and the village. The water that drained from the cellar had formed puddles below, but it wasn't completely flooded.

Ash swung down, landing gently on his feet. The passage was low, barely five feet high, but his light showed that although the passage was thick with spider webs and the odd fallen stone, it was otherwise intact. It snaked away beyond his light, the air stale and forbidding. He looked up at Theo. "I'm happy to go on my own. I'll tell you what I find."

"Are you mad? Of course I'm coming!"

Feeling sure he'd be quicker alone, Ash nevertheless helped Theo into the passageway and then set off carefully, checking around him with every step. The last thing they needed was for the roof to collapse on them. They'd managed to travel a reasonable distance when the ground shuddered. Ash paused, horrified.

He stared at the rounded roof, and saw a cascade of cracks splinter overhead, allowing a trickle of soil through. He was poised to run, but fortunately the trickle was all that came down. *But ahead?* He peered into the darkness. If there'd been a rockfall, he couldn't discern one from here.

"Not another bomb?" Theo asked, who like Ash, was frozen with horror.

Ash took in the old man's expression. He hadn't expected any of this. "It must be. Come on, let's get moving."

"*Towards* it? Are you mad?"

"You can turn back if you want, but my brother and Harlan are up ahead."

Hopefully still alive.

Through the slight gap between the door and the frame, Niel watched the slender form of Mouse jump over the parapet. She quickly coiled the lightweight rope and placed it in her backpack. The grappling gun device remained fixed to her arm.

Once she was ready, which took seconds only, she ran to the door and tugged it open. As the door opened, he stepped forward.

She gasped and whirled around, running back to the wall. But Niel was on her in seconds, grasping her shoulders, and spinning her around.

"Mouse, I'd recognise those eyes anywhere!"

She squirmed and kicked him in the shin. Then, in a move that baffled Niel, she gripped his arms and used them to lever herself up and then kicked him in the stomach with both feet. She vaulted backwards at the same time he staggered back, landing on her feet before sprinting towards the ramparts.

Niel regained his footing quickly, and virtually throwing himself across the roof, tackled her to the floor, face-down. His sheer bulk pressed her flat, but she wriggled like an eel, and he was very grateful that his brothers weren't there to see him struggle with a woman who was barely half his weight and size.

"Mouse! I just want to talk!"

"Then why the hell am I pinned to the ground?"

"You were about to run!"

"That's what happens when I'm ambushed by an enormous man with an axe!" She twisted her head to stare at him. "As I do recall, you were a little less handsy last time."

"So you remember me, then?" He felt ridiculously pleased to hear that.

"Of course I do." He couldn't see her face, as she had a mask on again, but her almond eyes gleamed with annoyance, and something that might have been humour. "I should point out that I rarely get caught, so the occasion was memorable."

"Good. This one should be, too." He edged back just enough to allow her to twist around, and now she lay fully under him, back pressed to the floor, her backpack a few feet away. He kept an eye on her grappling device, his hand pinning that arm to the ground. The rope might not be attached, but the hook would cause a nasty wound. Aware he could crush her, he supported himself on his other arm, his elbow pressing her arm into her side, effectively pinning her in place.

"Well, this is all very nice," she said briskly, "but what now? Are we going to lie here all night?"

There was nothing Niel would like better. Her musky, spicy scent filled his nostrils like a dream, but he focussed on the job. "What are you here for, Mouse?"

"Oh, please! Let's not dance around this. I need the Templar blade, and I intend to get it."

"Unfortunately, you can't have it. You see, it actually belongs to Theo."

"Theo can't always have his own way."

"In this particular instance, he will. What I really want to know is, who has paid for your services? The sneaky Greek, Nicoli?"

"Classified."

"I know he did it. A Greek man matching his description was in the library the day the documents he was looking at were stolen. Your doing?"

"Maybe." She stared at him, defiant. "Theo is an idiot if he thought no one else would be interested in Templar treasure and William de la More's dagger."

"And the bombs? Were they you, too?"

"Do I look like a bomber?"

"Hard to say. I can't see your face, which seems unfair. You can see mine." He was itching to pull down the mask, but he felt that would somehow be a violation. Ridiculous, really, when he was pinning her to the ground.

"I can assure you, I am not the bomber. You've attracted the attention of the Knights of Truth and Justice."

Niel froze. "Who are they, and how do you know?"

"Your team hasn't done their homework well enough. They have been searching for the treasure for centuries."

"A remnant of the Knights Templar?"

"Hardly a remnant. They are ruthless, organised, and violent when necessary." She struggled again. "Let me go, Niel. Well done. You've caught me. I need to leave now. Unless you're going to call the police." Her eyes held a trace of fear.

"No. That wouldn't do either of us any favours." He sat, still clasping her grappling gun device, and in a few seconds, unbuckled it, finally releasing her arm.

In seconds, she leapt to her feet, eyes darting everywhere, but she was trapped and she knew it. He wanted to fly with her, feel her arms around him, but she didn't know he was a Nephilim, and he wasn't about to tell her. Of course, Nicoli might have, but he wouldn't take that risk while he didn't need to.

She rubbed her wrist where he'd restrained her. "You're ruining my perfect theft rate."

"I take that as a compliment. I'll be honest, I'm impressed. You're very...flexible."

A smile creased her eyes. "And then some. You, meanwhile, seem as inflexible as a plank of wood."

"But I have other attributes."

"I'm sure you have." Her eyes travelled over him.

Yes. He definitely counted that as flirting. Niel decided not to push it, and instead held his arm out in the direction of the door. "After you."

"Aren't you letting me go?"

"Unfortunately, I can't allow you to leave. My brothers want to chat. I suggest you consider telling us who hired you."

"I don't know who did, other than Nicoli. It's pointless keeping me here. I can't tell you anything else."

"You can think on that while I escort you to meet Theo and Ash. I promise that they're very civilised." Shooting him another hard stare, she rapidly descended the steps that hugged the tower walls before they reached the top floor landing. "Keep going," he instructed her. But when they reached Theo's study, neither he nor Ash was there. There was no sign of a struggle, but a few papers and the hilt and key were gone. "Down again. They must be in the main keep."

The tower felt eerily quiet. On the ground floor, he saw a light in the laundry room through a half-open door. He grabbed Mouse's elbow so she couldn't run, and then pushed the door open. The room was large and lined with shelves that were filled with towels, sheets, and other furnishings. Shelving units jutted into the floor space, blocking the back of the room from view. The smell of dampness and rot filled his nostrils.

"That smells like the moat," Mouse muttered, her free hand flying to block her nose. "Has someone come in that way?"

Niel's finger flew to his lips and he listened. None of the household staff were in view and it was silent. He weaved through the shelves, and at the far end of the room saw a hole in the floor. Peering downwards into an inky black cellar, he saw puddles on the ground. A metal ladder was propped against the side, wedged into the earth below, and there was another hole in the floor.

Either Ash and Theo were down there, or someone had broken in and was now somewhere in the keep. *It had to be Ash, or else where was he?* Either way, he had to investigate.

"Sorry, Mouse. You're coming with me."

"You have got to be kidding me!"

"I'm not leaving you alone, which means where I go, you go. After you."

She was halfway down the ladder when the ground shuddered, rocking the ladder. Niel grabbed it to stabilise it, and Mouse glared at him. "I suggest we think of a new plan."

Twenty-Five

As soon as Nahum saw the grenade rattle across the floor and land at his feet, he knew they had only seconds before it exploded.

"Take cover!" he yelled at Harlan. With lightning-fast reflexes, he grabbed the grenade and hurled it into Henri's tomb, and with strength enhanced by adrenalin, booted the lid partway back on before diving for cover behind the next tomb.

With a deafening roar the grenade exploded, cracking the enormous tomb, and sending dust and debris hurtling into the air. For a second, he could see and hear nothing at all. The candles flickered out, and a high-pitched whine filled his ears. He peered around the tomb he was sheltering behind, and through the whirling dust, saw a figure running towards them.

It looked like the angel of death, but it wasn't wings behind him; it was a billowing black cloak. The figure wasn't bothering to hide, thinking he was hidden by the dust cloud. *Wrong*.

Nahum pulled his throwing knives from where he'd strapped them to his legs and forearms and hurled one after the other at their attacker. With a grunt, their assailant fell, clutching his leg as one of Nahum's knives found its mark.

Nahum struggled to his feet, shaking his head to clear it, and then dropped to the ground again as he immediately saw another cloaked figure at the entrance to the crypt. *Shit*.

Fortunately, he and Harlan were well down the crypt, and in the darkness they would be hard to spot. He still had another couple of knives, but the figure was too far away at present, and he wasn't advancing, either. He must have seen his companion fall and had edged inside to wait and watch. Nahum estimated they had seconds only before he decided to act. With luck the assailant wouldn't risk another grenade, but he didn't want to assume that.

"Harlan," he whispered. "Are you okay?"

"I'm alive, but *okay* is a stretch." He was crouching a few feet away, back pressed to another tomb. "How many?"

"One wounded, another at the entrance. We're trapped." Nahum risked peering around the tomb again. The fallen man—at least he was pretty sure it was a male, from the size of him—was nowhere to be seen. Neither was the man at the entrance. He was potentially edging towards them right now.

Candlelight bloomed on the other side of the crypt. *Bollocks*. His main advantage was the darkness, and now that had gone, but at least he had a rough idea where one of the men was. Unless someone else had snuck in while he wasn't looking, there were still only two of them.

He eased his sword from his scabbard and indicated to Harlan to stay put. He was going to circle around and kill their assailants. Keeping low, he ran to the next tomb, intending to edge his way forward. There was no other way.

Just as he had advanced a few paces, the unpleasantly familiar rattle of another grenade bouncing across the floor had Nahum whirling around again. Their attacker's aim was good. The grenade stopped a few feet away. There was no way he could get to it in time. He threw himself behind a tomb, using it to shield him from the blast.

But this time, there wasn't a huge boom of detonation. Instead, smoke hissed out, creating an impenetrable haze.

Excellent, the smoke would work to his advantage, too.

As soon as the boom shook the ground, Shadow made her move.

The knight that was her mark had turned slightly to look at his companion, and taking advantage of his distraction, she plunged her sword into the side of his abdomen, angling upwards. Unfortunately, it struck armour that was hidden by the cloak, deflecting her blade.

He whipped around to face her, sword swinging towards her, and she immediately parried, swearing under her breath. She should have anticipated armour. Their blades clashed breathtakingly quickly as they fought around the tombs. The knight's cloak billowed behind him, and his cowl hood fell back, revealing a bearded man. She caught details as they fought. He wore fitted, black chest armour much like their own that she had left in the keep, but it also had the large Templar cross emblazoned on it in silver. Sturdy leather gloves covered his hands, but his arms were bare except for armguards. He was brawny and big, but she was used to fighting men of that build. His size gave him brute strength, but he lacked flexibility and her quickness.

From the corner of her eye, she spotted the guards on the side gate come running. The others from the main lychgate would be with them soon. Close by, Gabe was fighting for his life. The clash of their swords was loud, and if they didn't end this quickly, very soon someone would hear it and call the police. Fortunately, she had fey speed on her side.

As she fought her opponent, he lost his balance trying to catch her. She capitalised on it, slicing behind his knees as he spun around. He fell to the ground with an agonized cry that quickly became a gurgle as she slashed his throat.

She turned to face her next opponent. Fire surged through her; a wild adrenalin rush she hadn't experienced in weeks. She'd missed this.

Niel waited for the repercussive shudder to stop. It was coming from his right; the direction of the village, or maybe the centre of the grounds again.

He pulled Mouse back up the ladder. "I agree. Change of plan. That was either another bomb, or the tunnel has collapsed." Both were nightmarish scenarios.

They looked out of the window onto the courtyard of the keep, both silent. There were no other booming sounds, or the flare of flames.

"I think it must have been underground," Niel suggested. "With luck, no one will have called the police."

"But if it's underground, where is it?"

"It must be the village. That's where some of my team is."

"And if there are people in the tunnel below?"

Niel was torn with indecision. If he headed down the passage to check on who he thought was Ash and Theo, he may get stuck there. But if they were in trouble... *No. Ash could deal with it.* Niel needed to find out what was going on, and that meant heading to the church. Nahum thought it had been cleared of bombs, but if he was wrong, he could be badly injured, and so could Harlan.

"If it's Ash, I have to trust that he'll be okay." He grabbed Mouse's elbow and pulled her out of the exterior door and into the small courtyard, one of the many that made up the warren of buildings and spaces around the keep. "You're coming with me."

"I don't think so!" She looked both outraged and amused at the same time.

He pulled his t-shirt off as he spoke, ready to unfurl his wings. Right then, he didn't care whether she knew he was Nephilim or not. "I'm not leaving you here, alone, to plunder the castle. You're coming with me to check on my brothers."

"Oh, really! You're going to carry me there? Over your shoulder like a Neanderthal?"

"You're not a Neanderthal," he quipped.

"Not me, you idiot! *You!*"

He grinned broadly at her, and then spread his wings. They took up most of the small courtyard.

Mouse stepped back, eyes wide. "I thought Nicoli was just spinning tales about you."

"Nope." He gestured in. "Come here."

She backed away, but her eyes lingered a little too long on his bare chest. "I don't think so."

"Mouse! I don't often offer people a lift. Come on."

She backed up again, but the courtyard was small, and in seconds he'd gripped her around the waist and lifted them both into the air. She squealed in shock, before clinging on tightly, and Niel swept across the sky towards the church. He was glad to see there were no signs of police or fire engines, and the police car at the drive entrance was still in position. But as he neared the church, he saw the fight below, and without a second's thought, deposited Mouse on the edge of the graveyard, and ran to join Gabe and Shadow.

Harlan was heartily sick of hiding behind a tomb and half choking to death on the smoke bomb. His ears still rang, and he wondered why he hadn't bothered to carry a weapon.

"Well, you weren't expecting the damn Knights Templar to jump out on you, Harlan," he muttered to himself. "You're an idiot! *Always* carry a weapon when working with Shadow and the Nephilim. They attract violence like a moth to flame."

The sound of a grunt and thud made him wince, and he hoped that was an injured knight, not Nahum. He wanted to help, but the memory of the long swords in the knights' hands made him reconsider. They would cut him in half just as soon as look at him. And then the sound of an uneven gait and a wheezing noise made him freeze. The wounded knight came into view as the smoke eddied. He was limping, his injured leg pouring blood as he headed towards the shattered tomb and whatever may be in it. He certainly wasn't looking for Harlan.

I don't think so, bud.

Seizing his chance, he grabbed a chunk of shattered stone, eased upright, and whacked the knight on the back of the head. He fell forward with a satisfying thump, landing half in the tomb. Harlan grabbed the back of the cloak at his neck, and dragged him backwards until he was on the floor.

Nahum staggered out of the smoke, winded and covered in blood. "I heard the noise! You're okay?"

"Better than you!" Harlan took in his bloodied state. "Are you injured?"

"All his blood, not mine." Nahum's hair was standing up in tufts, and he wiped the back of his hand across his face, smearing more blood over it. "I suspect they'll have reinforcements coming along soon. What's in the tomb?"

"Not sure. Was just about to check."

The lid of Henri's tomb had cracked into pieces. Half was on the floor, while the rest had tipped into the sarcophagus. Big cracks ran across the base, revealing a dark space beneath.

Harlan cocked his head at Nahum. "Something is under there." He sat on the edge of the tomb and supported his weight, before kicking the cracked slab. "It's not budging."

The sound of footsteps had them both whirling around, but it was Gabe and Shadow.

Harlan took in their bloodied appearance and slashed clothing. "I take it you found more knights?"

Shadow nodded. "Outside the church. Six of them. Niel arrived too, and he helped finish them off."

"All dead?" Harlan asked.

"Very," Shadow answered. She nudged the knight beyond the shattered tomb with her foot. "He isn't, though. Good. He might be able to answer some questions."

"You two had us worried after we heard that explosion," Gabe said, squeezing Nahum's shoulder. "Are you injured?"

"This isn't my blood," Nahum reassured him, wiping his bloodied sword on the knight's black cloak. "We had two to tackle down here. I presume Niel is keeping watch?"

"With Mouse." Gabe shrugged, amused. "Long story. What have you found? Please tell me you have something, because we found absolutely nothing in the old stables!" A frown creased his face. "Niel thinks Ash is in an underground passage." He quickly summarised Niel's findings.

Harlan was still perched on the edge of the tomb, and he pointed at the cracked base. "We definitely found something. There seems to be a hollow space beneath the sarcophagus. Maybe Ash has found another way to it." He indicated the irregular piece of stone he'd been trying to dislodge. "That looks to be the most likely piece to knock through."

Without another word, they all positioned themselves, and started to hammer on the stone with their feet. The jarring impact rocked through Harlan's body. The stone was wedged well into position, and it took several minutes before it finally dislodged and dropped into the space below. Harlan angled his flashlight downward, illuminating a chamber that looked about ten feet deep. And something was in there. Something blocky and tomb-shaped.

Shadow was pressing against him in an effort to see too, and she quickly said, "Me first!" Before Harlan could object, she wiggled over the edge and dropped inside.

Gabe called after her. "Be careful!"

Her muffled voice shouted back, "You're going to want to see this!"

Infected by Shadow's reckless enthusiasm, Harlan said, "I'm coming."

He wriggled down through the hole, fingers gripping the stone edge, and then dropped to the ground, narrowly missing landing on the huge tomb that dominated the space. He turned his flashlight on. "Well, at least we know why the two brothers on horseback was a clue. Something we got right!"

"But there's no treasure here!"

Shadow was right. The chamber was bare of ornamentation, but covered in fragments of rock and dust caused by the explosion above. A doorway in the wall led to another passageway. "There's another exit."

"I'll check it out in a minute," she said, preoccupied by the huge tomb.

The tomb itself was impressive. It was comprised of a series of stone bases, the lowest one wide and thick, stepping up by four levels to the sarcophagus itself that was on Harlan's eye level. The stone was richly carved with plants and swirling imagery, as well as Templar symbols. On top was another effigy, resting on his back, clad in full armour, a sword between gloved hands that ran the length of the tomb.

Written at the base, below the knight's booted feet, was the epitaph bearing William de la More's name.

He called up to Nahum and Gabe. "We've found William's tomb!"

In seconds Nahum swung down to join them. "But no treasure?"

"Not unless it's in the tomb with him. Or down there." He indicated the narrow passage. "What do you think?"

Nahum rubbed his bloodied jaw. "If someone has gone to all the trouble to hide William's tomb, surely you would at least make one route inside, and that could be the way Ash will approach—if he's in the passage. Let's face it, that grenade did us a favour. We'd never have found this place otherwise."

"You don't know that," Harlan disagreed. "We'd barely started examining the brothers' tombs before we were attacked. There might well have been a mechanism to get in. And what about the key in the hilt? That must have a use." There were still too many questions. Too many variables.

"While you two are arguing," Shadow declared, "I'm moving on."

"*Wait*!" Gabe's voice boomed from above. In moments, he dropped down, too. "I've just checked with Niel. It's all quiet up there. No police, no more knights. He's dragged the bodies out of the way for now, but we need to be quick—just in case."

"Easier to say than do, brother," Nahum said, turning his attention back to the tomb. "Unless there's treasure down wherever that other passage leads, this tomb must tell us where to go next, or why hide it?"

Shadow was already at the start of the next tunnel. "Gabe. Time to go."

Gabe nodded. "I'm coming. You two stay here and examine every inch of that tomb."

He left with Shadow, and Harlan surveyed the tomb with pursed lips. "I wish I knew what we're looking for. A keyhole, perhaps? Another mechanism? The tomb is elaborate, which suggests there has to be something else here."

"I agree. I'm going to get some of those candles and lanterns from above. Let's light this place up."

Twenty-Six

Ash used his sword to hack into the tree roots that thrust through the sides of the passageway, hoping that the whole place wasn't about to cave in on their heads.

They had just passed through a particularly tricky section of the tunnel, where a thick root had dislodged part of the rock wall. They had slid past the rockfall and earth, relieved to find that the rest of the passageway was intact, but from there, it had been slow going. It was clear they were under the wooded section of Theo's land.

"Do you think it's much further?" Theo asked, his voice muffled from the shirt he had pulled over his mouth in an effort not to inhale dust and debris.

Ash tried to estimate the distance they had covered. "Hard to say. I'm a bit disorientated. We just have to keep moving."

However, within minutes the passageway inclined, and just as Ash started to feel hopeful that they were within reach of their destination—wherever that may be—they reached an intersection where three passages diverged. One path ran straight ahead, the others went left and right. All were of equal heights and widths, and nothing indicated where they might lead.

He turned to Theo. "We should have known this wouldn't be straightforward."

"So which one do we choose?" Theo was filthy. Dirt was smeared across his face and clothes, and Ash knew he looked worse. His feet were still damp from where he'd waded through the filth of the moat beneath the tower.

"Got any matches? We could check for air flow. Or we could be methodical. Start with the left-hand passage and then try the next."

"Perhaps. It would help if we knew where we were. I suspect we're close to the village now."

"Me, too. One could lead to the church, one perhaps to the old inn. They're the two oldest buildings in the village. But the other?"

"There would have been other old buildings," Theo reasoned. "They've just been knocked down over the years. Or one could lead to a cave. We have no idea how far these will run."

Ash considered the possibilities. "I can't help but feel we should keep going down the centre one. It's the one that calls to me."

"Then let's do that. And let's hope the paths don't diverge again." Theo lifted a bushy eyebrow. "Or we might find ourselves lost down here."

Niel leaned against the side door of the church, surveying the graveyard, with Mouse next to him.

The bodies of the dead knights had been placed next to the wall, so that any casual passer-by couldn't see them. Not that there should be anyone passing by after midnight in a small village. The place was quiet, the inn closed, and the church was on the edge of the village anyway, providing some privacy.

The fight had sounded loud with the clashing of swords and grunts of engagement, but it was over relatively quickly once Niel arrived to help Gabe and Shadow. To Niel's surprise, Mouse hadn't escaped. He watched her, wishing he could trust her, but knew he couldn't.

"I presume you're waiting to see what we find," he said to her.

"Of course." She leaned against the wall, her face still covered by the black mask that revealed only those beguiling eyes. "I was employed to find the treasure. I intend to do that."

"Who by?"

"Nicoli. You know that."

"But who employed Nicoli?"

Her eyes lifted in a smile. "I don't know. I'm just a contractor. I don't ask questions."

"You don't care who you work for? Whether you're on the side of right or wrong?"

She rolled her eyes. "Who's to say who is right or wrong? Should Theo get to find Templar treasure that isn't his? Or should the rightful heirs find it?"

"You think that's who those guys are? The rightful heirs?" He nodded at the half a dozen dead knights. It seemed a strange word to call them, but having inspected their bodies, it was only fair. They all wore heavy black cloaks of good quality wool, and donned modern body armour of black Kevlar. Their swords were also quality, but the hilts were relatively plain, the blade lacking engravings or any ornamentation. "The Knights of Truth and Justice."

"From the insignias on their chests, I would say they are, wouldn't you?"

"I guess so." The silver Templar cross marked on the breastplate was interwoven with an ornate *T* and *J*. Beyond that, there was nothing to identify them. At least they didn't have tattoos and strange, metallic skin.

"Yes," Mouse continued, "I do think they have a claim. The Templar treasure was put aside for the *Templars*. King Philip of France and the pope stole huge sweeps of land and property. Men are no different through time. They are motivated by greed. Theo too, perhaps."

"I think he's thrilled by the chase rather than the monetary value. He said he'll donate it to a museum."

"It's not his to donate. What about you? Do you feel guilty that you killed them?"

"Yes, a little," he admitted, turning to study her expression. "But they were determined to kill *us*. They left us little choice."

Something felt wrong. Mouse protested that she didn't know who had employed her, but she seemed knowledgeable about the knights, and sympathetic to their cause. And it wasn't just her attitude that worried him.

Where were the knights based? There were only half a dozen men outside, plus a couple inside, from what Gabe had told him. There must be more of them if they were so determined to find the treasure first. *And Mouse.* Was there another connection, or were there really several groups interested in the treasure? Some would be interested in pure monetary value, for others there might be religious significance. Or Ash might be right. There could be esoteric knowledge hidden here somewhere. Eighteen ships had disappeared. *It couldn't possibly all be here, could it?*

A prickle of unease ran down his spine as a noise beyond the graveyard broke the night's silence. He wasn't even sure what he'd heard. *The crack of a twig? A footfall?* He stepped forward to try to see onto the lane beyond the side gate, and felt Mouse reach his side. He assumed that she was also looking to see what was going on, until he felt something jab his skin.

Pain ripped through him as his body spasmed, and the world went dark.

Gabe halted in the middle of the next chamber and stared in shock at the richly engraved walls all around him.

"What the hell are we supposed to do with this?"

"Maybe nothing?" Shadow looked as unconvinced as her voice sounded.

"No one goes to all this trouble for *nothing*!"

"Maybe the Templars and their descendants do. Sounds like they enjoyed a bit of pomp and ceremony."

The room they stood in was only a short distance from the tomb chamber, but it could not have been more different. As Gabe took stock of the place, his torch sweeping over the floor and the ceiling, he realised that not only were the walls carved, but the floor and ceiling was, too.

"I feel," Gabe said with a sinking suspicion, "like I'm standing in one of those Chinese puzzle boxes."

"What are they?"

"Don't you ever listen to anything? Ash was talking about them a month or so ago."

"Only when it sounds interesting. That obviously didn't. What about them?"

"They're intricate boxes that have things hidden in them. You have to work out what to press and move to open them up."

Shadow nodded as she prowled around the space. "I get it. The fey made similar pieces. Mystery boxes."

"Well, you know what I mean, then. Except we're on the inside. We need to figure out the right thing to press to reveal the prize—which is hopefully the treasure."

"And if we press the wrong thing?"

"Maybe you should stop walking, Shadow."

She halted, head cocked. "You think I'll trigger something?"

"This could be a test. Much like the Temple of Raziel. It's for the initiated." He hadn't moved from the spot in the centre, and now he wondered why he'd blundered inside. "We aren't even close to being initiated."

"But we have clues, and we're smart. Plus, we have a key."

"Not right now we don't." He groaned. "Bollocks. We should have waited outside."

Shadow's hands flew to her hips. "If you think I'm going to stand here like a terrified fawn, you don't know me at all, Gabe!"

"We need to be smart, Shadow. I know you're not terrified."

"We marched halfway across the floor and haven't triggered anything yet. You're just paranoid."

"Look around. We're surrounded by Templar imagery, as well as the Green Man, leaves, plants, heraldic symbols, and what appears to be a kind of history." A series of images caught his eye as he shone his torch around the room. It was hard to know what to focus on first. "And look. Ships on a river."

"Herne's horns." Shadow's voice rose in excitement. "This could be a map to all of the treasure. Perhaps that's what this place is! This isn't just a bit of it. This is the storehouse of knowledge!"

"You might be right. Maybe this is where Ash's key fits?"

Shadow pointed to another arched doorway opposite the one they had arrived through. "Ash must still be somewhere that way." She took a half pace forward and froze as something clicked beneath her foot. Immediately, a grating noise emanated around them. "Oops."

"Shadow! I told you not to move!"

"It was an accident!"

Gabe glanced at the open doorways wondering whether to run for it, but the doors were several paces away, and they might trigger something else on the way out. "Just don't move again. You must have opened something."

"But what?"

Both swept their torchlight around the room with increasing panic as the grating noise intensified.

"There! That stone!" Shadow's voice rose with excitement as her light showed a stone block moving backwards into the wall. As it dropped into position, everything fell silent. "Is that it? It's over?"

"Maybe?"

Then a whirring noise began, and with startling speed, doors slammed down into the only exits, and they were trapped inside.

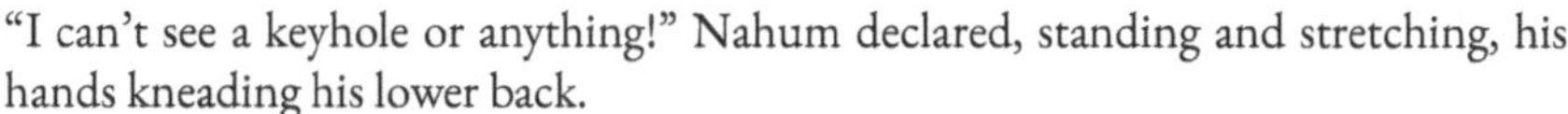

"I can't see a keyhole or anything!" Nahum declared, standing and stretching, his hands kneading his lower back.

"Neither can I." Harlan was still on his hands and knees as he examined the relief carved onto the lowest section of the tomb. "Intriguing, though. I think these reliefs tell a history. The words aren't Latin."

Nahum walked around to study the inscription. "No. Old French. They're all names. Probably the names of the English masters." The names made one big list around the lower level. All ornately carved in flowery script, and still reasonably crisp-edged.

"Wow. It's quite something, isn't it? To be looking at the final resting place of the last Commander of the English Templars. The end of a tragic piece of history."

"Why do you think their story has lasted so long?" Nahum asked.

Harlan stood and dusted off his knees. "Good question. I think it's the mystery of it all. Everyone loves missing treasure, don't they? And it was the swiftness of it. The shock. The fact that such a huge organisation could suddenly disappear in a matter of days."

"Although months is more realistic," Nahum pointed out.

"But still swift for such a powerful, far-reaching group. It's sort of a lesson, I think, that even the strongest and most powerful organisations are not immune to time, greed, and enemies. '*Look on my works, ye mighty, and despair! Nothing beside remains. Round the decay of that colossal wreck, boundless and bare, the lone and level sands stretch far away.*'" He cocked his head at Nahum. "Shelley."

Nahum smiled. "I've heard of him. I didn't take you for a poetry lover."

"I'm full of surprises. That was Ozymandias."

"Yeah, well. I'm living proof of those words." A wave of melancholy swept over Nahum. "Civilisations, organisations, dynasties, royal families...Gods. They all have their time, and then they're gone."

"The Igigi survived. And so have you."

"More by luck for us, and we are a fraction of the many Nephilim." Nahum shrugged off his mood. "No time for retrospection, Harlan. Perhaps we should go check on Gabe and Shad—" He didn't finish his sentence. A noise from above caught his attention and he froze, gesturing silence to Harlan.

A female voice with a hint of an accent, and a slight tease to her tone, called down to them. "So, that's where you are." Nahum leapt backwards, sword raised as she said, "Don't worry. No harm will come to you if you just do as we say."

Through the opening in the cracked slab, Nahum saw the veiled face of a woman, and clustered behind her, at least half a dozen knights. Ice filled his veins. "You must be Mouse. Where's Niel? I swear, if—"

"He's fine. More or less. And will remain so if you do exactly what I say."

"Are you bargaining with his life?"

"Yes. With all of your lives. Step back. We're coming down."

Nahum didn't move. "Prove he's alive first."

"When I'm down there. I can't do it from here."

Nahum knew he had no choice, not if Niel was in danger. He stepped back, Harlan retreating next to him, released the hilt of his sword, and held his hands high. "Fine."

The petite woman wriggled through the gap and dropped to the ground with the grace of a gymnast, quickly followed, with less grace, by three tall knights, clad in the familiar clothing of the Knights of Truth and Justice. All three swiftly bowed their heads and dropped to one knee before the tomb of William de la More before rising to their feet again.

"You trespass on hallowed ground, Nephilim," one of the knights said.

His shoulders looked broad, but that was deceptive. The cloak added width and bulk. His true build once the cloak was swept back showed he was wiry, his face thin, gaunt almost, marked perhaps with the fervour of a disciple.

"So do you," Nahum shot back.

The knight shook his head. "No. We belong here. The Dagger of Secrets was meant for us." *Dagger of Secrets?* He glanced around the tomb and then spotted the doorway. "Your companions are through there, I presume?" He gestured to his two associates who turned as if to leave.

Nahum stepped in front of them. "Show me proof that Niel is alive." He was prepared to fight to the death if Niel was dead. He wouldn't bargain.

The knight gestured impatiently to Mouse, and she held up her phone, showing Nahum a picture of Niel, unconscious, and trussed and bound outside the church. A knight stood over him. "There. He's okay, and will be released when this is over."

"But don't push me," the knight added, his voice gruff. "We have lost men because of you. I will not risk more if I can help it."

Nahum couldn't help himself. "You bombed Theo's grounds and threw grenades at us. Of course we retaliated!"

The knight clenched his jaw. "Enough. There will be no more bombs, but we *will* take the treasure."

Nahum glanced at Harlan, who nodded in agreement. "There's been enough bloodshed, Nahum. Let this play out."

Nahum hated being backed into a corner, but knew he had no choice. And all the talk of who was really deserving of the treasure made him consider their actions. Perhaps their team wasn't meant to find it. "Fine. Truce. But no more bloodshed or bombs, or that's all off."

The knight nodded, and his companions quickly exited the room, following Gabe and Shadow's path. As soon as they had left, he said, "Give me the dagger."

"We can't," Harlan answered. "Ash has it, and we don't know where he is. We think he's following a passage from under the keep."

"Ah, yes. Then we will capture him soon, too. Men are following them." He stepped past Nahum and began to inspect the tomb.

Nahum turned his attention to the woman, understanding why Neil was taken with her. She was slender, graceful, and had very pretty eyes. Unfortunately, those eyes currently held a steely reserve. "So, you're Mouse. We thought you were working for someone else, but you've been working with these people all along."

"It's just a job." She cast the knight a sidelong glance. "But I don't like bloodshed. I'm a thief. That's all. That's why your friend is still alive—because of me."

"Because of *me*," the knight retorted, eyes still on the tomb. "My decision."

Before she could respond, one of the knights returned, panic in his eyes. "Sire. The next room is sealed. There's no way inside."

Nahum and Harlan exchanged a panic-stricken glance, and regardless of Mouse and heavily armed knights, raced down the passage.

As soon as the doors sealed shut, Shadow heard the sound of trickling water.

"Oh, that's not good." She spun around, looking for the source of the noise, and with horror saw water streaming in through the dislodged stone.

Gabe was furious. "Herne's steaming balls! Now we're going to drown in here! I told you not to move!"

"And I told you it was an accident!"

"Well un-accident it."

She glared at him. "That's not even a word!"

Gabe strode over to the hole in the wall, thrust his hand through the water, and grimaced. "The bloody stone is gone. And the water is freezing!"

"You expected to find a plug?"

"Will you please do something useful, Shadow!"

Biting back a retort, she studied the block beneath her feet that had triggered the mechanism. She placed her blade down the side in an attempt to manoeuvre it back out, but it was pointless. Her gaze swept the room. There had to be *something* to reverse it. *Another mechanism? Maybe related to the river carved on the wall.* She studied it with fierce intensity. The freezing water was already sloshing around her ankles.

"Gabe, we need to be logical."

"Yes, I know. But we're running short on time."

"We have time!" She glared at him. "This is a slow trickle."

"We'll freeze before we drown." He marched to the doorway they had entered through, retracing his steps. "I'm going to try brute force—and summon help. Nahum!"

Leaving Gabe to try and batter his way out, Shadow tried to focus on the carvings, but it was impossible. Her thoughts refused to settle. There were so many images that it was hard to say what was more important. There were carvings of men being burned at the stake, men being tortured...gruesome images that told of the horrible demise of the Templars. But there was also a huge map of Europe and the Middle East carved onto one wall. Various posts were marked. *Centres of power, perhaps? Places where treasure was hidden—or where treasure had been found?*

Shadow was still unfamiliar with most of Europe, but she recognized France, Spain, Portugal, and the United Kingdom. Despite the urgency of their situation, she found herself fascinated by the story told on the walls. One thing was clear, though. She was completely unequal to this task.

"Gabe, I think we're going to drown."

"Not funny, Shadow."

"I'm not trying to be funny. I can't work out what we're supposed to do!"

Suddenly the sound of running water changed and slowed, and with a sigh of relief, Shadow looked at the flow. "Oh good, it's slowing…" She faltered. The clear water wasn't clear anymore. It was increasingly murky. And then a thin stream of mud oozed through the opening instead. "Oh shit, Gabe. I think we'll suffocate in mud, instead."

"What?" He turned to her, fists bloodied from where he'd been trying to release the door, and his eyes fell to the flow of ooze. "Brilliant. Just brilliant!"

"It must be a lake or something that silted up." Her spirits brightened. "This will buy us time."

"A delay to our eventual suffocation. And it stinks!"

He was right. The smell of rot filled the air, and Shadow pulled her t-shirt over her mouth again. *Herne's horns.*

She turned back to the images. Focus. Death was not an option.

Ash turned to Theo, head cocked. "Can you hear water?"

Theo stopped and listened, his face creased in concentration. "Yes. A weird gurgle. I think it's coming from the room ahead. *'The Chamber of Truth'.*"

They had just arrived in a small, square room that was half filled with rockfall and earth. Just visible over the mound was a doorway of solid stone, covered in carved reliefs. It fitted snugly into an arched stone frame. Carved into the arch, in Latin, was the name of the room that Ash had just translated.

Ash eyed the mound of earth and the unstable roof above. The fall looked to be a mixture of old and fresh, perhaps the latest triggered by the rumble they felt earlier. Or maybe this *was* the rumble they'd felt. Hoping the roof would hold, he was about to start cautiously clambering over it when a muffled yell made him stop.

"Did you hear that?" He stared beyond Theo, down the receding passageway, but couldn't see a thing.

"That was ahead, not behind us," Theo said with certainty. "Someone's in there."

Abandoning caution, Ash scrambled over the rockfall, Theo next to him, and shouted, "Hello!"

A muffled shout called back, but he couldn't make out the words. However, the voice was familiar. "Bloody hell. I think that's Gabe. He's in trouble."

"Would our key help?"

"The key! Brilliant thinking, Theo." Ash fished the key from his pocket. "Any sign of a keyhole?"

Over half of the door was buried in soil, and while Theo used his hands to dig the bottom half of the door out, Ash examined the upper portion. Dust lay thick in the folds and curves of the carvings, and he started to scrub it with his bare hand, holding his torch steady with the other. It was pitch black, and the air was thick with the smell of decay. The more Theo dug and the more Ash cleaned the door, the more choking clouds of debris flew up. Through increasingly gritty eyes, Ash made slow progress as the yelling increased in volume.

What the hell was happening in there?

"I'm trying to be as quick as I can!" he shouted back, almost losing his footing as Theo moved more and more earth. "Theo!"

"Sorry! This stuff is caked in, Ash. There are huge rocks in it."

Shadow's voice sounded close to his ear. "I'm going to drown in mud! What are you doing?"

"What do you think I'm doing, you crazy fey madam?" *Shit. He shouldn't have said fey.* Hopefully, Theo would think it was an endearing insult.

Ash wrestled a huge rock from the base of the door and threw it to the other side of the room, allowing Theo to move the earth more easily, then turned his attention to the door again. He wished there was no ornamentation. He was sick of ornate reliefs; beautiful or not, they were giving him a headache. There was still no sign of a keyhole, and he wondered if he'd got it all wrong. *Was there a mechanism instead?*

"Shadow, is there anything on your side?"

"I'm not a complete idiot! Of course there bloody isn't."

Gabe yelled, "Ash, time is pressing!"

"We're being as quick as we can!" While he searched, he asked, "What happened?"

"Shadow released something, and it trapped us inside."

"Who's us?"

"Just us two. The others are elsewhere—Niel, too." Silence fell, and then Gabe shouted again. "The bloody knights are on the other side! Get us out!"

Ash froze.

"Knights?" Theo asked, halting too. "Here?"

"That must mean they have the others," Ash reasoned. "Hurry!"

They both redoubled their efforts. And then Ash spotted it. The keyhole was in the centre, a part previously covered by the earth from the collapsed roof, placed within a carving of an eye. It had been plugged with earth, but as he scrubbed away at the door, a portion had fallen free, revealing the outline. He scrabbled at it with the end of his finger, but only succeeded in jamming it further in. Then he tried the point of his knife, but that wasn't much better.

Gabe bellowed again. "Ash!"

"I've found it. Give me a moment!"

"Here!" Theo thrust a small penknife at him with a tiny blade. "Will this do?"

Relief flooded through him. "Theo. You're a genius! Shine the torch on it."

In a few seconds, Ash managed to scrape most of the earth out, and inserted the key. It slotted in, and with a few wiggles, he felt it drop into place. With a deep breath, he turned it.

Nothing happened.

"It's stuck." Sweat trickled down Ash's brow and into his eyes, and he swept it away with the back of his hand. "I need oil."

"Sorry, I don't carry that."

"I think I need a bucket of it."

Shadow yelled again. "Use brute force, you giant oaf!"

"Shut up, Shadow. This is your fault!" Ash shouted back.

Theo sniggered. "She's really quite funny."

Ash continued to twist and wriggle the key. "See how you like constantly being insulted."

"It's a sign of affection. It's quite charming, really."

"Good. She can live with you, then."

"I can hear you!" she yelled, her muffled voice outraged. "You'll regret that when I'm out."

"If you still want me to teach you to drive, please shut up!"

Ash finally felt the lock give and the key moved a quarter turn. He jiggled it again, and with incremental movements, it finally twisted through the full turn. A mechanism started grinding within the door, and it shuddered to the right a few inches before sticking again. It was enough for a gap to appear between the door and the frame, and a foul smelling, thick slushy liquid oozed out. Gabe and Shadow's face pressed to the gap, Shadow's below Gabe.

"It's stuck!" Ash told them. "You need to help."

Between them, many fingers wedged into the slim gap, they forced the door open, and the sludgy ooze turned into a deluge. Ash recoiled, a hand flying over his mouth, as he and Theo backed up onto the mound of earth.

"Were you in a sewer?" he asked, trying not to heave.

For a moment, neither Gabe nor Shadow spoke, both of them scooting out of the door, looking almost green. They had been waist-deep in the filthy, muddy liquid, and now both of them were caked in it. It was smeared over their arms and faces, and Ash couldn't help but snigger as relief swept over him.

Shadow glared at him. "It's not funny. I could have drowned in effluent. I still might."

She was right; the mud was now rising in the antechamber. It was blocked by the fall of earth and was seeping into it, creating an even greater, sludgy mix.

Gabe leaned back against the wall taking deep breaths, but the air in the small, collapsed chamber wasn't really that fresh, either. "It wasn't a sewer. It might have been an old lake that's dried up now or something. I hope. Maybe it was a cess pit."

"That's the way I'd torment anyone who was raiding my tomb," Theo said, nodding. "I like their style."

Gabe suddenly took in the half-collapsed chamber. "Oh, crap. I thought we'd escaped. Where are we now?"

"Don't worry, there is a way out," Ash reassured him. "Back that way. We have two other options, but have no idea where they come out, or whether they're in a worse state than this. Did you say that knights are here?"

Shadow answered as she clambered up the mound of earth and rocks. "Yes. They must have followed us into the church, which means...*Niel!*"

"Don't even think it, Shadow," Gabe warned. "We'll go around, somehow, and find him."

Ash had a million questions, but they would have to wait. He scrambled back to the passage, already feeling the earth start to collapse under him, weakened by the muddy mix. He'd only gone a few short feet back down the tunnel when he heard voices and saw the flash of a torch.

He turned his own off, shushing the others to silence. But it was too late. A booming voice yelled down the passage. "Halt! Surrender to the Knights of Truth and Justice, now!"

"Back up!" Ash yelled, trying not to fall over his retreating companions in the cramped space. He pointed up to the already unstable roof. "We either fight our way out, or block the way completely."

Shadow groaned. "But then we're stuck in the chamber of death!"

"Gabe?" Ash needed his opinion. "I don't know how many knights there are, and to be honest, there's not much room for fighting."

Gabe nodded. "Retreat. The main chamber is the answer. We just—" he glared at Shadow, "need to be smarter about working it out."

"And if we can't?" Theo asked, eyes widening with horror. "We're trapping ourselves in a tomb."

"There's another way out, remember?" Gabe said. "It just has knights on the other side of it, too."

Without another word, they scrambled back over the mound of earth. This time Gabe balanced himself on the top, and started pulling at the remaining brickwork on the ceiling closest to the passage, as Ash helped him.

Together they pulled several stone blocks free and hurled them down the passage, and with an ominous rumble, the roof collapsed.

Twenty-Eight

"You know," Barak said, "I could get used to this. But weirdly, I think I miss my brothers."

"What about Shadow?" Estelle asked, amused.

"Even her!" He grinned and kissed Estelle. "But regular holidays like this may be the way to go."

They were seated in the *gîte's* living room, where they had set up the laptop on the coffee table. Both of them were seated on cushions on the floor, the remains of cheese, crackers, and olives on the table. Barak was drinking beer, Estelle wine, and both were tired. It was after midnight, and they'd been researching for hours. Barak's eyes were gritty, and his brain felt like a big knot.

"I'm not sure I'd call this a holiday!" Estelle gestured at the list of sites they'd made after their internet search. "We need to narrow these down, and to be honest, the internet doesn't have nearly enough detail. We need books! Maps!"

"I agree." Barak felt they'd barely scratched the surface of what they needed to know. "And we might even be completely wrong."

"Possibly. But it feels right!" Estelle raked her hand through her hair, her frustration and tiredness clear. "And I can't help but think on what Ash last said to you about the Templars."

"Don't bring that up again," Barak groaned.

"It's important. This is another facet of the count that we can't afford to ignore. It could well be tied into all of this."

Barak contemplated his conversation with Ash earlier that evening. Their latest job was delivering more than just a treasure hunt. It had brought bombs and subterfuge, and a new, unknown enemy that they feared was linked with the shadowy figure of the count.

Barak finally looked at Estelle. "I feel we're mired in darkness and cobwebs. That nothing's real. It's like..." he struggled to describe it. "Like trying to hold water with my bare hands."

Estelle reached for her glass of wine. "We can't forget yesterday's success. Finding Lucien and that facility was concrete proof of what they do. I know we've encountered their soldiers many times, but I feel we achieved a tiny glimpse into their inner workings. This potential Templar link just adds a whole new level of intrigue."

"But also another thread to pick away at. That's a good thing. However," he hated what he was about to say, because he loved spending time with Estelle, "I think we should return to England, and see Jackson at The Retreat. Thinking we could crack things from here is nuts. Fun, but nuts nonetheless."

"I know, but I like it here."

"I confess, I suggested it really just to be with you." He kissed her hand, happy to see her blush with pleasure. "I've loved every second of it. But, I'm a bit worried about Lucien." An uneasy feeling had been growing in him all night. "I don't know why, but I just am."

"You don't trust him?"

"I think I do. Maybe I just don't trust what's been done to him. He could be a ticking time bomb—metaphorically speaking. I think I'm going to phone Jackson."

"Now?" Estelle checked her watch. "It's late."

Barak reached for his phone. "I don't care. I have to. Hopefully things are okay." He shrugged, trying to make light of it, but he just had a bad feeling he couldn't shake. "Maybe Ash's news has made me paranoid."

"Trust your instincts. I do. I'll search for flights and get us on the earliest one. And for the record, I've enjoyed every second, too."

Jackson had been mired in a dream-filled sleep when his phone rang, and for a few moments he couldn't work out where he was, or what was happening.

Instinctively, he grabbed his phone, more to stop the noise than anything else. "Hello? Jackson speaking."

"It's Barak. Sorry. Did I wake you?"

Jackson groaned as he lay back on his pillow, staring into the darkness, and slightly dazzled by the light from his phone. There was no streetlight filtering into The Retreat, and the darkness was all consuming. "Yes, but it's a relief. I was having a horrible sleep. Is everything okay?"

"Just frustrated with our slow research, but we know we need to be realistic, and we can't justify spending weeks here. We're coming home tomorrow. But that's not why I called. I'm worried about Lucien."

Jackson sat up, his own fears rising again. "Why?"

"We don't know what they've done to him. I'm worried that something will trigger him. Something unexpected. Or *they* will. Something Lucien can't control...or won't want to."

"Like a sleeper agent?" Jackson couldn't keep the incredulity out of his voice.

Barak gave one of his deep, melodic laughs. "Something like that. I'm probably paranoid. I know I'm tired. I guess I just wanted to reassure myself that everything was okay."

Jackson rose from his bed, flicked the lamp on, and reached for his clothes. "He's in an observation room, and the team that extracted him is guarding him. It's not a cell, but we're being careful."

After a protracted argument earlier in the evening that Jackson lost, Lucien had been confined to the observation room rather than the bedroom that had been prepared for him. Miller, the team leader, had argued for caution. Waylen had agreed. Jackson had felt that every promise he'd made had been broken, but it was out of his control. Lucien had looked at him with barely concealed anger and disappointment, and maybe even fear. Fortunately, Layla had struck up a good relationship with him as she took samples and ran tests. Now they were just waiting for results.

"I'll get dressed," Jackson continued, "and I'll go and check on him. You get some sleep too, okay. You coming here tomorrow?"

"Yeah. I'll text you the time when I know it. Be careful, Jackson!"

"You too."

Jackson ended the call, and for a moment sat quietly, gathering his thoughts. The Retreat was utterly silent, but he was tucked down another side passage behind a locked door, and no one else was sleeping here. London could have exploded above him and he would never know. His room was large and comfortable, and like the rest of the headquarters, decorated in the Art Nouveau style.

Rubbing the sleep from his eyes, he got dressed, reached into the drawer for the service issued firearm he'd been trained to use, and strapped on his holster—just in case. Within minutes he reached the dimly lit corridor leading to the labs and the observation room, and heard shouts and thumping sounds from up ahead.

Shit.

He ran, and as he rounded the corner, he paused, horrified. The door to the observation room lay on the floor, light blazing from the room, and Lucien was standing atop it, the body of a guard on the ground at his feet. Lucien was clad only in his scrub bottoms. His feet and chest were bare, and his tattoos writhed in the light. His skin glowed like burnished copper, and as Jackson ran into view, Lucien turned unblinking, metallic eyes on him.

Jackson fumbled for his gun. The last thing he wanted to do was shoot Lucien, but there were no other guards in sight. *Where were they? Were they all dead?*

Lucien stepped off the door and over the guard's body, walking towards Jackson. He showed no sign of recognition.

Jackson's mouth was dry as he spoke. "Lucien! It's Jackson. I'm a friend. I'm here to help. Stop, or I'll shoot."

Lucien didn't stop, instead cocking his head at the gun before ignoring it. Jackson backed up, steadying his aim. If he shot at his leg, he wouldn't kill him, but that was a risky shot. He might miss.

"Lucien! I don't want to shoot, but I will. Stop *now!*"

He kept coming, and the only image that flashed into Jackson's head was the Terminator. Lucien wasn't going to stop until he was dead.

Jackson aimed for his legs, hoping the metallic skin didn't extend that far. Two shots missed and hit the wall, but the third found its mark—and didn't penetrate his skin or slow him down. Lucien blinked, and his eyes turned black before becoming metallic again.

Herne's balls. He had no Nephilim to save him now. He was screwed. Jackson raised his gun, aiming for Lucien's chest as he retreated down the corridor. His aim was true this time, but again, the bullets seemed to bounce off him. Jackson glanced to either side, wondering which was the best room he could shelter in, and he yelled for the guards on the main entrance. They were a distance away, but the sound should carry.

They needed an alarm system. If he survived this, he would insist on it.

Lucien's pace quickened, and Jackson fired again. He'd be out of bullets soon—not that they made the slightest difference. Just as he was about to turn and run, a figure crawled into view beyond Lucien and raised a weapon. At the same time, someone yelled from behind him. "Get down!"

Jackson turned and saw Miller with a rifle in his hands.

"Now, Jackson!"

Jackson threw himself to the floor and rolled to the side of the passage, just as Lucien broke into a sprint. Miller and the guard fired together, shots peppering Lucien from both directions. After a few faltering steps, Lucien dropped and thudded to the floor.

Miller raced to Lucien and stood over him, nudging his body with his toe. "He's out cold."

Jackson sat up, heart thumping. "Not dead?"

Miller grinned. "I wouldn't kill your prized asset, Jackson."

He stumbled over his words. "How? What?"

"Something the lab's been working on. Armour-piercing tranquilliser darts—especially designed for these guys. I wasn't sure they'd work, but I'm impressed. However, I'm not sure how long he'll be out for."

"Where are we going to put him? We haven't got any cells here!"

"We'll improvise."

Twenty-Nine

Niel's entire body ached, especially his jaw. In fact, it was clenched shut so tightly, his muscles felt locked in position.

For a second, he was utterly confused. Then his memory flooded back. He'd been attacked from behind. *By Mouse.*

Curse words littered his thoughts, but he didn't move or open his eyes, needing his captors to think he was still unconscious. He was lying face-down on the bare earth, soil and grit pressing into his skin. His hands were bound, and he heard breathing and felt the unmistakable presence of someone close by. A guard—most likely a knight.

He considered his options. His restraints were tight, and felt like rope, but Niel was supernaturally strong. However, he needed to be quick if he was to break free *and* overpower the guard. *But what had Mouse used on him?* The most likely option was a Taser or something similar. Ash had described his experience when he'd been captured by Black Cronos in the Igigi's cave, and it sounded the same.

It was a weakness, and Niel hated to be vulnerable. Had Mouse known about that, or was it just a lucky guess? A woman as small as she was needed to pack a powerful weapon. At least she didn't kill him. As he mused on that, his smouldering resentment became puzzlement. Why wasn't he dead? He must be a bargaining tool. Well, screw that.

He heard footsteps behind him and continued to pretend he was unconscious. A man joined his guard, and they both started to talk in hushed voices in a foreign language.

Portuguese. Interesting. Fortunately, Niel understood every word, and heard enough to know that Nahum and Harlan were also hostages, and that the others were stuck in another room.

In seconds, another voice joined them, and they all moved further away. The group was angry and frustrated. Their plans had been thwarted, and it sounded as if their other team members were in trouble. This was his moment to act, while their attention was elsewhere. Although his hands were bound behind him, his wings would not be impeded. He opened his eyes to slits, and saw he was a short distance from the church wall.

Niel flexed his shoulders and his wings expanded in one smooth, powerful move-ment. His wingspan was so great, he connected with a guard behind him, making him stumble. Using his wings as leverage, he bounded to his feet and ran, and seconds later was off the ground and flying to the bell tower at the top of the church. He ducked inside and sheltered within its thick walls.

His limbs still felt stiff, but he jerked his hands outwards, shredding the rope to free his arms. He didn't have any weapons except his bare hands, but they were good enough.

He dropped onto the church roof, ran across it, and peered over the side. One of the knights was searching the night sky for him, sword clenched in his hand. The other two had vanished. *To the tower perhaps?* With the other two nowhere in sight, Niel plunged over the far side of the church, ready to circle around and attack the knight. He'd been caught off guard once. He wouldn't be again.

Gabe took a deep breath. "Can we all focus, please!" He glared at Shadow, who was about to start arguing with Ash. "This is the place! The Chamber of Truth. Somewhere in here is a way to another room. Or a map. Or something."

So much for his motivational speech.

He continued, undaunted. "Now that we're in here again, we can't fuck it up. Concentrate."

"Is that aimed at me?" Shadow asked.

"Everyone."

"Well, if I can point out one important thing," Ash said in a low voice, "the mud has seeped into some rather interesting grooves."

They were all standing in the doorway, scared to set foot in the room again in case they triggered something, but Ash pointed to a series of grooves etched into the centre of the floor that weren't visible before.

Shadow grimaced. "Well, it's good to see that our brush with death wasn't all for nothing."

Ash ignored her tone. "What's through the other door?"

Gabe answered him. "Another antechamber, a short passage, and then de la More's tomb, right under the crypt."

"Anything in that?"

"We left Nahum and Harlan exploring it. The room itself was plain, the tomb huge. I have no idea if they found anything. They were attacked in the crypt, but won that fight."

"Okay." Ash nodded. "So this is called the Chamber of Truth. The dagger points the way to a treasure. We think. This room," he looked at it with trepidation, "is the answer. Look at how detailed it is. You already triggered one trap. We need to trigger the *right* mechanism."

"Another keyhole?" Theo asked, looking hopeful.

"Perhaps. We need to think like a Templar."

Shadow stared at him. "What do you think the grooves are?"

"They run along a set of slabs. I think they're a stairway." Ash pointed downward. "To another level. Let's face it—if there's another room, it's either accessed through the rear wall, or the front one. And that's where you triggered the stone that allowed the flood of mud, which has now mercifully stopped. There's already a room on that side and this side."

Shadow grinned, and in the torch light, and smeared with mud and blood, she looked like a demon. "I like it. You're right. You're good at this."

"It's just logical. We just need to work out what triggers it. Quickly." He nodded to the opposite door. "Before they find a way in. We also need something to bargain with."

Gabe wished they could fly. That would mean they wouldn't need to touch the floor at all. Unfortunately, the room wasn't big enough to allow any decent manoeuvrability. He studied the ground again, looking for patterns in the slabs, depressions, anything uneven. Ash was right. The remnants of the mud helped. It had coated the lower half of the walls, and still pooled in the corners, but it did highlight some of the reliefs.

"Ash, I think the key must have closed the flooding mechanism and allowed some of the mud to drain downwards, too." He pointed at the edge of some of the slabs that looked to have fine grills in them. "This place must have taken a long time to build."

"Well, the door jammed," Shadow pointed out, "so let's hope nothing else has failed over the years."

Ash stepped inside the room. "Follow me. I think the slabs marked with *Agnus Dei* symbols are safe. Can you see how they snake across the floor? They look the most stable of all of them. And there's more of them than any other."

"Well spotted," Gabe said, following him. The *Agnus Dei* slabs were clustered around both entrances, which had prevented them causing more problems earlier.

Theo pointed at one of the images in the wall. "That looks like the keep, and it's set within the grounds. And is that the village?"

"I think so." Ash stepped carefully on the designated slabs until he stood in front of it. "And there's the church. Is that a lake in the grounds?"

"Looks like it," Shadow said. "The one by the pavilion."

"But is it relevant?" Gabe asked. He was behind the others, as there wasn't room for him to get closer. He studied the church relief and compared it to the others spread across the wall. "The village is far more detailed than the rest of the carvings. You can see the individual headstones in the graveyard, the bell tower, the path—even the lychgate."

Ash nodded. "Too much detail to be irrelevant."

"The church cross!" Theo's voice rose with excitement. "It's sitting slightly proud."

"Isn't that a bit obvious?" Shadow asked, her voice filled with doubt.

"But look at how many other crosses there are," Gabe pointed out. "They're on all kinds of buildings spread across the map of Europe and the Middle East." It was the one constant of the images. Crosses were everywhere, large and small. Some were plain, others were ornate. "In fact, a few of them look as if they are sitting proud of the rest. Perhaps we need to press them at the same time."

"I doubt that," Ash said, but he sounded uncertain. "It makes more sense that the village church would be the trigger."

"For death?" Shadow asked scathingly.

"But what about the cross on Temple Mount?" Theo asked. "Or the ones in France. Wouldn't one of true significance be the one to try?"

"Surely Temple Mount is too obvious," Gabe reasoned.

"I agree," Ash said. "It's tempting to assume that, of course, but we're beneath Temple Church, next to William's crypt. It's logical to choose this one."

Shadow huffed. "Maybe that's what they want you to think."

Gabe was getting a headache. Trying to second guess someone else's reasoning, especially when they wanted to set a trap, was a nightmare.

Ash took a deep breath, in and out. "I'm going to try it." Ash laid his hand on the cross, hesitated for the briefest of moments, and then pressed it firmly. It clicked inwards and locked into place. Immediately, another loud grating sound resonated behind them, and Gabe spun around, ready to bolt for the door. *What could happen now? Pits of death? Spears shooting from the wall?*

Instead, to everyone's relief, the centre of the floor started to drop, revealing a series of steps leading down.

Gabe walked to the top of the them, torch shining into the depths. "These go down quite a long way. I'll lead."

Nahum stepped back into the shadows of the antechamber, beckoning Harlan to follow him.

"They're annoyed. We need to capitalise on it," Nahum whispered, while the leader, a man called de Moret, argued with another.

"How? We have no weapons, and that sneaky bitch, Mouse, is somewhere around here. Besides, if we act now, they could kill Niel."

"Just be prepared. And keep an eye on Mouse at all times!"

Harlan nodded, and Nahum studied the room for what felt like the hundredth time. After they had been captured, they had been hustled down the passage and into a small antechamber that must have been where Shadow and Gabe had been earlier. It was made of smooth stone blocks fitted tightly together, unadorned except that in one wall was an arched doorframe, a stone door sealing the way. The knights had tried to open it, but it was shut tight.

They were obviously wary of damaging it, so patience had won out over their frustration. More worryingly was the sound of Gabe and Shadow's muffled shouts on the other side. De Moret had tried to communicate with them, advising them of the situation and warning them to open the door, but they had told him they were trapped. Nahum wasn't sure if that was true or a ruse. Now, they had fallen silent.

Nahum wasn't sure what that meant. They could be dead, or they could have escaped. It was impossible to know. He decided to brave a question. "De Moret. You say you are Knights of Truth and Justice. Why haven't you got any information on how to open this?"

De Moret turned his deep-set eyes on him. "Because history has not been kind to us, and our predecessors chose to hide their treasure well. But we're close now. Too close to stop."

"Do you really think the treasure is here?"

"No. We believe another clue to the whereabouts of that treasure is here. The path has been hidden, so that only the true inheritors shall find it."

"How did you know to come here? To this church? Tonight."

"Theo Carmichael and Tower Keep have been under observation for a long time, as have many other places. We heard what he found. And what your companion discovered within it."

Nahum frowned, exchanging a worried glance with Harlan. "How did you find that out? He only opened the blade up hours ago."

De Moret smiled. "I have my ways."

"You have someone in the house."

"Perhaps. It is no business of yours."

Nahum wouldn't push it, but maybe Theo had employed someone new recently. Maybe it was even Owen, the gardener they had suspected earlier. He pressed on. "And you hired Mouse."

"An admirable assistant."

Harlan intervened. "I know your name. It's a Templar name."

"My ancestors were Templars, as were many of our other knights' forebears. Our order is old, dedicated. Determined. The treasure is ours. Not Theo's."

"You know, I am not unsympathetic to your cause," Nahum said, and meant it. "You were treated badly. I understand what drives you. Let us help."

"We don't need your help."

"Actually, I think you do. And we need yours. Our friends are on the other side of that. You need to get in. We have the key, too."

"No." De Moret cut him off and turned away. "We will get the key, and if you're lucky, you'll get to live."

"At least you tried," Harlan said softly. "Meanwhile, we're at a stalemate. The night is marching on, there are dead knights in the church, and soon it will be daylight. At least, I hope it will be. This night seems to have lasted for ever."

Another flurry of activity had them turning to the doorway, but Mouse had returned, carrying a bag. She ignored Nahum and Harlan and crossed to de Moret's side. "I've got the charges."

"Everything okay up top?"

"All quiet."

"Good. Let's blow this door."

"Woah!" Harlan stepped forward, alarmed. "You could bring the roof down and kill us all!"

De Moret glared at him. "I know exactly what I'm doing. Who do you think set the bombs in the lodge?"

Nahum was beginning to hate this man and his smug smile. Now he fervently hoped Shadow and Gabe had made progress. "You nearly killed my brothers."

"But I didn't. While I would rather not do this, we have to get in there, or all is lost."

Without another word, he turned his back and started to lay charges around the door. Mouse gave Nahum a fleeting look that was almost an apology. Right now, he hated her, too. For some strange reason, Niel had felt he could trust her. He took a deep breath and looked away. Anger wouldn't help him now.

Only icy calm would do.

Thirty

A huge, iron-bound door blocked their way at the bottom of the stairs, and Shadow waited impatiently for Ash to open it. They heard the repetitive clunking sound of several mechanisms releasing before it finally unlocked and revealed another room.

For a second, as their torches swept over the space, Shadow couldn't quite work out what she was seeing. Everything seemed to glow with a golden light.

And then she realised. It was gold.

"Oh, my God!" Theo said, almost breathless. "Is that what I think it is?"

"Yes!" Shadow said, grinning from ear to ear. The golden, twinkling light beckoned her. "At last, we have actually found treasure!"

"*Wait*!" Gabe's arm shot out in front of her to stop her from walking forward. "Can we just check the place out first, before we trigger some cataclysmic event?"

As one, they all shone their torches across the floor and around the rest of the room, discovering that it was designed like a church. The walls and floor were constructed of pale grey stone, but the central walkway was lined with gilded columns that soared to a golden roof, and at the far end was a huge altar. Throughout the entire room, heaped on pews and the floor, was treasure.

"Oh my goodness," Theo squeaked. "There's so much gold! Is it gilded, or solid?"

Ash whistled. "Surely not solid gold—or at least, not all of it."

"The floor looks safe," Gabe said, gingerly testing the ground beyond the bottom step. "I think we've passed all the tests now."

They slowly made their way into the church, torches flicking everywhere. Shadow spotted a series of arched recesses with candles and lanterns, and borrowing Theo's matches, she moved methodically along them, lighting them as she went. The golden light magnified and bloomed, and as it reflected off the surfaces, the light increased, revealing the true wealth around them.

Reliquaries of all shapes and sizes were heaped on the floor and on stone plinths, displayed to impress. Gold and silver crosses studded with gems, caskets inlaid with precious metals, gold coins, jewels, goblets, and so much more that Shadow could barely take it all in. The most impressive sight of all was the enormous gold cross mounted on the wall behind the altar. It was three times the height of a man, encrusted with jewels, and absolutely dazzling. She wondered how they had managed to get it down here. She had no interest in Christianity, but nevertheless, she appreciated that the cross was awe-inspiring, meant to drive the devout to their knees.

Gabe joined her, looking troubled. Uncertain. "I didn't expect this. I thought we'd find nothing! Or at best, a bag of gold."

"But this is good, right?"

"No." His mouth was set in a grim line. "So much hidden wealth is insane. And greedy."

"But you said you were once this wealthy. A prince with palaces, servants, and endless wealth."

"I was, but eventually it left me feeling uncomfortable. However, our God liked such tributes. It exalted him. And this type of worship clearly didn't change in all of the centuries that followed our demise. This should have been put to better use."

"To be honest, Gabe," Shadow said, trying to keep the impatience out of her voice, "the other Gods are no different. I don't know why you remain so disappointed by them all. You expect too much of them. I don't." *Especially after being conscripted into Herne's Wild Hunt.* "And I am not going to apologise for liking gold."

His eyes narrowed, and he headed to a pile of weapons. He clasped an ornate, jewelled hilt, and pulled it out of its scabbard. The edge of the blade was rusted. "This place is not immune from the damp of ages. The Templars' swords, perhaps?"

Ash joined them, abandoning his inspection of a gilded casket. "Or the weapons of those they escorted to Jerusalem. Remember, they acted as bankers—for royalty too, not just pilgrims." He stared up at the ceiling. "As above as below. Another layer of meaning. Another church below the one on the ground level."

"Didn't you say," Shadow said, recalling his earlier suspicions, "that this might lead to the Emerald Tablet?"

"Yes, I did. I wonder if it's here? Of all the items present, that would be of the greatest value to us—and to JD."

"Over all this gold?" Shadow was incredulous.

"Yes, and we can't take *all* of this!" Gabe swept his arm out. "It's impossible. And besides, it should be in a museum. Theo!"

Theo was still browsing the objects in a daze. "Yes?"

"You still aim to share this, right?"

"Of course. Can you imagine this displayed to the world? Or even this very room? It's magnificent!"

"But what about the knights?" Shadow pointed upwards. "And Harlan, Nahum, and Niel. We need to bargain with them!"

"There's no way, Shadow, that they will carry out all of this undetected," Ash pointed out. "I'm going to start searching for the tablet...just in case it's here."

Before he could say anything else, a dull boom resonated above them.

"Fuck it! What now?" Gabe asked, already jogging to the bottom of the stairs.

Shadow ran with him. "If they've blown the door, they could trigger something again!" Determined not to get stuck or half-drowned in mud again, Shadow sprinted past Gabe and up the stairs into the dust-filled room, yelling, "Stop! Don't move!"

A knight stood in the shattered doorway, sword drawn, and a grenade in his hand. His eyes glittered with fury in the pale light.

"*Stop!*" she yelled again. "If you don't want to destroy everything, I suggest you listen. We have found treasure. Lots of it. More than any of us will ever need. But if you make one wrong move, you could bring everything down on our heads."

His eyes raked over her and Gabe, before studying the room with its mud-blackened wall and floor. "What happened here?"

"A trap." She looked beyond the knight. "Where are our friends?"

His head jerked, and another knight pushed Harlan and Nahum into view. Both looked fine, but furious. A small figure was next to them. *Mouse.* "Your other friend is outside the church. Still alive. But he won't be if you don't guide me inside."

"Step only on the slabs marked with the *Agnus Dei*," Shadow instructed. "Nothing else."

"You're lucky that blowing that door didn't set anything else off," Gabe said. "Nahum! Harlan. You're unharmed?"

"Fine, brother."

"As well as can be expected," Harlan drawled.

The knight still stood in the doorway. "Who else is with you?"

"My brother, Ash, is downstairs, and Theo. That's all." Gabe released his sword hilt that he'd been clasping. "We need to work together. There's no point in fighting now."

"*I'll* decide that. Step back!"

Bristling with annoyance, but knowing they needed to comply for now, Gabe and Shadow made space for the knights to enter.

The knight pointed at Nahum. "You first. Join your friends."

Stepping carefully, Nahum studied the floor and crossed to the stairs, finally reaching Gabe and Shadow's side. "There you go, de Moret. It's all safe!"

Reassured, de Moret crossed quickly, and at the top of the steps, stared downwards. He summoned several knights to join him, but left Harlan and Mouse guarded in the antechamber. "Your friend will stay here as insurance for your good behaviour. Now, take me downstairs."

With Gabe at the lead, they headed down the stairs again, de Moret and his knights at the rear.

After a furiously intense fight, Niel killed the final knight he found at the bottom of the bell tower.

He had not intended to kill any more men; only incapacitate them. A courtesy, after they had spared his life. He had secured two of them, knocking them unconscious, and locking them in one of the church rooms, but the last knight refused to yield.

Niel was bloodied, too. His opponent, one of the most experienced swordsmen he'd ever fought, had inflicted cuts on his arms and legs, an especially deep one across his flank. He regretted the death. He would have rather spared him. Plus, killing someone in a house of God made him uncomfortable. He was under no illusions about the old God who had caused them such anguish, and he certainly owed him nothing, but for the many who treated this place with respect and reverence, he regretted sullying it. He only wished they'd come to their senses and make their own decisions, without recourse to old scripture that had no place anymore.

However, before he headed to the crypt, he stepped outside the side door and checked the graveyard. Shadowy figures were already moving through the gravestones. *More knights.*

Retreating inside, and hoping they wouldn't use any more bombs for fear of attracting attention, Niel shut and barred the door, and then wedged a pew behind it for good measure. He did the same with the main entrance, checked that the men were still incapacitated, and then headed downstairs to the crypt. He hated that they were now trapped inside, but at least they were secure. And they could escape through the bell tower, if needed.

Once in the crypt, it was clear where he needed to go. He relieved the dead knights of their weapons and dropped through the hole in the base of the tomb, landing lightly on his feet. Niel's stealth always surprised people. They assumed that because of his size he would be loud. However, all the Nephilim had been taught how to move silently. Their fathers had drummed it into them. It was part of their heritage. They might not have fey magic, but their angelic blood possessed certain unique qualities.

Progressing along the short passageway, he saw another chamber ahead and several knights facing away from him. Not knowing who or what was beyond them brought him to a halt. One wrong move now could be disastrous. He lowered himself to the ground, melting into the deepest shadows, and settled in to watch and listen.

Thirty-One

Ash was searching through the contents of one of the gold caskets when Gabe and Shadow arrived with Nahum, several armed knights behind them.

He straightened, placing his hand on his sword hilt, and moved closer to Theo, anxious to shield the old man from whatever the knights might threaten. He noted the lead knight held a grenade, and suspected they had more hidden in their cloaks. They'd be idiots to use them here, but Ash wasn't taking anything for granted.

Nahum acknowledged Ash with a nod before addressing the knights. "De Moret. You have found what you came for. There is no need for any more violence."

De Moret didn't speak. Instead, he strode down the central path and dropped to his knees in front of the altar, taking a few moments for a murmured prayer. Then he stood, hands on hips, studying the underground church. "Magnificent."

"Is this all of it?" Ash asked. "All of the lost treasure?"

"No." De Moret walked over to the nearest casket, picking up a gold cross with reverence. "There is much more hidden in other places. Somewhere in here will tell us where."

"Perhaps," Ash agreed cautiously. "Although, I think you may find the map carved into the Chamber of Truth above will be of more use."

"We will study all of it. And everything will be removed."

"You can't!" Theo clenched his fists and lifted his chin defiantly. "This is history! You can't take it all!"

"It is *our* history, and we most certainly will."

"How?" Gabe sounded irritated. "It would take a week at least to move all of this. The village would see you. And there are dead bodies in the churchyard, and a half-destroyed tomb in the crypt."

De Moret gave an icy smile. "But there is a convenient passage leading from here to Temple Keep. It may be blocked for now—oh yes, I have heard from my men. But we can rectify that. And no one visits the crypt. We will lock the door, clear the churchyard, and no one will be any the wiser."

"Except that you're talking about *my* home!" Theo said, outraged.

"If you want to live to enjoy it, you will shut up and let us work. Either that, or we'll kill you and let you rot down here. And that goes for the rest of you, too."

Gabe laughed. "Generous sentiment from a man of God. Have you lost your way?"

De Moret's lips twisted as he stared at Gabe. "I know what you are, and I do not fear you, or your fallen fathers, *Nephilim*." He virtually spat the word out. "You were cast out. You should have drowned. Perhaps I will finish all of you. Do the job the flood clearly failed at." He nodded at the knights. "Keep them quiet while we search down here, and then I'll decide what to do with them. The papers must be here somewhere."

"Papers?" Ash asked, unable to stop himself. "Surely they will have long since rotted. The swords down here have rusted. Maybe other things, too."

De Moret marched to his side and held out his hand. "I gather you have the key. Give it to me."

The key was the only bargaining tool they had at this point, and Ash hated to hand it over. However, Harlan was a prisoner, and he had no idea where Niel was, or how many other men were at de Moret's disposal, which meant the knights had the upper hand for now. Reluctantly, Ash handed it over.

De Moret held the key up. "De la More masterminded all of this, you know, but we never knew where the treasure's final resting place would be. We suspected that his close friends may have picked another spot, but it was here all along. As is his tomb."

"I thought his tomb was upstairs?"

"No. A false tomb for the uninitiated." De Moret smiled icily at Ash, before making a few swift adjustments to the key. In seconds, another key was in his hands, a small golden one that had been concealed within the first. "He was a clever man, as am I."

De Moret marched over to the huge, golden altar and started to search it, while Ash and Theo were escorted to where his brothers and Shadow were guarded by a ring of knights. Their weapons were collected and placed well out of reach, and for now, none of them resisted. Ash suspected that like him, his companions were curious as to what was about to happen.

De Moret was assisted by two men, and within a few minutes, they had success. He inserted the key into a place low down at the centre of the altar, and a section of it split into two, revealing a tomb hidden within.

Ash shook his head. "You were right about a puzzle box. This whole place has secrets within secrets."

"And there are bound to be more," Shadow said. "De Moret seems to know what he's looking for."

"Instructions that were passed down," Gabe suggested, "even when the map was lost."

A shout of victory ended their conversation, as de Moret held a package aloft and addressed his knights. "The lost papers of the Templars! The list of treasures of the ages. And this. One of the greatest treasures of all."

His companion lifted a bulky object and placed it on the altar. For a moment, Ash couldn't see a thing as his view was blocked by one of the pillars. And then a dazzling green light shimmered over the altar. Ash shifted position, heart in his mouth, knowing what he would see, and yet he still wasn't prepared for it.

The Emerald Tablet of Hermes Trismegistus was propped on the altar in its own support. A candle had been placed behind it, and the light dazzled outward, highlighting the words that had been carved into it. Ash could feel its power, even from a distance. *The block of emerald alone would have been priceless, but the information it contained...*

The men who were guarding them were a short distance away, distracted by their surroundings. They kept a cursory watch on the group, but most of their attention was on the magnificent church and its contents. Ash took advantage of it to address his companions. Keeping his voice low, he said, "We can't let them take it. It's too powerful in the wrong hands."

"But is it any better," Nahum said softly, "in JD's?"

"If we are to have any hope of understanding Black Cronos and defeating them, we need that tablet."

A hushed discussion was taking place at the altar, and furious glances were being cast in their direction.

Shadow's voice dripped acid. "We will not walk out of here alive, despite his smooth words and assurances. We have seen too much, and know too much. And he knows who we are, which suggests to me that they *are* linked to Black Cronos. We need to act now."

"You still have your knives, Shadow?" Nahum asked.

"Of course."

"They've hemmed us in well," Ash noted. They had been placed in a simple side chapel that echoed the design above them, with a low ceiling that would restrict their abilities.

De Moret finished his conversation, and one of his companions hurried back along the nave and to the stairs. He cast them a dismissive glance, and brought his hand down to their guards. It was the sign they were waiting for.

Shadow acted immediately. She jumped onto a pew, raced along it with a daring show of balance and speed, and before the closest knight could respond, placed her hand on his head and vaulted over him, slashing his neck with her knife with breath-taking speed.

Blood spurted out in a wide arc, splattering everyone as he fell to the floor, and the other knights scattered. The man heading for the stairs broke into a run, shouting to his colleagues above, and Shadow pursued him.

But that was as much as Ash could see, because the knights attacked, and he was suddenly fighting for his life.

Harlan heard the muffled shout from below and knew exactly what that meant. The closest knight turned to him, his eyes hard in the dim candlelight.

"Your time is up, American."

Harlan reacted instinctively. He kicked him in the knee and he stumbled backwards. But there were at least another three men clustered in the antechamber, plus the highly untrustworthy Mouse.

He was screwed.

In an act of horrible, ungentlemanly behaviour, he grabbed Mouse and pushed her into the knights, trusting they wouldn't kill one of their own, but frankly at this stage not caring one way or the other, and then faced the one remaining knight behind him. He ducked and rolled as his sword slashed at him, and then watched with surprise as the knight was dragged backwards, his shout of surprise ending with a blood curdled cry as his throat was slit.

Niel strode into view, blood-stained and covered in dirt, his eyes gleaming with a battle-hardened mania as he advanced on the others. Unexpectedly, Mouse jabbed her Taser into the man closest to her, and he fell with an agonised shout, his body bucking and twisting on the floor. In the confusion, Harlan jumped on the back of another knight, punching him repeatedly in the head as Niel tackled the others. Harlan and his opponent fell to the ground, rolling over each other as Harlan tried to dodge the long blade that had fortunately become tangled in the knight's cloak.

For a few minutes of grunting darkness and confusion, Harlan couldn't work out what was going on. All he knew was to keep punching and rolling, fearing he would feel the fiery sting of a blade between his ribs at any moment. Adrenalin made him stronger, and with a final punch that made the knight's head slam into the ground, his opponent finally slumped, unconscious.

Harlan was coated in sweat and blood. His knuckles were raw, every bone in his body seemed to ache, but he was alive. Most of the lanterns had been smashed in the fight, but the remaining light revealed that Mouse was pinned in the corner, Niel's long blade at her throat. Her mask had gone, and Harlan finally saw her face.

She looked terrified, her beautiful almond eyes open wide, her lips parted in a plea, her hands up, palms outwards. "I'm sorry, Niel, I had no choice earlier. If I hadn't incapacitated you, they would have killed you."

Niel didn't speak, instead he pressed his blade to her skin, and a spot of blood rolled down her neck.

Harlan staggered to his feet, using the wall to lever himself up. "Niel, she could have used the Taser on us. She didn't. She used it on him." He toed the man lying on the floor. "I must admit, she talked their cause up well, though, earlier."

"Because she's an accomplished liar," Niel growled, "who'll do and say anything to save her skin. But that's who you are, right, Mouse? You'll act for anyone who pays enough."

"That's not true! I have my boundaries, as do you. I had to make a choice today—for you and for me. I knew I had to wait for the right time to strike. I bought us time."

"How very convenient." Niel's expression was bleak. Hard. Harlan suspected he was at war with himself. He wanted his revenge, but equally couldn't quite bring himself to kill her.

"Niel." Harlan's voice sounded harsh in the hushed chamber. "Our friends are downstairs. They need our help. Remove her Taser, and let her go."

"No. There are other knights up there, and she may let them in. Search her, Harlan. Strip her of weapons. And be careful."

Harlan held out his hand. "Taser first."

Mouse didn't hesitate to hand it over, and he quickly strapped the pouch it was in around his waist before almost apologetically searching her. He found a small dagger strapped to her thigh, and one on her forearm, but that was it. She didn't even look at him. Instead, she stared only at Niel. Harlan felt like a jerk. Tension simmered between the two of them.

Securing the knives, Harlan stepped back. "All done. She's clean."

"Good. Where now, Harlan?"

"There are stairs to another level in the next room. Let me go first," he insisted. "I heard the instructions. Stick to the *Agnus Dei*."

Wondering what he was about to find below, he started across the chamber and headed down the steps.

Thirty-Two

G abe grabbed a gilded icon from the top of the small altar and hurled it at the advancing knight, taking advantage of the confusion caused by Shadow's attack. At the same time, he expanded his wings and charged, using his wings as another weapon.

The scene in the chapel was chaotic. His brothers were using anything handy as weapons. Icons, crosses, even the wooden pews, but the knights' long blades bought them space. Theo kept back, but added to the confusion by hurling priceless objects at their enemy.

Gabe picked up a pew and used it as a battering ram, running at the man closest to him. He pinned him to the wall with a blistering crash, and Gabe heard the knight's ribs crack. Gabe lifted the pew and slammed it into his head. It snapped back, hit the wall, and he slumped to the ground.

But Gabe couldn't celebrate yet. Another knight was already on him, his sword aimed at his gut, and he had no more room to swing the pew. Gabe swept around instead, his wings throwing his opponent into one of his companions, and they both went down in a tangle of limbs. Gabe needed a weapon. He lunged at an abandoned sword, which had slid beneath another pew.

Unfortunately, he wasn't quite quick enough. Another knight jumped over the pew, striking Gabe in his side, and he felt blood pump out, the sting of the blade like fire. Gabe scrabbled to turn, his long reach almost at the hilt, just as the man swung the blade at his outstretched arm.

Shadow raced across the nave, dodging caskets, icons, and other treasure, and with only seconds to spare before the knight was out of sight on the steps to the upper chamber, released her knife.

Infuriatingly, it struck the wall and ricocheted to the floor, missing her target. Before she could throw the next one, running footsteps indicated that another knight was already behind her.

She turned and took aim, and with grim satisfaction, saw this weapon hit its mark. It struck the man in the throat, and he fell immediately. De Moret was right behind him, his sword raised and hatred in his eyes. In the seconds she had spare, she raced to the pile of their confiscated weapons, grabbed her sword and Nahum's, and turned to face de Moret.

Nahum smashed at his opponent's sword with a large gold cross, using it to knock the blade out of his hands.

The irony of the situation wasn't lost on him. A Nephilim using a cross to battle the remains of a Templar order, whose knights had sworn to protect the pilgrims who wished to pay their respects to God. Would their fallen fathers be pleased at such a fight, or would they find something to fault in Nahum's actions? No doubt his own father, Remiel, would laugh. *Another point scored against the old God.*

Nahum blocked the thoughts from his mind as he swung the cross again, smashing the knight on the temple and sending him sprawling. Gabe was spreadeagled on the floor, a man looming over him, sword raised. Nahum smacked the cross into his arm, and with a grunt of pain, the knight fell awkwardly across the upended pew. Gabe grabbed the sword he'd been reaching for and immediately impaled the fallen man.

Nahum pulled Gabe to his feet. Several knights lay on the ground now, either dead or unconscious, and Ash was tackling the final one. Nahum ran up behind him and brought the cross down on his head. He crumpled to the floor.

Ash sighed with relief. "Thank you, brother." He turned to Theo. "Are you all right?"

To be honest, Theo looked a little green as he took in the bloodshed and injuries, but he nodded. "I'm fine, thank you. A little winded, but otherwise unharmed. But Shadow..."

His sentence was unfinished, his gaze beyond them, and they all turned to watch Shadow nimbly fighting de Moret, wielding both of her swords with an effortless grace and dexterity.

Gabe ran to the nave, the rest following, but it was clear that she didn't need any help. De Moret, for all his skills, was retreating. They bounded over pews, dodged around piles of gold, and leaped over caskets, the clash of their swords echoing around the church. Then Nahum remembered the knight who'd ran up the stairs. There was no sign of his body. He must have escaped.

Nahum yelled, "I'll head upstairs!"

However, by the time he'd reached the steps, a body was tumbling down to meet him, the smell of burnt flesh biting his nostrils. Nahum stepped back to watch the man's twitching body as Harlan descended the final stairs.

Harlan grinned as he waved the Taser. "I like this thing! I might have to get one."

"Looks like you already have," Nahum answered, peering past him to see Mouse, and then Niel right behind her. Ignoring Mouse for now, he said, "Niel. Good to see you."

"Brother." Niel's eyes were hard, his expression unreadable, except that Nahum knew him all too well. Niel liked Mouse, and she had betrayed him. "Is everyone okay?"

"Fine. Well, de Moret still fights, but Shadow has his measure." Nahum watched her for a few seconds, noting that Ash and Gabe circled close by her, in case she needed assistance. She didn't. If anything, she was holding back—toying with de Moret, like a cat with a mouse. De Moret knew it, too. Nahum could see the sweat on him even from a distance, and the knowledge that he was losing was clear by his increasingly desperate actions.

Nahum turned away and addressed Niel again. "Are they all dead upstairs?"

"Mostly. More were gathering outside, though."

"Then let's secure the survivors, and guard the doors. Harlan can watch Mouse."

"No. She's too untrustworthy."

Mouse spoke to the group for the first time. "No, I'm not. I told you, I'm on your side. I saved your life!"

Niel's gaze flickered and then hardened again, and Nahum intervened. "Niel, with me, now. I need you. Harlan?"

"I'm on it." Harlan gestured Mouse further into the church, the Taser aimed at her. He picked up the fallen knight's sword for good measure. Mouse didn't object. She walked, hands raised in surrender, and then took a seat on a pew, like a meek penitent.

Nahum heard Shadow's victory cry as he hustled Niel up the stairs. He didn't need to see de Moret fall. He'd seen enough bloodshed for one day.

Ash surveyed the fallen men and the blood-splattered gold, and wondered if it was really worth it. And then his gaze fell on the Emerald Tablet of Hermes Trismegistus.

This was worth it.

A splash of de Moret's blood marred its pristine surface, and Ash used the remnants of his torn shirt, damaged when he'd hurriedly expanded his wings, to wipe it clean. The candle still burned behind it, seeming to set light to the words carved on it. The chatter between Shadow, Gabe, and Theo, melted away as the words danced before his eyes. They were easily legible, and yet contained meaning that his special language skills could not discern.

The block of emerald was at least two hand-spans wide, four long, and several inches thick. The writing was cursive, ornate, and bewitching. Magic emanated from it, and yet it wasn't a grimoire. Nor was it a spell. However, it promised the secrets of the universe; the fundamentals of magic that Raziel had bound into his book, but in some kind of coded form.

Or at least that's what alchemists believed. Ash wasn't sure what to think.

Gabe's voice disturbed his thoughts. "At least we know that the count doesn't have it. It's been here for centuries. Half of me feels we should hide it again."

Ash sighed, and turned to face him, noting his bleak expression. "We can't keep hiding knowledge, Gabe. We're not gatekeepers. There's been enough of that already, don't you think?"

"I do," Shadow said, standing next to him to study the tablet. She shivered in its green glow. "Arcane knowledge is a dangerous thing. But it's even more dangerous to lock it up and pretend it doesn't exist. Besides, it might help JD, *and* help us defeat Black Cronos."

Gabe grunted. "Raziel's Book of Knowledge almost sent JD mad. Will this do the same?"

"It's a chance we have to take," Ash answered.

Theo looked dazed, but the battle seemed to have energised him. He took it all in. The room, the dead bodies, Gabe and Ash's wings, and Shadow's ethereal, Other-worldly appearance, as she had cast aside her glamour for now. "I don't know half of what you're talking about, and frankly," he gestured at their wings and Shadow, "I'm not even sure what you are, but I'm glad you're on my side. And Shadow is right. Part of me detests the Templars for the things they accumulated and then hid. They aren't custodians of knowledge, and neither are we. It should all go to a museum."

"Not that," Ash said pointing at the Emerald Tablet. "If you will grant us one request, Theo, other than your silence on our abilities, it would be to let us take this. The rest is yours to share with the world."

Harlan joined them, having ushered Mouse into a closer pew so that he could talk. They were both dusty and bloodstained, and Harlan in particular looked battered and bruised. "I've seen the defences that JD has on his house," he told them. "It will be safe with him. Anywhere else would place the tablet somewhere where the count could get it. We do not want to advertise its existence. I guess it depends," he turned to Mouse, "on what she will say, and what we do with her."

Mouse just glared at him. "You know me, Harlan. And you saw what I did up there. I was on your side!"

"Eventually. Zapping Niel has given me doubts."

"So, what are your options here? Are you going to kill me? Or lock me up forever?"

Shadow raised her still-bloody swords. "Killing you is just fine with me."

"No!" Gabe's voice echoed across the church. "No more killing." He stared at Mouse. "What about Nicoli?"

"I'll tell him that we lost." She shrugged. "It happens. I'll also tell him that everything that was found here tonight will be on the news." She lifted her chin. "I can keep secrets, too."

"Until they have a purchase price," Harlan pointed out.

"Then pay me more." Her eyes lit up. "Give me a piece of priceless iconography, and I'll keep this silent forever. I can disappear for a while."

"My blade can make that happen," Shadow muttered.

Ash smirked. Shadow was always consistent and economical. Gabe wasn't so amused. "Shadow, no. Mouse, we may need to work with you in the future, so I'll accept your terms. Harlan, choose her something, and then I'll escort her upstairs. I want to see what's happening up there. Make sure any remaining knights are retreating. I'll offer them a sweetener, too."

"Like what?" Ash asked. "They could be surrounding us even now, ready to mount another attack. And what are we going to do with all of these dead bodies? Prison won't suit any of us. We haven't got Maggie Milne or Newton to help us here."

"We'll offer them this." Gabe leaned down and picked up the package that de Moret had taken from William de la More's real tomb. "De Moret said it would lead them to the rest of the treasure—that this was just a small part of it. This should assuage them. Plus, it will be daylight in a few hours. They can't afford to keep fighting, and they will want to be out of here by then. They can take this and their fallen. I think they'll accept it. I would, if it were me. You learn to pick your battles."

Shadow nodded approvingly. "I like it. Although, I suggest we announce the discovery in another twenty-four hours. That will give us time to clean ourselves up, and all the blood, and move the Emerald Tablet to a secure location. The authorities will be so overwhelmed with the discovery that they won't question anything else. Theo? Harlan?"

Theo could barely contain his excitement. "Yes! Absolutely. I knew this would be my greatest find. *Our* find," he corrected himself. "Full credit will be made to The Orphic Guild, of course."

"Then it's a deal," Harlan said, grinning broadly. "Hopefully it will earn me the commission of a lifetime!"

While Harlan found Mouse a suitable item of treasure, Ash started to wrap the Emerald Tablet in de Moret's cloak. He felt a sense of loss as he concealed it, and the church seemed much darker.

He just hoped Harlan was right, and that JD could protect it.

Niel's side ached from the wound he had received, and his arms felt like they were on fire from the many cuts he had sustained. He sat in the pew staring at the altar, wishing he could be anywhere but here.

He felt like a fool. The memories of his earlier excitement at seeing Mouse stung even more than his injuries. Once he and Nahum had ascertained that the church was secure and that the knights had maintained watch around the church rather than advancing, weariness had swept over him.

For a while he kept busy to keep his thoughts at bay. He and Nahum had piled the dead next to the side door, keeping the two prisoners still trapped in one of the rooms, and then Nahum left him to his own devices, keeping watch through the stained glass window.

Nahum was a thoughtful brother. His only comment was that sometimes events weren't always as they seemed, and that time would probably tell. Niel was in no mood for platitudes.

Strident footsteps made him turn around, and he saw Gabe walk through the nave with de Moret's body over his shoulder, Shadow next to him. He stiffened as he saw Mouse's slight figure between them.

"What's she doing here?" he asked, rising to his feet.

"She's leaving," Gabe said.

"Like hell she is."

Gabe placed de Moret's body with the others. "I'm not arguing with you. The decision is made. Mouse has been compensated for her time, and she will keep our secrets. There are other services she may do for us in the future." Gabe turned to her, his dark eyes looking black in the shadowed church. "I will hunt you down and kill you myself if you betray us."

"I won't. I wasn't lying." She threw her shoulders back and lifted her chin as she addressed Niel. "I made a bargain. It actually wasn't a hard call. A Taser over a blade. I would do it again to save your life, Niel."

Niel couldn't bring himself to answer. Silence would impart his feelings more eloquently than words. His throat burned with fury and shame, but he wouldn't argue with Gabe.

Not here. Not in front of her.

"Are the knights out there?" Gabe asked.

"Yes, brother," Nahum answered. "Throughout the grounds."

"Good. We need to bargain."

Mouse appealed to Gabe. "If I walk out now, they'll kill me."

"Then I'll fly you away from here," Nahum said, immediately. "From the bell tower. Gabe, have you a plan?"

Gabe held a bulky package aloft. "I have. I will trade this. Wait with me while we bargain, and then take Mouse when we're done."

Nahum nodded, already opening up the side door.

Niel stayed back with Shadow, watching the proceedings, both armed and ready to attack if needed. Mouse kept her distance, her gaze averted from Niel, but he still felt her presence. He could barely look at Shadow, either. *Her teasing earlier was bad enough, but now...* He bristled, waiting for her scorn.

"You know," Shadow said softly, her lips close to his ear, "I would have killed her, but Gabe forbade me." Unexpectedly gentle, her hand touched his arm. "She doesn't deserve your regard, brother. If she crosses you again, just say the word and I will gladly kill her." Niel's throat tightened even more at her unexpected words. His mouth opened, but words refused to come. She squeezed his arm again. "I mean it."

He forced himself to speak. "Thank you, but I'll do it myself."

"I actually don't think she will betray you, for the record." Her voice lowered even more, and her breath tickled his ear. "Strangely, I believe her. I think she might actually like your well-hidden qualities." He glanced at Shadow, and saw a glint of humour in her eyes. "Us women are mysterious creatures. It's part of our charm."

His normal response reasserted itself as their banter slipped back into place. "If you say so, you wilful madam."

"I'm fey. I'm always right." She grinned and watched Gabe negotiate the deal.

Shadow never failed to surprise him with her unexpected, generous gestures. Niel squeezed her hand and whispered, "Thank you."

Thirty-Three

Jackson escorted Estelle and Barak to Lucien's makeshift cell, ensuring the door to the remote side corridor was locked behind him before they progressed.

They had arrived back in London after an early flight, and both looked refreshed. They also seemed close, as if they had reached an understanding between them. Whatever had transpired in France obviously suited them.

"You're not taking any chances, then?" Estelle asked as she watched him lock the door.

Jackson shook his head. "We can't afford to, after last night." He cocked his head at Barak. "Your call was uncanny timing. Although I might have been better off staying in bed. I ended up putting myself right in harm's way."

"Sorry. I had a feeling, and I had to call. I'm glad to see you're okay, though." Barak took in the corridor and other locked doors. "I take it that no one else is down here?"

"The great thing about The Retreat is its wealth of rooms and corridors. This one is now off limits for the foreseeable future. I hate that we're having to do this." Guilt at having gone back on his word to Lucien still ate at him. "We've turned an old office into a cell. We had to work quickly, but fortunately the tranquilliser knocked him out for hours."

"And now?" Estelle asked.

"He's fine, but chained up like an animal. We've had to draft in more guards." He pointed to the four men clustered outside a room up ahead, Miller being one of them. "I had no idea that the lab had been experimenting with tranquilliser darts. Thank the Gods they had, or things could be very different right now."

"Hold on," Estelle said, stopping him and drawing him aside. "The conversation we had on the phone was brief, to say the least. Tell us what's going on."

"Sorry, you're right." Jackson was shattered, but coffee had revived him. He hoped he sounded more coherent now. "Things were a bit up in the air earlier, but now we have a better plan. Sort of. We've stripped the room of everything except a mattress on the floor and a bucket in the corner. We've fixed chains to the walls, and Lucien is currently cuffed to them. It looks awful, but it's the only way. We've also left the door open so that we can see him at all times. I have to admit that I'm really happy to see you two. Miller was brilliant last night, but just knowing that you're here, with your abilities..." He trailed off, hoping to hear a favourable response to his earlier proposition.

Barak exchanged a wary glance with Estelle. "We can stop here for a while, but not indefinitely. Don't get me wrong, we want to help you, and it's important to us that you and everyone else here is safe, but I guess we need to know what your long-term plans are. What exactly is it you want us to do? Be prison guards?"

"No, not just that." Jackson leaned against the wall, hands in his jean pockets. They felt like they were hanging off him, like he'd lost weight, which wouldn't surprise him in the slightest. "Layla has run tests and we're waiting for the results, but we're just trying to work out what could have triggered his change. It seemed to come out of nowhere. We also can't decide whether JD should come here, or if we move Lucien there."

Estelle nodded in understanding. "But that means putting him in a van and risking him changing in there. Or he runs wild and kills JD."

"Exactly. I think the best plan is that we watch him for a few days, talk to him, try to understand the trigger. Maybe get JD to see him here, and then make a decision. If we do move him, I'd be really grateful if you helped us."

"We can do that," Barak agreed. "But have you heard the latest from Harlan or Gabe?"

"No. What's happened?"

"They've found the Emerald Tablet of Hermes Trismegistus."

"*What*?" Jackson pushed away from the wall with new found energy. "Where?"

"In the Templar treasure, beneath Temple Church by Theo's place."

For a moment, Jackson couldn't speak. "This could change everything!"

"Perhaps," Estelle said. "Or it could just add another layer of absolute confusion to everything."

"Does JD know?" Jackson asked.

"He will soon."

Wild excitement flooded through Jackson. "This is brilliant, but you're right, we can't get ahead of ourselves. We have to focus on the present." He said this more to himself than the others. "Are you ready to see Lucien?" They nodded, and in moments they were outside Lucien's room. He greeted Miller, who had refused to leave until he was happy with the arrangements. "Are we okay to go in?"

"Sure. Just keep your distance."

Lucien's feet and one arm were each attached to thick chains that were fixed to the wall. He was still dressed in scrubs, lying on the mattress and staring at the ceiling, but he sat up when they entered. Jackson felt a jolt of pity for the man. He looked haunted, and there were dark circles beneath his eyes.

"Hey, Lucien. I've brought you some visitors."

"You've come to watch the animal, like a zoo."

Estelle shook her head, her eyes full of compassion. "Not at all. We've come to help you."

"How? How do I control this?" Lucien looked down at himself, his face twisting with disgust as he looked at his tattoos. "I have no memory of last night. Nothing! It is a void!" He took deep breaths. "I was told I killed a man. I don't even remember that!"

Jackson closed his eyes briefly, as if he could block out the memory of the fallen guard, and then looked at Lucien. "It wasn't your fault. You had no control."

"But it *is* my fault. I did it! I can never undo it!"

Barak crossed the room, despite Miller's warning, and sat down on the edge of Lucien's bed. "I have killed men and other creatures. Lots of them. Some deserved to die, many did not. I will carry that always. But I cannot dwell on the past, and neither can you, Lucien. We must move forward, all the time. That is why Estelle and I are here. We will help you control this."

"How?" Lucien leaned forward to stare at Barak with doubtful, angry eyes, and Jackson saw Miller bring his rifle up. "You should have left me there! I'm a monster."

"You are not a monster." Barak laid his huge hand on Lucien's shoulder, unafraid and reassuring. "I don't know how we deal with this, not yet. And I won't lie. This won't be easy, but we will find a way. Your life will be different from now on, but it doesn't mean it's over. It's just beginning."

Jackson exhaled a breath he didn't even know he was holding, and for the first time in hours, he felt hopeful. They *would* find a way.

They had to.

Harlan helped himself to a huge serving of bacon and sausages, piled scrambled eggs on top, then sat at the table in Theo's dining room that overlooked the moat.

Only Gabe, Shadow, and Theo were there, also eating large breakfasts, as if none of them had eaten for a week. Thankfully, they had showered and changed clothes, although Harlan was sure he could still smell the stench of the awful mud that had flooded the Chamber of Truth. Nahum and Niel were still in the underground church, guarding the treasure and cleaning the place up.

He grinned at everyone. "I hope you all slept well. I slept like the proverbial log!"

"You're just thinking of your commission," Shadow said, amused.

"Well, that sure helps. And you're not?"

"Of course I am. I dreamt of gold. Lots of lovely gold."

Theo rubbed his hands together, a twinkle in his eye. "I'm just looking forward to calling the British Museum. I can't wait to see their faces. This will be the find of the century! I confess, I have no idea how this works, but it will be fun."

"Well, we'd better clean all of the blood splatter off today before anyone gets here," Gabe said, grimacing. "That will be a nightmare."

Harlan swallowed a mouthful of food. "Are Niel and Nahum okay?"

Gabe nodded. "I've just got back from seeing them. Everything's fine. The church is secure and tidy, the crypt is locked, and they've made a good start on the clean-up. We'll relieve them soon. Both of them will go with you to JD's."

"You sure you can spare them?"

"Of course. I know you don't want to risk transporting the tablet alone."

"No, I really don't." Harlan sipped his coffee, looking forward to seeing JD's face. He hadn't told him the news over the phone. He wanted it to be a surprise. But then something else struck him. "You know, JD will want to come here and see all of this before anyone else does. It wouldn't take him long to get here. Any objections, Theo?"

"I guess not—as long as he knows he can't pilfer anything else."

"I'll make sure he understands." Harlan could already see the avaricious glee in JD's eyes. He contemplated Nicoli's smug face, too. "I still suspect that Nicoli might try something."

Shadow shook her head and pushed her empty plate away. "I trust Mouse will keep her word. She'll tell him virtually nothing, and she certainly won't see him in his office."

"You trust her?" Harlan asked, surprised. Shadow didn't always mix well with other women, although to be fair, she did like the White Haven witches.

"Yes. She has a vested interest in our group." She grinned, her meaning clear. "And she was well paid last night. Don't *you* trust her?"

"I hardly know her," Harlan confessed. "Only by reputation, which is quite impressive. As you know, she's done work for us before. Which, by the way, brings me to another issue that's been troubling me." He turned to Theo. "Someone on your staff has betrayed you. I think you know who."

Gabe grunted as he forked up more food. "You're right, Harlan. Someone who can come and go in the house without anyone giving them a second thought. Someone who knew about the knife, and knew that you had found the key."

Theo's face fell, and it seemed his moustache became limp, too. "Oh, no. Not Chivers. Don't tell me the butler did it!"

Harlan laughed. "I think he probably did. Who else comes and goes as much as him?"

"It wasn't Owen," Shadow said. "I was wrong about him, and I'm happy to admit that."

"But we know Chivers is a gossip!" Theo said, appealing to all of them. "All the staff say so. Any one of them could have shared the information."

She gave Theo a wry smile. "You wanted him to retire, and he refused. He begged to stay. It has to be Chivers. It's time for him to go."

"Damn it." Theo thumped his cup down on the table. "All right. I'll do it later."

"Do it now!" Gabe insisted. "Before anything else goes wrong." He pushed his plate away and stood up. "I'm going to head back down to the church. There's more to see down there, and I want to make sure we haven't missed anything before anyone turns up. We need to explore the other tunnels, too."

"I think we should leave the one we blocked well alone," Shadow told him. "Otherwise, we risk bringing the church down on our heads and killing ourselves. What worries me, is that the church may say the treasure belongs to them."

"I would contest that," Theo said. "It is *under* the church, not in it. Although, it admittedly is their land."

"Potentially the money would be split between you and them," Harlan suggested. "And you did find it. That will count for a lot."

"*We* found it," Theo said, thoughtfully tapping his cup. "I couldn't have done it without you. I think that maybe the money should be split several ways. It will be worth millions! Plenty to go around."

Harlan stared at him, not quite believing his ears. "Are you seriously suggesting that, Theo? You hired us to help."

Theo brushed his fingers across his moustache, twirling the ends in his absent-minded way, before staring at them each in turn. "Yes, I'm serious. The more I think about it, the fairer it seems. We did this together, so we should all benefit. Plus, you fended off the Knights of Truth and Justice. No doubt they are on the trail of the rest of the treasure right now. We need to get our story straight on that," he said, nodding to himself. "Of course, we have no idea how long all this will take. It has to be valued. We might have to argue with the church, but either way, there's a lot of money to go around." He smiled, pleased with his decision. "Yes. I'm completely sure."

"Herne's hairy balls on a stick!" Shadow exclaimed. "We'll be rich! Mind-blowingly rich!"

Gabe had thumped back down in his seat. "Theo. Are you absolutely sure? Because I'm taking you at your word. A gentleman's agreement. Time to back out now if you have any second thoughts."

Harlan willed Gabe to shut up, but Theo merely shrugged. "No second thoughts. Let's shake on it, now. All of us."

Before Harlan could even take it in, they had all shaken hands on it. A decision to split three ways—Theo, Harlan, and Gabe and Shadow's team. With this kind of money, he could give up work. He could buy a yacht. He could build a palace.

But would he miss all this? The thrill of the chase. The uncovering of secrets. The unravelling of mysteries.

Yes, of course he would.

He stared at Shadow and Gabe, his comrades in arms, and couldn't keep the panic out of his voice. "Does this mean you'll retire?"

Shadow rolled her eyes and glanced at Gabe for confirmation. "No! Will you?"

"No!" He shuffled in his seat. "I quite enjoy all of this. Not the threats to my life, to be honest, but the rest of it."

"There you go, then." Shadow grinned, and raised her cup in a toast. "To our next adventure!"

IMMORTAL DUSK

WHITE HAVEN HUNTERS BOOK SIX

TJ GREEN

One

The clouds were heavy with the promise of snow over the narrow valley in the Yorkshire Dales, and Nahum was glad he was wearing a thick coat and boots. Especially seeing as Olivia Jameson, a collector employed by The Orphic Guild, had led him up a bleak hillside coated with frost to look over the small village nestled below.

"Couldn't we have done this in the car?" he asked her. "It would have been warmer."

"But less spectacular." She gave him an impish grin. Her cheeks were a rosy red from the biting cold, her face framed by the fur-lined hood of her jacket. "Besides, the exercise is good for you."

"I get plenty of exercise, thanks. Do I look unfit?"

"No. You look delicious."

Nahum laughed. He was used to Olivia's flirting and found that he liked it. However, that was all it was going to be. Olivia flirted outrageously with everyone—unless he'd become rusty with reading her signals. He shrugged it off. He had a job to do. "So, what am I looking for?"

"I just thought we could get a good impression of the place from up here. Make sure I wasn't missing anything."

"I thought we were planning on stealing from a vicarage, not a fortified castle?"

"I have learned from long experience that you should never presume." She frowned, her eyes narrowing as she studied the buildings below. "As you know, I have been searching for this reliquary for a long time. It has been very hard to track down. It's almost like it has a life of its own."

Nahum had flown to Leeds late the previous afternoon, collected his rental car, and met up with Olivia in the small town in the Yorkshire Dales. They had spent the evening in a boutique hotel they were both booked into, discussing Olivia's search for the reliquary, as well as answering her questions about his past. She was fascinated with the Nephilim and their history. In fact, they had spent more time discussing that than the job. Now he had a lot more questions. The reliquary was for one of Olivia's regular clients, but it had taken months to locate. She was convinced it was in the vicarage in the hamlet below, owned by the local vicar named Jacobsen.

He watched her profile, noting her tense jaw. "What aren't you telling me, Olivia? I sense that you are very capable, and I'm sure not averse to stealing from a vicarage. Why do you need me? Or should I say, a Nephilim?"

She cocked her head at him. "The more I've asked around up here—discreetly, of course—the more I've realised that this vicar is quite unusual. I'm wondering if he's a necromancer—or something of the sort. I thought backup might be important."

"A necromancer! You didn't think to mention this last night over dinner?"

She looked sheepish. "I wondered if I might be letting my imagination get away from me, but I've learned to trust my instincts."

Nahum hadn't wanted to pry too much into the background of the object they were stealing. It didn't seem necessary; it was just a job. As long as he understood the basic requirements, that was fine. Plus, he was only supposed to be there as a hired hand. The muscle. *But now...* "Why does it seem to have a life of its own?"

"The reliquary contains some of the remains of St Ignatius, an obscure saint who was originally from the Alps. He was a monk who preached the word of God in the surrounding villages, and lived in a monastery in the mountains, a small order that has long since gone. The monastery, too. It vanished, like many do. Anyway, he visited a village known for its paganism, and an angry mob turned on him and he was stoned to death. His body was collected and laid to rest in the monastery, and a while after that he was beatified." Olivia shrugged. "Well, his resting place became a place of pilgrimage. It was said he could cure madness. Draw out devils. His bones were split up and ended up who knows where, but his skull was placed in a highly decorated reliquary. Over the years it's been in different churches, and then a religious museum, but then it disappeared. Stolen, presumably. I managed to track it down by a lot of hard work."

"Revolting, of course, but that still doesn't explain why you say it has a life of its own."

"Well, now it seems that where the reliquary goes, madness follows. Odd outbreaks of violence or hysteria that the perpetrators can't explain. Not all the time, of course, just sometimes. I wonder if it's cursed or something, or can be manipulated by whoever owns it. Reliquaries are supposed to heal people, or offer solace..." She trailed off, perplexed.

Nahum stared down at the small hamlet with smoke pouring from its chimneys. It looked peaceful. "Has something happened here?"

"There's been a smattering of violence in the surrounding villages. Fights that came out of nowhere—pubs, schools, restaurants. A broad area—not small."

"Unfortunately, violence happens."

"But it all occurs around the area that this priest is in. It's not just the reliquary. He moves around, you see. Every few years he goes to a new church. Always small villages, remote, lonely. Attendance goes up, more convert to the church. I wonder if the priest is manipulating the reliquary somehow to swell his numbers."

"That sounds extreme! Besides, the monk, St whatever, didn't sound violent in life."

"Ignatius. No, he wasn't. Like I said, I suspect the priest is using it for his own ends. I've done a lot of research on this." A gust of wind whipped a strand of hair from beneath her hood, and she tucked it back inside again. "Let's walk a little higher."

Without waiting for his response, she led the way further up the steep sides of the valley, along a narrow track that weaved between heathers and ferns. Snow lay thick on the surrounding peaks, and suddenly the air seemed menacing. The wind tugged Nahum's hair and whipped his breath from his lungs. This was wild country. Remote, breathtakingly beautiful, and deadly if you misjudged the weather. If snow started to fall now, it would white out their surroundings in seconds.

Although he'd followed Olivia up the hill, he called out, "Olivia, wait! Let's turn back. There's nothing I can see up here that I can't from down there."

"Just a few more meters. Around the bend!"

Reluctantly he followed her around the rugged, boulder-strewn curve of the hill, and into the shadow of a ruined stone building. Immediately the wind dropped as they tucked themselves into its shelter. There was a small camping stool in there and the remnants of a camp.

Nahum laughed. "You've been spying on him!"

"Of course I have. It's sheltered, and I sit up here in the late afternoon and watch at night." She tapped her pack. "Night vision binoculars, as well as the usual."

"I'm impressed." He surveyed the area, the church a short distance from the village. "The vicarage is the old, grey-stone building by the church, I presume?"

Olivia nodded, binoculars already trained below. "He scurries to the church at night. Not every night, of course, but several. I see lights in the nave, long after everyone has gone to bed."

"That doesn't necessarily mean anything sinister."

She lowered the binoculars and clucked at him. "Really?"

"I'm playing devil's advocate."

Her eyes didn't leave his. "Something is very wrong here. I know it. I don't think it will be easy to steal this reliquary. I think he'll do anything to keep it."

"What does your buyer want it for?"

"To admire it, catalogue it, and fawn over it in private."

"Are you sure *he* doesn't want it for anything more sinister?"

"I've known Charles for a long time. He's a collector. That's all. I think it's better in his hands."

Glad to be out of the wind, Nahum leaned against the remnants of the stone wall, the roof long since gone. "Okay. Let's discuss the job. You think the reliquary is in the church or the vicarage?"

"I suggest we try the church first, but I think he moves it around. I should stress that it is not on show. No one actually knows it's here."

"So, we check out the church, and if it's not there, we go to the vicarage, make sure we keep Jacobsen secured, steal it, and go. The car will be close by, I presume?"

Olivia nodded. "Hire car, under a false ID. It's not my first clandestine hit. We drive out tonight. Job done. Couldn't be easier, right? If the worst happens, you use your fabulous wings and fly it out. I will escape in the car. Either way, we must get that reliquary tonight. I can't waste any more time on this. Besides, I've done my homework. I don't think there's much else to find out about this guy."

"Other than the possibility that he might be a necromancer, or using the reliquary to spread bad mojo, or something else..."

"Okay." She smirked. "I admit there's stuff I don't know, but I do know it's the right reliquary. I caught a glimpse of it. I've also tracked it historically—picked up where my client left off. As I said, strange events follow it. Unless you were looking for a connection—like me—no one would really know. And I've seen the priest. He's middle-aged, gaunt, not a physical threat. He'll be easy to deal with."

Nahum still wasn't convinced. He had an uneasy feeling about it, and it was obvious that Olivia did too, or else he wouldn't be there. But if the man was as odd as she suggested, and violence did seem to follow this reliquary around, then it was best they removed it. And he was a Nephilim. He could handle most things.

Finally, he nodded. "All right. Tonight, then. Now, can we get off this freezing hill and into a pub?"

Gabe watched Shadow put the final decorations on their huge Christmas tree in the corner of the living room in the old farmhouse in White Haven, distracted by her swaying hips.

"Can't we do something more interesting? Like, go to bed?"

She tossed her silvery hair over her shoulders as she turned to look at him. "This *is* interesting!"

"Not as much as your naked body draped over mine."

Niel groaned behind him as he entered the room. "Shut up! Other people are in the house."

Gabe grimaced. "I thought you were busy in the barn."

"I was, and now I'm here." Niel gave a malicious smile at seeing Gabe's disappointment. "Take it to your room!"

"Perhaps you should stop sneaking up on us!"

"I'm not sneaking! I can't help it if I'm naturally stealthy." He stared at the tree. "Please don't put an angel on the top of that thing."

Shadow had a mischievous glint in her eye. "Will it make you nervous?"

Niel's blue eyes turned to ice. "No. It will annoy me. As if my father would be watching over me benevolently!"

Gabe had already vetoed all angels from the house for Christmas decorations. Fortunately, Shadow had zero interest in deities of any kind, and was happy to dress the tree in a more naturalistic fey fashion. So far, branches of spruce and pine were festooned around the house. It was a huge fire hazard, but Gabe had to admit that it smelled good.

They were celebrating the winter solstice rather than Christmas, but like the previous year, they had agreed to exchange small presents...if they were even going to be at home. JD had called with a request—well, more like a command, because JD wasn't good with polite requests. However, Gabe had yet to break that news to everyone.

Reluctantly shelving the idea of spending a couple of hours in bed with Shadow, Gabe sat on the corner of the sofa. "Where's Ash?"

"Upstairs I think, researching the *Comte*—again."

Ash, always loving research and learning, had almost become as obsessed with the *Comte de Saint-Germain*, the man they believed to be behind Black Cronos, as JD and Jackson. He was helping in the search for possible bases, hoping to isolate a place that might be a centre of operations. It was Estelle Faversham and Barak who suggested that the *Comte* and Black Cronos might have an alchemical centre somewhere mystical, with history, energy, and power. A confluence of Ley Lines perhaps, or an old religious site. While that was a great idea, Europe and the UK were littered with such places. Some were easily dismissed; others, however, needed more careful screening. There were also hundreds of ancient castles around, many abandoned, but all offering discreet places to set up a secret headquarters.

Gabe's brothers were split doing various things at present. Barak was often with Estelle, in and out of London and The Retreat. Eli and Zee continued to work in town with the witches. The rest of them picked up occult-hunting jobs with The Orphic Guild. Currently, Nahum was helping Olivia Jameson, Harlan's colleague, steal a religious reliquary in Yorkshire. He was supposed to be there for only a day or two, but since yesterday, he hadn't heard a thing. Gabe, much to his annoyance, was being regularly contacted by JD, the demanding, immortal magician to Queen Elizabeth I.

Four months earlier, in the thick heat of August, they had found the Emerald Tablet belonging to Hermes Trismegistus in the Templar treasure hidden within Temple Moreton, and they had given it to JD. It was like all his Christmases had arrived at once.

However, after finding that vast treasure, they were still yet to receive any money for it. The collection was still being catalogued and valued, and no doubt there would be a lot of wrangling about money. Fortunately, Harlan and Theo were very good at dealing with the museum, something Gabe was glad to let them do. Shadow, of course, with her avaricious and shrewd, gold-loving heart, was also making sure they received their cut. He hoped they would, for their sake. Shadow was wont to exact retribution in any way she saw fit, usually at the point of her sword or the tip of her arrow.

"Why do you want Ash?" Shadow asked, her question drawing him back to the present.

"JD has a job for us."

Niel virtually growled. "I will not be experimented on!"

"Neither will I!" Gabe considered the weird conversation he'd had with JD about Alexander the Great and Hermes Trismegistus. "He wants us to go to Egypt. He thinks there's something there that will help him understand the Emerald Tablet."

He had Shadow's full attention now, her violet eyes wide with hope and excitement. "We're going on an adventure?" Her hands settled on her hips. "And you didn't tell me?"

"I just did! The details elude me right now, but once we go to see JD, I guess he'll explain everything. Just to be clear, I haven't agreed to it yet." And he wouldn't if he didn't like the job, no matter how much JD might sulk.

Niel still scowled. "Why can't he come here? Everyone runs after him!"

"He'll pay us. The least we can do is head to his estate."

"In a few months we won't need his pay."

"But we like the work," Gabe reminded him. "Unless you want to lounge around here all day, getting fat?"

Shadow marched over and poked Niel in his very flat abdomen. "Who knows? If he needs us to steal something, we may need a thief to help us. A small, petite thief..."

Any mention of Mouse, the thief who had captured Niel's interest only to seemingly betray him during their last big job, still made him scowl. "I think not. We can manage perfectly well without her. Besides, you're a thief."

Shadow grinned. "Just looking out for you."

"I'd rather you didn't." He turned to Gabe. "When are we going to see JD?"

"Tomorrow. Potentially, we'll fly out the next day."

Niel nodded, his gaze distant. "Fine. I'll tell Ash. I guess Egypt before Christmas will at least be warm."

Two

"Are you sure you're ready to go back to France?" Jackson Strange asked Lucien, seeing the uncertainty in his eyes. "If you want to stay here, that's fine. Barak and Estelle will manage without you."

"No! I am ready. I want to find the people who did this to me." The need for revenge was etched into the jut of his jaw and the tightening of his eyes. "I have mastered my changes now. I'll be fine!"

Jackson looked at Barak and Estelle, the only other two people in the room with them. "What do you think?"

Barak shrugged, the muscles across his shoulders rippling. "I think Lucien needs to get out of this place. Four months trapped in The Retreat is too long. Besides, I trust him."

"Me too," Estelle added. She sat in the chair in the corner of Lucien's room, eyes never leaving Lucien as he paced back and forth, nervous energy welling up in him. "He's already been here far longer than we ever anticipated." Regret crossed her face as she addressed Lucien. "I'm sorry, we had no idea how things would end up."

He finally sat down on the end of his bed. "I know. I don't blame you. I don't blame any of you. I blame only Black Cronos. The more I hear, the more I hate them. And the more I want to know."

Jackson knew that feeling well. The subject of Black Cronos was like a drug. It absorbed his every waking moment, and his dreams, his thoughts constantly circling them. He hated his own obsession, but couldn't shake it off, and understood Lucien's need to find them. He leaned against the wall, arms crossed, assessing the risks for what felt like the hundredth time. Since Lucien had been rescued by Barak and Estelle from beneath *Château du Buade*, he had been kept in The Retreat as a well-treated prisoner, with only the occasional trip to the surface at the beginning—accompanied, of course, by a security team. His semi-tattooed body had created unexpected and uncontrollable changes within him. Lucien had been as anxious to be kept safe as everyone else. His lack of control had terrified him.

Lucien had been studied, interviewed, poked, and prodded, and had endured all of it with good grace, as curious to understand the complex tattoos that had been etched into his skin as everyone else. Everyone was especially interested in the way they took over his mind, turning him into an automaton. Thanks to Layla, the team's doctor, the lab scientists, and the brilliantly irascible JD, they had made a lot of progress. The tattoos drew on astrology and constellations, all tied into Lucien's birth chart. It seemed that the tattoos connected him to the cosmos and the wheel of time. Jackson's head ached at the magnificence of it all. And thanks to an ingenious device designed by JD, Lucien now had control of his own body again.

As they grew to trust Lucien, the room they contained him in became a bedroom rather than a cell. Although, big metal brackets were still fixed to the wall, just in case they had to chain him up. It was also still in a section of The Retreat that was unused by anyone else. It had a small kitchen and bathroom attached to it, so his area was completely self-contained.

Jackson nodded at the thick metal bracelet on Lucien's wrist, a complex inter-weaving of metals that JD had constructed using alchemical means. The metals' magical properties had been enhanced and tuned to Lucien's energy frequencies. "Are you sure you're okay with that?"

Lucien's long fingers turned it as if for reassurance. "Yes. It has saved my life. I haven't changed at all without using my own will for almost two weeks. When I do change, I still have my reason."

"I still think it's too soon to be out there unaccompanied. It could be a blip."

Barak huffed. "He won't be unaccompanied. He'll be with us. And a big tran-quilliser gun."

"But, say you find Black Cronos—or maybe that rat, Stefan," Jackson continued. "What if he can override that device?"

"There are a lot of what-ifs and maybes," Estelle reasoned. "There are in life, all the time. Eventually we must trust that the progress we've made will work. I think we should head outside now. It's a crisp, clear day out there, and London is full of Christmas spirit. I think it will cheer Lucien up. Let's have lunch after a walk in Hyde Park. What do you say, Lucien?"

"Yes, please! I'm desperate for fresh air."

Jackson smiled. Estelle had been a revelation. When they'd first met, her guard-ed, prickly manner and sharp tongue had been off-putting. An attitude, he now suspected, that had been long honed to deter friendships and to protect herself. However, every time he saw her, she now seemed a little softer. There were still flashes of obstinacy, and sharp responses still bubbled out, but mostly she appeared happier, and certainly every time she looked at Barak, she seemed to melt a little more. As for Barak, well, the big man continued to surprise him. He'd stayed for weeks, on and off in The Retreat at first, making sure Lucien was okay. Even now he visited weekly, and stayed overnight to check on him. On Jackson, too. On the occasions when Jackson had barely left The Retreat, Barak had persuaded him to go out, and Harlan had backed him up. Jackson tended to shoulder all of this on his own, and knew it was unnecessary.

"In fact," Estelle continued, "let's all head out." She stared at Jackson, her tone brooking no refusal. "My treat."

Jackson nodded, thinking a pint and pub lunch sounded perfect. "Fair enough. We can discuss our next plan of attack."

"France again, you say?" Barak asked.

"Yes. But I want the usual surveillance on it first."

"You said that about the last half a dozen places." Barak didn't look angry, just resigned.

"I know, but I've changed my search parameters, and I think this one could be it. Sorry…"

Barak cut him off. "It's okay. We'll get there." He grinned, the flash of white teeth bright against his dark skin, but his eyes were hard. "I look forward to making them pay."

Harlan Beckett, Collector for The Orphic Guild, was mesmerised by the Emerald Tablet.

It glowed on its stand in JD's library, unaffected by the cool winter light from the window or the firelight in the grate. JD, the immortal head of the guild, stood over it, also bathed in its green glow, and the scowl on his face made him look demonic.

Harlan was standing several feet away, but the tablet exerted a pull on him even from there; he shuddered to consider the monstrous power and knowledge it contained.

"JD," he repeated. "Did you hear me? They're going to Montferrier tomorrow. Any advice?"

JD finally dragged his gaze away. "What?"

Harlan had arrived ten minutes earlier, and it had taken that long for JD to acknowledge him. Once he did, Harlan stepped back, unnerved by his ghastly appearance. "Holy shit, JD. Have you slept lately? Or eaten? Or even had a shower in weeks?" He tentatively sniffed, but the room merely smelled of polish and old books.

"Of course I have, you fool!" JD strode to the cabinet of drinks and poured a glass of sherry. "I have a lot on my mind, and can do without disturbances."

"Well, if you answered your damn phone I wouldn't be here!" Harlan's temper, normally mild, was always raised to boiling point within minutes of being with JD.

"Stop being so prosaic!" He swung his arm around and pointed. "Look! The Emerald Tablet of Hermes Trismegistus is right there! The man named the Thrice Greatest—Thoth, Hermes the God, Hermes the Scribe! It's older than the ten commandments—and I have it!"

Chastened, Harlan nodded. "I know." He'd averted his gaze, but he forced himself to look at it and instantly felt dizzy. The heart of it seemed to swirl, as if galaxies were trapped within it. "It terrifies me." He blinked, forcing his gaze back to JD. The room seemed dim by comparison, almost bleached of colour.

JD took a ragged breath, and the anger drained from his eyes. "Yes, of course. Sorry." Abruptly, he caught up a cloth from the table and threw it over the tablet, banishing it beneath thick, black velvet. "I have to do that just to think clearly. There's something in there."

Shivering, Harlan walked to the fire, and accepted a glass of sherry from JD.

"Sorry, Harlan. It haunts me. My every waking moment, my dreams, my plans... It's a drug. I both love it and hate it."

"I couldn't bear it near me. Isn't there somewhere else you can keep it? Somewhere behind thick walls and a reinforced door? Somewhere that contains its influence." He laughed. "Sorry. That sounds mad."

"Not mad at all. I've considered it. I think you're right."

"You said there's something in there. What did you mean? Hidden knowledge?"

"Yes. No. Something else..." JD turned his back on the tablet, focussing only on Harlan and lowering his voice. "I feel it's been shrunk, somehow. I've seen illustrations and read old texts that suggest it's huge. I thought it was an affectation, but now..." His eyes were wide, appealing to Harlan for understanding.

Harlan also lowered his voice, as if the tablet could hear them. "You mean as if magic has made it smaller?"

"Something like that. I believe that if I could make it bigger, I could actually see what swirls within it. I think I need to unlock it, somehow..."

Harlan's mouth was very dry, and he sipped his sherry. "That doesn't make me feel any better about it. Besides, you've had it for months."

"I could probably have it for several lifetimes and still not understand its mysteries. Alchemists have been debating the meaning of its text for millennia."

"How would you even go about making it bigger?"

"I don't know. I've been observing it for changes during full moons, new moons, the past equinox and solstice, as well as several planetary events, but the time I've possessed it is too short to see anything significant."

"I'm surprised it's not in your lab."

"It was for a while. It affected my instruments—all of them..."

Harlan stared at it over JD's shoulder, feeling as if it was sentient. "If you're going to try to make it bigger—and I'm not sure you actually should—you need it to be outside. Under a marquee or something." In the face of such weirdness, Harlan liked to focus on practicalities. "That way, at least its influence would be outside of the house. As long as it doesn't affect your defences, of course."

"It doesn't so far, I've already checked." JD nodded to himself. "Yes. A marquee is a good idea. I'll get Anna to organise it. Something robust on the far lawn."

Harlan decided to shift the conversation back to Black Cronos. "What about the latest castle Barak and Estelle will look into? Any suggestions there?"

"Not really." JD topped their sherry up and turned to the long table covered in books and manuscripts. He shifted several aside and picked up an old, well-read, leather-bound volume. "I've been reading my old notes again. This is my own research into Germain that I've added to over the years. In the light of new knowledge and our current theories, I've gained a fresh perspective on his activities, especially about his friendship with another alchemist, Melchior Figulus. He was an ancestor of the current family who own *Château de Bénaix*. Descendants of Cathars. I presume you've heard of them?"

"Sure. A religious sect that was considered heretical, and consequently persecuted."

JD flicked over a few pages, searching avidly for a reference. "Exactly. Figulus lived many years after all that, and was an average alchemist, at best. Ambitious, certainly, but lacking the intelligence to be truly brilliant." He said it matter of factly, without malice. "That's probably why he and St Germain became good friends. I'd forgotten him until Jackson mentioned the name. Germain collected people, but was never truly friends with anyone who was his intellectual equal." JD gave Harlan a ferocious grin. "It would have been hard to exploit or dazzle them."

Wow. JD really disliked the count.

"So, yes," he continued, "I think following up on the Cathars is a good idea. If that castle isn't the right place, it may be at least a step in the right direction." His gaze drifted to the velvet-covered tablet. "And if I can unlock some of those secrets, I may be able to help even more. That's why I need Gabe and Shadow."

Harlan frowned. "Do you? What for?"

"I stumbled on something I'd forgotten when I went through these notes. A thought I'd had on Thoth and the tablet."

Harlan nodded. "The Egyptian God with the head of an ibis."

JD fumbled for another book, already open at the relevant page. "Here's an image of him. God of writing and knowledge, who also wrote about the afterlife. The Greeks equated him with Hermes. Anyway, I think the key to the tablet is in Egypt. That's what I want Gabe for. I think I know where it is."

"The key?" Harlan could barely believe his ears. "After all this time?"

JD looked at him in absolute seriousness. "Of course. If it's anything like the tablet, it will be indestructible. I need it. Perhaps you should go, too?"

"Me?" Harlan blinked with disbelief. "I have cases to cover!"

"I think you'll be useful. Gabe is coming tomorrow for a briefing. Why don't you wait and hear all about it?"

"Why don't you just tell me now?"

"Because I hate explaining things twice. And right now, you're going to help me take the tablet into the garden. It can go in the greenhouse for now." JD gave him a pleading smile. "It's a bit heavy for me and Anna. You can stay here tonight, have dinner with me." He cocked an eyebrow hopefully.

"Okay, as long as I can read some of your notes on this other alchemist."

JD swept his arm expansively across the table. "All at your disposal."

"Deal."

Three

The warm pub that Barak and his companions had settled in on the edge of Hyde Park was festive. There was a Christmas tree in the corner, and lights were festooned across the ceiling.

Although Lucien's mood had brightened when they left The Retreat, his fingers drifted to the bracelet on his wrist as his eyes darted around the room. Barak kept a careful watch on Lucien's eyes. They were usually the first to change when what they'd dubbed "the Black Cronos effect" took over. First, they glazed over and Lucien became distant, and then his entire eyeballs turned an unearthly copper-gold, showing no white at all. The change happened quickly. After that, his skin shimmered with a metallic sheen that formed a type of armour.

Once he was drugged and tied up, they found that his skin was still warm and fleshy—just super strong. Barak patted the small tranquilliser gun in the inner pocket of his jacket, a subconscious need to check that it was there—just in case. To need to use it would be a disaster. Fortunately, Lucien still looked like any other person sitting in the pub with a pint and a burger in front of him. He'd been well cared for in The Retreat, but the lack of sunshine meant his summer tan had long gone.

Barak's gaze drifted to Estelle who, although eating, also kept a watchful eye on Lucien, and finally shifted to Jackson. "So, where in France are we heading? I'm hoping it's that Cathar castle in the Pyrenees." He and Estelle had found it with Ash's help about a month ago, and all three thought it sounded promising.

Jackson nodded, swallowing his food before he spoke. "Yes. I discussed it with Waylen and JD, and the more we investigated, the more we liked it. Although, there are a few castles in that region that offer promise, and many are linked to the Cathars." He sipped his Guinness before having another mouthful of his steak pie. "It's not a great time of year to be going there, though. It will be cold, and there'll be lots of snow."

Estelle shrugged. "If it's the place, we have to act, regardless of the weather."

"Slow down," Lucien instructed, glancing between them. "Where are you talking about?"

Lucien had not been involved in their conversations about possible bases for Black Cronos. They had all worried about his loyalty, especially Jackson, who suspected he may be a spy that Barak and Estelle had conveniently rescued. Barak understood Jackson's concerns. He and Estelle had endlessly dissected how they had rescued him from the underground lab, but nothing suggested that it was a convenient set-up. Especially the fact that some of the lab staff had been killed. Barak was sure that would not have been part of the plan. No, everything suggested that Lucien was a prisoner.

In addition, Lucien was genuinely distressed about his capture and the changes he'd been subjected to against his will. There was also his background to consider. Lucien had split from his long-term partner, a man called Davide, and devastated, had been searching for change and meaning to his life. Barak felt sorry for him. He had been vulnerable, and Black Cronos had taken advantage of that.

"Sorry, Lucien," Barak said, shuffling his position to look at him squarely. "We're getting ahead of ourselves. As you know, we're trying to find where Black Cronos is based. We looked at many remote castles, strongholds that might provide a base for the Count, and there are hundreds of possibilities, as we mentioned. We factored in that the count is immortal, with many powerful connections, particularly to royalty and nobility. Someone, or many people, supported him in the past. He had no obvious money of his own. But Estelle had the brilliant idea of focussing on places of power, or that have religious or astronomical significance."

He nodded at Estelle who said, "We know that the *comte* is—*was*—fascinated by alchemy, astrology, gems, angels, religion, magic, spirituality, and many other esoteric subjects. He thinks differently. He's subversive. A risk taker. Our investigation went wide and far, and we drifted to the Cathars."

"The Cathars?" Lucien shrugged. "Who are they?"

Barak continued. "A religious group of people who originated in about the twelfth century. They were considered heretics because of their beliefs. They believed in two Gods, not one." Barak paused, finding the subject odd because of the way it intersected with his own background. "They considered that the true God was the New Testament God, and that the Old Testament God was Satan. It's complex, I won't go into it all now, but they were linked to the Templars, and like them, the Church wanted them wiped out. Their beliefs were considered heresy. They had a huge power centre in the South of France, particularly the Pyrenees."

A smile of recognition crossed Lucien's face. "Of course. I remember the name, but I know little about them. They were a type of Gnostic, yes?"

"Yes, favouring personal growth with God over organised religion." Jackson snorted. "They've been linked to all sorts of subjects and people. Some of it seems inflated, but there's no doubt that they were hunted and their castles destroyed. The remains are littered across the Pyrenees, and one in particular looks promising. *Château de Bénaix.* It's privately owned and was rebuilt a couple of hundred years ago. It's positioned high up on a ridge and has astronomical links. Its chapel is aligned with the summer solstice."

"It's also," Estelle said, pushing her empty plate away, "remote and defensible."

"Who owns it now?"

"A family called Voland. They can trace their lineage back hundreds of years. Admittedly," Jackson said with a sigh, "there's only a tenuous link to the count through one of their ancestors who was an alchemist at the same time the count was '*alive*', but even so..."

Barak started to feel the stir of the hunt. Eager not only to find out more about the *comte* and the Cathars in the Pyrenees stronghold, but to explore a wild and mountainous region unknown to him. Somewhere he could spread his wings without city lights glowing below. And of course, another opportunity to spend time with Estelle.

"Where are we staying?" he asked Jackson. "I presume you've made arrangements."

"Yes. And it was very tricky at this time of year. The place is full of ski enthusiasts."

"I love skiing!" Lucien said, smiling. "I'm good at it, too."

"I'm so-so," Estelle said, wiggling her hands. "But hopefully cars will suffice for what we need."

"Well, courtesy of government connections, I've got you a house in Montferrier. A chalet, actually, on the slopes below *Monts d'Olmes* ski resort. It's big, too. I suspect some of your brothers will need to join you. *If* it's the right place," Jackson said, looking at Barak.

"That's fine. They're more than happy to help. Although, I think JD needs them and Shadow for something, and Nahum is tied up in Yorkshire for a few days."

Jackson's eyes darkened with worry. "That's okay. There's still more we need to find out before we act. Time for them to get things wrapped up and join you."

Barak nodded, hoping that Jackson's assessment of their time scale was correct. If they were right about the *château*, they couldn't handle it alone.

Darkness fell and the temperature plummeted. Nahum shivered, despite his warm clothing, but he adjusted the binoculars and focussed on the church below.

It was almost nine in the evening, and after a hearty meal, he and Olivia hiked back up the hill to watch the church. Olivia was right about this being the best place to watch. They had cruised around the area in the car, but it was hard to get close for a long period of time without it being obvious that they were watching. The church stood along a slight rise, surrounded by trees. Within the village, but slightly separate.

Olivia nudged him. "See those lights!"

"I see lights in the church. It doesn't mean anything."

"But it's a strange glow."

"It could be candlelight!"

"There's no service tonight."

"He could be praying. That's what vicars do."

She nudged him again, harder this time, so that he bashed the binoculars against his face. "Olivia!"

"He's walking from the vicarage. I can see him. And he's carrying something heavy. It's the reliquary."

Nahum adjusted his angle, watching Jacobsen, the vicar, trudge up the path. "I presume he doesn't keep it in the church because it's either too eye-catching and he fears it will be stolen, or he doesn't want anyone to know he's got it." He frowned, watching the awkward way he walked. "It's bigger than I expected." As soon as he said it, Nahum realised how weird that sounded. "Not that I'm overly familiar with reliquaries or anything."

"Some are big, some are tiny. It depends on what they contain. It's the gold and other precious metals and gems that usually make them so heavy. The more important the saint, the more ornate the container."

They'd changed their original plan. Olivia's car was parked in the village. Nahum would fly them in, and he would fly back out with the reliquary after tying the vicar up. She would escape on foot, and then meet him on the backroad out of town. It was so dark without city lights that he knew he wouldn't be seen.

He had tried to persuade her to let him steal it on his own, but she insisted on going. She wanted to make sure that up close the reliquary was the right one. Plus, it was her job, and she wanted to see it through.

Nahum lowered his binoculars as the vicar entered the church and studied Olivia, who was still watching Jacobsen. She was an attractive woman. Soft curves, long hair that was currently tied up in a messy bun, and very feminine, despite the heavy boots and camouflage clothing that she wore. "Are you sure you're happy to fly down there?"

She snorted and lowered the binoculars to stare at him. "Are you kidding me? Flying with a Nephilim? I can't wait! Are you sure you want to? It means stripping off, and it's freezing." Her eyes drifted down to his chest and back up again.

"I'll be fine. When I extend my wings, it banishes the cold. It's a weird trick of genetics. We don't feel the cold winds when we fly."

"Really? Interesting." Her lips twitched in a smile. "You'll have to promise me a longer experience some time."

He laughed. "Maybe you should see if you like it first."

"Fair enough. I suppose we should get started." She patted the pack at her side and smirked. "I have the ropes and stuff. Anyone would think I did this all the time."

He laughed, sure she stole such objects far more often than he suspected. "Don't you worry about being reported to the police?"

"He won't report it. These people never do. How would he explain owning something that was last seen in a museum in the 1840s? You don't look that concerned, either."

"I'm not. Although, this man does intrigue me. If what you say is true, he could be dangerous."

"All the more reason to restrain him quickly."

Nahum stood and stripped off his jacket, t-shirt, and jumper, and quickly extended his wings. He was used to people's reactions to his wings, but he still smiled at Olivia's wide-eyed expression.

"I know I've seen them before, but holy cow, Nahum. They are really something else…"

He opened his arms wide, aware her eyes were roving over his wings and bare chest. "Ready?"

"Am I ever!"

She placed her backpack on and stepped into his embrace. Her grip was tight, and after clasping his arms around her, he soared into the sky. She gasped and tightened her grip further. "Holy shit!"

"Shush! I'm just going to sweep around once before I land."

He took in the village, noting the empty streets, and the warm glow of lights coming from the pub, and then ensuring that the churchyard was empty, angled downward in a rush of flight. He landed soundlessly within the churchyard, close to the entrance, and for a moment just stood there, Olivia still clasped to him. He needed to make sure there were no traps or watchers, just in case they needed to leave right away.

The churchyard was deserted, the only light coming from the stained glass windows.

His skin prickled as he sensed ancient power he hadn't felt in a long time. He froze, Olivia still tight within his arms, the urge to flee strong. He fought down his panic, taking deep breaths.

"Nahum?" Olivia's question was barely a breath, spoken so softly only he could hear it. She eased back, hands on his chest as she looked up at him. "What's happening?"

"I feel something…unusual."

"Magic?" Olivia's pounding heartbeat echoed his own. "Should we leave?"

He liked that she didn't hesitate to ask, rather than insist they continue. But he had no intention of leaving. "No. Wait here."

He released her and edged to the main door of the church, the way the vicar had entered. With every step he took, the feeling increased. It was magic, but not of a kind he was expecting. It felt more like his own. Innate. Exalted. *Angelic…*

The huge door was shut tight, but he eased it open. Relieved it didn't squeak, he slipped inside quickly. Olivia, disobeying his request and just as silent, followed him inside and eased the door shut. They were in a small, square vestibule, and the glow came from the nave.

He withdrew his sword and edged to the nave's entrance. Only the altar was illuminated. A man was kneeling on the hard stone floor, a row of candles in front of him. The reliquary was placed on the altar. The candlelight reflected on its burnished surface and glinted off the gems inlaid into it. *Emeralds, rubies, sapphires. No wonder Jacobsen hid it.* It was certainly priceless. But it was what lay inside that troubled Nahum.

As yet the priest hadn't moved, still kneeling in wordless prayer. Nahum edged forward, keeping to the shadows. He should attack now, while he was occupied, but something delayed him. Curiosity, perhaps. Or fear.

He was aware that Olivia was staring as much at him as the priest, her anxiety climbing. He took a mental grip of himself and walked on. But halfway down the aisle, Jacobsen rose to his feet and opened the golden box. Instantly, he heard whispers; urgent, entreating, coaxing. They tugged at his memories. Demanded fealty.

And then the voice whispered a warning.

Jacobsen spun around, clutching something in his hands, and a wild-eyed look on his face. At the sight of Nahum, he screamed and dropped to his knees, face planted on the floor. An object tumbled forward, ringing loudly on stone as it bounced to Nahum's feet.

It was a thick, gold ring, inset with jewels.

Olivia had been crouched behind a pew, but now she bounded towards Jacobsen, taking advantage of his prone position.

Forcing himself to focus, Nahum scooped the ring up, the metal hot in his palm, and shoved it into his pocket before helping Olivia. He secured the blindfold on the vicar and bound his arms. Jacobsen didn't resist, so they were gentle. He was whispering about angels and God. Nahum laid his hand on his brow, willing him to be calm. He was no healer, but his father's blood still ran through his veins. If he wished, he could impose his will on others.

Instantly the man stopped fidgeting, but he still muttered softly. Nahum could imagine how he must have looked, lit by candlelight, his wings spread behind him. It was a wonder the man hadn't had a heart attack.

Olivia was crouched on the other side of Jacobsen, eyes wide in her pale face. She mouthed, "*Are you okay?*"

He nodded and stood, and together they crossed to the reliquary.

The inside lid of the golden casket was inscribed with angelic words and symbols, and on a bed of red velvet, was a skull. Next to it was a bracelet—a golden torc, beaten, inlaid with mysterious symbols. He could still hear whispers, and he asked, "Can you hear that?"

Olivia shook her head. "Hear what?"

"A voice." He pulled the ring from his pocket and compared it to the torc. "They match. They belong to a Fallen Angel." He threw the ring inside the casket and shut it. Instantly the whispers vanished, but the power emanating from it remained. "Let's get out of here. I presume this is what you were searching for?"

Olivia nodded. "Yes, but...it's not quite what I was expecting."

Nahum just wanted to leave. There was time enough for discussion later. His eyes swept the altar, seeing nothing else of note. Nothing unusual. "Are you okay to drive?"

"Yes. Are you okay to fly?"

He nodded. "See you in my room."

Four

O livia had calmed down by the time she returned to the hotel, and her hands had finally stopped shaking.

She might not have been able to hear the whispers that crawled from the casket, but she experienced a gnawing sensation in her brain, and an itching beneath her skin. She was just glad that the damn thing was with Nahum now.

But how was Nahum? His blue eyes had blazed when he saw the reliquary. A mixture of anger and bewilderment. *And maybe a trace of fear...*

She looked for him overhead, the memory of the flight vivid. His hard, warm body pressed to hers. The muscles she longed to explore further. The tantalising V that ran down to his groin. And the flight itself, of course. The rush of cold air. The feeling of space and freedom, and Nahum's power that he kept carefully concealed when his wings were folded away.

Of course, the reliquary itself was also emblazoned on her mind. She wasn't lying when she said it wasn't what she was expecting. She had been searching for only the skull, not the jewellery of a Fallen Angel. She needed tact for what was to come. Compassion.

She found Nahum in his hotel room, his blue eyes stormy, the reliquary sitting on the small table under the thickly curtained window.

"Nahum, I'm so sorry. I swear I didn't know what was in that. I thought it was just—"

He cut her off, his voice brusque with emotion. "It's fine. It's a shock, that's all. I'm not angry with you." He was less imposing with his wings folded away and his bare chest regrettably covered in a t-shirt—but only just. His height and broad shoulders still dominated the room.

"Would you mind if I opened the casket again? Does it hurt you?"

He laughed, a short, sharp bark of incredulity. "No, not hurt. Herne's balls, I need a drink. You?"

"Yes. Whatever's in that mini bar."

While he fixed the drinks, she studied the reliquary, shining the table lamp directly on it. It was definitely the one she had been seeking for her client. But it seemed more...*everything*. The gold shimmered, the gems sparkled, and now that she was close to it again, she could truly feel its magnetism.

"Why can't I hear the whispers that you can?" she asked when Nahum handed her a drink.

"Well, with the lid shut, they have quieted, but I still feel the power. Ancient power. As to why you can't?" He shrugged. "I'm Nephilim. The son of a Fallen Angel. I'd know that power anywhere. I was born with it. It runs in my veins, and it commanded me many, many years ago."

She noted his blue eyes had lost that stormy look, and it calmed her, too. "Can it command you still?"

"No. We threw that yoke off millennia ago." His eyes, which had been on her, now drifted back to the golden casket. "But it's unnerving to find that a piece of their jewellery is here. In the present. In this damn room. It should be under a pile of stone, or at the bottom of the ocean. No wonder people are going mad. Humans aren't meant to be close to it—not for prolonged periods, anyway."

"Well, *I'm* not going mad, or being destructive," Olivia pointed out. "Although, the itching under my skin is really annoying."

"Itching?"

"Like a crawling sensation, I suppose. Or a cold ooze of something."

"Some humans are more susceptible than others. Your body recognises something powerful, but can't place it." Nahum ran his fingers across the designs on the surface.

"Do they mean something?"

"No. These are just ornate, but inside..." He cocked his head at her. "Ready?"

She gulped a mouthful of neat gin. "Now I am."

He opened the casket and immediately the sensation under her skin increased. She shuddered. "You can hear the whispers? Many voices, or just one?"

He nodded. "Just one." He picked up the ring and examined it, turning it over, his long fingers probing it.

"I didn't think the Fallen had real bodies."

"They inhabited the flesh of men. Not for long, though. They burnt them up if they stayed in too long. But they liked precious metals, and adorned themselves with them." He shrugged. "Much like we did, at one point."

"I find that hard to believe."

He smirked. "It was expected of us. Gabe was draped in the stuff when he wasn't in battle, and Niel. So was Ash, come to think of it. The others, I'm not so sure. I saw less of them in our other life."

She could imagine them oiled and perfumed, resplendent in rich fabrics in their palaces once they'd bathed the dust and blood of battle away, something like the torc on their upper arms. She noted the small indentations that marked the torc's surface, and the perfect gems. Mesmerised, she reached in and picked it up.

Images suddenly rocketed into her mind—flaming eyes, alabaster skin, wings of grey feathers, and what looked like a palace in the stars. Her legs collapsed under her, and she stumbled and would have fallen if not for Nahum. His arm wrapped around her, and he wrestled the torc from her tightly clasped fingers.

"Bloody hell, Olivia! What did you touch it for?"

"I didn't think!" She felt breathless. Sick. A thrum of power tingled through her fingers and up her arm, and the cold, oozing feeling intensified. It was as if a river of slime flowed under her skin. She lowered herself to the bed. "Sorry, that was stupid…"

"It's my fault. I should have warned you."

A film of sweat had gathered on her brow, and she wiped it away. "I need water."

In seconds Nahum handed her a glass and she drank it down in one go, her mind and body slowly steadying. The torc was now looking innocent on the table.

"What happened?" Nahum asked, watching her intently.

She described the image. "An angel?"

"Perhaps. Probably." He frowned, clearly annoyed at the jewellery and its effects rather than her. "No more holding jewellery for you." Nahum placed it back in the box, shut the lid, and sealed it with the catch.

"What's written on the inner lid? I don't recognise the language."

"A mixture of angelic and Aramaic script. Protection to control the power of the contents. The symbols are protective, too."

Feeling steadier, and a little foolish at how much the torc had affected her, Olivia reached for her gin, cupping it in her hands. "Do you think Jacobsen will remember your face? I dived for cover as soon as he turned."

"He will hopefully think he was hallucinating. That he saw an angel. I can't believe I went in there with my wings still visible. I was so shocked at what I felt that I didn't think." He sat at the head of the bed, puffed his pillows, and then leaned back, legs stretched in front of him.

Olivia shifted to face him, cross-legged. "It's good you did. If he'd have seen a normal man, he wouldn't have dropped to the floor. Do you think he knew he had Fallen Angel jewels?"

"I was about to ask you the same question! You said you didn't expect the jewellery?"

"No. I've read lots about this reliquary, including the various churches and museums it was displayed in until it vanished. My client has been following it, too. Strange stories have always been attached to it, but there has never been any recorded mention of the jewels. Just the skull."

Nahum frowned. "The inscription? The symbols?"

"Also never mentioned."

"Which suggests someone added them to the casket years later. During its lost years. When did you say it vanished? Or when was it stolen, should I say?"

Olivia had reams of notes, but without them at her fingertips, she couldn't remember details. "Mid-nineteenth century, from a religious museum in Italy. Overnight it just vanished, but rumours surfaced every now and again. A visitor to a minor nobility's palace in Italy recorded seeing it in his memoirs. Then someone else said they saw it in a private collection in Austria. Then it was rumoured that it was in a church in France. Breadcrumbs only. My client has undertaken extensive research himself. He never mentioned jewellery."

"And the madness and violence?"

"Seems to be something that started happening only in the last hundred years or so."

Nahum watched her, eyes steady before they drifted to the casket. "Your client doesn't know about the jewels."

"You don't want him to have them, do you?"

"No." He looked regretful but determined, his jaw clenched hard.

Silence fell, the only sound coming from the hum of the heating, and the tinkle of ice in their glasses. It was a comfortable silence. Olivia felt safe with Nahum. But she also felt the pull of attraction. He was so alive. Virile. Sexy.

She should go to bed.

"He'll never know," she eventually said. "If you think you should, keep them. Especially considering the effect the torc had on me. Unless, of course, my client is keeping things from me, but I doubt it. I just hope Jacobsen will be okay." She considered his prostrate body on the floor. "But what was he doing with the skull and the jewellery? Was he being compelled? And if so, why?"

"That's a great question. I need to identify which Fallen Angel it is. That might help us. I'll take photos of the casket and the writing before you leave, if that's okay."

"Of course." She drained her drink, wanting another. "Thank you. And now I should go to bed. I need a shower. I'm dusty. And I need to wash *that* off me." She nodded at the casket. "I'm not looking forward to driving with it for hours."

"You drove up here?"

She laughed. "I can't very well put that on a flight."

"I'll drive back with you."

She smiled. He was a gentleman. Thoughtful. "You don't have to."

"I want to. Even if I take the jewellery, I won't know if they've left any residual energies. Besides, without the casket to protect everyone from their worst effects, I might send the whole flight mad. I can book another car in London and drive home."

The offer relieved her more than she expected. "I'd love that. But only if you're sure."

"I'm sure." He stood and stretched. "I need a shower, too." In seconds he had peeled off his t-shirt, once again revealing abs to die for, and that V that disappeared into his low-slung jeans. She knew she was staring. She couldn't help it. Didn't want to help it.

Olivia scrambled to her feet. She wasn't a teenage ingenue, but right now, she felt like one. "I better go."

His voice was rough. Hopeful. "I was hoping you'd stay. It's a big shower, and a big bed." His eyes darkened with desire. Those gorgeous blue eyes that glowed like sapphires against his olive skin. "No strings. No hard feelings if you walk away. Fallen Angels leave me feeling wrung out. I don't want to spend the night alone. But neither should you feel obliged to stay just because of that. I'm a big boy. I'll cope."

"I bet you're a big boy." It was out before she could control herself. "Oops."

"Is that yes?" He smiled and stepped closer, and desire shot through her.

No strings, no regrets, no second thoughts.

It was definitely a yes.

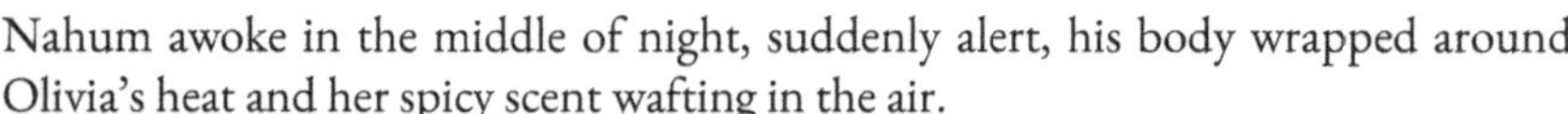

Nahum awoke in the middle of night, suddenly alert, his body wrapped around Olivia's heat and her spicy scent wafting in the air.

He froze, his senses on alert for strange noises or movement in the dark, but the hotel room was quiet, and his keen eyesight revealed that nothing was untoward. For a second he couldn't place what had awoken him, until the image flashed into his mind again. The flaming eyes that compelled obedience and obligation.

Once.

Was it the power of the jewellery that forced these images into his mind, or was it the angel himself, somehow connecting to him? Nahum would rather not debate it now. He would prefer to lie within Olivia's warm embrace. She was a bold and confident woman and knew what she wanted, and he was only too happy to oblige—despite his earlier reservations. He still wondered why he had suggested they sleep together. The idea had popped into his head as she sat cross-legged on the bed, her hair tumbling around her shoulders, testing desires that he ultimately gave in to. Maybe it helped that she was such a flirt.

But he hadn't been lying, either. The power of the Fallen Angel contained within the jewellery really had affected him.

Easing out of her arms, he rolled onto his back, staring up at the ceiling. He was pretty sure that he knew which Fallen Angel the jewellery had belonged to, but he needed to know more. If the pieces hadn't been in the reliquary to begin with, how had they got there? As much as he didn't want to leave the bed, he knew he needed to return to the church, and Jacobsen. There were still hours of darkness left, and tomorrow he would be too far away. He'd been far too surprised earlier to ask any questions. And he'd feared keeping Olivia there too long. She was recognisable, and vulnerable. He was not.

Nahum rolled out of bed and pulled his jeans on, then slipped out onto the balcony. The area was deserted, and within seconds he was flying high above the huddle of buildings and toward the next town. He wondered if the church would be in darkness, but a dim light still glowed behind the stained glass windows. *Curious. Was Jacobsen still praying?* That would at least save him from having to break into the rectory to wake him up and question him. Regrettably, he'd have to leave his wings out for show. It would frighten him again, but as much as he hated doing that, Nahum needed answers. With luck, he'd think he was having a vision.

Once Nahum was standing inside the door of the church again, he heard a low voice. But it was strange. There were gaps, as if the vicar was conversing with someone rather than praying alone. His voice rose with a plea. Frowning, Nahum edged to the door, seeing the church lit as before, candles on the altar, the vicar on his knees. At least the man had been able to free himself from his restraints. The ropes lay on the floor, cast aside.

Something, though, was very wrong here. The presence of the Fallen Angel was still strong. *How, though?* The Igigi had said they had restricted their movement on Earth.

Hating his decision, but knowing he had to make an impression, Nahum stepped inside the nave, extended his wings, and flew to the darkness of the roof. He then lowered his voice, injecting power that he hadn't used in years. "Jacobsen, I have questions that you must answer."

Emitting a startled gasp, the man on the floor squirmed, looking up in alarm. Nahum hovered, arms outstretched, knowing the candlelight made his feathers glow, and exploiting it. He dropped and hovered over the altar, his blue eyes pinning the man to the spot.

Nahum spoke commandingly. "Did you hear me, Jacobsen?"

Jacobsen's eyes widened with horror before cunning settled into them. "You're not Him."

"Who? God?"

"No! The angel I speak with. He told me you would return."

"You speak with him still? Even though I took his belongings?"

And then Nahum saw what he'd missed earlier. The clasp at the neck of the man's surplus that had been hidden by his fall—unless he hadn't been wearing it then. *Another piece of the Fallen Angel's jewellery.* Aware of Nahum's piercing stare, the vicar's hand flew to cover it. "It's mine."

"How can you wear it? Or even bear to touch it?"

"Because I have been *chosen*." Fire flashed in Jacobsen's eyes, and he staggered to his feet. "He says you drowned. That you have no place in this world."

A chill raced across Nahum's skin that had nothing to do with the cold church, and he unleashed his anger. "*I* have no place? And what of the one you talk to? He fell and was never supposed to walk on Earth. How dare he presume to talk with you?"

"I am His messenger!"

"Delivering *what*? Death? Madness? Cruelty? I met your supposed master once. I remember him because I fought his offspring. I won. You can remind him of *that*." Nahum withdrew his sword, a slow, deliberate hiss of menace as the blade whispered from its sheath. "Do I need to use it again?"

"You cannot hurt me!" But Jacobsen scuttled backwards, dark eyes uncertain.

"I most certainly can. Tell me how you found the jewellery."

"What does it matter?"

"I'm curious." Nahum landed in front of the altar, eyes darting everywhere, fearing some trick. "Tell me the name of your master."

"He won't let me."

Nahum laughed. "I'll make a guess, then. I'm sure I'm right. But first, tell me about the jewellery." He placed his blade beneath the man's chin. Jacobsen shot back so quickly, he hit the pew behind him and sat down.

"I found it in the casket."

"Liar. It never used to be there."

"I found them there!"

"In the reliquary you stole? That's not very worthy of a man of God."

"Neither is holding a sword to my throat, Nephilim."

"This *is* my job. You know that. I was the eyes and ears of the Fallen. The deliverer of rules, laws, and death to those who did not obey. Until I too rebelled. Give me answers." Nahum pressed harder, breaking the delicate skin beneath the man's chin. "If you think he will save you, you're wrong. Only your answer can save you now."

And as the man began to spill his secrets, Nahum knew he couldn't allow him to live. He contained too much darkness. Too much of his master—because he was in thrall, no doubt of that. Nahum had not envisaged having to dispense justice this night. He hoped Olivia would forgive him. And that her soft curves would drown it out afterward.

$\mathcal{F}ive$

S hadow was looking forward to the group's new job, but was far less enthusiastic about seeing JD. She tried to hide her impatience with him. She failed.

"You mean you haven't worked it out yet?" She gestured to the Emerald Tablet placed in the centre of the greenhouse in his extensive grounds. Due to the season, it was mostly empty, except for the plants kept in there to overwinter, and a selection of seed trays.

He glared at her, lips curling with disdain. "No! How many times do I need to explain this? It has hidden its mysteries for millennia, and no one has seen it since *their* time!" He jabbed his fingers toward Gabe, Ash, and Niel. "I'm brilliant, but not a miracle worker. Don't you ever listen?"

Refusing to be chastened, she shrugged. "I block out whining."

Gabe intervened with a pleading glance. "Shadow, shut up. This isn't helping. JD, focus please. The job? Egypt, you say?"

JD turned away from Shadow to face Gabe, his irritation still bubbling. "Yes. That's where I hope the key to this will be. I've done extensive research, and I'm sure of it."

"The thing is, JD," Ash started cautiously, "Egypt has been investigated by teams of archaeologists for years. How can you be sure that the key hasn't already been found? Or that it's there at all. It's a long way to go on a hunch."

"Not a hunch!" JD repeated, looking smug. "*Research*. Besides, it's already been found. I just need you to steal it."

Shadow's irritation turned to delight. "Theft is one of my favourite jobs! This sounds better by the second!"

Niel snorted. "It depends where we're stealing it from!"

"Ah. That's where this gets tricky," JD admitted.

"Of course it does," Gabe said with a sigh. "Go on."

"A few years ago, a team of archaeologists discovered an ancient pharaonic city built along the banks of the Nile. Many treasures were recovered, and one of them was a curious emerald disc with an ibis sitting proud of it." JD fished in his capacious pocket and pulled out a dogeared image that highlighted several Egyptian treasures, one of which was the disc. Unfortunately, the image didn't reveal much detail. "Not much has been posted about it since, but it resides in The Museum of Egyptian Antiquities in Aswan. It was once a private mansion, but now houses many Egyptian artifacts. I didn't give it much thought before. Not until I received the tablet. Can one of you help me turn it over?"

Niel was closest, and he waved JD away. "Let me."

"Put it on this bench—carefully!"

A soft velvet cloth had been laid across the wooden bench, and effortlessly, Niel picked up the heavy tablet and flipped it on its side.

JD tapped the base. "See? There is an indentation in it."

They all leaned forward to see better. A circle, about a handspan in width, was carved into the bottom of the tablet. In the centre was another shape, and if Shadow squinted, she could see a bird with a long beak. When it was upright, it was impossible to see due to the cloudy interior of the stone. The interior, that under a certain light, appeared to contain swirling clouds or stars.

Confused, she asked, "An ibis is a bird?"

"Yes. It represents a few things, including the Egyptian God, Thoth. He made the tablet."

Even more confused, Shadow said, "I thought Hermes did."

Unexpectedly patient, JD explained, "Thoth is also known as Hermes to the Greeks."

"Could it be a flaw in the emerald?" Ash asked. "It doesn't look that clear cut to me. The circle could just be a mount. Are you sure it's an ibis?"

"I considered that," JD admitted, reaching into his pocket again. "Until I pressed some plasticine into it. I made a mould." He withdrew a small clay disc. "I've considered making a gemstone replica, but I know I need the real thing."

Harlan whistled. "That's an ibis, all right."

Gabe nodded. "Okay. At least we know what we're looking for."

JD grimaced. "There are no details on the museum's website, or in fact any recent images at all. I just know it's listed as being on display. The museum has certainly not linked it to the Emerald Tablet. But it's just too much of a coincidence..."

"I agree," Niel said. "An emerald disc with an ibis relief that matches this. It has to be it." He eyed his companions. "It's worth trying, at least."

Ash didn't look convinced. "The ibis is a popular motif. It might not have anything to do with this at all. And there's no mechanism." He ran his fingers along the base of the tablet. "There's nothing to twist. No locking system. I mean, what could it do? More importantly, is it dangerous to put them together?"

Harlan folded his arms across his chest, a speculative eye on JD. "JD thinks the Emerald Tablet is supposed to be bigger. He thinks this key will magically make it grow. Perhaps it will. That thing is weird."

"Make it grow?" Shadow said, incredulous. "I suppose it could happen. Magic can achieve many amazing things. And the tablet is very odd. It has a compelling magnetism to it." Her eyes drifted to it, despite her attempts to look elsewhere. She noticed her companions were drawn to it, too. They glanced at each other for seconds only before their eyes slid back to the tablet.

"I have also seen the ancient images," Ash said, nodding. "Some do show that it is easily twice the height of a man."

"I heard stories about it way back," Niel said immediately. "It had a certain mystique, even then. There were whispers about its powers."

"And its size," Gabe agreed. "But I never saw it myself. But JD, why do you want to make it bigger?"

"That's easy. Because I sense there is something hidden in there that can only be seen when it's at its correct size." A gleam of desire kindled in his eyes. "I need to see what that is if I'm to even begin unlocking its secrets."

Secrets that perhaps might be better remaining hidden, but Shadow wasn't about to voice that.

Gabe addressed the team. "Do we want the job?"

"Of course we do," Shadow answered immediately.

"Not so fast, madam." Gabe stared at JD. "How big is the museum? Security?"

JD had the grace to look sheepish. "I'm actually not sure. It's a museum, so I presume that of course they take their security very seriously. I was rather hoping that you would find all of that out yourself..." He bristled. "It's part of your job."

Gabe nodded. "I guess that's true."

Ash was already searching on his phone, and he showed them a photo of a large, attractive mansion with a courtyard on the banks of the Nile. "It doesn't look like a fortress—unlike The Nubian Museum."

"I don't care how much security it has." Shadow grinned. "I love a challenge! I have fey stealth, you three have wings. How hard could it be?"

"Hold on!" Harlan said. "First of all, I will be of no help on this job, but I do know practicalities! How are you going to get it through airport security? If you're searched, you'll be in big trouble. You can put your weapons in checked baggage, but you can't risk that."

"All in hand, my dear boy," JD said breezily. "Years ago, I had a box made for me for just such events. I may have done a bit of smuggling in my past. I had a very nice witch friend of mine spell a box with disguising and hiding spells. It's very effective. You will take that." They all looked doubtful, but he just smiled smugly. "Trust me. You are far more useful to me out of prison than in. I have also arranged your transport through Jackson. You already have a flight booked tomorrow on a government plane. Some diplomats have business in Egypt. Please be discreet, and try not to cause an international incident."

Estelle admired the view that surrounded the chalet in Montferrier and shivered, despite the warmth of the house.

It was cold, brutal weather outside. The snow-capped mountains were spectacular but deadly. A night outside, without shelter, would mean certain death. The suspected stronghold of the *comte* would be high up and hard to access. Tackling this in the summer would make life so much easier.

The group had arrived only hours earlier, driving from the closest airport. Lucien hadn't travelled so far in months, and he was worried and wary, as were she and Barak. But the trip had gone well, and now Lucien was resting. It was something they had observed about him. When he was tired, he was more vulnerable to shifting into a super-soldier.

She heard the soft-footed approach of Barak moments before his arm snaked around her waist and pulled her against him. She smiled, twisting to look up at him, her lips seeking his.

"You're always so quiet!"

He kissed her and then grinned. "Always?"

"Well, except for when you're singing or laughing. Then, you're very loud!" Barak had an excellent voice and loved to sing, serenading her sometimes with the worst music just to make her laugh. And he had the best laugh. Loud, energetic, and infectious. She was lucky to have him, and that made her frightened to consider what they faced now. She would die to protect him; she knew that now. The intensity of her feelings shocked her. She had never felt that way about anyone else in her life.

"You're worrying about the job," he said, releasing her and leaning against the window frame.

"I'd be mad not to. Look out there! It's beautiful and harsh, and if we're right, we'll be fighting Black Cronos in their own space. They know it well. We don't."

His eyes drifted to the breath-taking view and the high peaks. "I know. But we can't afford to delay. They're already strong, and for all we know, are getting stronger. More unfortunate men—or women—like Lucien could be getting kidnapped and experimented on right now. At least we know that we managed to shut down one place."

They had returned to the *Château du Buade* a week after they had rescued Lucien with the rest of the Nephilim. At night, they entered by the rear doors that led to the lab, but the place had been cleaned out. It had been frustrating, but also a relief to know that base was finished. As for the *château* and the family, other than the placement of the base, there was actually nothing to link the family to it, other than the historical connection to the count. It might have been on their property, but there was nothing that would stand up in court. The family was so powerful that the local police refused to interview them without concrete evidence. It was a dead end. Jackson had used experts to investigate their finances, but everything was neat and tidy, and any pressure that he'd been hoping to exert from that side was a dead end, too.

Estelle sighed. "True, but how many more places are there?"

"Let's just worry about this one for now. We need to decide on our next step."

"Reconnaissance. But that will be tricky."

"Not for me."

"But you'll be on your own!" Estelle argued against him—again. They had discussed this earlier on the flight. Barak was going to fly over the old citadel to assess the activity there, and had refused to take her with him.

"I'll be swift, manoeuvrable, and high. I can fly just as easily in the cold as in the heat."

"And if they have lookouts with crossbows as they had before, and you're shot with poison?"

"They won't see me. I'll stay high. It's just reconnaissance." He held her gaze, his brown eyes steady and reassuring. "I'll be fine. The best way you can help me is by studying the map of the area. I think I hear Lucien stirring. There's a huge table in the kitchen, let's set up there. I'll cook while we work."

They had stopped at a supermarket and bought a mountain of food and drinks, and the kitchen was well-stocked. Barak had made his mind up, and on this she knew he wouldn't change it. He was being protective.

"Okay. Done."

Olivia was relieved that Nahum had offered to accompany her back to London, despite their night together that might have made life awkward. Fortunately, it hadn't.

Although the casket was in the boot of the car, she was aware of its presence, and she blocked it out by talking about anything and everything rather than the night before.

She knew he'd left in the middle of the night after she woke to an empty bed, and it was obvious where he'd gone. When he returned, he looked hollowed out, but she didn't say a word. She'd just opened her arms and comforted him. She knew that what they'd found that night had changed everything.

A Fallen Angel had found a voice.

It was now mid-afternoon, and they had stopped at a service station on the A1. Rather than eat in the café though, she had taken food back to the car. Nahum sat with the casket open on his lap, and as she slid into her seat, he shut it.

The insidious feelings were already trying to dominate her thoughts. She passed him his coffee and a pre-packaged sandwich. "I'll be glad to see the back of those jewels. However, I think it's time we talked about last night. The hour that you were missing."

He sipped his drink, eyes wary. "You'll hate me for what I did."

"I don't think I could ever hate you. What happened?"

He looked at her, his blue eyes once again darkening, but not with desire this time. Memories, more likely. "I killed him."

Olivia chose her words carefully. She could see that Nahum hated his actions. "You're not a monster, Nahum. You obviously felt that you had to. Tell me why."

"He was in thrall to a Fallen Angel. People were dying. It wouldn't have stopped. In fact, I'm sure it would have become worse. I couldn't reason with him, even though I tried."

"That's hardly surprising. You told me the Fallen are strong. *Were* strong." She tore off a piece of her sandwich, finding it hard to meet Nahum's intense stare. She forced herself to anyway. He needed to be heard. "We shouldn't have left straightaway. I should have been there with you."

"No way. I wouldn't have wanted you there. I had to go alone. But I only went back to question him. Get some details. But he was talking to the Fallen. He was in his head."

Recalling the insidious feel of the whispers crawling over her skin made her shudder. "I guess that can never end well. But we took the jewellery, so how could that happen?"

"Because he had another piece that we missed. A clasp on his surplus. It confirmed that the angel was Belial." The name seemed to hang in the air, a dark cloud between them. "Even though I took the clasp, I could see Jacobsen was still affected by him."

Olivia swallowed. "I think I've heard of him. He's bad news, I presume?"

"Very."

"Why?"

"He was one of Sammael's closest. Sammael's other name is Lucifer."

"As in the devil. Great…" She sipped her drink, but her hand shook, and she placed it in the drink holder. "So, we're facing some kind of Armageddon?"

"No. I wouldn't go that far." Nahum smiled and squeezed her hand. "Sammael had a bad rep because he caused the Fall. He was the first to walk out. He wasn't all bad, though. He just wanted independence. Belial, who has been conflated with Sammael over time, was meaner spirited. Freedom went to his head, and he exploited his power. All of the Nephilim that he fathered were the worst of all. They were known as the Sons of Destruction. The House of Belial. That's what the families were called, you remember? Houses. Remiel, my father, hated Belial. We were sworn enemies."

Olivia nodded. Nahum had told her about this over dinner the other night. "And you were of the House of Remiel. You had more brothers than just Gabe?"

"Yes. There were hundreds of us."

"And therefore, there were hundreds in the House of Belial."

He nodded. "We were armies, bringing destruction, until some of us rebelled." He flashed her a grin. "Rebellion runs in our blood."

"Mine, too. And the jewellery?"

"It was common for all of the Fallen to fashion some, but as I said, no human could sustain a Fallen Angel for long. But Nephilim also had jewellery made, and weapons fashioned to our design, with the emblem of our house upon them. All long gone of course, until now."

Olivia took another bite of her sandwich, and the food made her feel better. A memory suddenly struck her. "Not *all* long gone. The Temple of the Trinity had weapons there."

"You're right. I'd forgotten that! I guess because they were buried when the temple was destroyed. But it's surprising what parts of the past survive." Nahum finally relaxed and started to eat. "That's why museums are so fascinating."

"Which suggests that if Belial's jewellery has survived, others' could have, too. Jacobsen is dead, but what about Belial now that he has no acolyte?"

"Great question. We thought the Igigi had dealt with them, but Belial was always wily. Taking his jewellery might be the end of it, but I need to talk to my brothers—if I can get us all in the same room together."

"You still haven't told me how Jacobsen found Belial's jewellery. Or why a seemingly respectable vicar stole this priceless reliquary."

"He didn't. It was donated to him by a mysterious benefactor. The jewellery was already in it."

"Really?" Olivia squirmed in her seat to look at him. "You know, I don't often ask questions when I 'retrieve' objects. I can't, most of the time. My end objective is to get whatever it is and get out. However, I'm pleased you went back. This casts a whole new light on the situation. So, what now?"

"You give the casket to your buyer, and I..." he shrugged, "think about Belial and these *trinkets*."

Olivia liked the hunt, and she liked Nahum—not that she was expecting any more bedroom antics between them. The previous night would stick with her forever. However, she certainly didn't want to be left out. "But then what? Will you need help?"

He levelled his gaze at her. "I'm not sure this is something you should be involved in."

"Oh, Nahum. How little you know me. I already am!"

Six

B arak's raven-black wings blended in perfectly with the thick clouds that gathered over Montferrier, and after taking a moment to orientate himself, he flew to the *Château de Bénaix*.

These mountains were riddled with old castles, many crumbled ruins. He flew further than he first intended to take in the vista spread below. Thick snow blanketed the heights, making it hard sometimes to discern the true landscape. But the ruined buildings stood out, like a chain across the peaks. Defensible, tough, and remote.

Barak had read about the Cathars and felt sorry for them. They had been hunted only because they had strayed from the word of the Church. It seemed impossible that they had vanished into history after seeing these mountains and impressive buildings. He had never needed to fight in such extreme cold, but he'd certainly had to attack such fortifications before. They never fared so well when Nephilim attacked. Their angelic abilities were no match for men, although other paranormal beings certainly put up a fight—such as the Igigi and the servants of other Gods.

However, the Nephilim didn't have to contend with modern warfare. Although trebuchets hadn't been invented back then, spears were deadly, as were arrows when they came into close enough range. Of course, there were always paranormal weapons, too. *But what defences did the count have—if this was even the place?*

He swept around, approaching the citadel from the south. It stood on a steep-sided peak, a winding road meandering to a huge gate set into a thick wall. Within the walls were extensive courtyards set around a huge, sprawling castle, its many towers reaching towards the cloud draped sky.

Barak dropped lower, turning in a wide circle. The walls had broad ramparts, and where the walls turned, he saw lights in square towers, containing guards, no doubt. Lined up along the walls were huge bows and weapons that looked like cannons. That suggested they were correct in their assumptions. Whilst most occupied castles would surely have some kind of security, this seemed excessive. Especially when considering the remote location. A few guards patrolled the walls, wrapped up against the cold.

An area to the east of the building caught his eye. A large expanse that stretched to the perimeter wall seemed to have markings on the ground—all swept clear of snow. Barak had come prepared. He pulled binoculars from a pack strapped to his chest and studied them. It was a huge series of concentric circles, all marked with sigils and signs. It looked like JD's device, only it was vast in comparison. They denoted the astrological signs, planets, metals, the elements, and many other things. He recognised angelic symbology and ancient languages, too. And then he realised something else as he studied it further. *It was aligned to the compass.*

He felt sure he was looking at the centre of the *comte's* organisation, and that potentially there were layers of buildings, caves, and tunnels beneath the castle. The largest tower caught his eye next. A gleam of light shone within the highest window, and what appeared to be a communications array jutted from the top. He flew to it, far from the lights below, and settled into deep shadow. He could afford to stay here and watch for a while. See what scuttled below.

Gabe lowered his binoculars and considered their options. There weren't many.

The Museum of Egyptian Antiquities was set in a beautiful building with gilded courtyards and long balconies, all surrounded by large, landscaped grounds. These were also filled with sculptures and ornate walkways. And all of it was actively patrolled by guards.

Shadow wasn't put off. "I told you it would be fun."

"That's because you're nuts."

"You know I'm right. You love this stuff. We can afford to set off alarms and just fly out of there. They won't catch us."

"That's reckless and stupid, and I know that you are neither of those things."

She grinned. "But it would be so much fun! However, stealth is always best."

"And no deaths! *No one* needs to die. They're just guards doing their job. Understood?"

He loved Shadow, but there was no denying her ruthless streak. It was unnerving, and it was even more unnerving that he, a Nephilim, should think that.

"I'm not a complete monster!"

"No. Just a little bit of one."

She leaned forward and kissed him. "You say the sweetest things."

Their flight had arrived a few hours earlier, just before the museum had closed, and their team had managed to enter and see some of the halls. The problem was that they hadn't found the green disc of Thoth, and there were still many halls to search. With a deep sigh, he twisted in his seat on the top of the high wall bordering a neighbouring private garden, and turned to face the Nile. The rush of the current over the cataracts was loud in the still night. They were away from central Aswan here, out in the suburbs. He had never been here in his first life, as they all called it, but he knew Barak and Ash had.

Ash had studied the city with his cool, speculative gaze, his golden eyes taking in all the changes. His conclusion was that it was better before. Gabe was glad he had nothing to compare it to. Memories sometimes got in the way.

"Come on, madam. Time to go." He stood and opened his arms, and Shadow stepped into his embrace. He lifted her and she wrapped her legs around his waist. Even on top of a wall she stirred deep desire within him. But he launched into the air, wings extended, and crossed the warren of dark lanes to their rental car. Niel had been monitoring the area from above, and he swept down to join them.

"Anyone watching us?" Gabe asked. No one should be. This had nothing to do with Black Cronos—hopefully—but they were taking lots of precautions, regardless.

"Nope. All quiet around here. What's security look like at night?"

"As you'd expect. Patrols, guns, alarms, gates, lights. The works."

They joined Ash in the car, and Niel said, "Right now, I'm starving, but I'll come back later and watch for a few hours. Get an idea of patrol times and security patterns. That will help."

"Not if we can't find the disc in the museum," Ash said. He checked the mirror and pulled away. "If it's in storage, we're in trouble. Those places have endless rooms of stuff they haven't looked at in years."

Shadow huffed. "We haven't seen all the halls yet. That place is bigger than it appears. There are plenty of other areas it could be. Calm down. We'll find it tomorrow."

Her blithe confidence always amused and reassured Gabe. "You're right, there is still plenty to see inside. One way or another, we'll find it. We just have to be careful not to show our faces there too often. We'll visit once more tomorrow, so we need to be thorough."

Gabe watched the lights of Aswan sliding past the window, the streets becoming busier as they entered the main town. Aswan was a large city, the centre of commerce for old Egypt, and a popular place for tourists. Small islands crowded the river, as well as huge, abandoned temples and palaces. Many of the temples had been moved, brick by brick, years before. When the Aswan Dam was built to control the river flow, it had flooded part of the valley, creating the largest man-made lake, Lake Nasser. All of the old temples had been moved and rebuilt. Ash had had trouble reconciling the old with the new.

Gabe felt the familiar catch at the back of his throat that he'd felt in Mardin, back in Turkey. Here their own past was too close. Too raw. As much as he liked to visit these places, and to connect with cultures similar to his own, it was also too painful. Living in Cornwall, close to the quaint fishing villages, made life more comfortable.

"But we do the job tomorrow, yes?" Shadow asked, interrupting his thoughts. "There's no point in delaying."

"Yes. We do it tomorrow. The big question is, Shadow, will that box really hide the disc as we go through customs? If not, and we're searched, we'll be arrested for antiquities theft."

She patted his knee placatingly. "Have a little faith."

Niel just snorted. "I'd do better flying it out."

"Across how many countries?" Gabe asked, wishing Niel would be realistic. "It would take weeks."

"Just saying." He spread his hands wide as he twisted in his seat to grin at Shadow. "I'll grab it and make a run for it while Shadow gets arrested. Then you'd wish you'd gone with that plan." He winked at her. "I'd miss you—maybe..."

She scowled at him. "As if airport security could hold me."

Amused, Gabe let their banter wash over him. Niel and Shadow always bickered, winding each other up constantly, but he knew they would also defend each other to the death. They all would. He hoped it wouldn't come to that over the next twenty-four hours.

Harlan eyed Jackson over his pint of ale, noting how tired he looked. His shaggy hair needed a wash, his clothes seemed even more dishevelled than usual, and he had dark circles under his eyes.

"You need to get some sleep while you can. Lucien is out there with Barak and Estelle. He has control of his abilities now. Your babysitting time is over."

Jackson huffed into his Guinness. "Easy for you to say."

"Easy for you to do." He turned to Olivia, who was sipping a glass of white wine and looking preoccupied that evening. "What do you think?"

"I think as mere mortals, we need to trust them. We certainly can't protect them. Not in any physical way, anyway. You're exhausting yourself for nothing, Jackson."

Jackson shook his head, leaning back in his seat as he eyed the room. "I can't just switch off."

They were in a crowded pub near Hyde Park, and it was close to closing time. Conversation was loud, Christmas lights were twinkling, and festive music played in the background. Harlan's own mood was good. He hadn't needed to go to Egypt, which was a relief. As much as he would have loved some winter sunshine, getting arrested was not his idea of fun, and he certainly had nothing to offer Gabe's team. He'd left JD musing over the Emerald Tablet and returned to The Orphic Guild and his London flat. Olivia had phoned him earlier that evening and suggested a drink, and now they were all caught up on each other's news.

Harlan looked at Olivia. "So, your client didn't say a word about the casket's missing items?"

"They weren't 'missing,' remember?" She grinned. "No. He was very happy with the casket and the skull. But now I can't help wondering who gave the damn thing to Jacobsen."

"Someone who wanted to unleash a bit of devilry, obviously," Jackson said. "How long did he have it?"

"Close to five years. I'm surprised he hasn't gone completely mad in that time." She corrected herself, clutching her wine glass as if her life depended on it. "*Hadn't.* You saw the news, I presume?"

Harlan nodded. The news report had said a vicar had been found murdered in front of the altar in his church. The murderer had been decried as a cruel madman.

If only they knew.

"Nahum did the right thing, all things considered."

"What if he'd recovered over time?"

Harlan gave a dry laugh. "Like you just said, we need to trust them. Nahum is a good man. He considers things. He wouldn't have killed him if he didn't think he needed to."

"I know."

"So, what now?" Jackson asked her. "Will you follow it up?"

"I'm not doing anything as far as the jewellery goes. That's all on Nahum and his brothers. What could I possibly do, anyway? However," she paused, sipping her drink again, "I'll continue to make discreet inquiries into the casket. Based on the pattern of behaviour around it, I think the jewellery has been in it for some time. I really want to know who gave it to Jacobsen. And why *him*? I won't delve into the Fallen Angel side of it, obviously."

Jackson looked incredulous. "You can't separate the two! Leave it to the Nephilim."

A challenge flared in her eyes. "And what about you and Black Cronos? Like you can let your grandfather's disappearance rest! Or you, Harlan, and the business of the Emerald Tablet and how that might help the fight against Black Cronos? We're enmeshed in all of this, no matter how much we might want to disentangle ourselves. We can't."

Harlan was relieved he could discuss all of this with Olivia and Jackson. And Maggie too, when he saw her. He had formed an even closer friendship with her after the events with the Storm Moon Pack. A little band of humans in a paranormal world. *Their own pack*. He laughed at the idea.

"What are you sniggering at?" Jackson asked him.

"I'm laughing because I've just realised that you two and Maggie are my pack. I thought it was The Orphic Guild, but it's not. May the Gods help me."

Olivia raised an eyebrow, her eyes twinkling. "Who's the alpha? Maggie, right?"

Harlan was about to protest, then groaned. "Yeah, she so is."

"We should have invited her out tonight."

"Next time. It could turn into some kind of AA meeting. Like we're confessing our sins."

Jackson drained his pint. "Well, I'm going to take your advice and get some sleep. I might actually clean my flat, too. That can wait until tomorrow, though."

Olivia also finished her drink. "That's great advice. I didn't sleep too well last night." A trace of pink graced her cheeks, and she tried to appear a little too casual.

Harlan looked at her suspiciously. "Really? The theft?"

"Of course!"

Harlan didn't push, but he had a feeling he knew what that meant. Reluctantly, he also finished his drink. He may as well go home, too.

They were all heading for the same tube station and they walked together, still chatting, taking a short cut down a side street, when a large black van cruised into view ahead. Harlan's conversation faltered. Neither of his companions seemed to notice, and he told himself he was being paranoid. Black vans were everywhere in the city. It didn't mean they were Black Cronos.

And then he heard a vehicle slow behind him. He turned, mouth dry, hoping he was wrong. But there, at the other end of the narrow side street was another black van, and four tall men with broad shoulders were already climbing out of the side door. The gleam of copper and silver eyes was already visible.

Black Cronos had come for them.

Seven

The only two of Nahum's brothers still in the country were Eli and Zee, and both glared at Belial's jewellery.

They were in their farmhouse in Cornwall, on the moors above White Haven, gathered around a roaring fire in the living room. The Christmas lights twinkled, and a few presents were already waiting under the Christmas tree. Outside, the wind howled, and rain battered the windows. Nahum felt shut off from the rest of the world, but knew it was an illusion. Belial might be watching them right now.

"I always hated that devious bastard," Zee said, scowling. "I should have put money on him being the one to find a way past the Igigi's spell—if that's even what we call it."

"Whatever we call it, he found an agent to help him. If he were walking the Earth now, we'd know about it," Eli said. "He swaggered...liked to put on a show with his destruction."

"True." Nahum nodded. "There was no *show* last night, or over the years that his jewellery has been circulating. Just insidious madness instead."

Zee snorted. "There's nothing new in this world. That happened in our time, and it's happening now. The Fallen had nothing to do with madness or evil. Evil lies within the heart of everyone. Most suppress it. As for madness...well. Mortal bodies were always fallible."

"True, brother," Eli agreed, voice dropping. "But the Fallen were adept at manipulating weakness. Just as some angels were able to offer strength to resist it. It's the age-old battle of good against evil. All Gods and their acolytes have a stake in that."

Nahum ran his hand across his stubble. "You're both right, obviously. But now we have proof that Belial is manipulating again. I saw him and felt him. How do we find his agent?"

Zee looked confused. "You killed his agent, surely, last night. Jacobsen."

Nahum shook his head. "No. Someone gave him that casket. Delivered it right to his door. Maybe they thought that as a man of God, he would be more susceptible. Why *him* still eludes me. Something must have marked him as useful."

Zee was sitting cross legged on the rug in front of the fire, but he stretched his legs out as he pondered this. "Why not use the other agent, then?" he huffed. "This all sounds ridiculous. Unless..." Zee's eyes widened as understanding dawned. "Jacobsen was expendable. The other person was not."

"That's an interesting suggestion." Nahum knew this would get ugly. This was just the start. "If Belial has found a way, others will, too. Perhaps his true agent is another supernatural creature."

"Someone who will want Belial's jewellery back," Eli pointed out.

Zee grimaced. "He'll have more than just those three trinkets."

"Not necessarily," Nahum said, hoping time would have erased most of them.

"We need to ask Newton or one of his team to investigate Jacobsen's background." Eli leaned forward to study the jewellery, hesitated, and then picked up the torc. A shudder ran through him, but he didn't let go. "Its power has dimmed over time. I didn't think that was possible."

Nahum had thought similarly, but hadn't wanted to presume. "I'm glad you said that. That's good news. Something to work with. Maybe something about Jacobsen's belief made him more vulnerable."

"But again, why him out of all the holy men Belial could choose from?" Zee said. "Unless there are several out there."

Nahum felt steadier with his brothers around him. More in control of his emotions. Last night had unnerved him because it was totally unexpected, and in a moment of weakness he had sought solace with Olivia. That was unfair of him. She wasn't a tool for his enjoyment or to drown his sorrows in. He had once thought of women that way, but not any longer. He should apologise. Then he thought of the way her eyes and hands travelled down his naked body. *No, they were all square there.* Shaking off his memories, he turned to practicalities. "Let's ask the witches for help. A finding spell, perhaps. Or ask Alex to locate him."

Zee looked incredulous. "Are you insane? Asking him to connect to Belial! No way. I won't let you!"

"Alex is strong, and well used to crossing to other realms and dealing with demons and spirits."

"This is no demon. This is *Belial*. Alex is my friend—and I thought he was yours! I won't allow it!"

"*Allow?*" Nahum felt himself firing up. "You're not my master! I'll ask. It's up to him whether he says yes or no."

Suddenly Zee was on his feet, eyes flashing. "You'd risk Alex? What kind of man are you? Oh! I forget. You're *Remiel's* son. His house was always known to risk much to gain the upper hand."

Nahum leapt to his feet too, almost upending the coffee table between them. His ears were buzzing, and a need to exact violence and vengeance that he hadn't felt in years raced through him.

They were suddenly shouting and pushing, and the air was thick with anger.

And then Eli intervened, strange words looping in the air. Words of protection. Words of healing. The buzzing vanished, and reason returned. He found himself on the floor, Zee beneath him, with Zee's hands at his throat.

Eli pried them apart. "Nahum. You've spent too long around the jewels. We haven't been exposed to them in years. They got to you. Both of you."

As understanding dawned, Nahum stood and extended his hand to Zee. "Sorry. That was…"

"Terrifying? Yes." Zee took his hand and pulled him into a hug. "Time has weakened us, brother. Let us not let that happen again."

The jewels were now inside a swiftly drawn circle on the floor, a sprig of pine next to them. They looked innocent now, the Christmas lights bathing them in a rosy glow.

Eli glowered at his brothers. "Lucky I didn't lose my head, too, or we'd have probably killed each other. Are you all right now?"

Nahum ran his hand through his thick hair, tired and exasperated. "I will be. Zee, you were right. I can't expose Alex to those. They made Olivia feel weird too, and they were still in the casket most of the time. She touched the torc and saw him—well, elements of him."

"Actually," Eli said softly, sitting again now that the atmosphere had returned to normal, "I think we must ask Alex for help. Or maybe all of them. We need answers, and have no other choices. And if that fails, we have one other option that I'd rather not use, but there's no doubt they're powerful enough. The dryads."

Nahum laughed, and then stopped as he saw Eli's expression. "You're serious? The ones who have bound you to them for guardianship? What might they exact for *this* piece of advice?"

"I did say I'd rather not."

Zee grabbed his beer and took a long drink, then wiped his lips with the back of his hand. "That is the absolute last resort."

"I should call Gabe," Nahum said, reaching for his phone. "We have to speak to him before we do anything." He knew he wasn't planning on pulling off the heist that night, not after his earlier phone call. "Maybe he'll have a better idea."

Barak's limbs were stiff because he had been stationary so long, but at least he was warm. His wings were wrapped around him, blending with his black skin, and in deep shadow high up on the tower, he felt confident he hadn't been seen.

Barak just hoped the castle didn't have defences like JD's, or he'd either be zapped from existence or trapped if they were activated.

But his persistent watch had paid off. He had studied the number of square towers populated by guards, and had watched them patrol across the ramparts at regular intervals. Always two of them walked the castle walls before returning to their respective towers. Fortunately, most patrolled at the same time, and they didn't linger. No doubt the freezing temperatures were putting them off. They scanned the skies and the steep slopes and then retreated. They felt comfortable. Safe. The guards did not expect anything untoward. But he'd seen at least a dozen of them, and there were probably many more inside.

Just when Barak thought it was time to leave, voices echoed up to him, and he heard the slam of heavy doors. A couple of men walked across a courtyard below, vanished for a moment beneath arches, and then appeared on the periphery of the huge circle. They paced its perimeter, and one stopped to study the sky. The clouds were clearing, revealing the swathe of glittering stars above. Unfortunately, although he caught snatches of their conversation, he couldn't hear the words. Just mumbles. He wished he was lower, but that would be impossible.

After another animated discussion, one of them pulled a phone out and called someone, and within seconds a huge rumble broke the larger silence. Stone grated on stone as a couple of concentric circles started to move and realign. Light emitted from some of the sigils. Astrological symbols were aligning with the wheel of the year.

Of course. Yule was only a week or so away. It must have significance for them. Maybe a ritual that would give power.

And then a shaft of moonlight caught the face of one man, and Barak gritted his teeth. *Stefan Hope-Robbins.* The Oxford professor who had escaped from the Dark Star Temple and the Igigi's underground city. Barak studied his companion, noting the man's short hair and angular face. He was taller. Thinner. Barak didn't recognise him.

Stefan looked to the arches as another figure stepped into view and crossed the grounds to join them, and Barak's blood ran cold. She looked like the mirror image of The Silencer of Souls. Long limbed, lithe, and deadly, her hair a cascade of silk down her back. The first one had warned there were others, and here she was. *But why was she so similar? Was she a clone? Were they sisters?*

Barak was tempted to launch himself from the tower and try to kill all of them, but ultimately knew that would be a suicide mission. The tower guards would surely see him and attack. Not only would he risk death, but they would know their stronghold had been identified. He must wait. Now more than ever, Barak wanted to know what lay beneath the castle. If there were tunnels, rooms, and huge mechanisms, there would be other entrances, and they may not be as well guarded. Or at least as visible.

That was the next night's task, then. He would return with Estelle and Lucien to identify as many other entrances as possible, and hopefully his witch could veil them in an invisibility spell.

Olivia heard Harlan's warning shout on the narrow side street and looked around in alarm. She immediately saw the men exiting the black van ahead, blocking their escape.

Harlan tugged at her elbow. "There's a van behind, too. We need to move!"

"Where? I presume these are your bloody Black Cronos soldiers?" Unless they were Belial's agents, but she doubted that. Heart pounding, she spun around, looking for an escape route on the narrow lane. There were a few doors, but all were shut. "For fuck's sake. I was having such a good night!" She reached into her bag and found her pepper spray. It wasn't much to defend herself, but it was better than nothing. She didn't go anywhere without it.

Jackson, however, had pulled a gun from his pocket. "I really, really hate these guys."

"You have a *gun*?" Harlan spluttered.

"You know I do! I've just started carrying it more often."

"Thank the Gods for your paranoia," Harlan said, running towards the closest door and tugging at it. "It's locked."

Jackson fired at the lock without hesitation, the blast loud in the confined space. Rather than scare off the soldiers, they quickened their steps. As Harlan wrenched the door open, Jackson fired at the advancing men. Olivia was impressed. He was a good shot. A couple stumbled and fell, utter shock on their faces, but that's all she could take in as she ran inside the building. From the meagre streetlight, she could see a short passage and rooms ahead, and using the torch on her phone she ran onwards. More shots sounded, and then the door slammed behind them.

"Block the bloody door!" Jackson shouted.

"With what? My body?"

"No, you American moron! The bloody boxes!"

Olivia sought another way out. They were in the back of an upmarket furniture shop. She could see the store front to one side. It was large, a big glass window. *Oh, shit*. A shop near Hyde Park. *That meant...*

An alarm peeled out into the quiet night, the high-pitched whine painfully shrill. *At least that would deter Black Cronos...* She hoped. Unfortunately, there was only one other way out, and that was through the front door. Right on cue, half a dozen black-clad soldiers, a mix of men and women, appeared in front of the windows. They extended long, slender weapons from their palms and smashed the window. *So much for the alarm.*

She raced back to the corridor and spotting stairs leading up, yelled to the others, "Move it! Now!"

Olivia ran up the stairs, trying to ignore the sounds of splintering glass and thundering footsteps, and behind that the squealing of police sirens. They just had to keep moving for a bit longer. On the upper level, she skidded into another room.

Harlan was right behind her, and he yelled, "Jackson!"

They were in a storeroom, and there was furniture inside that they could use to block the door. But Jackson wasn't with them. She shot Harlan a look of pure desperation and ducked back into the corridor. "Where the hell is he?"

The alarm was insistent, and so loud she could barely think straight, but they both returned to the top of the stairs. With horror, she saw Jackson still at the bottom, firing his final rounds. "Jackson. Get your arse up here!"

But it was too late. A Black Cronos soldier tackled Jackson to the ground, and his gun tumbled to the floor. Olivia threw down the closest thing at hand to help, a huge glass statue. It fell short. Harlan followed it up with another. That missed, too. The soldier punched Jackson, and dazed, he fell limply on the floor. The soldier scooped him up and ran for the exit.

Only seconds before Olivia had wanted to barricade herself in, but all that was forgotten as she screamed, "*No!*"

They both raced down the stairs, desperate to save Jackson.

Harlan cursed loudly. "Stupid bloody man! What the fuck was he thinking? We're all going to get caught and turned into damn lab rats."

Another soldier was waiting in the doorway of the shop. His dispassionate silver eyes showed no mercy as he blocked her, intending to capture her, too. She unloaded most of the pepper spray in his eyes. Roaring in pain, he stumbled, and she kicked him in the groin. Harlan vaulted over him, racing after Jackson.

The sound of sirens was louder now, and it was the only thing that saved them.

The wounded soldier regained his feet and shoulder-barged into Harlan, knocking him into some furniture and clearing the way to the door. He staggered to the waiting van, and in seconds they accelerated down the road.

Jackson was gone.

Hot, sweet tea burned Harlan's throat. He would have preferred a large shot of bourbon, but this was better than nothing. *Screw this stupid British obsession with tea.*

Maggie was growling like a feral cat as she stalked around the furniture shop's kitchen. "You're both bloody lucky! You could have died!"

"They didn't want to kill us," Olivia told her, also cradling a hot cup of tea. "They wanted to capture us, just like Jackson. I'm so angry, I feel sick. If they hurt him…"

"Let's hope he's a bargaining tool," Harlan said, quickly intervening. He'd had those same thoughts, and wanted to push them away. "I've always been paranoid that they'll strike. Convinced myself I was crazy."

"Well, one thing is for sure," Maggie said. "You can't go home, either of you. You need to go somewhere safe. Perhaps The Retreat?"

"No!" Harlan shook his head. "They've been attacked before, and we don't want to lead Black Cronos back to their door again. We either hole up in my favourite hotel—"

Olivia interrupted him before he could finish. "The bloody Mandarin Oriental? Don't be moronic!"

"There's logic to hiding in plain sight! It's big and busy. Or, if you'll let me finish, we stay at JD's. Or join Barak and Estelle abroad."

Maggie finally sat down, eyes bleak. "You said they think they've found the count's base?"

"Yes. They're investigating the place now."

Maggie rolled her eyes. "You're a fucking idiot. First, you're moving yourself closer to their potential power base, which is insane. Secondly, you risk blowing their cover too, *if* they're watching you."

Dread ripped through Harlan, and he ignored her jibe. "What if they already *are* watching them? We're all spread out. Separated, and therefore weaker. Maybe the last few months of quiet have been to lull us into a false sense of security."

Maggie leaned on the table, her chin in her hands. "It's possible. Maybe you should start making some calls. Let them all know what's happened here."

"But it doesn't make sense to come after me," Olivia protested. "I haven't been involved in any Black Cronos stuff."

"But you have been working with Nahum over the last day or so," Harlan reminded her.

"Yes, but not on this stuff. He was helping me look for my reliquary!"

"You might have just been caught up in this because you were with Harlan and Jackson tonight," Maggie told her. "It could just be bad timing. Plus, if they've been watching Harlan, they know who you are and what you do. Seeing the three of you together might have been a big attraction. Maybe they think you're useful now. And all of that makes me feel very worried about us staying here any longer. I've got your statements, so you're free to go. I'll start following up with traffic cameras, looking for black vans. Unfortunately, I'm pretty sure we won't get far. They're too good. Any thoughts on where they could have taken him?"

Harlan shook his head. "No. We think they have multiple bases, but I guess logic dictates that he must be in England."

"Unless they have a private jet," Maggie pointed out. "Money does not seem to be an issue for them."

"Poor Jackson. This is a nightmare." Olivia raked her hands through her tousled hair, attempting to smooth it out. "But where will we go? And how?"

"I'll drop you off wherever you need," Maggie said, flashing a smile of reassurance that Harlan didn't even know she possessed. "I'd like to know you're safe. Even you, Harlan!"

He choked out a laugh. "Thanks. So, I guess I was right in saying I thought of you as part of our pack, earlier."

"Really?" Maggie snorted. "I could go for that. Only if I'm the alpha, though."

"Yeah. We thought that's what you'd say. But we're a member down right now. We need to find Jackson."

"Leave that with me. But warn the Nephilim!" She emphasised her message with a jabbing finger. "Now, let's decide where you should go."

While Maggie and Olivia discussed options, Harlan felt more and more uncomfortable as the shock of the attack wore off. He didn't want to go anywhere. He wanted to find Jackson. To do that meant they had to act quickly, so he interrupted their conversation. "I have a better idea. I found Jackson's scarf on the floor, and that means we can use a finding spell to locate him."

Olivia looked at him, startled. "That needs a witch. Who could we use?"

"The Moonfell witches." He cocked his head at Maggie. "What do you think?"

She held his gaze for a moment, and he could tell she was weighing up their options. She exhaled slowly. "I suppose that is a good idea. *If* they'll help."

"Why wouldn't they? They helped Maverick."

"Hold on!" Olivia intervened, puzzled. "The Moonfell witches? The ones you met last month? You hardly know them!"

Harlan shrugged, impatient to act. "Yes. The ones who helped the shifters fight the therians. We need a finding spell, and they're powerful. Our White Haven witch friends are too far away."

He had met the Moonfell witches the previous month when he'd helped Maverick Hale's Storm Moon Wolf-shifter Pack after one of the members had been brutally killed. The three Moonfell witches had helped find his killer. Moonfell was the name of their Gothic mansion situated near Richmond Park. Birdie was the oldest, nearly blind with cataracts, and she had two granddaughters, Morgana and Odette. Cousins, not sisters.

He pulled his phone out and found Morgana's number. "I had a long chat with them on the return trip from Wales. I like them. I'm sure they'll help. I'll happily hide out at JD's later." His Mortlake Estate was the only place with defensive systems strong enough to hold back Black Cronos without any other paranormal support. "Right now, I need to try to find Jackson while the trail is hot!" Neither Olivia nor Maggie liked to back out of a fight. He appealed to them. "You both know I'm right. And you, Maggie, are always saying how limited your resources are. Are you with me? I'll do this alone, otherwise." He squared his shoulders defiantly.

Olivia rose to her feet. "Of course. That's actually a brilliant idea. I met Morgana once, years ago, but I doubt she'd remember me. Let's do it."

That left Maggie, and Harlan stared at her, a challenge in his eyes.

Maggie huffed. "Bollocks. I just wish I'd have thought of them first." With her characteristic belligerence she charged out the door, yelling over her shoulder, "Don't forget to phone the bloody Nephilim!"

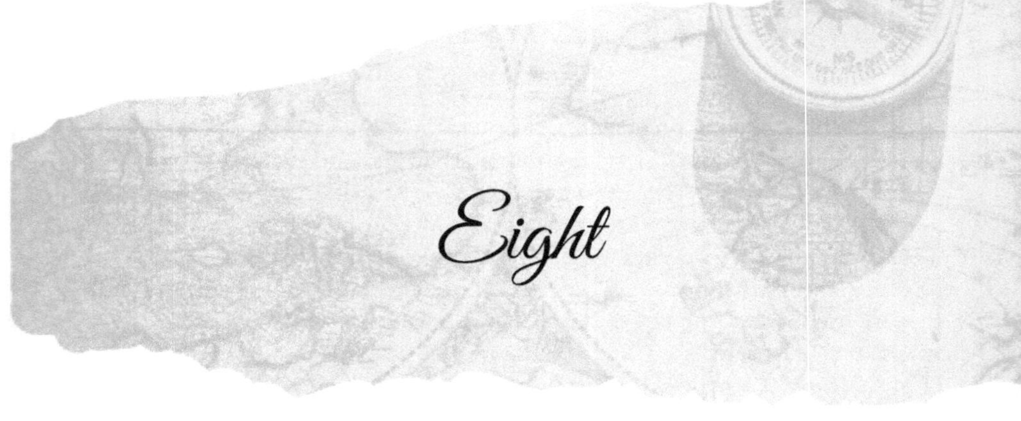

Eight

After Niel completed his survey of the museum, he settled on the roof of their hotel and admired the glittering vista of Aswan and the dark waters of the Nile. He knew he wouldn't sleep. Too many things swirled in his thoughts, and for once, one of them wasn't Lilith. Instead, it was the news of Nahum finding Belial's jewellery that worried him. He was sneaky, mean, and one of the most powerful of the Fallen.

When he couldn't stand thinking of Belial anymore, it was Mouse that preoccupied his thoughts. The thief with the beguiling eyes, slender body, and treacherous soul. He wondered what she might be stealing now. Maybe she was hanging upside down by a rope, or vaulting over a wall, or creeping through a silent museum. As long as it wasn't Aswan's Museum of Egyptian Antiquities, she could be anywhere she liked. But she wouldn't be there. No one except their own small group could possibly know their whereabouts. JD was more paranoid than they were.

However, he watched a black van crawl along the road in front of their hotel before shrugging it off. Lots of people drove black vans. Then again, it was almost two in the morning, and the roads were much quieter now. It was also the same make and model as those used by Black Cronos, and they weren't that common in Aswan. He cricked his neck and rolled his shoulders. *Could it be them?* He paced to the far end of the roof and studied the road below. The hotel was big and modern, sitting squarely at a junction. There was another van down there, too. However, no one emerged.

Unable to shake off his unease, he decided to keep watch. It was highly unlikely to be Black Cronos, and even it if was, it was madness to attack a big hotel. He pulled his phone out to call one of his brothers, just as it buzzed in his hand. It was Harlan. That cheered him up. He liked Harlan's dry wit, and the way he teased Shadow. "My American friend. You're up late."

His next words though were like ice. He listened carefully, and when he hung up, his thoughts no longer drifted. They were razor sharp. Jackson had been taken by Black Cronos, and they might be coming for all of them. No longer feeling so paranoid, he called his brothers, including Barak and those in Cornwall. In minutes, Ash, Shadow, and Gabe were with him. They had all been asleep, but were now dressed, alert, and armed.

Niel pointed to where the black vans had parked on the roads bordering the hotel. "Those two. No one has exited. It might be nothing, but…"

Ash pulled his hair into a ponytail as if preparing for battle. "And it might be everything."

Shadow shook her head. "It doesn't make sense. If it's them, it would have been better to attack us on the back lanes around the museum. Here it's just too busy."

"They're determined. Maybe they think a big hotel with people coming and going will be good cover," Gabe suggested. "Even at two in the morning, there are night staff and cleaners about."

Niel snorted. "They're soldiers. They don't look like cleaners!"

"Cleaners don't put up much of a fight though, do they?" Shadow pointed out. "And we're supposed to be tucked up in bed."

As Niel watched the road, he saw another black van pull up not far from the others. "There's another."

They all watched in silence, rewarded moments later when black-clad men and women exited the vans and assembled on the street. Seconds later they crossed to the hotel, some circling around the back to cover all exits.

"Damn it," Gabe muttered. "How the hell do they know that we're here? And does that mean they know *why* we're here?"

"If they steal that disc before us, we're screwed," Shadow said, watching the activity below. "Unless they're already there..."

"There's no way they know *why* we're here," Ash said, shaking his head. "We snuck that Emerald Tablet out from beneath the Templar Church, and no one knows about it except a very small group of people I'd trust with my life. This is an opportunistic attempt on us."

Gabe was still watching the last of the soldiers slide into position. "Which means we are being watched, and we didn't know. That's unacceptable. I feel like an idiot. And on top of that, there's Belial's crap to deal with. The farmhouse boundary alarms should work, but we still need to warn our brothers."

"I've already called, and so far, there's nothing going on there," Niel reassured him. He started to laugh, feeling like they might actually have the upper hand despite the nearly two dozen soldiers circling the hotel below. "They won't make a scene downstairs. They just want to find us, and we're up here. If they go in, guns blazing, the police will arrive. They won't want that. Let's leave them to it, and go steal the disc right now."

Shadow grimaced. "Damn it. Now I'm torn between wanting to kill lots of Black Cronos soldiers and stealing from a museum."

"My poor sister," he mocked. "Decisions, decisions..."

Ash cut in, moving things along. "There is no decision. Let them turn our rooms upside down. They won't find a thing there, and we have our weapons on us now. I think it's a great idea."

"But we haven't brought our packs with the other tools we might need," Gabe pointed out.

"I have my skeleton keys for the display cabinets, but I need a bag to put the disc in, and the packing," Shadow pointed out. "We can't risk it getting damaged."

"But we have pockets." Ash patted the fatigues that they were all wearing.

"Exactly. We'll improvise with the rest," Niel said, hoping he wouldn't regret the suggestion. "To go to our rooms now risks us being caught. Let's go get that disc."

Nahum, Eli, and Zee were still up, musing on Belial, when the calls from Niel and Olivia came through, literally within minutes of each other. They had immediately turned off the lights in the farmhouse, grabbed their weapons, and prepared for the worst.

"How much faith do you have in our new system?" Nahum asked his brothers as he stood at the window looking out on to the courtyard and the drive.

"A lot," Zee answered from the window to the rear of the house. "The witches did it, and they're brilliant."

"But Black Cronos are brilliant, too," Nahum pointed out. However, nothing moved outside, and only the usual night noises broke the silence of the countryside around their house.

A few weeks earlier they had decided to set up enhanced protection around the grounds. With their efforts to find Black Cronos intensifying, and after their encounter with the ancient Templar order in Temple Moreton, they had decided that they could be vulnerable to attack, especially as they were often spread out on different assignments.

They had debated putting in cameras and a standard security system, and had decided to place a couple of mounted cameras at the front and rear of the house, but for the larger area, they preferred something magical. The witches had been happy to help. They had warded the boundary of the fields immediately around them, and then added more wards within metres of the house. It had taken them several days to complete, and once a week one of them came over and reinforced them. Usually it was Alex or Briar. It was essentially a protection circle, enhanced with powerfully charged gemstones buried in the earth. The Nephilim, Shadow, and their friends could come and go with ease, but anyone else would encounter a type of forcefield they couldn't pass—they hoped.

Zee shouted from the kitchen, "The perimeter protection field has been activated!"

"I see it!" Eli replied.

Nahum left his own post—hopefully the last place that any intruder would get to was their front door—and headed to Eli's side. At the far end of the field, where Shadow had taken out several soldiers months earlier, a blue shimmer illuminated the oak tree.

Nahum nodded, already gripping his sword. "I see it. Damn it. I really hoped it wouldn't come to this."

"That they wouldn't attack us here again?" Eli huffed. "It was inevitable. But I think Niel is right. They know we're separated. This is a coordinated attack. And that means they've been watching us."

"Let's worry about that later."

Another spark of blue further along the field had Nahum marching to the kitchen, Eli on his heels. Zee was readying his crossbow, and he grinned at their arrival. "Time for some target practice. I'll head up to the roof."

Eli positioned himself at the back door. "If they find a way through, and they're spread out like last time, we're screwed. Unless we just take off. But that effectively means surrendering our house to them, and I won't do that."

"It won't come to that, I'm sure of it," Nahum reasoned. "Eli, what say we edge a little closer. Zee, watch the front of the house while you're on the roof."

He nodded and called over his shoulder as he left them. "Of course."

"I have one last suggestion," Eli said, just as Nahum was about to head out of the back door. "Let's take Belial's jewels."

"What?" Nahum spun around, Black Cronos pushed to the back of his mind for a moment. "Are you nuts?"

"There are only three of us. We could probably draw on his power to enhance our own—if needed."

Nahum hesitated, his normal revulsion at anything related to the Fallen pushed aside in favour of necessity. *Perhaps they could use Belial for some good, after all.* "Fine. But we need to be careful! He's strong."

"Brother. The time for care has passed. The time for battle is upon us." And with these most unexpected words coming from Eli, the lover and peacekeeper of their little family, he went to fetch the jewels.

Olivia liked gardens, and would have loved one of her own if she had any time available to spend tending it. She contented herself with a few pots on her small balcony. The garden at Moonfell, however, was very unusual.

Gravel crunched beneath their feet as they approached the Gothic mansion. High up, a window in a turreted tower glowed with a soft yellow light like a beacon. Or a lighthouse, warning them away from rocks that could kill them.

Huge evergreen topiary statues marched down either side of the drive, lit up by the occasional spotlight. Others revealed themselves in glimpses between the shrubs. A few were elaborate mixtures of round balls, spirals, and pyramids, but amongst them were shrubs sculpted into leaping cats, dragons, snakes, and what appeared to be sigils. *Someone was a very skilled gardener.*

Other trees—not surprisingly, considering it was mid-December—had bare branches that rattled together, sounding like cackling old crones. They reached towards the house, tapping the walls and windows as if announcing their arrival.

Olivia longed to explore, seeing fallow beds, and others with frost damaged plants wilting in the cold. She sensed secrets in this garden, and she shivered.

"It's watching us," she declared to Harlan and Maggie. "Assessing us."

"For fuck's sake," Maggie grumbled. "This place is weird enough without you making it worse."

"I can't help it!" Olivia kept her voice low, and wished the gravel would crunch quieter. "I'm a bit freaked out, but I'm excited, too. Have you ever been in the house before? Either of you?"

"Nope." Harlan shook his head. "Not entirely sure I'll be coming back, either. Now I wish I had called first."

"We did the right thing," Maggie reassured him. "It's harder to turn us away now that we're here."

The huge, wooden front door was made of thick timbers and set between two ornately carved pillars. The door knocker was a raven made of burnished brass, and what looked like a bone in its beak.

Saying nothing, but casting them a long look of apprehension, Harlan used it to rap on the door.

The boom was loud, and for a while, nothing could be heard inside. And then the door swung inward on silent hinges, revealing a huge staircase and a long hallway beyond it. All three froze on the covered porch, goosebumps erupting along Olivia's skin. No one was there.

Thick rugs covered the floor, the slim edge between rug and wall revealing ornate tiles in rich colours that glowed in the subdued light. Dim lights from open doorways lit the hallway in stripes. Incense hung in the air, and occult imagery lined the walls. Power resided here. And more secrets.

Maggie bristled with impatience, but Harlan smiled and said in an aside, "Arlo told me that Odette likes a dramatic entrance." With a firm voice he shouted, "Odette! It's Harlan. I'm here with friends."

A slender woman with shoulder-length hair falling in soft curls stepped from the room to the left and smiled, her teeth gnawing at her bottom lip with regret. "Harlan. Such a spoilsport!"

Maggie huffed and stepped in front of him. "DI Maggie Milne. Don't you have some dramatic music and the sound of bats, too? Maybe wolves?"

Odette's eyes sharpened, and she folded her arms across her chest. "Next time, perhaps, DI Milne. I remember you from Storm Moon club. You watched us treat Arlo. Is this a social call? It's quite late." And then she took a sharp intake of breath. "Darkness stalks you. Come in." She hustled them inside and shut the door. "Put your coats on the rack under the stairs and come to the kitchen. We don't stand on ceremony here." Then she gave a sneaky little grin. "Well, sabbats notwithstanding, and spells, of course. We have plenty of ceremonies for them."

"Odette," Harlan said, shrugging off his three-quarter length woollen coat. "This is Olivia, my colleague at The Orphic Guild, and a good friend."

Odette had cast only a cursory glance towards Olivia, but now she looked at her properly. Olivia noted her soft brown eyes ringed with amber set inside her heart-shaped face. She was beautiful, but her eyes reminded her of an owl. A predator. And Olivia was prey. For some reason Olivia couldn't explain, she felt wary around Odette, almost an instant dislike, and she couldn't fathom it. She had no problem with witches. She admired their magic.

But before she had time to consider her response further, Odette had frozen, transfixed, eyes looking deeply into Olivia's own. She grabbed her arms with her cool hands and pulled her under the light. Something within Olivia recoiled, and then flared in anger. A hard, jealous, resentful anger that craved destruction.

Odette's sharp voice was accusatory, like a slap. "By the Goddess. Something dark resides within you. What have you been doing?"

Olivia floundered, trying to push her weird thoughts aside. "I haven't been doing anything! Except being chased tonight, and almost killed! That's why we're here!"

"Chased by who? What I see doesn't seem possible!"

"Woah, slow down!" Harlan went to place a calming hand on Odette, but she flung it away. Chastened, he said, "That's why we're here. We encountered an old enemy. Well, a new one, actually. Is that what you see? Black Cronos? Alchemical monsters?"

Odette's face wrinkled with distaste. "No, that is not what I see. It's older. Far older." She focussed on Olivia, repeating her earlier question. "What have you been doing?"

Olivia suddenly felt very scared, and knew exactly what Odette could see. For some reason, however, she didn't want to answer. She had to force a response, her body seeming at war with itself. Her voice sounded gruff when she answered. "Nothing. I helped a friend, that's all."

"*No.* You lie. There is more than that. He's extending his influence, even now. It's a good job you came, Olivia. Before it's too late. To the kitchen, quickly." Her arm threaded through Olivia's as if she didn't want to let go, and she hustled her down the corridor.

The others scurried after them, Harlan calling, "Odette! What's going on? We came for help to find a friend! Will you help us?"

"Of course I will, but this is more important."

Olivia squirmed in her tight grasp. "Actually, it's not. Jackson is more important! He's been kidnapped."

"And you have a small splinter of a Fallen Angel inside you, and he's itching to get further in." Odette stopped again. Her amber-ringed eyes peered deep into Olivia's, and then beyond her, seeing something else. "Oh, my old enemy, I see you. But not for long." She blinked, smiling at Olivia, her thousand-yard stare vanishing. "He's hanging on by a thread, but he is tenacious. If we don't act now, it will be harder to get him out. But don't worry," she squeezed Olivia's arms again with her strong hands, her smile infectious. "I love a good battle, especially at midnight. The witching hour."

Nine

S hadow slid from Gabe's warm embrace and solidly muscled chest as he landed softly on the tiled roof of the museum.

She pulled her fey magic around her, embracing the dark night and the song of the museum's garden. The night sounds were different here, loud and voluble, despite the chill weather. Its exoticness reminded her of the Realm of Fire in her own world. But now was not the time to reminisce. They had work to do.

She adjusted her slim-fit leather jacket that moulded to her body, her fatigues tucked into sturdy leather boots, and extracted her daggers. Their cool familiarity calmed her nerves and sharpened her senses. She studied the uneven rooftop, its skylights and vents scattered across the large building.

Gabe folded his wings away and pulled on his jacket from his pack as Ash landed next to them. Niel still circled above. All three crouched in the shadow of the tower over the east wing on the roof. This was their way in. A couple of guards patrolled the high-walled perimeter, and the gates at the end of the drive were locked.

Ash's eyes were narrowed with worry. "This is a big building, and we barely saw half of it earlier. This is insanity. We have only a few hours before daylight. We should have waited."

"I think it adds an extra little fizz of fun to our endeavours," Shadow said, silently lifting the air vent's hatch and peering inside to assess the narrow space.

They had noted the vents high on the walls when they walked around earlier. They hoped they weren't alarmed like the doors and windows, but maybe that was naïve. If they were, they would just have to fight their way out. The east wing was one of the areas they hadn't reached during the daylight tour, and it seemed to have the easiest access, too. Although they had spotted cameras, they suspected that they weren't real-time monitored at night, and would instead record everything. They planned on disabling the system once they were inside.

"I'll go first to check the space." She eyed the two large Nephilim. "You might have trouble getting in. Perhaps you should wait here."

Gabe shot her an impatient look. "You can't search the entire place on your own. Carry on. We'll follow."

The next few minutes were hazardous and awkward, and she negotiated a long drop, which necessitated her walking crablike down the narrow vertical vent, and then having to slide into one that ran horizontally. It quickly became clear this was very difficult. From the grunts she could hear above, the men weren't faring any better. She shouted at them to back up, and in ten minutes they were all back on the roof, now very hot and grumpy.

Gabe looked furious. "I knew that was a stupid idea!"

"Well, at least it wasn't alarmed!" she hissed at him, aware their voices could carry to the guards.

Ash huffed. "That gives us very few options. We just have to break in, set the alarms off, and get out. We should have contacted Mouse for this."

Shadow scowled, not liking to be defeated, and even worse hating to think someone else could do the job better. "No! There has got to be a better way. We needed more time to prepare."

"Well, tough," Gabe said, still grumpy.

She knew he was worried about Belial. Once again, Gabe's fears regarding their fathers' interference in their new lives, after months of feeling like they had gone for good, had resurfaced. All of them were worried, actually. Ash and Niel had fallen into uncharacteristic reflection. At least this theft was a good distraction.

The soft glide of wings was barely perceptible in the brisk wind that was blowing off the river, and Niel landed next to them, dragging all of them down into a crouch. His blond hair was in a top knot, and his piercing blue eyes swept across them. "What the hell is going on?"

Gabe glared at him. "We got stuck. And you're supposed to be watching our backs."

"I'm watching you fail! But I have a solution. A pair of guards are heading to the museum's side door, I presume to patrol inside. I saw them enter that way last night, but hadn't realised they did it every couple of hours. I suggest you get down there now, let them disable the alarm, and then incapacitate them. North side, centre. Get on with it!" Without another word, he launched back up into the air.

"I guess that's option two, then," Gabe said, stripping to fly again. "Time to go."

"Drop me behind them," Shadow instructed. "I'll take one, one of you can take the other."

Ash nodded. "Deal. But wait until the alarm is disabled."

They circled high, spotting the two men that Niel had referred to. They were crossing the lawn along a path that snaked between sculptures, talking to each other and laughing. Gabe swept in low and dropped Shadow, and sticking to the deep shadows beneath the palms, she followed them silently. It would be far easier to just kill them, but Gabe was right. No one needed to die tonight—except maybe Black Cronos, who had forced their hand in all of this.

The side door wasn't as imposing as the front, but it had a security camera and a keypad, as well as a huge metal gate in front of a sturdy wooden one. Impatient, and as close as she could get, she watched them unlock everything and swing the door wide. A moment more, and she heard the beep of the alarm.

With lightning reflexes, she raced across the remaining short distance, knowing her fey glamour kept her concealed. One man was still on the threshold, the other just inside. She crept behind the nearest one, wrapped her arm around his neck, and pulled him backwards before he even realised what was happening. Using the butt of her dagger, she hit him at the precise point required to knock him out instantly.

While she silently dealt with him, Gabe landed and wrestled the other man backwards and out the door, leaving Ash to step inside and make sure the way remained clear. In seconds it was done, and they dragged the unconscious men inside.

"In here," Ash called from a side room. "We can lock them in."

After securing them as best as they could with what little they could find, they locked the door, hoping they would remain insensible for a while.

Once back in the corridor, Gabe said, "I'll find the camera feed and cut it. You two start searching. I'll join you soon. We have a couple of hours, at most," he reasoned. "Can you remember the different areas of the displays? We've searched the most obvious, but any ideas?"

"Let's just split up," Shadow said, impatient already. "We have no time to waste!"

"You're right, but thinking logically will be quicker," Ash reasoned. He was looking at her, clearly surprised. "You're a thief! Surely you're used to this."

"Usually I have more preparation time!" In the Otherworld, her team did extensive research before their heists, and Bloodmoon was the one who tackled all the security issues. She was relying on Ash and Gabe to do that now.

Ash sighed. "Fine. Let's just get on with it. The west wing is done, so I'll take east, Gabe go north, when you're done. Shadow, south."

"Suits me." She wiggled her phone. "I'll call."

"Do nothing until we're with you," Gabe warned her. She knew that he both admired and feared her headstrong approach to life.

She winked and blew him a kiss. "Later."

Zee liked his perch on the farmhouse roof. It gave him an unobstructed view of the countryside.

First, he focussed on the front of the house. The protective boundary was at its closest point to the house there, extending behind the barn and the outhouses to the end of their short drive. The last time they had been attacked, the soldiers had come at them from all directions. Their courtyard and barn had become a killing zone, and it had taken days to hose away the blood. Now, however, that way appeared clear.

So, what was Black Cronos's plan now? To kill them or capture them? They must have reasoned that approaching over the field was the less obvious route. He focussed on the edge of the field and the glowing points of light that showed where their attackers were trying to get in. Another fizz of blue illuminated an additional attempt.

Zee's unease settled. *This would be fine. Their defences were too good.* For several minutes, he watched their attempt to get in, debating whether to fly over them and take them out that way. However, that was pointless if he left the front of the house exposed.

Nahum and Eli were poised at the edge of the field close to the house, also watching their attempts, no doubt hoping they would retreat.

And then a loud explosion dispelled that hope. Rock and earth went flying, and a dozen soldiers dressed in black raced in through the breach. Zee raised his crossbow and fired, taking out at least three men before a strange *whump* drew his attention overhead.

A helicopter was approaching from the sea, and it was coming straight for them.

Black Cronos had obviously decided on another strategy to offset their lack of wings.

Zee couldn't be in two places at once, and he was loathe to leave his brothers. They were good fighters, but no match for another dozen men. Eli and Nahum were already running to meet them, weapons raised.

Black Cronos weaved across the field, their progress slow because of the mud, and Zee shot a few more. So far, no one approached the front of the house. But with the helicopter closing in, he had to deal with that imminently. He extended his wings and took to the air.

The helicopter swept closer, and he made out a couple of figures in the cockpit. He aimed his crossbow and shot, but the helicopter veered to the side, and his shot went wide. A soldier leaned out of the side door and shot at him in return, using one of their strange, silvery weapons that had almost killed Shadow.

Fortunately, Zee was more manoeuvrable than a helicopter. This was his natural element. He flew low and quick, raised his crossbow, and peppered the helicopter with bolts, once again dodging more fire from above as the helicopter swung wildly over him. He swept around the rear, soaring high above the enemy. Then, his wings behind him, he plummeted like a bird of prey, aiming for the side door.

Disorientated and confused, the soldier fired wildly, aiming below initially, before finally spotting Zee. But he couldn't aim in time. Zee sailed under the blades, hauled the soldier out, and promptly dropped him to the ground. He entered the cabin and found another three soldiers and the pilot.

This was going to get interesting.

Eli charged across the grass, sword raised. But he had only advanced a few metres when a flash of light arrowed straight for him.

He dived to the side, rolling in mud, barely having time to regain his feet before another shot had him diving for cover again.

Damn it. They had come armed with advanced weaponry. He knew they could target different energy signatures. It must be how they had finally shattered the witches' defences. It also meant they had a lot longer range than his sword. At this moment, he was pretty sure they wanted to kill them, not capture them. They were too deadly in their approach.

The soldiers spread out, advancing on him and Nahum.

Eli launched into the air, sword extended. His rise was so swift that their shots missed him, but the next singed his wings and burned his arm. Still, he advanced, aiming for the more vulnerable at the back, without the big fire power. But they still had crossbows, and a bolt grazed his side as he flew low, managing to kill one and injure another. For the next few minutes, he fought furiously, but was unable to make progress. He killed a few more, but couldn't get close to the ones at the front who had almost reached their house.

A boom resonated across the fields, and the loggia burst into flames.

The house will be next.

He flew high again, meeting Nahum up above the field, hoping they were out of range of their weapons. Nahum was bloodied and breathing heavily, but his eyes were sharp and focussed.

"Nahum, they'll destroy the house! We're outnumbered, and Zee is busy." He nodded toward the helicopter that was veering wildly over the moors. "We need to use the power trapped within Belial's jewels." He could feel it calling to him already from where he'd placed it in his pocket.

There was a flash of fear, but also resignation in Nahum's eyes. "I don't like this at all, but you're right. We have no other options."

"Then let's unleash Belial's power. Destruction and madness."

"And if *we* end up fighting?" He gestured between them. "Like earlier?"

"We stay focussed on them!"

"Since when did you become so willing to take such crazy risks, Eli? This isn't you!"

"Since I made White Haven my home. I fear our friends will be next. Ready?"

Nahum nodded.

Eli pulled the torc from his pocket and placed it around the bicep on his right arm as Nahum settled the ring on his finger. The power he had felt earlier magnified. It was a strange, compelling power rooted in the magic of the old God. Already it infiltrated his brain and altered his vision. A sharp, predatory hunger filled him, and a wild urge to destroy took root in his mind.

White flames raced across his body and filled his wings with incandescent light. His skin couldn't contain it. Neither could Nahum's. Both were like stars. *Fallen stars.* He could just about see Nahum's shape through the flaming white glow.

Vengeance filled his soul, and the certainty of inflicting death reigned. An old feeling he thought never to experience again. He arrowed himself downward, sword outstretched, with Nahum next to him.

Deliverers of justice, just as their Fallen fathers intended.

The next few minutes for Nahum were like a dream.

No, a nightmare.

In general, he took no pleasure in killing. It was a job, and he executed his opponents quickly, taking no joy in it. And yet, in those few minutes, there was a glorious feeling. The wash of blood, the mayhem, the screams, the satisfaction. The horror in the eyes of those they killed.

Black Cronos soldiers were not cowards. They were ruthless killers, but they visibly quaked as the brothers descended upon them. Their fire power was repelled by Belial's, or it burnt out before even reaching their bodies.

In minutes, their enemies all lay dead. Limbs strewn, blood draining into the mud. Nahum stood in the field of battle, having barely raised a sweat, covered in blood himself, and feeling nothing but vindication. Eli was a short distance away, face turned skyward, and together they watched the helicopter plummet, their brother leaping clear before it hit the ground and exploded, flames blistering the night.

Zee approached them warily, circling wide before landing a short distance away. He gripped his sword, the crossbow slung across his shoulder, his wings still outstretched. "Brothers. You're still glowing with Belial's power. I suggest you put it aside."

"I wish I could," Nahum said, breathing heavily as he sought to return to normal. It was like wrestling a snake into a match box. He looked at Eli. He was a vision from the Old Testament and all those illustrations. *Was that what he looked like? A weapon of God.* "Eli?"

Eli's warm brown eyes, normally so full of calm wisdom, were like burning coals, and when he spoke his voice was rough, the old language infecting his accent. "Brother. It feels odd again, does it not? Like slipping into our old skin."

"A skin you hated," Zee reminded him, stepping closer still, hand still gripping his sword. "Put it aside. You don't need it. The soldiers are dead."

Nahum wrestled for control, a madman laughing in his head at the power they had unleashed. It took all of his concentration and will, but finally the white-hot angel's power faded, and he felt like himself again. "Focus, Eli! Think of our friends. Newton will be here soon, no doubt about that. With his sergeants. Maybe the witches, too. You don't want to hurt them."

Eli nodded, his face contorting. His muscles corded and strained, veins visible across his skin as he sought control. Finally, the heavenly glow seeped away, and he sagged to his knees in the blood and the mud. He pulled the torc from his arm and flung it in front of him. "He's still in here." He tapped his heart. "I feel him. You need to get Briar."

Zee swallowed and nodded, eyes finally drifting to Nahum. "And you?"

"He's under my skin. Faint, but there. Just as Olivia said. Like an itch."

"Throw his ring away from you. On the ground, over here."

Nahum wrenched it off his finger and threw it at Zee's feet.

Zee took a breath. "I'll find something to put them in."

"You'll lose them."

"No, I won't. I'd feel them half a mile away." Zee cleared his throat, tension finally seeping from him. But only slightly. He pulled his phone out as police sirens sounded in the distance. "In the shower now, both of you. I'll call the witches and Newton."

Ten

E stelle paced the living room of their chalet, unable to settle as she waited for Barak to return.

He'd been gone for almost two hours, and with every passing minute, she worried even more.

"Estelle, please sit down. You're exhausting me!" Lucien remonstrated.

He was seated in an old-fashioned armchair by the fireplace, occasionally prodding the logs. He looked better after his rest, but his eyes were still haunted. Distant. Estelle could barely imagine how tumultuous the past few months had been for him.

"Sorry, I can't." She paused at the window and twitched back the curtains to look outside. The clouds were clearing, allowing the occasional shaft of moonlight to stripe the snow-covered peaks. It was charming and picturesque, but she wasn't really focussing on the view. She watched for Barak's return.

"You watching won't make him come back any quicker."

She finally turned away and sat on the sofa, reaching for the glass of wine that she'd barely drank. "I know. I'm running through our options if he doesn't return. Storming the castle with just us two isn't really an option, but I will if I must."

He regarded her silently for a moment, a sad smile on his lips. "You love him. That much is obvious. It's terrifying, isn't it? To love someone so much. When they've gone, you flounder. It's like your heart has been ripped from your body." His hand pressed to his chest. "I'm not sure mine has come back. And now I'm something else. Even if we were still together, he wouldn't love me now."

"That's not true! Love transcends everything." Even as she was saying it, Estelle wasn't sure she believed it. Her love for Barak was so huge, she couldn't imagine that he could love her as much. It seemed impossible. And yet, he constantly told her in so many ways. Her worry for him renewed, but she remained in her seat, wanting Lucien to reassure her.

He grunted out a mournful laugh. "You say that because your love is young and new. It feels invincible. I hope yours does last. Mine didn't." As if he sensed her fear, he said, "Don't worry. He adores you. He'd die for you. He watches you. Shelters you. Ignore me. I'm just jaded and heartbroken. Disillusioned. And then to be kidnapped and abused like this..." He gestured to his tattoos. "Well, it certainly tests your faith in mankind."

Estelle felt horribly selfish for her own preoccupations, but his observations allayed her fears about her relationship. "My family certainly jaded my faith, but it's not too late. My brother has decided to resurrect our faltering coven. I thought it was pointless. But, surprisingly, he's right. Things are improving." She smiled. "Life is never stationary. It ebbs and flows, and the tide will turn for you. Surely your time at The Retreat has restored your faith in people?"

"A little. Mastering my changes has helped too, of course. This is just a different version of me, right?"

"Exactly. The new you. And someone will love you for it."

He nodded, turning back to the fire. "Stupid that I should be worrying about that, right? We have more pressing concerns. Like ending these monsters."

"Unfortunately, I think that will be far harder than we imagine."

A noise outside the front door had them both on their feet, magic balling in Estelle's hands, but then Barak called out. "It's just me."

Her fears expelled in a rush as he crossed the room to the fire, carrying the scent of snow with him.

Estelle headed to his side, searching his face for news. "I didn't hear you arrive! You were gone a while."

"I settled on one of the towers to watch." He huffed, his jaw tight. "We were right, they are there. I saw Stefan Hope-Robbins and the new Silencer of Souls or whatever she's called—or at least one of them. They have a huge wheel of correspondence in one of the courtyards. It's enormous!"

"But that's brilliant! We finally found them!"

"Well, yes, it's good, but there are guards all along the walls, and no doubt below the castle, too. It's strongly fortified, and the only place I could land with any safety was a very high tower. I think it houses their communications."

Lucien had gone to the kitchen to get more beer, and he returned, passing Barak an uncapped bottle. "Yet, you don't look happy at finding them."

"Because I realise just how hard this will be. The reality of it. And how few there are of us in comparison."

"But we have time to plan our attack," Estelle reasoned. "To watch and prepare."

"Maybe." Barak's eyes settled on hers. "But the winter solstice is close, and I think they're planning something. Some ritual, perhaps."

"Why?" Lucien asked.

"Because while I watched, the wheel turned—or some of the rings, at least. There must be a huge mechanism underneath to move it. Some of the sigils lit up."

Estelle was very familiar with the solstices and equinoxes; the Sabbats, as witches called them. They were powerful times in the calendar of the year. Times of celebration, also used for spell work and rituals. "I guess that as an alchemist it makes sense that the *comte* and Stefan would utilise them. But they would use them regularly, just like witches do. It doesn't mean anything particularly untoward."

"Maybe not."

"So, what now?" Lucien asked, sitting in the armchair again.

"Now we explore the ridge that the *château* is on. I suspect there are entrances lower down. I didn't loiter, though. I didn't want to test my luck. I thought perhaps, Estelle, that we could use a cloaking spell tomorrow night."

"Absolutely. I have a few ideas." She'd been mulling on spells for weeks, honing the ones she thought would be useful.

"Good. I'll call my brothers tomorrow to alert them. Let's hope Gabe and the others can wrap up the theft quickly." He sat back in the chair, staring into the flames. "We'll need them. All of them."

Ash quickened his pace as he progressed along the museum's displays, all too aware of the advancing time, and the fact that other guards might come looking for the ones they had imprisoned.

He hoped that Gabe had found the set-up for the camera system. The blinking red light still flashed from the cameras, but hopefully they weren't recording anything. With luck, no one was watching from afar, either.

The weight of the past pressed upon him. Row after row of artefacts, sculptures, chunks of stone from long collapsed civilisations, and fragments of text. He scanned them all, fearful of going so quickly that he missed what they needed to find.

And then, after a few more paces, there it was. Or rather, there *they* were. Half a dozen discs of various sizes were displayed together, all made of precious gemstones, but only three were emerald. Several were the size of a small plate. Ash groaned. *Half a dozen of them?* JD hadn't mentioned these. *What if, for some weird reason, the missing piece wasn't made of emerald?* Some were completely flat with no raised area at all, and had different animals etched into them. However, three pieces had a raised circular area with the image of an ibis sitting proud. Two were made from emeralds. They were all described as decorative objects to honour the Gods, but no other function had been ascribed to them. There was certainly nothing to signal them as being important or related to the Emerald Tablet.

He searched the rest of the room quickly, but nothing else looked remotely similar. One of these had to be it. He called Gabe and Shadow, studying the glass case that protected the display while he waited for them. It was large, coffin-sized, clipped in place, and alarmed. The movement detector device was attached to one of the glass sides. Ash had read up on alarm systems, and there were many varied types that all essentially did the same thing. They detected movement inside the case. If the case moved, it would go off. It was battery operated and linked to a central system. Guards would be alerted immediately if disturbed. Unless, of course, Gabe had the key to the display cases among the bunch he had stolen.

The light tread of footsteps alerted him to the arrival of Shadow and Gabe, and before Ash could speak, Gabe groaned. "You have got to be kidding me! There are loads of them!"

"I know, right? What are the odds?"

"The Gods are screwing with us. Bloody typical!" Gabe glared at the display as if it was laughing at him.

"I have no idea which of those three could be the right one," Ash said, explaining his reasoning. "Although potentially it will have a quality to it that we'll recognise, much like the tablet has."

"And if it doesn't?" Gabe said, a frown creasing his forehead.

Shadow shrugged. "We have only one option. We steal all of them."

"And get them all in the box?" Gabe looked sceptical.

"Let's worry about that later." Ash pointed to the keyhole that would unlock the mechanism. "If we have the key, that will make life simple, but we can't isolate the alarm."

Gabe pulled the bunch of keys from his pocket, but it was obvious from their size that none would fit the cabinet. He huffed with disappointment. "I guess that makes sense. The guards just need the door keys."

Ash watched the entrances to the room, but no one appeared, and no alarms sounded. Nothing that they could hear, anyway.

Shadow rummaged in one of her pockets and pulled out her skeleton keys. "No problem, I'll just use these. I used them all the time in my world. Not this particular set, obviously."

"Wait." Ash put a restraining hand on her arm. "Let's talk escape plans. The alarm will go off anyway, I'm sure of it. We need to know the closest way out." He quickly consulted a guide of the museum they had picked up from the reception area the day before. The museum was an old mansion, designed around one large courtyard, with three small ones. Several double doors led into the courtyards, but he had noted they were locked and chained. "The mains doors are close, but there's another door to a courtyard two rooms along. That's the best way out. I'll check it first." He stared meaningfully at Shadow. "Just wait for me to give the go ahead. If it's impossible, we'll need another way."

"Fine! But hurry up!"

Gabe rolled his eyes, trying to quell his amusement. "Don't worry. We'll wait."

Ash crossed the gloomy rooms, lit only by bars of strip lighting under the displays. The statues and colourful masks looked lurid in the half light. He found the exit, but it was barred by another waist-high display. A chain looped around the inside bars of the courtyard doors, securing them together. If he tried to remove the display, he would set more alarms off. Then again, they were already setting them off, anyway.

At least he could break the padlock and unhook the chain first. He should be strong enough to do that. He gripped the padlock, twisting it within his strong fingers, only seeing the fine wires that connected it to an alarm system too late.

In seconds, the alarm sounded, booming overhead.

Niel groaned as the alarm erupted below him. *They had thought it inevitable, but even so...*

He circled over the museum, heading to the outpost at the top of the drive where the guards were stationed. It was a brick building, set into the tall stone walls that surrounded the grounds, and the solitary guard was already exiting, speaking into his phone. No doubt trying to contact his colleagues.

But there were no other guards, and no sign of the police yet. They would have to come from the main centre, and that would probably take at least ten minutes. After watching for a few moments more, Niel decided the man was waiting for the police. The huge gates were still closed, and he wouldn't want to leave them open. Perhaps he figured the thieves had nowhere to go.

He wheeled around and flew back over the museum. He groaned again. Huge steel doors had sealed off the front door. A quick scout around revealed every single entrance had been sealed with similar, shuttered steel doors.

Landing on the roof, he called Gabe, and when no one answered, he tried Ash. He figured that if Gabe was deep inside the museum, the signal might be poor. Hopefully they all weren't together. But his second call went unanswered, too. *Where were they?* Exasperated, he moved positions, flying lower, and was finally rewarded when he heard a dull banging from one of the courtyard doors.

He landed on the ground. "Hello? Gabe? Ash?"

A muffled voice shouted back. "It's Ash! I need help to lift the screen!"

Niel snorted. "You lost your strength, brother?"

"Clamps have sealed it in, you moron! Magnetic, I think."

"Sure! You keep telling yourself that. Stay back!"

Niel repeatedly smashed the frame at the base with his axe. It buckled and warped, and he put his axe aside and wriggled his hands under it. Ash's hands were immediately in the gap, too, and with a grating squeal of metal, they dragged the door partway up. He wedged the axe in place and propped the door open. Ash slid through, dust streaking his face.

"Where are Gabe and Shadow?" Niel asked, crouching to look inside.

"On their way, I hope. They're securing the discs in another room."

"Discs?"

"More than one, I'm afraid."

"Of course there are," Niel said, resigned. *Nothing was ever easy.* "Do they need help?"

"I hope not. I'll give them another few minutes."

"They set the alarm off, I suppose?"

"No, actually." Ash looked embarrassed. "That was me, trying to secure our exit."

"Nice, brother. You did well."

Ash gave him the finger in response. "I suggest we wait here—just in case something else takes us unawares."

"I'll leave that to you. The police are coming. I'll go keep watch." Niel took to the skies again leaving Ash to wait.

"Bollocks to the lock," Gabe said, growing more frustrated as the alarm pounded into his skull. "I'll smash the glass."

"No, you won't! Broken glass might damage the discs," Shadow protested.

She persevered with the pick, her nimble fingers turning the lock with practised ease. In seconds, the case was open, and she reached inside to grab the discs. As soon as she picked them up, another alarm sounded, and the whirr of a mechanism had Gabe spinning around. With horror, he saw a barred gate drop into place on both doors.

"You have got to be shitting me! Herne's fucking balls!"

"Go lift it! I'll get these!"

"Yes, of course! I'll lift it, just like that!" Gabe sprinted to the gate that led to Ash, relieved to see that only their room had been sealed off. He should have known it. Of course emerald discs the size of plates would have extra security. *Damn JD and his crazy requests...*

Gabe tried to lift the barred gate. It was solid, and brutally heavy. Knowing he was stronger with his wings open, as they enhanced his paranormal strength, he ripped his shirt off, and stuffed it in his pocket. With great effort he managed to lift the gate. He shouted at Shadow. "Hurry up!"

"I am being as quick as I can!"

"Shadow!" He glowered at her. "The guards are on their way, and I'm about to have a hernia!"

"It will all have been for nothing if these are damaged! Besides, the guards are Niel's job."

Gabe knew she was right. Heists weren't his forte, so he should just shut up and do as she said. Besides, he quite liked her being bossy. Not that he would tell her that, of course. If anything, it made her sexier.

In another few moments she raced towards him and slid under the gate. "Your turn."

With immense effort, he lifted the gate higher, braced himself, ducked under it, and finally released it with a thunderous clang. "That way!"

They crossed the floor and headed to the exit. The courtyard doors were partly open, and a mangled metal screen was warped beyond it. Gabe and Shadow slid through the gap and found Ash standing outside, gazing up at the stars, his phone pressed to his ear. "They're here. How's it looking, Niel?" He nodded, wings extending, and ended the call. "Half a dozen cars are on the way. Time to go. Got them?"

"Yep," Shadow said, a smug smile on her face. "Now we have to hope that Black Cronos has gone. Otherwise, where to next?"

"One problem at a time." Gabe opened his arms. "Let's go."

Eleven

"I still don't understand," Harlan complained to Morgana, "what a splinter of a Fallen Angel is! It sounds insane! Ridiculous." He tripped over his words, finally settling on, "Impossible!"

Morgana sighed heavily, eyeing him with impatience. She looked imperious in her flowing black dress with her hair loose down her back. "It's not impossible, because clearly it has happened. Although, perhaps splinter isn't the best word. It's hardly like Belial has a physical presence. Thank the Gods."

Maggie snorted with disdain. "Hasn't he? It sounds like he has to me. Him and his bloody agent. And the dead vicar!"

"But Belial has no physical body," Morgana explained. "He never had. He's all light and energy. All angels were. *Are,*" she corrected herself. "But their spirit was so powerful it was almost a physical presence. Nothing like a ghost."

They were in the kitchen at Moonfell. It was a large room at the rear of the house, half kitchen, half dining area, with huge, gothic arched windows that overlooked the garden. He and Maggie were talking to Morgana, while Odette worked on Olivia in the dining half of the room. A confused, slightly panic-stricken Olivia, who was clearly trying to remain calm.

Everything about this house is dramatic, Harlan thought, taking it all in while Morgana talked. From the three witches who lived there, to the house itself. The kitchen was modern, with black tiled walls and dark wooden cupboards and work surfaces. It suited the gothic style perfectly. A fireplace blazed at the dining end, and books, newspapers, and plants covered the table and filled shelves. Even though it was late, something bubbled on the large, five-burner hob top. He was pretty sure it wasn't food.

Beyond the windows, some of which had stained glass images depicting leaves and plants and the menacing grin of the Green Man, were the dark shapes of plants. Like the front garden, the occasional spotlight picked out the unusual topiaries. The scudding clouds revealed glimpses of huge trees with bare branches and big garden beds. It was all very intriguing. Everything about the house made him want to explore it. To uncover its secrets. His attention was drifting, as if the house was calling him. He shook his head and focussed on the conversation.

Maggie showed no evidence of being distracted. "So, what's a better word for splinter?"

"You're being very prosaic, Maggie. Magic and witchcraft are not paint by numbers."

"I'm well aware of that. Are you saying that an angel is magic and witchcraft? I'm not sure they'd like that!"

Morgana grinned and it made her look younger, more mischievous. "No, I'm sure not. They were servants to their God, one amongst many. They just threw their weight around a lot more. And there were loads of them." She opened a cupboard and started to pull out jars of dried herbs and put them on the counter. "It was when a few of them fell that the real trouble started. However, I prefer not to dwell on them. The Goddess who they tried to suppress is someone I have far more affiliation with. But, to answer your question, Belial has such a strong presence that he has buried a part of himself in Olivia. We must exorcise him."

Harlan thought he was hearing things. "You're exorcising an *angel*? Is that even possible?"

She turned her sharp, intelligent eyes on him. "Of course, with the right words. Besides, it's only a very small part of him. A fragment of his influence."

"Morgana!" Odette summoned her attention. "Olivia said her friend was there, and that he was influenced, too."

"But he'll be fine," Olivia insisted, eyes wide. "He's, er, not quite human. He'll be able to resist far more than me. Although, I feel nothing! I'm fine."

Odette shook her head. "You're *not* fine! That's Belial's influence. Fortunately, I can tell. One of my skills. Neither should we take your friend's ability to resist for granted. You must warn him."

"I can call him." Olivia reached for her phone, glancing nervously at Harlan as she did so.

"Good. Tell him to act quickly." Odette stood, leaving Olivia to make the call, and crossed to Morgana's side. "We need Birdie."

Morgana was weighing and mixing herbs, but she nodded. "Certainly. He'll resist, of course. Even a small part of him is strong. It's lucky," she said, glancing at Harlan, "that you came so soon."

Harlan nodded, feeling like the night's events were spinning out of his control. Being attacked by Black Cronos almost seemed a breeze by comparison. "But we came for a different reason. We need to find our friend, Jackson. He's been kidnapped by Black Cronos."

Morgana paused her preparations and stared at him. "Who are they?"

"An organisation that is obsessed with alchemy." He explained their previous encounters as succinctly as possible.

"Alchemy?" Morgana said thoughtfully. "How intriguing. It's one of my interests. An organisation with an immortal head..."

"We think," Maggie qualified. "Nothing is certain."

"Nothing ever is in this world. You have something that belongs to Jackson?"

Harlan nodded. "His scarf."

"Good. We shall try." She swept the herbs she'd prepared into a glass vial. "I need some fresh ones, too." She thrust a large jar of salt at her cousin. "Take them to the tower, please."

Odette nodded. "I'll start preparing the space."

"Where are you going for fresh herbs?" Harlan asked, not caring that he was being nosy.

Fortunately, Morgana looked amused. "The glasshouse. Want to come?"

"Yes, please!"

She handed him a small basket. "For the cuttings. Don't touch anything!"

Odette called to Olivia. "Time to go. Did you reach your friend?"

"No, but I left an urgent message." Olivia's face was creased with worry, and Harlan wasn't sure whether it was for herself or Nahum. *Maybe it was both.*

While Odette escorted Olivia and Maggie through a door in the corner of the room, Morgana led Harlan to a panelled door not far from the fireplace. In moments they passed from the warm kitchen to an ambient glasshouse lit by clusters of fairy lights. Harlan gasped at the sight of what appeared to be a faery garden before him.

The glass house was a half dome constructed entirely of iron and glass. The glass panels were a variety of different shapes—arches, hexagons, circles, squares, triangles—all designed with great skill. Within it were potted plants, gravel paths, and beds dug straight into the earth, as well as raised ones. A peculiar scent hung in the air. Something sweet and sickly.

"Are those lilies I smell?"

"There are some. The scent comes from many things." Morgana progressed down the path, aiming for a raised bed in the centre of the space. Harlan hurried next to her, hand reaching out to stroke a feathery frond. "Don't touch!" she shouted.

Startled, Harlan dropped his hand. "Sorry! I forgot. What is it?"

"Hemlock. Several beds here are full of poisonous plants. Prepared incorrectly, they will kill. Prepared correctly, however, and they will heal."

"Unless of course you *want* to kill someone," Harlan said, thinking it was a poisoner's dream.

Morgana smiled. "Of course, but I try not to kill my clients. Or send them mad or put them in hospital. Not often, anyway…"

From the twisted smile on her face, Harlan wasn't entirely sure that she was joking. "Would your clients ask for such things?"

"They might. I would say no," she said, pulling gloves on and snipping leaves from a large, bushy plant. "Vengeance is a poor man's game. I would rather give my clients the upper hand. There are other ways to do that." She didn't elaborate, and Harlan didn't ask. She dropped the plant into the basket Harlan carried and nodded. "All done. Time for some midnight magic."

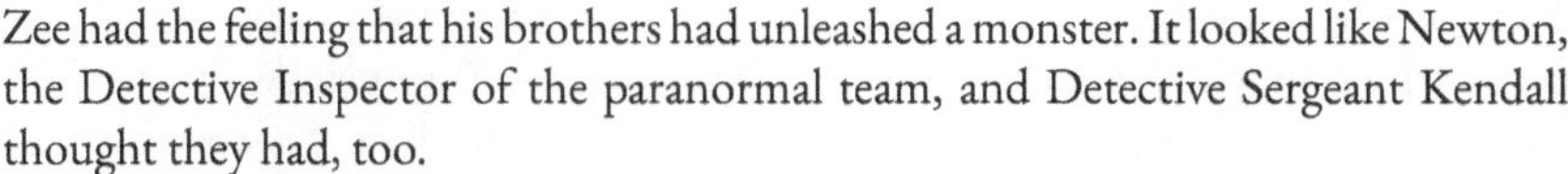

Zee had the feeling that his brothers had unleashed a monster. It looked like Newton, the Detective Inspector of the paranormal team, and Detective Sergeant Kendall thought they had, too.

All three stood on the edge of the field next to the farmhouse surveying the bodies of the dead. Again.

"Making a habit of this?" Newton asked, his tone sharp and sarcastic. "How did you three manage to kill so many?"

Zee sighed. "Like I said, Nahum and Eli had a moment of madness. They called on Belial's power. Through those." He kicked at the jewels that were in a box at his feet. "Don't touch them!"

Kendall, long-limbed and dark-haired, crouched and shuddered. "I won't. They have a presence, don't they?"

"Unfortunately, yes. Belial's."

"What will you do with them?" Newton asked. "If you let them get into the wrong hands, anything could happen."

"Anything has!" Zee said. "For a long time, they have been causing insidious behaviour, deaths, and madness, although it wasn't attributed to these until Olivia and Nahum found them yesterday. And tonight, well..." he sighed. "Tonight made things a whole lot worse. I think that by using them, the jewels have only become stronger. To be honest, though, if Nahum and Eli hadn't used them, we would all be dead. Or we'd have fled, and our home would have been destroyed." Like the loggia's blackened, fire-damaged timbers.

Newton dragged his gaze from the dead to stare at Zee. "They knew you were alone."

"Perhaps. Probably. But me and Eli have been alone many times, and we haven't been attacked before."

"But you said it was coordinated?" Kendall asked.

"Yes. Harlan, Olivia, and Jackson were targeted, too. Jackson has been kidnapped. And the team in Egypt have had their hotel surrounded. They're okay, though, as far as I know." Zee's thoughts were all over the place. He was worried about all of his brothers and Shadow. However, it seemed that although Barak and Estelle were camped out on the *comte's* doorstep, they were fine.

"And them?" Newton pointed to the smouldering helicopter in the distance, police cars, fire engines, and ambulance close by, the blaze of their lights bright despite the distance. DS Moore was with them, overseeing the investigation.

"Another team, come to block our air escape. I was lucky. I killed the pilot and managed to get out before it crashed." *Lucky might be a stretch.* One of their spears had pierced his side, but his body armour had protected him from the worst of the thrust. Even so, it ached.

Behind them, the sound of engines indicated the SOCO team had arrived. Newton sighed. "I'll deal with them, and then take your statement, Zee. Best do it now. Kendall, head inside and see what's happening with the witches." Newton waited until Kendall had left them. "How bad is it? Your brothers and Belial? Don't lie."

"It's very bad. They had so much power, they could barely contain it. Belial was the angel best known for death and destruction. Sammael's right-hand man. They were both lit up with his energy. It wouldn't surprise me if people saw them. They looked like falling stars, Newton. Bright! And deadly." He closed his eyes, but the image was burned on his mind. He opened them again, and found Newton still staring at him. "They killed all of our attackers, barely exerting themselves."

Newton clenched his stubbled jaw, his grey eyes unfathomable in the darkness of the terrace. "Were they in control of themselves?"

"Only just; even I kept my distance at first. I could see it in their eyes. The old bloodlust that our fathers had given us."

"I thought angels were supposed to be forces for good."

"Many were, but we're talking about the Fallen. There were many things they disagreed about with the old God, and one of the biggest were humans. The Fallen considered them a scourge on the planet. Of course, you know our role. We were their weapons."

"Because they couldn't walk on Earth."

"Exactly. Not for long, anyway. And then the old God came to see their side of it. He endorsed the destruction we unleashed. Until He had enough of all of it and sent the Great Flood." Zee sighed, fearing he wasn't explaining things well. "We all absorbed the powers of our Fallen fathers. We all could look like my brothers did tonight, if we chose. But it clouded our minds and judgment. We rebelled against that as much as anything. Their control. When we cast it aside, it diminished us, but left us whole of mind."

"I understand."

Newton looked through the kitchen window to watch Briar prepare her herbs at the counter. Her shoulders were hunched as she ground them, as if she were taking out her exasperation on them. The other witches were inside, all gathered in the living room. Zee should be there to protect them, just in case. He took a deep breath and tried to be rational. The witches could cope, and his brothers would not attack them.

Newton interrupted his thoughts. "Is this the start of something?"

Zee shrugged. "Honestly, I don't know."

Olivia couldn't help but be unnerved by Birdie, the small, wizened woman who was Morgana and Odette's grandmother. She was the epitome of an old crone, although she felt mean for even thinking that.

She had a tiny frame, shoulders rounded, her eyes milky from cataracts. But energy radiated from her as she directed Morgana and Odette's preparations. She was pretty sure neither of them needed her directions, but they acquiesced all the same. Every now and again, Morgana would suggest something, and Birdie would nod, and then Odette would offer a change, too. Between them, they completed their preparations quickly.

All the while, Olivia sat quietly, trying to subdue the rising panic she felt inside, and the insistent impatience and spite she noticed bubbling up along with it. Harlan sat next to her, a calm, reassuring presence, and she soaked him in. Despite her protestations, she knew that something was very wrong. Ever since Odette had called her out on it, the strange presence inside her—Belial, she couldn't deny it any longer—had become increasingly...alert. Maggie, however, was on the other side of the tower, watching every move avidly.

The round tower was a fascinating place, like something from a fairytale. Like the other rooms she had glimpsed, and the kitchen they had been in, these windows were gothic monstrosities of stone and stained glass, stretching up to the vaulted ceiling, the details lost in darkness. A fireplace danced with flames, and in the large space in front of it, the thick Persian rugs had been rolled back to reveal a pentagram scored into the stone floor. A large salt circle was around it. A couple of towering cases of books and armchairs were in shadows, witnesses to the events, but the rest of the space was empty.

Within the circle was a chair. Her place.

Birdie walked to Olivia's side, her gait slow and unsteady, her stick tapping the floor. "Time for you, my dear." She was so short that she was barely taller than Olivia, who was sitting. She peered into her eyes and muttered, "Enter the circle now. Don't hesitate, just do it. Give him an inch, and he'll take all of you."

Terrified, Olivia almost ran into the salt circle, feeling her legs drag with every step. But Birdie's words rang in her ears, and she didn't hesitate. She had visions of turning into a spitting monster of fire and light.

Morgana and Harlan entered with her, and Morgana said, "Sit down, Olivia."

But she couldn't. Olivia could feel herself rebelling, her limbs shaking as she disobeyed Morgana's order. And then a commanding voice screamed a language in her head that was so unearthly, she thought she'd go mad. The scream became her own, and she grabbed her hair as if she would tear it out, the voice along with it.

Harlan forced her into the chair, and Morgana uttered a word of command, her hand on her forehead. The room swiftly vanished, leaving only darkness.

Twelve

"What the hell have you done to her!" Maggie yelled, horrified, as Olivia slumped over in the chair.

"I've saved her from madness," Morgana replied calmly, as she helped Harlan tie her to the chair. "Good. Thank you, Harlan. Out of the circle. Now."

Morgana sealed the circle with more salt as they left Olivia alone in the middle, her head lolling onto her chest.

Maggie was horrified and fascinated. She had seen the flash of fire in Olivia's eyes before Morgana did...*something*. She rounded on the three witches. "You've made it worse! She was fine tonight!"

Odette, the most unnerving of the three in Maggie's opinion, with her strange, vacant expression that swept over her sometimes, turned to her. "She was *not* fine. He was lurking in there all the time. As soon as he knew I had seen him, he started to become stronger. Unfortunate, but inevitable. Left unchecked, he would have done so anyway. Better we tackle it now, before he's entrenched."

"But you said he was a splinter! How can he have grown bigger?"

"He's one of the Fallen, Maggie. One of the most powerful. An archangel. Even a splinter is enough in our weak bodies."

Maggie hated not being in control, and she was itching to boss everyone about and yell. But that was pointless. In this situation, she was powerless. She just had to shove her own annoyance and feelings of inadequacy aside, and help as best she could. And she couldn't deny the flash of fire in Olivia's eyes, or her shout in that strange language.

She took a deep breath and exhaled slowly, looking to Harlan for moral support. He shrugged his acceptance of the situation, eyes grim. This was harder for him. Olivia was an old friend. His colleague. One of his pack, as he'd called it earlier. A pack of which she was supposedly a member. The alpha, of all things.

It was as if Harlan could read her mind. His normal air of devil-may-care insouciance had gone. "We've lost one friend tonight, Maggie. I can't lose another. I trust them. You must, too. You can't deny what you've just seen."

Maggie huffed. "We have not lost Jackson. That is temporary. We will find him."

"Yes, we will. As soon as this is done."

"We haven't time for debate," Odette instructed. "Stand over there, by the book-case, and do not move, or try to help, no matter what you may see. It will be…difficult. Frightening. But exorcisms are my specialty."

"Even of Fallen Angels?" Maggie asked, ever sceptical.

"Hard, but not impossible. The Goddess will help."

Birdie cackled as she took her place around the salt circle. "The three aspects will come tonight. Crone, mother, maiden, embodied in us three. Then he will know what a fight is."

Of course, Maggie reflected as she stood next to Harlan, *the three witches were of the right age for the triple Goddess.* She may not know a huge amount about witchcraft, but she knew that much.

The witches, led by Odette, began their preparations, each taking a place around the pentagram, and each holding a staff that was as tall as the women. Every staff was different, with a strangely carved head inset with gemstones, and marks scored on the shaft.

Odette intoned a spell in her strange, sing-song voice that became even more hypnotic as she progressed. The language was unusual, of which Maggie only caught the occasional word she knew. As the words poured forth, the air thickened. A bowl of water in the circle that was filled with herbs, including the fresh leaves that Morgana had harvested, began to shimmer.

Odette's voice grew louder, the other witches joining in. She cracked her staff onto the floor and then lifted it, pointing it at the roof. The ceiling had been in utter darkness, but now sigils revealed themselves, fire racing along them. They reflected on the floor, revealing other sigils there. Maggie gasped and edged back, but the walls also filled with marks and signs, and she grabbed Harlan's arm. The whole room had become a spell.

Why was she even in here? They should be outside, surely. She felt as if she would be consumed.

The witches, however, didn't budge. Odette's voice grew stronger and more commanding with every word. The hairs on Maggie's arms stood up, and she felt Harlan's muscles clench. She didn't dare look at him. She was transfixed with the activity in the centre.

Suddenly, power cracked into—or maybe out of—Odette's staff as if it was a lightning bolt. It split, hitting the other two staffs that the witches carried, and suddenly they became more than just women. They were positively supernatural. A face was imposed over their own. Old, middle-aged, and youthful.

The Goddess is here.

Their voices weren't their own, either. They were all using one, powerful voice that resonated with magic, and seemed to be all around them and within them. The scent of blossoms filled the air, and a wild magic seemed to drag the breath from Maggie's body.

Only now did Odette address Olivia, pointing her staff at her. Again, the language was unintelligible, but the intention was clear. It was a command to leave. Olivia's neck muscles strained as she raised her head. Her eyes flew open, and they were filled with fire. Her face contorted, the muscles rippling, her mouth opening in a silent scream.

Maggie was horrified. Now she understood the true nature of possession. It was something she hadn't fully grasped before. *But why should she?* She hadn't witnessed it before.

Olivia's skin rippled with an inner fire, too. She writhed against the bonds that restrained her. Out of nowhere, huge fiery wings appeared behind Olivia, barely encompassed by the salt circle. Where the tips touched, the circle blazed into life. Inch by struggling inch, a creature of fire and light twisted out of Olivia. It curled around her in a wreath of smoke. But as the strange echoing voice continued its commands, the creature twisted upwards. A face blinked in and out of view, blindingly handsome and terrifyingly remote. The marks that the witches had drawn on Olivia's skin blazed with a white light, and the speed that the angel left her body increased. Maggie could hardly believe what she was seeing. A Fallen Angel, or a part of one at least, was twitching out of Olivia, pulled by the magic of the Goddess, summoned and embodied by the three witches.

A roar of anger seemed to come from everywhere, and Maggie shielded her eyes as the winged creature exploded with light. The room shook and glass exploded, and Harlan tackled her to the floor, covering her body with his own. It felt like an earthquake had struck.

And then in seconds, it was over. The longest seconds of Maggie's life.

Maggie finally lifted her head as Harlan eased off her. The sigils still glowed with a faint light, illuminating the room. The three witches were on the floor, their bodies twisted and twitching with spasming movements.

But Olivia was motionless on the floor, the chair she had been seated on splintered into fragments.

Eli felt strung out, as if he'd spent days drinking instead of minutes wielding Belial's power, but Briar's calming energy was restoring his equilibrium—slowly.

Briar was a petite earth witch, but her small frame contained a huge amount of power and knowledge. He had shakily made himself and Nahum a cleansing tea before she arrived, but as soon as she walked through the door, she had cast a palpable cleansing spell over them. Now she was working deeper magic.

They were seated at the kitchen table. The other witches were in the living room with Nahum. Briar had insisted on seeing him alone, even though he was worried that Belial's influence hadn't quite gone. He thought Briar was trying to demonstrate her trust in him. It was potentially dangerous.

"By the Goddess, Eli! What were you thinking?" She'd been in bed when she received the call, he could tell. Her long hair was loose, lightly curling as it spilled over her shoulders, and she wore minimal makeup. But her dark brown eyes were ringed with green fire, a sign of her agitation. Her hands ran over his body, bare millimetres from his skin. "Your aura is all over the place. And you feel..." she hesitated. "Violent."

"I was violent." He laughed. "I *am* violent. You know that. It's my nature."

"I know you cast it aside and spend your time healing now. You're an apothecary, remember?"

"I know. But it's still inside me. Normally, I control it better."

Briar sighed. "I know you use it to protect yourself and those you care about, and that's only right. What's the point of your abilities, otherwise? That's what happened today."

"That is *not* what happened today. I willingly absorbed some of Belial's power, using what he had bound into his jewellery. Jewellery I knew to be dangerous, because of what Belial is—was—and what Nahum had discovered. But I was so determined not to let Black Cronos win that I risked everything to stop them."

She lifted her face to his, so close that he could smell the sleep on her breath. "It wasn't about them winning. It was about them killing you and destroying your home. I'm so sorry this happened and that you were forced to make that choice."

He refused to be exonerated. "I had other avenues. I chose this one. Have you seen what I did?"

"You weren't alone. Nahum did it, too."

"It was at my suggestion."

"I saw the body parts and the blackened remains. There were many of them. It must make me horrible to say that I'm glad it was them and not you. Besides, what would your harem do without you?" Mischief sparkled in her eyes.

"Funny."

"Anyway, like you said, it's not the first time you've killed, and they deserved it. It's the manner of it, and what that means. I certainly don't think badly of you using something you thought would help. Admittedly, it was crazy, but sometimes desperation forces our hand."

Her warm presence reassured him. Invited confidences. He clasped her hands within his own. "It was almost like I *wanted* to experience it. Like a sudden craving for a drug I gave up. Maybe that's why I stopped doing this millennia ago."

"But you didn't use Belial's power years ago. You used your father's. You're getting maudlin, Eli. That's your out of whack aura talking."

"But he's still under my skin."

"Just his power, though, right? Not him."

"Yes. He can't possess us—although that feels like a very fine distinction at the moment. It's just residue."

"Then I'll keep flushing him out. I have spells and herbs for that." She smiled. "I'll give you the day off, too."

He then voiced the other issue that had preoccupied him for weeks. "I'm wondering if the dryads have some part to play in this. I think they have bewitched me."

A few weeks ago, Eli and Zee had made a pact with the dryads to help the witches defeat Wyrd and the mad wizard who had tried to change their fate. It meant he had promised the dryads guardianship. He had felt fine with that at the time, but now he wondered about his choices. Events had progressed quickly, and recently the dryads had escorted them to one of their sacred groves that only they could access, where the saplings grew. These were the trees they would plant in ancient forests across the country. But the dryads whispered in his dreams, where he wandered among dark forests that echoed with birdsong and streams and secrets.

Briar pulled her hands from his and reached for her herbal tea, studying him over the rim of the cup. "You're a Nephilim. I doubt that's possible."

"I'm not so sure. They are fey. Ripe with power that's rooted in the earth."

"So are you."

"We're different. Of air and flight."

"You've been listening to Shadow and her sylph theory."

"I know that angels, especially the Fallen, are not sylphs, but you know what I mean. Our magic and paranormal abilities are different. Lately I've been feeling as if they have seeped under my skin, too."

"They, or *she*?" She cocked an eyebrow, a knowing smile on her face.

There was one dryad they talked to all the time called Nelaira, and Eli would be lying if he said he hadn't had carnal thoughts about her, but equally, the idea terrified him. He loved women, so that was just weird.

"You're very discreet about your women, but it's obvious you like your relationships uncomplicated. I think Nelaira fascinates you. She is utterly unlike any woman you have met before. I think she has beguiled you, rather than bewitched you. Or maybe...it's love."

"Not funny, Briar."

"Is that so scary?"

"You tell me."

"*Touché.*" She smiled again, but it was brief. "Perhaps she fascinates you deliberately. It is their nature. Have you discussed this with Shadow?"

"No. It's the last thing I want to do."

"She knows dryads better than anyone. She must know about your pact."

"She was scathing." Shadow was horrified, actually, but maybe she hadn't told Briar that. She had berated him and Zee for weeks over their decision.

"Well, it's something to think about, but I honestly don't think you should worry about it too much. Belial worries me more."

"You look frightened of me." He hated that. Briar was gentle and kind, and he enjoyed working with her. She was a friend, and he had made a new life with her help.

"Not frightened, and not *ever* of you. But I am worried." She put her tea down. "More cleansing, I think, and then it's Nahum's turn."

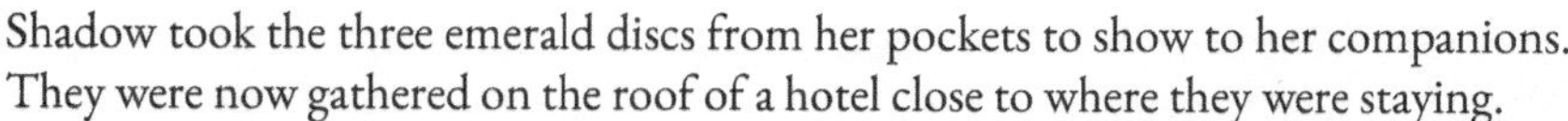

Shadow took the three emerald discs from her pockets to show to her companions. They were now gathered on the roof of a hotel close to where they were staying.

She tapped one specifically. "I think it's this one. It feels different. Not as powerful as the Emerald Tablet, but it has...vibrations."

Niel snorted. "That's great, but getting it out of the country now, after that fanfare of alarms, will be nearly impossible. Security in airports will be tight. Maybe one of us should fly them all the way to the UK."

"Niel!" Gabe looked incredulous. "Stop suggesting that! It would take *days*! Weeks, even! Weeks we haven't got."

Niel had bullish tendencies, and that's why they got on so well. Like Shadow, he just wanted to get on with the job. But in this case, he was wrong.

Shadow calmly wrapped the discs again. "Don't be ridiculous. JD's box and my glamour will work fine."

Niel folded his arms across his huge chest. "There are x-ray machines and scanners and all sorts of things. How do you know for sure?"

"Because I put my knives and a small emerald trinket in it coming over here—all in my hand luggage. A test. It worked."

Gabe glared at her, but Ash laughed. "Priceless. And if you'd been arrested?"

"It would have made the trip more interesting."

Niel, however, looked impressed. "You got your blades through? They didn't know?"

"Nope. JD's box works."

"So, Miss Smarty Pants," Gabe said, leaning against the air conditioning unit they were sheltering next to. "Where's the box now?"

"In our room, obviously! Like I had a chance to pick it up after we'd been summoned to the roof!"

"And if Black Cronos has taken it or destroyed it?"

A flash of fear constricted her heart. She'd never considered that. However, she put on a brave face. "What would they want with a wooden box? They might not even be in our rooms."

Gabe, always the planner, exploded. "Herne's fucking hairy balls! Without that box we're screwed!"

Ash cleared his throat, and they both stared at him. "So sorry to interrupt your cosy discussion, but perhaps we should also be worried about passports? In our haste to get the discs, we really didn't think this through at all."

"We're travelling in a government aircraft. That should have influence," Gabe said.

"But we'll still need passports just for ID," Ash pointed out.

Shadow groaned. "This world is so full of rules! It's tedious."

"Tough. Get used to it." Niel rose to his feet. "I'll check to see if the vans are still there."

After the elation and adrenalin rush of the theft, reality set in, and Shadow, Gabe, and Ash considered their options.

"Regardless," Shadow said, "of where Black Cronos is, we need to return to our rooms. For passports, the box, our bags…"

"And if they're there, we'll end up fighting," Gabe reasoned. "And that means deaths."

Ash nodded. "But if we hide their bodies—like up here, on the roof of another hotel—then it's all good. We could check into a new hotel, maybe next to the airport. Or Jackson can change our flight." He hesitated. "Shit. No Jackson. Maybe Waylen could."

Gabe was watching the sky, Niel a distant dot. "I doubt we can just hop on another government plane."

They waited impatiently, running through possible scenarios until Niel returned, looking hopeful. "There are no black vans, so they've either given up, or a team is lying in wait, which sounds much more likely."

"Let's hope for the former." Gabe stood and extended his hand to Shadow. "Ready?"

"Always."

Thirteen

Olivia woke to warm darkness, the only light a flicker of orange on the far side of the room. For a second, she couldn't work out where she was. However, she was lying on something soft, and she was deliciously cocooned.

She should be panicking, but Olivia felt so safe that the emotion never crossed her mind. She stretched, and then winced. Every part of her body ached. *What had happened?* However, the more she struggled to remember, the more her memory resisted. Despite the aches, she shot up in bed, her breath shallow.

"Woah! Take it slowly." Harlan's voice emerged from the shadows, as did he, rising from a chair to her right. He looked shattered. His normally neat hair had a rakish, ruffled charm, and his clothing looked like he'd slept in it for a week. He laid a calming hand on her arm. "I'm right here, and you're safe."

"Where am I?" She looked down and found she was wearing a cotton night slip over her underwear. "What the hell is going on?"

"Don't worry. I didn't undress you. The witches did. We're at Moonfell, remember?"

"Moonfell?" The name was familiar. "You said witches?"

"You're in a spare room in their impressively gothic house."

Olivia's eyes adjusted to the light. She was in a huge, four-poster bed on what felt like a feather mattress. The quilt and pillows were thick, and she smelled lavender around her. The room beyond the curtained bed had a fireplace containing a small fire, a huge window covered in thick curtains, and a few pieces of bedroom furniture. Oliva thought she'd gone back in time.

"But why am I in bed?"

He moved from the chair to the edge of the bed, watching her. "What's the last thing you remember?"

Something had happened. Something unpleasant. She remembered being in the pub with Jackson and Harlan. That was fine. *But then...* "Being chased by Black Cronos, and Jackson being kidnapped." She groaned. "Shit! We came here for help. But then..." There was something else; a buzzing in her brain that was evading her. She tried to think back before the drinks in the pub. She had worked with Nahum, and, *wow*, had slept with him. How could she have forgotten that? *And the reliquary.* "Belial!" she shouted.

Suddenly her breath seemed stuck in her chest.

"It's okay! Breathe!" Harlan grasped her arms and pulled her to face him. "He's gone. The witches did a *thing*."

She wrestled a hand free and patted her head and her chest. "I'm whole. But his eyes. I remember him. Like something lurking!"

"A splinter, apparently." Harlan eased away, giving her space, appraising her. "I have never seen anything like that in my life. For a splinter, he was insanely powerful."

"I have gaps," Olivia confessed. "I remember sitting in a circle of salt, in a strange tower, and then nothing."

"Oh, the tower. Yep. That *was* strange. And the three aspects of the Goddess. That was also something." He shrugged in his teasing, nonchalant way. "Yeah, you know, I saw a Goddess summoned today. She battled with an archangel and kicked his ass back to where he belonged. Somewhere beyond our realm! Yeah. Very cool. The windows have no glass now, the witches were half-dead when it ended, and me and Maggie had to shelter from a magical explosion. You were unconscious on the floor, after looking like you were about to explode. Normal, mid-week kind of stuff. What Odette called the witching hour. Yeah, that was something..."

He was making light of it for her, wondering what she remembered. "Sounds terrifying."

"Nothing more terrifying, though, than seeing you possessed. Those witches are really powerful. I will never underestimate them again."

"But all day I felt so normal!"

"Apparently, once Odette saw him, he grew more potent."

"I must thank them. Where is everyone?"

"In the kitchen. Maggie is making calls about Jackson." A shadow of worry crossed his face. "The witches are trying a finding spell for us later. They're recovering right now."

"I feel like I've been hit by a bus."

"I'm not surprised. You wrestled with a Fallen Angel." He pinched his thumb and forefinger together. "A little bit of one. Not a physical being, so I've been told. Just a touch of his spiritual presence."

Olivia plumped her pillows and flopped back onto them. "It was when I touched his jewellery. I felt him then. Like residue. That's probably an understatement, considering what just happened. Have you heard from Nahum?"

"Oh, yes. He and Eli had a moment of madness and used the power in Belial's jewellery to defeat Black Cronos who attacked them, too. They have the five White Haven witches treating them now."

Olivia sat up again, heart pounding. "Is Nahum okay? And Eli, obviously?"

"They're both alive. Chastened. Blood-spattered."

"I don't get it. Why voluntarily do that?"

"Desperation. There were three of them against a whole platoon and a helicopter." Harlan passed her a glass of murky water. "Drink up. Witches' orders. It has herbs in it and will help you. And then you should sleep some more."

Sleep was already beckoning, her lids growing heavy. "What about you?"

"I'll text Maggie, let them know you're okay, and then sleep in the chair. I don't want to leave you alone."

Olivia patted the bed. "Sleep here. I promise not to molest you. You can't sleep well in the chair."

"Damn it. No molesting? Where's the fun in that?" He winked. "Kidding. Are you sure? The chair is fine."

"I'm sure."

Olivia wanted to phone Nahum herself, just to hear from him what had happened, but it could wait. She'd call him in the morning. Right now, she just hoped that Belial's compelling eyes would not appear again, because if they did, she doubted she'd have the strength to resist.

Nahum stared at the three items of Belial's jewellery that were now stored in a wooden box protected with spells. They looked harmless, the precious metals and gems winking in the firelight. "I guess we're stuck with them forever."

"No volcano you can throw them in?" Reuben asked, deadpan.

Alex groaned. "Tit. It's not *Lord of the Rings*."

"It might work. You can unmake them." Reuben cocked his head, a goofy grin on his face. "If you unmade angelic jewellery, would the entire world melt down? Would we all be stardust again?"

"Herne's horns!" El, his blonde girlfriend and a witch, remonstrated. "Has your bloody familiar, Silver, been waxing lyrical again?"

"Don't think you can break our bond. We're like that." He kneaded his hands together. "You're just jealous, but there's room in my life for two."

Everyone laughed, and Nahum was glad of Reuben's humour. He was always able to add levity to a situation. Even one as grim as this.

The five White Haven witches, plus Newton, Eli, and Nahum were gathered in the farmhouse's living room. He and Eli had been cleansed, spelled, and declared free of Belial's influence, although Nahum wasn't sure he could as easily cast the memory aside. He felt more guilty and worried about Olivia, though. For some reason he felt responsible, like he had endangered her, when the reality was that it was no one's fault except Belial's.

"We can't get rid of Belial's jewellery, unless we can bury them at the bottom of the sea," Eli said. "No human should ever touch them. They're too dangerous, especially considering what we know about Olivia. At least *we* can't be affected like that. What worries me even more," he confessed, staring at the witches, "is what would happen if someone like you touched them. Could he manipulate your magic?"

Avery, the pretty, red-haired witch who was Alex's partner answered immediately. "It's very possible. It seems to me that Belial is after a slice of power again, and he'll try any means to get that. We would be a decent way."

"I don't get any vibes from them now, though," Alex said. "Those protection spells have worked."

"The reliquary must have been spelled, too," Nahum said. "The lid was inscribed with protection sigils and angelic words to help mask their power. I want to know who put them there."

"So do I." Newton had been listening to the conversation in grim silence. His sergeants and the SOCO team had gone home, much to Kendall's annoyance, who was keen to stay. "Was it a human who put them there, or another paranormal creature?"

"Whoever it was," Zee said, "that will have to wait. Black Cronos is on the offensive. We've beaten them back, but we're about to attack their base. We're needed in France."

Briar shook her head. "That seems like suicide."

"We're reaching an impasse. Jackson has been kidnapped, the rest of us targeted. JD has the Emerald Tablet, and hopefully Gabe and Shadow have the key. That might help us. Barak is on the count's doorstep, with only Estelle and Lucien to help. Right now, we're scattered and vulnerable. Black Cronos is either still tracking some of us, or all of us. How?"

"Maybe," Newton suggested, "it's as simple as monitoring your phone. Or maybe it's a spell. A tracking spell. Or a covert team. Or a mole…"

Nahum's immediate thought was Lucien, but he had been thoroughly vetted, and he trusted everyone else. "No. There is no mole."

"You sound very sure."

"Because I am. The only possible person would be Lucien, and he's out for revenge." They all knew his background, because the witches and Newton had been kept abreast of their business.

Zee shrugged. "The Order of the Midnight Sun thought the same, yet they had one."

"Barak and Estelle have spent months with him, and Jackson," Nahum reminded them. "They considered that, but he's clean."

"Maybe Jackson, then," Newton suggested.

"He's been kidnapped!" Eli said, all three Nephilim staring at Newton. "He has a desperate urge to find his grandfather."

Newton was unfazed. "Maybe he contacted them, somehow. In his desperate need for answers, maybe he made a deal. Frustration can sometimes have weird consequences."

"Like getting kidnapped on purpose?" Briar asked, confused. "How does that benefit him?"

"Maybe he offered up Harlan, Olivia and himself, and it went wrong. They put up a bigger fight than he expected."

Nahum considered Jackson's shabby, gumshoe appearance. It didn't seem possible. And yet, he knew where all of them were at any time, roughly. He was at the heart of everything. He'd helped them, advised them, recruited them. Had even been appalled and stressed when he found out about his grandfather's colleague. "No. I don't believe it."

"But he hid his involvement with the PD very well," Zee reminded him. "Harlan never knew. That says a lot."

"But Harlan didn't know Jackson that well last year. He just knew him as another collector."

"Until we encountered Black Cronos."

Eli sighed. "I don't want to believe it, but the kidnapping could be a ruse."

"Harlan and Olivia could have been killed! He wouldn't have risked them, surely?" Nahum asked, hoping they'd agree.

Newton looked regretful, but his eyes were hard. "Who does Jackson report to? Maybe whoever that is betrayed you."

"Waylen Adams? The director?" Nahum expelled a sharp breath. "It can't be him!"

"Why not? If he's the boss, he'll probably know everything. Unfortunately, all my years as a policeman have told me that people hide things, all the time. At this moment, I wouldn't discount anything or anyone."

Gabe crept down the staircase that led from the hotel's roof to their rooms, Shadow next to him. The team had two connected rooms. Ash and Niel were approaching from the other end of the corridor.

It was four in the morning, and they still had at least two hours of darkness left.

The hotel was quiet. No guests stirred, and the corridor was empty. Gabe had debated flying and entering through the window, but if the doors were locked and Black Cronos was inside, smashing glass would be loud. This way, they hoped, would be quieter.

He eyed the other doors as they passed, wondering if the soldiers were waiting in empty rooms, but nothing piqued their senses. Ash and Niel approached them, Ash shaking his head. No one was waiting from that direction, either.

They reached the doors of their rooms, and Gabe pulled the key from his pocket. *Did they enter the conventional way, or burst in?* Being loud meant alerting the guests. He looked at Shadow and his brothers. Ash placed a finger on lips and pulled their key out, too. *A quiet entry, then.*

In tandem, they swiped the electronic keycard, pushed open the door, and ducked. Nothing happened. No shots. No charging soldiers.

Gabe edged inside, Shadow next to him, all her fey glamour wrapped around her. He could barely see her. They had a large room, but it contained only the usual furniture, an ensuite bathroom, a balcony, and nothing else. The interconnecting door was on the right, and it was closed. There weren't many places that Black Cronos could hide. It took only seconds to confirm that the room was empty.

Niel threw the connecting door open. "No one is here. The room looks undisturbed."

"Ours, too," Gabe confirmed. "Check your passports."

"Well, this is unexpected," Shadow said. Her blades were in her hand as she checked the wardrobe and under the bed. "Maybe they're coming back."

Gabe headed to the safe where their passports were stored, sighing with relief to find them still in there. He put them in one of his pockets. "Let's just grab everything and go. Is the box still there?"

Shadow searched her pack that she'd left behind after Niel had summoned them to the roof. "Yes. But I don't like this, Gabe. Did they get the wrong room?"

Gabe didn't answer. Like Shadow, he couldn't fathom it.

Ash appeared at the connecting doorway. "We have our passports. This is too weird. We didn't imagine seeing those soldiers."

"Unless," Niel said, looming behind him, "there was another target in the hotel. But that would be an insane coincidence!"

"Maybe there's a bomb?" Gabe suggested, eyes sweeping the room, but this time slowly, looking for details he had missed before. "If they didn't know we'd seen them, they could have planted one, thinking we'd be completely unsuspecting."

"I like it. It's sneaky. But where?" Shadow asked. She'd frozen in place, like everyone had, suddenly scared to touch anything. "If it were me, I'd want my target relaxed. Maybe I'd wire the wardrobe, so that when I opened the door it would detonate. Or the bed. Plenty of places to hide a bomb under the mattress. Pressure sensitive, perhaps."

"Or a trigger. If they've seen us come in."

"Too unreliable," Niel reasoned. "They'd have no idea how long it would take to get to our room. Maybe a timer."

"While I hate to add to our list of possible places," Ash said, "our luggage is also a good option."

"I hope not," Gabe said, eyeing it warily. "Let's get out of here. We touch as little as possible, and then find another hotel."

"I like that plan," Niel said, vanishing into their room.

Gabe checked his overnight bag, while Shadow lowered herself to the floor, and looked under the bed, edging closer than she had earlier. She used her phone's torch to scan the base. "I'm pretty sure I can see something that shouldn't be here. A small, metal box."

Ash had been waiting at the door, watching her, but now he turned to leave. "I'll check under ours."

Gabe slid next to Shadow. She angled her torch for him. "See? Right there."

"Fuck it." The small box had a winking red light on it. They edged back, careful not to touch anything.

Ash called over. "Yep. Niel's bed is clear, but there's one under mine. We need to warn the hotel. People will die."

"Or we could set it off and pretend we're dead," Shadow suggested, rising to her feet.

"And still, people might die," Ash pointed out. "We could have neighbours!"

"I haven't heard a sound from that side for hours earlier," Shadow said, pointing to the left. "One of you could fly out and check the windows. Then we'd know."

"To be honest," Gabe said, annoyed and wondering why they were still in the room, "I'd rather we have this discussion outside, just in case someone pushes the trigger. Grab our stuff carefully, and let's get out and discuss this down the corridor! Ash, tell Niel to get moving!"

Shadow, like him, had packed light, and had barely taken anything out of her luggage. She grabbed her bag and her backpack and headed to the door, Gabe right behind her.

But they were barely through the door when a boom threw him into the corridor, through a wall, and the floor collapsed below him.

Niel was on the balcony, grabbing his pack from the table where he'd left it earlier, when glass and brick exploded outward, throwing him over the railing. He hurtled through the air, plummeting a couple of floors, dazed, before extending his wings.

He swept around and flew higher, keeping away from the flames that poured from their room. Although, there wasn't really a room anymore. Most of the walls had blown out, exposing their level and part of the floors above and below it.

Screams erupted, and ignoring the fact that the light from the fire would illuminate him, he tried to see through the thick black smoke to the inside of the room. *Where had Ash been? And Gabe and Shadow?*

Unable to get close due to the searing heat, he flew to a balcony a few doors down, smashing the glass door with his axe. The room's occupants were already in the corridor, shocked and terrified, running towards the stairs. Doors were thrown open, and loud screams and shouts filled the air. Heading against the tide of fleeing people, his wings tucked from sight again, Niel marched towards the flames that were greedily consuming everything in their path.

The area where their rooms had been was completely destroyed, the surrounding rooms obliterated, leaving ragged holes of plaster and metalwork open to the elements. Unable to see his brothers and Shadow, he clambered down over the rubble, the hot metal searing his skin, to the floor below.

He yelled, "Gabe! Ash! Shadow!" But it was impossible to hear anything over the screams and the roar of the flames. The building creaked around him, and another chunk of rubble crashed down.

A persistent screaming to his right had him running to investigate. It was a young woman, pinned by metal and brick onto her bed. Flames licked the ceiling, and it was so hot that it was hard to breathe. Niel raced in regardless, hauled the rubble off her, and lifted her gently. He took her halfway down the corridor and found a man running towards him.

"Here!" He thrust the woman at him. "Take her out. She's injured."

He didn't even wait to see what happened next. He headed back to the flames. Piles of rubble could be hiding bodies, and he started to haul chunks aside, shouting all the time. And then he saw an arm protruding from the dust, and he redoubled his efforts.

It was Gabe.

He dug him out, fingernails ripping and hands bloodied. Gabe merely groaned.

"Brother! Wake up!"

Gabe shifted and moaned, blood pouring from a wound on his head. Twisted beneath him was Shadow. Niel had never been more grateful for his strength. Some of the fallen masonry was in huge blocks, but adrenalin fuelled him, and he tipped them aside, allowing Gabe to crawl free.

"Gabe, can you get Shadow out? I need to find Ash! More of this building is coming down, and if I don't find him now..."

Gabe nodded, still dazed. "Go. I'll get her. I'll meet you on the last roof we were on."

Niel headed deeper into the destruction and then took stock, noting where the rooms were above him, and where Ash could be. Ignoring the flames that were licking all around him, he looked up through the hole to the floors above and saw columns of writhing black smoke. Ash could have been thrown upwards, rather than crashing down. Just in case he was wrong, he hurled a few chunks of rubble aside, but there were no bodies beneath. Niel headed down the corridor to the edge of the fire, and then started to clamber up again. The place looked deserted, and the screams receded.

He shouted again, all the while cursing Black Cronos. They were a disease, and they had to eradicate them. *If they had killed Ash...* He could barely contemplate the idea as he searched.

And then he heard a weak, "*Help!*"

Eyes adjusting to the flickering flames and darkness, he caught an odd shape high up on the wall, pinned behind masonry and huge pieces of metal. Flames were encroaching, and the smell of burnt flesh was strong.

"Ash?" He rushed forward, stumbling over a blackened body on the floor. For one heart-stopping moment he thought it was his brother, and then another faint shout summoned his attention. His head snapped up, and he saw that Ash was pinned to the wall, a huge piece of metal skewering his shoulder.

Ash looked to be in agony. He was half embedded in the wall, the masonry beneath his feet helping to support him. *At least the flames hadn't reached here. Yet.* But they were close, and the air was so hot, it was searing his lungs. Niel scrambled up the fallen masonry to his side.

Ash was gasping for breath and covered in sweat and grime. His golden eyes seemed feverishly bright. "I tried to pull it out. I couldn't get a grip." Ash's fingers were slick with blood.

"I'll get it. Don't worry."

"It's pinned in the wall. I think it's melted in."

"I don't care! I'll get it."

Niel was still bare-chested, and tearing his t-shirt in two, he wrapped his hands and gripped the piece of rebar. But it was wedged in deeply, and still hot. Ash's shoulder was blistered and raw, and his golden eyes seemed to dim.

"Ash! I swear if you die, I will never forgive you!"

"Leave me and save yourself."

"Shut up!"

Niel extended his wings as fully as he dared, aware that his smaller feathers were already smouldering. He braced his legs on either side of Ash, grabbed the jagged metal, and pulled, using his wings as leverage. The metal groaned, ripping through the skin on his hands, and searing his palms.

Ash yelled in agony. Niel didn't dare stop now that he had momentum. Inch by inch, he dragged it from the wall and out of Ash's shoulder. Finally, he flung it aside, catching Ash as he fell.

Another explosion sounded overhead, blowing the closest window out. Oxygen poured in, and the flames swelled, rippling across the ceiling. Niel flew out of the window, Ash in his arms, as the flames leapt out to consume them.

Fourteen

B arak paced the living room of their chalet, unable to sleep.

He'd spoken to Zee a short while ago and was still processing news about Belial. It didn't seem possible that his jewellery, his *tokens* as the Fallen used to call them, could have survived all these years. Especially considering that many Nephilim had actively tried to destroy as many of those tokens as they could, once they rebelled.

But like many of their things, they were indestructible. Made of precious metals and gems that were crafted to the finest qualities and imbued with angelic magic, it was probably surprising that more of it hadn't survived.

Unless they had. Advances in the field of archaeology meant that more of the past was being discovered every day.

However, Barak hadn't the time to think about that yet. Not until Black Cronos had been defeated. They were caught between the enemies of their past, and the ones of the present. While Barak hated to be negative, he doubted they could destroy Black Cronos entirely. They were too big. The count was too powerful. But they could weaken him.

Of course, it depended on what Black Cronos were planning. The more he thought about it, the more he was convinced something was going to happen on the winter solstice. That moved their timeframe up.

Barak knew he should sleep, curl around Estelle and let his dreams take him, but fearing he would toss and turn, instead he headed to the TV and put the news on. He'd been watching for a few minutes when he saw a breaking news headline.

An explosion in a hotel in Aswan.

He phoned Gabe, Ash, Shadow, and Niel. None of them answered. Then he phoned Nahum. After a few minutes of hurried conversation, they had decided only one thing. Barak needed to wake Estelle and Lucien and leave their chalet. They had to move to a new place.

The others had been compromised, and they could be next.

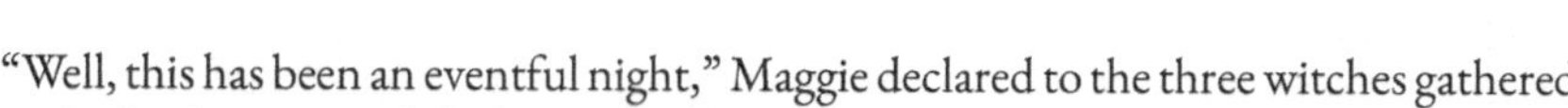

"Well, this has been an eventful night," Maggie declared to the three witches gathered in the kitchen around the large, wooden table.

She tried not to stare at Birdie, but like Odette and Morgana, she found it hard to look away.

Birdie looked twenty years younger now. Her eyes were bright, the milkiness of the cataracts vanished, her skin was tighter, and she was no longer a small, wizened crone. The other two witches had also been affected by the Goddess, but not as much. Morgana and Odette seemed to have a glow of youthfulness to their skin, and although Morgana still had a grey streak in her hair, her jawline appeared tighter. Odette, perhaps because she was the youngest, was the least affected.

Birdie laughed. Less of a cackle now. "The appearance of the Goddess always makes for an eventful night."

Maggie had so many questions that she didn't even know where to start. She had spent the last hour on the phone. First, she called Waylen Adams, the Director of the Paranormal Division, then Stan and Irving, her own two Detective Sergeants. She had rattled Waylen out of bed. She had done all of this in what she called the poison palace, keeping her hands well away from any plants, and eyeing the witches through the partly open door. She spent five minutes more in there than she needed, settling her nerves before returning to the kitchen.

She drank one large whiskey and immediately needed another. She didn't want to confess that she'd been scared witless by the night's events. Maggie had tangled with many paranormal creatures over the years, but she had never experienced an event like she had earlier. The news that Olivia had briefly woken provided some measure of reassurance. Maggie's hip still ached from where she'd crashed to the floor with Harlan on top of her. *Big lump. Sweet of him, though.*

Maggie reached for the bottle of whiskey and topped up her glass, glad that her hands were steady. She blamed the adrenalin, not nerves. "I take it," she said, addressing all three witches, "that you don't normally summon the Goddess?"

"No, and I didn't summon her tonight," Odette admitted. "I called upon her influence. That's very common in witchcraft. She came of her own free will." She cleared her throat, eyeing her relatives. "That's what we've been discussing while you've been plotting. We're wondering what it portends."

"Portends? Fuck me! That word makes it seem so much more ominous," Maggie said, scowling. "How, and why, are you younger, Birdie?"

"The Goddess gives, and she takes away." Birdie picked up the small hand mirror at her elbow and held it to her face, turning to see all angles. "I confess, I did not expect this. But we never expected her to come at all." Birdie was still petite, as her name suggested. Short, small-framed, and slender. Placing her mirror down, she flexed her fingers. "My arthritis has gone, too. I wonder if there'll be a price to pay."

"A price? But you didn't ask for this."

Morgana answered, her hands around a cup of tea steaming on the table in front of her. "No. But a gift such as this usually requires payment, even though I have been a loyal admirer of the Goddess all my life. All of us have. We have altars to her throughout the house. Even in here." She pointed to a collection of candles and winter branches on a shelf close to the fire. "She is always welcome."

Maggie rubbed her temples, a right royal headache threatening. She needed to go home, and yet the thought of leaving this house and crossing the cold garden to her car was not attractive. But she needed a few answers first. "What is the tower room?"

"A spell room, that's all," Odette said, shrugging nonchalantly as if everyone had one. "It's amplified by sigils and signs of protection, devil traps, and other useful things. It is where we work our most powerful spells. It was the only place we could have cast that spell tonight."

"And that spell was what, exactly?"

"An exorcism, just as I said, but a complicated one. It was not an ordinary spirit or demon. But you know that."

"I didn't think it was any kind of spirit at all. You said it was a splinter. An impression left on Olivia's mind. So how did..." She floundered for words as she considered the flaming wings and eyes that had manifested from Olivia. "How could Belial appear so real?"

"Because he is an archangel. Powerful beyond measure," Birdie explained. She frowned, her fingers drumming the table. "It was an example of what even a tiny influence of him could do, just by touching his jewellery. If I'm honest, I'm not sure any of us fully understand it." She glanced at the other witches, and they nodded. "But he imprinted himself on her. I think a curse would be the most appropriate explanation. I would like to see those items. I gather there were three of them. It might help us understand."

"I think that would be a recipe for disaster, and it's a good job Nahum took them," Maggie retorted. "Can he come back? Can he target you, or any of us?"

"No." Odette didn't hesitate to answer. "We broke his hold, although he resisted very strongly. The Goddess saw we were struggling and helped. There is no love lost between the Goddess and the angels."

"Why is that?"

Morgana huffed. "Don't you know your history? Or religion? The Christian religion suppressed all mention of the Goddess. It is a one-sided religion. It lacks balance."

"I suppose you're right," Maggie admitted, thinking she really needed her bed. There was nothing she could do about the Goddess, or her battles with a misogynistic God and his angels. "Dragging us back to more earthly matters, we came here originally needing to find Jackson. Our friend who's been kidnapped by Black Cronos."

"While I appreciate that it's important," Birdie said, "we are tired now—although my appearance may not suggest that. I think we should all sleep, you included, before we perform that spell. If we slip up, we could send you in the wrong direction. Besides, will you really charge after him tonight?"

"Unlikely," Maggie admitted. "However, my sergeants are following what scant leads we have. But you're right. It's late, and I'm shattered. I just hope Jackson is okay. I presume if they wanted him dead, he would be already. It's what else they may do to him that worries me." *Like alchemical tattoos that could change him forever.*

"You must sleep here," Birdie insisted. "I think we owe you a debt. Or I do." Her eyes sparkled with delight as she stood. "Thanks to you and your friends, I've regained years of my life."

"It's not our doing," Maggie protested, standing too. "Although, I'm pleased for you, obviously. And I can't stay here. I will go home. I can't impose."

Morgana gathered their cups and glasses and headed to the sink. "Nonsense. We have a huge house, and you'll just have to come back in the morning. We'll put you in a room next to Olivia and Harlan. I promise that you'll be safe." She looked amused. "Besides, I know you're very curious about us, DI Maggie Milne. This is your chance to find out a little more."

Maggie couldn't deny that, and the thought of falling into bed within a few steps sounded brilliant. "Thank you. I appreciate it."

As Maggie followed Odette upstairs, she just hoped that when she woke up the next morning, she wouldn't be a frog. And that Jackson wouldn't be partially transformed into an alchemical soldier.

The concrete roof felt cool beneath Ash's bare skin as Niel laid him down, and yet it still felt as if fire raged in his shoulder.

His memories were hazy. One minute he was in the hotel room, the next he was hurtling through the air, battered by rubble, and pinned to the wall by a piece of rebar. He had passed out, with only Niel's roaring voice dragging him back to consciousness.

"Here, let me," he heard Shadow say. His head was lifted and then lowered onto something far more comfortable. Something that smelled of summer woods. Shadow's face loomed above him, and her cool hand rested on his injured shoulder. "Brother. Let me help."

"Shadow. I hate to say this, but you look half dead yourself." She was covered in dust and streaked in blood, chunks of plaster wedged in her hair, but her eyes were bright.

"I may have been flattened by stone and Gabe, who is a considerable weight, but I'll survive. And so will you."

Now that his head was slightly elevated, he could see he was on the roof of a building, and Gabe and Niel were standing at his feet, locked in furious discussion. He glanced at his shoulder. It was an ugly mess of torn and blistered flesh. No wonder it hurt so badly. But Shadow's hand was still pressed against it, and a cool feeling passed from her skin into his wound.

"What are you doing?"

"Sharing my fey magic with you. I'm not a healer, but magic is magic, and it should help."

"It does. Thank you." He wriggled to get a little more comfortable, and then wished he hadn't. Everything ached. He had broken ribs, he was sure of it, and there were cuts and gashes all over his body. "Where are we?"

"On the roof where we rested earlier, but we can't stay here much longer. It will be light soon, and we need to get to the airport."

"I hear sirens."

"The street is full of police and fire engines. Our hotel is ablaze."

Ash focussed on the sky, and as his senses sharpened, he saw the red glow and thick smoke from the fire over to his right. "They really wanted to kill us."

"With luck, they'll think they have. Let's hope no one caught our escape on camera. Winged creatures will make a great headline."

"Is that likely?" Ash asked, horrified.

She gave him an impish grin. Upside down, she looked demonic. "Not really. We circled wide before landing. Everyone's focussed on the burning building." Her grin quickly vanished. "Death will suit our purposes well. I will kill them all for this."

"Maybe that's the trouble. Maybe we need to compromise—somehow."

"You think that will stop them from making alchemical monsters?"

"They don't see themselves as that. They are superhumans. Everything evolves, Shadow."

"I know that, but they're doing it to people without their consent. That's my issue."

She had a point; one he couldn't overlook. He was exhausted, and it was obviously addling his judgement. But the thought of fighting Black Cronos again seemed to sap all of his remaining energy. They needed to find another way.

Gabe and Niel ended their discussion and crouched on either side of him. Gabe regarded him with compassion, but anger blazed behind his eyes. Gabe would not seek a compromise.

"We need to fly again," Gabe told him. "I know it will be uncomfortable, but we must get off this roof. We're going straight to the airport. Niel will carry you. We'll find a quiet spot to land."

"I'll cope. At least I'm alive." He looked at Niel. "Thanks to you."

Niel's face was like stone, his blue eyes chips of ice. Niel wouldn't compromise, either. They were on the verge of war with a large, private army. However, now was not the time to discuss alternatives. He needed to heal, and then they would make plans.

Gabe was already moving on. "You and Shadow will return to London, as planned, with the discs."

"They survived all of that?" Ash asked, surprised.

"I'd put them in the box already," Shadow said. "My body shielded it. I have a box-shaped bruise on my arse now."

Ash laughed. "That's something, then. And the passports?"

Both Gabe and Niel tapped their pockets. "On us, and safe—if battered."

"Where are you two going?"

Niel answered for them both. "France. Barak needs us. He's on the move with Estelle and Lucien, finding a new place to stay. They found the castle, though. We'll take the battle to them."

Ash struggled to sit up, fearing an ill-thought plan would get everyone killed. "But you'll wait for all of us?"

"If we can," Gabe answered.

"You'll wait for us," Shadow told him, "or lose your balls."

"And our brothers in Cornwall?" Ash asked, worry growing by the second.

"That tale can wait for the airport," Niel said, already flexing his wings. "Let's move."

Fifteen

"So, what do you think?" Zee asked Alex at The Wayward Son, early on Friday morning before the pub opened.

"I'm thinking lots of things, and none of them are very good right now," Alex said, leaning against the kitchen counter in the small staff room. "You're playing a dangerous game."

"Not by choice." Zee hoped Alex wasn't about to wash his hands of them. "Well, not entirely."

Alex smirked. "You mean notwithstanding Eli and Nahum's crazy decision to invoke Belial's power. Herne's hairy bollocks, you guys really know how to liven up Christmas."

"At least you're smiling."

"I'm trying to make the best of a bad thing."

With the events of the last twenty-four hours, Zee had almost forgotten that Yule was only a week or so away, and that Christmas loomed after that. Although, with White Haven bursting at the seams with Christmas trees, lights, decorations, the Green Man, and the weird, wizened gnomes that seemed insanely popular, it was hard to ignore. Blood and guts around the farmhouse were apt to do that, though.

"But finding Belial by using his jewels, somehow, is that possible?"

"Bearing in mind we shouldn't touch them? You tell me!"

Zee winced. "I know. I'm sorry. And after what happened to Olivia, we absolutely can't risk you."

"Nice to know I'm not expendable. Coffee?"

"Extra strong."

Alex busied himself filling the coffee machine, while Zee, unable to settle, cleaned the work surfaces. He liked Alex, and considered him a good friend. *Did he even know that?*

"You know," Zee started, aiming for humour, "we don't want you hurt, or any of the witches. We just need a lead. I like my job. I don't want to kill the boss."

"Thank you."

"I mean it. Without you guys, we wouldn't be here at all, or have the life we have now. It's a life we don't want to lose. Finding Belial's stuff was a shock. He's a slippery bastard."

While the coffee machine chugged and steamed, Alex turned to face him again. "Just to change the subject slightly for a moment, Simon is leaving after Christmas."

"Simon the bar manager?" Zee spluttered, surprised. "He's been here years."

"I know. To say this is bad timing is an understatement." Alex raked his hands through his long, dark hair. "It seems that the paranormal activity around here has finally got to him. Last night's event was the final straw."

"The crashing helicopter?"

"The bright lights over the moors that looked like two angels. Christmas come early."

"Oh, no."

"We knew it was possible that someone had seen that spectacle. Simon phoned me at eight this morning. I'm hoping his call is not the first of many."

"Shit. I'm sorry, Alex." Zee dropped into a chair under the window. "What have we done?"

"Don't worry. It's just one thing amongst many. I can't blame you. I've been caught up in enough supernatural weirdness to last a lifetime. Guaranteed, Ghost OPS will be on the phone soon."

"Yeah, but they'll be happy."

"Anyway," Alex said, hands shoved in his jeans' pockets, eyes fixed on him, "I have come to a very quick decision. Do you want the manager job?"

"Are you serious?"

"No, it's a nasty joke. Of course I'm serious!"

"You'd trust me to do it?"

"Again, of course I would! I don't know anyone who I'd trust more. The staff like you, and so do the customers. They respect you, too. But equally, I know that you have a lot going on. No hard feelings, if not."

"No! Yes!" Zee crossed the room in almost one bound to shake Alex's hand. "I really want the job! I'd love the job!" He couldn't quite get over how much he liked the idea. It would give him roots. Purpose. A way to pay back Alex for all his help and trust.

Alex pulled him into a hug. "Good. Great, in fact. I have to advertise it, obviously, but it's yours."

Zee stepped back, overwhelmed almost by his excitement. "You know I just need to tie some stuff up first..."

"I know. Just don't get yourself killed. That will really piss me off." Alex turned aside to pour the coffee, and then handed him a cup. He chinked it with his own. "Cheers, and thank you. You need to go to France, I presume?"

"I was hoping they wouldn't need me, but after last night..."

"We reinforced the protection spell on your house, and will head back there later to add a few extras. I'm a bit gutted Black Cronos got through it."

"Me, too. I was feeling smug on the roof with my crossbow."

"How is Eli this morning?"

"Preoccupied. Nahum is looking into flights."

"And Ash?" The witches had still been at their house when Gabe called with news of the attack in Egypt.

"Stabilised. Not happy that he's going to London with Shadow, but he just needs to heal."

"Do you need Briar?"

"Nahum will drive her there later today. There are other witches he could see, but he only wants her."

"The ones who helped Olivia, you mean?"

Zee nodded. "A group of three family members. They sound fascinating."

"When you know more about them, you'll have to tell us."

"I will. So, Belial's jewellery? Will it help you find him?"

Alex cocked his head. "He's not human, and not on an earthly plane. It will be impossible. All we can do is limit his sphere of influence by potentially binding his power in the jewellery. Sort of muffling it. That will be *really* hard."

"But brilliant!"

"We might be able to help in other ways. Last night Nahum talked about the fact that there might be an agent acting for Belial. We could potentially find this person. *Potentially*," he stressed. "But it will take time."

"Excellent." Zee sighed with relief, feeling like they were making some progress, and shifted his attention to other matters. "What can I do today?"

"Nothing, just your shift. I know you need to pack." Alex's lips tightened. "Look, we really want to help you fight Black Cronos, but we can't. We hoped we could travel to France to support you, but we're all so busy at this time of year—"

Zee cut him off. "Don't apologise. It's fine. Besides, it's probably for the best. We don't know if Black Cronos will return, and it's unwise to leave White Haven unprotected." He shrugged, wishing the witches could help, but knew it was impossible. "You never know—Estelle might have asked Caspian. They seem a bit closer recently."

"I hope so. Make sure you don't give them an inch, Zee."

"We won't. We can't afford to."

One slip could cost them their lives.

Estelle studied the map of the area around the *château*, and the photos that Barak had taken, feeling overwhelmed at the task ahead of them.

They were in their new place that was now surrounded by protection spells, all three gathered around the kitchen table of the chalet they were squatting in. It was on the outskirts of a place called *L'Aiguillon*, one of the towns around *Bénaix*. Barak had found it in the early hours of the morning. He had set out after the phone calls with his brothers, none of them willing to take chances after Jackson's abduction. This place was furnished, secluded, and empty. *But maybe not for long.* If the owner turned up for a skiing holiday over Christmas, they would have a lot of explaining to do.

"Is there any shelter at all on the slopes beneath the castle?" she asked Barak.

"The valley is wooded, and some of the slopes are, but some of the sides are so sheer that it's just rocks. The base of the ridge is more exposed. That's why we need your shadow spell."

Estelle sighed. "I can absolutely use my shadow spell, but it means all three of us will have to stick together. That's probably safer anyway, now."

Lucien was on the laptop, also scrolling through images of the area. The *château* was one of many Cathar *châteaus*, all famous landmarks, and there were plenty of photos online. He tapped the screen. "Look how steep it is, though! No one would see us right at the base."

"Unless they have lookouts down there, too," Barak pointed out. "It was difficult to tell last night. My night vision camera didn't pick up anything."

"Bloody hell." Estelle shook her head at the sight of the craggy ridge. "They picked the place well. I can't imagine how hard it would have been to build there."

"I guess rich owners wouldn't care about that. We could wait and move at night again," Lucien suggested. "I realise we'll lose time, though. Is there another ruin or place close by where we could watch from?"

Barak frowned. "Like setting up a blind, you mean? Like for watching animals? Perhaps. Like I said, that wasn't my priority last night. I could have missed something."

"What about traffic in the area?" Estelle asked. "There must be cars around. We could sightsee. That's what regular visitors do, right? It was something we discussed."

"Absolutely. There are roads that wind through the valleys, and lots of hiking trails. They won't be used much in this weather, though."

Lucien leaned back in his chair, eyes clouded with worry. "Do you think they'll take Jackson there? I can't believe they've taken him at all. Or," he shot them a belligerent look, "that he would betray us."

Estelle had been trying to ignore her nagging fear about his safety ever since Barak had told her the news, but now it all came flooding back. "I don't believe he'd betray us, either. No way. He was too angry with them. He hated them. Especially when he found out about James Arbuthnot."

Barak ran his fingers over his shaved scalp as he gazed out of the window and onto the pine-dotted slopes outside. "Unless it's a ruse."

"What do you mean?" Estelle asked, confused.

He faced her. "Maybe he saw an opportunity to get kidnapped. I mean, it wasn't a set-up, but perhaps he just let them have him. Maybe he wanted to get inside."

"That's a hell of a suggestion," Estelle acknowledged, "and ballsy, on his behalf."

"And insane," Lucien added. "Look what they did to me! And it doesn't answer how they found him in the first place. Or Gabe and Shadow."

"That's easy. Magic," Estelle said. "Alchemists are magicians. That's what they called John Dee. They might not have natural witchcraft abilities, but they have a way of manipulating matter. They must have used a type of finding or tracking spell.

We've encountered them enough that they would have our blood or some kind of body matter. It's a horrible thought, but probable."

"I guess that makes me feel better," Barak said. "Better than thinking someone betrayed us or is tracking us some other way. Will your protection spell help conceal the house?"

"It should. I have brought supplies with me, and also have other spells I can use. I'll craft something more personal." Estelle hated to feel as if she couldn't cope, especially after all they had faced previously, but maybe more magical help would be a good thing. "I could see if Caspian will help us."

Barak smiled. He knew the issues she'd had with her brother, but Barak liked him. "I think that's a great idea."

"And your brothers?" Lucien asked Barak. "When will they arrive?"

"Gabe and Niel will be here as soon as they can get flights. I think it's proving harder than they thought. Shadow will come with Ash, hopefully today, but maybe tomorrow. She has taken the emerald discs to JD."

Estelle had heard all about the theft and the attack. The footage of the bombed hotel in Aswan had been on the news. Deaths had been reported, but no names had been released. She squeezed Barak's arm, hoping to reassure him. "I hope Ash will be okay."

"Me, too." Barak stood abruptly, anger and concern sweeping across his face. "I need to do something useful. Let's see what we can find below the *château*."

Harlan sipped his coffee while he sat at the scrubbed wooden table in Moonfell's kitchen on Friday morning. *At least the witches made great coffee.* Not that he'd seen much of them.

When he entered the kitchen at just after seven that morning, they had all left to do various jobs, including casting the spell to find Jackson, with instructions to make himself at home—with reservations. "Don't touch the plants in the glasshouse, and don't mix the herbs to make teas. "

Did he look like a tea man?

While he waited for Maggie and Olivia to join him, he reflected on the night's events, simultaneously envying the great gothic kitchen filled with state-of-the-art kitchen appliances—nothing old-fashioned about them. He wondered how long the house had been in the witches' family. Generations, he suspected. The place felt soaked in magic. Through the open kitchen door, other rooms beckoned. Harlan wished he had more time to explore. Or the energy to.

He'd spent a restless night at Olivia's side, worried about sleeping too deeply in case something happened, but also haunted by what had transpired. He was broad-minded, but the appearance of the Goddess had shaken him. And Belial, of course. Perhaps the spell wasn't quite on the scale of the Green Man making Ravens' Wood, but it was damn close. He'd *seen* the Goddess. Or was it *a* Goddess? *No matter.* She had fought Belial, banished his spirit, and saved Olivia. She had slept uneasily, too, tossing and turning, and moaning in her sleep. Nightmares, she'd confessed when she woke up.

It hadn't helped that they were in a great gothic mansion that was very unusual, far more so than Chadwick House. He and Olivia had found that place unnerving, with the dead collector's array of arcane objects, but it was nothing compared to this place. For a start, Moonfell was more castle than mansion, and although he was sure it was his overactive imagination, Harlan had heard creaks and groans all night. He blamed the heating system and old wood settling.

When his companions finally joined him, Maggie was as lively as a box of frogs. She had obviously slept well. Somehow, that did not surprise Harlan. He imagined she would sleep well anywhere; she was too stubborn not to. She was already texting furiously to her colleagues, her lips warped in a scowl and her hair slightly unkempt. Olivia was horribly quiet, in comparison. Her answers were monosyllabic, and her fingers played with the grain on the kitchen table. The witches may have banished Belial, but he'd left an impression.

Harlan's heart sank as Birdie entered the kitchen at Moonfell, her face grim. He'd been putting a lot of hope in the witches finding Jackson. *Too much.* Her long, grey hair was plaited and wound on her head like a crown, but wisps escaped, framing her face. He tried not to get distracted by her more youthful appearance, but it was disconcerting. Her shoulders were no longer hunched, and there was an air of determination in her step.

"Well?" he said by way of greeting as she sat at the table. "Did you find him?"

"No. Not a trace." She leaned on the table, her chin on one hand. "I've tried several spells, including using scrying, as well as more traditional methods. I'm getting nothing, and it's very frustrating."

"Is he dead?" Maggie asked, as usual striking at the heart of the matter.

"Not necessarily, although that is possible. I think they have just protected him well. You said they're alchemists?"

Harlan nodded. "Some of their group are. It's how they make the soldiers. They have labs, and alchemical wheels and things." He ended vaguely, feeling inadequately educated on the subject. He rubbed his face. "I choose to believe he's alive, or they would have killed him last night." He shot a smile at Olivia. "We have to hope, right?"

"Right." She nodded, but he could tell she wasn't really paying attention.

Maggie huffed, gearing up to her usual, belligerent state. "We'll rely on old-fashioned policing methods, then. I'll head back to the station and see how my sergeants are getting on."

"I'll keep trying," Birdie reassured them, "as will my granddaughters. I'm invested now. If you hear anything new, you must tell me."

"We will," Harlan said, finishing off his coffee. "Where are Morgana and Odette? I thought they were with you."

"Odette is appeasing the Goddess after last night. Morgana is preparing for the solstice, and probably creating spells for our clients."

"Not hexes, I hope?" Maggie asked.

"You came here for help," Birdie pointed out as she stood and walked to the sink with their empty cups. "Insulting me is not a good way to get it."

Harlan glared at Maggie, mouthing, "*Shut up!*"

She mouthed a silent, "*Fuck off.*"

Harlan had no desire to piss off a powerful witch. "Sorry, Birdie. Maggie has trouble with her big mouth sometimes. Ignore her."

"I'm trying." Birdie turned around and leaned against the counter, smiling. Fortunately. "She's hard to ignore, though."

"I'm right here," Maggie said, glaring at all of them.

Harlan had a feeling they were overstaying their welcome, and didn't want to see how much more insulting Maggie might get. "I think we should go."

"You two can," Birdie said, eyes narrowing, "but I think Olivia should stay. My dear, you look horrible."

Olivia blinked as if she'd been in a trance. "Do I?"

"Yes. I take it you had dreams?"

"Nightmares, really. Flaming eyes and wings." She swallowed, lips tightening. "Will he come back?"

"I doubt it. He'll be off licking his wounds somewhere. But, it has taken a lot out of you. Stay for another day. Let's get you right, first."

Olivia blinked. "Stay? But I have work to do."

Harlan intervened. "I can call Mason and update him on your current state. This is a result of work, anyway. He'd rather you be well." Mason liked Olivia much more than he liked Harlan. He turned back to Birdie, who was still watching Olivia. "What will you do for her?"

"Give her plenty of healing teas, and a little cleansing, too."

"But she'll get better?" Maggie asked, voice sharp.

"Yes. Think of it like the flu. Sometimes exorcisms take a while to shake off. Plus, she encountered the Goddess. Do you remember, Olivia?"

Olivia nodded. "I think so. A powerful female presence. It was like two people were at war inside of me."

"They were."

Harlan kissed Olivia's cheek and squeezed her hand. "I think it's a great idea. I'll see you later, okay? Once I've been to see JD with Shadow." She'd be arriving in a few hours, and he was acting as chauffeur.

"Okay. Don't forget." She offered him a wan smile.

After Harlan and Maggie had gathered their scant belongings, Birdie accompanied them down the hall. Once they were at the door, Harlan paused. "You're more worried about Olivia than you're letting on."

"It was a powerful spell. It has affected all of us. You two as well, I suspect, although in what way I'm not sure. Did you dream?"

"I tossed and turned," Harlan confessed, "but no dreams, not really."

"I slept like the dead," Maggie said.

"I think I'll prepare an amulet for you both, anyway. I can give them to you if you're dropping in later, Harlan."

"Great, thank you."

"Good. Later, then."

Birdie swung the huge door shut, leaving Harlan feeling diminished and exposed on the doorstep of Moonfell.

Sixteen

The previous twenty-four hours had been long and exhausting, and Shadow and the team had risked their lives to get JD's emerald disc. If JD didn't start looking more appreciative soon, she'd slit his throat.

"JD," she remonstrated, "we were almost captured by museum guards, blown up, and then Ash was skewered like he was a kebab! The least you can do is say thank you."

Actually, they would never have been captured, but JD really needed to understand the risks they had taken for him. Not only had the bombed hotel been on the news, but the museum theft was covered, too. The police suspected they were linked, but there was no hard evidence to prove it. They had announced the numbers of dead and injured, but no names had been released as of yet.

JD scowled. "I said thank you!"

"You mumbled it! Say it properly, or I swear that's the last job we ever do for you!"

He stepped back, hands raised as if in surrender, as she placed her knife at his throat. "Thank you! Very much! I am eternally grateful for your help, and as an immortal being, you'll know that counts for a lot."

"And say you are sorry that Ash has been horribly injured." She tickled his chin with the point of her blade.

JD's eyes widened and he stepped back again, hitting the long benchtop in the greenhouse in his grounds. "I am *very* sorry, but if I could just point out that I was not responsible for that..."

"Er, Shadow," Harlan interrupted nervously, "maybe it would be a good idea not to kill the boss?"

She didn't move, her dagger still lifting JD's chin, reflecting that Harlan should really hold his nerve for longer. "Just a grievous wound, then? A scar to remember this conversation."

"No!"

JD squirmed. "So sorry, Shadow. I forgot my manners. I was very preoccupied with the Emerald Tablet." His voice squeaked as he added, "Excellent thinking, too, that you brought several discs with you!"

"Well, I wasn't going back." Shadow finally lowered the blade. "And I avoided being arrested at the airport. Don't forget that."

Although she had every faith that the spelled box would hide the contents, it had still been a nerve-wracking exercise, even in a government aircraft. Their escorts didn't know what Shadow and the team had been doing there, and they didn't ask. If they had been caught, most likely they would be on their own. Friends with high connections were very useful, but only to a certain extent. Ash's injury also added to her worries. His natural healing skills meant he was already recovering, but it was proving to be a slow process. Potentially, Barak's healing capabilities might be able to help Ash, but as they hadn't tested that yet, they decided to play safe by using Briar instead.

"So," Harlan said, obviously wishing to move the conversation along, "what now with the discs?"

JD, after a final nervous look at Shadow, crossed to where the discs rested on the bench. They sparkled, even with the diffused light coming through the greenhouse windows. Shadow hadn't fully appreciated their beauty in the rush of having to steal them and then escape from the hotel, but all three were magnificent. And priceless.

JD rubbed his hands together as he studied them. "We now have to see which disc fits. This one looks and feels the most likely." He tapped the one that Shadow also had thought to be the right choice.

She nodded. "I agree. It has a certain quality to it."

"Are we going to try it now?" Harlan asked.

"I don't know." Perplexed, JD tapped his lip. "I'll run it across my alchemical wheel first. And perhaps move the tablet out onto the lawn. If it grows as I hope, it will smash the greenhouse."

"Then you'll have a huge tablet in the middle of your lawn. Has Anna arranged your marquee yet?" Harlan asked, cocking an eyebrow.

"I believe so." JD didn't elaborate. He picked up the disc. "Come on you two, bring the others."

Without a backward glance, he trudged across the garden, and they followed. The day was overcast, and a brisk wind carried an icy chill. They had already exchanged their news when Harlan had collected her and Ash from the airport and driven them to JD's. She'd offered to drive a hire car after successfully passing her driving test—and almost destroying Ash's will to live—but Gabe had broken out in a sweat and said, "*I wouldn't risk the roads in London. Leave it to Harlan.*" She liked to think it was out of concern for her safety, but suspected it was more to do with a fear of her driving. She was erratic; she couldn't deny it.

Harlan, however, was preoccupied with the disc he was holding. "Do you think he'd let me keep this if it's not the one?"

"Are you kidding me? First, of course not! Secondly, *we* stole it and should therefore get to keep it!"

"I suppose you're right. It would look great on my shelf, though!"

"And link you to a heist. Probably not a good idea for either of us to have it. No one is likely to raid JD's house. He probably has a vault somewhere for such things. Which is actually a great idea. Maybe we should get one." Visions of precious icons, weapons, and jewels filled her thoughts. *It really was a brilliant idea.* However, the sound of a car engine drawing to a stop on the far side of the house brought her back to the present. "Sounds like Nahum is here."

Rather than following JD into his lab, they accompanied Anna, JD's housekeeper, to the front door, but Ash had beaten them to it. He'd been resting in JD's sitting room, propped on the sofa and supplied with tea. He hadn't even argued, which was a sign of how much his injury ached. Anna tutted and eased him out of the way, but Nahum swept inside, giving him a half-hug, with Briar right behind him. "Ash! Good to see you! I was worried."

Ash smiled. "I was worried about you, too, brother."

"And Shadow!" Nahum enveloped her in a hug, too. He smelled of spices. "Good to see you here in one piece."

"You, too," she replied, grateful for his hug that made her feel part of the family. Even after twelve months with them, and her relationship with Gabe, she sometimes felt like an outsider. "Don't think we haven't heard about Belial."

"Who?" JD had appeared silently behind them all after emerging from the stairs to his lab. His face was red with fury. "Did you say Belial? One of the Fallen?"

Everyone froze and looked at him.

"Sorry," Harlan stuttered. "I don't think I mentioned that with all the fuss about the discs."

"God's breath! You're all idiots! Nincompoops! Boils of a pestilence! Especially you, Harlan! *Belial*?"

Amused, Shadow watched Harlan's mood erupt. "JD, seriously, after the night I had, you can stick your outrage up your immortal ass!"

Nahum pushed forward, eyeing JD with grim dislike. "Is there a problem, JD?"

"One of the Fallen makes an appearance on Earth and you don't tell me?" JD placed his hands on his hips, managing to stand his ground as Nahum loomed over him.

"Oddly, whilst I was fighting for my life last night against a horde of deadly Black Cronos soldiers, I did not think to call you. Or this morning when I was driving here, worried about my brother! I suggest we discuss this later. My brother's health comes first. Agreed?"

JD looked as if he might argue, but then swiftly thought better of it. "Yes, later will be fine! Anna will provide everything you need. Harlan, Shadow?" He gestured at the discs.

Shadow decided that ensconcing JD in his lab with hours of experiments would keep him occupied and out of their hair. "Of course, JD. Nahum, Briar, I'll see you soon."

Resisting the urge to kick him down the stairs, she followed him.

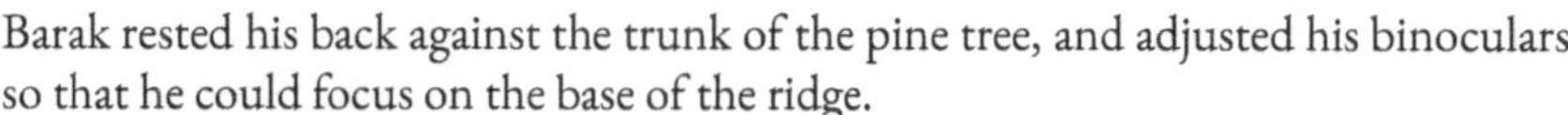

Barak rested his back against the trunk of the pine tree, and adjusted his binoculars so that he could focus on the base of the ridge.

He, Estelle, and Lucien had spent the morning driving through the valleys of the Pyrenees, admiring the landscape and taking photos like dutiful tourists. In the daylight, it was easier to see the contours of the land and the road that wound up the ridge to the *château* at the top.

From the base, it didn't seem as if there was any kind of security, but partway up, nestled under an overhang of trees, they saw what looked like a stone building and a gate across the road. They all assumed it was some kind of guard house. Driving around the neighbouring ridge, they parked by the start of a trail and walked to where they had a reasonable view of the castle.

While Estelle waited at the bottom of the tree, Lucien and Barak clambered up the trunk. Estelle had kept the shadow spell around them all, even though they were disguised by greenery.

"*Merde. C'est impossible,*" Lucien complained. "The trees are planted so thickly it's hard to see anything on the slopes. But there are tracks. For wildlife, perhaps."

"There are darker areas, though, on the eastern slope," Barak said, studying one spot in particular. "Could be caves, or maybe just a cleft in the slope. The trouble is, Lucien, if we investigate, and we're right, and someone is guarding it, we give ourselves away before anyone is here to help." He lowered the binoculars to look at Lucien, wedged on the branch below and to the right. "We can't afford to do that yet."

"No, of course not. We should keep identifying them, though. They are all places to investigate. I presume we'll split the team when we attack?"

"Yep. I prefer not more than three teams, but it depends how we plan to attack, and how many possible entrances we find." Barak studied the ridge for what felt the hundredth time. "A team could attack the top, but that's the most exposed, even though we can fly in. There are probably too many guards at the top."

"Unless we attack from the bottom, and distract them first."

"I doubt it will work like that. And who knows what strange weaponry they have here? This is their stronghold, after all."

"And there could be traps all over that ridge," Lucien pointed out. He lifted his binoculars to the sky. "I hear something."

The whump, whump noise of rotor blades announced the approach of a helicopter, and Barak was glad they'd parked next to other cars at the start of one of the hiking trails. The sleek, black helicopter headed straight to the castle.

"I wonder who that is?" Barak said. "I hope it's not Jackson."

"It might be the *comte,*" Lucien suggested. His voice grew thick with anger. "I really want to meet the man who changed my life forever."

"Be careful what you wish for," Barak said, starting to descend the thick branches. "I have a feeling he's the last one we want to meet. Let's get back to the house now, and then return tonight. With luck, Gabe and Niel will have arrived by then."

When the blindfold was removed from Jackson's eyes, he squinted against the harsh light. He hadn't seen daylight since the previous day. *If his abduction was even the day before.* He had lost track of real time.

He'd been knocked unconscious when he was captured, and when he'd awoke, he was blindfolded. His captors had barely spoken to him, except for issuing instructions. They had handled him roughly, but not cruelly, and he'd been offered water and basic food. He'd refused all of it, but that was hours earlier. Since they'd been airborne, they had said nothing at all.

When Jackson's focus returned, he saw a broad stone courtyard and an ancient castle ahead of him—a mass of towers, battlements, and thick stone. He knew exactly where he was. A mixture of fear and excitement flooded through him. *Château de Bénaix.*

They were right. This was the base for the organisation that had haunted his dreams for years. The fact that he was here surely proved that. Not that he would let on that he knew where he was, though.

His guards, two huge Black Cronos soldiers with impassive faces and muscles of steel, pushed him forward as the helicopter's engines cut out. He took the chance to orientate himself as he stumbled forward on numb legs that had been bound for hours. His hands were still bound in front of him, and a peculiar metal bracelet inscribed with sigils was on his wrist. Huge stone walls encircled the castle complex, guard towers placed at regular intervals. Vehicles were off to one side, as was a huge gate set into the wall. It was made of thick wood and bound in iron, looking Medieval in origin. *And perhaps protected by magic.* Sigils were everywhere. Giant ones were carved in stone and inscribed on metal.

Would Jackson find answers here? Or only death? *Or worse...* He eyed the soldiers that he knew were covered in tattoos beneath their winter clothing. *After all his raging and plotting against them, would he become one of them?*

He was pushed towards the huge entrance doors of the castle, also clad in iron and studded metal work. He was within feet of it when the door opened and Stefan Hope-Robbins appeared on the threshold. He hadn't changed. He looked mild-mannered in his tweeds and glasses, but still, Jackson faltered. The soldiers pushed him forward again.

Stefan smiled, but it didn't reach his eyes. "Mr Strange. Welcome to our *château*. We'd hoped to capture your companions, but you're all proving rather resourceful."

"We pride ourselves on it," Jackson said, lifting his chin defiantly.

The huge door clanged shut behind him, plunging him into the semi-darkness of an impressive entrance hall. A fire blazed in an enormous fireplace that was so huge a horse could stand in it. At least there was also central heating and electric lights; not everything was Medieval. Oil paintings and tapestries adorned the walls, and a huge double staircase led to the upper floors.

Stefan followed his gaze. "It's really something, isn't it? That's why I wanted to bring you through the front entrance. You need to appreciate all we have achieved."

Jackson stared at him. "Why would I need to appreciate that?"

"Because you need to see what you could achieve, too. Some of this wealth could be yours!" He raised his hands in a grand gesture. "You need only change your mind on your approach."

Jackson could barely believe his ears. "You want to convert me to your cause? You think I'm so pliable? I don't think you realise quite how much I loathe you and what you do!"

"Oh, I do," Stefan said. He removed the handcuffs from Jackson's wrists and led the way to a door on the right, his two guards dogging him. "Let's just say I have absolute faith in my abilities to change your mind."

They entered a much smaller but no less grand room. Another fire blazed in a stone fireplace, and the floor was lined with thick rugs. It was furnished in a mix of styles from modern to Medieval, a surprisingly pleasing juxtaposition. But it was the couple standing before the fire who Jackson focussed on. He drew a sharp intake of breath as he saw a woman who looked like The Silencer of Souls. The only difference was that her hair wasn't quite as dark, but her cold black eyes were exactly the same.

He faltered, confused. "I thought you were dead!"

It was Stefan who answered. "Your team killed her sister. There are several warriors who fulfil the role of The Silencer of Souls. Several have lost their lives in the course of their duties over the years. All consider it an honour. But you haven't met the most important member of our organisation."

Jackson's gaze shifted to the tall, slim man next to her dressed in an immaculately tailored dark grey suit. He looked to be in his mid-forties. He had light brown hair, tinged at the temple with grey, and his blue eyes fixated on Jackson like a hawk spotting prey.

"This," Stefan continued, his voice filled with pride and adoration, "is the *Comte de Saint Germain*. He has a proposition for you."

Seventeen

Ash winced as Briar deftly dressed his wound. Ash wasn't often aware of his height and build, but being next to Briar always made him feel like a giant.

She was petite and dark-haired, and for some ridiculous reason, probably the fairy stories he'd been reading to familiarise himself with different cultures, he had fixed her in his head as a kind of flower fairy. Seeing as he cohabited with a vicious fey warrior, he knew that was crazy. And yet, as she ministered to him, whispering healing spells while she worked, he had visions of her running through forests or meadows with flowers in her hair.

He must be delirious.

She looked up at him, the green ring around her brown eyes reminding him that she carried the Green Man within her. "You're very quiet, Ash. Are you okay?"

"I'm imagining you as a flower fairy. I think the pain is getting to me."

She sniggered. "Flower fairy? Herne's horns! And what do you mean, pain? You should be healing quicker than this. Although, I never saw your wound when it was fresh." He was sitting on a chair so she could reach his injury more easily, and she rocked back to look at him. "What aren't you telling me? Did something else happen?"

Ash hesitated, fearing to talk about what had preoccupied him for hours, ever since his injury. To discuss his fears aloud would make them more real. But they were alone in the ground floor bathroom. Nahum had gone to the greenhouse to study the Emerald Tablet again. Ash suspected he was putting off a discussion about Belial. Shadow and Harlan were with JD.

"Spit it out, Ash. What happened?"

He needed advice, and Briar was level-headed. "When the bomb went off, I was in the room that was ground zero. I should be dead, really. Anyway, I was blasted through the wall, with chunks of masonry and metal and furniture. Time can slow for us sometimes in moments of stress..."

"It can for us, too," she said. "It's weird, like everything's happening at a very slow speed. They say time is relative, right? Sorry, go on."

"Instinct kicked in, and I extended my wings. I smacked the wall in another room, and instantaneously was hit by lots of things, including the chunk of metal that pinned me to the wall. I retracted my wings, but they were damaged, and they wrenched, badly. Especially this one." He tapped his injured shoulder.

Briar frowned. "But your wings are magical, like you. Surely they've healed themselves?"

He summoned his courage. "I tried to open them earlier, in the sitting room when I was alone. The left one won't open." His fears came tumbling out, magnifying as he spoke. "If I can't use my wings, I'm not a true Nephilim. I'm some bloody half creature! I'm *useless*!"

"Shush. Calm down." Her hands cupped his face. "You are always a Nephilim, no matter what happens to your wings. They must have been injured before?"

"Minor only. Broken bones, burnt feathers. But this feels like something fundamental!" Panic filled him again. "It's not even like it hurt to use it. It won't manifest at all!"

"The body is clever. Injuries hurt because they alert us that something is wrong. To keep using a part of the body when it's injured is stupid! You will only aggravate it. Make it worse. Maybe your body knows better than you do. Perhaps your wing will stay safe where it belongs until it's healed. Wherever that is!"

He smiled, feeling ever so slightly reassured. The witches, and everyone else for that matter, always wondered where their wings went. It was hard to explain. They were always there, and yet, they weren't.

"Plus," she continued as she wrapped a large bandage around his shoulder and under his arm, "my magic works on many levels, as I'm sure your healing does, too. I suggest you don't try to summon your wing until you've healed a bit more."

"But that's the other issue. I should have healed more by now!"

"The bigger the injury, the bigger the shock to the body, and the longer it takes to heal."

"I've been stabbed by swords, spears, and daggers over the years!"

"But has your shoulder been pinned to the wall by a piece of red-hot metal?

"No, I guess not."

Briar tutted. "Stress slows healing, and all of you have been obsessed with Black Cronos, as well as being involved in other things."

"I'm a Nephilim. We're used to stress and fighting. We were bred for it."

"You are also half human! Honestly, Ash. How old are you? You know this! You're a scholar and a clever man."

"Not when it applies to me," he replied sullenly. He felt like a scolded child.

"Men! You're all alike." Satisfied that the dressing was finished, she leaned against the bathroom sink. "How does that feel?"

He flexed his shoulder. "Secure. Cool. The burning has subsided."

"Good. I used my special burn cream on it, and a few extras. The paste is packed with healing herbs, too." Briar hesitated, her teeth working on her upper lip. "I'm worried about all of you, actually. Especially after Eli and Nahum's behaviour last night. You all have your strengths and weaknesses. Niel is headstrong..."

"That's an understatement," Ash muttered.

Briar smirked. "So is Gabe, although he tempers it. That's his natural leadership quality, I guess. Nahum is more measured. Eli is a lover. Barak is a joker—and a bit of a romantic, I think. You are a scholar. Zee is a listener. What worries me is that those who I consider to be the more level-headed amongst you are being irrational! You're taking crazy risks! Stealing an emerald disc from a museum—several discs, in fact! Priceless artifacts that put you on the news! That's madness. Rash!"

"Finding Templar treasure put us on the news, too!"

"But that wasn't illegal. You were hired to do that! And," she continued, eyes blazing, "Eli and Zee made a mad pact with the dryads, which I appreciate was to help us, but even so!"

Ash saw her point. "Last night they were under attack with very few options, but I accept that it's been quite an interesting few months, hasn't it?"

"And then some. You're all scaring me a little, and the other witches."

"Scaring you? Why?"

"Because we care about you. You're our friends. Every single one of you. I know you arrived in this world under a storm cloud and things weren't easy, but look at what you've achieved! You must remember that you're not immortal—just long-lived, and yes, super strong and fast-healing. *But* you could still die, just like anyone else. You're surrounded by humans in a world where the paranormal takes a back seat. I understand that it probably clouds your judgment sometimes, but you're risking a lot!" He stared at her, unable to respond, because he knew that she was right—in part, at least. She sighed, humour once again returning. "That's it. Lecture over. I'm just worried, that's all."

He smiled. "Did you give Nahum an earful on the way up?"

"No. He was driving. I thought it might distract him."

"Lucky him."

"I say it because I care."

"Thank you. You're a good friend, Briar."

"I try."

"What will I do without you when I have to fly to France?"

Her impish grin returned. "Rely on Estelle. I'm sure she has a tender side."

He laughed. "Only for Barak! No, that's unfair. She's been good with all of us. She's even got a sense of humour!"

"A little love works wonders." A trace of sadness crossed her face, and Ash knew she was thinking of Hunter. "I'm just sorry we can't come with you."

"We'll be fine," he said, sounding as confident as possible.

As long as he healed. As long as his wings worked. The thought that he wouldn't fly again filled him with horror.

Nahum felt as if he'd betrayed his brothers as well as himself by using Belial's jewellery, and he suspected Ash thought so, too, which was why he was lurking alone in the greenhouse. He also sensed that Briar had been holding back her feelings in the car.

He tried to distract himself from worrying about their current troubles by studying the Emerald Tablet. Unfortunately, stray thoughts of Olivia kept popping into his mind. Her warm hands, smooth as silk skin, and soft, welcoming mouth. *Herne's horns. What had he done?* Belial had thrown him off his stride in more ways than one.

The trouble was, he had avoided sex ever since he arrived in this world. It had complicated his previous life; he hadn't wanted it to complicate this one. Unlike Gabe, his marriage was loveless, and he did not have children. His marriage was to unite the warring Houses of the Fallen. An alliance between him and the half-sister of another Nephilim. As he predicted, it had meant politics, manoeuvrings, arguments, and general annoyance. He had not been a faithful husband, but she had also not been a faithful wife. He continued to fight, drowning himself in blood, and then entered the courts of kings to negotiate peace. But the politics of that marriage had rumbled on.

That was one good thing about the flood—his marriage was over. He couldn't even say that he was scarred by it. He didn't harbour any feelings one way or the other towards his wife. Now, he sought to keep his life uncomplicated. And he was determined that it would remain so. Olivia was a woman of the world. He had stipulated the rules, and she had been happy to comply. It was fine. He probably wouldn't see her for months. *So, why was he so worried about her?* Because he was a friend, *obviously.*

"What are you talking to yourself about?" Shadow said, sounding amused.

He leapt around, sword drawn. "Herne's fucking balls, Shadow! Do you have to creep around?"

"I am fey!" She smirked as she leaned against the greenhouse door. He hadn't even felt a cold draught as she entered. "You were bobbing your head and muttering. You look quite cross!" She strolled down the gravel path towards him, hips swinging, dagger twirling between her fingers. "Are you chastising yourself for wearing Belial's jewellery?"

"Yes, absolutely." It wasn't a total lie.

In a split second her dagger vanished, and she wagged a finger at him. "I think it's more than that. Did something happen with Olivia?"

"*No*! What makes you say that?"

"Because you're all riled up, and you, Nahum, are never riled up." She prowled around the tablet, watching him, her figure sometimes blinking out of sight as her fey glamour soaked up the green earthiness of the greenhouse.

"I drew on Belial's power last night, in case you forgot. I was incandescent! Of course I'm annoyed."

"As insane as that was, I think it was a brilliant strategic move. You know he can't possess you. Unsettle you, yes. Worry he might have growing influence in this world, yes, but he cannot affect you unwillingly."

"No, but he's still powerful. He got under my skin, and he shouldn't have. And, it was horrifying to *feel* so powerful. I killed a lot of soldiers. I feel bad about it. They didn't stand a chance." As soon as he said it, he knew it was true. Killing vicious enemies was one thing, but they could barely respond to their onslaught.

"Bollocks! It was Black Cronos, and they were coming for *you*. They deserved what they got. They burned our loggia! But that's not what you're truly annoyed about, because you don't really regret killing them. Logically, you know it was right. So that means you are mulling over something else you did that bothers you a lot more. And you spent twenty-four hours with Olivia!" Her violet eyes sparkled with mischief.

"You are just obsessed with sex now that you're with Gabe!"

"Ha! I *knew* it! I didn't even mention sex, and that's the first thing you said!"

"You were implying it!"

"I implied *something*!" She leaned against the bench, arms folded across her chest as she grinned at him. "Well, well, well! Go you, Nahum!" She winked. "I bet she's like a wildcat in bed!"

"Shadow! Shut up! You can't speculate on someone's performance."

"People speculate all the time up here!" She tapped her head for emphasis. "Anyway, I don't need details. I'm just glad you're not denying it! In case you're wondering, Gabe and I have *great* sex. You probably don't need to hear that, but tough. Your brother—"

Nahum covered his ears with his hands. "No! Shut up! Shadow, you are exasperating."

Shadow was obviously beyond pleased with herself. She continued to grin at him. "Fine. I won't share details if you won't. She must have made an impression, though, or you wouldn't be so annoyed."

He lowered his hands, wanting to strangle her instead. "I would appreciate you not sharing this with my brothers."

"I have to tell Gabe, but fair enough. I won't tell the rest. You know they'll work it out, though."

"No, they won't. I am very discreet. It's only because you snuck up on me that you know anything at all."

"You're not denying that she made an impression, I notice."

"Don't push it, Shadow! We had fun, and that's all I'm saying. I'm worried because we're friends, and I don't want to ruin that. Sex can, you know."

"And obviously you're so irresistible she won't be able to keep her hands off you." She laughed, holding her own hands up to placate him. "I'm kidding! She's an adult, and very savvy. I like her. I can put up with her over Estelle anytime."

"You won't have to put up with her because we only have a working relationship. Nothing else."

"Fine. If you say so."

"I do! And, in case you hadn't heard, because of me, she ended up infected by Belial!"

"Harlan told me, but I'm not sure how it happened."

Nahum kicked the greenhouse bench in annoyance. "She touched his bloody jewellery. I didn't tell her not to quick enough, and to be honest, I'd forgotten how much it would affect her."

"I don't think I need to point out that it wasn't your fault," Shadow said, unexpectedly sympathetic, "but I understand why you feel guilty. What are we going to do about Belial?"

He smiled. "You want to help?"

"Of course! Gabe is furious about it all." Shadow's teasing manner vanished. "As soon as this business is over—Black Cronos, I mean—we will hunt for the agent who put his stuff in the reliquary. Although, you know that could have been done centuries ago."

"I suspect it's far more recent than that. But finding him, or her, won't be easy. And, by the way, I doubt very much if Black Cronos will ever be finished."

She shrugged. "You never know. The Gods might smile on us. Perhaps they already have."

"You never put your faith in the Gods. Or Goddesses."

"That's true." Shadow ran her finger along her blade. "I trust my companions and my weapons. And I include JD in that lot. Perhaps he will provide something for us that can make all the difference. But I was referring to Belial's very powerful jewellery. Maybe you found it for a reason. Maybe you're meant to use it on Black Cronos...again."

An uneasy feeling rippled through him. "I don't know if I, or Eli, would want to do that again, Shadow. It really shook him up."

"You don't have to. Perhaps Niel will, or Gabe. Maybe Barak?"

"I don't think they should, either."

"Nahum, we might not have a choice."

Harlan would rather not be hanging around in JD's lab. He would prefer to spend his time talking to the new arrivals, but JD seemed to want him there.

"You see," JD muttered as he adjusted his wheel of correspondences, "this is the alchemical signature of the Emerald Tablet. But this doesn't match it." He was referring to the emerald disc that they thought was the likely match.

"What does that mean?" Harlan asked.

"I don't know. Maybe it's not the one."

"Or maybe it doesn't have to match. Perhaps that's the point. It *adds* to the tablet. Enhances it, somehow."

JD gave him a sidelong glance. "That's an interesting suggestion."

"I know, right? I'm not just a pretty face."

JD tapped his lips while he stared at the wheel. "I noticed that the tablet has certain properties, but it's missing some that I would expect..." he trailed off, falling silent.

Harlan hated playing catch up. "Like what?" he prompted.

"Earth is missing. Elemental fire, air, and water are present, as well as a selection of metals. I won't bore you with the details." He went quiet again, but then yelled, "Ha! I am a fool!" JD moved the wheel slightly, making minute adjustments to all the concentric rings.

Harlan thought it a waste of time. "Why don't you just stick it in the base and see what happens?"

"Preparation is always the key!"

"But maybe you don't need to prepare anything."

Once again, JD didn't answer him directly. "'The power is complete when it is turned to Earth. Separate the Earth from Fire, the subtle from the gross, gently and with great ingenuity.'"

"What are you saying?"

"That is part of the script written on the Emerald Tablet. Alchemists have debated on its meaning for hundreds of years."

"You think it relates to the missing piece?"

"Perhaps. It could refer to many things. But no one has seen the tablet for, well, millennia. Only the script is known. So..."

Harlan nodded with understanding. "Everyone has debated its meaning, but it's intended for only one thing. The base!"

"Perhaps! One should not assume."

"And the other discs? Why are they so similar?"

"I don't know." He stepped back after adjusting the final circle. Nothing happened. He huffed. "God's pox."

"Not quite right?" Harlan ventured.

"No. Never mind, it was unlikely I would ascertain it's properties the first time around."

JD looked like he was settling in for hours of adjustments. All around him, jars bubbled and strange scents filled the room. One of these liquids could be JD's key to immortality. *Would he be so obvious about it? Would he share it if Harlan asked? Or did he assume, correctly of course, that Harlan wouldn't have a clue what it was, even if it was there?*

"I'll leave you to it then, JD."

"Wait." He focussed on Harlan properly for the first time. "What's this about Belial?"

Harlan groaned. He'd thought he'd avoided that discussion, but reluctantly outlined the issue as succinctly as he could.

"His power is in the jewellery? Interesting. True, angelic power, as close to pure as can be. I wonder if others could harness it?"

"The Nephilim did."

"I mean in another way."

"What about Olivia, JD? Does her health not matter to you? I witnessed something both amazing and terrifying last night. Olivia could have been killed! So could I!"

JD fixed his shrewd, hazel eyes on him. "I am very glad you both survived. But we shouldn't avoid these possibilities. I'll speak to Nahum about it later."

"I suggest you be quick about it. They're all heading to France soon. I'm hoping they find Jackson, because so far, it's as if he's vanished into thin air."

"Of course. They've done well to find that place. Interesting that it should be a base of the Cathars. They were considered heretics, you know." He scratched his nose with an ink-stained finger. "Which reminds me, I have something to share. Have everyone come up to my observation room in an hour."

Eighteen

Jackson didn't want to sit and drink tea with the *Comte de Saint Germain*. He wanted to punch him repeatedly in the face, but seeing as The Silencer of Souls was staring at him with fierce intensity, he settled for refusing to shake his hand.

The *comte* smiled, revealing white, even teeth. "Charmed to meet you, Mr Strange. It seems our organisation and yours have been at odds recently." His voice was smooth, his accent hard to place. It sounded vaguely European.

"Hardly at odds," Jackson shot back. "More like at war."

"Your term, not mine. I think you misunderstand our purpose." He sat, gesturing Jackson to sit opposite him. He crossed his legs, hitching his trousers as he did so to prevent creases. He was fastidious, and it instantly irritated Jackson even more. Unwillingly, he sat down. The *comte* continued, "I am an alchemist, pure and simple. I, like my colleagues, seek to understand the universe and the world we live in. How we are made. Not romantically so, as if we are stardust. No! Our essence. Our spirit! How we can all be a part of a greater consciousness!"

"Like the Borg?"

The count frowned. "The what?"

"Forget it! It's a pop culture reference."

"And that is the problem! Television. It's a distraction. I presume that is to what you refer?"

"Can you get to the point?" Jackson asked. "This is all rather tedious."

Stefan had disappeared after introducing them, but now he returned with tea in a fine, bone china teapot. He fussed and poured two cups, and then offered one to Jackson.

"No, thank you."

The count sighed. "I hear you have refused all liquids and food. That won't do at all. It's stupid, and you are not a stupid man. Have a drink."

"I have no wish to be poisoned."

"I am drinking it, too."

"You've probably acclimatised yourself to it."

"If I wanted you dead, you already would be," the *comte* snapped.

Jackson had to admit that his throat felt like sandpaper. He accepted the drink with a nod. *Fine. Let them play politely.* He was English, after all. It was in his blood.

"Perhaps you'd like to explain why you've kidnapped me and brought me here, wherever this is!"

"This place is my home, where I first found my love of alchemy." He expanded his elegant hands. "My spiritual home, and the base of my work."

Jackson stared around the room, drinking it in, and preparing to lie. "But where is it? The Alps? It's mountainous. We thought your base would be on Ley Lines or something. We've spent months combing places like that. Centres of power! We didn't expect this." He studied the count, eyes narrowed, attempting to goad him. "If I'm honest I expected something a little more magical."

"I don't need magical! I create my own magic by bending the universe to my will." He leaned forward, eyes hard. "You're trying to provoke me. You won't."

"But this is the Alps, right? Which part?"

"Let's talk about why you're here." The count placed the cup on the occasional table that looked like an antique. "Your team, the Nephilim, have killed many of my soldiers. They are, admittedly, formidable opponents, especially for so few. And the two women. Interesting."

It sounded like the *comte* was digging, but Jackson just sipped his tea.

"Our fields of interest are, for the most part, different," he continued. "I'm suggesting a truce. We can go about our business, and you can go about yours."

"Your business being kidnapping and torturing to make enhanced humans—against their will?"

"Some sacrifices are necessary, but not all are opposed to it."

"Lucien didn't think so." Jackson didn't dare mention his grandfather. It might cause him to lose control, and perhaps give away too much of his own interests. "Lucien has been fighting to regain control of his own body for months."

"Your little team of two interrupted a process of transformation when you stole him. It was highly dangerous."

"I think you'll find the word is *rescue*. He's not an object. He's a person! And he is not very pleased with you." Jackson decided to test the count's knowledge. "He's been near death several times. I'm not sure we'll ever help him recover."

The count laughed. "Come now, Jackson. That's clumsy. We both know that you have stabilised him." His eyes flashed with annoyance. "Quite ingeniously, I gather."

Jackson's stomach twisted with dread. "So, we have a spy." He wondered who the spy was. Surely not Waylen.

Please not Waylen.

The count continued, taking pleasure in Jackson's angst. "I prefer to call it a convert to our cause. I won't tell you who, but suffice it to say he's far happier with our recompense than yours." His eyes glittered. "Your friends caused a lot of expensive damage to one of our facilities. In fact, they have caused an incredible amount of damage to our organisation as a whole."

"You started it when you attacked The Order of the Midnight Sun."

"They wanted what was ours."

"You *both* had a claim to it. Perhaps you should have negotiated for that, too. And we shouldn't forget the Igigi. You tried to destroy an ancient race. Kidnap them, too. And Ash."

"Like I said, sacrifices must be made for progress. But," the count smoothed his suit lapels, preening, "as I said, we must come to an agreement."

Jackson smiled. "Because we're winning. You fear what we'll do next."

"You're not winning. You're like flies that we continually must bat away." He darted forward, like a cobra, and Jackson shot back in his seat. "Do you know how long I've been an alchemist? How old I am?"

"From my investigations, I estimate possibly seven hundred years old."

"A better guess than some have made. Closer to nine hundred, actually."

Jackson blinked in shock. *He'd suggested seven hundred as an exaggeration, but nine hundred...* "How do I know you're not lying? You could be someone pretending to be the *comte*. He courted controversy. People often thought him a liar."

"I courted controversy? Ridiculous! Many feared me, because of what I knew. Of the secrets I kept. Others, powerful men and women, sought to use me." He shrugged. "It worked both ways. I used them, too. Used their influence. Their money. And over all that time, I never met your Mr John Dee. I kept away from the Elizabethan court during his *actual* lifetime."

Jackson decided there was no point in lying. "He met you, in what he thought was *your* real lifetime."

That seemed to delight the count. "He met me, and I didn't know? Interesting. We're talking about the 1700s, I presume?"

Jackson nodded. "I believe so. He kept his distance after that. Thought you were a charlatan, actually. Until recently, of course."

"Oh, good. How nice to confound one's enemies. I've known about him a little longer, maybe a hundred years or so. We immortals have developed very good skills of deception. Of course, our longevity allows us to make money, and acquire the objects of our heart's desire. Eventually."

Jackson had always thought that he would hate immortality. "It must be a long and lonely life. Have you offered to make other humans immortal?"

"I have never liked anyone enough to do so. Some people become extremely tedious, very quickly. Others, I miss. However," he gestured to The Silencer of Souls, "Deandra and a few other soldiers live much longer lives than a normal human. She is over eighty years old, and some are older. The two soldiers at the door, your escorts, are over a hundred. Part of the process of their transformation." He shrugged, a callous gesture, as if they were inconsequential. "With each enhancement, they live a little longer. My earlier experiments lived only twenty or so years longer than usual. Stefan has added a great deal to our endeavours."

"They live longer because they have a purpose to you. You use them."

"Like you use the Nephilim? Your own little army." The count smiled maliciously. "We are not so different."

Jackson clenched his fists, willing himself to be calm. "We are *very* different."

"Delusional, but have it your own way."

Jackson wasn't sure what he expected of the count. He wasn't even sure that he existed at all, despite their speculations. But looking at him now, hearing his smooth words and reasoned explanations, he wasn't surprised at his tone. He'd spent hundreds of years doing what he wanted to do, reasoning his way through his behaviour and justifying it. He was a sociopath, no doubt about that. JD certainly had traits of one, as well. The need to achieve and succeed, regardless of the consequences. Despite his revulsion, Jackson was also fascinated by him.

Jackson put his empty cup aside, deciding he should find out as much as he could while he had the chance. "Why didn't you approach JD? Another immortal alchemist could have helped you."

"John would never have helped me. I could tell." He looked amused. "His ideals and mine were quite different. He worked with that angel summoner, Edward Kelly. Now, there was a charlatan! But there was no doubt that John was brilliant, even though he was susceptible in his desperation to speak to angels." His eyes darkened. "As a mortal, he had the ear of a powerful queen—for a while, at least. But John also made a few bad decisions. Ended up penniless. *Fool.* And then he died, or so I thought. When I realised he had achieved immortality, he had already set up The Orphic Guild. We competed several times over the years. I, obviously, made sure to keep my distance."

Jackson had a sudden flash of insight. *The count was jealous of JD.* He was a brilliant rival. A threat. He must have considered other alchemists the same. In addition, to offer anyone else immortality would also be a threat to his superiority. *How did Stefan feel about that?* To be used for his own brilliance in alchemy, but never trusted with that final step of never-ending life. Unless he was hoping to steal the knowledge, somehow—or make the breakthrough on his own, like JD and the count had. Stefan was watching their conversation in silence, Jackson noted. He hadn't been invited to participate in the conversation and drink tea. Like The Silencer, Deandra, he was standing. While Deandra was impassive, Stefan's eyes darted between them. *Perhaps Stefan could be a useful ally...if Jackson ever had the chance to talk to him alone.*

Jackson forced himself to relax, and leaned back in his chair. "Why did you make your super-soldiers in the first place?"

The count shrugged. "Because I could. The more I researched, and the more I discovered how the universe worked, of its design, I knew that given time I could manipulate it. It was a challenge, and still is. There are things I still wish to achieve, but can't." His eyes hardened. "Like giving my soldiers wings. That continues to defy me."

"Maybe you need angelic intervention," Jackson suggested.

"I do not need help. I will get there. Eventually. But that brings me back to my point. These fights with your men hinder me. They are a distraction. We either end this, or I end them."

"But you've tried and failed. They're harder to kill than you thought."

"Oh, I don't know. It seems we successfully killed four of them last night."

All of Jackson's hard-fought composure left him. "What? *How?* You're lying!"

He smiled maliciously. "Of course! You have been trussed up and unable to see the news! Your friends were in Egypt on business. Gabreel, Shadow, Asher, and Othniel. Yes, I know all their names—thanks to our spy. We planted a bomb in their hotel rooms, one of my own design. And now..." He threw his hands wide. "*Gone!*"

Jackson floundered, horrified. "I don't believe it."

"The rest will be dead soon." The count's hands tightened on the arm of the chair, his knuckles whitening. "There was an unfortunate delay last night, but we will strike again. Unless *you* negotiate peace."

Jackson noted that throughout the entire conversation, the count had not referred to Barak and Estelle's close proximity once. *Did he know? Was he holding it back to taunt him about later?* He hoped that Harlan and Olivia were safe somewhere. *And what about the other Nephilim? He said there'd been a setback, but what?* Jackson's head was whirling with questions, and he didn't know what to do. He certainly didn't believe that Gabe and the others were dead. But he couldn't discount the spy. *What if they were gone?*

Jackson was, however, very certain of one thing. "I will certainly not negotiate for peace with you! A man who tortures humans and changes them without their consent. Who makes bombs and weapons! You're not an alchemist. You're a monster. You won't change. You'll continue to do it, unchecked!"

"I told you, Stefan!" The count stood and turned to the professor, who straightened in anticipation. "I knew he would be stubborn. The misguided and self-righteous always are. Take him below." He gave Jackson a glittering smile. "You have no idea of the scale of what I have achieved. What you see may change your mind. Then we'll talk again."

Nineteen

Maggie showed her police identification to the security guards stationed at The Retreat's entrance beneath Hyde Park, huffing with impatience as they scrutinised her badge.

She tried to calm down. They were only doing their job. They were both humourless, although that wasn't surprising, seeing as they were stuck underground all day. She would rather shoot herself.

One guard lifted his gaze from the computer screen. "You have no appointment."

"I know. I'm the head of paranormal policing in London, and I need to see the director urgently."

"He sees no one without an appointment."

"He'll see me. It's about Jackson Strange."

She had decided to visit Waylen Adams, the head of the Paranormal Division, when her own enquiries proved fruitless. Irving and Stan had run into dead ends in their efforts to track down Black Cronos, and so had she. Their black vans had vanished, leaving no trace of Jackson's whereabouts, and she hadn't got the manpower to search through all the security footage in London. Nor would her boss sanction it. Not yet, anyway. And now, Waylen wasn't answering her phone calls. It infuriated her. His colleague and her friend had been kidnapped! The least he could do was answer his fucking phone.

Hence her grand plan to visit Waylen. She had met him once a few years earlier at an official police function. She couldn't remember exactly what it was for. He certainly hadn't been introduced as head of the PD then, but she knew his name from Layla Gould, the PD's birdlike doctor. She'd met her several times over intriguing investigations, and liked her a lot. Like Maggie, she was direct and forceful. Qualities she admired in anyone. That was her one and only meeting with Waylen, and she'd barely spoken to him since. Until the one call this morning to report Jackson's abduction. Fortunately, Harlan had visited The Retreat to see Jackson, and had told her where the entrance was located.

The second guard finally handed over Maggie's ID and then searched her bag slowly and methodically. Sarcastically, Maggie asked, "Do I need to bend over, too?"

Without missing a beat, he said, "No thank you, Madam. Your bag is quite sufficient."

While he searched, his colleague phoned Waylen. As far as she could gather, he didn't have a secretary. That seemed odd. Clearly, the PD did things differently. After a hushed conversation, in which the guard eyed her with suspicion, he finally nodded and ended the call.

"He'll see you."

"Thank you!"

He ignored her sarcasm. "Step into the scanner, please."

In another minute, after feeling like her privacy had been utterly violated, she was made to wait on a hard bench. With every passing second, she wondered if he would see her in the entrance and then dismiss her. She grew more and more angry, until a small, Indian woman walked up the long corridor, her heels clicking on the floor.

"DI Milne?"

"Yes!" Maggie leapt to her feet and shook her hand.

"I'm Petra. I've come to take you to Waylen. He's very busy, so sorry."

"So am I. If he answered his fucking phone, I wouldn't need to come!"

The woman stuttered. "O-oh! I guess he's been tied up." She walked down the corridor, looking at Maggie nervously. "I run the stats for England. I keep track of the paranormal activity in your area. We're all very upset about Jackson. Have you heard anything from him?"

Maggie softened slightly. "Not a thing. Those alchemically enhanced monsters have disappeared into the night. I need answers! Is Waylen always such a dick?"

"Er, no!"

"So, what the fuck is going on?" Maggie knew she was swearing a lot, especially at this young woman who seemed very pleasant, but she was exasperated. And the more annoyed she was, the worse her language became. She considered swearing a healthy exercise in reducing her stress levels.

"I honestly don't know!" Petra explained, darting nervous glances at her as they walked further into the labyrinthine interior of The Retreat. "I'm just an analyst. Me and Austin! It's all we do."

"You must see a lot, though."

"Only through reports," she persisted. "Jackson asked us to keep a particular vigilance for Black Cronos and their activities, but other than last night's attacks, they've been very quiet."

Maggie had been taking in the Art Nouveau features of the PD while they walked, noting side corridors, ornate mouldings, and inner, stained glass windows of what seemed like a lot of empty offices. There was a peculiar, hushed quality to the place, like it had just woken from a long sleep. It was nothing like a police station, with its ceaseless noise and bustle. Now, however, she stopped and stared at Petra. "Attacks? There were more? Where?"

"There was one in Cornwall. DI Newton's team dealt with it. Although, there was nothing much to deal with. Black Cronos's team was all killed in White Haven. There have been lots of reports of angels over White Haven recently. Christmas come early, according to some. A helicopter crashed there, too."

Maggie needed to call Newton. She'd been so busy that she'd barely paid attention to the news on the TV. "No civilian casualties?"

"None."

She ran through the events of last night, trying to work out what had happened. Olivia had phoned Nahum after they had been attacked, but couldn't get through. As far as she knew, he hadn't returned the call. Not that she'd heard, anyway. He lived in Cornwall and had returned there after dropping Olivia off. *Two attacks at roughly the same time...*

"Are you okay?" Petra asked.

"Just thinking what a strange coincidence two attacks are."

"I agree. It suggests prior knowledge of their whereabouts."

"Well, Black Cronos knows where the Nephilim live. They've attacked them there before. The Nephilim won that fight. However, I gather the Nephilim are split up at the moment." She huffed, feeling uneasy. "Let's see what Waylen thinks."

"He's in the lab at the moment, with Russell Blake."

"Who's that?"

"The Assistant Director, and head of the lab." She rolled her eyes. "He's becoming obsessed with alchemy. The alchemists in the lab are spending more and more time there. Russell asks me to update him on Black Cronos, too."

"You employ alchemists here? Why?"

"Because they're looking into Black Cronos and trying to understand their achievements." She laughed nervously. "It makes it sound like we have huge numbers of them. There are only two of them. They were just regular scientists who worked here, but when Black Cronos became more active again, they changed their studies. We have two labs, you see, side by side," she explained when she saw Maggie's confused expression. "One is more traditional, one is modern."

Maggie wasn't sure what she thought about that. It made sense, obviously, but she was starting to develop a dislike of alchemists altogether.

Petra continued to chatter nervously for the next few minutes, questioning Maggie on her job as they progressed deeper into the complex. Maggie knew the place was big, Harlan had said so, but this was vast. He hadn't fully relayed how big it was, although maybe he had and she hadn't been paying full attention. Hyde Park and Kensington Gardens were enormous. She really should have worked it out. They had passed the offices that were in use and had branched off down another passage when Petra announced, "Here we are. Layla works down here, too."

The noise of chatter and the hum of machinery replaced the hushed quiet of the corridors. They passed a series of offices, and then reached two well equipped labs with giant glass windows that were opposite each other on a broad corridor. It was obvious which was the alchemy lab. There was no fancy machinery present; instead, there was a dizzying arrangement of bubbling jars, tubes, and Bunsen burners. Yet, there seemed an air of sophistication to it. Huge white boards with scribbled symbols were on every wall, and a furious argument seemed to be taking place in front of the far one.

Petra hesitated. "Oh! This might not be a good time. Perhaps—"

Maggie cut her off. *This seemed like the perfect time.* "Who's Waylen arguing with, the guy with the rolled-up shirt sleeves?"

"That's Russell. He's been stressed lately."

"About what?"

"Getting results on Black Cronos's weapons. They seemed to be making progress, and then, all of a sudden, they weren't. Of course, that's made Waylen angry, too." Petra squirmed, seeming guilty about the admission. "It's been tense here lately, but I'm sure it will get better."

There were four others in there wearing white lab coats, three men and one woman. "Which ones are the alchemists?"

"The woman, her name is Lynn, and the man with the grey hair, Frazer. The other two are the regular scientists." Petra tried to pull her away. "Perhaps we should wait in an office."

"Let's not," Maggie said, and pushed the door open. The voices became louder.

Waylen Adams stood with his hands on his hips, glowering at Russell. "But I don't understand! You said you were making progress, and now it's failed? How?"

"This is alchemy! Like any science, there are upsets and failure."

"But we can't afford that to happen! We're playing catch up now, but we're actually getting further behind!"

Lynn interrupted him. "I must admit, I'm baffled. The latest run of experiments..."

"That's enough, Lynn!" Russell cut her off. "We'll just try again."

The woman looked outraged. "Russell! This bears debate! We've almost done a full U-turn!" She gestured to her colleague. "We were saying only a few days ago..."

Russell again tried to shut her down, but Waylen intervened. "Russell! Stop being so rude! I would like to hear Lynn's opinion!"

Russell looked furious and marched away, hands clenched. While Waylen questioned the woman, Maggie watched Russell. They were still only just inside the room, and no one had noticed them enter. She leaned close and whispered in Petra's ear, "Is Russell a scientist?"

She nodded. "Yes. That's how he got the job. He's been so weird lately, though. Grumpy. Short-tempered. The failures have been a huge issue. Especially after what they achieved with Lucien. Obviously, that funny little man called JD worked with them on that."

Maggie started to feel very uneasy. Black Cronos knew all about their enemy's whereabouts, and experiments were failing. She suspected that someone here was helping them.

"Any new staff here lately?" Maggie asked Petra, eyeing the scientists.

"No. They've all been here for years. Moved with us from the old place, after that was blown up."

"No breaches here, though?"

"No. But security is tighter. And besides," Petra shrugged. "No one much cares about us down here. The government mostly pretends we don't exist. Black Cronos causes issues, but they're not considered a national security threat, neither is any paranormal activity. It's just not big enough."

Maggie knew that. It echoed her own policing experience. "And Russell?"

"Been here years, too. He's Waylen's right-hand man. Knows everything about this place."

As the voices continued to rise and all the scientists joined in, Maggie said, "Time to intervene, I think."

She marched across the room, the strange smells and bubbling noises dogging her every step, as well as Petra. "Mr Adams! It's DI Milne. You agreed to see me."

Waylen turned, surprised to see her. "Ah, yes. You know, this may not be a good time..."

Maggie was potentially risking her job in challenging the head of the PD, but fuck it. "I think it's the perfect time. Jackson Strange has been kidnapped, I can't find him, and you're arguing about experiments. We need to talk." Maybe he didn't care because he knew exactly where Jackson was. *Christ. Had she walked into the lions' den?*

"DI Milne, I share your concerns, but this is important."

She met his stare with her own, refusing to backdown. "More important than your kidnapped colleague? We need to talk. Now. The sooner we talk, the sooner I'll be out of here."

An uncomfortable silence fell as everyone stared at Maggie. Waylen huffed. "Fine." He turned to the others. "I will be back. We have a major issue here that we need to get to the bottom of. We need a comprehensive investigation. Maybe an audit. I want a breakdown of every experiment on my desk by nine o'clock tomorrow morning."

As they gasped at the timeframe, he continued to rant, and Maggie was temporarily forgotten. She studied their faces, wondering if one of them had betrayed the PD. All she saw was anger and confusion.

Was she just completely paranoid? Had Black Cronos got to her, too?

Twenty

W hen Gabe and Niel finally landed in France, Gabe was tired and worried about his friends, as well as being furious at being blown up.

"It shouldn't have taken so long to get here," he complained to Niel.

"At least we *are* here!" he pointed out, as they walked through the airport to find the rental car companies. "I consider it a Christmas miracle."

"If it was a miracle, then we should have been here hours ago!"

The past few hours in Aswan had been a nightmare. After the bomb had exploded and they stabilised Ash, they had landed just inside the grounds of the international airport under the cover of darkness. Fortunately, the airport wasn't busy enough to be open twenty-four hours a day, and they hadn't needed to worry about incoming flights and control towers spotting them. It also helped that they were heading to the private area where the government jet had landed. Shadow had picked the lock so they could get inside. There they were able to patch Ash up, clean themselves up in the toilets, and wait until the place officially opened.

When they failed to reach Jackson on the phone they called Waylen, and he had been able to expedite an early flight for Shadow and Ash. He and Niel hadn't been so lucky. They ended up getting stranded for hours while Waylen tried to book them on a flight to France. They had kicked their heels, hoping not to get arrested for the museum heist, or somehow connected to the bomb that had gone off at the hotel. Security at the airport was tighter than ever. In the end, they flew from Aswan to Cairo, and then boarded another flight to Toulouse. They had a few hours of driving ahead now, but the Gods had finally smiled on them.

"We need clothes," Niel reminded him. "I am not wearing this all day. I look ridiculous."

Gabe laughed, relief finally winning over his temper. As soon as the airport shops opened that morning, they swapped their dusty, damaged clothes for tourist t-shirts and hoodies. Niel's read, *I Love Aswan*. But they really needed jeans or fatigues. They couldn't find anything big enough in the airport.

"You stink, too," Gabe told him. "Sweat and burnt hair. Sexy."

"You don't look much better!" He gestured to Gabe's sweatshirt that said, *I love Mummy,* with an image of an Egyptian mummy on it. "Shadow will find you irresistible."

"Of course she will!" Gabe grinned at Niel. "Because I am."

Niel rolled his eyes. "Brother. That still revolts me."

"I'll remind you of that when you're mooning over Mouse."

"I don't *moon*, and I won't be mooning over her!"

Gabe just smirked as they reached the line of counters that served the rental car companies. He decided not to push it. Niel was still sore about the fact that she'd betrayed him, but hadn't really, and that Gabe had let her go. He'd made the right choice, and Niel knew it. He just didn't want to admit it.

He changed the subject as they joined the shortest queue and pulled out his driver's license. "I suggest we look as responsible as possible to get a car. And then, our first stop is a hypermarket." He checked his watch. "With luck, we'll be with Barak by late evening—and Black Cronos will be none the wiser."

Olivia had spent a strange few hours with the witches. Ever since she woke up, she had felt out of sorts and tired. She was finding it hard to concentrate, and her surreal surroundings exacerbated the experience.

Moonfell was odd, and undeniably beautiful in its Gothic, almost stage-set manner. She felt like she had stepped back in time. The witches had been happy for her to roam about the house, as long as she drank the restorative teas packed with herbs every two hours. She hadn't wanted to abuse their hospitality, but she certainly took advantage of it. She investigated every room, her keen eye noting valuable paintings, tapestries, sculptures, statues, and books. Even some of the furniture could have been auctioned off for a high price. Most of it was antique, a mix of styles through the ages, as well as more modern pieces. Some of the items were well worn, the tapestries bare in places, their jewel-bright colours faded. Somehow, it suited them.

The peculiar, timeless quality of the place was enhanced by the gloomy grey day outside, and the array of lamps that littered corners and work surfaces. And despite the vast number of rooms—sitting rooms, parlours, several studies, numerous bedrooms and bathrooms, and spell rooms—every room seemed to be in use. It was as if the witches were determined to utilise everything. Olivia approved. She finally realised that the house had been divided into areas for each witch, so they could live separately under one roof. There were even other kitchens on the first and second floor, although they were nowhere near as grand as the large kitchen on the ground floor.

The guest bedrooms and bathrooms where she, Harlan, and Maggie had stayed overnight were on the second floor, all beautifully furnished. Odd little side passages and short runs of stairs led to numerous towers and turrets, including the one where the spell had been cast the night before. There were also a few locked doors that she desperately wanted to open, but she moved on reluctantly.

Her favourite room, however, was the huge attic on the third floor that stretched the whole length of the house. Half was lined with cupboards filled with old clothes, beautifully wrapped and preserved. Gowns made of silk, velvet, and taffeta, both embroidered and plain. There were also lots of old portraits of men and women painted in oils, acrylics, pastels, pencil, and collages. All were witches. They wore witches' hats and sweeping cloaks, and were surrounded by witchcraft objects and occult symbols. Olivia, comfortable as she was with the occult, felt a shudder of wonder pass through her.

The whole of Moonfell contained a history of witches.

Olivia was lost in her thoughts when a voice behind her made her jump. "There you are. I was worried you'd got lost. And you're late for your drink!"

Olivia whirled around. "Morgana! I'm sorry. I was side-tracked by your beautiful house." Morgana had brought up a tray loaded with a plate of sticky cakes and two cups. However, it was Morgana's appearance that held her attention. She hadn't seen her for a few hours, and she had changed her clothes. She was dressed in a long, Medieval-style dress in dark green made of plain, heavy cotton, and her long hair with the grey streak fell loosely over her shoulders. Her eyes widened with surprise. "I love your dress!"

Morgana smiled. "Sometimes I need to embrace my ancestors. Especially after nights like last night. Let's sit and talk." She walked to a small table surrounded by a cluster of chairs, arranged under an arched window. She placed the tray on the table and ran her hand over the two drinks. They immediately started to steam. "That's better. They had gone cold. Nobody needs cold tea."

Olivia sat and dutifully sipped it as warmth ran through her. "It's lovely. Different to the others. I taste honey and cinnamon."

"Yes, plenty of warming herbs to try and revive you. You're still not right. I need some, too, after last night." Morgana studied her, leaning in to stare into her eyes. "You're getting there. He took a lot out of you."

"But he has gone?"

"Oh, yes. Not many can resist the Goddess."

"Or you either, I would imagine."

Morgana smiled and swept her hand out to encompass the pictures. "Oh, I don't know. I sometimes doubt that we are as strong as some of these."

"Your ancestors?"

"Yes. Some of these people were extremely powerful." She pointed to a middle-aged woman with thick black hair and a widow's peak. "She was said to be the most powerful of all. She advised King Charles II, but no one knew. Her name was Eliza."

"She lived here?"

"Yes. Most of them did; a few preferred to live elsewhere. At present, there are other family members who choose not to live here for various reasons. The house was gifted to us hundreds of years ago by a very grateful nobleman." She cocked her eyebrow. "He was in need of an heir, and he got one."

"Your family did that?"

"Fertility is one of our skills. Mine, in particular."

"Do you see women here? Or couples? Are you like a private fertility clinic?"

Morgana laughed. "No! Nothing so organised. But yes, word gets round. I help where I can. I have been said to perform miracles!" She winked. "Really just herbs and a little magic."

As Olivia sipped her tea, embraced by the ancestors who looked on, she started to feel a little better. "What do the other witches specialise in?"

"Birdie is good at finding things and scrying. New spells, too. She has a gift for contacting our ancestors. Her familiar helps."

"Her familiar?"

"You haven't met him yet. Hades, her cat. He can be quite gruff, so I advise you to steer clear. He's suspicious of strangers. Once he gets to know you though, he softens. *A bit*. He's large though, so you'll have a shock if you see him. He's in the garden at the moment, stalking pigeons."

"Okay. I'll bear that in mind." Olivia hoped he wasn't tiger-sized, although honestly, nothing would completely surprise her in this house. "What about Odette?"

"Ah. She has the Sight, but slightly differently to some. She sees to the truth of things. She's uncanny. You can't hide much from Odette. It taxes her, though. She doesn't always want to, but things seek her out. She's resting now after last night. She saw things that she would rather have not. She saw Belial, for example, far more acutely than we did. And the Goddess, of course. I would imagine, though, that you saw more too, as you were in the thick of it."

"It's fading now."

Morgana picked up a sticky slice of cake. "Take one, Olivia, it will help your strength. They're made from honey and oats, and they're excellent when warmed, which these are."

Olivia had been so caught up in the conversation that she had forgotten the cakes, but she took a bite and nodded. "Delicious."

"Good. So, did Belial speak to you yesterday, while we were closing the window he had opened?"

"No. I just remember him not wanting to go. I felt like he was grasping on to every bit of my mind. It felt like I was on fire. Then I felt the Goddess arrive. She was like a cool breeze, in comparison. Does that sound weird? I smelled blossoms."

"No, that's not odd at all. There are times, like last night, that her generosity knows no bounds, but we do have to work hard for that. There are also times when she's terrifying."

Olivia focussed on the gifts. "Like your skin, Birdie's age..."

"Yes. She also confirmed something that I saw, too. I see it even more now, as does Odette." She stared at her, weighing her up. "This might come as a shock."

"What? Has something bad happened? Am I ill?"

"No. You're pregnant."

Shadow watched JD line up several metallic objects of varying sizes and shapes and knew exactly what they were. "You've made alchemical weapons!"

"You're giving away my surprise!" he complained.

"I'm still surprised, if that helps," Harlan pointed out, attempting to pick one up.

JD slapped his hand away. "Not yet!" He smiled at Shadow. "My deadly friend gets first go."

"Deadly? I suppose you're right," she admitted, a sly glance at Nahum and Ash. "I am fey."

Nahum rolled his eyes. "Shut up, Shadow."

Briar and Ash just laughed, and Shadow was relieved to see that he seemed to be improving already.

They were all gathered in JD's observatory on the top floor of the house. The room had huge, sliding glass doors that opened out onto a flat roof. The garden beyond was melting into early twilight, and mist was already rising as the ground temperature dropped. Despite the plunging temperatures, JD urged them all into coats and led them outside, carrying the weapons on a tray.

"We are going to do some testing," he said, an air of eager anticipation in his voice. "I have of course tested them myself, and then aligned them to some general frequencies, but this will be a better test. I hope that if you feel they are useful, you can take them to France."

"Will they get past airport security?" Nahum asked, eyes lighting up.

"They should do, but best to put them in your checked baggage."

"Can I have one?" Harlan asked. "I was attacked last night."

"Of course. I feel we should level the playing field, don't you? Although," JD cast a speculative look at Nahum, "it seems you may have beaten me to it there."

He said nothing more on that subject, although Shadow guessed he was referring to the angelic jewellery. No doubt he had much more to ask, but he placed the tray on a table and selected a weapon.

"I have set up targets for you to fire at." He pointed to the middle of the far lawn where a row of bottles and bricks were lined up. "As you can see, they're at quite a distance, and rudimentary. I thought it worth testing their maximum range."

"But what are they?" Briar asked. "Are they made with magic?"

"Trust the witch to ask that." JD smiled at her benevolently, and it was very unnerving. Shadow preferred his sharp, impatient manner better. "Of a sort. Alchemy. A manipulation of matter and correspondences."

Briar nodded. "Like the elements? The building blocks of life."

"Exactly. Something we could discuss later, perhaps?"

"Of course."

"Excellent." He pointed at the weapons. Some were oval, some round, others more cylindrical, all made from a variety of metals—silver, gold, copper, lead, and others no doubt. "The different metals carry different vibrations and qualities. But that's not all. They have been aligned with planets, moon phases and many other complex things."

"But they can be used at any time of the day or week?" Ash asked.

"Absolutely. It merely means they have certain characteristics. All are deadly."

He marched to the wall that edged the roof with his selected weapon, adjusted his stance, and fired. A pulse of light with a narrow circumference blasted out and shattered a bottle.

"Good shot, JD," Shadow said approvingly.

"It looks like a laser beam!" Harlan said. "I can't even get my head around that."

"It's not a laser beam. It's not even light. It's a different kind of energy."

Harlan scratched his chin, perplexed. "How does it work?"

JD opened his palm so that the oval silver weapon lay in his palm. "The power is in the tip."

Shadow leaned in. On closer inspection, she saw the oval did have a slight, almost imperceptible point, and its surface was engraved with unusual symbols. "May I?" He nodded and she picked it up. "It has a tiny gemstone in the point."

"Exactly. That's what releases the power." He beamed at them. "But who would know? It looks like jewellery, or just an object of beauty. They also align with certain qualities. That one is designed to be used by humans." JD whirled around and picked up a cylindric copper weapon, also palm-sized, and passed it to Shadow. "This one is for you."

Shadow examined it, noting different engravings and a cluster of tiny gemstones on the tip. Careful not to point it at anyone, she gripped it, feeling it almost melt into her palm. It was so light, she felt it would just float away. "How do I make it work?"

"Grip it with your fingers, line it up, and squeeze your palm *with intention*. Gently!"

Shadow wasn't sure what to expect, but did as he said. Immediately, a jet of coppery light shot out and struck wide, missing the bottles, but hitting the lawn. A patch of grass sizzled and blackened. "Herne's flaming bollocks! I missed." Annoyed, she steadied herself and shot again. This time her shot was closer, but still missed. "Damn it!"

"Think of it like your bow and arrow," JD instructed, moving closer. "You're tense."

Aware that the others were watching, and priding herself on her deadly accuracy, Shadow did as he suggested. Her bow, like her sword and daggers, was an extension of herself. *This should be no different.* She rolled her shoulders, took aim, and fired again. This time, the bottle shattered. She immediately fired at the next and shattered that one, too. She grinned at JD. "This is brilliant! *You* are brilliant!"

"Madam, I thank you." JD gave a small bow. "However, it has taken months to perfect, and I still feel I can make improvements." He turned to the others. "Come on. You must try yours, too. Even you, Ash. I know your shoulder is injured, but this should be easy for you to handle."

Ash looked uncertain but nodded anyway, and JD handed the weapons out, running through the instructions again. Even Briar was prepared to try. For the next few minutes, everyone practised. Initially, Briar was the most accurate, which surprised all of them.

"I don't know why you all look so shocked," she protested. "I do aim my own power quite accurately, you know." She arched an eyebrow at Shadow. "Events have been challenging!"

Shadow grinned. "Yes, they have, sister!" She pulled Briar aside as the others continued to practice. As of yet, she hadn't really had a chance to talk to her. "How is Ash?"

"He's worried that he's slow to heal, but he's doing fine." Briar's cheeks were flushed red with cold, her eyes bright. "I told him not to overdo it. A tough request, considering what you all will face over the next few days. I'm just sorry we can't go with you."

"It's fine. It's nearly Christmas, and you have your businesses."

"And we need to protect White Haven, in case Black Cronos returns. They have put White Haven at risk! I won't have that. My family is there. And my friends! But we feel terrible about not helping you. We'll never forgive ourselves if something happens to you."

"Please don't worry. We have resources, and new weapons. And as annoying as she is, we have Estelle. I gather she might be contacting Caspian for help."

"Good. We'll watch your home while you're away," Briar reassured her.

They were interrupted by JD, who summoned their attention by clapping his hands. "Any questions? Are you happy?"

There was a general murmuring of agreement and nods.

Harlan said, "I need more practice, but I'm impressed. Did the PD's lab help with this?"

"A little," JD conceded. "I worked with Russell Blake. He has a couple of test weapons there, too."

"Thanks, JD," Nahum said, turning his weapon over in his hands. "It's certainly effective. I still prefer my sword, but like you said, it offers us long range choices beyond Shadow's bow and the crossbows."

"Ah! That brings me to the ones I haven't shown you yet. Do you recall the weapons they could extend, as if from thin air?"

Shadow groaned. "I do! They seemed to make spears and swords out of nothing!"

"In that case, you'll be glad to hear I have made some of those, too." He turned to the small silver globes the size of tennis balls that they hadn't used yet. He placed one in his palm and swiped his other hand across the top of it. The metal stretched into a long spear, and JD twirled it like a baton. They all exchanged wide-eyed looks of appreciation, as well as perhaps some uncertainty. "Liquid metal, water, and air. I only have two, for now. These are works in progress. They're still too big. But these," he opened a large box that he'd set aside, "are game changers!" Inside the box were rows of silver balls that looked like golf balls. "These are grenades."

Shadow almost squealed with excitement. "Grenades!"

He picked one up, and they all leaned in. "See? They are in two halves. To activate it, you twist and lock it, and then throw." He turned and lobbed it into the grounds, and it exploded on his lawn. "Ten seconds to detonate, and the blast, as you can see, is big. Until activated, it's perfectly safe." He puffed up like a cockerel. "My own design. Another genius alchemical blend."

"Holy shit," Harlan murmured. "You could make a fortune in weapons manufacturing."

"*Could*, but don't want to," JD said briskly. "Besides, the set-up for mass manufacture would be exorbitant. However, what this means is that now I feel equal to meeting Black Cronos. And so should you, Harlan. You understand what this means?"

Shadow exchanged a nervous glance with Nahum and Ash, suspecting what he meant, but needing him to spell it out. "Not really, JD."

"If you've found the Count of St Germain's base, then I must come, too. I'm the only one who can truly understand his alchemical set-up. You need me."

Nahum stepped in. "You're not a warrior, JD. You're a brilliant scientist. That's a bad idea. You'll slow us down, just keeping an eye on you. It's about more than weapons. Taking them down is about strength, speed, and reflexes."

"And brains!" JD tapped his head, not the slightest bit offended. "I have plenty."

"But what about the emerald discs that we stole? Aren't you working on those?" Shadow asked, annoyed.

"That is still a work in progress!" JD pointed out.

Ash seemed as outraged as Shadow. "So then why did we have to get the discs now? We were literally blown up! We could have been with Barak sooner!"

"What if they were to be taken elsewhere, somewhere unknown? I couldn't risk that!" JD shook his head, utterly perplexed, and reluctantly, Shadow saw his point. JD continued, "You won't deter me. I'm coming, too."

"In that case, so am I!" Harlan said, although he didn't look half so eager as JD. "I need to find Jackson."

"*We'll* find Jackson," Nahum said forcefully.

Harlan huffed. "And defeat all of Black Cronos's soldiers in his fortress *château*? Come on!"

"We can't guarantee your safety," Nahum said quietly. "I can't even guarantee my own."

Harlan exchanged a look of solidarity with JD, unusual because they were normally at loggerheads. This time, it seemed they had common ground. "We know the risks, Nahum. We're coming anyway."

Twenty-One

J ackson presumed he would be led to a deep, dark dungeon and tortured, but instead he was escorted to a small, square room without windows that contained a single bed, a sink, and a toilet in the corner. Essentially, a prison cell.

However, he had no idea exactly where that was. He'd been blindfolded again, and all he knew was that there were twisting passages and lots of stairs leading down. He had been left there for a couple of hours, and had been provided with a basic meal and water. This time, he'd been sensible and consumed everything. If he was going to get out of there, he needed his strength.

Once he'd eaten, he examined every inch of his room. It had plastered walls painted white, a single, recessed light fitting set in a very high ceiling, and a concrete floor. Fortunately, it was warm. Placing his hands on the floor, he realised there was underfloor heating. *Interesting.* They clearly didn't intend for him to freeze or starve to death. He suspected he was in a cell that they usually kept their test subjects in. That didn't inspire confidence, either. And the place was very quiet. He couldn't hear anything. No footsteps or voices. The door was made of thick steel with a hatch in it. There was nothing he could use as a weapon, and no way of getting out. He threw himself on the bed, mulling over who their mole was, but despite his best intentions, drifted off to sleep. He was woken by the clang of the door opening.

Stefan stood at the entrance. "Time for a short tour, Jackson. Get up."

Jackson drank the last of his water, brushed his jumbled hair out of his eyes, and pulled his long mac on. "Is this the tour before I'm led to my death?"

"You're quite the dramatist," Stefan said, stepping back. "Deandra. The cuffs, please."

The woman stepped from the corridor behind Stefan, and with cold fingers, fixed cuffs on Jackson's wrists. They weren't normal cuffs, however; like many things here, they were covered in sigils, like the bracelet he still wore. Stefan had gloated earlier that it masked his energies, and that no one would be able to find him.

"No blindfold?" he asked.

"No. I think you're deep enough in the bowels of this place that you won't find your way out, anyway." He gave him a sly smile as he headed down a long corridor.

Jackson didn't bother to respond. He felt better after his nap, and he studied his surroundings, aware of Deandra behind him, monitoring his every move. He might be beneath a Medieval castle, but the corridors were plastered, and modern light fixtures were overhead. He passed multiple doors he assumed were other cells. It reminded him of how Barak and Estelle had described the lab beneath the *château* in France. All the doors were electronic, and cameras were mounted high on the walls. He looked up at one and waved.

"It's a sophisticated set-up," Jackson observed. "No expense spared at keeping your prisoners locked in."

"They're not prisoners!" Stefan said angrily. "The doors are to protect our *and* their safety. The process of transformation is not easy. You've probably seen that for yourself after stealing Lucien."

"Rescuing! You haven't convinced *me* of the merit of your cause yet, unlike your spy. Susceptible idiot."

"I confess, it always surprises me how little incentive some people need. It often comes down to money or recognition."

"It didn't do Barnaby Armstrong much good, did it?" He was referring to the secretary of the Order of the Midnight Sun. Another man who'd been swayed by the promises of Black Cronos. Now he was dead.

"Sometimes people outlast their usefulness." Stefan stopped in front of a row of three lifts and pressed the button to descend.

"Perhaps like you will, one day." Jackson watched his profile as he goaded him, but Stefan merely stared at the lift doors, waiting patiently. "You must work very hard for the count, and yet you seem to get none of the glory."

Stefan's mouth twitched into a smile. "I get to work in a properly funded alchemical laboratory, with access to precious metals, gems, an observatory, and a wheel of correspondences that, by the way, I enhanced considerably. My needs are well met. And," he stared at Jackson, "my skills are appreciated."

The doors of one of the lifts slid open, and they stepped inside, Deandra staying close to Jackson. He ignored her. "But you're not immortal."

"I have no wish to be."

"I guess you could discover the ability yourself, and then at least you'd have a choice. Sounds like the count guards some secrets very jealously indeed."

Stefan didn't answer, and the rest of the journey remained in silence. Jackson watched the number of floors they descended. They had entered on the floor labelled minus two, and were descending to minus five. According to the lift controls, there were another three levels. They must be in the heart of the mountain.

The lift shuddered and stopped, and the door opened onto a broad ledge that overlooked a huge cave. Despite his intentions to be unimpressed and coolly rational, Jackson's jaw gaped open. The cave was high-roofed and broad, making a huge, circular space. Within it were several large, intersecting, spherical metal bands that spun slowly.

Mesmerised, he walked to the wall that edged the broad ledge and looked down onto a vast series of concentric rings also made from a variety of materials, including metals. The largest was as thick as a road, and easily a hundred feet in diameter, set into a rim of steel. It was connected to the cavern wall at two points only. Within it, Jackson estimated there were about two dozen smaller rings, reducing in size to a circle in the centre. The metal bands passed around the giant wheel, continuing for some distance beneath it. Lights pierced from above, the whole range of the spectrum, and gemstones twinkled along the metals.

"I feel like I'm in an armillary sphere," Jackson said, barely able to breathe.

"Well done! That's exactly what it is. You're not a complete fool, then."

Jackson glanced at Stefan who was transfixed by the sphere's movements. "What does it do?"

"What any armillary sphere does—it models the objects in the universe, representing celestial longitude and latitude. This version is Ptolemaic."

"Which is what?"

"The Earth is the centre, encompassed in our wheel. If the sun was the centre, it would be called Copernican."

Jackson was stepping well beyond the bounds of his basic knowledge. "What do you do with it?"

Stefan dragged his eyes from it and looked at Jackson. He looked like he was drugged. "The rotating rings represent the Tropic of Cancer and Capricorn, the Arctic circle, the equator, the zodiac signs, the planets, and much more. It represents our universe. Many things that influence the alchemist."

"And the rings in the wheel?" He'd seen JD's, so he was pretty sure he knew what it was.

"Similar. A correspondence wheel. We can make many different alignments, and with the use of light, change energy. Create new life. And interesting weapons, too." He laughed. "I make it sound simplistic. It's not."

Jackson stared at it again, admiring the soaring metal rings, the shifting light, and its smooth movements. "It must have taken years to perfect."

"Hundreds. As man's advancements grow, so we incorporate the new with the old." Stefan warmed to his subject. "The metals are all slightly different. Some pure, some blended, all unique. All tested over years to make sure the proportions are correct. The crystals on them have been specifically chosen to enhance energies. When the wheel aligns beneath, we can manipulate energy. Matter!"

No wonder JD struggled to replicate the count's achievements. His wheel was impressive, but was tiny in comparison.

"We have a smaller wheel in the main courtyard," Stefan explained. "It's useful for simpler things, when we would rather work beneath the sun, moon, or the stars, but the true power lies here. This is the heart of the *comte's* genius."

"And beneath the wheel of correspondences?" Jackson strained to see below.

"Just the base of the sphere. The lift goes down to it for maintenance purposes."

Jackson knew this was what they had to destroy. *But how? Importantly, were Barak and Estelle and Lucien still alive? Were the others? Or did he somehow need to destroy it on his own?* "I presume the mechanism that drives it is down there?"

"Nothing *drives* it. It is self-driven, by the power of the universe that we have harnessed."

"And this is where you finalise your soldiers? Finish their transformation? Like with Deandra?"

She stared impassively. Her silence was unnerving. *Did she choose not to speak, or was she mute?*

"Yes, Deandra was a product of this. A combination of Mars and Venus, fire and earth, and other things. It is this which prolongs her life, too. At a certain time on the calendar, her powers are replenished."

Jackson's mind raced. *How could they destroy it? Un-align the spheres? Break the wheel?* But more unnerving was why he was seeing it. It could mean only one thing.

"I'm not here to negotiate, am I? The fact that you've shown this to me means you'll never let me go."

"Yes and no. We'd still like you to negotiate a truce. Call off your team. Explain the futility of their continued attacks. Under our guidance, of course. And then, this place," he extended his arms wide, "will be your home. If you behave, then you live. If not, then you die!"

"Transform, you mean?"

Stefan cocked an eyebrow. "Or that! Three options then, if that is your preference."

"Of course it's not my bloody preference!" Jackson exploded. "I want to go back to my life!"

"You think so small. Your existence is narrow, don't you see? You scurry away in your offices, chasing us around, and get outraged at our potential, when you could actually be part of it! This is what swayed Russell, in the end."

"Russell! Russell Blake?" *Fuck!* He had to tell Waylen. He was the PD's Assistant Director. "How did you get to him?"

"He was on holiday in September. It was a small matter of bringing him here."

"September!" Jackson felt an utter fool. For months Russell had been feeding Black Cronos information. *But what did he know of Barak and Estelle?* Jackson was pretty sure that he had only told Waylen where they were going, but what had Waylen told Russell?

Stefan laughed, a tight malicious grin on his face. "Yes. You think so small. That will be your downfall. Unless you join us, of course. Think about it for a few hours. I'm sure you'll come to your senses. If not, we have one more strategy to try."

"Why the hell do you care about my cooperation?" Jackson asked, clenching his fists. He desperately wanted to hit Deandra and Stefan, but knew that she would retaliate swiftly. Could he run somewhere? Hide? *No. He must bide his time. He'd find a way.* "What fucking strategy?"

Stefan smiled maliciously again. "You'll see."

Olivia felt as if a bomb had gone off under her. She stared at Morgana, utterly gobsmacked. "I'm *what*?"

"You're pregnant."

"I can't possibly be."

"I realise this is a shock, but I assure you that you are." Morgana narrowed her eyes. "I presume you have had sex recently? Or else this is way weirder than I expected."

Olivia immediately discounted Nahum. She had slept with him only two nights ago. It was far too recent. Three months earlier she had experienced a very enjoyable evening—actually, several enjoyable evenings—with a very handsome Italian man when she was on holiday with her friend in Italy. It was strictly a holiday romance, and they had used protection.

"It's impossible. I was careful, and besides I'm still having my periods. I can't be pregnant. I haven't put on weight, and I don't feel any different. I appreciate your skills and everything, but you're wrong."

"You're thinking this was how long ago?"

"Three months, when I was on holiday."

"Ah. No. It's more recent than that. This is a very early pregnancy, which is why you won't have noticed a thing."

Olivia froze, her drink forgotten. "How early?"

"A few days."

"How can you possibly know already? It's barely a collection of cells!"

Morgana smiled sympathetically. "I know, and so does Odette. She sees the truth of things, I told you. Yesterday, Belial was clouding everything else. Now that he's gone..." She hesitated. "It's rude to pry, but I presume there was someone recent?"

"Yes. A one-off night of very unbridled passion." She met Morgana's gaze and laughed. "It was the shock of Belial that did it. My conspirator."

Olivia stood, needing to walk and figure out what to do. She paced the room barely able to focus anymore on her surroundings. She had never planned on a pregnancy. Had never wanted children. Her career and travel were everything. *And what the hell would Nahum think?* He had promised nothing. It was a one-night deal. Would he think she had deliberately tried to trap him? No! What was she thinking? This didn't mean marriage! Or commitment. It was her decision. Or was it? She had to tell him. She owed him that.

"Fuck!" She turned to Morgana, who was still sitting and drinking her tea. "Are you sure?"

"Very. The Goddess saw it, too. It's a special baby, Olivia."

"Is it?"

"Yes. The father is...*different*, yes?"

Olivia didn't know what to say. She didn't know Morgana or the other witches. She'd met them barely twenty-four hours earlier. Although they'd shown her great kindness, and possibly saved her life, she couldn't tell them about Nahum. About who he was. That was too much. *Unless the witch already knew, somehow...*

Feeling foolish for standing in the middle of the attic and acting as if the witch ancestors were judging her, she sat down again, trying to compose herself. "Yes, he's a little different."

Morgana just sipped her drink and nodded. "I suspect that's why Belial clung on a little longer. Maybe he saw something, too. He craved that little window on your business. Best we got rid of him, for many reasons."

For some utterly irrational moment, Olivia felt afraid, and her hand flew to her stomach. "He knows? Can he harm me? Or the baby?"

"No! Rid yourself of that notion. He is spirit and air, powerless now to hurt you. Besides, you have gained our protection, and the Goddess's. If you choose to keep the child, of course. I don't judge, and can help you get rid of it safely if you choose to."

"I don't know what I choose. No, actually that's not true. But I'm confused."

"Go on. You can trust me. Olivia. I know you don't know me, but I am on your side."

Something about Morgana invited confidences. Or maybe it was the gloomy weather and the low lights that drew them closer together. Olivia felt like she was in a bubble. "I have never wanted children, but somehow, now, I can't bear to think of..." She struggled even to say the words. "Getting rid of it."

Morgana smiled broadly. "How lovely. Then it seems congratulations are in order."

Olivia felt a flutter that she thought was excitement, but it could have been dread. *Was she insane? Her life was going to change forever. There were so many things to consider...*

"Slow down," Morgana instructed. "I can see you're racing away already. One step at a time. All will fall into place."

But would it? Morgana sounded so sure, while Olivia was a whirling mass of emotions already. "I need time to think."

"And rest. Stay another night or two, please. For me."

The thought of being home on her own was terrifying. She couldn't even bring herself to tell Harlan or her best friend. Certainly not Nahum.

She found herself nodding. "Yes, please. That would be lovely."

Maggie huffed at the continuing argument in the PD's lab. Her attempted intervention had failed, and it seemed Waylen was avoiding her.

She turned to Russell Blake, wondering what his take was on all this, and saw that he was rummaging in a drawer. When he straightened, a strange silvery object was in his hands. He saw her staring, pointed the object, and fired.

Maggie dived under the closest workbench, wincing as a blast whipped past her ear and exploded some glass jars above her head.

Screams and shouts erupted, but she didn't have time to consider the others. She scrambled under the bench and out the other side, grabbing a stool on the way up. As soon as she regained her feet, she threw it at Russell.

Russell wasn't focussing on just her anymore. He was firing wildly at everyone. The scientists were running, Petra was screaming, and glass jars were exploding all around them. Hot liquid splashed everywhere, but Maggie stayed on her feet, grabbed a large metal pot, and hurled that, too. Both missed.

Unfortunately, one of the scientists hadn't been as quick to find shelter. The man was lying flat on his back, a huge, bloody wound in his chest.

Russell Blake was a murderer.

Russell sprinted for the exit, shooting wildly over his shoulder, and everyone ducked for cover. Petra froze in the doorway, and Maggie screamed, "Run!"

But it was too late. Russell fired straight at her, and she flew backwards through the door, into the corridor. Russell kicked the door shut, sealing them all inside. There would be no chase through The Retreat. Russell was planning to kill them all.

"Has anyone got a fucking weapon?" Maggie yelled. They had seconds only before Russell would methodically march around the room, killing everyone. This was not how she intended to die. Not trapped like a caged rat.

By now, benches had been upended to provide cover, and the scientists were cowering. That wasn't surprising. They weren't used to being shot at or attacked. But she was. She dodged around the corner of a sturdy metal bench lined with cupboards in the centre of the room and saw Waylen sheltering at the far end with the female alchemist called Lynn. He crouched awkwardly, clutching his hip, and Maggie remembered that he walked with a limp. He must have aggravated an old injury.

She summoned his attention. "Waylen? Have you got a weapon?"

"No!"

"I know where one is!" Lynn said. She looked terrified. "In the drawers under the window. There's an alchemical one."

More shots exploded above her, and more shouts erupted around the room. Russell Blake laughed maniacally. "You can't win! You're stuck in here."

Maggie hissed at Waylen. "Keep him talking!" Their only hope now was to distract him long enough to get the weapon. He sounded cocky, like he had it all figured out. And they were a long way from security down here. No one would hear them. "And throw things at him!"

Waylen nodded and shouted, "Russell! We are old friends. What are you doing?"

"Doing what I should I have done years ago. Getting ahead!"

"Getting ahead doing what? I don't understand!"

"Getting more money. Getting recognised for my worth."

"By betraying your friends?"

Maggie crept along the benches while they talked, seeing glimpses of Russell's legs as he stalked around the room. Every now and again she grabbed an object she found on the floor—forceps, scissors, jars—and threw them in a flurry all over the room as distractions. Lynn saw her and joined in, making Russell skip and dance back. Unfortunately, he also kept firing, even though he was talking to Waylen. *But what was he shooting at?*

Maggie risked lifting her head above the bench and saw that he was methodically destroying his own research. Glass jars exploded, one after another, flames shot high, and colourful steam drifted over the benches. Maggie hoped they weren't poisonous. Russell didn't seem bothered.

She managed to make it to the drawer Lynn had pointed out. She risked lifting her head again. Russell was glaring down at someone. He pointed his weapon as a man shouted, "Russell! No!"

A pot flew across the room and smacked Russell on the head. He stumbled back, raising his weapon as he fell, and fired wildly again. He hit a huge plate glass window and it shattered. Russell dived for cover too, and Maggie took advantage of the destruction to search the drawers. There was nothing resembling a weapon. She wrenched the next drawer open, and then another. There was just a solitary silver sphere nestled in a velvet-lined box. *What the fuck was that?*

A sound of grating metal made her spin around, and she saw one of the scientists pushing a metal counter across the floor like a battering ram, aiming at Russell. Being nearly shot was clearly a very good motivator to take action.

Unable to work out what was a weapon, she chanced her luck. She raced across the room, intending to tackle Russell from behind while his colleague was attacking him. Waylen was still talking, trying to distract him.

Russell yelled, "Shut up, Waylen!" He fired at his colleague, and metal hummed and smouldered.

Maggie was halfway across the room now. A few more feet and she'd be on him. She had threaded through the chaos of the destroyed lab and into clear space when Russell spotted her. He swung around and aimed at her. But there was nothing now between them. Nowhere to hide.

Then there was another shout, and another shot, and the back of Russell's skull suddenly exploded.

Maggie stumbled back, willing herself not to collapse. Her eyes darted around the room, wondering who had fired. *A counterattack? Another enemy?*

Then she saw Layla Gould standing at the shattered window, a gun in her hand. For a moment their eyes met, and she saw Layla's terror, but also her steel. Maggie raised her hands, hoping she was judging correctly. "It's over, Layla. It was just Russell. No one else."

Layla nodded and lowered her gun.

It was over.

Twenty-Two

Niel approached Barak's new address cautiously. He and Gabe still weren't sure if magic had been used to find their whereabouts and was being used to track them now. So far, Barak's team had been safe. They certainly didn't want to give them away.

"I've kept a careful watch on the road," Niel said, glancing in the rear-view mirror again. "No one has followed us."

"With Russell Blake dead, that risk should be eliminated," Gabe pointed out. "Bastard."

Niel grunted in agreement. Nahum had phoned them earlier with the news of his betrayal and subsequent death. *At least that was one less thing to worry about*, Niel reflected as he stopped the car on a rise, just off the road that wound through small towns dotted along the valleys, beneath towering peaks. The sky was clear, it was freezing, and snow sparkled on the mountaintops. "There's not much cover for us to fly tonight."

"But not many streetlights, either. You want to see the *château*?"

"Don't you?"

Gabe nodded, scanning their surroundings. "If Barak thinks it's safe enough. Let's get there and assess it." Gabe laughed, unexpectedly. "I don't know what I need first…a shower or food."

"A shower—you stink!"

"So do you!"

"The heat of the car doesn't help," Niel complained, cranking the window down just a little so he didn't have to smell unwashed Nephilim. "At least we managed to find better clothes!"

They had stopped at a large supermarket that stocked clothing, and bought plain black t-shirts, sweatshirts, jeans, underwear, and overnight bags to store them in. They also picked up toiletries. The thought of a hot shower and fresh clothing spurred Niel on. In another half an hour, after winding along frosty roads, they found the secluded chalet just outside the small town of L'Aiguillon. Here, the Christmas preparations were in full swing. Lights were strewn in front of houses and festooned the streets, putting into stark relief their own grim objective. Gabe had phoned ahead to warn Barak of their arrival, and he greeted them at the door with a hug.

"Glad to see you in one piece." He grinned at Gabe. "You have a bad habit of getting blown up."

"Not by choice, I can assure you!"

Barak laughed as they stepped inside the wooden framed and lap boarded house into a high-ceilinged hall. "This house was a lucky find, as most places are inhabited. Some of you will have to share a bedroom because it's small. I'm hoping no one turns up here tomorrow, or we'll be in trouble."

"Have you visited the original place?" Gabe asked.

"No. I thought best to keep away, just in case."

Niel sniffed at the rich scent of garlic. "That smells fantastic! Who's cooking? Doesn't smell like steak, so I doubt it's you."

Niel was always wary of other people's food, as his own standards were so high. Although, he had to admit that right now, anything would do. A burger at the airport hours ago didn't cut it.

"Am I that predictable?" Barak didn't look the slightest bit offended as he led them into an open plan lounge and dining area. "Lucien is cooking, and he's seriously good!"

"I expect nothing less from a Frenchman."

Niel and Gabe had met Lucien a couple of times, but didn't know him as well as Barak or Estelle. He was hoping they could trust him. Ever since their attack, he'd been wary of everyone outside of their tight circle.

Niel must have looked worried, because Barak said in a low voice, "I'm sure he's trustworthy."

"I hope you're right."

Lucien and Estelle emerged from the adjoining room that Niel presumed was the kitchen, and Estelle walked over and hugged them—an unexpectedly pleasant gesture. "I'm glad you're here. We're planning on going to the *château* tonight once we've eaten. Interested?"

"Of course!" Gabe dropped his bag on the floor and shook Lucien's hand, and Niel followed suit. Lucien hung back, looking uncomfortable, as if he shouldn't intrude.

"Nice to be out of The Retreat?" Niel asked. Lucien had changed since their last meeting a few weeks ago. His hair had been shaved then, and now it was longer. He had also put on weight and some muscle. He might hate his tattoos, but they actually suited him, and he had fire in his eyes now, rather than despair.

He gave a typical French shrug. "Of course. I'm not so sure it's nice to be so close to the count, though."

"It will be worth it to end this."

"And that," Estelle said firmly, "will be hard. Why don't I show you the available bedrooms, and we can discuss everything over dinner? We have photos to share, and maps. Tonight is just for reconnaissance, though. You've heard that the others will arrive tomorrow?"

Niel nodded. "Nahum called us. I presume he told you about Russell?"

"Bastard," Lucien said forcibly.

Estelle sighed. "We trusted him. He always asked about Lucien, but he was never allowed near him, for safety reasons, more than anything. Of course, we didn't elaborate."

"I can't believe he killed Petra," Barak said. "She was a nice young woman. It's giving me even more motive to destroy Black Cronos—not that I needed much more."

Estelle reached over and squeezed Barak's arm. "I've asked Caspian to help us, and fortunately, he agreed. He might even be able to bring one of my cousins. I've left him organising it."

Niel gaped at that revelation. "You've asked Caspian to come?"

"We may clash sometimes, but I'm not an idiot. We're attacking a fortress."

"That bad?"

"Guards, lookout towers, a gated entrance. The works," Barak confirmed. "You up for a challenge?"

"Always."

"Good. But could I suggest one thing first? You both stink, and need a shower. And frankly, those sweatshirts are awful. I think being bombed has affected your style choices."

"Having my clothes blown up has affected my style choices!" Niel lifted his arm and wiggled his bag. "You'll be glad to know we have fresh clothes now. Just point me to the bathroom!"

Estelle laughed. "You'd better follow me. Then we can start planning."

Harlan pulled up outside Moonfell, hoping that Olivia would be looking better. At least that would improve his mood.

After more target practice at JD's house, everyone had left except for their host, who was travelling to London the next day to catch his flight. Harlan had just dropped Shadow and Ash off at Chadwick House. Ash was still recovering, and Shadow had offered to stay with him. Briar had driven Nahum's car back to Cornwall. It seemed he had vetoed driving to London in Briar's tiny mini. Nahum was flying out of London with them tomorrow, and Eli and Zee would fly from Cornwall. The flights were numerous and messy, but at least they had all managed to get seats. After Nahum heard that Harlan was going to see Olivia, he had asked to go, too.

Harlan was also still reeling from Maggie's news. She had phoned him a couple of hours earlier to tell him about Russell Blake's betrayal, and they had passed the news on to everyone. It was all they could talk about in the car after they'd left JD's house. Harlan was now plagued with worry about exactly how much he knew, and what he'd told Black Cronos.

"You need to stop brooding," Nahum said. "There's not much we can do about his betrayal now."

"I can't help myself. The good thing is that I'm pretty sure Russell didn't know about the Emerald Tablet. Jackson kept that to himself. He didn't even tell Waylen why the team went to Egypt." Harlan shuffled to look at Nahum "You don't look that happy, either."

"I feel guilty for infecting Olivia with Belial. That's why she's here, in this gothic edifice, instead of her own flat." He peered out of the window. "You were right. It's a bit *Hammer House of Horror*."

"I promise that it's slightly less chilling inside."

"Only slightly?"

Harlan laughed. "I'm kidding. It's warm, and they're welcoming, if a little odd. And that house is as imposing on the inside as the out. But I like it. It has character, just like them. They are definitely weirder than your witches."

"The White Haven Coven? They're not *my* witches."

"You know what I mean. You have a badass coven on your side. That's great!"

"I know. I just wish they could help us now," Nahum admitted. "But it's also important that White Haven is protected. I don't put it past Black Cronos to strike again."

"Come on," Harlan said, and exited the car. "I need to get home and pack after this."

"Are you sure you want to come to France?" Nahum asked, as they strolled to the front door. "You didn't look quite as enthusiastic as JD."

"I'm not, but I must. It honestly seems wrong not to go. You have no idea what you're facing, and I need to find Jackson. Maggie said that he vanished into thin air."

"Of course, it's hard to question a dead man," Nahum said dryly.

"That's something else I need to do," Harlan said, making a mental note to do it before collapsing into bed. "Ask Maggie if the staff know anything. It was a bit chaotic when she called earlier."

That was an understatement. The call was hurried, and she was swearing a lot as she yelled instructions to others while also trying to talk to Harlan. He appreciated her updating them so soon. No doubt The Retreat was in a state of shock. He shook it off and focussed on Olivia.

Odette answered the door, her lips parting in surprise as she was introduced to Nahum. "Ah! I see it now," she said enigmatically.

"See what?" Harlan asked.

"Nothing to worry about." She smiled and beckoned them to follow her inside.

Instead of taking them to the kitchen, she led them down a passageway to the right. "We're in Morgana's sitting room. It overlooks the east moon gate," she explained, as if that would make any kind of sense. Harlan filed it away for another time.

The lounge was painted dark green, and one wall appeared to be a jungle. A squashy sofa took up a huge space in front of the roaring fire, but a couple of armchairs in differing styles flanked the other side, a coffee table in between. Curtains covered most windows, all except for double glass doors that looked out onto a spot-lit garden. Harlan barely took any notice though as Olivia rose to her feet from one of the armchairs, a book spilling off her lap and onto the floor. "Harlan, thanks for coming." She beamed, pleased to see him, until she also saw Nahum, and the blood drained from her face. "Nahum! I didn't know you were coming, too!"

Nahum crossed the room and pulled her to the lamp to examine her face in the light. "I was worried after I heard about last night. I'm so sorry, Olivia! Are you sure you're okay? I heard about an exorcism!"

"It's not your fault. And besides, I'm fine now. The witches did a great job of getting rid of him, and Harlan stayed with me all night."

"He did?" Nahum looked at Harlan, and for a moment, Harlan could swear he looked annoyed, before the expression vanished again.

"Sure, I did! I couldn't leave her alone after that. There was nothing funky going on! We're friends." Harlan couldn't believe he actually said that, but he felt like he should. *Just in case...*

Nahum floundered. "No, of course not. It's good. Yes. Very good." Nahum stepped back, and Harlan inwardly groaned.

How could he have missed it? Olivia looked awkward; Nahum looked awkward, and weirdly concerned. *They had slept together!* And Olivia hadn't told him. *Sneaky madam.* He cocked his head at Olivia, a knowing glint in his eye. "So, you're okay, Liv?"

She just stared at him. "I'm fine."

A cough came from behind them, and Harlan almost shrieked when he saw Morgana curled up in the corner of the sofa. "Holy shit, Morgana! You made me jump."

"I've been sitting here all along, Harlan. We're all just relaxing."

And then, as if out of nowhere, Birdie appeared in the other corner of the sofa. "Honestly Harlan, your eyes must be playing tricks on you."

He put his hands on his hips. "Oh yeah? I don't think so, ladies. Neat trick." Nahum was running his hands through his hair and shuffling like he was a child who'd been caught with his hands in the cookie jar. "Nahum, let me introduce you to the ladies of Moonfell. They have a rich sense of humour."

"Seriously, Harlan, I was just sitting there," Morgana said, rising to her feet. "The firelight casts long shadows. But you," she stared up at Nahum, "are hard to miss, even in a darkened room."

Nahum laughed. "I can disappear when I need to."

"Of course you can." Birdie also stood, appraising Nahum with her sharp gaze as she shook his hand. "Interesting."

Nahum's composure seemed to be returning. "I'm really not. We shouldn't have interrupted your evening." He looked at Harlan for support. "We won't stay long."

Odette, however, intervened, as she joined her cousin and grandmother by the fire. "Your wings are magnificent."

"My *what*?" Nahum shouted before calming himself. "Sorry, what?"

A smile played on Odette's lips, and her hands lifted. Harlan had no idea what she did, but in the next second, Nahum's wings were glimmering in the half light, fully expanded. There, but not there.

"What the fuck?" he twisted and turned. "How?"

"Odette!" Birdie reprimanded. "Stop being naughty. Poor Nahum is not used to us yet, and you have outed him." She addressed Nahum as his wings vanished again. "Sorry. But she's right, they are wonderful. Our house has never been graced by a Nephilim before." She then turned to Harlan. "You must stay for a drink. Come and help us prepare something. Tea, coffee, something stronger? No matter. We'll discuss it in the kitchen. And maybe some chocolate cake. That's always good for shock."

Before he knew quite what was happening, the three witches had whisked him out of the room, leaving Nahum and Olivia alone.

Nahum turned to Olivia, feeling like he'd been stripped naked. "What the hell is going on? How did that happen? And why are you laughing?"

She giggled as she sat down again. "Your face is a picture, that's why. They're funny, aren't they?"

"They made my wings appear! They knew!"

"No. Odette knew. The others just found you interesting."

Nahum sank into the armchair next to Olivia, relieved they were alone. His awkwardness vanished. "Sorry. I should have said I was coming, but I knew Harlan was, so..."

"It's fine. It's nice that you care." Her guarded face returned. "Honestly, I am fine."

"Harlan explained to me what happened. The whole Goddess thing, and Belial's expulsion. You should have called."

"I just felt so tired today, I could barely think straight. And after nearly being kidnapped, too." She curled her legs under her, reaching for a glass of water. "It was quite a night for everyone."

He nodded at her glass. "No wine?"

"No. Just herbal teas and water for now."

"Witches love their herbal teas," Nahum said, nodding. "I hope I don't get offered one."

"Don't worry. They like other drinks, too."

He mulled over how much he should say about his decision to use Belial's jewellery and assume his power. The fire crackled and popped in the silence, logs shifting as they burned. He needed to be honest about it. He didn't know why, but he felt like he should, especially after being so cut up about the discovery. It made his initial shock seem lame. Like an excuse to sleep with her. He didn't want her to think that, so before he could change his mind, he told her what had happened.

"You don't need to explain your reasoning to me, Nahum. Under the circumstances, you made the right choice. Sometimes our best intentions are undermined, and life just screws with us. You need to see his jewellery as a gift. It saved your life, and it might have even pissed him off."

"Maybe. Well, I just wanted you to know, so you didn't assume anything." He looked around the cosy room, the leafy wallpaper seeming to move in the firelight. "This place is amazing. How long are you staying?"

"Maybe another couple of nights."

His head whipped around to look at her. "You must feel worse than you're letting on. You look okay. Still not yourself, though." For a start, she hadn't flirted with him once, but maybe that particular part of their friendship was over now.

"Actually," she swallowed, "there's another reason I'm here. It's why they've left us alone. Poor Harlan must be wondering what's going on."

"Is something wrong?"

"Well, I guess it depends on your perspective." She shuffled again, uncomfortable. "So, what I'm going to say will be a shock, but I just want you to know that I don't expect anything from you. I don't even think this is a good time to tell you. I mean, you're heading off to fight Black Cronos tomorrow. You certainly don't need distractions, but I've been told I must. The witches are very insistent, and they're probably right. Because, you know, I don't know when I might see you next."

Nahum was starting to get worried. And confused. "Olivia—"

She cut him off. "I'm pregnant, and the baby is yours. I'm sorry. It's an accident, and I don't want you to feel..."

Time seemed to stop. "You're *what*?"

"Pregnant."

His mouth was suddenly very dry, and he stumbled to get his words out. "How do you know so soon? It was two days ago!"

"The witches. Odette, again. It seems it's impossible to keep secrets from her!" Olivia raised her hands as if to calm him down. "But I just wanted you to know. You don't have to feel obliged to do anything. I have money and resources. I certainly don't want to trap you. But you're the father, so you should know."

"Oh fuck." Nahum collapsed into the back of the chair. Being a father had never crossed his mind. Well, not for years. *And how the hell was he to tell Olivia that the baby might not survive?* Nephilim children never did. It was their curse. He looked at her face and saw a glow of happiness. "You want to keep it?'

"Yes. It's weird. I never thought I would. But as I said..." He could see her withdrawing, trying to be strong.

"No." He leaned forward, his hand shooting out to grab hers. "You misunderstand. I will support you. Of course, I will. I would never let you deal with this alone! Ever!"

"Thank you, Nahum, that means a lot. But I promise, I'm self-sufficient."

"Stop apologising. We did this, not you. In fact, as I recall, I started it."

"I didn't need much persuasion."

He gave a shaky laugh. "No. But there's something you should know, too. I don't want to tell you now, because just saying it out loud feels like a jinx, but in the spirit of honesty and all that..." He took a breath, feeling like he was gabbling. "Nephilim were not meant to have children. It was part of our making. For those who did, well...the children died young. All of them."

The blood drained from her face. "All of them?"

"As far as I know. Gabe had a child, and she died when she was three years old."

"How?"

"They become sickly, and just sort of fade away." Olivia released his hand and stared into the fire, her features showing a war of emotions. Nahum hated himself. He should have just kept silent. *He might be wrong, but if he wasn't...* "It might make you change your mind about going ahead. You could save yourself a storm of heartache later."

"Yes, there is that. But I'd also deny myself an experience I might never get again." She looked at him again, her eyes dark wells of pain. "What if this is fate, Nahum? And medicine is so different to how it used to be back then! The advancements are huge!"

"That's true, of course. But it's what we were told. How we were made. Can science and medicine change that?"

"Perhaps. Or magic might." She leaned forward. "It's what Morgana does."

Nahum desperately wanted her to be right, because despite his initial shock and misgivings, this actually did feel right. As for whether anything came of his and Olivia's relationship, that was something else. "My brothers will be in shock about this. It will rock every single one of them."

"Will they hate it?"

"Of course not! But it will start a flurry of debate, and bad memories for some of them." He groaned, unable to see the room anymore, only his brothers as he imagined the conversation he was to have. "I won't tell them now, obviously. I'll wait. You're right. It could be a distraction."

Olivia squared her shoulders, suddenly practical again. "You must put it aside, too."

"Tomorrow. Tonight, we'll discuss it with the witches. What about Harlan?"

Olivia's hands flew to her face, cupping her cheeks. "Herne's horns! What the hell will he say?"

"He'll support you no matter what."

"I know. Once he's got past taking the piss about us sleeping together. He knows already. He gave me a look!" She laughed, slightly maniacally. "Okay. We'll tell him now. Thanks for being so good about this."

"I'm not a monster, Olivia!" Nahum also hoped that Harlan wasn't about to turn into some heroic protector of Olivia, and question him about intentions.

And what about Belial? Despite his best effort, it was impossible to forget him. Belial could have more agents on Earth, spreading his destruction. *What if they found out about Olivia?*

What if they hunted her down?

Twenty-Three

Maggie had been in The Retreat for hours, and was now feeling seriously claustrophobic, despite its vast size.

How anyone could work down there all day, every day, was a mystery to her. But perhaps her experience was coloured by the catastrophic events of the afternoon. Three people were dead. The young woman, Petra, who had been shot at point blank range in the chest, the scientist named Ronald Larrington, who had been shot in the abdomen, and Russell Blake, the man who'd killed them, and had been shot by Layla.

The alchemy lab had been mostly destroyed, and the Scene of Crimes Unit had been picking through it, cataloguing everything. Russell's computer had been seized, and Waylen, despite his own injuries, had already facilitated a systemwide check on their computer systems and their staff.

The Retreat was currently sealed. None of the staff were allowed to leave. They were all gathered in the staff area, consoling each other, after Stan and Irving, her two Detective Sergeants, had interviewed them. All except for Layla Gould, who sat in front of Maggie in her own office, just down the corridor from the lab, and next to the mortuary. She was a small, elegant woman. Her hair, despite the events, still looked groomed, her makeup immaculate, and Maggie knew she must look unkempt in comparison. Layla had given a concise and professional statement, but had now fallen silent, staring at the wall. Maggie was sure she knew what she was seeing. It was a sight that haunted her, too. Seeing Russell Blake's brain splash over the lab.

"Layla," Maggie ventured, "I think you should join your colleagues in the staff room."

Layla shook her head. "I don't feel up to it. I shot Russell. I'm a doctor! These hands," she held them in front of her, "are meant to heal!"

"They also saved many lives, including my own. You're an excellent shot, by the way."

"Part of the PD training. I never thought I'd actually have to use it."

"Well, I am very glad that you took it seriously." Maggie had wondered if Layla's skills might be attributed to being a double agent, but had decided against it—mostly. Like Waylen, Maggie would do a huge amount of background checks. She suspected there would be big changes at The Retreat in the near future. Increased checks, maybe even increased staffing. Certainly new staffing.

With the formal part of the interview over, Maggie tried a different approach. "I'm really very sorry about your colleagues. Petra seemed like a nice young woman."

Layla nodded. "She was. An excellent analyst, too. I'm devastated, everyone will be. Especially Austin, her young colleague. They worked in the same office every day."

Maggie had seen him earlier. He'd been tearful, and then angry. She'd left him to Irving to deal with.

Layla continued, her voice faltering. "Jackson liked her, too. He'll be so upset—if he's still alive."

"I think he is, or they'd have killed him in the shop. I must admit, I wondered if Jackson might have been...*compromised*, security-wise. Now, I think not."

"I should bloody well think so!" Layla said, firing up. "He would never do that! Mind you, I also thought that about Russell. I saw him daily. I never suspected a thing."

"He was clever. You knew the dead scientist better than Petra, though?"

"Ron? Of course. Such a lovely man. Dogged, relentless. You say he was shot first?"

"Yes."

"Russell probably did that deliberately. Ron was the strongest. The most likely to tackle him." Layla's shoulders dropped and she started to cry. "He had a wife and children! Bastard."

Maggie gave her a moment to grieve. "What about Lynn? She seems smart."

"Very. The most capable alchemist out of the two of them. Creative. If Russell was destroying work, the chances are she can set it up again. She'll most likely have kept her own extensive records, too. She was meticulous."

"Good. I think Stan was interviewing her, so I'll check on that." Maggie stood. "Come on. You need to be with your colleagues, and I suspect they need you. With luck, we can release you all in the next hour. I'll arrange escorts to get you home."

Layla wiped her eyes and composed herself, and together they headed to the staffroom. Once she was settled with the others, Maggie walked to Waylen's office. The hushed silence of The Retreat had vanished as SOCO carried out their investigations. At least Waylen's office was in a main corridor and easy to find.

She knocked on the door and pushed it open. "Waylen? May I?"

"Of course!" He waved her to a seat. Waylen had cleaned himself up after being interviewed. He'd put a fresh shirt on and combed his hair, but he still seemed to be in pain. He sat awkwardly at an angle, favouring one hip over the other.

"I hope you'll be going to the doctor," Maggie said, again. She'd already nagged him about it earlier.

His response was the same. "I'll be okay. I just fell awkwardly. Old injury. It will be fine with rest and painkillers."

He was stubborn, and there was nothing Maggie could do about that. "Have you given any thought to my earlier question?"

"It's all I've been thinking about." Waylen huffed and leaned back in his chair, smoothing his hair automatically. "We've been friends and colleagues for years. It's fair to say that I'm devastated by his betrayal." He met Maggie's stare, his expression bleak. "But I can't for the life of me fathom why he did it, or pinpoint when it might have started. I keep examining every conversation, trying to see what I missed, but honestly, I don't know."

"Do you routinely check your security footage? I noticed cameras in the lab."

"No, but the feed will be stored electronically. Something else I shall have to start checking. If I had, I might have realised why we seemed to be going backwards, rather than progressing."

Maggie reached for her notebook, just to make sure she'd asked all relevant questions. "You suspect he has sabotaged the experiments."

"Unfortunately, yes."

"It makes sense. But wouldn't the other two alchemists have noticed?"

"Not if he was subtle. From what I gather, alchemy, like any science, requires extensive testing and minute changes to get results. It's utterly baffling to me."

"Which, of course, Russell would have known." She sighed. "Could he have brought anyone here with him? From Black Cronos?"

"No." Waylen was emphatic. "Security has been tight because of Lucien. It's meant that we've had an extra team in with him twenty-fours a day—until he left with Barak. Admittedly they were tucked away down a side corridor, but it still would have been too risky for Russell. One good thing, I guess."

"Did Russell have much to do with Lucien? Or Barak and Estelle?"

"Very little. Obviously, he knew that he was here. I've particularly agonised over that. The investigation into the latest *château* was firmly between me and Jackson."

"Why? As the Assistant Director, wouldn't he have known everything?"

"No. Absolutely not. He was very busy with the lab, and he had oversight of other paranormal activities. I supported Jackson with Black Cronos." He groaned, elbows resting on the desk. "Actually, he had been pushing to be more involved, but I refused. I didn't want him dragged into it because it's so distracting. I wanted him to remain focussed on the lab work. He was cranky about it, but I assumed that was the lack of progress."

"Good. Because hopefully that means that team is safe, and your entire operation isn't compromised." Maggie didn't know if Waylen knew about the team's job in Egypt. She knew they were up to something, but Harlan hadn't said what, and as it was nothing to do with London, she didn't pry. The less she knew, the less she had to lie about, too. She decided not to mention it. "Have you had any updates from Barak or Estelle?"

"Not today. I trust everything is going smoothly, or Barak would have contacted me."

"That's good, then." She packed her notebook away after jotting down a few points, and then stood up. "You need to wrap up here. My team will probably be here tomorrow, too. This is a big breach. You won't be allowed in."

"I'm in charge!"

"There have been three deaths. You can come back when we're done."

"But how can I help the team in France?"

"You still have a phone and remote access to your computer?" He nodded. "Good. For now, Waylen, that will have to do."

Estelle cast her shadow spell again, making sure it was strong enough to protect herself and her four companions.

The spell was normally simple, but the Nephilim and Lucien had strong auras of their own that threatened the efficacy of the spell. It had taken several renditions and a tweak to cover all of them. Gabe and Niel's presence had vastly complicated things.

"Okay. You're all done. Happy?"

"This is downright freaky," Niel complained. "I can't see myself!"

"That's the point!"

"I'm going to fall over my feet!"

Barak sniggered to her left. "Are you a toddler? You don't need to see your feet!"

"Piss off, Barak. You've had practice!"

Gabe groaned. "Will you both shut up! Will it protect us from infrared cameras or night vision goggles?"

"Hard to say," Estelle admitted, "but I've added a cooling spell into it. That's why you might feel colder than usual. I'm hoping to mask everything."

"Colder! *Mon Dieu*. My junk has shrunk!" Lucien complained. "I'm hardly a man at all right now!"

That elicited a belly laugh from Barak. "My friend, you need Nephilim blood. It's less of an issue."

"You might regret that," Estelle pointed out, "if he's invisible and you're not. Now," she looked around the forest that bristled with night sounds, "should we move on?"

"For the love of the Gods, yes please," Gabe said.

Estelle led the way through the tightly packed tree trunks, following the path they had discovered that afternoon. She had marked the way with a few spells just in case the darkness confused them, and she led them steadily towards the base of the ridge the castle stood on. Like that afternoon, they had parked by a walking track, and hidden the car beneath the trees and another shadow spell. It was well out of range of the castle, but all of them were wary.

They emerged out of the tree line onto a rock-strewn field, the base of the ridge only a short distance ahead. Estelle tipped her head back and craned to see the top. She could just about see the battlements, but that was all from this angle.

"That is one big ridge!" Gabe complained. "That's a lot of ground to cover."

"Which is why we can't waste time," Barak said. "At least the winter gives us long nights. If you look up and to the right, about a third of the way up the ridge, there's a darker area I thought might be an entrance."

"But there's no path to it," Niel said.

"Maybe that's the point. Maybe it's only accessible from inside. But for us, that's not a problem. I suggest that I fly myself and Estelle there and we check it out. You guys should check the rest of the base. The road is around to the west. There's guard activity there."

"I'll check that," Gabe said immediately. "They'll be the first people we should eliminate when we attack tomorrow. Niel, why don't you search further to the east and north with Lucien?"

"Fine with me. But if we're spotted?"

"Don't be!" Barak growled, "or we might find the place impregnable tomorrow."

Estelle tutted. "You know the risks, Niel."

"I meant, do I kill them? But I know the answer to that. Of course I do. Come on, Lucien. Let's hike closer, and then we'll think about flight."

"Let's say three hours, maximum," Gabe suggested. "We meet back by the car. And if you think you've been spotted, just leave."

The others moved out, and Estelle used her binoculars to check the area she and Barak would investigate. "It's hard to see anything in this light."

"Time for an aerial view, then."

She stepped into Barak's arms, and in moments they were flying up the face of the ridge. Even now, she relished his embrace and how safe she felt in it, but she focussed on the job. Up close, the vegetation was thicker along the steep faces than she'd realised. Shrubs clung to the sides, leggy and windblown in places, while straggling pines soared high, their roots buried deep in pockets of earth.

"Those shrubs could be hiding many entrances, Barak," she whispered close to his ear.

"I doubt it. It would make them too vulnerable, even though it would take a mountain climber to reach them. Anyway, we only need one, although two would be perfect."

They both fell quiet as they reached the narrow cleft. Nothing stirred, and satisfied, Barak moved closer. He hovered for a while, and she knew his eyesight would detect more than hers.

"All good," he murmured, as he swept in and landed on the lip of the cleft. He released his grip, and they stepped inside.

It was pitch black, and Estelle waited for her eyes to adjust to the light, desperate to use a witch-light, but knowing she shouldn't. Barak, however, moved ahead confidently. Not wanting him to be alone, she advanced, stumbling slightly. It was freezing in the cave, the walls slick with moisture and ice in places. The cleft was narrow with a high roof, the other end in darkness. But there was no sign of it being a lookout for the castle's inhabitants. Within only a few feet, the ceiling and walls tapered in and down, until she crouched to advance. She bumped into Barak.

He grumbled. "Damn it. It's a dead end. Can you detect anything behind the walls? Any tunnels?"

Estelle placed her hands on the freezing stone, working her way back towards the entrance, but all she detected was solid bedrock. "Absolutely nothing."

Finally, they both stood on the edge again, looking onto the valley. It sparkled under the stars, the peaks white with snow. It was beautiful in its starkness. It was hard to think they were beneath the *comte's* castle, in a place that had been part of a religious war. A place that was very fitting for Black Cronos.

"At least we've eliminated it," Barak said. "And we have plenty more hours left. Ready?"

"Ready." She stepped into his arms again.

Gabe flew around to the west and found shelter in a huge pine tree. He settled into its thick greenery, the branches creaking beneath his weight. Fortunately, the wind was picking up, and the entire canopy creaked back and forth as if he was on the deck of a ship.

He had a good view of the road that turned up the ridge to the castle gates. The road was as steep as he anticipated, following the natural dips of the rock face as it switched back and forth. Precipitous, certainly. He lost sight of it at points, as it wound behind the trees. There was no security on the lower part, but he quickly spotted what Barak had seen. A third of the way up, a light came from a lodge at the edge of the trees, and a huge, wooden gate blocked the road. He adjusted his night vision goggles and saw a camera on one corner.

That was something they had to take care of—or avoid.

He focussed on the lodge. It had two levels, with a door on the ground floor and barred windows on each level. Although it backed onto the trees, three sides were clear, with a good view of the road leading to and away from the gate, and the gate itself. That would be a problem for Gabe and his brothers. They could fly over it, but they needed to take care of the guards before anyone radioed from the castle for help. *But how many guards were there?*

Gabe needed to get closer. Knowing he was risking a lot, and with his own words of warning in his ears, he flew behind the lodge and perched in a branch a few trees back. That's when he spotted another large, single-story building beneath the trees. A pocket was carved out of the hillside, the trees blocking it from view. Voices came from below as a couple of soldiers crossed from the guard tower to the building. He heard a door bang shut, and the voices vanished.

Gabe eased downwards, hand over hand, branch to branch, until he had a clear view of the building below. It looked like a barracks. It was impossible to say how many soldiers it housed without getting closer, but if there were bunks, or it went underground, there could be between fifty to a hundred soldiers down there. If this was just a small contingent, and there were more in the castle, they were in big trouble.

They were going to need a lot more weapons.

"There!" Niel pointed to an area to the north of the escarpment, a quarter of the way up. "Where the waterfall starts."

"I can't see your arm, you idiot!" Lucien complained.

Niel groaned. "This shadow spell is annoying!"

"Actually, I think it's fading. I can see a little bit of you. You're like a ghost."

Niel blinked as if his eyes were playing tricks, but Lucien was right. He could see his faint outline. They had spent nearly an hour tramping around the north side, investigating various crevices, and he'd hoped the spell would last longer. "We'd better get on with it, then. Look at the waterfall! There."

"It's a trickle of water! Hardly a waterfall."

"By definition, it's still a waterfall! Besides, it's the exit that interests me. It looks broad, like the entrance to a cave. Could be a way in."

"Or it could be a quick way to get lost and die in the dark."

Niel glowered at him. "We won't know unless we check. Ready for a lift?"

"While I hate to doubt your strength, I'm a man. I'm heavier than Estelle. I don't wish to be dropped and die."

"I'm a Nephilim. I can handle it. Or do you want to climb? Or even stay here?"

"I'm not a goat or a coward. So be it."

Niel flew them up the steep rockface, battling the strong wind coming from the north that kept trying to drive him into the rock. The spray of the water was icy, but Niel ignored it, angled his wings closer to his body, and swept into the cave it emerged from. Up close, the stream was broader and deeper than he had initially thought, running down the centre of the narrow cave.

He landed on rocky ground to the right. Beyond the entrance the roof sloped up, and the cave stretched back. "Watch your step," he warned Lucien. "It's icy."

Treading carefully, they advanced further in, following the stream as it twisted into the hillside. It seemed that Lucien's Black Cronos changes had improved his eyesight, because he seemed to see as well as Niel. They proceeded in silence until they reached a metal-barred gate set into the rock. A large cave opened beyond it, a pool of inky black water in the centre rimmed with ice. And something else.

Satisfied there was no sign of soldiers, Niel whispered, "Can you see the mechanism over there?"

"*Oui.* I can't make it out, though. Is it a lift shaft?"

"A lift? Down here? Sounds nuts." Niel strained to see further in, but the cave stretched to the right, well beyond his view. "Perhaps it's a maintenance area? It would make sense that they have dug into the rock."

"But this is a long way down!"

Niel studied the thick gate. *That would take a lot of strength to move. And destroying it would make noise and risk a rock fall.* "This could be our only way in, down here. They must have more security than just this!"

"Listen!"

They both fell silent, pressing their backs to the rockface instinctively. Niel heard a low, whirring noise coming from above, and became aware of minute vibrations around them. The longer they stood, the more the weight of rock seemed to press in on them, but there was no doubt something was moving. Something huge.

One thing was certain. They couldn't go any further that night, but they would definitely be back tomorrow.

Twenty-Four

O n Saturday morning, Eli finished packing his bag to take to France, and carried it down to the farmhouse's living room. Immediately, he saw the box containing Belial's jewellery.

He could still feel the effects of Belial's strength, faint though it was. His sleep had been uneasy, filled with the images of one of the most powerful Fallen Angels in human form. Piercing blue eyes, long, white-blond hair, and high cheekbones that sculpted his face into ethereal beauty. An icy beauty, though. Unforgiving. His true, angelic form was spirit, not flesh, but the Fallen could always impose their will on the flesh of the hosts that they possessed. Belial was regal, tall, clad in armour that was richly engraved and moulded to fit his muscular body. Designed to impress and instil fear. And it worked. Men quaked at the sight of him. Usually before their death, from either his sword or madness.

Eli opened the wooden box the witches had spelled with protection. While he loathed Belial and all he stood for, his jewellery had saved their lives.

A footfall behind him announced Zee's arrival, and he said, "You should leave that shut."

"Should I? Or should we take it with us?" He turned to face Zee, seeing his brother's wary expression as he placed his own bag on the floor.

Zee's black hair was tied back, and he was dressed in black fatigues and a t-shirt, ready for battle already. "You know my feelings on it. I think you've been possessed by his madness."

"No. I have been blessed with self-preservation."

Zee crossed the room to his side. "Have you forgotten how much you needed Briar last night? You said you felt toxic."

"Of course I haven't forgotten. He's haunted my dreams. I still feel a tingle in my fingers, where his power flooded into my sword. But we are facing Black Cronos in their stronghold! Have *you* forgotten how you were nearly blown up in a crashing helicopter?"

"Hardly! Especially seeing as I can still smell burnt oil and hot metal."

"Then why are we having this conversation?"

"Because I saw you." Zee grasped Eli's arms as if to shake sense into him. "You were incandescent! You and Nahum. I'm your brother, and you scared *me*! I'm not ashamed to admit it."

"I would never have hurt you. I still knew what I was doing."

"Did you?" Zee searched his face as if he doubted him. "Because you looked lost to me. Drowned in Belial's power. And I almost got into a fight with Nahum last night because of the damn jewellery. You stopped us!"

Zee was right in some respects; he couldn't deny that. "It was overwhelming, but I was there all along. You know the feeling. We all experienced it millennia ago."

"That's what worries me. It narrowed our vision. Reduced our ability to judge."

"But we were still there. We were still us!"

Zee released his arms and stepped back. "We shouldn't allow them back. It might become a crutch."

"Like a drug."

"Exactly."

"But there is no *them*, only Belial." He smiled at Zee. "I'm a lover, not a fighter. When this is done, we find a way to dispose of these. Then we find the person who's behind their appearance."

Zee studied him, a wary acceptance in his eyes. "You are powerful in your own right. We all are. We do not need these trinkets."

"They're hardly trinkets."

"They are to me. We don't need them. We seven will fight together, and we won't need Belial to help us."

Eli knew Zee meant for the best, but he also thought he was short-sighted. "Would we have won last night without him?"

"Yes." But there was a flicker of doubt in Zee's eyes.

That was enough for Eli. He would pack the box, regardless.

Jackson stared at the soldier in front of him, wondering what new level of hell he was about to witness.

He was olive-skinned, broad shouldered, and brawny. His light brown hair was cut close to his scalp, and he had the usual impassive stare that all Black Cronos solders had. At least his eyes hadn't changed colour yet, which he hoped signified that he wasn't about to attack Jackson. However, he stood to attention, eyes fixed on the *Comte de St Germain*.

They were in a room in one of the guard towers on the walls surrounding the castle. The view was outstanding. Snowy mountaintops encircled them, their jagged peaks staggeringly beautiful in their own, deadly way. Their immediate surroundings were the lower ranges, a chain of castles stretching away. The last strongholds of the Cathars. He knew from his own research that many were now ruins, their inhabitants persecuted and slaughtered. Roads wound through the valleys below, and even though he couldn't see them, Jackson knew small towns dotted the landscape.

Everything below looked tiny and insignificant, cars like ants crawling along the terrain. At least they had stopped blindfolding him now that he knew his fate.

After his breakfast, Jackson had been collected from his cell and marched along the battlements. Jackson had counted at least a dozen guards stationed at various points, all armed, and all wrapped up against the bitter cold. He wondered who else inhabited the castle. There must be more staff he hadn't seen yet.

It was a grey day, the mass of clouds promising rain, or maybe even snow. At any point he expected to be threatened with being thrown from the battlements if he failed to join the count's organisation or agree to call Waylen. But they had asked him nothing so far. He had been escorted in silence. As usual, Deandra was guarding him, and Stefan was there too, looking far too pleased with himself.

"Good morning, *commandant*. No need to stand to attention," the *comte* said. "Take a seat." He gestured to the hard wooden chairs gathered around a table. When they were all settled, he said to the guard, "Tell me, how long have you worked for me?"

"Sixty years, sir," he answered in English, but with a French accent.

Jackson gasped. "Sixty! You look barely older than thirty!"

The *comte* beamed at Jackson. "As I told you yesterday, age means nothing as a Black Cronos soldier." He turned to the soldier again. "Tell our guest when you were enhanced?"

"As a child. I was three."

"Do you remember anything of the process?"

"No. It was painless."

"How would you describe your abilities now?"

The *commandant* gave a hard smile. "I am exceptionally strong. Bound to my guiding planet and all its associations. I call upon my strengths to fight." As he spoke, his skin and eyes glowed like dull metal.

Rather than withdraw, Jackson edged forward to study him. He changed so seamlessly. It was uncanny. Under the edge of his clothes, he could see the beginning of tattoos that glowed like fire. He had only seen Lucien change so close up before. Despite his fear, and natural abhorrence, it was fascinating.

"Can you still think for yourself?" Jackson asked, interrupting the interview.

The soldier looked to the count for permission to speak, and he nodded. "Go ahead. Answer him."

"Of course I can."

"So why do you stay here, bound to this monster who made you?"

"Because it's who I am." The man laughed, looking at Jackson as if he was a worm. "I am superior in every way to you. Here I use my skills fully, and I'm well paid as a senior officer."

"To kill people? How very noble," Jackson spat.

"If necessary, I do. Otherwise, I guard the castle and our new recruits. Our job is to help them acclimatise to their new world."

"And if they don't?" Jackson didn't expect the question to be answered, and he turned to the *comte* and Stefan. "It's one thing to groom a child for this lifestyle, quite another an adult. You must do something to them to make them stay. They will have left lives behind. Family!"

Stefan tutted with impatience. "Jackson. Many have nothing to go back to! We give them purpose. Some were already mercenaries. Now they have new lives."

Mercenaries? That explained a lot. "You prey on the weak, as we suspected all along. And I know that during the Second World War, and other wars, no doubt, you used captured soldiers to experiment on." Jackson had tried to remain calm, but he felt his fury build again. "Why am I here? Do you think I'll change my mind? You haven't warped my mind like you have everyone else's here. It's like a cult! A cult to monstrosities."

The *comte* banged the table with his fist. "It's alchemy and my genius! Not a cult."

"That's what all cult leaders say. All of this makes you feel powerful!"

"I *am* powerful." The *comte* took a deep breath and leaned back, his gaze drifting around the room. "I was here when the Cathars were attacked by the Albigensian Crusade. That was followed by the Medieval Inquisition. Men have always sought to destroy what they do not understand. Particularly the Church. The Cathars believed that humans were the sexless spirits of angels, trapped in the human body. Trapped in the realm of the evil God. You're aware of the two Gods of their belief?"

Jackson nodded, wondering where the *comte* was going.

"It was quite a time. I've always been open to different beliefs. You should have seen all the castles when they were new. Strongholds of might. That's what started my quest, you know."

"What?" Jackson felt like he was on a merry-go-round.

"The sexless spirits of angels. I thought that if angels were trapped in human flesh, it was a brilliant thing to transform them. Try to free them from their mortal shackles. I wanted to be their liberator. I thought they would help me find immortality." He smiled at Jackson benevolently. "As it was, I discovered that myself, and as the Cathars fell, I also discovered that angels are not trapped in human flesh. They exist in their own sphere, along with the other Gods and deities, demons, and spirits. So instead, I sought to elevate humanity. Why should we be trapped in flesh that decays in so short a lifespan?"

Jackson was now convinced the count was completely insane. "And yet you haven't gifted mankind with immortality, have you?"

"Of course not. The planet would be overrun. Most people do not deserve it. Only a few of us are worthy." He stared at his hands, his long fingers flexing and stretching. "My soldiers are worthy of longevity. Not immortality. I still strive for perfection, but you know that."

Stefan cleared his throat. "Perhaps..."

"Oh, yes. To business. I presume you still do not wish to bargain for a truce, regardless of what I have shown you. The scale of my operation. What you are up against?"

"No. Despite the fact you have wheeled this puppet in front of me."

"Puppet. Interesting." The *comte* smirked at Stefan. "I see the resemblance now, don't you?"

"Indeed. I'm surprised Jackson cannot."

Unease rippled through Jackson. "What are you talking about?"

The *comte* flicked a finger at the soldier. "Tell him your name."

"My name is Laurent Strange."

Blood thundered in Jackson's ears. It couldn't be his grandfather. This soldier said he was three years old sixty years ago. "Just because he has my surname doesn't mean anything..."

The count smiled. "I assure you, it does. This is your uncle. Now, do you see why I have introduced you? You wage war on us, and you risk killing your own family. Now perhaps you will make the call?"

By the time Shadow exited the car in front of the chalet that Barak's team was effectively squatting in, she needed to stretch, and hopefully release her pent-up energy by sparring.

The journey had only taken a few hours, but by the time she factored in waits at the airport, clearing passport control, and then retrieving their weapons from checked baggage, it had seemed to take forever. Then they had picked up the rental car to drive there. That hadn't been fun, either.

Harlan had volunteered to drive. Once again, everyone looked horrified at the prospect of her driving. She found it all rather insulting. And to make matters worse, the atmosphere was weird. Nahum and Harlan were quiet and preoccupied, and Ash was mulling on his injury. It had been tedious. She presumed Nahum was brooding about Olivia, even though he'd said she was fine. Nahum was clearly more invested than he was letting on. *Interesting*. She had no idea what Harlan's issue was. She charitably decided it was concern for Jackson.

Seeing Gabe was a breath of fresh air. He was dressed entirely in black, and his thick, dark brown hair was swept back, revealing his perfect face. Perfect to her, anyway. He bounded down the chalet's steps to the drive to help with their luggage, and swept her into his arms.

"You made it! I'm very relieved I won't have to break you out of prison."

"You will never have to worry about that, Gabe Malouf. You missed me?"

"Always." He kissed her, and despite her best intentions not to be overly affectionate in public, kissed him back, her hands threading through his hair.

That is until Niel yelled, "Get a bloody room!"

She drew back, still staring into Gabe's deep brown eyes. "Let me stab him. Just once."

"Best not. He'd only be worse."

"I can hear you, sister," Niel said, startlingly close. She whirled around to see he was at the back of the car holding a bag of weapons in one hand, and an overnight bag in the other. His blond hair was loose, and he had a rakish grin on his face. "Need to let off some steam with some sparring? Or would you rather be soppy with my brother?"

Gabe groaned. "Herne's horns. Do you two have to start already?"

Shadow cupped her hands around Gabe's face. "I love you, but I need to beat your brother's oversized ego into submission."

Niel laughed as he carried the bags into the house. "I give you ten minutes!"

Ash forced a laugh, and after a brief nod of greeting to Gabe, followed Niel up the stairs without a word.

Harlan just said, "I need a shower. Catch you later, guys."

Only Nahum was left on the driveway, and Gabe turned to him, frowning. "Are you all right? You look like you bear the weight of the world."

"It's been a full couple of days, Gabe, that's all. Finding Belial's jewellery, and then using it has taken its toll. I'll put some coffee on. Then I'll be fine." He picked up his own bag and Shadow's. "See you inside."

Gabe watched him walk up the stairs. "What's up with everyone?"

"I don't know." She lowered her voice, even though they were alone. "It was a solemn journey. Everyone was preoccupied. I can normally get a rise out of Harlan, but today? Nothing!"

"I guess we've all got things on our mind. I'll talk to Nahum later. This Belial business troubles me."

"But we'll deal with it, right?"

"Of course." He smiled and kissed her again. "I've missed you. I thought we'd be stuck in Egypt forever. Anyway, come and see the others before you and Niel try to kill each other. Eli, Zee, and Caspian are here."

She followed him up the stairs, shivering in the bitter cold. "How are they?"

"Caspian is fine. Eli and Zee, however, are as distracted as the others. I didn't help. Eli and I had words."

"Oh! Then it's a good job we have a mission tonight. There's nothing like a battle to clear the head."

"Weirdly, Caspian seems to have lifted everyone's spirits. Even Estelle's. And Niel is cooking, so that helps."

"Good." Niel was an excellent cook. "And Lucien?"

"Fine so far."

Fortunately, the house was warm, and although the chalet was rustic, it was comfortable. After Gabe had shown her their room, they joined the rest of the group in the large living area.

Once Shadow had greeted everyone, Gabe addressed them all. "We're only waiting for JD now, so I suggest that once he arrives, we discuss our plans. If you need to shower, eat, or spar, do it soon. And allow time for rest later! I don't see the point in delaying things. Tonight is going to be long and hard. We can't afford to get this wrong. We all know the consequences if we do."

He didn't need to elaborate.

Shadow thought she might pop if she didn't expend some energy soon. She caught Niel's eye. "Come on, then. Time to play. The rest of you should, too—even you,

Ash. The sooner you know your limitations with that shoulder, the safer you'll be. I do not intend to lose this fight."

"None of us do," Estelle pointed out, voice dripping sarcasm. She never disappointed.

Shadow grinned at her. "I've missed you. Care to join us?"

"It will be my pleasure."

Twenty-Five

s Barak watched his assembled brothers, Shadow, Estelle, Caspian, JD, and Harlan, he started to feel that perhaps they might have a chance at succeeding in destroying *Château de Bénaix*.

They were gathered in the chalet's living room, but Barak was worried about his brothers. Their moods were unusually grim. Zee was brooding about the jewellery that Eli had brought with them. Eli had weathered the storm of Gabe's fury on that subject, and now sat with Ash. Ash was clearly worried about his injured shoulder. He put Nahum's brooding down to finding and then using Belial's jewellery. Barak didn't blame him. He would most likely have done the same. Harlan seemed preoccupied too, and he figured that was nerves. Lucien, understandably, was worried about his own abilities, and about meeting Black Cronos again.

Caspian seemed his usual self. On his arrival, he greeted Estelle warmly and she reciprocated. For months, Caspian and Estelle had been at odds, but now they had reached a truce. For Estelle to have asked for his help said volumes. It was important to Barak that Estelle mended her relationship with him. He was not only her brother, but a good friend to all the Nephilim, and Barak was glad he'd agreed to help. Caspian would give her valuable magical support, and it eased Barak's concern for her. Because, despite all of Estelle's powers, Barak worried about her safety, and the thought that she might be injured or captured—*or worse*—filled him with horror. She returned his gaze, as if aware of his stare, and smiled. He winked in return.

Shadow had lifted everyone's mood. They had all had a vigorous and challenging sparring session in the chalet's garden that eventually left them hot, sweaty, and a good deal happier than they had been earlier. Shadow—bossy, exuberant, and as belligerent as ever—could always be relied upon to ignite the mood in one way or another.

And then there was JD. He had arrived on a later flight, which landed at a different airport, and he made his own way to them. At least he had brought new weapons that he had just finished demonstrating. Niel, who always loved weapons, was happy.

"JD! You have outdone yourself." Niel grasped the small, rose gold weapon in his large hands. "I prefer my axe, but this is next best."

JD preened. "It has a longer range. And these," he opened up a box containing silver balls, "are my own type of grenade."

Shadow grinned. "They are so good! I want one."

"Slow down!" Gabe said. "We need to work out who's with who, and who attacks where tonight. Then we decide who gets what weapon. Who has swords?"

There was a chorus of "I do" from every Nephilim, and Shadow. They had been able to travel with them in checked luggage after Jackson had prepared official government paperwork for them weeks ago. Niel had even been able to travel with his double-headed axe, and Shadow had transported her bow. It had made their life much simpler. And safer.

"How did you get those weapons through security?" Barak asked JD as he examined an oval, silver object like a squashed egg with a gemstone at the tapered end. It felt far too insubstantial to cause any damage, but after JD's demonstration, he couldn't doubt their worth.

"They're not weapons until they're activated. They just look like metal objects of art. Easy."

"And so unnerving," Harlan pointed out. "Bombs on board an aircraft. Just fucking perfect."

"You'll be glad of them later, I'm sure," Shadow told him.

"What about you, Caspian?" JD asked, fixing his intense stare on him. "You're a witch, you say?" JD had been sidetracked with his weapons and hadn't paid much attention to Caspian when they were introduced.

He nodded. "Yes. I'm Estelle's older brother, and I do not need weapons. I have my magic." He effortlessly conjured a ball of fire in his palms. "And I'm an air witch, so I can use witch-flight. Handy in tight corners."

"Witch-flight?" JD leaned forward eagerly. "What's that?"

"I can summon air and dissolve my body into it to transport myself somewhere else." Caspian frowned. "Not a great explanation. I'd best give a demonstration."

Caspian had been seated at the long dining table under the picture window, but he stood up and vanished in a swirling vortex of air, appearing again at the far side of the room.

"God's pox!" JD leapt to his feet and strode across the room to pace around Caspian as if he was a specimen in a lab. "That was magnificent! You use elemental air as a method of transport. Ingenious. I have never seen that happen before! In all my years..."

"Then you've clearly never met an air witch before. Or," Caspian grinned, "they've never trusted you enough to show you their skills. I assure you that I'm not unique. I can even transport others."

"Show me! How far can we go?"

"No more than a few miles, for safety's sake. It drains my power and might make you sick. Perhaps we should just cross the room for now?"

"Yes!"

By now the whole room was watching, amused, as JD pranced around like an excited teenager. Lucien was similarly awestruck. Caspian smiled at JD like an indulgent father, and he extended his arms. "Step close, then."

In another whirl of air that sent papers flapping, they transported to the other side of the room. Within seconds, JD was on his knees retching, and yet his eyes gleamed with a fervour that Barak was far too familiar with as Caspian helped him to his feet.

After enormous deep breaths, JD declared, "We must discuss this further. Your energies are clearly attuned to elemental air. Such symmetry. Such power."

Shadow rolled her eyes. "Beware, Caspian, he'll be running experiments on you if you're not careful. My affinity with earth magic had much the same effect on him."

JD threw his arms wide. "But this is what alchemy is about! The essence of life itself. And you embody it! Or an aspect of it, at least!"

Gabe coughed loudly. "Can we get back to the subject? We are planning an assault on Black Cronos! Or trying to..."

JD wagged a finger at Caspian. "We will talk later, young man!"

Caspian laughed. "Young man? I haven't been called that in a while, but of course." He turned to Gabe. "Sorry, should we sit down and plan our strategies? Time is marching on."

With a look of gratitude, Gabe sat, and everyone joined him around the table, stools taken from the kitchen when they ran out of chairs.

"Perhaps," Gabe suggested, "Barak, Estelle, and Lucien should lead this. Tell us what we know."

Between them, they outlined their months of investigations, and the recent confirmation that the *Château de Bénaix* was Count Germaine's base. What they hoped was the control centre of his operation. Then Gabe and Niel explained what they had found the previous evening.

JD stared at Niel and Lucien. "You heard a mechanism? Like an engine?"

Lucien shrugged. "Perhaps. It wasn't loud, unless the rock muffled it."

"I wonder," Barak suggested, "whether it works the alchemical wheel I saw on the roof. They moved some of the circles the night before last. I thought it might be to do with the solstice."

Niel frowned. "Perhaps, but we were two thirds of the way down the ridge. If the wheel is in the courtyard, surely that's too far beneath it?"

JD stared at Barak. "Set into the courtyard you say? How big was it?"

"Big! Fifty metres across, perhaps. I heard the grind of the stone moving while I watched. Some of the sigils lit up, too." He frowned as he recalled which ones. Like his brothers, he could speak any language and interpret signs and sigils. "The rune of Rowan, and the sign of Sagittarius, if I recall correctly."

JD worried his lip with his fingers. "A wheel like mine? The power that could generate would be huge. But if it's on the top of the ridge, then the mechanism would be beneath it..."

"Exactly," Niel reasoned. "I think that what we heard must power something else. There looked to be a shaft there, too, but most of the cave was hidden from sight. I'm more than happy to be part of the group who investigates that. But getting in will not be easy. The gate is made from huge steel bars set into the rock. I won't be able to get it out on my own."

Gabe nodded. "Okay. Barak, you found no other entrances?"

"Not one." Barak huffed with disappointment. "Just narrow clefts that went nowhere."

"Do you think we could have missed one?"

Estelle shook her head. "No. We were very thorough."

"Us, too," Lucien added. "Nothing northeast beyond what we found."

"It makes sense," Harlan said as he flicked through the photos they had of the castle. "No point in having an impregnable castle that features several entrances."

"Surely in the past they'd want an escape route?" Ash said. "Somewhere the women and children could use when they were under siege."

"I agree, Ash, and I have a theory," Gabe said. "As you know, I saw what I think were barracks behind the gate. What if there's a way into the *château* from there? The road loops around several times before it reaches the main gate. It would take a while to get to the top. Whereas a route underground would be so much quicker, and less dependent on weather, too."

"Sounds plausible," Zee agreed. "A separate barracks to supplement the one that must be in the main castle."

"There's plenty of soldiers there," Barak confirmed. "At least a dozen on the battlements, probably two, and plenty of buildings that could house them. The walls were thick. Six guard towers. Mounted weapons."

Eli looked puzzled. "I don't understand how you managed to get so close to see that, and not be shot out of the sky?"

"There was low, heavy cloud cover, and I kept very high initially. As the mist drifted in, I glided onto a high tower that looked to be some kind of communications nest. I think, for all of their available security, they are a little complacent here, or perhaps the cold has made them lazy. And of course, their elevated position offers them protection."

"No shadow spell?" Caspian asked Estelle.

"I wasn't with him. He has greater manoeuvrability without me. And I wasn't sure how long my shadow spell would last without me there. I did a lot of work yesterday to enhance it, and it still didn't last as long as I hoped."

Niel grunted. "Two hours tops, without you there to keep strengthening it."

"And I'd rather not be overconfident with it," Barak admitted.

"Okay, that's useful to know," Eli said, nodding.

"So," Gabe continued, "we have one sure way in. The *château* itself, which we can fly to, that has lots of guards. We have one way we *think* we can get in, the way Niel and Lucien found, but of course, that might be a dead end, too. And the barracks. Either way, all need to be targets. There are thirteen of us—let's hope that's lucky!"

"But what's our actual objective?" Nahum asked, stirring out of a deep, watchful silence. "To kill them, destroy the castle, or what? We all need to be clear on it."

Lucien answered quickly. "We need to stop them turning more humans into alchemical soldiers! If they have a master mechanism here, its destruction must be the goal. It doesn't matter how many satellite buildings they have, if this place is destroyed, they are no use!"

"Agreed," Estelle said, casting a dark look at Barak. "What we discovered was horrible. In all likelihood, we'll find more prisoners here, or at least a prison of sorts."

"And with that," Ash pointed out, "will come staff, kitchens, cells... There could be anything in that castle, or under it!"

"Are we insane?" Zee asked, looking around the room. "Thirteen of us to take on all *that*?"

"Maybe fourteen," Harlan reminded them. "Jackson could be in there. He could have been in that helicopter you saw."

"That's something else to consider," Zee said. "What if Jackson isn't there, and our attack jeopardises his safety? Hell, it could anyway!"

Barak knew Zee was trying to cover all angles, but Barak was cross anyway. "We can't back out now. We're too close. We may never have another chance again."

"I'm not suggesting we do!"

"We also have Belial's jewellery," Eli cut in. "That gives us the advantage."

"I thought," Ash said, "we were trying to avoid them in this life, not *use* them!"

An uneasy silence fell, in which everyone, including JD, eventually turned to Gabe.

He sighed, hands cradling the back of his head as he leaned back in his chair. "You know my feelings on the Fallen, but we can't ignore the power they give us. Who amongst us, the Nephilim that is," he shot Shadow a quelling stare as she bounced in her seat, "is willing to use it? There are three pieces."

"I will," Niel said immediately. "That sly, angelic, slippery little shit won't get the better of me."

"He didn't get the better of *me*," Eli pointed out forcefully. "But I won't deny that I didn't like the feel of him again."

"I understand, brother," Barak said, meeting Eli's eyes. "I think you made a good decision under the circumstances, but I also know the cost. I have done it before and came out unscathed. I can do it again." He turned to Gabe. "*If* I have to."

Estelle took a sharp intake of breath. "Barak!"

"I'll be okay, Estelle. Trust me." Her lips were tight, her eyes wary, but she nodded, and Barak knew they would have a much fuller discussion on the topic later that day.

"Then I will take the third," Gabe volunteered. "Nahum and Eli have done their share, and Zee has made his feelings clear – and I don't disagree. But Eli also has a point. So, now that it's settled, you're right, Nahum. We need to be clear about our objective. It is not to search every inch of that castle and kill every single Black Cronos member, it is to destroy their ability to make more of them. And of course, weaken their organisation as much as possible."

JD laughed scornfully. "If the *comte* still lives, he will simply replicate it. He has money, that much is clear, and knowledge. We should kill him."

Gabe shrugged. "For once we agree, JD. Cut off the head and hope the rest withers. I presume, JD, you will be of most use if we can find where he transforms his victims?"

"Yes, absolutely. I should at least understand the set-up."

"Then you will go with Niel to the cave. Hopefully you can find a way into the heart of the complex. If you can't, come join us at the barracks. Perhaps two more members for that team? What about you, Ash? Your brains could help there. I want two Nephilim on every team."

"No problem. I'm sure my shoulder won't hinder us." He rubbed it with his palm. "Briar's magic has made a huge difference."

"I can offer you some more healing," Estelle said. "We have plenty of time before tonight."

He smiled at her gratefully. "Thank you. But I was also wondering, Barak, about your healing power? From your father."

Barak was surprised. It was something he'd barely considered trying before. It had only seemed to activate when he was near death, and he hadn't even realised it. "I know it healed me, when I was least expecting it, but I have no idea how to use it to help others. Although," he hurriedly added after seeing Ash's disappointed expression, "I'm obviously happy to try. Maybe Estelle can help me to use it."

"Thank you. I really appreciate it."

Niel changed the subject. "We need something to get us through that barred gate. My considerable strength," Niel flexed his biceps, "will not do it. And don't even suggest using Belial's trick so early."

"Then you need a witch," Caspian said. "Plus, if there are alarms or cameras down there, I can disable them."

"Glad to have you on the team," Niel said.

"Good, then that's settled," Gabe continued. "So that's Niel, Ash, JD, and Caspian assigned."

Harlan interrupted. "What about me? I will be no good fighting Black Cronos. They are far too skilled for me, and I'll just get in the way."

"Then you go with Niel. You can search for Jackson once you're inside. Someone has to assume responsibility for that, so that works for me. Although, obviously, we must all keep watch for him. But," Gabe warned him, "don't go off alone!"

"Nope! Scout's honour!"

"Okay. Then I will lead the attack on the gate and barracks. I *am* aiming to kill as many as possible there, because when we attack at the top, they'll call for reinforcements."

"Hold on," Zee said, holding his hands up. "Do we even need to attack at the top? Maybe stealth is the key."

Shadow gave her usual, feral grin. "We need them to panic! The more places we attack, the bigger the team they'll think we have, the more likely they will make bad decisions. I think a three-pronged attack is the best. And the barracks and rooftop attack must be simultaneous."

"Or," Gabe countered, "we attack at the gate, hopefully draw some of the soldiers away from the castle, which means it will be easier for the team to fly in."

Nahum shrugged. "I don't think it will be easy either way. The minute they know they're under attack, they'll be on alert. I think a simultaneous attack is best."

Gabe huffed, hands on his head again. "Fair enough. There is no best way. But I also agree with Zee. Let's be as quiet as possible for the first few deaths. Take out as many as we can before they know we're there. If Barak is happy to lead the aerial assault," he looked to Barak for confirmation, and he nodded. "Perhaps, Zee, you should join him. You brought the crossbow?"

"Yes, both. I am very happy to kill as many as I can. Who wants the other one?"

"I'll take it," Nahum said. He gave a rueful smile. "I don't think my aim is as good as yours, but I'll try."

Barak turned to Estelle. "If I carry you, think you can take out a few with magic?"

She grinned. "Sure. Just get me close enough."

Barak eyed his three team members. "I'll go over the set-up of the castle with you later, and we can decide our best strategy."

"Great." Gabe sighed with satisfaction. "That leaves Eli, Shadow, and Lucien with me."

"I am very happy with that," Lucien said, nodding enthusiastically. "I'm more comfortable on the ground."

"Great. Shadow, there's thick tree cover by the barracks. You should get some good shots with your bow. Perhaps you or I can attack from the air, too," he said to Eli. "Are we all happy?" At their nods, murmured conversation broke out, and Gabe eased back from the table. "That arrangement also works well, because it means every team has a piece of Belial's jewellery. As to whether it's a curse or a blessing, well, I guess we'll soon find out."

Harlan pointed out the window at the darkening landscape. "I don't know whether anyone's noticed, but the clouds are building out there. I think we'll have snow. That's good, right? It will hide our approach."

Barak grinned. "It certainly will. With luck, they won't know what's hit them."

Twenty-Six

Olivia had spent a quiet, reflective day again at Moonfell, mulling over the events from the night before.

She had slept late, luxuriating in her four-poster bed, before descending the sweeping staircase to the main kitchen. None of the witches were around, but they had told her to help herself to breakfast and drinks, and treat the house as her own, so she had breakfasted alone. Huge copper pans, however, simmered on the hob, the rich scent of herbs drifting around the kitchen. Morgana must be somewhere close by, but Olivia was happy to be alone.

She spent time in Morgana's beautiful green lounge that seemed to rustle with her presence, even though she wasn't there. The fire crackled in the grate, and she found a leather-bound notebook and ink pen on the table by the armchair with a note. They were a gift from the witches, encouraging her to write a diary, and although she hadn't kept one for years, it suddenly seemed to be the thing that she wanted to do most.

Her day passed in a flurry of writing and reflecting on her current predicament.

Predicament! What a ridiculous word. She was pregnant! It wasn't something that would go away. *This was going to change her life forever.*

Her pen slipped from her fingers as she recalled Nahum's words about the Nephilims' curse. *Would she lose the baby before it even came to term? Or would it die shortly after?* It seemed cruel, and somehow impossible. *That might have been the case then, but now? Was he right? Should she save herself heartbreak and terminate it now?* She closed her eyes, unable to comprehend that. Already she felt so attached to it, and yet the idea hadn't entered her mind to even have a baby twenty-four hours earlier.

However, she had never been surer of anything in her life. It felt right. Thankfully, Nahum had been kind, thoughtful, and supportive. She wasn't alone. She laughed at the memory of Harlan's face. His mouth had dropped open, and he kept staring at her until he enveloped her in a hug that took her breath away. His words brought tears to her eyes. *"I'm with you every step of the way, Liv. Every step. And you,"* he'd whipped around to glare at Nahum, *"better not fuck up!"*

Nahum's answer was even funnier. *"Don't worry, Uncle Harlan. I won't."*

When she opened her eyes again, the flames were flickering on a darkened room. She turned to the windows, and saw that the clouds had thickened, bringing twilight early. The huge, arched windows looked out onto a wintry garden, the east moon gate framing a large topiary crescent moon beyond. She had never seen a moon gate before, but they were magical, seeming to offer a portal to somewhere else. The gate looked as it sounded. It was a circular opening separating one part of the garden from another, with no gate at all. The east moon gate was carved out of a thick yew hedge, and therefore entirely green. The arch stretched above the hedge by several feet, and a stone path, thick with moss, led through it. Olivia rose to her feet, thinking to explore it.

Morgana spoke behind her, making her jump. "I wouldn't, if I were you. The paths sometimes change direction at night. You might find yourself lost, and it's bitter out."

Hand on her thumping heart, Olivia turned. "You're very good at being silent, Morgana. In fact, it's a trait you all have."

"It's just the house. It absorbs our sound, like a hug. It can't help itself." She smiled, her face all sharp shadows in the gloom. "Sorry. I didn't mean to make you jump."

Olivia sat down again, hands rubbing her face. "No, it's just me. I'm all at sixes and sevens. And what do you mean, the house can't help itself? It's not alive! And surely paths can't actually change directions on their own?"

Morgana laughed as she sat opposite her. "I think you've been here long enough to know the answer to that. This house is unusual. Look after it, and it looks after you. We make sure to look after it very well. But enough about us. How are you?" Her gaze fell to the open book, and she beamed. "You're using it! Do you like it?"

"I love it! It's so beautifully crafted, and I found myself pouring out my feelings. It has actually helped. I feel better. Lighter."

"Good. It usually helps to share, even if only to the page. I often think it preferable. It's you and words, pouring out and filling space with hopes and fears and dreams. This is a new phase of your life. I think it's appropriate to record everything."

"But what about what Nahum said about the child's survival?"

"Something to consider, certainly. However, I have skills, and the Goddess has blessed you. We have powerful support."

Olivia felt like she was an actor in a play. "Why does the Goddess care about me, and especially about a Nephilim's baby if she hates Fallen Angels?"

"Because she hates injustice, and the Nephilim suffered it in spades. Plus, it displeases Belial, and that makes her happy, too. And no, for the millionth time, he cannot harm you or the child."

"Okay. Then I shall see this through." Olivia flopped back in the chair. "I need wine, and I can't have it! For nine whole months! I love my wine."

"It will pass soon enough. I'm sure we have something alcohol-free that tastes just as good, somewhere." Morgana settled into the corner of the squashy sofa, gathering her skirts beneath her tucked legs. "Tell me about Nahum. He's very good looking!"

"Isn't he? I'm a terrible flirt, Morgana, especially with him. But I never once imagined..."

"Oh, I'm sure you imagined plenty!"

Olivia sniggered. "Well, maybe."

"He's a good man, I can tell. Honest, reasonable. Brave. He'll make a good father. He has brothers, you say?"

"Six. All good men, all very different. Well, so I gather. I haven't met all of them yet."

"Interesting. Lots of uncles, who I presume would protect you to the death."

"Don't say that. Not even in jest."

"The Nephilim had a certain reputation, that's all I mean. And it seems Harlan is on your side, too. An interesting man."

"He's amazing." Olivia sniffed as tears threatened. "What a whirlwind few days. I feel better, though. I think I'll go home tomorrow. I need to start planning."

"You have room?"

"Enough. But I have money and can get a bigger place."

"What if Nahum wants you close?"

"We'll work something out. I certainly won't leave him out of this. But I also need to work. I enjoy my work!" She shook her head. "Actually, I don't want to think about that now." Her serenity vanished as she contemplated that night's activities. "They are all at risk tonight. They are fighting a powerful group. They have witches with them, and they're strong, but Harlan is human, and he's headstrong, and he wants to find Jackson…"

"It's natural to worry. All you can do now is trust in their abilities." Morgana lifted her chin, listening, and then smiled. "Maggie is here. That's good. You can share your news."

Olivia groaned. "What will she think?"

"She'll swear a lot and then defend you to the death." Morgana winked. "You're not alone. Never forget that."

Jackson glared at the count, trying to contain his icy fury as they sat in the middle of a well-appointed sitting room on the second floor of the main castle.

The count, however, looked at ease. He adjusted his cuffs as he said, "You have had several hours in which to think on my request. It's time to make the call."

Jackson looked at his mobile phone on the elegant side table and decided it was time to act on his plan. He had raged in his cell after seeing his so-called uncle, kicking his bed and desperately wanting to punch walls. He decided that punching the count would be far preferable. He did not believe for one second that his grandfather had willingly become a Black Cronos soldier. He had desperately tried to work out why he had an uncle at all.

Initially, he had steadfastly refused to believe the claim, but the count had offered photographic proof. Images of his grandfather in a Black Cronos black uniform. Despite his best efforts, Jackson broke down in tears. All his hopes had been crushed, his worst nightmares realised, and the count had observed dispassionately. He was a sociopath. There was no doubt about that. Jackson had flown at him in a rage, but The Silencer of Souls and his uncle had leapt in, and The Silencer's cold fingers had ensured he was unconscious in seconds.

But once Jackson was back in his own cell, he ran through potential scenarios again. He had to conclude that his grandfather might have been tortured and had eventually agreed. Or he had been brainwashed. He would never know the truth, which was the horrible thing. *Never.* And meanwhile the count, the monster, was preying on his own fears and anger. Jackson used his anger and started to plot. The count had also said they had killed Gabe, Shadow, Ash and Niel. He needed to ask for proof of that, too.

Now Jackson swallowed, acting nervous, eyes darting to The Silencer, who regarded him with her dark, soulless eyes before studying the count again. He sat comfortably, his snowy white cuffs on show beneath his elegant jacket, tailored to perfection. His too smooth skin was like a mask.

Jackson tried not to overplay his hand. "If I call, you must promise to enact a truce. You won't harm my friends?"

"No, if they leave us to our own devices."

"But what if they don't listen to me?" Jackson argued. "I'm not their leader. I don't control the Nephilim. They have their own agenda. You said you've killed four of their team. They won't take that lightly."

"They will if they want the rest to survive." The count's eyes glittered with malice.

"I think you're lying about that. You've never shown me proof."

The count picked up a remote control and turned on a TV mounted on the wall. "I thought you might ask. This happened two nights ago. When we kidnapped you."

Jackson watched the footage of the destroyed hotel in Aswan that he knew Gabe and his team were booked into. The report detailed the rooms and the floor that had been affected, and said they were still searching for survivors—or bodies. Jackson's chest tightened again. *That was the place.* Russell must have known, but hopefully he wouldn't have known why they were there.

Jackson's fury exploded. "You bastard. They were my friends!"

"And my enemies. There was an interesting theft from the museum just beforehand. Know anything about that?"

Jackson looked him dead in the eye. "My business is with you. That must have been another job."

"Well, their looted objects have been destroyed with them." He tapped the arm of his chair, his eyes never leaving Jackson. "Emerald discs. Very interesting, indeed. I wonder what their significance is."

Jackson held his nerve. "I'm sure I have no idea, or if they are even connected to Gabe. You're just guessing now. Their bodies?"

"I have no doubt they'll find them." He picked up Jackson's phone. "Unlock it for me. I have decided that I will speak to Waylen myself. I think letting you speak would be quite hazardous."

"Phone him yourself. You must have his number."

"I wish to use your phone, so he knows I have you, obviously."

"But what will happen to me? You won't keep me here forever."

"Forever is a long time."

"You'll kill me!"

"Not as a Black Cronos soldier. You may as well agree now. You will eventually. Your grandfather came to like it."

Jackson felt his rage building again. "Then why are you giving me a choice?"

"Because you will be far more useful to me that way!"

"Waylen will want proof that I'm alive, and a guarantee of my safety."

"I think the threat of more deaths will be a bargaining tool enough. But yes, I'll allow you to confirm you're alive. I'm sure we can come to an arrangement."

"Then it's not Waylen you need to speak to. It's Barak."

"Why?" the count asked suspiciously.

"Barak, one of the Nephilim, is leading the search for you. He's the one you need to convince."

"Excellent."

Jackson held his hand out and unlocked his phone, quickly bringing up Barak's number. "I doubt you'll convince him."

"Let hope for your sake that I do."

Twenty-Seven

B arak was still seething hours later at the memory of the count's smooth, silky voice that oozed menace.

He had made his intent very clear. None of them would be left in peace if they didn't back off. He had crowed about killing Gabe and the others in Aswan, and Barak, although shocked to speak to the count, had played along. He had argued and sworn and raged, of course. He had to make himself sound believable.

And then they bargained hard. Barak had argued for time to talk to his remaining brothers. They were to return the count's call at midnight. Barak aimed to deliver the message in person.

The good thing was that they knew he was with Jackson, and that he was alive. *But was he in the castle?* Jackson's message had been short. He'd yelled, "Forget me. Move on. I'll be locked up in his damn dungeons forever." Then there'd been the sound of a scuffle and the count returned with a promise to call again at midnight.

Barak was sure that message meant he was in the castle. It had to. He could have yelled anything. He could have pleaded for his life, or urged them to violence. Or even revealed the location that they supposedly didn't know. But perhaps that would have been too obvious. They wanted to do nothing to alert the count.

So, they had proceeded with the plan.

It was dark, and snow was falling as Barak led his team to the top of the ridge. They circled high above the castle, the wind whipping around them, Estelle tucked close to his body. Snow settled on the battlements and in the courtyard, helping it melt into the landscape. Only the glow of lights in the towers and the castle provided landmarks.

Nahum and Zee flew lower, crossbows ready. Unfortunately, the snow and bitter wind meant many soldiers were inside the towers, but half a dozen still walked the icy walls on their own.

Within seconds, they all lay dead.

No one had seen it happen. No other soldiers emerged.

"Damn it," Barak said in Estelle's ear, the wind whipping the words from his mouth. "I hoped they'd all come running and we could pick some more off. This means Plan B."

Estelle grinned. "Oh, goodie. I'll aim for the closest tower."

Before she could take aim, a muffled explosion sounded from further down the ridge.

Gabe's team.

Estelle released a volley of fireballs, bombarding the largest corner tower by the main gate. Stone blasted into the air, showering over the walls and courtyard. Seconds later, soldiers streamed out of all the towers, including the one that had been hit.

Immediately, Nahum and Zee took aim again, soldiers falling dead before they even realised what was happening. But that didn't last long, and they quickly manned the huge crossbows on the battlements, along with other more sophisticated weapons.

Barak swooped around and Estelle took aim, igniting fires along the walls and destroying the battlements and as many weapons as she could before a few fired in their direction. Fortunately, Barak was too quick, and as he swept away, Estelle kept firing, drawing their attention from Zee and Nahum.

A blast of energy sizzled past them, and a flurry of huge arrows almost skewered them. Barak flew into low cloud. When he circled back, Nahum and Eli had also been spotted, and were busy dodging the blasts from the weapons below. Despite the numbers they'd killed, reinforcements were coming.

All three Nephilim withdrew, disappearing into the ever-thickening snow. It was getting harder to see the castle, but that also meant it was harder to see them.

That is, until huge searchlights lit up the sky, a siren whined, and the volley of weapon fire began again.

Shadow had been thwarted in her efforts to shoot the guards at the gate. No one was stirring from the building, and the gate was securely locked, blocking the road.

It didn't help that thick snow was hampering her vision. *Time to use one of JD's grenades and hope it worked.* However, once she activated it, she would have seconds only to take the shot. She aimed her modified arrow that had JD's bomb strapped to it and adjusted her aim for the weight and the steadily increasing wind. Fortunately, her target was big. When she was sure of her shot, she activated the bomb, aimed at the window on the first floor, and released. The window smashed and a boom blew out the corner of the building. A fireball lit up the surrounding area, igniting the closest trees. *Herne's balls. What the hell had JD made that bomb from?*

As a second explosion ripped out of the sky far above, she knew the team up there had begun their attack, too.

Shadow focussed back on the guard tower. When soldiers ran from the building, and others jumped from windows, she took aim again, this time with her normal arrows, picking them off in the light from the fire. Shouts sounded from the building beyond the guard house where Gabe and the others were situated. She waited to see if any others would emerge before she joined them.

Movement to the right made her adjust her aim. *More soldiers beneath the trees. They must have evacuated the rear of the building.* She again picked them off. But then a flash of bright white light ripped out of the darkness by the gate and struck the tree she was perched in. With an ominous crack, it crashed to the ground.

Niel gripped the steel bars of the gate that was set into the thick rock beneath the castle.

"Any suggestions on how to get past this thing?"

JD frowned at the rock, hands on his hips. "We could try one of my bombs, but I fear it would bring the cave down on our heads."

"Yeah. Let's not do that."

"Or," JD persisted, "use my weapons to shoot it out. Aiming right at where the bars meet the rock. Effective, but not quite as destructive."

Harlan groaned. "I'm not sure I like that idea, either. We don't know what's around that corner! Anything loud could bring soldiers."

Niel nodded. "Agreed. Caspian?"

"I can try magic. Much quieter, too."

"What kind of spell?" Ash asked.

Caspian, like the Nephilim, was dressed in black, a change from his usual suits that Niel was so used to him wearing. "I've been thinking about that all afternoon. If only I'd have known, I would have asked El for her special blade that cuts through anything, but I'm going to try this."

Caspian laid his hands on the rock immediately to the right of the bars and murmured a spell. Cracks started to appear, and then the rock began to crumble. As Caspian pushed his hands further in, it was as if the rock melted at his touch, finally exposing the metal bars. But they extended deep into the rock, and the metal remained impervious to his magic.

Eventually, sweating and strained, Caspian pulled back. "The metal has been enhanced in some way. It's not responding as I hoped."

"And the rock is far too dense to make a hole through," Ash said. "It's at least four feet thick. It would take hours."

"Enhanced how?" JD asked Caspian. "By magic?"

"I can't detect magic. It's an unusual colour, though. Not just steel."

JD nodded. "A mix of metals, all alchemically done. In that case, we'll have to trust my weapons. I'll focus only on the bars themselves."

Niel was about to protest, but what was the point? They had to get in somehow, and he certainly wasn't giving up yet. "Do you need mine?" Niel asked him, reaching into his pocket for the strange metal object.

"No, thank you. I have a specific one in mind." JD had handed out most of his weapons, but he rummaged in his pack for the remaining ones.

Niel pressed his face to the bars, trying to see more of the space beyond. It was freezing cold and dark, but they'd risked using torches, or the humans wouldn't see a thing. Fortunately, the light had not attracted attention, and Caspian had thrown a couple of witch-lights in there, too. Small ripples disturbed the glossy black lake, and ice rimmed at its edge. A stream of water flowed out of the lake, across the floor and under the gate. Fortunately, their boots protected them from the icy cold water.

"What can you see?" Harlan asked him.

"Just the shaft as before, and bugger all else."

"Step back, everyone," JD instructed. "This will get hot."

A red beam of light shot out of the handheld device, and JD trained the beam on the edge of the bars, slicing down where they met the walls. The metal heated up and started to blister, the heat intensifying until everyone had to retreat several feet.

"Is that a laser beam?" Harlan asked, shielding his eyes from the bright red glare.

"No! Something much better, although, remind me to make a weapon that I can adjust in future."

Niel grinned at Ash. "I like this more every second. But I'd like it to be quicker!"

"At least it's quiet. Not that I think we need to worry this far under the castle. But," Ash shrugged and then winced and put his hand on his injured shoulder, "we can't be too sure."

Niel pulled Ash aside while JD worked. "Is your shoulder still painful?"

"It's not as bad as it was."

"But it should have healed by now."

"Brother, I think you forget how long some injuries take to heal."

It had been years since Niel had sustained a serious injury, and he'd never had a shoulder injury like Ash's. "I guess you're right. I take it Barak couldn't help?"

"No. He found it very frustrating."

"What about flight?" Ash hadn't flown earlier, insisting he needed to preserve his shoulder. They had travelled to their destination on foot, like the night before, and then Caspian had used witch-flight to take him and JD to the entrance, while Niel flew with Harlan. Flying with Harlan was nowhere near as pleasant as flying with Mouse.

"I'm sure it will be fine."

Ash's golden eyes met his own, but Niel saw doubt there. "What's going on?"

"Nothing."

Niel was about to question him further when JD's hoot of success drew their attention. He had finally succeeded in severing the barred gate from its moorings and it wobbled, threatening to crash to the ground. Caspian stepped in, and air whirled from his hands to cushion the gate. It landed as gently as a feather.

Niel pushed ahead, vowing to keep an eye on Ash. "Nice one, gentlemen. Stay close."

The cave opened to the right. It was long and low-roofed, the lake stretching for most of the cave. On the opposite side was the shaft he'd glimpsed earlier. Now that he had a better view, he could see the mechanism of hydraulics. The rest of the cave was empty, except for another hole in the rock wall at the far end, and a waterfall that streamed from the roof into the lake.

Harlan trained his torch on the shaft. "You were right. It's an elevator shaft." He stared at his companions, wide-eyed. "Is this for real? Can we just get straight in?"

"Maybe. But what's that?" Niel pointed at the round hole in the rock. "Another cave? A passage?"

"Perhaps, however there must be a natural spring somewhere in this rock," Ash suggested, focussing on the waterfall. "Very handy. A source of water during a siege. It might drive a mechanism further up. Or did, perhaps, years ago."

"Speaking of which," Niel said, "can you hear that hum?"

Now that they were in the cave properly, it was much easier to hear. Everyone looked up.

"It sounds big," JD mused. "Maybe it powers the castle. Their own turbine. That would be truly self-sufficient."

Niel quickly came to a decision. "Ash, JD, and Harlan, you check the lift shaft! Me and Caspian will check out the other exit."

He extended his wings and flew across the lake, landing mere seconds after Caspian, who threw a couple of witch-lights ahead of them. It was the start of a sloping passage leading upwards, hewn out of solid rock. Caspian walked up it, torch angled upwards. "It's pitch black. No lights at all. I imagine it's the way down, if the lift fails."

"But why dig this far into the ridge, anyway?"

"Perhaps there were natural caves throughout the rock, and they just added to them. Cathar strongholds would have needed places to hide. Places to store food and ammunition. Maybe the count has similar ideas. The question is, do we walk up, or take the lift?"

"The lift announces our arrival."

"But it's quicker, and we have no idea how the battle is going up top. If the fight has started, they won't be watching the lift," Caspian pointed out.

"Excellent point. Lift it is."

Zee swept around to the north of the castle, flying into the driving wind and snow.

The cold was exhilarating, as was the battle. The searchlights were powerful, but there was only so far they could penetrate, especially in a snowstorm. He let the wind take him, and as it drove him back to the castle, he angled his wings close to his body. He dived at the castle battlements, aiming for one of the search lights before it could swing around to see him.

He swept over it, wrenching it from its mount, and dropped it into the courtyard below. He swooped under the wall, so close that the soldiers had trouble seeing him, and then swept up again, picking a man up with ease, and dropping him from the battlements, too. He then decided to try JD's weapon. It felt clumsy despite his earlier practice, but he aimed at a soldier, squeezing, and firing with intent as JD had instructed. A blast cut through the air. He missed with the first shot, taking out only a chunk of battlements, but quickly adjusted and shot again. He hit the man square in the chest, catapulting him over the wall and onto the courtyard below. He then immediately sought cover as the rattle of gunfire split the sky.

The soldiers were shooting wildly. Estelle and Barak were still flying, and Estelle was hurling fireballs and glowing balls of energy with uncanny precision. He had no idea where Nahum was, but spotlights were being trained on the far side of the castle wall, and he guessed he was there. More and more soldiers were pouring out of the guard towers and onto the battlements. They had certainly drawn their attention. The newcomers immediately manned the remaining huge guns, swinging them up, and firing blindly.

Zee aimed at the entrance of the closest guard tower. As soldiers ran out, he shot the first few before they ducked for cover. He wheeled high again, the snow cloaking his movements. He flew around the north of the tower with nothing but the vertical face of the ridge beneath him, kicked in the window of the first floor, and threw a grenade inside.

Part of the tower exploded in a mass of rubble. Dodging the falling stone and debris, Zee decided to take the fight to the main castle and aimed for the yellow glow of lights leaking from the curtains covering a huge window. It overlooked the valley, not the courtyard, and there was no one firing at him. *Easy pickings.*

He hurled a grenade through the window, and in seconds the windows blew out and flames curled. It was only as he wheeled back to the fight above that he thought of Jackson.

Shit. Where was he?

Gabe's back was pressed to the wall next to the entrance of the barracks, waiting for soldiers to emerge. Lucien was on one side, Eli on the other, when he saw the tree that Shadow was positioned in topple to the ground. There was nothing he could do to help her.

The door to the barracks burst open, and half a dozen armed men rushed out, weapons raised. Gabe, Lucien, and Eli attacked them, Eli and Gabe slicing them down with their swords as Lucien used JD's weapon.

But the next batch of soldiers were more prepared. As the three turned to fight them, the soldiers' eyes turned dark black, and their skin became metallic. Lucien responded, his own skin and eyes changing as he drew on his enhancements. Gabe hoped he wouldn't turn on them. The next few minutes were chaotic as swords and weapons whirled, and the clash of metal and grunts of battle echoed through the trees.

Gabe knew they'd made a tactical mistake. They should have waited for more Black Cronos soldiers to emerge before attacking. That way they could have better assessed the numbers. But they had relied on Shadow being able to shoot from a distance, and that wasn't happening right now. He hoped that she wasn't crushed.

Flames crackled, and the fire spread. The main guard building was ablaze, flames and thick black smoke reaching into the sky. Potentially, it might set the barracks alight, and that wasn't the plan at all. They needed to get in to see if there was another route to the castle, and they couldn't even get close to the door. The heat was becoming unbearable. The smoke mingled with the snow, and visibility was poor. It was hampering them as much as the soldiers.

Gabe's fury and frustration grew as he saw his companions struggling, and heard the noise from the castle. He needed height and space.

Gabe extended his wings, seeing Eli do the same, and used them to beat a clear path around them. They crunched their attackers aside. Soldiers hit tree trunks, and flaming branches and ashes fell around them.

A spear seemed to come out of nowhere. He dodged it, but the sharp point grazed his ribs. A soldier emerged from the whirling snow, eyes flaming like the fire behind him, and flames rippled down the sword gripped in his hand.

That was new! Excellent. Flaming bloody swords...

Harlan studied the elevator shaft. Cables and rails ran down the walls, and buffers and a piston were on the ground.

"Damn it. There's no call button, and only the mechanism is down here. It's just the pit. We need to use *that*." He aimed his torch on the ladder that was bolted to a side wall. He stepped into the shaft and examined the space above him. The ladder extended a short way before ending at doors.

Ash stood next to him. "We can climb the ladders, open the door, and access the level above us."

"And if it opens on a nest of dragons?" Harlan asked.

"Then I'll be Saint George," Ash said, laughing. "Dragons? Seriously, Harlan, you need to get a grip!"

"I wouldn't put anything past Black Cronos."

JD had been examining the cables, but now he joined them. "Once we get through those doors, we can see how many levels there are. You're right about it feeling like a dragon's den, though, Harlan."

"*Dragons?*" Niel exclaimed as he arrived with Caspian. "You better be joking."

Ash laughed. "We hope we are. What did you find?"

"Another route up—we think, but we haven't explored it. Thought this might be quicker."

"We need to use the ladder and crank open the doors," Harlan explained.

Niel shouldered through and gripped the ladder. "Good. I'll go first and crank it open."

He quickly reached the door and used his axe to wedge the door open. When it was wide enough, he slipped his fingers in, pushed the doors wide, and clambered through the gap. "Come on. No dragons."

Harlan followed, hauling himself over the doorway and into a dark room. His flashlight revealed that they were in a storeroom that housed pieces of machinery. There were several shelves, and large boxes on the floor. He found a light switch and flicked it on so they could see properly. "There's a lot of stuff in here. Must be to maintain the elevator, and maybe other things for the castle, too."

"At least there's a call button here," JD said, pointing at the wall by the lift. "And no other exit here. That other way up that you spotted must bypass this one."

He pressed the button, and while they waited, Harlan gave the area a more detailed examination, but there was nothing that warranted their attention, and no cameras or alarms. None that were obvious, anyway.

They all waited, shuffling with impatience as the mechanism whined. The display above the door only showed a green light. It didn't indicate how many floors were above. Harlan gripped JD's weapon, heart pounding, but when the lift finally arrived, it was empty.

"Eight floors," Niel said, looking at the row of buttons in the lift. "Considering how far down we are, that's less than I expected. Where do we start?"

"Bang in the middle?" Ash suggested.

"Level six," JD countered.

"I suggest one by one," Harlan said. "There are only eight levels! Seven to go. Otherwise, we might miss something."

"That's slow!" Niel complained. Niel was all about mayhem and destruction; he wasn't known for his patience.

"We're here to destroy the damn place! We need to be methodical, or we risk screwing this up. And we need to find Jackson! Prison cells are likely to be low down. I am not leaving this place without him!" Harlan reasoned.

Caspian pressed level seven. "You're right, Harlan. Patience is a virtue. Let's see what lies beneath the *château* and bring the whole lot down."

Twenty-Eight

Jackson was lying on his bed, staring at the ceiling of his cell and debating his fate after his attempted escape earlier.

The minute he had shouted at Barak over the phone, Stefan had punched him, and taken his phone. By the time he had collected himself, The Silencer of Souls was looming over him, her lips leaning towards his. She'd miscalculated how conscious he was, so he punched her, and she had reeled backwards.

He had scrambled towards the door, but Stefan pulled a gun from his pocket and fired at his feet. "*Not one more move, Jackson, or you're dead.*"

The Silencer was snarling like a wild animal, ready to pounce again, but the count called her back. "*Wait, my dear.*" The count cocked his head, looking at Jackson like he was an insect. "*Was that an attempt at a clue? Foolish.*"

Jackson had staggered to his feet, wiping blood from his split lip. "*There are a thousand castles with a thousand dungeons. Was it really a clue, you moron, or was it just like I said? I'm not getting out of here…I know that now.*"

The count had stepped closer, his chilling eyes cold and dispassionate. "*No, you're not. I was prepared to let you choose your fate, but now I aim to break you. The winter solstice is in three days, and the team here is already prepping a new batch of soldiers. You'll join them.*" He then nodded at Deandra. "*Take him to his cell, and do not harm him!*"

And that was it. His fate was sealed. That was probably an hour or so ago. It was hard to calculate, with no watch and no natural light to go by. Then he heard voices down the corridor, and he rose to his feet.

The door opened and Stefan waited outside, flanked by two soldiers. "Time to begin the process, Jackson. Follow me."

He marched quickly down the corridor and Jackson followed, the huge, muscular soldiers barely a pace behind him. He'd rather be out of his cell than in it. This way, he could at least try to find a way to escape. When they reached the lift, Stefan took them down to another floor.

"You really are a fool," Stefan told him. "Thinking you can destroy us. This place is impregnable, and our organisation too big."

"Almost as big as your collective ego. Where are we going?"

"The lab preparation area, of course, for your tattoos, and…other things."

"The count said there were others. How many?"

"You'll see."

The lift shuddered to a stop, and they stepped into another corridor, but before they could progress, the ground rocked and a muffled explosion sounded overhead. All four froze and looked up, and then a siren peeled loudly as the corridor shook again.

Jackson laughed as hope leapt within him. "That sounds interesting. Or is it the count's armillary sphere?"

Stefan rounded on him. "What have you done?"

"I've been locked in a cell! What could I have done?"

Doors flew open along the corridor, and staff in lab coats evacuated. As the sirens continued to peel and panic spread, a couple headed to Stefan's side.

He had no time for them and yelled, "Get back to your work!"

A young man with slicked back, dark hair protested. "But the alarm! It's for an attack! We need to get in the shelter."

Stefan pushed him against the wall. "You'll do no such thing. Finish prepping everyone now!"

The crowd of outraged and panicking staff grew, and the two soldiers drew their weapons and pushed them back, their eyes already changing.

Then another dull boom sounded overhead, and the corridor shook again. The lab staff was spooked, and like a herd of elephants, ran for the lifts. Stefan was overwhelmed, and the soldiers started firing. But instead of being scared, the scientists were furious, and fights broke out as they yelled at the guards.

Jackson didn't wait to see any more. He took advantage of the confusion, pushed through the crowd, and ran into the closest room. He slammed the door shut and took stock. He was in some kind of central station with desks, computers, and observation windows that looked onto a series of open rooms. *Great. Lots of things to destroy.* He needed a weapon. But as Jackson advanced, he saw something far worse.

Lots of people strapped to beds.

Okay, change of plan. Rescue people, and then destroy everything.

Nahum took advantage of the havoc that Zee, Barak, and Estelle were causing on the battlements, and flew down to the courtyard.

The snow whirled in thick pockets, but as he descended, the wind dropped. He pressed himself to the wall of the castle. A few soldiers scurried out of the buildings and ran up outside staircases, but it was otherwise deserted. Nahum took flight again. He moved so quickly, and the sound of the battle was so loud, no one heard him. In seconds, they were dead.

Through the snow he saw a huge, dark shape on the ground. As he swept nearer, he realised it was a helicopter. It was unlikely that anyone would try to escape in it in this weather, but he decided to destroy it anyway. He hurled a grenade inside, and it exploded, showering hot, jagged metal over the courtyard. The blaze illuminated the huge, alchemical wheel a short distance away.

Shocked, Nahum realised it was already in motion. All the circles were realigning, from the large outer ones to the small ones in the centre.

This could not be good.

One by one the circles ground to a halt, and a section of sigils lit up with coppery red light. Beams shot into the air, forming a cone overhead. *No. A shield.*

Nahum blinked in surprise. Was he imagining it? If it was a shield, his brothers and Estelle could be caught in it. *Was it meant to kill them, or lock them inside?*

Or out, of course.

And then a bloodcurdling cry rose from above, and even though the thick snow and distance was hampering his view, he saw some of the soldiers change. Their skin was taking on the coppery red light. *Herne's hairy bollocks. Was this another enhancement?*

Nahum threw a grenade, but it evaporated as it hit the red light. *Shit.* He headed for the closest door. He needed to find the mechanism and shut it off.

Eli was cut, bruised, battered, and his wings were singed.

The battle was raging above them, and the snowstorm was getting worse, but they couldn't even get in the barracks to find a way to help. As he fought furiously, using his wings and every ounce of power and energy he had, he hoped that at least they were helping his brothers on the roof.

But then the soldiers' radios started to buzz with instructions, and a siren obliterated all other sound. Within seconds, most soldiers withdrew, leaving only a handful behind.

Eli squared up to face a huge-shouldered soldier with dead eyes, but an arrow whizzed past Eli's ear and struck his opponent in the forehead. He collapsed to the floor. *Shadow.* Lucien was fighting another soldier, but he was struggling. Lucien's skin may be metallic, but his fighting skills weren't as advanced. Eli was about to help him when another arrow killed that soldier, too.

Within seconds, all of their remaining opponents lay dead, and as Gabe, Eli and Lucien gathered together, Shadow dropped from a branch with lithesome grace and joined them.

She pulled twigs from her hair and grimaced. "Sorry. A fallen tree slowed me down."

"But you returned with a vengeance," Gabe pointed out. "And nearly burned the barracks down, too!"

"Don't blame me! JD's grenade had more of an impact than I expected!" She stared at the burning guard tower, a mixture of pride and regret on her face. "Remind me to get some more of those."

While Eli was relieved to see Shadow, his attention was on Lucien. He was taking deep breaths and seemed to be having trouble calming himself down. His skin and eyes still had a metallic glint. "Lucien!" Eli tried to keep his voice calm. "You're doing great. How are you feeling?"

"Uptight. I always struggle to bring myself back." He held his hands in front of him. "I can't switch it off."

"You don't need to right now, as long as you're in control. Are you?"

Lucien took another shaky breath. "Yes." He met Eli's eyes, and his normal eye colour returned. "Yes, I'm fine," he repeated. "I'm not as good as you guys. I can't keep up. But that was weird when I just...let go."

"You're doing great," Eli reassured him. "When all this is done, you should stay with us for a couple of weeks. A bit of sparring and training will help you in the future. But don't forget to use JD's weapon!" It was a reminder to himself, too. Using his sword was comfortable, but JD's weapons would give them another edge.

Gabe studied Lucien for a moment in silence, and then, seemingly satisfied, marched to the barracks' door and flung it open. "You'll do for now, Lucien. Don't beat yourself up. Stay close to us, and we'll help. Let's see where the others went."

They progressed through offices, a huge lounge area with sofas, chairs, a TV, and pool tables, all shockingly pedestrian. But then again, when they weren't enhanced soldiers, they still needed to be kept occupied. After that were some dormitories.

"So far, so boring," Eli concluded, throwing open doors to bathrooms and store-rooms. However, a huge steel door at the end of a short corridor beckoned, and he hurried toward it. It was sealed shut, and a type of electronic keypad was next to it, but there were no numbers or letters. "Down here!" he yelled over his shoulder.

Gabe and the others hurried towards him.

Eli pointed to the sensor. "That looked hand-sized to me. It must be activated by a handprint."

"Or maybe," Shadow suggested, "a signal from an enhanced soldier. You know, something alchemically weird. We could grab a dead soldier and find out."

"Or," Lucien said, pointedly, "why don't I try?"

He placed his hand on the black screen and it immediately lit up with a red light. He kept it there, focussing his intention, and his skin began to shimmer as he accessed his enhancements. The screen blinked between red and green and then settled on green. The door clicked open.

Gabe placed his shoulder to it and gripped his sword. "Well done. Let's be careful."

Shadow squared up with her bow, and Gabe threw the door wide, leaping inside.

The room beyond was lined with racks that probably once contained weapons. Now they were virtually empty. At the far end was another door. This one was wide open, and a corridor stretched beyond it.

While Shadow and Lucien examined the remaining weapons, Gabe and Eli checked the entrance to the corridor. The blinking lights of a lift beckoned them, and next to it was a doorway leading to stairs.

Eli was eager to move on and help his brothers. "Looks good. I suggest we take the stairs. The way this place is exploding, I do not wish to get stuck. However, maybe we should check how many levels there are." He pressed the button to call the lift.

Gabe nodded, yelling over his shoulder. "You two, let's move!"

Gabe's expression looked strained, which worried Eli. "How are you coping with Belial's baggage?"

"I'm okay. He's getting rather insistent. Especially when I'm fighting, but I can handle it. Can you feel him?"

"A little. The other two seem unaffected so far. Despite everyone's objections, I'm still glad we brought them with us."

Gabe lowered his voice, locking eyes with Eli. "I'm relying on you to keep me in check if it goes wrong later, okay?"

"Of course." The lift dinged and the door opened, and Eli checked the buttons. "There are only three floors marked. *Lab*, *Cells*, and *Ground Floor*. I guess we start with the Lab."

The seventh floor did not contain prison cells, Ash realised as soon as the door opened, but a view of the lower-moving sections of a giant sphere. As he stepped onto the rock floor of an enormous cavern, he felt like an ant.

As usual, when thrown into a situation he didn't anticipate, he swore in Greek. "Is this what I think it is?"

"If you think it's a giant armillary sphere, then you'd be right," JD said, advancing into the cave. "It's magnificent."

"It's freaky as hell!" Harlan complained. "What is it for?"

"Capturing the power of the universe on a massive scale." JD was transfixed, but to be fair, they all were. The biggest band of the sphere rotated above their heads, the others turning within it. It was mesmerising.

Niel gripped his axe as if he was about to start smashing things. "At least we know what's causing the noise."

Harlan looked up, head craning back. "But I can't see an engine."

Caspian gave a dry laugh. "That's because there isn't one. It's self-propelled. Can't you feel the magic? This is really something else."

Ash felt giddy and overwhelmed, but as he overcame his shock, he focussed on the details. Sigils and signs were not only etched on the bands, but on the wall and the floor, and high above him appeared to be a huge, metal disc accessed by walkways. "Up there. What's that?"

"Screw the lift," Niel announced. "Let's fly."

"Take me!" JD commanded.

"Sure, but don't struggle, or I'll drop you. Ash?" Niel cocked an eyebrow. "You up for it?"

Ash wanted nothing more than to fly, but he shook his head, terrified he might find that he couldn't. "I'll take the lift, but go ahead, I'll explore down here first. You can all go," he said to Harlan and Caspian. "I'll follow."

"I'd rather not," Caspian said, eyes narrowing with concern. "We shouldn't split up. But JD, is this the source of the count's power? Do we need to destroy this? Because that's a big ask that I don't even know how to answer."

"Destroy *this*?" JD looked outraged. "The thought is abhorrent."

"JD," Ash said, recognising the feral light of the fanatic in his eyes, "if this is what drives everything, then we have to!"

"I must assess it first!" JD's face flushed, and he clenched his fists. He was building up to one of his familiar rants.

Niel virtually picked him up by the scruff of his neck. "Let's go check it out, JD, and then we'll decide. And just to remind you, this is a group vote, so don't get ahead of yourself, or I might drop you from a great height."

Estelle had been so focussed on attacking Black Cronos, she hadn't realised she was freezing.

Although Barak's heat served to insulate her, the driving snow and wind was taking its toll, and she hadn't bothered to cast a spell to keep herself warm, preferring to focus her magic on the battle. She assessed the damage below.

Areas of the battlements were in flames, particularly some of the guard towers, but more and more men were arriving on the battlements to take control of the huge weapons. The good news was that the blizzard hid their position. The bad news was that it also hid the huge arrows and blasts of power emitted by the unusual guns. And she knew that Barak was itching to fight. So far he'd ferried her around, but he needed to do more than that. She was also becoming increasingly aware of Belial's jewellery in Barak's pocket, despite the fact that she'd cast a protection spell on it.

A strange glow below caught her attention. "Barak! Is the main castle on fire? What's that?" However, before he could answer, she felt the power it exuded. "Shit! It's a spell of some sort."

"It's coming from the wheel of correspondences! It's melting the snow—or am I seeing things?"

Estelle tried to sort through what it might be, separating the feel of the elements and magic within it. "There's air and fire, but there's also a lot I don't understand. He's harnessing planetary energies."

Barak flew wider to avoid it, but it advanced quickly, spreading outward like an umbrella. "It looks like a shield. I have a feeling if I get caught in it, we'll burn."

"And if we stay out of it, we'll be trapped outside for good."

"Inside it is, then. I hope Zee and Nahum have spotted it."

While Barak swept around and under it, Estelle scoured below for sign of the others. "I see Zee flying in from the north. I can't see Nahum at all, but the helicopter is on fire. Oh shit, and the soldiers are changing again! They're taking power from the wheel!" Despite all the havoc they'd achieved and the soldiers they'd killed, they were failing. The soldiers kept coming, and their power kept adapting.

"What say we dodge the fight up here completely and head for the castle?" Barak asked.

"I'll blast out a window."

As the coppery light bloomed above them, encompassing the battlements, Barak honed in on a window on the second floor. Estelle shattered it. Unfortunately, the blast drew the attention of their attackers, and with the narrowest of margins, Barak swept through the gap and skidded into a stately room beyond. They both rolled across the floor, landing in a tumble of limbs and wings.

"Keep running!" he yelled as arrows flew in through the opening.

Estelle rolled on her back and threw up a protective shield. Arrows thudded against it and fell to the floor. Barak hauled her to her feet, and they ran out of their attackers' view. Seconds later, Zee arrived, landing with a great deal more grace than they had, and ran to join them.

Barak gripped his shoulders, checking him over for injuries. "Brother! Are you okay?"

"Slightly singed, soaking wet, and covered in bruises and cuts after a few close calls, but I'll survive. You two look bedraggled."

"I feel it!" Estelle patted her head, and realised her hair was plastered to her scalp. Collecting her wits, she cast a spell to dry them all off, and delicious warmth oozed through her. "That's better." She took a deep breath and looked around the room. After the chaos of the previous hour, it was good to have a breather, no matter how short. Every part of her felt bruised. "So, we're in the belly of the beast, although, it looks very civilised in here. I suppose we should get moving, though. The question is, where to?"

Barak edged closer to the window and looked out. "That weird shield seems to be in place, so we're stuck here now. That means the count is, too, although I doubt anyone will go anywhere in this storm."

Zee nodded. "I agree. He won't abandon his castle, especially with his super-soldiers outnumbering us. We need to stop them from getting in. Block every door we can."

"I can do that," Estelle volunteered. "Simple sealing spells will work well."

"Good. Then, I suggest we head deeper into the castle and disable the wheel's mechanism. At least that means we can escape. Being trapped in here is making me nervous."

"I think Nahum may already be down there, somewhere," Estelle told him. "The helicopter is destroyed, so he must have done that."

"I'd like to find him," Barak said crossing from the window to the door. "It's not safe to be alone. Let's get moving, because we have only seconds before a stream of soldiers are at the door. Once we find Nahum, we go from there."

"Wait!" Zee studied Barak's face. "You're carrying Belial's ring. Is it affecting you in any way?"

Barak glanced at Estelle, then back to Zee. "I feel him, but I'm fine."

Barak normally had an open expression, his beautiful, dark eyes honest and guileless, but they weren't now. Estelle rested her hand on his arm. "Don't lie for my sake. I can add another layer of protection to it."

He considered her words, then shook his head. "No. I'm okay. Being aware of it all the time is not a bad thing. I'm fine, honestly!" He edged the door open and looked down the corridor. "All clear. Time to go."

As he stepped into the hallway, Estelle looked at Zee for reassurance. "Well? Should we worry?"

"You should always worry when Belial is involved."

Shadow gripped her swords, ready to fight. The staircase from the barracks ascended a long way, finally opening onto a small landing with another sealed door. The siren was louder on this level, and it was obvious they were in a more populated area of the castle.

Lucien released the door again, and they entered a series of offices. Even over the sound of the siren, they could hear shouting. Without speaking, they hurried towards the noise. Shadow motioned the others behind her and eased open an office door. On the other side was a corridor where a large group of people were arguing furiously. In the middle of them she saw two Black Cronos soldiers, Stefan Hope-Robbins, and a figure she had hoped never to see again. She ducked back inside and shut the door.

Shadow sighed. "The good news is that we have caused chaos. I think the staff are trying to get out. The bad news is that I saw The Silencer of Souls."

Gabe glared at her. "You couldn't have. I killed her."

"She promised there'd be more. She was right."

Eli was already crossing to another room. "Block the doors and leave them out there. Let's see what we can do in here."

Shadow wedged a chair under the door, and they headed into more offices and lab rooms. "This place is a maze!"

"Unfortunately," Lucien said, "it is horribly like the lab I was imprisoned in, but much bigger." He was pale and breathing heavily. "I hate it! We must destroy it all."

"We will," Gabe reassured him. "Let's keep going."

The next room they emerged into was a long, hospital-style room with beds on either side, all empty. Shadow barely had time to take it in when the far door burst open and a Black Cronos soldier appeared. He raised his weapon and fired, and

Shadow dived under the closest bed. Gabe landed heavily several feet away, but Eli and Lucien were trapped in the office.

The soldier shouted for backup and advanced. Under the bed, Shadow watched him approach. Pulling a throwing knife out of her fatigues, she rolled, stood, and released it. The soldier ducked with incredible speed and fired again. She hid beneath another bed as more soldiers arrived.

Herne's horns. Time to try JD's weapons.

Shadow whipped the small, silver device from her pocket and fired wildly over the bed. On the other side of the room, Gabe did the same. But the men kept advancing. Risking a quick look, she counted at least eight. Rather than aim at the soldiers, she fired at the wall above the door. The wall exploded, rubble shooting everywhere, and the frame collapsed. *At least no more would arrive that way.*

She rolled under the bed and fired at their legs. Unfortunately, a soldier had the same idea, and another boom of firepower whizzed past her head. *Great. No shelter under the bed or above it.*

Eli yelled behind them, "Back this way!"

Shadow hated to admit defeat, but she had no choice. She scrambled back to the office while Lucien released a barrage of shots from the doorway to cover them. When they cleared the entrance, they kicked the door shut and dragged a table in front of it.

"I hate being shot at!" Shadow complained. "I'd much rather fight with my sword!"

"I am sure," Gabe said, as they ran into the next room, "that will happen."

"Keep blocking the doors behind us," Eli shouted as he dragged a bed this time behind them, wedging the other door shut. This room was smaller with just two beds in it, but another door provided an exit.

For the next few minutes, they ran from room to room. The sound of shouting and gunfire echoed around them, and it seemed that they weren't the only ones fleeing.

"This place is huge!" Lucien said. "It's like a house of horrors. But where are the people?"

The next door they opened answered that. It was another hospital-like room filled with beds, but this time people were strapped in them. A lone figure at the other end was desperately trying to get someone up.

Jackson.

He looked up, alarmed, and then relief swept across his face. "Shadow? Gabe!"

But as they ran in, the door at the far end flew open and Stefan entered, The Silencer next to him. He took one look at all of them and shouted, "Kill them all! *Now!* I don't care what the count says!"

Shadow didn't hesitate, throwing a dagger at Stefan. The blade embedded into his chest, and he sank to his knees, hands clutching the knife uselessly.

The Silencer of Souls lunged for Jackson, who was closest, but he leapt over the bed, throwing any object he could at her.

Shadow vaulted over the beds, eager to meet her head-on, sword drawn. This was one fight she would relish.

Twenty-Nine

Niel landed on the giant metallic circle positioned in the centre of the armillary sphere, and set JD down.

He looked around, taking in the scale of the enormous structure. It was easier to appreciate it from the dead centre of the construction. Huge, concentric circles radiated out from the central circle, all manner of sigils on them, just like JD's. The metal bands were also engraved, and glowed with different coloured lights. Gold, silver, blues... It was beautiful, and they emitted an unusual energy that made his skin tingle.

"JD, what is it doing?"

JD paced across the floor, scowling. "Right now, it's maintaining a balance. It's ready for the solstice."

"How do you know?"

"From the signs. I think if we stood here long enough, we'd see it move, but it's so slight as to be almost imperceptible."

"Like a clock?"

"More than that, but essentially yes." JD stood in the centre circle, hands on his hips as his gaze swept the cavern. "This is definitely what he needs to change his soldiers. In fact, look!" He marched over to indentations set into the wheel. "Human-shaped, with hooks for restraints."

"To tie people in?"

"I would assume so. If you're going to change the resonance of a human, you would have to use something large enough to do it. This would be it. God's pox. It's brilliant." He looked up, gaze sharpening, and pointed to a set of steps leading from a platform above. "And that's how they get down here."

"It's horrific. Are we in any danger just standing here?"

"No. Not yet, anyway."

"As much as I know you want to admire this, we have to break it! Where is the mechanism to make it work?"

"I told you!" JD threw his hands up. "It doesn't need one!"

"But something makes the discs move. If you want to change someone, you must align it, right?"

"Something doesn't add up. I don't understand how..." He trailed off.

Niel flew to investigate the area the steps descended from, and found that it led to the lift. Right above him, another level up, was the lift again. It opened onto a maintenance platform that ran around the entire cavern. That made sense. He'd passed one below. This contraption would need maintaining, no matter how it worked.

Next, Niel flew to the top of the sphere, examining how the bands were connected. In the end, it didn't matter how it worked; they just had to break it. But that was easier said than done when it was so huge. They could lay grenades where the bands met, and also on the alchemical wheel. That would blow the whole lot up.

But where would the count and all his lab staff be while all this was going on? Surely, they would have to watch from somewhere...

And then he saw it. A large, glass viewing pane set high in the cavern wall, directly opposite the lift shaft. It had been hard to see at first because the room behind it was in darkness. He hovered outside it, seeing blinking lights and a panel inside. They were some kind of controls, despite what JD believed. Niel studied the glass. They could probably shatter it.

JD was pacing the circle, but Niel ignored him and flew down to Ash, Harlan, and Caspian. "I've found something. Some kind of control room, up there." He jerked his head up. "I think we should destroy it."

"What does JD say?" Harlan asked.

"He's pacing like a crazy man."

"He *is* a crazy man!"

"Have you found anything down here?"

Ash shook his head. "No. This is it. Just the fixing for the sphere."

"I could use magic to destroy the housing," Caspian suggested. "Or just blast it?"

JD shouted from above. "No! Touch nothing!"

Niel rolled his eyes. "Let me see what he wants. Why don't you come join us?" Niel flew while the others used the lift and found JD pacing again. "You have good hearing."

"Your voices carry! We can't destroy it."

"Why not?"

"Because the power of the universe that this whole thing draws on is too great! The spheres aren't just any metal! They are enhanced metals, forged using these very processes. Likely made using the wheel Barak saw in the courtyard. They are all protected by the very power that they carry."

"I bet I could destroy it using Belial's jewellery. It's throbbing in my pocket. I think this place is making it worse."

JD's eyes narrowed. "I feel it too, but using it here would be a mistake. Best not."

Niel was tempted to argue, but decided against it. Mixing angelic power with all of this could kill them all. "Okay, but we must stop it from working! *Forever!*"

"Let me rephrase my last statement. We will destroy it, but we magnify the power contained here to destroy the *whole* place," JD proclaimed.

"You can do that?"

"Of course I can! This is the same as mine, just on a grander scale. And I have a little something that will help." He marched to the central wheel and wedged a huge, clear stone into the middle. "Quartz." He said to Niel's unspoken question. He straightened. "You need to get me in that control room. And then we need to get out of here."

"Well, you can't set anything to happen until I find the rest of the team. They're above us somewhere."

As they spoke, a shudder shook the platform, multiplying Niel's concerns for his brothers. He needed to see what was going on out there.

"Oh no, you don't!" It was like JD had read his mind. "That room you saw. Get me in it!"

"I'll have to blow out the window."

"Why don't you use your precious axe? It seems to be attached to you."

"That's actually a great idea!"

Five minutes later, they were all in the control booth, crunching on shards of glass. Ash was only there because Caspian used witch-flight, and now Niel was even more concerned at Ash's refusal to fly. He wouldn't even try. Niel didn't want to make things worse, so he said nothing.

"I feel like I'm in NASA, about to watch a take-off," Harlan said, sweeping glass off a seat. "This is nuts."

"This is the best seat in the house," JD said, flexing his fingers.

A panel of buttons and switches was arrayed before them, and Niel couldn't make out heads or tails of them, but it seemed JD could.

"This door," Niel instructed everyone, "leads to what looks like a series of cells. Ash, do you want to stay to protect this pair? Me and Caspian will try to find everyone else."

Ash tapped his blade. "No problem. I've got this. Don't forget to use Belial if you need to."

"You know what? You should have it."

"*What?*" Ash stepped back. "No, you need it."

"I have full strength, and a witch at my side. You have an injured shoulder and a wing you don't trust." He dug in his pack and passed Ash the clasp. "Don't hesitate to use it if you need to."

He swept out the door, axe raised.

Nahum found the way to the mechanism beneath the alchemical wheel in the courtyard easily, but he also found several soldiers guarding it.

Nahum raced in, sword raised, fortunate to have the element of surprise on his side. With a few quick thrusts of his blade, the first soldier lay dead, but then it became a lot harder. The passages were tiny, Medieval in design, and certainly not meant to house enormous Black Cronos soldiers and Nephilim. In addition, despite the freezing cold outside, it was hot underground. Ahead of him, pistons screeched beneath the wheel.

The soldiers down here seemed to be affected by the weird cone of power emitted above. Their eyes flamed in the darkness, and real flames bathed the length of their swords. But Nahum could only think of one thing. *He was going to be a father.* It drove his every thrust of the blade, and with every sickening crunch of bone, it renewed his endeavours. In fact, Nahum moved as if he was still possessed by Belial. Perhaps assuming Belial's strength the other night reminded him of the true power he once possessed.

Stepping over their dead bodies, he raced under the wheel and turned off every crank and switch he could see. The great cogs spread beneath the wheel whined and ground together, their screams shrill against the backdrop of the still-whining siren. When they finally came to a shuddering halt, he heard pounding feet and saw another squad of soldiers racing down the narrow passage.

Nahum kicked the door shut and wedged a block of stone behind it, only realising too late that he'd sealed himself inside. Fortunately, he had grenades.

The circles of stone were mounted on metal rails, but the circle in the centre was fixed in place. The underside of it was scored with marks and cracks, and Nahum shoved the grenade into place, and ran to the far end of the room. The grenade exploded, and white-hot flames shot through the underground space. Nahum dived behind fallen blocks of stone that must have been used for its construction, flattening himself onto the ground.

The flames swept over him and then receded. Cold air rushed in, and with relief, Nahum saw snow. But the rest of the circles cracked and splintered, too. Only the rails were holding them up, and they were buckling badly. Ears ringing, and with stars in his eyes, Nahum dragged himself through the wreckage and into the courtyard, taking to the air just as the wheel collapsed beneath his feet.

But he couldn't stay airborne for long. The explosion had attracted attention, and once again, he was being shot at.

Then he heard yelling. "*Nahum*! Over here."

Barak's booming voice was calling him from below, and Nahum zeroed in. The huge entrance door to the castle was wide open, and Barak stood on the threshold. Nahum dived, wings close to his body, slamming through the gap and into the great hall. The door banged shut behind him, and breathless, he whirled around.

Barak's hands were on his hips. "You after bragging rights? You blew up the helicopter *and* the wheel?"

Estelle and Zee were next to him, laughing as they barricaded the door shut using furniture.

Once he had his breath back, Nahum laughed, too. "Sorry. I'm sure there's still plenty for you to do." He gestured at the half a dozen dead soldiers on the floor. "You've been busy, too."

"We were just coming to find you when we ran into these. The explosion caught our attention."

"And rattled every bone in my body," Zee added.

Nahum was suddenly aware that he was soaking wet and cold, and every part of his fatigues clung to his body. "Why am I soaking wet and you're not?"

"That's down to me." Estelle cast a spell, and a weird shimmer of warmth raced over Nahum until he was dry.

"Neat trick. Thank you." He took some deep breaths, observing the empty corridors and the continuing peel of the siren. "Where is everyone?"

"No idea," Zee said. "Every room is empty. No staff, no residents, no count, and no Stefan."

"And also no Jackson?"

"Nope." Barak pointed down the corridor. "But we found stairs leading down, and a lift. I suggest we get moving."

Jackson scrambled out of the way of Shadow's fight with The Silencer, fearing he would get killed accidentally. Or deliberately by The Silencer, who lunged for him every opportunity she could.

Gabe yelled, "Jackson, can you get to us?"

"Wait!"

He retreated to the far door that Stefan had arrived from and peered through it. So far, the room beyond was empty. With luck, the soldiers were still arguing with the staff. *Or maybe killing them.* Jackson didn't care; they were all monsters.

He wedged the door shut, and ducking and weaving beneath the beds and around equipment, finally reached Gabe. His huge bulk was reassuring. "How did you find me?"

"Sheer bloody luck," Gabe admitted, half an eye on Shadow.

"Do you think you should help her?" Jackson asked, watching the fight, too. They were both moving so quickly, it was all a blur.

"Are you kidding me?" Gabe said, appalled. "She'd kill me! Do you know the layout of this place? We blocked off the way we came, but there are soldiers all over the place, and we could be barricading ourselves in."

"I've barely explored any of this half," Jackson explained. "I came from back there. Is it just you two?"

"No. Eli and Lucien are behind us, defending our rear." Another explosion ripped through the offices, and black smoke streamed towards them. "What the actual—"

"Sorry!" Lucien came running. "Jackson! Good to see you. Gabe, problem! More soldiers. They blew out the door. But we've found more corridors."

"Of course you have! This is a damn rat trap." Gabe shouted at Shadow. "We need to move! Jackson, go with Lucien."

"No."

"What?"

"There are people here that we need to rescue." He gesticulated at the unconscious men and women in the beds.

"Not a chance. We have no way of taking them out of here. Nowhere to look after them."

Jackson appealed to Lucien. "Surely you understand. We have to get them out of here!"

"It's impossible, Jackson. We'll have enough trouble getting ourselves out."

"But if Barak and Estelle had left you, you'd be one of them now!"

"And perhaps I wouldn't know any better. I certainly wouldn't have had those agonising months."

Jackson stared at him in shock, struggling to find his voice, but Lucien didn't even blink. "You regret surviving?"

"Of course not! I'm glad to be here, stopping them. I would not wish anyone to go through what I have, but you could barely keep me safe, or everyone around me." Lucien gripped Jackson's arms. "Admit it! I terrified you. I probably still do! Where would you put them?"

Jackson closed his eyes, his hands over his face. Lucien was right. They couldn't deal with it. *But all these people...* He looked around at the unconscious men and women, some of them whimpering in their sleep. "We'll be monsters if we leave them."

"*They* are the monsters." Lucien marched over to the closest one, and pulled the sheets back. "Look at all their tattoos. They have far more than me! Barak and Estelle found me early on! *C'est impossible*! You know this."

Jackson's energy ebbed as the truth of the matter hit him. Lucien and Gabe were right. There were too many of them, and there was nothing they could do. Lucien pushed him towards the door as a sickening crunch announced that Shadow had killed The Silencer.

Shadow withdrew her blade, and the woman slid to the floor, blood pooling around her.

"About time," Gabe said.

"I didn't have the advantage of flight and gravity on my side," she replied archly.

They fled from the room and thickening black smoke, only to be met with a wave of soldiers charging on the other side. A door beckoned, but there was no way they would reach it before the soldiers were on them. Eli squared up to face the first one, and his blade sliced clean through his attacker's breast plate, piercing his chest.

Jackson gasped. "You cut through armour and their metallic skin?"

"We evened the playing field," Gabe shouted, pushing him behind them. "A witch called El enhanced our blades with magic."

Jackson retreated while the others fought, desperately looking for a weapon. He ran back to The Silencer and grabbed her fallen blade, then looked up in horror as the door was forced open at the far end. The soldiers had arrived from the other direction.

He staggered backwards, kicking the door shut and wedging it with a chair, before racing back to the team. "There are more coming."

There was only one way out of the room. The smell of smoke was strong, and he suspected that if sprinklers didn't kick in quickly, they would suffocate before soldiers could kill them. *Brilliant.* Gabe, Shadow, Eli, and Lucien were all battling furiously, and the door was being battered down on the other side.

"Gabe!" Eli shouted as he fought, "this could be the moment!"

"Not yet!"

"This is not the time to get cold feet!"

"I know!"

Jackson had no idea what they were talking about, but knew he was useless fighting with just a knife. "Has anyone got a gun?"

Shadow rolled and ducked, then threw a silvery object at him. "One of JDs. Don't point it at us!"

Jackson was familiar with JD's experiments. They had a couple of these weapons at The Retreat. He leapt on top of an empty bed and started firing at the soldiers. The door he'd blocked was kicked in and the others arrived. He had a good aim and hit the first couple before needing to retreat. There was no way they could fight all of these. It was madness.

And then a bloodcurdling cry rang out from the other room.

Barak stepped out of the lift into a full-pitched fight. No one saw them coming.

Barak knew they weren't all soldiers, but he didn't care, and neither did his companions. They dispatched the soldiers first, and as the staff ran, they killed them, too. They hunted through the rooms, chasing down anyone they found, following the sounds of battle and screams.

Then he heard Gabe's shout.

Barak yelled to his companions. "This way!"

They came upon a group of soldiers who were focussed on another room completely. Through the open door beyond them, he saw Gabe and the others, and with a mix of blades and magic, they fought the soldiers to reach their side.

By now Barak's blade was singing. He could feel it. It resonated up his arm and through his body. He wasn't wearing Belial's jewellery, but he could feel its effects anyway. Any empathy he might have felt vanished, and he viewed Black Cronos as dispassionately as they viewed him. Even the men and women on the beds. They couldn't afford to leave any of them alive.

He killed each one swiftly as he passed, wishing them peace in the afterlife. Anyone they left behind was a tool for the count. He caught Estelle's tight-lipped expression and tried to speak to her, but she shook her head. "Not now, Barak."

In another few minutes it was over, and they stood in the blood-splattered room, surrounded by the dead.

Gabe looked the same as he felt. Dead-eyed and impassive. Gabe clasped his hand. "You feel him?"

"I feel him."

"Then let's move on."

Barak noticed that everyone seemed to be eyeing them warily, even Shadow, but he didn't stop to consider it. He reached the rear door and looked into another corridor. "Empty. This way."

He marched through it, desperate to feel the slice of sword on bone again. He tried to shake it off. Maybe Zee was right. They shouldn't have brought the damn things. *But without them, would he have fought so well against such soldiers?*

A door burst open down the end of the corridor, and just as Barak was about to race to meet the enemy, Niel stepped out, followed by Caspian. "Woah, brother!"

Barak took a breath. "You found a way in!"

"We found a lot more than that. And so did you, by the look of it." Niel lowered his voice. "You used Belial's jewellery?"

"No."

"You look like you have. So does he." He jerked his head to Gabe. "What's happened?"

Barak shook his head. "A lot of death. A lot of fire. Have you found a way to end this?"

Niel looked warily at all of them, and glancing behind him, Barak suddenly saw what he did. They were all wild-eyed and bloodied, with torn clothes and smoke-blackened skin. Fighting Black Cronos had turned them all into monsters. But there was still more to do.

Niel addressed all of them. "We've found a way to destroy the place, but we need to leave now. Have you found the count?"

Barak shook his head. "There's no sign of him, but Stefan and The Silencer are dead."

"Thanks to me," Shadow piped up.

"Nice job, sister!" Niel congratulated her, "But I hoped we'd find him, too. There's no time now. Follow me."

Gabe pushed Belial's insistent beckoning to the back of his mind and focussed on the sphere. "You think that will blow this place up?

"I know it will," JD said. "We've already aligned the wheel. I just need to make one more adjustment."

Harlan nodded enthusiastically. "I've seen JD's weapons' system. It's ingenious. He doesn't have a sphere, but it's the same principle."

"So, when you set it off, how long will we have?" Barak asked.

JD shrugged. "Ten minutes at most, although it's hard to be specific. It will need to charge."

"I don't understand. It's not a bomb!"

JD wouldn't meet his eyes—or anyone's, for that matter. He stared instead at the dials on the panel, completely focussed. "I have made a slight alteration. It doesn't matter what, but when it blows, it will be big."

There wasn't time to question him, and besides, Gabe would never understand the details. "How big?"

"Big enough to blow a chunk out of this ridge. Although, I deeply regret having to do it."

"You shouldn't. We found a huge lab upstairs." Gabe tried to shake off what he'd seen. "It all has to go."

"Okay. Then we leave as we came in. Through the cave's entrance. Go ahead. Perhaps Caspian could take me when I'm done?" JD looked at Caspian hopefully.

Caspian nodded. "Of course. I can fly us straight there. The rest of you, carry on. Ash?"

"I'll go with my brothers, thanks, if one could fly me to the lift."

So, Ash still wasn't flying. That was worrying, but no matter. Gabe would talk to him later. And then a horrible little voice whispered that a Nephilim who couldn't fly was useless. *Broken.*

Gabe gritted his teeth, silently telling Belial to get lost. *It was a shoulder injury. That was all.* His meddling was the last thing he needed. Shadow's warm curves would dispel him. He opened his arms to her. "Let's go."

But when they clambered down the ladder into the chamber to wait for JD, they all had a nasty shock.

A dapper man, dressed in a suit and with the eyes of a sociopath, was waiting there with what seemed like a battalion of soldiers. They were lined up in front of their only exit beyond a shallow lake. A row of flaming torches illuminated the space, casting their faces into grim masks.

The count had found them.

He smiled. "I knew I'd find you here. It was logical. And Jackson, of course. Did you think you would escape? You're a fool."

Eli made to move in front of him. Jackson, however, wouldn't let him. "No. You're the fool for thinking that you could keep getting away with this! You can't keep experimenting on people! It's horrific. If we didn't stop you, someone else would. Some other government would find out what you do."

"No one has bothered us so far. Until you, of course. And there are so *few* of you." The count studied them all. "All seven Nephilim, I see. How unfortunate our bombs didn't kill some of you in Aswan. And Harlan, of course. I know *you*. We came so close to capturing you and your friend the other night. And there's the witch, and the fey. And my interrupted latest." His eyes flashed with annoyance. "The soldier you stole from me."

Lucien snarled. "My name is Lucien! I am not a faceless, nameless man! You stole my life."

"I gave you a new one." The count extended his hands. "I will give you *all* one. My lab will survive the odd fire. So will the *château*. It survived the Albigensian Crusade, and it will survive *you*. Fire cleanses, you know. But seven Nephilim, with my advancements...that will certainly be something." He cocked his head. "I don't know how enhancements would affect a witch or a fey, but it will be interesting to find out."

"I will cut your balls off and make you eat them first," Shadow said, already edging towards him. "Not even Herne could contain me."

That wasn't strictly true, but it sounded good. Gabe knew that in this light, she could disappear easily. But there were so many men. *Too many.* And not enough time. Belial's torc beckoned.

He whispered to Niel. "The exit is behind him, I presume?"

"The only way. He must have got down here using the passage over there." He nodded to the waterfall. "I knew I should have checked it!"

"Then we use what we have. Belial."

"I gave mine to Ash."

Gabe eyed his injured brother, wondering if he'd be prepared to use it, when Estelle laughed, drawing everyone's attention as she challenged the count. "You certainly can't contain *me*! Do you really understand my power?" She raised her hands. With an enormous roar, the lake of water rose in front of them, and Estelle shouted a spell that made Gabe's skin tingle. She brought her hands down, and the water crashed around the soldiers, sweeping some out of the door screaming, while others smashed into the cavern walls, carrying their dowsed torches with them.

Simultaneously, Caspian arrived in a whirl of air, depositing JD on the floor, and instantly summed up the situation. He whipped up the remaining water, sending it spinning across the floor, sweeping up soldiers and flinging them aside.

JD yelled, "What are you all waiting for? Run!"

Gabe sprinted for the exit, leaping over fallen bodies and making sure his team was ahead of him. The count miraculously was still standing, and weirdly still looking cocky. *He wouldn't be soon.* Gabe knew the explosion would kill him, but a niggling part of him needed to make sure he was truly dead. Although a group of soldiers were struggling to their feet to protect the count, Gabe aimed straight for him.

But then the count saw JD. He pointed at him, his hand shaking. "*You* are here! What have you done?"

JD stopped running and faced him, lifting his chin defiantly. "I recalibrated your machine."

"You can't possibly understand it."

"You always were a fool, Germain. You think because you're immortal that you're better than everyone. Well, you're not better than I am. I have drawn on the coming solstice. I beckoned darkness, and it answered. Mars and Jupiter are bringing their war horses. Capricorn and Sagittarius will also join the fight. And I placed a certain gemstone right in the centre of your grid."

Gabe wouldn't let him elaborate. The surviving soldiers were recovering their senses and moving to block their exit. A powerful whirlwind that blasted out from behind him showed Caspian was still there. In the ensuing confusion, he pushed JD through the exit and into the narrow tunnel, sorely tempted to pick him up and fling him across his shoulders.

He pushed Caspian ahead, too. "Take JD to the house!"

"Don't wait long, Gabe!" Caspian grabbed JD, and they vanished.

Gabe pounded down the tunnel to the entrance, finding Ash and Shadow waiting on the lip of the cave. Beyond it, the blizzard still raged, the landscape swallowed by snow and ice. "That's it! We're all out. Go!"

Shadow hesitated. "Ash can't fly."

"*What?*" Gabe stared at him. "Of course you can."

"I'm not so sure."

"Have you tried?"

"No. It feels wrong."

Gabe was dumbfounded, and again, Belial's voice sneered. *Broken.*

"I hear him, too," Ash said, his eyes filled with sadness. "He's right. Take Shadow. Go!"

"I'll take both of you."

"Yes." Shadow agreed. "He can. He's strong enough."

"Not tonight. He won't be quick enough or get high enough. Not in these conditions. You go."

Rage and fear filled Gabe. "Why didn't you go with the others?"

"Barak took Estelle, Niel took Harlan, Eli took Jackson, Nahum took Lucien, and Zee had already gone."

"You didn't tell them?" Gabe grabbed Ash and lifted him up by his breastplate. "I could kill you myself!"

"I know you're angry, but this is for the best."

"Gabe! Take him! I can scramble down," Shadow argued. "I'm like a goat!"

"You won't get clear in time!" Gabe pointed out, furious at the whole situation. He knew he must take both of them. He had to try. He didn't need to go far. "Shadow, shelter under my wings, on my back."

Before Ash could protest, he pulled him tight, and as Shadow grabbed him, he leapt into the storm, just as an almighty roar ripped through the ridge.

For a long moment, Ash thought that Gabe could make it, the blast helping to carry him higher and higher.

But then the snow and wind pummelled them, and Gabe plummeted.

Although he furiously beat his wings, carrying both of them in these conditions was too hard, just as Ash had known. And it was impossible to see where to land.

Ash fought free so that Gabe could save himself and Shadow, and then was suddenly tumbling, end over end, in a maelstrom of snow.

Another explosion sent out a second shockwave, picking Ash up and carrying him like a feather on the wind. Stones rocketed around him like cannon balls. As he found himself falling, thinking on his life and all he still wanted to do, he heard Belial's cackle.

Broken. Useless.

Instinctively, he ripped his armour from his body, extending his wings.

But he was right all along. Only one worked. He plummeted toward the ground, wheeling like a sycamore seed caught on the breeze.

Then that laugh rippled through his mind again.

Ash remembered the clasp. He felt in his pocket and gripped it, and suddenly Belial's power flooded through him.

Light bled from every pore of his skin, and suddenly the wing he thought was gone forever unfurled. He finally stopped tumbling, and the wild wind carried him higher and higher.

Through the hail and snow, the castle was a beacon of light. Flames blazed from it, and the ridge appeared to have been cleaved in two. The wind threatened to drive him onto it, but he steadied himself, and like a shooting star, headed for the chalet.

When he arrived there, he saw his friends gathered below, staring up at him. He was still incandescent. The light of the Fallen Angel leaked from him. He wanted to flee, but he didn't have the strength to. Instead, he wanted to sleep forever.

He lowered himself to the ground, wings outstretched, and let Belial's clasp fall away from him. But there was more than that. As the light faded, he realised his usual honey brown wings had changed, and were now as golden as his eyes.

Thirty

Harlan had hoped they would be jubilant after defeating Black Cronos, and yet the mood in the chalet was subdued.

He'd just indulged in a steaming hot shower, hoping the atmosphere would have settled by the time he emerged. It hadn't. He rubbed his hair with the towel as he stood on the threshold of the living room, watching the various groups who didn't see him in the doorway.

Ash leaned on the sill of the picture window that looked out on the valley below. It was still lost in the blizzard that seemed like it would last all night. Eli was with him, both talking quietly. Ash's magnificent golden wings had been folded away, but the memory of them was burned into Harlan's mind. As was his descent in the storm, to be honest.

He was used to the Nephilim and their amazing wings, but seeing Ash lit up like a Christmas angel was something else. But at least he could fly again. Gabe had told them what had happened when they escaped, convinced that he had killed his own brother, and he almost cried when Ash returned. He'd hugged him fiercely and Harlan walked away, feeling like he was intruding.

However, as the joy of beating Black Cronos and Ash's survival leaked away, the memory of Belial lurked. Niel had resorted to what he normally did when faced with a catastrophe. He cooked. Caspian was helping him. A clatter of pans, voices, and music leaked from the kitchen while they worked. The others were all gathered in the living room, taking a grim inventory of their injuries, relaxing, or cleaning their weapons. The room reeked of oil. The only one still celebrating was JD, who was crowing like a cockerel and pacing the room with nervous energy.

Harlan crossed the space to pour himself a bourbon, trying to decide how to lighten the mood, when JD did it for him.

He stood, hands on his hips in the middle of the room, glaring at all of them. "I will not tolerate you all brooding on the night we should be celebrating! We have destroyed the count! The immortal *Comte de St Germain*, who has plagued civilization for centuries with his deadly whims! I won't even presume to take credit." He shrugged. "I mean, I might have masterfully reconfigured his wheel, but you all helped! You killed soldiers, blew up guard towers, destroyed labs. Stopped the count from escaping—"

"I think the storm stopped the count from escaping," Barak pointed out from his armchair by the fire. "We just managed to kill a whole lot of people that might have been able to escape and recover. I must admit, the lab haunts me."

"No!" Lucien leapt to his feet. "You did the right thing. I know it! *You* know it. Look at the months I have struggled to survive. There were times today when I still wasn't sure where I ended and these enhancements began. It will be a struggle for months, if not all my life." His hands were clenched as he faced them all and his raised voice brought Niel and Caspian to the door. He took a deep breath, clearly forcing himself to calm down, and then turned to Barak and Estelle, who sat cross-legged on the rug in front of the fire. "I will forever be grateful to you for rescuing me, and to JD and Jackson for helping me in The Retreat. But I am sincere when I say I would not wish this on anyone. The people lying in those beds were too far gone. I could tell. You have nothing to regret." He sat down, collapsing in the chair as if the final bit of his energy had vanished.

"Well," Harlan said, "as much as I hate to agree with JD, he's right. We survived. We took out the count, and destroyed his base. There might be other bases, smaller ones, but we can root them out. Without him at the helm, we can all breathe easy. And as for Belial, he saved Ash's life!"

"Not willingly, I'm sure," Ash said, a rueful smile on his face. He shifted to look at the room properly, and his shoulders that had seemed so tight earlier finally appeared to drop.

"Even better, right?" Eli said to Harlan. "That's exactly what I said. But the thing is, Harlan, and you won't get this, I know, but he is one of the strongest of the Fallen. He is the Angel of Destruction, delivering chaos and madness. We'd be fools to ignore his power."

"But you're not ignoring it! You know exactly what you're doing," Harlan protested. "You used it to save yourselves. You didn't advance *his* power, you advanced your own." Harlan knew the Nephilim had a thing about the Fallen and their fathers. It haunted them. Drove them. He downed a slug of bourbon, grateful that someone in this *château* had thought to stock some. "You know, we all have family issues. My father was an uptight son of a bitch who wanted me to go to law school, not become Indiana Jones. He's never forgiven me. It's sad, but I've gotten used to it. Also, can I remind you all, we saved Jackson!" He raised his glass. "My friend, good to have you back. I was very worried."

"I was very worried for myself." Jackson sighed, and Harlan sat next to him on the sofa. "Talking of family, I found out what happened to my grandfather. They caught him, like James Arbuthnot, and turned him in to one of them. I found out he had children, too." Jackson paused, and it seemed the whole room waited. "I met my uncle. I guess he died in the fight. At least I hope he did."

"Holy shit." Harlan felt terrible. "I'm so sorry."

Jackson shrugged. "At least I know the truth. My grandfather died years ago, so I'm glad of that. I still don't understand how the count reeled people in. A kind of indoctrination, I guess."

JD leaned over and patted his arm in an uncharacteristic show of affection and empathy. "The process would have changed brain patterns, I'm pretty sure of that, especially now that I've seen the scale of his set-up. Your grandfather would have changed, and probably didn't even know it."

"I hope you're right. I really do." Jackson stared into the fire, lost in his thoughts.

"So, dare I ask," Harlan ventured, "where Belial's jewellery is now?"

"Locked back in the box and spelled with protection," Gabe said. He was playing with Shadow's hair as she sat on the floor between Gabe's legs, leaning into him, her eyes half closed. They seemed intimate, close, as if they were the only two in the room, but Harlan knew both were following the conversation closely. Especially Gabe. He watched and listened to everything. Most notably, Ash. "And they'll stay locked away until we are able to follow it up properly."

"And what about you, JD?" Harlan shifted to look at him. "What will you do about the Emerald Tablet?"

"Continue to test the discs, of course. I refuse to rush it." His eyes sharpened with the prospect. "After all this time, patience is the key. Besides, I think I need a break to enjoy Christmas. We all do."

Niel cheered from the kitchen where he'd returned to cook. "When we get home, I'll make eggnog! Hey Caspian, how many eggs have we got? I could make some now!"

This seemed a safer topic, and soon, everyone was chatting about their plans. Harlan took advantage of the renewed chatter to sit next to Nahum and Zee. They were seated at the huge dining table, polishing their blades with a cloth. The metal gleamed, and Nahum put his aside and picked up another from the pile stacked next to it.

"You two are quiet," Harlan observed.

"Just processing everything," Zee said. "Cleaning weapons is a mindless activity that soothes me. I'm enjoying the chat, too. Although, I'll be glad to get home."

"Yeah, me too," Nahum agreed. He glanced at Harlan, quickly focussing on cleaning again. "Will you spend Christmas with Olivia?" He asked it casually enough, but Harlan knew the truth of it all now, and he didn't know what to think. Olivia was pregnant. With Nahum's child. And at present, they were the only two people in the room who knew.

"Yeah, I guess so. Might even catch up with Maggie. She texted me earlier after she'd seen Olivia." Nahum stared at him. "Yeah, seems we have lots to discuss. I'll see if Jackson wants to join us, too. We'll unwind, let off some steam, swap stories. All the fun stuff."

Harlan liked Nahum, but right now he was angry with him, and he found his protective instincts kicking in. It was weird. It was something he needed to process.

Before Nahum could respond, Niel yelled, "Clear the table, food's up, and someone grab some plates!"

Zee gathered the weapons and moved them aside, shouting, "I'm coming."

Harlan took advantage of the moment and leaned closer to Nahum. "You need to tell them your daddy news. *Now!*"

"With everyone here? I wanted to tell my brothers alone first."

"Shadow and Estelle will know straight after. Estelle will tell Caspian, and I'll tell Jackson. And well, it's JD. He's a crazy, mad alchemist. He might be able to help!"

Nahum's eyes widened with surprise. "With a baby?"

Harlan leaned in. "I need to talk about this, and so do you! It's good news, right?"

Nahum sagged in his chair. "Yes, but I'm not ready!"

"Well, you better get ready, because it's happening!"

Nahum sighed and closed his eyes.

"Nahum!"

"Yes, all right!" He slammed the blade and oil onto the side counter, and after a frenzied few minutes of table setting and dishes being brought out, they all finally settled around the huge table.

Nahum cleared his throat and Harlan sat back to watch.

This was going to be fun.

After the meal, Estelle found Caspian out on the sheltered veranda that ran the length of the house. He was sitting on a cane chair, wrapped in a blanket and watching the snow, while cradling a whiskey.

"Here you are! I've been looking for you." She sat next to him and pulled her own blanket around her shoulders. "Mind if join you?"

The light from the room that overlooked the veranda illuminated his beaming smile. His eyes were warm, and a sheen of dampness was on his dark hair. "Of course not. I've been reflecting on the night, and this stunning view."

"There is no view. It's all snow."

"But it's still beautiful. We don't get snow like this very often in Cornwall, and we certainly don't get a mountain backdrop."

"Or Cathar castles scattered on the ridges."

"Thanks for asking me to help you. I don't like to crowd you...you know, with the Nephilim and Barak. It's important to you." He raised his glass. "It works for you. I've never seen you happier."

Estelle knew she could be prickly, but she'd been trying very hard lately not to be, and she loved her new lease of life with Barak and his brothers. Even Shadow. "Thank you." She chinked his glass with her own. "I've needed the space, to be honest. It's given me time to reflect on my life and direction."

"If you don't mind me asking, Barak seemed a little wild-eyed earlier. Was that Belial?"

That was an understatement. "Yes. I didn't like it. I haven't discussed it with him yet, but I will."

"Don't be too hard on him. I'm sure he's struggling with it, too."

"Perhaps. He seems to have put it aside for now. I'll make sure to keep that box the jewellery is kept in well protected." She turned the conversation to lighter things. "I also wanted to thank you for attempting to reinvigorate our coven. I think it might be working."

He shuffled in his chair to look at her. "I agree. Our uncle and cousins seem happier. I feel more positive. Less like I'm relying on the White Haven Coven for everything."

"Don't tell me you're abandoning them?"

"Of course not! They're still my friends."

"Good, because you need them, like I need this bunch of reprobates!" She laughed. "What a night. You really helped back there."

"I don't actually feel like I did that much in the end, locked down in the engine house of the castle. You were in the thick of it on the battlements."

"Of course you helped. You ferried JD around, and waited with him to do his thing—whatever that was. And of course, attacked the soldiers, at the end. Without that we might have been caught in the blast."

"But did you notice that the count wasn't affected by our magic? He was like the unmovable eye in the heart of the storm. My wind whipped around him, and the waves crashed over him, and yet he just stood there."

"Of course I noticed, but what does it mean?" She voiced what had been worrying her all evening. "Do you think he could have survived the blast?"

"It obliterated half the ridge!" Caspian sighed and stared at the swirling snow. "However, it makes you wonder. Perhaps he's just the master of illusion, too."

"Or the universe aligns for him. He is a brilliantly evil alchemist."

"If he has survived, it will take him lifetimes to rebuild, but I think he's dead. We're witches, and that blast would have killed us." He squeezed her hand. "He's gone. The count likes to get in people's heads. Don't let him in yours." His eyes suddenly gleamed with humour, "Why don't you tell me how it feels to be an aunt? Perhaps it might have given you ideas!"

Estelle laughed, throwing her head back at the outrageous suggestion. "You are hilarious, Caspian Faversham! *Children*. You must be joking me..."

With both of them giggling like schoolchildren, the subject turned to much lighter matters.

Shadow laid her head on Gabe's broad chest, listening to the steady beat of his heart, her head rising and falling with each breath.

"I know you're not asleep, Gabe Malouf. Are you all right?"

"I'm going to be an uncle."

She laughed. "And I'll be an aunt! I'll be great. I can teach the baby lots of skills. But I do not do nappy changing. I like Olivia." She tapped his chest with her fingers. "I approve."

Gabe groaned. "But you know our history—"

She cut him off. "Yes. I know it and I am very sorry for your tragic losses, but this is thousands of years later. Everything might change."

"Curses don't."

"The power of angels has waned. You don't know."

"You're trying to cheer me up, I know. I'm not convinced."

"Then we will find a way." Shadow slid off his chest, nestling in his arm instead.

"What's wrong with you? You hate kids."

"I hate other people's kids. This will be Nahum's. And he's excited. You must be able to see that."

"He's terrified."

"Underneath all of that, he's excited. So is Harlan. So are your brothers."

"Perhaps Olivia should move in."

"Don't be an idiot! She has her own life and a job that she loves. She will want to keep her independence. It's important to her."

"I know."

"And *I* know that your protective instincts are strong. This is your brother's matter to handle, Gabe. Don't crowd him."

He nuzzled her ear. "When did you get so wise?"

"I've always been wise. You just get distracted by my curves and swaying hips."

"Speaking of which..."

He kissed her deeply, and she leaned into him and let the night's events fall away.

Nahum stared at his phone, wondering whether he should call Olivia, the silence of his bedroom pressing in on him.

He wanted to see how she was feeling, and also reassure her that he had survived and would fulfil his promise to help her in any way he could, and yet...he didn't want to be overbearing. Intrusive.

At least the news of his impending fatherhood had been well received. More than that, actually. There had been whoops of delight around the table, and Niel had found champagne to make toasts. Even Shadow and Estelle, those two staunchly independent women, had been pleased for him. Shadow had immediately offered her coaching skills, which was frankly terrifying.

No one talked about their past issues. Everyone had focussed on the future. If they believed it could happen, then maybe it would turn out well. Refusing to second guess Olivia's response further, he called her, heart beating frantically like he was a teenager again.

She answered quickly. "Nahum! Are you all right?"

"I am. I survived. It felt as if I might not at times, but I did. We all did."

She sighed, her relief palpable, even over the phone. "That's so good. What about Jackson?"

"We found him. In typical James Bond fashion, he's shaken, but not stirred." He laughed. "Does that even make sense?"

"It's strangely apt. I'm so relieved."

"More importantly, are you okay? The baby?"

"It's still a little blob, and we are both fine. No official scans or anything of course until at least six or eight weeks. I've told Maggie. I needed to. I hope you don't mind."

"Of course not. I just told everyone here. Harlan made me. But they have been sworn to secrecy for now. They were very happy. We all drank champagne."

"Maggie is happy, too. She toasted us. I drank water." Olivia laughed. "So, it's official then. They all know. Wow. This is so odd. Is Harlan okay? He looked...shocked. And then he was all protective!"

"Ha!" Nahum recalled his intense stare. "He's fine. He's aiming to keep me on my toes. Make sure I fulfil my duties. I think he'll be the most fearsome uncle of all. But it's all good, yes? No second thoughts?"

"No. I should probably visit you in Cornwall at some point, just to meet all of your brothers. I've only met a few."

"They're eager to meet you. I guess I should meet your family, too, at some point." He rushed on to cover his nerves. "I know you probably have Christmas plans, but what about New Years? We have plenty of room. You wouldn't have to lift a finger."

"I'm barely pregnant. I can do plenty! But yes, that would actually be really nice." He could almost hear her relax, as if she was snuggling under her sheets.

"Are you still with the witches?"

"Yes. They've been amazing, but I'm going home tomorrow to re-evaluate my space. I'm excited."

"So am I." Nahum felt his heart swell. *This was unreal. Unexpected.* "I better let you sleep. I need to, as well. I'm shattered. I'll be in touch, okay?"

"Sounds good. I'll keep you up to date, too."

He ended the call and flopped onto his bed, feeling like he'd flown from one end of the Middle East to the other. He flicked the bedside lamp off and stared into the darkness. Everything was changing, again.

But it was a good change. New beginnings. And no doubt, new enemies.

The coming year was going to be a very interesting one, indeed.

BROTHERHOOD of the FALLEN

WHITE HAVEN HUNTERS BOOK SEVEN

TJ GREEN

One

Gabe settled himself against the curve of the church's domed roof, the starlit sky spread above him, and focussed on the shadow-filled courtyard below.

He was in Florence, Italy, with Niel, Ash, Nahum, and Shadow, waiting for the man they suspected was an agent for Belial, the Fallen Angel. It was the end of February; two months since they had defeated Black Cronos, and since then, this search was all they had spent their time on. Two months of achingly slow progress, with this the only lead. It was an opportunity that most of the team hadn't wanted to miss out on. However, despite their eagerness to participate, they all knew the importance of caution. Consequently, Eli and Zee were still in White Haven, Barak and Estelle were in Yorkshire, investigating Jacobsen's church again, and Lucien was in London, working with Jackson and Harlan as they continued to track down leads. They were all trying to keep Olivia out of it because she was pregnant, but she was not happy about it.

The patter of footfalls on cobblestone made him hold his breath, but the giggles of a group of girls made him realise the noise came from outside the church, bouncing off the thick stone of the surrounding buildings. The church was in one of the oldest neighbourhoods of Florence, at the centre of a spiderweb of streets, with small squares sandwiched in between the ancient buildings. The place was old, creaking with knowledge and secrets, this thirteenth-century church more than most.

It was after midnight, and they had been in Florence for two weeks, becoming familiar with the area and their quarry's movements. Only Shadow had been inside the church, the rest of them wary of being discovered and alerting their suspect, an elderly deacon called Salvatore Amato. So far, they were sure they hadn't been. Shadow, because of her natural fey magic and stealth, had followed his movements on foot at night as far as the entrance to the crypt, but was reluctant to explore further as she detected unearthly angelic power. Caution had won over curiosity, but it was enough to convince them to question the old man.

Niel's voice cut across his thoughts, through the earpieces they wore to keep in contact. "I see him now, approaching from the south. He's heading to the door that leads to the courtyard, just like normal. I estimate another few minutes before he arrives. Stick to the plan. Copy?"

The murmured responses from his brothers and Shadow confirmed his message, although Gabe knew Niel would have more trouble following that instruction than anyone. *Follow Amato, seize any jewels with Belial's power, and question him. Do not kill him.* Gabe carried a wooden box in his pack, spelled with protection, and designed to hold any Fallen Angel jewellery they found. Its weight reassured him.

Gabe glanced to his left. Ash was a short distance away, also perched on the roof, where he sheltered in the shadows of the ornate stonework. Shadow waited below, cloaked in darkness in a corner of the courtyard. Niel circled overhead, keeping watch, while Nahum looked out over the front of the church. They would both now adjust their positions to join them. *Just questions*, Gabe reminded himself. *Don't kill him, no matter how much he irritates the crap out of you. And be wary of Belial's trinkets.*

Gabe took a deep breath and exhaled slowly. *They were so close.* It was Jackson who had found Salvatore after tracking Jacobsen's movements—the vicar who had peddled around the reliquary that contained Belial's jewellery. He had investigated his various addresses over many decades and found that he spent a lot of time at this church in his youth. It seemed odd that a vicar of the Church of England should frequent a Catholic church, but something must have piqued his interest. That led them to do more extensive research, and they had found something very interesting. While many staff moved around, a few older members had worked here for decades, but Jacobsen had kept in touch with only one of them. *Salvatore Amato.* But what had confused them was that there were no sporadic outbreaks of violence in Florence. Another mystery, if Amato was an agent.

The click of the lock in the door alerted them to his arrival, and Gabe braced himself for flight.

The figure was slight, innocuous in many ways, but his movements were sure and swift as he locked the door and crossed the courtyard to the side door of the ancient church. *Just like clockwork.* Every Sunday, Tuesday, and Thursday night he would come here for at least two hours before leaving again. They waited for him to enter the church before swooping down, and then all four Nephilim landed in silence, although, Gabe noted again with a grimace, Ash's newly golden wings reflected the tiniest bit of light. An unexpected gift from Belial, and no doubt unintended. Shadow was already at the door, and they soundlessly followed her inside.

The scents of incense, cold stone, and a whiff of mustiness struck Gabe as they closed the door behind them. Amato had already disappeared, but Shadow led them down the passageway and into the nave. It was huge, a domed roof high above them, with rich reliefs on every single wall. At the far end was a spectacular altar, a gilded cross towering over it. There were angels everywhere. Huge, winged creatures that looked on from paintings and sculptures.

Gabe's skin prickled with unease, but he hadn't time to think about it. Shadow led them behind the altar to the choir area, then halted at the steps that led to the crypt. Gabe felt Belial's presence like a punch to the gut. He gently eased her aside, shot a warning look to his brothers, and led them down the steps.

The staircase descended further than he expected, the smell of dampness mingling with Belial's distinctive power. The ancient wooden door of the crypt was open, candlelight leaking through. A low-roofed space stretched ahead, filled with tombs, iron railings, niches, and statues. They faltered for a moment, still unable to see Amato, but light from a side corridor drew Gabe onwards.

With every step, Belial's power swelled around them, until Gabe was sure that he was actually about to face him. A palpable air of worry had settled over all of them, and Gabe gripped his sword for reassurance. Finally, they arrived at the threshold of an ancient round room with a domed roof, carved with hundreds of angels. A place of worship to a master who didn't deserve it. An altar dominated one side, an enormous marble statue of an angel with outspread wings looming over it. It was draped in jewels. A long, golden necklace with a heavy pendant rested on his broad chest, a silk-lined fur cloak flowed from his shoulders, and bracelets and torcs were fixed around muscular arms. In his outstretched hand was a real sword made of tempered steel with a rich, engraved hilt. *So much jewellery. So much power.* Amato was nowhere in sight, but he must be here somewhere.

Wary of traps, Gabe glanced down the corridor that continued past the small chapel, but it lay in darkness with an air of disuse. He tentatively stepped inside the room and had progressed a few steps only when he was suddenly struck by Belial's power. It was as if a giant weight was forced upon his shoulders, and unable to resist the unspoken command, he fell to his knees. By now everyone was inside the room, and his brothers followed suit. Shadow suddenly vanished. Panic swirled through Gabe as he struggled to master his movements, but he was utterly powerless. Unable even to speak.

Salvatore Amato emerged from behind the statue, black clothes billowing around him. His eyes glowed with a maniacal gleam. "It is fitting," he crowed, his thin, reedy voice swelling with the power of Belial, "that you kneel before him. You are nothing compared to his power and majesty."

Gabe's panic multiplied as he struggled to respond, his jaw tight, every muscle seized. *Idiot. Why did he step inside?* All four Nephilim were in a loose semicircle, darting eyes their only movement.

"You will swear your fealty to Belial or die," Amato continued, stepping closer. "I know who you are. You murdered poor Jacobsen and have used Belial's jewellery for your own ends." He shook his head as he paraded in front of them, then suddenly pulled a wicked, curved blade from his gown, glinting with angelic script. "And you," he paused before Ash, whose golden wings glowed within the candlelight, "even used his power to save yourself. You are already his. Perhaps I should ask you to kill your brothers. Stand."

Unexpectedly, and clearly against his will, Ash stood, sword gripped in clenched fist, muscles flexing. He towered over Amato, but the man stood before him, resilient, unyielding. *If he commanded Ash to kill now, would he?* Niel and Nahum were within easy reach, both furious and frustrated.

Trying not to let fear and anger overwhelm him, Gabe focussed on slowing his breathing and regaining control of his mind and body. He forced himself to look at the statue of Belial. He had no natural human form, but from his many incarnations, he recognised his narrow-eyed stare. The look of superiority. The vindictive smile. It might only be marble, but white fire seemed to flame behind his eyes, the skin taking on a luminous glow. His presence felt so strong, Gabe was almost convinced that he was actually contained within the statue, but that was impossible. And it was impossible that they should be restrained by him. He scanned the room, taking in the scored marks on the stone floor and its mirror image above them. He had been so distracted by the hundreds of angels that he hadn't seen it. A trap, but not for demons. For Nephilim.

Amato was toying with them, and despite all their stealth and care, the bastard had known where they were all along. But did he know about Shadow? And where the hell was she?

As soon as Shadow entered the shrine, she detected another level of magic, and it didn't come from Belial. It came from the sigils etched on the floor and roof, and she instantly knew what they were. Fortunately, they did not affect her actions, and she stepped into the dark, where the candlelight couldn't reach, and pulled her fey magic around her.

She felt an instant relief as Belial's insidious whispers muted, and the stone and earth around her offered her soothing comfort. *I am fey. As old as the Earth and her mysteries. I am not cowed by you, Belial.*

She was only just in time. As the four Nephilim fell to their knees, Amato stepped around the statue, and she moved silently behind him, back to the wall, assessing all other dangers. But there was no one else in the room. As well as the jewels on the statue, rings were heaped upon the altar amongst half a dozen candles. She also scented blood. Old, dried blood. *Sacrifices.*

Amato began to speak, his voice assuming power that was not his own. Shadow was torn with indecision. If she killed him now, they would learn nothing from him. No, she would wait and hope he would reveal more of his plans. He would not harm the Nephilim. *Not yet, surely.*

"Should I have you kill your brothers?" Amato asked Ash. "It would be so easy. You lift your sword, and you stab the one to your right." He raised his hand as he spoke, and Ash lifted his sword and struck at Niel, the blade missing his throat by a whisker. "If I willed it," Amato said, a thin-lipped smile creasing his face, "he would be dead by now."

Shadow flinched at the demonstration of power. She couldn't deny it was impressive. *But that was too close.*

Amato stepped back, and Ash sank to his knees, sweat beading on his brow. Amato whirled around, placing his dagger on the altar, then studied the Nephilim again. "I need answers. How did you find me? What else do you know? Who works with you? You!" he commanded Nahum. "Speak."

"Screw you, old man," Nahum ground out between clenched teeth. "You might control my body, but not my mind."

"Ah! The father of the Nephilim child. Belial is aware of it. She and her mother have the protection of the Goddess, which is rather annoying."

She?

Nahum stuttered, his blue eyes flickering with uncertainty and a flare of pride. "I'm having a daughter? I swear, if you touch her, I will kill you."

"You are in no position to threaten me, and certainly not Belial."

"Don't be so sure about that."

"You have no power here, so your threats are pointless."

Salvatore Amato looked utterly unconcerned. For an old man, he radiated health and vitality. In fact, he might actually be much older than they suspected. A gift From Belial. It would explain how he could assume the Fallen Angel's power and carry it so effortlessly. And this place certainly reeked of age. It was as old as the church above, maybe even older. Perhaps the church had been built over it.

He continued, his voice dropping and filling with Belial's power again. "How many others?"

"There are only us."

"Lies. Perhaps if I kill one of your brothers, you will speak the truth. With every lie, I kill one more." He studied the four prisoners. "Kill the golden-winged one."

Nahum unwillingly stood and lifted his sword, slowly advancing on Ash.

Shadow couldn't afford to wait any longer. She had hoped that Amato would give away some of his secrets willingly, but it was clear he would not. They would have to coerce him, and somehow break his power over the Nephilim.

She materialised out of the darkness, wrapped one arm around Amato's thin shoulders, and placed her dagger at his throat. "End it now, or I end *you*."

The old man roared in shock, and before Shadow knew what was happening, he seemed to swell in size as he emitted a blinding white light. It threw her off her feet and into the wall, her dagger falling to the floor.

Fortunately, it had thrown the Nephilim back, too. All four lay crumpled against the walls. But that was as much as she saw, because Amato snatched up his cruel-edged knife and flew at her with lightning speed.

She rolled to a crouch, her other blade already in her hand, facing him. "You are more than you appear, Amato. You must carry a trinket to have that much power."

"Who are you?" he spat. "How dare you enter my sanctuary!"

"I dare to enter anywhere I choose."

He flew at her, dagger slashing where she had stood, but she had already moved, keeping easily out of reach. "Release the Nephilim."

"I will kill them first."

Rather than lunging at her, he sprang at the closest Nephilim, all four still lying helplessly and unable to move. He reached Gabe first. His knife slashed his arm in a vicious jab. Shadow tackled Amato, rolling over and over across the stone floor, feeling his sharp blade slice her side. It was as cold as ice, yet it burned with the power of the sigils.

She landed on top of him, knee pinning his hand that carried the blade to the ground. She punched him repeatedly, his head striking the stone flags. But he was strong with angelic power. He rose up, trying to throw her off him, desperate to free his knife. With an unexpected surge of strength, he rolled, slamming her into the ground, blade slashing down. Shadow wanted to slit his throat and be done with him, but they still needed him for answers. Instead, she stabbed his arm, slicing through tendons, and with a horrified yell and a splatter of blood, he fell backwards, then scrambled away on hands and knees.

"Glad to know that you still feel pain, you bastard," she yelled. She struck again, cutting the back of his legs and slicing his Achilles tendons with another splatter of blood.

He screamed, eyes wild, foaming at the mouth as if with some religious ecstasy.

She edged back, knowing he couldn't move, and checked her team. They were still where they had fallen, limbs tangled. Gabe's arm was bleeding profusely. He stared at her, his emotions a mix of fury and gratitude. And confusion. Deep confusion.

Not surprising. This place was all kinds of unexpected, and so was Amato. The wound at her side ached, and she pressed her hand to it, trying to stem the blood flow. Amato was muttering something, eyes closed, his power building. Much like the unexpected surge of power when she had attacked him.

What now?

Two

B arak eased the door open and slipped inside the rectory that had once been Jacobsen's home, Estelle right behind him.

It was the first time they had been able to enter it after his death. There had been, understandably, a lot of press interest in the death of a vicar slain in his own church, and as yet there wasn't a new one assigned to the area. The weekly service was instead delivered by a visiting vicar. When the police investigation ended, they seized their chance.

"Do you feel any sign of Belial?" Estelle whispered.

"Not a thing." The loud ticking of a wall clock marked the time as Estelle threw a few witch-lights above them. They illuminated a short hall, and doorways to either side. "He'll have a study somewhere, a place where he would have written his sermons and seen visitors. Let's hope it's where he kept his secrets."

Together they opened doors and progressed through the house, investigating the living areas and kitchen before finding a large, square study at the back of the house overlooking the garden. The house was cold and dusty, and it was obvious that no one had been in since the week Nahum had killed him. A Christmas tree wilted in the front room, dead pine needles spread across the floor.

"Do you think he'll have a folder of co-conspirators?" Estelle asked, half laughing.

"Let's hope so. It will make our life easier." Barak shut the curtains and the door and flicked on the light switch. Fortunately, the house still had electricity, and light flooded the room revealing bookcases, a small fireplace, a desk and chair, and an armchair by the fire. "So far, so ordinary."

"It's hardly like he'll advertise his allegiance to Belial. Apart from the gigantic painting of an angel, of course." An angel in typical Biblical style was portrayed with spread wings, looking down at the Earth. "It's unnerving. I think his eyes are following me."

Barak laughed. "*Great*. A possessed portrait. That's all we need." He turned his back on it and started going through the drawers in the large, battered desk. Papers were spread over it, along with the remains of the powder the police used when dusting for fingerprints. "Old sermons, notebooks, pens, pencils. Just the usual crap."

"Is there an address book?"

"Not so far."

Estelle hunted through the bookcases, and for a while there was silence between them. Barak placed a couple of notebooks in his pack, but the desk otherwise held nothing of interest.

"Here are some more old notes," Estelle said, handing them to him. "We can check them later, and there's also an address book. Pretty scant pickings, really. All of the books are religious, apart from a few thrillers."

"What about those?" Barak asked, turning his attention to a few photographs on the wall. "He's young in them. Looks like he's fresh from religious college, or whatever they call it."

"A seminary, I believe."

"Let's take them, too. They might direct us to important connections."

Estelle was transfixed again by the oil painting. "We should look behind that. I have a feeling about it."

"I've learned never to ignore a witch's intuition." He lifted the painting down and turned it against the wall. There was nothing on the back of it, but set into the wall was a safe. "Time for your magic again." Within a few moments, the door swung open, revealing a bundle of pages inside, and nothing else. He flicked through them. "It's a manifesto."

"You're kidding me!"

"No. Some claptrap of bringing Belial's power to Earth. Bollocks." He looked at Estelle, seeing her confusion mirror his own. "This is bigger than we thought. Much bigger."

"Shadow!" Nahum drew her attention, relieved that he could still speak after Amato had lifted part of the spell. "Can you drag us out of the room? That's the only way we'll regain control. It's some kind of trap."

"What if I can break it?"

"I don't think you have time. We need to get out of here. Amato is summoning *something*."

Power was building again. The whole room resonated with it. It was so strong that Nahum felt sick, and he realised that the trap was making them more susceptible to it.

Shadow staggered to her feet, and grabbed Niel beneath the shoulders, the closest Nephilim to the door. But he was too heavy, and while her fey abilities gave her superior speed, they did not make her strong.

Shadow grunted. "I can't. You're all too big. Herne's fucking horns!" she yelled in exasperation. She slumped against the wall, blood pouring down her side again.

Amato cackled despite his pain. "You can't break the trap. It's burnt in by Belial, scored deep into the rock. He's coming now. He looks forward to seeing you."

"Impossible," Nahum said, sounding more certain than he felt. "He cannot walk this Earth again."

"He can through me." Amato pushed himself upright and dragged himself back against the wall, smearing blood along the ground. "This is one of his most sacred places. He's coming. I have called him. Even my death will not stop him. And when he sees you?" He laughed again. "You will all be recruited to his cause. You cannot resist."

Shadow limped to his side, unsheathing her Dragonium sword. "I'm willing to test that by removing your head. How many other sacred places are there?"

"You think I will tell you? Fool. Too many for you to find. There are more involved than just me and Jacobsen. So many more..." His voice was a rasp now as his strength finally started to ebb. Power continued to build, though, a pale glow seeming to light his skin.

Then Nahum spotted a chain around his neck. *Another trinket containing Belial's power.* "Get rid of his necklace. Don't touch it with your hands!"

She used her sword to slice through it, flicking the broken chain across the room, the ruby pendant clattering against the stone. A huge ring also adorned his finger, and she cut off his whole hand, kicking it across the floor, too. He didn't even scream.

"Shadow!" Nahum summoned her attention again. "Get the box from Gabe's pack, and put as many jewels in as possible! It should stop whatever is happening."

She hauled Gabe's pack from under him, rolling him awkwardly "Sorry, my love."

While Shadow raced around the room, sweeping as much of the jewellery as she could manage into the box, Nahum studied the trap. He'd be damned if he was going to die down here or become Belial's accomplice. *He was going to be a father. He was going to have a daughter. He would not leave Olivia to care for her alone.* Renewed hope surged through him. *There had to be a way to break the trap.*

"I can't get the rest of the jewels." Shadow gestured to the jewellery on the statue's arms. "Not unless I touch them. The box is near full, anyway."

"*No*! Do not touch them." Nahum's voice was sharp. "You are resisting all of this so far. We can't risk you succumbing to his power, too. What do we know about traps?"

"That if you break them in some way, then you interrupt their power. Strike out a sigil, or break the circle." She spun on her heel. "But Amato is right. These are scored deep. I'd need an axe, and even then, if they're made with angelic magic..."

"Niel has an axe."

She rolled her eyes. "It's huge! I doubt I can even lift it! It's almost as big as him, the big lump!"

Niel's only response was to glare. *If looks could kill...*

"Wait!" she said, almost jumping with glee. "JD's weapons! Why the hell didn't I think of that sooner?"

Nahum groaned with relief. "Of course! Belial is clouding our thoughts. There's one in my pocket."

"Don't worry." Shadow patted her fatigues and withdrew a sleek metal object from her pocket. "I have mine."

Nahum scanned the room again, deciphering the many sigils scored into the rough stone. As usual, the trap was circular, stretching to every wall. However, in the centre, was Belial's seal. Monstrous in size, it echoed the same design in the ground, and connected to all the other sigils. He pointed at it. "That one! Take it out, above and below."

"That sounds suitably alchemical."

Amato hissed. "*No!* You risk burying us alive!"

"Shut up!" Shadow commanded. "I'd rather that than be a puppet. However," she raised a sleek eyebrow at Nahum, "floor first! Close your eyes."

As Shadow retreated to the doorway, Nahum was relieved that at least he could close his eyes. His leg was buckled under him, and one arm was twisted behind his back. He lay half on top of Ash, and Gabe and Niel looked similarly squashed from the little he could see of them through his peripheral vision. *Please work.*

He clenched his lids shut just as Shadow blasted the seal with short, controlled bursts of the weapon. Rock and dust blasted into the air, pelting his face and body, and he knew he'd be covered in a myriad of cuts. The blasts continued for several seconds before it finally fell quiet.

"I'm done."

Nahum cautiously opened his gritty eyes and saw Shadow standing over the mess.

"It hasn't completely gone, but I've taken a chunk out. Round two." She took a breath, looking at all of them. "I'll make it as quick as I can." Her gaze lingered for a moment on Gabe, and then she headed back to the door again.

The next blast felt so much worse. Chunks of stone rained down, and rocks bounced over him, one striking his temple. Dust went up his nose and despite his best intentions, he swallowed some, too. He wished he'd thought to tell Shadow to cover their faces. *But what with?* Their clothes were in packs squashed beneath them. But then he realised that the air felt cleaner, and the sticky, cloying power of Belial had lifted. He carefully moved his arm and relief flooded through him.

Ash groaned. "That's my face. Ow!"

"I think I've dislocated my butt," Gabe said. "Is that even possible?"

"Sorry, Ash! Shadow, you bloody superstar! You've done it." Nahum brushed debris from his eyes and opened them slightly, but he could barely see anything. Dust filled the air, and he started coughing. "Are you okay? Why are you so quiet?"

"I think you should move. *Quickly.*"

"What the fuck have you done?" Niel bellowed.

"The roof is cracking, and so is the floor."

As if to emphasise her point, an ominous shudder shook the entire room.

Niel grabbed the stone door frame as the floor buckled beneath him. He was only just in time.

With an enormous *crack*, a chunk of rock dropped out of the ceiling and shattered the slabbed floor as it crashed through it. A section of the floor tilted precariously.

Niel flung out his other hand and grabbed Ash on his right. "I've got the door! Hold tight!"

In seconds his brothers had all gripped each other, forming a chain, but Gabe was the furthest from the door and was sliding towards the gaping hole as Nahum clung to him. A chunk of slab had upended, and Gabe braced himself against it as Niel gripped the frame with increasing desperation.

"I'm okay!" Gabe yelled. "For now. Shadow! Where are you?"

"Over here, trying to help Niel." She was flat on her belly, half in the corridor, arms wrapped around Niel in an awkward embrace as she tried to help, her legs braced against the frame. "The passage seems unaffected—so far, at least."

"Well, that's something, I guess," Niel complained, as her head wedged under his armpit to get a better grip.

"Can anyone extend their wings?" Ash asked, his voice strained. "I have no room."

"Me neither," Nahum said. "Where's Amato?"

Niel grunted as he twisted to see across the room through the settling dust. "I think he's under a pile of rubble. Yep, I can see his leg. At least the floor's stopped moving." He was trying to reassure himself more than anything. Although he was strong, he was carrying most of the weight of his brothers, with only Shadow and the slab Gabe was wedged against helping him. If he lost his grip now, Shadow would not be able to stop him from sliding.

"I might be able to open my wings," Gabe said, tentatively bracing himself more carefully. "I can't see into the hole, though. I don't know how deep it is. It might only be a couple of feet down."

"Or it could open into a cavern system, and we're screwed," Ash suggested. "But I guess we might be able to fly then."

"Bear with me." Gabe twisted again, testing his weight against the slab, and digging the fingers of his free hand into the cracks around him.

Niel took stock of the room as the dust cleared. It was a wreck. The altar and Belial's statue were covered in debris, and both were tilting precariously. The hole in the roof where the seal had been revealed a solid mass of earth and rock that could come tumbling down at any moment. *They had to get out of here.* He tentatively tested his strength, pulling against the door frame, but he barely moved an inch.

Gabe adjusted himself once more. "I'm going to open my wings really slowly."

It seemed that everyone held their breath as Gabe's wings carefully unfurled, catching chunks of stone as they did so. He slid for the briefest movement and then stabilised again, and finally they were fully extended. Niel felt the weight he was supporting ease. But they all knew the next step would be the hardest. The room was barely large enough to encompass his wingspan, and for him to fly he needed to move his wings.

Niel braced himself again, renewing his grip on the door frame and feeling Shadow tighten her grip around his chest.

Then everything shifted. Suddenly, Gabe was airborne, his wings filling the room, and the turbulence sent whirls of dust around again. Niel hauled himself upwards as the weight of his brothers reduced. Shadow squirmed backwards, helping to drag him to the passage.

It was impossible for Gabe to lift either of his brothers, and as Ash and Nahum started to inch backwards too, Nahum asked, "Can you see what's below us, Gabe?"

"There's a narrow seam in the bedrock, and it goes down a good way, from what I can see. It looks like the part you're on is solid. The weight of the falling seal must have broken through a weakened section. I think you're right, Ash. It's some kind of cave. Or it might even lead into old sewers or something."

Niel resisted looking at him, focussing instead on dragging them backwards, and with relief he cleared the door frame with his shoulders. In a few more minutes, they had wriggled clear and were wedged into the passage, covered in sweat and debris.

"That was too close," Nahum said, breathing heavily. "Gabe, is it worth trying to get down there? Could there be anything related to Belial?"

Gabe shook his head. "Unlikely. I don't trust the roof not to collapse further, either. But I want Amato, if he's still alive." He carefully landed on the more stable part of the floor and removed debris from the man's prone form. "Bollocks. He's dead."

"Is there anything we can salvage?" Shadow asked. "Anything on his body? Or can you get the remaining jewellery?"

He didn't answer as he patted the corpse down. "Just his knife. If the box is full, it's pointless for me to take the rest of the jewels."

"We can't just leave them here!" Nahum protested. "Others must come down here. Maybe more of Belial's disciples."

But the second the words came out of his mouth, the statue started to topple.

"Gabe! Move!" Shadow cried out.

Gabe had mere seconds to leap out of the way and take to the air when the statue crashed to the ground, taking another chunk of the floor away. With an ominous *crack*, the rock beneath them split again and the huge, winged angel plummeted into the gaping hole, Amato's body tumbling in after it.

"Time to go!" Gabe yelled, angling towards the door as everyone made room for him to land.

Without a backward glance, they all fled from the destroyed shrine, and Niel could swear he felt the ghost of Belial's presence pursue them.

# Three

"Two months," Jackson said, "and scarcely any leads."

"Did you honestly expect anything else?" Harlan asked, incredulous. "Belial has been here for centuries. Millenia, even. His agents are resourceful, and no doubt well hidden."

"You keep saying 'agents.' It's depressing."

"You know I'm right. It won't be just one person—or a paranormal *whatever*—supporting him. Belial will have backup. And besides, what we have is better than nothing. Stop being so negative."

Jackson ran his hands through his shaggy hair, making it even more messy than usual, and stared at the large world map pinned on the wall of his office in The Retreat, the base of operations for the Paranormal Division that sat beneath Hyde Park and Kensington Palace in London. "But it's so tenuous! This is like searching for Black Cronos all over again."

"Well, we found them, and we'll find these agents. At least Gabe and his team had some success last night. And Barak and Estelle found a damn manifesto! That's huge!"

"True. I'm just impatient." He sighed and headed to the shelf where he kept his tiny kitchen area to make a pot of tea. Knowing Harlan hated tea he asked, "Coffee?"

"Please. Strong."

It was Friday afternoon, and the working week was drawing to a close. Not that it meant anything to him or Harlan. Their hours were erratic, and although he'd take some time off over the weekend, he would continue researching. Both teams had phoned that morning with news of their overnight success. Amato's death was unfortunate, but at least Jackson could continue to hunt down his connections. Shadow and Gabe had gone straight from the church to Amato's city flat and searched it, knowing that the police would be notified of his disappearance very soon. Unfortunately, as at Jacobsen's house, there was little to find.

"I presume," Harlan said, "they'll investigate Amato's country house?"

"Heading there now." He handed Harlan his mug of coffee. "It will take them a couple of hours to get there, but they should arrive soon."

"And Belial's jewels?"

"Safely tucked up in the spelled box. I have a feeling we'll need one the size of a treasure chest next time." He dropped into the chair behind his desk, weariness washing over him. "The amount of jewellery there was worrying."

"Maybe it's a good thing. Perhaps most of it was there, and now some of it is down a very deep pit, forever." Harlan grinned. His relentless good humour was exhausting. "I mean, how much bling can an angel have, right? He sounds like a rap star."

Jackson laughed. "Well, that's one way to look at it, but I suspect that he has a lot! By the sound of it, the Fallen liked to preen. But we can't forget the manifesto." The mere thought of it banished his smile. "It's big. Organised."

"Not necessarily. Lone bombers have manifestos, too. If it was really so big, there'd be a lot more crap happening. I'm still convinced it's a small group who just love to spread unrest." Harlan sat in the chair opposite him. "We didn't even know about this until Olivia stumbled upon the reliquary. It's not great, but it's not huge, either."

Jackson sipped his tea. "You're right, I guess. I need a good sleep to get this in perspective. This place is getting to me again." He meant the unending corridors of The Retreat. Sometimes it was oppressive. It seemed especially so only a couple of months after Russell's death, the Deputy Director of the PD. He was killed by Layla Gould of all people, after Russell murdered two PD staff and was about to shoot Maggie Milne, the DI of the Paranormal Policing Team. "It's still unsettled here."

"Of course it is. You have new staff, increased security, and people are still grieving. Yourself included. You need to cut yourself some slack. *You* are still getting over the news about your grandfather too, never mind the scientist and that nice kid, Petra."

Harlan's statement depressed Jackson further. Petra *was* a nice kid. *Too young to have been murdered by Russell fucking Blake.* "I can't deny that their deaths haunt me. Petra's more than anyone's. I've convinced myself my grandfather wouldn't have known anything once Black Cronos changed him. But Petra? That's shit. I've seen the camera footage. She was screaming and terrified, and he shot her like she was nothing. Maggie and Layla are heroes for stopping him."

"So are you." Harlan considered him, a thoughtful expression on his face. "You need to get out of here. Maybe out of London. Strictly speaking, you don't need to be involved in the Belial stuff. Maybe you should pick up a case and work on something completely different."

"Waylen wants me to stick around. He's invested in finding Belial now, too. Plus," he gave Harlan a wry smile, "despite everything, I like it here. It's in my blood. And I owe Waylen. He needs me here. They all do."

Working for the government's Paranormal Division went back years in his family, and he had always worked for them in some capacity. Harlan didn't know half of it, although he suspected it.

Harlan nodded. "If you're sure. What's happening with the Deputy Director's job?"

"Waylen offered it to Lyn, the scientist and alchemist, but she refused. Said it would take her from the lab too often. Too much management crap that would get in the way of her research. He's disappointed, but understands her reasoning."

"Because Russell was a scientist, right?"

"Yes. So then, he offered it to Layla, and she said yes, but only until he has someone long-term. She says she's too old to deal with managing egos. It leaves Waylen with a dilemma. He doesn't feel the other scientists are up to the job, but he really wants a scientist who understands the lab and the research. He's very resistant to bringing in a completely new person for such a role. I mean, we have new staff, obviously, but not in such a senior position. So, he's considering asking someone else..." Jackson massaged his temple just thinking about it. "JD."

Harlan spluttered coffee. "You're kidding! JD? That grumpy bastard, managing people? No!"

"My sentiments exactly. I've objected—strongly. I suggested he keep him as some kind of special consultant instead. He could oversee the work, but not manage the staff. He likes that idea, and that has led to another scenario." It was another reason he didn't want to abandon Waylen and The Retreat right now. "He asked me to do it."

"That's amazing!" Harlan said, shooting upright in his chair. "Congratulations! You said yes?"

Jackson shrugged. "I'm thinking on it."

"What's there to think about? You'd be great! You're friendly, personable, balanced, and you know the PD well! Everyone likes you. This is a fantastic compliment."

Jackson ran his hand through his hair, feeling awkward. "But is it me? I mean, I'm a bit chaotic. Laid back. Scruffy." He meant it, too. Management to him meant suits and meetings, performance reports, and other such crap. "I hate evaluations and stuff. Just the thought of it is depressing! But it's very flattering, too, right?"

"Of course it is. He wouldn't ask you if he didn't think you could do it." Harlan smiled, his expression sympathetic. "I get it, though. You'd be responsible for others. But you know, you kind of do it anyway."

"I do? How?"

"You liaise with everyone. The analysts, Barak, Estelle, and Lucien. You brought the Nephilim in. You have contacts that Waylen doesn't. And you're relentless, my friend. You survived being kidnapped by the count! The more I think about it, the more I think you're perfect for the job."

Jackson was momentarily speechless at the unexpected response. "Really? I did not expect you to say that."

"You thought I'd talk you out if it? No way. Oh, man! Maggie will be so pleased to have the ear of the Deputy Director!" Harlan laughed, and once he started, he couldn't stop. He wiped tears from his eyes.

It set Jackson off, too. "Why am I laughing? It's not funny. She'll drive me insane."

"It's so brilliant. You'd even be JD's boss—kind of!"

Despite his initial reluctance, talking to Harlan helped clarify a few things. He did do all those things. "Perhaps I should say yes."

"Yes, you should! Do it now! Then we can celebrate. It's approaching beer o-clock!"

"Slow down. I'll give it more thought over the weekend. I can't drink too much, anyway. I'm meeting Barak and Estelle later. They're travelling back today and should arrive at Chadwick House soon. Lucien is already there, of course." Chadwick House used to belong to William Chadwick, until he was killed. He'd left it to The Orphic Guild in his will. Harlan's boss, Mason, was happy for it to be used by their contractors, and Lucien was living there for now. He was searching Chadwick's study for anything that might be relevant. As an occult collector before his death, he had many arcane volumes there, and they thought it prudent to check them all. "Want to join us?"

"I've got a date with a pregnant woman."

"Olivia? What are you two up to?"

"She's seeing Morgana for a check-up. I thought I'd offer some moral support."

Jackson noted his friend's earnest expression. "You're taking your uncle role very seriously."

"I can't help it. I'm worried, and with Nahum away, I don't want her to be alone. I know the Moonfell witches are great and everything, but, you know..."

"I know. She's okay, though?"

"She's great. Excited!"

"Even more reason to find Belial. Give her my best."

Harlan nodded, rising to his feet. "I will. If you find anything of interest in that manifesto, let me know. But accept the job! You'll be brilliant at it."

"Thanks, Harlan. I appreciate it." Jackson watched him leave, thoughts immediately drifting to Amato. He had a few hours to investigate his background. He'd see what else he could dig up.

"Are you sure she's all right?" Olivia asked Morgana, scrutinising her expression for anything that might suggest otherwise.

"I'm not lying!" Morgana pursed her lips, but then immediately softened as she ran her hand a few inches over Olivia's still-flat abdomen again. Olivia could feel the witch's magic like a gentle warmth. It comforted her. "She's perfect. Stop worrying." She stood back, her examination over.

"And still hardly a bump!" Harlan noted. He squeezed Olivia's shoulder as she sat up. "You look radiant."

Olivia adjusted her clothing, glad she could still wear her skinny jeans and silk blouses for a while longer, and then patted her stomach. "I thought I'd be feeling sick by now, but I'm fine!"

"That's Nephilim blood for you."

The three of them were in Morgana's private consultation area on the south side of Moonfell house, comprised of just three rooms—an examination room/office, a herb preparation room, and a bathroom. It had its own private entrance that was tucked into one of the building's many nooks and crannies. There wasn't even a door into Moonfell's interior. The better for privacy, Morgana told them. That explained why Olivia had never seen the rooms when she had wandered the house before Christmas. However, they were still decorated in Moonfell's flamboyant style. Morgana was a witch, after all, and used magic to help her clients, not science.

Morgana jotted a few notes into a file on her desk and then turned to face them. She looked a little less severe than usual. Her long hair was loose, and she wore a dark blue dress instead of her customary black, but it was still loose fitting and long, with a thick, colourful cardigan to add warmth, the sleeves rolled up to her elbows. "I must admit that I'm not sure what to expect of a Nephilim baby. Potentially, it could grow much quicker than a normal child, or will be bigger. I have chatted privately to Nahum about this though, and he reassures me that previous pregnancies have all progressed like any normal, human-fathered one."

Olivia recoiled in shock. "I didn't know you chatted to him alone!" Nahum certainly hadn't said so. It made her feel like a child. "You can tell me these things!"

"Of course, and I'm telling you now. But, if the pregnancy was moving along quicker than expected, we would all have had to adjust. I wouldn't have wanted you worried, or your energy depleted. Fortunately, though, all is as it should be." She smiled as she leaned back in her leather chair. "It's given quite the bloom to your cheeks."

"I know. Everyone keeps telling me how well I look, and they have no idea I'm pregnant. I haven't told anyone yet. Not even my best friend." Olivia felt horribly guilty about that, but thought it best to stick with regular time frames. "I won't tell either, not until the first scan. I'm hoping Nahum will be around for that."

She felt Harlan stir, knowing he was worried about their relationship. He'd become oddly protective lately, which was sweet, but unnecessary. And Maggie was being Maggie. Belligerent and forthright. Although, she had already brought her a pack of newborn baby clothes, unexpectedly revealing Maggie's tender yet practical side. Jackson was wonderful, like an indulgent brother, and that reminded her of Nahum's brothers. *Blimey.* They were something else, and her reception at New Years when she went to stay with Nahum at his Cornwall farmhouse... Well, she was treated like a queen. Not that they were together, of course. She had her own room, and he was courteous and solicitous, and very much at arm's length, when all she wanted to do was get him naked again...

Morgana's lips twitched with amusement, as if she knew exactly what Olivia was thinking. "I'm glad Nahum is being supportive, but I would expect nothing less. He's extremely charming. How is he? I gather he's off chasing Belial."

"They're in Florence, Italy. The team had a run-in with one of Belial's agents last night. He's dead now. The shrine was destroyed—accidentally, of course," she said, watching Morgana purse her lips.

"I'm not disapproving. I'm frustrated. Did they find anything out before he died?"

"Just that there are more of them."

"And," Harlan added, "that there was a lot of jewellery there. They managed to take some of it and place it safely in the spelled box that the Cornwall witches supplied, but some of it was lost forever. Well, we hope forever." Harlan ran through the events, and they coincided with what Nahum had told Olivia, which was good. At least he hadn't held anything back.

Morgana's eyes widened in surprise. "They were caught in a trap?"

"Yeah." Harlan huffed. "Seems to be the season for them. Shadow had to break it with JD's weapon."

"The priest, Amato, said that Belial had scored the trap into the rock?"

He nodded. "Do you think he was lying?"

"If he wasn't, it's very worrying! He's either found a way to act here, or it has been here for millennia."

"It was a very old shrine, hidden deep beneath a church," Olivia informed her, "so yes, perhaps it was that old. I think the shrine was hacked out of bare rock." She felt dizzy with it all. "If I hadn't found that reliquary, we would have known nothing. Surely that means whatever is happening is on a small scale? No one even knew!"

"No one knew about Black Cronos, either, and there was nothing small about that. But," Harlan said, "actually I agree, and as I said to Jackson, there's no reason for us to get panicky."

Morgana snorted. "Have you forgotten the night we banished him?"

"How could I? It's imprinted on my brain. But a few lone religious nutters spreading his word might not amount to anything."

"Bollocks to Belial!" Olivia was sick of hearing about him. "I'm pregnant. I want positive thoughts around me. Morgana, should I be doing anything? Or can you detect anything? Does the baby have wings?"

"Good grief! I hope not. You don't want to give birth to *that*." Morgana laughed. "It's a baby! Although, I will admit to feeling a strong spirit, and most definitely a whiff of Nephilim magic."

Olivia felt a fool for confessing, but... "I've never considered that they have magic. Not like you."

"Because it's not like a witch's magic, or fey magic, either. It's their own, angelic magic. Diluted, of course, being half-angel, and their human part is dominant, but supernatural strength, healing, speed—and wings—are all magic."

Perhaps this should have reassured Olivia, but instead it set off another wave of worry. "I'll have a magical baby! How can I be a mother to that?"

"Just like you would be a mother to any other baby. You will shower her with love, keep her warm and safe, give her boundaries, and educate her. Quite honestly, Olivia, I think you'll be wonderful. You're strong and feisty, and no one's fool. I doubt Nahum would have slept with you otherwise. I think he must have had a sixth sense that you were the perfect mother. Not that he was planning to impregnate you, of course."

"I'm not a test tube!"

"I meant that some creatures, paranormal ones in particular, know when they've found the right mate. That's all."

"But they are not *mates* like some fated mates bullshit," Harlan said a little too forcefully. "They are fuck buddies!"

Olivia slapped his arm. "One time does not make a fuck buddy! And please don't use that term again. It was a tryst! A late night comfort. That's all."

Morgana's eyes sparkled with intrigue. "Of course, Olivia. Just a tryst. Now, I have a packet of herbal teas that I want you to drink regularly. Just one cup daily will suffice. It will strengthen your immune system, help you sleep, and generally support the pregnancy. It's a slight change to the last mixture, just a tweak to adjust for the growing baby's needs. Okay?"

"Thank you." Olivia glared at Harlan once more before turning back to Morgana. "You're very kind. I feel much better for having your support."

"And mine?" Harlan asked.

"Sometimes! You can take me to the pub for dinner, and that will make up for slurs!"

With luck, it would also take her mind off Nahum, wondering what he was up to, and whether he was thinking of her at all.

Four

"It's unusual that a man such as Amato should have such a grand country residence, don't you think?" Nahum asked his brothers and Shadow as they finally located the building in the wooded valleys around Palazzuolo sul Senio, a small town to the northeast of Florence.

"I think it's probably his reward for decades of service," Ash said, staring beyond the locked gate and down the drive. It was dark now, close to seven in the evening, and the country lane was quiet. "It's impressive, without being overbearing."

"And very well concealed," Shadow added, craning her neck out of the window. "It's impossible to tell from here whether anyone lives there or not."

Gabe just huffed. "Another late visit, then."

"I need to get out and stretch my legs," Niel complained. "Two hours stuck in a hot car with you guys is driving me insane. No one will spot us."

Gabe obligingly pulled onto a grassy area just past the drive entrance, and they all exited on cramped legs. Nahum rolled his shoulders, taking deep breaths of fresh evening air and strolled down the verge, needing a little space to clear his thoughts. In the end, they had left Florence later than originally planned, after deciding they should stake out the church where Amato had worked and died. They had wanted to see who might be involved and whether anyone would arrive at the church that looked suspiciously upset and panicked. Unfortunately, or maybe fortunately, nothing untoward had presented itself.

They had carefully locked up the crypt after leaving the previous night, and nothing appeared to have been damaged on the upper levels of the church after the destruction below. They had hoped that with luck, no one would find his body for days. Maybe even weeks. His disappearance would be suspicious, but far less so than his death—especially in such a place and such a manner. Eventually, however, after the day proceeded as normal at the church, they decided that delaying any longer would be dangerous, especially since there was nothing else to learn.

No one talked much on the journey. They had all been shaken by what they had found, and they had barely slept when they returned to their hotel after their encounter and collective near-death experience. It was only now that they all seemed to be shaking it off. Belial, as usual, had slid under their skin. Nahum wondered what would have happened if they hadn't spotted the necklace around Amato's neck and the ring on his finger. *If Shadow hadn't removed them, would Belial really have manifested through Amato's body?* The glow of angelic light was real enough. His annoying cackle and superior laughter suggested inside knowledge. He knew who all of them were. *Was someone spying on them?* He glanced uneasily overhead, as if Belial's presence was close. It didn't help that they had a stash of Belial's trinkets in the boot of the car, either. They may be wrapped in protective spells, but they were like magnets, always drawing their thoughts. Well, Nahum's at least.

As always lately when thinking of Belial's trinkets, or whenever in fact his mind drifted at all, Nahum thought of Olivia and their child. *Their daughter.* Having that news delivered by Amato infuriated him. It wasn't as if he didn't want to know, but he did not wish to be told by *him*. Information Amato could only know through Belial. He had taken pleasure in revealing something Nahum should have learned with Olivia. He had phoned her as soon as he could with the news. It seemed only fair. Of course, he had checked with her before revealing the fact, but she had wanted to know, and could barely contain her joy. *A daughter.* Nahum closed his eyes, imagining Olivia's expression. The curve of her smile, the tease in her eyes, her smooth skin.

He had kept his distance at New Years. It was one night of passion. That was all. With lasting consequences that were unexpectedly good. *But once their daughter was born, what was he to do?* Unable to deal with that right now, he returned to his team and their conversation.

"Of course," Ash mused in a low voice, "if Amato had accomplices at that church, they may already know where to look for him."

Shadow nodded. "True, but would they want to make it obvious that they knew exactly where to look? I wouldn't. Someone will stumble on him in a few days, I'm sure. We should keep our eye on the news reports to see if anyone in particular found him. It might be another clue."

"Or, of course, no one will report the death at all," Nahum suggested. "His body did fall into a big hole. Or maybe they'll make sure it seemed to have occurred well away from the church."

"There's that *they* again," Gabe complained.

Ash laughed at Gabe's grimace. "He did say there were more of them. We can't ignore that. That shrine was significant. It could involve the entire church. There were a lot of angel motifs as decoration."

However, even as he was saying it, it didn't ring true to Nahum. They were all sure that Amato had worked alone there.

Niel, ever impatient, stripped his shirt off and extended his wings. "We should take a quick look around while we're here. If the place is empty, then we don't need to return later. If he has a housekeeper or someone else lives there, lights will be on now."

"That's logical," Nahum agreed.

Gabe considered the suggestion and then nodded. "Okay, if it looks deserted, come back and we'll join you. Be careful!"

"I'll come, too," Nahum said, stripping and extending his own wings, anxious to dispel his circling thoughts of Olivia.

"I'll move the car under that stand of trees," Gabe said, gesturing down the road. The forested slopes pressed closely along the lane, and the wind in the trees sounded like whispers.

"We won't be long," Nahum promised, and in seconds he followed Niel's lead and flew over Amato's grounds.

Amato's country house was a stocky building with a square tower and was actually much smaller than Nahum had anticipated. The grounds were heavily wooded, with the trees ending in a circle around the property. It would be menacing here even in midsummer, the air close and thick. And it was dark. No lights glowed in the windows, and there were no cars on the drive. They landed on the flat roof of the tower, and up close it was obvious why the house was deserted.

"This place is a wreck," Nahum said, noting the cracked masonry and general air of dilapidation. "I don't think anyone has lived here for years."

Niel peered over the parapet onto the roof of the main house. "I agree. Everything needs to be repaired. There are holes in the roof, and cracked windows. But why? What happened here?"

"Maybe nothing. Amato could have preferred living in Florence."

Niel scanned the woods, and then finally looked at Nahum. "There are secrets here. Or were once, at least. It feels ominous."

"I don't like it at all. I sense evil."

"We might as well investigate it now, then."

Nahum nodded, distracted. *What was it about this place that was so unsettling?* "Fine. You get the others. I'll wait by the main entrance."

He flew over the woods again in the time he had spare. There wasn't a break in the trees, or any sign of a building under the canopy. The grounds were obviously as neglected as the house. When he finally set down before the double wooden entrance doors, one was already ajar, the frame warped by the weather. He shivered, unable to shake the feeling of unease, and waited for his brothers to join him.

It was then that he spotted Belial's seal over the door, and felt a prickle between his shoulder blades. He spun around, sword raised. The dark woods presented an impenetrable wall behind him, but was something in there, watching him?

He turned his back, convinced that whatever had once been here was long gone, but Belial left dark shadows, and he did not relish stepping into them.

Lucien spread the manifesto out on the study table, the half a dozen pages lined up next to each other, and weighted their curling edges down with the objects closest to hand. A few peculiar glass paperweights, a brass hand, and a bronze egg in a stand. Objects he had become very familiar with once he had settled in at Chadwick House.

His attention, however, was on the manifesto, as was Estelle's, Barak's and Jackson's.

"It's handwritten," Jackson observed. "I didn't expect that. Old, too."

Lucien nodded. "An old-fashioned ink pen wrote this. It looks to be centuries old. I've seen similar papers that are stored in Chadwick's collection. Personal histories, some of them. Diaries of occultists. Not manifestos," he added hurriedly, in case anyone got the wrong idea.

Lucien felt very confident, compared to how he had been a couple of months before. Defeating Black Cronos had reinvigorated him, and he had mastered his shifts to a super-soldier. It also helped that he was now living at Chadwick House, with his own room and agenda, and no one watching his every move anymore. He hadn't really liked the house to begin with, but he had acclimatised well enough, and it was free to stay there. He had consequently immersed himself in the occult, researching Chadwick's collections, and familiarising himself with the study and the books it housed. He had grown to like it. The house's old walls creaked and moaned, but it was also secure and warm, and for the first time in months he relished his privacy. He felt that he had become the house's custodian. *Stupid, really.* Mason Jacobs, the Director of The Orphic Guild, was actually in charge, but only in name. He didn't live and breathe the house like Lucien did. Lucien had begun to think that this place was part of his destiny. He was a member of the paranormal and occult world now. He may as well embrace it.

Estelle agreed with his suggestion. "Yes, Barak and I thought it was old, too. It makes us think that Jacobsen must have been a valuable part of the organisation for him to own what looks like an original manifesto."

"Unless, of course," Jackson suggested, "this is an old copy of an even older manifesto. I need to study it properly, but the language is old-fashioned, the phrasing weird."

"Angels were always deliberately obtuse," Barak said, grimacing. "The more fanciful they could be, the better. It's tiresome, but at the time, it was just the way things were."

"You think Belial wrote this?" Jackson asked, eyebrows shooting up.

Barak shrugged. "Dictated, perhaps? I don't know. He was always fond of his own voice. I think it's likely he had a hand in it."

"Which means he had a strong connection to whoever wrote this." Jackson straightened up, gazing about the room but not really seeing it. "A mental connection, or was he actually, physically here?"

"I'd have said that was impossible," Barak said uneasily, "not for millennia, at least, but after what my brothers have seen lately, I'm not so sure."

Lucien rubbed his tattoos as he studied the manifesto, a habit he'd developed when he was first turned by Black Cronos. Now it just seemed to be something he did without thought. "I thought I'd got used to occult language, but that's gibberish!" He glanced at Barak, who like all Nephilim could read any language, but it wasn't the language at issue here; it was its obvious attempt to confuse and obfuscate. "Anything strike you?"

"No, other than the obvious. Ash might make more sense of it. Or JD, perhaps."

The manifesto started with a declaration, a promise to return the exalted Belial to his true position, after his selfless plunge to Earth as one of the Fallen. It stated that he had fought side by side with Samael, otherwise known as Lucifer, the devil, when he started Heaven's rebellion and left God's side. Together they sought to cleanse the Earth of the less than worthy, and reward those who were deserving. Those that followed him.

"That's bollocks," Barak said, pointing at the line that Lucien had just read. "He never rewarded anyone. He made them think he was going to, but it was all smoke and mirrors. He was a cruel, thankless master. Not many of the Fallen liked him. Unfortunately, you could never ignore him, either. His own Nephilim of course followed his every word, until they too finally rebelled."

"So, just to clarify," Jackson asked, "every Fallen Angel had his own Nephilim?"

"Yes, they all fathered lots of us. Remember, they could take the form of any man, for a while. Some women wouldn't even have known they weren't sleeping with their husbands, because the angel inhabited their skin."

"Which is horrific!" Estelle said, her hands clenching as if trying to contain her magic. "Treating them like a breeding machine!"

"And the men like a dedicated stallion," Barak pointed out. "Having an angel inhabit your skin was not pleasant, I can assure you. There were no winners in that scenario. We called ourselves Houses. I was from the House of Kathazel. Gabe and Nahum, the House of Remiel. As you know, my father had healing skills. Raphael was the most powerful healer. An Archangel. Kathazel was not as strong."

It was dizzying to hear ancient names uttered with such familiarity. Dealing with the immortal Comte of Saint-Germain and JD seemed strange, but this... Lucien focussed on the manifesto, and pointed out a few lines that were confusing. "What's this about angels of the First Sphere and the Second Dominion?"

"They were classes of angels. Belial was of the First Sphere. The most powerful of the angelic hosts." Barak grinned. "Even Heaven had a class system."

"The good thing," Estelle said, taking a seat at the table, "is that the manifesto seems unconcerned in general with any of the other Fallen. It only speaks of continuing Belial's work in cleansing the Earth by using his own brand of destruction—sowing the seeds of madness and causing destruction from within."

"A little hands-off for Belial," Barak stated. "He enjoyed getting his hands dirty, but he would like this, too. The insidiousness of it all."

"He does have a physical stake in all of this," Jackson reminded them. "His jewels that contain his power—his essence. How have they survived all this time? Gabe and the team found lots more beneath that church in Florence. That's what's troubling me more than anything. The manifesto is nothing without them. Just a bunch of words and promises that have no teeth without them. It's his trinkets, as you call them, that make the manifesto so threatening. You've read it. Does it give us any clues as to how they are here?"

Barak looked uneasily at Estelle. "There is a passing reference to the House of Belial, and the assistance they offered in distributing the jewels. Couched in flowery language, of course, but the meaning is clear."

"Are you saying that there are other Nephilim walking the Earth right now?" Jackson asked, face draining of colour.

"Not exactly! It suggests that there were at one time. That could have been hundreds of years ago. We are long lived, not immortal."

"But it's possible?" Lucien asked, shocked.

"Well, we're here, and the world is a big place," Barak conceded. He took a seat at the table as if all his energy had left him. "I've been mulling on it all day, trying not to see something where there is nothing, but it's in the manifesto. I don't think we can ignore it. It mentions certain jewels by name, too, and names his sword. They were names known only to his House."

"Why?" Jackson asked.

"Names confer power and knowledge. I mean, obviously I don't know if that *was* his sword's name. Someone could be making it up, but it sounds plausible. Especially because it's written in angelic script. It means *Justice Bearer.*"

"Have you told your brothers?" Jackson asked.

"No. I didn't want to unduly worry them until I was sure. I also wanted Ash's opinion. He's good at this kind of thing."

Jackson looked astonished. "I can't believe you haven't warned them after what happened last night."

"Dealing with other Nephilim is a walk in the park compared to Belial. We have all done that thousands of times. And," Barak held up a hand to stop Jackson interrupting, "I'm not worried. We would have seen signs by now."

"But if there are other Nephilim, even one," Lucien pointed out, as astonished as Jackson by Barak's decision, "who wields Belial's jewellery, like you all did, you know how it changes your abilities."

"They would not reveal themselves so soon. There is too much at stake for them."

Jackson snorted. "I hope you're right, Barak, because otherwise your brothers could be marching into a death trap."

Ash was as unnerved as his brothers as they searched Amato's abandoned country residence. Its obvious decay was surprising. *Why let such a place fall apart?*

"Perhaps something illegal happened here," he wondered aloud. "Maybe that's why he let it rot."

"You mean there might be bodies on the grounds?" Niel asked. "That wouldn't surprise me from the look of the place. Or under the floorboards, perhaps. Maybe even bricked up in the walls."

Ash rolled his eyes. "Good grief, you have a vivid imagination."

"Would you put anything past Amato, or any of Belial's acolytes?"

"I guess not after last night."

Ash and Niel were alone on the ground floor of the house, while the others searched upstairs. So far, they had found nothing untoward, but the place was undoubtedly creepy. Old furniture was shrouded in covers, including the paintings that hung on the wall. The air in the house was thick with dust, cobwebs cluttered the corners of the rooms, and there was evidence that animals had been inside, and maybe a tramp or two. Although the gate at the top of the drive was closed tight, the woods would probably provide a way into the grounds. The scent of decay was strong, and when Ash pulled the covers from some paintings, they saw that mould had started to creep across the surfaces.

"Perhaps we're assuming too much, and this was never a base of operations. It might have been an inheritance. Can you remember what Jackson said?" Ash asked.

"No, not really. All I heard was that there was a house we needed to check out."

They progressed slowly through the ground floor, investigating each room carefully, occasionally hearing their brothers and Shadow shouting to each other. There were holes in the ceiling where the joists had rotted, and Ash hoped that no one would come crashing through. The kitchen was still very old-fashioned, and it seemed it hadn't been updated since the early 1950s.

"Fancy cooking in here?" Ash asked Niel with a smile.

"Only if I wanted to poison everyone. It's filthy. I like modern kitchens, not clunky old ranges." He stood at the window and looked out on the dark forest, which seemed very close to the house at this end of the building. "Maybe Amato did inherit this house. He might have inherited his responsibilities to Belial, too. There's nothing to suggest it's not a family affair."

"True. The Fallen always liked to keep their Houses tightly knit. Maybe the same applies to Belial's human followers."

"I think," Niel said, pointing at the forest, "that something is in there. I think that's the start of a path."

"But you saw nothing from overhead."

"No, but look how dense it is. It's like Ravens' Wood. We're looking in the wrong place, I'm sure of it."

They exited through the side door into the wreck of an old kitchen garden, and followed the faint remnants of a path to the wood. When they reached the trees, they could see a faint trail heading away from them, although the start of it was overgrown.

"Well?" Niel cocked an eyebrow at Ash. "Looks likely."

"I agree, but let's wait for the others. I'll phone Gabe."

In a few minutes' time, the rest of the group joined them. "Nothing of interest on the upper levels," Shadow declared, "but I like the look of that path! I'm going first."

"Shadow!" Gabe started to complain.

She shushed him with a look. "I'm not susceptible to Nephilim traps, and the woods are my strength. Follow me, and keep quiet."

Ash knew better than to argue, and before anyone could complain, he squeezed through the undergrowth that she so effortlessly skirted, and followed her down the path, single-file. It looked like an animal track, and perhaps animals had maintained it, of a sort, all these years. Tiny tracks branched off it, and the hoots of owls accompanied them as they walked.

Shadow, as she always did, virtually vanished in the deep shadows beneath the trees, treading silently but quickly, her bow ready should she need it. His brothers, for all their size, were almost as quiet behind him. She led them unerringly onwards, only pausing once when a similarly sized path crossed the track they were on. She searched the ground, scratching away the earth, and then turned to follow the new path. Ash had no idea what had made her change direction, but he followed her up the gently sloping ground.

Suddenly, she halted and pointed, her voice soft like the rub of leaves on the wind. "There. A building."

Ash squinted. He prided himself on having great eyesight, but for a long moment saw nothing. Finally, he spotted a vine-covered column that looked just like a tree. "How the hell did you see that?"

"I am fey. I feel it as much as see it."

His brothers crowded behind them, and she waited until they had seen the column, and then progressed ever slower. In a few moments, more columns became distinct from the trees, and it was evident that they created a temple. A circle of them, now covered in moss and ivy, rose majestically towards the canopy, but there was no roof. The temple was open to the sky, although thick and twisting tree branches grew over the whole place now. The central space was sunken into the ground, a few deep steps leading down to a circular area, almost like a mini amphitheatre. It was hard to see its depth as it was filled with fallen leaves, but in the centre was a huge, winged statue of an angel.

"Herne's hairy bollocks," Niel whispered. "A temple in the forest."

"Ionic pillars," Ash noted. "Greek, not Middle Eastern. It might mean nothing, of course. Temple designs in England often lean to classical antiquity."

Shadow went to walk onto the upper step, when Gabe pulled her back. "Check the perimeter first."

"It's an old, abandoned temple, Gabe."

"Just listen to me for once!"

They fanned out, exploring the edge of the temple, finding stone slabs beneath the leaves that created a path around the columns, but many were cracked and broken, roots pushing their way through. Saplings even rose up through the central space, throwing the statue into deep shadow.

"Happy?" Shadow asked them all. When no one objected, she said, "I'm going to investigate down there, make sure there are no traps etched in the centre."

"Why is it abandoned?" Nahum asked, glancing around, hand clenched, like all of them, around the hilt of his sword.

"Places become unpopular. Newer temples supplant older ones. It's the way of the world," Ash said. "This place is creepy, though."

"It's on higher ground," Niel noted. "Might have had quite a view, at one point."

Shadow shouted, "It's all clear down here. No Nephilim traps or anything, just cracked stone. Marble, I think. The leaves are half a metre deep, sludge at the bottom, so it's slippery."

Ash waded through the leaf detritus and stood in front of the statue, checking every detail. "It's the same as the one in the temple last night."

Gabe was next to him, eyes lifted to stare at Belial's head. "I think you're right. It's uncanny. It looks just like him. It captures his haughty, heartless expression."

"His eyes are fixed behind us." Ash turned, looking in the direction that Belial faced, but the way was blocked with trees. "It's facing northeast. The same as yesterday's statue."

"Why is that important?" Shadow asked.

"I don't know that it is, but the fact that they are both facing the same way suggests it has significance. If it was just east, I wouldn't question it. Facing east was a common part of Christianity, and other religions, actually. It was Godly, the direction of the rising sun. But northeast?"

Niel stood next to him, also staring through the trees. "A direction for a reason, perhaps? To mark the way to somewhere of significance?"

"Perhaps."

Nahum was scrabbling about the base of the statue, moving leaves. "There's a big, square plinth down here, with an inscription. A large one." He pulled his torch from his pack and shone it on the surface, as one hand cleared moss from the words. "It's some kind of call to action. Lots of text."

Ash frowned. "A manifesto, perhaps? Like Barak found?"

Nahum looked up, surprised. "Maybe. Help me clear it."

Over the next ten minutes, they all cleared away the debris, scraping back moss to reveal the text that ran across the base, and Ash started taking photos. "I think it is. Whether it's the same..."

He trailed off, trying to comprehend what it meant.

"Niel," Gabe said, summoning his attention, "shine your torch straight upwards. I'll see if I can climb through the canopy and then fly. I want to orientate myself up there, see where he's looking."

"I'm going to explore further afield," Shadow said. "Check if there are other buildings or temples. Don't worry! I won't be long."

"Half an hour," Gabe instructed, "and then we're out of here. If necessary, we return in the light, tomorrow. There's nothing to worry about now that we know it's deserted."

Ash nodded, and once satisfied with his photos, focussed on the marble floor. He wanted to inspect every inch of this place, just in case something happened, and the wrath of Belial brought the place down over night.

Five

G abe peered over Ash's shoulder as he expanded a map of Europe on his laptop screen.

"So, we're where?" Gabe asked him.

"Here," he said, entering the name Palazzuolo sul Senio into the search bar. A small, red triangle popped up. "That's where we are right now. So northeast is roughly *that* direction."

It was Saturday morning, and Gabe, Shadow, and his brothers had just eaten breakfast and cleared the table in the small villa that Jackson had arranged for them to stay in for a few days. Nahum was phoning Jackson and Olivia with an update, and Niel and Shadow had returned to Amato's house to search in daylight.

Gabe nodded as he orientated himself. "Where is the church in Florence?"

"There," Ash said zooming out and scrolling across the page.

"Bollocks!" Gabe traced a northeast route from the church to their current location. "It's on the same line."

Ash swore in Greek. "I'd like a physical map to mark it out properly, but it's damn close."

"It must be significant, right?"

"I don't know. Perhaps?"

Gabe sat back, rubbing his stubble, and wishing he'd had more sleep. Unfortunately, his dreams had been plagued with memories and visions of Belial, and he'd slept poorly. "Two statues don't really make a case, do they?"

Ash turned to face him properly. "No, and as there was nothing significant to see—within easy view at least, last night—we're at a dead end for now."

Gabe had flown across the entire grounds of Amato's country house and then beyond it the previous evening, specifically searching the northeastern route, but nothing presented itself. No unusual buildings, or churches, or anything of note. "Potentially, there could be something that's miles away. Florence, after all, is an hour or two from here."

"There could be, yes. However, we should focus on the text for now." Ash pulled up the photos he'd taken the previous night and transferred to his computer. Then he accessed the photos of the manifesto that Barak sent. "The manifesto is convoluted and verbose, but there is that unnerving reference to the House of Belial."

"From what I can gather, Jackson was pretty cross that Barak didn't tell us about it yesterday, but I think Barak is right. Surely, we'd be aware of Belial's Nephilim by now." Gabe phoned Barak earlier and had a long discussion about what that reference could mean.

"Or maybe we're being naïve. Why should we know? We keep a low profile, why wouldn't they?"

"Perhaps." Gabe considered the implications of their use of the Fallen Angel's jewellery. "However, using his jewels has alerted someone to our presence. It certainly alerted Belial. He attacked Olivia, and had to be expelled. And Amato knew about us!" That had chilled Gabe more than anything. He felt under scrutiny again, as if Belial were watching him from afar.

"True, but no one has come for us. If anything, you would think his acolytes would go into hiding, but Amato didn't. He knew we were following him and set us up."

"But he underestimated us, and he—*they*—didn't know about Shadow."

Ash laughed. "Our secret weapon."

"Herne's horns! She loves that. It's no laughing matter, though, Ash. Without her, we'd have been stuck in that trap, and it did seem as if Belial was trying to manifest through Amato. How long do you think that temple under the church has been there?" They had barely talked about it afterwards, focussing only on searching Amato's apartment in Florence, and then his country house. Gabe had pushed it to the back of his mind, but he couldn't ignore it any longer.

"Hundreds of years, maybe over a thousand. It was old, hacked out of rock, deep beneath the church. Maybe something stood above it once, before the church was built. Or there was an earlier version of it."

Gabe voiced something else that had struck him. "It couldn't have been carved by Belial, though. It was hewn by hand. Belial would have made something like The Temple of the Trinity if he could." Memories of Raziel's temple still haunted him.

"Agreed. So it was carved by humans, or Nephilim."

"But that was after the Flood, so if they're responsible, some Nephilim must have survived."

"That's a reasonable assumption. It doesn't mean they're alive now, though," Ash reasoned.

"I think we have to consider the fact that they might be, however unlikely. Best to be prepared."

"Perhaps we should always carry one of Belial's jewels, just in case they are here."

"Perhaps." That was a last resort as far as Gabe was concerned. It had taken him only a few hours to shake off Belial's influence after destroying the count's castle, but it was long enough. Barak and Estelle had argued about it, and even Shadow wasn't impressed with the effect it had on Gabe.

"Come on," Ash said, turning back to the laptop. "Let's consider the manifesto and what's written on the base. They are similar, but the manifesto is much longer. They both essentially say the same thing, though. They exalt Belial and proclaim themselves his acolytes. But there is a different word used on the base of the statue in the woods." He pointed at a portion of text on the photo, difficult to read in the light of a phone torch, especially with dirt still ingrained in it. "It says *fraternitas*."

"Brotherhood. It sounds organised." Gabe sipped his coffee and then grimaced. It had gone cold. "We need to know more about that house and who owned it before. I want a proper history. I also want more information on the church above the temple in Florence. And we need more on Amato's contacts. Is there anything we can do in the meantime?"

"I will scrutinise the manifesto and inscription to make sure we haven't missed hidden meanings, but we should also explore places along that northeasterly line."

"So, we need a map. A big one." Gabe reached for his phone. "I'll get Niel and Shadow to pick one up."

Ash lowered his voice, looking through the partially open doorway to the hall beyond. "How do you think Nahum is holding up?"

"He's okay. Worried about Olivia, of course, and his daughter. It's a lot to take in, isn't it? Even now. And of course, we can't forget that Amato knew the sex of the child, either." Gabe raked his hand through his hair, exasperated. "I must admit that I'm worried, too. Nahum likes her more than he's letting on." *That much was obvious*. Over the New Year, he could barely take his eyes off her.

"I can tell. He's fretting, and that is very unlike Nahum."

"He's really excited by this whole opportunity. His past marriage was not based on love. He endured it, but this thing with Olivia... He says it was something that just happened, but it was more than that—for both of them. Now she's pregnant, well, that's something else."

Ash gripped Gabe's shoulder in an attempt to reassure him. "Olivia is strong and smart, and has plenty of friends who know the paranormal world well. If anyone can handle it, she can. I like her, and she fits in well with us. She already feels like part of our family. You know that I never had children?" Gabe nodded. He and Ash had known each other reasonably well in their old life. "It was never anything I missed, you know? But I am looking forward to being an uncle. These are strange times, Gabe." He smiled. "But good. We must not mess it up. We would all be devastated if anything happened to Olivia or our niece."

"I'm beginning to think one of us should be with her right now, considering what we know."

"Then send Nahum back to London. It should be him."

"He wanted to come with us!"

"Bravado. A need to be of use to us, and play down his feelings for Olivia, but I think we both know where he needs to be now. So does he."

Gabe laughed for the first time in what felt like months. "It could be quite a reunion."

Ash rolled his eyes. "They will dance around each other for days. Go tell him, I have work to do." And with that, he turned to the computer, and Gabe went to speak to their brother.

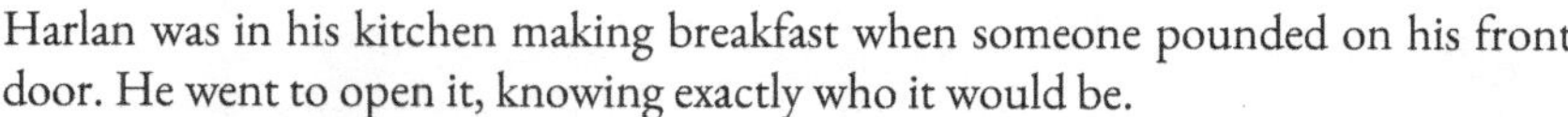

Harlan was in his kitchen making breakfast when someone pounded on his front door. He went to open it, knowing exactly who it would be.

"Maggie! I'm not deaf!"

She grinned, looking bright-eyed and cheerful. "You might have been lying in."

"And had I been, you would have woken me up!" He swung open the door to let her in. "As it is, I have already been to the gym."

She inhaled deeply. "Bacon! Delicious."

"Yes, there's enough for two." He led the way back to the kitchen. "To what do I owe this pleasure?"

"I can't just visit my friend?"

"Of course you can, but you don't." He started the coffee machine. "I presume you want one of these, too?"

"Yes, please. And you're very mean. We go out for drinks and coffee sometimes. It's not always about work."

He wagged a finger at her. "But it is today, I can tell." She had an air of purpose about her. And something else. "Did you go to Storm Moon last night?" A flush of guilt swept across her cheeks, and he smirked. "Yes, you did. Chat with Grey, by any chance?"

"I chatted with lots of people."

"And yet you look like a naughty schoolgirl caught up in a crush."

Her eyes narrowed. "What are you insinuating?"

"Maggie, it's okay. You like Grey. I can't blame you. He's a big, good-looking unit. Handy with weapons. Dry sense of humour. Doesn't mind prolific swearing, either. Just your type."

"I don't have a type, and no, I don't *like* him. I mean I do, but not in that way!"

"So why are you blushing?" He passed her a coffee, enjoying her discomfort. Teasing Maggie was always fun. Better, even, than teasing Olivia, and that was lots of fun at the moment.

"I'm not blushing!" She snatched her coffee, narrowly missing scalding herself. "I like Grey, of course, as I do all of Storm Moon's staff. It's a fun place to hang out."

"Has he asked you out yet?"

"No! He doesn't need to."

"You're a modern woman, why wait? Ask him yourself."

"Harlan! Pack it in!"

"But I'm enjoying myself."

"Fuck off!"

He roared with laughter, and then reached into the fridge to get more eggs. "I knew it!"

"We are changing the subject." Her sunny disposition had vanished, replaced by a scowl.

He wasn't giving up that easily, but he shrugged. "Shall we talk about what you want from me, then?"

"Peace and bloody quiet!"

"And?"

She stood at the kitchen window, sipping her coffee as she watched him over the rim. "I wanted to ask you about your Rome office. The Orphic Guild's, that is."

"Does this relate to a certain church and country house in Florence?"

"It might."

"I thought Jackson was looking into that."

"Jackson is looking into the church, and something about northeastern directions. I'm helping in my spare time. I have resources, but they're limited. I need more background on Amato's country house, and it's not the type of thing I can really ask the local police about. I have no connections there, nor with the local councils or whatever they call them in Italy."

"Herne's horns! I go to the gym for an hour, and so much is going on! You better bring me up to speed." He started to crack the eggs. "Scrambled okay? Your eggs, I mean, not your hormones."

Her eyes narrowed. "Harlan!"

"I thought that was funny!"

"It wasn't, and yes, scrambled!" She leaned against the counter and updated him on the statue and manifestos, and The Brotherhood. "So, we need to know more about that house! Who are Amato's family? Did he inherit the place or buy it? If so, who from? It has a bloody great temple on the grounds!" Her voice rose indignantly.

"Isn't this out of your area of jurisdiction?"

"Yes, but I want to help. It's important."

"I know. I have a couple of people I speak to in the Rome office, so I'll call once we've eaten. Then I'll chase up JD. I'm wondering if he's found anything that could help in his extensive library." He didn't mention the Emerald Tablet that JD was still experimenting with. Although he could trust Maggie, they were keeping the information about its existence to a very small group. Instead, he said, "He was obsessed with angels, and hearing about Belial has set him off again."

"Any little clue would be useful." Maggie had never met JD, and for that Harlan was grateful. They would be at odds, he was sure.

He plated up the eggs, bacon, hashbrowns, and mushrooms, his brunch treat after the gym. "All right. Let's eat, and then I'll make a few calls."

Shadow grimaced, hands on her hips, as she stared up at the statue of Belial. He looked imperious and patriarchal, and she already loathed him.

"I hate bullies," she said to Niel, who stood close by. "He must be one of the biggest. I thought Herne was, but I think Belial is worse."

"He was a nightmare." Niel had been clearing away some of the undergrowth with his axe, but he paused to catch his breath. "His Nephilim were the same. To be honest, we were all entitled, but they were nightmarish. Worse than Samael's followers."

Shadow nodded. He'd suggested as much before, and she'd had long conversations with Gabe about it. "We should smash his statue. I don't like to think it's still standing here, waiting for adoration."

"I like that idea, but perhaps we should take lots of pictures before we destroy it. Something about it might hold clues."

That brightened her mood. "You promise?"

"It's funny how the little things please you, sister," Niel said, laughing.

"You're the same," she shot back. "You and that axe are never apart."

"I'm not disagreeing. We have the same appetite for destruction and swift justice. I just temper it now."

"So do I, but it's hard when it's what you've done your whole life." She studied the statue's details. It was twice Niel's height, as was the wingspan's width on each side, and the feathers were painstakingly carved. "Someone took a great deal of care on this. Do you think it's the same one as was in the temple at the church?" The events had unfolded so quickly that she wasn't sure.

Niel paced around it. "The design is the same, I think, but this one is bigger. His features have been worn by the weather, too."

Belial was rendered with sculpted muscles, his chest bare, and a skirt low on his waist. He wore calf-length boots, and carried a raised sword as if ready to dispense justice. But he clutched something in his other hand. She pointed to it. "Niel, what's that? Is it a horn?"

"I think so."

"Did he usually carry one?"

Niel frowned. "I'm not sure. Perhaps. They were common, for some angels. A way to start a battle or summon a withdrawal of troops. Or just plain instil fear and awe. Their sound was unearthly."

Something else struck Shadow, and she clambered onto the plinth, and rubbed some moss away. "The jewels that were on the statue under the church are actually carved on this one. Look! The long necklace around his neck, the torcs on his arms, the rings on his fingers." She scrubbed at more of the moss, peeling it away to reveal the design beneath, and then dropped back to the ground. "And the sword looks to be the same as the one he was holding."

"You're right. That is interesting! Well spotted." He looked at her, eyebrow cocked. "Significant?"

"Perhaps. The only object I don't recall seeing that night was the horn. Admittedly, it was a bit chaotic in there, but I'm sure I'd have seen it on the table. I crept around the back while Amato was talking to you." She wasn't seeing the open temple dappled in half-light under the trees anymore. She was in the subterranean temple again, prowling around the perimeter unseen. The jewellery glittered on the stone altar, and she could scent the rich incense that hung about the cloak on his shoulders, cleverly arranged under the wings. There were a dizzying number of runes and sigils marked on the floor and roof, but no horn. "No, I'm sure of it."

She withdrew her phone from her pocket and started to take photos, working her way methodically around the angel. "Have you found anything inscribed in the marble flooring?"

"A couple of compass points on the outer perimeter. South and west so far. I'm heading to the northeastern part to see if anything is there."

She looked at the area he'd cleared. The marble was stained green and brown from decades of mud and leaf detritus, but south and west were clearly scored into the marble that formed the base of the mini amphitheatre. "Interesting. No altar, though, is there?"

"What do you think happened here?"

"It doesn't strike me as a meeting place. Belial's statue is huge. It hides big sections of the seating, especially on the upper levels, but it is imposing. The whole place, I mean. When clean, everything must have dazzled in sunlight and moonlight. Everything is made of white marble. Imagine walking up the path and catching a glimpse of Belial. Plus, you're right—it is on a rise."

"It's a place of initiation." Niel spoke with conviction, and he nodded to himself. "Yes, I'm sure of it."

"Really?" She looked around, considering his words, imagining the new believers being brought here and sworn to The Brotherhood. The steps that doubled as seats could have been for other members to watch. "It's possible, I guess."

Niel attacked the northeast quadrant with renewed vigour, and putting her phone away, Shadow joined him. They quickly cleared a large section to reveal the final two compass points, but there was nothing significant to mark the northeasterly direction.

As if reading her thoughts, Niel said, "You wouldn't spell it out, though, would you?"

"No." Something tickled at the edge of Shadow's mind. "A temple of worship, and this, a place of initiation. Could it be a sort of path of enlightenment, or some such bollocks? And maybe it's not northeasterly, but southwestern? You move from one point to another, through various tests designed for you." She shrugged, frustrated. "Do you know what I mean?"

"I think that sounds very interesting. Have you been spending time with Ash?"

"I am quite capable of working things out, too!"

He grinned, face smeared with dirt and leaves stuck in his hair. "You are so easy to wind up."

"Piss off."

"No, I think it has to be northeasterly because of the way he's facing, but I guess he could be looking back towards the beginning?" He huffed. "Lots to consider. Or, of course, we're seeing something where there is nothing."

"No, there's something. Can we smash it now?"

"I presume that's my job?"

"We'll do it together. Just a little push!"

"All right. Stand well back." Niel extended his wings and flew a few feet above the ground, until he was face to face with Belial. He gripped the head and rocked the statue back, roaring with effort. It wobbled off its plinth and smashed on the ground, cracking the marble underfoot. Chunks of the statue rattled across the rock, and something skittered out of the debris.

Shadow knew what it was, even from a distance. *Another piece of Belial's jewellery.*

Six

Niel carried the newly discovered ring back to their Tuscan villa that was tucked into a fold in the countryside, trying to ignore Belial's whispers and entreaties while they completed the shopping Gabe had requested.

They had smashed the statue into tiny pieces, Niel using his axe, Shadow using her Dragonium sword, eager to ensure they were leaving nothing behind. Fortunately, the ring was the only trinket embedded into the statue. It hadn't reduced their unease, though. They were both quiet on the journey home.

Ash was working on the computer when they entered the kitchen, but Gabe and Nahum were discussing flights.

Niel placed the ring, a huge ruby set within an ornate gold mount, on the kitchen table. "Another one."

Gabe and Nahum's conversation ended abruptly as Nahum asked, "Where did you find it?"

"In the statue that we smashed to pieces. There was nothing else."

Ash looked up, alarmed. "You smashed it? Are you mad?"

"We took photos beforehand," Shadow informed him. "Besides, isn't it good that we did? We found *that*!"

It pulsed with power. Niel could feel it, and felt sure if he could see auras, there would be a dark one around the ring. "It's just like the others. It whispers evil."

"We can hear it," Gabe said, answering for all of them. His jaw was tight, eyes fixed on the ring. "How many more will we find?"

"There could be hundreds more." Ash pushed away from the table. "I'll get the box."

"Why are you discussing flights?" Shadow asked.

"Nahum is returning home to look after Olivia."

Niel grinned. "Look after her? Is that what we're calling it now?"

Nahum glared at him. "Not funny. And not my idea!" His glare shifted to Gabe.

"It's for the best!" Gabe replied. "Look at what we're finding out. I don't think we should leave her alone right now. What if this bloody Brotherhood goes after her? Or do you want me to ask Lucien to be a bodyguard? Or Barak? Or Eli, perhaps?" There was a glint of amusement in Gabe's expression now.

Niel's grin broadened, and he expanded the tease. The ring was egging him on, urging him to unsettle Nahum. "I'm sure Eli would be only too pleased to comfort Olivia while you're away."

"I know what you two are suggesting, but I'm pretty sure that Eli wouldn't seduce Olivia while pregnant with my child!"

"But her hormones will be raging, brother," Niel said, "and she looked radiant at New Year. A good-looking woman! No wonder you couldn't help yourself."

Ash intervened, sweeping the ring into the spelled box as Nahum's hands clenched into fists. "Let's get rid of this, shall we? Before tempers flare."

The box shut with a bang and Belial's whispers instantly vanished.

Chastened, but only slightly, because Niel was enjoying getting his own back after all the teasing he had endured over Mouse, he said, "Gabe is right. All of us would hate for anything to happen to her. Maybe you should both leave London for a while. Find a place no one knows about."

Shadow smirked. "A love nest?"

"Shadow!" Nahum took a deep breath, a resigned expression crossing his face. "I know you think this is funny, and yes, you can tease me. Go ahead! I slept with her—*once*—and now she's pregnant. I didn't foresee this, and if I had known, well, I wouldn't have. I'm ruining her life." He sank into a chair, staring at the table. "The last thing I want to do is crowd her."

All of them stared at each other over his head, and compassion swept over Niel. He sat down next to him. "That's not true. You are not ruining her life. She could have chosen to abort her, but hasn't. She wants this, Nahum, and that means she wants *you*—and all of us, too—in her life. When she visited us, she was happy! She fitted right in. I think you're more worried than she is."

Nahum looked up, eyes locking with Niel. "What if I'm not father material? Or even a good partner, in whatever capacity that is? I've never done this before. My marriage was a sham. This life was supposed to avoid that."

"Then you would have been avoiding *living*. You cannot completely avoid connections, or love, or lust, or else you'd be dead! Or merely existing. And love and relationships are painful." He looked across at Shadow and his brothers, who had also sat at the table now, their mood sombre. "You all know about me and Lilith, but I wouldn't have missed all of that for anything. It's life, in all of its messy, glorious strangeness. It's what we fought to eradicate, and then fought to save. It's why we're hunting down Belial and his damn Brotherhood. It's meant to be, Nahum." He felt a bit emotional, as he always became when dwelling on such things. It's why he channelled his feelings into aggression half the time. It kept his ridiculous romantic side in check. "I want to be an uncle, and you will be an amazing father."

Nahum's eyes filled with tears. "Brother."

"Oh, you two," Shadow sniffed. "You're even getting to me."

"I'm serious, though," Nahum continued. "Should I suggest that I stay in a hotel room?"

"What good will that do?" Gabe asked, rolling his eyes. "You have to move in. I'm not saying forever, just for now! I could phone her, if that's what you're worried about? I'll tell her it's my idea, and she can't say no."

"No!" Nahum took a deep breath, pulling himself together. "No, I will. It's all taking some time to get used to. You know, how all of this will work."

Shadow's natural sarcasm returned. "You better get a move on. Seven months to baby time."

"Yes, thank you for that reminder." Nahum didn't move, though. "I can't just sit in London and do nothing. I must help in some way."

"I'm sure Jackson has a list of things to follow up. Or even JD," Ash said. "If I think of anything, I'll let you know. Maybe look at the map and pursue the northeasterly idea. Did you buy one?"

Shadow extracted the item in question from her pack. "It's the biggest we could find. Niel and I had a few ideas while we were smashing things. Ooh! And we discovered that Belial's statue was carrying a horn. Do you think that's important?"

Ash blinked. "A horn?"

"Yes, and jewels were carved onto the statue, just like the ones under the church. They were identical! It must mean something."

Ash turned to Gabe. "You must remember his special horn? It induced a type of madness any time he blew it—triggered a bloodlust among his Nephilim, as well as everyone else. It's what made his battles so...horrific."

Gabe narrowed his eyes, gaze distant. "I do, actually, but strangely I'd forgotten about it until now. I never heard it, though. I just heard about it through others."

"Have either of you?" Ash asked. Niel and Nahum shook their heads. "Well, I heard it. It was unearthly, and like his jewels it got under your skin and into your brain. If that exists here, we're in big trouble."

"Why?"

"Its sound carries for miles. It would have a far wider ranging effect than the jewels. It could be devastating."

"Surely that means," Niel reasoned, "that they haven't got it, or they would have used it already."

"Unless they have a specific time they are waiting for," Nahum suggested. "Although, I'm sure its effects would be devastating whatever time it was used."

Gabe stopped their conversation. "This is just supposition. We'll keep the horn in mind, but we focus on The Brotherhood." His phone started ringing, and he frowned when he saw the caller. "It's Theo! I'll take it outside."

"Theo?" Niel asked, excitement building. "It must be about the Templar treasure!"

Theo Carmichael was the rich owner of Temple Keep, and as the name suggested, it had once belonged to the last Master of England who served the Knights Templar. Theo had instigated the search for the lost Templar treasure, and they had found some of it deep beneath the church in Temple Moreton. Not without running into descendants of the Templars, however. After a fierce battle, the Nephilim had given them the instructions to find other caches, and Theo had generously agreed to split the money they would earn for the treasure. It had been in the British Museum for months since then, being evaluated.

Ash moved his laptop and spread the map across the table. "Perhaps they have come to a decision about money! That would be good news in the middle of all this. Now, let us search this northeasterly line."

He put a cross on the map where the church was in Florence, and then marked the position of Amato's house. "Okay, so roughly, if I draw a line to the northeast through these two points, and focus on the bigger cities, we cross the edge of Venice, head into Austria, skirting Linz, and on from there into the Czech Republic, and then Poland. If we go southwest, it will take us to Corsica, Algiers, and Morocco. After that it's the Atlantic, and north is Finland. Do those places suggest anything to you?"

Niel shrugged, "Not particularly."

"Perhaps," Nahum said, "they'll mean something to Jackson."

"We could at least research big churches and cathedrals," Shadow suggested.

"There'll be so many," Ash told her. "And there's no guarantee there will be any churches involved. We need more to go on."

Gabe entered the room, more cheerful than Niel had seen him in weeks. "Good news! The British Museum has agreed to an amount of money to award us, and we have Theo and his influence to thank for that. I think it would have taken a lot longer otherwise."

"How much?" Shadow asked, cutting straight to the point.

He named a seven-figure sum. "That'll do, right?"

"Are you for real?" Niel asked, the map forgotten. "That's huge!"

"The find was worth billions, and that's not even factoring in its cultural significance."

Shadow whooped, jumping up and down. "Lots of lovely gold!"

"Money in a bank account, actually, Shadow," Ash said.

"But I can buy gold with it, right?"

Nahum laughed. "You want a nest of it?"

"Could I?" Her eyes gleamed with the prospect.

Gabe shook his head. "Please stop giving her ideas. However, they need a signature from one of us. We need to meet Theo on Monday morning. Harlan too, because he'll get a share, of course. All of us and Shadow are all named as beneficiaries, so any one of us can do it. I suggest that you," he looked at Nahum, "or Barak go. Probably you, seeing as you want something to do, and Barak might have other leads to follow up. Or you can both go."

Nahum nodded enthusiastically. "Of course. Do we get to see the treasure again?"

"I believe so. Some of it, at least."

Shadow's mouth dropped open. "I want to see it!"

"Sorry, you're stuck here with us!" Gabe stuck his hands in his jeans' pockets. "I'm a bit gutted I can't go, actually."

"Why don't we all go?" Ash suggested. "It's a short flight."

Niel considered the jewels they had found, and the statues, and the likelihood that there'd be more. "I don't think we should. One of us should stay here. I'm happy to do that. Hopefully it won't be the only opportunity we get to see the hoard again. Plus, I want to get back in that house, in case there's something we missed."

"Unfortunately," Ash said, leaning back in his chair, "I agree."

Gabe nodded, disappointed but determined. "Yes, we'll stay here."

"Okay, then." Nahum headed to the door. "I'll organise my flights, and someone will need to take me to the airport. With luck I can get one this afternoon. I'll take Olivia with me on Monday. She'd love to see the hoard."

"I'll drive you," Niel told him. "What about the jewels? You may as well take those. We don't really want them with us." The spelled box would also get the jewels through customs without alerting anyone, much the same as the one they used to transport the emerald discs out of Egypt.

Nahum's lips tightened. "I'm not keeping them in Olivia's place. No way!"

"JD's house, then? Or The Retreat?"

"No!" Gabe's strident voice cut across Niel's suggestion. "Only *we* look after them. JD wouldn't be able to help himself."

"A trip to Cornwall too, then," Nahum said, nodding. "Leave it with me."

When Harlan arrived at JD's estate, Mortlake, on Saturday afternoon, he was buzzing with excitement that he knew even JD wouldn't dampen.

He'd be signing the paperwork on Monday morning to receive his Templar treasure finding fee, and would be seeing some of the treasure again. He'd been so overwhelmed when he first saw it under the church that he'd barely been able to take it in. Not helped, of course, by being captured and at great risk of imminent death. However, on Monday he would see it properly, with hopefully most of it catalogued. His imagination was working overtime just thinking about the stories the treasure could tell. It would be good to see Theo again, too. Out of courtesy, he'd tell Mason Jacobs, his boss. He would have to go during work time, after all. He had a feeling that Mason, who knew Theo well, would also want to go. He hoped The British Museum's staff would be accommodating.

Plus, he'd phoned his contacts in Rome, and had successfully talked to an Occult Hunter called Romola Falco. She had agreed to look into Amato's house and the family for him. Romola was a voluble woman in her mid-thirties, passionate about her work and effusive about everything Italian—food, cars, cities, fashion, and of course, its vast history. She was even named for the myth about Romulus and Remus who had founded Rome after being suckled by a she-wolf as babes, and then raised as shepherds. Romola was the female derivative of Romulus.

Harlan had kept the details about a Fallen Angel's jewellery out of it. He'd just said it was religious iconography that he was chasing down. She'd pressed him for details, and once she heard about the Florentine church, she'd told him she'd investigate that, too. He passed the good news on to Jackson, hoping that might encourage his friend to take time off, as well as Barak, Estelle, and Lucien. All of them had been obsessing over Belial for weeks, and this was a chance to rest for a while, and recover from their bruising encounter with Black Cronos, too. Like the rest of the team, he couldn't really believe that the count was really gone, but for now, he was enjoying it.

Since Christmas he had dedicated himself, more or less, to his job. He'd had a few old texts to track down, a rumoured cursed statue, and a few auction jobs to attend for clients. He'd only been sidetracked when a demon had rocked up in Wimbledon, courtesy of a witch who'd tried to fool the Storm Moon Pack. More fool *him*. Now that was over with too, and his thoughts circled back to the Emerald Tablet of Hermes Trismegistus.

Anna, JD's assistant, answered the door as usual, her gaze sweeping disapprovingly over him. He had no idea why she seemed to dislike him, but took heart in the fact that she looked at everyone except JD with that same tight-lipped air of intolerance. "He's in the marquee," she said, heading up the stairs and leaving him to find his own way to the garden.

"Thanks!" he called sarcastically after her.

He walked quickly through JD's Elizabethan manor, exiting onto the long back patio with the expansive lawns beyond. Right in the centre was a huge, white marquee that looked as if JD was preparing for a wedding. He wasn't, though. It housed the tablet.

Harlan shouted as he neared the entrance, not wanting to surprise him. "JD! It's Harlan. Okay if I come in?"

"Just watch your step! And shut the door after you!"

Warily, Harlan unzipped the entrance flap, pushed his way inside, and then stopped in shock. "Herne's horns! What the hell is going on?"

Electric cables snaked across the ground, and strings of lights were suspended overhead. Benches were set up in a circle around a central area, littered with scientific equipment that looked utterly baffling, like some kind of Frankenstein's circus, with JD as the ringmaster. Plus it was stiflingly warm from the array of heaters around the place.

"What do you think I'm doing, imbecile? I am testing the tablet."

Harlan ignored the insult. He was used to it. Besides, JD said it more out of habit than real meaning. That was what he told himself, anyway. "Now?"

"*Yes*! For about the hundredth time." JD was wearing one of his Elizabethan smocks that made him look like a mad Renaissance artist, and he turned, hand on hips. "In fact, to be precise, this is my one hundred and thirty-eighth test. It's all in there." He gesticulated to a large book on one of the tables.

"So many?" Harlan weaved through the tables, focussing on the Emerald Tablet displayed on a large, stone block. A wheel of correspondence was a few metres away, set up by some kind of control centre. "Is this the one from your lab?"

"Yes. I brought it all out here. Took a week. To make another one would take far too long." JD's beard was unkempt, and his hair was brushed rakishly in the wrong direction. "I've been testing since just after Christmas, once I knew we got rid of that old devil." He meant the count.

Harlan turned the pages of the book that JD had referred to, seeing reams of confusing notes and diagrams. "Why so many?"

"There are a million permutations of the wheel, but my investigations have narrowed down the possible combinations to several thousand instead. However, I am getting close. At least I know which disc fits now."

"You do?"

"It's already in place."

"It is?"

"Yes. It took a few attempts, but then I realised it had to be done at a certain time—planetary alignments, stars, etcetera. Well, one of several special times."

"How did you discover that?" Harlan was aware that he was asking an endless number of questions, but the last time he had discussed this with JD was weeks ago, and he hadn't achieved any of this.

"Mathematical calculations based on potential dates of its construction, the alignments of the cosmos, plus the properties of emerald, and the text itself, of course. It didn't make sense that it could just be resurrected at any old time. There needed to be a key, and not one that was accessible once in a thousand years, either. When I cracked it, it slid in like warm butter in a pan. You can't even see the edge where they join anymore."

"It's heavy! How did you manage it?"

"Anna helped me. So now I'm focussing various resonances at it using gemstones—much like I used in my weapons."

"Like a laser beam."

"If you have to use that term." Harlan studied the circle of tables again and saw that an array of objects was pointed at the tablet. JD followed his gaze. "Yes, I use all of them. I manipulate them using the wheel, and they direct energy at the tablet."

No doubt about it. JD was a genius. Harlan could feel the hum of *something* around him. "It could still take years."

"No. Days, I estimate. Maybe even today."

Harlan's mouth dropped open. "You mean that thing could grow *today*? Reveal its secrets?"

"Perhaps. There could be many stages, or just one. And whether I understand what I see... Well, that remains to be seen. Or, it might not grow at all!"

Harlan stared at the cloudy interior of the Emerald Tablet, considering the fact that it always reminded him of the solar system. Up close, it made him dizzy; at a distance, it just seemed threatening. "And what if the power it contains is like a nuclear bomb? Or even just a small bomb. You'll be dead, and you'll blow up the house."

"Or half the county. Or the whole country?" JD shook his head. "No. When I unlock it, it will be because I've done it correctly. It won't explode. I will have earned its secrets."

Harlan turned his back on it with a great effort. He'd forgotten how mesmerising it could be. "What about Belial?"

"Ah! Our Fallen Angel. Yes, I have found something. A reference in an old book written in the nineteenth century by another alchemist, actually. I believe it refers to The Brotherhood, although he doesn't call it by that name. He calls it The Consortium."

"That's great! Does it mention any names or places?"

"A *palazzo* in Venice—a grand residence. He had gone there on the invitation of a rich family who sought help with the object in question. A jewel that had strange properties." JD's eyes had taken on his usual, feral gleam. "I came across that book about a hundred years ago, back when I was still obsessing about angels. I followed that lead and came up against a dead end. I hadn't associated it with Belial. Now, however, things make sense. I'd forgotten all about it until this whole thing with Belial's jewels cropped up."

Harlan could barely contain his impatience. "Why a dead end? The house was destroyed? Family dead?"

"Oh, no. They were alive. But no one would answer my calls. In fact, I was hounded out of Venice."

"But what about the original alchemist that they invited?"

"Oh, he spoke very coyly of the object of power after the visit. He was Italian, too. I've left the book out in the library for you, with a translation. I don't suppose Gabe would let me see the jewels they have found?"

"Not a chance." Harlan already knew Gabe's view on that topic.

JD tapped his lip with an ink-stained finger. "I suspected as much. Well, if they need assistance, you know where I am. I will say, however, that they are probably far more dangerous than that." He pointed at the tablet. "But we shall see... Would you like to see my next test?"

"You know, I don't think I would." Harlan backed away. "Happy if I head to your library, though?"

"Of course. But stay the night, Harlan. I do want to show you a few other things, too."

Harlan wasn't sure how he felt about that, but he nodded anyway. He'd planned to meet up with Jackson, Maggie, and Olivia for drinks and a meal, but JD had a story to tell, and he needed all the details he could get on the mysterious *palazzo* in Venice.

Seven

Olivia had been fretting for hours, ever since she'd received Nahum's phone call telling her that he was coming back to effectively guard her.

He hadn't used those words, exactly. In fact, she couldn't remember quite how he'd put it. Something about how Gabe and his brothers had decided that with things being so uncertain, and with the latest developments, he had been sent to look after her. *Sent.* He hadn't volunteered. It was like she was a mission. *And that was fine,* she told herself. One night of passion and a child on the way inferred no obligation beyond what they had talked about already.

Nevertheless, it irked her, and she tried very hard to shove that feeling aside. She had suggested that Barak and Estelle could look after her if they were that worried, or Lucien, the super-soldier. *Surely, he was skilled enough to defend her?* But Nahum had hurriedly shot that down. So now, here she was, having cleaned her flat, plumped various cushions, and prepared the guest bedroom, as if royalty were coming to stay. She'd even stocked beer and nibbles such as soft cheeses and pâtés, the things she couldn't eat now that she was pregnant. *By the Gods, she needed a glass of wine. No, a bottle.*

She was just touching up her makeup, the barely-there look that smacked of time and effort, when the intercom buzzed from the main door downstairs. *Nahum.* She really needed to give him the code. She took a deep breath and exhaled, and then let him in. In minutes he was in her hallway, looking devastatingly handsome, and far more self-assured than she felt.

"I feel terrible that I've arrived so late," he admitted, following her into the kitchen. "Have I kept you up?"

"It's ten o'clock at night, not three in the morning! Besides, I'm a night owl. You know that." She smiled, trying to look relaxed. "I feel guilty that you've been travelling so late."

He shrugged. "Night owl, too."

"Beer?"

"I'd kill for one. Travelling is thirsty work. Sure you don't mind, though, seeing as you're not drinking?"

"The whole world can't stop for me. I'll sniff it and pretend."

"Thank you. You look well." He almost drank her in, and that set her to blushing.

She patted her stomach. "Yes, this little one is being gentle. I feel fine. But look, get settled first. I've put you in here." She opened the door to the guest room that suddenly seemed far too small for Nahum. It wasn't really, but his presence was so overwhelming. *Breathe...*

"This is great!" He put his bag on the double bed, taking it in quickly. He'd never been in her flat. Since her New Years visit to Cornwall, they had stuck to phone calls. "It's a nice place. Roomy."

"Well, I earn enough money, and I hate pokey flats. Come on, though. My room is opposite, with the ensuite, and there's a main bathroom, too—that's yours. And this is the living room and kitchen-dining area. All in one." She was gabbling and she knew it. She also had another room she could use as a nursery, but there was no way she was discussing that now. *Calm the fuck down!* For a while she bustled about, glad to keep herself busy. "I've bought lots of food. I know you eat like a horse."

"Okay. Rule number one. I pull my weight around here. I know it's your place, but I can cook, pour my own beer, make my own snacks." He gently took the can and glass from her hands, and the touch of his skin was like electricity. "I'm imposing, but well, things are weird..."

"You're *not* imposing! Please don't think that." She took a breath and smiled at him. This was Nahum. They were friends before their night of awesome sex. He was moving in for a while, and she couldn't deal with this awkwardness. "Yes, things are weird. But, like I said before, I wouldn't change a thing. This," she gestured between them, "will be something we'll work out. We're friends, right? We were before that night, and still are!"

"Of course. Friends." A trace of some emotion Olivia couldn't quite work out flashed across his face. *Relief, or regret?* "So, you have cases, I presume? I can help you with them. I really should be with you all the time, so..."

She made herself a cup of herbal tea to keep busy. "Yes, a few cases. The early stages of some, wrapping up others, but nothing urgent. I will have to go into the office at some point. I'm not entirely sure what I should say to Mason, though. No one at work knows I'm pregnant, and even if they did, I can't explain a bodyguard easily."

"But Mason knows all about us, and the paranormal. Does he know about when you were possessed?"

"Yes, actually. I had to have time off. He was very sweet about it." Mason could be prickly, but she'd always got on well with him.

"Just tell him we're worried he'll come for you again. That should suffice."

"True. I think I already have baby brain."

He laughed. "I'm sure you haven't. I've got a few things I have to do, actually, and wondered if you'd like to come with me. I need to go to Cornwall tomorrow to deliver the collection of jewels we found. My brothers will caretake them."

Her eyes widened. "You found more?"

"Yes, lots. I'll give you all the thrilling details if you want. It involved a near-death experience, so that was fun."

Her heart almost skipped a beat. "Near-death! Why am I surprised, though? Yes, of course I want to know!" *More jewels, and they were here.* "It might sound odd, considering what happened, but I'd like to see them. No touching, obviously."

Nahum shook his head. "No. Sorry. I don't want to give him any quarter at all. You and our daughter are too precious."

"I like being precious! It's gives me a fuzzy, warm glow." She couldn't resist a tease. It was in her nature.

"Well, it's true. My brothers will kill me if I let anything happen to you. And I'd never forgive myself." He held her gaze for a moment, and her brain emptied of everything except a desperate urge to kiss him. "So, do you fancy a trip tomorrow? It's a long drive, though. And we can't stay overnight," he rushed onwards, "because I have to go to the British Museum on Monday." He briefly outlined what had happened.

"I can go with you?" Vision of golden, jewelled treasures filled her head. "Holy shit! Yes, please! Templar treasure! An enormous finder's fee!" All embarrassment vanished. "Sit and tell me everything about what's going on."

"So, you see our problem," Zee said to Alex Bonneville as they were cleaning the bar of The Wayward Son in White Haven after a busy Saturday night. The other staff were well out of hearing range. "A box won't cut it anymore. We have too many jewels."

"Oh, no! What a terrible dilemma!" Alex shot Zee a wry grin. "So much gold!"

"Funny, if they weren't so dangerous!

Alex poured them both half a pint of Skullduggery Ale. "I'm kidding, obviously. You need another spelled box. Or a treasure chest, at this point."

"More like a bunker. Me and Eli have already prepared a place in the cellar. We've dug a pit. It was a rough brick and dirt floor anyway. We've lined it with slabs and made a trap door to go over it. Can you spell that?"

"Bloody hell, mate. How much stuff are you expecting?"

"Prepare for the worst, and all that." He'd already told Alex about what had happened to his brothers and Shadow in Florence. "There could be more. Weapons, too."

Alex's grin vanished. "I'd rather it be in your cellar than anywhere else. I'll come round tomorrow with the whole coven. We'll set up a protection spell."

Zee knew that Alex would help, but it was good to have it confirmed. "Thank you. I don't like us having them. Feels like we're sitting on dynamite, but like you said, better with us than anywhere else."

"You're sure you don't want to be with them? Your brothers, I mean."

"No! It's important that me and Eli are here to keep everything safe, and besides, I like my new job."

"Good, because you're great at it." Alex raised his glass. "And way easier to deal with than Simon!"

It had been two months since Simon, Alex's previous Bar Manager, had left and Zee had taken over the role, and he loved it. He also loved the fact that he had use of the flat upstairs. A partial sharing arrangement with Abigail Kendall, the DS on Newton's team. He was currently spending half his time there, and had debated whether to fully move in, but with more of Belial's jewels arriving now, he couldn't really.

"Cheers, Alex. That's good to know. Any idea what we can do with all of his stuff long-term, though? We can't keep it forever."

"There are a few options, I guess," he mused while he sipped his beer, "but the more you accumulate, the more overall power you'll have to contain. Digging a hole is a great idea. Maybe the best yet. However, with all your newfound wealth, you should have a proper safe installed. A big one."

Zee blinked in shock. "I hadn't considered that. The kind we can walk into, like in a bank?"

"Pretty much. You can then add spells to it, and you'd have double levels of protection. Make sense, right?"

"We could convert half the cellar!"

"Absolutely, if that's the best space. Reinforce the walls, etcetera. I bet Caspian can recommend someone. He'd know companies who could do that."

"That's a brilliant idea. Nahum is arriving tomorrow. I can talk to him and Eli, and call Gabe. He'll agree, I'm sure." The more Zee thought about it, the more he liked it. There would be no need for it ever to leave their house, and seeing as Gabe had bought the farmhouse and the land for all of them to use, it made sense.

"I bet," Alex added, as he put his beer down and loaded glasses in the dishwasher, "that your alchemist friend, JD, could recommend metals you could use for extra insulation, too."

"Alex, you really are a bloody genius! That's a brilliant idea."

Alex winked. "I know. I might not be able to search for Belial, but I'll do what I can."

It had been a great source of frustration that Alex couldn't use his magic skills to find Belial in other worlds. He couldn't touch the jewels, and even if he could, they couldn't risk him encountering such a powerful presence. It would kill Alex. Plus, there was nothing else they could use to find his agents. *Until now.*

"What about the manifesto?" Zee asked. "It will have been handled by people other than Jacobsen. Could you use that?"

"Of course, but isn't that in London with Barak? Why don't you ask Estelle to do that? It's one of her specialities."

"That's actually a great suggestion. I don't know why they haven't considered it. Unless they have, and it failed. I'll call Barak soon. He'll still be up."

"Hold on!" Alex held his hand up. "There'll be other spells you can use, not just finding spells. Objects contain impressions, and the stronger the emotion, the stronger the impression is. A manifesto will have lots! A skilled witch should be able to draw out the emotions of who was writing it, maybe even where. I have a few spells in my grimoire. They all vary slightly, but hopefully one will work." He grimaced. "I tried one on my own grimoire, but there are too many years, too many individuals to separate. It gave me a headache. The manifesto, however, could be perfect to try."

"Really? That's possible?"

"Perhaps. It's worth a shot if you're at a dead end."

"We are for now, but we're working on options." Zee forgot all about cleaning the bar, excited by the prospect of unlocking the manifesto's secrets. "Wow. If we could pin down who wrote it, even if it's years old, it would tell us something. Surely though, a psychic witch like you would have better results?"

"Maybe." Alex pulled his long, dark hair out of his top knot and rubbed his head as if it ached. "Confusing, isn't it? I don't know what hidden talents Estelle has, but she might have success. Or, what about the Moonfell Witches? Olivia was telling us about them when we saw her at New Years."

They'd had a big New Years Eve party at the farmhouse, and all of their White Haven friends had attended. The witches, Newton's team, the PCs from the town, Stan, and Ghost OPS. It had been epic. A way to celebrate after vanquishing Black Cronos, and to toast Olivia's pregnancy, of course.

"They saved Olivia," Alex continued, "and I gather Odette saw Nahum's wings. She sees the truth of things. It sounds like she works a little like I do."

Zee nodded. He'd never met them. In fact, the only Nephilim who had was Nahum. "I guess we could ask them if Estelle needs help—*if* she'll admit it!"

"She's not a fool. She'll ask if it will get all of you further along."

"I like working with you, though."

Alex laughed. "Thank you! We are glad to help, but they're closer, and I think you can trust them, too. You need all hands on deck for this."

Zee sat heavily on a bar stool. Everything seemed so big, with so many moving parts. He thought life might get less messy after Black Cronos, but it seemed even more complicated than ever. He felt like he was back on the battlefield, and could almost taste the dust and feel the sweat running down his face, and scent blood and death in the air. He took a deep breath to dispel it all. The images vanished, but it left him knowing something he'd rather not.

"We're going to become Belial's keepers, aren't we?"

Alex nodded and sat down, too. "If you mean you'll have to guard his shit forever? Yes."

"Forever is a long time."

"If you break up The Brotherhood, no one will know. You keep them in your big vault and forget about them. You think only of your future, which is for you to design as it pleases you. Like being here, for now."

"I've got a lot going on in White Haven. That stupid pact with the dryads with Eli. My flat share, my job, my friendships. A shit-ton of money coming our way, too!"

"Always nice!"

New resolve filled Zee. "Yes, we build a huge, fuck-off vault spelled with everything, and sit on it like big Nephilim dragons. And we make sure we celebrate everything else. Like pregnancies and weddings."

"Wedding! *Just one!*" Alex rolled his eyes. "That's enough."

"One for now!" Zee laughed, glad to change the subject. "Having fun with Reuben as his best man?"

"Fun is one word for it." He swept his hands down to his old rock band t-shirt, jeans, and boots. "Do I look like a suit man?"

"You have to wear a suit? Wow. Which means Reuben is wearing a suit for the wedding? *Wow,*" he repeated, unable to imagine Reuben dressed in anything so formal.

"Of a sort."

"But he wears board shorts all year round. Are you kidding?"

"No. So that means we have to start suit shopping."

Zee, on the whole, had stayed out of the handfasting discussions, mostly because Reuben wanted to surprise their guests. He normally exhibited an air of insouciance, but lately that had been replaced with distraction, and endless list ticking on his phone notes. Of course, his surfing habit remained ever present.

"So," Zee asked, now very curious, "this is going to be quite big, by the sound of it. I didn't expect that."

"Neither did El, nor Reuben, to be honest." Alex smiled. "He's determined to make this the best handfasting *ever*."

"So, where are you shopping for a suit?"

"I have no idea! But who does wear a suit very well?"

"Newton? And Caspian!"

"Exactly. I mean, I wore one for Gil's funeral, and so did Reu, but that's a funeral! This is very different—and Reu has *ideas*!" Alex made air quotes. "So, because I'm the best man and I can't duck out of these things, we four musketeers are going suit shopping. This fucking wedding is sprouting horns!"

"Oh! That's priceless!" Zee started to laugh. "But Reu is happy, and so are the girls."

"So happy." He drained his half pint. "Avery is only a bridesmaid, and yet we are knee-deep in bridal magazines! Even Kendall is involved!"

"I confess that I have heard some flower chat." Living with Kendall, it was inevitable. "But Kendall is being cagey."

"Avery is not cagey enough for me!"

"You, mate, need a night at the farmhouse, killing stuff on video games. It will do wonders for your soul."

"I might take you up on that."

"How long to go? A month?"

"More or less. The longest month of my bloody life."

"You love Reuben! You don't mean that."

Alex groaned. "No, I suppose I don't. I'll make him pay with my best man speech. I have many stories to share!"

Zee stood up. "Well, we better make sure most of this is under control before then, because I don't intend that I or any of my brothers or Shadow will miss that wedding. I'll phone Barak right now."

Eight

"I just wish I'd bloody thought of that," Estelle Faversham said, feeling cranky as she prepared a cup of coffee on Sunday morning. "Trust Alex to think of unveiling spells to use on the manifesto!"

"My love," Barak said, standing behind her and nuzzling her neck, "he's helping, and you should be grateful."

"I am! And that's even more annoying. I can't believe I'm actually friends with them."

"The dreaded 'F' word. Oh, no! You do know that you're coming to the wedding, right? With me."

"Yes." She giggled as his lips moved along her neck. "It's impossible to stay mad when you do that."

"I know. I can do it more often."

"Not in the kitchen!"

"No, not in the kitchen!" Lucien remonstrated from behind them.

Estelle turned around, laughing as she pushed Barak away. "Sorry. Barak is incorrigible."

"You don't normally complain."

"We don't normally have an audience."

"I'm not watching like a peeping Tom," Lucien said, horrified, as he headed to the cupboard to get a mug.

"I know! It's just an expression." Sometimes things got lost in translation.

Barak started to get food out of the fridge. "I was cheering her up, because one of our very good friends," he shot her sideways look, "has come up with a brilliant suggestion for that manifesto."

"Really?" Lucien was as frustrated with it as they were. "Like what?"

"Like a spell to unlock its secrets." Estelle checked her phone—again. "He's sending through some spells I can use on it. The only thing is, I might not have everything to hand here. Or it might be beyond my skill set. We may have to ask the Moonfell Witches for help—specifically, Odette."

"But you cast a finding spell," Lucien said. "Is that different?"

"Yes. The results were confusing." She had cast it the previous night, and watched the smoke trail across Yorkshire, and then over Europe and into Italy. But then it diffused, pinpointing nowhere in particular, and leaving her very frustrated. She had tried several different variations with the same result. Perhaps the Fallen Angel's presence had confused things, or maybe it indicated that several hands had designed it. Alex's suggestion certainly sounded intriguing. "This could tell us so much more, but I've never cast such a spell before. If I damage the document, then I might not be able to use it again. Magic can be tricky."

As she was talking, her phone buzzed with incoming messages, and she quickly scanned them. Alex was concise. He'd sent photos of the original spells and written transcripts.

"Have you got a printer here, Lucien?"

"In the study, upstairs. It's new, like the PC. The Orphic Guild installed it." He shrugged. "It's a sort of backup office here."

"Good. I need these printed off so I can study them better. Barak, will we be seeing Nahum today?"

"No. He's taking Belial's tokens to Cornwall with Olivia. Why?"

"In case I need the Moonfell witches. That's okay. He can phone them and tell them who I am. I hate to cold call." Estelle might be abrupt on occasions, but there were ways to do things, and rocking up on someone's doorstep asking for magical help as a stranger was not the way to go.

Estelle didn't often eat breakfast, so she left Barak and Lucien to it, and took her coffee upstairs to the book-lined study, filled with occult and arcane ephemera. She'd never met William Chadwick, but she had a sense of who he once was. Old-fashioned, obsessive, fastidious in his research, but chaotic in every other aspect of his life. He probably had his own, organised system that was confusing to everyone else. His occult collections in the series of rooms downstairs were meticulously displayed and organised, but here, in his inner sanctum, the place was a mess. Apparently, Mason Jacobs had started to organise the study, but hadn't got very far. From the piles of books on the floor and notes in Lucien's handwriting, it seemed that Lucien was keeping himself occupied by trying to organise the place.

After a few moments of fiddling with settings and Wi-Fi, she synced her phone to the printer and printed off the spells Alex had sent her. They were all long and complicated, and while she had the ingredients for one, she didn't have them for the others, and the herbs required were unusual. There were plenty of witchcraft shops she could buy supplies from, but that would take time.

Alex had also suggested spells that would reveal hidden writing. A message within a message. One used fire, but the other was far more unusual. Hating herself for doing it, she called him. After exchanging pleasantries and her thanks, she said, "You suggested a spell using Nephilim blood? Where did you find that?"

"I didn't. It was Avery's idea." Estelle rolled her eyes. *Of course it bloody was.* Alex continued, "She's good at making new spells, and she thought seeing as Nephilim are the sons of angels, their blood might unlock some secrets. It might not do anything, of course, but well…"

She finished the sentence. "It's worth trying."

"I found hidden messages in one of my spells once, unveiled by fire, which is my element. It worked. It was a bit risky, but seeing as you're dealing with Belial, they might have used the power in his jewellery to hide something. It's just a thought."

"It's a good one, too," she said. "It might even be why my finding spells aren't successful."

"But you should take all precautions. Set up a circle." He hesitated. "I don't like the idea of you doing that alone, Estelle. You're powerful, but Belial is a Fallen Angel. Who knows what weird crap might be wrapped in that manifesto. Can Caspian help?"

She shook her head, though he couldn't see her. "He's tied up with the business."

"We can't help, either. We're placing protection spells around a big hole in the farmhouse cellar today. A bunker for jewellery. Zee and Eli want to be prepared for anything."

She laughed, and the thought of the farmhouse, and Alex's Cornish accent, made her suddenly homesick. She had an urge to see the Cornish moors, and feel the cool air, and scent the sea. London was exciting, and travelling was fun, but it wasn't home. She shrugged it off. She had a job to do. "A bunker? I guess it's wise, all things considered."

"It is, and you should be careful, too. Ask the Moonfell witches. Don't do it alone."

"It had already crossed my mind."

They chatted for a few more minutes about ways to cast the spells, and potential issues, before ending the call. She walked over to the table where the manifesto was still laid out, and picked a page up, stroking the paper, and trying to discern what, if any, magic could be in it. The more she thought about it, the more foolish it seemed to presume that this was just a manifesto, despite the fact that it felt innocuous enough. The message aside, of course. The call of mad men to invoke more madness should not be taken lightly.

Their day was open so far. She would phone Nahum and get him to call Moonfell, and while he liaised with them, she could try a few spells, study Alex's spells, and generally prepare herself.

"You," she said, tapping the manifesto, "will tell us what we want to know, whether you like it or not!"

"Venice? How sure is he?" Gabe asked Harlan on the phone while he paced around the old attic in Amato's house.

"Very sure. I've read his diaries about it. You know JD. He records everything. It's worth pursuing."

"I have no doubt about that. I'd chase anything right now." Gabe gazed out of the dusty windows, not seeing the forest and overgrown grounds, but a *palazzo* in

Venice that might contain secrets of The Consortium. *The Brotherhood.* "You have an address? A name?"

"The family is called Lamberti. I contacted Romola Flaco yesterday, a friend who works in our Rome office. I had asked her to investigate Amato's house, so this morning I asked her to look into this place, too. But there's a problem. The Lamberti family is rich and powerful—she knew the name straight away—and there's no way that you can approach them directly. Romola will double check the Venetian house to make sure it still belongs to them, and that we are talking about the same family, but she strongly suspects it will be them. Apparently, they have used The Orphic Guild in the past. They like arcane objects."

"That's brilliant!" Ash looked over at Gabe's excited tone. "But will that be an issue? I mean, might Romola warn them of what we want?"

"I damn well hope not! They're a client, and they pay for our help for individual jobs, and then we move on. Unless Romola is on some kind of retainer. But she shouldn't be, that's not how we work."

"Good. So how long will that take her?"

"A few hours, maybe? She said she'd call you directly. Is that okay? I gave her your number."

"Sure. She doesn't know what we are though, right? Either us or Shadow?" Gabe liked to keep the fact that they were paranormal beings as quiet as possible, despite that Romola worked for The Orphic Guild.

"No. Not from me, at least. I doubt Mason will have told them, either."

"Thanks. I'll start looking for accommodation there. I think we've wrapped up here." Ash gave him a thumbs up sign. Niel and Shadow had continued to search the grounds.

"There's nothing else in the house?"

"Nothing useful. It's abandoned, and has been for decades. It's dusty, mouldy, and rotten. I can't help but wonder what happened to make them abandon it."

"Romola might be able to help there. Of course, even if the Lamberti family had an item of Belial's jewellery, it doesn't mean they still have it now. And one more thing. JD thinks he's close to unlocking the Emerald Tablet."

"How close?"

"Days, maybe hours."

Gabe sat on a dusty windowsill, the rotten wood creaking beneath him. "Seriously?" He turned the speaker on and beckoned Ash over.

"Is this a bad idea? I mean, could he unleash some kind of Biblical apocalypse?"

Ash answered him. "If I believed that, I wouldn't have given him the tablet."

"But did you actually think he'd unlock its secrets?"

Ash looked uneasily at Gabe, his gold eyes darkening. "Probably not, but we helped him get the disc, and we know he's resourceful. It was always a possibility. This soon, however..." He trailed off, and Gabe knew exactly what he meant.

They had given the Emerald Tablet to JD thinking it was the safest place for it, and believing it would be decades, maybe even centuries, before he could truly understand it, but now, a deep unease settled over him. However, other hopeful possibilities presented themselves, too. "Harlan, it's worrying, but it may offer a way to completely negate Belial's jewels. And anyway, is it likely that you could stop JD?"

"No, but one of you could."

Gabe shook his head. "No, like we said months ago, too much knowledge has been locked away. I won't gatekeep it again."

"But if it's as dangerous as Raziel's book?"

"Raziel was an angel who had recorded the world's first spells that underpin life. Hermes Trismegistus was not an angel."

"But," Ash said, "he was thrice Hermes, which meant he was Thoth, too, and Thoth is an Egyptian God."

"And the tablet," Harlan pointed out, "is supposed to contain the secrets of life and immortality."

Gabe sighed, seeing resignation in Ash's eyes, too. "I think we have to let this play out. For a start, he already knows the secret of immortality. If he opens it, it's because he's worthy of the knowledge."

"That's what he said." Gabe could almost hear Harlan's eyeroll. "Anyway, back to Venice. I can get you a place to stay there. Orphic Guild connections. Do you want me to organise it?"

"Yes, brilliant. Thank you."

"Will do. Okay, I've got to go. I'll keep you updated."

Ash sighed as Gabe ended the call. "I am sort of excited by the possibility, you know? The tablet, I mean."

"Say he does make it bigger. It doesn't mean he can understand it! That could just be one step of many."

"True." Ash walked over to his pack where the map was stored. "Let's focus on Venice. You know where it is, right?"

"Vaguely."

"I have a feeling," Ash said, unfolding the map and laying it across the duty floor, "that it's northeast. There!" He jabbed the map. "I was right. It's roughly northeast from here. About a three-hour drive."

"It must be related to all this!" Gabe didn't see the point in wasting time. "We've exhausted this place, right? Let's pack up and get moving. I'll call Shadow."

Nine

Harlan ended his phone call with Gabe and looked through the window of his first-floor bedroom at the enormous marquee that loomed out of the thick mist that had descended on the chill February day.

It looked innocuous enough, but it housed something so powerful that Harlan could barely comprehend that JD might actually unlock its secrets. He should get back to London and prepare for the week, but the marquee beckoned.

The previous evening, JD had delivered as promised. He had told Harlan of his conversations with angels—the celestial kind, not the fallen ones—and had looked so earnest, Harlan wanted to believe him. But he couldn't. Having read all about his dubious friend who had enabled his conversations, the man who history had decried as a fraud, the spiritualist Edward Kelly, he questioned everything JD said. He knew that Gabe had endured long conversations with him in the past, and that he doubted JD's experience, too, even though he had designed—revealed, perhaps—Enochian language. According to the Nephilim, though, that was not the language of angels that they were familiar with. It didn't mean that the angels hadn't taught him another one, though. One accessible to humans.

JD had also described his various quests for knowledge and outlined his visit to the Lamberti's. They lived in a centuries-old Venetian palace that sat on the Grand Canal. It was magnificent, apparently, with frescoed walls, ornate plasterwork, cavernous rooms, and decadent furnishings. Well, the part he had seen of it, which wasn't much. A reception area only before he was escorted off the premises. They had denied knowing anything about such a jewel, and accused JD of being a madman. *Nothing new there.* He had faced that accusation many times.

It must be hard, Harlan thought, *to be an immortal genius.* To have to live amongst people so less gifted than himself. No wonder JD was prickly and odd. He'd had to survive lifetimes of such experiences. Being around normal people, though, who understood him, was important. It grounded him. *Sort of...* Perhaps being a scientific advisor to the lab at The Retreat was a good thing. He was so isolated here. By choice, of course, but nevertheless... Harlan found he had enjoyed their conversation. JD talked to him properly for once, as if they were of equal intellect. It wouldn't last, of course, but his stories were fascinating. A window into the past, from someone who had actually been there.

Harlan decided to see his progress once more, and leaving his packed bag on his bed, headed downstairs. He was halfway across the lawn when the ground rocked, and a wave of *something* passed through him. It was so powerful that Harlan was blasted off his feet and onto his back, leaving him looking into the mist, and wondering if he'd lost his vision.

The wet grass soaked into his jeans and jacket, and the back of his head, and he could see the moisture hang in the air with crystal clarity. Time stood still. The power of the earth rose up and the crush of air pinned him to the ground, and yet he didn't panic. He could see so clearly. The millions of moisture particles hanging above him, both beautiful and surreal. He could feel them on his skin, and see them settle on his own eyelashes. And then the weight of air and the feel of earth vanished, and he floated, weightless, able to see and feel the minute breaths of wind as they passed over and under him. And the colours! He twisted like a kite on a breeze, seeing the garden spread below him, and the thick press of trees and shrubs, all with a strange, vibrant glow.

Wait... What?

His body was lying motionless on the lawn, and Harlan realised he wasn't breathing. *Holy shit. I've had a stroke. Or maybe a heart attack. I'm dead, and my soul is leaving my body.* Regrets raced through him. That he wouldn't be around to support Olivia. That he wouldn't see the Templar gold again. That there were so many places in the world that he still wanted to see. That he hadn't spoken to his mother recently.

His soul was leaving his body and going somewhere.

Then he saw the marquee that was glowing with a brilliant green light, and he knew instantly what had happened. JD had unlocked the knowledge within the Emerald Tablet and killed him. *That mad bastard!*

The knowledge triggered a visceral physical response, and he thudded back to the ground and into his body with a thump. He took a sharp intake of breath, sat bolt upright, and yelled. "I'm alive!" Struggling to his feet, his body feeling strangely familiar and unfamiliar all at the same time, he ran across the lawn, yelling, "JD!"

But as soon as he reached the door to the marquee, he skidded to a halt. From the outside the marquee looked as normal, but a strange, ethereal light was visible through a chink in the flap that served as a door.

"JD! Are you okay?" It was deathly quiet, with no sounds coming from the house or the huge tent. "JD!" Unzipping it as if it might explode, and half expecting to see JD dead, he peered inside. *"Holy shit."*

The Emerald Tablet had vanished, as had JD, and in the centre of the tent was a cavernous entrance to what looked like an emerald cave. The rest of the tent was unchanged—the tables, the scientific equipment, and even the wheel of correspondences were all still there. Tentatively, Harlan stepped inside and zipped the door shut. *Had Anna felt the ripple of energy? Would she come and investigate?*

Not knowing whether he should be terrified or excited, he crossed to the cave's entrance, feeling a wave of power emanating from it. A passage ran ahead, far too long to be encompassed in the marquee. It was a gateway. He called JD again, half wondering if his body had been turned to dust, looked back at the world he knew and might never see again, and stepped inside.

"I see what you meant about a bunker," Nahum said to Zee and Eli. "We could bury a body in there."

"Just being prepared." Zee winked at Olivia. "We put the bodies elsewhere."

"I don't believe that for a second," Olivia shot back.

Eli leaned against the wall, looking as usual, incredibly seductive. It was like sex just oozed from him. He gave Olivia a rakish grin and Nahum subdued a scowl. *No. He was not letting Eli look after Olivia.* "You should. The field out there was strewn with bodies just before Christmas. We had to put them somewhere."

"Oh, stop it!" Briar said, horrified. "The police took them all. Olivia, ignore them!"

"I try, but they're very naughty," she said, teasing. "Something I am already used to."

The farmhouse's cellar was crowded with the five White Haven witches, the three Nephilim, and Olivia. There was, despite the gravity of the situation, almost a party atmosphere. Nahum and Olivia had arrived about five minutes earlier and found their way to the cellar, where the witches had just completed their protection spell. It was good to be home again, and Nahum was looking forward to catching up with his friends and brothers.

Nahum placed the heavy, spelled box that contained the jewels on to the ground. "I should probably get this box back to Gabe somehow. If they find anymore of Belial's stuff, they'll need somewhere to store it."

"I thought they had a smaller box?" El said, confused.

"They do, but we're finding more of his crap than we expected." He studied the runes and sigils that had been burned onto the slabbed interior and sturdy wooden lid by witch-fire, reassured that it would suffice. "I'd like to leave everything in this one, though, as double protection."

Reuben, the water witch, pointed to the corner of the room where another spelled box was lying ready. "Already done."

A huge weight lifted off Nahum's shoulders. Carrying the box had started to bother him, even though it was spelled with strong magic. It was as if Belial's power could still leak from it, and even though he knew it wasn't, it was like his insidious whispers were in his head anyway.

"Fantastic. Let's do it. You lot, though," he gestured to the witches and Olivia, "need to go upstairs."

"Actually," Alex said, "I'd like to feel the effects once you open it. I won't touch anything, obviously, but it might help me get a feel for all this."

Zee was emphatic in his response to that request. "*No!*"

"You asked for my help, and what I can give is limited. We felt the effects of the other jewels and were fine. This will be stronger. It could help."

Avery shuffled uneasily. "Alex, we've talked about this. What if it kicks off one of your weird, psychic premonitions?"

"Which it could totally do," Eli agreed.

"It's my risk, and I'm used to managing psychic energy. You'll have to trust me on this. I won't do anything to risk hurting myself."

"You'd better not!" Reuben said, indignant. "We have wedding stuff to do."

Nahum exchanged worried glances with his brothers, and resigned, they both nodded. Alex wasn't a child. "Fine. But everyone else, especially you, Liv, out!" He had slipped into using the shortened version of her name, and found he quite liked it. She seemed to, as well. She was dressed informally today, in her jeans and t-shirt, and still looked good. *Focus.*

"I'm going." She headed up the stairs. "I'll make drinks."

"We should go to the pub," Reuben said, trailing after her. "The Wayward Son does a great Sunday lunch."

In less than a minute, only the three Nephilim and Alex were left in the cellar, and after casting a worried look at Alex, Nahum flipped the lid open. Immediately, Belial's insidious whispers seeped into the room, as if there were hundreds of him crammed inside, and his power radiated outwards, too.

"Herne's horns!" Alex exclaimed, staggering back as if he'd been punched. "That's insane."

"Are you okay?" Zee asked.

"I'm fine. Just taking a moment to shut my psychic awareness down."

Nahum and Eli lifted out the jewels, one by one. It was tempting to upend the box and throw them inside without touching them, but Nahum had made an inventory, and he wanted to check that they were all there.

Eli frowned as he lifted a necklace. "This looks and feels important."

"It was placed on the altar, and nowhere near as big as the one draped around his neck," Nahum explained. "Do you think he actually wore this?"

"Perhaps, on one of his visits. It makes my skin crawl." The huge sapphire mounted in silver filigree seemed to blink like an eye, and Eli lowered it into the new, larger box the witches had made.

Nahum quickly transferred the rings, loose gemstones, and bracelets, ticking them off his list. "The necklace on the statue ended up in the hole that opened up when the temple collapsed."

"Was it as bad as it sounded?"

"Worse. I've never been so powerless in my life. I couldn't move. Couldn't speak, even, except when Amato willed it."

"And this one?" Zee held up the broken necklace.

"Taken from Amato's neck. Shadow cut it with her Dragonium blade."

"Impressive, I didn't know it could cut through metal."

Nahum hadn't really stopped to consider it. "That's true. Neither did I, but I didn't take the time to consider it in all the drama."

"Her sword was undamaged?" Zee asked.

"Must have been, or we'd have never heard the end of it."

Alex crouched close by, careful to keep his distance. "It's a pure fey blade, right?"

Eli nodded. "Forged in the Otherworld. Dragonium is made from dragons. It's a pretty gruesome process. Makes the best weapons though, apparently. Even the dryads talk of it."

"You chat to dryads about weapons?"

Eli smiled. "About all things related to the Otherworld."

Alex just nodded, thoughtfully. "So, the fey blade can cut through angelic jewellery and not be damaged. Interesting. And Shadow went undetected by Amato."

"And Belial, I presume." Nahum sat back, glad to see Alex was coping with Belial. "When we first met Jacobsen, the jewels whispered that I was there. He turned and saw me. That didn't happen with Shadow. She was using her fey magic, of course. She kept to the darkness, and I couldn't see her, either. You know what she's like in her stealth mode."

Alex sat cross-legged on the floor. "She talked about Raziel's magic back when you found the temple. Of how the old God tried to stop others from using magic, and laughed. She said it was impossible. That magic is everywhere, especially in the Otherworld."

"I remember. She said writing it all in some big book and then locking it away was madness. She wittered about the elements."

"Yes, the fundamentals of life. The elements that we access." Alex smiled. "It's a weakness."

Nahum had been ticking off jewels and throwing them into the new box while they talked, but now he froze. "What do you mean?"

"I'm not sure, but I know it is."

Nahum went to speak but Zee shushed him. "Wait!"

Alex was quiet for a few moments. "They don't have control of it. Magic, I mean. Especially Otherworldly magic. It's wild, and not of our world. The world of fey is like magic on speed, right? That's how it almost seems to me. It's like having it on tap. Raw and unfiltered, unlike our world where it's hidden. Muffled." He laughed, eyes widening almost maniacally. "Oh, wow. They can't read it. Or could once but can't now. Or Belial can't, anyway. He's tuned to his own angelic magic, but that's different."

Nahum stared at his brothers, glad to find they looked as baffled as him. Well, Zee did. Eli laughed, too. "The dryads have no truck with Gods or angels. They are just other concentrated forms of energy to them. Dryads are a bit smug, actually. They consider their own magic the purest because it's of the earth."

"And the old God, the Christian God," Alex continued, "had no sway in the Otherworld."

Nahum nodded, seeing what Alex meant. "Shadow used to think that we're some kind of sylph, but now she knows we're not. They are air spirits. We're similar, but from a different mould. A different magic."

"The same root, but a different branch. He has no sway over Shadow at all." Alex grinned. "She's your secret weapon."

"But if she touched his jewels?" Eli asked. "We've been very careful to keep them apart."

"Probably wise, but I don't think they would have an effect on her."

Nahum had another idea. "Could her blade destroy these?"

"No. Break them, yes. But there'd always be pieces of them."

"So," Zee said, "we're back to being dragons again."

Confused, Nahum said, "Dragons?"

"I'll explain over lunch. Alex, are you getting anything from the jewels?"

"Let me sit quietly with them for a few minutes and I'll let you know. Then it's time for a pub lunch."

Ten

So, this was Moonfell, Barak thought, as the huge front door opened to a colourful hallway of rugs and burnished wood.

An older woman with a thick mane of white hair greeted them, elegant in a dark red dress, displaying a beaming smile and shrewd eyes that took them all in. "Welcome to Moonfell. Come in quickly, out of that nasty February cold." She shut the door behind them and shook their hands. "I'm Birdie. Estelle, I presume?"

"Yes. Thank you, Birdie. We really appreciate your help."

"A fellow witch is always welcome." She kissed Estelle's cheek. "Well, most of the time. We had an issue with one only recently. Anyway, you must be Barak and Lucien."

Lucien had been at a loose end and was as anxious as them to see the outcome of this visit, and the witches had welcomed all of them when Estelle had called for assistance.

"We're in the kitchen at the moment," Birdie said, leading the way down the hall, "the heart of the house, but we'll head to the tower room for the spell. Time for tea, first."

Barak followed her, soaking in the magic of the house. Now he knew what Nahum meant when he said the Moonfell witches were very different to the White Haven witches and Estelle's family. Although the Cornish witches had strong family histories of witchcraft, they lived fully in the present, especially Estelle and Caspian, who were doing their best to forget their father's influence completely. Already he sensed that the inhabitants of Moonfell kept a foot in the past, as well.

Birdie chatted to Estelle as she led them down the hall, and Barak observed the bohemian décor. He had no doubt that the characters who lived here were as colourful as the house. It reminded him of his old palace in Ethiopia. The wall hangings, the rich furnishings, and the sense of opulence. It was nothing like his ancient home, and yet it was, too, even down to the scent of incense that hung on the air. A wave of homesickness hit him like a blow to the stomach, and he stopped for a moment, images unspooling before his eyes like an old film.

Birdie turned and smiled. "It has that effect sometimes. It will pass."

She knew. "I'm okay. The past catches up with me sometimes."

"As does the heartache." She smiled at Estelle. "But that will pass, too. He has new things to love now. And you, Lucien, well, you have been through a lot. Morgana can help with that."

"You read auras," Estelle said, eyes narrowing. "I've never been able to do that."

"I can turn it off, but sometimes it's so strong that I can't help it. All of yours are strong. That's good, and to be expected from such powerful individuals. Now, here we are."

Suddenly they were in a large, spacious kitchen, with grey February light illuminating the shining surfaces of a very modern, yet still very Gothic kitchen. Two women were in there, one with long, dark hair who was making a pot of tea, the other younger, with thick, auburn, wavy hair, who was seated at the table reading a magazine.

"My granddaughters," Birdie announced. "Morgana and Odette."

Odette, the young woman seated at the table, rose to her feet, mouth falling open in astonishment. Her unblinking gaze seemed to see right through him. "Another Nephilim! By the Goddess, look at you! Your wings are like the wings of night. I can almost see stars in them."

Barak laughed. "My brother, Nahum, warned me about you. You have the Sight."

"Of a sort. And a sister witch." She moved around the table to hug Estelle. "You're not a hugger, I can tell, but you need one right now. And you!" She took Lucien in. "Metals course your veins and pattern your skin." It was like a storm swept over her clear features. "Such a violation. But you have mastered it. You are strong and will get stronger still. All will be well."

"Good grief, Odette," Morgana said, ushering them into seats at the table. "Let them get settled first before you blast them with your insights."

"I can't help it!" She smiled an apology. "Sorry. It's out before I know it sometimes."

"You can see the metals?" Lucien asked, face creased with confusion. "How?"

"*See* is the wrong word. It's a sense I have, really."

Barak could tell Lucien was itching to ask more questions, but they sat at the table as Morgana carried over a pot of tea and a plate of biscuits, and then set out the cups.

"So," Birdie said when they all had drinks, "you have a manifesto that you wish to prise secrets from."

Estelle nodded as she extracted it from her bag and put it on the table. "Yes, this is it. I have tried a few finding spells on it to work out where it could have originated from, or the person who wrote it, but I think I'm blocked somehow. Potentially by Belial himself, or perhaps by the power his agents wield. I know you saved Olivia, so you're familiar with him." She pointed to one of the cut edges. "That was my doing, where I took a portion for spells. I'm scared of doing that too much in case I damage it."

"Far too familiar, unfortunately," Birdie agreed, thumbing through the pages. "But I doubt you could damage these significantly." She closed her eyes briefly as her fingers ran over the paper. "Yes, I can feel angelic magic. Odette will feel more. But not yet, Odette," she said turning to her. "You will feel it more strongly, so I suggest we wait until we're in the protective circle."

"You're an empath," Barak said to Odette, certain he was right.

She nodded. "That, too. It's a strange mix of powers that I have."

"Do you think the spells that Alex has suggested will work?" Lucien asked as he sipped his tea.

Morgana answered as she too flicked through the manifesto now that Birdie had finished. "Perhaps, but using a protective circle is wise. If we lift the magic on the manifesto, there might be consequences." She smiled at Estelle. "It was wise to seek assistance. The circle is already prepared. We have added a few little extras to it," she eyed Odette and Birdie, amused, "after what happened last time."

"This will be nowhere near as dramatic," Birdie said.

Morgana laughed. "I'll reserve my judgement."

For a few minutes, while they drank tea, the witches questioned the group on their search. Barak felt relaxed around them, sure of their support and friendship. They were open and honest, and he understood why Olivia liked them. They had looked after her well, and Harlan trusted them, too. It was good, considering what they were up against. When Birdie was satisfied that they had all the background they needed, she led the way along passages and up flights of stairs, until they came to a curious tower room. The floor and ceiling were marked with a pentacle and edged with sigils and runes, as were the window frames and doorways. When Birdie closed the door, Barak noted the sigil on that, too. The only furniture in there were a couple of chairs, a small round table, a long table used as an altar, and a bookcase filled with old texts pushed against the wall.

"Wow!" Estelle said, clearly impressed. "A full protective circle. Permanent!"

"Our ancestors deemed it wise," Birdie said, gaze sweeping around it. "A seventeenth-century addition. All the glass was broken during our expulsion of Belial." She gestured to the huge, Gothic windows. "Cost a fortune to replace them."

"You couldn't use magic?" Lucien asked.

"We were exhausted," Morgana explained. "Plus, it would have taken too long. As it was, they were boarded up for a month. Besides, they were very old. It gave us a chance to eliminate the draughts properly. As you can imagine, it's an old place that requires a lot of upkeep, even with our magic."

"It's beautiful," Estelle said, relaxing for the first time since they had entered the house. She had been nervous about visiting, despite Birdie's assurances on the phone. Barak knew how self-reliant she was, and how she had hated to have to ask for help. "It has such a lovely feel to it. The entire house, I mean."

"It depends on the visitor." Birdie's smile was mischievous. "It likes all of you. Those whom it doesn't it has no time for, and they feel unsettled. Again, that was reinforced only too well recently. Anyway, let us prepare. Estelle, join us, please. Gentlemen, amuse yourselves."

With a word of command, the candles flared to life, casting the grey February light into a warm, yellow glow. The circular tower meant that there were no shadowed corners, and Barak paced the room's perimeter, half watching the witches' preparations as he looked out of the three windows.

The garden sprawled below in all directions. Unusual topiaries populated the grounds, along with shrubs and trees, winding paths, and flower beds, mostly bare at this time of year. He caught a glimpse of unusual moon gates, too.

"This place is amazing." Lucien spoke quietly at Barak's side, taking in everything. "I hope they let us watch."

"We wouldn't be here if we couldn't."

Lucien pulled the cuffs of his jacket back to look at his tattooed arms. "Can Odette really see the metals? They would be tiny specs. Powders!"

"But they have been alchemically enhanced, and they've changed you. That is what she must see. The traces of magic." He frowned at Lucien's discomfort. "No one else can see it. Don't worry."

"I feel exposed. Naked!"

"It wasn't intentional, although I feel exposed as well," he said quietly, unwilling to offend Odette. "She sees what others cannot. It must be unnerving for her, too."

The table and one chair were now in the centre of the circle, and Odette took her seat, the manifesto on the table. The spells that Alex had sent were in Estelle's hands.

Birdie carried another grimoire that she placed on the altar. "We also have spells that might work. One is very similar to what your friend sent through. That's an ancient text," she noted, head cocking as she looked at the papers in Estelle's hands.

"We all possess very old grimoires."

"Impressive. Ours are downstairs in our library. The texts in this bookcase are regular spells we use in here. Those of banishment, as well as protection. None to unveil. Perhaps we should remedy that." She looked across to Morgana who was placing out a range of ingredients for the spells on the altar. Gemstones, herbs, jars of what looked like oils, and more candles. "Ready?"

"Just the incense." Morgana lit a bundle of sticks with a word of power, and then proceeded to place them about the room. "For clarity," she explained to Barak and Lucien as she passed them. "I suggest you wait by the bookcase. Do not interfere, no matter what happens."

Barak nodded, but called Estelle aside, suddenly terrified for her safety, despite her power. "Are you okay? Really?"

She cupped his cheeks with her hands, her smile warm and reassuring. 'I'm fine. I've checked the circle. It's well constructed and will protect us, and I know we can trust these witches. I feel it." She reached up and kissed him. "Stay back, but watch carefully, both of you. We will be focussed on the magic, and you may see something we don't."

Reluctantly, Barak did as he was bid, joining Lucien by the bookcase. He stood, arms folded across his chest, leaning against the wall, as the witches made their final preparations. Three of them stood around the circle, the Moonfell witches carrying huge wooden staffs, but Odette remained seated at the table.

"Is Odette staying in the circle?" Barak asked, alarmed.

"Just for now," Birdie said. Odette's eyes were already closed, hands in her lap, the manifesto spread on the table. "She's going to get a feel for it with her senses and then touch. She has personal protection in place, but her response may be strong. It's hard to know. We won't perform any spells until she's with us. Don't worry." She considered her next words. "He may detect you—if he's hidden in the document. You are Nephilim, after all. Do nothing. Say nothing. Understood?"

"Morgana has already warned me. I understand."

Birdie looked into his eyes as if reading his soul, and then, satisfied, stood between Estelle and Morgana.

Barak took a deep breath after the intense scrutiny, and looked at Lucien. "You heard her. We do nothing."

"I'm okay with that, but are you?" Lucien asked, eyebrows raised.

Ignoring him, Barak focussed on the witches. Birdie raised the circle of protection, the sigils and runes that ran around the double ring flaring into light.

Odette's eyes were closed, but she could obviously tell the circle was complete. She leaned forward, not touching the manifesto, but running her hands a few inches over it. For a couple of minutes she did nothing but that, and her breaths deepened. "There are levels of magic here," she said, her voice low, but sure. "I feel it in the paper and the ink. There is a seal, too. Another level of magic. Angelic, of course. But it's subtle. It doesn't surprise me that you couldn't feel it easily, Estelle." She inhaled and sighed. "Myrrh. Sandalwood. Something else that evades me right now. I will touch it now." Barak braced himself following Odette's announcement. She opened her eyes and started with the first page of the manifesto, her fingers lightly brushing across the surface. "I sense many have had a hand in this—the making of the parchment, and the preparation of the ink. One scribe only. I see a dark, shadowed place, lit only by lamplight. A quill made from an angel's feather. Given willingly to impart magic."

Barak frowned. Surely not Belial's—or any angel's, for that matter. It could not have survived. *Could it?* He was desperate to question her, but it must wait.

"It is older than it seems," she said, continuing to the second page. "Ancient parchment and old ink stored in a sacred place for such an occasion, but written more recently. They are at least a thousand years old. The quill..." she took a deep, shuddering breath again. "Ancient beyond reckoning. The scribe is...different. Strong enough to handle an angel's feather. It is pure white, almost silver. A celestial light." She closed her eyes and drew back. "So bright!" Odette steadied herself, and opening her eyes moved to the final page where the seal was embossed in the parchment. Her fingers hovered over it. "The seal is where the power is strongest. Power is infused into the wax."

For long moments she did nothing, and Barak realised he was holding his breath. What she had seen seemed impossible, but she spoke with such conviction. *Was it a hoax?* Something to confuse them and send them astray. He could hear Belial's whispers again, so low, so insistent, he had missed their arrival. He shook them off. Belial was instilling doubt where there should be none. The room seemed dark now, despite the candlelight.

Odette placed the tip of her finger on the seal, screamed as if she was being tortured, and fell forward, motionless.

Harlan progressed slowly down the emerald passageway, fingertips touching the walls to reassure himself that they existed. The surface was rough, unpolished, and although he was no gemstone expert, he was sure it was raw emerald, glowing within from some unseen power.

He paused and looked back, relieved to see that the marquee was still there, looking reassuringly normal. But it was so far away. He took a deep, steadying breath. He was an explorer. He hunted occult objects. He was used to this. And then his inner voice rebelled. *No, you aren't, you moron. Not like this. You are inside the Emerald Tablet!*

The knowledge hit him like a blow, and he staggered backwards. *He was in the tablet.*

"JD!"

No answer.

He quickened his pace. Either JD was now dust as a result of the wave of power that had knocked Harlan off his feet, or he was up ahead. Within a few more paces, the passage turned and opened into an enormous cave, and he paused on the threshold, taking it all in.

"Herne's fucking horns! This is insane."

The entire cave was made of pure, polished emerald that reflected the lights of a thousand candles, torches, and lanterns. Hundreds of pillars filled the space, rooted to the ground and reaching to the roof high above. Some were square, some were round, while others twisted like spirals. The one thing common to all was the writing that covered every surface—script he couldn't understand, but that looked ancient. In addition, it was as if he'd stepped into a Middle Eastern bazaar.

The lanterns were made of silver, bronze, copper, or gold, designed with intricate patterns, with coloured and clear glass, and suspended on long chains from the ceiling or the pillars. Rich, Oriental rugs were scattered through the space, and occasional low seating was dotted throughout. It was so enormous that he couldn't see the far side.

One thing was clear, though. This was a gargantuan repository of knowledge.

He started to walk through it, noting the feeling of timelessness, but also of antiquity. The words on the pillars were inscribed in thick, bold, and curving strokes. Faultless and immaculate. And all of it waiting for the one who had the skill to open it.

"JD! Where are you?" Harlan's voice echoed back to him, and finally he received an answer.

"Harlan, I'm over here! In the centre."

The scent of incense and a bright, orange glow drew Harlan onwards, and he found JD staring at a column of flame that blazed from the centre of a six-pointed star inscribed into the floor in what looked to be pure gold.

"As above, so below," JD said, turning to Harlan with a beaming smile. "Can you believe it?"

"No! What the actual fuck, JD? What did you do?"

"I unlocked it!"

"I know that! But..." Harlan's gaze swept around once more. "This is insane. We're in a cave! An emerald cave!" His voice rose with indignation and shock.

"No. We are in the *Emerald Tablet*." JD spun on his heel, his arms stretched out. "Look at all this knowledge. A lifetime's worth. I don't even know where to begin."

"So, one of your calculations worked. JD, you really are quite brilliant."

JD's eyes had taken on a fervent gleam. "There will be a pattern to the knowledge. A system. I just need to work it out."

"Can you read all this?"

"Ancient Aramaic and Sanskrit are the two languages I've seen so far. Yes, I understand some of it." JD fixed Harlan with his piercing gaze. "I will look for angel-related information first, but if one of the Nephilim could help, perhaps?"

"Nahum and Barak are staying in London. Well, Nahum will be back from Cornwall tonight. They'll only be too happy to help, I'm sure." He reached for his phone automatically, and then saw there was no signal at all. *Of course there wouldn't be.* "I'll head outside. Do you think it's stable?"

"For now."

"That wasn't the answer I wanted!"

"It's all I can give you right now. The field is stable. Nothing should disrupt it. It has waited for millennia. Tell no one else, though! Just our small team!"

"Of course! I'm not a moron."

JD just nodded, his attention now on other things. "I need papers, pens, notes, filing supplies, all of it..."

Harlan left him muttering to himself, hoping the outside world was still there.

Eleven

L ucien was relieved to see Odette's eyes flicker open. "She's okay! Give her air!"

He had reacted even quicker than Barak when Odette had fallen forward in a faint. Birdie had dropped the protective circle, and Lucien had rushed in and picked her up, gently depositing her on the floor outside it. Her pulse fluttered faintly at her throat, and her eyes moved restlessly beneath her lids.

"Here, let me," Morgana said, kneeling at her side as everyone else stepped back. She laid a hand on her brow. "Odette, can you hear me?"

Odette's gaze was distant, as if her vision was blurred, and then she blinked and focussed on Morgana, and then Lucien on the other side. "I'm fine, thank you. Help me sit up."

"Water and chocolate!" Morgana commanded.

"All ready," Birdie said calmly.

Lucien smiled at Odette as he supported her weight. She was featherlight, almost insubstantial. "Take your time."

"Thank you, Lucien." She accepted the water and snack from Birdie, and after a few sips and a bite of chocolate, her colour returned. "Sorry, everyone. It was a strong image I saw from the seal. That's all. It was like a cobra strike." She gave a shaky laugh. "I feel a bit embarrassed now."

"Let's get her in a chair, Lucien," Morgana said.

After she was settled and had taken a few deep breaths, Odette smiled. "I'm fine. We can carry on soon."

Barak crouched opposite her. Everything about him was clenched tight—his jaw, his fists, and his corded muscles. "What did you see? Belial?"

"Yes, and someone else. The scribe. Belial was fleeting. A flash of his eyes and then he was gone. But the scribe was intense. I couldn't determine his age, but he was one of you. A Nephilim."

Barak's black skin turned grey. "Surely it can't be possible."

"I know what I saw. Not pure angel. Belial was his father, I'm certain."

"Of the House of Belial. That's bad news." Barak sat back on the floor heavily, looking at Estelle and then Lucien, absolute confusion on his face. "It shouldn't even be possible. You said the parchment and ink were old, but the manifesto was newer. So that means the scribe is of more recent centuries, too?"

"Yes. Well, I think so." Odette's gaze flickered to her coven and Estelle. "I don't see things with crystal clarity, but I can usually trust my intuition."

Birdie nodded. "Yes, she can. We have all learned to trust what she sees."

"So, what we—me and my brothers—have feared, is true. We had hoped it was just human agents that he possessed, but I suppose it was the only logical conclusion, really."

"Is it so bad?" Morgana asked, puzzled. "You are Nephilim, and you are here!"

"Well, human agents are easier to fight, that's for sure. Of course, we have battled other Nephilim many times over the years. That is not the issue, either. It's how he is here, now! We died in the Great Flood, and found our way back through an open portal. But him..."

Birdie nodded. "I see. He either survived for millennia after making it through the Flood, or was brought back another way."

"And if he did survive," Estelle said, meeting Barak's worried look with her own, "how many others also did?"

"Exactly." Barak regained his feet. "No matter. That is not for you to worry about. We will deal with that. It's even more important now to get more information from the manifesto. You've already told us so much, though, Odette. Thank you."

"It's my pleasure." She too stood up. "I'm afraid that fainting is one of my standard responses when I'm psychically overwhelmed. It's a defence mechanism that shuts down my psychic awareness. However, I am okay, and we can continue."

They settled back into their positions, this time with Odette outside the rune circle. While they set up, Lucien studied Barak. He looked preoccupied, his jaw tight, and he attempted to reassure him. "It will be okay. We will find them and stop them, no matter how many there are."

"Belial's sons fought dirty."

Lucien laughed. "So do we. And we have JD's weapons now, too."

"You want to help?"

"I'm here, aren't I? What else will I do with my time? I have all this strength and speed that I'm finally getting used to using, thanks to you."

His thoughts drifted as the witches cast the protection spell around the pentacle on the floor and started the first spell. Birdie led them, the High Priestess of the Moonfell Coven, and Estelle seemed happy with the decision. Lucien was used to her twisted lips that denoted disapproval. She had always been kind to him, but there was no doubt she was abrupt when things did not go her way.

The truth was that Lucien still wasn't sure how he'd live his new life, long-term. He wasn't looking ahead for more than weeks at a time. For now, he was enjoying his freedom, and enjoying living in Chadwick House. He could maybe ask The Orphic Guild for a job, or get a contract with the PD. Jackson had actually suggested it once, but he said he needed time. Now, as life settled down, it seemed like a good idea. He could get paid and find his own place. He couldn't live in Chadwick House forever. Or perhaps he could move back to France. Perhaps the Paris branch of The Orphic Guild could offer him a job there. Although, for now, London pulled him. He had friends who knew about his situation. That was worth more than anything.

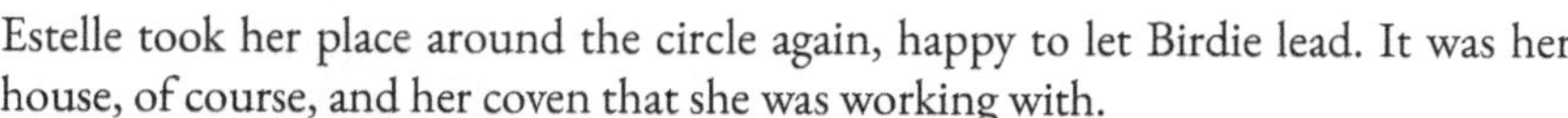

Estelle took her place around the circle again, happy to let Birdie lead. It was her house, of course, and her coven that she was working with.

For the next hour, the witches worked their way through the spells, first starting with Moonfell's own that Birdie and her granddaughters were more familiar with, and then moving to Alex's. She was used to working with other witches, and lending her magic to a spell, and this was no different—in theory, at least. Birdie's magic was rich, like a fine, aged wine. So far, they had extracted no further secrets from the manifesto. The pages lifted and turned sometimes, and once a spell caught them in a kind of whirlwind before settling the pages back on the table. Estelle became more and more frustrated, but Birdie calmly continued, moving steadily through the spells in the order she had chosen.

There was logic to her actions, starting with the familiar ones, and then the simplest, leaving the more complex to the end. Estelle was sure which one would work, though. She had been ever since Alex had sent it through. The one to which he had suggested they add Barak's blood. Finally, after another failed attempt, Birdie gave Estelle a long, measured look. "Blood it is, then."

She summoned Barak and pierced his finger with a sharp-bladed knife, adding a few drops to a potent herbal mixture that also contained herb oils and a thimble of potion, then smeared it on the edges of the manifesto before setting the circle up again.

They took their positions once more, at the four points of the compass, Birdie remaining at the altar in the east. As Birdie commanded the manifesto to unveil its secrets in Middle-English, the space within the circle darkened, as if she had conjured a storm. A haze descended on the pages, and they lifted into the air and hung there. The text lifted from the parchment and swirled like some sort of alphabet soup. Estelle's breath caught in her chest as she struggled to contain her power. The spell was drawing it in, like a giant sink hole.

Then Birdie shouted words of command again, and images began to form in the circle's centre, like a flickering film or a hologram, and finally the manifesto began to give up its secrets. A large sandstone cave, and then a temple, blazing with candles, an angel with outstretched wings and sightless eyes. A casket overflowing with jewels. A heap of weapons. A desk stacked with parchment. A library of scrolls. All passed by so quickly it was hard to keep track. A cityscape unfolded. Old buildings, undulating roofs, towers, and houses. Then the letters that had swirled aimlessly started to rearrange themselves into words.

Names.

Out of the corner of her eyes she saw Barak and Lucien scramble for paper. Birdie dragged her attention back, her voice rising as wind whipped up in the circle.

And then something exploded out of the images, shredding the manifesto and sending the letters tumbling. A wave of power rolled outwards, hit the protective shield, and rebounded like a wave. Out of the midst of it came the sound of a haunting, mournful call of a trumpet, accompanied by the flash of tawny wings edged with gold. Blinding white light exploded outwards. Estelle closed her eyes but stood firm. The circle would not break. Not while she still drew breath.

The trumpet sounded again, the white light pressing on her closed eyelids. She felt Birdie's steadying presence, and then Morgana and Odette's. The circle held firm, until the light vanished, and silence fell.

She opened her eyes, terrified she had plunged into a void, but the witches were still there, blinking in the candlelight, as half blind as she was. As her sight returned, she saw the table and chair in the centre of the circle were now splintered wood, and the manifesto was a confetti of tiny pieces spread across the floor.

She whipped around to stare at Barak and Lucien, who looked similarly dazed. "Did you see who it was, Barak?"

His features were mired in confusion. "It was Belial's commander. And he carried Belial's horn."

Olivia felt as if she didn't have a care in the world as she enjoyed a pub lunch at The Wayward Son.

A weak February sun illuminated the small backroom of Alex's pub, a fire crackled in the grate, and her food was delicious. It was the company, though, that sealed it. The witches were fun and welcoming, and the three Nephilim joked and teased Reuben about the wedding. Not his fiancée, though—El, the stunning, blonde-haired witch. But maybe that was because Reuben seemed particularly obsessed with it.

El smiled at Reuben affectionately. "Enough wedding talk before you drive us all insane! I can barely think straight!"

"That's all right, my love," he said, kissing her fingers. "I have it all in hand."

Alex rolled his eyes. "Yeah, right. As much as I'm pleased for you, no more midnight phone calls!"

"I had an idea!"

"Save it until morning!"

El sniggered. "And that applies to me, too."

Reuben gave Olivia a sly smile. "Yes, but if it's a killer idea, I can't wait, right?"

He was sweet for including her in this, and she smiled. "Maybe you should, though, just to keep your friends happy? After all, a few more hours won't hurt."

Reuben clutched his hand over his heart dramatically. "And I thought I had an ally!"

"You've missed your calling, mate," Nahum said, laughing. "Maybe you should swap surfing and your garden business for wedding planning."

Briar threw a piece of her bread roll at him. "No! Stop encouraging him."

"If anyone would be into this, I would have thought it was you, Briar," Eli said, teasing her.

A glint was in her eye. "Because I'm a woman?"

"Because you're excited. I see it every day! You can't fool me."

Of course, Olivia had forgotten that Eli worked with the earth witch.

"And the stack of wedding magazines on the table," Eli continued, "makes your enthusiasm very clear."

Alex snorted. "Not there, too! We have a forest of them at our place."

Avery batted his arm. "Shut up! *Men*!"

Looking lofty, Reuben ignored them all. "Just wait until it's your turn." He frowned at Olivia, and for one heart-stopping moment, she thought he was about to ask what was happening with her and Nahum. But no, all he said was, "Did we invite you to the wedding?"

"Er," she looked awkwardly around the table, "no, but that's okay. I mean, I barely know you!"

He waved her reassurances away. "Consider yourself invited. You're family now! I mean, you're carrying a little Nahum package, and they're all going to be uncles! I consider myself one, too—for the record!"

Nahum spat his pint out, showering his thankfully empty plate with beer.

Zee threw his head back and roared with laughter. "A Nahum package! Oh, that's priceless." He caught Olivia's eye, tried to stop laughing, and failed. "Sorry, but it is."

The whole table was laughing now, but Avery squeezed Olivia's arm. "So sorry. Reuben's mouth runs away with him sometimes."

Despite her blushes, Olivia laughed. "It's fine. It *is* a Nahum package. Mine too, though."

Reuben, clearly enjoying himself now, and with a big twinkle in his eye, suggested, "You should have a joint name. Like celebrities do. For example, me and El could be Reuspeth, or Elben. I think Reuspeth is better. Avery and Alex would either have to be Avex, which sounds like a car rental company, or Alery, and that's not much better. You two, though, could be Navia. Or Olivum." He grimaced. "Olivum sounds gross. Navia, however, is great! You could name your daughter Navia!"

Nahum was still struggling to get his breath after almost choking, his face flushed. He glared at Reuben, who ignored him completely.

Olivia tried to remain composed. "I don't think we've decided anything yet, but obviously we will consider it carefully!" What she didn't say was that mashed names denoted a couple, and that was one thing she and Nahum were not. She focussed only on the baby's name. "But thank you for the interesting suggestion! And the invitation, of course. I must admit, I do love a good wedding, as long as I'm not intruding." And by that she meant on Nahum's friendships. He might not want her there. She would discuss it with him later, and if he looked like he hated the idea, she would back out.

"Anytime. I'll send you an official invitation. Or I could just add a plus one to Nahum's invite." He cocked an eyebrow, amused, and now she knew he was shit-stirring, and so did Nahum, who looked ready to throw something at him.

"Perhaps," Nahum said, finally finding his voice, and shooting an apologetic glance at Olivia, "we should talk about our issues with Belial."

"Excellent idea," Alex agreed.

Reuben smirked. "If you insist."

"I do."

The conversation turned to Alex's theory about Shadow being impervious to Belial's power, and how to use that to their advantage. Olivia breathed easier. With no idea how their relationship was going to progress, the subject always felt awkward with others. Never when they were alone, though. Well, not once they had got past their initial awkwardness, at least.

Avery, however, the pretty red-haired witch who sat next to her, had other things to talk about, and she lowered her voice. "Sorry, Olivia, Reuben is a dreadful tease, and I hope he didn't embarrass you. I could hex him sometimes."

"No, of course not. It's a weird situation, isn't it? I can't deny it." She glanced around the table, relieved that no one was listening to them. "I'm sure everyone is wondering what will happen with us, but the truth is, I don't know. Other than of course being parents, and we'll make it work. Somehow."

"Of course you don't know. It just happened, as some things do. I'm a big believer in fate though, especially after our tangle with Wyrd last year. You two, and your baby, were clearly meant to be. Of course, it's impossible to say what will happen in the long-term, but you know," she hesitated and then rushed on anyway, "he watches you. In a nice way, obviously. And discreetly, of course. I think that says a lot."

"Like what the hell have I done, and how do I get myself out of this mess?"

"No! Like how do I make this thing work without scaring you off? Sorry, I shouldn't have said anything, because I'm interfering, but well..." Avery smiled. "I thought you should know. The men won't say anything. Maybe Zee would, but they wouldn't want to interfere directly. Reuben—obviously—is a massive tease. I, on the other hand..."

Olivia laughed, still feeling awkward, but she knew Avery meant it for the best. "Well, thank you, I'll bear that in mind."

Avery pulled back, leaving her to her thoughts, and Olivia was relieved when her phone rang. *Harlan.* She excused herself from the table.

"Hiya. Is everything okay?"

"No! Yes. I have news, Liv! Big news, and if possible, I need Nahum's help."

Twelve

Jackson studied the group of people gathered in Chadwick House's study, wondering how best to manage all the information they had to follow up. Initially they had struggled for leads, and now it seemed they had too many.

It was Sunday evening, and Nahum and Olivia had returned from Cornwall, Harlan from Mortlake with what was, quite honestly, shocking news, and Barak, Estelle, and Lucien, had cracked the manifesto at Moonfell. Sort of. All of them looked tense, not surprisingly. *It was too much.* However, they needed a plan, and they needed to stop arguing. Right now, Nahum and Barak were standing by one of the bookcases, locked in fierce debate as what to tackle first. Harlan and Olivia were in chairs by the fire, chatting quietly. Estelle and Lucien were seated at the table with Jackson, its surface covered with notes.

"Clearly," Jackson interjected, trying to calm Nahum and Barak down, "we must split things up between us, which includes the others in Italy, and Maggie, too."

"Which means," Harlan said, breaking off his conversation with Olivia, "telling her about the tablet. Is that wise?"

"I trust her! Don't you?"

"Sure, but it's the *tablet*! It's huge news!"

"So is Belial," Lucien pointed out, "and we trust her with that. She *is* the lead detective of the Paranormal Policing Unit."

"Plus," Jackson said, "we don't know what effect that tablet may have on things in general. It could carry paranormal repercussions. She needs to know, which is why I have invited her tonight. She'll be here soon."

"I have no problem with that," Nahum said, shrugging. "She's always helped us in the past. Like making sure we don't end up with criminal records, despite the body count."

"Good." Jackson massaged his temple. Keeping secrets was his job, but keeping them from his friends who could provide valuable help was annoying. He was tired of monitoring his conversations as to who knew what. "I suggest you get her up to speed, Harlan, when she arrives."

"Sure, will do. It will be a relief, actually."

"Well," Barak said, taking a seat at the table, "we must go to the British Museum tomorrow. That cannot be avoided. We have to sign the paperwork, and I want to see that treasure! We were holed up in France at the time."

"I want to see it, too," Estelle added. "It's not like we're wasting time. It'll be over by midday."

Jackson gestured to Harlan, Olivia, and Nahum. "You three are going, too?"

Nahum nodded. "After that, I will happily go to JD's place with Liv to see the Emerald Tablet that is now a cave." He stared at Harlan. "You're not winding us up, are you?"

"No! It really is a giant, emerald cave. I would never kid you about that!"

"Which means that we," Estelle said, including Barak and Lucien in that, "can focus on what we saw in the spell at Moonfell."

They had already updated all of those present with the images the spell had lifted from the manifesto. Jackson wished he'd been there to witness it. Everyone now took a seat at the table in the centre of the room, keen to formalise their plans.

Olivia tapped the loose papers covered in scrawled names. "These were in that spell?"

Lucien nodded. "Yes. The letters lifted off the page, rearranged themselves, and made the names. They just hung in the air! But it was too fast to catch all of them. We missed some."

"We missed a lot," Barak virtually growled. "There were dozens of them. Maybe hundreds."

"But potentially," Harlan pointed out, "that could be a list that has accumulated over decades. Centuries, even. They could be dead by now."

"Not if they're directly related to the manifesto we found. It's only a few decades old. Jacobsen's signature was on it."

Estelle drummed her fingers on the table. "That's an interesting suggestion, Harlan. The parchment and the ink are old and imbued with angelic magic. Odette said so, and I don't doubt her. One of the images showed piles of parchment on a desk, and scrolls stacked on shelves. Therefore, any individuals that contributed to their making, storage, or anything else, were probably part of The Brotherhood years ago, and could well be dead now. The spell pulled up everyone's names."

"It's a fair point, Estelle, but we shouldn't assume," Jackson mused. "Any names you recognise?"

"Amato's, but that's all," Barak said.

Harlan grinned. "I recognise one. The Lambertis. That's the family in Venice who own the fancy *palazzo*."

"The family mentioned in the old text JD found?" Olivia asked, becoming excited. "Which means we're on the right track."

Jackson made notes as they talked. "I'll let Gabe know."

"Let me," Harlan offered. "They should be in Venice now. I set them up in an apartment belonging to The Orphic Guild, and I want to make sure everything is okay. Plus, I need to chase up Romola." As he spoke, the doorbell rang, and he rose to his feet. "And that's Maggie, so I'll get her up to speed, too. Drinks, anyone?"

A chorus of requests rang out, and Harlan left them to it.

"I want to identify that city," Barak said. He stood and started to pace. He'd been visibly unsettled ever since Jackson had arrived. The big man was always so calm, but not anymore. "I have a feeling it's where Jiri is."

Belial's commander. "Why? It could mean anything," Jackson said, swivelling to watch him pace.

"Jiri was always in the thick of things. He wouldn't skulk in a country house, or a small village. He would want to be near entertainment, easy travel, everything."

Nahum nodded. "That's true."

"But it was an ancient-looking place," Estelle pointed out. "It could be long destroyed by now."

"There are plenty of old cities left, or old quarters, at least. It looked Middle Eastern, or Greek, perhaps. Maybe even North African."

Jackson sighed. "That still leaves a lot of cities. Tell me more."

"Red sandstone buildings, or red brick, at least. Red tiled roofs, too. A flash of the sea. Maybe even mountains," Barak said, struggling to recall.

"Sounds more Mediterranean to me," Olivia suggested.

Barak nodded. "Perhaps. Estelle and I could look along that north-eastern line the statues indicate. See if anything fits."

Jackson looked across to Lucien. "We could search through the names you've written down. It's a huge task, but we can't ignore them!"

"Of course. But I've been thinking about your offer, and my future."

Jackson smiled, knowing what was coming. "You want a job?"

"It makes sense, yes? I know The Retreat. I can help. Perhaps be a type of field agent. I have too many skills to sit behind a desk forever. Besides, I'd go mad. Hopefully, for now, I can continue to live here."

"Of course. We'll work something out." Jackson felt a renewed sense of excitement at his own job offer. He liked Lucien, and was keen to help him find a new role in his altered state. "I suppose that helps me make my mind up. I've been mulling over it all weekend."

Estelle spun around. "What?"

"I've been offered the Deputy Director role at The Retreat. I have ideas, and in that role, I could really develop them."

Olivia gasped with delight, ran around the table, and hugged him. "That's brilliant! You'll be so good at it!"

"Thanks Liv. I'm not so sure, but..."

She cut him off. "No! You will be great. How fantastic."

A flurry of congratulations followed, and Jackson was anxious to stop them. "Thank you. I guess it means my occult-hunting days will be at an end, for a while."

"Unless I help with that, too," Lucien offered.

"Thank you, but let's finish with Belial first. I'm still looking for the remnants of Black Cronos, too." *Always so much to do.* "Now that Maggie's fully on board, let's see if she can help with that list of names."

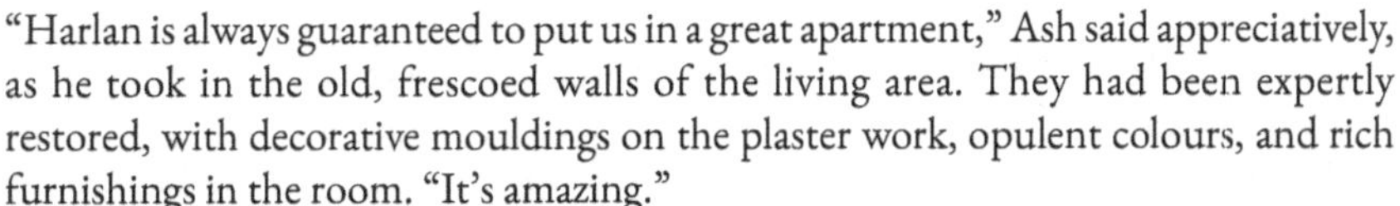

"Harlan is always guaranteed to put us in a great apartment," Ash said appreciatively, as he took in the old, frescoed walls of the living area. They had been expertly restored, with decorative mouldings on the plaster work, opulent colours, and rich furnishings in the room. "It's amazing."

"And the view isn't bad either," Shadow said. She was out on the terrace overlooking Venice's Grand Canal, her slender silhouette black against the lights of the opposite buildings. "A city on water. I like it."

Gabe stood next to her, his arm sliding around her waist. "We should explore later. Find the *palazzo*."

"And food!" Niel said. "I'm starving."

They had arrived only a short while earlier, after taking their time on the drive. Navigating Italian traffic was sometimes tricky. Their apartment was on the top floor of an old *palazzo* on the banks of the Grand Canal. The view was of the rooftops, ancient churches, and the winding canal that was filled with boats and gondolas. The sun had already set, and lights blazed across the city.

Ash left the sumptuous living area and joined them on the terrace. He leaned on the balcony, taking it all in. "There are lots of little trattorias on the back streets. We'll eat and then find the Lamberti's place." He checked the address and searched the map on the search engine on his phone. He took a moment to orientate himself, and then pointed to the left. "It should be that way. Not too far, actually."

"But what do we do once we find it?" Niel asked. He was lounging in a chair, already drinking a beer, his feet propped up on another chair. "I presume we'll break in later?"

"Perhaps," Gabe said, joining him at the table. "I'd rather scope it out tonight and wait for Romola to contact us. Getting some background on the family will be important if we're to avoid what happened in Florence."

Ash nodded. "You think we might encounter another Amato-style character. A vessel for Belial?"

"Perhaps. Or another temple in the cellars, and a Nephilim trap." He cocked an eyebrow. "I'd rather not go through that again."

Shadow played with her blade, sending it twirling around her fingers so fast it was a blur. "But I'm your secret weapon. Maybe I should go alone."

"No way!" Gabe scowled at her. "We wait. And we can't presume anything. After Florence, they may have found a way to detect your presence."

Niel huffed. "The mysterious *they* again. Don't we mean Jiri?"

They had all been updated on the latest events from London. The news that JD had unlocked the Emerald Tablet was shocking. Ash had honestly never thought he would do it. No one had. He was desperate to see it and help reveal its vast knowledge. However, knowing that Jiri, Belial's ruthless commander, was out there, somewhere, was a blow, and this had to take precedence. However, Ash had to admit that he was intrigued, too.

"How has he survived?" he asked. "Jiri, I mean. And I don't just mean the Flood! I mean all the years since. We don't live for thousands of years!"

"Unless," Niel suggested, "Belial's magic has sustained him. The use of his jewels, perhaps."

"He must have found a high mountain," Gabe reasoned, "and shelter. Somewhere to wait out the Flood and the years afterwards. Then he found a way to integrate himself into society, like us."

"Not necessarily," Shadow said, finally putting her blades away. "What if he escaped through a portal, like you? We know that witches can open them. They use them to communicate with Otherworlds, or summon demons. Or send them back! It's unfortunately common. We know that from Harlan because it happened recently, and Alex has done it a couple of times, too. Plus, we know that demon conjuring was very popular hundreds of years ago. You can't presume that you are unique."

"True," Ash said with a sigh. "He, and maybe other Nephilim, could have seized their chance, like we did."

"Or were summoned deliberately." Niel sipped his beer, eyeing them all grimly. "People are obsessed with angels, even more so in Medieval times and the Renaissance. Look at all of the art dedicated to them. If Belial was stronger in the past, he could have encouraged someone to do his bidding. And this place," he cast his gaze beyond the balcony to encompass Venice, "is very religious. Angel iconography is everywhere. In fact, the more I think about it, the more I'm sure that's what happened."

Silence fell, and Ash stared down at the dark waters of the Grand Canal, the cool night air ruffling his hair while he considered Niel's words. *Yes, that was the most likely scenario.* "Wait." He swung around to stare at the others again. "Belial's jewels. Where did they come from?"

"Perhaps Belial had news of the Flood," Niel suggested. "He always was a schemer. He had agents everywhere, even then. Maybe word reached him of the old God's plans, and he decided to plot for the future. He could have buried his jewels in a cave in the mountains. Left Jiri—and maybe some other Nephilim—with instructions of how to find them, should the opportunity arise. If he protected them with his magic, then they could have survived anything. He may even have assumed he could get them himself. I guess none of them foresaw what the Igigi would do."

Gabe nodded. "And remote mountaintops wouldn't be razed to make room for new cities. It's a good idea, Niel."

"You know," Shadow said, kicking out a chair and taking a seat on the wide terrace, "it's always bothered me as to why there were Nephilim weapons in the Temple of the Trinity. It made no sense. Why would Raziel have stored them there? You," she addressed Niel, "thought it was because he was screwing with you. What if he knew of Belial's plans, and he was offering you help?"

"Without any explanation?" Niel snorted derisively. "That would be typical!"

Ash exchanged worried glances with his two brothers. "It's a possibility, I guess. I never really considered why they were there. I was too worried about getting out of the temple at the time. And after, well... I didn't care."

Gabe stared at Niel. "You saw them better than I did. Whose were they?"

"There were a few different Houses. Tiril, Tumael, Baraquel, Meresin, and others I can't remember." He frowned as he sorted through his memories. "None particularly ominous. There were swords, shields, daggers. I considered taking a couple and then decided against it. Like you said, Ash. There was a lot going on."

The terrace was dark now, the last rays of the sun had dwindled while they talked, and only a dim lamp from the room beyond and the city lights illuminated them. Shadow placed her sword on the table, and pale light glinted along the blade. "Were they as strong as this is? Imbued with magic and special metals?"

"Not fey-made, if that's what you mean," Ash said, picking up her sword. He had handled it before. It was incredibly light for its size, and perfectly weighted. The blade was engraved, but the hilt was plain except for a curl of a dragon's tail engraved around it. "But yes, they had Fallen Angel magic. None were as fine as this, though."

"Forged on Earth, that's why," Niel said. "However, they were stronger than the weapons we have now, even though El has woven magic in them. I didn't want one though, if I'm honest. We carry enough of our past with us."

"A gift, nevertheless," Shadow said. "He knew, or suspected. He was arming you for a fight."

"Well, he should have left fucking instructions!" Gabe said viciously. "Damn angel games."

"It's done," Ash said, suddenly tired of the discussion. "Ultimately, it doesn't matter whose weapons they were, or why they were there. We have no access to them, and don't want them. What we have now is more than enough. As to how Jiri is here, well, no doubt we'll find that out when we find him. We should also assume that if he's here, others could be, too. It will make our job a little harder, that's all." He smiled at his brothers. "I take heart from the fact that they haven't achieved world domination, and Belial does not stride amongst us." He stood up. "Come on. Let's eat, find the *palazzo*, and scope the area. Then we should have a quiet night while we can get it. The beds look too good not to sleep in."

Thirteen

"I'm sorry about Reuben's teasing, yesterday," Nahum said to Olivia over breakfast in her flat on Monday morning. "He just gets carried away."

He'd mulled over Reuben's jokes all night, hoping Olivia wasn't about to run for the hills and decide to have nothing to do with him at all. Nahum had a good sense of humour, but he'd just felt awkward yesterday. It was stupid, really, because Olivia seemed to handle it well. Everyone liked her. And she'd been invited to the wedding. *As his plus one!*

"He's a tease," she said, laughing. "*Navia!* Cheeky sod!"

"He's always the same with everyone. He's a joker."

"He means well. He's not malicious. Just naughty. I like naughty." She gave him an impish grin, and his breath quickened. He still hadn't got used to seeing her in her silk pyjamas and bathrobe, bare of makeup, and with her hair tousled. Although, it was brushed now, and he could smell the minty toothpaste from across the table. It felt intimate with breakfast laid out between them. Breakfast he'd insisted on preparing.

"Please don't feel you have to go to the wedding, either," he continued. "I mean, of course you're welcome, but he might have put you on the spot."

"If I'm honest, I'd love to go. A hand-fasting! I've never been to one before. I can't wait. Are you sure you don't mind? I don't want to intrude. Our lives have become very enmeshed lately."

"Well, you are carrying my 'Nahum package.' They'll be even more enmeshed soon." He grinned. "Unless, of course, Reuben and my brothers have scared you off."

"They are all amazing. It's a long way off though yet." She patted her flat stomach, but her smile faded. "I must tell Natalie. She's my *best* friend, and I'm keeping everything from her. I won't mention what you are, but I have to say something. It's killing me not to."

"Of course you have to tell her. If she wants to meet me, I'll play normal."

"Thank you, but she'll pepper you with a million questions, so we'll put that off for a while. I need her to acclimatise first." She glanced around her eclectically decorated flat that was full of occult objects and treasures from her travels. "At least you haven't had to rescue me from anything yet."

"And won't. It's a precaution." He checked his watch. "We have a few hours before we have to sign the paperwork at the British Museum and we become insanely rich. Anything you want to do first?"

"Actually," she said, buttering her toast, "why don't we go to the museum early, and check out the displays? They have a huge amount of ancient Mesopotamian and Assyrian treasures, and also the Sutton Hoo treasure. I love it there. Who knows, we may even see something useful. They even have JD's old scrying glass. Mason has given me the time. I checked with him yesterday." She laughed. "I think he thinks that with me and Harlan there, we might get on the news and drum up more work for The Orphic Guild. He's probably right, too. I'm amazed he's not coming."

"Do you really think it will be on the news?"

"Today? Maybe. They could see this as stage one of their publicity plan. Having authenticated the treasure, they will be planning a huge display, and when they announce the news to the public, it will be enormous. Newspapers, TV. Everywhere! You found Templar treasure!" She stared at him, amused. "This has been debated over for hundreds of years, searched for by countless numbers of people, and you found a large part of it. In fact, I'm probably underestimating the impact this might have. It could well dominate headlines for weeks when it breaks. They've sat on it for months while they catalogue everything, but now? All bets are off. Knowing Theo, he might have organised some publicity, too. The village will be inundated with visitors. Are they opening the church vault where you found everything?"

Nahum looked at her, baffled. "I haven't even considered that!"

"If they've preserved the place, and I'm sure they will have, it will be a huge money maker. They'll probably open it for tours."

"Well, it's certainly possible to organise access from the crypt, but they'd have to make it more accessible, and yes, organised tours only, I'm sure. Wow!" Nahum sipped his coffee, remembering the fight with the Knights of Truth and Justice, the Templars' descendants, the huge, vaulted space beneath the church, the traps, and the riddles. "I've been so busy with Black Cronos, I hadn't considered any of it, but of course they will open it up. I'm sure Theo will have been working on it for months! I'm such an idiot!"

Olivia laughed. "Having missed out on all that fun, I know I must visit it! And I can't wait to see the treasure this morning. *If* they show it to us. They could be cagey about it, even now."

"I didn't consider that." He returned to her suggestion that they might be on the news that morning. "Say the publicity machine does start today, I'm not sure we should be photographed and splashed over the papers. We might be recognised by Jiri."

Olivia froze. "He knows you?"

"It's possible." Nahum shrugged, trying to cast his uneasy feelings aside. "Unlikely though, right? I mean, there were hundreds of us. It's not like we all knew each other. Sorry." He smiled, trying to make light of it. "I'm just paranoid."

"I might be wrong, too. There may be no press there at all. Besides, you will get to choose whether you want to be photographed or not. Theo will choose to be, I'm sure. So will Harlan. It means you're off the hook, as long as they have *someone* for photos!" She bit into her toast, chewing slowly and looking thoughtful. "As for The Brotherhood, it's unlikely they have photos of you. I mean, no one knows we were involved with Jacobsen's death. However, we can't forget that Amato knew about Gabe and the others."

"But Belial *saw* us," Nahum reminded her. He'd never forget the look on Jacobsen's face as he whirled around in the nave, eyes wide with terror. "Not like a photo, but through the connection with his jewels and Jacobsen, and he will have told Jiri and whoever else. He can connect with them, mentally. They would know what we look like. We have all carried his jewels." He tried to suppress the shudder that ran through him at the memories of using them at the farmhouse. He and Eli had channelled Belial's power and had become incandescent with his angelic magic, allowing them to crush many Black Cronos soldiers. *He would have known*. And Ash had survived because of Belial. "He warned Jacobsen that I was behind him, and he would have detected that his jewels were used. Plus, he obviously knows you and our baby. He possessed you!"

"But really," Olivia persisted, "would he have known what we looked like? He doesn't have eyes. He wasn't *in* Jacobsen, or Amato, from what you've said. He felt your presence. Our energy."

"But he's a Fallen Angel. He would see what others couldn't. They set a trap for us, under the church in Florence." Nahum glanced uneasily around the room as if he was watching them now. He rubbed his jaw, feeling the clenched muscle. He really was becoming paranoid and over analysing everything.

Olivia sat back, as thoughtful as Nahum. "He's the Angel of Death and Destruction. The bringer of madness. Maybe you feeling paranoid is exactly what he wants. I don't think he can know what we look like!"

"So how do you explain what happened in Florence with Amato?"

"Like you said. You touched his jewels, and he registered your presence. He alerted The Brotherhood. Perhaps they can attune to your energy if you're in close proximity? He clearly has a level of consciousness, which is why Jacobsen knew you were behind him in the church. And of course!" she said, rolling her eyes. "You said Amato was wearing his jewels that Shadow removed. He would have whispered to him as he did to Jacobsen, knowing you were watching him in Florence." She smiled, pleased with herself. "That must be right! You're the angel expert. What do you think? Logically! Let's not get paranoid."

He huffed, resigned to her suggestion. "Yes, that is the most likely scenario. When we carry his jewels, it's like we're wiring ourselves to him. An even better reason not to carry them. Now I'm even happier that they're in the cellar, under levels of spell protection. Hopefully my brothers are now invisible to Belial again, although I'm sure they are searching for us. I'm sorry that you were dragged into this."

"I was the one who dragged *you* into this! Anyway, it's done now, and we have to deal with it." She leaned forward, squeezing his hand. It was the first time she had touched him in days. Weeks, even. They had kept a wary distance, apart from an awkward hug in greeting. A hug that said, *I'm pleased to see you, but we're just friends.* Her touch was electric, and they both felt it. To her credit, she didn't pull back. "We're in this together, and I don't regret a thing. Not what happened between us, or our impending child. We'll get through it."

"Yes, we will. I promise." He wrapped his fingers around hers, fighting back the urge to lean in and kiss her. To lose himself in her soft skin and warm embrace again. He didn't want to think about how their daughter might not survive, or how he'd feel if the worst happened. How the loss would strike both of them like a blow. For now, their futures were entwined and ripe with possibilities and promise.

Silence stretched between them, their gazes locked, words bound behind their uncertainty, both unwilling to say more and risk everything. Then Nahum's phone rang, shattering the silence, and he wasn't sure whether to curse the interruption or welcome it.

Shadow studied their unexpected visitor, Romola Falco from The Orphic Guild, who Niel had just admitted to their apartment, hoping that they could trust her.

"We were expecting a phone call, not you in the flesh," Niel said, eyeing her warily. "Is everything okay?"

She beamed at him, eyes roving over his impressive physique before resting on his face. "Everything is great, but I decided that what I had to share should be said in person, rather than over the phone. All of this is fascinating! Especially the Lambertis." She tapped the leather briefcase she carried. "I have lots of information in here. Sorry if my arrival has upset your plans." She cast a quizzical look at all of them gathered in the lounge, watching her with narrowed eyes.

Shadow exchanged an uneasy glance with Gabe and his brothers. It was mid-morning, and they had risen late after a night spent exploring Venice and finding the *palazzo.* They had just finished breakfast and were actually debating whether to phone Romola when she had arrived, unannounced.

Despite her apology, she didn't look sorry at all. Romola was a striking woman with long, dark hair and flashing, intense eyes that were almost black. She had a light tan, and wore an elegant black trouser suit, tailored to fit her good figure. She was the epitome of an Italian businesswoman. Her smile was broad as she took them all in, no doubt noting all the details about them, too.

Gabe folded his arms across his chest. "It's just unexpected, that's all, and we take our privacy—especially in business matters—very seriously. But I guess that's why you just turned up. If you had asked to visit, I would probably have told you not to."

To her credit, she just laughed. "You've found me out! What's the expression?" she asked in her heavily accented English. "Sorry, but not sorry! And you'll be glad I did. Can I sit? Get a coffee? I'd love to go through what I've found, but I had an early start."

"Let me," Ash said, gesturing for her to sit and giving Gabe a look of resignation. "Nice apartment, by the way. I gather we have you to partially thank for that?"

"Yes, this place is one of our assets. Venice is packed with history and intrigue, so it's not surprising how often we have to come here to sort acquisitions of one type or another. Harlan," she said, placing her paperwork on the coffee table, "is very complimentary about you. We were happy to help a colleague." She sat on the sofa, at ease amongst strangers.

Shadow decided she didn't like Romola. It didn't mean they couldn't trust her, but she had dismissed Shadow with a tight glance, focussing all her attention on the men. A deliberate attempt to undermine another woman as she flashed her beaming smile around. Shadow had come across women like her before. She never liked them. They saw other women as a threat. To what, she wasn't sure. *Their feminine power? Their ability to control the room? Their wish to have all men's attention?* They were especially dismissive of other very attractive woman. Less attractive women could be humoured, but Shadow was good looking with a killer figure, and that would rile Romola more than anything. *That was fine.* Shadow liked being a threat, and was more than happy to play on such insecurities. She would remind her of her presence when it was needed. For now, she would stand back and watch.

"Have you been travelling all night?" Gabe asked as he sat opposite her. "You are based in Rome, I believe."

"Yes, but there's a fast train to Venice. A few hours' travel only, and very convenient. I caught the early train." She tossed her hair, leaning forward and beaming. "Is it your first time in Venice?"

"First time in Italy."

"And yours?" She turned to Niel, who had taken a seat, too.

"I came years ago. It has changed since I was last here."

"Same for me," Ash said, entering the room with a tray of cups and a pot of coffee. "I hardly recognise the place."

Shadow suppressed a smile. *Like several thousand years ago.* He had told her that Rome had just been a tiny village on a hill then.

"Well, I'm happy to take you all on a tour."

"Unfortunately," Gabe said, "we're not here for pleasure. We need to know more about the Lambertis. Then, we need to meet them."

Suddenly, Romola was all business. She lifted half a dozen sheets of paper and passed them to Gabe. "An outline of the Lambertis who have owned the *palazzo* over the years. I can confirm that Harlan was correct. The reference in the book that he found refers to the same family who own it now. I have focussed on *only* those who have lived there. The family is large and spread across the area. They were very powerful at one point. Now, less so." She wiggled her hand. "But still rich. They had connections to the Borgias once. Houses in Rome, the Amalfi coast, and Umbria. The *palazzo* here, though, was always considered the seat of the family." She accepted a cup of coffee from Ash, inhaling appreciatively. "Arabic?"

"Yes. It's how we prefer our coffee."

"Excellent. No complaints from me."

It was the one regular thing the Nephilim liked when they travelled, and they always packed a bag of ground coffee in their luggage. A quirk.

"Anyway," Romola continued, while Gabe and Ash scanned the list, "they have had less success over recent decades, and over the years a series of family deaths. I know because, as I said to Harlan, we have had dealings with them in the past. We all have our own clients, and the Lambertis aren't mine. Their contact within our branch retired years ago, and because we hadn't received work from them for years, they were never assigned to a new collector. Past purchases include religious statues and relics, mainly Christian but not all, old volumes of occult knowledge, nothing overly significant."

"And by that," Niel said, smiling, "you mean vastly expensive."

"Well, if you put it like that, yes. But over the years, it mounted up. Until twenty years ago. That's the last time they contacted us for anything."

"Any idea why?" Gabe asked.

"The son inherited the estate after his father died. The father, Enzo, was ancient. In his nineties. The eldest son, Tommaso, took over, and well, it seems he wasn't the collector his father was. He is now in his late eighties himself."

"You have been thorough," Ash noted.

"It's my job. Besides, we keep extensive records on our clients. The London office does, too. Anyway, I have decided to try to recruit them again. It will be a good excuse to visit them and get you inside." She smiled again, pleased with her ruse.

Gabe leaned back, the list ignored now that Ash had it. "I don't think so. We work alone. I'll pay you for your effort, of course."

Romola just smiled. "I know these types of families. You won't get in without having some kind of connection. I'm it. Although I'm sure they speak English, speaking Italian will also be helpful. Being one of them."

Gabe rattled off something in fluent Italian, and Romola gasped. There was a rapid exchange, during which Niel and Ash joined in, before Gabe switched to English again, for Shadow's benefit, of course. "So, you see," he said smugly, "communication will not be a problem."

"Well, aren't you dark horses." She turned for the first time in a while to look at Shadow. "And you?"

"Oh, I have my own hidden abilities."

Romola assessed her silently and then turned back to Gabe. "Nevertheless, you still won't get in without me. If you try and fail...well, you might not get a second chance."

"Neither might you if we go alone and upset them. I think your altruism is a ruse." Gabe leaned forward, elbows leaning on his knees, eyes locked with hers. To her credit, she didn't withdraw. Gabe wasn't being overtly threatening. He just was without even trying. "You need us, too. We only want information on one jewel. A ring. How will you help us?"

"I will ask about it, upfront. Say that we have been approached by a buyer who has heard of this ring and wants it. I will offer to broker a good price for it. One of you will be my assistant."

"Not the buyer?" Ash asked.

"No! We broker. We never introduce the buyer to the seller. How would we get our cut?"

Niel shrugged. "Sounds like a plan to me, Gabe. I presume we can ask questions, Romola?"

"Of course, although we should discuss what, first. We can ask to see it, too."

"He won't show it to you," Shadow said. "Not a chance. If they value it so much as they have in years past, he won't even admit to having it."

"We shall see, won't we?" Romola replied, gaze fixed on Gabe. Silence fell and she said, "I know what you're thinking. You're wondering if you could break in and find it. These *palazzos* guard many secrets, theirs probably more than most. We should at least try it my way first."

Gabe sidestepped the question. "What have you found out about Amato and his country house?"

"Ah, that! Well, that's where it gets interesting. It took a lot of digging, too." She reached for another set of papers. "It actually belonged to another member of the Lamberti family. One of Tommaso's nieces."

Gabe exchanged a jubilant glance with Shadow and his brothers. *Another connection.*

Ash set the list down and reached for the other set of papers. "Why did Amato end up with it?"

"I can't tell you *why*, of course, but I can say that the house belonged to her father, Tommaso's younger brother, for years. It passed to her the same year she got married. A wedding gift, I presume. That would have been forty or fifty years ago. But twenty years ago, just around when Enzo died, it ended up in Amato's name." Romola spread her hands wide. "I have no idea why!"

"Well, it can't be a coincidence that it was the same time that Enzo died," Niel said. "But why give away a house? A really great house!"

"Not just any house, though," Ash reminded him without elaborating.

A house with a temple to Belial in its grounds.

Gabe pressed her for more information. "For the last twenty years the family fortunes have been diminishing, according to you, Romola. Any idea why?"

"No." Romola eased back into her seat, legs crossed to give a flash of very expensive high-heeled shoes. "There's something you're not telling me. I can help—if you let me in on it."

Shadow was standing out of Romola's eyeline, and she shook her head at her brothers. Not that they needed her advice. Gabe was already answering her. "There's nothing to tell, other than this ring is rumoured to possess strange powers. Nothing you haven't experienced before in your line of work. It interests us. But more than the ring, we want to know how it came to be with the family in the first place. It connects to other avenues of our investigation."

"Your investigation," she repeated, her eyes sparkling. "This is getting more interesting by the minute."

"Nothing other than what you will have experienced before," Gabe reassured her. "And like I said. *Our* business. However, you have found out some great information, and we're very grateful. I take it your retired colleague couldn't elaborate?"

"I tried to contact him, but couldn't." She sighed with resignation. "Frustrating. I checked his files, of course. All paper, nothing on the computer from that time. However, there were no personal notes to cast any light on anything you asked me to find. My offer still stands, though." She looked at each in turn, Shadow included. "These old families are as cagey as you. They won't give up their secrets easily. As complete strangers, you won't have a chance. Me, with my connections, it's possible. I am used to keeping secrets. Just like Harlan."

Ash spoke quickly before Gabe could decline. "She's right, Gabe. We should accept her offer. We just need to decide who goes with her."

"I should," Shadow said, "for obvious reasons."

Gabe shook his head. "I know, but even so, I'm going. If we're not out after an hour, then you three come in and find us."

"Make that two hours," Romola said, shooting forward, eager to help, before Shadow could argue her point. "You can't rush these things. We will no doubt have to wait, then go through formalities. Niceties."

"Two hours!" Niel exclaimed. "That's nuts."

"Rich families like to keep people waiting," Romola shot back.

"An hour and a half," Gabe suggested. "A compromise. When do we go? Do you need to call to make an appointment?"

"No! That is one way to find our visit barred. We just go. I suggest this afternoon at three. A good time for afternoon coffee. It will give me time to shop for a gift. Something to go with a little present I already have." She smiled broadly as she stood up. "An artifact Tommaso won't be able to resist. A lovely religious icon I have been saving for a special moment such as this."

"You think of everything," Gabe said, unable to suppress a smile.

"I try. I'll return at half past two. I'm staying downstairs, in a smaller apartment, so nice and close. In the meantime, enjoy Venice."

Fourteen

"Theo! Good to see you," Harlan said, crossing to the old man's side and shaking his hand. "It's been a while. You look well!"

Theo beamed. "I've had plenty to keep me busy, and well, the anticipation of all this has kept me very happy!" He swept his arms out to encompass the Great Court of the British Museum. "We're on hallowed ground, old boy!"

Theo, despite his advancing years, was irrepressible. As usual, he was dressed in immaculate tweeds, no doubt bought at Saville Row, and his moustache and beard were oiled and groomed, his exuberant facial hair in sharp contrast to his bald head.

Harlan laughed. "I suppose we are. Any idea what we should expect today?"

"Aside from the large cheque, you mean? Hopefully champagne and a little publicity. My solicitor is already up there checking the paperwork. Can't be too careful!"

"You think the press will be here?"

"The British Museum's marketing team! I've been keeping in close contact, you know." He tapped his nose. "They have opening dates set for the summer. June, I think. Not sure which gallery yet. Guaranteed, though, this will draw a lot of attention. I intend that Temple Moreton will get lots of it."

"Won't that make your small, pretty village horribly busy?"

"We need the money. The church is desperate, and the local businesses will benefit from increased tourism. I will, of course, donate some of my money to the church for a new roof. We've already done some work in the crypt for accessibility."

Harlan had fond memories of the pretty village in the Weald of Kent, although not the fight with the Knights of Truth and Justice, or being held captive. Or having to cross the death trap that was the map room with the trick-slabs. "I must admit that it will be good to see the chamber well lit, without fear of my life."

"Oh, it's all safe now. The mechanisms have been disengaged. The access secured. We've even repaired the broken tombs." Theo's eyes shone with excitement. "It's quite something, you know. Obviously, it's not half as impressive without the vast quantity of treasure in it, but it's an impressive structure regardless. The other passage is still blocked, but has been secured with gates, and the roof has been repaired. Don't want anyone scurrying about under my keep!"

"So, you were able to reach an agreement with the church?"

"After a bit of wrangling." He rolled his eyes, and then his face cracked into a huge smile, directed behind Harlan.

Harlan turned to see Nahum and Olivia crossing the floor towards them, Barak, Estelle, and Lucien a few steps behind. Seeing Olivia and Nahum strolling side by side, relaxed and at ease, a certain closeness between them despite the fact that they weren't touching, he realised they were already a couple. They just didn't know it yet. He'd been worried that Nahum would do something stupid and abandon Olivia in a rush of fear or denial, leaving her alone. It had fuelled his own protective instincts. He now, however, realised how utterly stupid that was. Nahum wasn't going anywhere. It both reassured Harlan and left him feeling disappointed. He'd envisaged that he and Olivia might eventually end up together, their lifestyle aligning them, but that door had firmly closed now.

As for Olivia's job with The Orphic Guild, despite her protestations otherwise, that might well change, too. He smiled broadly as he greeted all of them, and he introduced Barak, Lucien, and Estelle to Theo.

"So, another brother," Theo said to Barak. "I take it you three were busy in France at the time?"

"*Oui*! Rescuing me," Lucien said as he shook Theo's hand. "You don't mind that I come to see the treasure?"

"Of course not. At least, I hope we'll see it. I take it that you," Theo addressed Estelle with a twinkle in his eye, "also have special skills?"

"You could say that." She smiled enigmatically, no trace of sarcasm in her tone. *Barak had indeed worked wonders.*

"Playing your cards close to your chest! Wise. Well," Theo said, all business, "now that we're all here, we'd better head to the main desk."

In a few minutes' time, they were escorted by a young woman through a door marked *Private*, along corridors, and upstairs, all well away from the public spaces, finally ending up in a large, spacious meeting room with half a dozen men and women gathered in earnest conversation. Reams of paperwork were stacked on the table, and a couple of men with cameras hovered nearby. Champagne and glasses waited on the side, and even a few select treasures were in the room, along with security staff.

Once the paperwork was signed, it was obvious that the marketing of the Templar treasure was about to begin.

"This is impossible," Maggie declared, throwing the list of names onto the table in Jackson's office, and glaring at Jackson. "I can't do anything about those! Have you lost your fucking mind?"

Jackson scowled. "I was hoping for some creative input!"

"I'm a police officer! I work with facts, not mumbo-bloody-jumbo!"

"They are not mumbo-jumbo! They are names of people who are involved with The Brotherhood!"

"Yes, Belial's bloody henchmen, I know!" She stabbed viciously at the page. "First name! Last name! Incomprehensible name! Do you think I have a list of bad guys in my desk that I can mix and match?"

Jackson rubbed his face wearily. "I know it's hard, but among those names we might strike gold. We already recognise the Lambertis."

"Well, jolly bloody hockey sticks!"

"Maggie! I argued to bring you in on this, the least you can do is stop ranting."

"And that's another thing! Why couldn't I be trusted with knowing about the Emerald Tablet?" That rankled more than anything. She had been so pleased to hear about it the previous night that she had just got on with it, but overnight she had seethed about it. "I should have been told straight away!"

"For fuck's sake, Maggie. Will you shut the fuck up and sit down!"

Maggie stepped back, gobsmacked. Jackson had never raised his voice to her before. He hardly ever swore, either. It was that more than anything that calmed her down. She had really pissed him off. "Sorry. I'm frustrated." She sat heavily in her chair, annoyance vanishing. "And thank you for arguing to include me. I just don't like being the last to find things out."

"You are not the last! Hardly anyone knows about this. It's The Emerald Tablet! Something of inestimable value and power. You don't just bandy it about in any old conversation. Your sergeants will never know about this, or I will never include you in anything again."

"Of course they won't! I'm not an idiot."

Jackson glared at her. "Are you done, then?"

"Yes. But I'm still right. That list is impossible. The best we can hope to do with it is recognise names as they crop up during research. Didn't you say that they could go back generations?"

"Yes." Jackson also sagged back in his chair, looking suddenly exhausted and defeated. "And span countries. They only recorded a fraction of them, too."

"I'm sorry. I really am. I know you've obviously put great store in these. Of course I'll bear them in mind, but Irving and Stan are busy on other cases. You've only got me. Let's focus on things I can do, like look at Jacobsen some more. Or look at the northeastern line, the direction the statues face. You say Barak wants to identify a city?"

"Yes, but that's insanity as well. I have nothing to show you. It's not like they took photos! Only Barak can help there."

"But, say that line is important. We can at least narrow down cities on it. Historical or current."

Jackson nodded as he pulled a folded map from the drawer in his desk. Like all the furniture in this room, it was of art nouveau design, complimenting the style of The Retreat. Maggie found the whole place suffocating, but the warm tones of the wood, and the soft light through the stained glass windows situated in the interior walls alleviated some of that. *Mostly.* When she wasn't ranting about stupid lists.

After clearing space on the coffee table, Jackson unfolded the large European map, and Maggie saw he'd already drawn a line in pencil partway across it. "This," he said, "is where the church is in Florence, and that spot is Amato's country house. I've extended it to Venice, but stopped in Poland when I hit the coast. I find it hard to believe anything will be so far north, but I could be wrong."

"Yorkshire is further north," Maggie pointed out.

"I know. It's not on the line, either." Jackson ran a hand though his shaggy hair. "I realise that Belial's agents could be anywhere, but the statues, I think, are part of something else."

"The root of everything," Maggie said, understanding his thinking.

"Yes. If we trace that line back, we hit Corsica. I thought it was Sardinia at first, but the line was wrong. Then we hit Algeria, Mauritania, and Senegal. I don't think we should focus there."

"Why not?"

"It feels wrong."

Maggie snorted. "*Feels* wrong? We need facts, not feelings."

"What can I say? I have a hunch. I think this is a European thing." He jabbed at Corsica. "I'd like to look there more closely."

"Why?"

"The description of the buildings that Barak saw makes it sound Mediterranean. It's French, but used to be Italian, and we have a lot of Italian links in this story."

Maggie patted his arm. "We work with what we have, and we don't make too many assumptions. We can't make our hunches fit facts that aren't there. That's one way to ruin any good investigation. It's called unconscious bias. You cast your net wide with Black Cronos. That's why you had success. We should do the same here."

Jackson gave her a wry smile. "Since when did you become so wise?"

"I always have been. Cheeky shit. Now, tell me about Corsica."

"Well, it's a French island..."

"Something I don't know."

"If you'd stop interrupting! It's the fourth largest Mediterranean island, and it has a long history of human habitation, the most notable being the Carthaginians and the Greeks. There's lots of prehistoric monuments there. The Etruscans were there for a while, and then the Romans took over."

"Wow. You have done your homework."

"The important thing is that there are old cities there. Maybe that's what Barak saw."

"Maybe. Let's not get ahead of ourselves. What about later years?"

"The Vandals and then the Byzantine Empire ruled. Then it became the Kingdom of the Lombards."

Maggie sighed as she settled into a chair. Jackson had become far too caught up in research and had lost track of his goals. "Let's focus on what we know, Jackson. Belial might be as old as the hills, and his jewels, but his agents are a more recent thing. At least as in the last few hundred years. That means we focus on closer timeframes. The church in Florence may have been a few hundred years old—"

"The temple underneath it, too, don't forget! The Nephilim said it was carved from rock."

"Yes, I know, but it could have been used for other things years ago and they repurposed it. The trap could have been added later, too. Amato's country house is also modern. Have you got a date?"

Jackson's face scrunched up as he considered her question. "No, but Harlan would know. I think three or four hundred years old, max."

"And again, whoever owned it could have been recruited at any point. Maybe even a hundred or so years ago."

Jackson smiled at her. "We focus on the last couple of hundred years, then."

"We consider it. No unconscious bias, remember. We also have to consider the relic that started this off, the one Olivia found. That's been around for hundreds of years too, but again, from the research that she did just to find it, she believes that the jewels were added only in the last hundred or so years. Why they picked that reliquary is still a mystery, but I guess that's something else we should add to the list." Maggie liked talking things through. It helped her thought processes. The more she talked, the more clarity she gained. She nodded at Jackson. "Yes. Let's focus on the last couple of hundred years. We won't exclude anything, but the facts are pointing in that direction. What might have happened a couple of hundred or so years ago to precipitate this?"

"Someone opened a portal and a Nephilim came through, if our discussion last night was correct."

"Perhaps. Why was there such a big hoard of jewels in the temple under the church?" Jackson just stared at her, puzzled. "I mean, why not spread that around, too? If the jewels are so destructive, why keep them there?"

"Maybe they hadn't found places for them."

"Perhaps. Or maybe they liked the collection of power there."

Jackson huffed. "Stop suggesting more things! This isn't helping!"

"It is. We must look at all angles." Her thoughts returned to their earlier conversation. "You say Romola gave Gabe a list of Lamberti family members?"

"Yes, and a list of a few other properties. Like Amato's place."

"Which we know was only passed to him twenty years ago."

"Yes."

"The names that Romola identified. Any of them on our list from the spell?"

"No."

"But that family is clearly involved. Or was. We know they were a couple of hundred years ago."

Jackson grinned for the first time in hours. "The alchemist. The one JD said went to the house about the jewel 'with strange properties.' That information is why we sent Gabe there now."

Maggie returned his grin. "Exactly! Now that's something tangible! Let's look at the dates in that diary." She stood abruptly, seized with conviction and the need to act.

"What? Now!" Jackson asked, rising to his feet, too.

"Yes. That family is involved! How did *they* get the jewel? And then why give the house away? They were involved, possibly deliberately, hundreds of years ago, and then something happened twenty years ago. Come on. We're going to JD's." Plus, she had an ulterior motive for going there. "Which means that we can see the amazing emerald cave, too!"

Fifteen

B arak smiled broadly for the camera, wishing he could put his fist through it instead.

The last hour had been tedious beyond belief. Guided by Theo's solicitor, who had examined the contracts in great detail for all of them, thankfully, he declared himself satisfied with the terms and amounts agreed upon. They had signed the paperwork, Nahum and Barak acting on behalf of the Nephilim and Shadow. Harlan and Theo each had their own identical agreements, as did the church representative from Temple Moreton who had arrived before all of them. Theo had been right. The amount of money involved—even for a portion of the agreed value, was astonishingly huge. They were all stupidly rich.

After the formalities were completed, the champagne flowed, and photos were taken. The museum staff were thrilled with the find. All of them who had been involved in its discovery were peppered with questions. There was a lot of lying involved. Of course, there was no mention of the knights and the near-death experiences, although the tricky episode in the map room was relayed—with reservations.

Even though Barak hadn't been there, he was part of the team who had, and of course Nahum had experienced the whole thing. Theo took centre stage, and that was fine with all of them. Barak posed for one final photo with Nahum and Theo and then retreated to stand with the others, who watched and chatted to each other, clearly amused by the whole event.

"I just want to get out of here," Barak confessed to all of them.

Estelle laughed. "Enjoy the champagne and the warm, fuzzy feeling of all that money, and just keep smiling."

He rolled his shoulders, trying to ease out kinks of knotted muscle. "I'm not a signing paperwork sort of guy."

"Neither am I," Lucien said, "but for that amount of cash, I'd stand here all day long. I was half expecting them to hand you a giant cheque, like on the lottery."

"Darling," Olivia drawled in an exaggerated tone, "this is the British Museum. It's far classier."

Barak smiled with his new sister-in-law of sorts. "Yes, it was just a big, whopping bank transfer to our account."

"Olivia!" Harlan called over. "Come and get a photo. A little extra publicity for The Orphic Guild."

She rolled her eyes, but clutching her orange juice, she crossed to his side. Nahum watched, face creased in concern. Barak understood his reservations. They were all paranoid about Belial and his agents, but that didn't mean they should put their lives on hold. Even though Olivia was pregnant with a Nephilim child. A first for thousands of years—or so they presumed. Lucien drifted away too, to examine the treasures laid out on a side table, and immediately a museum worker engaged him in conversation.

"You're getting as bad as Nahum," Estelle said softly, her gaze on Olivia, too.

"Are we paranoid?"

"Yes, but you have every right to be. I gather the Moonfell witches have made her an amulet, though. She's in good hands. And Nahum will keep her safe." Her dark eyes that glowed with passion for him alone now flashed with amusement. "He watches her like a hawk."

"I cannot find fault with that, or with the fact that he is falling in love. It's made me a happy man." Estelle's face flushed with pleasure. Barak angled his broad back to the room, hoping to put off anyone who might want to approach them, and leaned in for a sneaky kiss. "I've been mulling over that image of the city I saw in the spell yesterday. I can't place where it could be! Can you do anything to narrow it down?"

"No, unfortunately. The image was dragged from the manifesto, along with every other image that we saw. There's no way I can replicate it." She saw the disappointment in his face and squeezed his arm. "I'm sorry. I'm as frustrated as you. Why don't we focus on Jiri? What do you know about him that could help?"

She had asked this the previous evening, and he'd spent the night thinking over what little he knew. "Well, like I said, we didn't know each other, but he was based all across the Middle East. I was born in Africa, and I spent most of my time there, too. But that means nothing now. Look at us. We're in England!"

"True." Estelle huffed with disappointment. "The horn, then. Maybe we focus on that. There's nothing in the other images we saw that we can track down, interesting and informative though they were. Why did Jiri's image burst out of the manifesto, though?"

The flash of his wings filled Barak's vision again. "I think it was his power that was baked into it."

"You know, there is a group of very well-respected researchers behind you." Estelle nodded to the museum staff. "There are several different departments involved in the Templar treasure display. I doubt they'd have much to do with the time period we want. However, they might point us in the right direction."

Barak frowned. "You mean, someone might know about angelic horns?"

"They might. There are lots of Babylonian and Assyrian statues and art here. You saw them!" He couldn't miss them. It was as if he'd stepped back in time. "What if one of them knows about some special horn that was found on some dig?"

"That's nuts!"

She folded her arms, lips tightening. "Who cares? We should ask anyway. It would be stupid not to, now that we're here."

He too looked around at the gathered experts. "All right. I'm game. It beats kicking our heels while we wait to hear from Gabe."

They approached a middle-aged man dressed in a suit he looked very uncomfortable in. He ran his finger under his collar as he tried to loosen his tie. At the sight of Barak and Estelle approaching, however, he stood upright, beaming as he gripped Barak's hand. "I'm Samuel Dugan. I can't tell you how exciting this is. I have spent my life pouring over Templar documents. For you to have found a portion of the treasure is just breathtaking!"

Barak smiled and nodded, letting the man wax lyrical about the treasure before turning the conversation to more ancient matters.

Samuel frowned. "You're interested in ancient history? The Sumerians and Babylonians contributed much to our society. The true founders of the modern world. Not my specialty, of course."

"There is someone here, I presume, who we could talk to?"

Estelle flashed a huge smile. "Not in the room, we realise, but somewhere in the museum?"

He floundered for a moment at the change of subject. "Er, of course! We have a large department devoted to that era. Jenkins is the head of that particular team. I'm sure he would be happy to spare a few moments to speak to you."

They waited while Samuel called his colleague using a phone in the corner of the room. When he returned, he looked apologetic. "He can't see you right now, unfortunately, although he is thrilled to meet you! He suggests this afternoon. Would three o'clock suit? He can meet you in the main entrance."

Barak glanced at Estelle, and she nodded her agreement. "Excellent. This afternoon it is." Which would give him time to shake off the paper signing, eat lunch, and celebrate their enormous commission.

Gabe stood outside the main entrance of the *Palazzo* Lamberti, noting what he had failed to see the night before. That the old building was crumbling with age.

Romola clearly shared the same thought. "This place looks run-down. Neglected."

"Perhaps Enzo's death years ago precipitated a downturn in their fortunes."

"Perhaps. That could be why they no longer use our services." She wiggled the gift bag in her hand. "Let's hope that this is still well-received anyway."

They stood on a narrow street, one of many that laced through Venice, waiting for someone to answer the door. The bell had tolled deep within the house before falling silent. The Grand Canal was on the other side of the building, and Romola had told Gabe that the large entrances that many *palazzo*s had on the water were seldom used now. These small lanes crossed a multitude of narrow canals, and the scent of brackish water and dampness drifted around them. They stood in deep shade, the bulk of the surrounding buildings blocking out the light. Somewhere around them, well out of sight, were Shadow, Niel, and Ash.

The *palazzo*, however, despite its neglect, was magnificent. A mix of Byzantine and Moorish design, with embellishments over windows and doors. Gabe doubted that the interior would be as well preserved as their apartment, if the exterior was anything to go by.

Just as Romola lifted her hand to call the bell again, the door swung open, and a thin, sharp-eyed woman answered the door. She looked at them suspiciously before launching rapidly into a conversation designed to send them away. Just as effusively, Romola introduced herself and argued her point, before lifting the gift bag. Like any Italian conversation, it was voluble and full of gesticulations.

The woman sniffed, and then grudgingly let them in with an instruction to wait. Romola took a deep breath, sighing out her next words. "Well, that was harder than I thought."

"But we're in."

They stood in an imposing hall with a high ceiling. The plasterwork was detailed, and the paint was rich in colour. Deep reds on one wall contrasted with deep blue on another. But it was faded in places, and the glimpse offered through open doorways to either side showed that the rooms were devoid of furnishings. Still, it had a grand atmosphere that begged to be restored.

Romola explained, "The lower levels can flood, and were used for deliveries. They are hardly ever furnished. Everyone lives on the upper floors. Unless, of course, extensive work has been done. Flooding is an ever-present issue in Venice, as I'm sure you can imagine. St Mark's Square floods constantly. Have you been there yet?"

"We walked through it last night."

"You must visit St Mark's Basilica. It's magnificent."

Gabe wasn't sure he wanted to see such a monument to the old God he despised, despite its magnificent exterior that dominated the square, but he nodded anyway. *Perhaps he should. Beautiful artwork and creation should always be appreciated.* "Of course. We'll go before we leave."

He fell silent, both hoping and dreading that he should feel Belial's presence, but he felt nothing. A sharp voice called them from above, and Gabe realised that the housekeeper, if that's what she was, had summoned them. On reaching the next floor, everything changed. Opulent rugs covered sumptuously tiled floors, and oversized light fittings dangled from magnificently high ceilings. Furniture dressed in brocades, silks, and velvets was everywhere, as were the rich patinas of wood, Venetian mirrors, and huge oil paintings. Unfortunately, age tarnished everything, despite its cleanliness. There was visible wear and tear, and Gabe felt a pang of sadness for the house as it slid into decrepitude.

The housekeeper, however, was already leading the way down a long passage to a set of double doors, and with a peremptory knock, she threw one door open and ushered them inside. Gabe blinked in the bright light, taking a moment to focus after the dark corridor. Four tall windows overlooked the Grand Canal, and for a moment Gabe drank in the view before he turned and took in the rest of the space. This room was also richly decorated, the walls a beautiful, soft rose pink. For a moment, Gabe thought it was empty, and then he saw an old man seated by a blazing fire, a rug draped over his knees.

"*Signor* Lamberti," the housekeeper announced, and literally pushed them to the chairs positioned next to him. "I will bring coffee."

Romola hurried over, heels clicking on the tiled floors before sinking into the plush carpet. She kissed him on either cheek. "*Signor* Lamberti. Such an honour to meet you. This is my esteemed colleague, Gabreel Malouf."

Gabe shook his hand, trying to hide his shock. Tomasso Lamberti was a sick man. He was thin, gaunt even, his skin clinging to his bones, his eyes large in such sunken features. Gabe could feel his fragile bones in his hands, and he immediately slackened his naturally strong grip. "An honour, sir."

Lamberti nodded and wheezed, gesticulating to the chairs opposite. "Take a seat. Aria will be back soon with coffee."

Romola took the lead as she sat elegantly. She wore a different suit this time; a skirt, jacket, and silk blouse, and her heeled ankle boots were of supple leather. She crossed her legs, but leaned forward attentively. "Thank you, *Signor*. I realise that this is an imposition to visit without an appointment. However, I was in Venice on business, and..."

He cut her off. "No doubt you are in Venice on business many times. If I remember The Orphic Guild correctly, you were always here, trading secrets and occult objects." He nodded to the bag at her feet. "You want to trade secrets now, I warrant."

Gabe couldn't help smiling. The old man may be sick, but he was fully in control of his faculties.

Romola also smiled, barely missing a beat. "You know the game well. I should have come to see you before. Obviously, our business lost touch with your family when your father died. My condolences."

He batted a hand as if brushing her words away. "That was years ago. His contact there came to see me months later. I sent him away. I had no use for your business then, and no need now."

"And yet you let us in," Romola pointed out.

He smiled, revealing yellow, uneven teeth. "I was curious as to what *gift* you had brought. Besides, Aria said you were beautiful. I have always appreciated that."

Before Romola could answer, Aria bustled in with a tray of coffee and placed it on the small table next to Lamberti. She poured their drinks, slowly and deliberately, and Romola reached into her bag for the delicate biscuits she had bought. One of her many gifts. "To go with coffee," she said, smiling.

Once Aria had gone, the pleasantries continued. Gabe was amused by it all, and he sat back, knowing the conversation would take its own course, and there was nothing he could do to rush it.

"I take it," Lamberti said, "that there are more than just biscuits in that bag."

"Of course, but let's not rush," Romola answered. "I must savour your delicious coffee first." She glanced around the room. "I reviewed your father's records. A few of the items we helped him find are in here. I saw some in the hall, too."

Lamberti's face twisted in displeasure. "Yes, he spent a lot of money on such things."

"You don't approve."

"I like beautiful things, as you can see, but his obsession with religious trifles was annoying."

Romola's face fell. "Ah. In that case, you may not want what I have brought you. Nevertheless, it is a gift."

"I shall hold my judgement until I see it. I have no objection to religion as such, we were brought up Catholic, but he was obsessed. It was unhealthy. When he died, I sought to distance myself from such things." His eyes clouded over, and Gabe paid closer attention. *'Unhealthy' was interesting. Was this about the ring?*

"But," Romola continued, looking puzzled, "you still have some religious iconography here. If you wish to sell it, I can help."

"Oh, I got rid of some. But tell me about The Guild. Are you still busy?"

For a while, Romola chatted easily about the market and the work they did. They talked of old names known to both of them, and Gabe realised that like in England, this world was tight knit, and old families all knew each other, despite Lamberti's protestations that he had left it behind. Gabe remained silent, focussing on feeling for any signs of Belial. The Fallen Angel, though, was stubbornly quiet.

With a shock, Gabe realised Lamberti was addressing him. "You don't look much like the office type."

He smiled. "I'm a field worker. I have a specific interest in Venice."

"Religious iconography, too?"

Gabe decided to cut to the chase. There had been a lot of endless chitchat. "Of a sort. Fallen Angels, actually."

Lamberti's hand shook violently and the small, delicate cup he was holding fell to the floor and rolled across the rug. Romola was also shocked, but she recovered quickly and instinctively lunged for it. Gabe's attention remained fixed on Lamberti's face.

Lamberti's voice was hoarse. "I knew you had come here for a reason. What do you want?"

"I heard rumours of a powerful and unusual ring that your family was supposed to possess. I would like to see it."

From the expression of dread on Lamberti's face, frozen in masklike horror, Gabe knew he didn't need to elaborate. However, he tried to lie. "I have no idea what you're talking about."

"Of course you do. I can smell your fear. I have no wish to drag up bad memories, or to cause you any harm. In fact, I will do you a favour and take the ring away. It has no place in civilised society."

A measure of calm returned to Lamberti's face, and he wiped his brow with a fine linen handkerchief. "What makes you think such a ring is here?"

"Aside from your panicked expression? Something recorded in a diary, years ago." Gabe gave him a brief explanation. "The entry was about your family. And then, of course, there's the ex-residence of your niece, now falling to ruin in Palazzuolo sul Senio. The temple in the grounds is of particular interest to me."

Lamberti started wheezing, gasping for breath, his wizened frame buckling over.

Romola glared at Gabe. "Are you trying to kill him? Grab some water." She pointed to the jug of water on another side table, and then scrambled to help Lamberti upright.

Gabe, feeling horribly guilty, but also vindicated in their investigations, poured a glass of water and helped the old man recover. "I'm sorry. Take a moment."

Lamberti glared at him, sharp black eyes boring into his. When he finally spoke, it was with a whisper. "How do you know about that damn temple?"

"Someone tried to kill me. I take it very personally. I decided to get to the root of it. Why don't you tell me what you know, and then I'll leave you in peace." He sat down again, knowing his bulk looming over the old man wasn't going to help him relax. "I have no issue with you. I just want the ring, and to find out why you seem to be linked to Belial."

"Not me!"

"Your family, then."

Romola was now looking at Gabe with tight-lipped annoyance. Not surprising, seeing as he hadn't mentioned anything about Fallen Angels earlier. He'd rather she didn't know now, but needs must. Plus, it was a good test as to what she knew. *Not much*, he'd say so far.

Tomasso's voice had become a dry rasp. "If I tell you, will you leave me in peace?"

"Of course. But I want the ring."

"It's gone!" he huffed, outraged. "I sold it after my father died."

Gabe leaned forward. "Who did you sell it to?"

"One of my father's contacts. One of the..." he faltered. "A business colleague."

"I think you were going to say The Brotherhood."

Lamberti blinked. "How do you know that name?"

"I do my homework. If you have heard of them, then you know what that ring is and why it's so dangerous. I bet you know a lot more, too. Where is it?"

"Somewhere you will never find it."

"You'll be surprised what I can find."

Sixteen

"This is unreal," Jackson said, blinking as he took in the entrance to the emerald cave in JD's marquee. "I think I'm hallucinating."

"In that case," Maggie declared, "we both are. What the actual fuck…"

"Anna," Jackson said, whirling around to look for JD's assistant who had walked over with them, "have you been inside?"

She puffed up. "No! I have nothing to do with JD's work. I just feed him and keep his house clean."

"But this is The Emerald Tablet! He's actually cracked it! I mean, you saw it, right? You know what he was doing."

"Of course I saw it. It was hard to miss. One of his more impressive results, I admit, but when you've known him as long as I have, it just becomes one of the many things he's achieved."

She really was an interesting woman. To live and work with a genius, and yet have nothing to do with his work. It was its own form of madness. And yet, maybe she was the sanest one of them all. *Best to keep out of JD's business.*

"I'll leave you to it," she said, backing away.

Then it struck him. "Holy shit! You're like him. Immortal." Anna smiled, confirming everything. "For how long?"

"Long enough." Her eyes sparkled with mischief, and suddenly Anna, the dour and disapproving woman, became far more interesting. *Another immortal…* JD must value her more than he had ever let on. Refusing to elaborate, she exited the tent, saying, "I'll see you later."

Jackson looked at Maggie. "Can you believe that?"

Her hands were on her hips, lips clenched tight, her eyes boring into his. "Fucking *immortal*? How many other fucking secrets are you keeping from me, Jackson?"

"Oh, shit!" *Why had he forgotten that Maggie didn't know about JD?* "Oh well, one less secret to keep."

Maggie didn't budge. "Anything else, before we step inside? And perhaps some details now might be nice!"

"Er, can this wait until we've seen JD? I promise to answer all your questions later." *Fuck.*

"No! How old are we talking?"

"JD is about five hundred years old. Give or take."

"Five hundred!" Maggie staggered backwards, hands gripping the back of a chair. "How?"

"He's an alchemist. I have no idea! But clearly, he values Anna. And no, I have no idea how old *she* is."

"How long have you known?"

"Years. A few of us in the PD know. Layla and Waylen. Russell never knew." *Thankfully. Although, would it have mattered? The Comte de St Germain knew anyway.* "Olivia, Harlan, and Gabe and his brothers know, too. It sort of came out during the jobs we did with him."

"You owe me!" Maggie prodded him in the chest, fury rising. "The last to know about that, too!"

"To be fair though, Mags, you don't know him or work with him. Your paths never cross. So, why would you know?"

She regarded him silently, obviously wrestling with her emotions. "I suppose that is true. I know him by reputation only as head of The Orphic Guild. Damn it, I'm still cross, though! Is he someone famous? I would like to know before I actually meet him."

"Well, yes actually, you might know his name. It depends how much of a history buff you are." Jackson knew most people would never have heard of him.

"Try me."

"He's John Dee. He was Queen Elizabeth's court magician."

"Queen Elizabeth the first?"

"Well, yes. It clearly wasn't the second, you tit!" He presumed shock was addling her brain.

Maggie took a moment to gather herself. "Well, obviously I have heard of her! But him, no. I have no idea who he is."

"Well, don't tell him that. In fact, just don't mention it at all." Jackson was sure she knew that the Count of St Germain was immortal because she'd helped his research. Consequently he'd assumed she knew about JD, too. His head hurt just thinking about it. "Can we go now? The big, green cave awaits."

"Just give me a moment!" She sat heavily on the chair, looking like a smaller version of the Maggie he knew. "You've had a long time to get used to this news. It's a shock to me. I know you've talked about him, and the advancements he's made with alchemical weapons, and that he's been tracking Black Cronos, but I didn't know he is immortal!"

Jackson rubbed his face and sat next to her, suddenly weary. "You know, I'd actually forgotten you didn't know, and to be honest, in the course of normal conversation, it doesn't come up. It's just JD doing his thing! I'm sorry."

"I'm in your pack! Your alpha—according to you. I feel an idiot."

"Maggie, you're not an idiot. I forgot. I bet Harlan and Olivia forgot, too. Well, maybe not Harlan. It's like he keeps lists of this shit. But you can't tell Stan or Irving."

"Of course not." *Blimey.* She was so shocked that she'd forgotten to swear. "So, his huge library and diaries, and all of that stuff you've talked about...did he acquire it over his lifetime?"

"Of course. He was there for a lot of it, or was passing through places and then heard news about various things. It's why he's so smart. He was already a genius in his lifetime. Now, with hundreds of years of study under his belt, well..."

"Wow." Maggie took a deep breath and exhaled slowly. "Okay, I'm fine. Let's walk into the Emerald Tablet, shall we?"

He grinned. "I bet you didn't think you'd be saying that when you woke up this morning."

"Oh, fuck off you smug bastard! Let's get in there."

She marched down the green passage, leaving Jackson running to catch up. He'd meant to savour this moment, and now he was rushing. *Bloody Maggie.* He slowed, letting her race off alone, and examined the walls and floor, trying to commit it all to memory. It was surreal. Like walking through a dream. It was an even weirder sensation when he actually reached the cave itself. The pillars towered around him, covered with endless lines of text. *Incredible.* It stretched in all directions. Harlan hadn't fully described the enormity of it. *But how could he?*

A bellow from somewhere ahead of him made him sprint, but it was Maggie's strident voice that set him in the right direction.

"Calm down! I'm not a stranger!" she yelled. "I'm Maggie Milne, DI with the Paranormal Policing Team. I'm here with Jackson Strange."

By the time he found her, Maggie had her hands up, backed against an emerald pillar, while JD pointed one of his weapons at her.

Jackson shouted, "JD! She's with me! It's okay."

"It's not bloody okay! I could have shot her. I thought she was an enemy agent!"

"From whom? Your house is wrapped up with state-of-the-art defence systems. It took me ages to get Anna to let me in the gate!"

JD scowled and lowered the weapon. "You can never be too sure! You're a detective?"

"Yes!" she said, still annoyed.

"You should have warned me, Jackson!"

"How? Anna left us here and there's no mobile phone coverage. Now, can we forget the mundane and talk about this!" Jackson stretched his arms wide and spun around, the height and breadth of the cave overwhelming. "This is insane! And you look terrible." He studied JD up close. The light made him look sickly. "Have you slept?"

"A couple of hours, perhaps. I'm trying to map this out before I do anything else. I understand hardly any of it, though. I'm waiting for the Nephilim."

"Nahum and Olivia will be here soon. Is there anything here that can help fight Belial and The Brotherhood?"

"I doubt it! You'll be better off looking in my library."

"That's what we were hoping to do, actually. You don't mind? We want the diary you showed Harlan."

"It's all on the table. I found a few other things for him about that alchemist. There might be more entries about Lamberti, too." He groaned, looking uncomfortable. "I slept badly. It's this place, I think. It manifests a weird energy."

Jackson had been so shocked by the enormous emerald cave with its towering pillars that he'd barely noticed the atmosphere, but now that JD had drawn his attention to it, he realised there was a strange hum that was almost imperceptible. "I feel it. Where does it come from?"

"I don't know. Magic, perhaps? I have found no obvious source of power. No sign of habitation, obviously."

"What about the fire?" Maggie pointed to a column of flame a short distance away. "And the lanterns? I presume you didn't light them."

"No. All already lit when I entered. It's as if Hermes walked out of here and just left it, and then shrank everything into the tablet. Brilliant."

"Or terrifying," Maggie said, looking darkly at Jackson. "What if there is a strange power here? It could blow up. Take half the county with it."

"There is no 'what if!'" Jackson pointed out.

"You sound as bad as Harlan," JD complained.

Maggie was right to be worried. The longer Jackson stood there, the more uncomfortable he became, and the more eager he was to leave. However, he had one more piece of news to share. "JD, I've accepted the offer to become Deputy Director of the PD. Russell's old job."

JD's eyes narrowed. "Have you now? Good. You'll do an excellent job. I told Waylen as much."

"You suggested me?"

"Why not? Your family has provided great service in the past. Your grandfather included. You deserve it."

"Thanks, JD! I didn't know."

"It was logical."

"So, has Waylen mentioned about the lab?"

"No, but I can guess what's coming. He's dropped some big hints."

Jackson laughed. It seemed Waylen had been having a few conversations lately. "Will you help, then? Oversee the lab? I can't."

JD's features softened. "I will. But they'll need to pull their socks up. That Lyn should work out, though. Diligent. Organised. I like her."

"Good. Thank you." Another weight lifted off Jackson's shoulders. *This might actually work out.* "Well, there's nothing we can do to help you here. We'll leave you to it, JD."

JD just nodded, already distracted, and Jackson and Maggie left him to his thoughts. By mutual agreement, neither said much, both absorbed by the enormity of what they'd seen. Jackson led the way to the library, feeling the residual effects of the cave slowly leave him. On arrival, he headed to the large table in the middle.

"You're as disturbed by that cave as I am, right?" Maggie asked, when the door was shut behind them and they were alone.

"Of course! It's unnatural, filled with all sorts of arcane knowledge. However, just because we don't understand it, doesn't mean we should be scared of it."

"Yeah, well, I'll reserve my judgement on that. And on him!"

"As unconventional as he is, I've learned to trust him. Over the years he has been an asset to our country, time and time again. He destroyed Black Cronos's stronghold. The Nephilim couldn't have done it without him. He founded MI6!"

Jackson had worked hard to put his kidnapping behind him. He was still left with a few nightmares. Occasionally, he woke up in a cold sweat. Over the past weeks he had dedicated time to tracking down any remaining Black Cronos bases, but it was hard. Belial was actually proving a welcome distraction—sort of. A large stack of books was on the corner of the table, and he reached for a sheet of paper perched on top of them with JD's familiar scrawl on it.

"Yep, that's the pile of new information he found for us."

"With lots of helpful little stickers," Maggie noted, thumbing the first book on the stack. "This will take hours."

Jackson nodded. "It will be worth it, though."

"Will it, if the information is years old?"

"This is no time to get picky." Jackson slipped his jacket off and reached for a thick, leather-bound volume. "Best get started. By the time Nahum gets here, we might have something useful to share."

Seventeen

Niel sheltered in a shadowed doorway, watching the main entrance of the Lamberti house. Gabe had entered a while ago, and the intersecting lanes had remained generally quiet, the foot traffic light.

He scanned the street, knowing that Ash was situated close to the front of the building, and Shadow had clambered up the walls to find shelter on a narrow balcony. She'd climbed like a monkey, frighteningly quick, reminding him of that fact she was a thief in the Otherworld, and to be honest, was here, too. He had lost sight of her, and presumed she had entered the *palazzo*.

He was uneasy about this situation, and wasn't sure what he thought of Romola. He wondered where she and Gabe were, and hoped that Gabe would learn something useful.

Movement down the narrow lane caught his attention. Six men were approaching, and they looked far from casual. They wore dark clothes, and their eyes darted everywhere. Niel drew back further into the deep doorway, glad that the lanes were so dark. They paused outside the main door and waited. In moments, the door opened, revealing a glimpse of the housekeeper, and the men slipped inside.

Herne's hairy bollocks. Something was wrong.

As a precaution they had packed their tiny earpieces that connected to their phones, and he quickly called Ash. His response was worrying. "Two men are here, too," he whispered. "They are blocking the escape route to the water."

"You watch them. I'm going in," Niel said. "I'll warn Shadow and Gabe."

After a clipped confirmation from her, and a quick text to Gabe that he hoped he'd see in time, Niel used the skeleton keys that they were all now familiar with, and entered the cool hallway. The six men and the housekeeper were nowhere in sight, but he could hear two voices from somewhere on the ground floor.

The stairs took up the bulk of the entrance hall, and he edged around them. The room to his right was empty, but ahead was another couple of doors. One door was shut, but the other was partially open, and the voices were beyond that. A rapid, almost whispered conversation was taking place in Italian—a man and a woman's voice. Glancing uncertainly up the stairs, Niel reassured himself that Shadow would be investigating, and he crept closer until he was right outside the door.

He caught flashes of the conversation. Whispers of a ring. Betrayal. Weakness. Stupidity. The woman was furious. "I should have poisoned him while I had the chance. Old, decrepit fool."

"We had our reasons for keeping him alive, but no matter. It will be done today. He will die with the others."

"But we need to know who they are, and how they know!" The woman insisted. "He is not alone!"

"Don't worry. We'll find out. Although, we already suspect. We have had trouble lately."

Niel gripped his knife, JD's weapon in his other pocket. Much to his annoyance, strolling the streets of Venice with his axe was not okay. With the rapid conversation still continuing, Niel pushed the door open, revealing a virtually empty room. A narrow window allowed for a view of the lane to the side of the building, and a sliver of the canal. The man's back was to him, but the woman was facing his direction. She glanced at the door and her eyes widened in shock. Niel threw his knife before she could speak. It plunged into her forehead, and she crumpled to the ground.

The man spun, a knife in his hand, too. He threw it with speed and accuracy, but Niel was already running to the side, and it hit the plaster behind him and embedded in the wall. Niel pulled it free. The man raced towards him, crunching into Niel, and they both hit the floor hard.

Niel, however, was bigger and stronger, and although his opponent was quick, he was no match for Niel's paranormal strength. He rolled, smashing the man's head down on the hard, tiled floor. He straddled him, pinning him into position, and covering his mouth with his hand so he couldn't speak.

The man bucked under him, trying to move, but Niel smacked his head down again, and he fell back, dazed. Niel listened for signs of movement, but the house was ominously quiet. He needed to get moving and see what was happening upstairs, but the man could have valuable information. Killing him was not an option. *Yet.*

Unless Shadow kept one alive. He almost laughed out loud at that idea.
Idiot.

"It's your lucky day, you shit-bag," he said to the man. He punched him, hard, knocking the man out cold. He retrieved both knives, locked the door, and headed upstairs.

The tall double doors that opened onto the narrow balcony did not fit securely, and Shadow had eased one open and edged inside as soon as she accessed the balcony on the second floor.

The bedroom beyond was filled with dark, heavy furniture, and looked unused. She crossed to the door and explored the upper floor, hearing faint voices from downstairs where Gabe was talking with Romola. She assumed this floor was hardly utilised. It was clean, but dust sheets covered most of the furniture. She hunkered down behind the wooden balustrade, safe in the knowledge that the dark landing and her own fey magic would hide her. The woman who had let Gabe in hovered on the hall below. She was listening to their conversation. When she disappeared into another room and made a hurried phone call, Shadow wasn't surprised when Niel texted ten minutes later. *Six men incoming. I'll tell Gabe.*

She heard the entrance door open below and the faint carry of voices. After a few minutes, five men ascended the stairs, and she readied her blades. *Who were they? What did they want? And why so many of them?* They clearly did not mean for anyone to escape.

Shadow calculated her chances. She could take out a couple quickly, but not without alerting the others. They were too close to each other. But did she care if she made a noise? *Yes.* She needed to allow Niel time to enter. The main entrance was out of sight from her position. With luck, he was already inside. Four of the men progressed down the hall, leaving one positioned at the top of the stairs.

Shadow jumped down, vaulting over the balcony and landing directly behind him, as stealthy as a cat. The man was short and stocky. "Is there a problem?" she asked, blades already in her hands, back to the wall so she could see the room at the far end where Gabe was, and where the four men had already entered. She should give them a chance to explain themselves. Who knew? It could be another business proposition.

The man whirled around to face her. "Who the hell are you?" he asked in broken English, a slim blade appearing in his hands.

"Your worst nightmare. And you?"

"You have no idea what you're dealing with."

"Then tell me."

"I'd rather kill you."

She smirked. "You can try." She released her fey glamour, her otherness flowing out of her as she spun her knives dexterously. He staggered back, eyes widening in shock, but he quickly recovered and lunged at her. He was far too slow. She cut his throat and he crashed to the floor, blood pooling around him.

Worrying what was happening with Gabe, she turned to run to the door, just as Niel rounded the turn in the stairs. "Gabe?" Niel asked, reaching her side.

"That way."

They turned and ran together.

Ash decided not to act against the two men who had arrived in a small motorboat, killing the engine and drifting to the wide porch that led into the Lamberti house. Fortunately, there were stacks of mooring equipment and old crates outside, all damp and rotten, and Ash sheltered behind them and huddled down to listen.

The men disembarked quietly, watching the river in case anyone else approached, but they didn't seem worried. They stood close, conversing quietly, and their conversation was revealing.

Ash and his brothers had thought there was only one family associated with Belial and The Brotherhood in Venice—the Lambertis. They were wrong. There were at least two other families involved, maybe more, and they were worried. The Nephilim and Shadow had created trouble, and the smooth running of their organisation was threatened.

Then Ash heard something else that made his blood run cold. There was a meeting that night on the neighbouring island of Murano to discuss *the Nephilim issue*. They were presuming one would be dead before the day was out. *Gabe.* Ash glanced up, trusting that Gabe could hold his own before the others arrived to help. In the meantime, Ash decided he would gather as many details as he could without being detected.

It seemed that Venice was a nest for The Brotherhood.

When Gabe read Niel's text, he realised there were two possibilities here.

Either Lamberti was stalling and had sent for backup via his housekeeper, or Lamberti had no idea that half a dozen men had just silently entered his house, betrayed by the woman who looked after him. Then he added a third option—Romola was in on it, too. Either way, Gabe needed to move quickly. He had mere minutes to act, and Lamberti had barely shared anything useful.

"On your feet, Lamberti." He grabbed the man's thin arm and pulled him up. He was astonishingly frail, and Gabe flinched when he realised how thin he was.

Lamberti cried out, sinking back into his chair. "Stop. What are you doing?"

"We have company. Is this your doing?"

"W-what?" He stuttered, outraged, looking from Romola to Gabe. "What is going on?"

There was genuine confusion and pain on his face, and suddenly Gabe felt like a monster. "You don't know."

Romola looked equally shocked. "Gabe! What are you talking about?"

"The door in the wall behind you. Where does it go?"

"It's my bedroom." Lamberti's face drained of what little colour he had. "They have come for me. This is *your* doing!"

"They have come for all of us!" Gabe didn't have time to argue. He weighed his options, and decided he had to protect Romola and Lamberti. Once he had hidden them, he'd face the intruders alone. "Romola, get in that room and find a place to hide. *Signor* Lamberti, I'm going to carry you."

He scooped the man up like a child, aghast at how light he was, and ran into the bedroom, taking it in with one swift glance. Another door was on the other side of the room. Lamberti wheezed with pain.

"I'm sorry. Where does the other door go?"

"My bathroom. There's nowhere to hide in there. Or here! It's my bedroom!"

Romola had other ideas. "Gabe, the wardrobe. It's huge."

A monstrous, heavy wardrobe ran along one wall, deep enough to hide in. Romola had already pulled one of the doors open and started pushing clothes aside. Fearing the door to the other room would burst open in seconds, Gabe deposited Lamberti on the floor of the wardrobe. Romola clambered in next to him, pulling clothes over them, and Gabe shut the door, hoping he hadn't just locked Lamberti in with a killer. He then placed a heavy chair under the other exit, and ran back to the main room.

Gabe was just in time. He took his jacket off, prepared to unfold his wings if necessary, and unsheathed his short blades that were strapped to his forearms. He stood in front of the fireplace, facing the door. Four men entered, looking calm and composed, but their expression darkened as they saw Gabe waiting. All carried daggers.

The oldest man of the four, who had silvered hair at his temples but nevertheless looked fit and dangerous, paused just inside the doorway, and the others fanned out on either side.

"Can I help you?" Gabe asked. "I wasn't expecting anyone to join my meeting."

The man ignored his question, eyes darting around the room before settling on Gabe again. "Where is Mr Lamberti and the woman?"

"Busy. No introductions? Who are you?"

"Who we are is of no concern to you. You will be dead in a few minutes, as will the others. We *will* find them. I presume they are in the next room." He shrugged, his lips twisting into a grim smile. "It is just a matter of time." He stepped forward, the other men advancing with him, one heading towards the door to the bedroom.

"Not so fast." Gabe stepped across their path to block the door. "Ah, yes. Time. But *you* are running out of it, not me. I am on to you now. The Brotherhood. Or The Consortium, as you were once called. Your dirty little intrigues that are intent on spreading Belial's darkness. His tokens that you have sprinkled around. I will find them all."

If the man was surprised by Gabe's knowledge, he hid it well. "You pretend you act alone, but you don't. Is that how you knew that we were here? You have eyes on the building. No matter. We will find them, too."

Without another word he threw his blade with a deft flick of his wrist. His movement was so subtle, so smooth, that Gabe barely saw it, but he had faster reflexes than most. He dived to the floor, rolling behind the huge armchair that Lamberti had sat in. He threw one blade while in motion, aiming for the closest man. He struck him in the throat, and he crumpled to the floor, hands clutching at the hilt.

A flurry of knives followed, pinning Gabe in position. He picked up the chair, using it as a shield and a battering ram, and ran at the man who had been doing all the talking. Gabe crunched into him, knocking him to the floor.

Simultaneously, the door flew open and Niel and Shadow burst in. A short but furious fight followed. The men were agile and swift, but were ultimately no match for two Nephilim and a fey. Within moments, all lay dead.

"Fuck it," Gabe said, pulling his blades from the dead and wiping them on their clothes. "I had hoped to ask more questions. Where are the others?"

"I have one captive downstairs, Shadow killed another on the landing, but Ash is watching two more by the dock. The housekeeper is dead," Niel told him. "Where are Lamberti and Romola?"

"Safe, I hope. I'll check on them in a moment."

Shadow crossed to the window and looked at the Grand Canal below. "There's a boat down there. Must be owned by Ash's men."

"Go and check it out," Gabe instructed. "Be careful. Do not compromise Ash."

"You might need this," Niel said, throwing her the key. "I locked one room."

She nodded and vanished with her normal flash of fey glamour.

Gabe grimaced as he surveyed the dead. "I had hoped to avoid this. There must be others involved in Venice. Lamberti better start answering some questions."

Shadow avoided the locked room, and instead headed into the one next to it.

Its plaster work was crumbling, and the paint was faded, but one tall window looked out onto the small dock beyond. Two huge doors took up the rest of the space. It was a place to unload supplies. She crossed the floor silently and edged to the window.

Two men stood talking quietly as they overlooked the river. If she could open the doors, she could kill them easily, but the locks looked clunky and rusted, and no doubt that would make a noise. *Perhaps that wouldn't matter*, she reflected. *But where was Ash?*

Worried for his safety, she studied the shadows beyond the window. She doubted the men would have caught him off-guard, but where was he? The area was full of old crates, mouldering bits of rope, and other water-related paraphernalia. Fortunately, the men weren't looking in her direction at all. Plus, the windows were grimy, and the room was dark behind her. She pressed her face to the glass, peering to either side, and finally spotted a figure coiled in the corner.

Ash.

There was no way she could attract his attention. Any minute now, the men would be asking questions about what was going on upstairs. As she watched, one reached for his phone, and she heard the ringtone in the room next door. *Herne's hairy bollocks!* It belonged to the man Niel had knocked out. And it rang and rang and rang. The man turned, confused, and Shadow realised that he could hear it outside.

Not entirely sure what would happen, but fearing he might call for support, she acted quickly. She smashed the window with the butt of her dagger, and both men whirled around. She threw her knife at the man on the phone, and her blade plunged into his chest, killing him instantly. But before she could attack the second, Ash leapt from behind the crates and killed him after a very quick, muffled struggle.

Ash hauled the man behind the crates, and Shadow leapt through the broken window, helping him dispose of the other.

"I should have known it was you, Shadow. I was listening to them!"

"He could have been about to call for help!"

"You don't know that!"

"Oh, come on, the odds are strong. We've killed everyone except a captive. We do not want more turning up."

Ash paused, hands on hips as he surveyed the Grand Canal, but no one was paying any attention to their shadowed dock, deep under the overhang of the floor above. Shadow checked the dead man's phone, but it had stopped dialling, and she shoved it in her pocket.

"I guess not," Ash finally said. He lifted his chin, gesturing to the upper floors. "All dealt with?"

"Just the one next door that Niel punched unconscious. Want to help me take him upstairs? We have a lot of questions he could answer."

He nodded. "Oh, yes. I have lots of questions, too." And with that enigmatic response, he led the way back in through the broken window.

Eighteen

Estelle followed Barak, Nahum, Olivia, Lucien, and Harlan into Jenkins's office, somewhere in the labyrinthine passages of the British Museum.

He was a tall, rangy man who looked like he'd spent most of his life outdoors. He was, Estelle estimated, in his sixties, with tanned, weather-beaten skin and dark blue eyes surrounded by wrinkles. He had greeted all of them as if they were superstars, and they probably were to the museum community. Well, Harlan and Nahum perhaps, seeing as they had actually found the Templar treasure. Estelle was happy to soak it all up, amused by the excitement the find had provoked.

Before the appointment with Jenkins, they had all eaten a long, celebratory lunch, saying little about Belial, seeing as Theo was with them. However, once he had left them, Barak and Estelle had told them of their meeting, and the others had asked to join them. Fortunately, Jenkins seemed happy to entertain them all, dragging chairs from other offices to accommodate the group.

After some excited questions about the treasure, he said, "I understand, though, that you are interested in another type of treasure? Sumerian digs? Assyrian, perhaps?"

Barak took the lead. "I wouldn't know what age to categorise it, actually, but it is more Biblical in nature. It's regarding finds that have angelic symbols, or perhaps ancient jewellery—clasps, bracelets, rings of gold and silver, and other precious metals and gemstones. They would probably have been in a well-preserved state. Or maybe there was a horn? Something that you would use to call troops to battle. Potentially there would have been quite a hoard of jewellery, and it might have been found in the Middle East." He paused, glancing at Nahum, as if wondering how much to say. "Perhaps they would have had strange properties."

Nahum nodded. "Yes, as if they were cursed, like with Egyptian finds."

Jenkins leaned on the table, his hand stroking his chin as he considered their questions. "Well, as you know, Tutankhamun's tomb was considered cursed. I presume you refer to something like that?" They all nodded enthusiastically, but Jenkins frowned. "Are you on another treasure hunt?"

Barak smiled. "It's related to another case we're working. We're trying to find the source of a problem."

Jenkins cast Harlan a tight-lipped look. "Not planning on stealing antiquities, I hope? I know of The Orphic Guild's reputation."

Harlan sat back, affronted. "We delivered you Templar treasure! That's hardly justified."

"In *this* instance. I'm sure we both know there are others when you haven't been so forthcoming."

"That's unfair," Olivia said, glaring at Jenkins. "You have no idea what we do! Most things we find for clients are not significant enough for museums. And besides, you have so much stuff in your basement alone that will never be seen! Talk about hoarding treasure! Especially that which belongs to other countries."

Estelle winced. *Wading in on the Elgin Marbles debate was not the distraction they needed right now.*

Barak intervened, shooting Harlan and Olivia venomous looks. "We just want to know what has already been found, and what might be on display. You would know, I'm sure. A man of your vast knowledge and connections."

Jenkins rolled his eyes. "Flattery. You must be desperate." Estelle wondered if she needed to cast some glamour, something to oil his tongue, but Jenkins seemed to shrug off his issues with Harlan and Olivia, his interest piqued. He leaned forward. "There was a find many years ago that included just such treasures as you mention, and the dig was indeed believed to be cursed. It sends shivers through our community even now, over one hundred years later."

Estelle felt a stir of excitement, and leaned forward, too.

Jenkins continued. "The men on that dig ended up dead, all except for one, who disappeared."

Barak frowned. "They were murdered?"

"They went mad—or that was the theory, anyway, at the time. Some killed themselves, some killed each other. This find was in early 1800s. 1833, if I remember correctly. So, in the infancy of archaeology, when the profession was happy to trample over antiquities and raid other countries' culture." He shot Harlan and Olivia a narrowed glare as if daring them to contradict him. Fortunately, both remained mute. "It began when a rich Italian was touring the area and heard of an unusual cave that had intriguing markings on the walls. He hired a guide and went to visit it. Apparently, he was so excited by what he found that he harassed The Geographical Society, was given funding that he supplemented with his own money, and headed up there. He hired a group of men to dig. Not locals, you understand. They wouldn't touch it. A few reports were sent back, saying they had found a vast treasure of jewels. It mentioned a horn that was decorated with gold and silver leaf and had curious engravings on it. And then no one heard a thing. The Geographical Society contacted another group in the area—Turkey, actually—and they were sent to find them. It took weeks, of course, to get there. No planes and trains, like now."

"Where was the dig?" Nahum asked.

"Sorry! Didn't I say? The mountains of northern Iran. I can't remember exactly where. I could find out. Persia, of course, it was called back then. Anyway, when the expedition arrived and finally found the site, the team were all dead. The bodies picked at by vultures, and half rotted at that point. But it was obvious there had been a fight, and that some had killed themselves. One man appeared to have scratched his own eyes out. Evidence of the dig was still there—tools, implements, tents... And yes, there were indeed unusual markings on the walls of the cave. It went back quite a way. An ancient text no one could understand was inscribed on the walls. But there was no treasure, and the Italian man had vanished."

"How could they be sure?" Barak asked, exchanging a worried glance with Estelle. "Surely, decomposition would have confused things."

"Many of those there were Middle Eastern. It was obvious from their clothes. There were a couple of Europeans who had gone with the Italian man, but the Italian was older, and it was clear he was not amongst the dead. His body was never found."

Estelle's pulse pounded in her ears, and she was sure everyone had the same questions she did. "What was his name?"

"Beneventi. He never returned home, either. Well, at least no one admitted that he did." Jenkins threw his hands wide. "He had vanished. Poof!"

The group all looked at each other, their expressions saying everything. This had to be the source of Belial's jewels and his power. Beneventi must have opted to steal the treasure for himself, but the Italian name was unfamiliar.

"The horn had vanished too, I presume?" Barak asked.

"No, that was still there. Probably because of its size."

Harlan frowned. "How big was it?"

Jenkins held his hand apart. "A good two feet, and made of solid bone, mixed with ivory, pearl inlay, with gold and silver flourishes. It was filthy at the time! It had been covered by dirt for centuries. It took a lot of cleaning."

Estelle, aware her mouth was gaping open, quickly shut it. "It's on display somewhere?"

"Heavens no! It was taken to Turkey. That's where the team was heading back to. They already had an arrangement with a museum there. They hung around only to have the bodies moved, and then the locals sealed the cave."

It sounded exactly like the dig where the Igigi's underground home was discovered and the entrance was destroyed, but by the Igigi themselves to preserve their privacy. There, too, the locals had run in fear.

"Surely," Nahum asked, "The Geographical Society would have records?"

"I dare say they have, but with no one to report the actual events, I doubt that you would learn much," Jenkins qualified. "Anyway, the museum staff who cleaned the horn reported bad dreams. In the end, it was shoved in a box and packed away. No one wanted to touch it. Rumours were that it belonged to an angel." He forced himself to laugh. "A little far-fetched, of course."

The group was mute, fixed on Jenkins with rapt silence. *It had to be Belial's horn.* Estelle's mouth felt dry.

Nahum, however, was the quickest to gather himself. "Where is it now?"

"In the basement of The Oriental Museum in Istanbul. Or so I believe. No one mentions it anymore."

"So how do you know all this?" Harlan asked.

Jenkins gave a dry, almost embarrassed laugh. "Some digs develop an aura. A sort of myth. They capture your imagination, and the story becomes twisted. Your Templar treasure discovery will get a lot of interest, but when there's death and mystery, and talk of madness...well, that seals the deal. We curators gossip, you know." He smirked. "It's one of those things we whisper about over drinks. I got drunk one night with a Turkish curator who worked at The Oriental Museum. He told me about the rumours of strange whispers in their storage rooms, and how no one will touch the horn, even now. It even has an unofficial name. The Horn of Desolation. I have no idea if it's true, or whether he was just teasing me over drinks. I don't think he was, though." He laughed again, breaking the mood, and the spellbound listeners laughed with him.

Olivia scoffed to mask her probing for more information. "So, it's what? Just in a locked room where no one goes? Sounds highly implausible."

"Have you seen *our* basement? It's huge. I can assure you that it can happen. Half the time, museums even forget what they have. Or don't know. They obtain things in bulk, and no one ever goes through it for years! According to the curator, whose name I forget, it's on the lowest level and the furthest room. It's an old museum, set in an amazing building, so a warren of rooms in its basement is perfectly feasible."

Estelle's thoughts whirled, unsure of what to believe, but it was clear the story was beginning to fit together. *The question was, did they find the horn, or leave it safely buried in a museum?* One thing was sure. She didn't want Barak to have anything to do with it. She hated the effects that the jewellery had on him.

Jenkins addressed Barak. "Does that answer your question? No other discoveries quite like that one spring to mind."

Barak stood and reached over the desk to shake Jenkins's hand. "That does answer my question, thank you. It relates to another story we've been looking into. Unless anyone else has other questions, we'll leave you to it. I appreciate that you're very busy."

"It's been a pleasure." Jenkins smiled and walked to the door to see them out. "I felt left out of meeting all of you this morning, so it's great to have a private chat. I'll escort you to the lift."

After a few hurried thanks and reiterated goodbyes, they entered the lift alone. As soon as the doors shut, Barak heaved a long sigh. "So, who's going to steal the horn?"

Gabe pulled a chair close to Lamberti, glad the old man seemed to have composed himself after being shoved in a wardrobe, and then coming out of it to find dead bodies strewn around his house. He needed to resume their earlier conversation that had been interrupted.

Lamberti regarded Gabe with large, frightened eyes. His hands still trembled as he held a glass of deep red wine. "You have made enemies who won't rest until you are dead."

"That's okay. I aim to kill them first. But you need to get out of this house."

"No. This is my house, and I will die here. Either by their hands or God's. I will not be chased from my home. Those men," he nodded to the dead who had been dragged to the corner of the room, "come from big families. Powerful families. It is a miracle I am still alive after all these years."

Only Ash was still with Gabe. Niel and Shadow were watching for newcomers, either by water or land, and one of them was keeping an eye on Romola. Gabe wasn't planning on waiting around much longer. In fifteen minutes, they would be out of there. They had promised to dispose of the bodies first, as a courtesy.

Ash leaned forward, adjusting the rug over the old man's legs. "Did you know your housekeeper was working for them?"

"No, unfortunately. She was loyal at one point, I'm sure of it. But with our declining wealth and influence..." He shrugged. "Some people are easily swayed."

"Who are the other men?" Gabe asked. "I presume they were from the family you sold the ring to?"

"No, not these. Two families are represented here today. Arizzo and Carlucci. But there is a third. Marco Beneventi's family." He laughed dryly, and it set off a bout of coughing. "He leads all of it."

"Too big to dirty his hands with blood?" Ash asked.

Lamberti almost spat his wine out. "No. He has *plenty* of blood on his hands."

"I want details," Gabe said impatiently. "These dead men are in The Brother-hood?"

"Yes, along with the rest of their families, and Beneventi's, as I said. Four families set the whole thing up over one hundred and fifty years ago." He sighed. "My family was the fourth. They called themselves The Consortium then. I don't know why they changed the name. They exist to spread the word of Belial. The Angel of Death and Destruction. They are all consumed by him." Lamberti shrugged again. A pitiful gesture with his thin shoulders. "My father was obsessed with the whole thing. But me? I never saw the value of it all. I never touched the jewels, and I refused to be initiated. I distanced myself from it. My father was furious, but I didn't care. Beneventi has never had power over me. When my father died, I gave the jewel—the ring you asked about—to him. There was no sale. I wanted it gone from the house, and my obligation to The Brotherhood ended."

Gabe stopped him. "What kind of initiation was there?"

"You become eligible at the age of eighteen. There is a ceremony where you swear fealty, are draped in his jewels, and marked by him forever. It changes you. I see it in others. A sort of cunning behind the eyes."

"So they don't wear his jewels all the time?"

Lamberti shook his head vehemently. "No. It sends you mad. You touch them just once. That is enough. Only the truly devout wear them more often."

Ash exchanged a worried glance with Gabe. "How are you still alive?"

"I told Beneventi to kill me if he didn't like my ultimatum, but I warned him I had insurance. I said that if I died, information would get out about his deal with the devil." He smiled at Gabe's startled expression. "I know Belial is not the devil, but he's close enough. I also know he's behind the treasure that Beneventi's family and the others have spread across Europe over the last hundred years. I made it my business to know." He tapped his nose, a spark of malice in his eyes. "I have lists of where the jewels went, and where they could be now. I also have information on many of their dubious business dealings. That is what they are more worried about. I am the black sheep of the family, and glad to be."

"So Beneventi left you alone," Ash said, admiration in his eyes. "Well played."

"I was an idiot. It could have backfired at any moment. In the light of Aria's death and her betrayal of me, I suspect she has searched all over the house. I am not that much of an idiot, though. It isn't here."

"Hold on!" Gabe stopped him, needing to backtrack. "The ring that your family has owned for years is now with Beneventi?"

"Yes. It was a prized possession, one I'm sure he will have kept for himself. He's the descendant of the man who started it all. The man who found the jewels on a dig." Gabe exchanged a confused glance with Ash, but Lamberti hadn't finished. He took a breath and a sip of wine, and then related a fantastic story that left Gabe dumbstruck.

"Wait," Ash said, halting the old man. "They found everything in a cave?"

"High in the mountains of Persia. Everyone died, except for Beneventi's ancestor. He had a vision in which Belial told him to fake his own death and bring the jewels here. He was promised wealth. He formed The Consortium with three of his closest friends, and made a deal to spread the jewels far and wide. It became his personal mission for years. He spread the jewels around, planting them in religious objects. Icons. Places to infect those who already had religious faith, maybe even fervour."

At least now they knew who had planted the jewels in Olivia's relic, and no doubt many others. Gabe looked again at the once grand residence that now looked shabby. "By giving your ring away, you lost your wealth."

Lamberti nodded. "Yes. Our business declined. However, you need to know that there were many items of jewellery, many rings, bracelets, and other objects, but several were considered special. I don't know why. They all had influence. I could feel it. I refused to touch the ring we owned, though, as I said. I saw the effects it had. I told Beneventi to take it and he did. I presume it's in his house now."

"Here in Venice?"

"Murano, actually. It's more fortress than house."

"Murano?" Ash asked, excited. "I overheard a conversation downstairs. A meeting tonight on Murano. They have a problem," Ash's eyes slid to Gabe's before turning to Lamberti again, "that they need to solve."

"That will be Beneventi's home. You must have them worried."

Ash shrugged and said, "I'll tell you later, Gabe. How many people could be there tonight?"

"Perhaps twenty people, maybe less. The families are small now, but there are others involved. Acolytes, priests, and more. Not all local, of course. There are several spread across Europe."

"We'll deal with it," Gabe said. "Where is your *insurance*, as you called it?"

Lamberti sipped his wine again, and leaned forward, staring into Gabe's eyes. "If I tell you, what will you do with it?"

"I will hunt down every single object out there and hide them where no one will ever find them again. I promise."

"If you touch them, they will consume you."

"Not us. We are immune."

Lamberti studied him and then Ash. "I hope you're right. Okay. I trust you. You killed all these men, after all. My insurance is under the statue in the house my niece was forced to give to Amato. He is a dangerous and powerful priest."

"Not anymore," Gabe told him. He stared at him, looking for subterfuge. "Are you serious? Under the statue in the temple?"

"You've been there?" Lamberti's eyebrows rose in shock. "You have been busy. Yes. Under the plinth. It is the one thing they would never desecrate. I managed to hide it well, and I knew they didn't use the place anymore. They abandoned it years ago."

Shadow and Niel must have been so close when they destroyed the statue. Now they had to go back.

"But there's more," Lamberti warned them. "They raised more havoc. Beneventi, the original one who found the jewels, hired a conjuror to open a portal to the Underworld. He summoned a Nephilim. One of Belial's own. And he came." *Fuck.* "It meant that Beneventi wasn't in control anymore. He answers to Jiri. They all do. But Jiri lacks the one thing he really needs. Belial's horn. Beneventi found it on the dig all those years ago but when he went back for it, it had gone, and he had no idea where to. No one does. But when Jiri finds the horn that he has been searching for all these years, the *world* will answer to him."

Nineteen

Nahum took a long, deep drink of his pint of beer, and then leaned back in his seat, trying to absorb all the information that Jenkins had told them, and the news that Barak had relayed after a phone call with Gabe.

He, Olivia, Barak, Estelle, Lucien, and Harlan were now in a pub close to the museum where they had eaten lunch, and his companions looked as shocked as he was. Their mood was mixed with the excitement of discovering the root of where the Belial issues began, and the fact that they were now rich. The celebrations over their newfound wealth, however, would have to wait.

Barak looked thoughtfully at Nahum. "So, there's no doubt that the dig in Persia is responsible for the source of Belial's jewellery. The man who vanished matches the name that Gabe was given."

"I had my doubts earlier, but not anymore," Nahum agreed. "It all sounds right. It *feels* right!"

Lucien huffed and gesticulated in a way only the French could do. "Listen to you! Of course it is. They all went mad and killed each other or committed suicide. Plus, it cannot be a coincidence that there are Beneventis involved then and now."

Nahum laughed. "I'm actually relieved. We know the source of it! After what Gabe told you, Barak, we know that it's not some worldwide conspiracy. Just a few crazed families spreading havoc. It's still awful, obviously—people have died because of his influence—but we can manage it."

Harlan spluttered over his pint. "What about the damn Horn of Desolation that's locked in the basement of a museum? A horn that Jiri wants. If we know where it is, he might find out, too. And he's another Nephilim. Doesn't that bother you?"

"It worries me only because of Belial," Nahum said. "Nephilim are used to fighting each other."

"He could be juiced up on Belial's powerful jewels, like you were," Estelle pointed out. "That scares the shit out of me."

"And me," Olivia added.

"And me," Harlan and Lucien chorused.

"Okay!" Nahum huffed in annoyance. "I get it. Belial's jewellery has a weird effect on us, but we're still in control. If we have to use them to fight Jiri, then so be it. We'll even the playing field. I am sure that there will be more Nephilim, too. I can't believe only one is back. We just need to find their base."

"And unfortunately, I still have no idea where that could be," Barak said. Barak normally had a carefree attitude, and big laugh to match, but there was no evidence of that now. Nahum knew he was desperate to identify the city he had seen in the spell, but it was too hard without any landmarks or other clues. "We need to phone Jackson. With what Gabe has told us, maybe they should change their search in the references JD has found. We have other names to follow up. Maybe mention of Jiri and old cities."

Nahum nodded. "Good point. We should call them soon so they don't waste any more time on the Lambertis. Olivia and I will be driving there anyway, to look at the tablet. Or the cave? Whatever. We can catch up on their progress. What did Gabe say about the horn?"

Barak smirked. "He's calling Mouse. He wants a professional to steal the horn."

Estelle laughed. "Oh, Niel will love that."

"Yes, he will, because Gabe said he's going with her."

Nahum gaped. "To Turkey?"

"She can't get the horn on her own!"

"Why Niel?" Olivia asked, nudging Nahum. "I sense a story."

Nahum had forgotten she didn't know about Niel and Mouse. "He fancies her and she kind of almost betrayed him, but didn't really. This is Gabe's way of getting them together. I wish I could see his face when Gabe tells him." He laughed and winked at Barak. "We should put bets on it, like we did with Gabe and Shadow. And you and Estelle, too, actually," he added sheepishly. The brothers liked to place small wagers on each other's love lives. All in good spirits, of course.

"You *bet* on us?" Estelle's voice rose with indignation, and she drew herself upright.

Fearing she might cast a spell, he said, "Just for fun!"

Barak just laughed. "You might find that you're the subject of a little bet too, brother." He looked knowingly at Olivia.

"Well, you can bet," she shot back, "that I will do my utmost to confound all of you!" She looked triumphantly at Nahum. "We can all play that game."

Nahum felt another warm rush of affection and admiration for her—and maybe something else, too. To disguise his confusion, he just raised his glass to her. "Let's toast to getting them all to lose lots of money."

Harlan groaned, rolling his eyes at Lucien. "First, I want in on any bets. And second, just to get back on track, what can we do? Gabe and the others will be at Beneventi's place on Murano tonight. I feel like we should do something! The clock is ticking!"

"We need to find a way to neutralise Belial for good," Estelle said. "Even if you track all the jewels down and kill Jiri, the jewels still have power. How do we stop that?"

Olivia smiled. "The Emerald Tablet."

"What? We shrink it and wang it at his head?" Lucien asked sarcastically.

"No! It's a source of magic, right?" Olivia leaned forward, clearly excited, a flush on her cheeks. *She looks gorgeous*, Nahum admitted to himself. And he could see down her cleavage. He forced his eyes to her face. "Like Raziel's book, it lists the magic that underpins the world, right?"

"We think so," Harlan qualified. "That writing could also be an endless list of recipes."

Olivia poked her tongue out at him and continued. "Magic. Spells. As above, so below. Thoth was a God. There must be something in there about controlling angels. If the Igigi could do it, and Belial found a loophole, there will be a way to close that loophole in there. It's just a case of finding it."

"Holy shit!" Nahum said admiringly. "You're right!"

"No, no, no!" Harlan snorted. "You haven't seen that place. It's huge! Like half a dozen cathedrals, all mashed together. Thousands of pillars, with writing all over them. It's madness! It could take a lifetime to find the answer in there."

Barak shrugged. "We haven't got a lifetime. Like you said, we're on the clock. If Jiri's back is to the wall, he might well take matters into his own hands. I guess that answers what we can do. We are all going to JD's house to search the Emerald Tablet while we wait for further instructions from Gabe."

Niel's hand tightened around the handle of his axe. "You have got to be kidding me!"

"I'm not." Gabe folded his arms across his broad chest, not breaking eye contact with Niel. "I need you to meet Mouse in Turkey."

"*Anyone* could meet her. Ash could. You could. Or Shadow could. In fact, two thieves are better than one."

"No. I want you to go. The horn sounds heavy. Shadow and Mouse will struggle to lift it—and Mouse especially shouldn't touch it. You will not have such trouble."

"Neither would you or Ash."

"Ash is going to Amato's old place tonight to secure the paperwork that Lamberti hid there. Shadow and I will chase down Jiri—if we learn where he is after eavesdropping on that meeting tonight. He might even be there."

"There could be a lot of people there. We might make things a lot worse." Niel would have preferred Ash to be there too, but understood the need to secure the paperwork now that they knew where it was.

"Which is why we watch and listen," Gabe said. "You can leave first thing in the morning. I've already contacted Mouse. She's heading to Istanbul tomorrow. I'll let you know her arrival time when she tells me. Or, of course, she could tell you herself."

Niel put that suggestion aside for a moment. "You can't stay here, Gabe. They will hunt us down after today. No doubt Beneventi will have searched for the men he sent to Lamberti's place, and Lamberti could already be dead. He will have talked." Romola was safely out of Venice and heading to stay with friends in case anyone went looking for her. The old man, who Niel wasn't sure as to whether he was brave or stupid, had refused to budge.

"You don't know that."

"He's a weak, old man, and Beneventi will have tortured him."

"But he doesn't know where we're staying."

"It doesn't matter. It's a stupid risk to remain in Venice. You should have killed Lamberti. At least you would have made it swift and painless."

Gabe nodded. "I know, but I couldn't do it. He deserved to die on his terms, not mine. He knew what was likely to happen. As for leaving here, I haven't decided where we'll go yet. Maybe we'll leave Venice tonight, after we've been to Beneventi's house. We could book another villa and meet Ash somewhere. You, however, are getting on a plane tomorrow."

Gabe's dark eyes were almost unreadable. Except that Niel knew Gabe well, and understood just what he was thinking. He was fucking with him. "You are doing this deliberately. You know how I feel about Mouse."

"Yes, I do. That's exactly why I'm sending you. You like her. Your last meeting was just unfortunate."

"She electrocuted me!"

"To save your life." Gabe squared up to him, implacable. "I also know that you love to steal stuff."

"I love to fight more."

"And more than that, my friend, you love to *love*." Gabe's hard stare softened. "If you really hate the idea, then I'll send Ash, but I know that digging paperwork up is not your idea of fun, and that would mean you'd miss tonight's action *and* stealing from a museum. I also know that deep down, you want a chance to talk to her. Properly."

Bollocks. Gabe, infuriatingly, was right. He would love to see Mouse, both to gauge his own reaction to her, to see if he was misremembering how much he liked her, and also to see if Shadow was right. That Mouse did in fact like him. In this crazy, chaotic world of dubious morals they lived in, a little love would not go amiss. Besides, he would really like to get his hands on Belial's horn.

He sighed and walked to the balcony railing of their apartment to look over the Grand Canal. Darkness had fallen, and lights glimmered among the many houses, businesses, and boats. He and Gabe were the only ones outside. Ash was inside, preparing for the drive back to Palazzuolo sul Senio, and Shadow was checking their weapons.

Aware that Gabe had moved next to him, waiting for his response, Niel said, "Fine. I'll go. If we're successful—"

Gabe interrupted him. "You have to be."

"What if it's been moved to another location?"

"It won't. Not if it has a reputation. It will be there, and you will feel it."

"I guess that's true." *If the jewels gave off a wave of power and insidious whispers, what the hell would the horn do?* He shifted his position to look at Gabe, arm leaning on the railing. "What do I do with the horn? If it's that's big, I can hardly wrestle it on a plane."

"Can you destroy it?"

"With this?" He indicated the huge axe that hung at his belt. "I doubt it. This is not Mjolnir, Thor's hammer, and I am not a God. Except between the sheets." He winked at Gabe, his good humour returning.

"I am not even going to respond to that," Gabe said dryly. "Buy a big suitcase and put it on the plane."

Niel thought he was hearing things. "On a *plane*? Where its insidious whispers could cause the entire crew and passengers to have a melt down and we crash? I don't think so!"

"It might not have the same effect as the jewels."

"Barak told us they called it The Horn of Desolation. Does that sound harmless to you?"

Gabe clenched his jaw. "Now that we know where it is, we can't just leave it there."

"I know!"

Gabe turned away, also staring at the Grand Canal below them, as if seeking inspiration. Then he grinned at Niel. "Take a train across Europe. We're loaded. Maybe the Orient Express, or something else flashy. You could keep it in your cabin and bring it home. A train is better than a plane, right?" He put a search into his phone and started to scroll through the results. "Rough estimate, forty-eight hours of travel."

"Is that all?"

"Yep."

Niel felt the faint stirrings of possibility. *Maybe Mouse might want to travel by train, too.* "Okay. Something to consider. It will be even easier, though, if the others are successful in breaking Belial's power. Then the horn won't have any effect at all." Nahum's latest update had included an interesting idea. By now, all of their London team would be at JD's searching the fantastical emerald cave. "Or, we could ask Nahum to send the spelled box that he's not using anymore to Istanbul by special delivery. It could be delivered right to my hotel."

"Brilliant idea! Then, it goes in our bunker in the cellar."

"Are we really going to put a vault in?"

"Why not? Now that we're rich, are we going to stop treasure hunting?"

"I was thinking travel would broaden my horizons." Gabe just cocked an eyebrow, provoking a more truthful response. "Probably not."

"Then yes, we need a vault. Even if all of us end up splitting up and going our separate ways, it will always be our base." A maudlin mood seemed to have settled on Gabe.

"You think that's what will happen?"

"Of course it will. And it should. I mean, maybe not forever, but we're already drawing apart. Barak and Estelle spend lots of time in London—or in Cornwall, he'll be at her place. I'm pleased for him. Zee is already half moved out. Herne knows what will happen with Nahum and Olivia. I quite liked us all living together. It was chaotic, but fun."

"What about you and Shadow?"

"We like White Haven. We'll stay there, in and around trips and jobs, of course. I'm going to build, spruce up the outbuildings."

Niel smiled. "I like it there, too. I'll stay, around my own travel. It's home now. I don't think Ash is going anywhere yet, or Eli, with his bloody harem and his obligations to Ravens' Wood."

That seemed to cheer Gabe up. "I guess that's right."

"I like the witches, too. Plus, I want rooms in the barn."

"Done. You'll get to design them, too."

"Excellent. Besides, we still have a business. Shadow needs excitement, or she'll implode with boredom. So will I, for that matter. It doesn't stop us working together, even if we all start to do other things separately."

"True. But I guess we should focus on tonight. I meant it. We're *just* listening."

Niel felt the keen edge of his blade and sniggered. "Sure we are. And pigs are flying over Venice right now."

Twenty

Maggie snorted with derision, hands on hips. "Find a fucking spell to get rid of a Fallen Angel? You're all fucking mad!"

"Do you have to be so negative?" Harlan complained. "If the Igigi could do it, so can we!"

"The Igigi were half-Gods themselves, you oaf, you are not." She had only just found out about the Igigi, and she was pretty miffed it was the first she'd heard. *So many secrets.*

"But we have witches, and a bloody great emerald cave full of knowledge." Harlan swept his arms wide to encompass the cave they stood in. "And Nephilim, who can read any language in the world."

"I'm trying to be realistic."

"You're being a Debbie Downer. Or should I say a Moaning Maggie?"

"Actually," Jackson intervened, "in order to be grammatically congruent, it should probably be Maggie Moaner."

"Oh, shut the fuck up, both of you." Maggie glared at them, feeling overwhelmed and useless, which was partly the reason for her anger. She was also annoyed at having wasted hours looking for information on Lamberti, only to be told to search for Jiri and Beneventi references instead. Except, there were no mentions of Beneventi at all.

JD was making copious notes on an enormous roll of paper he'd spread across a long table in the centre of the cavern, close to the eternal flame, but he looked up then. "You have the mouth of a bawdy fish wife found in the back alleys of Spitalfields. It makes me quite homesick. If you threw in a few Elizabethan insults, it would be even better."

"Shut up, old man. You cock-wombling knave. Does that help?"

"Cock-wombling isn't quite Elizabethan, but I like it." JD wagged his finger at Harlan. "I like her. You can bring her back."

Harlan rolled his eyes. "Typical. I put up with months of crap from him, and you insult him and he likes it."

Maggie smirked. "I'm very charming, in my own way. So, you're serious? About the spell?"

"Yes." Harlan shrugged off his leather jacket and placed it over the back of a chair. "Jenkins gave us brilliant information. We know the source of the jewels now. It hasn't been an age-old conspiracy. Yes, there are a few families and their connections to track down, but now that Lamberti has told us where his list is, that makes things easier. Plus, we know where to find the horn, too."

"There's still a lot to do, though," Jackson said. He crossed to JD's side to look at the rough plan of the cave he'd started to make, and Maggie and Harlan followed him.

The London team, as Maggie called it, had arrived a couple of hours before, and searching and mapping the cave had begun in earnest. Jackson and Maggie had continued to read the selected books in JD's library, discovering all sorts of interesting snippets of information, but none particularly salient to their investigation. Reading JD's own notes from over a hundred years ago was weird. She'd also ended up searching for information on JD. He really had been the court magician to Queen Elizabeth I. Jackson wasn't lying. *Unbelievable.*

Their search had been fuelled by sandwiches and soup brought up by the immortal Anna. Maggie rolled the word around her mouth. *Immortal.* How weird would that be? *Lonely, perhaps. Or maybe exciting? So much time to explore and read and live expansively.* It seemed a very delicious thought. Maggie presumed that Anna must do more than cook and clean for JD, or she would have a very boring eternity. *The woman*, she decided, *had unknown depths.*

As had this place.

She'd been shocked earlier, and had barely taken the emerald cave in, but after hours spent buried in books, she and Jackson needed a break and had decided to see what was going on. Entering it again was actually intoxicating. She could lose hours here. Days, even. With no natural light, and with lamps burning constantly, and the smoky swirl of incense, she already felt disoriented. It was as if she had been transported back thousands of years. The rugs were of high quality, and she was sure the lamps suspended from the pillars and ceiling were of solid gold and silver. As for the flame in the centre, that was just weird. The place reeked of magic and knowledge.

"So," Maggie asked, inspecting the scrawl of JD's writing, "what have you found so far?"

"The cave is split into sections. Roughly. There are areas that pertain to countries, most of which have now vanished, or have changed their name, like Persia, for example. I guess Hermes would never have thought that Sumer or Assyria would vanish. There are areas that reference the elements, the base of everything and the root of all magic, and then there are histories. Endless histories." He sighed, his hands massaging his lower back as he straightened.

"Histories of who?" Harlan asked.

"Biblical figures. Adam, for instance."

Maggie was sure the room actually spun around her. "*The* Adam? As in Adam and Eve?"

"Yes. But, my dear, he was not the first man created from clay. Oh, no. Just a mortal who had evolved like all of us from the vast soup of the oceans. What the old

God granted him was knowledge. And a not very compliant wife, eh?" He winked at Maggie.

"Women are not meant to be compliant. What would men have to complain about?" she shot back. "We're here to remind you not to be so fucking self-obsessed. That was a giant fail."

JD threw his head back, roaring with laughter. "Oh yes, you can definitely visit more often."

Harlan cleared his throat. "Anything about angels?"

JD pointed to his right. "Nahum and Barak are examining an area over there. There are lists and lists of angels. Fallen and otherwise."

Startled, Jackson asked, "Are there spells to control them, or lessen their influence?"

"Give us a chance! I am giving you broad brush strokes only."

"Are Estelle and Olivia with them?" Maggie asked.

"Yes, taking notes. Lucien, too, I believe." JD sighed, eyes narrowing as he stared at the flames in the centre. "But whether we find a solution for our most pressing issue? I don't know. We've barely mapped a fraction of it. With Nahum and Barak, however, we stand a chance. The rest will take me a lifetime." He smiled at them. "It's a good job that I have many of them. How did you fare with those notes I left you?"

Maggie scowled. "Badly. That first reference to the alchemist was interesting, but he didn't really give any details, did he? There was no mention of Beneventi or the other names, other than The Consortium. It was all very secret squirrel."

"We alchemists like our secrets, and clearly Lamberti did, too. What intrigued me," JD said, "was that the alchemist, Alfonso, said if the power could be tapped, it would be phenomenal, and may have several useful applications. He never said what they were."

"We noticed," Maggie said grimly. *More bloody secrets.*

Harlan had been studying the plan, but now he looked up. "Lamberti knew those jewels—specifically his ring—belonged to Belial. That's why Beneventi formed The Consortium, after all. Why even request the alchemist's help?"

"Maybe," Jackson mused, scratching his head and making an even bigger mess of his unruly hair, "some of them were having doubts and wanted to get rid of the power, but keep the jewels. Or maybe they wanted to use the power for themselves without Belial's influence. It could even be they just wanted to understand how it all worked. Unfortunately, nothing else we found could tell us. There were other hints about The Consortium, but it was frustratingly vague. There was no mention of Jiri."

Something had been tickling Maggie's brain for a couple of hours, and now it struck her. "What if the alchemist had been asked to help them use the jewels to find Jiri?"

All three men turned to her, eyes narrowed. Harlan said, "But he was an alchemist, not a witch or a magician, or whatever you want to call it."

Jackson nodded at JD. "Our friend here used scrying glasses and talked to angels. What if Alfonso did, too? Maybe he was adept at summoning circles? Like you say, JD, you guys have vast and varied interests."

"It's very possible." JD nodded, eyes distant as he considered the possibility. "He did have an interest in demons as I recall from his other manuscripts and treatises. Yes, that could well be the case. Perhaps he did summon Jiri. Maybe others. However, we'll never know for sure, unless someone talks." JD took a deep breath and straightened his shoulders. "There are things we cannot know, therefore we must focus on that which we can influence. A way to bind Belial for good."

"In that case," Maggie said, having had enough of chatting, "I'm going to find the others. If nothing else, I can take notes."

She set off between the towering pillars to find the Nephilim and the WAGs, as she now liked to call Estelle and Olivia. Not that she'd tell them that. *Yet.*

Ash pulled onto the side of the road that ran past Amato's country house, making sure it was far enough from the entrance not to rouse suspicion. The lane was deserted, and within moments, he shed his jacket and t-shirt, extended his wings, and rose majestically into the air.

It was a pleasure to be flying again. Venice was beautiful but cramped, and he'd missed the night breezes that ruffled his wings. He gave a wry smile as he studied them under starlight. He still wasn't used to the fact that his wings were now golden, courtesy of Belial. He had wondered if the colour would fade, but so far it hadn't. Fortunately, in darkness, there was little light to reflect, but by candle or firelight, they gleamed, much like his eyes.

Fortunately, there were no other repercussions from his use of Belial's token. No lingering after-effects or power, or whispers in his head. His wings, and particularly his injured shoulder, had healed well. The phrase, 'Broken Nephilim' still rankled, even though no one except Belial had whispered it. He cast his annoyance aside to focus on the present. He flew high, circling the grounds to make sure no other cars were there. The entire place still looked deserted and abandoned, and no lights glimmered in any windows. However, as he aimed towards the woods, he saw a flash of light close to where the temple was.

Bollocks.

He carried his sword, as always, glad that they could now transport their weapons in the plane's hold, and he withdrew it from the scabbard. He patted his pocket, checking that he still had JD's weapon, and felt its sleek outline. He also carried a backpack over his shoulder with a crowbar in it. He circled wide of the light, gliding silently over the thick canopy. From this distance the light had vanished, and he wondered if he'd imagined it, until it winked into view again.

But where could he set down? The canopy was thick, the temple overgrown. He had been aiming to walk along the forest path, but that seemed like a bad idea now. Taking another few moments to get his bearings, he flew lower and partially alighted on an uppermost branch, his wings supporting his weight. He waited, trying to see the temple he knew was somewhere close, but there was no other light or sound. Fearing a trap, he considered his options.

The deaths of the six men in Venice were already all over the news. They hadn't bothered to hide the bodies. Instead, they had piled them into the boat with a tarpaulin thrown over them, and pushed it out of Lamberti's dock and into the Grand Canal. Ash had volunteered to swim under water, and had tugged it out in the middle of the waterway before abandoning it and swimming back to shore. They had hoped there would be no repercussions for Lamberti, but that was stupid. Of course there would be. *But had Lamberti talked, if questioned? Was he already dead?*

Wary of making loud noises, Ash flew to the start of the path through the woods that led to the temple. On foot, he progressed slowly and softly, wings folded away, sword close to his side. The place seemed as deserted as when they had left it the other day. Huge chunks of Belial's statue lay on the ground, the paving cracked, and there, in the centre, was the plinth beneath which the paperwork should be.

Ash waited in the shadows, his eyes now fully adjusted to the darkness. The soaring columns could barely be distinguished from the trees, and there was no light or sound now, other than the nighttime chatter of animals and the sough of the wind through the branches. *How long should he wait? Or was he just being paranoid?* Checking that once again JD's weapon was in his pocket, he stepped from the deep shadows by the nearest pillar and onto the top step, the central, sunken area beneath him. Most of the fallen leaves had been pushed around the edge, thanks to Niel and Shadow, and the large central plinth was bigger than he remembered.

After casting one more searching glance around the edge, he progressed down the broad steps to the centre, wading through leaves and stepping over chunks of the statue. Up close, he could see a large crack ran down the centre of the plinth, and a seam had opened where the base met the paving. He squatted to see it better. It was wide enough to get his hand inside, and he reached in, hoping to feel a box or a package. Unfortunately, the space within was empty. Frustrated, he adjusted his position, wondering if the paperwork could be accessed from the crack in the plinth, or if someone had beaten him to it. The movement saved his life. An arrow suddenly whizzed overhead, striking the steps behind him and clattering to the ground.

Ash sheltered behind the high base, eyes darting everywhere. A bare whisper of noise to his right made him dive for cover again, and another arrow whizzed past him. He scuttled to the side, still unsure of how many men were out there.

He hadn't imagined it. Someone was here, waiting for him. Lamberti must be dead, and he must have talked before he died. That meant they might be waiting for Gabe and the others, too.

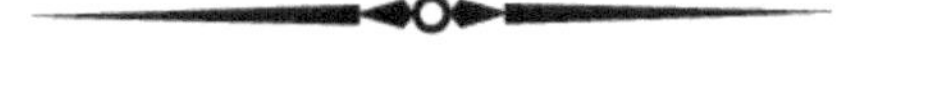

Gabe set Shadow down on the edge of Beneventi's grounds. *Lamberti had been right.* It was a large place, surrounded by high walls and thick shrubbery.

In fact, on first impressions, Gabe was sure that it had once been a religious building. A nunnery perhaps, or monastery. The main residence was built of old, thick stone, and cloisters stood to the side, a large statue of an angel with outstretched wings dominating the central space.

Murano was an island, one of several on the Venetian Lagoon, the second largest after Venice itself, situated very close to the city, and barely one and a half kilometres in size. It had approximately 7,000 inhabitants, and compared to Burano, it was nowhere near as pretty, but it was famous for manufacturing Murano glass. Not that Gabe would be buying any anytime soon. Beneventi's home was on the west side, bordering the lagoon. He wished he'd had more time to fly and explore. The lagoon was beautiful, serene, and he was able to take in the full scope of the area. It was also good to spend time with Shadow, alone, her curves pressed against him. He was determined that when this was all over, they would go away together, just the two of them.

Within moments, Niel landed next to them. "The roof is broad and shallow pitched. It will be a good place for one of us to hide."

Gabe studied the building. Several chimneys were on the roof, but one to the far end, closest to the cloisters, was the biggest. There was also a single storey building that edged the rear of the cloisters. *That could well be a good place to hide, too.* He nodded in agreement. "Looks good. That's presuming, of course, that they'll meet outside under that damn statue. If they do, I'd like one of us to get closer. On the ground, perhaps." He looked at Shadow, already almost invisible. "I couldn't get as close as you could get, though."

"But I won't understand a word they say, if they talk in Italian," she pointed out. "Let me enter the house, see if I can find the jewels in there. They will have stored them somewhere."

Niel shrugged. "Great idea. I'll circle overhead, and can drop down where I'm needed."

Gabe nodded. "Okay, but you must be careful if you find any jewels, Shadow."

"I'm not an idiot. Gabe, what exactly do we want to get out of this meeting?" Shadow asked him. "Names? Places?"

"I told you. I want to know where Jiri is, to get an idea of numbers involved, and to find their cache of jewels."

"But you don't want to kill them?"

"No."

"Despite knowing the danger they pose? The fact that they sent six men to kill *you*?" She cast Niel a long, sideways glance of disbelief. "Why not? This is the perfect time to strike." Shadow was beautiful and sexy, but she was also deadly. She had no compassion for those who had crossed her.

"They are enslaved by Belial. Not in their right mind. We might be able to save them."

"That's a big if, Gabe."

He bit back his annoyance, knowing Niel thought the same thing. They had argued about it earlier, and now it seemed they would argue again. "I don't care. If we're attacked, then go ahead, kill. But try to escape first. It may count in our favour later."

"And it may not. We should have killed Lamberti. He was weak and old, and whatever agreement he had with Beneventi before is gone now. They could torture him for information. They might know that we're coming here!"

Death did not sit so easily with Gabe as it once had. "He helped us, and that deserves our compassion."

"Beneventi will not agree. Six of his men are dead because of us."

The purr of boat engines out on the water interrupted their conversation. Like Venice, there were no cars on the island, and a series of pedestrian bridges connected the seven small islands that made up Murano. They had arrived as soon as it was dark enough, and Gabe expected they would have to wait for hours, but maybe not.

"Then we must be wary of subterfuge." Gabe nodded to the roof. "I'll find a spot to watch. Be careful, both of you."

With a single flap of his enormous wings, he soared high, watching a couple of boats pull up to the small dock. They had made it only just in time. Gabe wondered if this meeting might move indoors after the deaths earlier that afternoon, or even be cancelled, perhaps out of fear for their safety, but a couple of men were already in the cloisters, and a few lights illuminated the area.

Then, suddenly, lights were everywhere. In the garden, lighting up the house, and illuminating paths. He hoped Shadow had found a way into the house.

Twenty-One

Estelle placed her pen and notepad down and rolled her shoulders to ease the kink in her neck.

"I don't know about you, Olivia, but I feel useless."

"You shouldn't! At least you're a witch and have magic. I have nothing, except some expertise with hunting occult treasures. That's not exactly helping us now."

"Care to appraise this place?"

"You can't put a price on *this*!" Olivia brushed her long hair back from her face, her auburn highlights flaming as they caught the light from the many lanterns around them in the emerald cave. "I've given up trying."

They were both seated on large floor cushions atop a Persian rug that was spread in the centre of a group of huge, square pillars. It felt exotic, as if they were in some kind of Arabian tent, or palace. The light ignited the emerald columns, revealing flaws in the columns, and casting shadows on the archaic script. In the dancing flames, the elegant swirls of text shimmered as if they were alive. The whole place was intoxicating and mesmerising. She wished she had the Nephilim's skills with languages.

They were deep into the cave, the pillars running in all directions. Although Estelle couldn't understand the words, it was easy to see there was some kind of pattern to their placement. The pillars were grouped in shapes. Clusters of square columns, then plain round ones, fluted, spirals, thin, broad, gilded, unadorned... They all denoted segments of knowledge. The four of them had first spent time in an area that listed the thousands of angels, but then moved to another. This area talked about magic. Spells, to be exact.

Barak and Nahum were high above, inspecting the endless text that was written, well, everywhere. Both she and Olivia had started to make basic notes about the information on the pillars, but the sheer enormity of it was overwhelming. Eventually, Barak and Nahum had stopped shouting down information and had fallen silent too, except for short conversations between each other.

"Just think," Olivia continued, "what's written in here could rewrite history."

"And could destroy us all, too."

Olivia frowned as she sat cross-legged. "Do you think so?"

"People far cleverer than us could unlock the very material of our world. I'm not sure we should."

"Aren't physicists doing that right now?"

"You know what I mean. This is so much!"

"Someone could uncover the cure for cancer in here, or Alzheimer's, or all sorts of terrible diseases." Olivia's gaze drifted around the room. "It could change everything."

Estelle bit back her initial, scathing response. "You're so positive, Olivia. You see the good in things. I do not. Men would subvert this to their basest desires. Women, too. Wars, in fact, would be fought over this. We can never tell anyone."

Olivia looked as if she might argue, but then she just sighed. "I know. I can feel the tingle of it all on my skin, can you? It's like static electricity."

"That's the magic." Estelle stared around the vast cave again. "I can't decide where the source is. It feels everywhere. That seems impossible."

Olivia giggled. "We're in an emerald cave. That seemed impossible a couple of days ago. Men who didn't care for its secrets and knowledge would carve it up and sell it. We're in a billion-pound cave."

"I doubt it could be destroyed. I think the magic must protect it. Perhaps it would close itself up again and we'd be trapped inside."

"Would we know?" Olivia mused thoughtfully "Or would we be crushed to dust?"

"I guess if we weren't crushed, we would only know if we tried to leave to find food. We'd discover the entrance sealed, and we'd slowly die of starvation and thirst. Unless there's a kitchen here and an endless food supply we don't know about. Or if it granted us immortality and we'd never be hungry again." She laughed at her crazy suggestions. "I hope we don't have to find out."

"Well, I can absolutely say that hasn't happened yet." Olivia patted her stomach. "I'm hungry and thirsty. I might bring some food in for everyone. No one will leave here for hours. I don't even know what time it is."

They had realised some time ago that their phones and watches didn't work in there.

"Maybe we should check our messages, too," Estelle suggested. The cave suddenly felt oppressive, as if Estelle was in her tomb, and she wanted to leave, too. She looked up to see Barak soaring high above. "I'm surprised he hasn't complained about being hungry."

"He's obsessed now, like Nahum." Olivia hesitated, as if unsure of her next words, and then lowered her voice. "Is it really so bad when they use Belial's jewels?"

"Yes. I hate it." She saw Olivia flinch back in surprise and tried to temper her response. "They don't lose control completely, but it changes them. It gives them a hard edge. I see Barak's eyes change. He's not *my* Barak anymore. He's another man from another time. It's like I've lost him."

Estelle felt herself becoming tearful and tried to shake it off. She was never tearful, and she prided herself on it. But neither had she felt as comfortable talking to another woman before. She didn't get on with other women well, she knew that. The White Haven witches irritated her, and so did Shadow, although that was probably because they were horribly alike in many ways. Maggie was hilarious, and she respected her, but she wasn't sure they would ever be close friends. Olivia, though, was different, and she couldn't quite say why. Perhaps it was because they were of a similar age, and she felt no judgement from Olivia. Then again, Olivia had never seen Estelle at her spikiest.

"Sorry. I'm being stupid." Estelle looked up again at Barak, heart now thumping painfully in her chest. "I've never had anyone love me like he does. I don't think I could bear to lose it."

Olivia leaned forward and squeezed her hand, her warm tone reassuring. "You won't. They are...different, aren't they? They are like other men, and yet they're not. And I don't mean their wings and their strength that their half angel blood gives them. It's like this endless depth. I feel like I'm standing on a precipice, and if I fall in, I may never get out. I won't even want to get out."

She meant the precipice of love, of course. "It's worth it, Olivia. But yes. It's terrifying, too."

Olivia looked up at Nahum, and Estelle followed her gaze. He was hanging off another column, fingers gripped on some moulding, legs braced on the surface, his wings spread behind him, the lamplight burnishing his already olive skin as he studied a piece of text. His taut abs and muscled arms were more defined in the light. He was breathtaking. Not as breathtaking in her eyes as Barak, but these Nephilim were extraordinary.

She risked a question she wouldn't have dared ask earlier. "What will you do, Olivia?"

Her eyes never left him as she said, "I don't know."

Niel circled Beneventi's grounds, well above the reach of the garden lights.

They must suspect that he and the others would come here, or else having so many lights on was just a regular safety feature. It seemed excessive though, as did the number of guards. Men patrolled the dock, the area close to the gate, and the perimeter wall.

At least half a dozen boats were now at the dock, and people made their way to the house in small groups. Lights blazed at several windows, and there was a general air of hustle and bustle, and self-important posturing. Niel could also see more angel statues around the garden, but none so impressive as the one in the cloisters.

He wasn't sure whether the fact that the meeting was going ahead was a sign of utter naivety or sheer bullishness. Or a trap, of course. The cloisters, as they suspected, was their meeting place, and at least a dozen people were gathered there. He hoped Gabe could hear them from his position.

What Niel couldn't work out was why they weren't paying more attention to the sky. They must know that they were Nephilim. Belial would have told them. Or maybe their level of communication was far more basic. Perhaps The Brotherhood assumed that although he and his brothers had used Belial's jewels, that they also had a team of humans who they commanded, much like Jiri did them. Plus, according to Gabe, Lamberti had no idea that they were Nephilim.

Niel nodded to himself. *Yes, that sounded likely. Of course, only time would tell.*

Gabe lay flat on the roof of the single storey building that edged one side of the cloisters, watching the new arrivals.

The large, square space was edged with pillars that bordered a broad walkway, two sides of which were covered by a stone roof that backed up against the buildings behind it. The other sides were open to the gardens, partially shielded by trees and bushes. It would be a beautiful, restful place in the summer, with most of it in shade.

Half a dozen men and a couple of women were now in the cloisters. Belial's statue presided over them all, his wings spread wide, encompassing almost all of the enclosed space, but this time he didn't point anywhere. He carried a sword in one hand, and a huge horn in the other. *Interesting. Did this mark the last statue?*

A brazier blazed on the ground in front of it, and the group gathered in ones or twos as if they were waiting for someone else. Gabe wriggled forward so that he was close to the roof's edge, and voices drifted to him from the nearest pair. They were angry, speaking in Italian again.

A strident male voice that came from a portly, middle-aged man, said, "Amato's death has had catastrophic consequences! He must have left paperwork about, or else how could they have found Lamberti?"

"They are Nephilim," his companion, a tall, bearded man said, warming his hands by the fire. "Belial warned us that someone would know of the jewels' worth. They must have sent a team here."

"But *Nephilim*? How?"

"I presumed they were summoned here, just like Jiri was, but with no Fallen Angel to direct them, they are weak."

"They have smashed the statue in Palazzuolo! Stolen another ring! The temple beneath the church was destroyed! They are ruining everything!" Gabe's stomach turned. *So they knew about Palazzuolo already.*

"But they don't know all, my friend."

"They killed six men this afternoon, and pushed them into the canal on their own boat! You say they are no threat, but I do not believe it." His eyes darted about nervously. "They could even be here now."

"I doubt it, as Lamberti did not know of this meeting."

"But Lamberti knows about *us*! He could have told them everything."

The tall man leaned down, pressing his face close to the other man's. "Calm down. Armand does not like to see fear! It is why we meet tonight, despite their close proximity. At least old Lamberti is not a threat anymore. He is dead. Armand's nephew killed him. Not before he talked, though. We probably have his hidden paperwork already." The man scowled. "Armand should have killed him years ago."

"The risk was too great. The pact has served us well. We have thrived."

Gabe clenched his jaw, fearing Shadow and Niel were right. He should have killed Lamberti to protect themselves. He studied the people again, noting that although they wore jewellery, none seemed to be Belial's tokens. The men that afternoon hadn't wore them, either. *Interesting. It was just as Lamberti suggested.* He rolled onto his back, staring at the night sky as if he would see two glaring eyes watching him. He suddenly felt too vulnerable on the roof, and longed to crawl under cover. That was the thing with Fallen Angels. You were never sure how much they knew.

Then a door slammed below him, and a swell of voices carried to him. *Newcomers.*

A man spoke, his deep voice sounding older, mature. "Thank you for coming here on such short notice, especially after our losses tonight. Friends and family have died today. Aria must have been wrong. There must have been more than just one man and the woman there today."

"So, what are we doing about it, Armand?" a woman asked. "My son was one of those dead men."

"I know, and I'm sorry."

"Sorry doesn't help me! Belial is supposed to offer us protection! From *everything*. It's clearly a lie."

Even from the roof, Gabe could feel the tension. He adjusted his position, and caught a glimpse of the group. No one moved. It was a frozen tableau.

Armand, however, remained calm. "This is not time to lose faith, Emilia. The word has gone out. We are all on alert. Especially Jiri. Please remember that this is a relationship that has bound our families for years. We are rich and influential because of it. Of course there are risks, but..."

Emilia interrupted him. "Never risks like *this*! These men seem to have come from nowhere! They strike at the heart of us!"

"But they will not win. Georgio has the paperwork already, and they are waiting in Palazzuolo to kill whoever comes for it. We already are making headway on the others. They have friends and family, and they will die unless they leave us be. We have countermeasures. Whatever this is, it will be over soon."

Friends and family. His brothers, and maybe the witches in White Haven. Maybe even their London team.

Gabe's blood started to rage, the familiar, ancient bloodlust returning. He was insane for thinking that these people could be saved. They had all sworn allegiance to Belial, and no doubt had touched his jewels as some kind of initiation, just as Lamberti described. It was already too late to save them. They should just kill them all while they had the chance.

Belial was a cancer, and so were The Brotherhood. They had to cut them out, before they spread. *Change of plan.* As far as he was concerned, no one left here tonight. The house would become their tomb.

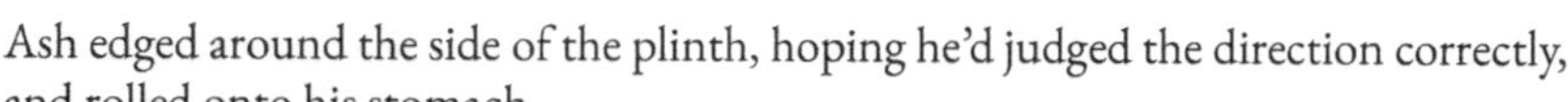

Ash edged around the side of the plinth, hoping he'd judged the direction correctly, and rolled onto his stomach.

He wriggled beneath the scant covering of leaves still left, now cursing the fact that Shadow and Niel had done such a good job of clearing the area. Abandoning the idea of using his sword, he pulled his alchemical weapon from his pocket.

Silence once again fell in the temple. He was a sitting duck, as the English so quaintly put it. Scarcely breathing, he focussed on the perimeter, and heard the crack of a branch. Another arrow landed within inches of him, embedded in the paving, but Ash had already spotted his attacker. He shot the branch above the dark figure and it crashed down, crushing him.

The flare of light from JD's weapon cast a harsh glow on the temple, partially blinding Ash. He used it to his advantage, trusting that everyone else out there would be similarly affected. He was on his feet in seconds, zigzagging across the ground to the edge. Arrows whizzed around him, all missing, and Ash ran up the steps and past the temple columns, then leapt over the fallen branches and the man beneath, using them as cover.

Keeping his body low, he reached between the branches, feeling for the man's pulse at his neck. He was sprawled awkwardly, but was still alive. Another arrow whizzed in his direction.

Ash shouted, "You risk killing your friend. He still lives."

There was no answer, only another arrow, this time very close. Ash cursed himself for speaking. *Idiot.*

He squashed himself to the ground, peering as best he could to try and see the second man, and hoping there weren't more. His assailant was either intent on killing him or was making his escape. If he had found the paperwork, he would have to follow him, but if he lifted his head to try to see him, he could die.

Another arrow flew above him, embedding in a tree.

Ash fired wildly, shooting haphazardly and not caring. He wanted to deter the assailant. Wound him, if possible. He had questions.

Then, in the flare of light, he saw why the other man was still attacking. There was an oiled package sticking out of the injured man's jacket, covered in leaf mould and dirt. *Lamberti's paperwork. It had to be.*

Ash gripped the fallen branch and reared up, using it both as a shield and weapon, just as a man came pounding out of the darkness. Ash ran towards him using the tangle of branches like a battering ram. He hit him with a huge crunch, and they both hit the ground hard. The man was still holding his crossbow, and the bolt flew past him, stinging as it cut his cheek. But that was the last thing the man did. He hit the ground awkwardly, his head striking the base of a pillar, and Ash knew he was dead, even before the blood pooled from his head wound.

Ash lay still, straddled across the dead man for a few moments longer, only standing when he was sure there were no others waiting. He strode back to the other man and retrieved the package. It was exactly what Lamberti had promised. A list of names, jewels, and where to find them, as well as business interests.

He crouched, moved the man's crossbow, and searched him for any tokens of jewellery, relieved to find there weren't any. The man groaned as he regained consciousness, and Ash put JD's weapon away and withdrew his sword. He placed it at his assailant's throat.

"Move slowly! I have questions for you."

The man took a moment to orientate himself, eyes on the sword. "I have nothing to say to you. You may as well kill me now."

He was young, maybe in his late twenties, and despite his bold words, he looked unsure of himself. Ash decided to try a different tactic. "You are a member of one of the three families who have vowed their lives to Belial, I presume?" His eyes flickered. "Or a friend, perhaps? An ardent convert? You have chosen badly. Belial is a harsh master, and he will kill you in the end, or send you mad."

"It's not like that," the man protested.

"Yes, it is. Were you promised wealth? A place of glory for spreading his madness?"

"He is one of the Fallen! To spread his power is for the good of mankind."

Ash sighed, withdrawing his blade by an inch. "I have seen the results of his power. People fight amongst themselves, or kill others, or are consumed by Belial himself. Have you touched his jewels?"

"Yes, months ago in a ritual when I was accepted into The Brotherhood, and I'm fine."

Then it was already too late. "Are you? Or did you see his eyes flash fire, and feel the beat of his wings, and hear the whisper of his voice? Can you feel him even now, as he sits deep within you? I think you can. He's whispering to you, isn't he? Urging you to act. Does he tell you who I am?"

The man's lips tightened as his gaze focussed inward. Then his eyes widened as he stared at Ash again. "You are Nephilim, like Jiri. Of the House of Raym."

A shiver ran across Ash's skin that had nothing to do with the cool night breeze. *So, Belial knew who he was.* "Yes, we fought against his House, and I know of Jiri." He spoke directly to Belial, knowing the sliver of his presence would register every word. "We will not rest until you are gone. You and Jiri, and however many other Nephilim are here."

The man writhed, eyes rolling back in his head, and suddenly his eyes flashed a pale, ice cold blue as he spoke in a voice that was not his own. A deep, commanding, and unearthly voice that spoke in the old tongue that Ash understood only too well. *"You will all fail. I will have dominion again."*

Anger blazed in his eyes, but Belial had no power outside of the man's body, and no tokens to draw strength from. The man's skin became mottled, his breathing laboured as his body failed to cope with Belial's assault. Ash saved him from a painful death and cut his throat. Blood splashed into the cool, damp earth, and his head fell back as the light faded from his eyes.

Another death, among many. And there would be more.

Twenty-Two

S hadow crept through Armand Beneventi's house, finding little to interest her.

He was rich, that was obvious; the furnishings were luxurious in a tasteless, overstated way, and the whole place felt claustrophobic. That was compounded by the men who guarded the exterior exits and patrolled the corridors, all armed with guns. She had successfully evaded all of them, her fey glamour and stealth concealing her. Frustratingly, she found nothing of use. No maps, no central area of command, only endless angelic and religious iconography. Neither could she detect any sign of power that would suggest there were more of Belial's jewels nearby.

Eventually, she left the house through an open window on the first floor, scaled a sturdy drainpipe, and made her way to the roof, where she spotted Gabe on the level below, atop the roof of the single storey building by the cloisters.

Keeping to the darkness, she dropped like a cat and edged towards him, trying to catch his eye before he tried to kill her. When he did see her, he edged back until both were at the rear of the building, well away from the gathered group. Gabe looked angry, his eyes sharp flints of obsidian.

"Something wrong?" she asked, her voice barely a whisper.

"Yes. We need to kill them all."

"So, I'm right?" She smirked. "Of course I am."

"Not the time, Shadow. They know who we are, who our friends are, and we need to kill them now while we have the chance. They have even set a trap for Ash, but I daren't warn him. Have you found anything?"

"Nothing of use. The jewels are either very well hidden, or elsewhere. But I agree with you. Let's tell Niel the new plan." Shadow looked overhead, hoping he was still up there. Her phone buzzed silently in her pocket, and she grinned when she saw his name. "Maybe he heard me."

"Spotted us, more likely."

He wanted an update, and she texted him Gabe's news succinctly, ending with, *We need to kill them.*

How many in the house? he asked.

Half a dozen. Maybe ten.

So, about thirty, maybe thirty-five in total. Nothing to worry about, then.

She rolled her eyes at Gabe. "He's cockier than I am."

"You're both too bloody cocky for your own good."

She texted Niel again. *Especially with JD's bombs.*

You've brought them?

Shadow sniggered, as Gabe looked over her shoulder at her message. *Of course! I'm not an idiot.*

I wish you'd have bloody given me some!

She turned to Gabe. "But that would deprive me of all the fun!"

"Tell him to wait until he sees us act, then he can, too. Where will he start?"

Niel's response to her typed question was swift. *At the dock, and then the gate. But there are many men on the perimeter, too.*

Gabe nodded. "We need to find where Jiri is first. Tell him I'll grab Armand out of the cloisters, and we can question him up there." He pointed upwards. "I reckon that will make him talk."

"Let's kill a few first, Gabe. He can see we mean business. Then you take him, and I'll clean up. Sound good?"

"Are you sure there's nothing in the house?"

"As much as I can be."

Gabe waited while she finished messaging Niel, eyes on the cloister again. Their angry voices carried to them.

Shadow pocketed her phone and checked her backpack. "I have ten bombs. Should be enough."

Gabe rolled his eyes. "You could take out half of Murano with that many. Let's not go mad, Shadow. A couple on the house, and maybe one in the grounds should do it."

"Fine. Spoilsport."

"All the more for later." He cracked his neck. "A few minutes just to listen to their discussion, and then we act. Ready?"

"Ready."

Niel watched Gabe and Shadow listen to the conversation in the cloisters for at least another ten minutes, and he hoped they had heard useful information. Then Shadow dropped to the ground with her usual grace, and Gabe leapt down with outstretched wings.

Niel flew down over the dock, coming in low and fast, and struck quickly. The two men guarding the dock were dead within seconds, neither of them even able to fire their guns.

He then flew again, but not for long. A couple of men patrolled inside the grounds, just beyond the gated entrance. He killed one, but the second spotted him, and a spatter of bullets broke the night's silence, one catching his wing and splintering the tips of his primary feathers, but Niel covered the distance between them, killing him as swiftly as he'd killed the others.

He had hoped the sight of his wings would intimidate the men, but it didn't seem to. *Perhaps they were used to seeing Jiri, and maybe other Nephilim.* The gunfire set off a series of shouts across the grounds, and more men came running.

Damn it. Sheathing his sword, he pulled out his alchemical weapon. As he started firing, screams reached him from across the garden, and he hoped that Shadow and Gabe were okay. The distraction cost him. A bullet grazed his arm, searing his skin, and he dived out of the way, rolling behind some bushes before taking aim. The noise would carry across the island. If they didn't get this finished quickly, the police could turn up, or curious neighbours.

He focussed his mind. *Kill, survive, and get out of there.*

Gabe killed three men before they even realised that they were in danger. Shadow struck quickly, killing another three. Both used their swords, despite the risk of gunfire. Swords were quieter.

The screams were not.

Gabe grabbed Beneventi, arms wrapped around him, and holding him close to his chest, he soared upwards, leaving Shadow to kill the others. There was little resistance—at least from the group in the cloisters. Despite the fact that six men had already died that day, they clearly were arrogant enough to believe themselves safe. Gunfire, however, was ringing out across the grounds, and there was only a matter of time before they reached the cloisters.

Gabe kept well out of range and hovered above the lagoon.

Beneventi hadn't said a word after the initial yell of shock. Now he was as stiff as a board, and mute with terror. Gabe gripped him under the armpits like a toddler, and held him at arm's length. He looked into his eyes, seeing a spark of cunning in them as his terror subsided.

"So," Gabe said, "you are a descendant of the man who found Belial's jewels." He was older than Gabe had first thought. Late sixties, perhaps. Maybe older. But he was tanned and slim, with an air only the very wealthy could cultivate. *Arrogant prick.* He decided to goad him. "You look smaller than I expected. Insignificant. I can only presume your ancestor was more worthy."

"You know nothing about me or the power I wield."

"Not *your* power. Belial's. Without him, you would just be a mean little man who likes money. I knew Belial. I imagine he must despair of you. No wonder he brought Jiri in to manage you all."

"How dare you! We serve him and he pays us well! We do not need Jiri! Besides, Jiri arrived before my time."

"Yes, so I gather. Your other ancestors must have been weak and pathetic, too." Beneventi tried to kick Gabe, and swung his arms wildly, but his kicks were weak, and Gabe crushed his ribs even tighter. "Like I said. Weak."

"Even now my men are searching for your friends. You need to leave us alone, or they will die."

Gabe smiled. "I don't think you've done your homework, little man. My friends are Nephilim and witches. Powerful witches. Oh, and maybe an alchemist too, for good measure. You have no sway with me."

"Even if he sends Jiri after you?" Beneventi's eyes narrowed with cunning. "With Belial's jewels, he is unstoppable."

"You forget that I have his jewels, too. That's how Belial knows of us. It didn't save Amato, did it?"

"Amato was one of the most faithful. Belial is displeased."

"I couldn't give a shit. I hope he's fucking furious." Gabe adjusted his grip as if he might loosen Beneventi, and he gasped, clutching Gabe's arms.

"We can come to an agreement. We have money—a lot of money!"

"So do I. I don't need his money or influence. You see, many Nephilim, me and my brothers included, cast off the influence of our angel fathers millennia ago. I will not be yoked again. Now, where is Jiri?"

"You may as well kill me. I'll tell you nothing!"

"Oh, I'll kill you, there's no fear of that. The question is, will I kill you swiftly or slowly? It's your choice." Gabe had no intention of torturing him; it was abhorrent. Killing was brutal enough, but he didn't have to tell Beneventi that. Gabe squeezed the man's ribs even tighter, and discomfort flashed across his face.

He continued to plead, trying to catch his breath. "You don't understand, which surprises me. You are a Nephilim, with angel blood coursing through your veins. How can you settle for so little?"

"So little? You have no idea how I live. Instead, you listen to Belial's whispers. His jibes and taunts, and you think you know so much. But you are the one who knows so little."

"This world," Beneventi said, spitting saliva with frustration and pain, "is corrupt. We are cleansing it of the unbelievers."

"You are the corrupt one, you fool! Belial is the Angel of Death and Destruction. He didn't pick and choose his victims. He was indiscriminate, and so are you. You spread his jewels and his influence, causing arguments, violence, and confusion all around. But I care not to debate with a madman. Tell me where Jiri is."

"He has a stronghold that you will not penetrate."

"I've destroyed a Cathar castle. I can handle Jiri, and even his few supporters."

"I hardly call twenty of the House of Belial few. They are the equivalent of a hundred."

Twenty? So many? Or was he bluffing? Or even under-reporting? Twenty Nephilim could easily overpower his two brothers in Cornwall, and maybe even the witches in White Haven. And the Moonfell witches, too. His human friends would stand no chance.

"Where is he?"

"You will never find him. He will find *you* when you least expect it. When we have Belial's horn, then the world will quake."

"His horn?" Gabe feigned ignorance. "That is dust now. It will never be found. You're pinning your hopes on a dream."

"It's here. Belial knows it wasn't destroyed, and my ancestor had it for one moment before it was lost. It's just a matter of time before we possess it."

Beneventi's bluster and arrogance had returned. Gabe flipped him upside down, ignoring his screams, and took a moment to check his house. A sudden explosion ripped out half the building, and another blast destroyed the statue. Gabe winced. He had intended to read the plinth first. He hoped Shadow had thought to do so, too.

The bright plume of flames illuminated Gabe and Beneventi, and out of seemingly nowhere, a bolt from a crossbow whizzed past him. Gabe dived further over the lagoon, and Beneventi smacked into the water before he lifted him up again. Gabe scoured the sky, but there was no sign of a Nephilim. There must be a soldier on the ground that his team hadn't found yet. Already, he could see lights and sirens on the island from whatever small police force there was, and boats were mobilising in Venice. They had to leave.

Beneventi was screaming and flailing again. Gabe dipped lower, immersing him into the water for several long seconds. When he lifted the man clear again, he was spluttering and shivering. "Jiri?"

Beneventi gave Gabe a ragged grin, and open his clenched fist to reveal a ring. A bright light flashed out with a wave of Belial's power, almost blinding Gabe. He must have been waiting for when he was closer to the ground. Gabe dropped Beneventi in shock, and he plunged into the lagoon once more.

The man's eyes were glowing now, as Belial awoke within him. Gabe wrestled the alchemical weapon from his pocket and shot him, the weapon virtually eviscerating him. Then Gabe fled to find Shadow and Niel.

Shadow ran into Niel in the depths of the garden, both bloodied and bruised from their fights, and Niel's hand was pressed to his side, blood pouring from it.

"Niel! You've been shot?"

"A graze. I'll live."

"It looks worse than a graze."

"Sister," he said, glaring, "I'm *fine*. As long as my pretty face is still intact for seeing Mouse."

Another explosion by the gate rocked the grounds. "Perhaps we should discuss this later."

Niel frowned as he looked over his shoulder. "You've bombed the entrance?"

"Seemed logical. It's bought us more time." She glanced anxiously overhead. "Where is Gabe?"

But Niel didn't need to answer. A huge, winged shape came into view, wing tips gilded by blazing flames, and Shadow released a breath she didn't know she was holding. Gabe looked fine. Better than fine. His burnished muscles glowed in the light, and she wanted nothing more than to shower him with kisses and straddle him right there.

"Duck!" Gabe yelled. He fired over their heads to a man who had snuck up through the bushes. The man flew backwards, dead, propelled by the power of JD's weapon. Gabe brushed his hair back, smearing blood across his face. "Time to go."

"Wait!" Shadow turned away from them both. "I've found something."

Niel scanned their surroundings. "Can it wait? The police are virtually at the door."

"No, idiot. We're not coming back!" She ran, trusting the others would keep up, until she was standing in front of one of the other statues in the garden. Two men lay dead beneath it. "I thought that this was another statue of Belial, but I was wrong. Look at his face."

It was implacable, just like Belial's, but the face was broader, and his body was, too. His wings were outstretched, and he carried a sword in one hand, and a curved scimitar in the other.

"Herne's hair bollocks," Niel said, aghast. "It's Jiri. I'd forgotten he liked to use a scimitar."

Gabe agreed. "The face is his, too."

"Look at the plinth," Shadow urged them, scanning the grounds while they did so. She was pretty sure most people were dead here, but she didn't want to take any chances.

Gabe gasped. "Is that a city carved on the base? It's wreathed in clouds."

"It has a name under it, too," Niel noted, getting closer. "*Aethalia*. I've never heard of it."

"I think," Shadow said, "that it's where he is now. I've taken photos, and of the other sides. There's writing on it, but you can read that later. I nearly destroyed it, but I didn't."

Niel snorted with surprise. "Wow. Wonders will never cease."

Gabe, however, just smiled and opened his arms. "Now can we go?"

"With pleasure."

Twenty-Three

Olivia was halfway across the cavern, heading for the exit with Estelle, when Maggie joined them.

"Had enough?" Olivia asked her. She was pleased that Maggie had been brought up to speed on everything, especially now that they were a pack, as she, Maggie, Harlan, and Jackson called themselves after one drink too many one night. The thought made her smile. Maggie was being so supportive right now, she didn't know what she'd do without her.

"I was looking for you two, actually. I thought you were taking notes," Maggie said, as she fell into step next to them.

Estelle laughed. "We need food and drinks. The boys are totally absorbed in reading the pillars, and until they find something of use, it's a waste of our time. And besides," she glanced around as they neared the tunnel that exited the cavern, "this place gets claustrophobic after a while."

"I know that feeling," Maggie agreed. "I'll come and help you."

Olivia had her own reasons for leaving. She needed distance from Nahum. He was like a drug. The longer she spent with him, the more addicted she became. Her talk with Estelle had both reassured her and terrified her. She felt she was losing herself in Nahum, and that was ridiculous. Absolutely nothing had happened between them after that one, fateful night, and he had only been kind and solicitous since, and yet there was a growing connection between them that she couldn't ignore. Every time they touched, it was electric.

As they stepped out of the marquee and into the garden, she took a deep, cleansing breath, and stared at the spray of stars above her. *Calm down. Don't get ahead of yourself. It will all be okay.*

And then she blinked as something seemed to block out the stars.

Something about her posture must have alerted Estelle, who asked, "What's wrong?"

"I thought I saw something. Maybe it was an owl." By now all three women were staring up at the sky, and Olivia shivered, drawing her jacket around her. "Sorry. I'm just tired."

Estelle didn't move. "No, something is definitely above us. More than one, actually. I don't think those are birds blocking out the stars. They're Nephilim." Olivia's head whipped up again as Estelle said, "Look how high they seem, and yet the wingspan is too big. I can barely see them, though."

"I see them, too," Maggie said, voice grim. She grabbed Olivia's elbow and yanked her back into the marquee. "Get back here, Estelle. They're gathering, probably watching us as we watch them. With luck, they might not have seen us yet."

Olivia's mouth gaped open in shock as she peered up, head peeking out of the marquee. The figures overhead circled, getting bigger and bigger with every pass. "Holy shit. Could it be Zee or Eli?"

"No. They would have called, and there are more than two," Estelle said with certainty. "These are not our Nephilim. Olivia, go get the others. *Now!*"

"Let me," Maggie said, leaping into action. "You two watch them, but run for cover if they attack."

"Oh, they'll attack," Estelle said softly, still watching the sky as Maggie ran back inside. "They're observing, for now. Well spotted, Olivia." She dropped her gaze and ducked her head back inside. "You need to go inside, too. The cave, I mean. This could be a general attack, or they could have come for you specifically."

Olivia's blood turned to ice. "But what will you do?"

"Hold them off. I think JD has got some sort of defence system here. I hope it's activated." The witch flexed her fingers, and a pulse of power crackled along the tips before she balled fire in her hands. "Fire is my strongest element," she told Olivia, "but I have plenty of spells to use, too. It just depends on whether they wield Belial's power."

Suddenly, everything seemed very real and frightening. "They're Belial's Nephilim?"

"Do you know of any more?"

"Sorry! I'm normally cool-headed, but," her hand flew to her stomach subconsciously, "I have other worries now. I'm not leaving you alone, though. What can I do?"

"Arm yourself with one of JD's weapons." Estelle pointed at the tables that were still in the centre of the marquee. "I saw them earlier. Careful how you handle them! Unfortunately, mine's in my bag in the cave."

Olivia already knew about the weapons. Harlan and Nahum had told her all about them, and she had seen Nahum's. He had even shown her how to use it. "Not a problem," she called out as she raced to the tables.

A blast of fire ignited the dark behind her, and Olivia whirled around. Estelle was already hurling balls of flames skywards. Turning her attention to the tables again, Olivia spotted a series of the ovoid weapons, and picked up a copper one. It warmed in her hands, and she took a deep breath to stop shaking.

An enormous tearing sound erupted overhead, and she looked up in horror as a curved blade sliced through the marquee's roof. Without hesitation, Olivia fired, almost falling over in shock as a searing flash of red light sizzled through the marquee. A roar of anger followed.

But then more swords slashed through the tent's roof. Olivia fired as accurately as she could, running to the cave entrance. "Estelle! Get back here!" But Estelle wasn't even at the marquee's door anymore.

Olivia's voice was lost in the noise of sizzling magic, and despite her numerous shots, a Nephilim dropped through the roof and onto a tabletop. He was dark-haired, with eyes of flames, and his wings were pure white. He was clad in silver armour, and he carried two swords, almost as long as he was tall.

And then he saw her.

He grinned wolfishly, bounded off the table, and raced towards her.

Estelle ran onto the wide lawn that encompassed the marquee, and quickly cast a circle of protection around her.

At least half a dozen Nephilim were winging out of the sky, most aiming for the marquee, others for the house. Estelle knew she'd have the best chance of attacking out in the open. All the Nephilim were armed with either curved scimitars or broadswords. One dived down at her. She threw a cascade of fireballs at him, so many that he couldn't dodge them all. But he was shockingly quick.

He wheeled around and attacked again, while another Nephilim tried to distract her from a different direction. She attacked with a jet of wind. Caspian had taught her how to harness air more effectively, and she put it to good use now. Mixing fire and wind together, she sent a flaming tornado up and out, and the Nephilim scattered—but not for long.

Standing in the open was leaving her vulnerable to attack on all sides. She brought her hands together with a clap, amplifying it with magic. The sound thundered across the grounds as she cast the spell. The closest Nephilim's wings caught fire, and he screamed in agony.

However, she couldn't distract the Nephilim from the marquee, and more were dropping through the roof now. *Where were the others? Where was Anna?*

Lucien was wandering the cavern on his own, lost in his thoughts, and mesmerised by his surroundings.

He was beyond grateful that he had joined the others, fearing that he would be left behind in London. He still felt not quite part of the group, despite everyone's welcoming attitude, but Barak had just said, "You're coming too, right?"

So, here he was, a super-soldier who had no idea how to fight as well as the Nephilim, surrounded by ancient magic in a palace of wonders. There was no sign of the others now, however. He had left them behind, and he was now at the far end of the cave. At one point he thought it would go on forever. It was easy to get turned around and disoriented. However, the columns had ended, and a towering wall of sheer emerald stretched ahead of him, like a huge ice cliff in Antarctica. He walked along it, determined to map the perimeter. It was shadowy here, the lamplight barely penetrating. A fine powder was on the floor, like sand, and it crunched beneath his feet as he kept the wall to his left.

He crouched, filtering the powder though his fingers. *Emerald dust*, he was sure. It was fine, like the gems and metals that had been ground and added to ink to make his tattoos. His skin tingled, and with surprise he watched his skin change to copper—except, he hadn't willed it.

"No!" he shouted in surprise, trying to brush the powder away, fearing he was changing without control.

However, he didn't feel any different, and as he focussed, his heart rate settling, his skin changed back to normal again. *What the hell was happening?* His finger traced the fine design of the alchemical bracelet JD had made for him, and as the emerald dust rubbed into it, the metals glowed, too.

Suddenly curious, rather than scared, he rubbed the dust over his arms, and this time actively willed his skin to change. The alchemical reaction was like breathing to him now. He felt stronger, and his vision became more acute as he transformed. Where he'd rubbed the emerald dust, his skin and tattoos glowed with extra brightness and hardness. It had enhanced him even more. He peeled his t-shirt off, rubbing more of the emerald dust across his chest, and immediately saw the change there, too.

He straightened up, seeing the cave with new vision. The pillars had light within them, and the script etched on the surface glowed with an Otherworldly light. He was somehow attuned to the cave. He saw a broad archway a short distance ahead in the wall of the cave. It was twice his height, and the longer he stared, the more it seemed to solidify and yet shimmer all at the same time. And then he saw more of them. There were more rooms here, hidden within the walls themselves.

Unable to contain his curiosity, he stepped through an archway into a room beyond, and found a cache of weapons. Shields, swords, and daggers, all ornate, all ancient. He grabbed a shield, hefting it on his arm. It was lightweight and seemed to mould to his body. *More alchemical weirdness.*

He needed to tell the others. However, he had progressed only a short way across the cave when he heard Maggie's anguished shout, and he ran.

Nahum flew through the cave as soon as he heard Maggie's shout for help, Barak next to him. They left the others far behind.

As Nahum reached the end of the tunnel, he saw the dark-haired Nephilim advancing on Olivia. She fired JD's weapon at him as she retreated, upending chairs in his path, but he moved like the wind, his speed supernatural.

Fortunately, the intruder was so fixated on Olivia that he didn't see Nahum until the last moment. Nahum angled over her, slicing his sword at the Nephilim's head. With impossibly quick reflexes, his opponent's head whipped up, and he blocked him with one sword, while striking with another. Nahum wheeled around, using his wings as a weapon, dropped onto a table top, and pivoted on the balls of his feet. He launched at him again, keeping his attacker's focus away from Olivia. He glanced around, assessing the risks, and saw that Barak was tackling another Nephilim who had broken through the roof of the marquee. But more were arriving now, swords flashing as the marquee's roof was slashed to ribbons.

Nahum didn't know his opponent, but he recognised the insignia on his breast-plate. *The House of Belial.* He didn't appear to be wearing any of Belial's tokens, though. But that was as much as he could take in. They met with a fierce clash of swords and grunting aggression. Fortunately, Nahum was used to fighting warriors after months of battling Black Cronos, and the Nephilim was distracted by Olivia, who was still firing at all the newcomers. Their armour was obviously enhanced, as they seemed impervious to JD's weapons.

"You will die here!" Nahum yelled. "Leave now while you have the chance."

"And leave your spawn behind in the human whore? I think not." His eyes sparked with malice as he slashed at Nahum.

Olivia shouted in outrage. "*Whore*? Who the fuck are you calling a whore? Get back, Nahum!"

The searing red light of the alchemical weapon sliced down the Nephilim's wing, leaving it shattered and broken. He roared in pain and shock. *Clearly, not everything was impervious.* Olivia struck again, hitting the other wing and making Nahum dive for cover behind a table. Her aim was scattered in her fury, but she had already caused enough damage. Nahum knew that the pain of severed wings would be immense. He leapt in and ended him, forcing his blade though his neck to behead him.

Then he swung around, ready to face another attacker.

Harlan sprinted towards the cave's entrance, flanked by Jackson, Maggie, and JD. The two Nephilim were already way ahead, and he had no idea where Lucien was.

"I have to get to my control tower," JD said, trotting to try and keep up with the others.

"Aren't your defences already on?" Harlan asked in horror as he contemplated the alternative.

"Only the ground ones! That will be of no use if Nephilim are attacking from the sky."

"Well, why the hell weren't they on already?" he asked, exasperated.

"Because of the birds, you bloody fool! They would be eviscerated!"

Chastised, Harlan fell silent, instead focussing on withdrawing his alchemical weapon, something he'd taken to carrying with him always now. *Thank the Gods he was paranoid.* "Maggie, you should stay in there!"

"Not a fucking chance!" She sprinted next to him, JD falling behind. "We need all the help we can get. I just need a weapon. We'll need to escort JD to wherever the fuck his control centre is."

"The roof." Harlan remembered the glass-walled control centre well. *The farthest damn point from here.* "Jackson, are you armed?"

Jackson nodded. "I have my handgun."

JD wheezed behind them. "I have some of mine on the tables out front."

Harlan slowed in disbelief and dread when they all reached the end of the cave's tunnel. Olivia was firing wildly, destroying tables and igniting the marquee, while Nahum and Barak battled with four Nephilim. Another was already dead on the floor, his wings shattered and smoking. Harlan wanted to shoot to try and help them, but all of the Nephilim were fighting so quickly they were a blur, and he feared he'd accidently hurt his friends.

"Olivia!" Harlan shouted. "You're a terrible shot! Stop!"

"Screw you, Harlan. I helped kill that one!"

"And you'll kill Barak or Nahum next, the way you're going. Come with me and JD. We're heading to the house."

"No! I'm staying with Nahum."

"No, you're not," Nahum yelled, grunting as he fought. "You go with them."

Jackson had already sprinted to the marquee's entrance, after weaving through the fighting men. "It's not looking any better out there. Estelle is fighting off more Nephilim. At least three."

"Help her!" Barak commanded. The big man was a blur of darkness, his huge wings sweeping tables and chairs out of the way as he fought. The marquee that had seemed huge before now felt far too small with the battling Nephilim in there.

"They must not get into the cave," JD said, wringing his hands. "They might destroy everything!"

"JD, we can't wait. We have to get to the tower, or we'll all be dead, and there'll be no one left who cares about the damn cave!"

And then Lucien suddenly appeared behind them all. "I will protect the cave. Go."

Harlan turned, and almost staggered back in surprise. Lucien was carrying an enormous shield, and he was a super-soldier once again, his skin glowing like burnished copper. But he looked different.

"Lucien? Where did you get the shield? What's going on?"

"I found something. Now go! I have this!"

Harlan nodded. "Thank you. Come on, Olivia."

"No!" She stuck her chin up, defiantly. "I'm staying!"

Harlan had known Olivia long enough to know when she wouldn't budge on something. "Fine! Lucien, you better protect Olivia, too!"

Harlan spotted alchemical weapons on the ground where they had fallen from an overturned table, and grabbing them, he handed them to JD and Maggie, saving one for Jackson. "Let's go. Maggie?"

Maggie cast an anguished glance at Olivia. "I'm not sure whether to go or not."

Olivia pushed her ungraciously towards Harlan. "Harlan is right. JD has to get to his tower. Go!"

"Be careful, Liv!"

Harlan led the way through the fighting Nephilim, and out onto the lawn.

Jackson didn't wait for the others. He sprinted across the lawn, firing his gun upwards as he ran. More and more Nephilim seemed to be arriving now, wheeling across the sky like huge bats.

Estelle was encased in a protective circle, three Nephilim trying to get close but failing as she attacked them relentlessly.

"Estelle. Get to the house! I'll cover you."

"But Barak is in there," she said, not stopping her attack.

"He's okay! Get moving." He fired at another Nephilim, and then rolled across the ground as one dived at him. They were too vulnerable out there. He looked behind him, relieved to see Harlan, JD, and Maggie closing the distance between them, firing wildly overhead.

Estelle didn't budge. "I'll wait until the others are close to the door."

As much as he admired Estelle's power and stubborn resilience, he knew she was wrong. "No, you'll end up stranded." He fired upwards again, most shots missing in his haste, and then glanced to the house to assess the distance. *Damn it.* A huge Nephilim had landed by the door, and was waiting for them. His outstretched wings blocked the door's entrance, and he twirled his swords as if taunting Jackson.

Harlan caught up and passed him an alchemical weapon. "Use this. Target their wings."

Jackson made a sudden decision as he blasted at the Nephilim on the door, combining his timing with the others. "You go. I can't leave Estelle. Run!"

It was growing increasingly dangerous on the lawn. All of them were firing at the Nephilim. A few were still flying, while others were advancing across the grounds. The alchemical weapons gave them a slim advantage, and were the only things keeping them alive. Jackson realised that staying out there was insane, but he couldn't leave Estelle alone.

Harlan knew it too, but he also knew they couldn't wait, and he ran, dragging Maggie and JD with him. "Stay safe, my friend."

Estelle yelled, "Get in here now, you bloody idiot!" He glanced over his shoulder, seeing Estelle slice open her protective circle with a cutting motion. "Now!"

He stumbled backwards, just about getting inside as a Nephilim took advantage of the lull in magic to attack. Estelle grabbed him by the collar and yanked him backwards, sealing the circle again with a word of command.

Instantly the noise muted, and her power crackled around them. *They were safe, but for how long*, he wondered as he studied the charging Nephilim.

Barak fought with increasing rage, aware that Estelle was outside fighting deadly Nephilim. He was not comforted by the fact that their friends were with her. They were all human and therefore vulnerable.

He needed to help her, but Nahum and Lucien were fighting another couple of Nephilim who had dropped through the roof. *Surely there couldn't be many more of them?* Four already lay dead on the floor, killed by a mixture of blades and alchemical weapons.

Barak caught sight of Olivia hanging back in the cave's entrance, desperate to fire JD's weapon. His anger at the assault fuelled his strength and increased his speed. These Nephilim, for all of their size, had clearly not fought like this in a long while, unlike he and his brothers, and they also had the advantage of JD's weapons that the Nephilim clearly weren't expecting. Barak had to thank JD later. They had definitely gifted them the advantage. And for some reason, their attackers did not carry Belial's tokens.

"Does he not trust you to wear his jewels?" Barak sneered as his sword sliced his opponent's arm before he danced out of the way.

"What we do," he replied, breathing heavily, "with his tokens is none of your business."

Barak smirked. "Perhaps you have run out because we have found them all."

The Nephilim lunged, and Barak stumbled back under his onslaught. He grabbed a table and used it like a shield. "You are a fool if you believe that, Barak of the House of Kathazel."

Barak was so shocked that he knew his name that he stumbled again, almost allowing his blade to reach him. "Have we met before?"

"No. Belial has his ways."

Barak was about to ask more questions when a sizzling, red beam of light struck the Nephilim in the neck, blowing a hole right through it. Barak followed up with a swing of his sword and beheaded him, even though he was already dead.

He looked around to see Lucien holding the gun, and Nahum breathing heavily as his opponent also lay dead at his feet. "Thanks, Lucien. I need to find Estelle. Can you stay here?"

"Of course. I have this. You too, Nahum. I will guard Olivia."

Nahum looked torn with indecision, but Barak checked the marquee one more time, and relieved that no one else was dropping though the roof, he nodded. "Thanks, Lucien. Get back down the tunnel. You'll defend the entrance easier than being here."

Lucien herded Olivia ahead of him. "Don't worry, I will."

Barak ran outside and immediately flew, taking in the scene, and Nahum joined him. He sought out Estelle, and found her in the middle of the lawn with Jackson, surrounded by a protection circle of shimmering, blue light. A few Nephilim were dead, while more still circled them. Others were trying to stop Harlan, JD, and Maggie who were almost at the door to the house, a dead Nephilim sprawled across the threshold, his body smoking from the many wounds that had been inflicted on him.

Without a word, they dived down to help.

Maggie sidestepped the Nephilim's body and threw open the back door of JD's house, her alchemical weapon raised.

A figure shouted, "Stop or I'll shoot!"

"For fuck's sake, Anna! It's me, Maggie. Are you okay?"

"Of course not!" Anna stepped into the light, looking terrified, her hands trembling as she held a shotgun.

"Get back. We're coming in." Maggie unceremoniously shoved JD inside. "Go. I'll follow." Harlan was still firing on the other Nephilim, and she was relieved to see Barak and Nahum fighting nearby. "Harlan, are you coming?"

"No." He glanced at her before firing on the diving Nephilim again. "You go, though, and make sure JD gets up there safely. And be quick! I suspect there will be more coming."

Maggie pounded down the hall, following JD who was barking orders at Anna as he ran for the stairs. "Head to the lab and grab the bombs. You know where they are."

"JD, you know I hate those weapons and your lab."

"I don't care! Get them, and take them to Harlan."

"I never signed up for this, JD!" Anna looked furious.

"Neither did any of us! Now do it. I have to activate the grid."

Maggie felt sorry for Anna, but JD was right. She had to pitch in and help. "Actually, Anna, bring me a couple of bombs, too."

Anna just huffed and headed down the stairs to the cellar lab.

Maggie shrugged it off as she followed JD, both wary, and with their weapons raised. Fortunately, it seemed there were no Nephilim in the house. On the first floor, JD went to flick the lights on, and Maggie stopped him.

"I wouldn't. It will alert them to where we are."

"They know we're in here."

"But not *where*, and," she added, catching a glimpse of the fighting through the hall windows, "I'd like to keep it that way."

In a few more minutes they arrived in the huge attic space. One wall was glass and opened onto a roof terrace. JD opened a door in the panelling and led them upstairs. *So, this was the control tower that Harlan was wittering about.* It was crazy. Like the controls of a spaceship—or so she imagined. It gave a perfect view of the grounds, and Maggie watched with increasing horror. Nahum was tumbling end over end, locked in a deadly embrace with a Nephilim. Three other Nephilim were still flying, frustrated at not being able to get close to Estelle and Jackson, but Estelle had gone very still, as if summoning her power for another assault. She couldn't see Harlan at all, and she realised he was still out of view, close to the house.

"Can I help, JD?"

He didn't answer, concentrating on flicking switches on his console. Lights flickered on the edge of the grounds.

"JD," she prompted, "did you say that you're activating a sort of dome?"

He kept working while he said, "Yes."

"How high will it be?" She kept an eye on the Nephilim flying outside the window, almost at their level.

"It will cover the whole house, obviously, another twenty metres above."

"So, Nahum and Barak have to keep below that?"

"Oh, yes. If not, they'll be caught in the beams and die."

"Do they know?"

"Well, they should," he answered grumpily.

"But they're fighting, which means they're distracted!"

"Well, you better tell them, then."

And that also meant any Nephilim still alive would be trapped inside with them. *Bollocking, fuckity fuck!*

The glass control tower was in darkness, but the flashing lights inside were drawing attention, and Maggie swore loudly. "For fuck's sake! I think they've seen us. Is there a window here?"

"Downstairs. You can get on to the roof through the sliding doors."

"Okay, I'm heading outside. How long will you be?"

"Two minutes at the most, just charging it all now."

Maggie raced back down the stairs, thudding into Anna at the base. Anna thrust what looked like an eggbox at her. "Here are your bombs."

"How do they work?"

"I don't know!" She was already bolting to the door.

"Anna, you're a bad liar. You must know!" Maggie wanted to slap her, immortal or not.

"You twist each half, in the centre." She mimed the action. "Ten seconds, and they blow."

"Thank you!" Maggie's voice dripped with sarcasm as she raced to the roof terrace. "Although, this is your home. Perhaps you should fucking help!"

The cold night air was bracing, and the battle cries were loud. Maggie fired at a Nephilim who flew at the tower, sending him wheeling. A bomb exploded below, and a Nephilim was thrown backwards. She fumbled for a bomb, too, planning to throw it at the Nephilim in the air.

However, in seconds, Anna was with her. She extended a hand, jaw tight, eyes full of fury. "Give me one."

Maggie smacked one into her palm, and with startling speed, Anna activated it and hurled it under the Nephilim that Maggie had fired at. It exploded below him, not quite underneath him, but close enough, and he shot skywards.

Impressed, Maggie passed her another. "Great shot!" Then she shouted to Nahum and Barak, gesturing with her hands, hoping they would understand her. "Nahum, Barak, keep low!"

What was taking JD so long?

Then Anna pointed upwards. "What's that?"

Two bright lights like shooting stars were hurtling towards the house from far above.

"Holy shit. They're Nephilim wielding Belial's tokens. They'll kill us all."

"Then we need to slow them down." Anna grabbed a catapult off the table on the terrace, twisted a bomb to activate it, and expertly fitted it into the catapult's pouch. In seconds, the bomb was hurtling upwards to meet the descending Nephilim. It exploded with shocking brilliance, the shockwave sending Nahum and Barak tumbling to the ground.

"Well, you're a dark horse," Maggie told her.

"Who do you think helps test these damn things?" She fired another with surprising accuracy, the shock of the explosion almost knocking Maggie off her feet. The flaming Nephilim slowed to divert around it. They were so close now that Maggie could see them in all their glory. Their outstretched wings were bathed in an almost incandescent white light. She could see the murderous intent in their eyes, and the flames dancing along their swords.

Another explosive kick of power rippled across the house and grounds, like a localised display of the Northern Lights. JD had activated his shield. Of the two Nephilim wielding Belial's power, one was caught in it, and he vanished, vapourised, the other was stuck on the outside.

For a brief moment, their eyes locked, and Maggie felt the full brunt of his anger. It was so palpable that she fell backwards into a chair, his eyes feeling like they had burned a hole in her head. He lifted his sword and pointed it at her, as if promising what was to come, and then he turned off whatever power he had used, his incandescent light diminishing, examined the view below, and in seconds, he flew away.

Estelle raced across the lawn to the last Nephilim she'd brought down. He lay on the ground, wings smouldering, his skin badly burned by the fire balls she had released.

Barak was also running over, his sword raised ready to dispense justice.

"No!" Estelle shouted. "Wait!"

Barak stood over the injured man. "Why?"

"Because we need him to tell us where the others are."

The Nephilim spat at her feet, barely hanging on to his consciousness he was so badly wounded. "I will tell you nothing!"

"Careful," Barak warned, sword at his neck, "or your death will be slow. Help us and I will show mercy."

The man laughed, blood staining his teeth. "I doubt that."

Jackson had followed her, and he asked, "How will you get him to talk?"

"Glamour. I need you all to hold him down—just in case." Although she doubted he'd mount much resistance.

By now Nahum and Harlan had arrived, and without argument, all four pinned the Nephilim down. Estelle crouched beside him, aware of the other dead bodies close by. She hated all this death and destruction. Excitement and treasure hunting was one thing, but this was something else. When this business was over with Belial, she wanted a new direction with Barak. She hoped he would want the same. This was not what her magic was for. For a long time she didn't know how she wanted to use it, she just knew she needed to use it to its full potential. But now... Well, this wasn't the way.

Pushing her objections to the back of her mind, she cupped the man's face in her hands and stared deep into his eyes. The pain he suffered was enormous. She had inflicted that. She took a deep breath and cast her glamour spell, feeling its power roll into the fallen man. Nephilim were generally too strong to succumb, but this man was near death. Nevertheless, he tried to resist.

"Tell me where Jiri is."

He ground out words through clenched teeth. "Screw you."

Estelle decided to try another angle before she recast the glamour spell. "Belial's time is at an end, or should be, and you know it too. Is this really what you wanted when you came here? To be doing his bidding once again? Or did you want true freedom, like these Nephilim have?"

He gave a grim laugh, blood speckling his chin. "Belial does not offer freedom. Death is my only way out."

"It is now, for you, but not for the others. What if we could work together and defeat him? Would Jiri help?"

"Jiri would never help you."

"Would the other Nephilim help?"

"And betray our commander? Never."

Barak's deep voice rumbled a request. "Forget commanders. Forget rules! Make your own."

The Nephilim's eyes flickered with what looked like hope before it vanished again. "It's not possible."

"Yes it is, because we did it."

Nahum nodded, adding his own support. "Yes, we did. We have long lives, too long to live under the yoke of Belial."

Estelle turned the man's face so he was staring at her again. "Tell us where Jiri is, or who we can contact who will help us." She reinforced her glamour spell, and added one to dull his pain, but tried not to confuse him. Regret was the man's overriding emotion though, and she appealed to that. "Who would help us? I know someone will. I can see it in your eyes."

"Ozan. There will be a few others too." He gave the name up easily this time.

Estelle felt Barak flinch in surprise, but she didn't dare break eye contact with the injured Nephilim now. "Where are you based?"

"Cabo." His speech slurred as he slipped away, his eyes glazing.

"I need more details! Where is that?" Trying to keep him with her, Estelle asked, "What is your name?"

"Emre."

"Thank you, Emre. We need a number. A way to contact Ozan."

But Emre was already dead.

"No!" She groaned, head falling forward with disappointment. "Damn it!"

Harlan however was searching the man's pockets, and with a cry of triumph, he shouted, "Yes!"

He had found Emre's phone.

Twenty-Four

Ash opened the door of the rented villa for his brothers and Shadow at two in the morning, taking in their dishevelled appearance, and cuts and bruises. They all stank of smoke.

"Good journey?" he asked, leading them to the small living room.

"Quiet. No one followed us." Gabe shrugged his jacket off and threw it on the sofa. "We took a circuitous route, just in case."

"Too bloody circuitous," Niel complained. He was streaked with sweat and ash. "We could have been here half an hour ago."

"Oh, stop whining," Shadow said, shutting the door behind her. "At least we're safe for a while."

"I take it," Ash asked, amused, "that you created a little bit of trouble?"

Gabe snorted. "We created havoc, although we made a clean getaway. At least, I think we did." Gabe pulled Ash into a hug. "I'm glad to see that you're okay after your own fight."

"It was touch and go for a while." Ash was bare chested, wearing only his jeans that he'd pulled on in a hurry, and the scratches on his arms and back were obvious, as was the graze along his ribs from the crossbolt.

As agreed late the previous afternoon, the group had decided that Ash needed a place to stay after his long drive to find Lamberti's paperwork, somewhere that Gabe and the others could get to easily if needed. It was obvious that staying in Venice for much longer was not an option. So, prior to leaving the Venetian apartment, Ash had made a short-term rental booking of a villa partway between Palazzuolo sul Senio and Venice, along with a second rental car for his own use. Fortunately, they had managed to secure a big enough place, deep within the countryside and far from neighbours. Not even Romola knew where they were now.

He rubbed the sleep from his eyes and brushed his hair back from his face as he headed to the kitchen. He had managed a couple of hours' sleep, far too tired to examine the paperwork he'd retrieved, and had placed it under his pillow.

"Coffee?" he asked.

"Very strong, please," Niel said, leaning his axe against the wall. Flecks of dark, dried blood still marked the blade. "I'll head to the shower first. I won't be long."

For the next few minutes, the group cleaned up and changed their clothes, and after making the coffee, Ash retrieved the paperwork from his room. He carefully opened the pages, relieved to see that the oilskin package had kept the information safe. He scanned the list of names, noting that Lamberti had even listed the type of jewel for each piece, whether it was a ring, torc, clasp, necklace, or even short, jewelled daggers.

Gabe took a seat in the armchair and poured himself a coffee from the pot on the table. He'd showered and was wearing clean clothes, although he needed a shave. Stubble lay thick on his cheeks, and his damp hair was unruly. More than anything, he looked tired, but he also looked hopeful as he saw the paperwork in Ash's hands. "Anything useful?"

"Plenty. Whether they're still where they are listed, though, is another matter. This is dated about five years ago. There are, I estimate, about thirty people that we'll need to track down. Have you found out anything?"

"Shadow did." Gabe looked up as Niel and Shadow entered the room, both wearing loose trousers and t-shirts after their showers. "We have a clue as to where Jiri is, but the name is unfamiliar to us. However, Estelle also managed to give us useful information. I take it you haven't heard from Barak or Nahum?"

Ash sat upright, alarmed. "No, why?"

"A dozen Nephilim attacked JD's place. It was touch and go for a while, but they're okay. Mostly. No serious injuries." Gabe outlined what had happened.

Ash felt terrible. His night had been nothing compared to everyone else's.

"I can't believe they attacked. Estelle did well to get Emre to talk." He could see the scene only too well. *The blood. The fear.*

"Very well," Gabe agreed. "If Emre is right, and some of them will help us, we can win this!"

"Have they called Ozan yet?"

"They're trying to decide on the right time." Gabe closed his eyes briefly. "Tomorrow morning, perhaps."

"If Ozan was a good friend to Emre, he won't take kindly to the call."

"He will if it gets him his freedom. But just in case, we need to find out where they are." He looked across to Shadow. "Show him the photos. If we can identify the island, maybe the place name that Estelle was given will make sense."

Shadow sat next to Ash on the sofa, and after accessing the images, she handed her phone over. Ash frowned. "Another statue?"

"There were several in the garden," she explained. "Most were of Belial, but this one was different. Gabe says it's Jiri. That's the base."

Ash enlarged the images. "If Jiri has his own statue, it must mean they consider him very important. Is that a cityscape?" The image showed the relief of a range of buildings, their silhouettes standing proud of the stonework.

"Looks like one, doesn't it? On the other side of the plinth is what looks like an island. Very stylized, with waves around it."

Ash kept scrolling, reading the words carved into the base. "It exalts Jiri as Belial's commander. It's a bit grandiose."

Niel grunted. "He was always a pompous ass."

"The text," Gabe says, "describes him as returning to the base of his power, where he will centre his command. A place called Aethalia. We don't know the name, so I've searched for it. It's the name of a few boats and tankers. That can't be right!"

"Aethalia." Ash frowned, knowing it sounded familiar. "It was the name of an island. It's Greek."

Niel had been slumped in the chair, but now he perked up. "A Greek island?"

"No, but it was in the Mediterranean, though." Ash was still tired, and his eyes felt dry. He needed more sleep. However, he handed Shadow her phone and accessed his own, quickly pulling up a map of Europe. "It was in this area, I think."

"Could it be anything on that northeasterly line?" Shadow asked.

Ash glanced at her. "That's a great suggestion. It can't be further north from here, so we must have to go south. Just off the Italian coast is Sardinia, Corsica, and..." He frowned as he enlarged the image. "Elba."

Niel looked confused. "Elbow?"

"No! *Elba*. It's where Napoleon was exiled. That's it!" Ash felt more alert as excitement welled. "Look at the shape of it compared to what's on the base. It's the same."

Everyone crowded around as Ash showed them the image. Then he did another search of Elba and grinned. "I knew I recognised the name! It was called Aethalia by the Greeks. It was famous for its mines."

Gabe took the phone off him and scanned the details, while Ash looked at the photos of the statue's base again.

"So, we've found him?" Shadow asked, eyes sharp.

"Looks like it," Gabe answered, "if he hasn't moved. But why advertise where he lives on his statue?"

"It isn't so much where he lives, it's just about him! Of course," Ash said, as more memories returned, "I remember rumours that whispered while we had palaces, he had a bloody island. It was under his dominion for a while before the Flood. It all adds up."

"So, the statues pointing in one direction originate from Elba?" Shadow asked, confused. "Again, why?"

"Maybe they like games?"

"Maybe," Niel suggested, "they didn't think anyone would notice the statues aligned in one direction. I mean, they were supposed to be private. So, what now?"

"We have to go there," Gabe said. "If that's where he's based, we go to the source. The name that Emre gave Estelle was Cabo. Let's see... There's a place called Cavo! Could that be it?"

"Perhaps," Ash said. "You said he was dying. He could have mispronounced the place's name. Unless, of course, he was lying and just pretending to help. I'm certain of the island, though."

"Good. The rest," Gabe nodded at the paperwork that Ash had found, "can wait until afterwards."

Ash leaned back, hands behind his head, thinking through their options. "Did you kill all the humans tonight?"

"Most, I think," Gabe said. He looked uncomfortable. "I didn't want to, but they talked so remorselessly about their plans that I couldn't stand it. It was like a game to them, and Beneventi said their aim was to cleanse the Earth of unbelievers. He was deranged. There was no way to save them."

Shadow nodded in agreement. "If they had all been initiated as Lamberti suggested, they were already possessed by Belial's madness. It struck me that they were his eyes. He'll be weaker without them."

"Not weak enough." Niel poured himself more coffee. "He still has his Nephilim. Well, some of them. Even less, if Ozan will join us."

Ash hated putting his faith in others he didn't know, but if they had someone on the inside, it could change everything.

Gabe continued. "We stick with the plan. Tomorrow—or rather, later today—Niel, you meet Mouse in Istanbul, and we'll fly to Elba. Estelle, Barak, and Lucien will join us. Everyone else will remain at JD's for protection, while Nahum will stay to help with the translations. Zee and Eli will remain in Cornwall. I don't want those jewels to go missing. Then, if we can contact Ozan, well, we go from there."

"Which means," Niel said, darkly, "I can't join you in Elba, because I have to get the horn back to Cornwall."

"Exactly. You cannot bring it to Elba."

"If I don't find it, though, I'm coming."

"Fair enough. And Ash, there's more news." Gabe looked at Ash again, his expression unreadable. "They found something else in the emerald cave. Something weird."

Olivia sipped overly sweet tea in the wreckage of the marquee, wishing she could drink hard spirits like everyone else.

She wasn't sure why they were all in the marquee instead of JD's house, but it seemed everyone wanted to be close to the emerald cave and have a good view of the garden to ensure their attackers wouldn't return. They had righted tables, swept broken glass aside, and lit a multitude of lamps. The dead were on the lawn. Most of their team were injured. She had cuts and bruises from where she had rolled across the floor and dived under broken tables. Nahum and Barak looked the worst. They were covered in cuts, grazes, and ugly gashes. Nahum had an especially deep cut along his abdomen. It was now bound and dressed, and Estelle had cast a little healing magic. Fortunately, his own naturally accelerated healing was already having an effect. Barak had glowed from within, his healing abilities different to Nahum's, and it had healed an ugly cut across his forearm in no time.

Lucien had fared better. His weird, metallic skin rebuffed even the heaviest blows, and their Nephilim attackers had looked at him with ill-disguised unease. Estelle remained the least affected, but she was drained after using so much magic. Olivia also suspected that killing Nephilim had taken its toll. She looked defeated, despite their success. *At least they were safe.* The grounds hummed with power now that JD's weird dome had fully activated, and it was invisible, thank the Gods, after its initial pulse of green.

Nahum was sitting so close to Olivia that she could feel his heat, and her skin tingled as his arm brushed hers. He was solicitous, unconcerned about his own injuries. She felt loved. Seen. She liked it. But he didn't love her. He was just being Nahum, and that thought pained her more than anything.

Her thoughts were all over the place, but she focussed on the conversation as Jackson asked JD, "How long will the dome thing last?"

"As long as I want it to. It's a source of constant power. But, as I said, birds will die, and I don't like that."

"Better them than us," Harlan drawled sarcastically. He also looked rumpled and bruised after the battle on the lawn.

"They won't come back," Maggie said with certainty. "That remaining Nephilim, the one who was lit up like a bloody star, knew he couldn't cross your barrier. Unless they find a way, of course. Have you warned your brothers in Cornwall?"

Barak nodded. "The witches are confident that their protection spell will work. Plus, they might not have identified our home. With luck, this will be over in a couple of days if Ash is correct about where Jiri's base is, and Emre wasn't lying. Let's hope we can contact Ozan tomorrow and make a deal." They had accessed Emre's phone using his fingerprint, and found the number of the Nephilim they hoped would help them. Barak stifled a yawn. "I need to go to bed and get some sleep if we're to be rested for our flight later today. JD, are you sure about having beds for all of us? You don't exactly own a hotel."

JD waved off his enquiry airily. "A couple of you might have to share, but it will all work out. Anna is organising it now."

"She is wasted as your housekeeper," Maggie said. "She's a mean shot with the catapult."

"Ah, yes." JD smirked. "She's helped me test things over the years, but she doesn't like violence."

"Well, she sure steps up when she needs to. With a little provocation," she added slyly. She cocked an eyebrow at Olivia, who laughed. There must have been a lot of swearing on Maggie's behalf.

Nahum spoke up. "Before we sleep, I really want to see what you've found." He directed this solely at Lucien. "Your shield was once a Nephilim's."

Lucien nodded. "I thought as much. Follow me."

They crossed the enormous cave and reached the back wall, where Lucien led them to a dark, shadowy area where the lamplight didn't reach. He pointed at the wall. "Can you see the archway leading to another room?"

"Archway?" Nahum asked, puzzled. "There's nothing there. Are you seeing things?"

Lucien just laughed. "Look at this." He bent down and gathered up a handful of emerald dust. "You've all said that I looked different. That my enhanced abilities looked, well, even more enhanced than normal. Look at this." He rubbed the dust up his arms and onto his bare chest, and as he did so, his skin bloomed with a metallic hue. "I can't explain how, but it enhances me even more. It's like adding a double layer of metal skin."

"Herne's hairy bollocks," Harlan said, reaching forward. "Can I?"

"Sure. But it still feels like skin."

Harlan ran his fingers along Lucien's arms, pinching slightly. "It's so weird. But what has this to do with an archway?"

JD and Jackson were already tapping the wall.

"It's changed my sight," Lucien explained. "I seem to see with extra depth perception. The Nephilim we fought, even you two," he said to Nahum and Barak, "look odd. I can see your energy, the flow of angelic magic in you. As for this this cave? Well, everything is glowing. The pillars seem to have light inside them, and I can see that there are other rooms here." He laid his hand on the wall, and it shimmered and then vanished, leaving a doorway into a room beyond.

Rather than rush inside it, everyone hesitated at the threshold. Olivia shivered, suspicious that it would seal her inside somehow. It was twice as tall as she was, the archway oriental in design, the pillars that formed the frame, fluted and ornate.

"God's breath!" JD exclaimed, examining the entrance closely. "How did you open it?"

"I don't know, but the emerald dust makes all the difference."

JD stared at him, absently stroking his trimmed beard. "You must be attuned to this cave through your alchemical enhancements. This place is, after all, made through alchemical means, too. I was never able to completely determine exactly what gems were used to make your tattoos, but emerald must be one of them. It has interesting qualities."

"Such as what?" Olivia asked, intrigued.

"Well, it's always been popular in alchemy. We believe that it helps to manifest visions, and it also shields against conjurations and malevolent spirits. It provides inspiration and balance, enhances creative and mental abilities, and more importantly, increases psychic sensitivity and clairvoyance. What you are experiencing right now," JD said thoughtfully, eyes narrowed as he assessed Lucien, "is exactly that. You are seeing beyond the veil of normality."

"Will the effects last?" Nahum asked.

"Perhaps." JD shrugged. "Time will tell. I suspect, though, that once away from this place for a while, it will not. Unless you take the emerald dust with you." He patted Lucien on the shoulder. "Don't worry. None of it is bad. Now, let's see what's inside."

Harlan laid a hand on JD's arm, stopping him from crossing the threshold, his concerns echoing Olivia's own. "Is it safe? I don't want to get stuck in there."

"I'll come in with you," Lucien said, confidently, "just in case."

The room was circular, again carved from pure emerald, its surface polished to a glassy shine, and once again covered in lines of script. And there were heaps of weapons, much like in Raziel's Temple. They were piled on the floor and displayed on shelves carved into the walls. Everyone started to pick them up, examining the engravings and quality. They were in good condition, polished and untarnished, as if they had been stored there for hours rather than centuries.

"Herne's horns," Barak said, lifting one of the shields from a haphazard stack of them. "There are so many. I don't understand why they're here."

Nahum ignored the weapons and instead read the script. "Ancient Aramaic," he noted with a frown. "These are lists of Fallen Angel Houses and their Nephilim."

"All of them?" Jackson asked.

"Perhaps." Nahum scanned the walls. "There are hundreds, maybe thousands listed here. Unlikely that there are weapons for every House, though. There's nowhere near enough."

Barak nodded in agreement. "This is a sample. Why?"

"Thoth, or Hermes, or whatever the fuck you want to call him," Maggie said, "must have collected them. If there were as many of you as you say all those years ago, it would have been easy, right?"

Olivia nodded in agreement as she examined a richly engraved dagger with a polished horn handle. "This place isn't just a place of learning. It stores history, too." She glanced up, aware that the others were staring at her. "What? It makes sense. The lists of angels, the histories of Biblical figures, and probably those we've never heard of except in myth, and there's so much more here that we don't know about yet. It's like a museum!"

JD's mouth fell open in shock. "I hadn't thought of it like that, but yes, you're right!"

"Which means," she said, as she studied the hoard of weapons, "that these aren't here for any threatening reasons, they're here as a reminder of Nephilim might and power. That's all." She smiled at Nahum, noting his tension seeping from his shoulders. "You could use these, if you wanted. Maybe that's why they were in Raziel's cave, too. He must have known that it would take a Nephilim to enter. Perhaps they were a gift."

Jackson laughed. "I much prefer that theory." He nodded to the doorway, "It's still open. I suspect it will remain open, now that Lucien has activated it. We have earned the right to enter. I also suspect, JD, that you would have worked it out yourself, given time."

"Of course I would," JD declared imperiously, making Olivia suppress a smile. "Come, Lucien, let's open up the other rooms, too."

Twenty-Five

N iel landed in Istanbul at three in the afternoon. He'd showered off the stench of blood, alchemical weapons, smoke, and death, and was rested and wearing clean clothes, ready for adventure. For a moment he stood blinking in the sunshine, as the scents and sounds of Istanbul cast him back centuries.

No, he mentally urged himself, *do not get lost in memories*. This city did not exist in his time, but nevertheless, it triggered memories of other, similar places with equally evocative buildings and inhabitants. He hailed a taxi, and was soon threading through crowded streets that he longed to explore.

Unfortunately, time was short. Mouse had already been sent details of their plans, and he trusted she had researched the best means of entry. He adjusted his jacket again, and caught sight of his face in the rear view mirror. He looked fine. *Better than fine, actually*, he thought, grooming his beard.

Stop it. She nearly killed him. This is just a job, and then it's done. He wouldn't need to see her again.

He had texted Mouse a couple of times, deciding to organise his plans with her directly. He didn't need Gabe acting as a go-between. Besides, he knew his brothers and Shadow found it amusing. *Screw them*. He would rise above it. From Mouse's tone—if texts even had a tone—she was being just as professional.

He checked into his hotel, pleased that he'd organised it himself. It was a small, boutique place on a side road, and lowkey, just as he liked it. It was luxurious, though. He may as well enjoy their newfound wealth. According to the last message from Mouse, she was already there. Pausing only to unpack his scant belongings and observe the view from his window, he called her. Minutes later, he was heading up to the next floor, where her room was situated.

He knocked on her door, and then realised he'd never seen her face before, only her eyes. For some reason, this made him more anxious. He set his jaw, prepared for anything. Or so he thought.

The door swung wide open, and a startlingly pretty woman looked up at him. Her eyes were exactly as he'd remembered them. Almond shaped, dark pupils, teasing. But her lips were fuller than he'd imagined, her smile broader, her cheeks rounder. Her eyes darted to the hall. "Niel, you better come in."

"You arrived without any problems, then?" he asked, wondering why he was asking such a lame question. *Of course she fucking had.*

"Actually, I was a bit worried I might not get through passport control. I've had issues here in the past." She raised a groomed eyebrow, amused. "It seems my new passport is just fine."

"Great! On Europe's Most Wanted list?"

"Something like that." She walked to the coffee machine and kettle in the corner, and he took the opportunity to appreciate her figure. She was dressed in slim-fitting jeans and a fine knit jumper that hugged her petite, lithe figure. "Tea, coffee, or beer? My fridge is fully stocked."

"Beer, please." He studied her room. It was a mirror image of his own, and had a narrow balcony that looked over a side street. The furnishings were rich in colour, and he had another ache of homesickness before it vanished. Standing on the balcony, he said, "This is a little more sheltered than mine. If I have to fly, I can land here."

"Planning escape routes already?"

"I always like to be prepared."

She smirked as she handed him his beer and kept one for herself. "Aren't you the boy scout?"

It stung, for some reason. Like she was patronising him. It made him want to strike back. "Well, seeing as you electrocuted me last time, I always like to have options when working with you. I have a healthy sense of self-preservation. If it wasn't for Gabe, I wouldn't be here."

Her amusement vanished. "I told you, I did that to save your life."

He shrugged. "When you could have just included me in your plans."

"That was impossible! You are infuriating!"

"So are you. I'm still pissed off about it, so get used to it. I presume you have a way to get inside the museum?"

She glared at him for a moment longer as she swigged her beer. "Yes, actually. We're heading there very soon and strolling right through the front door."

"Why?"

"Because I have stolen from there before, many years ago. It was a nightmare. It has an excellent alarm system and a large number of guards. Our best bet is to walk in and hide until it's closed. Even then, we'll have to avoid the guards."

"Are you insane?"

"No. The museum closes at six, and I will get us into the staff areas. I know the place quite well, having spent hours in there just appreciating the displays."

"And the private areas?"

Mouse's arms were crossed, one hand gripping the beer bottle, a challenge in her eyes. "Less well, but I have a rough idea of the layout." Her fingernails were short and unvarnished, gracing slender fingers that were devoid of jewellery, and they tapped the bottle repeatedly. "Would you rather break in at night?"

He dipped his head in a sarcastic bow. "I will do whatever you advise, but if you set me up, I won't be half so accommodating with your health as I was before."

"I am not setting you up! We walk in there together, and we walk out of there together. You will need to take a backpack that's big enough to get the horn in. Maybe a change of t-shirt. They search bags on the way in, so no weapons."

Niel frowned. "Why a change of t-shirt?"

"Seeing as we're staying there overnight, I'd like to look different if we're spotted on camera. We'll emerge into the morning crowd and exit."

"Stay overnight? That's hours, which means ample opportunity for the guards to find us! Are there cameras?"

"Lots in the museum, but nowhere near as many in the staff areas. Especially in the old storage rooms." She seemed very confident.

"How many times have you been in the staff area? Really."

"Three—no, four times. The guards rarely open the locked rooms. We just need to get in one and hide. Then we explore later."

"And you stole an item every time?"

"Every time, undetected, from deep in the basements."

Niel drank his beer, watching her as he did so. It was a good suggestion, but being in the museum for so long, especially with The Horn of Desolation, didn't sound like a good idea.

Mouse picked up on his hesitancy. "If you have objections, say now, but this is the best option."

"Do you know what we're stealing?"

"No. Just something old and weird and bulky."

Niel kicked a chair out, putting aside his animosity, and sat at the small table. "Have a seat. This is no ordinary item. You've heard of Fallen Angels?"

"Of course. You're a Nephilim, and they fathered you." Her pretty eyes flitted over him, staring at his shoulders. "I haven't forgotten that, or your wings. It was a memorable night flight."

He wanted to add that he was always memorable, but decided against it. "Well, we are stealing a horn that belonged to one of the biggest and baddest. It's quite a story."

"Is it long? Because we have to go soon."

"I'll make it quick, but trust me, you'll want to hear this."

Nahum studied the script on the twisted stone columns, wishing Ash was here instead of him. These words were gibberish. He rubbed his eyes, blinked, and tried to focus. *Damn alchemists and their weird speech.*

"Are you okay?" Olivia asked, calling up to where he was studying, halfway up the column.

"Fine. I don't think this is what we need. I'll be down in a moment."

Olivia was another reason for his ill temper. She had shared a room with Maggie the previous night, and he hadn't had a chance to talk to her alone. He'd had some romantic notion that she might need his protection, and he could angle an excuse for sharing her room. Instead, he'd been relegated to a room down the hall. *At least he'd had a bed.* Lucien had slept on a sofa, admittedly a large one, while Harlan and Jackson had shared a room. Of course, Barak shared with Estelle, and both had already left for the airport with Lucien. He was worried about their safety and wished he could go, but someone had to stay and find a way to stop Belial for good.

When he finally flew down to the ground, Olivia looked pensive. "Nothing useful?"

"No. This is madness. Finding what we need could take years."

Olivia nodded absently as she took his news in. "Look, if we don't find a spell to negate Belial's power right now, it will be okay. The jewels have been around for years without causing outright destruction. We'll root them out."

"And my brothers? And Shadow and Estelle? If Jiri draws on Belial's power, it won't be a fight, it will be a slaughter."

"They have JD's weapons and bombs."

"It's still an unequal fight."

She swallowed, casting her gaze to the floor. "It's my fault. I wish I'd never have found those damn things."

He reached forward and lifted her chin so he could look her in the eyes. "It's not your fault. It's Belial's and the damn Brotherhood."

She nodded. "I know, but..."

"No buts. Where are Maggie and the others?"

"Maggie is dealing with the dead bodies. Her team is on the way, with Layla. Jackson is helping her. Harlan is with JD, working on other strategies."

He took advantage of their privacy, and stepped closer. "Are you okay after last night? I haven't really had a chance to ask."

"It was a bit of a shock to be attacked, but I'm fine. I need to improve my aim. It's shit."

He laughed. "Well, I didn't want to complain, but you almost killed me a couple of times."

"I had to try!" She scowled. "Harlan was extremely insulting. He almost wrestled the weapon off me!"

"Good. I owe him a drink. Probably several."

"You're both very cheeky. But how are *you*? You were fighting for your life." Her hand tentatively rested on his abdominal wound, and her touch was electric. A flare of desire raced through him, and he didn't dare touch her hand. *Or should he?* Her lips were parted as she stared up at him, a flush on her cheeks. *Fuck it.*

He took her hand in his left one and turned it over, the thumb of his right hand stroking her palm. Her breath caught in her throat, but she didn't pull away. Instead, she stepped closer as he said, "It's healing already. Don't worry about me. Look, Olivia, I don't know what the future holds, but I think..."

But before he could say anything else, JD yelled, "I've found something! Come and see!"

Nahum ignored him, his attention solely on Olivia, "I've been thinking about our living arrangements. I don't want to be away from you or our daughter at all. It feels wrong!"

"You want to move in? With me? All the time?"

"Is that so horrible? You're having my child. I'm excited and terrified all at the same time. And I think... I *know* that I'll miss you."

She smiled as she leaned into him. "You will?"

He lowered his head, desperate to kiss her, when JD shouted again. "Come on! It's important."

Nahum's jaw tightened. "I wish he'd shut up."

Olivia didn't speak. Instead, both hands reached around his head and pulled him towards her, kissing him with fierce intensity. His arm wrapped around her waist and pulled her closer, losing himself in the breathtaking kiss. He couldn't think straight. All he knew was that this felt right. When they broke away, he was breathless, his desire stoked, desperate to revel in her nakedness.

She spoke first. "Let's talk later?"

"Sounds good." He held her gaze for a few meaningful moments, hopeful of some kind of future together, and then after another annoyingly insistent shout from JD, led the way across the cave.

JD and Harlan were in one of the side rooms that Lucien had opened up before he left. He'd found another dozen that Nahum had barely glanced at, but it seemed JD had deemed them important enough to study further.

"Oh, good!! JD said eyeing them with annoyance as he turned to the doorway. "You took your time!"

Harlan snorted. "I think I know doing what, too." He motioned towards Nahum's lips. "You missed a smear of lipstick there, buddy."

Nahum grinned, refusing to be embarrassed as he rubbed his finger across his lips, and wanting to tease Harlan after putting up with weeks of his overprotective behaviour. "It was more fun than translating old text."

Harlan just rolled his eyes as Olivia poked her tongue out at him.

"Is anyone interested in this?" JD asked, hands on hips. "I might have found a way to stop Belial!"

Nahum focussed on the text inscribed on the walls of the cave. It was roughly the same sized space as the others, but this one was carved in the shape of a six-pointed star. "What a weird room. Aramaic script again."

"A language I understand reasonably well," JD said. He looked wild-eyed this morning, and Nahum realised he'd had little sleep. His hair was tangled and untidy, and his eyes looked red from too much reading. He scowled at Nahum and Olivia. "Does the shape of this room seem familiar?"

"It's the Star of David," Nahum said.

"And also," Olivia added, "it represents the alchemical sign meaning as above, so below."

"Exactly!" JD pointed to the main cave behind them. "There is one on the ground in the centre of the cave. This room is all about that sign!"

Harlan grinned at Olivia like a naughty schoolboy. "It's the key!"

Nahum frowned, confused. "To what?"

"The star on the floor, dummy!"

"And the wider cave," JD added, now bouncing on his toes with excitement. "It's the map room!"

Olivia traced a section of script with her fingers. "It's the map to the whole cave?"

JD pointed to the ground. "That is."

Nahum had been so focussed on the walls that he hadn't looked at the floor. He studied it now, JD and Harlan retreating to the walls to allow a better view. Patterns of dots in bronze were marked on the ground, and he realised they represented the columns. Seen from above, and at this scale, it was easy to see what they had missed in the larger cave. The columns were also arranged in the shape of a large six-pointed star, which explained why some areas of the walls did not have pillars close to them. In the centre was a smaller six-pointed star, representing the one in the cave that had the flame in the centre.

He shook his head. "I can't believe I didn't see the pattern!"

"It's too big to take in, even though you can fly," JD said, shrugging it off. "But now, it's obvious. The text on the walls maps out what is where. We were right with what we have found so far, and this gives us more details. There are sections on astronomy, geology, the Gods, Goddesses, the movement of planets, their correspondences, some in far more detail than even I have discovered. Some," he smiled smugly, "I already found out myself. And the mathematics here...breathtaking."

Clearly outraged, Olivia said, "So why hide it away? We could have made progress much quicker!"

"It's all about proving your worth. Knowledge is locked away behind layers of meaning. Lucien provided a shortcut, although I would have worked it out in time."

Nahum didn't doubt it. He scanned the text. "You said you have found out something to help us with Belial?"

He nodded, exchanging a nervous glance with Harlan. "I think so. The flame in the centre is the key. It seems that when used in the right way, it can undo great magic. Unravel it. But it might be dangerous."

"There's no *might* about it!" Harlan remonstrated. Unlike JD, Harlan looked refreshed and groomed, with no trace of stubble on his freshly shaved cheeks, but his eyes were shadowed with worry. "It essentially sounds like it breaks apart matter."

"As in 'unmakes' something?" Olivia asked, forehead creasing with worry. "Is that even possible?"

"No." JD jumped in quickly. "'Unmake' is the wrong word. Matter is matter. It can't go anywhere. But it can be rearranged."

Nahum's head was already hurting. "Like when you melt down metals to make something else?"

"No, that is still metal. Instead, you make something else entirely."

Nahum suggested something ridiculous. "Like cheese?"

"Yes, sort of. You change something fundamental. That's what one branch of alchemy is all about. Changing base metals into gold, amongst other things. It's what

I did," JD added cautiously, "when I became immortal. I unlocked something at the cell source in my body. I gave it renewable energy. I switched aging off. I didn't turn myself into cheese or a chicken, but this formula here—" he tapped the wall, "suggests that is possible."

"Transmutation. Isn't that what some witches in fairy tales can do?" Harlan asked. "Become a frog or cat? Can any witches we know do that?"

"Not as far as I know," Olivia said, but she looked excited by the idea. "I'll ask Morgana!"

JD sighed. "I am, of course, explaining this at its most basic level, and clearly not very well."

"Because we're dumbasses," Harlan explained.

"Because it's complicated!"

"Hold on!" Nahum held his hand up. "Belial's jewels contain his power. How does that help us with them? Are you saying you have found a way to remove his power?"

"I think so. But I would need everything here to assess and try, because I need the eternal flame to do it. Even then, well, I'm not sure at this stage where his power goes..."

Nahum rubbed his forehead. "I think I'd rather leave it contained where it is until we know more. A bloody great cloud of Belial's power just wafting about sounds toxic. Like a cloud of nuclear waste."

"That is the issue," JD admitted. "We can melt down metals and destroy his jewels, but it's his power that creates them and holds them together." His eyes narrowed as his gaze sharpened, exacerbating his ferocious intellect. "Months ago, I talked to Gabe about the Igigi. He said that they used the Stone of Utu against the angelic horde, restricting their abilities. That precious stone contained the power of the sun, and unfortunately, I have no such thing, but we have an emerald cave..." He trailed off, thoughts clearly elsewhere.

Harlan regained his attention. "JD, you have harnessed the powers of gemstones in your weapons. Can you use gemstones in a similar way to make one that will destroy Belial's weapons, and diminish his power?"

"I've already considered such a thing, but the eternal flame could help. You know, what has just struck me is that this place is—as Olivia says—a repository of knowledge, but Hermes was an alchemist, too. If you're going to go to the trouble of making such a magnificent place, wouldn't you work in it? I wonder..." He paused, eyes vacant, and then spun on his heel and marched out of the cave.

Harlan rolled his eyes and then ran after him. "JD, I wish you'd finish your damn sentences!"

Olivia started to follow them, but Nahum grabbed her hand and pulled her back to him.

She looked confused. "Aren't we going, too?"

"In a minute," he said, pulling her close and wrapping his fingers in her hair at the nape of her neck. "I want another kiss first."

Twenty-Six

Gabe paced the terrace of their villa in La Calcinaia, a province of Elba where Cavo, the resort beach town, was situated.

Elba was a small island that was very popular with tourists, and Gabe was thankful that they were travelling in February, when tourism was low. Not only were there beautiful beaches and a pretty countryside, but there was also a huge amount of history and many ancient sites on the island, too. They had been able to pick up their accommodation through an online booking site at short notice, and the place was perfect for their needs. It sat on a hilltop with a huge swimming pool and a commanding view of the countryside and surrounding sea. Other villas and hotels were dotted about the hills, and Gabe wondered how close they could be to Jiri.

Darkness had already fallen, despite the fact that it was barely six in the evening, but the pool lights illuminated the paved area next to it. He was preparing to ring Ozan again, the third time he'd tried that day. He vowed this would be the last time. Either Ozan couldn't talk for some reason, or wouldn't because he didn't know Gabe's number. He didn't want to call on Emre's phone. It seemed cruel to offer Ozan hope that he was alive. Perhaps the deaths of the Nephilim who had attacked JD's house had caused major issues. Gabe knew the devastation it would have caused if his brothers had died, but perhaps Jiri's team was not like theirs.

Barak, Estelle, and Lucien had arrived only an hour after them, and all were inside, swapping stories with Ash and Shadow. As for Niel... Gabe checked his watch. He would be in the museum by now, and it would be closed. With luck, he would have hidden somewhere safe. It was pointless to worry about Niel; he could look after himself. Gabe had more pressing needs. Knowing he couldn't put it off any longer, he called Ozan again, running through his rehearsed conversation as he started to pace. Within only a few rings, a deep male voice answered in Italian, his tone short and clipped.

"Hello? Oz speaking."

Gabe was so shocked, he almost stumbled over his words. "Oz, my name is Gabreel, and I was given your number by Emre—don't hang up!"

"Emre? How do know him? Who are you?"

"I'm a Nephilim, like you, and I'm calling to make you an offer."

He didn't answer, and Gabe heard shouts and raised voices in the background.

"Oz! Please, hear me out."

"Wait!"

The background noise diminished, and Gabe imagined that perhaps Ozan was, like him, pacing a terrace on his own. He looked at the stars, paranoid that he might be ambushed, before shaking it off.

"I can talk now," Ozan said quietly, his tone dripping with menace. "I know who you are. You are in the group that is pursuing Belial. You are lucky not to be standing in front of me, or I would kill you for what you have done."

"I didn't kill Emre, if that's what you mean. I wasn't there."

"He is dead because of you."

"He attacked my friends, not the other way around. They defended themselves."

"If you hadn't started this stupid hunt, they would all be alive!"

"And hundreds or thousands of others would be killed by Belial's poison."

"Emre was my brother. You know the way of the Nephilim. Have you called to gloat?" His voice was hard, but Gabe detected a trace of tiredness. Of regret.

"No," Gabe said softly, "I have called to make an offer. He and all of the others are dead because of Belial and Jiri and their stupid need to destroy. You have been recruited to a cause that yokes you to them and stifles your independence. You know I'm right."

"I know that as a member of the House of Belial, that it is my duty."

"Is it? Or did that end with your death millennia ago?"

"Duty never ends."

"It ended for us when we decided to make our own rules. Many Nephilim did, but you know that."

"Belial is not your father."

"They all had their moments, mine included." Gabe heard the man's heavy breathing over the phone. His grief and anger. "Let us end this by stopping Belial's influence."

Ozan gave a dry laugh. "You speak madness."

"Do I? Or do I actually make sense? What do you and the others get out of this arrangement?"

"Life. Money. Power. The chance to live again. Like you."

"But are you free to do what you want?"

"Of course."

"So, you could leave right now and tell Jiri you want nothing to do with this?" Ozan didn't answer, and Gabe continued. "Or are you a soldier again, deployed to go wherever you're needed? I bet Emre didn't have a choice yesterday."

"We know the risks."

"You seriously see that there is a point to this? Does this make you happy, to know that you are spreading Belial's madness? That already happened once, a long time ago, but you do not have to play a part in it now. Especially seeing as his power is already diminished." Gabe had absently paced to a low wall while he talked, and he sat on it, overlooking the hills. The lights twinkled in the distance, and he could see boats out at sea; he suddenly felt very weary. "It's a waste of a life. It's wasting mine right now. I'd rather be doing a million other things than fighting you and trying to stop Belial. I think Emre gave us your number, because deep down he felt the same way, and knew you did, too. And others. Am I right?"

"It is not so simple."

"It can be, if we work together."

"Humour me, for a moment, Gabreel. How do you spend your life when you are not chasing us? Is it really a life of peace? You would be bored, I know it."

"I can't lie. We are violent men—it is our nature. There have been occasions when we have had to fight, but only to defend ourselves. We choose to spend our time hunting treasures and helping others, when we're not living in the countryside minding our own business. That's what I want to be doing right now."

"Then do it."

"I can't, not until this is done."

"And this is what you suggest I do? Hunt treasure?"

"You can breed pigs for all I care. It will be your life to do with as you choose. I can promise there is work for men like us. We have skills that not many have, and a paranormal community to welcome us."

"How many men have you?"

"How many have you?"

"So suspicious. All right, I'll start. Now, with so many dead, barely twenty. Jiri, his second-in-command, and the rest of us."

"There are five with me, others that I can call on if needed." Gabe didn't elaborate about witches and fey and enhanced super-soldiers. "How many of you would join us? If we work together, we could end this for good." Gabe hesitated to talk about Venice, but he sensed Ozan was interested in his proposal. "We have already killed many of The Brotherhood in Venice."

"We heard. It is fair to say that Jiri is displeased."

"Just displeased?"

"Fucking furious. He is raging right now with his innermost circle, deciding on what to do about you."

"Then there is no better time to strike."

"It is not that easy. It would take time for you to be here."

"It depends where you are. Are you saying," Gabe asked, feeling the tentative beginning of hope, "that you would help us end this?"

"I need to talk to the others who may want to join me. Maybe."

"So Emre was right. You do want out."

He didn't answer, instead saying, "I will call you back. One hour."

"Wait! I need to know where you are, just roughly?" Gabe wanted to finish this tonight. He was sick of it all, and he knew the time to strike was now. He could hear it in Ozan's voice, too.

Ozan was cautious. "I don't think so. Not yet."

"What if I guess?"

"By all means."

"You are on the island of Elba, off the Italian coast."

Ozan swore prolifically. "Emre talked."

"We picked some clues up, too. We're here already. If we attack tonight, while Jiri is angry and irrational, we can finish this quickly."

"Even though he has Belial's jewels? You know their power."

"We have options."

"Enough. I will call you." Ozan ended the call abruptly.

"So," Niel said to Mouse as he hunkered down in the back of a storeroom in almost complete darkness, "this is afterhours in a museum. Fun!"

"It's gets better, I guarantee."

"Good, because frankly, this is tedious."

Mouse smiled, amused. "Keep your voice down. The staff can hang around for hours."

"Even down here? In the bowels of the Earth?"

"Less so, fortunately." She paused, holding her hand up for silence. The light from a narrow window over the door illuminated her eyes, almost as if she had a mask across her face again. She was dressed all in black, as usual. "Guards."

There were two voices, conversational and relaxed as they rattled door handles and moved on.

Niel took comfort in the fact that so far, everything had gone smoothly. They had entered the museum an hour before closing time and wandered the halls and galleries, and occasionally Mouse held his hand, or looped her arm around his elbow. She had smiled playfully and said, "Let's pretend we're lovers."

His loins stirred again, even at the thought. His response had been harsh, though. "I'll pretend, but your nasty habit with a Taser has soured my ardour." A shutter had fallen across her eyes, and he kicked himself for his response. But she had been true to her word. She had accessed a staff door in a crowded corner of a large hall and snuck inside, pulling him along a short corridor and down a flight of steps until they were on the level they were hiding on now. They had passed no one, which seemed like a miracle. She obviously knew her way around well.

They waited until silence fell before Niel spoke again. "How much longer?"

"Another ten minutes. Normally, the guards settle into a routine. They'll come back this way, and then won't return for another hour or so."

Niel adjusted his position, stretching out his legs between tall stacks of shelving. A variety of boxes were stored on them, some were labelled, others were unmarked. "Do you know what's in this room?"

"Fragments of pottery, jars, vases, pots, some animal bones, sculptures, and figurines." She shrugged. "Most of it is uncatalogued, and nothing looks vaguely interesting to me. I picked this room to hide in because it's one of the biggest and the most unorganised. In fact, from what I can tell, most of the rooms on this floor are."

They were two levels below the ground floor. "All from archaeological digs, then?"

"I think so. The lowest level has the most interesting finds. The big ones." Her eyes gleamed.

"Like what?"

"Huge statues, massive stone blocks from digs, half destroyed pillars. Some were donated. I read the inventory when I can find it."

"You really are a little mouse, aren't you? Scurrying into dark corners. How did you get into this line of work?"

"Stealing, you mean?" Niel nodded. She intrigued him, even more so now that he was getting to know her better. "I had a poor childhood and was unattended for hours. It was a fun way to pass my time. And lucrative."

"How come you work for others?"

"Certain people always need a good thief, just like you do."

"But clearly you do get caught, which worries me, or else why do you need multiple passports?"

"It's an occupational hazard. Besides, I've never been truly caught. Just suspected. That's very different. Shush." She held her finger to her lips, and he heard the bang of a door from further down the corridor.

They both fell silent, and Niel used the time to try to feel for Belial's horn, but there weren't any tell-tale whispers or strange hums of power. After another few minutes, the guards returned, and eventually Mouse stood up. "Time to go."

She progressed stealthily to the door and peered into the corridor; satisfied, she stepped out and headed left. "The stairs to the lowest level are this way."

They passed several locked doors, finally reaching a lift with a staircase next to it. They ignored the lift and headed down the stairs. The lowest level was in darkness, and both accessed the torches on their phones.

"It's supposed to be in the end room," Niel said, wondering which end of the corridor that would be. Mouse had run through the layout earlier, but he was slightly disoriented now.

"There are two set of steps down here," Mouse told him. "One at the other end, close to the more populated areas of the museum, and this one. I suggest we try right, away from the steps. That way leads to the big service lift."

"Fine by me." He scanned every door they passed, noting that the place was a warren. Several smaller corridors led off the main one, and his spirits dropped. "This will take hours if the horn isn't where I expect it to be."

"We'll just be methodical," Mouse suggested. "Otherwise, we'll forget where we've covered."

They reached the huge doors of the service lift that opened onto a large, square area. "This is where the biggest pieces are stored," she said, gesturing to the rooms behind them. She accessed her skeleton keys and opened one. "Look."

The beam of the torch showed a large room filled with enormous stone sculptures, broken columns, and what looked to be the remnants of old temples.

"Holy shit," Niel said. "It looks like an ancient site."

"Probably several. Come on."

In a few minutes they reached the end room down a side corridor. There was nowhere to go from there. Mouse opened the door and Niel stepped inside, expecting to feel a blast of power, or something insidious, but still felt nothing.

"Bollocks." The room was a mass of boxes and shelving, and he progressed down them, looking into bigger boxes, and ignoring the rest. "It's not here. I'd feel it anyway, I'm sure."

"Okay," Mouse turned to the door. "I suggest we check every room in this corridor, and then head to the far end of this level. At least then you've checked the end rooms, as your source suggested. Then we work our way from there. We could split up, if you'd like?"

"No. I don't trust the horn, and if we're discovered somehow, it's best we're together."

It didn't take long for them to ascertain that the horn wasn't in their corridor, and with a weary sigh, Niel said, "The other end it is, then."

Twenty-Seven

Harlan watched the last of the local police leave with Anna, feeling very relieved that Maggie was there to liaise with them.

He'd grown bored of watching JD investigate the central area of the cave, and desperate for fresh air had headed into the grounds for the latest news. There had, not surprisingly, been several reports of noise from the neighbouring houses, and a few reports of fireworks that would be the interpretation of the incandescent angels that attacked them.

"Is that it?" he asked her, as she turned back to him and Jackson.

"For now. They were a twitchy pain in the arse." She rolled her eyes as she pulled her jacket around her. It was another cold and misty day, and JD's grounds were barely visible. It was with the greatest difficulty that they had kept the police out of the marquee. Jackson was responsible for that. He'd flashed his government badge around, which had not impressed the local police at all.

"You two," Harlan said to them, as they headed back to the marquee, "make an impressive power couple."

Jackson exhaled, sounding resigned to the issue. "They didn't like being restricted, but Waylen pulled a lot of strings. It was still tricky, though."

"Fuck 'em," Maggie said with feeling. "No one sees that emerald cave except us. I don't care how much they complain."

"What did Layla say?" Harlan asked. She had arrived much earlier, when he'd been with JD.

"She'll do the autopsies on the Nephilim. She's quite pleased, actually, having obviously never done one on them before."

Jackson laughed. "It's a strange world we live in." Then his laugh was replaced by a frown as he looked beyond Harlan, pointing to the flower borders by the house. "Is there something in the grass over there?"

Harlan turned. "I can't see anything."

Jackson strode across the grass and other two followed, Maggie almost running to keep up with his long stride.

"There!" Jackson said, triumphantly. "That's a ring."

The ring was battered, its metal dull and the gemstone cracked, but it still exerted a trickle of power. Enough that Harlan could feel it, anyway. Jackson stepped towards it, but Harlan pulled him back. "Don't touch it! It must have fallen from the dead Nephilim."

Maggie's eyes widened with horror. "The one that died in JD's protective field? I thought it was destroyed!"

"If it was that easy," Jackson pointed out, "we'd be throwing them all at the shield. I need something to put it in. It could help JD."

Maggie pulled an evidence bag out of her pocket. "Use this."

"No." Harlan grabbed a stick from the shrubbery. "Use *this*. I wouldn't even touch it through plastic. Just poke it inside and hold only the bag. You two must be able to feel it, too. No whispers, though, which might mean it was affected by JD's alchemy last night."

Maggie nodded. "I feel uncomfortable. Like it's trying to draw my attention."

"It will be interesting to see what Nahum and Olivia think of it," Jackson said. With careful manoeuvring they swept the ring into the bag, and Jackson carried it gingerly in front of him, as if it might explode.

Their find subdued their mood, and when they entered the marquee, Maggie swore. "Herne's bloody horns! This place looks even worse than I remembered."

"JD lost a lot of equipment last night," Harlan observed. They had cleaned the place up, but many of JD's instruments and alembic jars were smashed. Fortunately, his alchemical wheel had survived, although it was covered in blood. "Not that he cares right now. He's too caught up in there, especially since he's discovered the map room."

Jackson cocked his head. "A map room? You didn't mention that."

"It's hardly a conversation to have with the police around. He thinks that there are instructions to find a hidden laboratory in there."

Maggie frowned as she led the way down the cave's long entrance passage. "What makes him think that?"

"The fact that so much information is in there, and that Hermes was an alchemist. I see his point. You'd want your lab close to all the knowledge. It's like being in the midst of a vast library or museum. He thinks the six-pointed star is the key."

Jackson stopped. "Can you feel something? Like a hum?"

"You can't feel a hum!" Harlan pointed out as he and Maggie stopped, too.

"You know what I mean. It's like the air is vibrating. Like there's a giant beehive somewhere."

"That's a really weird suggestion."

Maggie scowled. "If he's unleashed killer bees somehow, I'll never fucking forgive him. Fucking lunatic."

Harlan increased his pace, curious to see what the noise was about. "I applaud your imagination, guys, but surely not even JD is that nuts. And he's a genius, Maggie, not a lunatic."

Despite his reassurances to the others, Harlan couldn't help but feel trepidatious as they entered the cave. The humming sensation became more insistent, a dull throb, like a pulse. *Had JD released power, somehow?* Knowing that Nahum and Olivia were inside too, Harlan increased his speed, suddenly terrified at what he might find. However, when they reached the centre of the cave by the eternal flame, all three stopped dead in their tracks, eyes wide.

"What the hell has JD done now?" Jackson said, breathless from shock and the run.

The six-pointed star in the centre of the floor had risen out of the ground by about three metres on metal struts, leaving a gaping hole beneath it. Harlan stepped warily to the edge and saw stairs leading down to a large room, most of which he couldn't see, with more alchemical symbols inscribed in the floor, all arranged around the base of the flame. JD, Nahum, and Olivia were exploring the space.

"Herne's hairy balls, JD, you were right," Harlan said as he reached the bottom step. The chamber reached under the main floor by some distance, a dizzying number of symbols everywhere, and lots of tables filled with alchemical paraphernalia.

"Holy shit in a bucket." Maggie breathed out the words in a rush. "A lab?"

"Hermes's own, it seems," Olivia said, eyes sparkling. "I mean, find of the millennium, right?"

"I should think so," JD said as he handled some alembic jars. "There's still no sign of how the flame came to exist, though."

The flame's base was in the centre of the lower level, a round stone table encircling it, with a space for access. Close by was a three-legged stand holding a huge crucible. Harlan blinked as he tried to take it all in. It looked as if Hermes had just stepped outside, much as it appeared on the upper level, and Harlan couldn't help but wonder what other things the cave could be hiding. It was like a Russian doll. If anything, JD looked wilder than ever. His groomed beard and hair were dishevelled, and his flowing shirt was creased and stained with tea and ink.

"When I left you," Harlan said, studying the room in disbelief mixed with a degree of dread, "none of this had happened! How did you do it?"

"The map room, dear boy. It's the key to everything. After you all became bored and left me to it, I found the lock to opening this. The surrounding columns held the information, but I didn't fully understand it. Then something I read in the map room unlocked it all. There was a series of alchemical triggers I had to perform. Once I did that, this place revealed itself." He swept his arms wide, "It's the key to stopping Belial."

"How?"

"By removing his influence from his jewellery. Maybe all of it."

"Speaking of which," Jackson said, holding out the plastic bag, "look what I found in the garden."

JD's eyes lit up and he swooped on Jackson like a magpie on gold.

"Not so fast!" Nahum scooted in front of him, taking the bag from Jackson. "You didn't touch it, I hope?"

"Nope. I did not wish to end up possessed by Belial. Although, we suspect its power is muted."

JD bustled around Nahum. "Let me see!"

Nahum held it high out of reach. "No!"

His hands flew to his hips. "I just want to look."

"And that's all!" Nahum lowered it, and they all crowded around. "I think you might be right, Jackson. It does feel less powerful."

Harlan felt a little aggrieved. He had pointed all that out, not Jackson. "No whispers, right?" he added.

Olivia was behind Nahum, almost using him as a shield, but she nodded in agreement. "No whispers."

JD clenched his hands, a maniacal gleam in his eye again. "That means that I'm already on the right track. Good. I need to experiment—with your help, Nahum." He pointed to the floor that was inscribed with alchemical symbols. "Do you notice anything?"

Harlan frowned. "I see a lot of symbols."

JD tutted as everyone looked confused. "The patterns?"

"It looks," Jackson suggested, "geometrical."

"Just one design, or many?" He tapped his foot impatiently. "Use your eyes! God's pox, you all walk around with your eyes shut! The world works in harmony. There are patterns everywhere. One of the keys to life. Beneath our feet, many of these patterns, geometric nuggets of wisdom, are laid out and interlinked. It is a well of knowledge!"

"It is?" Harlan asked, his head already aching.

"Sort of like your wheel of correspondences?" Olivia asked.

"Far more complex. I have worked with geometric designs, obviously, but this is a work of brilliance. And have you noticed what the designs are made up with?"

"Looks like precious metals," Nahum said.

"And?" JD had become a mad professor. "Use your eyes!"

"Gemstones," Maggie said, frowning at the floor. "And some of them are pretty big."

"Exactly. We are standing on an infinite web of power that feeds *that*!" JD pointed to the eternal flame.

Harlan could see it now. If he squinted, it helped him see the interlinked circles and geometric shapes. He crouched down to examine the design in greater detail, and saw fine metal grooves. "JD, do these move?"

"What?" Jackson asked. "The floor?"

"Yes, I believe they do." JD started striding around the room again. "It's just a matter of finding the key."

"Another one?" Olivia asked, hands on hips as she watched JD. "This is insane! I don't understand how you can understand all of this already!"

"Harlan, tell her!" JD demanded, now completely sidetracked.

"Me?" Harlan wasn't sure whether to be flattered or annoyed. "Well, JD has been studying this for five centuries, Liv. He's a genius. Especially a mathematical genius. Geometry is math."

JD puffed up like a strutting pigeon. "Exactly. I am what used to be called a savant. Mathematics are easy to me. It's order and purity, and so much more. Like the elements, it's the root of all life."

"No wonder I fucking hate maths," Maggie complained. "What are you looking for? Can we help?"

JD didn't answer, instead focussing on the area around the eternal flame. After studying the ground for a few moments, he pressed his foot on a large, round gemstone, and a section of the floor started to move. Harlan leapt back, and Nahum pulled Olivia out of the way.

"Bloody hell," Jackson said crossly. "You should warn us."

JD was unperturbed. "I wasn't sure it would work. I'm wondering if there are walkways through all this." The section of floor continued to move, rearranging the circular table, and swinging the three-legged stand over the eternal flame, including the large crucible. "Ah, good. I was hoping that would happen. I suggest," he said, looking up at all of them, "that you leave me to it. I'll work it out better if I'm uninterrupted. You, Nahum, need to get your brothers to bring the jewels here. I think I know how to release them from Belial's grip. Or I will when I practise on *that* one."

"All of them?" Nahum had tipped the ring into his palm, but now he looked up, shocked.

"Why not?"

"I'm not sure I like that idea, JD. It's a long drive. If the other Nephilim come back..."

JD turned to him, lips pursed. "But it's all in a spelled box, right?"

"Yes, but—"

"Then it's fine."

"It really isn't. If Jiri and his bloody team are watching the house, they could pounce on them."

"I doubt it. They will have gone to lick their wounds. Besides, you said they didn't know where you live. "

"I don't think they do, but we didn't think they'd attack us here, either!"

"Do you want this to be over?"

"Yes, of course..."

"Then get them here. Now!"

"Are you saying you could do this tonight?"

"I thought you said the sooner the better? Aren't Gabe and your other brothers about to fight Jiri?" JD's foot was tapping the ground again, and Harlan wanted to throw something at him when he was in this mood.

Nahum remained calm. "Yes, they hope to."

"So, no time to waste!"

"But," Harlan interjected, "don't you need to experiment, or practise? Or just make sure you know what the hell you're doing?"

"Harlan, you blistering nincompoop, what have you just told Olivia? I have been studying alchemy my entire life. I am not coming at this blind! And this place offers me all the tools! I can do it. I know I can. Are you sissying out now?"

"Will there be consequences?" Harlan stepped closer, refusing to be intimidated by JD.

"To us, probably not. To Belial, yes. At least I bloody well hope so!" He looked at the group's uncertain expressions. "Well? Do you want to just sit around and twiddle your thumbs?"

"JD," Olivia said, laying her hand on his arm, "what you're proposing is big. We hoped that it would happen—we just didn't expect it so soon. All of this is incredible. I feel like I'm in a fairy story, or Aladdin's cave. It's the speed of everything that is so unnerving. You have to remember that we're not as brilliant as you."

JD liked Olivia far more than he did Harlan, and his expression softened. "Sorry. I know, but this is tremendously exciting. This is an alchemical playground for me, and it's exactly what we need. The important question that you must ask yourselves is whether you trust me, because there's no way that you will understand anything of what I will do." He stared at each one of them in turn. "I'm on your side, you know that. I helped you destroy the count. I will help you do this, too. And then," he grinned unexpectedly, "I wish to be left alone for months so that I can study this place properly, without interruption. Does that sound fair enough?"

"Well, I trust you," Jackson said, "and you're right, I have no idea what the hell any of this does. However, I'll help you in any way possible."

The rest of the group agreed with him, and Harlan smiled. "You're a mad old bastard, JD, but you're our mad bastard. I'm in."

"Wait!" Nahum demanded. "You can't handle the jewels. Belial will possess you. I won't allow it."

"Then you will have to help me. I have no intention of being possessed, thank you very much!"

All eyes swung to Nahum. He sighed, and then reached for his phone as he headed for the stairs. "I'll call them."

JD wafted his hands at them. "Shoo! Everyone else out, too. But be ready for my instructions!"

Harlan was the last one up the stairs, and he took a last look at JD exploring his new workshop. *What the hell were they getting themselves into?*

Shadow studied her brothers. She had rarely seen them so tense, but this wasn't any ordinary meeting they were waiting on. It was a meeting with Ozan. The Nephilim had phoned Gabe, and they had arranged to meet at a neutral location.

They were on the terrace, scanning the surrounding area, and checking their weapons. Shadow wished Niel was with them. She had absolute faith in everyone there, but Niel was a useful addition to the team.

"I suggest," Shadow said, "that only Gabe and I go. If it's a trap, then at least we won't be caught. Not that they'll catch me, of course. I am fey."

"Being fey," Estelle said with a bite to her voice, "will only get you so far."

"But I'm your secret weapon." She knew that statement would irritate Estelle, and although they had come to a truce, she couldn't resist teasing her. "Belial does not see me, and his tokens have no power over me." She tapped her long bow. "Plus, I have this. I can stay far enough away so that I am not seen, but still be close enough to be deadly if Gabe is compromised."

Barak shook his head. "I still think we should watch from above, but we'll keep our distance. I bet he'll have backup, too."

Gabe nodded. "Yes, he probably will. But just Barak. The rest of you stay here—including you, Ash."

"If you're not back within an hour, I'll come looking for you," Ash promised, "and I won't spare anyone if you're hurt."

"Where are you meeting?" Lucien asked.

"There's an old, ruined fortress on a hill, in the east," Gabe said, pointing across the dark landscape. "We meet there. You can't miss it, apparently, and I've looked it up on the map. We'll meet in front of it."

Estelle pointed at Shadow. "Where will you be?"

"Either on the roof, or in the trees. We'll assess it once we're there. Sound good, Gabe?" Shadow had no intention of giving Ozan any leeway, either. "If he steps a foot out of place, or you're surrounded, I'll take them all out."

"He won't. I could hear it in his voice. He wants an end to this, too. It sounds like others do too, but he didn't want to commit until he'd met me, which I understand. I want to meet him, too." Gabe rolled his shoulders, checked his weapons, and called Shadow over. "Let's do this."

In seconds, Shadow had wrapped herself around Gabe, legs around his waist, her sword in her scabbard, and her long bow slung across her back. He dived off the terrace, swooping down the hill before rising on a current of air. Barak followed them.

"You seem different, Gabe," she said, lips close to his ear. "Worried."

"I'm over all this, that's all. I want to spend time with you. Proper time, in which we're not killing people."

"Forever?" That sounded appalling.

He laughed. "Do you think just treasure hunting will fill your excitement void?"

"I suppose so. As long as you are with me, I can handle anything. I think it would probably be nice not to be fighting for a while."

"Good. There it is," he said, changing the subject abruptly.

She twisted in his grip and spotted the ruined building down below. A large courtyard was in front of it, partially surrounded by a stand of trees. "Put me down by the trees. I can shelter in the branches."

"Let me circle for a moment more."

Shadow spotted Barak hanging back, much higher than they were. In the opposite direction, she saw another winged figure. "I think I spot Ozan."

"Me, too."

Gabe angled around and down, the wind whistling through his wings, and he landed at the rear of the yard. Shadow nimbly unwrapped herself and kissed him quickly before heading into the trees. She took a moment to check her surroundings, back to a tree trunk, wary of anyone who might have had the same idea as them. Nothing moved, and she scrambled into the lowest branches, ensuring she had a good view of the front of the fortress, her bow loaded and ready.

Gabe stood in the centre of the courtyard, and within a few moments another Nephilim landed close by. In the far distance, a second Nephilim hovered on the air. Not Barak. Ozan, too, had brought back up.

Gabe focussed on Ozan. Like all Nephilim, he was tall and muscular, and he wore his dark hair long. It reached well past his shoulders, and he had braided part of it, so it was pulled back from his face. Like Gabe, he was Middle Eastern, and his wings were dark in this light. Gabe could not detect any sign of the power of Belial's jewels now. It was odd to be seeing another Nephilim besides his brothers. He hadn't thought it possible. Part of him was glad. There should be more of them. It was an abomination that so many of them had died.

Both kept a wary distance from each other, and Gabe called over to him, his voice loud in the still night air. "Ozan, I presume. I am Gabreel Malouf."

"Ozan Bakir." He glanced up above to the distant figure of Barak. "I see you brought another."

"As did you. I understand why. I hope you bring good news."

"You are committed to doing this, tonight?"

"I am committed to this any night. If you refuse to help, then we will be enemies, and I will find out your hideout one way or another. If I'm honest," Gabe said, stepping closer to Ozan, "I would rather not fight at all. It is as I said on the phone. I am tired of this, but equally I cannot let Belial continue to spread his madness."

"There are many in our House who will not know how to live without Jiri or Belial, and that is the simple truth of it."

"But there are others who feel the same way as you."

"Yes. There are six of us who want this to end. However, there are another dozen who do not." There was pain in Ozan's gaze, and now that they were closer, Gabe could see scars on his arms and chest. It was rare for Nephilim to scar. Those injuries must have been bad.

"Then the numbers are evenly matched."

"Jiri always wears Belial's ring, as does his own second-in-command, Pirro. They will use his power without hesitating. You know the consequences."

"Only too well." He wished he had some of the jewels with them, and cursed his weird moral decision not to carry them. Although, it was out of a sense of self-preservation, too. A need to hide from Belial. "Who were the Nephilim who wore his tokens yesterday?"

"Karim was one, Mikal another lieutenant. Mikal's death whilst wearing Belial's token was unexpected. It has caused much unrest. No one believed that it could happen. Or, in fact, that the team Jiri sent could die, The Brotherhood could be attacked so effectively, and the list of jewels discovered and stolen. Jiri has already instructed that all his jewels are to be moved again. You have caused havoc."

Gabe cursed under his breath. *Of course they were moving the jewels.* There would be no easy retrieval of all of them. He should have expected that. *Fool.*

Ozan stepped closer, examining Gabe as if he was hiding something. "I am as surprised as them. The Brotherhood has hid effectively for years, until you made it your business to find them. How did you destroy Mikal and my brothers? What weapons do you have?"

"I can't explain how Mikal was killed. The man we work with is a genius. As for the others, my brothers are hardened warriors. We have had many fights recently. It has honed our skills."

"While we have languished and fought only each other, not thinking that we would be fighting anyone as powerful as another Nephilim." *That explained a lot,* Gabe thought. It was what Nahum and Barak had suggested might be the cause. "But do you have more of that weapon? I ask," he explained as Gabe hesitated, "because it is that which swings us to help you. For the first time in a long time, we can see a way out of this. There is no way that we can walk away otherwise."

Ozan was a strong and powerful Nephilim, but there was no doubt that he was worried. Fearful, even. No wonder he wanted to meet Gabe. If he didn't believe him, he would walk away. "Yes, we have smaller versions of these weapons. They are very powerful. I don't know if they could kill Jiri once he summons Belial's power, but it's possible. And there are other options." *Like bombs.*

Ozan took a sharp intake of breath. "Then it is true. This could work."

"I take it that you are not allowed to wear Belial's tokens?"

Ozan gave a dry, mirthless laugh. "No. Jiri rules by fear, like in the old days, and he is paranoid. He does not trust us, and with good reason. I would absolutely kill him. But I hide it well, as do the others. We bide our time, and that time is now."

Silence fell as Gabe contemplated his offer. The wood was quiet, and he trusted that Shadow watched them. Barak circled overhead, opposite to the other Nephilim, and it seemed as if the world hung on his decision. The ancient fortress that had no doubt witnessed many battles would now witness once more a pact between warring Houses. But Gabe trusted Ozan. He could see Ozan's need to rebel and find freedom, but he was just as worried at the prospect of betrayal. However, there would be no better time with Jiri angry and irrational, and weakened by the knowledge that he could actually be defeated.

"Agreed." Gabe stepped forward, hand outstretched. "Let us shake on this and plan our strategy."

"But there is one more thing you should know," Ozan said, gripping Gabe's hand between both of his own. "There are women at the villa. Human women. Playthings that he has...*acquired* in recent months, despite some of our protestations."

Gabe knew exactly what that meant, and his anger intensified. "Then I'll save them, too."

<h1 style="text-align:center">Twenty-Eight</h1>

As soon as Niel stepped into the dusty and neglected room at the end of the narrow corridor, he knew The Horn of Desolation was in there.

"Keep back," he warned Mouse. "It's here."

"Oh!" She followed him inside and shivered. "I feel it. It's like there's a presence here. A ghost."

"Ghosts are far preferable," he said, weaving through the crowded metal stacks full of boxes. It was clear no one had been in this room for a while. Dust lay across all the surfaces, eddies of it swirling around as he walked. He ignored it all, drawn to the horn like iron to a magnet. Despite his warning, Mouse kept following him. "I said to keep away."

"I can't. I have to leave here with you, and I need to know what we're dealing with." She looked up at him, a challenge in her eyes, a slight pout to her full and very kissable lips. "I'm not a wilting flower, Niel, despite my size."

"I'm well aware of that." He pushed his desires aside, annoyed that he still liked her despite the fact she had tasered him, and followed the trace of... *What?* It wasn't power, not like the hum the jewels gave off, or the insidious whispers. It was far subtler. An effect on his mood. It made him wary, suspicious, and paranoid.

A large box on a high, top shelf beckoned, and he clambered up the metal shelves, able to brace himself on the opposite shelving system, since the path between them was so narrow. He pulled the box towards him, noting it's weight. If the horn was as big as the box suggested, it would be too big to carry it out in his backpack.

"Pass it to me," Mouse instructed.

"It will squash you."

"Niel, it's a horn, not an anvil!"

"Be careful!" He handed it to her, still supporting much of the weight, but she helped enough to enable him to scramble down again. "Right, let's see what it looks like."

While Mouse held both of their phone torches, Niel used his blade to unseal the wrapping on the battered box. Inside was a nest of packing material, and he dug into it with his fingers, finally feeling the horn inside. It felt cold to the touch, almost like ice, and as he lifted it free, the precious metals that decorated it glittered in the light. The horn was, as he suspected from the size of the box, larger than he'd initially expected. It was about three feet in length, but the flared bell was narrower than described. It curved like a scimitar, and the entire length of it was decorated with precious metals in a curling design, inlaid with gemstones. The horn's material was thick, what little of the surface he could see, polished to a glossy finish. At least, most of it was. A section was still covered in a reddish dirt, and it seemed the museum had abandoned their attempt to clean it.

His feeling of unease intensified, and he looked over his shoulder, half thinking someone was watching him, even though he knew no one had followed them into the room.

"Ugh!" Mouse said, nose wrinkling in disgust. "It looks amazing, but it smells funky."

"Does it? I can't smell a thing." He lifted it to his nose, scenting at first only old bone and packing material. And then he detected a trace of musk in the binding of leather near the mouthpiece. Niel had a moment of complete dizziness, and he staggered back, assaulted by images of battle and bloodshed, and the keening war cry of Nephilim.

"Niel!" Mouse grabbed his arm, and her touch returned him to the present. Her pupils were large in the light, and she look scared. "What happened?"

"A flashback, that's all."

"It must have been intense."

Niel didn't answer; instead, he put the horn down and breathed deeply, trying to find fresh air, but only finding dust and mustiness. Finally, when he felt steadier, he asked, "You said it smelled funky. Like what?"

She gave a tentative sniff again. "Smells rotten. Like a rotting carcass, or...death, actually."

"Well, this horn has certainly been responsible for that. Do you feel odd?"

Mouse shrugged, looking around the room for a brief moment. "A little unsettled, as if we're being watched." She stretched her fingers towards the horn, but Niel grabbed her wrist.

"No! You can't touch it. I don't know what effect it will have." He pulled his backpack off his shoulder, but it was obvious that the horn was too big to fit in it. "Bollocks!"

"That is a rather large horn."

"Yeah, well, Belial always liked to boast. I can't exactly walk out the front door with it. Neither do I wish to sit in this room all night with it, either." His feeling of unease was growing, and he knew Mouse's was, too. She looked jumpy, and kept glancing over her shoulder. It wasn't just unease, either. He felt the creeping urge to be violent. To smash things, or people... He had to get out of this room. The confined atmosphere was making it worse. He had expected humans to be affected by it, but thought he would be okay. He shoved the horn back in the box and headed to the door.

"Where are we going?" Mouse asked, running after him in alarm.

"You are staying here, as planned, and leaving in the morning. I am finding another way out of here."

"No! I'm coming with you."

He quelled the urge to snap at her, internally cursing Belial. "It's dangerous. I can feel this damn horn's effects already, and it will intensify. You don't want to be around me then."

Mouse swallowed, and he knew how he must appear to her. He had a wild look in his eye already, he just knew it, and his jaw was clenched. Despite that, she said, "Actually, I think you need someone to keep you on an even keel. That's me."

"That's stupid. You're already twitchy, and you'll only get worse. The men who found this and the jewels killed each other, or themselves."

"But you are a Nephilim, and I trust you. I will remind you of that, and I'll keep you grounded, too. You can do the same for me." She stepped close, hands gripping his arms, eyes locked with his. "I can already see that you should not be alone with this thing."

"I can be a very dangerous man."

"I know, but you won't want to kill innocents. You need me. Besides, you hired me for the whole job. It's not over yet."

"I'm okay with that."

"I'm not."

Niel wanted to argue and shout, but knew she was right. He did need her around. He was reasonably sure he could control his violent urges, but with Mouse at his side, he'd try even harder.

He nodded. "All right. Any exit suggestions? I was thinking we should head up to the ground floor, and I'll just smash a door down and leg it."

"So sophisticated!"

"As long as we get out with this thing, I don't care!"

"I have a better idea that will be a lot stealthier. But it's also dark and damp." She pointed downwards. "There are extensive ancient water cisterns in Istanbul—huge, stone arched chambers and waterways. Most of them are abandoned now, but some are open to the public. This museum sits over one of them. I suggest we leave that way."

"Why the hell didn't we come in that way?"

"Because the entrance is impossible to get through from the other end. It's chained and padlocked on this side, and it's...tricky. I know because I checked once, years ago. You'll see."

"My way sounds easier."

"You're a smash and grab kind of guy, aren't you? No. You'd set alarms off, men will come after us, and it will create waves. We do this my way. That's why you hired me. And we have time. We found this pretty quickly, really."

He grudgingly had to admit she made a lot of sense. "Fine. Lead the way."

"The access is in the centre. I think I can remember which room." She pulled her mask over the lower half of her face again, eased the door open, and immediately frowned. "I hear something. Voices on the main corridor. I think the lights are on at the end, too."

She snuck out, padding silently up the narrow hallway, Niel right behind her. He felt like a giant in comparison. Carrying a backpack and a box wasn't helping.

"Well?" he whispered.

She turned to him with a look of resignation. "They're bringing in a delivery through the service lift."

"Now?"

"I told you, they work at night sometimes." She turned and glanced down the main corridor again. "Okay, only the area around the lift has lights on, and it's a good distance from here. We need to head about halfway down, and then duck into one of the side passages."

"One of them? You mean you don't know which?"

She glared at him. "I'll know it when I see it." She looked down the corridor again. "Okay, let's go now. They're out of sight."

He followed her as she sprinted down the corridor, quickly ducking into another passage just as a group of half a dozen men entered the big square area by the lift. Most boarded the lift, but one remained behind, returning to the room they had exited. Niel presumed it was the big one that Mouse had shown him earlier.

That meant only one thing. They were coming back.

Mouse didn't speak, she just continued, examining each corridor briefly before finally turning down one, just as the lift doors opened again. Niel saw the men wrestling a huge statue inside on a wheeled dolly before he followed her. He waited, wondering if he'd hear shouts or evidence of pursuit, his agitation and worry abnormally exaggerated because of the horn, but fortunately he hadn't been spotted, and he found Mouse entering another storeroom.

"This is the one, I'm sure."

He waited by the door while she searched the room. It was similar to the others they'd seen, containing big cabinets and long shelving. In here, though, there weren't any boxes. Instead, a range of textiles and paintings in frames were stacked haphazardly. *What a waste.* So much art going unseen. He should just smash it all. *That would teach them.*

Niel gasped in shock at his thoughts. *Damn Belial.* He was certain that being surrounded by old objects was intensifying his experience, but perhaps that was just stupidity. It really shouldn't make any difference at all.

"Niel! Over here!" Mouse summoned him with a raised whisper, and he hurried to her side.

A large, round metal cover was set into the floor, a padlock securing it in place. It was also partially covered by a long worktable. No wonder they couldn't have entered that way.

"I'll unlock the padlock," Mouse said, already on her hands and knees, lock picks in her hand, her face covering removed once more, "while you move the table."

Preparations complete, Niel lifted the heavy cover with a grunt of exertion, and edged it aside. Below was blackness, and the pungent scent of damp welled up to them. He flattened against the floor, gripped the edge, and peered inside, and as his eyes adjusted to the light, saw the reason why it was so hard to enter.

"For fuck's sake, Mouse," he hissed, "we're thirty feet off the ground!"

"I know." She crouched opposite him. "There used to be access, a ladder, I think; however, this cistern was dug very deep, and it's been built on over the centuries. Now there's just a big drop, but seeing as you can fly—"

"How do you know that there's a way out? It could be our tomb!"

"I found a way in through the other end. We're actually very close to one of the cisterns that's open to the public. We can exit to the street that way."

Niel didn't speak as he once again assessed the space. Below, he could discern the inky sheen of water, and enormous stone columns emerged from it to support a vaulted roof. There was plenty of space to fly, at least in the area he could see. The hatch he was looking through was set into the roof at the side of the room, and he could see evidence of where ladders had once been fixed to the wall.

He looked up at her, suddenly amused at the situation. "Are you sure you want to do this?"

"I want to get out without being chased or arrested. Yes!"

"You're plucky, I'll give you that. Potentially insane, but that works, too." And at least he'd have an excuse to hold her again. "Okay, I can't get in this hatch with my wings visible, which means I'm going to have to hang from the rim, then extend them. There is no way I can carry the box and you, so the horn will have to be wedged into my backpack. You will hand me the pack, then you have to clamber down and wrap yourself around me. You face me, and wrap your legs around my waist. Then you can make sure the backpack doesn't fall off."

"I have to hold the backpack and you?" She looked down at the drop and then at him again. "That's a big fall if lose my grip."

He smirked, feeling like he was getting his own back for the Taser incident. "Don't you trust me?"

"Yes, or I wouldn't have suggested it!"

"But the reality of it is becoming clear, right? Don't worry, I'll hold you. Whether I keep holding you when I think of what you did to me is another matter."

Her lips twisted with annoyance, and she jabbed him in the shoulder with her finger. "I told you, I did it to save you! When will you listen to me? I could wait here, let you exit in a blaze of fucking glory upstairs, and sneak out tomorrow, but no, I'm here, helping!"

That poke in the shoulder was enough to give him a thrill of desire again. *Oh yes, he liked Mouse a lot.* She was feisty, and the urge to kiss her was strong. Plus, she'd apologised plenty of times, so maybe it was time to move on. Time to flirt, instead. "You're just wanting to wrap yourself around my bare chest again. I get it. I look great naked."

A gleam of amusement flashed in her beautiful, almond eyes. "Perhaps we should talk about that another time."

"I like the sound of that." He leapt to his feet, stripped his jacket and t-shirt off, and then pulled the horn from the box again. Its touch slithered over his skin, but he ignored the sensation and quickly wrapped it in his clothes and stashed them in his backpack. He couldn't zip it closed completely, and the wrapped horn stuck out of the top, but it was reasonably secure. "Pass it to me when I'm ready."

He clambered into the open hatch, fingers gripping the rim, muscles straining as he hung from it. He unfurled his wings carefully, angling slightly backwards so he was almost horizontal as he looked up at Mouse's pensive face, because his wings extended above his head. This was far trickier than he'd expected. He couldn't even use his wings to brace himself. The columns weren't close enough.

"You're going to have to wear the backpack," he told her.

She didn't question it, instead securing it tightly. "What now?"

"Lower yourself onto me, and grip very tightly."

"This is insane. You're taking up most of the space."

"Too late to change your mind now, so please, just get on with it! And just so you know, I'm going to drop pretty quickly."

Mouse rolled over the hatch, wrapped her arms around his neck while her legs braced on the rim, and said, "I can't get my legs in!"

By now, despite his considerable strength, the weird angle was proving too tricky to maintain. "Hold on tight, and when you can, wrap your legs around my waist."

Her face was inches from his, her eyes wide with genuine terror. He dropped, leaning backwards to allow her legs to slide through the gap, and they plummeted through blackness together. His arms wrapped around her body, clutching her to his chest as she screamed shrilly in his ear. With a flap of his huge wings, he suspended their fall, and she tucked her legs up like a gymnast, gripping his waist.

"Fucking fuckery!" she said, breath hot against his ear. "That was insane."

He adjusted his grip, so that his arms were wrapped around her and the backpack, the swell of her breasts tight against his chest. "It's okay. I've got you. Are you ready? It's going to get twisty."

Fortunately, the columns were set far apart, and he weaved through them, heading towards a tunnel that was lower than the vaulted roof. The columns seemed sturdy enough, but moss lay thick in places.

"How can you see where you're going?" she asked, her breath coming in quick, sharp bursts. "This is terrifying."

"I can see in the dark. Don't worry. I'm aiming for a tunnel lower down—is that the right direction?"

"Yes." She steadied as she talked. "I think you can fly through it. There is water on the ground, but it's shallow. It leads to another cistern, just like this, and then there's another tunnel that's gated at the far end. That connects with the next cistern that opens to the public."

"And you travelled through here on foot? On your own? I'm impressed."

"You don't know half of what I get up to."

"I'd like to," he said, lips brushing her ear.

She didn't answer, but she seemed to settle more closely to him, legs tightening around his waist. Then again, she was hardly likely to pull away.

He flew through the tunnel, which was just wide enough to accommodate his wings, eventually soaring into the next cistern. It was as stunning as the last one. It seemed incredible that humans had designed such beautiful places that were just meant to be filled with water. He wished he could linger, but focussed instead on getting them out of there. When they finally reached the gated entrance, he dropped to his feet, finding that the water came up to his knees.

"Let me open the lock again." Mouse slid down him, her breath catching. "Give me some light."

He took the pack from her, and in a few more moments they were through and Niel relaxed. He'd become used to the horn, and the effects seemed to diminish. Perhaps it was the circumstances, and he suspected it wouldn't last, but he'd enjoy it while it did. He took a moment to orientate himself, noting how this cistern had been cleaned, and walkways erected. Columns stretched ahead, and he couldn't see the way out.

"Where now?"

She pointed across the chamber using her torch. "That way. There are steps up to street level. We'll have to break out of the main entrance, but it opens on to the road, and then we can return to the hotel. But first, I want to show you something."

Rather than fly, they walked, using torches to highlight the details, and a peculiar feeling of peace descended over him. They were almost out. He'd secured the horn, avoided pursuit—for now—and he was with Mouse. And neither of them was unduly influenced by Belial yet.

The cistern was huge, and she chatted while they walked, talking about the cistern's history. When they reached the top of the steps, she flicked a bank of switches, and light bloomed through the chamber.

"Herne's horns!" Niel gasped as he took in the colourful, floodlit display. Shades of blue, green, red, and yellow illuminated the columns and the clear water at the bottom. The vaulted roof was also visible. It was breathtaking. "This is incredible."

"They spent years clearing this out. Amazing, isn't it?" Mouse's eyes shone in the light. "It's one of my favourite places in the world. Especially in private. Normally, it's full of people."

"Then I'm happy I get to see it like this, with you."

She smiled up at him. "You've forgiven me, then?"

"I guess I have. Shall we have one last flight while the lights are on?" He secured the pack over his shoulder and opened his arms wide.

"I sincerely hope it's not my last flight ever," she said, wrapping her arms around him again.

He lifted her up so she could slide her legs around his waist again, and he rested his hands on her slender hips, wishing he was cupping her pert bottom instead. He launched off the platform, hearing her breath catch again, and took a slow, circular route through the cavern, wishing he could spend hours with her instead of just minutes. When he finally landed again, his loins were aching with desire.

She didn't jump down straight away, instead extending her arms at full length so she could look at him, and circled back to his earlier question. "Do you really want to know what I get up to?"

"Yes. I want to see more of you—in all ways."

"You barely know me."

"I know. That's the point. I want to get to know you. You intrigue me."

Mouse leaned forward and kissed him, hands on the back of his neck and threading through his thick hair. He pulled her close, turning so that her back was to a stone column, and pinned her to him, kissing her like he hadn't kissed anyone in years, all thoughts of Belial's horn forced into submission. He wanted to drink her in. Actually, he wanted to take her right now on the floor of the chamber, in this place of light and water and stone. Instead, he eased back, both of them breathless.

"I think," she said, lips full, skin flushed, and her pupils wide with desire, "that we should continue this discussion back at the hotel. After one more kiss."

"Done."

Twenty-Nine

"I hope this isn't a set-up," Barak said to Estelle as they approached Jiri's sprawling villa.

It was several miles from their own place, but was high on a hill overlooking the sea. The coast spread below them, the lights of Cavo in the near distance. Ozan was meeting them all on the roof with another couple of Nephilim, and then they would split up to fight the others.

"Gabe is a good judge of character, and so are you. You felt you could trust him. Plus, he wouldn't have told him about the women."

"He would if he thought it would motivate him. It has certainly motivated me." Barak was as furious as Gabe at that news—all of them were, actually. Except perhaps Estelle, whose incandescent rage had settled into cold, determined intent to rescue them all and kill the Nephilim responsible. Barak had eventually been summoned to join the discussion at the ruined fortress, along with Ozan's friend, Nibal. Shadow had remained in hiding. "I believed him, but now I'm second-guessing myself. I know what Gabe saw though, because I saw it too, and we've both seen it too many times in the past. And experienced it, of course. Ozan and Nibal are trapped, and they hate it." He remembered the hollow sense of being unable to control their destiny, and how it ate away at him until he seethed with frustration and impotence. "I felt smothered."

"Much like I did with my father. We are doing them a service, as well as us."

Barak smiled at her words. Estelle was fierce with her enemies. She had a true warrior's soul. Her energy had been skewed in the past. Warped by frustration into taking out her pain on others who did not warrant it, but her balance was returning.

"Don't put yourself at risk, though," he warned. "I want a life with you after this."

"Same goes for me, Barak. Be careful."

He kissed her neck as he flew down to land on the roof of the small, round tower. "Always."

"Liar. If you see Belial's jewels, you ignore them, or I'll fry your balls. And you know I mean it."

They'd had a fierce argument after destroying the Cathar castle, and he wouldn't forget it easily. "Yes ma'am."

He spotted Ozan with Nibal and another two Nephilim, and checking his brothers were close by, they all landed together, Gabe with Shadow, and Ash with Lucien.

There was a wary silence as they landed, the two Nephilim they hadn't met before hanging back with worried expressions. They all looked beaten into submission, eyes hard with suspicion, as if this was another trap. All had dark hair, and were very similar in appearance to Ozan.

Gabe stepped forward confidently, hand outstretched to Ozan, and Barak followed suit with Nibal. They needed to settle nerves and instil confidence—as well as assess the others. This was not the ideal time to put their faith in people they didn't know. Shadow hung back as was her way, sweeping the surroundings with her sharp eyes, and looking over the tower roof. It was a big building, all encompassed by a high wall, more fortress than villa. She finally joined them as they were introduced to each other.

"There are a few changes to our original plan," Ozan said cautiously. "Jiri is still with Karim, his lieutenant, in his War Room, as he calls it. A glorified study, really. But following Mikal's death, another Nephilim called Pirro now has Belial's ring."

"So, once more," Barak noted, "there are three Nephilim with tokens now?"

Ozan nodded, and Barak glanced at Gabe and Ash, noting they looked as disappointed as him. Despite the fact that they had lost a ring, Jiri had others, as they suspected. They had planned to approach all the other Nephilim and attempt to sway them to their cause. If that failed, they would have to fight. However, with another ring in the mix, that would be hard.

"Pirro," Ozan continued, "is in the main hall with the rest of our team, and my other two brothers who are with us are there, too. They are organising who to send to Venice. There are still some of The Brotherhood there, and they are deciding where to go from here, and how best to regroup with the survivors. They have every intention of continuing, and of course there are members spread further afield."

"Despite what happened in Venice?" Gabe asked, incredulous.

"Even more so, now," Nibal answered. "Belial, through Jiri, is determined he will not be thwarted. But," his eyes gleamed, "Belial frets and rages, and he takes it out on Jiri. That is why Jiri is so angry. Of course they discuss how to deal with you, but all we have achieved has to be restarted. Belial commands it. He is working on a bigger strategy right now."

"No," Gabe said abruptly. "This ends tonight."

"Jiri will do as Belial commands, and the others will follow."

Gabe squared his shoulders. "Take me to Jiri. I want to discuss it with him. I'm sick of sneaking around."

A ripple of unease ran through the other Nephilim, and Barak wasn't surprised. "Gabe! Are you insane?"

"No." Gabe turned to him. "Perhaps we can reason with him."

"You have clearly," Ozan said, amused, "never met Jiri. To parley signifies weakness, and to set foot inside his War Room will be suicide. You need to persuade him of your intent. Attacking him here, in what he considers his stronghold, will be another blow."

Shadow interrupted. "We need a way to draw them all out and cause maximum confusion. I suggest a bomb at the front door."

"Isn't that more likely," Ash said, "to get them to retreat behind closed doors?"

"No. That will definitely bring them out," Nibal said, "but our brothers must not be harmed."

"Why aren't they with us now?" Lucien asked.

"To listen, to watch. To ensure they all remain in one place. And to ensure the women stay together."

"Where are the women?" Estelle asked, her tone as hard as her eyes. "You need to take me to them."

Nibal studied her. "We didn't expect women would be part of the team. Neither of you are strong enough to fight."

Shadow didn't answer, only rolling her eyes, amused. Barak knew that Estelle did not want to reveal her power until she had to, and he respected that.

Estelle said, "Let me worry about that. Where are the women?"

Nibal glanced at Gabe, as if seeking approval. He said, "I suggest you answer her."

Nibal shrugged. "I will take you to them. They are safe, don't worry."

"Safe is a subjective word. Why isn't anyone keeping watch?" Estelle asked, as she observed their surroundings.

"Because they believe this place is still a secret." Nibal smirked. "Jiri is arrogant."

"Let's get on with this," Barak said, impatient to end it. "We do as we originally planned. Lead us to the room where all the Nephilim are gathered, and we will try to get the others to join us. If not, we fight. Pirro will die first. As for Jiri?" He cocked his head at Shadow, who was fully kitted out with sword, daggers, long bow, bombs, and JD's weapon. "Perhaps bomb his precious War Room."

"My pleasure." She pointed at a Nephilim called Dorian who hadn't spoken yet. "You can take me."

"Then I'm with you," Gabe said to her, clearly still determined to talk to Jiri. "Barak and Ash, you're in the hall with Lucien. Estelle, do you need assistance?"

She shook her head. "No. I just want to make sure they're safe, and then I'll join Barak."

Gabe nodded, then gripped Barak and Ash's arms, reinforcing his message. "Let's try and talk first, get them to come around. Help Ozan make them see sense. Especially if we negate Belial's power! They have nothing to fear, and everything to gain!"

Barak nodded, returning Gabe's strong grip with his own, and wishing he had half of his optimism. "We'll try our best."

Nahum met Eli and Zee at the entrance to the emerald cave. They carried the large, spelled box between them, and placed it down on one of the trestle tables to catch their breath. Anna left them to it with barely a backwards glance.

"An uneventful trip, I hope?" he asked his brothers in greeting.

"Unexpected, but yes, uneventful." Eli's lips were compressed into a thin line with resentment. "I had to dump my date."

"You're always dating, I'm sure she'll recover," Nahum said, smirking. "A new addition to your harem?"

"No. A regular."

"Lovely. I'm sure she's thrilled."

Eli gave him a slow, knowing grin. "Not all of us are a one-woman man. How's that going for you?"

"Just fine."

Eli leaned against a table, arms folded across his chest. "Just fine?

Nahum knew they were winding him up, especially as Zee had a goofy grin on his face, too. He arranged his features to an impassive stare, sure that guilty pleasure was radiating out of every pore. He'd eventually tell them that things had progressed, but not now. He wanted to luxuriate in their privacy for a while. *If Harlan kept his mouth shut.* "Yes. Fine. That's all I have to say on the matter."

"Oh, brother," Zee slapped him on the shoulder. "We'll just have to assess for ourselves. I take it," he cocked his head at the cave's entrance, "that used to be the Emerald Tablet?"

Nahum massaged the bridge of his nose, glad of the change of subject, but knowing it wouldn't last. "Yes. It still is! It's even crazier in there than when we first went in. JD has found the original lab, and it's nuts."

"The actual lab of Hermes Trismegistus?" Zee asked, almost scoffing in disbelief.

"Yes. And in the intervening hours since I called you, he has tested various alignments—I have no idea what to call it other than that—and has replicated the protective dome's effects and blasted Belial's ring again. He's weakened it further." He had already explained some of it over the phone hours earlier. "He's making a few minor adjustments, and then we'll try again."

Zee and Eli were both silent with shock, but Zee recovered first. "Are you saying he can negate Belial's power?"

"He has already weakened it. He's trying to eradicate it completely."

"So, we don't have to be dragons forever?"

"Hopefully not. Not to *his* treasure, at least."

"And what about the other tokens out there?" Eli asked.

"Herne's hairy bollocks! I don't know. Seems like a stretch, but ask JD."

They followed him into the cave, carrying the box between them, and after allowing them a few moments to gasp at their surroundings, he waited for more shock when they saw the lab.

"I must admit," Eli said, when he finally put the box down on the stone table in Hermes's lab, "I really have seen everything now."

Everyone was gathered down there after leaving JD alone for hours. Some had caught up on sleep, Olivia included, but Nahum had continued to explore the cave, trying to ignore the booms that emanated from the lab.

"Guys! Good to see you." Harlan marched over and shook their hands, and Nahum introduced his brothers to Maggie, JD, and Jackson.

"You've brought the box of tricks, then?" Harlan asked, eyeing the box as if it would bite.

"Everything we have," Zee confirmed.

Maggie, normally a stalwart in every situation, eyed up Zee and especially Eli. "Well, you two are a sight for sore eyes. Do you stir up as much shit as your brothers?"

"Sometimes," Eli confessed with a wink.

Nahum rolled his eyes as Eli exuded his normal charm. Fortunately, Olivia didn't seem the slightest bit interested. Instead, she watched Nahum out of the corner of her eye, and every now and again she gave him a teasing, shy smile that was for him alone.

"Whatever!" JD interrupted them. "Open the box. I need to see it all."

"In your dampening field first," Nahum reminded him. JD had set one of the geometric grids up with a protection field. "This packs a powerful punch."

"I really need to feel it first, if I'm to assess it properly." His stare was implacable.

Nahum relented, knowing it made sense, and addressed the humans. "Cover your ears. It will help a little."

Zee flipped the lid, and immediately Belial's power rolled out. Actually, *roll* was the wrong word. It reared up like a jack-in-the-box, and everyone except the Nephilim recoiled. Insidious whispers assaulted them like spears, and Zee quickly snapped the lid shut again.

"Enough?" Nahum asked JD, who looked pale with shock.

He swallowed. "They're more than I expected."

"I did warn you."

JD waved his concerns away. "I had to know." Wrinkling his nose with distaste, JD pointed to a hexagonal area to the right of the eternal flames. "Put it there for now. You all need to stand over there." He pointed to an area on the far side of the lab. "There's a line of pure obsidian. Stand behind it. I have one more test to make on the sample ring."

JD had made several alterations to the lab, and now had his mass of strange, gemstone-powered beams pointed at another octagonal shape laid out on the ground made only of precious metals. The ring they had found in the garden was at the centre, and JD had erected a forcefield around the whole area.

Everyone shuffled nervously back, and Nahum stood next to Olivia, ready to protect her.

"Er, JD," Harlan asked, "is it safe for us to stay?"

"Absolutely. But perhaps," he pointed to a box on the table close to where they stood, "wear those to shield your eyes."

The box contained dark-tinted goggles, and JD pulled a pair out of his pocket and set them over his eyes while the others followed suit. Immediately, the room was plunged into muted colours. Odd fields of energy were visible in different areas of the lab, and the obsidian line presented a dark shield in front of them. Nahum was well out of his depth. Nothing in this room made much sense, and only Jackson seemed to have some knowledge of what JD was talking about.

After a few moments of nervous anticipation, JD activated his beams that were directed at Belial's ring and a corona of light exploded around it, contained within the grid.

"What the actual fuck is that?" Maggie yelled, staggering backward into Jackson. "It's like a frigging bomb went off!"

No one answered, because no one knew, and JD was far too absorbed in his work.

The light swelled and receded, colours radiating with changing intensity as JD manipulated his instruments. For a brief moment, a writhing figure seemed caught in the glow, and then it blinked out as the light pulsed and then vanished completely.

JD whooped. "I did it!"

"Stay here," Nahum told Olivia, before racing after his brothers. He felt deflated, as if more should have happened. "Was that it? Belial is gone?"

JD had entered the grid, and he picked up the warped metal ring with tongs. The gemstone had utterly vanished, and the metal was cracked and charred. "What do you mean, was that it? Have you any idea of the power I used to do this? Yes! He's gone!"

Zee reached forward, plucking the ring from the tong. "Holy shit. He *has* gone. No Belial. JD, you're a bloody genius."

"I know."

Nahum couldn't quite believe it, and he took it from Zee. The ring was completely inert. "How?"

"The right combination of gemstones, set at the correct frequency, a combination of planetary energies, and the right conjunctions on the grid. A certain celestial combination. It's complicated."

Eli was flushed with excitement. "So, you can really do it? You can do the same to those?" He pointed at the box.

"I can indeed. But," JD wagged a finger, "this ring had already been weakened by the immensity of my field around the house. Those have not been. And there are a lot of them."

"So we do them one at a time," Zee suggested.

"Oh, no." JD shook his head, a spark of excitement kindling in his eyes. "We don't want a trickle effect. I thought you wanted to knock Belial off his perch?"

"Yes, especially seeing as Gabe and the others are attacking Jiri's stronghold tonight." Nahum checked his watch, fearful for their safety. "Right now, in fact."

JD rubbed his hands together. "Then let's tackle them all together."

"But will deactivating those affect all the others?"

"If we do it in one big strike, perhaps. Probably." JD nodded with conviction, eyes on the box.

Nahum felt renewed hope surge through him. *This could be the solution to everything...if they didn't bring Belial's fury down on all of them.*

His brothers, however, did not look reassured, and Zee asked JD, "Is it safe?"

"God's balls, no! I suggest we add a couple of extra protective fields, just in case."

Thirty

G abe rested his hand on his sword hilt, eyeing the door at the end of the first-floor corridor.

"Describe the room's layout," he said to Dorian, who had escorted them.

"It's windowless. The desk is next to the wall on the left, and there's a seating area in the right corner, and a pool table on the right, too. It's a big room."

"A pool table? In his War Room?"

Dorian grimaced. He was leaner than Gabe, but still muscular, his dark hair tied back at the nape of his neck. "It's his private space for him and his lieutenants. He dangles it in front of us as some kind of private club. I want no part of it."

Gabe knew the type only too well. He loathed Jiri already. "And there's definitely only him and one other in there?"

"Yes. Karim, who was at your friend's place last night. He is also furious—and scared. It shook him up, although he hides it well."

"Perfect." Shadow readied her bow, a bomb in her palm. "Then let's rattle them some more with a bomb."

"No," Gabe stayed her arm. "I still want to talk to him."

"Gabe! You're insane. Let's really unnerve him."

"That bomb could kill him."

"I think Shadow is right," Dorian interjected. "Jiri won't negotiate. He's half-possessed by Belial after all these years."

Gabe felt sorry for Dorian, and that was hard to do with Nephilim. They had a presence, and were usually full of confidence. Dorian projected it, but it was a façade. He was over all of it and wanted his time with Jiri to be finished. *And he was scared,* Gabe suddenly realised with a shock. *Jiri ruled by fear.*

Gabe, however, was determined, and although worried about the use of Belial's tokens, he refused to be cowed by the possibility. "I don't care. I'm going in. Shadow, I'll open the door and head inside, but I'll keep out of the door's entrance and leave it wide open. If I come out running, send a bomb in. Dorian, you stay out of sight."

"My pleasure," Shadow said, adjusting her stance. She had become frighteningly efficient at loading her arrowheads with JD's bombs. She had spent weeks perfecting how they were carried.

Gabe marched down the corridor, took a deep breath, and threw the door open. Two big men, brutish in their size, were standing next to the pool table, hands resting on their pool cues, deep in conversation. They were halfway through a game, balls strewn across the table, and the room was low lit. It was obvious who Jiri was. There was a dominance to how he stood, hard eyed, staring at the man who was his lieutenant. *Karim.* Both were olive-skinned and dark-haired, and Jiri's hair was oiled into a long plait. His cleanshaven face was all sharp planes.

Gabe took it all in with one swift glance and stepped inside. "Jiri. It's time we talked."

Both men looked around in shock but recovered quickly, Jiri's face settling into a scowl. "How the hell did you get in?" He looked beyond Gabe's shoulder, but his angle was such that he couldn't see down the corridor, and he gripped his pool cue like a weapon. "No matter. I will find out and kill them—after I kill *you.*"

"I want to talk," Gabe said, hand on his hilt, and stepped to the right of the doorway. "You need to walk away from Belial. I can help you do it."

Jiri walked slowly around the pool table, eyes not leaving Gabe's, his prowl like that of a lion stalking its prey. "Why would I want to do that?"

"Because this is another world, Jiri. Belial has no place in it, and you are free to build the life you choose." Gabe kept his eye on Karim, who circled the table in the other direction, watching Jiri as much as Gabe. Both wore gold rings, large emerald gemstones flashing in ornate settings. Gabe could feel their power from across the room.

"I wouldn't be here if it weren't for him. None of us would. I am loyal to my father."

"It's time to grow up and see him for what he is. A bully. You follow his orders like an automaton. Think for yourself for once!"

Jiri never stopped moving as his lips twisted into a smile and his eyes glittered viciously. He oozed danger. "I am thinking for myself, you fool. We have power here, spreading Belial's influence amongst the sheep in this society. I aim to continue our work of cleansing the weak for a long time." His eyes travelled up and down Gabe dismissively. "And you won't stop me."

"We stopped you last night." He switched his attention to Karim, and noted his fear that he tried to hide. "You saw it. Your brothers are dead. Even Mikhal, who drew on Belial's power. His time is over, and so is yours."

"It is not over," Jiri roared, "until I say so. And I say never!" He sprang towards Gabe, his pool cue raised, ready to swing, and Karim did the same. Gabe had expected as much. It was clear that Jiri was a power-crazed bully just like his father. He ran for the door and dived to the side.

An arrow whizzed above his head, and he scrambled to his feet to run up the corridor, looking back over his shoulder. He'd barely made a few paces when the bomb exploded behind him.

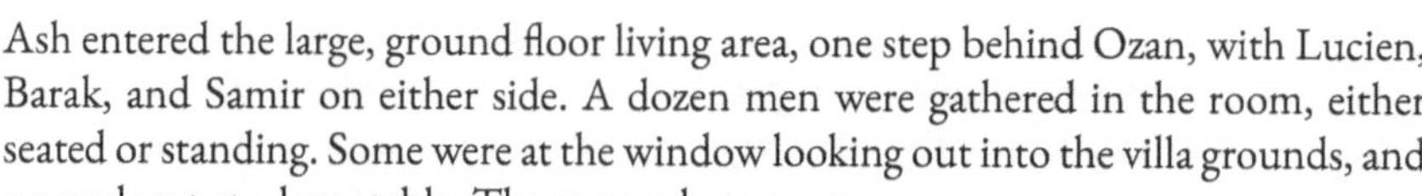

Ash entered the large, ground floor living area, one step behind Ozan, with Lucien, Barak, and Samir on either side. A dozen men were gathered in the room, either seated or standing. Some were at the window looking out into the villa grounds, and a couple sat at a large table. The atmosphere was tense.

At first, no one took notice of their entrance, and then a couple looked around and immediately rose to their feet. The movement drew everyone's attention.

Ozan spoke quickly, arms outstretched in a gesture of appeal. "Brothers. I am here to make a proposition. I suggest we leave Belial behind and forge a new life. This can be easy if we choose it to be, even for you, Pirro." He directed this at a Nephilim with high, sharp cheekbones and a clenched jaw.

"And who," Pirro asked, stepping forward with oily grace, "have you brought with you? Our enemy, I presume."

"They are Nephilim who want to live in peace, just as we should, without fearing Belial."

"Yet they are armed, and you have brought them into our home." Pirro's lips curled back. "You have betrayed us, you and Samir, and who else?" His eyes darted around the room. "Where are Nibal and Dorian?"

Ozan ignored his question. "We are on the wrong path, and have been for years. I am sick of it, and so are many of us. It's time to change direction, Pirro. That trinket on your finger is poison."

Ash watched the other Nephilim, spotting two who seemed to stand apart from the rest. He presumed they were Habib and Jabril, their co-conspirators. Ash leaned close to Samir, voice low as the other two talked, his eyes darting to them. "Those two are the ones on our side?"

Samir gave the briefest nod. Ash's hand was on one of the bombs in his pocket, ready to throw it to the far side of the room now that he knew who to avoid. Even though the Nephilim were in their own living room, all were still either armed or within easy reach of their weapons.

Pirro unsheathed his sword, pointing it at Ozan. "I have worked hard for this token, Ozan. Don't tempt me to use it. Stand down now, and you will survive. You too, Samir. Your friends won't, of course." His gaze swept over them all, and Ash knew, if given half a chance, Pirro would make them all suffer before death.

Ozan laughed mirthlessly. "If I stand down now, you will kill me. You have always been a liar, Pirro." Ozan withdrew his own sword, and the others did the same, all except for Ash, who cupped the bomb in his hand, judging when best to activate it. Ozan addressed the other Nephilim. "Make a decision quickly. I know some of you are with me. This is no life anymore. It is a gilded prison, and we are chained to a cruel master."

Most Nephilim, however, fell in behind Pirro, armed with swords and daggers, and a couple of guns too, Ash noted.

"Have it your own way," Pirro said with a sneer. "I will kill you myself, but the others I want alive!"

A distant boom rang out across the house, just as Pirro charged. He halted for the briefest moment, confusion etched across his features, and Ash threw the bomb under the window. He'd timed it to perfection, and in seconds it detonated. The windows exploded and rubble flew everywhere, but Ash and his companions had crouched, braced for the explosion, and they regained their feet quickly.

Time to get to Pirro before he summoned Belial's power.

Estelle's rage increased as she observed the half a dozen women kept in a secure area of the villa. They were young, some barely out of their teens, and they all looked scared.

The series of small rooms were in the basement area, windowless and cramped, and the whole place stank of sweat and fear. A lounge area and TV comprised one room, and a bathroom was to the side. Through a partially open door, she saw that beds were lined up, dormitory style. A couple of other bedrooms with double beds were to the side. It wasn't hard to imagine what happened there, and rage welled up again.

She subdued it for now, far too worried about the women to be angry with Nibal at her side. "It's okay," she said, holding her hands up. "Do you speak English? I'm here to help."

The women had all jumped up and cowered back when they entered, but when they saw Nibal, they appeared to calm down. That reassured Estelle—slightly. One of them nodded at her. "Yes, I speak a little English."

"I am getting all of you out of here today, understand?"

The woman's eyes darted to Nibal and back again. "They're letting us go?"

"No. *I'm* letting you go." She glared at Nibal. "This is horrific! And you let it happen!"

"I was in no position to free them, but you can tell, they do not fear me."

She looked at the woman who had spoken. "Is that true?"

She nodded, eyes downcast. "Nibal is one of the kinder ones."

Fire flared along Estelle's palms as she said to Nibal, "But still a rapist?"

"No! Never. I feed them. I check their injuries. I try to keep them safe."

"He's right," another girl said. "He tries."

Estelle spelled Nibal back against the wall with a word of power. "It's not enough."

"I swear, I did what I could." Sweat beaded along his brow, pupils dilated with shock. "Are you a witch?"

"That's my business. When these girls are safe," Estelle said through gritted teeth, wishing she knew a spell to shrink testicles to dried walnuts, and penises to withered, flaccid skins, "I will burn everyone to ash."

"And I will help you, I swear." Nibal had flattened himself against the wall, hands raised. "They are all here. All safe, for now. We need to help my brothers."

An explosion rocked the building, and some of the girls screamed. Estelle was worried for Barak, but nowhere near as worried as she was for these abused women. She wanted to kill the men responsible, but it was clear it wasn't Nibal. She dropped her spell. "Tell me the best way to get them out, then you can help your brothers." She turned to the women. "Grab your belongings. It's time to go."

Nibal stepped onto the corridor and pointed up the stairs, back the way they had entered. "Turn left at the top instead of right, and you will find a series of short passageways and a few other storerooms. At the end is a door to the courtyard. It's locked on the inside." He thrust keys at her. "There's a way into the garage; there are cars there, and the gates out to the road." He flinched as another *boom* shook the building. "My brothers!"

"Fuck your brothers. Are there any traps on the way out?"

"No! Just locked doors. Lots of them."

She thrust the keys back at him. "I don't need these keys, only the car keys. And I want cash."

"The car keys are in the garage. Cash is all over the house."

"Down here somewhere?"

"The room above this one. There's a safe in the wall."

"You better not be lying, Nibal, or I swear I will kill you before all others, and it will not be swift."

"I'm not lying."

She nodded up the stairs. "Go. I will find you when everyone here is safe."

Nibal fled and she returned to the room. Most of the women were hastily grabbing clothes and toiletries, but two were just sitting rigid with shock. The other women were packing for them.

Estelle approached the woman she had first spoken to. She was young and pretty, but her eyes were shielded, and bruises marked her face and arms. "What's your name?"

"Chiara."

"Good." Estelle realised she was radiating power, and she took a deep breath and calmed down. *These women were scared enough.* "Can any of you drive, Chiara?"

"I can, and a few others."

"Are you all Italian?"

"No." She shook her head. "Some are Spanish, German, French... They took girls travelling alone, mostly." She clutched Estelle's hand. "We have nowhere to go, and no money, although," she glanced at her bag, "I still have my bank cards."

"I will find you money. Lots of it. You'll have to look after each other, but I swear that I will help. How long have you been here?"

"A few months, I think. I've lost track. Others have been here longer. They took our phones from us."

Estelle gave Chiara her own key and phone, after entering the directions to their rented villa. "Head here. It's about half an hour away. It's safe, and no one else is there. We will return there soon, and I promise to help you. Now, follow me."

In a few more minutes she had led them up the stairs as Nibal had directed, using magic to open locks, until finally they reached the garage. The half a dozen women squashed into one large four-wheel drive, the stronger women rallying the younger ones along. Estelle opened up the gate and leaned in through the window to Chaira again. "I'll be with you soon."

"Will you call the police? I don't think we can face that."

"We'll dispense our own justice, don't worry about that. Tell me, though…did these men hurt you?" She listed the names of Ozan and his friends.

Chiara shook her head. "It was mainly Jiri, Mikal, Karim, and Pirro. Nibal wasn't lying. He was kind. So was Ozan." Her eyes filled with tears. "No one crossed Jiri."

Estelle nodded, her resolve strengthening as she watched them leave, the car lights disappearing as they rounded a bend, and then turned back to the house. Now, she would unleash her vengeance.

Shadow rose from her crouched stance as the flying debris from the bomb settled, and cocked another arrow as a weird, hushed silence fell.

She spotted Gabe lying sprawled on the floor, half covered by the door that had been blown off its hinges. Another man had been blasted out of the room, too, and lay in a muddled heap. Dorian was at her side, still dazed, but she was clear-headed. She edged forward, seeing Gabe move beneath the rubble, and motioned to Dorian. "Move the door and help him up. Who's that behind him?"

"Karim." His voice was scarcely a whisper.

There was still no sign of Jiri, and keeping her bow aimed and steady, she kept moving forward. Karim groaned and sat up, his groan becoming a growl as he saw Shadow. She had a clear head shot, and she didn't hesitate. Her arrow pierced his forehead, killing him instantly, and he fell backwards.

Still no Jiri. She stepped around Gabe as Dorian dragged the rubble and door off him. The doorway was only feet away now, although less door and more hole. The room smouldered behind it and flames danced in patches, but where there had once been a wall was now a big, gaping hole to the outside, and Jiri was nowhere in sight.

Shadow ran to the gap in the masonry, scanning the area. A figure lay spawled on the ground, one arm at a strange angle. *Jiri.* But he was still alive, and he sat up, glaring at Shadow. She shot a volley of arrows, but it was already too late. Jiri was glowing with an incandescent white light, and his wings were unfurling behind him.

She couldn't stop him. He had already summoned Belial's power. She grabbed JD's weapon instead and fired.

Maggie had very little idea of what was going on, other than that things were about to get serious.

The level of worry and nervousness had escalated as the group in Hermes's lab watched and attempted to help JD's preparations. Now, it seemed, he was ready.

"Right," he declared, clapping his hands. "Time to play."

"I'd hardly call this *play*!" she remonstrated. "We might all die!"

"Hush woman, you nagging old rump-fed runion, it's all in hand. Back behind the obsidian line now. Well back."

It seemed JD had decided to use his choicest Elizabethan swear words on her. She found it quite endearing. "Screw you, you jumped up knave with a badger's arse."

"Nice retort, madam." He winked at her. "You may leave if you're worried, but I assure you that you will miss a treat."

"I'm not going anywhere!"

He flapped his arms at all of them. "Back!"

Harlan, Jackson, Zee, and Eli retreated with her to the back of the room. Nahum and Olivia had been banished to the garden, well away from the lab. Olivia had been worried about the effect on her baby, understandably, and so had Nahum. JD had fiddled with geometric grids, and adjusted his instruments that he hauled in from his old lab with their help, and now the place hummed with power, including that of Belial's jewels, of course.

They were heaped in the centre of the grid, and their strange energy had been temporarily dulled by a forcefield of JD's own design. Nevertheless, with hands clamped over their ears and the dark goggles on, they huddled at the back of the room. It was madness to stay, really, and they all knew it, but neither could any of them drag themselves away. Once her glasses were firmly in place, Maggie saw another three fields rippling between them and Belial's jewels. JD had retreated behind the second one.

His back was to them now as he held his controls, and he held one hand up, counting down from three with his fingers. With a terrifying display of light and noise, his alchemical weapons fired their beams at the jewels. The pressure built in the room, and Maggie's hair stood on end, even on her head. So did the others', their hair floating in a nimbus around them before settling again. The hum of power was still discernible despite the fact that they had their ears covered, and it wavered in volume, like musical pitches.

Then a boom rattled across the room.

They all staggered and jostled together, keeping each other upright. And then another boom resounded, and a rainbow wave of light flashed from the far end of the lab so brightly that Maggie closed her eyes and ducked her head. The pressure continued to build as her hair once again lifted off her skin. She felt breathless, terrified, and somehow exalted... As if in the presence of something great.

Exalted?

She lifted her head, blinking against the light, and saw an enormous figure almost as white as the light surrounding it, wrestling as if trying to break free. Wings caught in rainbow hues, and Maggie gripped Harlan's arm. He too lifted his head.

"Holy shit," she gasped out. "Is that a fucking angel?"

Eli was on her other side and leaned close, arms around her shoulder in a protective gesture. "Not just any angel." She glanced at him, but his eyes were fixed on Belial. "He doesn't want to let go."

"It's just like with Olivia," Maggie said, "although, that battle lasted for far less time."

JD fiddled with his controls as he staggered back. The play of light changed, and this time it was like the Northern Lights again, as a ripple of vivid green flashed across the room.

The writhing figure, wings outstretched, emitted a keening note of despair that Maggie knew she had felt more than heard, and then there was another enormous boom. The shockwave it released pulsed across the space, slamming through one protective wall after another, until with a dying ripple, it washed up against the obsidian shield and faded.

She closed her eyes tightly, and when she opened them again, Belial had vanished.

As the light dimmed, and the pressure decreased, Maggie tried to see JD. *Where was he? Was he dead? Unconscious? Pulverised into dust?*

She blinked with surprise as her focus returned. JD was none of those things. He was dancing a mad jig, kicking up his heels and crowing like a cockerel as he cavorted around.

"Well," Harlan drawled, "I guess it's a success."

But Maggie couldn't celebrate yet. "Has it worked on the other jewels, though?"

Lucien had turned into a super-soldier, confounding the fighting Nephilim, and that had worked to his advantage. With the addition of JD's weapons and the bomb blast, the fight quickly became uneven.

When the bomb exploded, Pirro had been thrown off his feet, and Barak had leapt on him. Lucien aimed at the men with guns. Both had been thrown across the room by the blast, but one still gripped his weapon. Lucien shot him before he could recover. The other man scrambled for it, but Jabril was already on him. Another Nephilim fought Habib, while Ash took on three of them all at once. Lucien ran to help him, shooting one with his alchemical weapon, battering the other with his Nephilim shield. Samir was also fighting his brothers, and it was ugly and brutal.

Lucien glanced over to Pirro, and with horror saw him stab Barak in the abdomen. He fell to the floor, hand pressed to his wound as blood poured from it. Pirro ignored him and started to glow with the incandescent light of angels that Lucien had been warned about. It summoned everyone's attention, and they all fell back.

Pirro roared with pleasure as his wings unfurled and his sword filled with light. "Now you will feel Belial's might!"

Ash grabbed Lucien, pulling him back as the two fighting teams disengaged. *This is it*, Lucien thought. *I am going to die at the hand of a Fallen Angel and his mad disciple.*

He didn't even think to use JD's weapon, watching instead with admiration and terror. His breath caught in his chest. Ash fortunately kept his head and shot at Pirro instead, but now that Pirro was drawing on Belial's power, the weapon had little effect.

And then something weird happened. The light faded, and Pirro's face turned from a mask of victory to one of confusion. "Belial!" he roared, face upturned to the sky. He looked down at Barak, incensed with rage, sword flashing as he slashed wildly at him. "This is your fault!"

"No!" Estelle cried out from the doorway. She hurled a barrage of fire balls at Pirro, and he burst into flames as his body was propelled across the room.

Estelle was consumed with fury, that spiteful expression that Lucien hadn't seen for so long etched onto her face. Magic radiated from her, and she turned her attention to the rest of the room. Noticing they had now split into two groups, she laid their enemies to waste with her power.

Gabe reached Shadow's side, pulling her back from the window as Jiri's glowing figure filled the view.

Jiri was airborne now, wings fully open, completely in possession of Belial's power. Gabe could see Belial in him, could feel him even, just as he had when Gabe had carried his token in the Cathar castle. Jiri's blades danced with angelic fire as he hung there, glaring viciously at Gabe.

"It's too late," Gabe said, drawing Shadow close. He had imagined a future for them, especially as she had returned from the Otherworld at Yule, choosing him over her other life. Now it all seemed futile.

Jiri would win.

"It's never too late, my love," Shadow said, breaking free of his grip. In a split second, her bow was armed with a bomb, and she fired directly at Jiri.

It hit his chest, and the explosion sent him cartwheeling over the grounds. He roared with fury, recovering quickly, and he flew with unbelievable speed towards them. Shadow fired again, and again, and again, driving Jiri back.

"It won't last," Gabe said. "It can't. He'll keep coming."

"Then at least I'll buy us time!"

Jiri was laughing manically through his fury, caught by some bombs, dodging others with lightning reflexes, until Gabe realised his glow was fading.

Jiri knew something was wrong, too. He twisted and turned, looking skyward as if for assistance, and then he stared at Gabe, arms outstretched as he held his two swords. "What have you done?"

Gabe felt the faint stirrings of hope as Belial's power faded. "We have friends. I think they've found success in your ultimate demise."

Jiri hung there, just a Nephilim, deciding whether to fight or flee, when Shadow made his decision for him. She released another arrow loaded with a bomb, too swiftly for Jiri to avoid. It hit him dead on, and Gabe averted his gaze as Jiri exploded. Shadow, however, didn't move. She watched, drenched in his blood and flesh.

Finally, she looked at Gabe. "It's done."

Thirty-One

"So," Niel said, rising up on his elbow to stare down at Mouse—a very naked Mouse, who was covered with the finest Egyptian linen bed sheet, "Belial is defeated, and I have a long train journey to look forward to. Would you like to come with me?"

"Well," she traced a finger down his bare chest, "you could catch a flight now. The horn has no influence."

Niel had texted his brothers to tell them of his success as soon as they arrived at the hotel room, and later had found out that they were fine. After that, he'd put all of them out of his head again. At some point in the night, and he couldn't honestly say when, Belial's power had vanished. By then, however, he was having far too much fun with Mouse to give it much thought. He had found out her real name was Anouk, and it suited her perfectly. It was Hebrew, and meant grace and favour.

"A train journey with you," he told her, "in a small room dominated by a bed, sounds much more fun. I have decided that I want to take my time returning home. I might even spend a few days in Istanbul first. It's unlikely they'll spot the theft for a while, or know we're associated with it."

"Those rooms are rarely used. They might not even notice the opening into the cistern for months."

"Good." He glanced across the room at the gilded horn. "When I get home, that's going on my wall."

"A trophy?"

"Yes. And a symbol of freedom."

Her fingers skimmed over his abdomen, stirring his desire again. "I admit, a train journey across Europe with you has its attractions. I'm not sure if I want to go to London, though."

"Where do you want to go?"

"I live in France. Provence, actually. I want to go home."

He caught her finger in his hand and pulled it to his lips to nibble it. "But you travel the world. Don't you fancy a trip?"

"You don't live in London. You live in Cornwall. You'll go home."

"Not forever. I like to travel, and we make a good team."

Her deliciously full lips curled into a smile. "We've crossed paths three times. I hardly think that's enough evidence."

"Yes, but this time surely proves it." He ran his finger down her breastbone to her navel and beyond, pleased to see a flush to her cheeks and hear her breath catch. "We work together very well."

"Are you suggesting some kind of partnership, beyond the physical?"

"Yes." His brothers had their own lives, and while he had no intention of leaving Cornwall for good yet, he needed to explore his options.

Anouk smiled again and pulled him close, and he rolled over her, pinning her beneath him, as she said, "I am open to negotiations. A train journey would be the perfect place."

"Excellent."

Barak prepared coffee in the rented villa on Elba, listening to the chatter of the women they had rescued in the other room. His wound ached, but was healing, thanks to his father's power. He had refused Estelle's help, wanting her to focus her time and skills on the women.

Estelle was still seething with anger, but her vengeance the previous night had assuaged much of it. However, once they were alone, in bed, after the women had been tended to, he held her as she cried. Huge, wracking sobs that encompassed her own experiences as well as the women's. He wished he could do more, but instead he just held her close. She had said only one thing before she slept, and that was, "*I want to do more for women like this. Will you help me?*"

He'd kissed her head. "*I will do anything you want me to.*"

She had cupped his face with fierce intensity. "*Thank you.*"

He shook the memory off, knowing they would discuss it further, and carried the tray containing the coffee and mugs out to the terrace and placed it on the table. Chiara and the others they rescued had already finished their breakfast and coffee. It was a cold but sunny morning, and the team were all keen for fresh air. The view across the hills was spectacular, especially with the sea sparkling in the distance. Spring was creeping closer. It was certainly warmer there than it would be in Cornwall; nevertheless, Barak was eager to be home. He needed time to decompress, to breathe again without fear of Black Cronos or Belial. He had no doubt that they would encounter other problems eventually, but for now, he would enjoy the peace.

Lucien, Ash, Estelle, Shadow, and Gabe were on the terrace too, debating their next course of action, especially how best to help the women, and Ozan had arrived to argue his point. He looked like a different man this morning. He stood taller, his expression hopeful, although right now, he was desperate to get Estelle's approval. It seemed Oz, as he liked to be called, and his companions wanted to help the kidnapped women, to atone for the others' treatment of them. Estelle was reluctant to let them near the women. Barak understood that. Their priority was to get the girls home. After that, they could go home, too.

"I see your point, Estelle, I really do," Oz said, leaning forward in his chair, "but we need to help them. We could do nothing at the time, and I hated it."

"You could have tried."

"It would have got us killed."

"Exactly. You favoured your own life over theirs."

Barak felt sorry for Oz, but equally he saw Estelle's point.

Oz wasn't done. "We took them extra food, and we gave them toiletries and medications."

"You mean to help with the wounds your brothers gave them."

"Do not call them my brothers. They were not."

"If I might intervene," Lucien ventured. "I experienced capture and degradation myself. I also want to help them, and Oz, I see that you want to help too, but it's not right. You have to walk away from this. We," he glanced at the others, "will do this. There are enough of us to make sure the girls get home or go wherever they want to."

Estelle smiled at him. "Thank you, Lucien."

Shadow reached for the coffee and poured herself a mug. "I agree with Estelle. We will deal with this. If you want to make amends, Oz, help us track down The Brotherhood."

He nodded, resigned, and accepted a mug of coffee that Barak offered him. "All right. We can do that. We know most of them, between us. Although, if the jewels no longer have power..."

Gabe glanced at Ash and Barak as he said, "We find them anyway, just in case. You know where they have been moved to?"

"Yes, mostly." A renewed determination settled over Oz as he said, "Yes, I like that idea. We will do that, and then chase up any remaining members of The Brotherhood in Venice."

Barak asked, "What about the dead Nephilim?"

"They are already in the sea. We carried them far out last night and dumped them. Nibal and the others are cleaning up the villa today. It's ours now, to do with as we please. Jiri bought it years ago, when he tired of living in Portoferraio." *The capital city of Elba – the city that Barak had seen in the images at Moonfell.* "It's a good place to rebuild."

Barak mulled over what he'd briefly discussed with the others the previous night. "Oz, it may be that we can put you in touch with someone who can offer you work, if you need it. It's not always honest," he said, laughing, "but I think you'll find it more honest than what you have been doing. We'll have to discuss it with our contact, but his organisation might want to use your skills."

Harlan might want to discuss it with Romola, too. They would see how they would fair with The Brotherhood first. See how trustworthy they could be. From his brief interaction with Oz, though, they all felt they could trust them. They had, after all, helped them defeat Belial.

Oz smiled, and it transformed him. "We would appreciate that. We have some money, but we'll give most of it to the women. Then, yes, we'll need work. Thank you. We are all curious to see this paranormal world you speak of."

Ash shook his head, perplexed. "You really haven't met many other paranormal creatures?"

"Very few. Jiri didn't want it. It's been an isolated existence, for the most part."

As the conversation changed direction to talk of the paranormal and the life they led, Barak realised they had been lucky with their new friends, and he wondered how his brothers were faring in London.

Zee pushed his empty breakfast plate away and reached for his coffee. The noise around the table was loud.

Everyone except JD and Anna was present in JD's dining room that overlooked the rear terrace and the battered marquee, and a range of conversations were taking place. Harlan, Jackson, and Maggie were debating how old Anna might be, whether the emerald cave would send JD mad eventually, and if he would ever actually leave it to help Jackson at The Retreat. Certainly, he had showed no sign of separating himself from it yet.

After their success at breaking Belial's control the previous night, they had helped JD put the slightly battered lab to rights before he shooed them out. He was a peculiar little man, no doubt, but Zee felt he owed him a debt that he could never repay. They couldn't have banished Belial alone. Now, Zee was eager to get home.

He and Eli would leave soon, needing to return to work in White Haven, but it seemed Nahum was staying in London for a while. He sat next to Olivia, and they leaned into each other; it was clear that they had come to some sort of accord. *The early beginnings of love, perhaps.*

Zee spoke to Eli, keeping his voice low. "Do you think Nahum will ever return to Cornwall? For good, I mean?"

Eli shrugged, smiling as he watched him. "Hard to say. Right now, I think not. Shame, really. I'll miss him, but change is good."

"But if the worst happens..." He didn't need to say what that would be. Eli knew. The death of their daughter was a distinct possibility. Sooner or later, it happened. It always did.

"Then we deal with it, but let's have a little hope, brother."

"I have a lot of hope, and so do they. That's what bothers me."

"They have Morgana and JD. Having met him, I now think he could do anything. But we have work to do when we get back, and I don't mean with the witches. The dryads need us. It's spring soon. Ostara. Nelaira has plans."

Zee nodded. Their promise of guardianship over Ravens' Wood was making demands again. They would honour it, of course. They had to. Eli also had his own reasons for helping Nelaira. An obsession that he kept under control, most of the time. More and more lately Zee suspected that Eli slept with other women to assuage his need for Nelaira, and he wasn't quite sure how that would play out.

"As long, brother, as it doesn't clash with a certain wedding." Reuben would be devastated if they weren't there, and so, in fact, would Zee. He was looking forward to it.

Eli laughed. "I'll make sure it doesn't."

Zee sipped his coffee as Maggie demanded Eli's attention. It would be almost a week before Niel returned home, and most likely Gabe, Barak, Ash, and Shadow, too. Nahum would return for the wedding. Zee decided to take advantage of the lull, and prepare to move into the apartment above The Wayward Son properly.

It was time to see to his own future, too.

It was a week after the fight on Elba and Jiri's defeat when Gabe finally walked into the farmhouse in Cornwall.

It was now March, and there were signs of spring everywhere. Early daffodils nodded at the base of hedgerows, and crocuses peaked from borders. Here, on the hills that surrounded White Haven, the fields and moors were fresh with green growth, and it soothed his soul. The courtyard was clean, and Eli—at least he presumed it was Eli—had been planting and tidying up the drive and courtyard. The house was clean and quiet, and it welcomed him. *And*, he thought, inhaling the scent of spiced meats, *Niel was home and in the kitchen*.

It hadn't been an easy week. Returning the captive women to their homes had been satisfying but traumatic. There were times when he felt ashamed to be a man, but it was done now. Oz, Nibal, Dorian, Samir, Habib, and Jibril, were fresh on their quest to end The Brotherhood for good. He had taken to calling them the House of Ozan. Oz was their undoubted leader, and they seemed to have forged a new strength together after the end of the House of Belial. They had all sustained injuries, some of them quite bad, but like all Nephilim, they healed quickly. Their mental injuries would no doubt take longer.

Ash nudged Gabe as he entered the hall behind him, carrying his bags. "Get on with it, Gabe."

"Sorry. Lost in my thoughts for a moment."

"Glad to be home?"

"Very."

Shadow followed Ash inside, silent as usual. She poked him. "I can't wait to tease Niel."

Gabe smiled. Shadow, as always, had rebounded from their situation with her usual ebullience. If it wasn't for her stubbornness, he might not be here. "After you, madam."

She kissed his cheek and wiggled her hips as she sashayed up the hall. She tossed her hair as she looked back over her shoulder at him and Ash. "I believe I won the bet, too! I haven't forgotten."

She meant the bet on Niel and Mouse. Gabe grinned as he and Ash followed her. "Some things never change."

Niel was surrounded by food when they entered the kitchen—bowls of salads, platters of breads, sweetmeats, and other delicacies. He looked up as they entered, a smile spreading across his face. "You're here already! I thought you'd be hours yet!"

"We caught an early flight," Ash explained. "Niel, you've outdone yourself."

"Well, it's going to be the first time we've all been together in months. It's a proper Middle Eastern celebration. And," he nodded to the fridge, "we've stocked up on champagne, too. I don't believe that we've all toasted to our newfound wealth yet."

"Or," Shadow said, "your successful liaison with Mouse."

He refused to be rattled by her double entendre. "Her name is Anouk. Mouse is her professional name."

"Oh. So nice you know details now."

He grinned. "Isn't it?"

"Hold on," Gabe said, confused. "What do you mean, we're all here?"

"Barak arrived last night, and Nahum this morning." He smiled at Gabe's confusion. "Barak came back from Estelle's place and Nahum has decided Olivia can cope alone in London—for a short while, at least. They're out there."

Gabe looked out of the window and gasped. "The loggia's been repaired."

"That's down to Eli and Zee. They're out there, too."

Gabe dumped his bag in the hall and headed out of the back door, Shadow already peppering Niel with questions about Anouk. His brothers were all seated around the table, and the barbeque was smoking. The scent of Arabic coffee came from the pot on the table.

Nahum stood and hugged him. "Good to see you, brother."

"You, too. Everything okay with Olivia?"

"More than okay."

Nahum was composed, always level-headed, but today he had an elevated level of calm and contentment that Gabe hadn't seen for a long time. "Good. You'll be going back, though?"

"Yes. I have to. I *want* to. But that's for another time. Today, I wanted to be here with everyone."

He and Ash greeted the others and Gabe settled at the table, looking forward to catching up with everyone's news, but a strange mix of sadness was tinged with it, too.

Change was coming for all of them. He may as well embrace it.

Thanks for reading this multi-volume set. Please make an author happy and leave a review on a retailer of your choice, but I would especially appreciate one in my shop, Happenstance Books.

Newsletter

If you enjoyed this book and would like to read more of my stories, please subscribe to my newsletter at tjgreenauthor.com. You will get two free short stories, *Excalibur Rises* and *Jack's Encounter,* and will also receive free character sheets for all of the main White Haven witches.

By staying on my mailing list you'll receive free excerpts of my new books, as well as short stories, news of giveaways, and a chance to join my launch team. I'll also be sharing information about other books in this genre you might enjoy.

Ream

I have started my own subscription service called Happenstance Book Club. I know what you're thinking! What is Ream? It's a bit like Patreon, which you may be more familiar with, and it allows you to support me and read my books before anyone else.

There is a monthly fee for this, and a few different tiers, so you can choose what tier suits you. All tiers come with plenty of other bonuses, including merchandise, but the one thing common to all is that you can read my latest books while I'm writing them – so they're a rough draft. I will post a few chapters each week, and you can read them at your leisure, as well as comment in them. You can also choose to be a follower for free.

You can comment on my books, chat about spoilers, and be part of a community. I will also post polls, character art, share rituals and spells, share the background to the myths and legends in my books, and some of my earlier books are available to read for free.

Interested? Head to Happenstance Book Club.

https://reamstories.com/happenstancebookclub

Happenstance Book Shop

I also now have a fabulous online shop called Happenstance Books where you can buy eBooks, audiobooks, and paperbacks, many bundled up at great prices, as well as fabulous merchandise. I know that you'll love it! Check it out here: https://happenstancebookshop.com/

Substack

"Where the Witches Gather," is my new Substack newsletter, and offers content from my previous blog and fresh, exclusive material. I'd love you to follow me there.

YouTube

If you love audiobooks, you can listen for free on YouTube, as I have uploaded all of my audiobooks there. Please subscribe if you do. Thank you. https://www.youtube.com/@tjgreenauthor

Read on for a list of my other books.

Author's Note

Thank you for reading this multi-volume set in the White Haven Hunters series.

I wasn't sure how many books would be in this series, but it feels right to end it now. I love all of the characters, and although it's bittersweet, I believe that with so many of them pursuing their own lives, to try to wrestle them all into one book is madness. It won't be the end of the characters, though. They will continue to pop up in my other series, and some characters may well get their own short stories and novellas.

I have other books and series to write, and I'm looking forward to diving into them. I'm about to start writing the first full length Moonfell Witches book, and there will be more White Haven Witches and Storm Moon Shifters too.

If you'd like to read a bit more background on the stories, please head to my website, www.tjgreenauthor.com, where I blog about the books I've read and the research I've done for the series. In fact, there's lots of stuff on there about my other series, too. I have two websites, just in case you wondered! My other site is my shop, www.happenstancebookshop.com.

Thanks again to Fiona Jayde Media who keeps producing such fabulous covers, and thanks to Kyla Stein at Missed Period Editing for sorting out my knotty sentences.

I must also thank my wonderful Happenstance Book Club members who read an unedited version of this book before anyone else. I loved hearing their feedback as I was writing it. Please join one of the tiers if you want to read early versions of my work, as well as receive other goodies!

Thanks also to my beta readers—Terri, and my mother. Their reassurance as they read each new book always soothes my nerves. Also, thank you to my launch team, who give valuable feedback on typos and are happy to review upon release. It's lovely to hear from them—you know who you are! I also love hearing from all of my readers, so I welcome you to get in touch.

I encourage you to follow my Facebook page, T J Green. I post there reasonably frequently. In addition, I have a Facebook group called TJ's Inner Circle. It's a fab little group where I run giveaways and post teasers, so come and join us.

Finally, just a reminder to sign up to my newsletter, either through my shop, or at www.tjgreenauthor.com/landing.

About the Author

I am a writer, a pagan, and a witch. I was born in England, in the Black Country, but moved to New Zealand in 2006. I lived near Wellington with my partner, Jase, and my cats, Sacha and Leia. However, in April 2022 we moved again! Yes, I like making my life complicated... I'm now living in the Algarve in Portugal, and loving the fabulous weather and people. When I'm not busy writing I read lots, indulge in gardening and shopping, and I love yoga.

Confession time! I'm a Star Trek geek—old and new—and love urban fantasy and detective shows. Secret passion—Columbo! My favourite Star Trek film is the *Wrath of Khan*, the original! Other top films—*Predator*, the original, and *Aliens*.

In a previous life I was a singer in a band, and used to do some acting with a theatre company. For more on me, check out a couple of my blog posts. I'm an old grunge queen, so you can read about my love of that on my blog: https://tjgreenauthor.com/about-a-girl-and-what-chris-cornell-means-to-me/. For more random news, read: https://tjgreenauthor.com/read-self-published-blog-tour-things-you-probably-dont-know-about-me. To read about my journey as a witch, read: https://tjgreenauthor.com/leaning-into-my-witch/.

Why magic and mystery?

I've always loved the weird, the wonderful, and the inexplicable. Favourite stories are those of magic and mystery, set on the edges of the known, particularly tales of folklore, faerie, and legend—all the narratives that try to explain our reality.

The King Arthur stories are fascinating because they sit between reality and myth. They encompass real life concerns, but also cross boundaries with the world of faerie—or the Other, as I call it. There are green knights, witches, wizards, and dragons, and that's what I find particularly fascinating. They are stories that have intrigued people for generations, and like many others, I'm adding my own interpretation.

I love witches and magic, hence my second series set in beautiful Cornwall. There are witches, missing grimoires, supernatural threats, and ghosts, and as the series progresses, weirder stuff happens. The spinoff, White Haven Hunters, allows me to indulge my love of alchemy, as well as other myths and legends. Think Indiana Jones meets Supernatural!

Have a poke around in my blog posts and you'll find all sorts of posts about my series and my characters, and quite a few book reviews.

If you'd like to follow me on social media, you'll find me here:

facebook.com/tjgreenauthor/

pinterest.pt/tjgreenauthor/

tiktok.com/@tjgreenauthor

youtube.com/@tjgreenauthor

goodreads.com/author/show/15099365.T_J_Green

instagram.com/tjgreenauthor/

bookbub.com/authors/tj-green

https://reamstories.com/happenstancebookclub

Other Books by T J Green

Rise of the King Series
A Young Adult series about a teen called Tom who is summoned to wake King Arthur. It's a fun adventure about King Arthur in the Otherworld!
Call of the King #1
The Silver Tower #2
The Cursed Sword #3

White Haven Witches
Witches, secrets, myth and folklore, set on the Cornish coast!
Buried Magic #1
Magic Unbound #2
Magic Unleashed #3
All Hallows' Magic #4
Undying Magic #5
Crossroads Magic #6
Crown of Magic #7
Vengeful Magic #8
Chaos Magic #9
Stormcrossed Magic #10
Wyrd Magic #11
Midwinter Magic #12
Sacred Magic #13

Storm Moon Shifters

This is an Urban Fantasy shifters spin-off in the White Haven World, and can be read as a standalone. There's a crossover of characters from my other series, and plenty of new ones. There is also a new group of witches who I love! It's set in London around Storm Moon, the club owned by Maverick Hale, alpha of the Storm Moon Pack.
Storm Moon Rising #1
Dark Heart #2
Wolfshot #3

Moonfell Witches
This series features the mysterious and magical witches who live in Moonfell, the sprawling Gothic mansion in London. They first appeared in Storm Moon Rising, Storm Moon Shifters Book 1, and then in Immortal Dusk, White Haven Hunters Book 6, and features characters from both series. However, this series can be read as a standalone.
The First Yule - Novella
Triple Moon: Honey Gold and Wild #1
Amber Moon: Secrets, Ink, and Firelight #2

www.ingramcontent.com/pod-product-compliance
Lightning Source LLC
Chambersburg PA
CBHW061027310726
48969CB00004B/870